IRON ANGEL

THE FRENCH YEARS

Book I

A Novel

By

P.F. BUSCH

To Carl, my love and my pillar of strength.

Acknowledgments

To Jeri Smith, your excellent suggestions were invaluable. Thank you kindly Jeri.

Also great appreciation to the historians and general staff at the Nationale Archives and at the Bibliotèque Nationale in Paris and the Louisiana State Museum in New Orleans.

To Todd Engel, artiste extraordinaire, thank you so very much. Engelcr@att.net

Warm thanks and great appreciation to my family for your unconditional love.

And to my friends, your encouragement and support touch my heart.

France 1830-1869

1830 July Revolution *Les Trois Glorieuses* Charles X from the House of Bourbon goes in exile in England. Louis Philippe from the House of Orleans is crowned.

1836 Charles Louis Napoléon, the future Napoléon III, tries unsuccessfully to initiate a Bonapartist Coup by taking over the French troops in Strasbourg. He is arrested and is sent into exile in Switzerland.

1840 Charles Louis Napoléon attempts another unsuccessful coup. He is sentenced to life imprisonment in Ham. He escapes to England.

1848 February Louis-Philippe is deposed. A Republic is established.

1848 Charles Louis Napoléon is elected President of the Second Republic.

1852 After a Coup d'État in 1851 Charles Louis Napoléon declares himself Emperor.

1853 Georges Haussmann is charged with the reconstruction of Paris.

1854 France and England declare war on Russia and defeat her in Sebastopol in 1855.

1855 Exposition Universelle in Paris. Courbet defies the Salon and sets up his Pavilion de Réalisme across from the Académie des Beaux Arts.

1859 King Wilhelm of Prussia accedes to the throne. Otto von Bismarck is appointed Minister/Imperial Chancellor.

1859 France defeats Austria. Nice and the Duchy of Savoy is ceded to France.

1859 February Capture of Saigon by Admiral Charles Rigault de Gernouilly.

1859 Darwin publishes his <u>Original Species.</u>

1861 Construction of the Palais Garnier begins—the new opéra house.

1861 April American Civil War begins.

1862 France invades Mexico

1862 Indochina is ceded to France

1862 Manet *The Lunch on the Grass*

1863 Salon des Refusés. Another venue from the French Académie de Peinture and Scuplture, the Salon of the Rejected artists was instituted by Napoléon III to satisfy the bourgeois taste and essentially to gain their political support.

1864 Prince Ferdinand Maximilian of Austria is crowned as Maximilian I of Mexico with French support.

1865 Napoléon III meets with Otto von Bismarck.

1865 Monet *The Bodmer Oak*

1865 April Robert E. Lee surrenders to Ulysses Grant at Appomattox.

1865 April 14 Lincoln's assassination

1867 Maximillian I is executed by the Republican forces led by Benito Juares. Return of the French troops from Mexico

1867 Exposition Universelle in Paris

1867 October 22 Garibaldi marches on Rome to oust the Pope from his lands—the Papal States.

1867 October 28 French troops arrive in Civitavecchia to protect the Pope against Garibaldi. Garibaldi is captured.

1867 The poet Baudelaire, the Great Flâneur dies in December 1867.

1869 Suez Canal is opened. De Lesseps is a hero.

1869 Summer of 1869 Renoir and Monet paint together near Bougival *La Grenouillère*

Chapter One

"Opéra is a strange mix of poetry and music where the author and the composer, both embarrassed to be in each other presence, have massive amount of conflicts and dilemmas to create a horrific spectacle."

Charles De Saint-Évremond (1614-1703)

Paris France September 1867 L'Opéra De Paris

Mesmerized and enthralled by the supreme beauty of the opéra De Paris, Gabriella De Conte Thornsen sat regally in her loge next to Maître Lauriot, the famed music maestro. Her eyes lifted to the heavens. She prayed fervently that Jean-Louis-Pierre De Pleyssis, Duke de Bourbonne would be in attendance tonight yearning for her presence.

Libiamo, the famous aria sung in Verdi's La Traviatta, had been the catalyst to their passion. The orchestra played the lively music that normally convinced opéra aficionados to sing, dance, drink and be merry. Instead, Gabriella was devastated. The music brought back reminiscences of the formidable moments spent with the Captain on *La Tempète*, his private vessel, and of the passionate nights in the south of France. She called to memory the Grand Gala in Monte Carlo in the company of the Prince of Monaco, Jean-Louis' great friend. The Russian Ballet's awe-inspiring rendition of Swan Lake had enchanted her. That very same night their lovemaking had ignited Jean-Louis-Pierre powerful body as he'd gathered her to him. "I want to erase all connection that you might have had, Gaby. I want you to live for me and me alone," he'd whispered in a moment of rare passion. "I adore you, too, Jean-Louis," she'd gasped. At the time she'd presumed that the passion they sensed for each other would become the love story of the century. She was confident then that he adored her as well. The following morning he'd presented her with a stunning emerald necklace and had clasped it around her neck. "They match your eyes, Gaby," he'd murmured as he'd kissed her eyelids shut. "I feel complete when I'm with you, chérie," he'd shared.

Out of her *rêverie*, dreaming, she lifted her hand to her throat and felt the stones. Five months had passed—did he still feel passion for her? She doubted it. He had not given her a sign of life. Young girls' fairytale stories . . . her heart lamented for days gone by.

She sat, regal, in a white and gold satin bergère looking down at the *Grand Monde*, high society, as they filed down the aisle to their assigned seats. Her mind raced, frightening thoughts fired and immobilized the young soprano and plantation owner from New Orleans who had been admitted at the Académie de Musique in Paris. If by any great chance an encounter with Jean-Louis should arise, would he engage her in conversation or feign not to recognize her? The sisters at the convent in Grenoble had prepared her for the disappointment. They knew all too well the culture and treatment of tainted women.

Her beloved cousin as well, Cardinal Philippe Thornsen had failed to convince her to return with him to Rome to ignite her musical career. "Milan, Rome, Venice—you'll delight in the artistic scene, my dearest Gabriella. Italian cities have commanding National Académies de Musique—the very best, you know that, dear cousin," the cleric had assured his cherished first cousin with all the love he possessed for her.

Lost in her unfulfilled dreams, Gabriella nodded.

"I presume that it would be enlightening as well, Philippe," the astonishingly beautiful, raven-haired young girl replied without much enthusiasm.

"You'll flourish under illustrious maestros, Gabriella. Jean-Louis, as you so familiarly call him was a mistake. You're too perfect. Don't compromise your future my dear Gabriella. You'll be cast out like a commoner. For God's sake . . . let me clarify," he sighed and cleared his throat; his magnificent face softened as he invoked the Lord's name in vain. "Bear in mind your dreams, your laughter, your dislike for society women of your time. Remember your independence, it used to be the only thing you lived for. What happened to all that Gabriella?"

She nodded and smiled sweetly to her beloved gentle cousin.

In a last attempt to convince his stubborn cousin to accompany him, Cardinal Thornsen appealed to her sense of logic.

"Your plantation and privileged background and standing in New Orleans will not appeal to his aristocratic roots. You're aware of that, Gabriella," the ecclesiastic exclaimed bluntly. "Entertainers make good courtesans, but my dearest, you want more and you deserve more, a lot more. In my eyes you deserve the world, my dear cousin."

He'd kissed her lovingly on her forehead and he'd gathered her tenderly to his chest to absorb the pain and bring a sense of reality to her conflicted mind.

"Dear Philippe, I love you immensely, as well," she'd responded, knowing all too well that she could do no wrong in his eyes. However, she had chosen another path.

While traveling to Avignon with Philippe, she'd visualized a joyous life that had taken hold of her optimistic spirit once more. The original plan to return to Paris and lead the life she delineated for herself in New Orleans was back on track.

Through Jean-Louis in the south of France, she had encountered influential men in both Nice and St. Tropez. The Prince of Monaco had been impressed when Jean-Louis had told him that she had been accepted at the Académie Nationale De Musique. Life would shine upon her. After all, she was no stranger to set back. Her whole life had been one difficult decision after another. She had learned to turn defeat into victories. She knew how to make herself happy. Filled with confidence, she had told Philippe of her plans to return to Paris.

Three weeks later, however, in the City of Light, her *joie de vivre* vanished. She felt vulnerable, weak at the thought of an encounter with Jean-Louis. She had seen him two days earlier in front of his mansion on the Quay De Bourbon, but her pride forbade her to confront him. Now, she pondered in her loge where the euphoric sensations of a few weeks past had gone.

What would be Jean-Louis' reaction to her ordeal? That is, if he even deigned to speak to her. Why had she taken so long to share with him the tragedy in Grenoble? Would she take the leap and confront him? He had a terrifying sense of pride. Would he empathize? No. Jean-Louis never empathized with anyone. Had he forgotten her? The thought alone filled her with despair.

At this most opportune moment, when her heart sank and her mind told her to flee, the orchestra began the prelude. The acoustics were phenomenal. Momentarily, the magnificence of the music absorbed her entire being. She was lifted into another world, a world that she adored, and one where she always found refuge. Thank heavens, music always assuaged her distraught mind.

Gabriella lost track of time. She had entered her own private world filled with euphonious sounds she knew so well. One day soon she would be the lead soprano singing on that very stage.

* * *

In the intervening moments, just as conflicted but for other reasons, Jean-Louis-Pierre De Pleyssis, Duke De Bourbonne, or Jean-Louis, as Gabriella commonly called him, stepped down from his carriage and walked up the steps leading to the foyer of the opéra de Paris. His Grandmother waited in the reception area with her long time *ami*, friend, the Count D'Ardienne. Hats were removed as he passed along the crowded halls. Smiles and cleavage flashed from lovely ladies clad in satin and voile evening gowns, who might have known the Duke in more private venues. His enigmatic smirk responded to all greetings. He knew quite well what society murmured under their breath this evening, the great De Pleyssis, the worst of rakes, brought an American Southern Belle to France and now the sweet young thing had disappeared—nowhere to be found. A colonial had tossed the Grand Monsieur aside like an old rag. The story would feed the gossip mills for the rest of the opéra season.

Nevertheless, le *Grand Monde*, the aristocracy, noticed the celebrated Captain and rushed to his side. To see and to be seen with a man of his stature and influence in both the political circles and the world of high finance was the favorite pastime of many. His life and victories, fighting along Admiral Charles Rigault de Grenouilly in the colonies and his exploits during the American Civil War had become a legend. All around the French nation, and particularly rampant in Paris, gossip alleged that Louis Napoléon himself had recalled the Duke to the *patrimoine*, native land, to negotiate the final treaties dealing with the complete reunification of the Papal States to the Kingdom of Italy.

Of all nights, Jean-Louis-Pierre De Pleyssis was reluctant about wasting his time on entertainment. However, his Grandmother had extracted a promise from him. It was her eighty-seventh birthday and the Duke recognized that nothing would please her more than to attend the opéra at the arm of her grandson. He had assured *l'aïeulle*, grandmother, that he would accompany her to the gala. A little distraction would serve him well. He just wished it had not been at the opéra.

Playing over and over in his mind were visions of the stunning American girl who had stolen his heart on that fateful journey home from America. He recalled her expressive face, as she looked up at him, stunned, when he'd entered his cabin on the Tempète, at midday. Gaby had unwrapped the bindings from her breasts, and she'd let her wet, mahogany mane stream down her décolleté. She had been pretending to sing her heart out as she rehearsed silently the necessary acting skills of a diva. Wrapped in 'his' burgundy coverlet, her opulent breasts teased his gaze. The expressive emerald green eyes shot sensual sideways glances at him. Blinded by her imagination, she'd extended her hand elegantly while she danced around his desk on light feet, gracefully holding on to a bottle of Cognac—the imaginary partner. How charming the pose had been. He recalled how she feebly smiled at first, and then shock and discomfiture had overtaken her formidable flawless complexion, first turning her cheeks many different shades of pink, and then crimson. He should have taken her in his arms then and continued with the fantasy waltz as her real partner.

She had fallen off the face of the earth and all the efforts in finding her whereabouts had been fruitless. What had happened to the little mischief? There lay the mystery. There were more questions than answers.

His Grandmother brought back reality to his distant thoughts. She guided him toward a group of intimate friends on the first balcony. Obediently he followed her and flashed his inscrutable smile. The social ballet had begun.

* * *

Four months ago, his ship, as planned, had anchored in Brest. He'd sent word to his secretary that he would be in Paris within days. The message was to be relayed to Gaby immediately. He had spent over a month of passion-filled days with the beautiful young American. She stirred up emotions, he didn't know he was capable of feeling. The sense of loss he felt when they had to part ways at the height of passion in Grenoble had shaken his stoicism. Yet he had been consoled by the idea that they would reunite weeks later in Paris. Never would he have imagined that she would go missing. The reply had returned promptly stating that no one knew the whereabouts of Mademoiselle De-Conte Thornsen and that she had neither registered, nor attended her courses at the Académie.

The search for Gaby had started immediately. Now just before leaving his home for the opéra, a missive had reached him. There were clues about the whereabouts of the beautiful soprano.

After so many disappointments, he was doubtful that she was in Paris. He was almost certain that she had returned with her cousin to Rome. Next week he would travel to Rome once more. He was going to get to the bottom of this sordid affair. The suspense had to end.

Chapter Two

Enthused by the splendor of the highly decorated opéra house along with its superb acoustics, Gabriella missed the entrance of the Duke De Bourbonne. His Grandmother at his arm, he slowly walked to his grand loge overlooking the stage. She recalled how he'd teased her during the crossing.

"Gaby, I will do you the honor. You'll attend your first Gala night at the Opéra De Paris with me, ma chère." It now seemed but just a faint image.

During the intermission, she remained in her seat and glanced at the audience as she searched for his tall frame and dark brown hair. Everyone appeared to be of short stature in Paris. Jean-Louis surely would stand out in any crowd.

Predictably, in one of the loge one level below hers she caught a glimpse of his distinctive profile. He sat next to an older woman who glared at everyone through her *lorgnette*, opéra glasses. The dowager's gaze froze on Gaby, who at this very moment could not for the life of her peel her eyes away from the Duke.

An exchange of words between the regal dowager elegantly dressed in a blue satin dress with large white roses sewn on the shoulders and around her décolleté, and Jean-Louis seemed to be taking place. Lazily, with his sensual smile, he turned as he glanced upward.

His indolent glimpse suddenly turned into a look of incredulous disbelief. Instinctively she recoiled. For lacks of knowing how to better respond, she returned the gaze, waved and fluttered her long-gloved fingertips.

Abruptly, without interrupting his defiant glare he stood up and cast a skeptical stare once more—no it was not a mirage! Briskly, he stomped out of the loge.

The same urge enveloped her. Without a word to the old maestro, who gawked at the scene that unfurled before his eyes, she elegantly peeled away from her *fauteuil*, armchair, dashed up the three steps leading out of the loge and ran out the door into the highly decorated hallway. In the excitement of the moment, she lost all sense of direction. Where would he be coming from? She froze for an instant at the top of the staircase. It was a dream. By enchantment in this fairy tale castle, a breathtaking familiar voice called out her name— powerless she glanced down.

Jean-Louis stood, dashing, bigger than life, clad in a black formal waistcoat with a snowy white shirt that enhanced his olive skin and magnificent blue eyes.

Gabriella paused, terrified. Jean-Louis was striking in both look and demeanor. Suspended in time, she prayed with every last fiber in her body and soul that their storybook adventure would be eternal. *God, don't fail me now*, she fervently asked the Master up above.

Gracefully, she glided down the stairs onto the platform where he stood. The reflection of a thousand Jean-Louis and Gabriellas manifested in the gigantic mirrors that framed the staircase. She flew in his arms.

Oblivious to the crowd, who had left their salons to watch delightfully the play develop before their very eyes, Jean-Louis-Pierre De Pleyssis took her fully in his arms, lifted her off the floor only to hold her as close as it was humanly possible. His passionate kisses landed ardently on her lips and on every inch of her uncovered bosom. Unmindful of where he was, who was looking and what the gossips were going to trade the following days, he collected her close to him for interminable minutes, not willing to let her go for fear of losing her forever. The world closed in on both of them, Gabriella lay immobile in his arms, afraid that she might wake up from a formidable dream.

After a long embrace, unaware of the large crowd now standing on the balconies and the staircase, gawking at this most unusual encounter, Jean-Louis-Pierre gently set her back on the stairs and gazed in her eyes.

"Where have you been, Gaby?" he whispered in a voice meant only for her. I searched for you incessantly." His body ached with an overwhelming desire.

"In Paris . . ." she began to explain as she felt his body go rigid.

"In Paris?" he interrupted loudly. "The entire time?"

Her mind raced as she tried to find the right words to calm him.

Simultaneously men and women strained their necks; some gasped. Gabriella looked upward.

"I can explain," she murmured. "I can Jean-Louis . . . please let me," she reiterated.

Instantly the reality of the situation hit him. She had not been hurt. She had not been missing. In fact she was intentionally hiding from him. Gabriella's desperate attempts to explain became distant background noise and an untenable fury grew inside him.

He looked around, the gawkers were all ears, drafters' pencils scrolled on their pads.

She sensed the change in his demeanor. As quickly as he had gathered her up to his body, he took a deliberate step back. She watched his gaze change from one of unabashed passion to an icy glare. His square jaw clenched with flawless determination.

She searched his face for answers. Did he still love her? Would he ever forgive her? No. She sensed a tangible seething fury set in. Her heart broke. He would never want to see her again. As he started to turn away Gabriella caught a glimpse of pain.

Chapter Three

It was the first time she missed Mardi Gras in New Orleans. Gabriella De Conte Thornsen conceded somewhat gleefully that her singing would be missed at the prestigious Krews balls. However, memory was short in these fashionable circles. As soon as the season ended, she would be history. The grand of the city had forgotten her beloved cousin, Philippe, now Cardinal Thornsen, when he'd travelled to the Vatican.

Gabriella never took anything for granted. The young plantation owner had lived well and independently for the past twenty years because of that very philosophy. She reveled in the knowledge that her voice was special, an incredible God-given gift that she cherished. She was forceful, diligent, and very much aware that in the world she lived in, she only had herself to trust and God to rely upon. Her singing talent had been honed to near perfection; now she needed additional professional support and she was on her way to get it. She had been accepted to the Nationale Académie De Musique in Paris.

The Frigate that would take her to France waited, anchored at the port. The crew stood in attention, awaiting orders from the Master.

While she stood alone on the cay, her cognac-colored valises held shut by large white leather straps next to her, she silently watched the heavy-set and very muscular longshoremen. In oversized beige cargo pants and dirty white sweaters with rolled up sleeves, they lifted and carried away the remaining trunks inside the cavernous suites of the ship. Clad in a black and white, ankle-length suit, she gazed at the ship and the mast towering over her as she waited to be taken across the ocean to a faraway land.

An overwhelming sense of nostalgia took hold of her as she recalled her childhood, her friends, and the sisters at the convent. She sighed. The tinge of sadness toward the past would never supersede the great satisfaction she'd derived from not meeting the coward, her father, during the opéra season. All the false pretenses of affection and fondness he professed toward his daughter in front of the grand society, his friends, were a farce. That was one horrific act she would not miss in Paris.

On the cay, ready to climb on that fateful ship that would change her life forever, she lifted her gaze to the heavens and prayed.

The ship across from her waited in New York harbor—for her. She had traveled five days to get here, with stops in Washington and Philadelphia. The crossing to France would be an extraordinary experience and by God she was ready for the challenge.

Less than an hour later, a mariner came to escort her up the wooden plank where the Captain, an Italian seaman, Master Capello, stood waiting to greet the passengers arriving on deck.

Gabriella noticed that she was the only female on board. Just as well, she thought. She had brought a large amount of reading material. Tranquility, she valued. Had she ever experienced a time in her life when a responsibility to something or someone had not been a pressing issue? No, she could not recall the instance.

The Captain of the ship went out of his way to personally welcome her on his vessel. Short and stout, Master Capello's uniform fit tightly around his rotund abdomen so that the fabric around the buttons was stretched to its maximum and coming undone. *Un bon vivant*, she promptly thought. The Captain possessed a charming voice and a great sense of old world niceties.

"I am thrilled, Signorina, to personally welcome you on my vessel." He was seemingly enthralled when she shared that she spoke fluent Italian.

She greeted the Captain and the other travelers that would join her in the crossing. After a polite salutation to all, she filed into the designated room.

The crossing would take approximately twenty-eight days. She looked out upon New York Harbor from the porthole above her bed and was frightened by the dark billowing cloud that covered the pane. Momentarily, a long, thundering noise shook the furniture in her room. It blasted from the ship's chimney. The great road onward had begun. She'd followed her dream by taking a giant leap forward.

* * *

The first few days of the passage were quiet. She sat reading in her cabin, thankful for moments of pure silence. Almost two years had passed since the end of the Civil War and the Reconstruction was not going well. The War of Secession had left its indelible prints on Southern society. The federal government had ordered federal troops to stay in the slave states for another fifteen years to protect the former slaves, Freedmen. Sherman's rampage on her Southern lands had been horrific and the deaths inflicted on the population while he marched on to Savannah were unbearable. The very thought that the federal government could protect a polarized population appeared bleak.

White women did not fare much better, Gabriella thought. In her eyes, now that the men had returned home from the war, the independence that many of her friends had acquired during these troubled times vanished. Rare was the master who returned from war, who asked his wife, sister, or mother how his land should be managed.

It was a debacle and she presumed that it would take many years, perhaps decades to soften the pain inflicted. She was pleased to have taken the decision she had envisioned years ago. Self-determination was the means to attain her goals; she possessed financial independence and self-reliance. Consequently, her happiness did not depend on being taken care of by a man. Marriage was not on the table for her. She had the means and determination to make herself happy. Most of the women she knew had very little control over the lives they led.

A bottle of red wine, a pewter pitcher of water and a book were placed on a mahogany desk. She walked over and picked up the book given to her by Edgar De Gas when he visited New Orleans. She fell on the tweed eiderdown of the large wooden frame bed and expertly propped up the pillows behind her while she reclined lazily with book in hand.

The book was enveloped in a soft yellow parchment like cover. It brought to mind the encounter with the great painter of everyday lives. Degas had changed the spelling of his last name, not willing to share with the world his doubtful aristocratic background—his father's lineage was not as pristine as the old man would have liked it to be. The family had money since they were involved in the European banking system, and Edgar had a most privileged childhood. His love of depicting simple people in their working lives captivated her. Of all places, they had met at the Cotton Exchange in New Orleans; he had been painting the scene. His mother, Hortense, had been a close friend of her mother. She was a Southern socialite who loved balls and festivities. Unfortunately, after marrying the Old Man, as Edgar's father was known, in effect, he was thirty years older than his young impetuous wife, they had moved to Paris with the family. Deprived of her friends, status and social life, Hortense slowly died of boredom and despair. Edgar was only sixteen when his mother passed and perhaps because of this traumatic event in his life, he had developed a cynical view of life. His icy remarks often enraged many would-be friends. Essentially, the man lived for his art and frankly he was not the worst off for it, Gabriella thought. That familial proximity and their similar background—Gabriella's mother had been married in a loveless marriage in Italy at an early age and had been forced to America by her husband who sought to expand his fortune in the New World—Edgar had shared his world with Gabriella and asserted that she would absolutely love Paris. A fortnight hence she'd written to him announcing her arrival. The answer had been prompt: "Why have you waited so long?" Yes, she thought, why had she waited so long?

Later that day the Captain came to meet with the young girl who'd showed up on deck to glance at the sunset.

"Miss De Conte, I would be honored by your presence, if you chose to join us for dinner this evening," he demanded gallantly. "You are the only woman on board, so please feel free to talk to my commanding officer and request whatever is needed. We do not have the pleasure of female companionship often enough. Dinner is usually served at seven. I would be honored to have you as my guest anytime you so desire."

"With great pleasure," she responded. A bit of social activities might make the long voyage less tedious, she thought. She gladly accepted the Captain's standing invitation.

She strolled back on the main deck, and got closer to the railing. Porpoises frolicked on the large gray mass of water that slowly formed and broke in white crests on the steel arches of the bow.

"Hello, Miss Thornsen," one of four men she had met earlier on the ship approached her. "We're having a mid-afternoon nibble and we were wondering if you'd consider joining us. At this time of year, the sunset falls mighty quickly; we have a perfect perspective from our seats in the enclosed dining area."

"That would be great fun, thank you," she replied as she followed the tall and lanky man who seemed delighted by her quick acceptance. They entered a small but lovely dayroom. The walls were covered with a dark paneling, but the view from the windows was spectacular. She stopped at the entrance mesmerized and soon came to recognize the four other fellows she had met on deck earlier that day. In that very manly setting with five gentlemen sitting and drinking around a heavy wooden round table, she thought of excusing herself and returning back to the cabin, but the need for company and conversation got the best of her and she decided to sit and watch the sunset on the horizon. A spirited conversation ensued on the merit of traveling at sea on an Italian passenger boat. The food was scrumptious, they all agreed.

It would be a very nice passage, she concluded after returning to her cabin.

The following night she accepted the Captain's standing invitation. Four of the men she had met the day before were in attendance. She was the only Southerner onboard; naturally the conversation seeped in areas that were still tender to both camps. Far from shying away from politically incorrect verbiage, Gabriella exposed her view as a Southern social observer assertively.

Sitting at the right of the Captain, she had been listening to two men who discussed how to do business with Italian merchants on the Old Continent. And just as quickly, one of the men turned to her as if he had wanted to make a statement about her Southern roots all evening.

"Miss De Conte-Thornsen, how do you reconcile the perverse attitude toward humanity that the South has conducted for the past two hundred years, before we placed a stop to it?" The tall and slender man called Melville Brown asked haughtily. He was a Bostonian minister, involved in some sort of business venture in Europe, and he had been drinking heavily.

"I don't reconcile anything, Mr. Brown. I never practice this infamy on my plantation. We had servants—paid servants, that is." Gabriella emphasized just as testily. "As a matter of fact, two of these servants were instrumental in my upbringing. They not solely attended to my physical needs as a young child, but they instilled in me from an early age integrity and myriad of valued moral lessons, sir. Yes, the South was wrong about slavery. It certainly went against every fiber of society." She concluded on a more conciliatory note.

"Interesting," mused his companion, squirming, visibly uncomfortable with the gist of the enduring conversation. He smiled at Gabriella.

"I am pleased that you feel that the North was correct in pursuing this largely humanistic war. I wonder how many of your compatriots," he stopped for a moment and most likely realize that there was no longer a national division between the states, "would argue otherwise," he concluded.

"I'm unable to speak for all Southerners, sir; however, not everyone looked at the practice as benevolent. My mother was a fervent abolitionist. She hung for it, Mr. Brown."

Both the Captain and the hefty man called John Henry La Tourte pushed away from the table at the same time. The conversation was inappropriate and the amiable Miss De Conte-Thornsen surely would take offense. Furthermore, she most surely would deprive the other passengers of her lovely presence by spending the rest of the journey in her cabin. The Captain was about to interrupt when the articulate minister/ businessman intent on proving his point preempted him.

"Therefore, this conversation is moot, Miss De Conte-Thornsen. You have just demonstrated that most Southerners were hostile to free their slaves. The North served a highly mighty purpose in this war—the fight for human rights for all people." The gentlemen from Boston continued.

"Hostile or not, sir, the South was built on the free services of our Freedman, women and their children included. I will give you that, sir. It's been a way of life; even some free slaves purchased and owned slaves once they got their freedom papers. I'll grant you that the practice itself was horrific, but the Freedmen who have fled to the Northern cities have not gained much in terms of prosperity and acceptance."

"Let's agree to disagree," the Captain stated in a conciliatory tone.

"What gives you this idea?" The man continued agitated, oblivious of the discomfort his controversial speech produced among the Captain's guests. "Being free is an innate right. That alone is primordial, I'd rather be starving in a Northern city than owned and fed on a Southern plantation."

Knowing that the conversation was inappropriate, especially the second day of the crossing, the Captain chose this point to put an end to the supper.

"Miss De Conte-Thornsen, gentlemen, I thank you for your graciousness. Unfortunately, my men need rest and so do I. I hope to see you tomorrow. I can only hope that the weather will be as pleasant and fair as it has been these past two days. Good night." He stood up and waited for his guests to do the same and take their leave.

Brown was visibly disturbed that he had not been able to pin down the pretty plantation owner. Involved in politics, he liked making a point that could not be refuted. Gabriella realized the situation and as he tried to continue the same line of conversation in the sitting room, she bid good night to all and strode to her cabin.

Stay away from these disturbing conversations, she concluded, nothing good can ever come out of it, especially with men as narrow-minded as Mr. Brown. No matter how lopsided a story was, both sides required to be explored and understood so as to not repeat the errors of the past. Mr. Brown was not the man to speak to. She promised herself she'd stay close-mouthed on questions of race, politics and religion the next time she met him.

The following two days were nauseating. The seas were rough and Gabriella stayed in her cabin. Just the idea of eating was appalling. Finally, on the third day of the crossing, the ocean calmed down and she walked on deck to feel the cool breeze on her face. February was not a good month to travel across the Atlantic.

Once more Mr. Brown and Mr. Balludeca—a half-Spanish, half-Italian businessman—were sitting on two of the four lounge chairs the crew had set up for the travelers.

"Good morning, Miss De Conte-Thornsen, you look mighty perky after the storm. I presume it did not affect you, personally I don't recall such high seas and yet I sail these routes fairly often. Please sit with us the fresh air is invigorating."

Reluctant, Gabriella acquiesced to the man's request, hoping he would not start up on the subject of slavery once more. Less than ten minutes later the topic was brought up—yet again.

"I felt cheated the other evening, the Captain did not let you respond to our lively chat. You mentioned something about the well being of the Freedmen in our Northern cities?" he asked.

"Well …" She was going to tell him to forget the issue. It was the past. The war had changed many traditions but then she changed her mind and went straight to the point. "My feelings, Mr. Brown, are quite opposite to yours. I feel that the white Anglos responded in two ways, neither correct nor appropriate. Out of pity or guilt, some would bend backwards to assimilate the Freedmen into the white man's society in our Southern cities, they fell to recognize that 'freedom' was not a quick fix for things like illiteracy, poverty, and business savvy. They overlooked the frustrations the newly freed slaves were facing. The paper-thin golden cover I call it Mr. Brown. I don't quite know how you see it, but in my eyes it is far from being an egalitarian gesture toward a newly free individual."

"That is a serious charge Miss De Conte-Thornsen," the dismayed Mr. Balludeca stated, visibly shocked at such an impertinent remark especially coming from a young woman who would do well to think about her wardrobe and marriage to an honorable man. The businessman cast a glance of displeasure at Gabriella. His companion, however, wanted closure on the subject, and woman or not, this young Southerner was the only one he could vent his frustrations upon.

"Are you speaking about your culture, the people that you know, Miss De Conte-Thornsen, or do you have the audacity to accuse us for the problems that the South brought upon all of us as a nation?" He questioned trying to assuage his comment with a sarcastic laugh.

"Since you are being so candid, Mr. Brown, please allow me to do the same. Trust that I found the practice appalling, however, your elevating the Northern cities as the epitome of fairness and good wages is largely exaggerated. This ambiguous philosophy is professed by freedom-loving members of the society who often appeared to have fallen in love with the sound of the word freedom!" she concluded extremely annoyed.

"Inconceivable. So you shame the North for its admirable effort while trying to lessen the wrongdoings committed by people in your part of the nation?" he said incredulously.

"I simply want to state that it is not in my view what is needed. We have appalling issues as well in the South. Many former slaves owners either despise the free blacks or worse—yes, worse—they just do not care. Care at this time would be a good thing, indeed. The newly freed slaves need care and compassion, not rhetoric. For many, it is their place of birth. Why should they flee to the North? They have worked hard to make the South their home, now they require financial and educational support to learn how to rebuild their lives, how to retrieve their family members, how to rebuild their cultural heritage. As slaves, they knew where food and shelter came from to feed their loved ones. The practice of oral history went a long way on the fields and houses they toiled in to retrieve lost family members. However, as Freedmen they have to fend for themselves in a world mostly hostile to their plight, or at the very best indifferent to their situation in life.

Flabbergasted at such outrageous comments, the Bostonian did not try to hide his displeasure. "Miss De Conte Thornsen you are dead wrong and history will prove my point. I am just too sad that I will not be around to appreciate its value. Good day." He stood up, red-faced, while Mr. Balludeca follow suit. They both left the deck. The

Captain had watched from afar the altercation. The poor man did not appear too enthused to settle a dispute especially one as sensitive as the conflict between North and South. The sweet little Gabriella was not so sweet after all, he concluded.

Meanwhile, Gabriella had been amused at the reaction of the Northerner. Internally she was divided on the issue. Listening to some of her mother's friends, the ones involved in the abolitionists' movement, one would think that the issue was already settled. They could foresee an integrated South in less than a generation. She remembered thinking at the time that these people most certainly believed in Santa Claus.

As the men walked out, she watched them climbing up the stairs to the main deck, she also noticed the Captain, a stern look on his face. He must have been privy to her remarks. Perhaps she should have walked away from the tense conversation. These types of altercations never served the purpose intended; instead, they aggravated and polarized the parties involved. She would have to control her responses from now on. Meanwhile, unwilling to return to her cabin, she walked closer to the bow.

Gabriella stayed up on deck reading for a long while. Often she would lift her head and stare at the horizon as moments of sadness in leaving behind her beloved New Orleans, her plantation, her servants, and her Country, flashed in her mind. The conversation with Mr. Brown had re-ignited her melancholy. She was proud of the great new power the United States was quickly becoming, but she looked forward to fulfilling her dreams somewhere else. It sounded so right. Why was she feeling so conflicted and egoistical?

She had worked very hard after all to keep the plantation profitable during the Civil War. She was a teenager then and she had achieved a miracle. After the war, her plantation, which had been left intact because of her father's Irish ancestry, had become one of the few lands still financially viable. She had been the sole financial administrator. In essence, her business savvy and practical negotiation style had served her well.

Many of the old influential sugar brokers had lost immense fortunes in the war. To them, Gabriella had suddenly become an alluring partner. Single-handedly, Miss De Conte-Thornsen—the Voice, as she was commonly called in the New Orleans musical circles—had re-established her plantation as a financially sound and working land.

God had blessed her again and she looked forward to a wonderful life, one that she, as a young woman had chosen. She had been accepted at the Nationale Académie De Musique. That was the reason she was sailing to France. Very few women had this sort of opportunity.

Her earlier heartaches, that of not being loved or nurtured by her parents, had worked in her favor after all. Her unanswered prayers had been the real blessing. And there she was, standing at just five feet and one inch tall— she never forgot those last two-and-a-half centimeters ready to take on Europe with her supreme singing.

"Good afternoon, Miss De Conte," she heard from behind. "Terribly sorry that I was not able to put an end to your conversation with Mr. Brown earlier," the Captain said in a heavily accented English.

"I have heard it all before, Captain; do not worry. I am thrilled to sail to Europe. I look forward to the European life, my singing career, traveling through Europe, hopefully performing as the lead soprano of major opéras with my sublime gift." She smiled charmingly. She wanted to sing and share her gift with hundreds, maybe thousands of people with different cultures, set of beliefs and mores.

"I was not aware that you were a singer, I had been told that you were a business woman. I thought you'd travel to France for pleasure." He smiled, just as charmingly. Austrians and Italians understood music and its many layers of texture that truly changed the spirit of those who let themselves fully surrender to it.

"I have been accepted at the National Académie De Musique, Captain. That is the reason I'm sailing to France. As an artist I feel that music is a force that touches everyone at every level of society, bringing real pleasure, and to many it gives a sense of tossing every negative force out of the window," she responded.

She would learn it all. Yes, she would crown her career at the Scala in Milan. That was one of her long-time goals. Singing was her passion, always had been, the one talent she relied upon to bring her happiness and a sense of hope. The gift was always there to take her mind off the hardships she had experienced and faced. Singing would transport her to a different world, a world of dreams where she could feel secure and truly happy. Through the study of music she had met fascinating individuals who also shared this freakish passion of nature felt solely by a few chosen ones.

Her own parents had financially supported her music lessons—her singing having been a source of pride for them. Mind you, not of pride in their daughter's accomplishments, oh no. That was unthinkable on both of their sickly, soiled minds. Rather, in their perverse, egotistical thinking, they actually attributed her skills as their own accomplishments, a trait passed on genetically to their child. She had to forget and forgive those two horrific souls. In any case, it was her past; her bright future lay ahead aboard the Italian frigate.

The Captain of the ship was both surprised and perplexed with the young passenger. She looked awfully young, maybe twenty-one or twenty-two years old. At odds with her youthful appearance, her language skills and demeanor appeared much older than her youthful smile. It betrayed her. He took upon himself to invite her often to his table. She was not the prissy type, deathly sick with every rolling of the sea. He had inkling that the forces of nature would not deter her steely demeanor. It was quite attractive.

Later that day he made a point to meet her formally. Gabriella De Conte Thornsen kept to herself, studying her music books. The first time in her young life when she had no other chore to oversee or accomplish, she savored the moment. She had no other thing to think about but her one passion—her music. She lived that moment and loved living it, as she constantly reminded herself never to lose sight of the happiness she so richly deserved.

The Captain would find her often, late in the afternoon sitting in one of the great big chairs on the deck, which almost engulfed her tiny body. She was almost invisible when she placed her feet Indian style under her large bouffant skirts. What could she be telling her secret diary? Was she writing her daily events or perhaps keeping a journal? Lots of young women of this era kept great journals, he had read quite a few from Southern ladies who had described in their writing, real, gut-wrenching, factual events that occurred during the divisive Civil War. They passionately described the sadness experienced by the widows that had been left behind—the forgotten ones.

Besides lean and straggly Mr. Brown and fat Mr. Jerkins, a few of the other gentlemen sailing on the ship had tried to engage her in conversation, but to no avail. She was polite but cool. She had learned her lesson, the old Captain grinned.

Four days had gone by, the sea was calm and beautiful, unusual for February. "You must be my guardian angel," the Captain had told her yesterday, as they passed a French ship that had communicated with them earlier. The Captain of the French ship, the Duke De Bourbonne was returning home after almost five years spent in the United States. He had fought on the Union side, although France had had an inkling of supporting the Confederacy in 1862.

"He was seduced by the new free world," the Captain explained, "and he remained in Boston and purchased a home in the aristocratic Louisburg Square, in historic Beacon Hill. The area is the Bostonian's answer to the English blue blood society. One never falls far from his roots."

"That's interesting," Gabriella, replied, curious. "Why is he returning to France?"

"Perhaps the women in Boston are too prudish for his affinities, Jean-Louis-Pierre De Pleyssis, Duke De Bourbonne is a dashing young French aristocrat with a reputation for leading the fast life. He loves danger, challenges, fighting, and women. He accumulates as many of the above mentioned experiences as is humanly possible." The Captain laughed happily.

"He sounds like a nice fellow," Gabriella retorted sarcastically.

"The fact is that if one should travel across the Atlantic Ocean, it is a fabulous omen to have his ship sailing nearby. It means that protection is at hand. His personal ship, *the Tempète*, is magnificent and equipped with cutting edge technology, most powerful armaments, and the toughest and boldest soldiers who share their

Captain's love for dangerous world situations and unconventional challenges. An invincible force," the Italian seaman declared.

"I was under the impression that the crossing was relatively safe," Gabriella stated, concerned.

"Very safe, Miss De Conte Thornsen, not to worry," the Captain replied calmly.

In reality, Captain De Pleyssis had communicated to him earlier that a pirate ship had slipped in the sailing routes and that it had already pillaged two passenger boats. Be aware, the old mariner had been told.

For two days, the Italian Captain had taken precautions, placing his crew on high alert, and then he had relented. It was quite difficult for the passengers to stay indoors. It was not good for business.

At exactly 12:03, the seventh day of the transatlantic passing, l'Escalina was attacked and rampaged.

Shock struck Gabriella sleeping all alone in her cabin. Screams, clanking of swords, and gunshots blasted above. Fearless and without one iota of self doubt, she fled her cabin, grabbed the outfit of a dead sailor laying outside one of the Captain's door, and slipped into his uniform. She quickly noticed two large trunks that had already been looted. She stepped in the larger and deeper trunk and hid under a heap of men's clothing and burgundy like silk curtains. She listened intently and was almost sure that she'd heard someone shouting orders in French. She sank deeper into the trunk and waited for either death by drowning, death at the end of a sword, or maybe with a bit of luck, the French Captain who appeared to have entered in the battle would find her alive.

For what seemed to be forever, shrill shrieks from prisoners begging for mercy to not be killed or tortured, seeped through the planks. Some begged to sail for the new Captain, change banner, so as not to be thrown overboard. She lay quietly and motionless as screams and gunfire and the clatter of barrels rolling and crashing down the stairs terrified her. A human must have rolled close to the trunk where she hid, for squeals of terror and moans of extreme pain echoed in her trunk. The moans turned to a piercing screech and seconds later silence reigned. Fighting, swearing, the bumping and rolling of bodies, hollow splashes from humans falling or being thrown overboard continued above on deck. What seemed to be hours of complete terror and torture persisted and quite suddenly the shouts tapered and quietness returned to the vessel? She was alive. What was next?

Her clever tactics worked so far. After several loud cannon shots and the cries of battling sailors just above her, the war above seemed to die down. She had read somewhere that the large trunks belonged to the master of the vessel. Therefore, with a bit of luck, she would be delivered to Master Capello or the French Captain if his forces vanquished whomever had tried to board the vessel.

In hindsight, she was still flabbergasted at her reaction. She had often thought that heroes acted out of fear and responded with integrity to the demands of human survival. Her personal skills at self-survival had been sufficient to make her act like a hero in her own eyes. Let compliments fall where they are deserved.

All of a sudden she heard footsteps and someone lifted the trunk where she hid. She prayed that she would not be tossed out to sea. Maybe that had not been such a great idea after all.

She was rolled around for what seemed an eternity; the trunks were going to the Captain's room she heard someone say in French. She bit her lips not to scream in pain when the trunk was lowered and then roughly dropped on the hard wooden planks.

A while later, a door closed and silence returned. She waited a few minutes. As quietly as a mouse she peeked in between the slates, not unlike a gator that surfaced silently from the murky waters to take hold of its surroundings.

She had been lifted to another ship, one that displayed an elegantly decorated cabin with much comfort. An empire desk in the middle of the room was scattered with documents and maps and a half-eaten meal rested on the ink blotter. The bed was massive, the man lying in there must be gigantic she told herself. She slowly lowered the lid to its closed position and curled in a fetal position once more. Tasting horror—total despair beset her. She sunk in deeper in the trunk as dread inculcated itself in the deepest layers of her mind.

Someone tapped his boot against her trunk. A fearsome cavernous voice, loud, harsh, devoid of emotions shouted to another to search the trunks and to toss everything overboard if no precious metals, papers or money was found.

"Tell the sailors unwilling to conform, that they will be killed and thrown overboard. They'll come around quickly." The brute opined.

Her hope of finding someone who would understand her plight evaporated. If he gave her a chance, however, she would tell him that she was being sent to France because she wanted to join the Ursuline Order in either Grenoble or Paris. Her cousin, a Cardinal would take care of her as they disembarked. He would gladly pay for whatever expense she might incur since her own fortune had been taken from her.

Damn, what type of scenario she imagined. God, she was at his mercy. Extreme fear engulfed her whole being now. She would have preferred to die or be sunk with the ship. What were they going to do with her? Rape her, torture her, kill her? She heard the clanking of the boots once more on the wet planks and the screams and shouts of the mariners who were supplicating their captors to save their lives. A detonation of gunshots discharged. Minutes later the begging ceased. *Oh, dear Lord*, she thought, she should surrender all hope and prepare to die.

She heard another voice. This one decidedly had an Irish accent.

"Captain, what should we do with their Captain? He is still alive"

"Throw him in the brig. If he refuses to cooperate—starve him. In my view handing him over to the authorities is absurd. These scoundrels do not deserve prison; they should be shot on sight. We found four sailors who had been impressed by these brutes on four different docks in different lands. One I happen to know vaguely, a connaissance of my friend, Luke. For years, his family searched high and low for the chap. I understand that he would have gambled all of his family's fortune given half a chance, not much of a find, I'll give you that, but nevertheless the pirates should be eradicated, not paid off like so many monarchies and empires are presently doing."

Both men entered the cabin and the Captain spoke once more.

"What are these trunks doing in here?" he shouted.

"They were found next to the travelers' cabins, Jean-Louis-Pierre. Gold and silver was spotted in one of them. Before our mates decided to tear them open, I decided to have them brought in here first."

"Look through all of them, Cunnan, and give what is unnecessary to the crew. Jewelry, coins belong to the Empire. You can leave the trunks piled up against the wall for now."

The man called Cunnan started to rummage through the trunks. Gabriella froze. Nothing was processing through her nervous system. The first and second trunk had been disposed of and pushed aside. The third, her own, the larger of the three was being opened. Brutally, the mariner grabbed all the silk drapes, and then he discarded the mound of men's clothing and stopped as he stared at the nightgown she'd discarded before donning the mariner's uniform.

Cunnan, the commanding officer, hesitated and wavered, he must have been processing the feminine attire since she had been the sole woman on the Italian frigate.

"I wish we could have gotten there on time," he muttered, "but the old seaman flippantly chose to preserve his business ventures instead of taking precautions against pirates' attacks. Damn, we warned about the real possibility less than seventy-two hours ago, for God's sake. He had to learn the hard way," she heard him whisper to himself.

The female attire still surprised him, as he continued his monologue pondering at the possibility that maybe these were gifts for girlfriends or wives. He dug deeper. When his hands squeezed her breasts, she let out a sharp screech. The large man looked down, astounded to find two green eyes staring back at him in horror. He let out a curse as she heard loud footsteps walking over toward her hiding place. The first mate was astute enough to realize that this was neither the time nor the place to let the master know that a young lad disguised as a 'matelot' was hidden in the trunk. She shot a supplicating look in his direction. For an instant, she thought that he would pull her out and let the wrath fall where it may, but with a smirk and a tilt of his head, he related to the Captain that besides a gigantic candelabrum and a few other silver items, no coins were found. Uninterested, the Captain retorted that he would remain in his study. He had had a full day and wanted some sleep. Tomorrow was going to be disagreeable and he needed some rest.

Cunnan waited for the Captain to reach his study and calmly returned his attention to his new guest. "You need to stay in there, lad. The Captain is in no mood to deal with you now," the old sailor placed his finger over his mouth to demand silence.

"I was going to France to enter the order of the Urseline in Paris, my cousin is a Cardinal waiting for me in Nice," she whispered.

"A girl! Good God, please don't say another word," he whispered. "Later I'll bring some food when the Captain leaves his cabin. I'll leave the trunk partly open and hidden behind the others. Please don't disturb him. Stay in and keep quiet." He looked backwards towards the Captain's cabin and he returned his intent stare upon her. With a deep sigh, he closed the trunk and pushed her trunk further back toward the wall.

It was getting more and more challenging by the minute. Gabriella relaxed a bit, at least the mariner seemed to have taken pity on her plight. But her life depended on the monster asleep in the gigantic bed in the next room. Better be quiet and endure another night. She needed rest, as well. Who knew what future lay ahead for her? She curled up once more. Thank God for her ballerina training, flexibility and pliability had come in handy these past frightening hours.

Chapter Four

Gabriella listened intently. The Captain must have left earlier; everything was quiet. To orient herself, she softly lifted the top of the trunk a tad more and gazed at the empty cabin. She moved like a cat, rounding her back, then she finally got on her knees, raised her arms above her head and she fully lifted the lid as she stood up and stretched the stiffness out of her body.

"Get out!" a voice roared.

A boding evil giant with dark shoulder-length hair, a bushy black beard that spread down from his temples, and piercing blue eyes that stared right through her, was towering over her. The man wore tan, form-fitting suede pants and a white, loose tunic shirt.

"Please, dear God, don't hurt me, I'm a nun!" Gabriella shouted before the man could utter another word. "No... no, not quite, but I will be. My cousin is a Cardinal; I have money, some connections, well, not a lot, but I'll be good, my cousin will pick me up when we reach France, please, oh please, have mercy, I'm in love with God . . . I want to go to the convent. Please don't throw me overboard. I'll shine your boots. I will be your servant, I'll poison you if I cook, but I can do other things..." Out of breath, she stopped.

"What other things can you do?" The giant stared down, immobile.

"I can sing, or read you books or tell you stories about my plantation. I have money, I have a plantation, I own it. It's true. I will not need it if I become a nun or an opéra singer. You can have it all, if you spare my life." She babbled, terrified.

"What?" he frowned, "an opéra singer or a nun? That's a real stretch, mademoiselle. How are you going to accomplish all that?" He asked looking a bit confused.

"Well, no . . . but I'd like to study music. No, no I am going to sing with the nuns in their chorale at the convent." His voice had not reassured her. Better lie a bit more.

"Well, mademoiselle, I was thinking of something else."

"Tell me, I'll try."

A smile tugged at the corner of his mouth.

"Please spare my life, but if you don't want to, please, please do not leave me alone with the mariners down below, I beg you, I read many books on that, I know what they do to young women, please shoot me first and then throw me overboard. Oh dear God, please spare my life . . . I'm young, very, very young; I'm sure you have a daughter or sisters my age, everybody does." She begged in one last desperate attempt.

"Do you?" he asked.

"No, not sisters, but most people do, I have lots of half-brothers on my father's side. I want to live, please. I worked hard all my life to sail to France and study music at the convent. Please spare me. I will be most appropriate and kind and I promise, on my life, not to disturb you. I'll work for you. There has to be something a woman can do on this ship. I'll be happy, no, thrilled to do it. Captain, do not kill me," she implored as her beautiful green eyes widened.

If she was truthful and truly intent on cloistering herself what a pity for manhood that would be, he reflected. She had been quite adamant about doing anything on board to save her life. Obviously this pretty young thing was experienced—perhaps she was trying to expiate for previous sins, he thought. Looking at her with amusement in his eyes, he walked to the desk and perched on its corner. Did he look that old to have a daughter her age, he quietly asked himself? She had stopped babbling and he noticed that she returned his stare and was studying him now with a serious, analytical gaze.

"Do you always ramble on like that when you are caught at sea by honorable men?" he smiled a long sensuous smile.

Still fearful and tense, she forced herself to relax her small stature and straighten fully.

She must not have been more than five feet tall, at that, he judged, but the large green almond-shaped eyes looking at him now were mesmerizing. Helpless, standing less than ten feet away from him, wearing an oversize mariner's outfit, way too large for her, dark hair pulled back and tucked away under a cap, she alternately looked like a little girl masquerading as a sailor or an under age beauty, with eyes

29

that could challenge any French or English courtesan anywhere. Suddenly, she flashed a half smile, which revealed pearly white teeth, and sheepishly, she raised questioning eyes in his direction.

"Well, the last two times I was kidnapped at sea by honorable men it worked quite nicely," she tentatively forced a smile, "I thought I would try it one more time." She smiled awkwardly at first, a reserved grin, as she sensed her fears evaporate she bravely continued, "never two without three, as the French saying goes. Isn't that what the French state? You sound French, Captain."

"I'll ask the questions, thank you. So, you were the noise last night?" he inquired.

"I'm afraid so, sir."

"Get out of that box, and tell me your story in thirty seconds or less." He came closer and gallantly lent his hand to pull her out of the trunk.

"Well, please give me a minute. You said you were honorable? I have spoken correctly, Captain? And—and—you don't want me to ramble on, I do have a lot to say, Captain." She eyed the breakfast he had left on his desk.

"Can I have something to eat? I'm very, very hungry and thirsty. I'll pay you for your crumbs, the ones you left on your desk." She pitched her chin toward the desk. She needed to buy time; she thought an honorable man would not deny her that privilege.

The girl was direct and thought promptly, he pondered amused. He liked spontaneity.

"How much?" he asked

"How much what?" she questioned, surprised.

"The crumbs? How much are you willing to pay for my crumbs?"

"Well, Captain, I'm at your mercy, and I'm sure you'll search my trunks if they have not been rampaged. Take what I have."

"You must be hungry. Very well, it's settled then I'll take it all."

"Oh, that's highway robbery," she retorted in good spirits "I mean high seas robbery." He walked closer. She froze.

"Do not be frightened." He smiled at her. "You are safe with us now. I'll have Cunnan, my commanding officer, the man you obviously met last night, bring an extra breakfast." She stepped back.

"I have to get back on deck. Meanwhile, please do not leave the cabin unless one of us has authorized you to do so. Clear?"

"Crystal clear," she responded.

"We will talk this afternoon or tonight." He turned to leave and promptly turned on his heels.

"I will ask my commanding officer to bring a cot in here, as well. I don't want the mariners to know we have a woman on board."

She nodded.

"Can you read?"

She shot him a look of fury.

"I'm happy you don't have bullets in your eyes. I probably would be talking to my maker right now." He responded with mirth.

"Can I read? Yes, in three languages, French, Italian and English; I have studied Latin. Good God, Captain," she proclaimed angrily and pretentiously, obliterating her precarious situation. "Guess what, I can even read music and I can sing—very well, that is. I can write poetry, quite movingly I have been told. I can hunt and I'm good with a pistol …" She discontinued her tirade promptly. Once again, she reflected that she had revealed way too much about herself. Why did she always ramble when she felt insecure? She was pretty, she knew that, but because of it her intelligence was often overlooked; consequently she placed way too much emphasis on her magnificence. Unfortunately, instead of feeling better she always felt the worst for it.

"You are good with the pistols, hum … lock up the guns Cunnan," he said ironically. Cunnan had just entered the room.

"I see that no introductions are de rigueur," Cunnan acknowledged.

"Well, my chère, what else can you do, can you cook, mend, wash clothes?" the Captain continued. "You have many talents. I can see none that could help us much on the ship except the one with the pistols. Now if real pirates attack us, you will come in very handy. The rest—well, I don't see any rabbits or fox nearby; I don't think that the mariners would truly appreciate a good aria although I agree with you," he said as he recalled the entertaining moments he'd spend at the old opera house in Paris, "opéra is addictive. And finally, honestly, I don't think that many mariners speak Latin, it may be problematic with communication.

Gaby realized that she had lost control of her temper once again—not a very smart in such a risky surroundings.

"I'm sorry, Captain, it was absurd of me to elaborate on my accomplishments, I truly apologize. The servant who raised me always said I was a quick study. So, although I am not a very good cook, I could learn to wash or clean or mend quickly." She rambled once more, hoping to improve on the gaffe she just committed, "I'm a fine card player; my cousin Philippe always said I could make a killing on one of the gambling riverboats on the Mississippi. In all due respect to your rank, sir, I would have loved to strip bare some of the Captains that came to pick up our products from the Justine, my plantation. They deserved to be beaten by a woman or by black men. I would have liked that, a condescending crowd they were, always trying to cheat me."

The two men looked at each other, confused. The Captain wondered if her babbles were genuine or had her acting skills been honed to perfection? He stared at her while he appeared to contemplate the power beauty afforded a woman. She was absolutely beautiful, her face anyhow, she could have weight in at one hundred kilos, for all he knew, under all that fabric, but, one thing was for certain, had she not been so pretty to look at, he certainly would not still be here listening to her absurd nonsense. He took his guns and handed them over to Cunnan. Better safe than sorry.

She quickly noticed the men gathering the arms with great amusement. They did not leave anything to chance, she thought. □

"So tell us, mademoiselle, you play cards—solitaire?" The Captain turned toward her again, seemingly interested.

"No, no, I can play poker," she stopped as if she had sinned.

"Do you drink brandy and smoke cigars, as well?" Cunnan questioned good-naturedly.

"No," her pretty heart-shaped face turned crimson, I'd like to try though," she murmured. "Maybe when I get to France, I will. I understand from the writing of Mr. Adams and his wife Abigail that French women are very open about their sexuality, their rights as equal partners in risqué conversations, and that French men really listen to their ideas and concepts. My cousin told me so." Too late, she realized she had been caught in a lie.

"I thought you were going to a convent?" the Captain smirked as he cut her off.

"Well, in reality I will be living in a convent when my cousin is in Rome, but when he returns to Paris he'll install me in his apartments. He has a home on the Isle St Louis. You know where it is?"

Cunnan looked at the Captain.

"It is very nice. I'm sure that you will like it." The Captain persisted, "tell me, Mademoiselle, what are you going to do in Paris?"

"I have been accepted at the Conservatoire, the Académie De Musique, to study voice," she proudly stated.

"You must be good," he said with a hint of admiration in his voice. "It's a very difficult school to gain entrance to."

"I am good, Captain and it did not hurt that I had a few connections as well."

Suddenly she was no longer a spontaneous child but a very mature and assertive woman. As she gained more assurance, her voice took on a more confident tone.

"All right, I really have to go now." He shot a look at Cunnan and he cleared his throat. □

"Lock up the guns and bring her some warm blankets; it gets cold in here."

"Thank you very much, Captain," she replied. He noticed the euphonious American accent. *This should be novel*, he thought to himself.

"By the way, what is your name?" he questioned as he neared the door.

"Gabriella De Conte-Thornsen"

"That's an odd combination."

"Italian on my mother's side, Irish and English on my father's side." She replied quickly.

"Oh, what a long name for such a petite woman. A little angel on our ship—bearer of good will, I hope. Gabriella, I am Captain De Pleyssis."

"Nice to meet you," she responded, nodding her head slightly.

He looked intently at her once more. He then turned on his heels and decidedly strode to the door. It slammed hard behind him. He was gone.

She promptly turned toward Cunnan.

"I'm sorry, sir, I tried very hard to follow your advice. It had been quiet for so long, I thought that the Captain was gone. I was in so much pain. I hope that I did not get you in trouble." Her apology touched his heart.

"Do not worry your pretty little head," he gently took her hand and taped it reassuringly.

She had seen many fathers give emotional support to their offspring with such reassuring gesture.

"Jean-Louis and I go back a long time. I knew his father very well. We have another twenty-one days on the ship—you will be fine. Just stay out of his way. If I can be of some help, please let me know. I'll have some food brought in." Have a good day," he retorted gently.

"Likewise, thank you."

The Captain returned later and obliterated her presence as he marched into the cabin. A deep frown hardened his features, or what she could see of them hidden under the heavy beard. Finally, he must have retrieved what appeared to be maps on his desk. He grasped the yellowish parchment package, walked around his desk and sat behind it in a large, velvet, burgundy armchair. With quill in hand he sat silent, reading.

To be polite, she felt obliged to enter in some kind of light conversation.

"Thank you for the meal and blankets," she started awkwardly.

He nodded, without looking up.

"I stood by the porthole, and could not believe the darkness of the sea." She continued, "the last few days before you boarded my ship, the weather had not been very clement and the seas had been quite rough, I should say, so I have not been on deck for quite some time, any chance, Captain, that I could climb on deck anytime soon?"

He looked at her annoyed.

"No."

"Very well," she walked toward the desk and she tried one more time at light conversation. "Well, is there a predictable theory that can forecast the weather and the state of the seas for the remnant of our voyage?" She questioned. She paused her palms against the mahogany desk and she leaned forward on it to watch for a reaction.

He straightened up his long torso and glared at her harshly. She could feel by the way he looked at that moment that she annoyed him but she did not expect the verbal trashing that ensued.

"Gabriella, this ship is a working vessel. I emphasize 'working.' I don't have the time or the liking for your polite conversion, so I would ask you not to talk to me. Answer the questions that I ask of you in a yes or no mode, that's all I hold you responsible for. There are as few rules of courtesy on this ship as is humanly possible and secondly, I'm not interested in your babbles. You can enjoy my hospitality and do whatever you did when you were alone on that other ship we so rudely boarded, save our good intention of saving a stupid man, his crew, and his ship. Check with Cunnan or myself, first—that is all. You are dismissed." He lowered his head and continued working with ill-conceived annoyance.

Mortified was an understatement; she wished she could have sunk into a hole forever. For a long while, she remained quiet, and then once more her pride got the best of her.

"My apologies, Captain, I will remain quiet from now on unless asked to speak, as a proper young girl should do in the presence of older, wiser, honorable man of your standing. However, if you are ever in need of astronomical advices, I read the stars and know most of the constellations quite well. I read whatever is available on the subject—us mere silly females who can read, that is. Please feel free to use my services; I would love to return your hospitality with substantial information that can be of service to you."

The flippant little ingrate, he couldn't resist thinking, with a smirk.

"Thank you mademoiselle, we'll converse tonight. Maybe then I'll listen to your timely advice."

She looked up and executed a French salute touching the side of her forehead with her palm down and she walked away. She felt his gaze upon her as she circled around her cot twirling her hands. Quickly she turned, stared back and gave him a subtle smile. A smile lit his icy blue eyes. Not knowing what else to do, she retrieved an oversized leather chair and sat down quietly.

'Older, wiser, a daughter her age,' if she had not lied to him earlier, he concluded, she proclaimed to be twenty-one years old; in essence that would make them a little over nine years apart. The beard must have made him look older. The little witch was unusual, and as they said in France, her tongue was not locked away in her pocket. Was she really that accomplished or just a good chatterer? Unusual chit. He continued mapping the sea routes for a short while and then left the room.

Later that night, the Captain returned. Cunnan had already brought supper. They had dined together on fried cod, small red russet potatoes, and French green beans. Dessert had been a dish of chocolate tapioca. It was great fun having someone to talk to. After all, she had been silent for four days; the bad weather had kept her in her cabin prior to the ransacking.

Concerned about the first night on the vessel and her sleeping arrangement, she shared with the old seaman the afternoon friction. She asked Cunnan about the ways of the Captain—namely, how not to annoy him. The older man grinned.

"You'll be just fine, Gabriella. The Captain is a gentleman. He has been raised well," he proclaimed assertively. Cunnan loved to talk and she just listened to the exciting life he had led.

After a while she recounted to him tales about her life and her love for Tita and Gustav, her beloved servants that had been given freedom papers by her mother. The former slaves had practically raised her. They had taught her substantial lessons of life. She missed them both.

The Captain walked in and found the two of them sitting around his desk in deep conversation.

"I was looking forward to having a partner to share dinner with—pre-empted I was. What a pity," he interrupted, oblivious of his rude behavior earlier that day. "I'll have to come in earlier tomorrow evening. I presume, Cunnan, that we should change the crew's eating habits so as to accommodate our new guest." He shot a sharp glance at Cunnan.

The old man laughed. He admired the young De Pleyssis much more so than he had admired his father. Jean-Louis-Pierre reviled the behavior of his aristocratic peers; nevertheless, he was an aristocrat to the end of his fingertips—so accustomed of having everything his own way.

"Well, my friend, she is all yours now, that is if she is willing to talk to you after your purported rudeness at midday."

Gabriella was mortified. She wished she had not said anything.

"I'd be more than happy to sit with you and you certainly can do the talking. I'll listen," she answered graciously. I have been remiss in thanking both of you. Please accept my deepest gratitude and appreciation. I'll be forever indebted. This afternoon, I thought about your earlier statements, Captain De Pleyssis."

A bit perplexed, the Captain raised his eyebrows and looked at Cunnan, both men smirked. Again their guest was on one of her rambling tirade, politely they listened.

"I certainly can help," she stated self-assured, "I cannot cook at all, it would not be a wise idea especially on a working vessel," she looked up in the Captain's direction. He gazed straight in her eyes, but she wouldn't let him stare her down. "But, I can clean, well, not exactly, but keep everything in order. I can find a place for everything, maps, and papers, anything you wish. When my mother was on the plantation, she was not too keen in having me around, so instead of provoking her ire, I would go outside in the kitchen with Tita. She was my dear servant, Captain," she explained to Jean-Louis who had not heard her life story yet. "I would help her with the cleaning, she always had me wear a pair of white cotton gloves and put everything away in its proper place. 'Order un-clutters the mind,' she'd proclaimed. Actually, she'd purchased these pretty gloves for herself in New Orleans to attend the Sunday religious services on the Hill. The Hill, as it was called, was the location where the slaves used to congregate for mass and prayers on Sunday. She gave them to me, stating that my elegant and graceful gestures would go unnoticed when I curtsy, if my hands looked rough and red. Perusing through the trunk, you brought to me this morning, one of the few things that were not tossed at sea," she looked crossly at first, and then with a sweet smile at Jean-Louis, "were my gloves. You must have known, Captain, such female attire might come in handy to place a young girl to work."

"Eh bien, Gabriella," the Captain interrupted, "show us that knockout curtsy'"

"Oh, but I can't gentlemen, I need to keep in my mind your station in life, Captain, *absolument pas*, absolutely not, I familiarized myself with the mores of the citizenry, consequently, no curtsy for military officers, only kings, dukes, and Emperors," she proclaimed with hilarity.

Her voice and laughter were crystal clear. *It could shatter glass*, he thought. For an instant both men were mesmerized by it, and then Cunnan took the lead.

"Well, well, lucky, lucky us. The Captain here is a Duke, great Bourbon lineage, centuries of good manners," Cunnan asserted with a pronounced Irish note.

With an ironic simper, she kept quiet for a short while and quickly broke in a hearty laughter. "Well, your grace" she employed the proper title given to Dukes in England, "I do not know how to address a Duke in French, or do you still use titles? I know there were lots of changes after the revolution. Do you?"

"Never mind, Gabriella, show me that reverence."

She could not help but to denigrate his behavior earlier today.

"Let me think, Captain—I am an American. I believe that we went to war with England to erase all form of subservience, including the reverence to titled men and women." And just then she recalled his coarse behavior earlier that day, "I wonder about all these years of good breeding, Captain. Either years in America or my own callous demeanor caused you to obliterate centuries of good breeding. You came quite close to demand silence from yours truly, earlier today." She walked closer to him with a playful grin in her eyes and a determined chin, "admit it, admit you were going to, Captain. I am correct *n'est-ce-pas*?"

"I'll pronounce myself happily on our earlier encounter, that is exactly what I had in mind, how succinct of you to have noted my tone. I'm happy to hear that you will not repeat your earlier behavior." Intent on testing her verbiage, he persisted.

"Mademoiselle, please implement that curtsy."

"Very well." She came much closer to him. With the most disarming and elegant bearing, she bent quite low and executed elegantly a most charming curtsy. She showed her proper education as to even take the required three steps backward required of the noble during the reign of the absolute monarch Louis XIV. She also made certain not to step on the oversize material of the mariner's pants. He could not help but to look down at the overextended mariner's shirt. No, definitely not, he thought, she did not fill the mariner shirt that she was wearing—her breasts were non-existent. He helped her up. Both men clapped.

"Your slave was right, mademoiselle."

"My servant," she interrupted, "although my mother was less than maternal towards me she had grand ideas about human equality. Too bad she did not extend these ideas of love and compassion to her own daughter. Well, gentlemen, I have done it again, rambled a bit too long, I'll wash up and turn in with your permission. By the way you can talk all you want; I'm a very sound sleeper."

Both were amused. They did not answer and left her to her toilette. The Captain returned way past midnight. The place looked liked the Arc De Triomphe on the fourteenth of July. She had left all the lights on. He smiled.

She heard him walk in, drop his clothes, and fall into bed. Quickly she turned her back so as not to be faced with his nakedness.

"Good night, Gabriella."

"How did you know I wasn't asleep?"

"Your breathing became quite irregular after I took off my clothes, and you turned your back toward the wall, sorry, I—"

"Years of good breeding do not show in your demeanor, Captain, good night." She pulled her blankets over her head and tried to fall asleep. He had turned off all lights. Fear and anxieties returned. Finally fatigue overcame her anxious mind. She woke up early. It was his turn to be sound asleep. Quietly, she tip-toed in the adjoining room, and in the process, she bumped her knee hard on the hard corner of a wooden hassock, she held her breath, bit her lips so as not to be bothersome and counted to twenty, before she started again toward the highly decorated secretary where she had set her book down yesterday. She picked it up and returned cautiously to her cot.

Mr. Franklin was a great writer; she loved to read his amusing anecdotes on France and on the French people. He seemed to really love it. The women especially appeared amusing, witty, and always ready to explore controversial subjects. She wondered how she would fare in that Parisian society. She sat and read and watched the sunrise out of the porthole. The Captain's coffee pot was close by and although she refused to touch anything of his, she could not resist. She tiptoed to the large water tank as quietly as she could and poured the water in the coffee pot. The brewing was loud. Afraid he'd wake up and be angry, she made an extra cup in case he wanted one as soon as he awakened.

She was reading one of the captain's books, Ben Franklin's thoughts on the Parisian social life, when he sat up in bed and contemplated the pretty creature in front of him. She stood relaxed, perched high on her cot, close to the porthole for light with his mug. He noticed that her bottom was nicely rounded as she stood on her cot to reach the light. From what he could perceive, he appraised that her ankles were slim and her lower legs shapely. He could not discern if she had a small waist. Damn, his head was in the trash bin. He chastised himself for thinking about sex. Mon Dieu, what could he expect? Was she a virgin child? He highly doubted it. She either was a terrific actress or she was as pure as a gold ingot.

"Tell me, Gabriella how old do you think I am? And can I have a cup of the coffee you just brewed?"

"Good morning, Captain; I hope that I did not wake you," she sweetly responded, shaken by the loud voice. "I tried to be very quiet, but I could not stay in bed another second, I get very restless. I usually ride my horse in the morning. I wish I could have taken him with me. Challenge will be the only one I'll miss."

"Your plantation is quite large then. Who is manning the fort while you're away?"

"Yes, it is. It will be managed while I am away by a dear friend recently married to a woman he adores and who adores him. That's quite unusual these days." She raised her shoulders and nodded her head. "Well, Lisette, his wife, will be riding Challenge. I'll buy a horse in Paris when I settle down. According to Franklin, the Bois in Paris have excellent equestrians trails."

He seemed to be evaluating her with his piercing blue eyes. It was hard to see if he was handsome under the bushy dark beard, but he possessed striking, vibrant eyes that were difficult to ignore. Actually, she surprised herself at the feeling of comfort she experienced in his presence. In reality, it was quite nice to wake up next to a virile man, to sleep in close quarters with an absolute stranger. His scent was everywhere, even on the leather bound book she had been reading. She liked it. *Gabriella, beware of your heart,* she cringed; the sheer thought disturbed her. Without answering his question, she poured the coffee as nonchalantly as she could manage.

"I have been reading Ben Franklin's thoughts on French, namely Parisian society, Captain. He has a lot to say, especially on women. Is your wife as independent, clever, and witty as the description of the French feminine soul depicted by Mr. Franklin?"

Silence reigned. She felt it was a cue for her to continue.

"I chose France to study music for that very reason. Italy would have been wonderful as well—it was a difficult choice. Why Paris? I'm not quite sure? I love the language and the French. England had been one of my choices as well, but in retrospect I do not think I could handle British high society; I am much too spontaneous and direct" she mocked. "The king would have thrown me in a dungeon or ordered me beheaded!"

She walked to the side of the bed where he lay and handed him the coffee.

"I love coffee. I think you'll like it if you like it strong."

He took the silver mug from her hand and sipped the dark liquid. She sat at the foot of his bed, anxious for conversation, oblivious to the underlying silent statement.

He waited a few minutes and said thank you, staring at her sensually as he sipped the coffee.

"I'm not married, Gabriella." She quickly hopped off his bed. "Consequently, I would not know what my wife would do in the situation Franklin describes, but I know a few ladies vaguely and I think you'll fit in just fine." He lied; he did not want to place any doubt in her and have her change her spontaneous nature to prepare herself for the role of *précieuses*. She was cute, innocent, and a lot of fun and the next twenty days might be novel and fun—he hoped.

"But you lied to me again, Gabriella," he said reproachfully, "I thought you were entering the convent, I did have some serious reservations, knowing that such a lively personality would never be seen or heard from again. What a loss to the secular world."

"Are you being sarcastic? I talk your head off, Captain." She countered with a chuckle.

"No, go on."

"I did lie to you, I'm sorry. I will be staying at the convent while attending the Conservatoire in Paris. My cousin Philippe, who is a very influential figure at the Vatican, has rented an apartment in the convent Du Sacré-Coeur on the Ile St. Louis. I will then be able to attend my music classes in Paris, protected, while he is not there and move in with him when he returns back to Paris. Perhaps I'll get tired of the atmosphere and I will move into my own place but it is most practical, now."

"In effect, mademoiselle, you are very well connected. Tell me about your cousin, the Cardinal. What does he think of the Nationalistic movement unsettling Italy and the Catholic Church?"

He thought at this point that he would have her cornered. She would either divulge helpful information or she would retreat to her cot politely waiting for her breakfast. He received a reaction he did not expect from a woman—her expressive eyes reflected delight; they were filled with anticipation. Within seconds she climbed back on his bed, as she begun a lengthy opinion on how the Nationalistic movement in Italy might affect the Industrial Revolution in Europe.

"Louis Napoléon is correct in thinking that a push toward the full reunification of the Italian States, including the Papal States, would be welcome by other European nations. As more trade routes are opened, modernization will be well under way and a new class of citizens could develop skills needed not only to feed their families but also to bring prosperity and peace to Italy and frankly the rest of Europe. What concerns my cousin is the insistence of Victor Emmanuel on his appropriation of Rome. He appears to want to annex the city along with all that he has already taken from the Papal States."

The Captain kept quiet. Surprised at her right on, as they said in the United States, deduction. He heaved a long sigh.

Since the captain had not responded, she pursued, " granted it would permit more trade, especially from the Asian routes. It just appears to me that it is always easier to deal with one entity. I know from my own dealings with my suppliers on my plantation. It also makes sense to significantly reduce the influence of the Church. The Catholic Church, in my opinion, should embrace less political power throughout Europe. They would then truly be able to concentrate on providing spiritual and monetary help to the poor and downtrodden, while at the same time encourage a deeper faith. I know that for thousands of years, the Church has played an immense political role in Europeans affairs. Frankly, it was not the intention of the original Founder."

"Very good, Gabriella. I know what you think, now what does your cousin think about the reunification of the Papal States to the Kingdom of Italy?" He persisted, knowing full well that a man of the cloth might see it otherwise.

"He is torn, but Philippe is one of the few visionaries in the Church. Politics fascinate him and he would love to use his vast knowledge on the subject to better the treatment of the have-nots. This, you see, Captain, is not necessarily the philosophy of his Church. Le Droit de l'homme, as you say in France, is a great viewpoint; however, wealth and titles have so much power over the poor soul who has very few resources. It is often hard to lead a spiritual life when surviving from one day to the next. Making the next meal is the only constant. To answer your question, I do not believe that he would be distraught if a solution could be consolidated between the Pope and his Princes and Victor Emmanuel II.

Personally, I do understand that Rome is a primordial location for an Italian Capital. Florence is landlocked."

"Interesting. Your cousin should not be too vocal about his perspective on European politics while engaging the Pontiff, Gabriella." The Captain retorted pretentiously.

"Philippe is a brilliant man, Captain. I have nothing to suggest to him," she replied just as haughtily.

"I stand corrected, Gabriella, but how do you expect government to advance toward modernization without placing even more demands on the poor? It has to be done. Economically, one generation needs to prepare the road for the future—to sacrifice. We are at this crossroad, aren't we?" he questioned, surprised by her analytical skills but baffled that he would even ask a political question to a woman. She was no George Sand. Nevertheless, he was curious and furthermore he wanted to keep her on his bed. He listened politely.

"Well, naturally my American background affects my thinking and response to the European dilemma, and I will give you that we are a youthful country with lots of resources besides . . . the moral strength of our citizens "

She was always sheepish about the Southern flaw, he noticed. He wondered how her Southern brothers and sisters felt about this 'resource'—no need to ask, he knew. He let her continue.

"I always felt it was much easier to start on a blank page, rather than to try to use old material to affect a change or to integrate a new policy. America has a very short history. It is easier to implement changes, I'll grant you that. In Europe you have culture, classes, long held traditional views, and old standing jealousies and rivalry between countries; it certainly adds to the complexity of your problems. That is not to say that we Americans are conflict-less; our Civil War certainly showed our divergences and we paid dearly for it, but, then again, the separation between Church and State was the wisest policy implemented." So as to make her point, she placed her cup on the nightstand and moved closer to him.

He could feel his manhood swelling under the comforter as she spoke passionately. He sat up and pulled up the blankets to cover his backside and to bring her closer to him. She fell forward in his arms.

In one smooth motion, he placed one hand on the back of her neck while the other applied pressure to bring her body toward him, closer to his face. Stunned momentarily, she did not respond. Sensations traveled all over her body as he pulled her closer to him and gently brushed her temples with kisses. His warm breath searched for her lips. With a sharp push backward, she jumped sideways away from the bed and gasped.

"Oh, my God, what have I done? No, no, you don't understand. I was wrong to sit on your bed. My cousin and I . . . we sit and discuss world politics all night. I'm sorry I gave you the wrong impression."

He let her go, angry with himself. He had not been with a woman for quite a long time. That was it, he thought . . . but Gabriella was but a child.

"Let's forget about this moment, Gabriella. I was wrong and I am sorry." He asked her to turn around as he got up.

She quickly ran back to her cot, pulled down the mariner's cap over her forehead, and for countenance she looked out from the porthole and stared. Minutes later, he returned to his desk with his coffee cup, he finished his coffee, replaced it on his desk and marched out.

Later that morning, Cunnan came in with her breakfast. She was so upset she could not eat.

"I see that you have learned how to brew coffee. I know that the Captain will be most appreciative."

"I love coffee as well," she said shakily.

"Good I'll have the cook prepare a full sack so that you can enjoy it during the day. She could have hugged him except that after what had occurred earlier this morning, she wouldn't dare. Instead she offered him a cup, which he gladly accepted.

"Sugar?" he asked

"Yes, of course, I *own* a sugar plantation on the river," she smiled.

"Sorry, mistress, no flogging." Cunnan tested.

"You damned Irish, your retorts are worst than the Yankee's," she snapped back.

Jean-Louis chose this moment to re-enter his cabin to retrieve some materials.

"Thank heavens you are not entering the convent," he teased. "That coarse reflexion would have gotten you on bread and water for a month."

She smiled sheepishly. She needed to stand tough for a few more weeks. He had all but forgotten the incident. She would, as well. At sea, different rules applied and she was not going to be difficult.

"I was telling Cunnan, Captain, that all the workers on my plantation had been given freedom papers long before the amendment was signed by Mr. Lincoln and they earned good wages as well, Captain. I know, I do my own bookkeeping and pay for all medical bills. If Congress looked at my plantation, Reconstruction might work, you know."

"Yes …" He replied absently, grasping a cup, filling it with coffee while he added a couple jigs of liquor in it. He ambled to his desk.

"Should I continue, or am I annoying?" she asked with a questioning gaze.

"Go on," he smiled.

"As I was saying, I do not know how the South will take care of its new citizens. It is worse now for the Freedmen especially since the Federal troops will not stay forever. Hate groups might be on the rise as the economy flattens.

"It had started to flatten even before the Civil War, Gabriella." Cunnan remarked.

"True. It is much worse now, obviously. In the South, many of the large plantations are folding up from bad management and lack of consideration for the help."

Jean-Louis looked up from his desk, listening to her comments, surprised at the assertive observations. Gone was the ingénue who had seemed so confused when he had tried to kiss her, she was more man-like than he had ever expected her to be and, furthermore, she made sense.

"Well, Mademoiselle I'll talk to President Johnson to see if you could be his running partner in the next election." He spoke ironically, as he retrieved his male superiority. "Your analysis of the Reconstruction, however, is quite succinct," he scoffed with a wink.

Straightening, Gabriella shot him a glance replete with disdain. It surprised him.

"Your disparaging statements, Captain, are not well taken, it may not be such a bad idea to have women running for political office to soften the male ego. After all, we are accustomed to negotiate, for we have to beg for everything we get. Yes, women in politics, that's what the world needs—that is if we ever get the right to vote." She snapped with blazing eyes.

He glared.

Suddenly, self-preservation piqued her spirit and she shot in his direction a warm, beautiful, sensuous smile.

"I'll have to soften my words lest I want to be tossed at sea, such is the fate of burdensome, wily, lowly females."

He chuckled.

"I'm happy we've seen this side of you, Cunnan and I will be expecting a good challenge when we return tonight and take your plantation away from you in a game of poker. Could we play the part of two Southern gentlemen intent on your wealth?" he said as he prepared to walk out the door.

"Good day, gentlemen." She waved them goodbye and returned back to the one music book spared in the rampage. She'd noticed his well-stocked library, surely he would not mind sharing some of his titles.

Most of the day she waited anxiously for them to return. Perhaps they might ask her to play a game of poker, she looked forward to the game. As it was, Cunnan returned late. He looked fatigued. The seas were rough and the Captain did not want to leave the deck.

There had been a couple of fights at the midday food break and it had been hard on Cunnan. One of the mariners that he liked enormously had been banished to the brig. The captain as usual in these instances, had not been willing to hear either side, both guys had been thrown in the same cell for three days. As Cunnan solicited a less severe punishment for the one mariner, the Captain finally told Cunnan that his decision was irrevocable and asked him to leave the cabin.

The Captain was inflexible and not well liked. She had deciphered that much. Some unflattering comments filtered through the door. She was happy he liked her and she'd make sure of that, short of having sex with him. What a terrifying creature he was when angered, she posed.

Gabriella, who had already placed the cards on the table, slowly backed away in her little corner toward her cot. The less noise she made, the better off she'd be, and maybe he'd forget she was even there.

"Have you eaten, Gabriella?" he asked in the same loud imperturbable voice.

"Yes, I have, thank you."

He looked up at her. "Are you afraid?" he continued.

"Well, no—well, yes... The last time I heard you speaking like that, I was in the trunk praying that the Captain would spare my life. You had begun to speak of throwing people overboard and starving the Captain and commanding officer of the pirate ship. I was petrified and I'm petrified now. I'll let you cool down if you don't mind, I'll stay quietly here. Although, if you want my advice on what I have just heard, I'd side with ..."

"Hush. I don't want your advice. No changes will be made."

"You. I'd side with you on that issue," she twirled herself in a blanket, covered her small body with the eiderdown, and turned her back to him.

He ate his meal alone, reading the maps, but glanced toward her sometimes. He hated to admit it, but he kind of liked having her around. She was entertaining. He could see her trembling under the blankets.

"Are you cold, Gabriella?"

"Freezing," came the fast reply, as she longed for more blankets.

"You are too close to the wall. Come here, you will catch pneumonia."

"Where do you want me to come?"

"Climb in my bed"

"In your bed? Not after this morning I don't think so, I'm truly fine here, maybe... if you have a few extra blankets."

"You said it yourself, Gabriella, I could be your father. Come here, all bundled up. I will not try to kiss you, if that is what you are afraid of. Besides I have to work late into the night."

"No, really thank you."

He got up from his chair, came to her cot, picked her up and placed her, blankets and all, on his bed.

Angering the giant now would not have been very reasonable. She rolled toward the far end of the bed, looking for an excuse to return to her cot, and then she noticed that his back was turned as he resumed his reading. It was getting nice and toasty in there; she would roll off when he decided to turn in. She was a light sleeper. She turned off her anxiety button and quickly fell sound asleep.

The Captain climbed in his bed late that night. He was very much aware of who he had next to him, remembering the act itself, he thought of gently taking her. She had not fought him much this morning. The thought disturbed him again. He rolled to the other side of the bed. Eighteen more days, he counted.

Gabriella found herself lying next to him the following morning. Good God. She bolted up and swiftly scampered to her little cot. Thank goodness the sun was rising. She prepared the coffee and stretched silently.

Never again, she chastised herself. The incident was way too close for comfort. *Come to your senses, Gabriella*, she scolded. This is a man who will not easily take no for an answer. You are not dealing with the young New Orleans society courtiers. Don't push your luck. She seared at the thought of agreeing to sleep in his bed last night. What a fool she was. Thank God nothing had happened.

All her agitation had not been lost on the Captain.

Catching her body moving so gracefully, he rested quietly, watching.

"You are very flexible, Gabriella." He observed in a low throaty, disconcerting voice.

Speechless at first, she turned to him. She did not acknowledge his comments and promptly retrieved her fast retort.

"Good morning, Captain." She tried to appear calm, cool, and collected and to display some zone of comfort in her otherwise frightened and apprehensive demeanor. She forced a monologue.

"To audition well, all art forms are involved and used in opéra. It is imperative to have some ballet training. Acting, ballet, singing, and one's background can bring passion and reverence to the lyrics. Also the knowledge of history and of the cultural data of the time and the setting displayed on stage, all these aspects are most important to wring the gut out of an audience. Naturally, working the voice is the utmost duty of a soprano, but to set your mind at ease, Captain, for the next few weeks, I'll keep it to a murmur," she continued.

He nodded silently.

"Actually, I'm very diligent—a perfectionist in my trade. I need to do everything to perfection, with passion and perfect timing. In my life, both of these characteristics have served me well, Captain. A little rest will do me well if I learn to keep quiet. I have the strange feeling that it might please you, as well."

He smiled at her.

"You do not annoy me, Gabriella. As a matter of fact, you're an interesting young woman," he candidly stated. She had a cute, vulnerable girlish voice that she could switch on quickly to the grave, intimidating sound of an iron woman. He had not met too many in this world. The ones he had met with this specific trait were manlike; he wouldn't have touched them if they had been the last women on earth. Gabriella however was appealing, half child, full woman, quite a powerful combination.

"Did you sleep well?" he asked.

"*Admirablement, merci*," she replied in French with that adorable accent. "With your permission, I'll use it this afternoon for my nap—a full bed all to myself? It's been a while since I've enjoyed that particular comfort." She pursed her lips into a sensual pout.

He shot her a knowing look.

"I could make it even more comfortable, mademoiselle, if you let me, but no matter how much I like you, giving up my bed is too much to ask," he bit his lips. "Feel free, however, to stretch all you want, especially in my direction."

She flirted and he had caught her at the game. This man certainly was not the sort of dandy she'd flirt with casually in the salons in New Orleans. They would always remain courteous and polite, liking the game as much as she did. Her roommate did not play. He acted decisively. Better not entice him in anything she was not ready to handle. Mon Dieu, had he not tried to kiss her just three days after the incident? It had to stop now. She played with fire. He responded to her sensually and quite directly. She quickly changed the subject and while he was still in a good mood, she asked for another favor, this one out in the open.

"Captain, it's a bit lonely down here and I know I'm talking your ears off, making absolutely rude demands on you, can I walk up to the bridge?"

"No." The curt answer was given without a thought.

"Turn your head, Gabriella," he commanded.

She turned toward the porthole. He got up, put on his clothes, grabbed the coffee, and was gone. She had angered him. She would return to her little cot tonight and stay there. Meanwhile, she'd relax today, peruse through his well-stocked library … write perhaps. It was only 8:00 a.m. She had a full day ahead of her.

Chapter Five

Boredom set in. The last two days had been calm. She had spoken to the Captain a few times at mealtime and had nearly frozen the night before. She would have to remember to ask for more covering lest she'd wake up as a stalagmite.

She walked to the porthole and lifted herself onto the steel frame of the window to see if other vessels or schools of fishes were in sight. Most of her books had been tossed out to sea upon the attack and the only two dresses remaining were a bit too risqué to wear on the ship. Consequently, she had kept her mariner's outfit and the little beret came in handy to hold her heavy mane. She would ask for another outfit as well. He could not refuse her if he had extras.

Tired of reading and doing vocal exercises that obviously were pointless as she was unable to reach the hight notes required to truly work her voice, she took a vacation from her diligent daily routine. Done correctly, her musical routine would enlighten the mariners that a woman lived in the Captain's cabin. Some probably already knew that. Extra food was being brought in daily, but the Captain and Cunnan mentioned not a word, the least said the better. She would have loved to climb up on deck. Oh well, beggars couldn't be choosy. The alternative was still horrific to her every time she considered it. Therefore, at this point she was not much better than a beggar. Although her clothes and books had been thrown overboard, she'd been smart enough to place her money in her bosom under the heavy binding that she still wore.

Cunnan and the Captain had eaten with her last night and played cards for an hour. It had been a lot of fun and this time she had been quiet. Although millions of questions popped in her mind, she did not want to be thought of as a blabbermouth. She had accomplished that much quite well the first few days after the take over.

Perched on the porthole, she watched with amazement a school of porpoises frolicking right outside the window. These incredible mammals were performing for her as if they knew that she was bored.

They'd follow the ship for two straight days now. They sense my loneliness and they are bound on my entertainment, she grinned.

"Hello, Gabriella." the Captain entered the room. Oblivious, he searched for his midday meal that had been left in front of his door. He picked it up and he glanced toward her.

Gabriella had grabbed one of the chairs and had placed it on top of the cot so as to reach the porthole. Still too short to reach a comfortable stand and good view, she stood on her tiptoes while she held on to the oval steel cover that surrounded it. Her wide mariner's pants were rolled up to her knees. He discovered a pair of beautifully formed calves and very slim and feminine ankles. It was hard to tell if the rest of her was as feminine engulfed in that huge suit. He'd ask Cunnan to obtain a smaller outfit. He stood up behind his desk, his two hands placed firmly on the leather surface as he admired the sight at hand.

"Hello," she glanced back and placed a finger over her mouth. "I've observed a school of dolphins all morning. One seems to have noticed me," she whispered as she turned her pretty little head toward him.

A long brown wavy curl escaped from her beret. For the last few days, she had kept her hair in a tight knot, but today as she woke up her scalp was enflamed. She detached the pins from her hair and placed the heavy mane of mahogany curls loose under the cap.

While he marched to the porthole, intent on finding out what she was so entranced about he wondered how long her hair truly was? He stood behind her and placed his two arms on either side of her, as he flippantly leaned on his forearms and lowered his head close to hers to stare down at the ocean.

Gabriella froze. His presence on either side of her frazzled her. His virile scent and his warm breath on her cheeks, immobilized her while hot sensations engulfed her body. Quickly she moved sideways to breathe. Unfortunately the chair tilted to the right on the mattress' unsteady surface. She lost her balance hitting his right bicep. By a miracle solely due to his quick reflexes, she landed in his arms instead of on the cabin's wooden floor. He held on to her waist so as to stabilize her and instead of an immediate release, he held on to her a while longer. He gently pressed her to him along his hard length and kept her there for what appeared to be an eternity. Without warning he quickly pushed her back and planted her on the floor.

"I'm sorry, Gabriella," he murmured apologetic.

"I'm not," she heard herself respond.

Stunned at first, and then apparently amused, he smiled that long, sensuous smile that had been the demise of so many. Slowly, he walked back to the desk, sat down, and started eating. The De Pleyssis' touch was still powerful, he thought amused.

Stunned at her inappropriate response, Gabriella would have loved for the sea to part and engulf her forever. Her face burned and she stood where he had left her, her hands dangling by her side like a schoolgirl.

Amiably the Captain invited her to sit with him to have a déjeuner—to convey an atmosphere of normalcy, she presumed.

Spineless, she shouted inwardly, but she obeyed, thanked him, and started eating. Her mind was blank and she could not think of one subject to make conversation.

He realized it and politely asked if she was comfortable.

"Well—yes—indeed—you know the climate is quite warm and humid in Louisiana. I know I will have to get accustomed to the colder, dryer days, but it would be greatly appreciated if I could have a few extra blankets . . . and can I also borrow some of the books in your library?"

"Very well, mademoiselle, I'll ask Cunnan. Meanwhile, use whatever is on my bed." He stood up and walked to the cabinet where many classics were placed in order that they had been written. She followed closely behind and chose one by Montesquieu. Montesquieu had done a wonderful job at delineating years earlier the basic tenets of the American Constitution. It would feed conversation, she thought quickly.

He smiled at her as she returned with the book she had chosen. He closed the bookcase and locked it up again. Then he turned on his heels and walked toward the door.

"I'll make sure you'll have some warm blankets tonight."

"Thank you," she responded. Terribly embarrassed about her response, she found it difficult time to concentrate on her reading. She read the same line over and over again. She would tell him tonight that her response was very unlike her; she did not know what had happened. With everything that had occurred lately she probably felt a needed human touch. No, absolutely not, this was ridiculous. He would try something else soon. Was she crazed—a man and a woman in the same room with living arrangements such as theirs? This was an invitation for trouble.

The remaining of the afternoon she tried to no avail to concoct a response that would be appropriate and would absolve her lack of control. Fortunately he did not show up for dinner. Well, maybe tomorrow, the morning would bring fresh thoughts. Cunnan brought in four blankets. She'd sleep well tonight. After turning on the light and tossing and turning, she finally fell asleep.

The Captain did not enter the room until past midnight.

He looked toward her cot. The blankets covered her completely except for her cap and face. He walked over and stared down at her pretty profile. It was cold in that corner and the freezing air seeped through the steel of the ship. The cot was close to the floor. Without a bit of guilt, he picked her up, blankets and all, and placed her on his bed. She woke up immediately wide-awake.

"No!" she shouted.

"No, what?" he questioned.

"No, I will not sleep with you." she exclaimed loudly. □

"I had no intention of forcing myself on you," he responded sarcastically. "Gabriella, what were you thinking?" He laughed out loud reproachfully. "It's much warmer here. You will sleep better without catching pneumonia. We do not have a doctor on board. Better to keep you healthy. Now go back to sleep, I have to rest for a few hours myself."

Bolting out of his bed, while she held on to all of her blankets, she returned stubbornly to her little cot. It was much colder, granted, but she suddenly felt that it was the best little arrangement she had ever had.

"Suit yourself, mademoiselle, however, it is too cold over there." He walked over one more time and pulled the cot close to his bed on the opposite side of his desk. "Like it or not, you'll sleep here from now on."

She did not reply and lie down quietly. She pretended to enter a relaxed state. That could not have been further from the truth. All twisted in knots, she thought of millions of awful scenarios. What if he decided to remove his clothes by the bed? She had to turn over and face the desk. She heard him get into bed. He had the politeness to enter from the other side. She relaxed a bit. Ouf. Oh, no, Mon Dieu, now he had turned off the light. The past few days she had had the luxury to fall asleep before him, now the darkness terrorized her. She could not sleep without the light on.

"Captain, would it be too much to ask to leave the light on until I fall asleep?" she asked with sugar cubes in her breath.

"Yes," came the curt response.

"Please, I cannot sleep with . . . " She persisted with the sweetest of voice.

"No," he replied in the low, guttural sound that he usually displayed when he was annoyed.

His voice had a finality that she did not want to question further. She rested on the mattress; her eyes wide open, praying that some unexpected turn of weather would require his presence on the bridge. Her wish did not come to pass.

He woke up at four in the morning, got dressed, and left the room. She had not slept a wink. Relieved, she quietly looked at the closed door and just as quickly got up and turned on the light. Then, too exhausted to stress about everything that was going wrong in her life, she fell asleep thinking that twenty more days were not the end of the world. She could have been dead, killed, raped or whatever. Her spirit unwound, her body yielded, and she fell sound asleep.

A few minutes after she returned back to her cot, the Captain quietly open the door. He was right, he pondered. She had turned on the light as soon as the door slammed shut and now the little annoying angel appeared to be resting comfortably.

Chapter Six

Gabriella was having dinner with Cunnan who expanded a little more on his experiences and the relationship he had with Captain De Pleyssis.

Apparently, Jean-Marc-Louis De Pleyssis senior and Cunnan had been great friends. They had fought together in two wars and both had returned to their countries and married the love of their youth, an oddity in theses times of arranged marriages. Both had been widowed while still in the heat of passion. When Jean-Marc-Louis had lost his beloved wife, Cunnan had returned to France. Their one and only fall out had always been over the upbringing of the young Captain, an only child who had lost his mother at birth. Jean-Marc-Louis had been a strict disciplinarian and years later he had re-married. His new bride, however, ignored the child.

"A son or a daughter would have been the love of my life after the death of my wife," he candidly shared with Gabriella. "I never understood the peculiarity of the situation."

"Was the second marriage passionate?" Gabriella inquired curiously. Society gossips in New Orleans always said that her own father had fallen madly in love with his new wife and by all accounts was an exemplary father to his new brood.

"No," came the curt reply. "The lovely Armande De Fronteleau married the Duke for his titles and vast estates, but frankly," Cunnan said "the relationship had been mutual. Armande pleased the Duke. She was pretty, witty, and she adorned his halls nicely. His one true love had been the Captain's mother and no one, not even his son, could lessen the pain that he suffered until his untimely death."

"At one point," Cunnan proceeded, "many in the old man's entourage thought that he would kill himself, but his great sense of responsibility to country and family probably saved his life. However, his only son, who should have been an ode to that great love, was instead a constant reminder of his loss. Jean-Louis-Pierre is the spitting image of his mother. So instead of showering the child with all the love in the world, he distanced himself from him, and when they were together, Jean-Louis-Pierre would be held accountable for perfection in everything his father got him involved in."

"What about his stepmother, was she heartless as well?" Gabriella questioned.

"His stepmother could not have cared less. The more time the old man spent disciplining the child, the less time was spent on her shortcomings. Armande loved life, Parisian life, and all the men that paraded in her boudoir. Jean-Marc was as perverse as she was when it came to other women. They managed an easy relationship—they both did as they pleased. That's the European nineteenth century tradition you will be faced with, my dear Gabriella; keep your chin up and control your heart." Cunnan said in a fatherly voice.

Gabriella nodded, well aware that her own Southern culture did not differ much from its European cousin.

"How did you come to travel with the Captain, Cunnan?" she questioned. She enjoyed his company and did not want him to leave.

"I never remarried and my wife and I were childless. Therefore, after her passing, I continued sailing the world and I searched the China Sea for exciting challenges. Years later while I visited a friend in London, I received a note from Jean-Louis-Pierre who had been studying in England, he wrote to acknowledge his father's death. Jean-Marc-Louis had died in a duel after an altercation with a neighboring Count over the land that divided the families' castles in his native Loire. Jean-Louis-Pierre had not expanded on the full situation at the time, but it appeared that a bit of mystery surrounded the event. Jean-Louis-Pierre had not reacted much to his father's death; frankly, he did not care. He had not spoken to his father in years and although he was now the sole inheritor of his father's vast fortune that expanded over two continents, he handled the day-to-day business from afar. Less than a year later, I received a letter from the young man asking me if I wanted to sail round the world with him in search of adventures. These were his exact words." Cunnan smiled recalling the event. "I did not hesitate. I always loved the lad, and in essence he is the son that I never had. Jean-Louis-Pierre's rambunctiousness comes from a highly independent soul."

"He was alone a good part of his adolescence. It promoted independence and strength of spirit," she concluded, well aware of her own situation. Her aversion to the Captain began to lessen.

"The Captain always follows the rules of society that are demanded of him, but he was, and still is, quite good at extricating himself from a lot of social demands. He spends a good deal of his time outside of France, and small increments of business-oriented ventures in Paris. The relationship has worked very well for the past eight years and then more recently we were allowed to help in the Civil War in your country."

"I understand his steely demeanor a bit better now that you shared part of his history with me. Thank you, Cunnan," Gabriella replied.

She and Cunnan dined together often now. He brought her meals and the past three days he had dined with her. She loved the visits. He was an interesting man and she had opened up to him as well. She had an ally on this ship. After the rude encounter with the Captain, she had seen him only once—late at night. He must have turned off the light and she had woken up suddenly. As she rolled in his direction, she had caught an eyeful—he dropped his pants, of all things. She'd rolled toward the paneled wall and struggled for breath. He must have heard her gasp, for he laughed.

What a rude beast, she'd thought to herself. She felt no pity for him. She had been raised quite alone as well, and yet she still respected the rules of society. He turned off the lights and he rolled into bed. She was not going to beg again.

Good riddance, she thought when he was called out in the middle of the night. That same afternoon she heard him shout at the top of his lungs at a poor sailor who apparently had misplaced his favorite boots that were to be shined to a mirror-like condition everyday. He opened the door, and then slammed it shut. The bang of the door resonated so loudly that she was certain it would come off its hinges.

She sat further back in his large leather chair hoping that she would not bring any attention to herself. Bad luck struck. She had borrowed the maps on his desk without asking his permission. At first, she hoped that he would not notice—no such luck. She watched him angrily search for something that was not in its proper place.

Bravely, she rolled out of her chair, ready to face the music, no need to exasperate his highness.

"Captain, my apologies," she whispered. "I borrowed the maps; I just wanted to get my bearings." He looked at her, no rather through her as if he would momentarily leap over his desk and toss her out of his room.

"I'm sorry," she repeated, "had I known you were so possessive about your things, I would never have allowed this faux pas." She tried to humor him with a half smile. She had been told her smile warmed the heart. She certainly hoped it would melt his a bit right this minute.

He stared at the large expressive emerald green eyes gazing at him. His roommate really had a beautiful face he thought, and a *sang-froid*, composure, that was admirable. At any other time but on his ship he probably would have pulled her to him and kissed that smile off her face. Now, however she stood next to him almost touching him with her non-existent breasts, defiant, poking fun at his character—his possessiveness. Stunned by her impertinence, he smiled at first and started laughing—a clear guttural, manly laugh.

The constant hardness that seemed to delineate his features softened. He flashed pearly white teeth that contrasted with his bronzed and piercing blue eyes.

He was intimidating her, he thought.

On the contrary Gabriella was not at all intimidated, she was mesmerized by the discovery that the Captain with his dark hair and bushy black beard looked young, much younger than she had previously thought. Perhaps he was in his early thirty's, but then she caught him off balance.

"You should laugh more often, Captain; you appear more compassionate, incredibly attractive as well, indeed." She spoke sensuously.

Piqued by what he had thought was intimidation and fear, he retorted harshly.

"I laugh plenty when the situation is right, Gabriella. I don't find any of your quips too amusing, although your arrogance is laughable.

Give me back my maps and do not touch my things again," he glowered.

His arrogance and his lack of even the most basic polish shocked her. She could not stomach his impertinence. She took one step backward so as to get a better look at his face.

"My arrogance?" she said snidely. "Your impertinence is quite uncanny, Captain. I do recognize that it must be terribly inconvenient for you, not to have your own privacy—particularly with a woman in your quarters." But then she recalled his lack of shame and his cruel laughter at her prudish reaction when he undressed the night before. "Although I don't see you trying hard to be private," she slammed back.

Her reference gave him fodder to mortify her even more.

"I didn't know you were looking, ma chère," he icily remarked.

Ignoring his crass comment, she continued her tirade.

"It was your decision to keep me here with you, so that I would not cause trouble. A little civility between us would make my passing a bit more enjoyable. My only sin was trying to be friendly, to show you my gratefulness and appreciation. But now," she paused for too short a time, "I really don't like you. Tell me, Captain, what do you expect me to do all day? I love my music, but some of your books were of interest to me, that's all. A small change of pace, I …"

He was livid. How dare she speak to him in that tone of voice? His glare spoke volume.

"Frankly, Gabriella," he clipped. "I don't care whether or not your passage is pleasant or horrific. If it were not for my crew and my vigilance, you would have been fish food last week. Now return to your cot and kindly stay away from me when I come in. Don't ever think of touching my things again until you are off my vessel. Understood?"

His tone was menacing by now and she compliantly turned away from him, picked up her diary and pen and returned not to her cot but instead came to sit in his large overstuffed leather chair.

He stared at her now, incredulous, disbelieving her bravado.

She stared back. Knowing he would not relent, she turned her eyes away as if he had suddenly become obsolete.

He grabbed the maps she had returned to his desk and he turned once more to take her in his sight. He walked out with a smirk on his face.

No grown men would dare stand up to him when he was enraged. The impertinent little brat had done a pretty good job. He liked her.

That same night, the Captain returned while Cunnan and Gabriella were having dinner. She pretended not to see him although she noticed from the corner of her eyes that he was holding on to something bulky. Unable to withstand her curiosity she looked and recognized the object—a phonograph with records on top of it all. All her madness melted, she ran to him, watched him deposit the musical box on the side table and then she remembered what he had told her earlier. Not taking the chance of fueling his anger when he held such a treasure in his possession, she stood a few feet behind him.

"Captain, can I see it? Does it work? Will you please, oh please, play it for me?" She almost begged.

"It's yours, Gabriella. Decipher its usage and don't play it when I'm asleep." He smiled, looked down at her pleased, and ambled to the side bar by the door.

Nonchalantly, he walked back to the table, sat, and poured himself a brandy.

Philippe had given her nice presents, but never had a stranger buy anything other than flowers and candy for her. This was the very best of all—ever.

Presumably that was his way of saying sorry, someone had told her long ago that powerful men never apologized. Instead, they showed their repentance with pleasant actions that showed they cared. The pretentious Duke De Pleyssis had done just that.

Before he could change his mind, she had brought down the big box onto the floor to examine it and read the *mode indicatif,* set up directions. Sitting Indian style, she got it to work quite quickly the Captain and Cunnan acknowledged, and she lowered the volume as much as possible, so as to not annoy the Captain. Her right ear was placed on the phonograph where the sound piped through, and the two men watched and admired her pretty profile. Totally entranced, the Emperor of France could have entered in the room, she would not have noticed. Her power of concentration was pretty intense, the Captain thought.

For close to a year now, she had wanted a phonograph. The nuns at the convent of the Ursulines in the Vieux Carré in New Orleans had received one. It had been sent to them directly from the Vatican. She had asked and paid to receive one imported from Italy as well, but it had not arrived with the ship.

The men watched her. Part of her curly hair had fallen out of the tight bun that seemed to be glued to her head. Now she tried in vain to fit it all back under the cap. That strand reached down to the middle of her back. The Captain wanted to know at this moment what she looked like without the stupid bun. *Bon, eh bien,* he spent way too much time thinking about this girl. He had to run a ship but it was a pleasant diversion, he admitted somewhat reluctantly.

"Gabriella, will you bring me the two books on the floor directly across from you?" he ordered at first and quickly shot her a kindly smile, "please?" he added.

Rapidly she twisted and leaned forward from her waist with her two hands pushing off the floor. She looked up at him sarcastically.

"I'm not allowed, remember? All of your things are off limit to me, Captain."

He smiled again. When he was nice to her, the Captain had a very expressive, manly face.

"Most obedient, I like that in a woman." He got up, and walked to her. He hovered over her amused.

"You have no fear, do you?"

"Fear of you? No, not really, I was petrified of the pirates and your first reaction to me when you ordered me out of the trunk. But since then, you've been beyond rude to me, but not cruel. All of your shouts are more posture, I hope, and that does not frighten me, either. I'm quite accustomed to it as well."

He looked at her questioningly. It gave her confidence to explain.

"René Du Bois, our overseer would ramble on with fearsome shouts to the workers on the plantation, but he would always be the first one to bring a warm bowl of soup or mutton cutlet to the workers and their family members when someone was ill or indisposed. So shouts do not cause me any anxieties. You can shout all you want, Captain as long as it is not directed at me. You can be certain, I very much appreciate being alive and on my way to Paris. Whatever I do that annoys you is not done consciously to make your life miserable, so just tell me when I irritate you—nicely—and I'll promptly amend my pestering ways." She smiled.

Well he had been told with sugar to put up and shut up. All five feet of her showed him her assertiveness.

"As a matter of fact," she continued, "you have been quite generous—with my life, good God. You let me share your room, your food and now this incredible gift. The best I have ever received."

He looked and raised his eyebrows as if not quite believing her.

"No, really Captain, I don't recall getting gifts. Maybe when I was small, I don't remember."

"What about your parents, Christmas, your birthdays?" he asked to help her remember.

"No, no, I'm not complaining. I get what I need. I buy what I want for myself, but you see my mom was always a very busy woman at the plantation and she was gone a lot and then in her later life, she was extremely involved with the anti-slavery movement. My servants did not have any money to spare although they both gave me great love and magnificent memories and instill great values and integrity in my personality. Priceless gifts these were," she nodded with a gentle smile. "With Philippe, we give ourselves small presents at Christmas, but it's mostly books or outings, things of that nature, nothing like that." She looked lovingly toward the phonograph. "No, really it's the first and most wonderful present I have ever received. Thank you," she quickly beamed as she reached over to grab the books he had asked for. Looking up, she handed over the pile.

He thanked her for lack of a better response.

"And let it be known, noticed, and certified that you, Captain, asked me to touch your things." She shot him a sideways smile while she held on to his gaze.

At this moment he felt downright horrible. And he thought he had had a severe childhood? She was a young girl, for God's sake. Not a present ever. He continued, wanting to know more. "What about your father?"

She was quite direct when it came to him and made no excuse.

"Well, he does not like me, never has. He has another family in New Orleans. But from what I hear, he is quite decent with them. Not a very nice man, Captain. I'd rather know a mean man than a coward! Frankly, I'd rather not lower myself nor waste my breath on my father," she finished with a tone that would not allow any more questions on the subject.

He noticed a somber shadow overcast her pretty features; very much like a rain cloud that forms out of nowhere, then a heavy silence projected a sense of doom. He expected a downpour, but before he could react, her pretty smile reappeared.

"So, thank you, Captain, thank you very, very much. It's extraordinary, I love music, and I'll cherish it for many years to come. In less than a week you saved my life, and now my first gift ever, one that even I couldn't have wished for. Two momentous events in my life."

Once again, he felt a bit sheepish when he remembered what he had spent on some of his paramours. Gabriella was happy with a bauble that he had been given. The best gift ever, she had said. He smiled back at her. She was really sweet and awfully adorable to look at.

She sat in a ballerina's split on the floor, her legs appear long and slim through the stretched mariner's pants, although she lacked a woman's charm on top, she was a cute girl, he thought, fearless, too. She had not budged when he had come in raging mad this morning. What a combination, she was mysterious and yet very candid, even a bit too candid at times—not mincing her words. He had experienced first-hand her curt directness. By all accounts her life must not have been too easy, either—the more power to her. Never a present from anyone, he incredulously thought. No one had seen that bright-eyed happiness peer through when he had given her the phonograph. He pledged he'd try to be more tolerant from now on. □

"You are very sweet, Gaby," he told her.

"My name is Gabriella, I have no surname," she replied, with a great big smile.

"Good, now you have one, another momentous event in your young life. Never two without three, ma chère, as you so aptly recalled the French phrases."

"Gaby," she repeated aloud, "it sounds quite French. Very well, every one appears to have a surname in France, isn't that so, Captain? I like it. I'll keep it." She beamed.

He lapsed into silence and return to the table to finish his meal.

"Have a good night, Gaby," he said before leaving the room to regain the bridge.

He did not return until late that night and she was happy to have had dinner with Cunnan. He played a mean game of chess and laughed easily. A big teddy bear, she thought with mostly red hair, a heavy red beard with large strands of white hair sprouted from his temples. The Captain appeared to respect him greatly and she felt she could trust him as well—a good accomplice. He had told her that the Captain would stay away tonight as well. Their only stop would be in the Canary Islands—cargo check, she had been told.

Gaby was surprised how happy she was, albeit she was kept in a state room most of the day. It could have been a disaster had the Captain not shown up during the attack. Thank God, she was alive. He might change his mind later during the crossing and let her wander out on the bridge, but she was not too sure she felt secure walking on deck. These men may not be accustomed to passengers, especially a woman. No, she was just fine down here. In any event, the Captain might be willing to open the door that was concealed and bolted shut behind heavy velvet burgundy drapes. It gave way to a small deck. Well, they were finally getting along. She would make her demands later during the week.

She walked over behind his desk. He had an incredible library with priceless volumes of past and present great writers. She decided to pick one of his books. He would not know the difference if she picked one of his novels from the top rack. She proceeded to pull the ladder to the en-walled bookcase and picked Diderot, <u>the Human</u> <u>Encyclopédie.</u>

As luck would have it, the Captain walked in and caught her red-handed borrowing 'his possessions'. This time there were no shouts, instead he just looked at her and within seconds she climbed back up the ladder and tried to replace the book in its proper place.

"Not there," he corrected. Surprised by the loudness of his voice, the book fell from her hands and she was forced to step back down to pick up the stupid thing that landed at the bottom of his long legs. He did not budge to pick it up, forcing her to kneel down, his glare following her every move. She lowered herself down to the floor, picked up the book and replaced it back on the shelves angry with herself. She shot him a deadly stare.

What was wrong with this crazed man? Was he mentally challenged? One moment he gave her presents, the next, she was sure, he was angry that he had. She hated to share as well, but she had compassion. It was not out of being thrifty, just possessiveness. Consequently, if someone in her entourage wanted something that she had, she just would go out and purchase a new item for the person. But with the Captain, that was just plain mean-spirited. He loved the control he had over her and would take any chance that presented itself to remind her that she was on his ship and she had to abide to his will. Well, what could she do? She hoped that not all Frenchmen were that intransigent.

"I hope that you savored seeing me on bended knees. This forced curtsy will not be repeated, I assure you," she hurled, as venom spewed in her emerald eyes and she held his glare with animosity and anger. "What is it that pleases you so, Captain, about watching a young, assertive woman heel to your orders, or are you like that with every other female? I detect a bit of insecurity on your part when you are dealing with women of substance. A trait of fragility and frailty in your grand personality." She quickly stood up and was about to turn her back to him, when a strong hand clasped on her forearm and turned her willfully toward him. She noted disbelief in his eyes. For an instant, she could decipher a glance of admiration.

He waited a moment, silent, as he glared down at her. She stared back. Two great wills are trying to impose their victory on the other, he thought. Then he spoke, "Ask my permission if you want to peruse through my library," came the curt and explosive reply.

Better leave it at that, she thought, and she walked away toward the porthole. Maybe the school of dolphins she had been following might still be there.

He watched her for a while and took a seat behind his desk. He wished he had not been so abrasive with her. The little brat did not know her place. Just yesterday he had told her to leave everything as is. What part of 'do not touch my belongings' she did not understand?

He worked, he read, he ate for a long time, and then at one o'clock he left.

She did not engage in conversation. He would not return until late. Good riddance. She wished he could find another cabin to sleep in.

That was his cabin that he was sharing, she suddenly mulled over, amused. Well, never mind. Why couldn't he give her another cabin? Not all cabins were taken, she surmised. She would not disturb him, then. Instead, he took pleasure in making her life miserable. She would bring up the subject of another room tonight with Cunnan. 'Better be lonely than in bad company' always had been her motto. She would stick to it.

Once more he came back to the room late, seeing that she was twirling in her blankets, back in that miserable place close to the floor and the outside wall. He took pity upon her again. Although he did not look forward to sharing his bed again for more than one reason. He needed some sleep tonight. However, feeling selfish, he heard himself say, "Gaby, come here. You can share my bed. I'll work for a while longer. You will freeze over there."

She did not reply and pretended to be sound asleep.

"Do you hold grudges, too?" He spoke with a smile in his voice.

"I have no grudges to hold, I'm just thankful for your hospitality but indifferent toward you," she concluded.

He walked closer to her cot. She was shivering. He threw his heavy fur-lined leather jacket on top of her tiny, curled up body. Only her gorgeous face was peeking out from under the blankets. He felt warmth in his lower body. She was hard to resist. Suddenly angry with himself for wanting an insolent colonial, he brusquely turned and started to undress.

She heard him wash up. Would he try to seduce her? Had she gone too far? Did he mull over what punishment to inflict? With the great and mighty Captain De Pleyssis, no one knew what would set him off.

He said nothing. Instead he picked up the maps he had studied this morning, made a few adjustments on the parchment, turned off the light, and climbed in bed.

She turned in her little cot, forgetting her pride.

"Captain, can you please turn the lights on, just until I fall asleep. It will not take me long. I'm very tired."

Silence reigned in the room for what seemed to be an eternity. Then the great man pronounced himself. "Frankly, Gaby, I don't care if you shudder all night, just don't utter another sound." He murmured fury in his voice.

Subsequently, he rolled toward the wall and within minutes, she heard his heavy regular breathing. The king was asleep.

Gaby lay in her cot, petrified once more. A warm stream of tears rolled down her cheeks and she cried long and hard. Finally the intense rolling of the seas and her sad heart must have lulled her to sleep. She woke up early the following morning, freezing cold, but pleasantly so. She felt strong and refreshed.

Thank God, Blue Beard still slept in his toasty bed. She walked over past his desk and glanced at the maps. She could not help but notice the changes he had made on the parchment. It appeared that they were now going southward toward the Coast of Africa. Why? She walked closer to the desk and studied intently the new markings on the parchment. Entranced as she tried to decipher the new route, she felt his body heat. The master stood in front of his bed, glaring down at her. She jumped back and quickly dissuaded herself from any statement that would start the day on a negative note. She even apologized, not meaningfully, but apologized nevertheless for having had the audacity to peer over his maps.

"I experienced a leg cramp, just now," she cracked awkwardly. I was just holding on to your desk—for support. I did not touch—" Suddenly, an insurmountable anger flashed. She twisted back with wrath in her huge green eyes and she marched the length of the desk that separated them. She came close; the mariner's rough cloth she wore touched his loose tunic.

Surprised, he stood immobile, incredulous of the enduring drama.

"No, I was looking at *your* maps, I tried to decode how many more days I'd have to suffer incarceration in this prison cell!" she hollered.

"What?" he responded, "disbelieving?"

"You heard me. Your only goal is to intimidate me. What have I done to you? Well, you may have heard me cry last night, but don't feel too happy and proud of your accomplishment quite yet, I cry at the slightest disappointment."

"I have no reason to try to intimidate you, Gaby, you have done nothing to truly displease me, just a few inconsequential annoyances. I do not understand your anger towards me. In my circle of friends, I am courteous and usually liked by women," he responded, skeptical.

"Courteous . . . even liked by the women in your circle of friends? That's a joke. You must hang around Europeans from mentally challenged sanatoriums. If a person doesn't get slapped, it is considered a kindness!" She shouted back, ready to smack him.

Flabbergasted, he did not reply. Instead he stared at her beautiful face and admired her fiery character. Then he burst out laughing, a long, loud roaring laugh that melted a bit of her anger.

Now she felt downright ridiculous. She had let him get the best of her. She proceeded to back off and move away.

"Come back here." He reached for her arm while he forced her back toward his desk. He placed her small body in front of him and bent over her head to explain the changes to her.

"You noticed the changes, didn't you?" he asked knowingly.

"Why are we going toward Africa?" she asked not overly polite, but mindful of her manners.

His torso lightly leaned on her back; his warm breath on her neck truly annoyed her. She was responding to his closeness in a sordid physical fashion that, she hoped to God, he could not divine. If he did, he did not let on and continued his explanation. Gaby had not heard a single word of the lecture. Never had she felt so physical before in her whole life and God knows she had been the envy of many a men— young and old.

Unwilling to let him know the effect he had on her, she moved away and bowed down under his arm to escape his chemistry.

"Thank you," she said and walked to the water closet to wash and to flee his heady presence.

When she came out he was still there, this time with two cups of coffee he had obviously brewed himself. He offered her a cup.

"This is as close to a peace pipe as it is going to get. Are we friends once more?" he asked.

"I did not know that we were friends."

He laughed again that hearty, manly, cavernous laugh she'd liked a few days ago.

"Gaby, you are willful and abrasive. Here are the keys to the library. You have my permission to use it whenever you wish."

He proceeded to take her hand and to place the keys in her palm; he pressed her fingers shut over the metal piece so as to keep it from falling to the floor.

"I'll see you tonight. Have a good day, Jeanne d'Arc!" He trailed a last admiring glance toward her as he walked out the door.

Stunned, she glanced down at the key and unconsciously caressed the area where she still sensed the warmth of his touch.

Chapter Seven

The following day was dreary. The sky was dark and menacing and after lunch she decided to practice her voice and some acting. Might as well, he never showed up in the afternoon until quite late, therefore she could wash her outfit and unbind her breasts as well. His eiderdown was warm and very light. She picked it up and enveloped herself in it. What a wonderful feeling it would be to let her freshly washed hair down, and let her body breathe. These poor souls in China, with bounded, deformed feet, unable to walk anywhere, a sign of royalty and privilege she had read somewhere, too divine to walk on earth, these women were transported like human cargo. What was it in the male population that gave them the right to subdue those weaker than them? Because they could, she pondered. She walked to the hidden door behind the burgundy drapes and tried to open the lock to no avail. Either way, bright light sparkled in the cabin. She began her vocal exercises, humming her preferred arias, she let her creativity run freely. She reached for bottle of unopened brandy and begun singing Libiamo. She visualized herself on stage, dancing and gesticulating to the cadence. Her small willowy body, pretended to speak to her imaginary dancing partner and her expressive eyes flirted with the bottle. It was as this most inopportune moment that the Captain chose to cross the threshold.

Frozen in space, her arm extended forward, she tried to move quickly to explain her confusion at his sudden apparition, all to no avail. Disaster loomed. He stared at her, no, not at her, at her breasts peeking out from under the heavy wrap. His sweeping gaze progressed on over her arms and back to her breasts with a surprised smirk on his face. She lapsed into silence. As she tried to retrieve her stability she inadvertently stepped on the lengthy eiderdown that hung behind her like a train. All happen in a flash, first the bottle fell to the wooden planks, the glass shattered in millions of pieces, the brown liquid slowly sipped out onto the floor, Gabriella tripped furthermore, and for one propitious moment, she grasped on to the top of a bookcase and struggled for breath. This moment lasted for a few short minutes as disaster loomed once more—in the mirror she noticed that the coverlet slipped away, down her legs. She desperately pulled the eiderdown back over her shoulders in an unsuccessful attempt to cover her opulent breasts, which by now were showing their magnificence. She paced forward. Mischance had it; she forcefully stepped on large shards of glass and screamed in pain as she inadvertently released the grasp on her cover. The coverlet fell onto the floor. Stark naked, she bent forward to retrieve the blanket but the shards on the planks perforated the skin on the sole of her feet. Blood seeped out of the wound.

The Captain reacted quickly at the sight of blood. He gallantly grabbed the eiderdown, wrapped her in it, picked her up, and sat her on his bed. He rolled the coverlet back to her knee, and gently pulled out her ankle as he applied pressure on the cut with a rolled-up handkerchief. Anxiously, he paused for a long moment and looked up at Gaby's painful stricken face. Calmly and sensuously, he smiled.

"You'll live, beautiful." His eyes rested once more unabashedly on her breasts.

She quickly pulled the cover up to her neck, holding it there for dear life. She had been embarrassed yesterday, but that last event took the cake.

He smiled at her at first and then roared with laughter.

"Eh, bien, Gaby, I have a new name for you. Trouble. Yes, that's it, Trouble."

She did not respond. She could not respond her frazzled nerves took control of her emotions. She burst out laughing as well, a euphonious crystal clear laughter that left him mesmerized.

At this most awkward moment, the Captain looked young and—beautiful! That finding comforted her. After all, young people had the tendency to act inappropriately at times. He must certainly have understood her predicament. On second thought, no, the ogre of a man that faced her had never been young. She jerked her gaze away.

"I am so, so very sorry, Captain for causing such a havoc in your cabin. I will be more careful from now on, no more pretend acting scene." She could have sworn he did not hear a word she uttered.

He glanced at his bed first then looked up. He discovered that his room had been redecorated. Heavy cotton tan bindings were hanging down from one bedpost. Her mariner's outfit hung on the opposite post.

As she followed his glance, she started again.

"You never come in, not in the afternoon, Captain, I needed clean clothes." Seeing no reaction from him but the same silent stare, she tried to roll off the bed to clean up the mess but to no avail, his non-negotiable stare immobilized her.

"Stay," he ordered and he marched on over to the cot where one of the book she had been reading yesterday lay. He picked it up and brought it back to her.

"Stay put, Trouble, I need a few hours of rest and you probably do, too." He pulled down the bindings, tossed both on the floor. "We will get you a change of clothes later. Then assertively, he took off his shirt and sprawled on the bed next to her.

It was her turn to be mesmerized. She stared at his broad torso rippled with huge muscles bulging out from under his tan skin. She had never seen a white man built so strongly!

He turned his head in her direction and noticed her staring. Sensuously, he rolled onto his side as he gazed up at her.

"You are a very beautiful girl, Gaby, *trés jolie*, very pretty, indeed." He fell back on his back, his arms folded under his head with his eyes open.

Gaby did everything in her power to avert his gaze.

Women in Boston were more puritanical, he thought. After all, the city was the seat of the Puritan Movement and he had not expected otherwise from the many women he had met. Virgins were not his type, however. He wanted women who felt secure in their sexuality and who were willing to experiment.

In France, he never felt too guilty about taking married women to bed. It was their decision and besides, ninety-nine-percent of the marriages were arranged for money, title, land, etc... no problem there. Once a woman had given her husband a male heir, they essentially were off the hook if they showed a certain amount of deference and privacy! He was usually courted by such women; the married women in Boston were more reserved. However his stay in Boston had been good—once these women strayed, they really strayed. He smiled, reliving a few too close to call escapades. In the South, customs might be different. Gaby was passionate and quite enticing. If she was as passionate in bed as she was when she discussed politics, they'd have a real good time this afternoon, he evaluated. More to the point Gaby's feminine assets were hard to resist, especially now that all had been revealed. She had done a pretty good job at hiding this most sensuous part of herself. Thank God, with breasts like that he would have taken her to bed that very first night. Delighted with the turn of events, he calmly continued to stare at the ceiling. Feeling the burning sensations in his lower half, he recalled her singing and cavorting with the bottle. He smirked at all the improprieties that had taken place in his stateroom recently. Taking no for an answer was not in Gaby's demeanor. What a tenacious little spirit she was—afraid of no one. It's not as if he had been courteous with her as was his customary inclination with all the women he met. No, he had been plain difficult with her as he attempted to place her, like everyone else on his ship, under his control. She had followed his demands more out of politeness and recognition for his hospitality, but she always had a disparaging word to make him aware that in any other situation, he would not have had the last word. Her stare spoke volume when he displeased her.

This arrangement had been a new situation for him as well, he had never lived with a woman, maybe in vacation for a month or so, but no one had been allowed in his immediate entourage or his domain, as he liked to call it. He had paid for his paramour's lodging, but his home was his and sharing did not fit in any of his plans. But with the pretty woman lying next to him, he did have to admit that he looked forward to seeing her at night, and in the morning she made a fabulous cup of coffee. Now his trip back to France had gotten even better. He wanted her and the look in her eyes told him that she desired him as well.

Why couldn't he fall asleep instantly? Her mind raced. Helpless in the far corner of the bed, she thought of jumping over him and running out the door. She sensed real trouble approaching.

And it did. He turned toward her, and he slid his hand under the cover, letting it rest on her abdomen. His large hand on her naked skin sent shivers up her spine. He had just touched her in a way that could not have been more explosive. In his eyes was the purposeful intent look she had come to recognize when he willed an outcome. She pleaded with her treacherous body that she would not become the outcome.

Misunderstanding emotional paralysis for pleasure, he took pleasure in her reaction. Quickly he pressed closer to her. As he acknowledged the warmth that his touch produced, he placed his full body on hers. At first, her acceptance of his advances surprised him. New Orleans must have been a more emancipated city. The Southern women, after all, had had to tow the line and defend their plantations once their men went off to war. War had a way of lowering sexual discipline. After a war, most humans wanted to experience life to its extreme in food, drink, and sex. Gaby had survived the war and preserved her plantation while bringing it back to its original lucrative state. She must have had to deal with a number of nasty, shady characters.

He felt her move underneath him. She felt heavenly, soft, voluptuous, hot. Furthermore, he was now convinced that she wanted him just as much as he did her. He lowered his head, pulled the blankets away from her body and kissed the firm roundness of her breast. The areola around her tiny excited buds was a most tender shade of pink. He had yet to find an area of imperfection. Everything from her flawless heart-shaped face to the tip of her round and fleshy toes was pure perfection. The right amount of shapely flesh, he admired. He placed his arms on both sides of her head and kissed her fully on her mouth as he placed more pressure on her lips to enter and interlaced his tongue to hers. She was hard to resist.

"Kiss me, Gaby," he whispered in her mouth while the heat of their bodies rose a thousand degrees.

Obediently, she linked her arms around his neck and pressed her mouth and body to his. The only thought crossing her turbulent mind at this tense moment was that she did not want these sensations to end.

She was ready, he thought, he caressed and kissed her to insensibility then unable to restrain his passion, he quickly rolled to the side of the bed and remove his pants.

Without his warmth, the cold air stung her as she slowly woke up to the fact that she had been lying with the Captain in a most inappropriate mode. His bare bottom stared at her. Her mind ordered her to flee, her body still mesmerized by the sensations traveling through the length of her spine wanted more.

He turned to her.

Faced with a gargantuan naked man sporting a giant instrument of love, reality struck. Good God, what had she gotten herself into? In an explosive move, she grabbed the eiderdown, covered herself with it and started the unsteady walk across his sprawling bed. The scent of their burning bodies radiated in all directions.

He caught her trying to move away from him and gently reached his long arm to her as he rolled her back gently but firmly back in his arms. He leaned and kissed the shoulder closest to him as she drew near. Her resistance was nil. He lifted her up off the bed. Suspended in his arms, he pressed her taut abdomen to his enlarged manhood as he encircled her small, helpless body in his strong arms. Relentless, he pressed his torso onto her breasts and brushed his lips to hers. Her skin begged for his touch, her mind traveled outside of reality while her body desired fervently the formidable vibrations that ran up and down her bare body. She loved his kisses and all the sensations it evoked. She observed herself kissing him back. She placed her arms on his chest, not pushing away but caressing, just like he had done to her. She ran her hands on his back. She held on tight.

Her mind knew how to avoid a bad situation, cerebral decisions, evaluating, analyzing were a cinch—sensually she fell apart. She now realized that her body wanted that sensation to continue, a warmth permeated her body, she had never felt these fabulous tingling in her entire existence. She stopped trying to pull away and let herself be fully engaged in giving and receiving.

As if he approved of her denial of self, he kissed her temple and he picked up her legs and replaced her softly on the bed. Calm and restrained, his entire body swayed on top of hers.

Somewhere near her mouth, she heard a faint no, but conscious of what was to ensue and unwilling to let go of the idyllic sensations every single cell in her body craved, she continued to let herself be loved. She curved her arms around his shoulders and held him forcefully to her as she lifted and pressed her mouth to his.

His startled reaction confused her.

"You're so soft," he murmured in her ears as he gradually bent his head to the middle of her breasts. "You feel wonderful, Gaby"

Resistance was no longer a word she knew. There was no stopping now. She sollicited the passion she craved. She placed both hands on the back of his neck and pressed him to her tightly. Her world was all sensations. She would not stop him. He continued to please her, lowering his kisses to her abdomen, waist and hips. She was sexy and she sensed it.

He reclined in bed and pulled her on top of him. It was getting harder and harder to resist the act.

"You are sweet, Gaby, very beautiful indeed," he murmured, his head burrowed in her hair.

"And intelligent as well," she gasped.

His laughter scared her and brought her back quickly to reality. Afraid that she might change her mind, he rolled her over under him once more and no longer refrain his restraint. With one powerful thrust, he entered her forcefully only to be paralyzed by her screams and painful moans. He froze. Gaby . . . a virgin?

"Gaby you are pure," he sheepishly admitted as he drew a swift breath.

"What made you think I was not?" she gasped.

He pulled back entirely and held her head to this chest. He did not answer her, but kept on holding her.

At first, she did not dare move and then she looked up at him, questioningly.

"Why does it matter," she panted, "I did not stop you."

Shocked by her response, he finally retrieved his words.

"It is not in my habits to rob a woman of what appears to be a most precious gift ... to most women." He was the one on shaky ground now.

She did not respond, instead she pressed her body against his side and kissed it. She confidently stared up at him—a mesmerizing look that he had no difficulty to decipher.

He paused, fixed his glance on her long hair falling heavily on his chest, and gently he pushed her away. Catching the lust in her eyes, he pulled her up on his chest and looked questioningly in her eyes. He expected a response of some sort, but she held his glance steadily. He sighted heavily and gently forced the cascading mane of brown locks further down his chest. He brushed his lips to her hair, intent to stop the act. Instead, transparent pearly beads moistened her rosy cheeks. She pulled herself up and gently moved her lips on his. The sexual passion that her lips ignited was too much to resist. Dazed with passion, he rolled her once more on her back and no longer able to sustain his desire, he joined her in the momentous act.

Nestled in each other's arms for a long time, both were quiet. He had never met a woman like her. At times, a pure spontaneous young girl and this afternoon she had shown him what she wanted and had not felt embarrassed at the result—secure in her sexuality.

She looked up to him, her pretty face rested on the pillow close to him. He could not decipher her thoughts. Frankly he did not quite know what to make of it. He kissed her and gathered her back to him tightly, feeling a heavy fatigue brought on by the act certainly, but also by the incessant schedule he kept, he assured himself. Quietly he fell sound asleep in her arms.

Later that evening, he woke up with Gaby sound asleep in his arms—like an angel. She looked so very content that he hated to move, afraid of waking her up. He touched her lips softly and she opened her gorgeous eyes. God, he wanted her again. Restraint, he told himself.

"Gaby, I have to return back on bridge. I'll be back late this evening. We will talk," he whispered softly, kissing her eyes shut.

She nodded. Tenderness in her lower abdomen reminded her that she had just experienced a momentous time in her womanhood—something she'd remember forever. She wished he could have stayed a while longer. She felt glorious and protected in his arms. She straightened her back and slowly rolled out of bed onto the floor. She enveloped her body back in his coverlet. He stayed in bed a while longer, watching her graceful body move about as he smiled at her.

A momentous day, indeed. He stood up, walked to her, and placed his hands once more under the cover to feel her warm body. A frisson shook her body. Shaken, she flushed. "I have a most powerful effect on you." He smiled and sensually kissed her.

"You do, indeed." It was her turn to measure her words now. She did not feel embarrassed, just awed at what had happened to her.

He left her side and strode to the washbasin. He splashed water onto his face and neck and quickly he got dressed. "You are beautiful, Gaby. I'll see you tonight," he said nonchalantly, as if nothing of great importance had happened. She swallowed hard and nodded smartly. Left behind, she finally let herself sink fully in his leather chair. It was like having him here all over again. His scent was powerful as well. Not wanting to think about anything, but helpless in her attempt, she conceded that her world had now become incontrollable. Fear, shame, and painful sensations in her womb tumbled in complete chaos. Well, she'd always comparmentalized her thoughts and actions.. His kisses still warm on her lips, she tossed all innerving thoughts away from her mind and returned back to the warmth of the bed they had just shared as she fell soundly asleep.

* * *

As Jean-Louis walked the bridge, he was particularly pleased at the turn of events. What a way to spend an afternoon at sea. He chuckled. Fifteen more days before they reached Villefranche. Why rock the boat? He would set things straight after they landed. He'd accompany her to Grenoble so she could meet her cousin. After all, he thought, she was right. They both were consenting adults. She was almost twenty-one, not going to the convent after all—an independent American girl, he surmised as he tried to placate his guilt in order to rationalize his absolute awful behavior.

What had he been thinking? He shamed himself. She was a virgin. He did not recall the last time he had deflowered a young girl, probably in his youth it had happened but to whom was a complete blank. He would apologize and keep her away for the duration of the crossing. That was the honorable thing to do. Now, pleased with his decision, he tried to banish the thought of holding her soft, curvaceous body again tonight. Walking up to the wheel, he silently took over the watch.

Meanwhile Cunnan and the first officer, the only two mariners who knew for certain that a woman lived in the Captain's rooms, were talking about Gaby, namely about her intellect—a strength quite unusual in women. She had surprised them the night before when she compared the lives of some of the slaves in the plantation to servants throughout Europe. After all, many were able to work and sell their vegetables outside of their owners' plantation, she'd told them. From what she had read in books, servants in Europe did not fare much better.

"Captain, is Gabriella still speaking to you?" the first officer called out. "She was intolerant of your statements as I recall. We were quite pleased that she did not have bullets in her green, velvety eyes; none of us would have survived last evening if she had," he continued amused.

The Captain smiled, thinking of her warm curvaceous body pressing passionately against his.

He did not return to the cabin that night, the seas were rough and rugged and since they were getting closer to an area infested with pirates, the more people on deck, the better prepared they'd be if a troublesome situation should occur. He had not expected the urge that he felt to see her and hold her by the time the next morning arrived.

Chapter Eight

Upon entering his cabin the following morning, the Captain was intent on telling his roommate that sex was more a physical need than an emotional state. He came close to her and sweetly caressed her temples, a lazy grin swept across his face.

"Gaby," he murmured sweetly, "I believe that we need to talk, what happened yesterday afternoon ..."

"Jean-Louis, I am not a naïve young girl," she interrupted, calling him by his first name for the first time and shortening it to boot. After all, they had gotten as intimate as intimate could be. "Your experience with women must be either limited or you must choose helpless non-intellectual women. You have nothing to explain," she noted duly. She now had a better appreciation for women who fell madly in love after giving themselves for the very first time.

Stunned first by being labeled by his Christian name—he had not instructed her to do so—and then secondly by her countenance, he frowned. She did not beat around the bushes, as they said in America.

"Please, Gabriella, don't be shy. Be as direct as you wish," he retorted sarcastically with a smirk on his face.

"Very well, then. Jean-Louis, as I was saying, I do not see what there is to talk about. I may have been a virgin, but I am not as innocent in matters of the heart as you might think. I read many classical works that describes the act of lovemaking quite succinctly and if you recall, I made an obvious conscious decision. I am a businesswoman after all. Not that I like it, but I have had to be. I did not fight you, nor push you away, nor did I ask you to stop. I know very well what has happened to me sexually, although I may not know as well what has happened to me sentimentally," she finished in a whisper, almost thinking out loud.

Good. She was taking it well, he surmised. Why complicate matter by having a discussion that he had thought at one point necessary? It facilitated all other sexual encounters they would have. She was mature and seemed to know the difference between matters of the heart and the needs of the body. So far, so good, he thought.

"Very well. So tell me, Gaby, why are you still awake? Waiting for me?" he added sensually.

She tried to change the subject and injected absurd statements to calm her frazzled spirit. "I don't know," she began insecure, "I just could not sleep and later I became curious. I wanted to know how long you could stay awake? Twenty hours, I envy you. If you did not return to the cabin while I dozed off here and there, that's quite impressive. Do you do it often?"

"The seas are rough and four eyes are better than two." He politely answered, understanding her awkwardness. "But tell me, why are you back in your cot?"

Her cheeks were hot. She crossed her hands on the mariner's outfit and fiddled with the fabric. Be direct, she thought—you do not know how not to be. She always remembered what Tita had told her long ago, "never think you know something and act upon that assertion without first asking a direct question to the party involved. Their answers might surprise you. It may save you days of unhappiness, of sorrow, of disappointments and of uncertainties," her loving servant had advised.

"I did not know how you'd feel finding me in your bed, if by chance I would have been able to quiet my mind and fall asleep."

"Why would I feel anything but pleasure?" he questioned, as he stared into her eyes, well aware that he placed her in an embarrassing situation.

Her cheeks turned crimson.

"Well, I'm happy to hear that," her smile widened and her eyes became alive.

What a temptress she was, he thought, his lower half once again talked to him.

"Come here, Gaby," he continued.

She let it register, waited, looked at him, and then regally crossed the room. Her years of ballerina training inculcated in her posture and appearance never let her down, whether she was walking in a ballroom or she was frightened out of her wits—as she was right now.

Jean-Louis sat in the large overstuffed leather chair and gazed at her. Not specifically at her approaching body, his gaze boldly starred at her unbounded breasts, small waist, small ankles and sexy peachy feet peeking out from under her uniform.

"You walk like an angel, Gaby," he stood up and met her half way, reached for her waist, pulled her in his arms, and kissed her first tenderly and then hungry for her caresses his mouth opened over hers.

"I love kissing you. You're so responsive, Gaby," he whispered in her mouth stunned at the effect the spontaneous five-footer had on him. He took her in his arms and placed her tenderly on his bed, kneeling on the bed at first as he stared intently in her gigantic, expressive eyes. He tried to make sense of the odd sensation he was experiencing besides lust. Mon Dieu, he was much too tired to think, a very pretty and willing young woman lay next to him. He did not need to think. He turned away from her long enough to sit on the bed to pull off his boots, to take his clothes off and to roll in next to her. Thinking was not on the agenda.

Unwilling to appear too eager, nor letting her know that she had some odd control over him, he kissed her forehead and relaxed fully on his back, his hands behind his head. He cast a skeptical glance, the thought about the comments to Cunnan earlier, the part about explaining to Gabriella the desire of the flesh and the need to control it until they reached Villefranche.

All this could wait until the following day. Right now he wanted her and he needed a few hours of sleep—in that order.

She pushed herself up in a sitting position against the headboard; one of her leg brushed his bent arm. Irritated that she'd moved away, he looked up at her, clasped both her legs, and willfully he rested his head on her thighs.

A warm, sensuous sensation ran throughout Gaby's body that evoked a young girlish dream that she had had years ago—an image of a man, his head positioned on her lap while she read. She'd thought at the time that arrangement to be terribly romantic. Oddly enough, she experienced this pleasurable moment now as sensual emotions toward the stranger who had delivered her from an awful fate at the hands of marauding pirates developed against her will. The Captain had saved her life and given her refuge, she thought, but it had come at a price—her virginity. How fantastically wacky her world had become.

Naturally, at that time she'd never expected that making love to a man could be so titillating and simply wonderful. Odd times required bizarre responses. Maybe it was the extended hours she'd spent all alone in his cabin that made her reach out for closeness and warmth? Maybe it was a feeling of belonging—something she had yearned for all her life. Maybe it was just a great release of all the pent-up emotions she had repressed since her very birth.

The Captain was terribly attractive. She had read somewhere that chemistry was one of the most influential factors in a relationship. She wondered if he felt it too. It certainly was an odd encounter. She had lost her virginity, consciously, no need to fret over spilled beans, as Tita would say. Now she wanted to make love with him all over again.

She repressed all guilt and elegantly bent over his head and kissed him fully on his mouth.

His response was immediate. His hands reached behind him and around her waist. He looked up momentarily as she bent over him like a willow branch curved downwards by strong winds.

"How can you do that?" he murmured. "It's impressive."

She laughed and straightened her right leg away from his head. Elegantly, she moved her upper torso toward her thighs and held the position as she turned her head toward him and winked.

"I can do that, too." She pleasingly moved her upper torso back to him. She stretched a tad more, held his gaze a while longer and kissed him again on his mouth, "and that as well."

She really was adorable and unusual, he thought, full of spunk. He liked her personality and never had he met or been with a woman so direct, real, and secure, certainly not in Paris where he was considered part of the Grand Monde. French women with great lineage in his circles of friends were a lot more submissive with him than this short, voluptuous, and very sensual young girl.

He did not know what classics she had read, but had she not been a virgin, he certainly would have wondered about her life in New

Orleans. But no, she was real and alarmingly secure in her sensuality. He moved his head back on the bed and pulled her down next to him.

"I'll dislike you greatly in a few hours when you'll be fast asleep and I'll be back on deck," he grudgingly mumbled.

"Can I come up with you and get a bit of fresh air?" She demanded

"Absolutely not. Come here," he smiled and reached for her. He kissed the arm that had landed on his stomach.

"Continue what you have so delightfully started."

Hours later, still nestled in his arms, wide awake, she felt him roll away from her. She pretended she was asleep when he bent down, tenderly kissed her, moved her curls away from her face and pulled the cover over her bare shoulders.

If one could have read their minds after the love interlude, an understanding of men and women's values toward sex could have explained centuries of pleasure and guilt.

Jean-Louis left the cabin, deeply pleased and satiated as he smiled inwardly to himself.

What a way to start the day, he thought.

Gaby, in contrast, was overwhelmed by feelings of having been bad, senseless, and not at all proper. What about all these years of religious education? Why had she let her emotions control her physical world? What annoyed her the most was that her little voice whispered softly that it was right. She hoped she would not be punished for the impure act she had just committed. Ah, religion, why was it that it always made the woman suffer, when it usually was the man who took the initiative to be pleased. Because of a man's desire, a woman became a sinner.

He had not expected the urge that he felt to see her and hold her by mid-morning. He asked Cunnan to take over for an hour as he pretended to get more maps. In fact, why did he have to pretend anything?

He walked down a few steps into his cabin, which was located right outside the Captain's bridge. Gaby was still asleep, in a very sound dreamland, where he hoped he had sent her. He gently bent down, and nipped at her lips.

"It's twelve o'clock, my chère. Time to hop out of bed or better yet to stay there for a while longer." He wanted her again. He lied down on top of the burgundy satin coverlet next to her.

"Can I have some coffee, please?" she lazily asked turning her back to him.

"No, but you can have me." He smiled.

She reached for the covers and pulled them over her head. He burst out laughing.

"Is that a way to treat your savior? You should be like a Musulmane at my beck and call sleeping on the floor like a submissive wench. Never mind taking over my bed, keeping me awake all night, and sending me back to work during the wee hours of the morning."

She sleepily peeked her curly dark mane out from under the covers then turned her pretty face toward him. She rolled her eyes, and sunk in deeper under the blankets.

"I presume I'm no longer a frightening, powerful, commanding figure in your eyes, Gaby," he remarked amused. "I'll have to come in with tea and biscuits the next time I want to bend you to my will."

She nodded. He kissed her warm little body and returned on deck. The little angel was a brat. He did not join her for dinner, the seas were rough and the crew and its officers were on the alert. Near the Azores, special care was de rigueur.

Chapter Nine

Jean-Louis had been gone for almost two days straight. Gaby had spoken to Cunnan on several occasions when he brought her dinner, but both men had been kept on deck almost continuously because of the weather.

The once proud and fiercely independent Gabriella De Conte Thornsen had fallen madly in love with the Captain of the *Tempète* and to her dismay could not seem to think of anything or anyone else. Concentrating on her life in France or her music was unachievable, for his great stature figured in every single thought she formulated. Good heavens, why now, she asked the bright and brilliant blue sky? She wished she could go up on deck and be with him. No need to dream about it. He would not allow it.

The sky was still dark when she heard the heavy clanking of his boots down the steps. The center of her obsession had just entered the cabin. She stayed in bed.

"What is wrong with this scenario, Gaby? For the past two days every time I come in, you're asleep. Have you turned into a hibernating grizzly?" he questionned, totally unaware of the early morning hours.

"Take me, take me and let me be and sleep. It's three o'clock in the morning. I wait and wait, I feel like a medieval Princess waiting for her Prince—the one that never returns."

"Well in your case, my love, your Prince has returned. Move over, I'll follow your kind advice and pretend to be Sir Lancelot." He rolled in next to her and pressed her small warm body next to his.

"You're sweet, Gaby, I'm pleased that you're here," he whispered.

A loud crystal clear laughter broke the silence; he realized what he had told her and brushed his lips to her temple.

"What pretention. You make fun of me? Your impertinence may lend you with your friends the dolphins, out there," he motioned to the porthole.

"Never in a million years, I know so, your arrangement is quite palatable. Deny it, Captain?" she retorted ironically.

"Touché, Gaby," he smiled and enveloped her in his arms. "It's freezing in here. I don't know, Gaby. No food, no fire—what have you been doing all day? You need a sound correction," he laughed, momentarily recalling the offensive expletive she'd used toward the overseer of the plantation next to hers. The horrific being would beat his wife when he returned from the fields if his dinner was not on the table. And then she'd rambled over the incapacity and the lack of control women experience in her time. She was happy she was financially secured with a career that she hoped would bring her happiness and the means to continue her independent lifestyle. He also recalled how she had looked to him when she'd proclaimed loving her independence. There had been a short pause of longing, or so he had thought at the time—for one of his comments. Maybe she would have liked to hear that not all men showed their superiority with the stick and that a loving, egalitarian relationship was possible between a man and a woman. Instead, he'd smiled and had not commented one way or another. Both of their lives were going to be different once they reached Paris. He would miss her. She had been a most delightful companion.

"Eh, bien, Mademoiselle, we are getting closer to the straight of Gibraltar. Always a difficult area namely with Spanish and North African pirates." He got out of bed and walked to the porthole.

"You know, Gabriella," he pursued, "we will be neighbors in Paris. I'm sure we will meet in the capital," he remarked kindly.

What was he saying? Was he preparing her for their eventual break-up? They were closer to Europe.

He looked back at her and was about to remark that it was not uncommon for a woman to get more attached than a man when sensual relations had been breached, but he noticed a painful gaze in her eyes. He walked to her and gathered her in his arms. He was going to miss her, too.

"The opéra season will be just beginning. I'll introduce you to the Parisian Grand Monde," he said.

Why not? The break would be easier for her in Paris. "As a matter of fact, you may want to come with me all the way to Brest, and we will travel to Paris together. You are now quite accustomed to a mariner's hard life, beauty. It will be a while before your cousin picks you up in Grenoble. I have to stop in Villefranche. I'll be meeting with several Sardinian dignitaries sent by Victor Emmanuel II, and then we will ship out again. Meanwhile, I'll show you the southern coast of France. It is beautiful. The people are warm and very friendly contrary to what your compatriots levy against them. But more importantly the food is out of this world."

She shot him a frightened look.

"No, Jean-Louis, I cannot. I need to start at the Académie on time. Philippe will wait for me in Grenoble. No, I would love to, but I can't. What would people think of me? I'd be ostracized by the students; I have been disparaged sufficiently throughout my young life. No fault of my own, you understand. No I want to start a new chapter in my life," she emphasized. "You understand—do you?"

"Yes, Gaby, I understand, come and eat." He stood up once more, reached for her hand and led her to the table. "We will discuss and arrange your return to Grenoble in a timely manner when we arrive in port. As it appears right now, if we continue on our path, we will arrive in Villefranche earlier than predicted. We will have plenty of time to make the proper arrangements for your prompt and safe return."

"Thank you." She looked up with such conflicted emotions in her pretty eyes that he changed the subject promptly.

"So tell me, beauty, what prompted you to come to France and become an opéra singer?" He knew that subject was close to her heart and she would forget all her silly comments and questions if pressed in that direction. That was a sure start for she talked about her goals and desire to leave New Orleans and everything she had known for a more adventurous life.

He listened to her intently and although she rambled on, she was interesting and fun to listen to. Her expressions, her thoughts, and her demeanor everything made her an individual, an original. He could see how people wanted to stay in her entourage, she had a magnetic power that few men had, never mind a woman of her times.

She seemed to think that what made her different was really her financial security, that gave her independence, but in reality it was the full package. She was appealing, fun, and witty—very witty—nothing was sacred with Gaby. She made fun of everything and anything excluding herself. She did not take too well to criticism and he had never heard her once disparage herself without emphasizing her great qualities that always superseded her avowed shortcomings. She was sweet. He liked her way too much. He might take her out in Paris. His life from now on was going to be structured, dangerous filled with unresolved challenges. He would never involve a woman in his adventures. Not even a woman with Gaby's qualities.

Chapter Ten

Storms battered the seas and the Tempète was swaying heavily across the ocean. Gaby began to feel the effect of the rolling waves. She was reading The Count of Monte Cristo by Alexandre Dumas *père*, father, a novel that Jean-Louis had let her choose from his extensive collection.

"His grand mother was an African slave in San Domingue and although his grand father's lineage was aristocratic, his mulato appearance caused him a great deal of grief as a young man. Alexandre is a talented man, my father shared years ago but always in search of approval." He'd explained.

"Approval is a hard emotion to inculcate, especially if a parent or loved one has not instilled it as a child," she'd reflected almost to herself. She'd let it go at that, although it provided fodder for her own decision to seek fame on another continent. No she loved music. It was her passion. The European stage had been her ambition since she was a child. Surprisingly, when they were together, Jean-Louis shared a lot of his knowledge with her. He seemed to like to delve into history.

"You seem to know a lot about your culture, both the military aspects and the cultural and literary tidbits, Jean-Louis." She'd observed.

"Eh bien, Gaby I have had to. My family ties are wide-ranging. My father was a very accomplished man. In other for me to become my own man, I decided long ago that I would exceed my father's varied accomplishments and outrank him in my military endeavors and responsibilities. I believe that I did," he'd responded gravely.

Absorbed in the lecture, she sat in his great leather chair, heavy blankets surrounding her, life was great she fancied. She had fallen madly in love with Jean-Louis and she did not want for this trip to end.

The seas were getting rougher by the minute. She had never experienced that feeling but liked it immensely. She let her body go and enjoy the sensation.

Jean-Louis walked in.

"The seas are rough," he proclaimed in a commanding voice. "Put on the protective gears." He waited a few seconds and then seeing no immediate response, he became annoyed that she was taking her sweet time.

"Gaby, get your life jacket and put it on—now. He shouted loud and clear.

"I will Jean-Louis, in a while, I just want to finish the chapter. Don't worry about me. I'll take care of myself." She returned her attention to the book, thinking that he had just come in to inform her of the thunderstorm.

Incensed now by her laissez-faire attitude, coupled with the stress of the storm's fury, the Captain lost his composed demeanor.

"Don't you dare question my orders—ever?" He walked over to her and within seconds she was in his arms, book and all, and placed none too gently on the hard mat against the wall as he pulled the life jacket over her head, buckling her to the wall like a butcher preparing his meat.

She knew better than to say anything now, but she would not forget that tone soon.

He continued to tie her up and placed some padded earmuffs around her head.

"I came down to make sure you were safe. Now do as you are told. Tie up the rest of the jacket and stay put. Understood?" He was right in her face.

She would not give him the satisfaction to shy away from his stare.

"Gaby, answer me!"

She did not utter a word and kept her burning green eyes to his. All bundled up in the life jacket by now, she obediently proceeded to tie up the rest of her protective gear without a word. Not letting him enjoy his victory, she stared back with fury.

"Tell me, Gaby, are you trying to stare me down?" He was also unwilling to let her triumph in her small, pitiful way. When he gave an order, no one, including her, dare question it.

Silence still.

"Because if you are . . . "

At that very instant, a strong wave rocked the boat, crushing Jean-Louis in between his desk and bookcase. He lost his footing temporarily.

Gaby followed his fall with her eyes. An ironic leer cracked her lips.

He returned back to her, lightning in his icy blue stare.

"God help me, if I return to this cabin and find you anywhere but where you are right now . . . Do you understand me?"

Silence again.

Finding humor in her expressive green eyes starring at him, defiant even in that silly costume, he straightened up and in a moment of affection, he turned back and shot her a fatherly glance.

"The forces of nature have to be respected, Gaby," he explained gently.

"Don't be condescending toward me," she shouted back sharply.

He strode back toward her, fiery anger in his voice now.

"Gaby, are you trying to show me how tough you are? I'm not impressed. You are lucky that you are a guest in my cabin and not a mariner. You'd be freezing, naked in the brigs, fearing the moment until I dealt with you when the weather became more clement. I'm in charge here, understood? My orders are followed without questions at once, now answer me."

He was now a bit too close for comfort. He was a big man, after all, and could do some damage.

She nodded and looked down, straightened up her torso, and picked up the book that had fallen on her knees. She started reading, obliterating his image.

Inflamed, he took the book from her hand and tossed it hard on the wall next to her.

"In your own lingo, Gaby," he continued his tirade, "since you seem to have difficulties with spoken English. This is my plantation and I am the Master. Clear?" he shouted.

She did not answer him, did not even look his way. He had become an unknown entity. She would not give him the satisfaction to assert his will and break her against her own will.

"Clear?"

Once again, silence reigned. She pulled herself up once more, bound on both sides of the small mat located between two steel girders with handles on each side. She looked round and stout, her small body surrounded by life jackets from head to toe. She reached for the book that she had been reading, now on the floor, and submerged herself in the lecture once more.

At this particular moment, he could have strangled her or held her into him so tight so as to absorb her small body into himself. He looked at her one more time in the hope to elicit an answer, an expression of some sort. No chance there. She gave him neither. He walked out. He pitied the poor soul who would need to spend the rest of his life with her. A reckoning force—a mighty force at that.

The storm raged overnight, but by early morning the winds died down and a clear blue sky replaced the enormous black clouds.

The Captain sent Cunnan down to look on Gaby. She must have been deadly sick, the little witch, he thought. No, the answer had been, she was fine, tied up, hanging on for dear life, but no sign of stress from Iron Angel down below. They stayed on deck a few more hours and then Cunnan decided to walk down and take care of Gaby.

The two were having a cup of coffee when Jean-Louis entered his stateroom.

"Jean-Louis, I'm happy to report that Gaby, here, took care of me these past few hours. I fell asleep when I realized she had withstood this wicked storm without even an upset stomach. An amazing little woman. I was even served a cup of warm coffee when I woke up. Gaby, you are an angel. I have never known a woman with all your qualities. I'll get back on deck now, Jean-Louis. You must be exhausted, get some sleep."

Jean-Louis turned to her with an ironic smirk. She jerked her gaze away. With a grin, he fell on his bed, hands behind his head. She was still furious he could see that. He turned in bed hoping to fall asleep quickly. It did not happen. He liked her warm, willing body next to his. He would have to take the first step and start conversing, for he was certain she wouldn't. He sat up in bed and stared at her.

She picked up the book again. She suffered his gaze on her shoulders.

He would throw that book in the stormy water the first chance he got.

"You are a formidable woman, Gaby, I thought for sure, you'd gagged in your vomit, looking deliciously vulnerable, albeit with your mask on your face. Instead, I found a woman that served impeccable coffee to my commanding officer, who by the way, had been sent down below to take care of your needs. In its place, you watched over him while he slept.

"Jean-Louis," she sliced back, "I am a woman who has gone through hell and back, and yes, I had to rely on my iron will, as you say, to re-emerge from a sea of despair—more than once. You may have experienced sadness and loneliness in your privileged, aristocratic youth, but I have had to rely on my will to survive through both physical and emotional upheavals. Small defeats are a known entity for me. I have lived through it and came out the stronger for it. Major failure I have never experienced and never will. I have the tools to deal with the unimportant debris that are strown my way," she stared at him with disdain, "early on before it gets overwhelming and ready to engulf me. You have strength, courage, and intellect. I have might. It encompasses all of the above."

He looked at her amazed at her voice and her words, and quite certain that his apologies would remain hollow, consequently with a most sensuous smile, he rolled out of bed and walked to the large leather chair where she was ensconced. He wanted her more than ever—now. "I'll exercise that strength since it is the only lever I have against you?" He bent down, picked her up, and placed her on his large sprawling bed.

She rolled away as far back from him as possible toward the wall.

"Leave me, I have no desire to even be close to you."

"You are a formidable soul, Gaby," he stretched toward her and rolled her back in his arms. Not uttering another word, he placed his heavy legs on her hips, he gathered her to him ever more tightly, he reached for her breast and inclined his head in her hair—within minutes the powerful and influential Duke De Pleyssis was sound asleep. She lay awake, unable to move, furious at his commanding tone this morning. Maybe she had been a bit flippant about Mother Nature and its rocky temper, but tying her up like a trapped animal and speaking in such a disrespectful tone—no, that was plain outrageous. She would talk to him tomorrow morning. Then, it was her turn to fall soundly asleep. The seas still lolled the couple around on their bed, but the Captain had a hold on her. She could not go very far.

He woke up first and was looking at her when she wakened.

"Good morning, beautiful. Are we on speaking terms this morning?

"No," came the curt reply. "Let me go."

"No," he kissed her hair. "Oh, mighty one, had I known what a fierce combatant you were, I would have thrown you out to the fishes weeks ago."

She burst out laughing. That crystal clear laughter that he loved. She amused and interested him.

"How long are we going to be on the war path?"

"Until you apologize for your absolutely rude and unnecessary curt comments yesterday morning."

He followed her orders obediently. God, he really liked her. She was the first woman who could evoke such fury. *Quelle femme*, what a woman, he would miss her immensely.

Chapter Eleven

Gaby waited a good part of the day and now dusk was setting in. She pranced once more in front of the mirror—clothes, French clothes, at that. How would he react to her new look? She couldn't wait to toss these old mariner outfits. Well, perhaps she'd keep one as a souvenir.

"Captains are always the last ones to leave the ship," he had told her last evening as she packed the few personal things not sunk in the take over.

At three in the morning, he had awaken her, kissed her, and repeated all the instructions he had articulated a good many times before. In essence, the message was—let Cunnan handle all concerns and wait for me in the Villa, which has been placed at my disposition by my friend, the Captain of the Port, Monsieur De Massa and his young family. My house should be ready to move into the following day.

Gaby felt sadness at the thought of leaving the cabin. It had been home for the past four weeks and had changed her life forever. Gone was the ancient and seemingly firm belief that she possessed full control over her sentimental life. She had fallen madly in love in less than twenty-one days—so much for what she thought was her exclusivity and self-control over feminine emotions.

She pushed her few belonging in a green hemp bag and walked to the table where the phonograph was located. Again she pushed the square box down as far as she could, the bulky earpiece kept on sticking out of the vagabond pouch. She gave it one last shove. Achieving her goal, she pulled on the cordon laces. Good, the bag was closed. She was ready. Her oversized mariner's outfit back on her small stature, she waited for Cunnan to come and get her.

One last time, she sat on Jean-Louis' oversized leather chair. She recalled all that had happen. Delighted that her journal was current, it described the entire momentous event, but furthermore the minutest details that had developed in the quarter had been noted down diligently.

What was next? She was a tad morose at the realization that she'd have to share Jean-Louis. But she was confident that many more memories would be created in the future. She was sure he had fallen in love with her as well. He did not have to say anything. She sensed it and her intuition was never wrong. A knock at the door brought her back to the present. Cunnan walked in.

"Well, mademoiselle, ready for the continent and its adventures?" the old seaman asked.

"Oui, Monsieur, I can't wait." She pulled her hair in a tight bun, placed a few barrettes in strategic places to hold the heavy mass of curly hair she had washed earlier today, and she fitted the mariner's cap around it. The hat covered her forehead. Her huge green eyes and firm lips were overwhelmingly in focus.

"Dear God, you are beautiful, Gabriella," Cunnan said, looking at her a little longer that he would have liked.

She smiled.

"On our way, sailor," he said, as he opened the door and placed her heavy duffel bag on one of her shoulder.

"My Lord, Gabriella, what are you taking with you, the silver?" he questioned amused.

She grinned, and he gave her a great big hug. Looking at the shape that her 'things' had formed, he knew exactly what she had packed.

They both walked out of the cabin and started climbing up the wooden steps. The cool breeze hit her face, loosening the cap. Quickly she readjusted the hat and looked around for Jean-Louis. A cacophony of noises surprised her. Some sailors already stood at attention waiting to be dismissed; to hop on another ship or to stay with the Captain all the way to Brest. Only a few mariners were not part of Jean-Louis' crew. He paid well and although tough and intransigent, he was fair and respected by the ones who sailed under his command.

She turned to look at the magnificence of the small town. A fortress stood on the border by the sea. It had soldiers keeping guard on its perimeter. A marching band appeared to be forming on the cay.

The small port was located at a bottom of a steep hill. A medieval-like castle stood alone halfway up the hill, overlooking the marina, and to the right of the ship, gray buildings stood grim.

There was no sign of the Captain. Where was he? Everybody and their brother appeared to be on deck except Jean-Louis. Had he gone to shore? She was afraid to ask questions lest someone recognized her as a woman. The secret had been kept—no need to reveal now.

She walked obediently next to Cunnan and followed his command when he directed her to the beginning of the third row of sailors in line to disembark. Barges waited to take the sailors to shore and Cunnan had instructed her on the proper way to stand in attention and how to salute the Captain. She was prepared as she took her place in line.

The band, far away had started with La Marseillaise, the French National anthem. A sideways glance revealed that Jean-Louis had stepped on deck with his first officer. The tension in the two mariners standing on each side of her rose a hundred degrees.

Curious, she must have cocked her head to catch a glimpse, just to be reminded in no uncertain terms by a sous-officier, to keep her head straight and expressionless unless "he" wanted to spend a few extra days on the ship—down below, that was.

Good try, she told herself, but she nevertheless straightened as quickly as she could, marching her pupils to the right to watch for Jean-Louis.

He must have heard the summons for he looked over in her direction and for a short pause their eyes locked and a smirk widened his lips.

The load on her shoulders was getting heavy. She relaxed a bit and took a first ballet stance and waited. Her small stature and third row position saved her for another half an hour.

What in the world were they waiting for? She would tell him tonight. Why put these poor fellows in such mode of anticipation. It just was not right, she thought. She must have slacked in her attention posture once more, a sharp jab to her right side, and then again, an elbow on her left side almost made her shriek. She shot a killer glance to her partner and he nodded toward Jean-Louis marching their way.

The poor fellow was pleading with her with his eyes to straighten up lest they would be stuck on board all day.

She came to perfect attention stance—or so she thought. Jean-Louis was babbling something to each of the sailors who were then released after saluting the Captain. Her row finally came to his attention. She was next. She had all to do to keep from laughing.

He looked down at her. Without an utterance, he untied her heavy bag and looked in to see what in the world she could have in there that was so bulky. Faced with the mouthpiece of the phonograph—her first gift, he thought—he felt touched and embarrassed at how much emotion she placed on this simple item. His eyes smiled at her. He tied the load once more. He wanted to inculcate in his mind every bit of her appearance.

It had been a whole lot of fun. Damn, she was adorable. He cast an up and down glance once more and he noticed her first ballet position. Placing his heavy boot against her oversized shoe he gently pushed it back into a position of attention.

"Watch that step, sailor, lest other Captains think of you as a ballerina. You'll find yourself having to pay for a return. Words of that nature get around quite quickly."

She smiled up at him and afraid that she might retort a sly response, he dismissed her.

"Godspeed sailor." She saluted him making sure to make it the French way touching the side of her temple with her palm down, and then she turned decidedly toward the ladder and the barge in the water. With her bag, oversize sailor outfit, and boots, she walked down the ladder, sat down, and looked up.

The last mariner was now in the boat. She turned back as she took her seat next to two large men. Jean-Louis watched. She winked. Surprised, he smiled back and quickly swept toward the bridge. She followed him with her eyes as long as she could, but he never returned in her field of vision.

The sun shone brightly and the sea was calm. The fishermen's boat quickly moored to the pier. Cunnan waited patiently. Without a word he nodded toward her and whisked her away quickly. They passed a marching band at the beginning of the Chemin De Ronde, the path that bordered the castle on all sides.

Jean-Louis was an important personality for such a show of force to be displayed. She would have loved to have been able to stay and watch as a large group of soldiers in full uniform followed a stout man with rolled up, ram-like mustaches. No doubt they were celebrating Jean-Louis' return. Cunnan had told her that he was an influential man in France. Well, that certainly was no exaggeration. She was suddenly brought back to reality. Two horses were waiting.

"You can ride, Gabriella, correct?" Cunnan questioned.

She nodded.

"Good, let me have your bag, it will be faster this way."

She looked back one more time. Quite a few people were on the Condamine, the place where the border patrol checked mariners and merchants alike for piracy items or unwelcome traitors. The security around the ship was unyielding. She hoped that Jean-Louis would not be too late.

Faced with his bigger than life stature on the deck, she had a hard time believing that she had been in his arms this morning. She recalled his tender ways and sweet words just before his departure. The giant man she had observed on the deck frightened her. She could not wait to get to know him out of that environment. Certainly the different social scene would add or maybe detract from their relationship, but she had told herself she was up to the challenge. Now, she was not quite as sure.

Cunnan rode with her, up to the top of the hill. They had contoured the fortress and as they bypassed the town, she'd noticed quite a few little shops.

"Oh, please, Cunnan can I stop? I would like so much to purchase a few things to wear. Look Cunnan, the stores, can we stop for just a few minutes? Perhaps they'll let me buy the dress displayed on the window?

Cunnan wanted to arrive at the villa, rest for awhile before taking leave of the couple, and depart for Monaco where he had some dear friends, namely his adored late wife's cousin that waited for him. But Gaby looked so excited over the dress that he decided to stop. He remembered what pleasure shopping for clothes had been for his wife when they visited Paris—and also the financial burden it had been for him.

They stopped on the Place Emilie Polonaise where a number of *buveries,* bars, had outside terraces. She was off that horse in minutes. Reaching inside her duffel bag, she pulled out a small reticule. Quickly she came next to him and encircled him with her arms and kissed him on both cheeks.

"You see," she said, "I have already picked up on the French way of greeting and showing appreciation.

Cunnan hugged her back. He could not believe how he had grown to love that child. She had a way of making people love her. He had adored a woman only once—his wife, but this child surely had touched his heart. Why she had been rejected by both of her parents was his dilemma.

"Gaby, I will be in the Maison Audibert just here outside. Call me if you need anything. I have French money, which you will certainly need. Here." He handed her a burgundy velvet purse filled with gold coins.

"Oh, I had forgotten I will pay you back as soon as I can get some change. Thank you, I will shop wisely." The United States had begun to use paper money only five years ago although the Massachusetts Colonies had used paper money since 1690.

He watched her go. She entered the shop she'd pointed to earlier. Half an hour later, all smile, she walked out of the shop with two large packages. She returned his coins.

"They accepted my dollars after I told them I was staying with the Duke De Pleyssis. I think I could have charged his account for a lot more." She laughed. "Anyway, thank you so much. I hope I did not make you wait too long." She took a seat next to him. "Can I have a small collation? I'm dying of thirst."

She was taking everything in and asking all sorts of questions to the waiters, striking conversations with some of the fishermen who had stopped for *un ballon de vin rouge*, a small glass of ordinary red wine, before they returned to their barges.

Cunnan realized that it was getting late. They should really continue the climbing to her new surrounding. They stayed there, longer than expected. She was horse savvy, he could see that. She did not need his help to mount and now she attached her packages to the back of the saddle expertly. A real cowgirl, he thought. How different from all the other women Jean-Louis had had relationships with? He hoped to God that Jean-Louis would not hurt her. She was too perfect of a human being to be pained.

Invigorated by the cold beer and lemonade called a panaché, she rode fast up a hill, past a cemetery, and up towards a magnificent villa called the *Léopolda*. It belonged to the king of Belgium and the view of the bay and the Cap Ferrat was impregnable. Their stables were filled with magnificent stallions. Jean-Louis had told her that while his house was being readied overnight they would spend their first night in the King*'s palace*.

"You will be more comfortable after such a long trip, Gaby," he had said with a tinge of sadness, "but we will return to my house first thing on Saturday morning. We have arrived earlier than anticipated. Everything should be ready for us by then. She nonetheless wanted to see his house. After all, she did not want to keep on moving and she knew that he'd made these arrangements on her account.

"Cunnan," she asked after seeing the opulent estate, "do you think that Jean-Louis would be greatly disappointed if we returned to his house? It is not cold. I would like that very much since I will have to leave on Monday. Besides, we can easily ride or walk to town from there."

Cunnan had mentioned to her that Jean-Louis' home was close to the Darse, walking distance from the pier where the commuter's barge moored. There was a zoo nearby that belonged to a Russian scientist, a ship repair owned by a certain Monsieur Radouble, and on the other side of the dry dock was the rather large pink house that Captain De Massa, the Chef de Port occupied.

Jean-Louis' palace had to be reached by steep stairs that went up the hill into the *propriétée*, estate. The stables were well equipped and she was close to town.

"So why not stay there?" Gaby asked.

Cunnan agreed. Jean-Louis would be pleased, as he had not skimped on anything so as to have complete modern comfort. She had been shocked by the opulence of the villa which looked liked an old medieval castle with round turrets and high steeples. Cunnan shared that the architect who had helped Jean-Louis with the design had wanted to characterize the house with a history of his lineage, which essentially went back to the high Middle Ages. The architecture showed this span of time. The interior was ultra modern with only a few magnificent pieces of epoch furnishings in each room, huge windows on the perimeter of the propriétée bordered by large terraces on each of the three floors. A party house, she thought.

How many other women he had bedded in this gorgeous place? She pushed the thought out of her mind. After all, Villefranche had opted for a French government in 1860, and Jean-Louis had been gone for almost seven years. He could not have spent much time here, if any. She tossed her jealous thoughts away.

Cunnan had returned to the pier. She watched him out on the balcony. He spoke to a sailor who quickly turned around and walked along the pier to embark on the commuter launch. He must have given instruction to the sailor to inform the Captain that he should return to his home.

Cunnan returned.

"Gabriella, I'm off to dreamland. Ask the servants for whatever you need. I have spoken to the butler. They will show you to your room and provide everything you need. Will you be fine or would you rather I stay?" he asked kindly.

"I'll be perfectly fine." She walked to him and hugged him tenderly. "Thank you so very much for all you have done for me. I will never forget," she proclaimed solemnly as she laid her head on his heart. Sadly, she pushed away. "I'll see you in Paris. Goodbye, Cunnan. Have a wonderful time in Monaco."

"Goodbye, Gabriella. Keep Jean-Louis-Pierre in line. See you soon."

By two o'clock, Gaby was ready for Jean-Louis to come back. She could see a lot of activities on the Cay, but the Tempète had not budged from its original mooring far in the bay. Consequently, Jean-

Louis would be late. She looked through the telescope, the Captain's gig was still attached to the back of the ship, and she watched him stride on the bridge. What a magnificent instrument. I'm spying on him, she concluded amused.

She looked down the port and a clever idea popped in her mind. She could finish her shopping in Madame Metzera's shop. She had seen so many beautiful dresses. After all, she had the time. Why not? She walked down the stairs and asked the stable boy for the quickest way to the fishermen's village.

Mounting one of the stallions, she departed on her merry way. She had been smart enough to purchase boots and a riding habit. It would be essential these next few days. Now she wanted pretty things. She was lucky her small size permitted her to purchase things that had been made for display, although no good aristocratic French or English woman of means would ever buy off the rack. How common, she would often hear. But now, she was the happiest woman and Madame Metzera's was more than pleased to accommodate her with everything that needed a little adjustment. She returned back to the house with five day-outfits and four beautiful gowns with matching satin heel slippers. Jewelry lacked. She told herself she would have to wait, maybe in Nice, tomorrow.

She tried on everything she had purchased and twirled in front of the mirror. Oh, Lord, how she loved clothes. It gave her such a pleasure to dress in magnificent dresses. When she sang she had teased the director of the New Orleans' opéra house that she derived true joy not from singing but from the clothes she wore while singing on the stage. He had given her such a sarcastic and arrogant look that she still laughed about it when she recalled the moment. What a pompous man he was, but he was a splendid actor and now director of one of the most appreciated opéra house in the United States. It was strange for her to think of her home as 'the United States'—two years after the end of the war she still felt that a Southerner was a breed of its own. Maybe one-day things would change. Her life had been a whirlwind for a little over a month.

It was almost five o'clock and Jean-Louis had not arrived. All dressed in a magnificent shapely satin yellow dress with a matching ribbon in her hair she walked down in the foyer where the sitting room with the telescope was located. She looked again and this time the Captain's gig was no longer attached. She wondered about his reaction upon seeing her all dressed up. She had bought him—with his own line of credit—a gold razor and had placed it on the rim in his bathroom. Well, at least she had not forgotten him. Would he shave his beard?

The Captain landed on the Condamine. All vessels needed to anchor near and attend to the laws of the new frontier. Arriving on a non-military port, it was usual for the guards to mount the ship and check its cargo. The Tempète carried live cargo as well. Some of the prisoners of the pirate ship had been handed over to the authorities.

The Captain was the last to disembark.

Jean-Louis was enthralled. He had not seen the finished product of the house in Villefranche and could not wait to show it to Gaby. He wondered, as he mounted his horse that would take him to the villa, how Gaby would acclimate to her new life in France? She was different from most women he had met. That was fine with him. He liked her that way. However, the world that she would enter, although far from having the strict aristocratic rules he had to abide by, was nonetheless quite constricting. He envisioned that she might be excluded from many activities, unless of course she became someone's mistress. The thought disturbed him. He swallowed hard and tried to inculcate a bit of reality in his thinking. What should he expect? She was beautiful and he certainly could not make any commitment with the type of life he had delineated for himself. He would try to introduce her to his world in Paris. That alone would be more transitory for him and her. He would quickly retrieve his cavalier lifestyle. He was pretty sure of that.

She in turn would be devastated at first. But he had met and played with quite a few dancers and sopranos and their lives were richer than most; some had quite independent lifestyles as well. Gaby's upbringing had prepared her for the self-reliance she would need if by chance she'd have a difficult time forgetting the romantic interlude they had just spent on the *Tempète*.

Pleased with his deductions, he quickly galloped toward the hill. He could see the house standing like a small castle in the fishermen's village. He had chosen this very location upon his trip with Louis-Napoléon and Eugénie. It took in a perfect view of the fingerlike projections of the Mediterranean coast while presenting a fair view of the vessels entering the bay. It was also an excellent lookout of the marshes at the very far end of the bay where pirates lived and hid their loot.

The short ride to the castle whet his desire for the woman he knew waited anxiously for him. The domestics awaited his arrival. He entered the foyer grandly and cast a look of great delight at the finished work.

A large concave window overlooked the bay. He shot a quick glance toward it and stopped.

"Gaby . . .? He remarked, with lust in his voice. "Where did you find?"

"I've been in town with Cunnan and returned later this afternoon when I realized that you'd be kept on the vessel longer than I expected."

He frowned.

She smiled and twirled around.

"You have not commented on my very feminine apparel. How come?" She asked chagrined.

"You look ravishing," he smiled. "That is the very reason why you will stay by me from now on. No trips down to the village by yourself. Understood, beauty?"

"*Trés bien*, very well, Monsieur," she flew in his arms.

He held her head close to his heart for a long time.

He had fallen in love with her as well, she told herself, she was certain.

The bath had been drawn. In his naked splendor, Jean-Louis stepped in the marble tub. His tired body felt the heated water. He moaned.

Momentarily, a timid knock at the door stopped Gabriella on her way to rejoin him.

She turned back, marched to the door, and opened it. A pretty blond young maid, with large innocent blue eyes stood behind the white double-paneled entrance doors. □

"Pour Monsieur," she said as she tried to enter the room.

Gaby stopped her and extended her arms to scoop up the soap, scented oil, and beige horsehair glove from the young girl's hands, but the dark haired gangly maid standing behind her refused.

"Monsieur requested our presence and services, mademoiselle."

"Attendez ici," wait here, Gaby replied. She hurriedly walked to the bathroom where Jean-Louis appeared to have dozed off.

"Jean-Louis, there are two young maids outside your bedroom door who persist on wanting to wash, no, to rub you down," she exclaimed with disbelief in the heavily accented voice he had grown so fond of.

Annoyed by his lack of response, she placed herself in between the massage table and marble tub, shooting an inquisitive glance at the tall statuesque man she adored.

"Let her in, Gaby. That is one of the many pleasures being back on firm land in France presents. Unless you are willing to do their soothing work, let them come in. I am in need of a massage and as a matter of fact, I'm looking forward to it. You can stay if you wish," he said lazily.

"I can stay if I wish," she replied, furious. "First, I will ask her to go away in no uncertain terms and never to return and secondly, I will give you whatever you need. What strange customs you have here," she replied, scurrying toward the door. The maid looked surprised but nevertheless she handed her the oils, salts, and brushes and both left promptly obviously pleased to have been relieved from another assigned job.

Gaby returned with all the toiletries in her arms.

"What else am I going to be alarmed and shocked about in the next few days?" she mumbled half to herself.

He heard her and smiled.

"I'll try to be proper and abide by your puritan values, my chère, now come in and relieve my tired muscles that you so impolitely abused." he continued amused.

"Do butlers give rub-downs to the mistress of the house?" she asked.

Now it was his turn to look horrified. He glanced at her as if she was mad.

"Ah, non, it just would not be proper, ma chérie," he proclaimed.

She shot him a scandalous glare, and then kneeled by the tub and kissed his beard.

"Are you going to shave off your beard?"

"Would you like me to?"

"Yes. Today."

He laughed and lingered in the tub while she lovingly lingered on all parts of his body.

"Well, Jean-Louis," she asked "tell me—could I get a job as a gentleman's maid if my singing does not open up a lucrative and comfortable way of life in Paris?" She finished with a sexy smile.

He looked at her surprised. It was the first time she had spoken about Paris or about the new, independent life she was about to lead. Although she had been independent in New Orleans, that was before she knew him and before she had known about lust and great passion, he evaluated sadly. A possessive, jealous sensation brought him back to reality. She, after all was going to be in Paris before his own arrival. Just as well, he thought sadly, he needed to prepare her for an eventual separation. He sat up in the tub, reached for the towel she was holding up to him, and looked at her.

"Over my dead body, mademoiselle. You are too superior for the many wimpy aristocrats you will encounter in the capital. I'll hire you myself."

She laughed, her beautiful crystal clear laughter, which moved and provoked him every time he heard it.

"You beast, I better never catch you with a lovely maiden scrubbing that back!"

He reached for her, his strong, muscular chest warm from the hot bath. His arms enclosed her small body and he pressed her against him. He held her as tight as he could while his thoughts reminded him how much he would miss her after he left her in Grenoble.

She stayed cradled in his arms.

What about in Paris? He would surely see her, introduce her to his friends, la vie Parisienne, but then they'd part and go their own way. At the realization, he cringed and his body must have flinched for Gaby turned her pretty face to him. Smiling down at her, he tried to envision her with another man. None of that ever fazed him much with all of the other women he had left behind, but Gaby . . .?

He had to face reality. He would return to his own cavalier life once in Paris and then he'd leave for Italy or the Germanic states. Bismarck was the one to watch—not his little escapade. Of course, things would fall into place. He was just tired and could not think straight. He just needed to make love to her now and sleep.

He looked down at her beautiful face, resting calmly on his chest, content, as if nothing before or after this moment mattered. She enjoyed the moment at this precise instant. Jean-Louis knew that his life had changed. Gaby would have to be given up. For the first time in his life, leaving a woman would be difficult. Too tired to think anymore, he raised her chin toward his face and rubbed his beard on her cheek.

"One more night sleeping with an ape, ma chérie." He took her passionately, restricting all movement and allowing just moans of pleasure—that's all he wanted to hear, to retrieve some control of his ever more entangled life.

She felt his renewed passion or was it just the comfort of being in a comfortable bedroom with no concern of anyone eavesdropping. He held her for a long time and then placed her on her side and with one of his heavy hand on her breast, he pulled her body closer to his chest. He wanted to absorb her completely in him, and then he fell sound asleep.

In sharp contrast, Gaby could not sleep. The immensity of the ordeal, of her lost independence, became all too real. She had let her guard down and had fallen in love. She was confident that Jean-Louis cared for her—but how much, that she couldn't tell. He had said he would introduce her to his friends in Paris, but would they be lovers?

Did he have another *amour*, love, in Paris? All these questions for which she had no answers re-surfaced. She could not settle her mind. Finally, as the early morning hours crept into full daylight, she turned and kissed Jean-Louis' shoulders. She would make every second of the present count.

It was past one o'clock in the afternoon when they decided to say hello to their first full day in the small port. Both were famished, the sweet scent of freshly baked flaky croissants permeated throughout the house. She looked up at Jean-Louis. His piercing blue eyes stared down at her.

"A couple of engagements this evening, Gaby, and then the next two full days are ours to do whatever we wish. I want to show you this splendid area. It's magnificent, a wonderful way to end our adventure."

She shot him a look that held all the sadness in the universe.

He added promptly.

"Before your return to Grenoble to meet your cousin." A relaxed sense of relief suddenly illuminated her gorgeous face. This was going to be harder than he' previously thought.

"I'm famished," she proclaimed, frightened of what he would say next. "Let's eat, get ready and visit the town." She quickly got up and he followed her slowly and started for the sink.

Chapter Twelve

Jean-Louis had gone out alone early in the afternoon and Gaby prepared for the trip to Grenoble. They were to leave in two days, and her heart was heavy. Six weeks was a long time before they would meet again. Nonetheless, her positive nature had taken over once more. She would have time to get situated, along with her singing lessons and her new home—maybe even by then she'd have sealed a few friendships.

Philippe waited for her in Grenoble. He always brought such happiness and he was a wonderful and forceful influence in her life, standing behind her every decision, her business, her voice, and her travels. She adored her cousin and everything that he stood for. She was positive that Jean-Louis and Philippe would get along extremely well and in no time they would become the best of friends.

Luck had once again shone upon her. *Thank you, God*, she whispered to the heavens. How dare should she feel sorry for herself, for leaving Jean-Louis for two months? Some women did not see their lovers and husbands for three, four, even five consecutive years. Remember the Civil War, Gabriella, she reminded herself.

They were going out tonight. Jean-Louis had shared that they had been invited to a reception in Nice given in his honor. Cunnan had told her that Jean-Louis was highly in demand—sought after, were the exact words he used, and extremely powerful. She heard him walk in and promptly she left all the packing behind to join him downstairs.

"I'm here," she called out. The place was so vast, if all of his homes were that grandiose, she understood why his shouts were downright frightening. It was a good thing her voice projected well.

Jean-Louis was amused. In her candid, girlish demeanor she was absolutely sure that his world revolved around hers. She believed that she was forever in his thoughts. He must be in hers constantly, he deduced.

What had happened to his independence? He thought as he walked in, dressed smartly in a gray overcoat, matching vest, long dark pants, and a white cravat. He never liked being in the presence of the weaker sex longer than it was needed to be pleased. These long trips at sea had softened his disposition. He did not want to hurt Gaby, but soon there would not be time for their romantic interlude. He had to start preparing her for the eventual break up. Talks of his eminent trip to Italy had been approached today.

"Well, well, Miss Stowaway. You look ravishing. Come down and keep me company. I'm famished. I could not stay away from you any longer, I wouldn't even stop for a déjeuner with some former colleagues," he said half-joking.

The sun shone on her face, radiance and sheer delight gave her a bewitching aura as she flew down the stairs.

"What grace you possess," he noted regally waiting for her at the end of the marble staircase, his hand resting on the balustrade. He loved watching her step down the stairs. She looked like an angel.

"Jean-Louis, after supper I want to share something with you."

"Our bed?" he retorted, smiling.

"No," came the sharp response. "You have a one-track mind, my friend. Now that we are on land, the world is ours to explore, no more somber stateroom where you kept a vital American woman prisoner in seclusion for your own desire and pleasure.

"Please remind me of these charming moments now," he reached for her waist, pulled her close and kissed her.

"Jean-Louis, be serious," she declared solemnly.

"What is it you want to show me, Gaby?"

"Well I needed more towels." He continued to touch her lips as she tried to explain about her strange finding. "I noticed the maids busily walking in and out of rooms, so I decided to help myself without having to disturb anyone. I roamed around looking for linens. Well, I must have mistaken the floors, for I actually walked in a music room adorned with spanking instruments." She roared with laughter, her pretty features animated as she pulled her hair away from her face. Detecting his shocked expression, she tried to regain her composure.

"You walked where?" he repeated, incredulous.

"I walked in a room that must have been designed as a music room. Did you include plans for a music room?"

He nodded. He recalled faintly that he had approved a theatre.

"The walls are all made of wood with rounded corners for the sound to bounce back to the audience, but Jean-Louis, the amusing side of this sordid finding is that it's been transformed in some type of erotic utility space where I found myriads of martinets, carpet beaters and straps all arranged neatly on shelves. What should I use to beat my husband or servants today, let's see?" She pursed her lips and glanced at the ceiling.

The Captain looked at her with a distressed expression on his face.

"Jean-Louis you will have to forgive me. I presume that I'm a bit too candid. Nothing is sacred with me," she regained her mischievous grin. "Well, I can see that it is not amusing to you. I'm sorry. I know the tenant was one of your good friends. He must have forgotten to clean up his act before he left your saintly dwelling," she tried to humor him once again plainly. He was not amused.

"I was out of line. I take back everything I said. It was not meant to be an insult to your culture nor to your friends. I know the maids use these cleaning contraptions to beat the carpets," she theorized gravely, "we have the same thing on my plantation."

"It figures," he muttered haughtily.

Her facial expression changed from skittish to downright grave. It was his turn to regain a bit of seriousness. "I mean the carpet beaters for the stables and such...."

She shot him an icy look.

"Cease your insinuations, Jean-Louis. I feel as opposed to our old customs as you are, but I can't undo history and although I loathe my mother, I still have great respect for the stand that she took against a great portion of her peers. We did not own slaves. She gave them their freedom papers way before the war. But we had servants just like you do and frankly they had a wonderful life on my plantation in sharp contrast with what I have just noticed in this household."

There was coolness and a show of strength on both sides of the great divide. The tension could be cut with a knife and finally he was astute enough to break it.

"Very well, Gaby," he said softly, in a conciliatory tone, "tell me about my erotic theatre. No more lecture—I read you."

"It is not important. I was being childish and insensitive to your mores. But you will have to admit, it is an oddity to transform a music room, and a wonderful one at that, into a—laundry closet. But since you have never been fortunate enough to hear my beautiful voice, I can't help but to invite you to the spanking room to hear me sing!"

He chuckled. His face showed pleasure to be in her company.

"Gaby, I will not do you the dishonor to listen to your great gift in such sordid place. I will just have to wait until we meet again in Paris."

"Anything not to listen to my euphonious voice. Your loss, Monsieur." She shot him another hard glance.

"Gaby I would be honored to hear you sing in the—music room, but chérie, what were you thinking, snooping on my friend's positively perverse sexual demeanors? How ungrateful of you to demean a man's warm hospitability?" he retorted haughtily.

She shot him a murderous glance. "Off with your head, you pretentious aristocrat. I just wanted to make you aware of your friend's habits when you are away. The Catholic Church might expropriate you from Villefranche. I can see that you have been in your country just two days and your arrogance, and that French aloofness your countrymen are so famous for, is flaunting its burgeoning buds. I will have to drill you into enjoying the simple things in life when you arrive in Paris. Or—are there any simple things in Paris? Why are the French so complicated?"

He looked at her amused with a curious grin on his face.

"Gaby, what makes you so sure that our life will be the same once in Paris?" He continued teasingly, "maybe a young wimpy aristocrat will court you and you'll have forgotten all about me by the time of my arrival." He laughed.

Gaby stopped smiling. She had not inculcated the rest of the sentence and her beautiful green eyes filled with tears that she fought hard not to shed.

"I never thought of it, Jean-Louis," she said candidly. She turned away and looked up toward the ceiling so as to hide her tears. "Do you have someone special waiting for you in Paris, Jean-Louis?"

"Don't be absurd," he gathered her close to his chest, "I have been gone for seven years. With the culture of modern Parisian women I wouldn't seriously court one of them for a day."□

"But so, there was someone, Jean-Louis," her voice cracked.

"No, Gaby, there were many liaisons, not one mattered, chérie."

"Do I matter to you, Jean-Louis? You matter to me," she said candidly.

"Yes, you do, Gaby, but I also know that our relationship might need to adapt. It will experience some changes and I want you to use your keen sense of logic. A new life may be ahead for you—new experiences, new friends." He held her tightly as he pressed her close to his body.

Her beautiful sad face stared back at him. She held back an ocean of tears ready to stream down her cheeks.

"I love you, Jean-Louis with all my being and I know you love me, too. I know you do." She held the lapel of his dove gray jacket as if to convince and console her sad spirit. "I do not understand why it is so hard for you to tell me so."

He smiled. She paused and tightened her hold on his broad stature.

"I presume I'm feeling a bit insecure. I do not know anything about French traditions and—and after your last statement, I'm getting confused and very, very sad."

"Gaby, the only thing that I meant to say is that things will be somewhat different. Your studies, other people around us, our living arrangement, your new friends, mine, our social commitments, I think that it's only fair that we should think about these new surroundings and responsibilities. Our lives and responses will change—our relationship will change, Gaby. We must be reasonable." He was pleased that he had touched on the subject. It was only fair. She was sad, but he had planted the seed. And that was the right thing to do. He now retrieved his gaiety and lighter spirit.

"Now, come with me, I'm famished," he commanded.

She followed him absently. She had been shocked and torn apart about his logical response but something deep inside her told her not to take it too seriously. He loved her. She was certain of that—then

117

doubts began to unveil themselves. She slowly walked with him into the dining room that had been set up for an early dinner.

"I accepted an invitation for this evening in Nice. We will spend the night in Nice in a beautiful hotel overlooking the Bay Des Anges. I thought it might be a bit reckless to travel back here at night. So pack lightly just a few extra things for tomorrow morning. We should return late tomorrow afternoon unless you simply adore all my friends and prefer the social life that Nice has to offer during this period of festivities. I'm very pleased, Gaby, because you will be meeting quite a few individuals which will be great contact points if you were to need anything before I arrive in Paris, chérie."

"I'm well taken care of, Jean-Louis. I'll do well either way." She replied sadly but assertively.

During their déjeuner, she was quiet and did not touch her meal, save a few blueberries. She asked all the right questions about his day but her joie de vivre had left her adorable little face. He tried to cheer her up.

"Eh bien, I'm ready for your heavenly arias, my beautiful diva."

"Another time, perhaps," she said with a polite smile.

Guilt pains tortured him now. Why had he been so direct, so logical with her? He'd hurt her he knew that now. He had just been trying to ease the separation and make her understand that their relationship might cool off once in Paris. She had been so sure that their romantic interlude might extend into the future. He had just wanted to insert a bit of reality into her girlish dreams. On the other hand, he cared and liked her tremendously. He loved her tumultuous nature, a true chameleon. He never quite knew what to expect from her. She always surprised him with her romantic, artistic nature in stark contrast with her sense of economics and athletic abilities. On horseback, she'd nearly beat him on their way back to Villefranche yesterday. She was an accomplished rider, never afraid to go against all rules of feminine etiquette whenever she felt that proprieties were entrenching upon her right as an individual.

He looked at her, wanting to offset his harsh comments with compliments that she knew were real. He saw her staring at the ceiling across from the table. Her green eyes filled with tears that he knew were difficult to contain. He placed his napkin on the table, stood up and he reached for her hand as he forced her to stand next to him.

"I'm sorry, Gaby, I've not meant to anger you, I was . . . "

"I know exactly what you were trying to do, Jean-Louis. You did not anger me. You made me very sad." Her voice trembled. She paused. He pulled her to his chest, but in a sob-staggered voice, she continued.

"We have only two more days together and I don't want to talk logic and reason. I want to keep it the way it's been for the past few weeks. I want to remember it perfect, Jean-Louis. Let me go. I want to go upstairs, cry freely, talk some sense to my crazy self and come back down and be ready for the night—full of merriment."

She broke free of his embrace and ran upstairs. Her small body shuddered with sobs shouting for release.

Helpless, he observed her up the stairs as the lacey, body-hugging tunic trailed on the thick red carpet. He watched her open the door and slam it shut behind her. He returned back to the dining room and sat in a red velvet deep chaise—his appetite had vanished. Why had he been so blunt? It's that partnership 'thing', as she called it, which had developed between them that was the culprit. He never intended to hurt her so deeply. He had not expected her stricken reaction. After all, she was an innocent twenty-one year old girl. Although she was accomplished in areas that most women totally ignored, her youth and innocence with men of his sort had worked against her. He was going to make it up to her.

It suddenly downed on him that her absence was going to be difficult for him as well. He missed her even at this very instant. This romantic interlude might be bigger than he'd ever imagined in his wildest thoughts. He had caught himself a few times with a vision of Gaby in his house in Paris waiting for him, entertaining together. Now, his life had been filled with many liaisons, some lasting longer than others, but—and that was a huge but—his home was always his domain to be shared with no one. He had bought a few apartments and had two hotel particuliers that many of his mistresses had used but never his Saint-Louis' mansion—that was his personal residence.

He pushed away the thought and walked in the study to evaluate and approve some of the charting routes his officers had drawn up for him. He decided against accepting two diplomats who would be traveling to Italy with him. He was going to have to work with these fellows—at the very least for one year. He needed a zone of comfort. A while later, as he re-entered his room to get ready for the soirée, he was surprised to found that Gaby was not there.

"Oú est Mademoiselle Thornsen?" he asked.

"Getting ready in her boudoir, Monsieur, "the young maid replied.

Suddenly, he recalled the maids were probably helping her. He could smell her sweet perfume as he walked toward the bed and once again the thought of being away from her for two months distracted him. He gave himself time to reflect over the past month. Had he been a romance novelist, the storyline could not have been more outlandish. He got ready all in black coattails and a crisp white shirt that showed off his deep tan and piercing blue eyes. How lucky the little brat downstairs was! He poured himself a scotch and Gaby walked into the room.

"Voila, Monsieur le Duke," she exclaimed in her beautiful laughing voice, *votre escorte est finalement prête," your escort is finally ready.*

As he tuned around, he was faced with an absolutely alluring beauty who had been coiffed in a very Parisian style, her gorgeous mahogany mane placed high on top of her head with ringlets falling softly around her heart-shaped face. The rouge and make-up her maid had used showed off her refined features and the low décolleté of her vanilla satin gown hid very little of her shapely, voluptuous breasts. Jean-Louis swallowed hard giving her an approving look lingering on her breasts and small waist.

"Well, Mon Cher," she remarked with an insolent glimpse, "will the young and wimpy aristocrats you referred to this afternoon give me a second look? Do I have your fatherly approval?"

"If they even come within three feet of you, Gaby, I'll kill them in a duel."

She obviously enjoyed the visible effect she had on him.

"In retrospect, it is coming back to me, I recall having quite an effect on the male population—not that it ever mattered at the time." She smiled and looked at him with loving eyes, "Not until I met this one fellow on a ship who completely dazzled me and threw my innate logical reasoning and sense of self-realization out to sea."

"You are remarkable, Gaby, never hiding your feelings so as to play little cat and mouse games. I like that, chérie," he bent down and kissed her. "If I linger longer on you, I'm afraid we will not attend the soirée.

He asked for her cape and off they went to beautiful Nice. The road to Nice although short, a mere seven kilometers, was quite bumpy, but Jean-Louis regaled her with gossips on many of the Grand Monde they were about to meet. She asked a few questions on certain rules of proprieties that applied to women.

"Don't ask you'll never follow any of them," he replied sarcastically.

"No, I will. I do not want to embarrass you. Knowledge of what is proper in a culture is always most important."

Taking into account her own knowledge of the Southern etiquette in the honorable circles on Charles Street in New Orleans, she surmised from the two days in Europe that the rules of etiquette in France were stricter and practiced without any interruptions.

"Do as you wish, Gaby. You are perfect, chérie, ahead of your time perhaps, but perfect as an individual. No one expects perfection from you and if they do, I can assure you that they will not say anything to embarrass you. You are with me. You should be proud of all of your gifts and accomplishments. Be yourself, chérie—you will be adored."

Armed with such words, she felt very confident and her spirit lifted. She was going to show him that her wit, intelligence, and good looks were researched as well.

Upon arrival in the Grand Ballroom of the hotel, the couple was mobbed. Jean-Louis had not exaggerated when he advised her to enjoy herself and to touch base with him at regular intervals. She had been so happy that he had reserved a room in the hotel. He instantly became the focus of awareness—old men, younger men, old ladies, and young, beautiful, elegant temptresses who at one point without so much as an apology nearly pushed Gaby out of his way to gain access to his greatness—le Duke De Bourbonne.

She had been surprised. No one called him Jean-Louis. Jean-Louis was the name she had become accustomed to. Gaby was disappointed. She had counted on two things that would serve her goal of making him realized he adored her. First she had felt her looks and spirit would make him the envy of all his friends—yet no one paid attention to her. Actually there were so many beautiful, elegantly clad women that Gaby's small stature did not rival the elegant standard of the French women. Secondly, since no one paid attention to her, she could not shine with her intelligent and spirited conversation.

Thank heavens for splendid French champagne. Vive le Dom Pérignon! She picked up her third flute and moved away from the circle where her lover clearly was the man of the evening.

She walked across the grand foyer thinking that she might as well return back to their room but she spotted the game rooms on her way. Roulette, baccarat and all sorts of gaming tables stood in the fabulous hall and groups of tense looking men, surrounded by statuesque women, their good luck charms, were placing large sums of money on the table.

While she pondered if it would be proper to enter and watch, someone placed his arms under hers.

"Mademoiselle, would you do me the honor. It would please me grandly to show you *la Salle de Jeu*," the casino.

She twisted to the right, stunned that someone had been so bold as to touch her so daringly. It felt good.

The tanned god standing next to her smiled. He had perfect features on his sun-tanned face, dark-brown eyes, and a drop-dead smile that showed off pearly-white teeth. She learned later that most women would lie down when asked by this sensual man to sit down. Thus the French motto, *les horizontales*, when one spoke of women with less than perfect virtue. Renaud De Beauvaur was not too tall, perhaps his only imperfection. He was just beautiful, such perfection was unusual for a woman, and it was breathtaking on a man!

"Do you play or just enjoy watching?" he asked while he led her away from curious onlookers.

"I like to play." She smiled back, a bit sheepishly.

"Good, so let me do the honor." He reached for her elbows and led her toward the Roulette table.

Momentarily, Jean-Louis who towered above the crowd, searched for Gaby. He noticed her just in time to see her being led away by De Beauvaur. Unfortunately, the Emperor's envoy had just arrived and the two men and their aides moved away from the crowd into a more private and secluded room on the second floor.

Hours passed pleasantly. Gabriella was following Jean-Louis' advice—having a jolly good time while she flirted with Renaud De Beauvaur. She had not engaged with another man in quite some time.

The seductive De Beauvaur was a very wealthy aristocratic landowner from Provence, financially rooted in the construction of the new railroads projects. Recently his business savvy had taken him to the Orient where his fleet traded in oriental decorative arts highly valued in France.

According to Monsieur De Beauvaur, the French Emperor wanted to set in motion this monumental development not solely to unify Europe, but to make France the leader of the economic and industrial revolution looming over Europe. No expenses were to be spared to achieve his goal. His name in history would depend on his diligence to further that very cause.

For the time being, Renaud was charming. He knew the American South quite well and was one of the few Europeans who did not hold most of the Southerners in contempt.

"Well, mademoiselle, what are you doing in Nice, especially in the company of such a bad boy as Jean-Louis-Pierre De Pleyssis," he said sensuously as he looked into her eyes.

She smiled. "A bad boy?" The champagne was working its warmth and as the evening wore on, she opened up to him about her musical dreams, Paris, her life in New Orleans, her plantation, and about her decision to follow her dream and study voice in Paris at the Conservatoire.

"I heard the sordid story about your encounter with Jean-Louis-Pierre. Tell me it's a lie."

"No, sir, it is all true. What about yourself, Monsieur? What do you do? I deduce from your statements that you are one of the few persons here tonight that do not hold the Duke in high esteem. What has he done to you?" she concluded candidly.

"Stolen the love of my life," he laughed, "I intend to make myself so agreeable to you that you'll drop him tonight for forcing you to face le Grand Monde all alone. You are invited to spend the rest of your vacation in Nice as a guest of mine. I'll gamble with you and show you one of the world's greatest winery in the world."

"So your trade is making fine wines?"

"And much more, Gabriella, but wine has been a hobby in my family for hundreds of years and I would love sharing some of its secrets with a witty and beautiful woman such as yourself."

Gaby was amused. It felt wonderful to be light and flirtatious.

"Well, Monsieur, if you beat me at roulette or any of the games available here I will seriously ponder your offer."

She let him point the way toward the gaming tables. Sitting next to a portly man and his beautiful companion, she waited anxiously until the wheel stopped.

The croupier called *faites vos jeux* and she placed her bets. Forty minutes later, her winning accumulated. There was no end to her luck!

Both were now out-betting the rest of the Salle. She was playing her win against his and laughing as if she did not have a care in the world. She was now the only one left taking the win so frivolously, silence reigned and even Renaud was getting less talkative.

"No more banter, Monsieur De Beauvaur? Are you now taking me seriously?" She questioned ironically.

He smiled at her in astonishment. She winked back at him, pressing her lips together in a threatening fashion.

This last gesture was not lost on Jean-Louis who had just entered the room after friends had told him that *his petite amie, his young girlfriend,* was intent on breaking the bank.

Renaud could afford it. Gaby should whip him he smirked. As a matter of fact, he would have loved for Gaby to teach the insolent imbecile a lesson, but the wink—that he had not expected and he became annoyed instantly. What was she doing with him? They had gotten quite chummy in just two hours. Renaud was smart, handsome, and extremely wealthy and women liked his personality.

The croupier watched the small white ball come down on the riveted edges of the number two. The crowd gasped—Gaby had won again.

She was intent on winning again. The focused expression on her face showed that she intended to do just that. The croupier was giving her the chips as he once again pronounced himself.

"Messieurs, Mesdames faites vos jeux."

Jean-Louis became irritated. Gaby was getting a whole lot of attention—mostly bad. He could hear snide remarks about American women from women and men in his entourage.

"Ces étrangères, la-bas en Amérique sont trés évoluées, n'est ce pas? Where did you meet her, Jean-Louis-Pierre? These American women are emancipated? But then as soon as he was out of earshot, gossip ran rampant. Jean-Louis thought that they should look further at the 'emancipated' behavior of the Merveilleuses?

"This is outrageous, a most impolite behavior, *voyez- vous cela*? What poor image, this . . . this circus gives to our well-mannered spouses. Women have already invaded our suites and salons at the opéra in Paris," others concluded. "I recall when well-behaved women stayed in their loges watching the opéra, recital, plays, now they pursue us everywhere. We have no more privacy. What calamity! Hopefully this last outrage with the colonial will not be remembered in Paris."

"I just do not understand Jean-Louis-Pierre," a tall, impeccably-dressed, white-haired man with a lorgnette interrupted the rest of the group, "his Grandmother must be beside herself. Imagine that, bringing back a mistress from America with all the beautiful, polished, distinguished women we have in our beautiful France."

The gossips went on and although irked by the wink, it was in his nature to go against all rules of proprieties. This affair suited him just fine. He walked away from the main entrance of the game room, away from the gossip, and he positioned himself at the opposite side of the croupier. With a good view of both gamblers, in between betting, his loud, distinct, cavernous voice resonated throughout the room.

"And I thought I was saving a nun! Saving and protecting this saintly child from marauding pirates bent on deriving pleasure from the innocent, was my honorable intent. I was bringing her back to the convent of the Sacré Coeur, an act of *bienfaisance* on my part—to mend my evil ways. Mon Dieu, instead I saved an incorrigible gambler with her heart set on breaking the bank. My apologies, Mesdames and Messieurs."

The room roared with laughter.

Surprised at his apparition, Gaby quickly lifted her head. How long had he been there? The statement struck her fancy, a crystal clear laughter surprised the room and she continued the hilarity as she stared in his smiling eyes.

"Faites vos jeux," the croupier started again.

Gaby paused and surveyed the large crowd gathered around her waiting for the next number to be played. She stared at her lover once more and summoned his words on the fleeting nature of French women sexual mores and financial interests.

"Voila, fini," she proclaimed, "the Duke is absolutely correct. My saintly and virtuous nature fed by deep-seated spiritual convictions forbids me to remove the obvious pleasure that I have so rudely deprived each and everyone of you. Sinful, indeed, I offer my most sincere apologies. I retire forever from gambling."

She picked up her winnings, straightened up her torso, tidied up her dress, and turned abruptly around. Self-confident and poised she walked to Jean-Louis. She had won on all fronts, she thought. Thank you, dear God. She removed the scarf that she had draped over her shoulders to conceal her voluptuous body as she bent down to play the game. She dropped all her chips inside it. Decidedly she walked over to Jean-Louis and extended her arms to show him the considerable amount of yellow and red chips she had won.

It reminded him of a little girl anxious to show her father her day's pickings.

"Gabriella," Renaud interjected, "you can't do that. The pleasure is ours, trust me. I can assure you that watching your beautiful features and your formidable *chance, luck,* at the table gives us all a great amount of pleasure. Everything comes alive right in front of our eyes. It is worth all the chips on these tables. Jean-Louis-Pierre convince her to continue!" Renaud shouted.

Jean-Louis lifted his hands up as if helpless in her decision.

"She's an American, De Beauvaur. Haven't you heard what they've done to the British? No, I'm not going there." Once again the room roared with laughter.

"Thank you, Renaud, for an unforgettable evening." Gaby said politely. "It was a lot of fun," she remarked spontaneously.

Once again the laughter from the room soared. Renaud was known as an intense and incorrigible gambler, spending thousands of francs on the casino tables in Nice, Monte Carlo, and Deauville. He never thought of gambling as plain fun—decadent, suspenseful, and addictive, yes—but never as fun.

"When will you reach Paris, Gabriella?" he questioned.

"In about three or four weeks. I start at the Conservatoire le deux Juin."

"I'll look you up in Paris. I'll show you Paris before Jean-Louis gets there. We will get you acclimatized to la vie Parisienne very quickly. Good night, Gabriella, au plaisir."

"Good night, Renaud," she responded courteous. She turned on her heels and strode sensuously towards Jean-Louis who was looking at her from the far end corner of the table. She smiled sweetly at him as she rounded the game table. Without any deliberation she offered him the shawl filled with winning tokens.

Questioningly, he smirked, astonished.

"I don't know where I can cash it. Help me please," she posed.

He took the makeshift shawl, grabbed a basket, tossed the winning inside it, and led her to the cashier.

"Come, I want to show you Nice by night?" he said in English as he stopped momentarily to pick up a couple flutes of champagne.

Quickly he guided her to the second floor on a balcony that overlooked one of the most magnificent bay she had ever seen.

"The view is magnificent, Jean-Louis," she murmured mesmerized.

"This is the Bay des Anges, Gaby." He pulled her out of sight from the gawking crowd.

"In an enchanting sort of way, the two land masses that encircle the bay appear to be the arms of a lover gathering his loved one," Gaby murmured romantically.

He smiled down at her.

As they slipped out of view from the crowd, Jean-Louis reached for her waist, pulled her close to his chest, lifted her chin between his fingers, and kissed her. She saw lust and desire burning in his eyes. His hands dropped over her shoulders and her back. His kiss became demanding, passionate in an odd needy sort of way.

Momentarily, she lost her balance and had to grasp his velvet vest to regain her footing. This move fueled his lust and passion and he continued to kiss her ardently. Out of breath, she pushed him back gently.

"Please remind me to always give you all my winnings whenever I gamble—always—always. Let me rectify, I was only joking when I publicly announced my retirement from gambling."

"You insolent little brat," he said, nipping on her lower lip. "Now listen, you'll only have one chance to accept. I have a deal for you," he continued kissing her cheeks and brushed his knuckles along her chin up to her earlobe. "I have changed my itinerary. How would you like to spend an extra ten days here in the south of France? I'll take you to Grenoble later and we will send a messenger just in case your cousin arrives earlier than expected. There are lots of beautiful places to visit. I want to show them to you. What do you say, chérie?"

"What do I say? I adore it. I just adore it. It's just marvelous. Will it be just you and me, a vacation? How did it all come about?"

"I met with some people earlier today and gave myself a well deserved holiday. However, Gaby, if you wish to meet more people before your arrival in Paris, we can have a social calendar every evening until we leave for Grenoble. I will have to attend the Carnival du Mardi Gras and the Bataille des fleurs. I'm the guest of honor. However, the rest of the time, I rather spent it with you."

"I don't really care what we do, being with you is sufficient for me. I don't quite know what it is that I have done right to deserve such happiness, but I've never been so content and joyous about life—ever." She smiled at him and she kissed him tenderly. Her passionate nature took over and even Jean-Louis was no match for her lovemaking.

He would have loved to run upstairs, Gaby in his arms, and spend the rest of the night loving her, but more serious business discussions needed his attention downstairs. Frustrated with himself that she possessed such a big chunk of his life, he regained his composure.

"I'll walk you back to the room, chérie, I still have quite a few annoying meetings."

"But Jean-Louis, I can stay downstairs. I met a few people. Really, I do not mind being left alone. The music is euphonious and I am not sleepy—at all.

"Good, then wait for me in great anticipation, didn't you say this afternoon you wanted it to be exactly like it was on the ship. I'm giving you the chance, sweetheart, I answer your every wish."

"Scoundrel, you just do not want me to interact with anyone." She raised his hand to her lips and she kissed the soft warm spot inside his palms.

"Don't be too long, darling, there is much too much excitement downstairs," she winked.

They reached the large apartment that had been reserved for him. He let her in first. At first she could not quite make out what he was going to do. Why did he have to attend to all these meetings? One thing for sure he made it crystal clear that he did not want her downstairs—jealousy, she hoped.

"Not a bad idea after all, I'm very tired. Have a good time."

He brushed his lips on her forehead.

"I'll see you soon," he said as he passed the door.

Left alone in the magnificent room she walked toward the ornate balcony. She parted the heavy white and gold curtains to the side, hundreds of blinking lights bopped on the Méditerranée as fishermen on their barges dropped down their nets for the daily catch. She stared at the picturesque scene without really seeing it. Instead, she thought of Jean-Louis. How exciting, she now had another ten days to enjoy this beautiful locality with the man she loved. He had said a vacation. Her mind whirled with beautiful thoughts of the two of them visiting exciting places.

A hard knock at the door brought her back to reality. Who could it be? Quietly, she re-entered the room from the balcony where she had been dreaming. Her suspicious nature re-enforced by the trauma she experienced when pirates had overtaken the Italian frigate, now placed her in grand alert. She walked inaudibly toward a black trimmed with gold Directory table where a tall and heavy crystal vase was posed. She lifted it and silently advanced toward the door.

"Who is it?" she asked more severely with her pronounced accent. There was no response. A key inserted in the golden lock turned the doorknob.

"Jean-Louis, is that you?" she forced out. The key turned a second time into the lock. The knob twirled in her hand as she tried to stop the rotation. The door ajar, she was shoved backwards against the wall. She held her breath and waited.

Jean-Louis entered and stared at the empty bed and the still open window.

"You frightened me!" She raged.

Swiftly, he turned on his heels and stared at her terrorized expression. He smirked. She had been the force behind the door.

"Do you own a gun, Gaby? He questioned amused.

"You might be lying face down on the floor if I had my gun!" She retorted uncompromising.

He ambled across the room to her. He grasped her writs and clutched her to him forcefully as he silenced her anger by pressing his lips insistently against hers. With total control, he paused and stared at her beautiful startled face while his gaze strayed down to her breasts. He bent down and kissed the very spot where his eyes had wandered. Now passion dictated his every move, he placed his two hands on each side of her décolleté and he ripped the satin frills down to the top of her hips. The dress began its slow, fluid descent onto the carpet while only her white satin underwear stood in the way of his resolute muscular stature.

Flabbergasted, Gaby pulled away and shot a sideways glance at her naked body in the mirror.

"I presume you did not like the dress?" she gasped.

"Not particularly," came the terse reply. He pulled her down with him on the divan, and smiled at her shaken expression. Gaby's bosom arched against his body desiring all the sensations that tortured her body. She yearned for more of everything he allowed her to feel.

"Ever since we left the propriétée this evening," he murmured, breathing heavily as passion raked his body, "I ached for this very moment." Lust controled his core.

Gaby needed no explanation. He'd already sent her in a world of overwhelming sensations.

After the release, he held her close to his heart—very close. There was another dimension to his embrace. She could not pinpoint it, but she knew that tonight something had clicked in his mind—in his heart. It was good.

He continued to hold her for a long time.

"I am very happy that we have these extra days together, chérie. You make me very happy, Gaby."

Amazed and blissful at the revelation, she took his hand, kissed it tenderly, and lay motionless in his arms afraid to break the spell. She hoped that he was here to stay, and that he would not return to the meetings he had told her earlier he had to attend.

"Up, my gorgeous lover," he said almost brusquely, "I need to return to my duties."

Jean-Louis had hoped that having a sexual release would relieve him from the constant urge he suffered from incessantly wanting her near him. She took too large of a place in his life.

"I can't, I can't move. You have taken my strength and resolution. Will you take me to bed?" she replied in English, too exhausted to even attempt to make sense in French.

"Again," he scoffed, "Don Juan belonged to another era, my chère. They don't make them like him anymore."

"Let me refresh your memory, my darling, I was not the ravenous vulture this evening." She snapped with blazing eyes

He picked her up and gently lowered her on the bed. He laid her pretty brown curls on the white satin pillowcase.

"Sleep well, chérie," he countered as he looked down at her sternly.

"Jean-Louis," she said sleepily, as he bent further down toward her to listen to her murmuring voice, "please don't be too late, I don't like sleeping alone in strange beds. It's a bit frightening. And don't turn off the lights."

"*Eh bien*, a consoling thought, indeed. That's a very comforting comment to entertain, as you will be away from me in a forthnight."

"Hush," she responded sleepily as she rolled on her side.

On the spot, Jean-Louis summoned all the control he possessed not to roll in bed very close to her and gather up the infernal brat in his arms for one more romp. Instead he buried his head in the curly mass of shiny hair. He nudged her for a long moment and assertively he straightened, and walked to the dressing room to re-assess his professional stature. Within minutes he was gone—again.

This time he did not return until the early hours of the morning, Inebriated, he plopped into bed completely dressed. He placed one leg on top of her hips, drew her closer to him and rested his face in her hair. She sleepily took his hand and clasped it to her breast.

Hours later Gaby woke up, full of energy, ready to take on the French Riviera. She untangled herself from his clinching legs and walked on over to the balcony as she took in the breath taking *Bay des Anges*.

"Jean-Louis, wake up," she called out to him, "it's magnificent. Everyone is on the Promenade, along the beach. Oh, please." Silence reigned. Minutes later, she strode back in the room and approached the bed. The staggering sound of a large cannon would not have wakened him up. She came closer to him and kissed him.

"Were there other women with you? You smell awfully good, scoundrel!" She remarked jealously.

He rolled away from the sunshine, and went right back to sleep.

As the sunshine shone through the thick, cream and gold satin drapes, she decided not to wait around. Jean-Louis was going to sleep a good part of the day. He had shown up at six this morning.

She took the money she'd won at the gaming table the prior evening and decided to visit the town and shops. She might be very lucky yet again—just like in Villefranche. She loved clothes. To be able to purchase the actual French fashion in France made her feel wonderful. She left a note for Jean-Louis on his burgundy, leather-bound appointment book that he checked assiduously and told him about her shopping trip. She probably would return before he awoke.

The gray suit she had purchased from the Italian seamstress in Villefranche fit her in a most alluring way. She liked what she saw in the mirror. Off she went.

The concierge observed strangely, probably tongues wagged. She was now known as the woman who gave up breaking the bank—or Jean-Louis-Pierre De Pleyssis' mistress—she just did not care. She was happier than she had ever been. The doorman stood by the revolving door and nodded politely as she walked out and stood mesmerized facing the breathtaking Méditerranée. She decided to walk along the beach near the water before shopping. There were no waves, very little surf, the water looked like undisturbed oil. A gentle rustling sound pleased and soothed the soul. She looked back and lifted her eyes to the room where the man she loved lay asleep—or here again there was a strong possibility that he was talking to the ceramic God! She giggled at such an ordinary thought.

The next ten days would be idyllic. She missed being on his ship. She did not have to share him in their small cabin—not with other women.

The small boutiques where couturiers and tailors were busy at work sewing, pleasing, adjusting, and creating were filled with wealthy people who perused and bought all sorts of pretty things. She entered many such stores on the Promenade. Money flowed in France. She had not seen any beggars or ruffians—so prevalent in New Orleans. Although, Jean-Louis had mentioned, while in Villefranche, that pirates still loomed in their niche at the far end of the bay where heavy vegetation grew wild. The fingerlike projections facing the Cap

Ferrat provided a perfect setting to hide their loot. They at times came into the small fishing village to rape or to steal or both. A lot of people, according to his assessment felt that the pillaging had contributed to the movement to rejoin France.

Gaby sat in a café, she wrote down her impressions and all the history Jean-Louis had shared with her while still on the Tempète, on a brand new leather-bound cognac escritoire. *The villagers hoped that the Count of Savoy would shelter them from the marauders, she wrote and the Duke Dolmans had mentioned that there could not be a stable Provence without a protected Villefranche and Nice. He had begun to leave troops in the Citadelle in Villefranche.* She needed to write everything down lest she would forget some important event. A large number of the guests she had met last evening with Renaud appeared in the historic anecdotes Jean-Louis had recited. She wandered why he had not introduced her to many of them?

The French were not the friendliest people. Many of her questions were often ignored. The people who did answer her questions were curt and rarely smiled. No one seemed to show any interest to a stranger who was most intent on learning about their country and their culture, she mused, incensed. Oh, well, she would soon be part of that society whether the natives wanted her to or not. She had helped the local economy with all the purchases she allowed herself.

Several times, people had lowered their voices when she entered the stores. She would have loved to know what these rich-looking, beautifully dressed ladies spoke about. Many men had smirks on their faces and even flirted with her while their lady friends were trying on bonnets or purchasing gloves. What a place!

She strolled in front of the many hotels that lounged the beautiful Promenade des Anglais. Suddenly someone called her name. She looked toward the terrace of the hotel and noticed Renaud who sat nearby. She waved. He appeared to be surrounded by a large group of friends, all enjoying an aperitif. She waited on the sidewalk as she watched him leave the group and march to her.

"Hello, Gabriella, where is the grand Monsieur?" He asked.

"He was not a bit interested in showing me the stores in Nice. I left him in his room reading," she lied.

"I bet," Renaud replied with a good-natured smile, while two of the ladies in attendance glanced sideways.

"Eh bien, Gabriella, what about *un déjeuner*, a lunch?"

She accepted gladly.

The lunch was mouthwatering. All enjoyed a salade de tomates, with myriad tomatoes tossed scrumptiously in olive oil and vinegar with eggs, cold green beans, radishes, endives, anchovies and tuna. Naturally baskets of ficelles and baguettes accompanied the lunch. She listened to the conversation at hand. Gambling in Monte Carlo was the evening's plan.

"Would you like to join us, Gabriella," Renaud asked.

"Oh no thank you. Do you recall Renaud, I swore off gambling!" she giggled. "But I'll take a rain check on your kind invitation to show me beautiful Paris upon my arrival. I would like that very much," she countered. She appreciated Renaud's company immensely.

"Consider it done, Gabriella. Eh bien, since you will not join us this evening, can I guide you through Nice?

She was about to refuse. "I will get you back to Jean-Louis-Pierre quickly, but please do me the honor," he implored.

"Thank you, I'd love to," she replied enchanted to have such a charming guide showing her the city.

Renaud took her in an open carriage and guided her to the old Nice with its colorful flower market and hard working patissiers, pastry chefs, boulangers, bakers, butchers and more. On one of the side streets, she noticed a church and a convent.

"Oh, please, if I could spare just a few minutes of your time."

"With pleasure, I presume that you are a religious young lady. The gossip about lying to Jean-Louis-Pierre about your coming to Europe to join the convent has some truth to it after all, Gabriella?" He questioned amused.

"Well, yes and no. I will live in the convent . . . or perhaps in my cousin's home in Saint Louis when my cousin is in Rome—for the time being, anyway. But I . . ." she paused, somewhat embarrassed, "I always stop by a convent before or after a shopping spree."

Millions of questions erupted on his gorgeous face.

Not willing to give him any more details, she had taken a large sum of money to donate to the nuns in preview of her spending activities the following weeks.

She hopped down gracefully from the carriage and stepped into the large courtyard. She turned back, and held on to the open door for an instant.

"I always donate half of what I spend on clothes, jewelry, and furs to a charitable organization," she explained, "I like the convent. The nuns do so much good. I am extravagant when it comes to buying clothes and I feel so guilty about it. So, in this instance, I do a bit of good."

Renaud appeared stunned at first and then disconcerted. Perhaps she should be less candid, she thought. Her guilt after all was nobody's business.

She returned to the hotel later than planned. Renaud was a lot of fun, although in a sarcastic sort of way. She wondered what he was going to say about her, for he had an amusing anecdote for everyone that either nodded or saluted him. She'd spent a lovely three hours with him and as she climbed down from the carriage, she promised to contact him when she reached Paris.

She entered the room followed by a bell captain who pushed a tall rolling bronze rack stacked high with all her purchases.

On the balcony, Jean-Louis sipped a cup of coffee while reading the local paper. Two or three pages lay shuffled in disarray at his feet.

"I'm back, darling, how do you feel?" She walked over and threw her arms around his shoulders and kissed him.

He was livid but did not let on. He had seen her climb out of De Beauvaur's carriage.

She continued her usual babblings with every imaginable detail.

He turned her off and cut down her tirade to a quarter of all the things she had heard, seen, and felt. Nevertheless he was surprised to realize that he had missed her and was happy that she was back. Gaby was a breath of fresh air.

His beautiful temptress had fine shopping skills. Good heavens, they needed another room to store all the things she had bought. He was impressed to see that one of her bag contained books; he was about to ask her about her literary interest and decided against it. Mon Dieu, he surmised, it would be another two-hour lecture on the author, the subjects, the shop owner and whatever else she would talk about.

"I can see that you are still under the weather, my friend." She exclaimed sarcastically.

"What?"

She laughed.

"You are not looking very fresh, that is you look sick from too much imbibing, my dear. I'm glad. You deserve it. You should have returned to me, immediately, *immediatement*," she emphasized in French. Instead you gallivanted with beautiful women, while I waited patiently for my man," she burst out laughing again and came back into the room wearing a gorgeous yellow dress, her décolleté was so low that he gave her a second look with a smirk.

"You are not getting out of this room with this attire."

"I bought it just for us," she sweetly whispered in his ears.

"Come here, Gaby. Why didn't you wait for me to wake up?"

"I was restless," she sat on his lap "and I thought I would return before you woke up. □

"Don't go anywhere without telling me." He ordered. His tone did not leave much to question.

"But Jean-Louis, I did, look," she walked on over to the table where his escritoire lay untouched. She grabbed it and showed him her notation.

"All right, let me rephrase it. Don't go anywhere without me while we are here. Understood?"

"Crystal clear, Captain." She replied amused.

For a moment he pressed his lips together and his skin tightened around his finely chiseled jaw.

"Very well," she retorted sensing the tension. Pretentiously she turned up her chin and took a seat across from him.

"Are there any dangers I should be aware of, Jean-Louis? Or are you just angry that I would have taken leave of your company," she smiled at him gently.

"Both. Now, Gaby, prepare a few outfits, leave all of your things in Nice. We will return in three days for the Bataille des fleurs. But meanwhile, let's take some time to visit the countryside, I think you'll love it."

Although his controlling voice annoyed her, she remained quiet. She had learned that much during the crossing. Never retort anything when he was irritated. He got over his anger quickly if he was obeyed.

"Jean-Louis, how long will we be gone for? How fun, are we leaving today?" She questioned sweetly.

He looked at her surprised. "If you wish, I presume we could leave later this afternoon."

"Very well, then it's settled, *à moi La Côte d'Azur*." She began to move away from him

"Come, Gaby," he murmured. He stretched his arms to her, and pulled her back to him. He encircled her small body and forced her back on his laps. "Not so fast. I haven't had breakfast yet." He smiled.

"Jean-Louis," she started again, "do you recall when you spoke about our relationship in Paris and that changes should be expected?"

He did not move nor answer.

"Well, my heart was broken, but do you also recall that I told you I needed to go upstairs and talk to myself? Well, I did, and you were right."

He lifted his head and looked at her seriously. A morning with De Beauvaur and she was already talking about her independence. He removed his hand from her lap and reached for the newspaper that had dropped on the carpet.

"No, listen to me," she said as she gently grasped the paper and folded it in her lap. "I don't want to look into the future because it will tarnish my present and the perfect happiness that I now feel."

"Yes?" he said, not particularly interested.

"I don't really understand, Jean-Louis, why I spoke of long term. I presume that love affects people in ways they could never imagine. Cupid had me in his sight. I've always been afraid of losing what I had already gained—the perfect look, the perfect relationship, the perfect note. I remember feeling this way with Philippe or Tita or Gustav when we experienced an especially wonderful moment. I've always been afraid that I could not duplicate moments of true happiness. Consequently, I have always concentrated on the present and it worked, *magnifique*, because one has control over almost anything in the now, as long as there is a vague idea of where a person wants to go into the future."

He looked at her with interest now. He wanted to know where she was going with her revelation.

"I was slapped in the face by fate, Wednesday, Jean-Louis, I will not let it happen again. The pain is too great when I get disappointed. You feel close to me now, but I'm starting to realize and understand your life. I can presage how returning to Paris will be and how my life will be different as well. I have a good handle on all that, now . . . I think," she said pensively to herself and then assertively, "I'm prepared for whatever our relationship will be when we get to Paris. But . . . let me down easily, that's all I ask of you."

He was going to reply sarcastically that a morning with the Count had changed her thinking rapidly, but that was until that last sentence. He gathered her to him, instead.

"I'm sorry that I hurt you, Gaby," he said, holding her head close to his heart. "Very sorry," he bent down and kissed her neck. "I think you're a rare jewel."

She did not answer and he didn't pursue his thoughts. He just held her, retrieved his newspaper on her lap, and kept on reading.

She picked up some of the newspaper sheets that had been strewn on the carpet and began reading the political articles. He looked over her shoulders; her choice of reading impressed him.

That certainly was a first for him, he thought. He sat like a grand-père, actually enjoying reading the paper quietly and happily with a woman in his arms. He moved awkwardly to dismiss promptly thoughts of endearment he showered on Gaby—thoughts that had plagued him these past few days.

She looked up at him, distracted, seemingly annoyed that she had been disturbed.

"Sorry, Princess," he smirked.

She nodded and continued her reading as she reclined in his arms and lifted her legs sideways over the armrest.

Thank heavens he was returning to Paris. This young American really got to him. Paris would set him into a new mode. After all, he had to think about his future trips and political responsibilities in Italy.

Shocked at his reaction, he asked her, "If I recall correctly, you speak Italian fluently. Do you read and write the language equally well?"

"Mon Dieu," she laughed out loud, "and I thought you only listened to one fourth of my babbles. Your memory is well honed. I do read and write the language well. My mother made sure of that. She never truly accepted my father's great admiration of colonialism; this is how she took her revenge. I feel that I know Italy and the Italians better than my own culture and myself. You know, I'm not quite sure why it should happen now. I always harbored loathsome feelings towards my mother, but since my encounter with you and the French, I'm starting to better understand her motives and feelings. I feel closeness to her, which is both pleasing and harmonious. I wonder what she would think if she could see me now. Unconsciously, perhaps, I display a lot more of her character than I previously thought. We were never close. No wonder my father wanted nothing to do with me."

"Your father must be a very foolish man, Gaby, to let you go and not appreciate your great qualities."

"He is, Jean-Louis," she said gravely without remorse. "I presume men are less attached to people and things than women. I would have fought this thought before I met you, Jean-Louis. The idea that anyone could be so attached to someone so as to give up their own potential for another human being was totally absurd and incomprehensible to me back in New Orleans. But truly, I'm like every other woman, Jean-Louis, whether I like to admit it or not." She looked up at him for a short moment and smiled, the momentous cloud that seemed to engulf her at times momentarily returned, but just as promptly she was all business once more. She returned back to the article she was reading.

"Jean-Louis, what do you think is going to happen to the Nationalistic Movement in Italy? What about France's role in it?" she asked him out of the blue.

A knock on the door gave him pause to hold on to his answer. Room service was rolling out a gorgeous table, adorned in the center with a crystal vase that displayed magnificent yellow, rounded buds of soft mimosa that suddenly vaporized the room with its heady scent. The food, oh, the food was wonderful and beautifully prepared. Gaby peeked at the dessert; they had not forgotten her strawberry tart.

Jean-Louis loved watching her. She never gave his mind a rest. From her sharp intellect— she was well versed in politics and her questions were succinct and engaging, and often she was not abashed about her vulnerability. She was the perfect partner in more ways than one. He had already noticed that on the ship, but now he also realized that she read quickly and could evaluate a situation well. She was curious, too much so, he thought. She never ceased to ask questions, but what made it interesting to be with her was that she truly enjoyed knowing both sides of an argument. Gaby was an active listener. She wanted to know all sides to a story so that she could deduce her own conclusions—in essence a good conversationalist with a sharp intellect, qualities uncommon among women.

He reclined further back in the fauteuil and the next two hours were spent eating, and exchanging lively opinions not solely on politics, but culture, emotions, and music. Gaby was vital and amusing without really knowing it.

"I'd love to be humorous. I treasure the times I spend around funny people," she told him.

She seemed to think that it was not something that could be learned. You either had it or not. According to her assessment, De Beauvaur had it. Surprise, surprise, he hated it when she spoke of his friends.

"I think you're spending way too much time thinking about the chap." He smiled half-heartily.

"A bit of jealousy, perhaps," she beamed.

She noticed his 'how absurd' glance and quickly changed her tune. "I was only teasing," she said.

He let it go, thinking that once again she had read his mind—or his heart. He was enlightened by many of her repartees regarding the assessment of the current political situation in Europe. She answered his questions or statements with an eye fixed on the American political system. It could not apply to Europe, now, but her ideas rang true in the greater scope of cultural development—ideas of modernity and of the Droit de l'Homme—basic human rights.

She was proud to be an American and a Southerner. He personally was not too fond of the Southerners, the ones he had met personally in New Orleans, but the progressive spirit she possessed toward basic human rights truly amazed him. *Ah, Gaby, why didn't I meet you five years from now*, he thought.

Chapter Thirteen

Earlier than anticipated they left for St. Tropez—to be alone and away from the crowds, to enjoy riding, the beach, the food, and their love.

Located on a hill near a medieval castle with rounded turrets, a wide moat and a drawbridge, the hotel stood magnificent with a full view of the port and of the village down the steep hill. The legend told of an American couple that made their home in this charming town to live their passionate life. Gaby was amused at the romantic nature of the French. Thus far, all professed to be above such inconsequence. Yet, she had not visited a town or village that had not its own romantic interlude. Maybe one day, the Gaby and Jean-Louis' story would be told to countless visitors and tourists. They, too, would become immortals.

Another palatial apartment awaited the Duke De Bourbonne. As they strode in the hotel, she noticed that beyond the gardens to the right of the piano bar were several tennis courts where mostly men played. She walked closer to the terrace while Jean-Louis took care of business. Aghast, women dressed in mid-calf dresses tossed the ball back and forth over the net. They played as well as they could, considering their cumbersome attire. *That would be great fun*, she thought. Oh, she would love France!

Four messages had been handed to Jean-Louis. She hoped he would not have to return to Nice.

Their suite faced the Méditerranée's magnificent coast with its projections of rose-colored landmasses and immense forest of yellow mimosa trees. The scent filled the air with its sweet, pungent perfume; unfortunately, their heady blossoms had a short-lived course. While the carriage clattered on the road, she'd asked the coachman to stop and she'd run down the hill to cut off a sprig of mimosa that she'd pinned to her waist.

At first, Jean-Louis had balked, but it dawned on him that she never asked for much—as a matter of fact, she'd never asked him for anything. He had been shocked that she'd purchased her own clothes today. After all, his name alone would have afforded her a line of credit that even she would have had a difficult time to spend. None of his other paramours had passed on the incredible chance of endless open accounts. He made it a point to send her flowers upon arrival at the hotel.

As they settled in their room, a sumptuous lunch had been prepared for them on the balcony overlooking l'Esterel, the chain of mountains that bordered the Méditerranée. A bouquet of red roses, mimosa, and baby breath placed on the table with a bottle of Dom Pérignon encased in a massive silver bucket was left as well. The perfectly ironed, heavily starched, white tablecloth brought about a most sensuous thought. Had there not been colossal pieces of silverware and delicate, white, bone-china plates set on it, she would have gladly wrapped herself in it and offered herself as the *premier déjeuner* of the day to her lover. Instead she read the note politely, caressed Jean-Louis' scholarly writing and tucked the note neatly in the satin pocket of her reticule.

She wondered how she even repressed the sensual, highly sexual feeling she experienced with Jean-Louis. She had been a virgin for twenty-one years with absolutely no desire of sexual closeness with any of the young men she had met. She recalled being terribly amused when some of her socialite friends would venture their inner thoughts about the person they loved or lusted after. She was so proud, then, that she was different. It serves me well, she'd assured herself. Love, in many a young girl's life, made them behave like wet rags, too pliable, lacking in wit, spirit, and logic—in essence, they forgot themselves in order to delight the object of their passion. She was not about to take that path, she'd decided early on. Oh, non, mon Dieu, doubly so after she'd accepted the invitation that the Musique Académie had offered. That was then.

In France she had heard that men did not take no for an answer. Had she chosen England, mothers protected their daughters' virginity, although it would not have helped her situation—she had no mother.

Philippe, she thought as an afterthought, he had myriad of wonderful contacts, but he would not be around much. Moreover, Philippe had always needed her protection. That intelligent, gentle soul, who adored her, always depended on her strength of spirit. Whatever she lacked as a child served her well. She was strong, independent, very smart, and doing what she wanted to do.

Jean-Louis was a wonderful dream. Well if he was, she did not want to wake up from it—not now. She would have time while in Grenoble and Paris to sort things out for herself.

She turned and looked back at Jean-Louis who'd flung his thin, beige, linen shirt off on the bed. He was coming toward her. She knew that look. Lust. It would creep up from the corner of his well-defined full lips and radiate in his piercing blue eyes. His body was strong and muscular. She adored his well-cut upper arms every time he rolled up his sleeves. She stood on the balcony, her back against the black wrought-iron balustrade, ogling intensely at Jean-Louis while she was still clothed in a pretty yellow dress that she had worn for the two-hour trip to the village of St. Tropez. She appraised his good looks lingering on his lips, chest, and lower body still encased in an impeccable fitted pair of tan gabardine trousers. What a perfect specimen he was—virile, sensual, powerful, fearless. She adored everything about him. She heaved a long sigh. Her risqué judgment must have shown on her face.

"Gaby, maybe I should be the one wearing that pretty yellow gown. I've just been appraised like a frisky, fierce stallion whose knowledgeable horse breeder evaluates, after approving the purchase at a most outrageous prize!"

"What a singular, evil thought! You just compared me to a man, in view of the fact that I took special precautions early this morning to make myself as pleasurable to you, Monsieur, as I possibly could. I take your sarcasm as an insult—good heavens," she huffed. "Eh bien, since I've been compared to Adam, I will, therefore, take this unique opportunity to do what a man usually does so well. I will seduce you, mon cher. If you resist, you will leave me no option but to beat you unmercifully into submission!"

He raised and waived his two hands toward his chest. "Please Gaby, do as you please, I will submit to your outraged treatment!" He cast a skeptical glance and winked.

She sexily ambled away from the balcony and into the bedroom. Her naked arms extended toward him while her long and elegant fingertips landed on his chest. She bent and pressed her lips to his taut abdomen and continued a shower of kisses around his navel. Slowly, teasingly she lifted the buckle of his thick leather belt and begun to blow bubbles of air inside his waistband.

"Gaby, you're a devilish partner." He smiled arrogantly, "I taught you well," he murmured as pearly white beads became visible on his forehead.

"Why does it always have to be about Jean-Louis-Pierre De Pleyssis?" she replied, incapable to hold back her mirth.

Oblivious to the sweet tasting Cordon Bleu déjeuner that had exclusively been prepared for them, he clasped her to his chest, lifted her up in his arms and placed her gently down on the light gray and pink satin coverlet. Momentarily, he gazed intently at her. God, she was beautiful. Yellow was an amazing color on her. Being out in the sun these past few days, her sunburned face emphasized her incredibly expressive green eyes. He kept on looking at her as he detected her restless stare.

She sat up and grasped his wrist. She forced his fingers to unfurl and she pressed her rose-stained lips in the center of his palm. "You've been branded my friend," she declared softly as she left the imprint of her sexy pout on the handside of his rugged hand. □

"Hey partner, how about joining me and pleasing me, instead of standing there and meditating on my womanly attributes?" She proclaimed in the most grave and guttural voice she could muster and out of the blue, she recalled Renaud's wildly interesting take on Indian's cultural traditions. "Jean-Louis, have you ever been to India, I understand that there are men who actually place themselves in trances whereas not even the pain incurred by walking on hot coals break their mental state. Do you believe we could place ourselves in such trances while we make love, consequently reliving for hours that special moment of ecstasy?"

She would have kept on asking questions about his trips to Asia had he given her an answer.

Instead, he unfastened his waistband, stripped off his pants, and placed his long, heavy body on her voluptuous curves. She parted her lips to receive his kisses.

They made love a good part of the day, slept, and then woke up ravenous just in time for dinner. They devoured the cold meal that had not been taken away. The busboy most certainly had thought it wise not to disturb them after countless unanswered knocks on the door.

The powerful man and his assertive American girlfriend ran toward the table and snatched the still delicious *salade de tomates à l'huile, quiche aux crevettes, fresh tuna in herbs with an anchovy sauce, and cold langoustines with lemon,* that had been set up for them five hours prior. They laughed uproariously as they watched their reflections in the mirror.

"Jean-Louis what were we thinking—not eating first?"

"My view precisely, mademoiselle."

"Scoundrel, I'm compartmentalizing this statement for future reference. Understood, my dear?"

He picked up a small red plum and tossed it at her. She ducked promptly and charged toward the raspberry Melba, now melted in one giant white creamy sea with little purple pebbles swimming in the porcelain bowl. She gulped it down, keeping an eye on her lover, who frowned in disapproval.

"I'm not saving any for you; real men don't eat *Framboises Melba,*" she said, shaking her head. She turned her back to him, stole one last apple tart from the pastry tray and bolted to the magnificent marble bathtub in the dressing room.

She settled in the warm, scented bath she had drawn for herself just minutes ago. The dream would continue, she murmured to herself.

Meanwhile, Jean-Louis walked out of the room and down the carpeted staircase to ask the concierge to make a reservation in a small-secluded restaurant he knew well.

Chapter Fourteen

They arrived at the restaurant at around nine-thirty that evening.

The owner, Monsieur Nestouli, knew how to delight and entertain his guests.

The restaurant had many private dining rooms, some had dancing, others showcased comedians that denigrated politicians and every newsworthy event. They called themselves the *Chansonniers,* political observers, and their lines were truly the soul of France. No one was above the disparaging commentaries.

Since he had just arrived in France, Jean-Louis thought that they most probably would not have found enough material to tear him apart. He would take Gaby to their repertoire. Nothing was sacred with this group. Gaby would probably like it and it might prepare her ever so slightly for the reality of *la vie Parisienne with him.*

Again, a delectable romantic dinner had been prepared for them and Jean-Louis was amazed at Gaby's knowledge of sauces and their ingredients.

"You said your cooking skills were right out of a slave's ship mess. How do you know so much about the culinary arts?" he asked incredulously.

"I just never learned how to cook, but I love good food. I can't paint, but I certainly appreciate art. I love witty individuals, yet I cannot tell a funny joke and get some laughter. You either have the skill or you don't. I'm sure I could improve on all the things that I do not do well, but I'm certain I couldn't excel in any," she replied in a condescending tone.

"Touché, I'm very pleased that you excel on the arts required to please me. You must have had a wonderful instructor." He chuckled.

She turned crimson and promptly reverted her eyes back down to the menu. Well aware that the table next to them had heard his rude comment and had seen her turn all shades of pink, she shot him a sideways glance that amused him greatly. She was about to retort when the chef and Mr. Nestouli walked to their table to engage Jean-

Louis in a light conversation and ask about his travels. It was good for business to seek out influential clients. The men had spoken for a while about common friends and then Jean-Louis had interrupted him and turned to the chef.

"Mon amie ici," he started, "believes that she knows the ingredients in your *escalope de veau*, veal cutlet."

"Ah, Mademoiselle Thornsen, do you know how many guests have guessed but none have divined," Nestouli returned haughtily.

"Would you tell me, Monsieur, if I guessed correctly?"

"Of course not. First, you cannot possibly guess the right ingredients, and secondly, I would loose my confidence in my skills if —"

"Eh bien, let me try," Gaby cut him off. "First, *naturellement*, I do not think that there is only one particular ingredient which gives it such a scrumptious taste. There are a combination of herbs, but I would bet my winning last night—and it was a lovely sum," she smiled devilishly, lifting her head to the chef and nodding, "—the prevalent taste that gives the escalope its lingering and distinctive flavor is butter of anchovies," she stated flatly as she stared at the renowned chef.

The chef's startled look gave it away. She had touched a sensitive cord—the right one, she was certain. Just like the first time she reached the highest of note, no one believed her and she repeated it and duplicated it many times afterward.

It suddenly made her sad to think that Jean-Louis had never heard her sing. She was going to make him listen to her when they returned to the *propriétée* in Villefranche.

"Well, mademoiselle," she heard the chef say, "your sense of grande cuisine is well developed but non—you are wrong."

Quickly, he changed the spirit of the conversation.

"Lucky for you, Monsieur, we are expecting Le Duke Of Roicevoy this very evening, his friends, the Earl of Edinbaugh, and their respective amies, Elise De Maintgassie and the talented Mademoiselle Georgette Lerry. *Vous connaissez,* you know, the painter? They will be here as well. Have you seen them, yet?

"No, but do tell them to join us when they arrive, Nestouli," Jean-Louis asked the old restaurateur.

"Avec plaisir, Monsieur. Did you know," the owner of the famous restaurant continued, "Mademoiselle Lerry painted this delightful view of my herb garden and the perspective surrounding it? People do not stop asking me about the artist. I understand that she is now spending most of her time in Montmartre avec les Impressionistes. She came last month with a Monsieur Manet who kept on looking at every women that walked by, visually disrobing them, on account of his artistic eye. He almost had a duel over it with a Russian Prince. Ah, you have missed a lot, Jean-Louis-Pierre these past few years. I understand Paris is most enchanting these days with the work of Count Hauffman. The Count was here recently with the Emperor; they are doing great by the wealthy, bourgeois, and aristocrats. His ideas of bringing France to the political and cultural forefront of Europe with the use of the railroads, and his drive toward the full reunification of Italy will change our world—I'm sure for the best," the restaurateur flatly asserted.

"I'm certain that it will be so, Nestouli," Jean-Louis responded surprised at the candor.

"Many here in the provinces do not agree, *vous connaissez la force catholique?*"

Jean-Louis did not respond. The restaurateur politely nodded his head and left.

Gaby was just delighted. It was great being with Jean-Louis and conversation was never boring. He knew a lot of interesting people and the French loved giving their ideas about everything and anything. Reserved, they were not, not in the circles she had been introduced to. After Nestouli left, Jean-Louis complimented her on her culinary knowledge again.

"Really good, chérie. Nestouli was shocked and a bit startled for a while. I have never quite seen him in that light."

"Tita taught me a lot. Before coming to our plantation she was owned by a French man in Haiti who had come from the Provence. His wife hated the colonies and to please her he had brought along with him many of France's best chefs so that she could continue her social life in Haiti. I understand that during their heyday, there was no greater honor than being asked for *souper,* dinner, over the Du Grangeais. Everything was imported and I understand the ships coming to the colonies always stopped by their plantation first before coming to the United States to bring a bit of the old world to our New Society.

"What were their names again, Gaby?

"Les Du Grangeais. He was killed during the uprising along with a large number of his French staff, which I understood were a hard, cruel lot to work for. However a much darker and sinister fate awaited her. Someone found out, or perhaps papers were falsified—anyhow, she supposedly had black blood in her and I understand the surviving former slaves sold her to a trafficker in the slave trade between Haiti and Natchez on the Mississippi river. Tita also heard that she had purposely drowned herself while on the boat. Well, in truth no one really found out. Truth, rumors, or lies we never heard of the family ever again and their wealth vanished as mysteriously. The plantation was taken over by the new government. Voila that's all I know of the family."

"Interesting, the name sounds familiar. Perhaps I heard of the family while I passed through New Orleans." His eyes focused on the white napkin as he tried to recall something about the family.

Gaby did not give life to her story. A cool reaction, or awkwardness always surfaced every time the South was mentioned.

A large group of mostly men entered the room, inebriated and loud. Jean-Louis stood up, the group walked to their table.

"Jean-Louis-Pierre, my friend, I'd hope to meet with you Friday in Nice. When did you get back, Captain? Shame on you, not even one little contact upon your arrival?" The tall red-haired fellow with an English accent scolded Jean-Louis as he gripped him to his chest and tapped him on the back. "Eh, what do I see over here?" the man persisted while he gazed at Gaby. "Not bad, mon cher. Now I know why we have not heard from you, a little tryst before returning to Paris? The colonies and America have not changed you much, my friend." He smiled at Gaby. "Alors, introduce us, Jean-Louis Pierre!"

Jean-Louis still walked around the group of men and women who had just been ushered in their semi-private salon. Interesting, she thought, these fellows, all with British accents except for the two women with them called him Jean-Louis-Pierre as well.

The man called Ribaud marched to Gaby, who now sat alone at the table. He came close and touched her hair. Crudely he placed his hand on her shoulder as he bent down and whispered in her ear in a heavily accented but perfect French.

"*Alors petite, vous êtes bien belle*, you are very pretty, The Duke De Bourbonne has not changed his taste when it comes to beautiful women. Are you in town for long? I'm available tomorrow. *Une petite soirée, n'est ce pas*, when Jean-Louis-Pierre leaves? We will be in town for a full month. *C'est oui*, mignonette?" he asked. His breath smelled like Courvoisier.

Gaby shoved his hand off from her décolleté.

"Oh, oh, easy," Ribaud snapped out loudly. "That is odd," he smiled, "my friend always shares his women with us. Don't be afraid, he will not be upset, my dear. The more the merrier, don't you think?"

"I have no idea what you are talking about, and when it comes to sharing—I never share." She retorted coolly. The fellow was inebriated. She understood that—but still. Luckily, Jean-Louis returned to the table and to her horror he asked for more tables to be added to theirs.

So much for their private romantic dinner, she thought. The whole group was obnoxious and the women even more so.

"You are American?" the one called Élise asked with disgust in her voice. Jean-Louis-Pierre, what were you thinking, my friend?"

Jean-Louis chuckled, but Gaby was no longer amused. He saw that somber look in her eyes and promptly changed the subject recounting her background and the reason for her trip to France. That did not go along too well, either. Both the British and the French demonized her Southern roots. Jean-Louis was busy talking to his other friend, who appeared a bit more serious, but equally drunk. She had to endure the excoriations alone, unwilling to be viewed as flippant by his friends. Unfortunately, they were his friends. Gone were the light banter and the snide remarks behind their backs. Jean-

Louis laughed heartily WITH them! She recognized readily that they were on the same social level and rude as can be.

She kept quiet and listened. A pretty good perspective of what to expect in Paris, she mused. She wondered about the rosy picture Jean-Louis had described to her. At least all of them loved the arts. She could tell the excitement in their voices when they spoke about the salons they attended, who was great writer and why, who painted with their souls, who slept with whom . . .!

The woman called Elise begun a long tirade on all his previous paramours—about their new lives, new husbands, new trends. Jean-Louis seemed to enjoy all the gossips and when they asked him to rejoin them on a boat in the harbor in Saint Tropez, he gladly accepted.

Her disappointment must have registered on her face for he took her in his arms as everyone stood up for the next engaging good time. He pressed her to him.

"It will be fun, Gaby. I want to go. I have not seen these friends in quite some time." He whispered in her ear.

She nodded.

Ribaud and Luke arrived first. The yatch moored on one of the piers already had guests on its illuminated decks.

As the door of the carriage opened and Jean-Louis stepped out, he was surrounded. He reached for Gaby's hand, and he pulled her quickly on the ladder leading to the large vessel. An orchestra played very loud music and she noticed couples waltzing on the highly polished wooden planks.

Jean-Louis left her to get some drinks and naturally he must have been stopped and questioned by friends who had not seen him in a while, she thought angrily.

Aware that he was not about to return too quickly, she walked to the bow of the ship and looked inside the many portholes to see if she could catch a glimpse of her celebrated lover. He had vanished. She walked to the railing and observed and absorbed the society at hand.

"Gabriella, what are you doing all by yourself?" Ribaud commented. "Come with us. Jean-Louis is busy. You know how these things go." She did not know, but she'd be damned if she let on about her lack of savoir vivre in France. She followed Ribaud reluctantly.

"So tell me when will you be in Paris?" One of the men who had been at Nestouli questioned, getting a bit too close for comfort. "I will have to take you out and show you what they mean by gay Paris," he slipped his hand across her lower back and led her back inside in a room crammed with people of all ages engaged in—.

"Take your hands off me!" she shouted as loud as she could in the room filled with smoke and cacophonous sounds.

She shoved him away hard and he fell, got up to his feet, and was about to say something when a blonde Amazon caught his attention. He began touching her instead. Awed at the spectacle, Gaby watched the woman approve of the caresses that Jean-Louis' friend bestowed on her. As she spun on her heels, longing to get back on deck, she was handled simultaneously by both a man and a woman who wanted a little more from her than good conversation. As her eyes acclimatized to the dark, she moved away and looked for an escape—there was none. Shocked beyond words—everyone appeared to be enjoying one another—and not verbally. Hands and mouths darted out at her. Some pulled down at her décolleté, others lifted the hem of her dress, while others caressed her hair. Was there a way out of this hellish place?

"Gaby, my love, where have you been?" Ribaud had re-surfaced now with two women in his arms.

Ready to ask him about Jean-Louis' whereabouts, instead she decided otherwise. His less than polite demeanor did not inspire trust. She extricated herself from his claws and crawled out of the place on hands and knees, eluding as many couples or threesomes as she could. Finally, she reached the small ladder leading to the main deck and climbed up as quickly as she could. As if nothing was happening downstairs, couples and groups of friends gathered drinking, gossiping, and dancing. Where was Jean-Louis? She wondered. Could he have been down below? What did Ribaud mean, when he spoke about sharing in Nestouli? Was he speaking about women? Oh, God, what did she get herself into, she quickly thought. Readjusting her dress and curls, she moved in between the crowd, intent on taking his carriage back to the hotel. She finally reached the rail leading to the dock. Grasping the railing with both hands, she felt a familiar hand around her waist.

"Gaby, where have you been? Jean-Louis asked. A woman nearby looked at Gaby curiously.

"Where have I been?" she stated incredulous. "Your friend dragged me in an orgy down below while I patiently waited for your return."

"And?"

"And . . . nothing. I can't even come to term with this question. Either you are totally out of your mind inebriated or perverse beyond imagination. I'm leaving. I can't take all the excitement."

The mysterious woman walked closer to the couple. She placed her elongated delicate hands on Jean-Louis' shoulders.

"You see, Jean-Louis, she has different mores than we do. Come back with us, chéri. We missed you so." She kissed his forearm and began to press her body into Jean-Louis'.

Gaby's eyes must have turned into large green orbits for Jean-Louis burst out laughing and he gently lifted Caroline's arm away.

"Shocked, beauty?" he asked.

She did not bother to answer and waddled with her new heels down the gangway. He followed close behind and wiggled the passerelle hard.

Gaby screamed certain that she would land in the water. Instead, Jean-Louis lifted her in the air into his arms.

"Welcome to the grand parties of the Grand Monde, chérie."

"Jean-Louis, I almost was raped down below. Don't you have anything to say about that?"

"Gaby these people are harmless, trust me; no one would have taken you against your will. It's just a different way to play—if you are willing." He placed a few kisses on her cheek.

"What? You would have let yourself go . . .?"

"If you had been my main partner, maybe."

"I have heard and seen enough. Take me back to the hotel," she replied flabbergasted.

He followed her quietly in the carriage. The ride back was silent. He tried to kiss her. She pushed him away. He gathered her forcefully in his arms and kissed her temples.

"Wouldn't you have been upset if by any chance someone might have gotten his or her way with me, Jean-Louis?" she asked, incapable to extricate herself from his embrace.

"You wouldn't," was his stark answer.

"What makes you so sure of that?"

"I know. You are not ready for that, might never be ready for it. It's not as grand as some would like you to believe. Just another experience, that's all. I'm perfectly happy with you and only you?" he responded candidly.

"Do I please you that much?" she questioned bluntly. After what she had seen in the cavernous bottom of the yacht, she had her doubts. Sensations seem to be the name of the game.

"You please me that much and a whole lot more that you could ever imagine."

Incredulous, she raised her eyebrows and her gorgeous green eyes to him.

He raised his eyebrows back to her and nodded.

"I'm that good?" She laughed.

"That good." He smirked. A difficult impasse had been crossed. He was glad he had redirected her thoughts away from this crazy *soirée*, an entertaining evening. He had forgotten how wild he had been in his youth.

Gaby reclined in his arms calmly. Damn, he wished he could keep her a while longer. He dared to wish upon a star.

Chapter Fifteen

Gaby had woken up much earlier. Jean-Louis was still sound asleep. It was one-thirty in the afternoon and she extricated her body from his.

What a night! She crawled out of bed and nearly stepped on a crystal flute. Dom Pérignon bottles were strewn all over the carpet. She remembered it well. They'd poured champagne over their naked bodies and tasted each other until their inebriated senses were satiated with alcohol and raw sex. She wanted to erase all recollection of what they had done to each other. It had been a different kind of hungry and angry love. She surveyed the room. His leather belt was still hanging loosely on one side of the huge poster bed. Her cheeks were burning with embarrassment at the barbaric way they had taken each other.

What about the occupants next door? Had they heard their muffled screams, laughter, and lewd remarks? The idea alone made her wish she could disappear under the heavy Aubusson rug covering the parquet floor.

What about the servants? Oh, she should have placed the "Do Not Disturb" sign on the door. She'd beg Jean-Louis to leave today. Everyone and their brother seem to vacation in St. Tropez; if they left within the next hour, she would not have to face anyone she might meet again in Paris.

All of sudden she was so ashamed of her lewd conduct. The thought of facing Jean-Louis when he woke up made her want to flee.

Surely, she would have to listen to another one of his logical lectures about sex.

"Whatever pleases you Gaby sex is the great equalizer. We are all brought down to the same level, an animalistic behavior . . . all of our inhibitions are revealed, unveiled, and hopefully our hunger satisfied. There is no upper or lower classes, no social or intellectual standing with sex. That's why it feels so good," he had told her a million times.

She looked at her sleepy lover spread out, naked and beautiful, his powerful and strong body rested so peaceful and content. God, how she loved him. She wished she could see it his way—but she could not. What infuriated her was that she had instigated a lot of their amorous behavior. Go figure, in her drunken state last evening, maybe she had not wanted to disappoint him after the revelation. She'd wanted to be all and even above what he had revealed about her sexual prowess. How idiotic. She had to quit drinking. Imbibing much too much of that murderous Dom Perignon turned her into a perfect pervert with a capital P!

She reached for the light satin coverlet and wrapped herself in it. She picked up the bottles, the broken glasses, the belts, the satin panties, the curtains tiebacks dropped next to their sprawling bed— anything that could reveal roughness and inappropriate behavior.

She walked to the terrace facing the ocean and sat there, her legs pulled tight in her abdomen and her chin resting over her knees. The warm sun on her slightly clad body was delicious. She prayed that he would not remember last night completely, another guilty thought, now she prayed for the lewd act she'd committed. Had she lost all sense of propriety? Unfortunately, she recalled every minutes, every second of their early morning orgy and she cringed at every flashing thought.

Loud knocks on the door brought her back to reality, *le petit déjeuner avait été monté,* breakfast had been served. Jean-Louis called out to Gaby to open the door. She stayed on the balcony, recoiling from view.

Angry, he got out of bed, pulled on his pants, walked to the door, grabbed the plateau, gave the boy a tip, and rolled the beautifully dressed table inside himself.

The windows were open, and the light glass curtain flayed with the morning breeze. He noticed Gaby hiden on the terrace. Frustrated, he marched toward the balcony, annoyed that he had had to get out of bed when she was already up. One look at her rosy cheeks brought back vivid memories of their loving interlude. He came up behind her sweetly, he kissed her temples and brushed his lips down her earlobes, a move that drove her wild—fast—he had learned.

"Should we start off where we left off last night, Gaby? I like it when you're mean to me," he teased, his kisses tumbled lower on her neck and breasts. "I think you could have handled those pirates single-handedly last month," he murmured.

"No, Jean-Louis, I think that it was wrong," she almost shouted, her expressive eyes showing great concern and guilt.

He straightened up, irritated at her response.

"Gaby, cease, chérie, we both knew that if you stopped liking it— enjoying it," he emphasized, "I would have stopped. It's just a different way of enjoying each other's body and obviously looking at your response last night it will happen again if we both wish it. That's all. Come back down to earth, chérie, and quit this prudish behavior. Come and have breakfast."

She did not budge from the safety of the balcony and kept on looking at the water. He sat inside by the breakfast table with the paper for a while as he sipped a cup of coffee. Understanding that she would not rejoin him, he returned outside, kissed her naked shoulders, unbuttoned her satin peignoir and lowered his mouth to her opulent, warm and sunburned breasts. He felt a slight tremor.

"Trés bien, since my companion is not responsive nor very talkative, I'll search for better company downstairs."

He placed a light linen white shirt on his tan torso, took the paper, and walked out. She heard the door close behind him.

She was stunned that he would not listen to her. Not paying heed to her furious response enraged her.

How arrogant! Well, she was not about to go downstairs, even if she had to stay in this room all day. He would surely return. He had told her last night he would not touch any of these beautiful women, even if they were the last girls on earth.

"They no longer appeal to me, Gaby, why should I when I have the sexiest and most complete woman this earth has yet to know." He'd reassured her in the carriage as they returned to the hotel.

He could bend her any way he wished, and he knew it too. She was sad that they even had an altercation. She picked up a cup of coffee and suddenly heard the crystal clear laughter of Elise, who was calling out to Jean-Louis to join her along with some of the people that had been in attendance last evening.

His friend Luke was there, *il cuvait son vin,* sleep off one's drink, he looked dismal. She pried on them through the holes of the barrier on the balcony. She watched Jean-Louis walk over to the large table where the group was having breakfast; he pulled out a chair, sat, and reclined while a butler filled his cup with coffee. Elise came around close enough to hug him and kiss him on both cheeks and went further as she brushed her lips to his.

What audacity! Gaby could still feel his kiss on her breasts. Irate, rage replaced her shame. To get a better view of the scene, she leaned on the balustrade overlooking the pool and outside patio. She caught Jean-Louis' glance toward the balcony with a half-smile hanging on his lips. She fluttered her long and elegant fingers in his direction.

To hell with shame! In this country of loose morals, everything was possible. She was not about to hand Jean-Louis over on a silver platter to Elise or any other woman down below.

She marched in the luxurious bathroom, washed up quickly, colored a bit of rouge on her bronzed chin and lips, and ran out the door.

She wanted to appear as relaxed and sensual as all of his other friends. She paused and took a deep breath. The world stage is waiting, she confided to her heart. Minutes later, she began her grand entrance.

Looks of approval from both men and women gave her much needed confidence. Well aware of her appealing allure, she had chosen to wear a white piqué embroidered cotton dress; the décolleté was low with a sweetheart notch very much in vogue in France. Her minuscule waist and fabulous ballerina posture showed off the beauty of her shapely arms, shoulders, and swan-like neck. She had pinned her dark tresses on the back of her head and pulled back every stray curl except for a few wispy curls on her forehead. The magnificence of her heart-shaped face showed off her spectacular features, a beautiful sight to look at, un *objet d'art,* as the French called it. This beautiful woman who walked nonchalantly towards him with a smile would have melted the heart of the most hardened celibataire.

As she passed by the bar, Ribaud who had left the group to visit with another English friend, did a double take and begun his walk back to the group, a few steps behind her.

"Gabriella," he called out, "how are you this afternoon? You are quite a beauty, my dear."

"Very well, thank you," she responded without much enthusiasm and she kept on walking.

Ribaud, unaccustomed to her haughty behavior, suddenly was piqued at having been shunned—ignored by the American. The impolite colonial from the South had snubbed him. This girl did not know her limitations. He was going to talk to Jean-Louis-Pierre. She definitely was not for him.

Jean-Louis followed Gaby hungrily with his gaze. The English man regrettably recognized that the unpolished little colonial had a definite effect on him. Ribaud hoped he was not too late.

Sensually, Gaby walked to the table. Close to Jean-Louis, she bent down and kissed him on his lips, shocking everyone in the entourage. He placed his hand on the small of her back.

Following close behind her, Ribaud saw his friend completely taken by this gorgeous girl. He rudely and arrogantly called out to Gaby.

"Well, my dear, better know your friends and enemies quickly. Remember to pay heed to my attentions. Jean-Louis-Pierre and I go back a long way. We are childhood friends and have always taken care of each other in love and war. Gabriella, we always win. Better embrace and enjoy my polite attention, mademoiselle; it will serve you well with Jean-Louis-Pierre, and that goes for Elise as well."

Jean-Louis had an ironic smirk on his face and said not one word to rescue Gaby from the rude comments uttered by his friend.

Elise continued. She grasp at the chance to make a point with her friends.

"Frankly, Gabriella, if you dislike us so, found us so repulsive, how can you stand Jean-Louis-Pierre's company? Or are there some interests that we are unaware of, ma chère? *L'argent parle*, money talks," she haughtily continued "*et la position sociale, peut être*? His social standing maybe? *Òu peut-être encore ses connaissances à Paris*?" or maybe his contacts in Paris?

Looking at Elise sadly and disappointed that Jean-Louis did not come to her rescue, Gaby placed no brakes on her fury toward this group of society leaches. What else was she going to found out about Jean-Louis? Was that the bad boy image Renaud had referred to two nights ago? Was she wrong about him or was he just trying to let her fight her own battles? She had pestered him so about unassuming, meek women; was he trying to see if she buckled under pressure? Well, she was not about to let herself be humiliated.

With Elise, she did not want to lower herself and respond to her mean-spirited statements, but with Ribaud it was different. She had done nothing to him. He wanted to show his superiority and abase her—that she would not tolerate.

Clearing her mind, she indifferently sat on the arms of Jean-Louis' chair, and focused on Ribaud with disgust in those fiery, green eyes.

"Frankly, my dear Ribaud," she retorted eating part of Jean-Louis' brioche, in between well-enunciated American words, "your statements are rubbish to me. I don't give a damn about your thoughts and advices on my relationships, nor about your childhood connection with Jean-Louis."

Ribaud looked surprised. She had caught him off guard.

"Pardon me, your lordship, a little advice to you—save your breath! I really do not think you have my graces, intelligence, and charm and furthermore, I do not believe that Jean-Louis holds you in such high esteem that he would want you in his arms." She continued icily, "you don't appear to attract him in that way, if you know what I mean."

And then like a torrent of water tumbling down a waterfall, she plastered him in place with her virulent tirade.

"You were insolent, arrogant, pretentious, vulgar, and extremely out of line last evening while inebriated. I gave you a second chance today, however your sober state is far more insulting than you unconscious one." She stopped, drank a sip of Jean-Louis' pineapple juice. "I do not care a bit about you; you're definitely not a person with whom I would care to spent a minute, no, another second in your company." She now looked directly down at Jean-Louis. "Furthermore, if your influence on your dear friend, your old childhood friend, is so pervasive, I'm no longer quite certain that I want to socialize with the likes of any of you. It's repulsive."

Jean-Louis opened his eyes wide, digesting her words. He smirked up at her.

"I can see that you neither like my company, nor that of my friends," he remarked in a conciliatory tone, "but you love my food."

She finished the last of his croissant and look daggers. Could he change that much overnight? What had happened to the stern Captain she had fallen head over heels with? Men changed quickly after a sexual romantic interlude. Was she in for a terrible heartache?

Elise continued and picked up on what she thought was a window of opportunity.

"Oh, mon Dieu, how vulgar and ordinary Jean-Louis-Pierre, but where did you find her, mon chéri? You always seem to have discreet and polite petites amies. Have they changed your taste so much in the colonies? Thank God, you have returned to us." Then she turned to Gaby tossing her blonde curls off her shoulders as if to finalize the tirade.

"We have been friends forever, mademoiselle, and your behavior is not accepted in our circles. You will do well in your circles of entertainers, some of them are quite racy and this ordinary behavior will be enchanting to them. *Ah, oui,"* she professed laughing, *"le circle des artistes est parfait pour vous."*

Gaby looked through Elise.

"Elise, I'm a wealthy young woman," she said calmly, condescendingly, degrading the poor woman with every word she pronounced, as if she was talking to a small, unimportant child. "I possess a keen business sense, a vocal gift that will enchant the crowds and the likes of you, ma chère. Furthermore, God gave me charm and intelligence, as well, a well-rounded modern person, that I am," she continued on a maternal patronizing tone. "I will grant you that French and English old world culture are quite different than ours in the United States. In my view, the old world leaves a lot to be desire. If I need to make an estimation by your behavior and your disparaging words, your kind is on the decline." Then swiftly she turned her head back, as if Elise was now inconsequential and she faced Ribaud who had been shocked by this calm young woman with venom in her breath. His friend was in trouble.

"Jean-Louis-Pierre, my friend, rein her in." Ribaud exclaimed.

With an ironic smirk in his eyes, Jean-Louis gazed calmly in Gaby's eyes.

She hated him. How could he not say one word, one small word in her defense? She fumed as she immediately stood up from his armchair where she had perched. Not surprised, he promptly grabbed her hand to keep her close.

Encouraged by the warmth of his grasp, she stood, still hopeful for a kind word. Instead, he floored her by saying, "You are taking all these silly remarks way too seriously, Gaby. Ribaud here is solely making a humorous remark. You have just met him, give him—"

"I think you are absolutely right, Elise," Gaby said sarcastically. "I hear a wonderful performer in the next salon—my racy circles of friends are awaiting me. I'll feel a lot more at home with artists, rather than in this stifling high and mighty aristocratic entourage." She turned and faced Jean-Louis, peeved that he had not come to her rescue. She pulled her hand brusquely from his and as tears swelled up in her eyes, she shot him a disdainful gaze, confident now that he would not come after her.

"Please don't bother to come, I'll do quite well on my own. Good day," she said haughtily, not fully able to hide her fury and pain.

He raised his shoulders and laughed, looking at her affectionately as she turned quickly and strode with regal elegance toward the covered bar where a black performer enchanted the audience. Around thirty or thirty five years old, the man sang the blues. The early afternoon crowd, unaccustomed to the melodious sound of Cajun melodies, sat mesmerized at the new rhythm. Gaby walked into the room and paid little attention to the rest of the couples sitting at the tables, she directed herself to a small round table closest to the performer, oblivious that she was the only woman sitting alone at a table.

She sat there quite a while, not aware that the waiters asked everyone else if they needed drinks, but that she was being passed over. The Maître d'hôtel had noticed her with Jean-Louis and his friends earlier. Consequently, he had not asked her to leave.

As she turned back to call on a waiter, her eyes locked with a man that she recognized from New Orleans—Christmas Eve at the Beauregard. Chance had it that the United States' vice-ambassador and his mistress had walked in earlier for a *petite salade niçoise* and some good New Orleans sound. His roving gaze strayed on the alluring brunette that sat diagonally from him as she faced the stage.

He first looked surprised but quickly bent down and whispered a few words to the gorgeous red-haired woman sitting next to him. He paused for another second, as he seemed to search his memory.

"I'll be darned," he proclaimed out loud. That's Gabriella De-Conte Thornsen—the voice." Immediately he walked over to her table, as his mistress sat alone, not knowing whether she should sit or accompany her friend.

"It is such a pleasure to meet a fellow traveler from New Orleans Parish in this paradise. I'm Michael, Miss De Conte-Thornsen," he exclaimed not quite sure that she'd recognized him.

For the life of her, she had forgotten his last name. She looked intently at him.

This time, he seemed to understand her precarious position.

"Pardon me, Miss Thornsen," he repeated politely. "I'm Michael Striker, our Country's vice-ambassador to France, and I recognized you immediately. You filled my Christmas with deep pleasure and admiration when you sang the Ave Maria in the Cathedral in New Orleans. How did you ever arrive here in St. Tropez?"

"Naturally, what a lovely surprise, Mr. Striker, I have been accepted at the Académie de Musique in Paris and I decided to vacation in the South of France prior to meeting my cousin Philippe in Grenoble, before I regain Paris."

"Cardinal Thornsen? May I join you for a few short moments?"

"Naturally," she waved her arm toward the rattan chair across from her. The two Americans sat and conversed about their old acquaintances for a long time. Totally oblivious of his mistress, who was livid as she waited for him in the far corner on the terrace. He called out to the barman for drinks.

Meanwhile, back in the courtyard, Jean-Louis listened to his friends who still denigrated the provocative foreigner.

"Jean-Louis-Pierre," Ribaud called out, "come back to your senses, my friend. She is *infernale*, nightmarish, rein her in, she'll rule you. What's got into you, starting up with someone so opinionated, so prim and proper, and a colonial?"

Jean-Louis grinned as he remembered the previous night. They would not have thought of her as prim and proper. "I have learned to like the independent spirit of the Americans," he replied. "Not unlike us, they are chauvinistic about their nations, extremely independent, and pride themselves on their new-found freedom. I have the feeling that when this new Country becomes powerful, and it will, we will have a great amount of admiration for the Americans."

"Come, Jean-Louis-Pierre, Europe is the seat of the Enlightment, they have not had a Jean-Marie Arouet as of yet, although Mr. Franklin tried his best to supplant Voltaire's observations."

"They believe that they are superior and that they are applying the spirit of the Enlightenment in their politics; something that we talk about but have not been able to enforce because of our love for everything that is impractical. What we call substance in Europe is in fact a combination of love and hate for everything that is polished and royal—the aristocrats versus the populace. First, the hatred for everything that places another person in a superior rank just because of a lucky birth, and the flip side of it being, that every bourgeois would cut off their right arm to be little replicas of us—the aristocrats. There is a great divide in our nation over this issue—one that no Frenchman even truly understands, but feels. Non, we are a nation of complicated spirits in constant conflict with our past history and our longing for the modern world. Mark my words, Ribaud," he concluded calmly.

"I don't fully agree with your philosophy or your politics, Jean-Louis-Pierre. We've always differed about the idea of freedom of spirit for all. An overstatement. Even your friends there in the United States believe in heavy-handed leadership. Didn't they have a civil war over it? It appears to me that a large part of their working population was not considered human but chattel and still many of the common people are not allowed to vote. Not everyone in society has the power, or the intelligence to govern. That is, however, an affair we never quite agreed on, and I presume that your years in America have reinforced your own ideas of empowering all governed. But this affair with Gabriella—"

Jean-Louis started to push away from the table, not willing to talk politics so early on in the day. Besides, he was in vacation and right now the little episode with Elise and Ribaud served its purpose. It made Gaby forget the shame she felt over their sexual interlude earlier this morning. And furthermore, it helped to toughen her spirit as well. He was very impressed with her and her responses. She would need that sangfroid in Paris before his arrival, especially if word got out, which would surely happen, that she was romantically linked with him. He stood up, and Ribaud stopped him in his tracks.

"Listen just for one minute, mon ami. Elise and I are convinced that you are quite taken by l'étrangère. Be aware, Jean-Louis-Pierre, don't lose your head or you'll lose your heart. I can see it. We have never seen you smitten before, Jean-Louis-Pierre. Watch out, she's a sorceress of the first rank, and unfortunately you have nothing over her. Not money, not status, well maybe, but she does not appear to crave it like most women we know. She is intelligent, bold, witty, assertive, totally sure of herself—all awful traits for a woman. Except for her spirit and perhaps her prowess in bed, what do you see in her?"

"The same thing you saw in her this morning while you trailed behind her, as you attempted in vain to win her over with your charming compliments. She saw right through you. Then you had to belittle her after she rebuked your polite advances and parlayed you back in your place for not apologizing for your awful performance last evening."

"She's bewitching Jean-Louis-Pierre that I will grant you. Although I never was attracted to short women, her elegance and demeanor are compelling, indeed. Oh, well, my friend, don't tell me I did not warn you. You are treading on unknown, dangerous territories. This is not the Lewis and Clark expedition, my friend, these are challenges that men like you welcome, but a five-foot colonial controlling your life—that's perverse."

Chapter Sixteen

Oblivious to his friends' advice, Jean-Louis reasoned that although the last episode prepared her for her new life, what was sure to follow in the day room where the piano player entertained was another situation. He would not allowed anyone to embarrass her by asking her to leave the table, or worst have an imbecile refuse to serve her if she asked for a collation.

In many well-heeled establishments women were to be accompanied by a male escort. Although archaic, the practice was very much de rigueur in the South. He would never want to see her belittled in that manner. After all, she had asked him questions about the culture and the behavior she should follow in her new land. That is the least he could do for her. He promptly walked toward the room where she obviously had been sitting since he had not seen her return to the room or walk on over to the beach. Instead of finding a poor innocent soul waiting for her knight in shining armor, he found her in a very animated conversation with, of all people, Michael Striker, the assistant to the U.S. ambassador to France. The man was from the American South. They might have known each other in New Orleans.

Jean-Louis paused a moment in the shadow of the dark mahogany bar to assess the situation. And he thought she had learned a lesson, sulking over the acid words she had articulated without much effort to his friends? Eh bien, instead of sulking, there she was, very much involved in conversation with Michael Striker, while his mistress *attitrée* was green-eyed. Wrong again, he ironically thought. She certainly had not learned a lesson. Instead, she very probably was incensed with him. Gaby was a challenge. He was starting to learn about her ways of dealing with life. She was magnetic. Every time he was set on retrieving his independence, pushing the bar up a notch and let her be, he found himself struggling to make her fit in his existence.

He had to admit that independence was not what it used to be. He was very much attracted to her, to put it mildly.

169

He had to tread carefully with this new challenge. Staying close to her would be wise; reaching for her waist, no, that would not be smart. She would push him away and tongues would wag. All in all, that was a very fortunate encounter at best. He felt assured that Gaby would be well taken care when the Parisian crowd found out she already had some political clout other than his. He would speak to Michael, although it meant to step a ring closer to a more permanent relationship. Well, he thought, to reassure himself of his honorable motives—that was the only right thing to do. Poor Gaby, after this last episode with his friends, she needed to be protected, especially if word leaked that they were romantically involved. He would tell Michael that Gaby would reunite with him in Paris in his St. Louis' home. No woman had ever been allowed that privilege before. He did not care about *entretenir ses amies, kept them financially set,* but his home, that was his kingdom. He hoped the little brat would appreciate the concessions he was making to make her stay in Paris agreeable and safe.

Jean-Louis smiled as he entered the bar and sauntered into the room. The ambassador's friend, the tall redhead, noticed him. Instantly, her angry pout turned into a charming smile as she began to trail behind him. Beatrice De Beaunharde was an extraordinary beauty, who at the moment was showing great displeasure with the spontaneous encounter. She and the Duke had had many short dalliances and her heart palpitated every time he walked in a grande soirée or at the opéra, she'd shared with many common friends. Their loges had been next to one another, but then with not as much as a farewell, Jean-Louis-Pierre had left for America. Although he had broken her heart several times, she always reserved a soft spot for the incredible force of nature that was Jean-Louis-Pierre De Pleyssis. He walked past her. His focus was on the short brunette and the Ambassador. Both reached the couple at just about the same time.

With impeccable assurance, Jean-Louis approached the twosome.

Gaby continued her conversation with the American Ambassador. She had noticed Jean-Louis-Pierre's entrance into the dayroom but paid him no heed. He had hurt and embarrassed her earlier, but worse he had not taken her side in the least when confronted with such outright insults by his own best friends. The great De Pleyssis' loyalty was shaken at best and maybe shattered forever. She did not need him, she surmised, and turned ever more lovely toward Michael Striker.

Beatrice took this moment to show her allure and grace to the Duke.

"Jean-Louis-Pierre De Pleyssis, you are back, mon cher. Paris has not been the same since you left. What are you doing in St. Tropez?"

Jean-Louis stopped momentarily to acknowledge the statement. Damn, for the life of him, he did not remember the beautiful redhead's name.

"A pleasure to see you again. I see that our friends have mutual acquaintances, a small world, indeed." He walked next to Beatrice until he reached Gaby and Michael.

"I have been in France for two full years now." Jean-Louis heard Michael share with Gaby. "The lives of my friends appear so distant, Miss Thornsen; tell me all you can about New Orleans." Michael asked Gaby.

"Once a Southerner, always a Southerner," he told Jean-Louis as the Duke approached their table. "Welcome back to France, Jean-Louis-Pierre. When did you return? I heard from very good sources in Paris, that you have been recalled to the patrimoine and that your ship was expected in Brest," the ambassador remarked extending his hand to Jean-Louis.

"Hello, Michael. There was a change of plans," he answered, his eyes focused amusingly on Gaby.

Michael's knowing smirk was not lost on Gaby.

"So tell me," he pursued, "how did you two meet? She must have enchanted you with her voice. I have never heard anything quite like it. Christmas in New Orleans will not be the same this year without your *cantiques*, Miss Thornsen."

Gabriella smiled.

"Well, we are giving a party this evening in the Villa; it would be such an honor if you could grace us with your presence?"

Gaby looked at Jean-Louis. He was non-responsive, so she took the lead. "I would love to," she responded gaily. "And furthermore, I will be happy to sing a few arias with the sopranos and tenors this evening, Michael—for old time's sake," she added with an enchanting smile.

The Ambassador's could not keep from showing his immense pleasure. He quickly tried to regain his countenance.

"Pardon me for not asking earlier. How is your father?" As soon as he saw Gaby's tense expression, Michael seemed to remember the rumors about their rocky relationship. The legal fight over her plantation had been the talk of the parish for almost two years. He promptly continued, "how wonderful to have you here with us this evening. You said you were on you way to Paris? I'll send a driver to your home. We have some wonderful guides at the embassy, and one in particular is well learned in the arts and history of the city. You will love him. What great pleasure. What great pleasure," he repeated. "And where will you be staying?" Michael questioned.

Before Gaby could answer, Beatrice, now standing next to Jean-Louis, tried to engage his company.

"Eh bien, tell me Jean-Louis-Pierre, will you be in Paris for a long period of time? I hope to see you in more comfortable surroundings," she murmured gazing sensually at him.

He smiled but did not answer. Knowing that she'd heard the advance, he stepped closer to Gaby, and slid his arm around her waist as he took this opportunity to formally introduce her as his mistress.

"Gabriella will be staying with me in my home in St. Louis. I know that she will appreciate your offer—until I return that is. Thank you, Michael." Jean-Louis answered, pleased at the development.

She felt his sleeve on her bare arm. While staying friendly so as to not let gossip run rampant, she tried her best not to acknowledge his presence

"Ah, Jean-Louis-Pierre," Beatrice said as she flashed an ironic smile toward Gaby, "another singular aspect of our similar personalities—our dedication and affection toward people so far removed from our world."

Gaby was now acutely aware that Jean-Louis was a person of influence in France. She was no longer certain that she could withstand the amount of attention that he received, but she would not embarrass him publicly, although she would have liked nothing better. How could he have been so flippant with her? She couldn't fathom his behavior earlier. She would have fought tooth and nail for him had any of her friends tried to mortify him in the way that she had been a little more than an hour ago.

"Please join us for lunch," Michael asked.

"Thank you," Jean-Louis replied "but we already have plans."

What plans? She was not aware of any.

"Good bye, Michael, we will see you this evening. *Enchantée,* Beatrice," she said, as Jean-Louis spirited her away. She politely pulled away, knowing that all eyes were on them and decidedly walked toward the beach. He did not fight her.

"I know that you are fuming about my laissez-faire attitude earlier. However, I was impressed with your responses, Gaby, you did not let anyone tear you apart. You will need this aplomb once you get to Paris." As they pass a secluded area, he tried to take her in his arms, but firmly she pulled away. He let it go at that.

"Don't you dare patronize me! Your condescending statements have no place in my life. I can handle myself quite well. It just would have been nice if you had said one word in my favor. I want to go back to Villefranche after the party this evening and I will start my trip to Grenoble on my own. I do not need anyone, and certainly not you. I have found out many things that I dislike about your personality, and I have way too much pride to be treated with such impertinence. I personally do not care about aristo—"

He grabbed her forearm forcefully and pulled her to him.

"Enough, Gaby, cease. I get your message and frankly it does not matter what you think on that subject. I was right. Yes, this experience will prepare you for my world in Paris. You asked what you needed to know about the French etiquette. You learned it first hand. You can choose whatever path you wish. Some would have been more pliable, more compliant, you chose not to and I respect and applaud you for standing up to this tough crowd. However, remember, I came to you when you committed an etiquette gaffe, as you entered and sat in the dayroom without a male escort. I would never let anyone embarrass you in this instance."

She was shocked. Frankly, she could not see the difference between the two.

"I'm sorry, if you felt let down." He was contrite over their first real argument.

She pulled back looking at him for a while and smiled.

"You run around with a wild bunch, Jean-Louis-Pierre De Pleyssis. I don't think that I'll like them very much, no matter how hard I try," she replied softly, aware that he had save her from a real embarrassing situation if she had not met Michael Striker.

"Thanks for coming to my rescue," she said looking up, her anger completely gone from her pretty face. She gave his hand a quick squeeze. "Some of my friends would be in stitches if they knew that Miss Prude was taken for a high-class harlot. The music was enchanting."

She pulled away and began walking to the beach.

"I recall Michael vividly, now," she said pensively. "He and his wife, when she was alive, gave the most fabulous soirées in Charles Street. He took the post after she died of viral pneumonia. They were so lovely to look at. Beatrice just does not fit the mold. Jean-Louis you are so powerful and in great demand. What is it that you do beside fighting wars and being a Captain? Everyone appears to be in awe of your personae. I know that your charm could enchant any woman. I do not think however that every man is infatuated with you."

He let it pass and returned the subject to Beatrice.

"Get accustomed to this kind of couple, Gaby, you will encounter many like Beatrice and Michael in Paris."

"Beatrice's snide remarks towards me were uncalled for. She made herself available to you, not the other way around. I have the strange feeling that she was trying to explain her relationship with Michael to you. Her spiteful remark toward Michael as well made the two of us appear like two colonial fools. Did you feel that as well?"

"Maybe, darling, but that was fine because he will take care of you when you get to Paris."

"I do not need to be taken care of," she replied sternly. "I have a home, school, money, and a few acquaintances. I'll be just fine, Jean-

Louis, I assure you, she replied curtly. Now I'm famished." She pressed her body toward his to force him to turn left, back into the courtyard toward the dining room.

"Can we have breakfast just you and me?"

"I'm hungry, too, Gaby, but neither for croissants nor for brioches." He grasped her waist and led her toward the grand foyer and up the elevator.

"But, Jean-Louis, I'm so hungry. Please, after last night . . ." Without much of a fight, she let herself be led upstairs.

In the elevator, he turned her around so that she would face him. He held her tight in his arms. The cabin trembled, balancing from one cable to the other. Jean-Louis looked down at Gaby's expressive eyes, no fear just excitement and anticipation. She was the only woman he had ever met who courted and liked danger. While riding to Nice two days ago, she'd followed the hardest of trails, explored the darkest of ravines and pushed her horse so that she could ride next to him.

"You like that?" he chuckled.

She smiled, nodded, and lifted her lips to him to receive his kisses. As they walked to their room, Gaby was still intrigued why Jean-Louis had not said anything to defend her during their midday meetings.

"I can't buy your defense," she said aggressively. "Tell me the truth. Were you embarrassed to stand up to your dear friends? Did I embarrass you? Why? They were vicious, Jean-Louis. And why, all of a sudden, did you have a change of heart and come in to save me from the maître d'hôtel in the day room?"

"You're being absurd, Gaby. I told you before, I wanted to see how you'd fare in the face of heavy banter and harassment. You did well, chérie; you'll need that skill in Paris. In the case of the restaurant, I knew that you were not aware of the etiquette and that some imbecile would embarrass you. That, I did not want to see happen."

"You know, Jean-Louis, I feel a bit confused about the French culture. It is quite difficult for a foreigner to really know what to expect. At times one feels devastated, shocked, overwhelmed by the amount of frankness and the open libertine spirit that is pervasive in this part of the world and yet there are certain undeniable, unspoken, illogical rules that every Frenchman and Frenchwoman appear to know and are not willing to share. They seem to enjoy making foreigners appear like outcasts!"

He laughed, "Don't denigrate my country, *mon étrangère, mon ange de fer.*"

"I'm not excoriating. I'm just stating facts," she responded haughtily.

He tapped her backside and stood by the door. He waited and looked at her, smiling that ironic, sensual smirk that devastated her.

"Well?"

"Well what?"

"Let me let you in on one of our illogical rules. You see, chérie, had you been a Frenchwoman, you would have known, without my asking you to, the underlying *of my nature.* You should have removed your clothes at once and then walked, no, run to bed waiting for your master to come and take you."

"Mon Dieu, what rubbish!" Instead she raised her shoulders disdainfully and walked to the table that was still standing with cold fruits, pastries, a basket of French bread, and croissants with butter and raspberry preserves. She grabbed a croissant and looked back over her shoulder at Jean-Louis who had just started to take great strides toward her. She shrieked and ran behind the table. In one swift shove, he pushed the table aside. Confused she threw herself in his arms, laughing that crystal clear laughter of hers that always melted his resolve.

"You win, you win, *maître de mon destin*, master of my destiny. I'll do anything for you, anything a French sensual woman would do and more, much more."

He picked her up and threw her on the bed while he placed his long sturdy body on hers. He held himself up on his elbows, facing her, her head in his hands.

"What am I going to do without you these next few weeks when we are apart?"

"Miss me so terribly that you'll get to Paris, retrieve me, marry me, and keep me barefoot and pregnant forever—totally controlled, under your thumb! Or in an awful scenario, you'll realize how sweet your freedom from the étrangère really is. You will then send me packing, and break my heart in the process." She laughed her heart out. Nothing could seem to stop her theatrics.

"Infernal brat!" he shouted. "I will have nothing less than ten children and you will be sent packing if you dare balk at that."

They both fell in each other arms laughing, kissing, nipping, licking, touching, and loving one another. They stayed in most of the day enjoying the beautiful sights from their room while loving each other whenever the urge arose.

Later that night they prepared for the Ambassador's party and left for the Villa in Cannes at around nine o'clock. In the carriage, he asked candidly.

"Gaby, are you really going to sing? You do not have to you know that? As a matter of fact, I would rather you not."

"But Jean-Louis, I love to sing. I may not have practiced much, but I have an exceptional voice, you will be pleasantly surprised. Besides, I am not worried about the other singers, it's quite difficult to top my voice." She was so secure and self-confident in her assertion of her gift that he did not press on.

One hour and a half later, they entered the breathtaking estate with the long driveway bordered by white pebbles and gigantic, symmetrical pines.

Gabriella looked stunning—ravishing Jean-Louis had told her earlier. Her short, voluptuous body enveloped in a lemony-yellow satin dress that hung low to her waist in the back. The front of the gown uncovered the mound of her magnificent breasts with a low décolleté. Her heavy curly mane was lifted by diamond barrettes and weaved in a long elegant bun. A few tendrils fell on her forehead, temple, and on her long delicate neck. Jean-Louis looked at her before leaving. She was perfect, he pondered, but in addition to her beauty there was in Gaby, a *je ne sais quoi* that made one want to keep on looking.

Everything in her demeanor fitted like a jigsaw puzzle and yet she displayed a playfulness and impetuosity that distinguished her from most women he had ever encountered. She was truly beautiful, knew it, and yet not an ounce of pretension showed in her personality. She was who she was and never affected to be anyone else or hide her vulnerabilities. He hoped and prayed that no one tonight would hurt or try to intimidate her with her lack of knowledge of the old European culture.

He had dated quite a few women in Boston and one in particular that he enjoyed being with. However, these women, although different, less affected, and more prudish than the European women, certainly did not possess Gaby's charm. All were more reserved, more fearful, hiding a lot of their wishes or desires, and accepting the status quo. Maybe the Southern Belles, as they were called, were more animated than their northern sisters or maybe she was a rebel even in her hometown. He would find out a little more about her background tonight at Michael's house. The vice ambassador had asked about her father but quickly had changed the subject. He should not be too surprised. Gaby did not hide the fact that she detested him. Amazed at the curiosity she'd posed—he had never been curious about his paramours families, usually the less attached women were to their parents the better he liked them.

Gaby must have had a difficult childhood. She had told him that the only relative she liked was her cousin, the Cardinal, and his best friend, who was a lawyer. She loved the two slaves, freedmen that had raised her, and that was about it. She never wanted to expand on her parents, but obviously they had a home in New Orleans if she sang in the Cathedral and attended some of the parties Michael had attended. Lost in his thoughts, he suddenly felt her warm hand searched for his.

"Don't leave me alone tonight," she said, unabashed to ask for his protection.

"You do not have to sing, Gaby, if you feel uncomfortable," he repeated. She had told him her voice was exceptional and although he had heard some extremely harmonious sound from this beautiful girl, tonight she was in the company of top tenors and sopranos. Michael had said she sang like an angel, but had he ever heard true angelic voices in America?

His earlier warnings had gone astray. Flippantly, she'd responded that she doubted that anyone tonight would be in her league. He would be there to soften the blow. No one would dare mock her if he stood by her—not in front of him anyway.

"I'll be there for you, Gaby," he murmured so seriously that she barely kept from laughing out loud. She just pressed her body closer to his.

A large crowd awaited the announcement of the couples and dignitaries present. Jean-Louis and Gabriella were treated like royalty. Gaby conversed easily; she was articulate even in French and his presence had greatly improved her speech and pronunciation. She spoke mostly French with him and most often he responded in English. He could see that she surprised quite a few people, her spontaneity, lack of pretension and knowledge of French etiquette brought a few smirks on many a face. Grimaces, mostly, from the ladies, and looks of approval and approbation from the male population. She did not leave his side, even when the ladies retired in their own sitting room. He knew that he should have told her to mingle with the other women, but he had the strange feeling that she knew that already. After all, in many of the southern plantations there were two entrances—one for the male population, the other for the women. He felt she did not want to play that role and he was not about to force it upon her. They would make social history.

Jean-Louis was tall and impressive in his dark evening attire and snowy white shirt. Women devoured him with their eyes and Gaby was not about to let the competition spoil her night with the man she loved.

Dinner was served. A wonderful repast of *grives*, thrush, en sauce, au vin rouge, and naturally the crustaceans du pays was abundant. There was even a dish called *la petite friture du pays*, tiny little fishes that looked like minuscule sardines served with lemon wedges. She had noticed a few people eat the whole fish, head and tail alike. Gaby stopped a few seconds between each entree. There was new silverware that she had never seen before. All were so practical to properly remove the meat from the shells or discard the spine of the fishes. The French really loved to eat and everything seemed to serve the purpose to truly enjoy and make the process pretty and enjoyable. She would have loved to imbibe in the wonderful wines that were being served. She sipped a bit, trying all the different varieties presented. There were so many glasses, she was lost in the choice of what to drink with what dish. She just looked at Jean-Louis coyly and copied his every choice. Her knowledge of wine was red for meats, white with fish, and bubbly for desert.

Well, all these wonderful choices had blown her minuscule knowledge on wine degustation. Knowing that she would sing a bit later, she just sipped and left it at that.

She knew that her singing would surprise Jean-Louis. The scoundrel had never even asked her to sing for him these past few days. She could have been downright awful or mediocre. He was totally disinterested, his gaze was on her and she shot him a sideways murderous glance. He reached for her elbows.

"What have I done?" he whispered.

"It's what you have not asked, mon cher," she said out loud.

A few amused and knowing looks were directed at them. The crowd surely thought of a marriage proposal. She laughed heartily. He laughed as well. He seemed to know why she was laughing—or did he? It was just fun and special to pretend that they both had a telepathic relationship.

Jean-Louis did not know what she was referring to, but with Gaby he never quite knew what to expect. He wondered why he laughed? Probably because she'd laughed. Her laughter was insidious and catchy; he was just happy and fulfilled around her. She was adorable and so in love with him, he thought arrogantly, yet a dark shadow overcame him when he thought of leaving her behind in Grenoble. His thoughts came to a stop. She squeezed his hand sharply.

"I will leave you, my handsome escort, but for a few short arias." She spoke dramatically. I have just been called to perform. Her small stature moved gracefully toward the music room where she assertively took her place. He watched the entertainers discussed with her, chords, music theory, and songs. The pianist stood up and bowed politely. Gaby smiled and shook her head in an affirmative. The tenor and lead sopranos shot a sideways glance at one another as if to dismiss what she was purporting. Gaby held their glare bravely and confidently. It was not lost on Jean-Louis.

He was beginning to doubt her wisdom to accept a singing invitation with such luminaries. Why had he not discouraged her or intervened somehow? He would walk toward her in a few minutes and tell her not to proceed. Ribaud reached his friend at that very instant.

"Well, well, my friend, your beautiful Gabriella will make a spectacle of herself, indeed. I'm surprised that you are letting her, Jean-Louis. Why?"

"Good question, Ribaud, I was just thinking along those same lines and yet I don't think that she would obey my request. Let's just see," Jean-Louis responded with a worried frown.

"I don't like the chit much, a bit too assertive for my taste, my friend. But I have to give her that, she is gutsy, like they say in America. Refreshing, indeed."

Both stood silent, waiting, expecting the worst, hoping for the best, and then the music started. Gabriella stood behind the lead singers, hands behind her back, her voluptuous breasts heaved rhythmically with every musical movement. If anything, Jean-Louis thought, her stage presence evinced the other three performers.

Libiamo, the aria by Verdi warmed her vocal cords, then another choral ensemble seemed to take her to another level easily, and then another high note ignited so quickly that the roomful of revelers were stunned. She exploded onto center stage and took over the performance. Her mannerism, voice undulations, roucoulement, and theatrics were divine. She held the audience in captivity.

Shocked at the strength, volume, flexibility, and agility of her voice, he gazed expressionless. He had always loved opéra and could not believe that he had been living with her for a month and a half and he had never heard the magnificence of her voice—didn't even know it. She shot a sideways glance at her lover and winked as if to say, didn't I tell you so?

After the end of her solo from Mozart, Le nozze di Figaro as Countess Rosina Almaviva, Ribaud elbowed Jean-Louis. "I now know why you feel for her," he said. "Quel canary! Good heavens, Jean-Louis-Pierre, le tout Paris will be asking her to grace their parties with her roucoulement." Jean-Louis remained silent. He was angry at himself, at her, at Ribaud, at Michael. Michael had told him about her precious voice—how Gaby and the cousin had mesmerized a church full of music lovers for many years, but he just did not expect this performance. Besides, the people Michael spoke about were colonials. He'd listen a bit more closely to the Americans this time around. They had surprised him already in more ways than he could count. He loved Boston and suddenly wished that he and Gabriella would be on their way to 'bean town' rather than Paris with all its pleasure and haute society. Perhaps in a few more years . . . he mused pensively.

Gaby came back to him, surprised and alarmed at his distant look. She took it as a disapproval of some sort.

"Un sou for your thoughts," she asked, viewing the obscure gaze. "You were disappointed, Jean-Louis? I thought I did well. Not wonderful, but well. I have not practiced in over seven weeks, perhaps that's why," she clipped flatly.

"Gaby, you were magnificent. Your voice is one of the most enchanting I have ever had the pleasure to enjoy. Look at the crowd. They have not recovered yet."

Indeed, this short, cute colonial with the curly, mahogany mane and expressive, green eyes had overwhelmed the crowd. Everyone wanted to talk to her, to find out about her past, her present—and her future.

Jean-Louis realized all that quickly before Gaby. He let her bask in her instant fame—even the soprano came and congratulated her.

She could feel Jean-Louis getting cold and more distant as more and more groups approached her.

She loved fame and approval of things she did well. She planned to continue to excel. However, at this time in her life, music and everything that she held dear to her heart became second fiddle. She wanted Jean-Louis to love her as much as she loved him and to that end she would not stop until he admitted his love for her—for she was certain he adored her. He was her life. She cared very little about anything else and as usual, her persistent fear of losing it all because she was so happy resurfaced time and time again. She walked through the crowd of admirers and she reached for Jean-Louis' hand.

"Can we walk on the balcony? From the stage I could see the magnificent view. I want to share it with you."

"It's cold out there, Gaby; it may not be the best for your voice."

"Jean-Louis, are you displeased with me? I sang well, I don't think I embarrassed you in that light."

He looked down at her and smiled.

"I told you, Gaby, you were magnificent, ma chérie," he continued in a neutral tone.

They stopped momentarily to gaze ahead of them as their eyes adjusted to the darkness, they then ambled on the balcony.

For a short while he leaned on the concrete pillar examining her. She pressed her back against the cold marble of the balcony and returned his gaze.

"You are looking at me like a street vendor. Could it be, Jean-Louis, that you are jealous of my love for music or of my wild appeal from your countrymen?"

He pushed off the pillar and straightened.

"Gaby, get a hold of yourself. No, you're absurd. You are coming to Paris to pursue your musical interests. Why would I even entertain such idiocies?"

Her cheeks turned crimson and she posed her hands on the silk sash of the gown for countenance.

"Jean-Louis, I am young and inexperienced when it comes to men and their moods and feelings. I know what I feel and I think that you might feel the same. You know my only true friendship and experience is with my cousin, Philippe. He is highly dedicated to the church and his vocation, therefore I respect and do not worry about his changing moods because I know he loves me in a way that is pure and sincere."

"And you think I'm impure and insincere? Even to you, Gaby, doesn't it sound ridiculous?" he said in his haughty style. He picked her up and placed her on the wide balustrade of the balcony.

Now eye-to-eye, she did not bat an eyelash and just held out her hands to hold on to his forearms.

Another thing he liked about her, he thought. She felt completely secure and protected in his presence. Most women would have screamed, shouted, uttered words of fears of being dropped or of falling four levels down into the bushes—not Gaby, she held on to him, apparently secure that he would protect her or would not endanger her well-being for any reasons.

"So tell me, Gaby, why are my feelings towards you insincere?" he smirked as he retrieved his insouciance.

"Jean-Louis, you are putting words in my mouth. I just said that I was inexperienced with men, with you and your moods. I feel very young and immature at times, especially when I compare myself to some of the French women that surrounded you tonight. That's all I said."

"Well, you are right, but that is exactly what I like about you, Gaby—your vulnerability, spontaneity, and your pure and sincere nature."

She forced him toward her and kissed his lips. "My purity? Oh, please, you beast. You took it from me. Thanks for assuaging my fears and insecurities." She nipped at his upper lip. "I love you," she said as she placed her arms around his neck, "I love you very much, Jean-Louis." She kissed him again not expecting any response.

Damn, she was a force of nature. He could feel desire surging and he wanted her to himself—not adored by everyone in this room who were in awe of her gift.

"Let's get back to the hotel. We made an appearance, which was polite. They will take care of you before I arrive. You may be more popular than Parisian bread and Beaujolais before my return!"

"Ordinary and vulgar, mon cher, I would have preferred to be compared to a Renoir painting, something to look at and enjoy, not something for degustation, darling."

"Too many weeks aboard a ship surrounded by vulgar, ordinary people," he retorted.

"Hush, let's go," she replied in English as she slid down from the balustrade.

He placed his coat over her shoulders, took her hand, and they bade their hosts farewell. He knew he would meet the same boring group the day after tomorrow at the Bataille des fleurs in Nice.

Chapter Seventeen

The Carnaval was grandiose and elegant in Nice, unlike the Mardi Gras festivities in New Orleans. Gaby was thrilled and amazed at all the honors and medals Jean-Louis received. He had been honored as a great statesman. From what she perceived, it appeared that the French officials expected a lot more of him that he was willing to give. He was a lot more than a petty French Captain, adventure seeker and swashbuckler. The French looked to him as a future leader of their country, or so it appeared to her, but here again she was not acquainted with the culture and it may very well have been a way of honoring his long lineage and his accomplishments in Asia and in the United States.

She did not care. They were back in Villefranche and life was glorious. Ecstatic to have returned to the picturesque village by the sea with its emerald water and luxuriant verdant banks, she perceived it as one of the most spectacular, natural beauties she had ever laid eyes on. She never tired of its splendor. What a place to be in love, she murmured lifting her eyes to the heavens.

The Tempète was moored on the quaint port they called La Darse. Jean-Louis had left very early, and she had not asked when he would return.

The inhabitants of the village were quite pleasant and willing to grant her every wish. She had gone out without telling Jean-Louis yesterday and had ridden one of the mares on the ramparts of the old Citadelle, which had led to a dark, cold, and humid street built as a continuation to the fort. It was properly named the Rue Obscure, the somber street. On one of the side streets, she had found a little shop with a charming seamstress, Gaby had picked up some pretty dresses and the woman had been willing to alter everything at no extra cost.

She could not wait to show Jean-Louis. He'd promised her he would take her to town this afternoon. She wanted to take him to the Old Church, to the townspeople's *buverie*, a gathering place where men and women congregated to drink their *ballons rouge,* glasses of red wine, and to meet their friends. He had told her that the Church might have originally been built as an old fortress. Apparently, the steeple might have been a dungeon. She had seen the Sculpted Christ chiseled in fig wood by *Le Gallérien,* an anonymous prisoner sent to the local gallows located near the docks closer to Nice. She could not wait to show him everything she had discovered in the upper village. Jean-Louis had warned about marauding pirates at the far end of the bay who sometimes came to town disguised as merchants to stake out the women population and the many places to loot. But this part of town appeared very safe. She'd return quickly to the elegant villa in the Darse. Having been locked in for twenty-eight days, she now wanted to see, learn, and love.

Upon her return, she promptly dismounted and attached her horse to the wooden rail just outside of the stables. She snatched up her riding skirt, ran up the steps, marched into the villa, and continued her flight towards their room. The heavily carved wooden doors were slightly ajar. She ran to the bathroom counter, washed her hands and face, and then quickly donned her new purchase. In her rush, however, she had not noticed that from the foyer, Jean-Louis observed her every move. Dressed and perfumed, she looked out to the bay from the tall windows and sat on a damask divan inserted between the wide windowpanes. She then noticed the driver pulling Jean-Louis' horse back in the stable. Quickly, she sprung out of the divan and into the hallway, looking down from the top of the golden banisters.

"Gaby, where did you go?" Jean-Louis asked loudly.

She turned, stared down to the bottom of the stairs where Jean-Louis was now standing holding on to the massive bronze globe of the balustrade.

"Oh, I'm sorry, I did not see you," she turned about and started downstairs once more. "When did you get back? I rode like a crazy woman hoping to return before you did," she replied, gasping for air.

"It is the most beautiful, the most picturesque, the most romantic little village I have ever been in," she continued. "I love the people, the fishermen, Jean-Louis they work so hard, up a good part of the night, returning with *la pêche,* the catch, at five-thirty in the morning. Meanwhile their wives weave these long and knotty nets for their men all day, it's back-breaking work sitting on these low-to-the-ground rattan stools mending away all day after cleaning the fishes and selling it to the locals. Yes, a hard life indeed. Will you come back with me this afternoon? There is so much to see in this little town."

She failed to notice the quiet anger that twitched his jaw.

"You're not going anywhere. Didn't I tell you it is not safe for a woman alone in town," he retorted angrily.

It was the third time he had used this intransigent tone of voice towards her. She clearly remembered the very first afternoon on the Tempète when she had annoyed him with all her polite talk . . . and then again during the storm. Was he angry because she did as she pleased or was it real concern for her safety? Either way, she did not like being spoken to that way. She voiced her thoughts aloud.

"Both," he retorted with an air of finality that did not expect to be questioned.

"Well . . . I do not like it when you are angry, especially when your anger is directed at me, but my first flaw you will just have to live with, because there is not much I can do about it. I'm my own woman, Jean-Louis. I have been independent from a very young age and I do not take to orders readily or well. If you are concerned about my safety, I'm truly sorry I worried you, but truly there is nothing to fear. I felt quite safe until I realized I was being followed in the rue du Poilu, the soldier street. I quickly ascended the steps that led to the Church. The man followed me inside the Church. I was a bit concerned until I realized he was the resident priest. Since he was dressed like a painter, I could not have known." She laughed and his anger dissipated.

"You irreverent little witch, come here. Have you no reverence for a man of my social stature? Where did you say that spanking room was located?" He walked to his desk and sat behind it.

She marched up to him and tried to turn his chair away from the desk to sit on his lap—to no avail. □

"Need to lose some weight, Captain," she teased.

He pushed away from the desk and pulled her down to him. She reclined in his arms. Her hair dangled down the armrest of the chair as she looked up at him.

"Will you come back with me this afternoon, please?" she murmured sweetly.

He nodded, and then bent down and kissed her.

"Tell me, Jean-Louis, what did you do this morning? Why did you leave to go to Nice? Why so early? Did you meet anyone you knew—from your past, maybe?" She remembered the first night that he had spent away from her in the hotel in Nice.

"You're asking too many questions, acting too much like a wife, my dear." He bent down and kissed her again.

"Did you see any one from your past? Did you?" She anxiously stared at him.

"Of course, Gaby, hundreds of people from my past."

"Any women from your past?" she directly questioned.

"Naturally. I met many women from my past since our arrival. I was not a choirboy, nor did I enter the seminary at an early age, chérie."

"Well . . .?"

"Well what, Gaby? I'm here with you, right?"

"Right. Do not tell me anymore. I don't want to know, but why are you so well considered. People truly admire you I can see that. It appears that you appeal to everyone, poor and rich alike, and everyone knows you?"

"What a question? You see, Gaby, you should be more in awe of the wonderful, powerful man in your bed. You should recognize and give homage due to a great person like myself. Consider yourself lucky, my dear, that you are allowed time to spend with one of the great figures of our time."

"I do, Monsieur, but now allow me to take leave of your greatness, to leave your humbling company. I'm tired, very tired all of a sudden. Watching the sunrise over Villefranche and Beaulieu was breathtaking, but I did not sleep much after your departure." She had grown accustomed to the sweet taste of the brownish-gold liquor, but it put her to sleep. Besides, now she wanted him to come up with her.

He threw a pillow at her.

"Back in your revered hands" She picked up the pillow reverently, curtsied and politely handed it back to him. "For you my lord." She burst out laughing and ran out of the library.

In front of the immense windows overlooking the bay, she let her body fall and sink on a day bed covered in green and gold silk. Sexually driven, he followed her and sauntered in the magnificent living room. Her profile turned to him, her body willing, she sensually tapped her fingertips to the seat next to her. He obliged.

"Would you like to walk down and go swimming later tonight when we return home?" she asked.

"Although the days are balmy and clear, Gaby, the sea is chilly." His lips widened in a half smile. "Where do you find your energy, Miss Thornsen?" He got up and strolled towards the side bar.

"Well, you kept me as a prisoner on your ship for twenty-eight days, your Majesty," she replied reproachfully, sarcasm in her sensuous voice. "Now I need to react to all that pent-up energy."

"Good. Come here, angel, spend all that creativity on me." His grin widened. "It does not look too comfortable over there. I'm a big man."

"Non, come closer, next to me, Jean-Louis. It's beautiful. Grab your paper and come here next to me. It will be extremely comfortable. I'll make it so . . . please?" She patted the place next to her again.

Slowly, he reached the sidebar, poured himself a cognac, and returned to the divan where he placed the glass on the side table. He sat down, turned his body sideways, and lay down on the sofa with his head on her lap. He grabbed hold of the paper. For the second time in his life, the Duke De Pleyssis loved feeling like an old lover with his long time adored mistress—his head lying on his lover's lap while the paper tickled his interest. He reached for her hand and placed it on his heart.

"You are sweet, darling, very sweet," he murmured.

She bent down and kissed his forehead and then his lips as she basked in total happiness.

"I love you," she whispered. He smiled a long sensuous smile but did not reply.

* * *

Later that afternoon they rode into town. This time they left their horses outside the moat in the *fosses*, ravines, of the Citadelle and walked romantically on the Chemin de Ronde, the path where soldiers watch for strange ships that sailed into the bay under a clandestine flag. Pirates, she had been told were a huge problem. Unfortunately, the two Citadelles had an inglorious past. On two occasions, they had been forced to capitulate—to abdicate to the Franco, Turk and Spanish force in 1543 and then to the invading French and Spanish force in 1691. It had been devastating for the region, in consequence a third Fort had been built on top of the hill. It was said that the Provence could never again be subjugated if Nice and Villefranche were secured. Well, both times the Citadelles had failed but hopefully this time France was going to keep this region. The people had voted to be part of France in 1860, and Jean-Louis fully expected the port to play a huge part in the next few years as he consolidated power in Italy and used its vast bay to accommodate trade and obviously to continue tourism with the various vacationing royalties.

They walked hand-in-hand, stepping on the large stone slabs that bordered the walled fort. He had shown her how to unclasp the minuscule mollusks from the rocks immersed in water and ate the arapedes's meat raw like an oyster. Meaty and salty, she developed a taste for sea treats. They looked for flat rocks on the beach; she was good at making these large flat rocks jump on the transparent water.

He liked the sound of her laughter. Gaby was always happy. She was authentic. She loved the simplest things so much so that her *joie de vivre,* love of life, was catchy. Always she impressed and surprised him. When he thought he had her all figured out, she caught him off guard.

Just two days ago he had taken her to La Napoule, a lovely small town sporting a dilapidated castle on the other side of St. Tropez near St. Raphaël. Essentially he'd wanted to verify her purported 'good' shooting skills. She had been right once more—she was a sharp shooter.

"I would not want to be your enemy, Gaby," he had told her admiringly. "It's just so out of character with your personality. You never cease to amaze me."

Gaby had hung on these very words for the last two days.

He liked being with her. She was smart, witty, assertive, and she loved challenges and danger—a bit too much for a woman. It could get her killed. But yet mice and being in the dark could send her into folly. A fairly large rat crossed her path while they were shooting in La Napoule, instead of aiming for it, she'd begun to run away from it with her gun loaded. He had had to run after her, grab her and her gun and gather her body close to his. In return, she'd folded her arms around his torso in such desperation that her body trembled and her face expressed pure horror. For a minute or two, he'd almost felt like a savior, until he realized he had saved her from a rat! Minutes later, she timidly giggled. Her laughter was contagious and beautiful.

"Well, Gaby, you are very good, chérie, as long as you keep your rat phobia under control. If you are ever in a situation like that, shoot the bad guy in the heart or head. Never look down on the ground."

"I wish that I was not afraid of rats and of the dark. I have tools to deal with darkness; I sleep with the lights on. As far as rats, well . . . " she'd responded, helpless.

He noticed that sometimes she would have moments of sadness or maybe melancholy. It would happen suddenly. She'd zone out for a moment or two and then catch herself and retrieve her zest for life. She was mysterious in her own way, and yet so open, so easy to live with, loving, candid, and great in bed.

He was having a very good time with her. They had finally reached the old town. A place called Amélie Pollonnais sported an incredible boulangerie. The sweet smell of French bread and brioches filled the air. They walked in to choose a pastry and Gaby showed him what she had been enticed to purchase earlier that day. They called it Pissaladière, onion-covered Foccaccio bread smothered with onions, olives, and anchovies. Gaby had to have it, so they purchased and collected their snacks and then walked back down to the Rue Obscure. She was mesmerized by the lives of the fishermen's wives.

"It's almost like their own lives are not important." She'd said sadly, they dedicate themselves to everyone in their families but themselves.

They walked up by the old church, St. Michel. Jean-Louis knew the area well because the Commissariat De Police was located right across from the great Church on the Place de l'Eglise. He had attended mass once in the impressive church. The wooden Christ was an amazing work of art and the organ dated from the 1790s. The Brother Gondia had built it. They had been commissioned for three thousand francs to build it. The choral, as he remembered, was well established in the parish.

A long line of women and children lined the side of the Church. He suspected a wedding. Well-wishers were waiting for the party to march out and be congratulated. Pulled in the middle of the crowd by the darling girl next to him, he towered over everyone and felt foolish.

"I have never seen a French wedding, can we watch?"

He was about to tell her that all weddings looked the same everywhere, but she looked so cute and anxious that he reached for her waist, pulled her in front of him, and waited for the couple to come out.

Gaby had asked the girl next to her if she could have some rice to throw at the couple. The mother of the girl had given her some and she shared her portion with him. The simplest experiences animated her and her enthusiasm was contagious. She acted like a child at times, so very vulnerable, and yet she could stomp you with her intellect and cut you down to size with her sharp power of deduction, logic, and analysis. He liked speaking politics with her. He could count on her with accounting, rarely erring, and she was well versed in music, its history and its theory, and naturally her voice—her voice was superb.

"Jean-Louis, are you ready?"

"What?" he responded distracted.

"They're coming out. Are you annoyed . . . bored?"

He shook his head.

"I am with *you*, Gaby; how can I possibly be annoyed or bored?"

"Oh, look there they are. She is beautiful. Oh, my God, Jean-Louis, he could be her father. Oh, how sad." She coolly declared in English.

The procession made its way down the long parvis, and happily and with gusto she threw her rice at the newly married couple.

"Well?" she turned to him, waiting.

"Well, what?

She looked at the rice in his fist and nudged her head and eyes towards the couple.

"Oh, that." He complied.

The priest noticed Jean-Louis. He walked briskly towards the young couple and blessed them. Gaby was on the verge of tears as the cleric introduced himself to Jean-Louis.

"All of France is depending on you, Monsieur, les Bourbons are admired in our devoted provinces, " he pronounced formally, ending the short conversation as he returned calmly to his priestly duties.

By now everyone stared at them. Gaby turned to him and she passionately kissed him fully on his mouth. "To seal the blessing!" she murmured. The crowd started clapping.

At that very moment, Jean-Louis almost ran after the priest and asked him to marry them—right then and there, on the spot. She would not have to go to Grenoble. She would return with him on the ship, he considered. The eminent separation disturbed him. He pressed her ever more tightly to his chest and he wrapped his hands around her waist. Better to just kiss her, he reasoned, than to do something so irrational and unreasonable as marrying someone he had just met. They must have stayed in each other's arms for quite some time, for when they disengaged, the crowd had dispersed. The ones that were left looked at them with knowing smiles. A love story unfurled in front of their eyes.

"I love you, Jean-Louis. I do not want to think of the day that I will be going to Grenoble. It's coming too quickly," she murmured.

"Come back with me, then, on the ship. You know life on board well by now; we will send a note to your cousin. He will meet us in Paris."

She was tempted, oh so tempted, but she could not, she just could not. Philippe would be devastated. She did not answer him. He did not push.

* * *

Jean-Louis had discovered the beautiful port when Villefranche had voted to bear arms for the Empire in 1860. He had come back to France for a short while and had traveled south with the Emperor and the Empress Eugénie. They had landed in the Darse and Jean-Louis had fallen in love with the picturesque village that had one of the largest and deepest bays in the world.

The Imperial Russian Navy had had a strong influence as well. They'd moored their battle ship in the bay of Villefranche while they vacationed in Nice. The area called Cimiez was a popular escape for the Russian aristocracy who escaped their frozen homeland during the brutal and long winters. They owned quite a few villas on the hills surrounding the Bay Des Anges and would arrive in the dead of the winter months to soak up the sun and enjoy the gambling in Monaco and Nice.

Villefranche, however, was decidedly a significant port for the Russian Navy. Russian scientific researchers had also set up a small zoo at the end of the Darse, Le Petit Port, to research animal behavior. Nevertheless, Jean-Louis had decided that the town was far enough away from French society and furthermore he could moor his ship closer to his home.

The first villa he had purchased in Villefranche he'd let his many friends use throughout the year. However the small palace he had built just above the Petit Port in the Darse—he truly cherished. He had worked closely with a Parisian architect that had refurbished and modernized his ancestral castle in the Loire to bring about a modern look inside the walls of the vast propriétée.

Gaby was delighted when he had shared with her that the provincial castle was like his domaine in the Ile St Louis in Paris. No paramours had been entertained in this home.

"I'm the first one who has stayed with you in this room?" she hesitantly questioned.

"You're the first one who has share my lodging and a greater part of my life contiguously for five weeks." He laughed in return.

"Good, very good," she nodded pensively, "but now, my dear Jean-Louis, if you are not ready in half an hour, I'll go riding without you, my lord," she teased. "Voila, follow me or be left behind—the ultimate ultimatum!"

"Maybe I'll think of coming with you, beauty, but first you'll have to please me. Come here, Gaby." She quickly walked to him. He relaxed, reclined in one of the great lounge satin chairs that overlooked the bay. In Louisiana they called those fainting divans. One of his long muscular legs hung down the arm of the elongated fauteuil, the other was folded with his boots crushing the delicate fabric of the sofa, a book lay on his groin.

"Come here. Tell me, where do you want to go, darling?"

"I want to leave now Jean-Louis. Look I'm all dressed up and the horses are saddled. They're waiting for us at the bottom of les Escaliers de Verre, the glass stairs. Come, there is so much to do, so much to see. I want to ride down the Rue du Poilu, the street of the old soldier—it's charming. There are all sorts of buveries. We'll have a collation somewhere there. The Church St. Michel is very close and we could ride through the Rue Obscure on our way to the new train station. I'll need you to be with me there. It's like midnight in the middle of the day. I would get scared in there all by myself," she said almost as an afterthought. "Did you know that the station was built almost exclusively to welcome and accommodate the Emperor and Empress of Russia? They refurbished the station, building a lovely enclosure for high-ended personages."

"Like myself," he said haughtily.

He was not kidding, she recognized.

"I presume," she answered, unimpressed but feeling on shaky ground, "they will not let laborers ride on the new trains. You know that, do you? I have a difficult time placing you in this same unfortunate lot of people, Jean-Louis."

"That is unfortunate, Gaby. Most people would think otherwise. I'm willing to bet that even these poor laborers you spoke about would disagree with you. They would love to have my chance of birth."

"Yes, I know," she murmured cautiously.

"You were speaking of the difficulty of life of these fishermen's and their families earlier. It is that same chance of birth, darling, which propels me to do the work that I do, to use my full potential including my great wealth to represent many of these people who work so hard and have no time, no means to make a difference in their lives and those of their children. The future of humanity relies on people like myself who have the means, the intelligence, and potential to make a difference for the well-being of the populace. I owed that much to the spirit of the enlightenment so well loved and proposed by Voltaire. I think this is the time in history when his philosophy and dream can become a reality, Gaby. That does not mean that the poor of our times will not keep on struggling. They will and even their children might be in the same precarious situation years from now." He paused and resumed, "however, *les fruits*, the benefit of my work might become apparent in the third generation—our grandchildren, Gaby."

She goggled him wildly.

"The grandchildren of our generation," he promptly clarified. I can't give up now, there is too much at stake." He looked away.

Stunned by the revelation—much of which she did not comprehend, but she was certain that it weight profoundly on his mind. She would venture a few more precise questions at a later time. She slowly reached the divan and looked at him as she bent down and lifted his loose white tunic. She placed her delicate hands on his sunburned skin and kneeled down between his legs as she faced him squarely.

"You are an honorable man, Jean-Louis-Pierre De Pleyssis. I'm glad that I have met you."

"Good. Now, ma chérie, appreciate all that I have to give you. Continue to honor me with your feminine charms, Miss De Conte-Thornsen—a mouthful, that name." He chuckled and held her head close to his chest while he smoothly took her hand and placed it below his belt.

She knew what he wanted her to do, but . . . she was in a tormenting mood.

"Tell me, darling, do you ever lose control?" She brushed kisses slowly down his taut abdomen.

"Never chérie. I'm always in control." He laughed once more, "Don't force your luck."

She waited a few extra critical minutes making the most of her feminine charms, as he called it, knowing that by now he was pretty damn close to losing control.

"Well, wonderful, my darling, you'll need all that control now." She stopped kissing him and bolted towards the door giving his oversize manhood an ironic sideways glance as he was left perplexed and incensed.

She no longer feared him. As she ran out of the room, she winked at his distressed face. He'd be on her trail as soon as he'd recover from the insolence.

"I'm on my way to the train station," she said as she blew a kiss in his direction and passed the double-doors into the upstairs foyer, "I hope it will not take too long to regain your self-proclaimed self-restraint, darling."

She dashed down the thousand steps from the villa and leaped on the saddled horse and galloped hard towards the old fortress. The coachman was left with two hands on his hips, as he watched the young girl race toward the town.

Unfortunately, as she neared the Citadelle, the large portals were closed. She assumed that the soldiers were practicing their shooting skills. The path along the sea, Le chemin de Ronde, guarded by the soldiers twenty-four hours a day to protect the castle, was the only viable conduit to the town. She vaulted the horse around and noticed Jean-Louis hot on her trail. Not an easy task, she thought, to steer the horse away from him now. She slowly, submissively, rode the horse toward him. He came close, too close. He attempted to reach the bridle of her horse.

"To no avail," she shouted as she preempted his gesture and bolted the opposite way, down the steep hill that meandered around the steps that led to the sea where the boats moored. Instead of waiting for him, she shot straight ahead to the Grand Port where the fishermen would unload their fishes at six a.m. in the morning.

She glanced back quickly and noticed amused that he was following full throttle now. She heard his horses' hooves clanking on the paved stones. He probably no longer sported a smirk on his face, she mused. She didn't dare look back. She had ridden up to Place Amélie Pollonais where Cunnan had waited for her at the buverie, past Madame Metzgera's boutique. She rode along la rue du Poilu, paused for a frightening second before entering the Rue Obscure, the dark, ominous, stone-covered arched street where light never showed its pleasant face. She felt the insidious courage that one gets from aggressive athletic activity and rode full speed in the corridor. Jean-Louis is following close behind, she told herself. Toss your fears away. Unfortunately, at the very end of the winding street the horse's hooves caught the Pas de l'Ane. The Pas de l'Ane was a significant trench dug in the dirt. Donkeys and beasts of burden used it as leverage so as to not fall backwards and loose their footing while carrying heavy loads. She looked back just in time to see Jean-Louis come right alongside her mount as he reached for her bridle.

"Scoundrel," she shouted, "I almost made it."

The street was deserted. He dismounted his horse and led her horse easily up the trench and out in the open countryside.

Gaby could not hold her mirth.

"You ride well, Jean-Louis. Had I known about the Pas de l'Ane you would not have caught up to me?" She proclaimed assertively.

"Don't be too sure of that," he replied, amused by her boldness. "But now that I did catch you, down you come." She dismounted proudly. He grasped her wrist none too gently and led her in a small clearing where an olive tree had grown in between a patch of soft green grass. He sat down next to the tree trunk and pulled her down first next to him, and in a swift motion, he bent her over his knees and proceeded to pummel her bottom.

"That's what happens to disobedient girls."

"How dare you!" she shouted. "You horrific, cruel, controlling soul," she screamed, gesticulating to avoid his hands.

Amused, he turned her over while still holding her knees under his thighs. Her eyes shot darts, ready to strike. He thought it wise to place and hold both of her arms and hands behind her back. Her opulent breasts protruded insolently under a light linen blouse. He bent his head to kiss her jaw and gently pressed his lips to the softness of her sensual décolleté. Slowly he released her arms and placed them on her abdomen as he held her like a small infant. He stared down at her with lust in his eyes.

"You know, Gaby, that's a French man's trait to control," he said softly.

"Well, thank you. Remind me to never marry a Frenchman. I don't do well with control."

He roared with laughter. One could not possibly be bored with her.

"I can see that. Eh bien, Gaby you may have blown your chances with me."

"But, Jean-Louis," she snapped back, "this retort was devised especially for you, mon cher."

Flabbergasted at first, but quickly retrieving his good spirit, he continued to chuckle.

"What happened to the pliant, obedient, respectful, young beautiful woman on my ship?" he asked.

"And smart, Jean-Louis; you forgot smart and conniving. Now let's see, I was on your ship, *your* ship, in *your* stateroom—tell me, what other choice did I have but to show you my pliable nature. The alternative was horrific—being tossed at sea or thrown in the brig with no lights. No, in retrospect, my tactics were very smart, indeed."

"You mean to tell me you lost your virginity to save your life?" he said, stunned at her boldness.

"What do you expect? But of course I would have, if it came down to that." She regarded him as if he was mad, then quickly realized that this insouciant banter might have cost her a more permanent relationship. She smiled and encircled his large stature in her arms, forcing his lips down on hers.

"I hope you did not pay too much heed to my rude comments. In my eyes you are the most formidable man I have ever met. You are just perfect in every possible humanly way . . ." She lifted herself up to kiss his lips. "I love you—very much.

"Is that another ploy, to achieve your freedom from my embrace, my dear? You have no alternative to extract your will now. You are here in my arms until I decide to let you go." Jean-Louis said assertively.

She looked up at his gigantic stature towering above her, and down at his heavy muscular thighs that still held her prisoner.

"No, I presume not. Logic tells me now that I have been vanquished, totally, that is completely," she whispered as she fully reclined in his arms.

He cautiously lightened the pressure he placed on her hands and gently rolled her fully in his arms, close to his chest. He wanted to hug her, not solely to give her pleasure and security or to make up for the insensitive statements he had shared with her a few evenings ago in the spirit of enlightenment, but mostly to satisfy his own urges of sensuality, sexuality and affection. His feelings for her were getting a bit too uncontrollable. God forbid. He was tormented. He needed to return to Paris. Being with her gave him infinite happiness, and yet he loathed the lack of self-discipline it brought about. To retrieve some of the lost self-control, he took her hand and placed it squarely in his pants. Seeing her surprised glance, he shot her a sideways smile.

"Well, Miss Independence, please continue what you so wonderfully started and so rudely interrupted. Voila." He kissed her intensely as she lost track of time and space. In years to come, she would learn that direct confrontation with Jean-Louis De Pleyssis would never bring her victory. Sympathy, rarely, humor, at times, gentleness, often, but when it came to the battle of the wills—never. He was the most tenacious man she had ever encountered.

This time he held on tight to her as if he had been caught once but would never make that same mistake twice. She pleased him and after the act, he pressed her close to him for a long time. He wanted to prolong the intimacy.

Gaby loved his ways. She had heard of men taking their pleasure and then rolling around and leaving their partner unfulfilled and frustrated, but not Jean-Louis. He always encircled her in his muscular arms and stayed there until she moved. He then would roll her possessively close to him and place his leg over her hips and his hands on her breasts. It felt wonderful to continue the closeness after the sensual lovemaking was over.

"Jean-Louis, I never imagined this region to be so breathtaking. I'm just flabbergasted at the perfection of the coast, the vegetation, and the clarity of the water. I think I'll go swimming when we return."

He looked down at her disarmingly. "Do you ever think of including me in your plans? Please notice, I have respected your independent spirit."

"I'm sorry, I'm back on land in my own backyard, sort of speak—horses, water, and my independent spirit of doing what I want to do, when I want to, and how I want to, my spirit has returned. I have never shared my life with anyone. I would love it if you could, if you'd want to join me." She hesitated. "You know right across from your castle there is a platform where we can dive from, I believe this area was used by the ships that left the prisoners at the end of the port, behind the house of the Chef de Port."

They were so much alike in so many ways. He hated to admit it. She tried hard to compromise, but he noticed how difficult it was no matter how much she professed her love for him. She was accustomed to doing things her own way and waiting for permission to be approved was not in her line of thought. Too bad, she'd just have to learn.

"Maybe, let's see what time we'll return," he answered as he glanced sideways at her and remarked her annoyed pout.

After their promenade in Villefranche, he acquiesced to her wishes. They left hand-in-hand to enjoy the still quite cool Mediterranean water. They had waited until the sun went down for Gabriella did not have a swimsuit. Thank God there was not a soul in sight. That's all he would have needed if the press had followed their escapades like they did when he was in Paris. Gaby swam well. She was fearless and inhibited. He reached for her waist and they slowly walked back to the house.

Chapter Eighteen

Now let's think of Monaco," he said. "You will love it there. It's a Principality. In fact, the sovereign will receive us. I know him quite well.

Gaby did not listen to his speech. Instead, the movement of people on the platform intrigued her.

"Jean-Louis, this train is only for the aristocracy? They say that it was built for passengers of *Haute Classe*. Look, they have special wagons in the back. Oh no, these poor souls, with all these unoccupied seating, they will not be allowed to board." Outrageous, you know, everyone here excoriates the American Southerners and their slaves, the class division in Europe, from what I have seen here these past few days, is quite pronounced as well."

"Except, Gaby, that here they are paid. However small their wages, they are free to move to Paris or the Kingdom of Italy and to take their families with them. Huge difference, mademoiselle."

She did not respond but looked up at him mordantly.

He stared right back as he gazed at her, waiting for an answer.

She turned her expressive eyes away and looked at the bay.

"Wait for me here and don't get into trouble. I will return shortly." He proceeded toward the carriage that had brought them there and said something to the coachman and then walked back to her.

"Have you made a reservation?" she asked.

"No," he replied curtly.

She curiously looked at him whereas he adorned his arrogant glare.

"You are with one of those deserving the title of *Haute Société*, ma chère. We will have the wagon of honor all to ourselves.

"Really?" She looked up to him, incredulous.

"Yes, really," he said, taking her elbow as he walked to the attendant of the cabin.

Sure enough, courbettes upon courbettes, curtsy, and everything in between was granted to the illustrious and powerful Jean-Louis-Pierre

De Pleyssis, Duke de Bourbonne. They sat in an exquisite salon with deep red velvet upholstered cushions.

"I presume I have said it way too often recently, but I am impressed and a bit intimidated by the amount of influence you exert in your country. Sometimes all this power moves me and frightens me at the same time," she said.

"Excellent. You need to feel a bit insecure at times. You're a bit too assertive for a woman, ma chérie. Realize what I can do to you?" he smiled, "if you do not grant me my every wish. Do you recall what my countrymen did to these bothersome little ladies who ate too many brioches?"

She was munching on a raisin and sugar brioche she had just purchased at a patisserie near the station. Gaby looked up, mirth and laughter in her divine throat.

"You mean the ones that got shortened a little bit when they ate cake?"

"Precisely"

"Be serious. I feel insecure. Did you have many long-term relationships, Jean-Louis? Do women like you for who you are or your prestige or . . .?"

"What demeaning questions. What are you driving at, Gaby?" He shook his head in disbelief, although by now he should not, he thought.

"No, I mean that—I know where I come from, who I am, and what a man may or may not want from me. I know about well-heeled men who would have loved to marry me merely for my name and my financial status. The status of a man in society counts for quite a bit in both of our world—even more so in France. Whether the man is worth the attention because of his integrity, charm, or what have you, makes all the difference. You seem to be very recherché, in demand, like they say here. I mean—I don't know what I mean and I do not want an answer. Let's change the subject."

"With pleasure."

They were quiet for a while and then she noticed that he observed with interest a boat that rounded the Cape Ferrat closely. The area displayed fingerlike projections of land that could give cover to all sort of unsavory activities.

"Watch closely Gaby," he told her as he caught her glance. He pointed to the boat. "You see," he repeated, "this is what I mean about dangers lurking the coast. Do you see this ship lounging the coast as if she wanted to hide? If I'm not mistaken it's a pirate ship—Olbeireado or one of his family members. They have been in the piracy business for over a hundred years, Gaby. Victor Emmanuel II, a strong and powerful leader that governed the area before us, was the only one who fooled him. Olbeireado had promised to leave Villefranche and Nice alone if he could have Emmanuelle's wife as a trophy. Victor sent one of the ladies in waiting. Not noticing, the pirate stuck to his deal for ten years and pillaged every other port and villages but Villefranche and Nice.

"So you see darling, I'm safe. I stayed with you when we were in St. Tropez and la Napoule and I just took my leave in Villefranche and Nice where I have carte blanche," she replied quickly.

"It's not amusing, Gaby. His sons do not always respect the treaties. They have been known to pillage and rape when their father is gone on one of his frenzies. There has been more than one horrific act committed by these marauders over time. They lurked the Rue du Poilu, and especially the Rue Obscure, where they hide at La Porte des Boeufs, close to the slaughterhouse in the vicinity where I caught up with you yesterday."

"La Porte des Boeufs at the end of the Rue Obscure? No wonder the stench was awful when I rode past it."

"You were there?" he blazed.

She recognized that tone. "No, no, remember the other day? We rode past it," she lied, not willing to reveal that she had wandered through the area just to become acquainted with the old street. Fishermen's wives pulled their nets on the cobblestomes to straigten the lines. She'd followed slowly behind.

"Yes, Gaby," he continued, not quite certain if she had told him the truth, "that's the perfect vantage point—easy to jump unsuspecting travelers. More than one unfortunate soul was killed in this impasse."

She cringed and removed his hand from her lap nervously.

He now knew for certain that she had gone there alone. He had to keep her on a tight leash. "You see, he said, "once the guards have gone home, they land their ships below the balcony of this building and they walk up to the street. They have pillaged and ransacked restaurants so many times, that the poor souls had to close their doors. They wreck havoc in the drinking places located at the end of the street.

I was in there with a few friends and mariners one evening, prior to my departure for Asia, and these unsavory fellows attacked us. They took the lives of two of my men. None of them lived to talk about it.

Looking somber and shocked, Gaby turned her eyes to his.

"You killed them?"

He glared down with a questioning pause that seem to say, "What other alternatives were there?"

"I'll stay close to the *propriétée* from now on," she said gravely. "Were you with women friends as well?" she asked hesitantly.

"No, darling. Thank God." He gave her a long hug.

She lay in his arms, delighting in the moment. After all, it had been given to her to enjoy. What would it prove to feel guilty about her state of life? It's not as if she had planned it. This heavenly ordeal had been willed. She reassured herself that it would be sinful not to appreciate its glory.

Suddenly for no apparent reason, fear took over her whole being. What if he left her? Once in Paris, his life would return to normal— his friends, his work—whatever an aristocratic Captain did during peacetime. Maybe he would even renew some of his old liaisons. Oh, mon Dieu, what did she get herself into? She tightened her grip on his chest.

"Did I frighten you with the pirates' story, beauty? From now on you'll stay close by from your own accord and grant me all that I wish in return for my supreme protection."

"Hush. I was not really thinking about the pirates, there are ugly and mean spirited people everywhere, Jean-Louis." Abruptly she changed the subject, what will you do after you leave me in Grenoble?"

"I'll return back here. I have my ship, remember? Then we'll sail to Brest and then on to the Loire for a few days. I have our ancestral home in Artoise and I need to attend to some affairs. And then on to Paris, where you will be waiting for me—waiting anxiously—unless you fall madly in love with a young Parisian and drop me like a wet noodle. I'll have guards who will keep a strict surveillance on your whereabouts, Miss Thornsen, until I arrive. They will bring you to your classes and keep you sequestered all night, just like if you were in a harem."

Gaby felt sick and unsecured all of a sudden. Why did he have to joke like that? Something weird was happening to her body. She probably rode too hard this morning not letting digestion take its due course. All those exercises after twenty-one days at sea wreaked havoc with her body. She experienced bizarre mood swings these days.

"Jean-Louis, I will not stay in your home when I get to Paris."

He looked down at her surprised. "Why not, Gaby?"

"Well—I have told you that at times I felt isolated in New Orleans, out of the loop. I want to start anew in Paris. No one knew us on the ship and in Villefranche I was your friend. But in Paris, like you said, my life will be different. I need to appear proper and remarkable in all ways. I'll study with new people that will surely judge me. I will need to prove myself. I understand that talent is not enough. It is whom one knows, who likes you, I do not want to make any enemies or be looked down upon from the very start. To move in your home without you—no, I just would not, I could not."

"Have it your way, Gaby," he replied proudly, miffed. "It's your decision, but remember, I am one of these people you will need to impress. My family has been the largest and oldest contributor to the Nationale Académie de Musique since its very inception. We have kept it afloat and alive for many years." He straightened, removed his arms from her shoulders and placed it on the back of the double burgundy bergère.

She did not move. She knew that she had angered him, but she also knew that she was right in making this difficult decision, no matter how much she wanted to be with him. What kind of a first impression it would present to the circles she wanted to interact in? Besides, Philippe would have been devastated. To be qualified by the company she kept was one thing. However, to be qualified as the new mistress of the Duke De Pleyssis was quite another. Her vocal gift and artistic demeanor would be abased or looked at for the wrong reasons. They would go out, she hoped, fearful now. She looked up anxiously at him. His gaze was fixated on the blue horizon. She pressed her body against his chest tightly, eager for some response, some reassurance, but none came.

Finally, the chef de train came in.

"Monsieur Le Duke, the next stop is Monaco. A carriage will be placed at your disposition, Monsieur."

"Thank you. We will take the offer. Make the arrangement." Jean-Louis stood up. He did not help her up and showed no emotions.

"Where will you stay?" he questioned.

Surprised, Gaby did not know where she would stay in Monaco.

"I—I thought we were staying at the castle?"

"In Paris."

"Oh, Paris. Well, I do not really know Paris, but Philippe has a home in the Ile de la Cité. I have a choice the convent or his home."

"Stay at the convent. It's just one block away from my home. It is a safe area and I'll sent word to place a carriage at your disposition. I wish you could change your mind. What is wrong with this picture? You know Gaby, I have never made an offer like that to any other woman and trust me there has been quite a few." He shot her a cruel glare and moved away and then returned to her.

She stayed mute.

"Very well, Gaby. I do not really understand your motives, but it is your life. From what I have seen until now, you delineated it incredibly well for a person your age. In your own soft and charming nature you have an iron will, a woman to be reckoned with. It's impressive." He smiled and brought his arms to encircle her small body once more. He held her tight and brushed his lips to her temple.

"I want to do everything perfectly, Jean-Louis. I have dreamed to be in the situation where I stand today and now that I am, I would give my whole lifetime not to have anything changed. I never in my wildest of dreams thought that I could have been that happy. It frightens me as well, Jean-Louis. The old demon of being afraid of losing these moments of perfection still haunts me. I do not want to capitulate to it by giving up all my dreams—my professional life, that is. In a sense, I'm afraid of you and of these torrid *bourasques,* these hurricanes, which stir my body and mind. After all these years of denigrating my friends and their romantic interludes, minimizing their intellect and sense of self, it frightens me that I am ready and willing to give it all up. It terrifies me." She paused and looked to him. "I can't—I'm afraid of being hurt and rejected."

There it was again, he noticed the dark cloud that overwhelmed her whole being. Something in her background she did not want to divulge crippled her, he thought. But just as quickly, the sunshine reappeared.

"Non," she pronounced categorically, "it is the right and logical thing to do. I will still be waiting anxiously for you, but instead of a debutante opéra diva, you will retrieve a ravishing, artistic, and enchanting Parisienne *insousciante,* without any care."

He tightened his embrace. "Stay as you are, Gaby. You are sweet, smart, spontaneous, and a whole lot of fun." He kissed her locks.

"You forgot 'beautiful'," she interrupted jokingly. "I am pretty you know; men find me attractive."

"That is an understatement, chérie."

She gazed up at him, searching for his usual smirk when she complimented herself. There were none. After all, if she did not give herself a few compliments here and there, who would? She always wondered why people never complimented her? She would have appreciated a few words of awe. As it was, individuals always had a difficult time complimenting women, in particular, women that were accomplished. After all, they were just as insecure as others, she surmised. Excluding the necessary acquiescence that was de rigueur after a job well done, an accomplished person received no kudos. Instead, she would always have to be aware not to let her faults surface. Jokingly, she'd assert a disparaging retort about her shortcomings in passing. Unfortunately, people attached such importance to it, and never a moment passed in the many soirées she'd attended at home without a verbal assault directed at her limitation. It was as if they wanted to remind her that she was not perfect nor above their own mediocre nature.

Another thing she adored about Jean-Louis was that his compliments were not forthcoming, but when he admired something in her personality, he was forthright. She knew he felt it. No one had ever treated her like that before. Philippe had, of course, but Philippe did not see her as she really was. She was just perfect to him. She loved him so. He gave her his unconditional love. Jean-Louis could learn a thing or two from her dear cousin.

The train had come to a full stop. She watched him as he regally stood up. She knew all too well that he still mulled over her decision.

She walked to him and reached for his hand. This time he did not pull away. He took it and gave it a sharp squeeze. Then he looked down at her, smiled, and paused for a short moment. She saw love in his eyes. Jean-Louis loved her, she was certain of that. The problem with men like him, she had surmised years ago while listening to many of her girlfriends or reading about her literary heroes, they, unlike many women, denied it to their loved one, to the world, and also to themselves. They compartmentalized their emotions so tightly in an obscure corner of their mind, that to call these emotions back to memory became a hardship, especially if they found other companions to please them sexually. He had not told her about his plans upon arriving in Paris, but she sensed that responsibilities to name and country were paramount in his world. He had not counted on falling in love.

They rode from the train station to the Rocher, the hill that rose above the port of Monaco where the Prince's castle was located.

Jean-Louis had not seen the Prince in ten years. He had been an acquaintance of his son Albert Honoré Charles. The young Prince had been madly in love with his cousin, but word had it that the relationship had turned sour. He had had to return to the Monaco and focus his thoughts on the future governance of the Principality.

Although in 1861, the Franco-Monégasque Treaty had been signed, the defense of the Principality was the responsibility of France. The Grimaldi governed, but France kept a tight leash and was responsible for the defense of the Principauté.

Jean-Louis liked the old Prince, Charles III. The Casino of Monte-Carlo bore his name—the Mount of Charles in Italian.

Upon their arrival at the Rocher, Gaby looked in amazement at the Carabiniers keeping twenty-four-hour guard of the castle. She had never seen so much pomp and was enthralled by it all. One man having so much power over his subjects was quite frightening, she mulled over. Jean-Louis was revered. As the large and heavy irons gates opened for their entrance, the old Prince himself held out both of his arms to greet them.

"Ah, Jean-Louis, what an agreeable surprise. I heard that you had stayed in America—married to an American woman, mon ami." He turned courteously towards Gaby, and bent down to kiss her hand, which she elegantly extended.

"Enchanté, Madame." He greeted her politely, visibly mesmerized for an instant by the intensity of her regard. □

"Non, Votre Altesse, mademoiselle," she replied quickly. Her heart sank to a new low, but she did not let it show. She would have to ask about the other American woman. What had happen to her? The other woman was most certainly a Bostonian. Obviously Jean-Louis had left her . . . she had to push back all these questions in the back of her head until later.

"Jean-Louis, introduce me to this beauty," he heard the young Albert called out. The Prince laughed heartily. He was not tall but quite handsome, with intelligent, expressive brown eyes and a powerful body that indicated he was an avid sportsman. Jean-Louis had told her how the Prince loved the sea and its challenges and the sporting activities it provided. He was gregarious. The men walked in front of her reminiscing on days gone by.

A lavish magnificent late brunch had been placed in front of the Prince and his guests. The view was incredible again; the beauty of the area took all her senses. She was asked if she wanted a tour of the surroundings. She would have loved for Jean-Louis to come with her, but seeing that it was not in the cards, she gladly accepted the offer. The Principality had staying power. The Grimaldi had reigned and asserted their authority since the late 11th century—a tour de force in these times of great upheaval throughout Europe.

She had always thought that negotiations and comprises were the key to peace and development of a country and its people. Monaco could teach the high and mighty a few good lessons!

She returned to the balcony. The men had not budged; however, the content inside the bottle of Eau De Vie had significantly been reduced. She was certain they had discussed her charms. Had they discussed the 'girls' with their different personalities? Probably, she thought. In any case, she was the one here with Jean-Louis.

Later that evening they attended a grand gala—the Russian Ballet enchanted the crowd. It had been held in Monte Carlo, the opposite hill facing the castle where the celebrated Casino de Monte Carlo was located. The lavish soirée came right out of a fairytale book. L'îsle Enchantée by Sullivan had been danced in a way like she had never seen the like. In the opéra house located inside the Casino, the classical architecture of the building and its magnificent terraces overlooked the Mediterranean directly across the illuminated castle. It made this town appeared enchanted and populated by good fairies.

What a night of grand pleasure—the food, the wine, the company, the spectacles, and the formidable dancers. They had ended the evening back in the castle, satiated with all the finer things that life could offer. The Prince could not do enough for Jean-Louis.

At around five in the morning, they strolled in the immense residence on the ground of the palace. Their lovemaking took on a different take. Jean-Louis was a lot more passionate than he had ever been before. His powerful body felt as if he wanted to absorb her into him, to remove all of her connections to anything but him, to live for him and him alone. It was a most blissful moment before the eventual end of an idyllic ten days.

Two more days and he would return her to Grenoble. He fell asleep on her. She tried to roll away to no avail. He would not budge. They could not have been any closer physically and she would not have it any other way. Was she living a dream or was it real? To bring herself back to reality, she forced herself to think of the Bostonian. He must have left her, too.

Why did he not want to tell her he loved her? He acted as if he adored her. He was apparently disappointed that she had turned down the invitation to live in his home. Jean-Louis was brutally truthful, God bless him, a tad too frank at times.

"Je suis réaliste, Gaby, c'est tout" he'd proclaim nonchalantly. Oh well, it was too complicated, she discarded all negative ideas from her spirited mind, hugged him tightly, and fell asleep.

It was later in the afternoon when she finally woke up. Jean-Louis had woken up before her and was admiring her beautiful body. She laid on her back, totally serene, her gorgeous hair splayed on the white embroidered cushion. Gaby would be the perfect model for a Manet painting, he thought. Everything about her was perfect. Her magnificent expressive face, her voluptuous breasts, her tiny waist— he could hold it in his hands—her hips, her bottom—a man's dream. Yes, he thought, a perfect woman for a priceless painting, although he would never allow sharing her with anyone even on an artistic level. He had to admit to himself that for the first time in his life he had let a woman touch his heart. There was something about her that titillated him. He missed her when she was gone.

Consequently, he thought, the separation was needed. Romance had no place in his life. He needed to return to Paris and experience his normal Parisian lifestyle before making any permanent decision. Then, it occurred to him that she might have a say in the matter. After all, she had refused his lodging, the arrogant brat. He sweetly caressed her shoulder and kissed her cheek. "Wake up, beauty," he called out softly.

The following evening was just as fantastic and simply magnificent. They had once more attended a lavish soirée. She had not taken any formal attire. No crisis—she had been given three magnificent gowns to choose from. She had chosen a golden satin furrow that had been adjusted to her by the court's tailor and then two estheticians followed with all types of rouge, powder, and eye makeup that she had never seen before. They even brought in a wig that she tactfully declined. She hated having anything on her head even while singing opéra; it constricted her every movement. Gaby felt like a canvas, two women were pondering with their palettes what color would best match the tone of her golden gown and dark green brilliant eyes.

Jean-Louis walked in. With the woman contouring her lips, she glanced sideways, catching his eyes. Lust in his eyes, he shot her a look of approval. Gone was the beautiful ingénue. Facing him instead was a sophiscated beauty who gracefully twirled and rolled her neck backwards in a charming motion that invited a man's kiss. He caught her and did just that. He nodded for the two women to leave.

"Let's forget the ball this evening. You can play the role of a beautiful courtesan." He chuckled and gathered her to him.

"As you please, mon cher," she responded flirtatiously. "I missed you. We are returning in just two days, let's not stay away from one another anymore—please?" In a smooth motion he pressed her to him and searched his jacket pocket for an elongated black velvet box. He opened it and placed a stunning diamond and emerald necklace on her neck. She gazed at it in disbelief. □

"How magnificent, I have never seen anything so exquisite." Her crystal clear laughter that he adored erupted. "It will be hard to leave the dresses and the crown jewelry behind. Do you think the Prince will mind if I keep a few of these baubles?" She teased.

"I do not know about the dresses, Gaby, but the necklace and the bracelet," he was taking out another square box and pulling out a matching bracelet, "are yours to keep." Seeing her bewildered look, he smiled. "I'm happy that you like the setting."

Speechless, she placed her hand on her throat where he had placed the magnificent jewel. She turned away from him and glanced at herself in the mirror and then turned back her voice filled with emotion.

"Thank you, it's stunning," She looked up to him with a gigantic smile as her arms extended to him. "Kiss me now and my day will be complete. A man I love, princely outings, boat rides, balls and jewelry—I must be in heaven."

He laughed at her and tapped her on the backside.

"You should be kissing me," he said as he pulled her to him and admired her pretty face and sexy mouth. "I feel complete when I'm with you, Gaby," he said very seriously. He kissed her again, more passionately this time. She knew that it was as close as she was going to get to an 'I love you.' Moments later they left for another sumptuous evening.

That night they'd fallen asleep in each other's arms on the large canapé, exhausted. Once again Jean-Louis had woken up earlier and once again he had not woken her. He admired the beauty next to him. For over a month now they had been together. Her monthly flow had not started. Could she be pregnant? He wondered. Shocked, he had not winced at the thought. Instead he thought of her lineage. Her mom was Italian, probably small-statured people; her dad was Irish and probably a bit larger and taller. If she expected a boy, he hoped that his own lineage would supersede hers. His family, including his mother and grandmother, were fairly tall with a sturdy frame. Although he was unusually tall and large-boned himself, he hoped a boy would be more like him—a girl could be exactly like Gaby.

She opened her eyes, rolled a little closer, and kissed a spot close to his heart.

"Good morning," she whispered. He felt his desire for her rise again.

"Well, gorgeous, are you ready for another day of riding, learning, and discovering? He repeated the same words she had told him yesterday.

"We are fishing today on the Prince's ship, so up, up," he chuckled, his hands gravitated to her bottom and pulled her to him, "or should we just stay in bed all day. Your call." It always took forever to wake her up. Stroking her body, he whispered more seriously. "Gaby, you have not menstruated since we have been together . . ."

Suddenly wide-awake, she raised up on her elbows.

"Well, it—it should not be anything too worrisome. It happens that I stay months without having my—Tita used to say, it was because I rode too hard and too long."

"Good," he said silencing her once more by placing his lips on hers. Happy to have planted the seed in her head, he let his passion take over.

When they finally rolled out of bed and out of their room, they were told that the Prince was waiting for them on his ship. They went out past the Carabiniers in their small cement and stones guardian houses, down the road to the pier. They had chosen to walk and naturally guards were following them and escorting them down the hill where they reached the fishing vessel.

A magnificent cruiser was waiting and the ship set out for the fishing expedition. Jean-Louis stayed nearby at all times, teaching her how to pull in the large tuna fish. She had lost two large ones already. Large schools would travel the deeper water facing the city. It would not be long before another one would catch her line. She loved being at sea again. The day was just grand. She pushed herself in the chest of this giant man who had changed her life forever and just stayed there letting him do the work.

"Gaby, what happened to all your grand talk about fishing and pulling your own line?"

"I'm tired." She laughed. He continued pulling in the fish and she stayed nestled in his arms.

They had spent an extraordinary afternoon fishing tuna and exploiting the magnificence of the Mediterranean and the small French villages that bordered Monaco on its borders. That night they turned in early after dinner with the Prince.

Gaby was exhausted and retired to the apartment soon after dinner. The men chose to have a private meeting and Jean-Louis appeared anxious when he returned to the room.

The Prince had breakfast with them, promising Gaby to meet in Paris shortly. The following morning, they left Monaco.

Gaby had heard the two men talk about political upheavals in Europe. Jean-Louis appeared unsettled. She asked him about it, but he did not want to elaborate. She left it at that, hoping to press him on the issue a bit later.

Their return to Villefranche was fine. They stopped in the Rue Du Poilu for a drink on the place Amélie Pollonais and then instead of going around the path outside of the walled city through the old city wall, being that it was Sunday, he brought her to the Bal De La Jeunesse. It was a small place above the town cemetery where the youth would dance to the rhythm of a mechanical piano. She was so delighted to sit there, drinking, watching everyone having fun that he sat with her much longer than he had anticipated, just watching her become alive, listening and responding to all her amusing anecdotes.

They would start their trip towards Grenoble tomorrow and as dusk descended on the now quiet village; they slowly walked down to his propriétée in the Darse.

Chapter Nineteen

Their ten idyllic days on the French Côte d'Azur had come to an end. Grenoble was the next destination. Gaby's sadness overwhelmed all who came in contact with her.

"Stay, Gaby, come back to Paris with me," he'd asked earlier today.

However, she felt responsible for meeting her cousin. They had gotten up fairly early, and although she tried to stay alert and fun—her heart was heavy. They would leave for Grenoble at two o'clock. Now she wanted to make the most of the morning. They had gone riding toward Nice and she looked over one more time the splendid city where she had spent idyllic moments with the man she adored. They'd returned to Villefranche. Down the steps from the Villa, a stone dock had been built for the awaiting prisoners arriving on their respective gallows from many destinations. These men would descend on the dock and arrive in Villefranche to spend a miserable life, expiating for the sins they had committed towards society in the early part of the century.

Marks were engraved in the wall of the prisons, and the heavy metal rings the prisoners were attached to at night left the grimly impressions that the ghosts of these men were still there. It was said that they had gotten what they deserved, and for many of them it might have been a right punishment, except that the prison served more than one jurisdiction. Consequently, what was considered in France a major offense, for another man in another country, the offense and its punishment could be quite different. Criminals had been incarcerated there for murder and rape, but also some prisoners had been sent to the gallows for adultery or tax evasion. One could never know what had occurred, but one thing was certain—they had left their imprints on the town as well. One of them had sculpted the wooden Christ figure in the Church Saint Michel in town. This era was filled with inequities and Villefranche sur Mer did not escape its conflicts.

Jean-Louis and Gabriella lay on the concrete, basking in the warm winter sun, holding hands, letting the sun warm their bodies. "It's been wonderful, Jean-Louis, the most magnificent, unforgettable days of my entire existence. Was it the same for you?"

"It was wonderful, Gaby. I will miss you immensely. The Tempète will never be the same without its gorgeous Southern stow-away."

Shocked at his polite but emotionless tone of voice, she just laid there, embarrassed. The response had been so cool, like tying up the end of unfinished business.

"All right, darling," he continued, getting up and pulling her up to her feet. "Time to go. The carriage will be here shortly. You still have to pack. Do not overburden yourself. I'll take a lot of your *vêtements,* clothing. But then again, perhaps I should leave everything here in the Villa. Now that I have a better understanding of your shopping habits, you will toss out most of the things you have purchased here once you get to Paris."

She'd felt plain awful at his cool retort a while ago, but this last statement gave her some comfort, there was some permanence in his voice and it reassured her. They went back, made love, ate, and then the carriage arrived.

"Jean-Louis, I want to go to Church once more. I have time, right?"

"Yes, of course," he replied politely.

They both went back and Gaby prayed hard, making all sorts of vows, promising God all sort of assurances that men and women usually ask the Almighty when their future is uncertain and out of their control. "Please God," she prayed, "grant me a permanent relationship with Jean-Louis. Oh God, please," she continued to pray, "I will get married, I will bring him back to this small town if he ever asked me to marry him." She prayed long and hard to the statue of the Immaculate Conception, located next to the Sacristy. Then, knowing that everything would turn out well, she stood up, crossed herself, kneeled down in front of the altar, and then turned and walked out. God had already granted her wish—she just knew it.

The trip to Grenoble was long. They stopped in a picturesque inn for the night and continued their trip the following morning. He had taken her sexually in the carriage.

"Jean-Louis, is it normal for couples to have relations or to want to have relations as often or as passionately as we do?" she wondered aloud.

"It is normal for us, that's all that is important. Why do you need to know what the rest of the world thinks or does?" he asked cautiously.

"Curiosity, I presume. How would I know what others do?"

"Why does it matter?" he asked.

"It does not, I was just wondering, that's all."

Finally, in the late morning, the narrow door that was the entrance to the convent faced them. She could see the façade with the climbing ivy. She discovered narrow elongated windows where the nuns probably lived. It looked drabbed from the outside and Gaby had a sudden feeling that she should stay in the carriage with Jean-Louis' warm presence. Everything was somber and frigid about the building.

He must have caught her distressed profile as she looked out the window.

"Stay with me, chérie; we will leave a message for your cousin to meet us in Paris."

She tapped the window to let the coachman know that she wanted him to halt the coach.

He took a lot of courage for Gaby to unlock the door. She stepped down and directed herself toward the convent.

A cheery nun with a large amount of radishes and green beans in the folded pleats of her black habit greeted her. A large cross-hung on top of the vegetable as if it was blessing the harvest carried by the smiling nun.

"Oh, we have been expecting you, Miss Thornsen," she said in English with a very heavy French accent. Your cousin should be arriving tomorrow afternoon. We heard that he has been detained in Arles. But please, everything is waiting for you, come to the salon. Monsieur, you can come as well, the Mother Superior will be with you shortly. What a happy *rencontre*, mademoiselle."

Jean-Louis and Gaby followed the old nun down a somber corridor and up a stern hallway and then finally both were led in a sumptuous room with a grand piano. A large and stern desk overlooked a small window. The Mother Superior recognized Jean-Louis immediately.

"Monsieur Le Duke, Mademoiselle," she pronounced in a most respectful tone of voice devoid of emotion.

Jean-Louis started speaking first. He held Gaby's hand—it was cold and clammy.

"Very well, we will not abuse your hospitality. We have been told Monsignor Thornsen will be arriving tomorrow; consequently, we shall take our leave and find an inn outside of the convent while we await his arrival. It was very nice meeting with you. We will meet again tomorrow."

Gaby had not said a word. She was shocked at the immensity of her decision. A premonition stared her in the face. Stay with Jean-Louis, it told her. Jean-Louis had realized her uncontrollable fear and had spoken the exact words she would have uttered had she not been so frightened. She squeezed his hand tightly. She knew deep down she would follow through, but she was thankful that Jean-Louis had taken the lead today. She could not have gone in cold today without someone she knew for comfort.

The Mother Superior was shocked at first but unwilling to cause distress between two powerful people, she walked them back to the gate and recommended a few hotels with good standing in town. Gaby still held onto Jean-Louis' hand for dear life.

"Take hold of yourself, mademoiselle. You are in a convent, not in front of an executioner, chérie," he teased, amused.

"I visualized it differently. I—I don't know what came over me. There was a feeling of doom, of desperation that I resented. It was awful. What happened? How silly of me." She was still feeling uneasy and she slid her hand under his coat around his waist tightening her grip as if she did not want to let him go.

"Good, I have the feeling that you are returning with me."

"I think so, Jean-Louis, but can we stay another day? I would like to explain it to Philippe," she said. "He should be here late tomorrow afternoon."

"Well, yes, I presume we may have to take the train back down, darling. Something different, it will be fun," he replied. Quite pleased that things were looking up, he pulled her even closer to him.

The afternoon was a total delight, the area was pretty, picturesque and pastoral. That was the first time she had seen shepherds leading their herds up the hill for grazing, and although it was still quite cold, the sun was bright and the fields of lavender offered their fragrant delight to the lovers.

They settled in a lovely hotel overlooking a lake where a large tributary threw itself in a large lake. France was quite beautiful, she thought. She had noticed in just one full day such diverse settings from the warm beautiful Mediterranean coast to the breathtaking hills of the lower Alps. Small villages settled at bottom of ravines with fortifications that appear to have diverse architecture. All looked different except the ever-lovely church and its tall steeple. Gaby stopped in every church in every village she visited.

"*Pour une petite prière*, for a short prayer," she would tell Jean-Louis.

"You must have a lot of wishes or you are most sinful, ma chérie, all these little prayers," he replied, but still he followed her. She wandered if he also prayed when he knelt next to her. The whole experience was titillating. It was fascinating traveling with Jean-Louis. He knew so much about the political and historical situation of the area. They had an incredible lunch of pâté de foie gras and pâté de campagne in a warm, crusty sheepherder bread. They hiked high in the mountains and returned late, tired, and happy. The inn smelled of soup that the cook had placed on the cauldron just before their departure for the hills earlier that day. Like two young children, they sat on the wooden benches in front of the fireplace, warming their hands and freezing feet. Jean-Louis made fun of her about her horrific reaction to the convent.

"What huge sin have you committed and hiding from me, Gaby?" he teased. "Maybe I should take you to confession to the local priest.

An unusual reaction I should say for one who was going to wait for your saintly, pure Cardinal at the Convent of the Sacré Coeur."

"Scoundrel, that you are," she responded, "you are the cause of all my sins." They laughed late into the night. He was pleased she was returning with him and she felt confused and disappointed with herself for letting her fears and stupid intuitions rule her life. Of course she wanted to be with Jean-Louis, but she was giving up her long life dream to enter the conservatory for she could not be able to reapply until the following year. What would she do once she got to Paris? What if she did not get accepted again? Long after Jean-Louis was fast asleep, she could not for the life of her come to terms with the decision she had taken yesterday. She would reverse herself tomorrow, she finally decided. It was the responsible thing to do. She had made a decision long ago, although she'd love nothing more than to become his wife and continue her singing career, she knew that she'd would be giving up too much. Jean-Louis had not spoken about permanent ties. Anyhow, he would understand.

The following morning, Jean-Louis did not understand. It was the first time she had seen him so forceful with her and that set her mind to do the opposite of his wishes even more so.

"No, I have delineated to you the reasons for my change of venue, I'll stick to it this time."

"Gaby," he said angrily, "you make no sense. I'll get you in. I know the director and administrators. No one will say no to me. Mon Dieu, I have built and sustained the place."

"Precisely, Jean-Louis," she replied, as inflamed as he was, "you are not listening nor comprehending anything I have just said. I got in without any support; I got in on my own volition, by my own accomplishments. Why would I need special reference? It's just a matter of a few months of separation. I love you, and my love will never cease to be, maybe you will realize you love me, too."

"That is an absurd reason, Gaby. I hope that it is not the incentive behind your reasoning."

"No, I just wanted to hear those words coming from your mouth before we parted."

He smiled and pulled her close to him, knowing that he had met his match. She would not relent this time no matter how much he patronized her. Haughtily, he assumed defeat.

"Right, let's get ready and go. You already have all the addresses you need to contact on my behalf when you arrive in Paris and I'll sent word as soon as I reach land."

While her luggage was taken off once more from the carriage, they walked hand in hand to the convent. Silence reigned. Both knew and felt that somehow their decisions were wrong. Jean-Louis had the urge to take her and place her back in the carriage, screaming and shouting. She'd get over it, he thought, but his many good years of good upbringing let the moment pass without such action.

Gaby wanted to change her mind, feeling that it was the wrong decision, but instead she silenced her inner voice.

This time, the convent had opened the wide wooden doors that faced a large garden. She looked for her cousin's carriage; it had not arrived yet. Two young novices were putting her suitcases on the steps to be taken to her apartment.

She turned to Jean-Louis just outside the doors, and snuggled in his arms, her head landed on his chest where she could hear his heart beat. "I hope all these beats are for me, darling," she said, her eyes filled with unshed tears Unable to control herself, she burst out in long, uncontrolled sobs.

"Why in hell are you doing this to yourself?" he asked, distress in his voice. "What are you trying to prove, Gaby?"

She pulled away and looked up, waiting for his kiss. He bent down, held her close, and pressed her body unabashedly close to his. He kissed her long and hard. She rested her forehead on his chest a while longer and then pulled herself away and smiled.

"I love you, Jean-Louis—so much." She raised her eyes to him once more to impress his face and stature in her mind, and then she decidedly turned and walked quickly but gracefully away.

He stood still, his lips pressed together, still feeling her warmth on his body. Before walking up the steep staircase, she turned once more, placed her fingers to her lips, and blew him a kiss. Minutes later, she was gone.

He stayed there a while longer hoping she would come back. It was not in the cards. He turned on his heels, stomped the short distance to his carriage, and then he stepped in and closed the door. As she watched him from the balcony the carriage slowed down, paused, and she saw his hand tap the door of the carriage hard. They drove away until it was just a minuscule dot on the horizon.

She cried long and hard and then talked to herself. Her behavior was utterly ridiculous. They'd be back together in a few months. Certainly the relationship could outlast the separation. If it could not, then it was not worth putting all that energy in it. He had never told her he loved her but he'd share that he felt complete in her presence. This reassured her and she remembered the wonderful feeling she had felt in the Church in Villefranche. Everything was going to be just fine. She consoled herself and started unpacking a few things she would need for the trip to Paris. Philippe would arrive later in the afternoon and they would sit long and late into the night. She would tell him everything. She would spend a few more days in Grenoble and then they would leave for Paris.

She cleaned up a bit and walked along the narrow and stern corridors to rejoin the nuns. Might as well make new friends, she thought. She heard angels sing as she walked in the refectory and followed the beautiful melody that led her to the chapel. It was afternoon vespers and the nuns were singing like angels. She sat on the wooden bench and was transcended.

Chapter Twenty

Finally, at three o'clock the following afternoon, Cardinal Thornsen arrived. Gaby ran down the staircase to the garden as she saw the black carriage with the ecumenical coat of arms enter the courtyard. The coachman brought down the steps and she flew into his arms. Her embrace was passionately returned as the cleric gathered his cousin to him. The curious and highly offended eyes of the Mother Superior and the convent nuns did not make an iota of difference as he tightened his embrace unwilling to let her go.

They spent the rest of the afternoon together and declined dinner at the convent for a walk outside the walls. They stopped at a lovely inn near the river and had dinner, before returning late to the convent where a richly furnished apartment had been placed at his disposition. She spent a great deal of the night confiding to Philippe her idyllic romance. Being a religious man but having ambiguous feelings towards his dear Gabriella, Philippe had come to the conclusion that she should go on with her life. After all, this short interlude had been so shocking, so intense, and so quick that poor Gaby must have been traumatized. He thought after the attack and her rescue that she certainly must have been in need of tenderness. Yes, surely that was it, he persuaded himself, and wisely he advised her to take a little time and to reflect upon the ordeal.

"Put on your thinking cap, dearest. Listen to the Mother Superior. She is surely a person to trust and confide in. She appears to be quite modern, Gaby. You know she hears that sort of thing all the time from the women that seek solace and comfort in the convent after affairs gone sour.

Gabriella laughed at his face.

"My romance has not gone sour," she mimicked, "Jean-Louis is in love with me, Philippe. I know that our passion will continue in Paris!" He could not stand having her make fun of him. She'd always win and he would follow her in a fit of laughter and usually align his feelings and thinking with hers. She was rarely wrong. Gaby was smart, an iron personality that never let her sense of self and business down. He had never seen her so—so flighty. For a second he wished that her passionate nature would be directed toward him and then full of shame and guilt, he looked down and stare at the large chimney.

When it came to Gabriella, he could never reach a balance between his love for God and His law, versus her happiness and well-being. He always wanted her happy and why not, he adored her. Why shouldn't the Duke? He bent his head and then she pulled it back up and kissed him tenderly and continued to banter with him.

"Come off it, Philippe—asking a nun for sexual and sentimental counsel? What are you thinking of, my dear cousin? The idea alone makes me blush and you know quite well what the response would be."

He already knew the Mother Superior's response. She had spoken to him about Gabriella and the Duke. The fellow certainly did not have a very good reputation, but after all, Gabriella was an exceptional girl. He no longer knew how to counsel her.

On this subject, Gabriella thought, the Directrice's thoughts were skewed. Throughout the centuries Mother Superior in convents had seen so many women that came to expiate their sins in the saintly walls, starting with the King's mistresses. Thoughts of Madame De Levallois, who had been devastated to the point of losing her mind when Louis XIV the Sun King had chosen Athenais de Montespan as his new lady. She had had her lovely blond curls cut off and had follow with dignity the very strict and stern life of a cloistered nun.

This example stood out in her mind, but there were hundreds of these ladies who had adorned the veil after having wrecked their lives and dreams. Not that there were too many dreams for women to pursue in this world, but if one did not choose the vocation, life in the convent was hard and devoid of life's niceties.

The difficult part with Gaby, Philippe calculated, was that she had delineated her life in Paris. So telling her to return with him was not in the cards. She just would not. Besides, she was not asking him his advice, she was just sharing her love and happiness with him. Why not embrace her happiness? The City of Lights would welcome her electrifying rendering of melodious music. After all she had aristocratic blood, she was wealthy in her own right and could return to life in New Orleans if she chose to do so. No, he was really worrying for no reason. It was just that he had never seen her out of control, and she appeared quite smitten with the Duke—to his own dismay.

He had taken an extra month to visit the area with her. Perhaps she'd change her mind. They had had a wonderful time, but her mind was set in stone. She was going to Paris and he had to head back first to Avignon and then Rome. He would return to Paris in four months.

The day after his departure, she stayed behind and packed her things. She would leave the following day. She had cemented some wonderful friendships and she had truly enjoyed singing with the nuns. It had gotten to the point where she never missed the cantiques.

That night, unfortunately, the drama came to pass. Every evening after dinner lately, she felt unusually fatigued and nauseated. She had been spoiled with Jean-Louis. The food had been excellent. She disliked everything they fed to her in the convent. Her travel to Paris would require sitting for long periods of time the following two days. Afraid of ill health she decided not to show up for dinner.

The anticipation to be reunited with Jean-Louis was overwhelming. He must have been close to Brest by now, so there was no need to delay her departure for Paris. She would meet him at the Convent of the Sacred Heart. She missed him so much and she wondered if he lay awake at night as she did and dreamt of having her in his arms, feeling the passionate nature of the love that they had shared.

She did not want to understand, nor evaluate what was happening to her. She was in love with a man who had taken her virginity. Well, she had handed it over with lustful passion to a man who had never spoken of marriage, of a durable future, and yet she wanted nothing else but to be reunited with him. She smiled inwardly at herself. Wherever his location, he probably wanted her just as much. She did not recognize herself. How often she had laughed at all the debutantes in New Orleans. Many of these young women and their mothers were waiting for the mother-of-pearl engagement fan. What a farce that was, she recalled flippantly telling Philippe. "A fan, for an heir and a fun social life—how lovely!"

She was not the marrying kind, she had told herself then. There were so many exciting activities to experience, so many sights to see. Why burden oneself with a man who would place all sorts of barriers on a woman's happiness. She was proud of being a fast-thinking realist, and even though her parents had never given a hoot about her, they had given her a sense of independence. Now that she was an adult, she knew that she had the means and the knowledge to achieve whatever she set her mind out to do. Indirectly independence had set her free. That was an immeasurable offering.

When she had decided to go to Paris to further her opératic studies, she'd made sure that her plantation was striving and in good hands. Her father would surely have tried to take it from her while she was in Europe. She had employed every imaginable ploy to keep the plantations in her name, and although the legal process had taken a little more time than anticipated, she had finalized her plans and embarked on the Spanish Frigata. "Watch out for what you are praying for," she'd often heard Tita say. Well, her dream of studying voice in Paris had materialized. She recalled fluctuating between France and Italy. After all, Italy was the crown queen of opéra where the likes of Verdi and Rossini composed ardently in its milieu. She had studied Latin for that very purpose, the language of the long vowels and smooth consonants set melodies afire, and furthermore, sopranos could sustain a prolonged sound by singing at many diverse pitches. But Philippe was in Rome, so she would be more independent in Paris, she'd thought. Moreover, Louis Napoleon III had authorized Count Haussmann to give the architect Charles Garnier the contract for building a brand new opéra house on the Grand Boulevards in Paris. Consequently, the decision to study at the Académie de Musique in Paris had been solidified.

Sitting on a burgundy settee, she looked at the tall trees that surrounded the convent. Autumn's crisp winter air made her shiver as she watched two lovebirds perched side by side on a long branch that touched the rim of her windows. Maybe they sensed that she was madly in love as well. She smiled, everything these days reverted to love with her. She wondered what they communicated to one another. The long winter might alter their communication forever. Smiling as she contemplated her own life, there she was, madly in love, in lust, in passion—not being able to think of anything else but of Jean-Louis-Pierre De Pleyssis. She should be ashamed of herself. After all, she was in a convent how could she lust after a man she had just met a little less than two months ago. What a funny turn of life! Two lonely souls who cherished their independence above all, who desired nothing more than to achieve their given potential in life, tumbled in one another's life and shared an incredible passion that might very well engulf their lives.

The crystal clear voices of the sisters singing the *High Cantiques* reached her open windows. She would resume the practice of the cantiques with the sisters at the four o'clock mass for the last time. Everything was going as planned. A little incident now and then, one that thwarted her path, was nothing new. She knew she had the tools to veer away from trouble.

The tragedy started that very night. She woke up with stomach cramps in the early morning hours. She dashed down the stairs to the kitchen's pantry, entwined in an eiderdown. The carpet lining the long and stern hallway had been rolled up the night before, darkness all around her she inadvertently slipped and rolled down the marble staircase. She shrieked as a warm, sticky substance slid down between her legs. Nauseous and burning hot, she tried to grasp the balustrade, but instead she lost her balance and dropped unconscious to the bottom of the staircase in the foyer. The following morning she awoke with part of her life erased, surrounded by women in black and white habits. There were also two men—one sporting a long black chasuble, his face as white as the cloth around his neck. He stared haggard and anxious, the other man sitting next to her on the bed sported a brown coat as he held an instrument to her heart. Who was she? Why was she here? She could not for the life of her remember anything about her past. Was it just a horrible nightmare? Sternly, the physician, the man who sat on the bed and who had examined her recounted the ordeal. She understood what had happened to her but not a trace of her past was familiar. The physician told her that with time, her memory would return. He had been correct.

Days had passed and slowly recollection of certain events in her past flashed vividly. By the time Philippe returned, he had been recalled to her bedside, she'd retrieved most of her mental faculties but alas not the child that she had been carrying.

The Mother Superior, along with her favorite sister, Sister Andrée, were wonderfully kind and understanding as they reiterated the incident and what she could expect in her ambiguous situation. They knew how to handle these situations. Many aristocratic women had passed these convent halls. The doctor was more severe and informed her in no uncertain terms that the probability to conceive again was less than twenty percent. She could not imagine that she and Jean-Louis had actually conceived another life. She wondered how he would react to the news. Not well, the sisters replied unequivocally.

A man of his rank expected an heir. Upon that realization, her dreams shattered. Gaby's world collapsed. How childish of her to expect anything more than a short, passionate affair, or perhaps a long enduring one—but not as his wife. She'd secretly wished that they would marry. Was it in a woman's genetic make-up to want to be owned? She should tell him the truth. He deserved it and she had to accept the decision that he would make concerning their lives. Her mind made up, she was going to Paris, she would explain and the chips would fall where they may.

By the week's end, however, she gave up her assertive ideals and chose to follow Philippe to Avignon and Rome and to pursue her studies in Italy.

Being rejected was a challenge she could not fathom. The sisters were correct. In her present vulnerable state she probably would agree to anything and everything and that was not her true nature to suffer or to be found an annoying object, as her mother had often called her. No, she was going to Rome, and she would find happiness in her work. At least she had experienced passion and the pain would subside throughout the years. Time healed all pains.

A distraught Philippe no longer knew what to think. He had never seen Gaby so subdued and sad. His pretty cousin, *l'Ange de Fer*, Iron Angel, as he playfully referred to her in New Orleans, had turned into a malleable weather vane. He took three months away from his duties so as to give her the needed support. Gaby had finally made her final decision last evening.

"Philippe, I just cannot face him. I'll return to Rome with you. Perhaps I should return to New Orleans," she said doubtful of any assessment she had to devise for herself.

"You will love Rome, Gabriella. It should have been your first choice, my dearest. I know lots of good-hearted individuals who will guide your career superbly. Trust me, Gabriella, you know that I have never let you down."

"That's because you have never made a decision when it came to our lives. Remember?" She smiled and threw herself in his arms.

"You need me now, dear cousin; I will not fail you."

She needed time. What bothered Philippe more than anything else was that no one had tried to contact the convent? Maybe the Captain had been detained at sea longer than anticipated. But if not, he should have been in the Loire by now. This was the only sticky point as far as he was concerned. She seemed to know it as well. He would not counsel her to return back to Paris. Explaining her sordid affair to someone not intent on listening or caring would be detrimental and could only cause her more pain and insecurities. Two days later they began their southern descent to Avignon.

They left early after the doctor's approval of the trip. It would give them ample time to reach the city so as not to fatigue Gabriella's already-shaken constitution. He was not quite certain that her decision had been the right one. He had told her that perhaps she should go to Paris and face Jean-Louis, but after she'd pronounced herself, he'd joyously bent to her resolute will. He adored her.

Chapter Twenty-One

While the ordeal in Grenoble took place and followed its sad turn of events, the Duke returned down to Villefranche to take the Tempète back to Brest. On his way to his final destination, Jean-Louis was detained in Gibraltar and the delay caused his ship to arrive at its homeport later than projected. He sent some messages to Paris to the Convent Du Sacré Cœur and felt assured that everything was following its course. After a short stop in Loire in the ancestral castle, he was anxious to reach Paris. They were to meet at the Pensionnat Du Sacré Coeur. He had gone to the convent prior to reaching his town home in the hope that she would willingly come to live with him. These past weeks had been particularly lonely. The decision had been taken. The young Southern Belle had stolen his heart and he wanted her to share his life. Whatever the future held for them, they would face it together.

Unfortunately, at the Convent, no one had heard of the young soprano. The Mother Superior knew of Cardinal Philippe Thornsen, her cousin, the influential prelate who was now attached to the Vatican and yes in effect, they had been told that he was to have visited Paris a few months back, but no one seem to have seen or heard from Gabriella.

How could she have disappeared from the face of this earth? Even her music instructor could not give him the same answer twice. At first he'd heard she was coming, and then she had decided otherwise, and then an envoy from the Cardinal had contacted him stating that she would not attend his courses.

After having exhausted all of his searches, the baffled Duke decided to return to Grenoble. After all, he had spoken to the Mother Superior and she was aware of their plans to meet again in Paris. Nuns did not lie. She would tell him what had happened to Gabriella.

Gaby, having second thoughts about their liaison? Never, he thought. She adored him, he asserted haughtily.

He arrived in Grenoble late in the day. The Mother Superior would not see him for two full days on pretense that she had taken to bed with a bad case of the flu. On the third day he pushed himself on the frightened novice and climbed the treacherous marble staircase to the Directrice's office. Without any introduction, he unlocked the door and strode right in. The nun sat composed behind a large desk, her back to him, staring at the vast gardens below. She turned slowly, placed her two hands flat on her desk, and evaluated him unperturbed.

Flabbergasted at the nun's calm demeanor, he marched closer to the desk.

"I was expecting you, Monsieur," she pronounced assertively.

Outraged at the insolent remark, he did not put on his gloves to bring her back down to reality.

"Madame, I found it outrageously impolite and less than religious to take cover under a lie. You appear quite well. I doubt that you'd recover from the many malaises you experienced yesterday that promptly. Obviously, you are aware that I am looking for Gabriella De Conte Thornsen. You knew of our plans. Where is she? What has happened to her?" He blazed.

"Monsieur, I am unable to tell you her whereabouts. Her cousin, Cardinal Philippe Thornsen, came for her some time ago and I was asked to keep their whereabouts confidential."

"I will go to the Vatican, Madame, if I have to. You are aware of my influence in the Europeans circles. I pray that you disclose to me what has happened to Miss Thornsen, immediately."

She looked at his distressed face and she knew then, that perhaps her advice to poor little Gabriella might have been an error. But, she reflected, what kind of embarrassment and gossip would Gabriella have been made to suffer in Paris if she had once again started her liaison with the Duke? Most surely, a man of his stature would require an heir and after the miscarriage there were doubts that Gabriella could conceive again.

After weeks of rest and long defining talks with her and a few other confidents, the Mother Superior recalled as she stared at the powerful man standing across from her, Gaby had decided to follow Cardinal Thornsen to Rome. Once there, she would continue to pursue her opératic studies under the Cardinal's protection. The Cardinal adored his cousin—his dedication to her needs was astounding.

"There is nothing I would not do for her," he'd candidly told the doctor at the convent. "She has always been there for me. Whatever Gabriella asks of me, I will comply to her wishes."

The candid remarks had stunned all the attendants.

The Mother Superior focused hard on the handsome man. She recalled how long ago, a man not unlike the man facing her had broken her heart. No, she had made the right decision, she assured herself.

"Gabriella's decision in the long run was best for both of you," she, in the firmest of voice, unceremoniously told Jean-Louis. "I personally approved the final separation."

Jean-Louis had to surmount anger never felt before. Mon Dieu, he seethed. A woman that wore the habit of a religious order had the impudence to interfere with his private life. Years of etiquette and good breeding did not come undone so promptly. He straightened up to his full height and shot her a disdainful glare.

"Madame," he began, measuring his words, "your approval or disapproval of my personal affairs is of no concern to me. Be aware, however, that this ordeal has only just begun. I will find Gabriella and I hope that your help will be forthcoming when I need it, for otherwise I will personally see to it that your role as the Mother Superior of this good and saintly establishment is terminated immediately. Intrigues and the hiding of fair maidens is no longer tolerated under the law—for any class, Madame, religious or not." He turned on his heels, walked to the hallway and slammed the door behind him. Returning from matins, nuns and novices stood in the corridor, flabbergasted at this new turn of events.

He returned to Paris and immediately sent couriers to the Vatican to find out about Cardinal Philippe Thornsen. He had a plan. He would travel to Rome, if need be, for relying on his security had been fruitless. He would act. His greatest concern was for Gaby's safety. The Italian conflict concerning the reunification of the Italian Papal States to the Kingdom of Victor Emmanuel II was taking so many innocent lives. He worried that their carriage might be stopped, and that being accompanied by a Cardinal might endanger her life. Their passionate liaison could not end in such a sordid way. Their lives had crossed path for a bigger purpose than just a few passionate and sensual days, he reminded himself.

Chapter Twenty-Two

Gabriella had changed so much, the Cardinal sorrowfully observed—teary-eyed a great part of the day. He was frightened that she would not surmount the inner pain she experienced. They had had dinner in an adorable small auberge in the Haute Savoie. She, always so talkative and spontaneous, was now calm and serene, her spirit tortured. On the fifth day of their travels, as he sat waiting, he noticed her coming down for breakfast with a happy bounce in her graceful allure. Her morose mood had dissipated. She came round and kissed him on the cheek.

"I'm returning, Philippe. I have never escaped from my duties, emotions, and responsibilities, so why should I act cowardly, now. Jean-Louis needs to know. I have my own life and I will return to it. I just hope that my silence and long absence has not contradicted or cancelled out all of my chances of entering the Conservatoire. Resuming my career is what I have to do. Anything less and I would never forgive myself. I'd always have regrets."

"Gabriella, I really think you should try Rome for a year or even for the duration of the opéra season. I will introduce you to many who will appreciate your gift. Think again, my dearest," Philippe implored.

"No, my mind is made up," she pronounced solemnly. Jean-Louis conveyed that he would pledge for me. I do not believe that he would renege on his offer. Even if I cry for years, I will not let these dark and obscure thoughts that have been tormenting me destroy my life."

Philippe relented and agreed with her—again. He never disagreed with her. They both left for Grenoble once more. This time they would stay with his dear friend, Count de Beauvernes, and his family.

"Why haven't I heard about the Count, Philippe?" Gaby asked.

"We met in Naples in a music camp when we were just ten years old," Philippe said, "except that the Count's father kept his son whole. He wanted many heirs to his lineage. We kept in touch for many years and when I returned to the Vatican, the Count was studying philosophy in Rome. We renewed the close friendship and I officiated at their marriage. You will like them, Gabriella."

By the fire, reminiscing of tender times long ago, Gabriella and Philippe had spent their last evening in the Palace of the Popes in Avignon. Early the following day, after a hearty breakfast, they had ridden straight through, reaching their destination at around two. Upon their arrival, the Count entertained them grandly. By chance, the Count and his family were returning to Paris to take pleasure in *the Season des fêtes* in the capital in just two days. "We would love for Gabriella to accompany us back to Paris," the Count assured the Cardinal.

Gabriella agreed, although she would have much preferred to regain Paris on her own accord, but poor Philippe would be distraught, she pondered.

For his part, Philippe decided, he would return to Paris in a few months. He would have loved to share all the pleasure of Paris in the fall with her, but for now, almost five months had gone by, his return to the Vatican was primordial. Returning to Paris with his friends would force Gabriella to socialize and to not overly meditate on her sad story. She would know what to do once in Paris. She had retrieved her will if not her heart. She would experience a brand new life and certainly she would meet hundreds of people who would fall in love with her, even if the Duke rejected her.

Poor Gaby everyone always loved her, except for her father and mother, the Duke would probably fall in the same category, the sordid moron, Philippe grumbled, as he prepared to return to Rome.

Just before leaving him, she asked one more time if there had been any inquiries on her behalf at the convent. The Cardinal had celebrated vespers the evening before. By now, she understood that Jean-Louis should have tried to make some contact, unaware that Philippe had told the Mother Superior not to divulge their whereabouts once a couple months had passed. He deemed that once her decision had been made to pursue her singing career in Rome there were absolutely no reasons to place more doubts in her pretty little head. She would be close to him. De Pleyssis had had ample time to show his arrogant face.

"Why is it, Philippe, that the persons that I love most always desert me?" Gabriella asked her cousin. It had broken his heart.

"I never deserted you, Gabriella," he responded in such a loving tone that she went around her chair and came close to him, hugging and kissing him tenderly, just like when they were children and their hearts were sad. Dear God, how he wished he could show her his love in a manly demeanor. Alas, he reflected.

Philippe left again the following day for Rome.

Count de Beauvernes taught a course in philosophy in Paris at the Sorbonne. Gaby enchanted him. She continually asked questions about French history and its cultural movement. Jean-Louis had taught her a lot. The old Count was mesmerized by the information she was privy to. They stopped in Beaunne in a magnificent old castle that also served as an inn. The Bourgogne wine flowed and the food was out of this world. Everything they ordered was delicious and for the first time since the miscarriage Gaby ate heartily. Jacques De Beauvernes ventured good-naturedly that Mademoiselle Thornsen would save herself for only the best in this world. Wrong again, she thought. She thought that Jean-Louis had been the very best. If he intended to pursue their relationship, he should have given her a sign of life by now. It had been almost five months. No, he must have returned to his carefree life in Paris. He had said that their paths would encounter many obstacles for a long-term relationship. Her dream of his undying love for her had been just that—a young girl's illusion.

The closer they got to Paris, the more frightened she became. The last night in Beaunne she could not fall sleep. When was she going to meet him? She had lost a lot of weight and felt a lot less attractive. Perhaps she should wait a few weeks? Just some extra time to adapt to la *vie Parisienne*. She wondered if he missed her? Had she dreamed that he had fallen madly in love with her? Probably, was the sad answer. He had not tried to make contact with her.

She thought of contacting the Mother Superior during her short stay in Grenoble. After all, the castle was less than two miles from the center of town. But the old woman was astute and Gaby was much too proud. Why hurt oneself unnecessarily, she asked herself. She just wanted to forget. Surely Philippe would share with her any inquiries.

Finally, by six o clock in the morning, she fell soundly asleep, but unfortunately was woken up two hours later when the last leg of the trip to Paris had begun. At three o'clock in the afternoon, they reached the capital.

The carriage left her in front of Philippe's apartment and the butler, the doorman, and the valet helped with the few articles of clothing she owned. She did not have much. She would have to either meet Jean-Louis or follow his advice and go shopping for the unexpected cold weather. She chose the latter. All of her dreams to jump in with great gusto into the Parisian life went out the door as soon as she reached the city. She would do what she came here to do, she told herself. It would just take a tad longer than anticipated.

Ten days later she ventured to the Académie where the Maître de Musique was shocked to see the young American. He wanted to call the Duke. Jean-Louis and his family before him had been the greatest benefactors of the Opéra. She practically had to beg him to give her a few extra days. She was frightened to meet him.

The request placed the music master in a difficult position. One, he did not want to anger the Duke by not revealing Mademoiselle Thornsen's whereabouts and two, he did not want to anger her, knowing that if they ever got back together, anything that would cause her pain would eventually fall back on his shoulders.

Better to entice a fortuitous meeting at the opéra in case the Duke attended a performance. He would check with the ticket office. They knew of his coming because of the extra security it entailed.

"All of Paris knows that Monsieur is looking for you, Mademoiselle Thornsen. I'll go along with it, but frankly, unless you hide in the catacombs, I do not see how you will be able to live in Paris without his knowledge. Someone will be on to you quickly— very quickly. I do not know your motives, mademoiselle, however the Duke is very recherché, sought after. I do not understand your decision."

She understood it herself. That's all that mattered.

She stood by her decision and thanked him for giving her a short period of time to figure out her next move.

"*Trés bien*, mademoiselle. I see that I can't change your mind. But an exceptional presentation of La Traviatta will be presented next Thursday night, a gala night. I'm taking a few students. It would be lovely if you could join us. The Directeur of the Académie will be there, I'm sure you'll be able to talk to him and explain your recent delay. It is always nice to meet him during a social function, he is much more approachable that way."

She thought about it, frightened that Jean-Louis might be there with another woman. She stood her ground. She needed to face the music.

"Thank you, *avec grand plaisir*, I would be delighted."

The following day she attended her first lesson de Musique with the maestro. Later in the afternoon, she walked for a long time along the quays of the river Seine. Entering the impressive Notre Dame de Paris, she burned many candles under every possible saint statue and prayed for a long time. This time she would not relent, she promised herself. She crossed the short bridge that led to the Ile St Louis and she paused on the Pont Sully. To lift her spirits, today she had purchased a dark brown mink coat with matching hat. She felt feminine, confident and very warm. Paris was dreadfully cold in the winter. She was pleased that she'd decided to use Philippe's townhouse. The clergy owned the magnificent mansion, although dark and formal, it was decorated with supreme good taste. Salons and her own rooms were filled with sublime works including paintings from Raphaël, Da Vinci and Michelangelo and myriads marble statues of the Virgin and the Infant Child. There was a large courtyard with a magnificent fountain that lulled her to sleep at night and a carriage had been placed at her disposition.

More relaxed, she found the convent where Philippe had told her she would find support if she needed it. In effect, Jean-Louis had told her it was very close to his townhouse. And that it was.

She began to amble down the quay, forcing every step forward. Steps away from where she stood an immense wooden gate opened. The loud clunking of hooves on the cobblestone momentarily left her breathless. She stood frozen as Jean-Louis appeared. She watched him run down the marble staircase that led to the vast gardens facing his home. Within minutes, two coachmen dressed in white and gold livery lowered the golden staircase to the magnificent black and gold carriage that had been drawn forward. In his usual hurried pace he climbed in. His hand tapped the window of the carriage. Quickly it began to move out of the courtyard onto the street. She stood motionless on the sidewalk holding on to the *parapet*, cement wall that bordered the Seine. She stared immobilized as the carriage pulled away from the entrance and filed in front of her. It could not have been more than a couple of minutes, but it seemed like a lifetime to her. Her heart beat painfully in her chest and she felt faint. She could not move. She had not realized the proximity of the convent, less than a five-minute walk. He certainly could see the entrance to the nunnery from one of his upstairs windows.

She wanted to rejoin her cousin in Rome. The fear of being rejected immobilized her as she tried to relax. The maestro had told her that Jean-Louis had been looking for her. Well, he did not try too hard. If he'd really wanted to see her, he would have gone back to the convent in Grenoble.

What would she say to him? Should she even say anything? He would get it out of her. What if he had gotten over her? Would he ostracize her? No after all, Jean-Louis was a polite man and except for the emeralds he had given her in Monaco, he had taken a lot of her belonging.

Maybe next week she'd find the courage to talk to him. She needed time to think things over. The apparition had shaken her. She walked home very slowly and of course could not eat nor sleep. Expiating for my sins, she thought.

* * *

Jean-Louis recently had received positive feedback as well. The Vatican had been contacted—her cousin was on his way to Rome. But more importantly, he'd received word that Mademoiselle De-Conte Thornsen had been seen in Beaunne with the Count and Countess De

Beauvernes. The family was returning to Paris for the season. He did not know exactly where she was, but after five months . . . finally there was some movement.

Last week he had promised his Grandmother that he would take her to the opéra for the season's opening gala. He recalled telling Gaby that she would be his escort. Five months later, she had disappeared from the face of the earth! What had happened to the arrogant little brat? He reviewed in his mind the incompressible turn of events.

After his departure from Villefranche, his ship had finally anchored in Brest. He'd sent word that he would be in Paris in less than a week. Relay the news to Mademoiselle Thornsen, he had written to his secretary. The news had returned overnight that no one knew the whereabouts of Mademoiselle Thornsen and that she had not registered, nor attended her courses. She had never shown up at the Académie.

The search for Gaby had started immediately, and now, just before leaving for the opéra, a message reached him stating that they had some definitive ideas on the whereabouts of the beautiful American soprano.

After so many disappointments he was certain that for some unknown reason she had returned with her cousin to Rome. Next week he would travel to Rome. He was going to get to the bottom of this sordid affair. The suspense had to end.

Chapter Twenty-Three

Counts, marquis, and even a few members of the wealthy bourgeoisie were in attendance, either engaging or trying to engage with the Duke. Politely, he returned all the niceties, as he pretended great interest in the story at hand. In actuality, his spirit was miles away. The performance was second nature to him.

Prior to entering the corridor that would bring him to his loge close to the Emperor's, he wondered again how he would handle this rendition of La Traviata. His greatest wish would have been to have Gaby next to him tonight. How had he fallen so madly in love with Gaby? His life no longer made sense without her presence. Why me, he wondered? His responsibilities to name and country had always been his primary focus. Crazy to get Gaby back, the distraction ruled his life. He had missed two conferences called by the Emperor. Frankly, he would be pleased if the position of chief negotiator for the French delegation in Italy would be offered to someone else. His life and its emphasis had taken a different turn. Gaby had given him a joy he had never been privy to. Gone was his incessant search for adventure and danger. Instead, flipping flat rocks in the Mediterranean on a calm evening night with Gaby had provoked in him a sense of great joy and contentment and he wanted more of it—now.

* * *

The Paris opéra house on the Grand Boulevards was spectacular. Charles Garnier, the architect, had had a vision that he had presented to the Emperor and Count Haussmann, and with great gusto the dream had been realized.

Enthused by the splendor of the highly decorated stage along with its superb acoustics, Gabriella missed the entrance of the Duke De Bourbonne with his Grandmother on his arm as he slowly walked to his grand loge overlooking the stage. Instead, her thoughts recalled the blissful days on the Tempête. Jean-Louis had wanted to take her to a gala night at the Paris Opéra. He had teased "Gaby, I will do you the honor, you'll attend your first gala night at the Opéra De Paris with me, ma chère."Alas, the gala night was at hand and their world had veered on different paths. Scalding tears burned her eyes. Opéra was to lift one's spirit, to wrench a person's gut with emotions, but not to calm a broken heart. She smiled sadly.

The warmth of the candelabras soared upward. In the loge next to hers, the old man who had been gazing during the performance at many of the lovely ladies in attendance, cleverly lifted his arms to his head to re-adjust his monocle. She looked to her right to the maestro. He was staring at her questioningly along with her friend—Jane Victoria. She nodded to both and slightly bent forward to view the orchestra. During the intermission she remained in her seat and she glanced at the audience searching for Jean-Louis's tall frame and dark brown hair.

She leaned further forward toward the velvet-trimmed balustrade and suddenly caught a glance of the Duke's distinctive profile, in one of the loge one level below hers. He smiled at an older woman who seemed to gaze at everyone through her lorgnette. The dowager's glimpse froze on Gabriella, who could not peel her eyes away from the Duke.

An exchange of words between the elegant looking lady and Jean-Louis seem to be taking place. Lazily, with his sensuous smile he turned sideways and searched the loge where the older woman focused. His indolent glance suddenly turned into a hard and alert glower on Gabriella, who for the lack of knowing what to do, returned the stare and waved. Abruptly, without interrupting his glare, he stood up and walked out of his loge.

The same urge enveloped her, and without a word to the old maestro, she pulled away from her fauteuil, dashed up the three steps leading out of the loge, and ran out the door—only to be immobilized. In her exhilaration, she'd lost her sense of direction. All was glassy. Where would he be coming from? She froze for an instant at the top of the staircase. Baffled by enchantment in the fairytale building, a marvelously familiar voice called out her name, and she glanced down.

There he was, clad in black with a snowy-white shirt, striking in both look and demeanor. Gabriella paused, terrified and suspended in time. She prayed that her fairytale story would continue to be heavenly. God, don't fail me now, she implored.

Gracefully, she rushed down the stairs onto the platform where he was standing. A thousand reflections of Jean-Louis and Gaby manifested in the gigantic mirrors framing the staircase—she flew in his arms.

Oblivious of the crowds who watched delightfully the live play unfurling before their very eyes, Jean-Louis De Pleyssis took her fully in his arms, lifting her off the floor, only to hold her as close as it was humanly possible, kissing her passionately, unmindful of where he was, who was looking, and what the gossips were going to state the following day. He kept her close to him for many minutes. The world was closing in on both of them. She lay in his arms—silent.

In this rapturous moment it was Jean-Louis who rapidly became aware of the brouhaha that this encounter had engendered. Men and women alike were curiously pulling their necks forward on the railings and balconies to stare at the unlikely couple. Gently he set her back on the stairs and gazed in her eyes as if he was dreaming, and then he asked, "Where in God's name have you been, Gaby? Le tout Paris has been looking for you across Europe. Don't tell me that you've been in Paris all this time?"

"Yes—" she could not talk, tears choked her, "in Paris—" she began to explain and felt his body go rigid.

"In Paris?" he interrupted loudly. "The entire time?"

Her mind raced as she tried to find the right words to calm him. Men and women strained their necks and some gasped. Gabriella looked upward.

"I can explain," she murmured. "I can, Jean-Louis. Please let me."

In that instant, the reality of the situation hit him. She had not been hurt. She had not been missing. In fact, she was intentionally hiding from him. Gabriella's desperate attempts to explain became distant background noise and he could feel the fury growing inside him. He looked around and saw the gawkers.

She sensed the change in his demeanor. As quickly as he had gathered her up, he took a deliberate step back. She watched his gaze change from one of unabashed passion to an icy glare. His strong jaw clenched. She couldn't help but appreciate how striking he was even during this horrible unfolding of events. She searched his face for answers. Did he still love her? Would he ever forgive her? All she saw was a seething fury that was tangible. Her heart broke. He would never want to see her again. He started to turn and just before his stone-set face turned toward the entrance, Gabriella caught a glimpse of pain.

"Let's leave, he commanded, completely oblivious to poor Maître Lauriot, who was standing with myriad of curious onlookers. By now, the crowd surrounded them and hundred of curious eyes were directed towards the Duke and the beautiful brunette with the striking green eyes. Without another word, he led her down the next level and within minutes, both were out of sight. He directed her outside down the long stairway leading down to the Grands Boulevards where his carriage was waiting in front of the opéra.

"Slow down, Jean-Louis, I cannot keep up. I'll fall." He glared, and in one swift movement, he picked her up in his arms and all but ran down the stairs. His name was going to be all over the newspaper tomorrow morning. One more *faux pas* would not make any difference.

"I'm freezing," she pressed her body closed to his, "oh, I forgot my coat."

He stopped, took off his own coat, and placed it on her bare shoulders.

"Whoever will find it will need it more than you do, Gaby."

His carriage was waiting. As he placed her inside, he noticed one of the security men run toward his carriage.

"Monsieur De Pleyssis, *Nous avons trouvé mademoiselle Thornsen. Elle est ici, à l'opéra ce soir.* We have found Miss Thornsen, she is here at the opéra, this evening."

The Duke blasted such an inflamed stare that the poor fellow retreated immediately in the shadow of the entrance.

"I'll talk to you tomorrow. Mademoiselle Thornsen is inside my carriage."

As he climbed in his carriage, his anger at the security he had assigned to her rose once more. If they could not keep track of a five-footer in a convent in the province, how in the world could they protect his men and the French delegation in the forthcoming negotiations with the Italian states? Heads were going to roll.

"Where are you staying, Gabriella?" he questioned wryly.

"My cousin's residence."

"To the Cardinal's residence," he ordered the coachmen and tapped the vignette forcefully.

The carriage began to wobble speedily on the uneven cobblestones.

Jean-Louis sat opposite of Gaby, his long legs spread apart, his shoulders square with one arm extended over the undulated spine of the headrest. He glared through Gaby.

"Alors, in Paris, Gaby?" He straightened his back and pressed it back against the seat.

"Yes, but not for the full duration," she begun, utterly confused. "Please let me explain, Jean-Louis."

He interrupted her as he forcefully grasped her wrists and pulled her to him. He gathered her body to him and hungrily reached for her mouth and breasts. Utterly confused, she tried in vain to push him away to explain, but the same sensations that emanated from her soul minutes ago on the staircase of the opéra as she'd flown in his arms overwhelmed her violently. She pressed her body to him and caressed his cheeks. Boldly she returned his kisses and gathered his body closer still. She sensed the uncontrollable spasm that ran through his body as he tightened his hold on her. He loved her madly. All would be well, she thought. She let herself be loved to oblivion. For a long time the lovers reveled in the sensual passion they had craved for five long months, as the carriage traversed Paris back to Saint Louis. Suddenly it came to a complete stop. Gaby gasped and Jean-Louis gently pushed her away as he straightened, sighed, placed her back on her seat across, and gently rearranged the white silk that border the décolleté of her dress. He sat back and swallowed hard. His icy blue eyes were moist and he wiped a flagrant tear that glistened down his cheek. He continued to stare at her as if for the last time.

"We have arrived," he murmured, and waited an instant as he looked through her once more." I will send for your wardrobe first thing tomorrow morning, Gaby," he said, more assuredly as he quickly tapped the vignette.

Hurriedly, the valet appeared and opened the door.

"Show Mademoiselle Thornsen to her door," he ordered.

Stunned, Gaby did not utter a word. She stood up slowly and shot a deadly glower as she passed in front of him. "Adieu, Gaby," he murmured, gazing in her eyes. She snatched up her dress and flew down the three steps to the street.

"I will need no help," she exclaimed to the valet.

The man looked to his master, confused. Jean-Louis nodded him back to his seat next to the coachman. The carriage waited until the large gates opened and the Cardinal's doorman, valet, and butler had come to greet her. As the door closed behind her, she heard the rumble of the wheels starting up again down the cobblestones quay.

Dazed she walked up to her apartment. She swallowed with difficulty as sobs collected in her throat. The nuns had been right, she thought distraught. A future with Jean-Louis had never been in the cards.

The following morning, as she prepared to call for her carriage, she noticed the iron gates opening as an elegant shiny black coach rolled into the courtyard. She parted the heavy burgundy curtains and watched as the two footmen and the gatekeeper exchanged words. Jean-Louis had made good on his promise.

Not surprised at the denouement, she determinedly hurried to her upstairs apartment and gathered the emerald necklace and bracelet he'd offered her in Monaco. She ran back down to the foyer before the men had the time to lift her trunks out of the coach and onto the marble platform. Calmly, she stepped outside and called out the coachman and gave him the heart-shaped jewelry box. "Please return these items to the Duke and communicate to him that the clothing can be given to the poor. One last thing, remind him that his carriage will no longer be admitted in my cousin's courtyard," she snapped with a contemptuous tone and then quickly spun on her heels and turned her back to the servants as she regally re-entered the townhouse.

The love story was over. Her spirit and determination had returned. From now on, she would concentrate on pursuing her musical career.

Chapter Twenty-Four

The last days of autumn in Paris were magnificent. Leaves swirled down on the banks of the Seine, carpeting in brown and gold the new sidewalks and large avenues that Louis Napoléon and Baron Haussmann had devised for the new Paris. It was finally a capital the Emperor could be proud of. As an added benefit, the large avenues enabled troops to react quickly to the incessant rebellious republican skirmishes.

Gaby loved to stroll along the cays on her way home. She knew that it was improper to walk alone without a chaperone, but she was an independent working American girl. Furthermore, her carriage and her cousin's devoted coachman were never far behind.

Yesterday, she had been given her first major role in the opéra, *Les Pêcheurs de Perles* by Bizet. As she had known it would, the old maestro had noticed her voice immediately and he had added extra private lessons to her artistic curriculum. He'd even introduced her to Bizet who as a young man had attended the Conservatoire. She had replaced a lovely chorus singer almost immediately after her arrival at the Académie, and had become quite friendly with another foreigner, a beautiful ballerina and accomplished concert pianist from polish lineage, Jane Victoria Pregelinski. Jane Victoria was madly in love with a very married Count from Provence who would come to Paris a few times a year to visit with her. Gaby had befriended her as she sobbed while waving goodbye to her lover's carriage. Over hot chocolate at the neighborhood café near the opéra, Gaby had comforted her and candidly the young woman had revealed her sad story. But Gaby realized to her great surprise that Jane Victoria was not one to cry for a long time over her sad lot in life, instead she had interesting friends, she attended many intellectual salons, and frequented in Montmartre the *Café Guerbois* and *la Nouvelle Athénes*, where many new artistes-peintres, poets and novelists came to discuss the cultural dilemmas of the new Paris and drink absinthe—the green fairy as it was commonly called. Furthermore Jane Victoria loved Gaby. She had become her mentor into French society.

Naturally, everyone in Paris had heard of the short lived passion the Duke de Bourbonne had had for the American soprano and although Gaby refuse to divulge anything about their affair, she knew that they were still the talk of the town. Maître Lauriot had told her that more than once he had been asked to point out the new singing sensation that had taken the Duke's heart. The old maestro was accustomed to aristocrats who promised the world to young, unsuspecting girls only to deflower them and toss them aside at the arrival of another pretty face. It was a reputation she loathed, but had to endure.

She had not seen Jean-Louis, but there was not one ball or play she attended where his name was not mentioned. She had seen his coach trailing hers on several occasions, but she reminded herself that the town houses were located very close to one another.

Philippe was due in Paris over the Christmas holiday and she missed him. He was the only soul she could open her heart to. He would be proud of her, she thought, smiling at the thought of her cousin's gentle face. She could do no wrong in his eyes.

Weeks later, Gustave Flaubert, the prolific French writer of Madame Bovary extended a dinner invitation to Gaby and Jane Victoria. Edgar Degas had been given the task of asking Gaby to sing a few arias. Maître Lauriot had given his permission, saying, "A little more recognition is all that she needs in order for her to be recognized as the supreme soprano that she is. The clarity and agility of her voice is incomparable. Let me know how her singing is received in recital," the old man solicited.

Two nights later, Gaby and Jane Victoria arrived at the lovely townhouse on the Place des Vosges. To her great surprise as the guests gathered around the long table to find their seating arrangements, she noticed with delight none other than Renaud De Beauvoir. Stunned at the appearance of the man who had guided her through her first French social affair in the Casino in Nice, while Jean-Louis attended to business, she smiled grandly at him. A sexy grin swept across his perfect face.

"Gabriella, my lovely, what a magnificent pleasure. I heard that you're taking Paris by storm." Renaud came closer and politely kissed her hand. "Your name is on everyone's lips, including stories and pictures of you on the Figaro and the Gazette. I've just returned from a trip to Bombay." He noticed her questioning gaze. "Just business, ma chère. It is *magnifique* to be back in Paris and doubly so now that you're here in our magnificent capital," Renaud concluded with a chuckle. He had not spoken about Jean-Louis, obviously word had gotten out and for that she was thankful. His gaze wandered to the long-legged blond next to her.

"Renaud, this is my friend, Jane Victoria, we met at the Académie. Jane Victoria is an accomplished concert pianist and ballerina." He stared at both women and quite charmingly slid his hands beneath their respective elbows. "Gustave," he called out "you will not separate me from these two formidable ladies. Besides, Gabriella and I have a lot to talk about. Are you aware that she nearly broke the bank in Nice?"

"You gamble, Gabriella?" the surprised host inquired. All eyes turned to her. She smiled lazily and with an aura of quiet control she started toward the dining table without an appropriate response.

The evening was marvelous and it pleased her to have reconnected with Renaud. As they parted, Renaud asked if he could come and call for her the next day. She quickly accepted and told him that she was staying at her cousin's home on the Isle Saint Louis.

"Riding in Fontainebleau tomorrow at one o'clock Gabriella," he beamed, laughter lighting his dreamy blue eyes as his carriage pulled away.

Weeks later, the two had become inseparable. To Gaby, he was the best friend she could ever have. He was smart, spontaneous, keen on all the activities she loved, plays, opéras, riding, and he loved giving lavish parties. Unfortunately, his love for gambling overrode all of that. He took her to Deauville in Normandy and she had had to endure seeing him fighting a streak of bad luck. Discomfited by the loss, she had tried to lift his spirit but to no avail. The following day he had departed for Nice to try his luck somewhere else. Weeks had passed before he'd call on her again after one of her performances at the opéra.

Meanwhile, invitations to balls and lavish soirées never ceased to arrive at the townhouse and although gossips about Jean-Louis and his new paramours swarmed around her, she had not encountered her former lover since that last faithful night at the opéra. In mid-December, however, at one of her performance, she saw him in his loge with a fiery blonde as he lowered his head to listen to a possibly amusing anecdote. He leaned back and suddenly broke into laughter. That first sighting with another woman affected her immensely. Tears collected in her eyes and shrieked for release. She was not quite sure if she could continue. This is the life of an artist. She'd silenced her tormented heart. Once on stage, the show must go on. Use it to infuse emotion in the role. In fact, she had been splendid in the role, but as she left the stage with dozens of roses in her arms, the bouquets were used to hide the stream of tears cascading along her cheeks. She vaulted up the stairs into her dressing room, closed the door on all the courtiers, and fell miserably in a large chair. It was bound to happen. After all, Jean-Louis was part of Paris' society, but the knot in her stomach tortured her for days. From that time on, she saw him everywhere. Once she had a glance of him in the salon of his loge during one of her rehearsals on stage; another time his coach had followed hers all the way home. She saw him at the Tuileries' weekly garden concert in the company of the Emperor and Eugénie, talking, of all things, to La Castiglione, the Emperor's cherished young mistress who was breaking the Empress's heart. She had thought that these encounters would be less and less painful, but the grief she experienced with each meeting did not abate.

Early one morning, as she disembarked from her coach, she observed Jane Victoria on the sidewalk approaching hurriedly, her hands waved in front of her face, pressing Gaby to tap the vignette for her groom to hurry and lower the steps.

"Gabriella, please forget my insistence and lack of compassion, but Juliette has fallen ill—to pulmonary consumption they say—and word has it that you are in line to assume the role of Leila in the Pêcheurs de Perles this season." Jane Victoria came close to Gaby and held her hands between hers. "Oh, Gabriella, I hear that Maître Lauriot is waiting for you in the grand salon. Come quick."

Flabbergasted, Gaby followed promptly. Should she grieve for Juliette or let the anticipation of the moment fill her heart and soul? They had been practicing for the Pêcheurs de Perles for three weeks now and she knew she could take on the challenge. In the foyer the old Maestro waited for her.

"Mademoiselle De-Conte Thornsen, we would like to speak to you in the salon; please follow me," he said sternly.

Jane Victoria squeezed Gaby's forearm. "Bonne chance," she whispered.

The opéra administrators had chosen wisely. They began to plan large-scale productions and the American soprano was unstoppable. She breathed new life into the opéra classical repertoire and always infused the heroine with emotional flames that intensified their tragic destiny. Her reputation preceded her and her sober arrival in Paris as the adored but passing mistress of the great Jean-Louis-Pierre De Pleyssis was now of no consequence. Myriad invitations arrived daily and she had had to hire a secretary to keep track of her appointments. Gabriella De Conte-Thornsen had taken Paris by storm in less than a year.

* * *

At one of the late night parties given by her friend Renaud De Beauvoir, she'd promised Renaud a few arias. Jeanne Victoria played magnificently in the salon where many women sat discussing the latest Parisian gossip. The ballroom was ablaze with lighted chandeliers and mirrors that spanned three stories. As usual, Gaby stood at the very top of the curving staircase and surveyed the ballroom below as butlers in full livery followed the guests with silver platters filled with champagne flutes. Le Beau Monde was at its best in this setting. She knew so many people and yet after all these months her heart fluttered each time a tall, dark-haired figure walked into the room. Gossip abounded with tales of his new conquests. He had been seen vacationing in the south of France, in London, in

Normandy . . . She wondered what the Beau Monde spoke about when Jean-Louis had been in the United States. Her name was called and she watched as interested gazes shot up to where she was standing. Gracefully she begun descending the long sweep of stairs and on the very last step, she reached for the marble banister. A large crowd of admirers gathered to encircle her. She held on lazily to the shiny rose-veined Italian marble balustrade as she answered a multitude of niceties. A side-glance revealed a mocking gaze she knew all too well. Jean-Louis eyebrows flicked and he flashed a devastating smile. Momentarily sweetness filled her heart but his lazy grin began to wander down the length of her body as he softly placed his hand on hers. "Hello, Gaby" he murmured sensually. Stunned for a few short seconds, she stood immobile. The recent past and his paramours exploded in her mind immediately. She pulled her hand away, lifted her chin, stalked right past him and proceeded toward the dance floor. Her heart beat frantically as she pulled away and fought to bring her apprehension under control. She had not been prepared for the encounter. Tonight he had brought Hilaire Roquebrune, one of his many old paramours. She was beautiful, well traveled, and, unlike many of her contemporaries, well educated. Gaby had met her at one of Madame Manet's weekly salons. Her sister was a pianist and Jane Victoria knew her well along with Suzanne Leenhoff, Manet's wife, who had come to Paris from Germany as a piano teacher and had landed in the Manet's household. Stalked by myriad of admirers, she forced a fake smile that she would have to affect for the rest of the evening. Renaud was nowhere in sight, but his whereabouts were well known—the gambling salons upstairs. She recognized one of the tenors from the Académie and quickly sauntered toward the performing artists circle. Of all nights, she wished she had not promised to sing. She just wanted to disappear.

"Gabriella, have you been hiding from me?" Renaud called out as he offered her a flute of Cristal, her favorite champagne. "I opened this bottle just for you" he said sweetly, as he tucked her gloved hand in the crook of his arm and proceeded to ask one of the butlers to hold on to the bottle. "Let's dance. Everyone is green with envy, Gabriella, I am the luckiest man alive," he said gaily as he drew her with him on the dance floor. "Marry me, Gabriella," he asked, staring in her shocked emerald green eyes, gathering her body a tad too close. She tipped her head back unable to control her mirth. "Never," she exclaimed terribly amused, well aware that there was no sentiment in his proposal. "I'm not the marrying kind."

Suddenly, a third voice chimed in. Jean-Louis chose to interrupt the waltz and murmured a few words to Renaud while nodding to Hilaire. He promptly played on the surprise of his move and Gaby stepped into his arms as he whirled her around and away from her partner to the enthralling music. Hilaire and Renaud stood aghast momentarily and to save countenance they began to dance once more as if this little incident had been premeditated.

As he whirled her around the ballroom, Jean-Louis lowered his lips to her ears. "Let's try again, Gaby," he said sweetly. "I miss you so," he whispered in English.

It was her turn to stop short on the dance floor. She gave him a scornful glance as she straightened fully and pushed away.

"There will be no other time, Jean-Louis, not now—not ever," she asserted, glowering at him before she spun on her satin heels and walked elegantly off the dance floor.

All eyes were now on Jean-Louis, who affably relaxed, sauntered slowly away from the dance floor with a knowing smirk on his face. He stopped for a flute of champagne and headed for the gaming rooms upstairs.

Victoria Jane, who along with a large crowd had noticed the unusual scene, dashed after her friend and caught Gabriella's gloved elbow. "You should not act so—so flippantly, Gabriella. After all, the Duke is a grand Monsieur, ma chérie; it will hurt your career," the beautiful ballerina pleaded with her stubborn American friend.

"Let me be, Jane, I need to locate Renaud. He asked me to sing a few arias later for a small group of friends after the ball. Let me step upstairs for a breath of fresh air. I need to think clearly before I return to the foyer," she concluded.

With sophistication, she smiled sweetly at all the reproachful stares directed her way and then dashed to the third floor veranda. It was bitter cold; no one would follow her outside. Humiliated and heart-broken, she had not expected to be so disturbed. She advanced on the balcony, unaware that Jean-Louis was following close behind. Taking in a deep breath of fresh air, she reached the parapet that overlooked the magnificently manicured gardens down below and realized that most of the leaves on the trees were gone. A lonely squirrel scurried onto the half-frozen ground. She shivered. In her business a cold could ruin a career. She brought both of her hands to her throat and heaved a long sigh. A door opened and the gay laughter and cheerful conversations from the grand ballroom woke her from her rêverie. Heavy footsteps behind her forced her to turn around and face the last person she wanted to see.

"Gaby," Jean-Louis murmured, brushing her naked arm as he came closer to her and placed his jacket over her shoulders while he leaned on the parapet, "I really think that it is time to talk," he continued sweetly, taking her stunned expression for one of agreement to engage in dialogue. "We both have had time to reflect on what has happened . . ." He came closer and begun to gather her to him only to be shoved away by a mighty blow.

"Talk to you? Never again Jean-Louis. I'd be the happiest woman if you could disappear from the face of the earth!" She turned on her heels and started toward the door. Not one to accept defeat, he reached for her arm and pulled her back into the shadows of the garden. Inflamed, she lifted her arm as she turned to face him and slapped his face as if that was the last act she would ever perform on this earth.

"Don't you ever, ever, touch me again or God help me!" she shouted as she stormed out of the room.

Astounded Jean-Louis did not react. The little hellcat, he smirked as he patted his reddened cheek. He wished he had been less decisive the night of their first re-encounter at the opéra. Eh bien, he was going to have to try harder. Whatever occurred after his departure from Grenoble, he now doubted that Gaby had intentionally tried to avoid him once she'd reached Paris. Ribaud entered as Gaby exited. "Hello, Gabriella, I like your—" She shot him a virulent glare and elegantly lifted her skirts to clear the few steps that lead to the upstairs foyer.

Both men looked toward the double doors. As they slammed shut the golden knob fell on the hard marble and rolled to their feet.

"It's going to take some time," Jean-Louis shared with Ribaud. "The one thing I do not have much of."

"Did the Emperor set a firm date for your departure?" Ribaud questioned, not comprehending the effect that Gabriella had on his friend.

"No, but you can be sure that within the next eighteen months, my life will no longer be my own." Jean-Louis calmly replied. "I want to reconnect with Gaby as quickly as possible; whatever it takes for the little mischief to hear my side of the story—I will comply."

"Very well, my friend. I do not understand the perverse attraction you have for Gabriella, but I'm with you." The two men walked away from the Garden and into the foyer just in time for Ribaud to notice Jean-Louis' Grandmother marching imperiously toward them. "That is, when it comes to Gabriella," the Englishman nodded conspicuously to his friend. "But you're on your own with the Duchesse." He smiled to the dowager as she dismissed him with her fan.

Jean-Louis stood still waiting for his Grandmother. She directed him toward the empty salon.

"Have you forgotten who you are, Jean-Louis-Pierre—your family name, our impeccable lineage? What is wrong with you? Le tout Paris is amused, hundreds of women of good standing are waiting for an invitation from you and you only have eyes for the Thornsen, a vulgar singer. Have you lost your mind? Cease this carnival immediately! It is obscene Jean-Louis-Pierre. Remember your illustrious ancestry. France expects a lot out of you, my child," she reprimanded and then departed with much rustle from the many layers of her overly bouffant satin gown before Jean-Louis could reply.

He returned a sympathetic smile without answer nor rancor, well aware that she lived on the edge of new social mores and that she would not ever give up her traditional ways. But that had no importance, he thought, now he was obsessed with the reason for the long separation. He'd replayed thousand of times Gaby's first words at the opéra, "I can explain Jean-Louis, please let me." He wanted to know now what had happened during their separation. Gaby's fame had climbed phenomenally and she now had many friends who could not wait to show her Paris and all it had to offer. But romantically she was approachable to no one—his security knew every minute of her whereabouts. That was good. He just wished he had been more understanding with her on that fateful night.

Back in the safety of her opulent carriage, Gaby disbelieved what had just transpired. Reading people well had been her strength. Good God, everything had been wrong with Jean-Louis. Enough wasted moments on this man, she thought. Her career would take her away from Paris soon enough into the major opéra houses of the world— that was the reason behind her trip to Europe. One day soon, Jean-Louis would cease to exist for her.

* * *

Later that month, Edgar Degas, Auguste Renoir, Fréderic Basille, Camille Pissarro, and Claude Monet invited her and Jane Victoria to a boating party near and around Argenteuil and Bougival. They'd stopped by the Grenouillère, a bourgeois' paradise where bathers and sinners played. Auguste, Camille and Claude, had been working on the borders of the Seine, which meandered along the picturesque villages, all summer long. They painted at the same place, often sitting next to one another at different times of the day with a different palette.

"You will understand the new Paris better," Edgar explained. "Everyone, Gabriella, rich, poor, aristocrats and us les artistes, dear Gabriella hang out on the Camembert, drunk out of our mind, but we return to Paris with a light heart, filled with new dreams, new colors, new pigments to mix, and new ideas on how to depict our times, our lives in the moment, Gabriella." Degas had a difficult relationship with many, but with her he was the perfect gentleman. Perhaps their New Orleans roots touched him. Lately they spent quite a bit of time together. His new interest had gone from horses to wood workers, to the *repasseuses*, women who ironed clothes, to hat makers and now he could only think of dancers. He would paint them in the most unusual positions, but they were as real as real could be and there lay his great talent—to catch an instant in the life of his models.

They zigzagged unsteadily on the narrow walking path that led to the noisy Camembert where couples sang and danced to the lively music. She noticed Hellen Andrée stare at the riverbank. Curious Gaby turned to see who had piqued the famous actress' interest. Flabbergasted at the apparition that flashed from a side-glance to the mainland, Gabriella noticed Jean-Louis with a large group of friends jumping out from one of the barges. Her heart fluttered and her merry demeanor vanished for there was only one way to reach the land and Jean-Louis had started on the narrow bridge that crossed the river. Gaby swallowed hard and let out a heavy sigh. She watched Jean-Louis sensuous smile as he approached. Unconsciously she gracefully lowered her umbrella as they prepare to meet. The glass of Absinthe she had sipped earlier lowered her inhibition. She was ready to trip the Grand Monsieur casually into the water as he passed next to her. Her sly movement was not lost on her former lover, the half-smile turned into a glacial glare as Jean-Louis kicked the tip of the umbrella away from his path. Gaby very nearly lost her balance. And had it not been for Claude she would have made a spectacle of herself—right in the water along with all the male bathers. She swallowed hard and smiled winningly at Claude and Edgar and continued on her cheery way to quickly rejoin her friends.

"Better let things go," Edgar whispered. He reached for her hand and tapped it gently. She candidly questioned his statement with a flick of her braided hair and wide-open eyes, while she replaced the fashionable yellow straw hat on her pretty head in a very feminine demeanor.

"Where to, *les amis*?" she gaily exclaimed taking in the exact area where Renoir sat, while painting one of the barges attached to the pier. She would let things go, she promised herself. Her reputation already tainted, she had joined the dozens of ballerinas and singers who had fallen prey to the libertine demeanor of the aristocracy. Her untamed spirit reminded her that her mother was part of that very aristocracy that she scorned.

In late October, the soprano who was to sing for the first gala of the second opéra of the season had fallen gravely ill and could not perform. There were talks of consumption again and although Gaby knew that it was the malaise of the century, she doubted that the diva would have been able to carry on with her schedule. Consumption or not, Marie Laise was addicted to absinthe. More than once Gaby had had to take on her demanding role on a day's notice. There were five more performances of Verdi's opéra, *Les Vépres Siciliennes and* Maître Lauriot asked her to sing all five. Picking up another lead in the opéra De Paris after just a season was unheard of. The opportunity she had been given held no equal. She promptly wrote a few lines to Philippe and she sealed the envelope with a grain of salt and hot wax and gave it to the courier. She then proceeded to share the news with Jane Victoria.

"Gabriella," Jane called out "I have been meaning to talk to you. Rumors have it that the Duke sits in the salon of his loge as you practice. Is there something that you want to share with me, ma chérie?" she questioned.

Stunned and unwilling to show the slightest of interest, "No, my dearest," Gabriella scoffed contemptuously, "his paramours are uncountable. A young singer or dancer must have caught his eye." She glanced promptly at the maestro and walked rapidly in his direction.

* * *

Her first night singing in Verdi La Traviatta in the role of Violetta at the Theatre Lyrique in Paris had placed her at the epitome of classical performances. All of Paris spoke of her crystal clear notes that she reached rapidly with great emotions and perfect theatrics. Her picture adorned all newspapers and kiosques in Paris. Adoring admirers pressed invitations upon her and the Emperor Louis Napoléon and Eugénie would attend the Christmas Eve Gala. Philippe in Rome had heard of her fame and although she had been terribly disappointed at the news that he had had to cancel his trip to Paris, she could not wait until they could reunite. Her goals had been hastily reached. She wished she had never heard of Jean-Louis-Pierre De Pleyssis. She stopped by Notre Dame de Paris on her way home and kneeled on the heavy mahogany Prie-Dieu in front of the Immaculate Conception. She smiled as she pleaded with God to make her forget Jean-Louis. She repeated the same prayer every week as she stopped to pray and lit a candle in the spectacular medieval Cathedral. To date, her prayers had not been answered. Perhaps someday soon the pain would subside.

Meanwhile, the advent of the holiday's season was phenomenal in her adopted city. She'd purchase a tree, a manger, myriad gifts for the children at the orphanage just a few blocks away and she'd spent a great deal of her time honing her singing and acting skills. Jane Victoria was morose. She missed her Count for he spent the holidays with his family. She had lost her joie de vivre and could not wait until the New Year. Often, Gabriella thought, that her episode with Jean-Louis had in some obscure approach turned out for the best. Had she become his mistress in Paris, Jane Victoria's sort would have been hers to endure. She now quite clearly understood that great things were expected from him, not least of all a marriage into a good family to secure many heirs. Her mother came from Italian aristocratic blood, but providing an heir was now unattainable.

She returned to the townhouse, her coach filled with packages. The gatekeeper presented a small but heavy package to her. She asked her footman to bring it in and to place it under the tree. Alone or not, she would open presents tomorrow morning with the servants. Now she needed to rest for the gala performance tonight. The Emperor would be in attendance.

With elated anticipation, Gabriella surveyed with Maître Lauriot the arrival of the Imperial Court. Louis Napoléon III in full regalia along with Empress Eugénie and five of her ladies in waiting all formally entered their loge. She listened to the ahs and the ohs and the dramatic acclamation of her troupe, but quickly her gaze jerked to the left of the Emperor. Jean-Louis had just stepped in his loge, and he quickly nodded to the Emperor. His Grandmother sat next to a bold, older man. Many medals adorned his jacket and with his monocle pressed to his eyes he inspected every pretty woman that walked in the loges across from him—and down below in the orchestra. Slowly after each inspection he would lean over to the Duchesse De Bourbonne and he appeared to be giving her a complete run-down of his impressions. Gaby smiled—the French and their obsession with beauty.

Her furtive gaze focused on Jean-Louis perfectly clad in black evening attire. He stood while he conversed with three women and two men. He nonchalantly shrugged off his black evening coat. She recalled that first social night in Villefranche when he had shaven his beard. Childishly, she had told him how beautiful he looked. She heaved a long sigh. After all, it was Christmas Eve. A little sadness for happy times lost was permitted. She lapsed into silence. It would help with her performance she told herself as she cast a last skeptical glance toward her audience. The orchestra began the prologue. The lights dimmed. The chorus stood ready. The curtains parted and she walked regally on stage.

As she danced and flirted with her partner, her voice writhed emotions seldom heard before, women and men both were crying. The Duke sat mesmerized, moving his elbows onto the painted wood of the balcony to see her more clearly. His companion elegantly placed her long gloved fingers on his arm hoping for a kerchief. None was forthcoming. Gabriella captivated Jean-Louis. Along the couloirs, drafters were drawing pictures of the Duke mesmerized by the beautiful soprano who enthralled her audience. Journalists wrote on their yellow notebooks. Every movement of the Duke's companion trying in vain to interest him were recorded and photographed. When the tenor sang, heads turned to glimpse the man who had ruled Paris' society for far too long. The newspapers would have a blast with it tomorrow. Le tout Paris would talk about it for days and Jean-Louis, usually so aware of his surroundings could only think of having her in his arms again. Nothing mattered any longer. Even his loyalty to name and country could not let him forget Gabriella De Conte-Thornsen. She had to listen to him again. He'd grovel. He would make sure of that after the performance. Proud of his decision, he relaxed in his fauteuil and suddenly realized that all eyes were on him.

Diane De La Rochelle, one of his companions this evening, was livid. She turned her head away as he turned to her and smiled. Ah Gaby, what have your reduced me to? He smirked amused.

At the end of the performance, she stood exhausted in front of her audience as she tried to catch her breath. Not a word was uttered. A sense of awe spread through the spectators before they broke into a loud applause that would not cease. She knew that she had no peers in her delivery. She had rendered an electrifying performance. Proud of herself, she turned and faced the Emperor. All were standing and many ladies held white handkerchiefs to the corner of their eyes. She had touched their hearts, she thought. Good, that's why she had come to Europe. After countless standing ovations, she left the stage. In the couloirs, photographers and graphic artists were taking pictures and sketching her every move.

"Mademoiselle De Conte Thornsen, une rendition merveilleuse . . . splendide . . . *vous nous avez fait frissoner*, you made us shiver, mademoiselle," she heard from all sides. She wished Joyeux Noël to all and she quickly marched to her dressing room that was already filled with hundreds of rose bouquets. Her maid was waiting to remove her wig and comb her hair and she quickly changed into a long dark green satin gown designed with a Japanese landscape. Her throat was quickly wrapped with a warm cotton towel and her manservant massaged her shoulders. She lounged for a few short minutes until a knock at her door made her open her eyes.

"Mademoiselle, the Emperor is here to personally congratulate you," her maid told her. They all knew what to do and within minutes all was cleared, wingchairs were brought in the salon, and Gaby stood up. The Emperor walked in.

"Mademoiselle, I wanted to personally congratulate you. Your performance this evening touched all our hearts. France thanks you for sharing your gift." She smiled and reverenced. But it was the person next to the Emperor that commanded her attention. Jean-Louis stood serious as he calmly walked to her.

"Gaby," he spoke softly with emotion, "your voice is exquisite. I have never heard such magnificence." She slowly raised her flushed face to his, clearly shaken. For many long minutes their eyes locked, silence reigned, and the world and its constant state of agitation came to a standstill. An aura of extreme passion swept the room. Suddenly, the side door swung open and Renaud stomped in.

"Gabriella," he exclaimed. The spell was broken. It was then that he noticed the Emperor. Quickly he came around and paid his respects. The moment was lost. Gabriella flashed a grand smile to her friend and her countenance returned. Jean-Louis clenched his jaw, remained still for a short while and politely bid goodbye to all as he strode out of the room. A few more niceties were exchanged between the Emperor and Renaud and Louis Napoléon excused himself.

"Eh bien, mademoiselle; the Emperor himself came to congratulate you, Gabriella. What a great honor, you were splendid tonight. Get ready, we'll . . ." He noticed her sad expression. "What is wrong? You should be ecstatic. Do you miss your family? The holidays are always difficult. You will love my Maman's feast tomorrow. I will pick you up at around twelve o'clock."

She nodded, smiled and leaned back on her day bed.

"It does not have anything to do with Jean-Louis-Pierre," Ribaud questioned, curious as he reached the door and left it halfway open.

"Renaud, of course not," she scoffed. "I am exhausted. You know how hard I have worked for this performance. I just want to go home and wake up tomorrow morning and unwrap all of my presents. I've always loved Christmas. Joyeux Noël."

"Joyeux Noël, Gabriella."

* * *

Furious Jean-Louis bolted down the stairs and into his carriage. He had planned on basking with her in her aura of fame and taking her home tonight once and for all. With Gaby, he never knew what would unravel. He wondered about De Beauvoir. Yes, they were seen everywhere together, but he had it from good sources that there was no romance between them and certainly after tonight, he had felt her loving eyes upon him. Gaby still loved him. His patience was growing thin and yet he wanted her to come to him willingly. Tonight she would have been ready to listen to reason if that moron De Beauvoir had not walked on his parade. A false move with her and she would detest him for months. He no longer had the leisure to wait for months. Time was precious. He had to make her understand.

Chapter Twenty-Five

Gaby's friends waited for her in front of the opéra house. All would attend the decadent masked balls so cherished by the Emperor and Eugénie to celebrate the night away and to rejoice in the coming of *La nouvelle Année,* the New Year. Although exhausted, she preferred to be entertained until the wee hours of the morning, rather than spend New Year's Eve all alone in her cousin's townhome. She descended the steps to the foyer and noticed the flickering lights of the coaches waiting for the last revelers. Lights illuminated the Place de l'Opèra and the Grand Boulevards—Paris was splendid. She continued down the stairs and noticed Jean-Louis' magnificent black-lacquered carriage with the gold De Pleyssis coat of arm encrusted in its doors. She froze and quickly glanced behind her. The carriage came to a stand still across from her. She had not seen Jean-Louis in his loge, but perhaps he might have wandered around during her performance. Men had the tendency to spend a lot of time in the halls of the opéra house talking about everything but the Opéra at hand. Instead, Jean-Louis opened the door himself and stepped out of the coach as his footman scurried to let the steps down. He walked decidedly to her as if he had been anxiously waiting for her appearance, a white mink coat wrapped on his arms. He quickly placed it over her gold satin cloak, gathered her in his arms, and lifted her in the carriage. Gabriella found herself sitting in front of a smiling Jean-Louis as the carriage negotiated rapidly around the crowd. The coachman bawled the powerful white horses down the Boulevards. The whole episode could not have taken more than a few minutes.

"I wished we could have spent Christmas together, Gaby, but the New Year will have to do," he said, gazing down at her, "I am sorry about the way I behaved when we met at the opéra," he began rapidly, fearful that she'd jump out of the flying carriage. With Gaby, one never knew. "I do not know what happened to you after I left you in Grenoble, and Gaby, I do not need to know. You were right in Villefranche, Gaby. I love you more than life itself and I know that the feeling is mutual." He paused for an instant to assess her reaction. She was stunned. "Why are we playing these games?" he said as he looked down, grasped her hands, and pulled her to him.

"Talk for yourself," she gasped, trying to extricate herself from his embrace, "I've gone on with my life and my world is absolutely marvelous—without you in it. I have everything I have ever dreamed of and much more, so now please let me go and return me to my house immediately."

He smiled without releasing her. Instead, he tightened his embrace and lowered his lips to her long, graceful neck.

"I love you," he reiterated with all the passion he felt for her. "Be patient with me, chérie. Whatever happened during these long months of separation, I now could not care less about—they're totally forgotten."

She shoved him hard, unclasping her hands from his.

"Oh, thank you immensely, Cher Duke for your regal forgiveness," she retorted, eyes ablaze. "Except that I was the one who was wronged, Jean-Louis and had it not been for Philippe and the nuns I probably would have returned home to New Orleans—my dreams never realized, nor recognized." Drained in resentment, she straightened her torso. "Let me be clear. A month after you left me in Grenoble, I woke up in the middle of the night feeling deathly ill. I lost consciousness while I tried in vain to call for help. I—I lost all recall of my life." She had been on the verge of disclosing the loss of their child but could not bring herself to risk pity. "This is what happened to me, Jean-Louis. What are your excuses? Cruelly, you never came calling or tried to inquire about me, I could understand a short delay, but three months?"

He was shaken, that much she could tell. Tears collected in her eyes as she recalled the incident. He reached across and pulled her to him again. He clasped her head to his chest and held her intensely close to him.

"I looked for you from the moment I set foot in Paris, Gaby," he murmured. "Three times I returned to Grenoble. I was sent to Avignon only to be told that you and your cousin were on your way to Rome, and when I arrived in Rome, Philippe's office said that the

Cardinal had been delayed in Arles. I was leaving for Rome the following day the night we met at the opéra. One of my contacts had sent word that your cousin had resumed his religious duties. I was certain that you had returned to Rome with him," he said, holding on to her so tightly that she gasped. He released his embrace just enough for her to take a deep gulp of air, so afraid was he that she'd slip away once more.

What she heard stunned her. Jean-Louis had flaws, egotism, arrogance, and control issues, but he never lied.

They stayed in each other arms for a very long time, neither one of them wanted to break the spell. Both wondered why the people they loved the most had tried to separate them. He no longer wanted to talk. He took her in his arms, looked intently at her, and letting his urges get the better of him, he kissed her mouth passionately.

"How I missed you, Gaby," he finally said as he gently pushed her away to gaze at her once more as if to reassure himself that she was really there.

Utterly confused, she stayed ensconced in his comforting embrace. It was New Year's Eve, she'd think of something tomorrow.

* * *

The next morning he'd woken up early. He lay next to her watching the woman who had stolen his heart at the most inopportune time in his life. He smiled and pulled up the coverlet over her naked body. Her disheveled mahogany mane cascaded down over his pillow. He cuddled next to her as his hands wandered on her warm breasts.

All night she had touched his arm, squeezed it, raised her head and kissed his lips as she nestled closer to him in between their many loving interludes. "It's not a dream, Gaby," he'd told her. She had smiled and reclined, secure in his arms. He was dismal over the pain and confusion she must have experienced all alone. Damn this whole ordeal. Of all people the ones surrounding her were a cluster of virginal nuns and a Cardinal. Not even a woman, an experienced woman, to give her some emotional support. He was going to talk to Durand, the family physician; she needed a top doctor to examine her.

Her fighting spirit had returned her to Paris. He wished he could take back his dismal demeanor at the opéra. Recalling her love of sleep, he decided to get up and attend to her security now that she would share his dwelling. He made a note to increase his own private security, especially now that Gaby was here with him. She could be in danger as well. No need to let her know. He would have enough people watching her every move. Without her knowledge, Gabriella De Conte-Thornsen had taken her first step in a political world marred with unparalleled conflicts on the European theater. Her flagrant whereabouts in the south of France had helped the French intelligence to tighten their security. It would prove to be a good thing.

He looked down at her one more time and covered her small body with a heavier coverlet. He stole one last kiss and strode out quickly. He would be back before she re-opened her fiery emerald eyes.

Less than an hour after his departure, Gaby tossed in bed and she rolled toward Jean-Louis. Where was he? She opened her eyes quickly. She was in a strange house—his house. She drew herself up and pulled the covers away. Her eyes glanced down to her gown that lay ripped on the thick carpet. She had not one piece of clothing to wear and Jean-Louis was nowhere in sight. She looked around and noticed a dark burgundy satin robe thrown haphazardly on a chair. She grabbed it and wrapped her small body in it by tying it up at the waist. "He's not even here?" she said aloud.

Her anger mounted and then her insecurities returned. Had he changed his mind? No, Jean-Louis did not require much sleep; some events must have needed his attention. But still, she mulled over. Ten minutes later, she decided to wander about. She had no clothes and her coat must have been left downstairs. As she walked down the long corridor, she stopped in front of a particularly lovely oil painting of a young boy—Jean-Louis at probably four or five painted by the great portraitist himself Jean-Auguste-Dominique Ingres. He looked so susceptible and loving; his big blue eyes had been caught in a moment of vulnerability. She stood staring at the painting forgetting how displeased she was with him for leaving her to fend for herself like a *misérable*. She couldn't fathom the harsh treatment his father and stepmother bestowed on such a loving child. There was love painted all over that face, she pondered, mesmerized by the picture.

Come on, Gaby, she reminded herself, as she recalled his demanding and authoritarian attitude on the ship. Perhaps he was a little demon that tyrannized the whole household with his impertinence. This was just a painting—something his parents perhaps wanted him to aspire to.

She walked down the impressive hall. It was formal and awe-inspiring. Antique secretaries, Bellini sculptures, and Master Italian paintings, mostly from the late seventeen hundreds adorned large rooms and walls. Beauvais tapestries hung from walls in one of the large library she passed by. She walked inside in awe. One that had attracted her curiosity was the Italian village scene—*The Hunter with Girls with Grapes*. She stood mesmerized in front of it as she tried to decipher every angle of the silk tapestry. Clocks, watches and scientific instruments were displayed on walls and alcoves in the hallways. Surprisingly enough for these types of grand old houses, it was light and airy with large glass openings in the vaulted arches of the ceiling where the warmth of the morning sun diffused subtly in the rooms. She glanced at the immense fireplaces that lined the walls of the emerging rooms on each side of the hallway. Suddenly, she heard greetings and the large entry door opened.

Emerging in the impressive foyer down below, she watched Jean-Louis as he entered his home, giving hat, coat and leather briefcase to the butler. Immediately, his glimpse shot up in her direction. He cast a skeptical smirk at his satin robe that was trailing behind her and smiled as he ran up the stairs. She looked annoyed as he encircled her body and pressed it along its length.

"Why did you leave without telling me?" she exclaimed anxiously.

He grinned and kissed her nose.

"Hush, I did not have the heart to wake you. You slept so well. I thought for sure that I would return before you awoke."

"Tell me from now on," she replied curtly. He looked down at her surprised, but did not reply.

"I'm sorry," she echoed quickly, as she placed the side of her face on his chest. "You will have to be patient with me for a little while longer. I have made great progress since the incident. I have never been so confused, so overwhelmed with decision making." She lowered her voice to an embarrassed murmur, "I am so scared and insecure about the smallest event in my personal life."

He held her tightly. Surprised to have her divulge her insecurities in view of the fact that she was the picture of independence and self-worth for a large bastion of Parisian women.

"Take your time, Gaby, everything will fall into place. Right now the only thing you need to do is to enjoy the ride, ma chérie. I'll take care of everything. Think of us, your music, and our future." He bent down and kissed her. "Even in an oversized manly robe you look ravenous. Come, I surmise that you did not talk to Maude. Come with me." He reached for her hand and led her to a room next to his.

"Voila, mademoiselle, your boudoir."

There were five Degas, his ballerinas at Garnier, the opéra de Paris, and a few from his New Orleans period at the cotton exchange. The room was decorated in a most feminine tone, unlike the rest of the house. A woman must have inhibited this area, she thought.

"I thought you told me, no woman had ever been allowed in your *domaine*—your home here in St. Louis. I have difficulty imagining you in this frilly atmosphere," she responded, jealousy mounting.

"Absolutely right, Gaby. It was a study before I had it redecorated for you. Notice the Degas. I had hoped to change your mind. I doubt that the convent or your cousin's somber residence would have competed with this room. I was not aware however, that it would cause me so much pain as the months of our separation accrued."

She looked at him incredulously.

Knowing quite well that she doubted his comments. He marched to a mirror-covered wall and slid a golden pad down; a huge walk-in closet opened in front of him. "Come and see," he smiled and enticed her to walk closer to him. Jean-Louis had a charming boyish grin that he turned on quite easily when he meant to have his way. The wardrobe she had purchased in Nice and had given to him to take back on the Tempète was here. On one of the chairs lay a black mink coat with matching hat and *manchon, a muff*. "This one is to replace the one you left on my account at the opéra." Astounded she walked in after him.

"All that to convince me?" she asked, still incredulous.

"Yes, Gaby, I stop at nothing to get my way. You should know that."

"I will admit that was a perfect ploy knowing how obsessed I am with clothes. Did you give part of your spending to charity as well?"

"No, Gaby, I just paid the workers well."

She smiled.

She turned and faced the room, staring in space, pensive.

Jean-Louis walked away from the closet and came to sit on a plushy gold and white satin sofa. "I understand your response, Gaby, and even the nun's, but you said your cousin is a man of the cloth—a Cardinal at the Vatican? He must be an intelligent man to have achieved that status. What was he thinking? Is he that clueless?"

"No, Jean-Louis, when it comes to my well being, Philippe will forgo all logic and accept whatever I feed him. I have always been the one who took decisions for our lives, never the other way around. He just went along with my feelings and whatever the doctor and Mother Superior told him. Philippe is an exceptional man. You will like and respect him, I'm certain. There is nothing he would not do for me, Jean-Louis," she answered sweetly as she recalled Philippe's sweet face.

Jean-Louis did not answer. He disliked the Cardinal, perhaps because she adored him. The power he allowed Gaby to have over his emotions was mind-boggling. Eh bien, in the end, everything had turned out well. He did not have to fight her to move in with him. These long months of separation had been hellish, but in the scope of a lifetime, the frustrations had been a drop in a bucket. □

They had a wonderful leisurely breakfast in his house and they spent a good part of the morning and afternoon roaming through his house. It was filled with priceless paintings, antique furniture, and books. Gaby felt like that she was discovering a museum with each room he brought her to. One could choose from a First Empire-decorated study with original documents, to salons and dining areas with Louis XIV and Louis XV originals decorative arts.

"How could you have left this *domaine* for the Tempète?" She posed, amused.

"A strange intuition that a charming American young woman would require my help at sea at some point in my life obliged the adventurer in me to roam the world awaiting the apparition of the heavenly maiden from New Orleans—the love of my life." He took her hand and they strolled to his library where a butler was rearranging the logs. He took her in his arms and was kissing her tenderly on the large sofa facing a huge fireplace, when she recognized the ever-questioning gaze.

"Yes Jean–Louis?" she smiled.

He lifted her gently and then sat her on his laps.

"What happened, Gaby?" he demanded, but just as quickly he checked himself and added sweetly, "I would like to know."

She quickly recognized the non-negotiable tone. Secretly, she wished he had not asked. She now had to tell him the truth. He deserved it. She had been less than candid with him. Pulling away from his warm embrace, she paused and looked at his face noting the taut demarcation of his jaws. He looked at her intently with curiosity.

"It's an involved story, Jean-Louis." His eyebrows flicked, he seemed to say go for it.

"Well, less than two weeks after you left me, the sisters had fixed some sort of dish that I disliked greatly, some type of blood sausage called *boudin*. I therefore decided to fast that day and to wait for the following morning to have a larger petit déjeuner. Crazy, but in the middle of the night I could not sleep and felt an urge for condensed milk. I had seen a tub in the pantry, so I decided to walk downstairs to satisfy my sweet tooth. I did not want to wake anyone, so instead of looking for my peignoir, in my less than patient nature, I instead wrapped myself up in the coverlet that lay on my cot.

Intently staring in her mesmerizing green eyes, he remembered the fateful afternoon across the ocean on his ship. He gave her a gentle squeeze. "You did it again this morning. Is life too sweet, Gaby? Are you looking for trouble?"

She heaved a long sigh. "It had gotten me in trouble once before. I should have known better. Anyhow, I fell and I rolled down on the marble staircase. I must have created an awful loud noise because as I came back to life, the sisters, the doctor and even the parish priest were all looking down over me. The trouble was that I could not remember their names. I did not know that I was in France. I could not remember my name. The fright I experienced still makes me shiver."

He was about to gather her back in his arms when she began once more. "Well, to make a long story short, I recovered and weeks later, although still a bit weak, I resumed my activities. Philippe arrived and soon we traveled to Avignon. He wanted me to see the city that had been the seat of Christendom for almost 100 years in the 1300's. Upon our return to Grenoble we stayed in one of Philippe's great friend's home, the Count De Beauvernes."

Now, it was his turn to look down at her not knowing what to make of the story.

"According to the story that you have just told me, Gaby, this whole episode happened months ago. You've been in Paris for quite some time now and you've handled your professional life quite succinctly. Did your memory return and leave you again or is there more to the story?" he queried, sarcasm and disbelief in his tone. He felt her body tense up. He should forget everything that had happened, he concluded. Whatever her reasons, she would tell him someday soon. No need to bother with it now when the only thing he wanted to do was to make love to her again. He leaned over and reached for her.

She stood her ground and pushed his arms away as she stood up and crossed the room before she came to rest in a large chair across from him, her enormous green eyes filled with tears. She looked at him anxiously.

"No, that's not all Jean-Louis—that very same night . . . I lost our baby." She was staring at him now, studying his reaction, her teary eyes evaluating his every move.

He reached across and tried to pull her next to him. She resisted. He was shaken, that she could tell, but his next sentence confounded her.

"Gabriella, what do you expect me to say? Why don't you let me hold you? I had an odd intuition when my coach pulled away from the convent that I shouldn't leave you there by yourself. But why didn't you come back to Paris? Why couldn't we have gone through it together? Why did you have to keep me at large—that I don't understand? Gabriella, what in God's good name made you think that I could not handle this awful incident? You know how much I wanted you to come back to Paris with me."□

"But, Jean-Louis, you don't understand. I may never be able to have a child, your child, any child. I have to come to terms with that. I don't usually run away from my responsibilities or hardships, but emotionally I was in total disarray. I didn't know what to do, where to go? It was as if my world had come to a sudden halt. The nuns and Mother Superior advised me not to seek you out. I prayed very hard that I would somehow meet you. I did not know how or when, but a feeling in my heart told me something wonderful would happen and reunite us. I had been in Paris a fortnight when I saw you getting into your carriage, but I was immobilized. Do you remember the rice in front of the Church of St. Michel in Villefranche at the wedding? Do you recall that I threw rice at you and you gave a small sack of gold to the little girl next to you for a handful of her rice and you threw it back at me? Do you remember?"

"Yes, Gaby, I do," he answered. Where was she going with the rice now, he thought? How could he forget that passionate moment that had shaken him so. He had wanted to recall the priest so that he could marry them immediately. In retrospect, he should have. He let her continue to ramble. God, she should be a writer, he thought, she would give some concurrence to George Sand.

"Well, I thought at that moment we had been touched by Cupid. Love and luck were in our cards, so I knew deep down that it could not end like that. For a while, I entertained the idea of following Philippe to Rome and it came to pass. I did go with him. In the back of my mind, however, while traveling to Avignon, I knew that you were to negotiate some treaties in Rome. Consequently, I felt that perhaps fate would place us on the same path as it did on the Tempète but in a different world, in different times and our love would rekindle. I'm a student of romanticism through my musical gifts." She pulled her head to the side, nodding sideways as if embarrassed to have disclosed such a conniving adventure.

Jean-Louis looked on. Smart women analyzed and evaluated immensely. If only superstition and self-doubt would not rob them of these pertinent faculties, they would make a great contribution to this world. On the other side of the coin, he now realized why men of his time liked absurd beauties rather than having to deal with women with an active intellect; they were much easier to handle. He was going to tell her to let him take care of everything. For once, she did not have to plan her life for the next year. He could easily handle that, but in retrospect he changed his mind and reached for her and this time he held on and pulled her against her will towards him.

"You have no control here, chérie. A lively intellect cannot compete with sheer strength."

"You think?" she responded, unable to retrieve a fast retort.

"I know, always." He gently pressed her to his chest. "Gabriella, listen—I love you more than words can tell." She looked up at him with disbelief in her expressive eyes. She had lost a lot of weight and her eyes seem to overtake all her finely sculpted features.

"Can you repeat that again?" She hesitated as if she had misunderstood.

"Would it have made a difference if I had said it in Grenoble?"

"Most certainly."

"Why?" he demanded.

"I don't know, I knew that you had fallen in love with me, but—"

"You knew?"

"People usually do when I let them get close enough to know the real me, but, like any woman that is placed in this situation, we doubt ourselves and it's this self-doubt that swallowed me up so many times, Jean-Louis. I listened to the nuns. I knew that they only had my well-being in their mind and heart. I was insecure and my pride and fortitude of spirit prevented me to face the possibility of rejection."

She seemed to have finished. He could feel her heart beat below his hand and he decided that his latter decision to place the sword on her court would be wiser.

"Gaby, I have heard, through my Grandmother that often women in your state of spirit, after the loss of a child, need rest. You think, evaluate, and analyze way too much. Look at you. In less than a year, you have taken Paris by storm. Let me handle our affairs, your affairs, for just a short period of time. We deserve to enjoy one another."

She could feel herself melting and yet she knew that she had to finish what she'd started to divulge. She assertively interrupted him.

"Jean-Louis, look at your station in life and what is expected of you. You will need an heir." She paused. She had said it. "And I may never be able to give one to you. What has occurred to me, the sisters told me, may have left me infertile—barren. I did not doubt your fortitude, I was so into our love, our passion, that it never occurred to me that you might want—may need—to marry and I did not want to be your mistress. That is why I did not return to Paris immediately." She stared at him intently.

"And now?" he demanded.

"Now, I don't know. I feel so weak when I'm close to you. I do have a flourishing career to fall back upon." She stopped and looked fixedly in his eyes. But one thing is certain, the day that you decide that you need to marry, I will leave you, no matter how much it will hurt. I know that I could not see you go into the world with someone else. I would be devastated." She shuddered at the thought of the pain that it would cause her.

Placing his fingers on her mouth, he bent down and brushed her temple with a kiss.

"As I was saying before you so rudely interrupted, I want to forget about these frustrating months. Let's start where we left off, Gaby. All the explanations you have given me matter no more. We are back together, let's make up for lost time. I want to show you Paris. I want to introduce you to my friends. I want to take you to the opéra." He smiled. "You pre-empted me." Then he laughed, thrilled that she had not fallen in love with someone else while he acted like a fool for much too long. "I want to take care of us, completely. Will you let me, Gaby?"

She nodded, letting herself sink in his arms, listening to his voice.

"Buy clothes, furs, jewelry . . ."

"I don't need any." She chuckled, amused.

"How many men would love to hear such words coming from their stylish wives?" He mocked, but Gaby most certainly could be tempted with clothes.

Her singing career and fame had not been taken into consideration. Of course, she would have to give it up, but now was not the time to bring up potential discord in their conflicted lives. They had time.

"Jean-Louis," she fumed disappointed, angry that he reduced her state of melancholy to a walk in the fashionable Faubourg Saint-Honoré.

"Eh bien, whatever you want to do, or enjoy doing, as long as you love me," he concluded.

She looked up and slid her arms around his large torso. Unable to envelop him in her arms, she reached up and placed her two hands on his cheeks, looking straight into his eyes.

"I adore you, Jean-Louis, you know that?" She looked at him questioningly. He had that ironic sideways smirk on his face.

"It would have made a huge difference, Gaby, if you'd stated that in Grenoble."

"I did—hundreds of times," she replied, amused.

"I adore you, Gaby," he whispered, "don't ever leave me—ever again."

He accompanied her to her classes the following week. All eyes had been on him as he helped her out of the carriage. Her friends had come to meet her, obviously all hoped to learn about the latest development in their relationship, but regal and self-assured she had not uttered a word about their liaison. She had not even turned around and waved good-bye to him. The brat, he thought.

Now her popularity knew no bounds. He tightened security around her and he attended all her performances. Some came to hear her incomparable voice. Others just came to bring back some fine gossip at the next salon. Her artistic schedule was annoying and Jean-Louis was in constant fear that she would succumb to over-exhaustion or consumption. He had wanted Durand to talk to her and perhaps even examine her, but one glacial glare from Gaby had ended the possibility right then and there.

Durand, the family physician, had told him one evening at the Cercle over brandy that perhaps a trip to Normandy might be a lovely idea. She would have time in between performances. He did not recognize Jean-Louis-Pierre, for that matter few did in Paris. Yes the young American soprano had a magnificent voice but to be so taken by her? He looked forward for an invitation to meet her. The day arrived sooner than expected. Jean-Louis-Pierre had instructed Durand to approach the idea that perhaps after her horrific ordeal, she should rest a lot more. The physician's own wife had not been able to bear children, so he knew a lot on that subject. Poor Durand had tried in vain to relate his own story, but to no avail.

"Miss De Conte Thornsen," the doctor politely said in accented English. "It is a real pleasure to meet you. Le tout Paris is mesmerized." The doctor made polite conversation to place her at ease. The dinner had been pleasant enough and as they entered the salon for a last cognac, the physician pressed by Jean-Louis had touched on the tender subject.

"I am sorry that you had to experience such a horrific suffering in Grenoble, Miss Conte-Thornsen. My father and I have been in the service of the Duke and his family for many years and Jean-Louis shared with me your—"

Fury took hold of her and Durand stopped in mid-sentence. Gaby was inflamed at Jean-Louis for sharing such private ordeal. She knew damn well what this fellow had been asked to do—poke her in every possible way and then tell her the inevitable. She wanted to forget it all, not be reminded of it.

Very polite but very cool, she shot murderous glances at Jean-Louis that he chose to ignore. Unable to stand any more, she stood up. "Pardon me, doctor. Please excuse us, I need a moment with Jean-Louis."

Had he been standing on the gallows, she would have tightened the cord around his neck and kicked open the trap door beneath. Without looking at either of the men, she stood up and marched to the side bar to fix herself a brandy. The butler tried to preempt her to no avail. She poured the brown liquid into a small crystal glass and waited for him to join her.

Jean-Louis stared at her gorgeous face and did not move. Poor Gaby, he thought. Her life had been so well defined before he met her. After their chance encounter, all hell broke loose. He turned to Durand, who was now standing up and confused, the physician wanted to be anywhere else but where he stood. Jean-Louis nodded toward the chair and the old man sat back down.

"Miss Thornsen," he began shakily, "when I was studying medicine at the Sorbonne, my wife became pregnant and lost the baby. We have five adopted children that we adore, but we were unable to have one of our own."

"I'm sorry," she replied politely, wanting to end the conversation and leave Jean-Louis forever.

"Do not be. We have the most wonderful children any parents could ever dream of. I was just asked to make you aware that if you needed someone to talk to, my wife could answer many of your questions."

"Jean-Louis-Pierre, why don't you take Miss Thornsen to your Chateau in Normandy? The air is so pure and I know for certain that Madame Perideot will add a few extra pounds to your slight frame. Did Jean-Louis tell you the story, Mademoiselle Thornsen?" The physician politely continued.

"No," she replied with some curiosity.

To establish an area of comfort with Durand was Jean-Louis' goal. He smiled, as he remembered his nursemaid.

"Eh bien," Durand sat back in the chair and lit his pipe. "Madame Perideot is, or rather, was Jean-Louis' nursemaid—a woman who never married with no children of her own. Needless to say, Jean-Louis was her adored child. The summer of his sixteenth birthday, he returned from Normandy, a foot and a half taller. Mind you, he was already tall but always quite lean. Eh bien, he returned to us with forty extra pounds on his gigantic frame."

Gaby stared at him, unconscious of her flippant expression. "Anyhow," the old man braved on, "we were sitting having dinner, when his father chose this moment to announce that Jean-Louis was going to study medicine at Oxford University. His father, confident that Jean-Louis would follow his every order, smiled down at his son only to discover the ironic smirk that you now must know very well. Instead, Jean-Louis stood and as he was towering over the old man, he calmly announced that this was not the case. First, he had sign on with the French Navy and furthermore, he was going to study law in the Sorbonne afterward. De Pleyssis senior dropped his jaw. I thought I was going to be called to his side. You just had to know Jean-Marc-Louis De Pleyssis, Gabriella. Can I call you Gabriella?" he asked sweetly with tenderness and concern in his voice.

She nodded. The old physician perceived a slight interest. He continued enthusiastically.

"He was always so regal," the old doctor continued, "so domineering, so severe when it came to his son's behavior, demeanor, and future. I remember that moment so well. He looked sideways and down at his son and smiled—a sour smile that spoke volume. Jean-Louis-Pierre stared him down. The old man sat back down, speechless for a while, toying with his food, and then, not able to contain his ire anymore, he finally released his outburst."

'We will have to see about that,' the father shouted. 'Follow me immediately to the library, Jean-Louis-Pierre.' As they left the room, the tension between the two men was indescribably hostile. Everyone at the table turned towards the great windows to observe the battle of wills that fired between them. Jean-Louis will tell you the gist of what occurred. The story in Paris went around for months, and as weeks passed, it elevated the power of Madame Perideot's magical cuisine. The boy had acquired his boldness through his nursemaid's magical cuisine. Few would go against the senior De Pleyssis'will. His son had just demonstrated that he had gotten his mental strength from the old man and had surpassed it." The physician stared at the burning logs as he recalled the vivid picture. "I think that her name is still linked through her culinary arts, incorporating assertiveness and strength of spirit to body and soul." The old physician grinned and reclined in the large chair. "So Gaby, make friends with this lady in the next few weeks. Better having her on your side than against you." Durand smiled again. He was proud of himself. Although the situation had been awkward at first, he had served Jean-Louis-Pierre well.

Gaby smiled politely again. "I will try, but next week is unfeasible." She looked at Jean-Louis questioningly. "I do not think that Maître Lauriot will look upon my absences positively. I have concerts to perform. No, maybe early spring."

Durand looked at Jean-Louis, amused.

"I'm sure that I'll convince your Maîtres to let you go to Normandy for ten days. If they can't abide to my wishes—I'll fire them."

She first looked up at him outrageously, and then quickly realized that he probably had the power to do it.

"Very well then, just let me do it." She laughed, a crystal clear mirth that mesmerized Durand for a moment. Jean-Louis reached for her and kissed her hair.

"You are learning fast, my little plantation owner." He pulled her to him and kissed her.

Durand took his leave. Fernand, the butler accompanied him back to the foyer.

Alone together, she walked closer to him and looked intently in his eyes.

"Thank you," she said calmly, taking his hand and kissing the inside of his palm. "You know Jean-Louis, it's been more difficult than I like to acknowledge." Her voice had a tone of finality. He would leave it at that.

Chapter Twenty-six

Jean-Louis had a well-stocked library. There were books that dated back to the early 1600s, even a signed copy of *Candide* signed by the master himself, Voltaire, before his exile to Switzerland. It was immense and sumptuously decorated. A bit too ostentatious for her, she mused ironic. Nearly every day she got lost in the many rooms in the three-storied Mansion. His Bourbon ties dated back to the Middle Ages encompassing many illustrious kings of France, including Louis the XIV, the Sun King who had given France its taste for conquest both literally and figuratively. The King also had left a very French legacy that included the nation's taste for luxurious goods, for all refined forms of arts, the theater, music, paintings and sculptures—in essence for the timely enjoyment of everything magnificent.

"The powerful lords of the time had succumbed to the galas, theater, banquets, and salons of the magnificent Versailles, away from Paris' dreariness and their castles in the provinces. By and by, they had softened in the King's claws and cowered under his absolute power. The poor and downtrodden were left in the rat infested, garbage-collecting streets of our stinking overcrowded capital." Jean-Louis asserted.

"I visited Fontainebleau and the Chateau du Vaux Viconte, Jean-Louis, I am always amazed that it took such a long time for the populace to rise and unseat the Kings. And I'm doubly stunned that after the Terreur and the cultural and political conflicts that Napoléon Bonaparte brought to France during the *First Empire*, the French still allowed three monarchies to govern their country. It's almost unbelievable," she exclaimed.

He looked at her curiously.

She was about to question the Second Empire, but decided to listen instead.

"Baron Georges Haussmann," Jean-Louis continued, oblivious to her observation, "Louis Napoléon's architect, the portly fellow you met at the ball last night, two hundred years later somewhat adopted the same philosophy—but in reverse. Instead he evicted the poor outside of the city and let the wealthy and their servants enjoy the beauty and fruit of his travails."

"Renoir told Basille, that his parents had been pushed out," Gaby said. You know he worked in the Sèvres factory, painting pastoral scenes on their magnificent china. I believe that although he loves being part of the new independent painters, Renoir is more of a romantic painter. Have you seen him copying at the Louvre?

Jean-Louis shook his head. "I don't have the passion for the arts that you possess and display Gaby." He was about to divulge that he paid little attention to artists, except that Gaby was one of them and she happened to be quiet close to Degas and Manet. Let's leave it at that, he thought wisely.

"While Monet looks out of the windows to paint the outside world," she continued, "Renoir sits in front of a Delacroix, dreaming." She smiled as she brought to mind the picture. "I learned a lot about Paris from them, Jean-Louis." He did not respond. "As I was saying, Renoir's parents' home was razed to make way for the beautiful gardens of the Tuileries where we now attend our weekly concerts."

Not to be outdone by the painters, Jean-Louis responded quickly. "Paris was essentially a dirty, overcrowded city before Louis Napoleon came back as president in '49 and a year and half later crowned himself Emperor. He spent some time in exile in London. Upon his return, he was determined to make Paris a worthy and beautiful capital—one that he could be proud of when he received the many dignitaries that seek his friendship. His ambition is to create a path toward a modern Europe with France at its epicenter. I support him in this endeavor. I don't know that it is going to work this time, Gaby. There is a whole lot of division in France. If the Emperor survives, it will be the beginning of a better world."

They continued their political chat late into the night.

Chapter Twenty-Seven

Time flew for Gaby in Jean-Louis' company. Her days were always occupied. She'd leave for the Opéra around ten in the morning and more often than not, Jean-Louis would meet her for lunch and then again would wait for her. The time that she spent with her friends was now scarce.

Jean-Louis wanted to handle everything. The first week had been a week of passion and both had taken time from their own busy life to rekindle their liaison. Later, she thought it appropriate to move back into Philippe's home just two blocks away.

"You are not allowed to think," he'd remarked assertively. "Let me do the thinking for a while. Just love me and pursue your musical interests. That's all I will allow you to do now."

"What a controlling soul you have become," she'd laughed and went about doing just that.

She loved seeing him off in the morning and being home to greet him at night. The social life he had spoken about had not started yet and she was pleased about it. No need to be anxious about anything. She was one hundred percent happy. After all the doubts and anxieties she had experienced, the decision to return to Paris had been the right one after all.

Today, after her return from the conservatory, she'd settled in the downstairs library. Mahogany-encased bookshelves were filled with leather-bound books too numerous, she thought to focus on just one period, one writer, one philosophy.

She never realized how erudite Jean-Louis really was. Up to this point, their relationship had been mostly amorous. Recently however, he had begun to confide in her. Last night, they had discussed at length the plethora of philosophies that involved the political issues that rocked Europe and the United States. He had told her much about French thinking and its reaction to upheavals, dictatorships and wars—and also about his world—the European aristocracy and the cultural differences between France and America.

He was well versed in opéra as well. He knew the history behind the great thinkers and the moods that prompted wonderful musicians to write scores, scripts, and arias.

They had not touched upon literature. Had he really read most of these bound books or had they been purchased and handed down through generations to fill the mahogany walls of the vast library? Why had he given up his privileged lifestyle for the life of an adventurous Captain? He detested everything that smelled of aristocracy and yet, there was the dichotomy—he could not get away from his good breeding.

As she walked out of the library, she suddenly heard rumbling in the foyer. Men spoke loudly and assertively and one thunderous voice distinguished itself from all the others. She stood still in the entryway to the foyer. Jean-Louis walked, boisterous, the ever-present arrogant man she had been frightened by on his ship, had re-emerged. Not willing to get involved in his business, she retreated in the doorway.

Gaby's assertive resolve had not yet resurfaced. She became very insecure at the least displeasure he displayed and was always ready to move back in her cousin's home. Durand had drilled him on the emotional frailty many women experienced right after a miscarriage. Jean-Louis recognized that precarious state and he tried his best to control his temper when she was around. Today, unaware that she'd returned home earlier than usual, he continued his verbal assault at several, severe-looking older gentlemen over an internal political issue. It concerned the radical republican movement heralded by the realist painter, Courbet.

Fernand announced Mademoiselle Thornsen was in the library.

The man must have eyes behind his head, she thought.

She marched in the foyer. Why was Jean-Louis talking to government officials in such an irresponsible manner?

"Jean-Louis, I'm here," she exclaimed coyly.

Although the newspapers wrote incessantly about the couple since their last reunion at the opéra, none of his colleagues had seen them together—certainly not in his home.

"Well, perhaps let's pretend that I'm not," she said quietly, as she caught his less than ecstatic stare. She began to retreat in the comfort of his large library.

Hearing her dismayed tone, he turned back and retraced his steps. "You came home early, Gaby?" He spoke quietly and his stern expression took on an amused grin. He approached her and bent down to brush a kiss on her lips.

"Should I disappear now and let you go on with your ranting and raving?" she murmured, aware that the men were watching them.

He burst out laughing. "Eh bien, perhaps." Then he quickly changed his mind. Gaby could meet up with her friends, *les artistes*, as he preferred to address them. Better invoke his Grandmother.

"I will have to work late, Gaby, but you may want to go with my Grandmother. She, like you, is quite fond of the theater and she rarely misses a performance. You will find her to be an aficionado," he said. "I will admit that she knows quite a lot about it. She passed on all that information to me when I was young—whether I wanted it or not."

"Without her knowledge, she was preparing you to please me." Gaby replied. Unfortunately, she was not too fond of his Grandmother. "No, I prefer to stay here with you. You'll have supper later. I'll see you then. I longed for many long months to be in the very position that I am now, waiting for you, just like I did while on your ship. I will not deprive myself this small pleasure, my darling. I love, no, I adore waiting for you." She turned her on her heels as if she was about to leave, but instead she cast a sidelong glance as if to say, "Do not leave me waiting too long."

He did not show up for dinner but terminated the meeting earlier than expected, joining her in their sumptuous bedchamber.

"What took you so long, Jean-Louis? I know that you work closely with the government; I don't understand your rude behavior toward many of the Emperor's advisors. Why is the reason for your celebrity?"

"My wit, my extreme good looks, and prowess," he responded.

He came closer, took her in his arms, and kissed her. □"All that talk about waiting patiently for your lover to return to your side was short-lived, my gorgeous mistress."

She shot him a mortified glance. In effect, she was his mistress and *la haute Société* knew it and called her by that very name. The realization was painful.

"Your mistress? Is that what I am? Is that what your friends and colleagues call me, Jean-Louis?"

He looked down at her questioningly.

"I hate that word and the connotation behind it. It sounds so fleeting and filled with unreality, unfulfilled commitment, and frivolous behavior. It lacks substance and depth. Certainly nothing close to what I feel for you. Besides it's an awful word, I'm not your lap dog!"

He smirked and pressed her to his length. Slowly he took her with him as he lowered himself on the canapé and teasingly begun to stroke her back. She bolted upward.

"Do not even joke in this disparaging way."

He reached for her and forced her back down. This time he encircled her waist so as immobilize her small voluptuous body.

"You were saying?" he questioned.

"I don't know that I want to continue; my thoughts have suddenly changed. No, seriously, I dislike the term, I'd rather be your—"

Jean-Louis interrupted her abruptly and begun to impart some Parisian realism in her thinking.

"Gaby, be real, my darling. You are living in my home, le tout Paris knows that I searched for you relentlessly for many long months, and more recently ever since the New Year you have not left my side. Unfortunately for you, my reputation as a wanderer is well established. I assure you that I would have a real difficult time to convince Paris that my attentions towards you are purely sentimental and pure."

"You could try at least, for my sake."

"Unsuccessfully, Gaby, I don't believe into placing any energy in tasks that have no purposeful value, you know that."

"You spent a lot of energy and resources in trying to locate me," she questioned, not quite knowing if she could accept his candor.

"You were purposeful value to me. I would have found you wherever you hid. I have connections and purpose, darling. Don't even think of escaping," he warned.

Uneasy at the threat at first, a surge of warmth and happiness permeated through her.

Jean-Louis stood up, picked her up and placed her under him on their bed.

"Besides, Gaby," he continued, "ninety percent, no, probably ninety-nine percent of marriages in France have no emotional commitment to one another. It is just a practical legal document that joins family names, fortunes, and lands. It has the advantage to legalize procreation within one's class. There is very little affection, never mind love in any of these relationship and to further confuse you and to disprove your erroneous point, the mistress is usually the one most men are emotionally, sexually connected and committed to. Do you still feel the same about the connection, Gaby, now that I have enlightened you into the perverse French etiquette of the 1800's?"

She continued to listen to his tirade "these numbers are disconcerting indeed, yes, but," she looked at him and in her usual transparent mode, "I still intend on becoming your wife. Furthermore, I will have it only one way, in a strict monogamous relationship. I'll make your life a living paradise." She shot him a bewitching smile and boldly kissed his lips.

Shocked, he raised up on his elbows, his body weight on hers and both of his upper arms encircled her pretty face. "Don't be shy, Gaby," he ventured, a smirk on his lips, mesmerized by her assertive expression. "Please don't hold back. Be as direct and candid as you please, ma chérie."

"That's the only way I know how to be, Jean-Louis. Although these numbers are disturbing, we will just have to make history." She answered, delighted.

"Gaby—"

She interrupted his thoughts by forcing herself on his right forearm. Off balance, she rolled her body onto his and placed her lips on his invading mouth with wild kisses. Desiring to control everything that was his, to own it, she caressed his inner thigh slowly and gently, looked for the mass that would grow, warm and throbbing in her burning palms. She reached for it with her left hand, encircled it, and stroked it deep and meaningfully.

"I love you, Jean-Louis. I do not want to talk about it anymore," she gasped in between kisses, now she caressed every place accessible to her. She knew he would lose control, and she was on the cusp of losing it as well. She peeked up at him through her long thick curly lashes, but to her surprise he was not in the ecstatic state she had expected.

He pulled her upward and then rolled her once more on her back. He stared intently as if he tried to read her and then with an ironic tone of voice, he placed her roving hands above her head, pinning her to the bed.

"So tell me, Gaby," he said, "you want to be a Duchesse? Duchesse De Bourbonne. You'd wear the title well."

She laughed.

"Do you really think, Jean-Louis, that I am impressed by all the elegant crowd you surround yourself with? No, darling, I would not know where to start on how to be a Duchesse. I still have everything to learn about French etiquette. When I think that I have reached a comfort zone, I commit another faux pas. I just want to be your wife—forever. To me, a mistress connotes the other woman, sinful in a way, one that can be loved but dropped at anytime. Marriage—my kind of marriage—will require commitment on both of our parts. Otherwise, we will just have to part. I could bear almost anything from you, except deceit with another woman."

"But, Gaby, wait—many mistresses are cherished. It is usually the wife who's being cheated on. Marriages are arranged for financial reasons, for family connections and titles, for an heir," he reiterated stunned at her flagrant honesty.

All of a sudden, she looked devastated and became silent.

"I agree," he quickly inserted, "from my perspective, it's dismal. Arranged marriage for financial reasons are the most common and as I said earlier, the most pathetic." He had lost her. A shadow overcame her beautiful, candid profile as she turned her head sideways, gazing at the great fireplace.

"I presume," she said calmly, having lost her festive and assertive mood, "if it came to having an heir, then in my case it would be a huge obstacle. I'd be the Joséphine De Beauharnais of the late 1870's. I can see your point, Jean-Louis."

He took her face in both of his hands.

"You only see absurd reasons, Gaby. You are perfectly fine. You are young, and trust me, many woman have experienced your trauma—no, our trauma. Once and for all, Gaby, I could not care less about heirs. I have ten nephews that would love the title. I want to return to the United States once my work here in Europe is done—with you."

"Then, Jean-Louis," her face brightened up again. "Then the other reasons you mentioned are inconsequential. Money is not an issue with us. I am wealthy, educated, and I have a wonderful career," she replied with clarity and boldness.

Jean-Louis looked at her in disbelief.

"Wait, are you telling me that I should ask you to marry me?"

"I'm telling you," she retorted, "that I want you to kiss me and to take me passionately, Monsieur le Duke." She raised her lips to his and held firmly onto his shoulders while pressing her breasts firmly to his naked chest. "What do you say to that?" she laughed in his mouth.

He nodded, laughed, and went about her request in a most dutiful demeanor.

"You may just have your way one day," he replied candidly.

The marriage question did not resurface for a very long time. Gaby did not care. She knew he would marry her—one day.

Chapter Twenty-Eight

Meanwhile they had become the talk of the tout Paris once more. All knew that she sang like no other. Her lessons at the Académie had lasted less than a month before she was chosen to sing in a full-blown performance. No other soprano had attained such fame in so short of time. But what type of lineage did she have? Was she an American courtesan? There was some aristocratic blood on her mother's side, but her father, it was quickly leaked, was an English or Irish commoner. Then it had gotten out that she was a plantation owner. That alone had given high hopes to the young aristocratic girls looking at Jean-Louis as a prospective husband.

Jean-Louis-Pierre De Pleyssis would never allow himself to marry a commoner and entertainer, it was said. It was just a passionate liaison that would fade away, the Beau Monde claimed. But then he'd introduced her to Louis Napoléon. The rumors mills had regained their intensity.

Gaby had the most disarming American accent that charmed the most hardened bachelor. She also possessed immense, green, innocent eyes that mesmerized with just one look.

Jean-Louis had not underestimated the effect she produced on people from her first night out in Nice. To everyone's shock, he was always at her side. No one could dance with her, especially young men. Speaking to the beautiful brunette for any extended time was frown upon. In her loge at the opéra, myriad securities would screen everyone not on the Duke's list. And unfortunately, the list comprised only a few intimate friends. It was said that the former rake tightly controlled her. Furthermore, he did not allow her too much time to meet other women. At the Conservatoire, she befriended her friends, *les artistes*, namely the ones she rehearsed with, but even her outings with Jane Victoria had been severely curtailed. The Duke controlled her life. She realized it, but did not resent it.

For the first time in her existence, she enjoyed being taken care of. In the past she'd had to make decisions for herself and hundreds of others. In Paris, with Jean-Louis, her only concern was to please him. He drove with her to the Conservatoire in the morning, although he complained about the early hours she kept. "Servant hours, for God's sake," he'd moaned daily before his first cup of coffee.

"Well, darling, artists are the servants of the well-heeled like yourself. Maybe one day if you get your way it will filter down to the populace. We are the bearer of creativity, happiness, and laughter. That is what we do and thank God, some of us have that very spunky outlook. Life would be most desperate in this city if it was not for our gifts."

At other times she'd retort, "Stay put, I'll attend to my own needs." But he always followed her, grumbling. Most afternoons he'd pick her up and they'd go out riding, her favorite activity. He loved getting out of the city. The woods outside of Paris were magnificent. They would ride until dusk, arriving at the house weary but happy. So different in their professional lives and yet so alike, even their reading choices were similar. In less than a week they'd purchased three of the same books.

Gaby had learned early on in life to appreciate every little happiness life threw her way. Tita had taught her never to take anything for granted.

At the conservatory, the Maîtres were enthralled and fearful that the Duke would put an end to her singing. The adored mistress of the influential and powerful Duke De Bourbonne was not the most malleable student. She knew her talent and would not let anyone distract from her performance. At first she had had to work harder than most French and Italian students to just be heard and then her talent had shown through. Her sense of theatrics was enigmatic and most appealing. Her recollection of voice intonation, movement, and breathing was exacting, and her voice was a gift from God that needed a very limited amount of practice. Le Maître never had to remind her of a correction. She was *charmante* and witty.

For most, it was hard to imagine the liaison. Two individuals so less alike—background, culture, language, personality traits, it defied all odds. There was no common ground, it was said, and yet when one saw them together, love permeated the many layers of their personalities. The giant and the dwarf were happy—not a small task in this day and age. They walked the streets as if no one watched. The Duke haughty, doing his duty for country without much tolerance for the populace, and Gabriella, the brilliant performer, who loved anything that had artistic value. Painting, sculpting, drama, ballet, and of course her beloved opéra—she loved and supported it all with great gusto. Her passion, enthusiasm and zest for life were captivating to anyone who had the chance to befriend her. How could they be so in love? This was the enigma. And in love and lust they were.

Weeks passed and the trip to Normandy had not resurfaced. She was pleased. She loved Paris and did not want to ask the Maître for special favors. One Monday morning, without much fanfare, however, Jean-Louis returned from the Palace of the Elysée and stopped by the Conservatoire. She'd walked down the long narrow street on her way to the Patisserie, a block down from the great hall, to purchase *une petite barquette,* pastry*,* and a cup of hot chamomile tea.

Upon seeing his carriage coming down the street, she wondered what might have happened. Was he sick? It was not in his habit to disturb her schedule in the middle of the day.

She stood in front of the conservatoire with a worried look on her face waiting for the carriage to come to a halt. Jean-Louis descended quickly. "What are you doing standing there?" he questioned, surprised. "They let you out early?"

"I was about to ask you the same question, darling. No, I was starving." She laughed back.

"Hop in Gaby, we are leaving for Normandy."

"No, be serious Jean-Louis, I can't. Not these next two days, I'm preparing for Violetta. You know that we practice for—"

"Let's go, Gaby. Gerome will let your instructor know that you will be back in ten days."

"I can't"— she started.

"You can and you will, ma chérie," he interrupted rudely. He reached for her waist and placed her gently in the carriage without much protest from his beloved.

"That is very rude, Jean-Louis. They will brandish me *une Americaine ordinaire* on your account. No one will ever let me live that one down. They forgot that I was from the other continent. Please let me go in and explain."

"No," he took her in his arms and kissed her tenderly on her mouth. "Good practice for you. You will have to learn how to take criticism. You are smart, beautiful, endowed like a goddess, charming, and my adored mistress. You will be criticized even if you were a saint."

She looked at him with a grin on her amused face. "I thought that I was a saint." she responded ironically. "Oh well, I'll have to start out again at ground zero. I hope that your influence, Monsieur le Duke, will make my return the more pleasant. You told Gérome to tell the director that it was your idea, correct?"

He shook his head negatively.

"Jean-Louis how can you be such—such a pretentious aristocrat? You talk a nice talk, but your walk is crooked."

He laughed. "I do enough for the populace of this world to allow myself a few impertinences. Now, Mademoiselle, do you want to go or not?"

She shrugged her shoulder a few times and then sunk deep in his arms and lay there. "When I regain my strength, I will recoup the temerity to fight you. Meanwhile, take me where you wish." She languorously sunk even deeper in his chest. "I love you," she whispered.

They did not utter another word upon the return to his magnificent Hotel Particulier on the Cay Bourbon. They did not have to.

297

Chapter Twenty-Eight

"You will love Normandy, Gaby. The castle is quite beautiful. I loved it growing up. Madame Perideot, as you heard Durand describe her, was sent there to watch over me during my summer vacations. She innervated my stepmother. It is most probable that my father's young wife must have realized that her health seemed to deteriorate every time she came to the castle in Normandy. She would have one liver crisis upon another. You know about the frailty of the French liver? By some perverse culinary preparation, it appeared that Francoise was always ill whenever Madame Perideot was in charge of the cuisine. I never got to the bottom of it, I was way too happy to spend my summer vacation in Normandy with Madame Perideot," he recalled pensively.

Gaby listened intently. It was not often that Jean-Louis talked about his childhood.

"One early spring, my father had tried to fire her for her lack of disciplinary sense when it came to my upbringing. She had no problem correcting everyone else on the staff and because of that approach she had made some enemies—namely, my tutors. The three tutors approved of her dismissal. My father sent packing a woman who had been in our household for over thirty years—all her adult life really. It was a blessing that it was close to summer vacation, and that I was old enough to understand that in this particular game, niceties and politeness would not work. I became a demon. First, with my stepmother, who already was obliged to spend the summer in Normandy to replace Madame Perideot and to oversee my well-being and to supervise the instructors and tutors. She hated it. My father's disciplinary actions did not work either and finally they came to the proper conclusion that Madame Perideot deserved to be punished for her bullish insolence toward her mistress. Keeping the insubordinate devil—me—all summer would be her *Calvary*. She was asked to return, she accepted promptly, and we both were left without supervision to expiate for our sins. I made sure to be difficult during our trip, so as not to take any chances with the coach driver. God forbid he would return to the Loire and tell my parents and tutors of our laughter and grand old times."

She looked up to him tenderly. "Your childhood must have been difficult?" she questioned.

"Madame Perideot made it lovely," he replied as he cast a faraway look, "I sincerely hope that you will like her, Gaby."

Like her? I will adore her even if she was a witch, thought Gaby. It was rare for Jean-Louis to be so sentimental about anyone. Thank God, the former governess was now in her late sixties.

"Besides," he continued, "Luke's and Ribaud's castles are nearby. Summer made up for all the inadequacies of *l'année scholaire,* scholastic year. It was a blast, as you say in America."

"Ribaud has a castle near you? Will he be there with Elise?"

"Ribaud and Luke will be there. I have received word."

"I do not know Luke, but meeting him does not send burst of happiness running through my veins, albeit you had a blast with him as a child. I do not have fond memories of Ribaud and Elise, either. I wonder why?"

"Hush, you do not know them. And yes, they will be there—Luke and Ribaud anyway. Elise, it remains to be seen. I have sent invitations to many friends, good friends. Many will bring their petites amies, as well. Deem it our first soirée. You will glamorize my halls, beauty."

"That I will," she responded a bit disappointed. She had thought they would spend two weeks alone.

He read her mind.

"I want you to meet my friends, Gaby. The men, I know to be friends, the women, eh bien, just go along with the game. It will be fun, anyway." He looked eager. She would try her best. After all, the 'entertainment' as he called it, was to last just three days. Three long days if all were like Ribaud.

They arrived late in the afternoon. Naturally, everyone was aligned in front of the entrance of the impressive castle. Madame Perideot was the first to break rank and walk toward the couple.

The old lady only had eyes for Jean-Louis. She had not thought about asking Jean-Louis about the nursemaid's stature. Unconsciously, she had presumed that she would be a large, robust woman with heavy breasts and a white apron tied haphazardly around her rotund stomach. Although not short like herself, Madame Perideot was smaller than average height and skinny, very skinny—like skin and bones. She did not have the soft features and warm smile that Gaby had imagined. In fact, she was downright severe, with a long pointed nose, small eyes, hardly any hair on her bold skull, a yellow complexion that made her look jaundiced, and her hands, oh, dear God, they were deformed. This woman had been the cherished nounou of Jean-Louis-Pierre De Pleyssis. The poor darling, he was lucky he had not developed a taste for young men, Gaby mused.

Everything in his childhood looked dreary and cold. Even this magnificent castle was lifeless, she thought. She looked up at Jean-Louis. He had taken his nursemaid in his arms, giving her a great bear hug. He should be aware that she could crack, she grinned. Finally, it was time to be introduced and to Gaby's surprise, old scraggly bones had the most beautiful smile. She had large, meaty lips and an extra wide mouth that made one forget how scary she appeared at first encounter.

"Enchantée Mademoiselle De Conte Thornsen," she said in a polite, elegant voice. She looked at Gaby intently.

So that was how a mother-in-law looked at their son's prospective bride. Her friends had told her about the alarming glare. That dreaded look of disapproval, of condemnation, most often came from the mamas' side.

The two women sized up one another. Gaby did not know what to make of it. Surely Madame Perideot had heard about the saga. According to Jean-Louis, he had been there a few times during her long absence. She was still being looked over and then finally, Madame Perideot turned back towards the waiting servants and asked all of them to return promptly to their tasks. Gaby was surprised, usually a nursemaid did not have that type of power in an aristocratic household. She would have to ask Jean-Louis later.

"This castle is run like a perfectly timed clock, Gaby."

She nodded. Well, she had yet to be told whether her first impressions had been positively glorious. For some odd reason she did not think so.

Their luggage was brought up to their room and they fell in each other's arms.

"Well, Gaby, your first impression, ma chérie?"

"It is impressive, Jean-Louis. I never imagined this grandiose of a setting. How many other castles do you own?" she asked, stunned.

He smiled. "Quite a few in France and a few abroad."

"I feel foolish about having gone on with my plantation," she laughed. "I can't wait to see the grounds tomorrow. You are quite close to the sea as well, right?"

"Right, we will go out early tomorrow morning. It's breath taking. The schedule I have had to keep with you these last few weeks has officially inducted me into the early bird society. This weekend we will hunt with our guests."

She loved the 'our' in his sentence. She would have loved nothing better but to fall with him on the white satin dawn coverlet. But she didn't. He was starved and wanted her to sample la cuisine de Normandie. So down she went and sat with him. An hour later she was thrilled that she did, for the meal was incredible, including heavenly creamy sauces, and sweet blueberries in some delicious tarts. The wine and the liquors were outstanding. While the meal was being served, she looked around to see if old Hawkeye was surveying the situation. She was. Consequently, she asked Jean-Louis to switch platter with her.

Taken aback, he questioned her action and understanding her actions, he leaned back against his chair and burst out laughing loudly. He remembered what he had told her about his stepmother's 'liver ailment.'

"Come here, I love you?" he said spontaneously. She obediently walked over to him and kissed him and sat on his lap. He proceeded to feed her from his own plate. "How long will I have to endure this outrage," he murmured in her ears?

"If you feel fine for the next few days and do not develop any 'liver ailments,' I will start to nibble from my own plates. Until then, you're the guinea pig."

They spent a few hours playing chess in the library. It was during that time that she noticed Madame Perideot watching her from the side bar. Gaby had the urge to grimace, but she controlled herself begrudgingly.

Jean-Louis followed her stare and he noticed his former nursemaid.

"Venez nous joindre, Marie, join us," he continued in French asking specific questions about the household and its needs. It was quite rare to see this tender side of him directed to a servant. This woman meant a lot to him, of that she was certain. One astounding question shocked her. Jean-Louis had mentioned Italy a few times while in Villefranche but it had always been in vague terms. Marie Perideot had just asked him point blank and he had answered that his trip was inevitable and that he was preparing for it.

"Jean-Louis what is this Italian trip that you are contemplating?" She asked him later when they were alone.

"There is nothing to tell, Gaby. It is most probable that I will be asked to go. It does not concern us right now. When the time comes, I will make a decision."

"And me? You will not leave me behind?"

He thought about it a while and then decided to keep it on a back burner.

"We will talk about it, if and when we need to." He shunned another question, not willing to continue on these lines. Instead, he took her in his arms and kissed her, a smile parted his lips.

She was about to pull away and ask more questions, but she felt him relaxed and happy. She decided to relent for the moment. Clearly, he had said they would talk about it. Jean-Louis had always been upfront. She was the one that had been less than truthful in that relationship. However, she hoped they would have a few months of cherished peace and tranquility. They deserved it.

The next day, they spent visiting the magnificent countryside. He took her to Cherbourg where they visited one of his friends, Boudain, the father of the painting outdoor movement. Claude Monet had spent many a summer learning the new techniques from Boudain. He and his wife Camille spent long hours on the white and sandy beaches of Cherbourg where the new wealthy bourgeois rode northward by train from the overcrowded cities to uncover the magnificent northern coast that bordered the Manche. Often the tourists would ask Claude to paint a small painting in remembrance of their vacation. He would abide gladly, since his family, save his aunt, was less than pleased with his living arrangement. His parents had opted to cut their financial responsibilities, only to change direction and relented when Camille Doncieux had given birth to their son.

Jean-Louis made her discover France and she loved it. And slowly but surely she tried to open his eyes to the new artistic movement that was taken place. She had seen some of Degas' exhibits in New Orleans and had adored this new spirit in painting. Painting life with its unspecified contours, with its myriad lights, with its approach in displaying the mores of working people in their natural state. It was all titillating. She remembered that in Saint Tropez, Nestouli, the restaurateur, had spoken about Monsieur Manet and his love for depicting the naked female body, nothing novel in art of course but Victorine Meurent, his favorite model in the Déjeuner sur l'Herbe had a modern flair, one where SHE held the gaze of the art lover! Last week in Montmartre at the Café Athenée, Jane Victoria had shared that the Impressionistes had discussed quite openly a possible exhibition at the *Salon des Refusés*. The Emperor had facilitated the display of new avant-garde paintings not accepted by the French Académie de Peinture and Scuplture with a new artistic venue. In actuality the new modern paintings received high marks from the new bourgeois and the untitled Parisians. Was it to assuage the bourgeois and to gain a much-needed political support or perhaps to abase the critics of the annual Grand Salon? Gaby thought it was a bit of both. The group could no longer be ignored. Naturally, members of the Académie judged the Grand Salon. Anything short of the classical style with its rigid rules of showing scenes where only the learned and erudite could appreciate the art, was denigrated by the Académie and most art critics, Louis Leroy being his most vocal in the Charivari.

"You know Gaby," Jean-Louis proclaimed while riding, "the Emperor's approval rating is in decline. To assuage the moods of the have-nots by approving of the Salon Des Refusés—a show where essentially the rejects of the Grand Salon can display their art is a good political move."

"The institution of another Salon d'Art is good Jean-Louis. It gives another outlet to artists." She had not told him that she had gone to Montmartre after attending one of the literary salons. Better leave it at that, she pondered.

Gaby thought of how wonderful Jean-Louis truly was. He had friends in all circles of life. It was great fun to be with him, but to her dismay quite a few women also found him quite exciting as well. Often, her jealousy fired her up. She told herself there was not much she could do about it. He always included her in everything he did and she was the mistress of his Rue Saint Louis en Ile apartment, he snidely reminded her when she questioned him about a particular rumor that linked him with so and so in such and such time. She would make herself crazy if she hung on to every bit of rumor about him. There were daily articles on his whereabouts and his many political and cultural affairs. He could not have hidden very much from her even if he wanted to—it would be all over the newspapers. What Gaby did not know was that she had her own personal surveillance service and that she could not have hidden much from her well-connected, influential lover either. He had known about her escapade in Montmartre but had let it go at that as well.

They stopped in one of France's largest stables. He had taken her to the Camargue while in the south of France, but these corrals were more spectacular. Gaby fell in love with one horse in particular that had taken to her. As they departed, the owner came to her. "I know you will adore *Tempête,* mademoiselle. She intuitively appears to have a connection with you." Gaby stared at Jean-Louis.

"You know how much I dislike sharing my things. You chose my favorite horse this morning." He laughed.

"Another present, Jean-Louis? You will have to stop. I'll become spoiled." She placed her hands around his waist and squared off in front of him. "I love you, Jean-Louis," she said softly. Suddenly that morose, far away look reappeared. He had forgotten about it. A dark cloud overcame her pretty face and she frowned as if she was seeing something awful in her mind.

"Gaby, what is happening? I have seen this look before. Why? Is there something, some fears?" he questioned.

Almost instantly, she quickly retrieved her naturally happy demeanor.

"I don't know, Jean-Louis, it's just a passing feeling, but it's very dark. Maybe I was born with it. Maybe some unconscious fear frightened me during the war. I truly do not know and thank God they are *moments passagers*, fleeting moments, like you say in France. Let's not talk about it. They pass quickly."

He realized that there were a whole lot of things that he did not know about Gaby.

They arrived at the castle very late, fatigued and starved.

She reached for his hand and brought it to her lips.

"Today was grandiose, thank you," she whispered.

Upon their arrival, Ribaud was already waiting in the library. He had arrived a day earlier and had been looking for the couple all day.

"Well, you two love birds, an ungodly hour to arrive home, I should say." He smiled at Gaby. "A real pleasure to see you again, Gabriella. How do you like our youthful summer playgrounds?"

Reserved, Gaby shot him a distrustful glance.

"It's absolutely magnificent, Ribaud. We had a glorious day. When did you arrive in Normandy?" she asked politely.

"Late last night. I drank a bit too much last evening." He looked toward her sheepishly, remembering her pointed comments at the terrasse of the Hotel in Cannes. "I did not want a repeat performance of our slight disagreement in Cannes. Instead, I wanted to be on my best behavior to make you aware of my polite and reserved nature and to show you my gentle manners." He smiled sweetly.

"What a long way you take to say I'm sorry," She laughed and walked to him, extending her hand. He pulled her to him and kissed her on both cheeks.

"That's the French way, Gabriella."

"But you're English, Ribaud," she responded amused.

"Ah, but when it comes to you, I wish I was French."

Jean-Louis marched toward his friend.

"I'm glad you did not show up last night, I would have had to share Gaby, today. By the way, did you know that Boudin is in town? The exhibit was a disaster, I understand; all the attending artists were quite upset. It's too bad for the ones that have families. It makes it hard for them to coalesce to their true art ideal. We will have to go to Montmartre and take Gaby when we return to Paris. She had a fabulous time today."

The three of them sat on the red velvet sofas in front of the fireplace.

"Have you met Madame Perideot, Gaby? Your opinion?" Ribaud questioned.

"She appears to be very dedicated to Jean-Louis." Gaby replied, reserved.

"And . . .?" Ribaud pursued.

"And—she has been very nice to me." She did not want to disparage Jean-Louis's favorite old lady.

Ribaud laughed.

"Watch her, Gaby. He is the only one that counts in her life— always has, always will. Some advice: do not reprimand him while she's around—I know your fast retort, I have experienced it first hand—lest you want to remain in bed with the runs for the rest of your stay in Normandy." Gaby looked around to see if Hawkeye was around before smiling at Ribaud statement.

"I see that you learn quickly. Another asset to your incredible personae," he replied.

The men spoke about the invited guests and naturally gossiped about the *guests' petites amies*. She wondered why Elise was not coming, although she was delighted about it. One less insolent to deal with, Gaby thought.

"Is Elise in Normandy as well? Did she accompany you?"

"No," Ribaud looked at Jean-Louis questioningly. Jean-Louis shook his head. "I presume that we should tell Gaby." Ribaud started once more.

"For the past ten years, Elise has been madly in love with a maniac—a mad man. Elise loves life and men, I should add as well, and the Count is an obsessively jealous old goat."

"Not again," Jean-Louis interrupted. "She sent out a note about a month ago and she did not make any allusion to Gillet. I thought they were fine. Besides, I was so consumed with Gaby's whereabouts that I really did not pay much heed to her calling. What happened?"

"As usual, at a gala she was giving in Paris for her birthday, inebriated to the hilt, he reverted to his sordid accusations, in front of his wife and many friends he indicted her as Paris' most famous harlot. It did not stop at that. He named many in the room who had shared her bed and divulged many sensual notes that she had written to him and flung all of them on the dance floor. I saw her a couple days ago. She could not show her face here, for certain. Naturally she talks the talk, she rages that she will press charges this time, this time she will not relent, she says—you know, the same story," Ribaud explained sadly.

Gabby was stunned.

"Are you talking about Elise, your common friend?" she asked.

"Yes, unfortunately." Ribaud continued. "Gaby, we have done the utmost. Jean-Louis put him in a hospital for more than a month when it first happened. She returned to him and worse, visited him to comfort him in the hospital. After all, it was his jealousy that made him react to her *petite aventure,* like a raving beast. That's been her explanation time and time again. The second and third time I almost killed him myself, but the explanation is always the same—she has to change, she says, be less flirtatious. After all, 'he adores me. He is a gentle heart who does not know how to handle his love for me' and so forth you know where I'm going. This has been going on for ten years, Gaby, and although it breaks both of our hearts—she is a childhood friend, now we just go with the flow. There is very little we can do."

Gaby did not say anything, but her eyes spoke volume.

"She has no recourse with the government?" she asked.

"With the government? Gabriella, you are in Europe. Married men have rights over their wives, unless there are extreme cases of battery. Elise is just a mistress. What right would she have?"

Gaby kept silent.

"Often the laws on the books are overlooked, sad but true. So the right of a *maitresse attitrée* does not hold much weight."

"I presume I'm taking the high and mighty road, but I should not be much surprised for battery is a common form of assault on married women in the United States as well."

Jean-Louis changed the subject and wanted to know who was coming with whom.

"Do you know who will be in attendance tomorrow on the women's side?" Ribaud asked. "Sorry, Gabriella, but I'm single and still looking for a good time."

She smiled. "As long as you don't expect Jean-Louis to follow in your footsteps!" She shot him a hard look.

"You mean to tell me we cannot follow him in your bed chamber?"

"Ribaud!" she exclaimed shocked. "You were being amusing, correct?" She demanded half jokingly, recalling the scene on the yatch in Cannes.

"Not really, Gabriella. I find you absolutely gorgeous, so if Jean-Louis wants to share some happy moments with his best friends—I'm ready and willing."

Gaby's eyes opened so wide that Jean-Louis realized that all the warm friendly feelings she was developing for his friend were soon deteriorating into contempt and hatred.

Not a good move. Ribaud did not know when to stop. They had had some wild times in these rooms upstairs and downstairs. But now, Gaby was the new player in that duo and she totally sufficed him sexually. The idea that she could be sexually involved with someone else than him—he could not fathom. He'd kill the fellow. He was getting old. He laughed and put a stop to the nonsense.

"Ribaud, you are destroying, *à grand pas,* quickly, the efforts at character rehabilitation you worked so diligently at, these past two hours. Be aware that you may become a persona non-grata in our household. Gaby may not allow me to spend much time with you, my friend." Jean-Louis retorted.

"You were teasing, Ribaud?" Gaby smiled, half suspicious.

"But of course, ma chère. Who do you think we are, part of the ordinary populace? We have a name and lineage to represent, Gaby. Alors." This last ironical sentence was pronounced with some sadness in his usual jovial tone of voice.

The men continued to talk. Italy surfaced again, but by then Gaby was having a hard time staying awake. Jean-Louis had taken her in his arms and she was waking and sleeping. He did not want to take her upstairs, she felt so sweet and vulnerable in his arms. However, he looked forward to a long night with his friend. Ribaud wanted to talk. The party and the drinking had just started.

Looking at Gaby, Ribaud asked how her health was.

"Well," Jean-Louis responded calmly.

"Is your love as intense, now that you are living together? Any doubts?"

Jean-Louis did not verbally answer. He shook his head instead. Awaiting a response, Gaby looked up at him and caught him off guard.

"Yes?" she asked.

"You little witch, you were pretending to sleep so as to listen to my most private conversation with my friend." He retorted shocked at her coyness.

"It cannot be that private, if it involves me as well."

"I should have known better and talked all about my sensual liaisons in Paris to teach you a lesson.

"You did not answer Ribaud's question," she pursued, wide-awake by now.

"No, Gaby, I have no doubts, you're here to stay," he said simply.

"Good, I love him too, Ribaud." She replaced her sleepy head back on his chest, her long hair spread on his torso. He caressed her dark brown locks and kissed it.

She woke up in their bed. He was sound asleep, his heavy leg over her hips holding her prisoner. For a long time she did not move.

Instead she let her fingers rest on his thigh as she pressed her back closer to his body.

By eleven o'clock the servants were already transporting trunks from some of the arriving guests.

Jean-Louis had checked the stables. He had asked a few questions about the preparation for the hunt the following day. Everything was ready.

One thing that Gaby was not aware of was that one of Jean-Louis' long-time paramours Simone De Goffaut was coming with one of his closest friends. She had first started a light flirtatious relationship with Jean-Marie Boucautier mainly to get some news from Jean-Louis.

Simone was witty, amusing, and Jean-Marie was terribly in love with her. Jean-Louis personally did not care either way. He had deep ties to Jean-Marie and knew him as a man of integrity. That was fine with him; the couple seemed to be happy. He was pleased for his friend. Simone was a nice girl, very understanding but a bit conniving and sticky. He hoped Jean-Marie had not gotten in over his head with her. He did not want to see the few male friends he possessed to be taken advantage of. Jean-Louis was quite protective when it came to their happiness. The women, well, he liked them all—in bed. Until Gaby, the clout that the little witch had on him was just as astonishing to him as the rest of his acquaintances, until they got to know her. He was going to think long and hard before leaving her behind when time came to depart for Italy.

He needed to stay close to Gaby. The very articulate Simone was always ready and willing to humiliate a few members of his close circle with her keen understanding of the human soul. With Gaby, the venom would flow as well. Poor Gaby, she had gone through enough difficulties these last few months, no need to make her sad in his home. In their home, he corrected his thinking. He needed to—no, he wanted to think in these lines. The introductions had already taken place and everyone was having a jolly old time eating with relish an absolutely scrumptious lunch.

The women had decided to do the pastoral thing and pick apples. The farmers had extended large white sheets below the trees so as to facilitate the pickings. She remembered apple-picking times in

Philippe's orchards. They would run like wild monkeys from tree to tree and throw down as many apples as they could. Tita and Gustav would then make applesauce. Well, this well structured activity was downright dull, she thought.

She finally left the group and walked away from the ladies. She climbed on one of the trees that had two large trunks and sat on the converging branches. It did not have many blossoms or fruits, but it had a killer view of the river and further down the line she could see La Manche, the North Sea. She must have been there for a while, for who should show up with Jean-Louis but Simone De Goffaut. The couple was coming down the majestic alley leading to the orchard.

Gaby thought that she would die. She was immobilized. Both walked toward the gigantic tree with the double trunks and as fate would have it, Jean-Louis and Simone decided to sit on one of the trunks directly below the area where she was perched high in the tree.

"Jean-Louis, I do not understand your rationale. You certainly recall what we had. You adored me or maybe," she said softly, "I adored you. But we belong to the same world, we laugh at the same things, our culture, our language, we have a connection. We know about each other, you know I never held back on your freedom, your escapades, as the press called it. It would be the same now, Jean-Louis. You could have the little colonial as often as you wish. But we had a wonderful relationship. Mon Dieu, Jean-Louis, she has been caught climbing trees, Françoise just told me, she saw her with her own eyes. You're in love with an ordinary monkey. I just don't understand. She will stain your name. It will get old very soon, I assure you. I know you too well and this time I will be gone. I will not wait for you," Simone said assertively.

"Simone, go and have a good life. Jean-Marie loves you. I doubt very much that Gaby was climbing trees, but even if she was, she is here to stay. I truly love her and there is no changing that," he concluded candidly.

"Very well," the beautiful Simone said, "if the colonies have changed you that much, then you have become as ordinary as they are. Stay with your southern monkey. You are absolutely correct. I have wasted my youthful years waiting for your return." She left in *an effete of* frilly jupons, petty coats and many layered skirts.

Perched high up on the canopy, Gaby wandered how to climb down without being noticed. Thank God she wore beautiful tailored pants with high leather boots. She waited until Jean-Louis almost disappeared and then began the slow descent on the opposite trunk. She had almost made it down to the ground, when she realized that Ribaud had noticed her and was walking towards her. She placed her fingers over her mouth, her eyes supplicating him not to appear to walk her way. He understood right away, and passed right by the tree, feigning not to see anything out of the ordinary. She quickly directed herself towards the reeds on the bank of the river, and stepped into a small barge. God she was safe. She hoped that Ribaud would not make fun of her in front of the other women and certainly not tell Jean-Louis. She watched him rejoin the group and no one looked back. He had not said anything to the women and for that she was ever so thankful. Years later, she would have a lot more to be thankful for, but meanwhile, she considered him her best friend.

Jean-Louis returned toward the house looking for Gaby. He found her calmly returning from the river. A big smile on her face, she opened her arms and ran toward him.

"Where have you been?" she asked lovingly.

"Let me ask you the same question. Everybody is looking for you. I've been told you were climbing trees."

"Jean-Louis, seriously, what lies are being pounded into your head, you surely don't believe that. Of course not, I decided to take the barquette to understand what Boudin stated yesterday when he was explaining to us about light and the new landscape painting."

"I wish you would stay close to me, Miss Explorer."

He took her forearm and pulled her to him.

"Are you enjoying the guests?" he asked.

"Extremely so. You have wonderful friends, except for their boring ways of picking apples. I would have rather been with your good friends. Was the hunt fun?"

"It was, chérie, I'll take you next week. We will go, just you and I."

"What is next, Jean-Louis?"

"A moment of respite from our guests. Everyone is doing their own thing." He took her in his arms and led her back toward the river.

"I missed you, Gaby." He bent down and kissed her temple. As he stroked the long mahogany mane, his fingers felt a prickly thorn. He gently swirled her around, sure enough she had thorn and white blossom flowers along the long curls flowing down her back.

"Gaby, you lied, you were in the apple trees." He was flabbergasted.

"Jean-Louis, stop, that is absurd, what would I be doing in a tree? I may be spontaneous and a bit too reactive or proactive, but truly, climbing trees in front of your guests. Unthinkable, chérie."

"Gaby, you're a great actress, but I don't believe a word. My friend Ribaud would say, "proof is in the pudding. You were in that tree, admit it," he laughed with great gusto as he fanned her hair out in front of her eyes. You little devil. Your mane is filled with thorns and white blossoms."

Caught in the act, she stopped pretending.

"I'm so sorry, Jean-Louis. I was so bored I hid in one of the trees and then I saw the boats in the ocean. It reminded me of Biloxi, Mississippi, when Philippe and I would go and visit his aunt Miss Sadau Lirette. Her home was right next to the Beauvoir's House. It was a wood plantation at the time; it later became Jefferson Davis' home after the end of the Civil war. The poor fellow—even his own daughter married a northern abolitionist.

"The home was located right on the coast, overlooking the Gulf of Mexico. We would sit on a semblance of beach early in the morning. A myriad of birds would wake us every morning at around 5:15. It was like a symphony that neither of us wanted to miss. It was our daily fix. Maybe our sense of music developed into a full-fledged talent there. We would sing our hearts out, right there on the beach with only the pelicans as our audience."

"Did you know that in 1720 Biloxi was the administrative capital of the original Louisiana Purchase?" he questioned curious.

"Yes, before it was moved to New Orleans, I believe. But anyhow we sat on the jettee, all in a row, watching the horizon for the return of the shrimp boats. All the boats had their nets pulled up toward mid-ship to keep the shrimp inside, away from the scavenger birds. Incredible memories indeed," she sighed. "The fishermen would throw out their nets early in the evening. This was our routine, you know, we also pointed ourselves on the beach at around eight or nine o'clock at night. The fishermen would sail their boats from the small harbor in front of the lighthouse and then one by one would come out, their nets extended like giant dark witches extending their black cloaks to catch as many sinful souls as they could. We adored watching these boats at night. Before nightfall, the nets would be held high in the air and dropped late at night with only a few lights illuminating the dark waters of the Gulf. Then the fishermen would lower their nets—the moment of retributions had arrived. I was mesmerized every night."

"I can see where your theatrics developed," Jean-Louis retorted, impressed that she had shared all theses memories. She rarely spoke about her childhood. "You have the ability to take pleasure in the smallest of wonders. A Captain in my own right, I probably would have gladly cut the strings of those annoying shrimpers. Knowing how you romanticized these simple men, I will never excoriate the values of these fishermen."

She smiled, a wide, kind, beautiful smile. "It brought back wonderful memories, Jean-Louis, I couldn't tear myself away from the sight."

Jean-Louis looked down at her gently. Gaby was an artist in the true sense of the word. Everything rang a bell in her pretty little head, even the simplest manifestation of life. She truly lived and that was one of the incalculable reasons for his great love for her. His past life appeared empty when he looked back upon it. He adored her. Where had she been? He felt that somehow she had always been present, maybe a spiritual connection. Thank God, she was younger than he was. Some of the wild times he had practiced, namely in this town, in this castle, with his friends, had been *ennivrant*, intoxicating.

In retrospect, he was looking at another version of himself. An uncontrollable one—one that could not be repeated nor truly continued, he no longer aimed for that type of thrill. However, it was his past, it was going to be left at that. He'd tasted it all, the good, the bad, and the downright ugly.

Now, Gaby was with him and the world had changed. He wanted to have an impact in the world. His goal was to help shape Europe's into a modern society where the continuous wars of the past could be replaced with trade amongst the major players on the continent and abroad. All played a part in the scheme of things. Listening to his adventuresome lover, he'd realized he'd have to keep a muzzle on her. She had it in her to do wild things and she was fearless. In Italy however she'd become indispensable. Her cousin's close relationship with the Pope was propitious. Besides he loved the total surrender of her body, "on a golden platter" she'd teased. It would be an attractive distraction.

He would take her to Villefranche. If the negotiations took longer than required, it would be easier to travel there both by boat and by carriages. Besides she loved the area and security would be easier to handle than in a larger city. Yes, that is exactly what he would do. Her music, well, that would be hard in the south of France. He would talk to the Prince of Monaco. She might be able to get involved in the art community in Monaco. Yes, Villefranche it was.

"I will never do that again. I swear, darling. I'll never embarrass you again." Her voice was sweet and apologetic.

"Gaby, I found it hilarious. My only concern with your impetuosity rests on these idiots' reactions. I do not want to see you embarrassed when you are by yourself in Paris."

"No one will embarrass me, Jean-Louis. I will not let it happen. I will not socialize with anyone I don't like. I'm not too fond of many of your friends and they do not seem to think much of me, either, but I can assure you of one think, my voice will always mesmerized. I will still pack most of them at the opéra!"

"Except, Gaby, you will be asked to go to events on my account, on my behalf. You do not have to go, chérie, but it may be fun."

"Jean-Louis, I really do not need all this *beau monde*. I have my own life and goals."

He did not reply, but he took her in his arms and kissed her temple, her cheeks, and her neck.

"Your job, your goal is just to love me, Gaby," he murmured in her ears.

"That job, I take very seriously, darling. I always will."

She bundled her tiny body close to his and pulled on his shirt to giggle in his mouth.

"I love you with all my heart."

He kissed her nose. "Grow up, Shorty." They ran back to the castle and raced to their room like two kids looking for candy.

All these long evenings were taking their toll on her wakefulness. She felt dead tired and when he woke up later in the afternoon, she could not pull herself out of bed.

"Jean-Louis, will you handle all formalities with your friends for a while longer. You wore me out, darling."

He walked downstairs. She could hear the maids greeting him and Madame Perideot asking about her health.

"Just perfect," she heard him say with a voice that did not leave much room for extra comments.

Gaby fell back soundly asleep.

Later in the afternoon, she dressed and went downstairs. The halls appeared quiet and she decided she was going to wait for their guests in the salon. Their guests—she liked the sound of it. Madame Perideot passed by in the foyer and gave her a forced smile, which she mirrored, giving her a dazzling pearly white agreeable expression that said, 'I want you to like me.'

The old woman did not give Gaby the illusion that her wishes had been granted. She was always polite with her and as of today she had not been poisoned. Jean-Louis was fine as well. The old woman was on her best behavior. Gaby decided that she would continue her acts of kindness to this less than malleable woman. In retrospect, she may have been the perfect stalwart to prepare the great Duke De Pleyssis for the less than conformant mores of his American lover.

To her surprise, Ribaud was in the salon, drinking brandy and reading the paper.

"Ribaud, you gave up on all the activities as well. Only the French, I suppose, are able to show us up. I was exhausted after this morning." She smiled coyly. "I owe you. I was petrified that you would use my less than feminine hobby as a mean of humiliation with the others, especially Jean-Louis. Thank you. He found out on his own after all."

Ribaud flashed a gentle, sweet smile back and walked back toward the side bar.

"Would you care for a brandy, Gabriella?" he asked politely.

"Yes, that would be wonderful." She had never seen Ribaud with a morose expression on his face. She followed him on the sofa and sat on the other side. To her surprise he took comfort in an Indian style arrangement on the plush velvety couch, his legs and feet crisscrossed in front of him. This position did not fit the atmosphere of the room. Something was wrong with the picture. Comfort was not the aura that the room imposed on the spirit of the onlooker. She sat directly across from him on the soft plushy red velvet cushion. Prim and proper as a perfect little lady should.

"So you like to climb trees, Gabriella? I loved watching your sheepish expression, this morning. Although I do not know you well, I assume I am one of the few who has seen it. I presume it is not in your nature to beg. You appear to be a woman who gets what she wants, when she wants it, and how she wants it. Therefore, I treasure that expression doubly. I will have to place it into my little pocketbook of paybacks."

"You scoundrel!" she grinned unwilling to affirm his comments, instead she changed the subject. " I assume that it is not in your habit to look so glum," she replied with a smirk, "May I ask what is bothering you?"

"These days, it does not seem to be too diverse. I am deadly in love."

"Deadly? What a way to describe this incomprehensible sensation that does not bypass anyone."

"Sometimes Gaby, I wish I could die. The feeling takes over my entire being. I'm in love with someone that I cannot have, nor will ever allow myself to marry."

"Why?" The statement sparked her curiosity. What was it with these aristocrats? They had the influence, the power, and the financial assets to achieve all they wished for in their society and yet they thrived on placing stumbling blocks on every stone that they walked on.

"The young, beautiful woman that is, and has been the subject of my attentions for years, will marry next year. She has become betrothed to an older man and will move out of London in the countryside, near Edinburgh. She will become a true country bumpkin. Away from me, from our amorous life, and there is not a damn thing that I can do about it."

"She has fallen out of love with you, Ribaud?"

"No, we adore one another, that is not the issue nor the problem. She has turned down many suitors over the years, but now, her father has died and there is pressure for her to marry and start a family."

"I don't quite understand. Let me get this right—you love her, she loves you, you are both single—what is the problem? You do not want to get married?"

"Yes and no, Gaby. I would like to, but I can't. We come from dissimilar backgrounds. My lineage is perfect and highly in demand. For all our money and influence, we still have to follow the rules of society. When we grow up, we wait until the last possible moment to decide on this momentous event that is marriage. In a family like mine, I need to find a family whose name and fortune equals mine, whose status equals mine. My only duty in life is to accumulate power, wealth and mostly influence on the Royals. Certainly, Berthe could have continued on as my mistress. It is not uncommon in England. However, the woman I am to marry would probably make Berthe's life a wretched mess. Berthe has chosen not to take this path after all and frankly I have known for quite some time that I would not, could not, put her through this emotionally charged ordeal. She chose the high road. She is absolutely correct in that sense."

Gaby was astounded at what she was hearing. To some extent, the explanation applied to her as well. The nun's speeches in Grenoble mirrored that very same thinking. She lost her polite composure and placed both of her feet on the sofa with both hands encircling her bended knees. She faced Ribaud, her expressive wide eyes staring with curiosity. She listened intently to his explanation of the English aristocratic culture, knowing damn well that the French traditions could not be far behind. Very much aware of what she was thinking, he looked at her and grinned. Gaby was adorable, charming, he understood that, but also very intuitive and smart. Her intellect was far beyond most women he had met. He knew many witty, charming, artistic women, essentially the women he played with. Gaby, however, was a *mélange,* mix, of both. She had the capacity to delineate, evaluate, and quickly diffuse a proposed situation. That very same capacity could be used to inflame, as well. He had been at the receiving end of her sharp, acid-like retorts in St. Tropez. He had deserved her pointed remarks and she had not been shy at dishing them out. But here, he'd opened up to her for he knew she could relate and she appeared to be non-judgmental. He had the feeling that she could be trusted and could empathize.

Ribaud was a handsome fellow. Women must like him, she thought. She did not want to think of their wild times with Jean-Louis, nor of the consequences that may be luring around the corner.

"Ribaud," she said assertively, "you are a very handsome man, and influential at that. Explain to me why is it so important to deprive yourself of emotional happiness? Times are changing. Look at me and Jean-Louis," she stopped and paused a while longer.

"Do you think your sort in life is the exact one that is awaiting me? Do I believe in Papa Noël? Santa Claus, as we say at home?" Large tears appeared in her gigantic, communicative green eyes.

"I know where you are going with that, Gabriella. However, I also believe that our situations are worlds apart. You see, I am an only child and unlike Jean-Louis, I revere my family. Besides Berthe, my love for my parents and my grandparents is immense. My role, the one I eventually will have to submit to, will be the continuation of the lineage within the rules of the English peerage, Gabriella. You see Jean-Louis has no allegiance to his lineage. It drives his Grandmother mad. His allegiance is to humankind. This is where your chance of success in your relationship lies with Jean-Louis. He will take the risk of his lifetime with you, without even thinking for a second about his responsibility to name and family. His goals are more grandiose, on a larger global scale than any of us present here in this great ancestral castle."

Gaby was astounded at his perspective of her timid future. *He will take you to Italy, malgré all the rhetoric he professes.*

"Italy? What do you know?" she questioned.

At this inopportune time, Jean-Louis walked in the room, irked at seeing the woman he adored and his best friend together in such a chummy atmosphere. Never mind Villefranche, he was taking her to Italy. They would just have to double the intelligence and security if they wanted him. He might even marry her if it came to that. Irritated by seeing both of them so animated and not noticing his entrance, so involved in their conversation, his annoyance showed in his tone of voice as he walked to the side bar.

"I'm terribly sorry to interrupt such an intense tête-à-tête," he haughtily proclaimed.

She turned her head to watch him walk to the bar and then back toward them.

"Ribaud was sharing with me the malaise of your aristocratic century. I realize that with all of your influence, power, and worldly goods you are truly prisoners of your lives. You should follow in Jean-Louis' footsteps, Ribaud. Go to America. You have a lot to learn from us."

The two men, flabbergasted at such a response, pondered on her directness and then on what she had alleged.

"Gaby, I can't believe that this type of situation is seldom seen in the United States. After all, I know many Americans who come to England and France. They do not seem too different than us. They like women, they like a good time, and from what I have seen, their sexual diversion is as perverse as ours—married or not. Look, Gaby, the rumor ran rampant that Jefferson himself had brought his black mistress to France with him. Come on, not all is rosy on your side of the Atlantic."

"You are correct, Ribaud, and I do realize that I am fortunate. I am of good lineage, as you say, although nothing compared to yours." Neither knew if she was kidding or being facetious. "The difference lies in my financial independence and also of having displayed in a most consistent manner my manly qualities—that of being a good businesswoman. Do not be mistaken, however; being married to someone to coalesce family wealth, titles, or influence is certainly well regarded and coveted by many fathers. However, I was not ostracized because I decided otherwise. That, to me, is an enlightened spirit. We call it freedom in my country. Granted, it is just a beginning, we still have a long way to go. However, the trend has started. Do you understand? I just can't fathom you renouncing your love, your emotional ties to someone, because you need to bring in more money, more land, and more titles to your family. It sounds absurd in our day and time."

"Well, it's not that absurd, Gabriella, even in your liberated America," Simone said as she entered the room. Gaby saw Hawkeye watching the scene from the entrance of the side bar. "Passion and love last but a few short months at the masculine level." She glanced at Jean-Louis. "One can be affectionate with almost anyone who has the same background, cultural mores, interests, lively spirit, and language. Therefore, why sacrifice all of the above mentioned by our dear friends for a few months of perfect bliss. Men have emotional and carnal moments countless times throughout their lives. Clearly, we women are at the losing end of the stick. In these circumstances, our lack of rights in our society is a curse on our sex. I understand you are well read. The literary *ouvrages,* books that you have read are not all lies, ma chérie."

Gaby looked up calmly at the statuesque blonde.

"My point precisely, Simone, Ribaud here, is a man of means and culture. Maybe it is his responsibility to show the world that he has been touched by the works of Voltaire and Diderot and Mallarmé, to enlighten England and his contemporaries there, so to speak." She looked up coyly at Jean-Louis, and then back unperturbed at Simone. "Jean-Louis and I are doing our share." These last words were pronounced ruthlessly as if icy boulders were rolling down uncontrollably on thick icebergs.

Usually witty with the retorts, Simone was silenced. The tension could have been cut with a knife.

Madame Perideot to the rescue. She walked in slowly and politely asked Jean-Louis about the ball this evening. The wheater was clement, could the servants set up table and collation in the gardens. Jean-Louis smiled at her, pleased that his dear nounou came to the rescue at this most uncomfortable gathering of conflicting minds.

He stood up, indicating that the party was over.

"It sounds wonderful. Come, Gaby let's go upstairs. See you later, Ribaud. Good day, Simone."

Without so much as a word, he reached for Gaby's hand, pulled her up from the couch, and led her away from the salon. The little brat was going to cause a world war. As they left the room, he reached for her and kissed her.

"I have more pressing things to do right now," he added, she looked up questioningly, "like controlling you." He laughed, picking her up in his arms and walking upstairs.

He bent down and kissed her cheeks and lips one more time.

"I love you, Gaby."

Jean-Louis took Gaby to bed. Undressing first, he rolled next to her, pulling her loose peasant shirt away from her shoulders as he began to fondle her bare breasts.

"You have the most perfect body, chérie. I love it that you do not wear brassieres, jupons, and petticoats. I want you way too often to fend off these niceties."

"Should I just walk around stark naked all day, a sex slave to the service of the great Jean-Louis De Pleyssis, waiting impatiently from minute to minute to comfort his soothing and comforting habits, my darling?"

"Wonderful idea, Gaby. When our guests leave, we will start a new routine."

She softly threw the pillow over his head.

"Tell me, Jean-Louis, I want to know about Italy, it appears to be the talk of the town. I know what you said the other day and I had no reason to doubt your words. However, if everyone is aware of whatever is going to happen in Italy, I find it only reasonable that you should talk to me about it."

Pulling her hands away from his buttocks and placing them over her head, he turned her over and lay heavily on top of her.

"I don't want to talk about it now, Gaby. When the time is ripe, we will. That's all." He kissed her gently on the lips and the tip of her nose. Seeing that she was not finished on the subject he silenced her with a passionate kiss. She pulled her face away from him, to the side.

"I want to know, Jean-Louis, tell me, I will not relent. Are you planning to take me? You will not leave me behind, will you?"

Rising on his elbows, Jean-Louis voice hardened.

"Gaby, cease immediately. I said I did not want to talk about it. You will not end my silence now, if that is your intent."

"It has nothing to do with power. I want to know your intentions. It is my future as well after all. I must know."

He did not answer, but his anger showed through.

She remembered the day of the storm on the ship when she had not obeyed his order. She presumed returning to the easy life of *la vie Parisienn,* had not changed him much. The Duke had a short fuse.

He let himself down on her cruelly, as if wanting to silence her by affecting her lung capacity. His lips pursed and with his expression devoid of any emotion, he pushed her thighs apart with his strong pelvis, preparing to enjoy the moment.

She was quite sure that he did not want her to enjoy this moment, however she pursued assertively.

"I want to know, Jean-Louis—are you taking or leaving me behind? Don't expect me to be waiting for you if you leave me behind," she countered with a long quavering breath as she shot a sideways cold stare in his eyes.

"Don't threaten me, Gaby. That has never worked with me and never will, not even if the threat comes from you."

"I'm not threatening, Jean-Louis. I'm stating a fact, my life will be affected by your decision." She replied forcefully, not letting him off the hook.

In one clean sweep, he rolled away from her, pulled on his pants, and headed towards the door.

Gaby turned on her stomach and watched him stride through the room.

Before exiting, he glared at her once more. For a split second she witnessed surprise in his eyes and thought that he would return. He didn't. He turned on his heels, walked out, and slammed the door behind him. Unperturbed, she climbed out of bed, got dressed one more time, and picked up the book that Ribaud had lent to her yesterday afternoon. Mallarmé had written it about his friends, the Impressionists. She hoped she would meet him soon. Oblivious of the time, she climbed back on their bed and started reading.

Jean-Louis returned to the room two hours later, surprised to see her in the same position he'd left her in but clothed and with a book. He did not utter a word. He undressed fully, sat next to her, untied the back of the blouse and unbuttoned the back of her skirt. In one swift motion he ripped it off and placed his naked body on her back, his hand pressing the mound above her womb to him. He pushed his lower body deep inside her. She moaned and let her face fall on the book. He kissed her cheeks, his breath reeked of alcohol.

"I'll take you with me," he murmured and kissed her smiling mouth into oblivion. "By God, I'd die if I had to be away from you once more."

She smiled. She was getting quite good at getting the grand master to see things her way.

* * *

The couple could hear the household come alive when they woke up from their afternoon nap. They both readied up quickly and went downstairs to meet their guests.

"Gabriella, will you bless us with your magnificence? Ribaud asked. "The orchestra is ready for you."

"Very well, I would love to," she replied gaily.

Madame Perideot nodded to Simone. What were these two concocting, Ribaud asked himself in passing. He had caught the look of complicity between the two women.

Small rosewood tables held drinks and scrumptious hors d'oeuvres: Beignets à la Normande with bottles of Mâcon village white wine, asperges en sauce à la crème with a terrific wine coteaux de l'Aubance that she liked immensely, champignons de Paris with cream and for those who preferred fruits and sweets, ananas au Saumur and bavarois de Framboises au cassis, naturally flutes of Cristal covered many silver platters as butlers passed the dry champagne around. It was Gaby's favorite.

"Did you know Gaby, that it was created for a Russian Tsar Alexander II, it has an equal mix of the finest Pinot noir and Chardonnay grapes?" Ribaud told her.

"No, I did not Ribaud, but frankly I don't care!" she responded flippantly after she drained the flute.

"Ah Gaby, you're one in a million!" He'd countered as he'd brought her crashing against his chest, unable to contain his mirth. The episode was not lost on Simone and Madame Perideot.

Jean-Louis walked toward one of the large chairs that had been set up around the ballroom. He sat down, one of his long legs crossed sideways over his knee. He reached for a brandy while a butler bent over to lit the Duke's cigar. The expensive scent of the Havana cigar permeated the sitting room. He had a difficult time accepting Gaby as an artist. And yet, that was the reason why she had come to France. Among his friends, he was more accepting of her art. She enthralled with her singing—surely she displayed the most beautiful voice he had ever heard. She should keep it for him, then, he thought. He would truly appreciate it. There was no need for the world to see her as an entertainer. He could foresee conflicts in their relationships over her artistic nature. Perhaps he should build a theater in his home. It was all the rage in Paris. She then would have no reason to perform at the opéra, he deducted. In his home, he could choose their guests. Quite pleased with the novel idea, he watched her walk with confidence toward the orchestra. She spoke to the maestro for a short moment. Jean-Louis admired her demanding profile. He could tell that the leader of the orchestra was giving her advice that she did not like. It was perverse. He loved that look of stubbornness, although he had wanted to strangle her a few times because of it. But she had substance and an indomitable character—a bit too much for her own good.

The orchestra, and then the tenor and sopranos began the musical program. And then, not unlike the performance in St. Tropez or at the opéra, Gaby focused her melodies to first attract attention to the aria. Again, she was splendid. Sensually, he watched her amble away from the group, her insolent gaze focused on him. The aria "Habanera" should have been written for her, he thought.

He smirked. She threatened. Passion emanated from her person, she had taken over the stage. All in the ballroom stood silent waiting for the enigmatic brunette's next roucoulement, instead her unremitting flare for emanating drama sparked as she marched to the beat inches away from him. She tapped her heel fiercely on the parquet floor and immediately flicked her castagnettes as she snatched her multi colored skirts up and above her knee. She stared him down with a knowing glance and quickly jerked her gaze and body away in an effervescent shrill of frilly satin skirt. At the end, she retreated rythmically back toward the orchestra.

The guests, entranced with her voice and expressive dramatics, again stood silent to take in what had just happened and then they broke into loud, "Brava, Brava!" She was astonishing as she basked in her glory, Jean-Louis thought, annoyed. She bowed her head elegantly and proceeded to return to her position next to Jean-Louis.

"One more, Gabriella," many guests solicited.

She heaved a long melancholic sigh, glanced at Jean-Louis, and burst out laughing.

"Another time, perhaps. Jean-Louis took me to Normandy to rest."

"Eh bien," Madame Perideot exclaimed, "Jean-Louis' great concertos could be next. You would enlighten the life of an old maid who has eyes only for the great Jean-Louis-Pierre De Pleyssis," she requested shyly.

Stunned, Jean-Louis shook his head. He had not seen this one coming.

"That is sinful, Jean-Louis-Pierre," Simone exclaimed. "Madame Perideot learned how to play solely to help you practice. Do you recall, Jean-Louis, your father was not too friendly towards entertai— artists." She glared at Gaby who did not lower her emerald gaze.

"Surely, certainly," Simone advanced, "you have not forgotten the warm, lovely moments we shared around the old grand." Simone walked slowly, sensuously toward Jean-Louis. She reached for his hand that was now nonchalantly resting on the armrest of the chair.

He smiled at her and his old nursemaid as he stood up and sauntered to the piano. He sat on the embroidered armless bench. Simone sat close by and hummed the hymn she wanted him to play.

Jean-Louis began Beethoven's Fifth Symphony. Ludwig van Beethoven, he was not, Gaby mused, but quite impressive, nonetheless. Simone was in seventh heaven and Gaby walked toward the piano, mesmerized by the music and also by her lover's musical gift.

The scoundrel, she had wondered why the piano held the place of honor in his home in Villefranche. He looked up to her and winked.

She waved her elongated fingers and continued to look at him adoringly. Gaby was not the only one looking adoringly at Jean-Louis. Simone touched and rubbed his back, lowering her face to his ears as she hummed the melodious pieces. He quickly interrupted the opus, stood up, and walked to Gaby. He reached for her hand, gathered her in his arms as he ambled back with Gaby in tow, and nodded to the coveted place next to him on the bench.

Mortified by such a lack of nicety, Simone angrily pushed away and strode out of the room, not to be seen again for the rest of the evening. Jean-Marie followed right on her heels.

Perideot evaluated the situation with a knowing gaze. Simone was out. Gabriella De Conte Thornsen was in. She needed to make some adjustments—quickly. On a lighter note, she was just thrilled to listen to him play. They would have some lovely musical evenings. The old maid quickly revised her plan of action.

"You are wonderful darling, I never in my . . ." Gaby begun.

"There is a lot that you 'never in my life' don't know about me," he said, brushing his lips to her earlobe. She trembled. He did it again and this time she stayed close.

"What would you like me to play?" he asked.

"Schuman, *Arabeske*."

Jean-Louis smiled. He knew well why she'd asked for Schumann's most reflective work. Schumann composed most of his piano music for his wife, Clara Wieck, who was a most accomplished pianist in her own right.

Jean-Louis had played the piece well and at the end he nodded to the orchestra and let the slow, romantic tunes of the violins take over while taking Gaby in his arms and kissing her passionately.

"God, I love you," he whispered, while their friends surrounded the couple.

"Jean-Louis," Ribaud called out, "we know what you will be doing when we leave. Playing the piano most surely." Jean-Louis grinned as he drew her to her feet and whirled her on the dance floor. The crowd followed.

Later that evening, Berthe Morisot, a good friend of Mallarmé, the symbolist poet, took a seat next to Gaby.

Gaby had wanted to meet with the impressionist painter. She had seen and admired her work earlier that week. Furthermore, her name had been mentioned quite a few times in Paris in the café in Monometer, as an up and coming dedicated impressionist who, unlike her sister, had persisted in following her dream. She was an artist like herself, but she had noticed the French aloofness surfaced when they had been introduced weeks earlier. Tonight, Berthe had made the first step.

"You sing with such passion, Gabriella. I'm mesmerized, completely taken by your rendition of Carmen. I could hear and visualize beautiful changing images such as the changing mood that I at times try to portray in my pictures. I loved it. I will call on you when you return to Paris. Meanwhile, visit with us while you are here in Normandy. It would be my great pleasure to have *un petit déjeuner* with you, Gabriella."

"The pleasure will be mine, Berthe," Gaby replied politely.

This was an informal gathering and many rules of etiquette had been thrown out the window this weekend. The food was fabulous and Jean-Louis's arms were glued to her shoulders.

Seeing Jean-Louis basked in his glory, it was hard to remember him on the Tempête, stern, downright mean and controlling at times.

He was a different person here, one that she liked and loved all the more.

The entertainment was about to start in the ballroom and outside.

"The François Vatel of your chateau has prepared an exquisite feast *digne* of a Prince," Gaby joked to Jean-Louis.

"I am wealthier, more powerful, and I have a better lineage than most kings and Emperors in Europe, Gaby," Jean-Louis retorted with aplomb and confidence.

Astounded, she remained silent for a few minutes as she absorbed his response.

"Seriously?" she ventured.

He nodded.

"That's terrifying." She shot him a sideways glance and then looked away. "Let's rejoin the guests," she replied sternly and began walking toward the ballroom where everyone imbibed freely of the flowing Dom Perignon.

Jean-Louis was by her side. He reached for her hand, pulled her to him, and brushed a gentle kiss on her temples.

"Two steps behind me, Miss Thornsen," he chided.

She shot him a murderous look and walked quickly to catch up to him. They entered the ballroom again. A boisterous crowd greeted them.

"Gabriella," she heard Ribaud call out to her, "enchant us my dear with your compelling voice once more. I have been dreaming of you all these months."

She extended her hand to him as he bent his head to kiss her hand, but to his utter surprise, she sweetly gathered him to her and kissed him on both cheeks.

Unconsciously, he stepped backwards.

She chuckled and burst out in a crystal clear laughter.

"I love the fearsome effect I have on you, Ribaud,"she murmured. "I bet you thought I was coming close by to bite your ear."

"Well, my dear lady, we never know what to expect with Americans. Your compatriots display mercurial behavior. Look how you repaid the British Crown for its patience with the colonials."

The crystal clear laughter echoed once more.

"I should have taken your ear off after all. Well, my friend, I will assuage your great longing for my magnificence. I will sing again— your favorite aria," she responded flirtatiously, giving him a sideways glance. Her pearly whites gleamed in a fabulous smile that seemed to mock him.

Chapter Twenty-Nine

The feast had been grandiose and for all the guests leaving Normandy this day, waking up had been a difficult task.

Gaby and Jean-Louis were standing on the large impressive marble staircase. The carriages were beginning to align. All or most had had a wonderful time and Jean-Louis had been proud to have Gaby at his side. The only glitch had been *l'histoire* with Simone. Arranged marriages or not, significant affairs were always difficult especially if the one who had been betrayed still had some tender feelings for the significant other. The couple had left without too much fanfare. At least the ordeal had been settled. Upon their return to Paris, life would be significantly easier.

He was happy that Gaby had been established as his *maîtresse attitrée.*

No doubt Simone and her friend would continue to be invited and to attend the parties in the Grand Salons. They were great fun, after all.

Now he wanted Gaby to socialize with the society, to meet, to chat, to gossip, to evaluate the great literary works of the time. She would love that type of activity and it would keep her away from her artistic ventures. He hated to see her so involved with her art. Why couldn't she enjoy watching the performances? Why did she have to be part of this lowly entertaining world? He would have to deal with all these issues later. Gaby brought him out of his dilemma.

"Jean-Louis, do you believe that Simone still cares about you?"

"It is really of no concern to me, Gaby," he responded. "I have been gone for seven years. In these types of situations, the person left behind feels a sense of loss. I presume that Simone was mortified when I left. It's really a question of posture, of not wanting to let go of someone that never belonged to you in the first place. Furthermore, I am '*recherché*," sought after, a grin lit his deep blue eyes. Again he gathered her to him and smiled down at her pretty face. Although you do not seem to care one way or the other, Miss Thornsen, others do, so watch it, ma chérie."

The guests had all left, even Ribaud, who had promised Gaby that he would seriously think about her comments on personal happiness in an impersonal world. Jean-Louis knew that Ribaud would not even entertain the idea, but he would not deliberate the issue with Gaby. It was way too close for comfort.

* * *

Since last evening, Gaby had been thinking about Italy. Jean-Louis had mentioned in no uncertain terms not to approach the subject again. It would actuate soon enough, he had said. She felt uncertain about his response. After all, Jean-Louis had been inebriated. She proceeded with her thinking, knowing quite well, that she was on shaky ground.

"Darling, I truly understand your stance on what you said to me last evening about Italy. However, now that it's bright and early, can you repeat it one more time?"

"Gaby, don't even go there," he responded with anger in his voice and an icy glare.

"But, I need to. Will you please, just one more time?"

He turned suddenly and out of self-preservation she fled. Unable to run inside for fear of being caught, she ran down the marble steps onto the large alleys that bordered the entrance and ran for dear life to the stables.

The grooms astonished at seeing her run so quickly toward the stables, opened the doors wide, unwilling or fearful to slow down her attempt at getting to the horses. Whatever she was contemplating, they would be honored to help.

"Don't bother to saddle Tempète, I will do it myself," she shouted as she bolted toward the stall of her newly purchased horse.

Jean-Louis was astounded at her capacity for flight. Where did she think she was going?

"Gaby, don't you dare," he called out. "We don't know anything about the horse."

She did not bother to turn back. He was right there on her heels. She picked up the heavy saddle that was lying on the wooden stall divider and threw it on the horse's back. Without any embarrassment, she hitched her frilly long skirt above her knees, mounted the horse and within minutes she was out of the stall, passing at more than a prudent speed her stunned lover.

He looked up at her as she passed by, flabbergasted, too slow in his intent to grab the bridle. For a moment he looked at her, as she sped down the alleys leading to the hills.

She quickly looked back to watch his reaction. He was bewildered at her behavior. A smile tugged at the corner of her lips. She kept on at breakneck speed on her way to the river.

Jean-Louis soon followed, his anger rising with every lounge forward. Thinking that the dense forest facing her would slow her down, he took a deep breath, knowing that he was about to strangle her now if he did not reason with his temper. He slowed his horse down. She did not slow down. Instead, placing her face down low on her horse's neck she took on the forest at full speed.

This time, fully aware of her escape abilities, he rode to return her to the castle. He finally caught up with her in the clearing, rode close to her, snatched the halters, and slowed the horse down to a full halt. He dismounted his horse and in one swift movement, he reached for her waist and brought her down.

He was incensed. She in contrast, let laughter dance in her emerald eyes.

"It felt so wonderful, so delightedly awesome!" She articulated slowly. "She is wonderful and understood my every move, Jean-Louis, I..." Gaby turned and gasped as she took in his anger.

"Are you annoyed with me?" she questioned candidly.

"Annoyed? No, Gaby—I'm livid with fury!" He shouted. "Are you trying to kill yourself?"

"No, I just love speed and demanding terrains. It's a lot of fun. I haven't ridden like that since I was home." She was breathing hard and pulled out of his reach to talk to her horse.

"You're a wonderful horse," she whispered in the horse's ear, kissing him on its neck. "We will be great partners, Tempête."

Jean-Louis reached for her again and pressed her head on his chest.

"You love danger, Gaby. It titillates you." He said it almost to himself.

She beamed, close to his heart.

"I do, Jean-Louis, just like you."

He smiled down at her.

"I'm a man, Gaby. It comes with the territory for me. But you, mademoiselle, you will find yourself locked up in my room tomorrow morning when I have to leave for an hour or two."

"You can't," she said, amused. "You forget my monkey-like abilities. Didn't you notice that the tree curls up to the balcony? It will be a cinch for me to climb in and out of there." She smiled coyly. "Find something else," she pursued with brilliant eyes, waiting anxiously for another task to disprove.

"Yes. I will sell your horse."

"I have plenty of money to buy my own," she answered flippantly. "Your money and influence does not help there, besides Jean-Louis, your stables are well stocked."

"Hum, all true. Well then, I can only see one last mean of control." He picked her up, walked to a large tree stump, sat down, and put her over his knees. "Who will win this contest, Gaby?"

"Stop, stop, you beast." She was laughing so hard that she was unable to speak. "You won," she gasped, "on physicality only, no cerebral response on your part, Monsieur" she shot back.

Shaking his head, unable to put down the impulse, he turned her over. His eyes told her he had formulated a harsher plan, one that she might not be able to top.

"Let me see, I'll have to talk to the pied piper and ask him to re-direct his rats not out of town but towards my castle. And when he does, I'll have the servants take away all of the candelabras. Is that controlling enough? Am I in charge of your pretty little personae?" He winked at her, knowing that he had touched a chord. He did not however expect the effect that his off the cuff comment received.

The black cloud fell upon her face once more. She grabbed his torso tightly, pressing herself fully into his body.

"Hold me darling, don't say that, I get very scared—just the thought is horrifying."

"Gaby, ma chérie, don't take it so seriously. Chérie, please, I was teasing. Why do you display such a sense of dread when the lights go off and—

She cut him off.

"I don't know, something happened during the war. I'm not sure, but I have been like that for a while." She lay in his arms like a helpless child. Minutes ago, she was this fearless goddess, an Amazon, and now she cowered in his arms. He would call on Michael, the American ambassador. He needed to find out a bit more about her background—her father, especially.

"Gaby, I love you. I will always protect you. Always Gaby. Don't be afraid, I'm here with you I will not leave you. You're safe, " he murmured sweetly saddened that he'd inflicted such fears.

Her heart still pounding, she lifted her eyes and looked up at him like a sad doe that had just lost her Bamby.

"I will be fine very soon." She paused, took a deep breath, and let go of the tight grip around his torso. She forced a timid smile and took another deep breath as she pushed herself away and stood up. He followed her.

"Let's ride a little longer, Jean-Louis; I wanted to reach the river." She pronounced with melancholy. He did not contradict her and followed quietly.

They continued onto the steep hills and spent most of the afternoon riding and taking pleasure at the sight of the pastoral landscapes. Later that day, they stopped in a small inn and had dinner. Jean-Louis had noticed that Gaby had retrieved her peachy coloring, although still quiet thin, the few extra pounds she now sported looked well on her.

She was experiencing firsthand the influence his name produced. She had heard of all his honorable acts in peace and in battle.

"Why is it Jean-Louis, that these people know about your exploits in my country and yet I never read about you anywhere during the war? Could they be exaggerating the great undertakings of the Duke?" she teased.

"Possibly. Are you overwhelmed? Is it annoying, darling? All that influence is frightening, you said?"

"No, not really, what is frightening to me is that your power might affect my independence. I hope that it will not stifle my whereabouts to the point that living with you will become like living in a prison."

"Gaby, please, don't mince your words," he replied offended. What you have just advanced is outrageous!"

"Jean-Louis, I'm young. I came to France to study music and work my voice and I found myself involved with the most powerful man in Europe. Innocently, I fell in love with the temperamental Captain of the Tempète and I realize now that you or the security that works for you will probably know and watch my every move—my whereabouts. That is a bit threatening even you can admit to that."

"This is who I am, Gaby; get on with the program," he replied sarcastically. Quickly he stood up, came around the table, offered his arm, which she took, and led her outside to the stables. He did not wait for the stable boy to bring their mount. Darkness had set in and she asked if she could ride in front of him. He grasped the bridle of Tempète. The way back to the castle was quiet. He did not respond to her light conversation. She reclined back.

They finally arrived at the castle. Without much fanfare, he walked to the library, asked for his brandy, sunk down in his overstuffed chair, and started reading. The omnipresent Madame Perideot waited and glanced knowingly at her adored Duke. She shot a quick glare at Gaby and retreated to the back foyer.

Meanwhile Gaby felt plain awful. She did not quite know what it was that she had said that irritated him so. She decided to found out. Walking close to him, she picked up two cigars, a gold lighter with his initials engraved on it, along with a small dish filled with his favorite chocolates. She approached and came to sit next to him. With a sweet smile she reached for his hand, turned one over and filled his palm with the sweets.

He gave her a stern look and quickly replaced the chocolate on the delicate secretary closed to his fauteuil.

"I'm tired, Gaby. I want to read. Go on to bed. I will be up later."

"No, I want to know what is bothering you. I'm miserable. You hardly said a word since we left the inn."

"Go on upstairs or stay down here and be quiet." he replied.

"Are you angry at my statements, the ones about my concern for my independence?" She came closer to him and took his book away.

"You are pushing your luck right now," he said angrily.

Not afraid, she sat on his lap.

"Don't push me away, Jean-Louis. I articulated my feelings strangely at the inn. You know how at times we react to an overwhelming situation in a bizarre sort of way."

"No, I do not, Gaby." He grasped his book away and glowered. "What do you mean by resenting me . . . I'm young?" he blurted, his grave voice filled with disbelief. "What is it Gaby? After just two weeks together you want your sexual independence? An open relationship? It's not going to happen in my home. Why, do you like Ribaud? Do you want to make history with him? I saw your flirtatious smiles. Don't tell me that I do not satisfy you sexually." She detected anger and disbelief in his tone as he pushed her off his lap none too gently.

"Jean-Louis, stop. Take me in your arms. You're overreacting in a bizarre sort of way. I expressed something that I was feeling at the time. You have to understand that your personae can be overwhelming for a person like myself. I do not belong to your world. We are worlds apart and yet we only feel complete when we are together. I only want you and always will. I loved you before all this," she elegantly arched her hand over the splendor surrounding them. "Your wealth and your power do not impress me; they terrify me—a great deal."

She received no amiable response from the great Jean-Louis-Pierre De Pleyssis, so she continued persistently.

"These past two weeks have been heavenly. I'm willing to share my life with you and accept your position, wealth and power," she waved her hand around the room again. "Just be patient with me and love me."

He first looked at her severely and then cast a forgiving gaze as he pulled her back onto his lap. "Kiss me, we will resolve all our differences tomorrow. On second thought maybe we never will. We might as well enjoy the ride."

He kissed her long and hard, taking her small body and absorbing it into his. And she thought her life had changed, he mused dreamily. How easy it would have been for him to get back in an easy relationship—Simone no, but someone not unlike her, who'd be willing to let him live his life as he saw fit. Well that was not in the cards. He had fallen madly in love with a girl who had a mind as stubborn and independent as his own. God help them. Taking her to the couch and placing his heavy body on hers, he gazed deep into her eyes.

"I love you, Gaby." He felt an insatiable urge for this young American. As his body hardened and the urge to take her mounted, he felt her giggle in his mouth.

"I love you too, Jean-Louis, more than the sky, the stars, the moon, and the whole universe." She closed her lips and waited for his tongue to force them open. That small conflict felt delicious. She would fight as long as she could and then would take his tongue deep in her mouth, knowing that his hands would knead her breasts forcefully, knowing that she would arch her back to give him all he wanted as her nipples became hard and sensitive to the slightest of touch and finally knowing that his penis would penetrate forcefully deep inside her. All these sexual and sensual games would come to a vibrant end with both lovers interlaced in each other's body—never wanting to be anywhere else but in the present.

They woke late in the middle of the night intertwined in each other's arms on the sofa.

"I presume that we have not taken the habits of old married couples, yet." He picked her up and brought her upstairs to their room.

Chapter Thirty

Upon their return from Normandy, Gabriella was now recognized as the Duke's great love. *C'est le grand amour*, it's the perfect love, Gaby would often hear as she passed by in her lavish landau or more often in the powder rooms of the balls they attended.

She continued her happy life, exactly like Jean-Louis delineated. Foremost, she loved him more than heaven and earth. Her music came in a close second. Life in The Garden of Eden must resemble her present life, she envisioned.

After an extraordinary day at the Académie, she returned home, elated. Jean-Louis was waiting for her by the fireplace with a scotch in his hand.

"How was the day of the most beautiful woman in Paris, who at this exact moment appears to be walking on air?"

"Oh, Jean-Louis, it was splendid, Maître Lauriot called me in the *grande salle* today, and," she paused and then almost shouted, "King Wilhelm of Prussia has extended an invitation to his just completed Hohenzollern castle. He wants me to sing for his son's birthday in the newly renovated opéra house in his private castle. He was told of my superbly agile and seductive voice." She copied the Prussian accent amusingly as she told him the terrific news. "You know I have been improving admirably. I must say, rest has proven to be therapeutic, my voice continues to have its vast vocal range but I have added conviction and individuality in my theatrics. She came closer to him and timidly murmured, "between you and I, I still think I'm the most communicative of all the sopranos I have heard and studied since I landed in France," she concluded. She twirled her supple body wrapped in a green frilly skirt and landed on his lap. "I'm thrilled, life is magnificent."

Overly ecstatic, Gaby did not notice his anger as she gleefully contemplated her achievement. She walked to the sidebar and poured a flute of perfectly chilled Dom Perignon, and she turned her loveliness just in time to hear his low, ominous voice.

"I will not allow it, Gaby. It will not happen," he declared assertively. "You can continue your art here in Paris, everyone adores you in the capital. Take all the lessons you wish. You can transform your apartment in your private conservatoire. We will attend as many opéras as you wish and finally you can throw as many soirées with opératic themes as you see fit, I will go along with any of the above. However, and this is final and not negotiable, you will not, I repeat, you will not be paraded on stage in another country!" He clipped in a non-negotiable tone of voice.

Flabbergasted, she stood in front of him, speechless. She had thought that he would be happy for her. She'd even believed at one point that the invitation might have been conveyed because of his connection. Resentment mounted.

"You are mad, giving up such opportunity. This is why I came to France, Jean-Louis. Surely you are not serious. You know how much I love to sing and how I adore sharing my gift. No, tell me that you are just jesting, please." She looked squarely in his eyes.

Understanding the disappointment that he was causing, Jean-Louis stood up and strolled close to her. He gazed in her clear, expressive eyes.

"No I am not, Gaby, you will not sing on a foreign stage. That is final. I have great difficulty as it is to accept your performances at the opéra here in Paris." He scoffed.

"I am not your wife. How dare you order such an unthinkable response," she countered inflamed. "Furthermore, after this controlling statement I don't know that I ever want to be. To refuse such an honor is not feasible. I will perform. It is my decision and mine solely," she protested. Controlling her anger was too demanding. She turned on her heels and sprinted toward the door to hide her tears. She was not about to let him see her disappointment at the cause of their first altercation.

Jean-Louis followed instantly and none too gently grabbed her by the waist and turned her around. He placed his huge hands around her wrists.

"I am not amused, Gaby. You will write Lauriot, and tell him that you are turning down the invitation. I don't care what excuse you use, but you will do it. Otherwise, I will, and I won't mince my words. He knows our situation. He should have known better than to make you such an offer, the imbecile."

Gaby was devastated, her face drenched with tears, anger, sadness, disappointment, all rolled into one. She was shocked that he did not share her joy. She was always happy when he shared his accomplishments with her. It was way too simple to cry, she chewed over, suddenly her strength of character returned. He had a way of completely dehumanizing her womanhood and artistic nature. She would threaten to leave him. He loved her as much as she loved him. He'd relent if she did not stand powerless like a doormat—sobbing her heart out!

"Please, let go of my wrists, you are hurting me. Your order is out of the question I will proceed with my decision since you did not give me any reasonable nor acceptable rationale for not doing so." She defiantly pulled her wrists out of his grasp and straightened up to her full height.

"Suit yourself, Gaby. I'm on my way to the opéra," he said in a pitiless tone. He turned on his heels and stormed out of the room.

"Jean-Louis, don't— " Her words were lost notes in the beautiful salon.

She heard the double doors open and the sound of his voice calling for his horse to be brought forth. She thought of running after him and forbidding him to go. Her sentimental nature wanted the servants to think that all was splendid with their idyllic relationship.

Nonsense, she quickly told herself. She was leaving him—that was it. No she probably would not, but why was he so jealous of her other love? Music was not another man after all. She lamented.

Dejected, she ambled back inside the salon close to the great fireplace and sat in his large, leather chair. She watched the bursting orange and gold flames leap from one large log to another, engulfing first the outside layers of the wood and then vengefully scorching the deep cognac-shaded center of the log, dissolving it to gray ashes. She observed the fire for a very long time, lost in her thoughts. She wished they could have discussed it. He probably was talking to the Maître now, how terribly embarrassing. Why were opéra singers, ballerinas, and actors held in such low esteem by the same society who promoted them financially? How many of these aristocratic men kept ballerinas and opéra singers in the lovely Hotels Particulier in Paris? They were not ashamed in the least to parade them whenever they had a chance. Family life and love of family had taken a turn for the better during the later part of the 19th century in Europe, her friend Lilianne at the Académie had told her. However from her viewpoint, men had not ascended to giving up their beautiful *petites amies*. This cultural inclination was still a huge part of married life. Most men in Europe and probably quite a few titled women as well, were reluctant to give up their *amours,* love. Granted, many of these artistically inclined, very talented men and women were not the most cerebral. She often found herself looking for subjects to talk about other than the usual codicil of their respective arts, beauty, and fame. Involving oneself into the lives of others often played tricks on an entertainer's mind, making them forget who they really were, obliterating the self when they were not acting. Most actors went to their death not knowing who they were. Acting to the end.

At times she felt that the entertainment world was the great egalitarian. She often went as far as thinking that the less education, the less cerebral an actor was, the better it was for the director to advise and to control the production. The less personality, the less questioning an actor had, the better to mold them into roles of real credence by a director who had a vision. Education increases the productivity of the curious mind, she mused. Curiosity and intelligence prod questions. The fewer questions an actor had about deep, thoughtful issues, the more room for superficial creative energy. Intelligent thought takes time to be mulled over, she mused. The erudition of an Aristotle was not required to act.

Although embarrassed about this crude thought, Gaby sensed that most actors were really better off being dumb. The problem arose when many of these uneducated dimwits, but incredible, gut-wrenching artists started to look down on others who had not achieved the same status in life. She had met quite a few since her arrival. The prima ballerina excoriated the lesser dancer. The exquisite soprano often acted like an entitled queen and the talented tenor espoused complexes of superiority, Maître Lauriot had confided in her. She smiled, recalling their conversations. They were granted passage in society all right, the salons sometimes, but mostly the bedrooms, he had declared. She had written to Philippe amusing anecdotes about her colleagues who often forgot to finish sentences, using the *précieuses verbiage* still so very popular in the salons, berating the very fiber they came from—the ones they ran away from. On the other side of the coin, many aristocrats felt that entertainers were not at their level. At their level of what, she speculated—chance of birth? If that was the case she knew a lot of aristocrats who left a lot to be desired on the intelligence topic—her mother, for one.

The only thing left was on social class and that, as well, did not have any thump. So what if actors borrowed from the characters they played, comportment that pleased them, that helped them to be happy, and to live a financially and socially sound life, the more power to them, she thought

What people suffered to be liked, was always a paradox to her. Why was it so difficult to enjoy another creature without prejudging them, they were members of society and for that they should be given credence, they had as much right as any other individual on this earth, to express their simple thoughts.

Why was it that only aristocrats should enjoy the niceties of life? Individuals sufficiently wise to become financially sound and live reasonably happy lives should not be detested just because they were ordinary, in the Gallic sense, meaning rude and unpolished. A person emotionally in touch with their inner self and able to portray it and give great pleasure to others should be rewarded. Everyone in this world had their strengths and finding them and pursuing them was the real accomplishments. So why lower the artistic accomplishments of these talented men and women? Did society really need cerebral people playing other lives?

She understood not wanting to spend much time with people who were shallow and not interested in deeper issues that affected the lives of a population. True enough, she did not research the friendships of individuals she had nothing in common with. But the immense difference lay in that she did not look down on anyone because of his or her standing in the social strata. And that was exactly what Jean-Louis had done when he forbade her to sing publicly. She could not expect miracles from him; he had, after all, been raised in a most limiting world and yet had extricated himself from almost all ties to his background.

Gaby had often thanked God that He had given her a good, working brain. She was intelligent, charming, and in love with the most wonderful man in the world. He must have had his reasons to feel so strongly about her singing outside of France.

She adored him. In retrospect it was not the end of the world. Given the choice between Jean-Louis and her music, she would not give any credence to singing. He came first, far beyond everyone and everything else in her life. It was the way he gave her the order that irked her whole being. She would explain all this to him later.

Pleased with her analytical perspective of the altercation. She sat back down and picked up a music theory book. After all, Jean-Louis had said that she could sing when they entertained their friends. He did not forbid her to attend any of her classes or to perform at the opéra. It was a small sacrifice that he had asked, she pondered. Perhaps he did not want her to be away from him for any extended period of time. After all, she was going to Italy with him.

Fernand, the butler, knocked and walked in the room with a huge bouquet of her favorite white roses; they were called *les jolies Marie-Josée.* How thoughtful, she thought, Jean-Louis remembered everything she had told him about her likes and dislikes. She was about to tend to the bouquet when she noticed her name written on a beige parchment envelope written in his scholarly handwriting.

Jean-Louis had had guilt pains ever since he'd left his house. She had been thrilled about the invitation. She must be furious by now he deliberated. He took the time in his note to explain to her his partial reasoning. He could not tell her that because of his station in life, her own precious life would be endangered in Paris if she became too visible. In a foreign country the risks could quadruple.

By now, most of the Parisian society were well aware that the Duke De Bourbonne adored his mistress. Their engagement and their wedding plans, although there weren't any as of yet, were the talk of the tout Paris. *L'étrangère* is his weakness, people whispered behind his back—probably his only one, it was said. Jean-Louis had her under constant surveillance without her knowledge. He loved her independent spirit.

He stopped by his office and sat behind his desk. Paris was divided between a run toward modernization versus the revolutionaries who kept on dreaming about a Republic, he evaluated. Courbet, the realist painter, led many of them and especially in Paris a strong Jacobin current re-surfaced. He certainly could at times sympathize with a lot of them. There were excesses during the Count Haussmann's years, as this era was often referred to, and much of the populace had been relocated to the outskirts of Paris. Montmartre was the new cesspool of these new thinking radicals.

Poverty was rampant in this part of the city. Hate, crime, and the black market flourished, but these vulgar streets also forced the appearance of a new look at life through a different lens. The impressionists often worked there. They depicted, such as Degas did, the predicament of the everyday working girls, such as the *repasseuses*, women who ironed for a living, the milliners, women who formed men and women elaborate hats, and the dancers. The old opéra was located in Montmartre, and likewise, the studio Guerbois was not too far off. La Belle-Athénée, the coffee bar where many artists met to discuss their art, also was located in Montmartre. Consequently, a spirit of modernity seeped through these quarters. He truly admired the work of these new painters who saw their world in a different light.

The avant-garde movement of the impressionists painted life as they saw it, with light and shade and smiles and laughter in the present. Movement and light were the rage, from the childish innocent looks of Renoir's women, to the bold exotic nudes of Manet, to the grace and finesse of Degas' ballerinas; these artists depicted life as it appeared to them, the history of their times.

A grand success, they were not, but a handful of art critics gave the movement some credence and viability. The artists that were married often continued their classical and romantic paintings. The ones, who had the leisure to paint without financial worries, dedicated themselves solely to the movement. They would meet in the café on the boulevard Saint Michel on the left bank and gave each other support for the new genre, that of expressing their world on canvas with different strokes and a distinctive palette.

Rich and poor craved modernity. To act foolhardy, to forget the conflicts of the past with *débaucheries* and *grande vie,* these experiences were rampant throughout France. Ah, what a dangerous time they were living in.

He had chosen the voice of the future, he thought. Unless France and Europe industrialized, more of the same was to ensue. He was an aristocrat with a vision for the future. He had traveled to the United States and study their Constitution, a document he held dear to his heart and was in awe of. The United States Constitution worked and it would work even better now that the Civil War was over, he deduced. Why not export some of the same ideas to France, he had told Gaby. De Montesquieu's book on the Spirit of Laws, asserted that for a democracy to work, a balance of powers was required. Consequently, he expressed great sentiment for the tripartite system of government. The works of Montesquieu had been an inspiration for the Founding Fathers, why shouldn't the French capitalize on the same ideas that worked so well on the North American continent?

Now was the time to ask for gigantic sacrifices from the population. He knew well that the poor and the needy of his nation would become the first one to suffer the advancement of modernization but human rights ideals for the future was no small victory, he deliberated.

"The people in the United States, the ones I know anyhow, have an admirable sense of belonging, of being enlightened with freedom in the truest sense of the world," he had said to her one evening while they took an evening stroll on the Cays of the Seine. I purchased a lovely home in Boston in a beautiful area on the Charles River named Beacon Hill. I'm looking forward to take you there, Gaby." He'd told her

"But I'm a child of the South, Jean-Louis. Acceptance in these circles will be difficult for me. Listen to my accent," she'd laughed.

"By then you'll have a French accent," he'd retorted. "Anyhow, that lovely picture belongs in the far distant future. We have much to accomplish before. But, I know in my heart," he recalled confiding in her as he'd gathered her closely to him, "that we will finish our lifelong journey there, with children or not. It does not matter to me as long as I have you, Gaby." He now wished that she remembered these words.

Enough thinking, he was heading home. He rounded his desk and walked out.

At the florist Jean-Louis had tried his best to delineate his reasoning in a most loving and tender tone. Only writing could do justice to the love he felt for her.

Returning later than he expected, he braced himself for her cold shoulder. To his unrestrained joy, she was waiting for him and waived from the balcony overlooking the impressive entrance. He climbed the marble steps leading to the front door held opened by Pierre as he noticed her running towards him in the foyer in her elegant graceful trot. She stopped a few steps away from where he was standing and quickly threw herself in his arms. Affectionately, she slid her small hands under his coat.

"I should stop at the florist more often," he grinned.

He picked her up in his arms and brought her inside.

"What do I owe this sudden change in attitude, chérie?"

"Frankly I'm not quite sure. I should be on my way back to New Orleans." She smiled. "Maybe the flowers, and surely your romantic note which turned me inside out only two hours after our altercation this afternoon. It is also true that I did not want to anger you. She looked up at him from top to bottom. "You are after all twice my size and I live in your house." She paused, winked, and bit the inside of her lower lip while surveying his reaction.

He winked back, raising his eyebrows showing stern approval of her succinct assessment of the situation.

She waited a few more moments and candidly proceeded with the truth.

"But mostly, the realization that I always used singing as a mean to happiness, to forget whatever sadness I experienced. Well, with you I am always splendidly happy and I know you are too. I am never sad. I thank God that I have found you every instant of my life so why all the disappointment over a part in an opéra. Voila. Am I entitled to more goodies?"

He threw his head back and laughed heartily.

"Maybe, mademoiselle," he reached in his side pocket and brought out a beautiful black velvet box. It could not be a ring, she thought, the box was long and rectangular, certainly a bracelet.

"Seriously, I'm an awful negotiator, Jean-Louis. Had I waited, you would have apologized profusely and then you would have bought my forgiveness with more jewelry if nothing else worked."

"That you are, my darling, an awful negotiator that is, and yes, precisely that was my intent."

"You scoundrel," she laughed. "All the jewels in the world would not assuage my anger if I had not decided that I was a bit foolish after all. I want to know why." She opened the box. The dazzling flash of the diamond bracelet took her breath away.

"Oh, it's beautiful, Jean-Louis." She picked up the brilliant row of diamonds and placed it on her wrist. She loved yellow diamonds for they offset her green eyes. Before leaving for France, she had bought herself a pair of beautiful, yellow diamond heart earrings. Naturally, the jewelry had sunk down with the ship she had been sailing on. She walked to the man she loved, pulled on his lapel and kissed him fully on his mouth.

"I love you so much," she said passionately.

He laughed.

"Me or the diamonds?"

"Both the same," she said with an ironic sideways glance.

Shaking his head from side to side, he picked her up again and started walking upstairs to their room.

"Where are you taking me?" she asked coyly with a glance over her shoulder, folding her arms around his neck.

"Upstairs where I need to undress, and hopefully where I will be thanked in proportion with the sensational gift I have just presented to you."

"Well, let me think. Just a bracelet, fairly nice I must add, but no matching earrings, no necklace, and no brooches—a few light kisses should render you quite joyous my love," she retorted perversely.

He held her far above their bed and let her fall unceremoniously on the thick satin down coverlet. "For your impertinence, mademoiselle."

She opened her arms and legs like a young child trying to delineate an angel in the snow and stopped and gazed amorously in his eyes.

"I love you, Gaby," he whispered.

"I love you more, Jean-Louis."

That was too much to bear for Jean-Louis. He undressed by the bed. Soon his tall, muscular body emerged and his engorged manhood appeared. She knew her hair was cascading on her back and she felt sexy and beautiful. She rolled out of his reach

He tried to grab her body, but she had gracefully landed on her two feet on the other side of the bed.

She sexily undressed. At first, she asked him to unbutton her dress and then changed her mind. She pulled away from him at a safe distance from his wandering hands. She slowly removed the one shoulder from her dress then the other. The dress fell to the ground but the short white chemise was still there.

"Off with it. You are driving me crazy, chérie. Come join me," Jean-Louis said, his voice low and sexy filled with desire.

She turned around walked away even further from their bed. She knew how frustrated, hot and bothered he'd become. She continued to turn around, fully showing her firm round bottom.

"It appears to me, Jean-Louis . . ." she glanced over to him and realized her lover had jumped out of bed and was directing his large frame toward her. "Jean-Louis . . . don't," she shouted. She dashed out of his reach to the other side of her room. Naturally she was no match for his speed and after a few strides, he pounced, grasped her waist, and he covered her voluptuous body with his own. He kissed her to oblivion and without restrain gave her what she moaned for. Both of them exploded with ecstasy.

She fell limp on his chest, her right arm reaching for his neck, his arms resting on her backside, and his lips on her curly raven mane.

They both fell soundly asleep, thanking God that they had found one another.

Chapter Thirty-One

Jean-Louis had shown the world in essence, that she was no longer a young, available woman. She was happy. She had the person that she adored and her singing. Singing had been a wonderful part of her life—past and present. She recalled waking up at the crack of dawn in New Orleans to ride over to the convent for the five o'clock mass so she could join the angelic voices that made up the convent's choir. Her voice had been her surviving strength. Tonight, they were attending a grandiose soirée at the Count Devinnette, one of the political men who would accompany Jean-Louis and his delegation to Italy. She had danced with many while Jean-Louis was in the segregated salons.

Before he took his leave, she'd teased him unmercifully.

"You only pretend to be involved in detailed business affairs. I just think you want a rest from all of us. What is so important about men's privacy, anyway?"

"Grand secret, Gaby, one that you will never know," he'd retort, as he was spirited upstairs behind large double doors engraved in gold moldings. She'd turned on her heels and shrugged her shoulders.

Hours later, Jean-Louis returned to the ballroom and myriad beautiful friends accosted him. What were these women thinking, Gaby questioned? Promptly, she'd ask her escort to return her back toward Jean-Louis's circle of friends.

She walked slowly to him, touched his broad back and reached for his hand. Without missing a beat, he pulled her to him and continued the conversation he was engaged in.

She tugged harder on his fingers and then placed her hand on his elbow, squeezing it gently.

"You were saying, mademoiselle?" He looked down at her with his sensual inquisitive gaze.

She held her pretty head in gracious acknowledgement.

"I was hoping that you'd ask me to dance, that's my favorite waltz." She asked with a most bewitching smile that melted everyone she came in contact with.

"And if I don't?"

"Others will cher Duke!" She squeezed her brow and pouted as she began to spin on her heels.

He quickly grasped her elbow and directed her towards the dance floor. He was going to have a wonderful time this evening, he thought. God only knew what the future held for both of them.

He looked down at her as he questioned his recent decision to take her with him. Should he leave her behind within the French confine? To place her under such imminent danger was cruel, although—Gaby did speak fluent Italian. No, taking her with him would be too risky. She came to France to study music, mon Dieu. Then again, La Fenice, in Venice, was a magnificent opéra house. Verdi had written La Traviatta in its honor and the first performance of the opéra had taken place on its fabulous stage. Stop trying to convince yourself that it could be worked out, he told himself. It could not. Gaby would stay behind, that was that. Lost in his conflicted thoughts, he looked down and smirked—the little brat had gracefully but intentionally stepped on his foot. He straightened up as he clasped her waist and weaved through the crowd to the sweeping music.

"Jean-Louis, I understand you went to the Bois de Boulogne yesterday, why?"

"I wanted to see you and flirt with you, but most of all, I wanted the *Tout Paris* to see me court you—properly, that is."

That delighted her. Not solely because he had made the decision on his own merit, but furthermore because she did care about what people thought about her. Obviously he respected her enough to go along with the proper etiquette.

Yesterday at the conservatoire, her voice instructor, Rosette La Hague had mentioned in passing that Jean-Louis had been seen with Jocelyn De Harcourt, one of his former paramours. She had not said responded. Jean-Louis had many friends, including women. She'd come close to breach the subject but had been unable to find a proper moment.

Asking flat out about the remark from the always well-informed Rosette was not to her liking. Instead, she chose to ask leading questions. As they twirled on the dance floor she glanced at him and smiled.

"I know that your life was quite diverse before you met me and returned to France, chéri," she nonchalantly remarked. "Have you met anyone from your past recently?"

"Gaby, you might as well ask about Jocelyn. Coy questions are not your forte, my dear." He gazed down at her with a fatherly look. "Yes, yesterday I met an old friend, and yes, she asked about our status, as you say in the United States."

"And?"

"And I told her that I would not stray or something like that, maybe less explicit, less direct," he concluded a tad annoyed.

"What do you mean less direct? Did you give her any hope for the future?"

"Gaby, cease this utterly boring conversation, I do not stray and I apply the same standards to your friendly relationships."

She sweetly smiled and quickly changed the subject. She would meet Renaud next week. He had just returned from England.

"Will you come and visit me at the Bois again? I would like that very, very much," she instead pursued.

He laughed and kissed her tenderly on the forehead.

Why did Jean-Louis have such an incredible effect on her? There was a magnetic energy about him and she felt fabulous when he was near. She had the tendency to overanalyze, but with Jean-Louis, everything fell into place really quickly. She was sad when he was gone and in heaven when he was nearby—as simple and mundane as that. An astonishing chemistry, she pondered.

The following week there had been no lunches. Time was of the essence. She had taken serious lessons from an Austrian maestro and he had shown interest in her from day one. Not that it would make much difference as far as a live performance in his country. Jean-Louis was adamant, but it felt wonderful coming from someone whom she knew was not coerced by her lover's influence. The week had been exciting and she'd stopped by the Fouquet's after the many performances the Austrians had presented. She loved the famous restaurant on the Champs Élysées. Artists and theatergoers as well would congregate after the shows. Journalists would give their critiques. They were always ready to listen, inquire, and note down all the gossips so as to smear it all over the papers the following day. "That is their motto, Gaby. Watch your words in public," Jean-Louis had told her.

But tonight was special. Jean-Louis had taken her, with many of his friends, inside the private rooms set up for certain members of the elite. Austrians were a gregarious, amiable people, an unruly bunch that played hard.

Now alone, the press had cornered Gaby. She was astounded by the directness of the probing. Six journalists surrounded her on all sides as they shoved their pads at her. By now she knew how to advertise her performances, but tonight the questions focused on their relationships.

"Mademoiselle Thornsen, will you follow the Duke to Italy? We have heard that the trip is now imminent? Is that correct?"

"Mademoiselle, will you stay in the house on the Ile Saint Louis?"

"Mademoiselle, you speak Italian, we hear that you may be an asset to the Duke and the mission—professionally or otherwise?"

"Mademoiselle, will the Duke marry you?"

She remained silent. One of Jean-Louis' cousins came to her rescue and he led her beyond the dance floor and into the De Pleyssis grand salons in the theater. She quietly chose a light pink bergère and sat with members of Jean-Louis' family.

His Grandmother always had a half smile on her face and appeared regal, reserved, and aloof. The dowager had boundless energy when surrounded by her friends. She knew it all and needed constant attention. Listening to her was a requirement. Gaby had learned to acquiesce a lot. She copied Jean-Louis' demeanor in her presence. The poor fellow, no wonder he took to the sea at such a young age. She wondered what would have been worse, being attentive to a talkative Grandmother for hours on end or being raised alone as she had been?

The food was delicious and Gaby endured the conversation. She was going to give Jean-Louis an earful for leaving her behind.

"Gabriella, what did you think of the Australian soprano?"

"She was quite good. I was impressed by—"

"It appeared to me that her theatrics took away from her voice. I feel that it took her much too long to reach and sustain the high note, althought that might have been the reason for the expressive features. Even then, I would say that it was not natural for the role she played."

Gaby listened. She knew from previous attempts that she would not be able to get a word in edgewise. At first, she thought that the old woman just thought of her as stupid and uninteresting. However, as the months passed, she realized that everyone was treated to her long discourses on every possible subject—the ones she knew and the ones she did not. Her questions were really statements and they always seemed to veer into condescending tirades. God forbid someone would teach her something.

Marie Josée, her best friend smiled. Gaby just could not understand these two women having such a close relationship. Marie-Josée was petite, vivacious, and always ready to amuse with comical anecdotes. She needed it with a friend like the grande Duchesse. Gaby had discovered a warm and engaging heart—everyone loved her. A few weeks back, Gaby had attended one of Marie Josée favorite couturier's new winter collections. On her way home, to Gaby's surprise, she had asked the driver to stop in front of a bakery and as Gaby watched from inside the carriage, she saw her give a sack of gold coins to the woman tending the store.

"Her young daughter is ill," she'd said, as she'd noticed a questioning look on the young American face.

Since her arrival in Paris, while observing all things and everyone, Gaby had learned a very important lesson into the behind the scene emotions of the 'quiet society.' One could almost discern the personality of the high and mighty by glancing at the people who served them. Gaby could see that Marie-Josée was loved by her domestics or at the very least respected.

A smile tugged at the corner of her mouth. On this aspect Jean-Louis did not fare too highly. Respectful demeanor would accompany his majesty, but love or deep affection, only Madame Perideot displayed these traits toward the great Jean-Louis-Pierre De Pleyssis. She smiled.

Marie-Josée however was just plain adorable. She had even extricated from Gaby the profound love that she felt for her adored Jean-Louis. She had the knack to ask the perfect question and she displayed the tolerance to accept whatever came her way.

That night as they were riding back toward his house, she asked Jean-Louis about the mission. She shared with him the reporter's questions.

"What were your responses, Gaby?" he asked

"Nothing, I pretended not to hear."

"Good. Tomorrow is Sunday. I made plans with Luke to go to Chatou. I know you'll love it there. We both need a little fun. This week has been exciting but stressful for both of us."

Fatigued, she reclined in his arms and fell sound asleep.

The following morning, she looked at the sleeping giant next to her, kissed him, and began to roll away, and then she felt his powerful arm pulling her back into bed.

"I accompany you to the conservatoire at an ungodly hour every morning. If you force me to get up at this ungodly hour on Sunday, I'll send you back to your cousin's place." And he rolled her under and imprisoned her body beneath his large musculature.

Chapter Thirty-Two

Later in the afternoon, they met his friend Luke who was being entertained by a fascinating but utterly wild woman. Her sensuality and not a care in the world attitude were appealing. She was not what one would call pretty, but she had an enigmatic demeanor that Gaby liked from the start.

Montmartre was a crazy suburb filled with art, furor, rage, and unrest. The revolution against the Empire spewed its controversial ideas across France. The new artists' fervor for the depiction of these decadent quarters where love, passion, addiction, prostitution, poverty, was unveiled on their canvases and came to light in these less than safe streets.

The less than guarded behavior of these painters did not help the critic's perspective of the new art. Renoir loved to paint frivolous women with innocent looks. He never missed an occasion to deflower his innocent subjects who were attracted by his tender voice and his drawings of pure genius. His bed was often filled with beautiful ingénues.

Manet adored shocking the new bourgeoisie. His darling model, Victorine Meurent stark naked in the Bois de Boulogne flouting the viewer, surrounded by men in full suits eating and picnicking as if that was a common sight in the Bois had caused furor in the Salon. The painting had not been accepted at the Salon. Edouard had been devasted but had not given up his subjects. Two years later the masterpiece Olympia was exhibited! The sensuality of love, beautiful women, and food in these ordinary outside settings where light was paramount, depicted a generation of painters thirsty for the modern, for something wild, sensuous and different from the old historical paintings. It was a new world, and although after Charles Louis Napoléons' defeat in Mexico, the people were suffering, there was in Paris an emergence of modernity difficult to rein in. The artists depicted life as it was lived. The fun times, the times of despair, the simple activities of everyday people became alive on canvas and celebrated.

These artists seemed to know that the world was in transition and would not regress to the critically acclaimed artistic ideas of the past.

Jean-Louis understood that he had to push through the changes to his world—the aristocracy. Many of Gaby's friends changed the culture of the bourgeois through their artistic gifts. He had to change minds at the political level. There were times, however, that the fear of losing Gaby, of being separated, somehow made him longed for his peaceful life in Boston away from this present folly. He believed in the movement—in modernity. Paris after all was experiencing a facelift as well.

People never learned from history, he heard over and over again. But how could they? The world was changing—culture, art, class division—everything was constantly evolving. Regardless of how attractive the old adage of learning from history appeared, it was world events that shaped a generation's thinking. And the reaction to that thinking would never be the same. Men did not seem to learn how to negotiate conflicts without fighting one another. Was this the lesson from history that men were supposed to learn from? If this was the consensus, then the whole human race was obtuse. It was not hard to decode that a country that had been colonized forty years ago could not be overtaken today with the same principles of the past.

As a general roadmap studying history was satisfactory—constructive at best, but truly never the answer. However, forceful nations that wish to advance civilization toward a more peaceful world for themselves and the world at large needed to comprehend the present state of affairs, the present culture of a population, its needs, its wishes for its children to really make it work, for at the very least three quarters of its population. There was Jean-Louis' strength and he knew it. Unfortunately, all this modernization was being built on the back of the poor. They had been pushed back toward the edge of Montmartre. So much poverty, kids were going to school to keep warm and eat a few crumbs of stale bread, and drink a bit of black market milk thanks to the teachers who had dedicated their lives to these downtrodden. Everything they had was because of the black market operating in Montmartre. Men and women negotiated with the epicures and the bakers of the area.

Jean-Louis stared at Gaby. He was part of this atmosphere. He believed that this particular generation might have to sacrifice for the good of posterity. He reached for her hand, squeezed it, momentarily placed it on his heart and pushed her along the streets to the Moulin De La Galette. There, sadness and poverty was forgotten, love, passion, and absinthe stupor were rampant, couples frolicked to the latest tunes, poor and rich alike mingled to enjoy and to forget themselves in this moment in time.

They stayed very late and were escorted back to their carriage by both his private and the state security. Luke had gone home with the intriguing beauty.

Meanwhile back in the heart of the city, their lives was a whirlwind of activities—the plays, the theater, the soirées, the walks and concerts in the Jardin des Tuileries, in Boulogne, Vincennes. Jean-Louis never missed a chance to come and see her.

Springtime was lovely in Paris and the banks along the Seine where filled with old and young alike enjoying the pleasant days at hand with great enthusiasm as if knowing that the worst was yet to come.

The age was changing as well. The impressionist movement in the Rue Trieste was getting more and more vocal; they wanted a larger representation in *the Palais d'Exhibitions*. Reality was in vogue, lightness and liberation of the old ways through the Industrial Revolution. France was diligently working toward a change of path.

Gaby could not believe her happiness. Never in a million years could she believe she'd be so happy. A man she adored and who adored her, voice lessons with Maître Lauriot that had improved her artistic gift greatly, her new friends at the Conservatoire, exposure to the greatest minds of the time, and a man who was sufficiently liberated to let her pursue her dreams and encourage her artistic nature Well, with a few barriers now and then.

She had noticed a frown on his face when she spoke to him about her progresses, the students she encountered, the gossipy, tumultuous lives of tenors and sopranos, and the jealousy that reigned supreme in the corridors leading to the audition's room. She shared her world, her anxieties about sustaining the clarity of voice she so diligently try to produce on a consistent basis, and the excitement and fears of living her dream in one of the world's most creative capitals.

Tonight she shared with him her critique of Puccini. She had heard he was being pressured to write a new Opéra, *Tosca*, based on the novel by Victorien Sardou.

"How did you found out about Puccini, Gaby? I heard that it was a well-kept secret."

"I have friends in high places," she responded cheerily. Her association with artists that frequented Montmartre brought out another frown on his handsome face.

"I hear it all darling, the Conservatoire possesses the most knowledgeable gossips of our time. Trust me, Jean-Louis, we are at the epicenter of all the verbal carnage. I am not immune to it, either. I often am at the receiving end of many scornful looks from certain *Mamans* who volunteer on the board. I presume I am not a model for their precocious young daughters. All in all, I no longer care," she candidly told him. "For the first time in my life I have no dreams, no goals. I am living both of my dreams—total dedication and commitment to you and to my music. In that order."

Later that week, while waiting for her friend, Lilianne, sitting on a bench, she watched Jean-Louis arrived on his horse. He dismounted, and searched the banks of the river for her. She watched as many young beautiful women smiled and tried to engage in conversation with her sensual lover.

France hated liking aristocracy with a vengeance. At the same time, the man in the street despised everything his social structure stood for. But there was the dichotomy of a nation at odds with itself—the simple man admired the polish of the rich and noble and tried to duplicate the *grand monde's antics*. The revolution had slapped down the monarchy all proclaimed, and then in the usual French approach, everything had returned back to its original sorry state. The populace cried that they had taught these aristocrats a lesson. The aristocrats predicted that the worst was past and it was time to return to the status quo.

However odd the process appeared, there was no continuation of thought or focus in any of the political ideas presented. The process of solving an issue never was set in motion. As a result, the problems always resurfaced and the despicable state of affairs never moved forward for the benefit of the populace.

Napoleon III had been a breath of fresh air after the years following the reaffirmation of the monarchy under Louis Philippe. But his loosening of power, his arrogance toward many of the Europeans leaders, and the defeat in Mexico had created a broken man both politically and emotionally she concluded.

Jean-Louis hoped to change all that without having to serve as president of a Third Republic—a task too difficult to avoid in view of the latest developments. She wondered how she would react to such an imposition on her frivolous life. The wife of a political man would weigh heavily on her artistic nature. Perhaps his forthcoming trip to Italy would change the turn of events. Perhaps not.

Jean-Louis looked again, this time more carefully.

He noticed her watching him and extricated himself from the ladies who'd surrounded him. After ten years abroad, he was still a wonderful match. Power, money, virility and an adventurous character—what a combination, she thought, and she was the lucky receiver of all these gifts. Why had he fallen for her? She often wondered. What was the magnetism that she possessed or was there a master plan they were not privy to?

"How can such a beauty be seated all alone?" he proclaimed while looking down at her with hungry eyes.

"I think the answer to this question is fairly easy to respond to. You made it quite clear the other night at the ball that I was not to be spoken to unless you were by my side."

He smirked. She touched his boots with her slippers and slowly stood up next to him. She loved being near him.

"I never felt so loved in my whole life. I could stand here next to you forever."

He took her in his arms and kissed her tenderly on the forehead taking her hands and walking toward the banks of the river where a wide oak tree was spreading its branches, providing both privacy and shade. He sat her down next to him.

"Chérie, are you happy here in Paris?"

"I was just thinking that I have never been happier, Jean-Louis. Why do you love me so much?"

Surprised, he looked at her expressive eyes for a split second.

"Why not?" he asked stunned.

"I see you're so researched, influential, you could have anyone of these women," she waved her shapely arm in the direction of the many landaus crisscrossing the Bois. Many I know are quite qualified to be your wife. They are intelligent, have charm and status in life, and most would probably give you something I probably will never be able to—a child—so why? Why are we so attracted to each other? We cannot be further apart in culture, likes, language, background—"

"Am I being given the boot, Gaby? What prompted these crazy thoughts you have been entertaining, chérie?"

"No, seriously." She sat motionless amused that he had not even contemplated the idea.

"Darling I don't know and frankly it is not a subject that keeps me awoke at night."

He changed the subject after kissing her. "Let's talk about important things. I am taking you to London. I have some business and I'm hoping that Luke and Ribaud will have returned from Monaco where I understand they have traveled to recently." He saw her frown. "You don't seem too eager, my love. Why? Would you have rather stayed in Paris with your new friends?"

She knew that he was referring to her friends from the Conservatory. She could tell from the sound of his voice that he was less than pleased about her choice, but she was an artist at heart and all artistic issues were of great interest to her.

"No I just don't know about Luke and Ribaud. My first impression in the south of France was not too positive. I liked Ribaud in Normandy. Together, I have not yet made up my mind. They will not try to pull us apart, will they?"

"Gaby, you will get to know them better and you will like them. I am certain of that. They are my closest friends. Give them a chance."

"When is this trip taking place?"

"We will leave next Monday."

"From Brest?"

"No, we will take the ferry across, not as comfortable as our ship, but it will do."

It sounds wonderful, and then bothered by the statements of Jolette and Murielle, two singers from the chorus, who had been sitting with her the last hour, she continued.

"Jean-Louis, how do you feel about having an heir? How important is it to you?"

"Gaby, what is going on? Whom have you been talking to?"

"I have not been talking to anyone. Except . . . that while waiting, I was sitting with Jolette Du Caysne and Murielle Durot. They said that it was impossible for an aristocrat not to produce a child, that a bastard would be better than none! The family would apply too great a pressure on anyone who tried to lead a childless union and that essentially Societée would make their life miserable."

Women have a mean streak, he thought. Maybe the lack of control in their lives immersed many with bitterness. In their deprecating eyes a woman like Gaby who essentially had it all needed to be brought down a notch or two. He wrapped her in his arms and kissed her tenderly on her eyes, her cute little nose, and sexy lips.

"All right, sweetheart, once and for all—I never want to hear this question again. Now, Gabriella, I have nephews, the passing of the title is settled. Think about it this way, Gaby, you have six other siblings, which I'm sure would jump at the chance of owning your land. Don't you think so?"

She nodded, "but I fought long and hard to deprive them of that pleasure, Jean-Louis, the land belonged to my mother. She passed it on to me. And that is settled now." She replied cold as ice.

Stunned he recalled what Michael Striker recounted to him just a few weeks past. During the war Gaby had turned away her father and his family who sought refuge in her plantation from the destruction of their home in the city. He had not paid much heed to the passing comment then, but now curious he breached the subject now.

"All true," she replied without emotion. "He's a mean and manipulative man, Jean-Louis, I'd prefer to leave it at that. My plantation is mine." She looked up and smiled. She would not say more. Just as well he thought, save the Cardinal, Gaby was his and his alone. He liked that.

Her inquisitive glance begged him to continue.

"Eh bien, I would love children with you, but if we never have any, it would not lessen my love for you. I do not intend on spending my old days on the Loire. I love America and I want us to return and live in Boston. I like the American spirit. It's a country that engenders hope and freedom for all. I know that for a woman, having a child is the crowning glory, but frankly, children are not that exciting to me. They would take too much of the time you now devote fully to me. I'm quite pleased with our life. I truly need no one else besides you. But if we do have children, we will manage and find a way to be just as happy."

By then she was in tears and she reached for his shoulders, then his face, and then his lips, bathing his face with her tears.

Chapter Thirty-Three

Gaby had taken the day off from the Conservatoire for she had a sore throat. She had some wonderful friends that were going to the Bois, so she decided to follow along. She sent a note to Jean-Louis to meet her there if he could. He had not replied. While everyone returned back to the Conservatoire, she lingered a while longer. She sometimes felt lonely in that big house all by herself and lately she had placed the stores off limit. If she continued to buy, her wardrobe would push him out of his dressing room!

Paris had been the site of her emancipation. She compared herself to many of the young women surrounding her. Quite a few appeared much younger than she was and yet at such tender age many of these young ladies were either married or about to be married to men twice and even thrice their age. Many had had their lives decided at their baptisms or in the foyer of the opéra. They had been chosen just like cattle. Her mother always said the country where one was born was either a one in a lifetime chance or a complete demise.

She looked up and she saw Jean-Louis arrive. She observed as he dismounted Boyer. She loved the horse he was riding. He returned the salutations of men and women crossing his way. Today his meeting must have taken him to a restaurant near by, *L'orée du Bois* perhaps. It was nestled on the periphery of the Bois. She sat cross-legged on a bench in a pensive mood as she twirled her umbrella above her head to shade herself from the bright sun. Finally he noticed her as she sat by herself. Eluding the Beau Monde, he reached the bench where she was sitting. He bent down and brushed his lips on her forehead.

"Un sou for all of your thoughts," he smirked.

"They are perverse, my love; I would not divulge them to you."

"You must, it's a French custom. Nothing in a woman's head should be left to one's imagination."

She stared at him. How she desired him. How she loved being held in his powerful arms. How lucky they both had been. Not many couples could pride themselves to be in such situation.

Desire burned her body. Dazed with passion and longing and aware that he'd divined her thoughts along with the rest of the walkers observing her demeanor closely, she heaved a long sigh. A pink shade crept up her cheeks.

"What are you concocting?" he questioned, a lazy grin tugged at the corner of his mouth. Should we take a walk in a very woodsy and private area of the Bois? I think the latter," he said with a hearty laugh. "Your eyes betray you, Gaby." She gently tapped his arm with the tip of her umbrella and started her beautiful, crystal-clear laughter. Grasping the umbrella, he pulled her up to him and casually led her to a more secluded area. Close to a small stream that cascaded over a stony riverbed that led to the Seine, he stripped off his jacket and threw his coat down on a grassy area shaded by two large trees. Clasping his hand, she forced him down with her. Lazily he moved in next to her and kissed her swan-like neck before he expertly unbuttoned her frilly white shirt and moved down to her opulent breasts. He waited for a few short minutes and admired the beauty who lay next to him. He bent down and kissed her gently, and then again and many more times, until fully aroused he threw his body on hers, forced her to recline and teased her womb with forceful thrusts.

"Is that what you want from me Gaby?" He thrust his manhood through her bouffant lacey skirt.

She giggled. Her mouth wide open, she spoke in his mouth, unable to control her mirth at his decisiveness and arrogance.

"Can't I hide any emotions from you, *Monsieur*?"

"None, absolutely none."

"I'll have to use my splendid theatrics to fool you so as not to appear perverse."

"Darling, you can be as perverse as you wish, everything works as far as I'm concerned" he looked down at her with adoring eyes, "and it is genuinely encouraged," he smartly added.

How embarrassing it would be if they were caught. The *tout Paris* would never let them live it down. All these embarrassing thoughts did not deter Gaby. The place was terribly romantic and she wanted him. They could hear the distant murmurs of the boaters on the Seine and the birds singing in the trees. She was an American—to hell with

Paris' society, she gathered. Spontaneously, she responded passionately to his touch.

"I'm glad I came at the right time today. Who knows what would have happened if I had not shown up. All that sexuality bottled up and oh, so many chaps. It should teach me to be more attentive to the beautiful and very sensual Miss De Conte Thornsen. Tomorrow, same place, same time," he murmured in breathless anticipation.

He had time in between meetings today and he lingered over her most of the afternoon. They watched the boaters and he told her about all the new developments that were taking place in Paris and once again the discussion of the reunification of the Papal States including Rome resurfaced.

"Gaby, I want you to come with me to Italy. I will play an instrumental role in the negotiations leading to the reunification of the remaining Papal States to the kingdom of Italy."

"The Papal States?" She retorted stunned. "I just don't understand, French troops are there already protecting the Pope? Will Philippe be involved?"

"He might be." Jean-Louis responded soberly.

"Well, of course I'm coming, you are not leaving me behind when and if it happens. Do you remember, you promised me in Normandy? I thought that was settled. You mean to tell me you have had second thoughts?"

"No," he replied lying, "and yes it will happen."

God, he had never been so happy and he dreaded to disclose that their dreamy lives in Paris might come to an end faster than expected. He would marry her—concern of respect when involved in Affairs of States. Primarily her safety was paramount. His security would be more inclined to protect and serve her if she was his Duchesse. In Paris, it did not make any difference. In Italy it might.

He thought of the challenges—a new country, new people, a cat and mouse game—all would have been titillating to him had he been single. But Gaby was his life now, how she'd handle the change in their private lives that was unknown territory. He could count on her stubborn spirit. Consequently, he would just have to prepare her for all eventualities.

He had requested his ship to undergo a modernization process for his future bride. There had been some ironic looks, but few had dared to question him.

"So, Jean-Louis-Pierre, you will take the beautiful American with you. What a lovely companion," General Arsique had sarcastically told him.

The intensity of the glare he received forced Arsique to spin quickly on his heels and found another target.

Jean-Louis did not like any of these men. He found them a bit too influential with Louis Napoléon. All possessed a rosy idea of the state of the French military. Jean-Louis was brutally candid with the Emperor in their presence.

"The lack of military preparation could cost you the Empire!" He'd retorted angrily as the Generals and advisers to Louis Napoleon vented their military advantages. "Let's not forget that France could found itself surrounded by the Prussians if Emperor Wilhelm prodded by Bismarck decides to place a Hohenzollern on the Spanish Throne left vacant by Queen Isabella. Are you prepared for a Prussian invasion? If it occurs, the Papal States become secondary, we will need the French troops that are protecting the Pope to return. You will need me here!"

"Naturally De Pleyssis, you spent too much time in America," the general responded sarcastically. We are very well prepared although your deduction is absurd," he continued, "why would the Prussians want to invade France? But if they dared, our troops are ready to inflict a decisive defeat." The three generals stood up and after the usual courtesy took their leave. Jean Louis stayed behind.

"I do not trust Bismarck, the old Emperor might be willing to let his grand son take on a more combative stance. I for one do not believe that Bismarck will let him. Be aware. We need more communication and diplomacy with Bismarck." He had reiterated to the Emperor.

These men when pushed for a plan spoke of the grandeur of the military and its readiness in the Capital and all of the French provinces. They were ready on all fronts, they proclaimed in the likelihood of an altercation with Otto von Bismarck of Prussia. Many took the Prussian Chancellor too lightly, Jean-Louis deliberated, and he thought that they should negotiate their positions rather than drain the French purse with needless wars.

"I'm concerned" he shared with Gaby, "Bismarck is a fox, he might try to ruffle some feathers that will be wrongly interpreted by the Empire."

"He appeared sufficiently tame at the masked ball I attended a few months back," she answered curious. "What kind of trap are you foreseeing?"

"Not quite certain Gaby, but Bismarck is an ambitious man, I found it odd that he would not tempt to lure Louis Napoléon and his pretentious cohorts into a political scheme of his own making. Placing a Hohenzollern on the Spanish throne, would greatly affect France's security."

"How would the Emperor react?" she questioned anxious.

"That is my dilemma Gaby, I am concerned that during my absence the military will control Louis Napoléon's response. His health is failing and Eugénie is easily convinced. They are liable to present the Emperor with a plan of attack that could assure total defeat of the enemy within days. The ideas are well conceived on paper. The reality is *autre chose* . . . the men are not well prepared. Many are poor, often hungry. Insubordination and disorganization are huge factors in the lower ranks." He stared at the boats pensively.

"The French army is tired and all the ostentatious plans on paper have no back up?" She questioned candidly, shocked.

"Something like that," he replied preoccupied. It was no great surprise to anyone in Jean-Louis' circle that there was no love lost with some of the Emperor's generals. Years from now he would suffer the consequences of his arrogance.

He looked down at her again. Life was going to be difficult for Gaby. She was accustomed to doing whatever she wished, when she wished it. However, on his ship he was Captain and he would not tolerate any insubordination from her or anyone else. To do so would place everyone in jeopardy. He could foresee a tremendous amount of conflict. She would fight him constantly. Life might be very harsh for her while he needed to be in complete control. They could handle it, he tried to reassure himself. She was smart. She probably would abide most of the time.

"Do you remember, Gaby how it was on the ship coming to France?"

"Yes, very well, every single minute of the crossing Jean-Louis. What an odd question."

"Do you recall that we were apart a lot? This trip will be pretty much the same, Gaby. The negotiations might last more than a year. Are you ready for the challenge? I will not take the assignment if you are not up to the task. We are happy here in Paris, after all."

"I want to, Jean-Louis, I really, really do." She had hoped he would offer marriage, but that did not seem to be forthcoming. She did not want to bring it up again. She wanted him to ask her.

"Tell me, Jean-Louis, when would we depart?"

"Nine months to a year, I presume, maybe less than that."

He still had plenty of time to bring up marriage, she thought.

Chapter Thirty-Four

The soirée at the townhouse of Gérard Louvier was splendid. All of Jean-Louis' English friends and Parisian crowd were in attendance. Jean-Louis had been called back upstairs. She hated these long nights. Everyone always appeared to have a great time but often the man she loved along with a few others would disappear from sight for hours. She usually danced the night away awaiting his return.

Tonight however a wonderful surprise awaited her. Renaud De Beauvaur had just returned from India. He was tan, magnificent, and flamboyant as ever. A lovely French trait—once a friend always a friend, she mused watching him talking, laughing, surely telling myriad exciting adventures that all craved to know. Their gaze crossed. She waived to him. Minutes later he nodded to all, he touched the elegant gloved elbows of a few ladies and kissed a couple of hands extended to him and hurriedly he crossed the ballroom towards Gaby.

"Gabriella, I have missed you so!" he proclaimed loudly. "I have so many wonderful stories to share with you. Let's have a déjeuner next Monday that is if Jean-Louis-Pierre will let you out of his sight!"

"But of course," she good-naturedly replied. "It will be great fun. I'm terribly happy that you are back in Paris, next week it is." A crowd gathered around them. Months before Jean-Louis and Gaby's reunion there had been talk of a romance between the Diva and the very wealthy aristocrat. They had been inseparable until his departure to India. He cast a skeptical glance at the guests surrounding them and quickly took hold of her elbow and whirled her around on the dance floor.

"You look beautiful Gabriella, I presume the grand Monsieur is treating you well?"

"He is Renaud, I'm extremely happy." She replied sweetly knowing that it was not the reply he wished for.

"What is it that I hear Gabriella, that you experienced amnesia in the Convent in Grenoble, the reason for your late arrival in Paris? My ears have listened to absurd scenarios on the subject of your reunion with De Pleyssis."

"Some things are better left unsaid," she proclaimed, a smile lighting her emerald eyes. "Mystery is a great source of curiosity. As an artist I need to have questions raised about my behavior, my life, my dreams, and my man. People will keep on wanting more, inventing more, this is the price one needs to pay for fame, Renaud."

"I do not think that Jean-Louis would appreciate your comments. You know how he loves his privacy. But not me, Gabriella. I adore all the brou ha ha. I knew from the first time I met you that we were made for each other," he flirtatiously teased as he gathered her to him and gracefully continue the waltz to the sweeping music.

"Well, Renaud, anytime Jean-Louis works late I would be flattered to have dinner with you." She replied amused.

"Run that by your lunatic lover, Gabriella," he laughed. "He truly is a lucky fellow. By the way, how is everyone treating you at the Conservatoire—now that you are a grande Dame? Caroline and I heard you practicing au Petit Conservatoire. You are an angel, my friend. Why hasn't Maître Lauriot placed you in all the performances? I was in London recently, and I understand that the Paris' opéra is the only venue allowed to you by De Pleyssis?" he questioned sarcastically. "What is that all about Gabriella, rumors I hope."

"Oh, that's another story, Renaud." She swallowed hard and heaved a long sigh. "Jean-Louis is not too keen on having me strut my stuff, as we say on stage, although I still have the right to practice, rehearse, dance, perform on stage now and then, perform in our home, and actually teach some of the younger students. This is an experience I have never had the pleasure to appreciate. I really like it. By looking at others' mistakes and or areas of strength I see where I can improve. And then . . . sometimes I do miss performing live," she confessed. As the words blurted out, she wished she had not shared that last piece of information.

Renaud De Beauvaur certainly should not have been her confidant as she revealed her ambivalent discontent with her present lifestyle— it was such a minimal sense of loss. She'd gladly given up her career as a soprano at the opéra. She led an exceptional life ... again she wished she had not divulged her sentiments. It must have been the champagne and the knowledge that her singing was spectacular. When she compared herself with the sopranos who'd just finished their arias, her heart sank.

The all-knowing Renaud perceived a touch of resentment in her voice. He did not let go of it. After all, Jean-Louis-Pierre was an adversary in business, in political influence, and certainly, in love. Renaud would have no problem instigating sentimental conflicts in their relationships if he chose to do so. He'd professed his plans clearly the first time she'd met him in Nice.

"Eh bien Gaby, I sense a bit of umbrage. So you miss performing?" he concluded with a grin.

"Well, no, not at all," she said. "I'm perfectly happy to perform in recitals for our friends." She justified not very enthusiastic.

"Eh bien ma chère all that could change suddenly if you will it. I'm back and still very much enamored with you," he proclaimed haughtily with a wink and a chuckle.

She chose silence.

The orchestra took a well-deserved break and quickly Renaud led her to a more secluded area.

"Your glass requires attention, Gabriella" he scooped a flute from the barman that he gallantly handed to her and he asked for a scotch. Quickly a group of friends rejoined them and the conversation continued.

Having been told that his beautiful American was dancing happily with De Beauvaur, Jean-Louis stepped out of the meeting almost immediately. As he hastened out of the room, two of the men laughed heartily. "Who would have thought?" An older man with a long blond curly moustache decried with ill-conceived annoyance.

Jean-Louis glared darkly at Renaud as he located the couple from the upstairs foyer. Someone leaned toward Gaby and murumured in her ears. she glanced upward and noticed him. A smile and a waive from her gloved fingers rewarded his reappearance. Quickly he began to scale down the long formal staircase as she turned back politely to the circle of friends who had just joined them.

"Well, I see that the Master was advised that we were having a jolly old time!" Renaud murmured in Gaby's ear. "Bonsoir Jean-Louis-Pierre," Renaud clipped as the two men faced one another.

"Bonsoir Renaud, I see that you did not loose anytime to reignite your friendship with Gaby," he clipped back. "When did you return?"

"About a week ago, I spent some time with my mother in Deauville and I returned back to the capital pronto. I'd hoped to catch one of Gabriella's performances at the opéra. I understand that it is no longer feasible" Renaud curt reply resonated in the great hall.

Jean-Louis clenched his jaw but nevertheless he tried hard to appear good-natured about the fait accompli.

"Eh bien, it was a delight to see both of you." Renaud countered with an exhalation. "I look forward to our déjeuner next Monday, Gabriella."

"Likewise," she responded joyfully. Renaud quickly turned on his heels and departed with three women following him. He nodded to a group of friends in the sitting area across from the dance floor.

Gaby shot a sideways glance to Jean-Louis. None too pleased was he. Well, well she huffed silently amused, a well-deserved consequence for leaving her to mend for herself. Actually she was thrilled that Renaud had returned. Essentially he was her only great friend in Paris.

"Eh bien Jean-Louis are you going to ask me to dance?" she questioned coyly.

He did not respond. She stepped in his arm and let herself gather close to his body for a short minute before he whirled her on the dance floor. The next hour was pure delight but as usual the politically influential men attending the soirée this evening lured Jean-Louis back into their circles. Once more four economists, two bankers and several advisers to Louis Napoléon surrounded him. She tapped his back gently and whispered, "I'll be back shortly." He nodded as he watched her climbed the few steps to the powder room.

If she was a journalist, this is the very place where she would seek out stories, she pondered. All the gossips of the Haute Sociétée originated in these beautifully decorated rooms. While she rearranged a couple of diamond barrettes in her curls, she heard someone call out her name. She moved closer to the wall that divided the two rooms and listened intently. It was Juliette De Beujeot, a socialite, Jeanne-Eloise De Forge, another amusing gossip on this side of the North Sea, and Caroline Lloyd who was in Paris for the season. She had met her in England with Jean-Louis last summer. The woman was a wealth of knowledge on London's history, but her salacious comments on everybody's lifestyle on both sides of the channel was vile. Consequently, Gaby stayed away from her. Caroline, unlike many women of her time, was highly educated and actually quite fun. Unfortunately, people emptied their souls to her; she would then spread the scandalous comments in every salon she attended.

Jean-Louis's name and the Faubourg were mentioned. She drew a bit closer. Apparently Jean-Louis had bought an apartment close to the Elysée where he worked. She had not heard of it.

"Eh bien, that is one thing one can say about Jean-Louis, he is a formidable and amazing man. Thank God the love affair with the little colonial is coming to an end or at the very least appears to be waning. I have caught him looking at other women with his usual roving eye."

"It was absurd. What is it that they had in common?" Marie-Hélène scoffed.

"She is brilliant, that I can attest to, but since when did Jean-Louis-Pierre like intelligent, brilliant women. He just has one thing on his mind, and it is certainly not conversing about the inequities of our social classes with women. He likes long-legged blondes who have a reputation of conducting themselves well, preferably with no inhibitions in bed, if you know what I mean," retorted Carolyn, looking auspiciously toward Catherine. Gaby had caught the expression in one of the mirrors.

"Well we have heard nothing of her promiscuous nature, but she is pretty, even stunning, for her diminutive stature. Her demeanor, however, is so unpolished, so spontaneous, it is hard to understand what Jean-Louis-Pierre sees in her. I do have to admit; I have seen something in him that I never thought I would ever encounter in his kind. There was, for a short period of time, a look of perfect adoration pour *la petite*. He looked at her the way he had never looked at any one of us. Sorry, Caroline, not even you." Juliette commented wryly.

Astounded, hurt beyond words at the revelation, she wished to flee but felt immobilized by the pain.

"As I was saying," Juliette continued, "I understand from Charles De Louvet, who used to cavort with him and is still his right hand man in the State Affairs, Jean-Louis-Pierre has bought a magnificent apartment close to the conservatoire. It is close to his office in the Elysée as well. His love nest, he referred to it," Juliette laughed. But you know him well, Caroline, isn't that his trademark? The pretty American is on her way out. Charles says the place is absolutely magnificent with the latest, most modern niceties. Well, you know with all the brou ha ha, he needed to spoil her a bit more than the others."

Gaby could not budge. She was devastated. She straightened to her full height and took in a deep breath. Walk on stage, she murmured to herself. She strolled past the group of women, looked haughty and glanced at the cruel bunch with a pretentious glance that only the French could understand.

"What rubbish, Mesdames," she smiled, nodded and strolled out of the room swallowing the tears mounting in her eyes.

Walking out of the room, she walked straight out to the garden for some fresh air. She was getting sick and could not force herself back in the ballroom. Every time she tried to return, she could feel tears swelling in her eyes.

Jean-Louis wandered around the room unable to find her inside. Finally he found her outside, sitting dejected on a cement bench surrounded by her favorite roses.

"Mademoiselle, you look picture perfect in that setting," he turned the corner and noticed her face drenched in tears.

"Gaby what happened? Why . . . why are you crying? You looked so happy an hour ago? Someone hurt your feelings?" Although Gaby was resilient, arrogant and mean-spirited remarks from his circle of friends would often devastate her state of mind for hours. Gaby was too candid to hide her pain; he would detect it immediately if someone caused her some sadness.

He pulled her up to him.

"Tell me darling, why the waterfall?" he laughed. "No one here can be taken seriously. You know that, why do you let it affect you so?" He pressed her to him, kissing her temples. "Come, Gaby, tell me."

She had promised herself not to question, but . . ."

"Jean-Louis did you purchase an apartment in the Faubourg?"

He was surprised that she had been told—but disinclined to divulge the secret.

"Who purported this bizarre idea? I'm quite happy with my home. And you, Gaby?" An unwillingness to lie to her outright kept him from asking more in depth questions.

"I love your home; the view is impregnable, and the servants, well, I fell in love with them, too." She replied timidly.

"Good, we are both happy, forget all the absurd comments you hear. I'm happy, you are devastatingly happy, so why look for things to be sad about?" He bent down, kissed her lips, and turned her around back to the ballroom wiping her perfect features with his handkerchief. "Mon Dieu, Gaby, you are so beautiful. I have never seen features so refined, elegant and just so plain damn perfect."

She smiled. For a moment she obliterated all that she had heard.

He turned her around and brushed his knuckles along her chin up to her temples.

"You are all congested and teary-eyed, beauty. Let's walk and be alone for a while."

Jean-Louis had been drinking heavily as well, although he was not one to shy away from what he wanted, he never let his inhibitions get the best of what he willed. The brandy was working its warmth and magic on his sexual desire. He wanted her.

They followed a long winding path where a lovely and hidden rose garden concealed a secluded sitting area where the mistress of the house and their guests no doubt must have enjoyed the magnificent aromatic garden.

Jean-Louis clasped Gaby's waist and pulled her to him, kissing her passionately and drew her breasts away from her gown.

"I love you, Gaby. I have never in my life felt a need to have a woman close to me at all times. I often think that you possess the missing chip that makes me whole—in there." He pointed to her heart-shaped diamond locket. "You keep it locked up away from me to keep me in constant need of your company."

"You have been drinking way too much, mon cher, concocting such things? You've said yourself time and time again, that sex is just a need. I'm sure you could find a long-legged blonde as desirable and fulfilling as myself when it comes to satisfying your needs, Jean-Louis"

"Of course, Gaby, that's a given. Many could satisfy me. But it is the connection, the feeling of completeness when I'm deep inside you that I experience only with you." His hands traveled up her thighs and into her warmth. She shivered with anticipated passion. He continued to caress her breast with his free hand. Desire mounted and spread all over her body.

Unwilling to care about anything that would cause her pain, she reclined in his arms. She probably was wrong to believe these horrible creatures. Why would Jean-Louis profess his love so tenderly if he had any inkling of shooing her out of his home? She threw herself just as passionately into her lovemaking. She adored him, he adored her, and that was that. She had to stop listening to every gossip that the tout Paris concocted about their affairs.

He sat her down on his engorged penis and rocked steadily deep inside her for a long time, as he kissed the back of her neck. A wonderful warmth engulfed her body. Keeping her close to him after the moment, he brushed his lips to her eyes and closed them. They stayed entwined in each other's arms for a very long time.

"I think we need to return before they come and get us, chérie. Up, beautiful. Lucky lady, you have been verbally comforted, your tears erased with kisses, your womb warmed to a passionate and languorous height by the most wanted and desired man in all of Paris. It is now time to perform your duties as the great love of the Duke De Bourbonne and show your great strength—cerebral and artistic, I mean—the reasons why I so adore you."

Her beautiful crystal laughter echoed in the garden and hand in hand they slowly climbed back to the main floor. As usual, he was soon called away. She directed herself toward Renaud and his friends. She'd miss him.

"Alors Gabriella, will you enchant us with your melodious voice." Renaud stared sensually in her eyes. She pursed her mouth and looked up at his very manly face.

"Maybe," she retorted amused. "Are you ready for the performance of your life?" She loved flirting with him. He was *un homme recherché*, very much like Jean-Louis. There was no end in sight to his vast fortune, he collected lovers and paramours and was most generous, but his most ardent passion was reserved for the casinos. Renaud was a hardened gambler and his passion had no end in sight. Their glasses were refilled and the conversation turned to the glamour of Paris.

"I miss the capital immensely when business takes me away to another continent," he remarked candidly. Suddenly she noticed Renaud's gaze leveled across the room. She jerked backwards. Leaning back on a pillar, a lazy grin swept across his face, Jean-Louis watched her while surrounded by a crowd. She beamed, and returned his leer as she touched her diamond locket with her gloved hand. She tapped it a few times before cupping it and holding it down firmly with her hand. She heaved a long sigh.

Gaby works her magic on everyone that knows her he seemed to ponder. She hoped that she was right. She sipped several gulps of champagne and regally strolled closer to the pianist. They exchanged a few words. She lifted one hand to her throat and elegantly lowered it down on the instrument.

"Eh bien, Juliette" said Carolyn, "I think our little story needs to be tossed to the wind. Look at him," she whispered to her friend. "Poor Lou-Ann, she will probably have to wait a while longer. He still appears quite taken by Gabriella."

Gabriella De Conte Thornsen began the chosen aria.

The enchanting voice rose in the great hall. Silence fell—all were transfixed. She teased her audience with her passionate theatrics. Reaching the end of the aria, she sensually grasped a red rose from a crystal vase set on a rosewood table nearby and bit the stem of the flower as she danced wildly to the cadence of the orchestra. The guests began clapping to accompany her theatrics that she never failed to include even during a recital. "Une artiste incroyable, an incredible artist" the guests cooed. Once again the audience was mesmerized. It was Jean-Louis who retrieved his senses and walked across the ballroom, taking her in his arms and onto the dance floor. He nodded to the orchestra. They begun La Valse Du Désir by Beethoven.

"I'm going to take you home and beat you," he laughed.

"Oh the perfect evening! I have been wined, danced, comforted, and passionately made love to by the most eligible bachelor in Paris and now I will be spanked. Mon Dieu, I marvel at my tremendous great fortune."

He held her closer. "I can hardly be called a most eligible bachelor, chérie. You certainly have placed a lid on that one."

"Pardon me, you said it yourself less than an hour ago."

"I told you I was the most wanted man in Paris. I happen to have this exotic beauty at my side from morning to night."

"I hope you appreciate it, Jean-Louis," she responded sexily.

He swept her expertly across the room. Not taking their eyes away from one another, they danced as if the world ceased to exist. It was not until the wee hours of the morning that the awaiting servants happily saw the Duke and his cherished lover ambled in the mansion.

The following day was Sunday. They rode out of the capital fairly early to the suburbs and returned back to Paris very late.

"What is your schedule this week, Gaby?" he asked while they strode back from the stables.

"The same as last week." She retorted exhausted.

"Good, let's keep tomorrow morning open. There is something I want you to see." The rest of the night he kept her close to him. He had planned on showing her the apartment later in the week. Nevertheless De Beauvaur was to pick her up for a déjeuner tomorrow. He would take her there tomorrow. She'd have to send a note.

Upon their late return home, Jean-Louis had been passionate as usual. Surely he was right. She just should not let these women spoil her own happiness. It was insane. And yet Chouvet knew Jean-Louis well. Jean-Louis must have his reasons for not telling her, but then again he did not deny it and what about tomorrow morning. Was he going to ease her away from him slowly? Why didn't he acknowledge the apartment? Did he have un petit amour, another love?

Jean-Louis woke up and watched her staring at the ceiling wide-awake.

"Is there anything wrong?" he demanded. She shook her head and moved in closer to him, taking his arms and placing his hand on her heart.

Gaby was acting strangely, he thought. He watched her wander around the house as if it was the last time she was looking at it. Maude and Pierre walked in to ask if they could enter their bedrooms and bring in their breakfast. She touched Maude's back affectionately with a heavy sigh. What was she concocting? Then he began to wonder. He had seen her talk to Renaud last evening. Had she develop sentiments towards him? No, this was absurd, he concluded. Gaby adored him.

"Are you ready, mademoiselle?" He asked.

"Yes," she said, trying hard not to show her melancholy.

"I presume that I should go to work on Mondays. You appear annoyed by my presence."

She walked to him and encircled his face with her arms affectionately. She pressed her head on his chest. No, it could not be the end of their love affair, she told herself.

He turned, drew her down on his knees and swept her hair from her face, "I love you, Gaby," he said with great emotions and kissed her.

"I love you too, Jean-Louis."

They stayed in each other's arms for a long time.

"I should figure out a way to get you involved in the French political system. You would be with me at all times. I'd like that," he said sweetly.

Breakfast was then served and half an hour later the two of them were on their way out. Gaby was silent in the carriage.

They were going toward the Faubourg. They stopped in front of a magnificent building, the concierge let them in, and the elevator stopped at the fifth and last floor. He produced a set of keys in the large foyer facing the door of the apartment and then he entered.

Gaby was livid. The gossips had been correct. She was kindly being escorted out of his house.

Clueless about the sadness that he inflicted on his lover, Jean-Louis was elated. Except for his house in Boston whereas Bullfinch had been commissioned and the small castle in Villefranche, he had inherited all of his properties. The castles, the one in Normandy, the one in the Loire, the estate right outside of London and the mansion in the Ile Saint Louis all had been the De Pleyssis' estates. But this one had been his choice, just for them in downtown Paris. She loved the Madeleine. She often prayed there. She would be within walking distance of the Church and all the shopping areas, the Champs Élysées, the theatre—everything was near by. They could both rest here at midday if they wanted to and furthermore, he had built for her the most modern of dressing rooms. She would love it, he thought, delighted. Had it paid closer attention to Gaby's facial expressions, he could have predicted the coming storm.

Sadness had disappeared. She felt betrayed and her deep-seated survival skills re-emerged. She was no longer sad but firm, strong, and now sure of what he had concocted these past two months.

"So, Gaby, what do you think of your new waterhole?" he shouted on the threshold between the bedroom and the salon where she stood. He had spent a lot of time and creative energy in accommodating the most modern apartment. All looked perfect as far as he could see.

"The apartment is magnificent, Jean-Louis," she said stoically cold. "You will enjoy it, surely. Don't expect me, however, to live here. I do not need to be weaned from your home."

He flipped facing her, flabbergasted, not quite understanding her words. He thought she would be thrilled; their own little place close to his meeting places, the stores, the opéra, her church, a thoroughly modern music room, which would be the envy of the director of the opéra himself. He walked out of the bedroom.

"Gaby, I have spent nearly two months decorating, summoning contractors, finding the right marble for your tub, of all things, and you are telling me you will not step your precious little American feet in here?"

"No, I will not, Jean-Louis. Remember I'm a wealthy woman, I do not need to be bought or assuaged or weaned from your home, or any home. I thought that you would have been a bit more creative when it came to me, darling, I presume you want to resume your life as a bachelor. Two years are starting to weigh on your aristocratic shoulders. Well, mon cher, you can keep your trademark for your future paramour. I can afford my own!"

She walked right out of the large sitting room toward the foyer.

He did not quite know what transpired, but it had something to do with the ball they'd attended a few nights past. Following on her steps, he reached for her forearm and then her waist, flipping her around none too gently toward him.

"Explain that gibberish to me, Gaby? Are you thinking that I am pushing you out of our home so that I can be *a célibataire* once more?"

"Aren't you doing just that, Jean-Louis? I have been told so. I overheard Caroline Lloyd, Juliette, and Marie Hélène saying that Chouvet told them you had just purchased a love nest. Come on, Jean-Louis, I am no innocent moron. He is one of your best friends and your trademark, as they say is—"

He did not let her finish." That was it, last night, right? Admit it."

"There is nothing to admit, Jean-Louis, these women are never wrong. Cruel, brutal, pitiless, vindictive, yes, but never wrong. So save your lies and deceitful words. I want nothing from you."

She pulled her arm out of his grasp and ran to the door. She was already down the staircase when he started after her.

"Gaby, come back," he shouted until he became aware that someone in these elegant dwellings would surely recognize them. He began running after her. Damn, the little witch was light as a feather running down the stairs at lightning speed. Her sobs were perceptible, as he got closer. He caught up with her on the final step and expertly reached for her upper right arm and drew her back to him.

"Don't touch me," she shouted. He picked her up and intercepted the elevator that had been called down below.

"Hush, we need to talk."

"We said it all already. I want to go home and—to go to your house and move everything out, now, Jean-Louis."

"Gaby, stop. You are ridiculous." The elevator stopped on the floor where they stood. His gesticulating mistress in his arms, he marched in awkwardly and slammed the wooden gate behind him.

"Let me go! I hate you. You're a deceitful—" At this very moment the elevator stopped—a shocked, elegantly clad old man with a cane, waited patiently. He paused for a moment and watched in disbelief as the Duke De Bourbonne carried his sobbing mistress out of the elevator.

Jean-Louis walked on the platform and realized that he'd locked the keys inside the apartment. Still holding Gaby in his arms, once more he spirited the elevator right in front of the old man's face.

So much for neighborly pleasant relations, Jean-Louis thought. Gaby tried to disengage when they reached the lobby.

"If you annoy me one more time . . . Gaby, my patience has its limit!" She kept quiet without letting go of her repulsion directed at him. She was serene now. Nothing would change her mind. If he thought he could see her at his leisure, while returning to his guilt free lifestyle—well certainly that scenario was not in the cards. Commitment was primordial—the very aspect she would never relent on.

Jean-Louis called out for the concierge to open the door of the apartment. Through the service elevator, the servant reached the floor faster than the quarreling lovers.

The man with the top hat still waited as they reached the top floor. Unlike the reaction of most Frenchmen in such a precarious situation, he observed calmly. His reserved demeanor and stiff upper lip displayed an ironic expression on his face.

"Is everything fine, Monsieur Webster?" the concierge called out.

"I believe the Opéra is over. Please call the lift." The man responded in a haughty English accent. A sarcastic smirk hung on his lips.

The couple re-entered the apartment. He sat Gaby on the chair, walked to the bar, poured two glasses of brandy, and walked back to her.

"Drink!" He ordered as he placed the crystal glass inches from her face

"No."

"Drink!"

She grasped the glass and set it on the table near by. He pulled one of the chairs close at hand and sat facing her. She returned his stare.

"Gaby, what brought on this moment of foly? Let me in because I'm at a loss."

Hesitant now about the veracity of the comments she'd heard.

"You explain," she shot back. Quickly anger rousted her once more. "What made you think that I would even move here, Jean-Louis? Are you mad? Do you find me so desperately in love, so vulnerable, that I would lower myself to such a despicable living arrangement?"

"Despicable living arrangement?" he exclaimed, "are you mad?"

"Yes, despicable. I don't need you, not in that way. Just let me go!"

Finally, it dawned on him that she was under the impression that the apartment was a parting gift. He leaned his head back, reclined in the large overstuffed leather chair and laughed uproariously.

Incensed, she bolted from the settee and slapped his face as hard as she could. She spun on her heels and promptly marched with great pride to the door.

Immobilized once more, his mirth veered to rage.

"If you open that door, Gaby—God help me!" He shouted loud.

She opened it and bolted across the threshold.

This time her agility was no match to his reaction. He ran behind her, reached for her arm, pulled her back in the residence, and with a swift kick he slammed shut the heavy door. Taking hold of both her arms with one hand, he lowered his head to her mouth.

"You are infernale," he shouted. "Stop, for God's sake, Gaby. I bought it for *us* as a love nest, not as our permanent residence," he roared incensed. I'll think twice before I'll present you with another superb surprise. I'm selling it—it's a nightmare!"

The revelation troubled her. "Why would you want to have another place in Paris? Your house is across the river?" she retorted less forceful.

"Well, just for that reason. We would have had a place closer to our workplace to unwind, to be alone, to meet in the middle of the day without having to cross Paris."

Still with a slight touch of doubt in her voice, "It is a fabulous place," she murmured sheepishly, as she moved closer to him. "I thought you wanted me out of Saint Louis," she revealed.

Her honesty always touched him. "No, Gaby, I called it a love nest before, but now I will call it a lion's den if we keep it. As I said earlier, chérie, it's yours and mine, if you so wish." He swallowed hard, his anger now assuaged he gathered her to him as his lips grazed her ears. "Gaby, listen once and for all, I intend to spend the rest of my life with you. I will never release you. You are my air, my water, my very breath, and the missing piece of the puzzle that makes me whole. I hurt when you are not next to me. I love you."

She rested in his arms, silent, and faced the opposite side, "if you truly intend to spend the rest of your life with me, why not marry me?" She whispered to his forearm, embarrassed to bring up the subject at such a junction.

Stunned, he stopped kissing her and brought her even closer to him. "I will, darling, when the time is ripe. And the way it stands right now, it will probably be sooner rather than later.

She pulled away and looked up intently at him. "That is an awful way to speak of our union, Jean-Louis. I'm no ball and chain . . . ripe? Ripe for what? It is not a business deal that I want."

"I know Gaby, it would make you happy." He looked down at her less than idyllic expression. "You would be ecstatic, wouldn't you?"

She did not answer and her face did not reflect adoration!

What was it with Gaby? He could be so sure of her reactions and at times when he expected the least commotion on her part, she would place doubts in his mind about everything that pertained to them. Damn, he thought, his assertiveness shaken, at times he felt in total control of their relationship and yet just one glance from these giant green eyes would fling the control out of door! Falling in love with a doormat would have been so much easier.

"Gaby, look at us now, our wedding would take months to prepare. Our privacy would be intermittent at the very least—our life in Paris less than personal. I am a famous and influential man and I am expected to have a huge marriage. My Grandmother has friends in every part of the world and I would not break her heart, but if we were called to Italy, Gaby, the transition could be immediate. We could then handle our wedding on our own terms, personal, intimate or just the way you want it. I do not want it to become a matter of Church and State. Personally, I'm comfortable with our situation. I do not need a piece of paper that reminds me that I adore you. I never will."

She let herself fall back fully in his arms. He was right. It would be truly wonderful to be his wife. Man and woman were so different, she pondered. This feeling of belonging to someone, to show off to others that she was the one—the chosen one. A lot of good it did to many wives in this day and age; they were cuckolded at every opportunity their husbands possessed. Well, whether she liked to admit it or not, she would love to be his wife, but she had lowered herself enough today by asking outright and his answer had been less than passionate.

She turned in his arms and kissed him with all the love and passion she felt for him. He pulled her down on the sofa. She missed a step and fell on the new Aubusson. He kept her there, kneeled down, and then laid his body on hers.

"Let's try out our new rug," he grinned.

Chapter Thirty-Five

In Paris, Louis Napoléon's complete control of the city's many institutions became more and more contested. Haussmann, the architect of the City of Light, was under fire for taking bribes and many of his colleagues had to resign. Some had even been fired and were now being prosecuted. In this spirit of discord Louis Napoléon decided on a new Grande Exposition. He wanted above all to enlist the help of the Russian Tsar. This particular accord would assure France a partner on the East of the Prussian States. Jean-Louis had warned of the less than compliant Count Bismarck. Years later, in 1894, the Treaty would be signed, but unfortunately for the last French Emperor, the Magnificent Fair along with its illustrious guests were to be the last hoorah of The Second Empire. Less than two years later, France would declare war on the Prussians, and its armies would be defeated in a matter of six weeks.

* * *

Amidst the spirit of cordiality between Italy and France, the Italian Ambassador had given a grandiose soirée in his palatial townhome. The following morning in their sumptuous bedroom, propped up upon mounds of white delicate lace pillows and rumpled coverlet, Gaby tossed her mahogany mane backwards and uncovered fully the magnificence of her porcelain-like breasts. She winked and shot a seductive smile his way. Desire flashed in her emerald eyes.

"When will we leave?" she questioned amorously.

"Sooner than expected," the Duke answered with sadness in his grave voice, as he walked from his dressing room to the massive bed where she lay. He knew all too well that their lives would take on a different turn. He stood over the bed, looking down at the woman he adored. He pulled over the wrinkled sheets and moved in next to her, his arms encircled her small body.

The ball last evening had been grandiose and they'd reveled in all the festivities. They'd returned in the early morning hours and most of the day had been spent in bed. Later that evening they walked downstairs to the library. In front of the impressive fireplace, Gaby in a frilly gray and white dress sat on the Duke's lap and read the Gazette. Jean-Louis encased her waist in his right arm while his other hand held documents that he was intent on evaluating before the long voyage. Last night, talks of their trip to Italy circulated in every social circle. The planning for his professional life was laid out. Time was of the essence, now he had to prepare for his personal life. He gathered her closer to him to catch her attention. It worked, the paper fell to her knees, and she looked up to him, curious.

"Gaby," he said nonchalantly, "I have gotten our marriage licenses; it is necessary that we get married fairly soon. Choose a date and place. I'll take care of the nuptial and social arrangements." He caressed her hair and placed a kiss on her temple.

Had he looked down at her shocked grimace, he would have known from the onset that he had committed a grave error. But, clueless, as often men are about women's sensibilities, he continued his trend of thought. "As I predicted, our mission to Italy materialized sooner, rather than later. I have decided to proceed. I want you to be my wife, share my name for safety and status' sake. I want everything in order. Louis Napoléon knows that you will accompany me—on this particular point there was no negotiation." He smiled and held her even closer.

"I beg your pardon?" she interrupted, flabbergasted, disbelief in her voice.

"Happy chérie?" he questioned, not presaging the tempest that agitated her.

"Happy?" she repeated, outraged. "You are joking?" she snapped, as she still entertained the elusive dream of a formal demand in marriage. She looked in his baby blue eyes and the realization that he was absolutely serious stunned her.

"Have you no compassion? No understanding of a woman's mind? Of a woman's need?" she shouted. "We have been together for two years, I thought that you would understand my passionate and romantic nature. I have never been asked to marry, but a demand in marriage is not a statement of fact," she retorted angrily. She grabbed the documents he held in front of her abdomen and tossed them angrily on the rug. Heatedly, she removed herself from his lap. "You are asking, no, *telling* me to spend my whole life with you without even a pretense of romance, a special moment that I could hold dear in my heart forever. I'm not a slave that you will to yourself."

Caught by surprise, he heard the words come out of his mouth. "Don't be absurd, Gaby. We made that decision long ago."

"Not that I'd say no," she continued, oblivious to his insensitive statement, "but I just wish you could have asked me to marry you in a very special way." She softened her voice. "Like telling me you'd love me forever. Every girl wants to hear that."

She walked away toward the sidebar and fixed herself a brandy to steady her nerves.

Jean-Louis was shocked, first, by the tone of her voice, second, by the absurdity of her rationale. They had been living together like man and wife for close to two years now. He had thought that she would be delighted. How unpredictable.

She shot him a glacial look and went upstairs.

What had just transpired was incomprehensible. Perhaps Gaby did not want to get married? For God sake, he fumed; he probably was the most passionate lover in Paris. She certainly could not complain that he was not romantic enough. Was there someone else in her life? He speculated despondently.

His first impulse was to follow her upstairs to mend the altercation and to have her explain her bizarre reaction to a married life with him. But, instead, he consciously remained ensconced in the large leather chair.

He ate alone and later that evening he heard her magnificent voice resonate throughout their home. Gaby must have spent a good part of the late evening in her music room. He decided to join her. "Music and singing has a way of making me forget all sadness," she had told him one night.

As he entered her world, she turned and looked up to him as she continued her singing. He took a seat on the piano bench and listened. Always, Gaby would stop all her activities as he entered her room, he recalled sadly and, radiant, she would run in his arms. Not tonight, the night he had told her of the pending marriage ceremony. She had shown no emotion and she continued to do so. Instead she looked through him, his presence as transparent as a Baccarat flute! He lingered on the pink-flowered satin bench for a long time, ignored, as he anticipated a reversal of mood. Gaby showed no sentiment. Even the aria she sung showed no compassion.

Devastated with her odd response, he went to bed and waited anxiously. He could not latch on to her bizarre behavior. Very late, she walked into their room and slipped quietly into bed. He rolled to her and held her in his arms. "I love you, Gaby," he said, on tenterhooks for a response. But none came forth. She had not returned his kisses and furthermore, she had pushed him away and rejected his advances. Stunned, he lay awake as a million questions surfaced throughout the night.

At the breakfast table the following morning, he asked about the motives behind her conduct.

"Gaby, you seem so angry, I just do not believe your claim of romanticism. What is the real reason behind this anger? Mon Dieu, I asked you to marry me, not to burn on the cross!"

Angry, she retorted, "I'm enflamed, livid. Why don't you ask your friends how they asked their wives to marry them?" She walked out on him again.

In effect, it was just the romance, he contentedly deducted. Thank God, he thought, it hit him, like a large boulder rolling down a steep mountain slope. He had never really thought of how important romance was to a woman. He had made that transition early on in their living arrangement. He treated Gaby as an equal on account of her keen intelligence and logic. They both were made for each other and he adored her. He had forgotten how romantic she was. He'd hurt her. Knowing damn well that if he ever had been wide of the mark in their relationship it was now! He was dead wrong. He stormed out of the breakfast verandah, determined to do something grand to atone for his lack of compassion and insensitivity. He caught her in the foyer and he reached for her waist, gathering her small body to him. His lips landed on her sensual throat and then her lips. Momentarily, a frisson shook her shoulders, but she did not respond and she pulled away as she turned and returned to the verandah toward the sidebar, seemingly oblivious to his presence. He hated it when she behaved in such a haughty demeanor. Mon Dieu, she was not French, how could she be so good at it. He smiled.

"I'll return soon, chérie." He tried again enthusiastically, desiring a response. Another long silence, and then she left the room.

His impulse was to run after her and kiss her. He decided against it. He had to seek penance and make some important arrangements. He called Fernand to have his carriage drawn to the entrance. Without waiting for the servant to hand him his coat, he grabbed the long gray overcoat and walked out of the house.

The family jeweler in the Faubourg was located on the Right Bank. He stopped and chose a modern setting for a large emerald, and later, he summoned his secretary to reserve a table in the Café La Belle Athénée in Montmartre. Her friends, Manet, Monet, Degas, Pissarro and especially Frederic Basille—Les Artistes, as he commonly called them—surely would be there to discuss all the new gossips of the several salons they attended, but more importantly, all were there to discuss their new modes of painting Paris and its suburbs, as it appeared to them—in the now. No more classical themes, no more romantic motifs, and no more mythology, but the present was foremost in their thinking and to their credit the moment had never been more enthralling. Napoléon III, himself had founded a new salon for these artistes of modernity, called the Salon Des Refusés, the Salon of the Refused, since many of them had been refused at the yearly Paris Grand Salon, founded by Louis the XIV in 1668. Gaby adored the new colors and themes. He was quite fond of these artists as well. The Manets had been casual friends of his family and he liked Edgar as well. He entered the very fragrant and beautifully decorated store of the florist, Madame Devoreau. Surprised, the florist straightened to her full height behind her counter, she shoved her bright red hair away from her face and brushed her apron.

"Monsieur, quel honneur, your visit enchants us. How fortunate, the favorite roses of mademoiselle have been sent to us from the provinces. Yvonne, my young helper just retuned from Les Halles.

We all love the central new market that our Emperor so wisely chose for our beautiful new Paris, the new nuances in color are splendides, Monsieur, they will arrive in your townhouse in less than an hour. A bientôt, je vous remercie."

Pleased, he walked out of the small store, and later that day, after a lengthy lunch at the Cercle, he picked up the ring and the emerald necklace he had chosen earlier. His family had used this jeweler for more than one hundred years and the *bijoutier,* jeweler, knew her taste and size. Happily he hurried home.

As he entered his vast townhouse, Gabriella was nowhere to be found. He knew she had seen him arrive. She peeked through the parted white lace curtains of her boudoir when his carriage entered the courtyard.

Climbing the staircase three stairs at the time, he found her in her dressing room, looking at herself in the mirror.

She glared at him as he walked in and did not even say hello. The flowers, which had arrived earlier and appeared everywhere in the large boudoir, did not appease her mood very much, he thought.

He walked decisively toward the pretty brunette that now totally ignored him. He collected her to him and forced her pretty face to him as he covered her mouth with his ardent kisses.

"No escape until you hear what I have to say." He kissed her once more to assuage her demeanor, as he picked her up and placed her on the sofa near the fireplace. The difficult little witch needed to loose her control and now that all of his insecurities, those about the possibility of another man in her life, evaporated after her candid confession this morning, he was happy to attend to his manly duties to amend for his sordid deportment.

The urge to take her to bed was renounced. His sexual discomfort would make him sound even more passionate, he judged. Not so easily he stood up.

"I'm sorry, my chérie, truly sorry. You are so smart, beautiful and charming. I take all these charms for granted and I'm totally repentant." He knelt before her, a contrite smirk on his handsome face. "Will you ever forgive me?"

She caught her breath after the passionate interlude and sighed. Something close to a grin cracked her sexy pout and she stood up from the sofa, enjoying the physical superiority. He attempted to straighten up but she abruptly brought him back down to his knees, her long and graceful fingers resting on his broad shoulders. She stared down at him as she placed more pressure on his shoulders.

"Stay down and expiate a while longer. I'll tell you when you may rise." She turned her back to him and started once more towards the dressing area.

In a split second he was back on his feet, with Gaby in his arms.

"I'm taking you to a favorite place of yours for a chat with your friends, les artistes. I think you will like it."

A grin hung from her pretty mouth. She wished she could hold a grudge. She told the servants to help themselves to the food as she walked in her new redingote held by Fernand. The coat was to die for. She had fallen in love with it while in a store in the Faubourg. It was the latest rage in Paris, all white with pretty gold buttons that encircled her tiny waist. She sensed that she was very attractive.

He looked at her, kissed her a long and passionate kiss, and did not let her go until he felt her body respond.

"This coat looks beautiful on you, Gaby. Is it new?" he asked with great interest.

She smiled. Jean-Louis never noticed what she wore.

"When I look at you, Gaby, I ask myself what have I done right to deserve such an angel?" He noticed a faint smile on her face, so he continued with a sexy and sulky voice as he kissed her just below the earlobe.

Quite aware that the reason beyond all the compliments he showered upon her now was to mollify his rude statements on marriage, she fought his advances a tad longer. He deserved it! She could have asked him anything she wished for now, but she could not think of anything—she had it all. She knew that he adored her; it showed at the balls, at the opéra, at the theatre. He could not help but to keep his hands or his gaze off her. Actions spoke louder than words, she was well aware of the old adage, but last night his nonchalance toward matrimony had hurt her. That was one of the most important moments in a couple's life for God's sake, she thought.

She kept her distance in the carriage and appeared cooler than usual. He knew he had hurt her and he could not bear to look at her disappointed face.

How could he have been so callous? He chastised himself. That was beyond reasoning. Gaby never forgot anything, not his birthday, the day that they met, or the day that they first made love. She would leave love notes on his dressing table, poems on the seat of his carriage, and stay by him night and day when he was ill. She shared with him romantic passages in the books she read. "Isn't that well said, Jean-Louis?" she would ask.

For him, life as a couple had been cemented the first night she had spent in his home in the Rue Saint Louis en Ile. Inculcated in his brain forever was the very first night they had formally entertained. He could not keep his eyes off her as they formally received their guests in Normandie. The pride and overbearing love he felt for her was still overwhelming—even now. These two moments had been momentous in his life. A real union had been consummated.

How foolish of him not to see marriage as the epitome of their life. She had told him a month after their reunion in Paris, and again last year when he had bought the apartment in the Faubourg that she wanted to be his wife. How heartless and pitiful on his part.

They finally arrived at the restaurant in Montmartre. They stayed a while in La Nouvelle Athenée and they strolled over to Le Moulin de la Galette. Close by was Renoir sitting with his friends. Lots of diners, drinkers, and dancers were cavorting to the music. They served her favorite dessert, *la tarte Tatin*, a caramelized apple tart that she ordered whenever she noticed it on the menu. The music was lively and fun to dance to. The artsy scene that surrounded her softened the edges of her anger and disappointment. She was beginning to talk and laugh with him. Jean-Louis came around the table and for the second time today, knelt in front of her and took her hand.

"Mademoiselle De Conte Thornsen, puis-je avoir l'honneur de passer le restant de ma vie auprès de vous? May I have the pleasure to spend the rest of my life at your side. He smiled, still on his knees, when from the corner of his eyes he noticed the reporter of the Gazette, *eh bien*, he thought, it was bound to happen. He continued.

"Mademoiselle, are your tears joyful or are your tears streaming down your cheeks, over the loss of our former arrangement?" She touched his cheek and bent down to kiss him.

"Joyful," she replied.

"Can I assume that the answer to my question is affirmative?"

She nodded and looked for a kerchief that he gallantly provided. Her voice could not utter one word.

He opened the small velvet box that he spirited out from his coat pocket and reached for her hand. He kissed it and quickly placed a splendid diamond on her finger. She could not speak before—now she was mute. He stood up, pulled her up and kissed her tears.

"Thank you, my love," he whispered in her ear.

While the courtship was happening, no one paid attention, people enjoyed these free and fanciful moments, dancing, flirting, discussing new books, new artists. What a wonderful place Montmartre was. Unlike the bank of the Seine where literally dozens of painters sat and painted the new colors of the season, Montmartre still captured the caché of Paris. The wild and exotic life, the seedy café and circuses where Mademoiselle La La, a young black American hung from her teeth from a trapeze as she performed her acrobatic theatrics, and naturally the Moulin Rouge, where artists and courtesans sold their wares.

Degas and Renoir had taken her there more than once, late at night after the opéra. That was the very place where she first had a glass of absinthe. Naturally she had not said a word about her escapades in this sleazy part of town. It was just that Manet and the boys, as she liked to call them, wanted to show her the Café Athenée where Charles Gleyre, their art instructor conducted art and cultural lessons on painting life as it was. The scent of wickedness wafted through the small square gray houses where cries of pleasure and vulgarity converged and could be heard from the street. Concierges shouted their displeasure at the debauchery that took place in their buildings while pimps dressed in black with straw canotiers hats guarded their meal tickets like marauding hawks. The foundation of the Basilique of the Sacrè-Cœur was almost complete and the crooked streets that debouched on the butte were replete with tenements that housed most of the Parisian proletariat that had been displaced from the city center. High Christian morals rivaled the most sordid dissipation in the new capital. To add softness to this picturesque scene, little pots of red geraniums hung on the railing of the upstairs windows.

"That is the true Paris, Gabriella," Edgar repeated over and over again as he pointed toward the workingmen and women he liked to paint. In the present he could not get enough of the hat makers, the milliners, sewing ten or twelve hours a day the new bonnets that no aristocratic or bourgeois women could do without. Bars and cafés were everywhere on these streets and at night the lively voices brought drunken men and women on the dance floor, dancing à la Musique of the time, their bodies touching as they cavorted on the dance floor.

Paris in spring was for the first time in the city's history filled with a marvelous scent that floated from the newly planted trees along the banks of the river. The bateaux-mouches did their round up and down the river bringing much needed provisions for the newly constructed restaurants that entertained the new bourgeoisie. Anywhere else, the world would have stopped and they would have been the center of attention and gossip. As it was, nothing of the sort occurred. She took his hand, held his palm to her lips and kissed it tenderly and as she gently tugged on his lapels to force him down, she took his face in her hands and kissed him passionately. Time passed. She savored the moment. The afternoon ran into early evening. They strolled in Montmartre, as they admired the paintings, and socialized with several artists friends that they both knew.

These avant-garde men and women were fascinating—the new take on life, titillating. In a world of poverty and harshness, for the impoverished, the artists let the sun shine in. Tired after such a long day, they slowly started for home. Nestled in his arms, she was where she ought to be.

"I want you to call me Duchesse after our marriage," she said haughtily.

He grabbed the hood on her fur hat and pushed it down over her face.

"Remember, Gaby, on the notorious day of our marriage, I will have some rights over you." He laughed heartily.

"Such as?" she questioned.

"The right to victimize you if I so choose, if you disobey my orders, wives have little rights in France outside of their homes, you know," he teased unmercifully.

Her eyes glared at him. She half seriously started to remove her ring.

"Stop, Gaby, I was only joking. You have way too much power over me, chérie, I'll be the one who ends up being tortured."

The carriage left them in the courtyard and Jean-Louis insisted on entering through the main entrance. He took her hand and pulled her tired, achy body behind him. She dragged slowly up the marble staircase when he finally picked her up and entered the foyer. As she looked on, the hall was covered with white roses, the lights turned on as if they were giving a grande soirée. Without her knowledge, over seven hundreds guests had been invited. His friends were in attendance and her artist friends provided music and entertainment. She smiled, crimson.

His Grandmother cringed at the sight of her future daughter in law—an American no less! Instead of acting regal, and walking royally down the elegant marble staircase to be introduced formally to the Grand Monde—as the etiquette of such an illustrious family would have it—the chit made her first formal entrance in her grandson's arms, hair disheveled, and dressed haphazardly. No class, no tradition, her son would have gone mad.

"Where did Jean-Louis develop such a flavor for the tasteless," the dowager whispered to her long time companion, Count Henry. The old distinguished man smiled and tapped gently the wrinkled hand that rested on his arm. It was beyond her understanding. Well, now at least, she probably would have a little more influence over Gabriella. She'd rein her in, if Jean-Louis did not care to, she thought.

Flabbergasted, Gaby looked up toward her fiancé.

"Jean-Louis?" she uttered, confused. She quickly slid down from his arms and smiled shyly, greeting some of the guests. Damn, someone had called in the photographers. Tomorrow their cavalier pictures arriving from Montmartre would be all over the newspapers. She did not like conventions, but she knew proper etiquette, and mostly she wanted him to be proud of her.

"Yes? Is that enough fanfare, Mademoiselle De Conte-Thornsen?"

She quickly asked her maid to come up to help her dress and left Jean-Louis with his friends. But before she ran upstairs, she looked for him, found him, and sweetly reached for his hand and kissed his fingertips.

"I love you so much," she whispered, "you can torture me all you want—just like today," she whispered as she scanned the room with a graceful gesture before she disappeared upstairs to bathe and change.

Everything was already in motion in her dressing room. She stopped, thrilled. On her bed lay a beautiful green fourreau dress that she had considered a while back and a pair of matching satin slippers at the foot of the bed. He had been to Madame Gauthier, surely. Her favorite champagne chilled in a large Christofle silver ice bucket was on display. She poured her favorite bubbly in a St. Louis flute. Jean Louis would come up. She quickly bathed and combed her hair and quickly wrapped a towel around her body.

Jean-Louis had asked Cunnan, Luke, and his Grandmother to oversee the guests for a while. It took Gaby forever to get ready. As he walked in, she ran to him—in her birthday suit.

"I knew you'd be stalking me upstairs," she said as she encircled his waist in her arms and pressed her body into his. "I have never been happier, thank you." She smiled at him, waiting for his kiss. As he bent down to reach for her lips, she placed her hands in the back of his pants and smoothly moved forward.

"Gaby," he laughed, "get a hold of yourself. We have seven hundred guests down in the ballroom." His desire for her however was lit.

"Darling, they've waited this long, I'm quite certain an extra twenty minutes will not matter. We will not be missed," she continued, as she began to remove his belt.

399

He could not fight the urge of making love to her—nor did he want to. He placed his large hands on her breasts and teased the aroused nipples. Excitement and desire ran through her veins, the glass of champagne made her a bit heady, and without too much fanfare, she pulled him to her and kissed him tenderly. "I love you, darling and I'll always will."

"I love you too, Gaby." With one swift motion he placed her none too gently on their bed, intent on tasting every bit of her sweet body. She came to climax quickly and then rolled away from him, winked, and rolled off the bed.

"Up and away, it's high time we meet our guests." Frustrated pain shot through his longing body.

"Gabriella, you are not sending me downstairs like that, you little witch, engagement or not."

"Chut, not one word, darling, you forgot," she laughed heartily, "it's all about me today."

He reached for her, missed her and just as she stood up he quickly pinned her down on the Aubusson rug.

"In your sweet dreams, ma chérie."

Twenty minutes later, they forced themselves up from the carpet. It was excruciating to get up and get ready once more, she thought. But by now, she knew most people had been aware of the couple's absence.

Before they left the room, he held her close to him tightly, sensually. "I love you, Gaby, and I'll always will."

"I adore you Jean-Louis, I never, never want to argue, ever again. It's so painful."

"Oh, I'm sure that we will, you came quite close to hurling me to that warm place down below merely twelve hours ago."

"Right again. I was so sad, but how could you have planned such a perfect day, so quickly?"

"I took your advice. I asked a few of my close friends yesterday at the Cercle how they had asked their wives to marry them and I upstaged their own engagement by one hundred percent. He kissed her one last time.

"Now, our engagement has turned into a business transaction?" She sent a dark glance in his direction.

"Gaby, I am not the most romantic person," he sighed. "Everything that is real and beautiful, I have learned from you. Give me time, darling. I adore you," he pronounced solemnly.

She stood watching him and came closer. "Tonight will be inculcated in my mind until the day I'll die. It's the second most beautiful day of my life," she murmured.

"Second?" he replied curiously.

"The first was when I met you." She brought his hand to her lips and held it there as she laid her head on his chest.

A short while later, they walked to the large foyer overlooking the grand ballroom and all their guests. They stood a short while looking down at the now silent crowd awaiting their hosts, and then regally, the Duke and his fiancée stepped down the impressive marble staircase leading to the ballroom. As the music once again started to greet the influential couple, Gaby squeezed his hand. He looked down at her, smiling.

"I hope," she whispered, "that we will have a very, very long and happy life together."

"We will, ma chérie, eternally," he responded gravely.

The following weeks, she noticed that Jean-Louis was really making an effort at romance. Naturally, their busy social life continued and now that she was betrothed to him, everyone wanted to see the ring over and over again, as if le Grand Monde wanted to assure the veracity of the future wedding of Jean-Louis-Pierre De Pleyssis to the beautiful American soprano, Gabriella De Conte Thornsen.

Chapter Thirty-Six

A week later Maître Barandi, became ill. He sent word that if his students wished to practice, they would find him in his studio in Montmartre.

Most students delighted in the rare cancellation. In contrast, Gabriella was disappointed.

On stage, waiting for her friend Marie-Louise, inadvertently her gaze shot up toward her fiancé's loge. From this vintage point Jean-Louis' loge was perfectly situated. She walked slowly to center stage and visualize herself singing, the flowers covering the planks after her performance . . . the audience in awe . . . she even loved the scent of the grande salle! Ah, she hoped that Jean-Louis realized what she had given up for him—an immense part of herself. A few weeks ago, he'd made love to her during an excellent rendition of Mozart's Magic Flute. First, the door had been locked and the exquisite brocade curtains had been pulled down for privacy. She'd chuckled at the shocked expressions of the gentlemen who had come to call on him during the interlude. At the very first knock, Jean-Louis promptly had pulled the cord to reinstate the curtains in their places on each side of the golden sconces and tapestries. She'd watched him sigh, stretch fully, and button up his rich black velvet jacket as he ran his hands through his thick wavy dark hair. He'd looked as respectable as he could have under the circumstance. His regal demeanor indicated that this act had been practiced to perfection. The scoundrel, she grinned.

Slowly he'd opened both doors as he'd glanced back at her. In connivance she'd winked. He'd chortled as she sat deliciously upright looking perfectly proper. She'd pretended to be fully engaged in the performance unfurling before her eyes. Perfect theater it would have been had her elaborate curls and diamond studded chignons had survived their passion. Instead her hair was disheveled, cascading over her curvaceous shoulders while the golden ribbons that previously held her mane lay scattered on the thick carpets along with many diamonds and a few baby breath petals. "Worthy of the grand composer." Jean-Louis had whispered.

Most men never listened to a full opéra, they wandered from loge to loge, they visited their mistresses, or they stood in well-lit salons to be seen conversing with the grand of their world. Women had just started the same practice. For years, the dictate had been to stay quietly and happily in their seats while their spouses and lovers gallivanted amongst friends, their bankers, or their lawyers. Recently, a few wise women had taken the initiative as a group; they'd begun to walk around as well and although it had raised a few eyebrows among the old society, the practice kept up with the times and everyone appeared to be happier because of it except for the tenors and sopranos whose art, they said, was no longer appreciated.

The jaunt had gotten massive amount of hype in the Gazette the following day, prompting Jean-Louis' Grandmother to call upon him.

"I know that you are running about with an entertainer, however, Jean-Louis, need I remind you of your proper upbringing in the world's most noted capitals."

"Need I remind you, Madame, that Gabriella will soon be an integral part our illustrious family? I am astounded at your sudden interest in the gossips of the Gazette. I recall the days when you excoriated the very individuals who peruse through this trash in the kiosques of the Boulevards." No response had been received and Gabriella had given her future mother-in-law the most innocent of looks at their next visit at the Manet salon.

Later that day, she and Jean-Louis had laughed over the perceived importance of his pedigree for hours while they play cards and drank Dom Perignon.

"A real ordinary and vulgar practice for a well-bred woman," she'd ironically retorted. "Oh, mon Dieu, I have spoiled the little choir boy. What a pity that you had to fall in love with an ordinary, unpolished woman born and raised in the wild colonial world of America. I truly wonder, Jean-Louis, why she faults me for all of your awful behavior?"

Uproariously laughing, Jean-Louis had walked to her while he'd tugged her down to the sofa." I am a man, need I remind you that in this world, men rule—always my dearest." He'd kissed her hard to suppress another tirade on the oppression of women.

She scanned the opéra house from the stage, one last time. Back to reality, she told herself, as she brushed her hand over her satin skirt. Instead, she continued her vision of a full house. Goodness, it was so real. She missed it so.

Gaby felt warm lips on her cheeks. "Bonjour, Gabriella, *tu rêves,* you're dreaming, *ma chère?*" Lilianne asked appropriately.

"Bonjour, Lilianne. I'm most frustrated. Maître Barandi cancelled his lesson. He is too ill to travel to the opéra." She looked intently at Lilianne who was just as disappointed. "He has given his permission to meet him in his studio in Montmartre. I think we should go, Lilianne. Jean-Louis has taken me to Montmartre," she pursued. "I have an excellent sense of direction. I'll get us there quickly."

Lilianne hesitated. She was not the most liberated woman in the troupe, but she was smart, very smart indeed, one of the few in that circle of artists. Gaby truly enjoyed her company. They never ran out of subjects to talk about and fun things to do. Very much like Gaby, she could lose herself in museums and she regularly attended lectures and discussions in many salons. Sometimes Jean-Louis lectured at the *Académie Francaise*, the fame *Institut De France*. The French persisted in keeping intact their beautiful language and famed history. They honored its spirit. She admired that trait immensely.

Lilianne had been raised as a poor aristocrat in the Haute Savoie and had left her family estate to follow her married lover. He'd placed her in a luxurious townhome in Aix-En-Provence, but as the outrage from both families mounted, it had proven to be too difficult to keep up the affair. An impresario had spotted her in a rendition of *Swan Lake* at the local opéra house and had offered to further her art at the *Maison des Arts* in Paris. Lilianne had jumped at the opportunity. Her lover promised to help her financially and in less than three weeks she had left for Paris to seek fame and financial independence. The scandal in Aix had gotten so out of hand that her father had disinherited her and had forbidden her mother to ever contact her. Her sister would visit her a few times a year and these times were always special. She had not been allowed to return prior to her mother's death—a guilt she could not seem to surmount. She had achieved fame at the Nationale Académie des Arts as the first ballerina at the

Paris opéra—no small accomplishment. However, her love life was chaotic.

"Gaby I do not think that we should. Poverty is rampant in that part of town and crimes against women and children go unnoticed," Lilianne warned, knowing that Gaby had made up her mind and that her statement was just a matter of polite askance.

"Trust me, Lilianne, I am accustomed to danger. New Orleans is a most treacherous town. I have learned to navigate and keep *mon sang froid*, my fortitude, in these type of settings," Gaby replied forcefully. "We will be just fine. Besides Jean-Louis took me there a few weeks ago. It was perfectly fine."

Lilianne nodded.

"Come, it will break up our daily routine," Gaby remarked, terribly pleased that she had convinced her friend to join her. Before Lilianne could change her mind, Gaby started toward the door and they left.

The crowd in Montmartre was a bit different than the one she'd experienced with Jean-Louis at the Café Guerbois. The two women were looked over in an aggressive fashion and stared at unabashedly by passersby. Both knew quite well that all in this quarter saw unaccompanied women without a carriage as common workingwomen. Earlier today, Gaby deducted that her own carriage was much too ornate with Jean-Louis's coat of arms encrusted in gold on the doors. Lilianne had called for a simple landau. However, upon arrival, both felt a bit uncomfortable and out of their element, especially after asking for directions. Gaby bent down elegantly and touched the boot where she inserted her handgun daily.

"Music teacher, hein?" some sneered. "How about a few baguettes or some milk for our starving kids. Your filthy money won on our back could help out humanity," an angry, dirty looking man responded.

Out of nowhere, a very tall and secure in his demeanor mendicant came closer to the girls and pushed the man who had accosted and insulted Gaby and Liliane.

"Let them be," he snapped out loudly and with a cane he began swatting away at a small group that had gathered, obviously looking for mayhem.

Quickly without a word the assemblage dispersed. Gaby wondered about it but Lilianne's trembling body returned her to the task at hand. She jerked her gaze away. "I'm feeling faint . . . a malaise, Gaby, let's return" the dancer expressed frightened. "We'll be just fine, Liliane," Gaby proclaimed firmly. She grasped Lilianne's hand and slid it under her elbow. Interlaced the girls quickly turned on their heels. "We will be just fine," Gaby reiterated, determined to arrive at the Maître's dwelling.

"Although I am not a Parisian, I know about the Republican Movement that inflame many young men and women in this part of town. Many hungry souls have been pushed back on the periphery of Paris because of the re-construction in the capital—" Gaby begun.

"Gabriella, perhaps we should return quickly. It will be late when we get back," Lilianne pleaded.

"No, of course not, it will be a wonderful lesson, Lilianne. We live such an affluent life, it is good for us to experience first hand a world that is deprived of basic needs and that suffers. I'll have to talk to Jean-Louis," she murmured almost to herself.

Lilianne was silent. She hurried the pace with ill-conceived annoyance.

"I just have a different outlook because of my background." Gaby deliberated. The war was frightening, Lilianne, but I survived it and it gives me strength knowing that I have. In addition, I lived in New Orleans and I spent time with friends from school in one of the plantations in Natchez. The buff was quite nice, but down the hill from the domaine, the seedy elements of the city resided. Murder and rogue living was prevalent, I have a small gun inserted in my boot. Jean-Louis has instructed me to do so. I have it with me at all times. I feel quite safe and secure."

Lilianne held on ever so tightly to Gaby. The ladies finally arrived at the apartment and had to find the *porte cochère*. Maître Barandi's studio was on the third floor and the girl decided to walk up since the 'monkey cage', the word that Gaby had coined for the elevators in France, was in service.

The Maître was first surprised and then extremely pleased to see that his two most talented students did not want to miss a day of his wonderful coaching.

"Ah, Mesdemoiselles, how I wish the Duke would let Gabriella sing Violetta, in *La Traviatta* this fall," he proclaimed dramatically. "I have rarely heard such clarity, such strength of voice and oh . . . the control of the notes! Perhaps you could convince him, Gabriella, just for the gala performance."

He offered the girls some tilleul with honey. Eagerly they accepted. As they sat on the burgundy settee, the Maître commenced his usual tirade about the ill effects of all milk products on the rendition of the vocal sounds. Gabriella did not bother to listen to him and poured a large amount of fresh cream in her tisane.

"You do not appreciate your gift, Mademoiselle Thornsen," he chided. In a few short years, it will sound like a badly tuned piano— brassy. *Quel Malheur*! What calamity!" He whined.

Gaby looked at her friend and sighed. Ironically she rolled her eyes to the ceiling. Both stood next to the piano. A very ornate grand sofa and two golden satin fauteuils were placed nearby as they reviewed notes and nuances. Although she was a magnificent ballerina, Lilianne loved to sing and she never missed an occasion to attend a voice lesson if Gaby asked. A woman shouted just outside the door and the clanking of boots echoed on the wooden staircase and then in the corridor.

Barandi, Gaby, and Lilianne looked toward the entrance door. A deafening bang knocked the bronze tapper to the wooden parquet floor. Barandi's butler was pressed in the salon against his will. An instant later the door flung open and Jean-Louis, too tall to fully stand in the archway stood bent forward. He surveyed the dimly lit room and quickly located Gaby.

"Jean-Louis, do not fret, darling, we came for our lessons, I remembered the lay of Montmartre to the Butte quite well," she beamed. Without as much as a nod, he marched straight to her.

She was about to thank him for coming when she noticed the angry, no, murderous glare displayed on his expressive face. She remembered that look. The very same one that flashed on his face when he had forbidden her to travel to Prussia when the Emperor Wilhelm had expressed a deep interest in her interpretation of the many opéras he loved.

He definitely was not a happy camper. She crossed the room slowly to cajole with a seductive smile.

"What are you doing here without my permission?" he exclaimed ominously.

She tried hard to stay calm after his demeaning statement. No need to wash their linens in public, she thought. She would deal with him at home. Still smiling, she kept up her pleasant demeanor.

"Well, what does it look like? Maître Barandi was ill, so we came to him," she retorted. "How did you find us, Jean-Louis?"

He lapsed into silence, but her cape was thrown on her lap.

"Put it on now. Lets go," he raged.

"I beg your pardon . . . your demeanor is outrageous," she responded, incensed from the embarrassment she could no longer contain.

Once again, she received no response. Jean-Louis marched close to her. He clasped her delicate fingers with his steely grasp and drew her none too gently toward the door.

As if years of good breeding briefly took over his callous attitude, he turned gallantly to Liliane. "Liliane can we take you back to your apartment? My carriage is waiting downstairs."

Lilianne was petrified, for herself and for her friend. In a moment of self-preservation, she acquiesced. Walking home alone to her apartment on the grand boulevards was a more terrifying thought.

"Oui, merci Monsieur Le Duke, I would greatly appreciate it."

Gaby was irate. He was offensive to her but he treated her friend with deference. How demeaning, she thought. Reluctant to cause a scene in front of the Maestro and Lilianne, she glanced at her teacher. He smiled condescendingly. He must have been accustomed to these scenes. He did not appear at all surprised.

"Thank you for the tilleul, Maître," Gaby remarked politely as she tried to regain her composure. Jean-Louis held her forearm firmly. She disengaged of the offending hold.

Unwilling to ferment the situation, she kept quiet. Countless times she had told Lilianne to leave her lover, who was jealous, brutal, controlling, and very married. What a hypocrite she was, her friend surely must be reflecting.

She shot a murderous glance at Jean-Louis. He shot back a steely glare that frightened her. Gaby decided to ride out his mood. She lifted her shoulders to her ears looking to her right at Lilianne. The poor girl had been shaking since the encounter.

"*Je ne sais pas*, I do not know," Gaby ventured with that charming American accent that would have melted the most hardened heart. Jean-Louis however was in no mood for her niceties.

As they waited in front of the carriage for the footman to bring down the steps, Gaby noticed that Jean-Louis nodded imperceptibly to a group of men facing him. At odds with the movement but too concerned about Jean-Louis' irreverent behavior, Gaby climbed inside followed closely by Lilianne.

"What is your address, Lilianne?" Jean-Louis demanded. The ride to the Grand Boulevard was ominously silent. Jean-Louis looked out the window, not uttering one word. His fury was assuaged now that both women were safe in his custody.

In contrast, Gaby was fuming. She could not wait for her friend to be brought back to her apartment, so that she could unleash her furry. She would tell him in no uncertain terms that his behavior was not acceptable.

Lilianne knew that their behavior today had been less than lady like. She did not utter a word, either, although Gaby proposed many open-ended statements. The ballerina could not hide her pleasure when they finally arrived at her place of residence.

"Merci beaucoup," she said, relieved, as the carriage came to a sudden stop, Lilianne bent down to kiss her friend. She squeezed her arm as if she could comfort and strengthen her in the face of adversity. Seconds later, with the help of the footman, she scurried out of the carriage and into the street.

"I will see you tomorrow, Lilianne. Have a pleasant evening." Gaby called out.

Jean-Louis did not even bother to acknowledge a courteous remark. Although he hated to admit it, he was an innate aristocrat. He would never have behaved in this boorish demeanor if Lilianne had been his equal. Class division was forever engrained in France. It alarmed and depressed her. She wondered if her American status placed her lower or higher in the class hierarchy than Lilianne's. Letting her curiosity take the best of her, she was about to ask Jean-Louis about it, but she took note of his tightened jaws. She would approach the subject at a later time. How long was he going to hold on to his anger? His behavior was innerving, she mulled over.

For his part, Jean-Louis was ready to strangle the little witch. Of all people, he knew about the old maestro's reputation and so did Lilianne and her friend Marie-Louise. The old man took sexual advantage of all of his pupils, dancers, and singers—anyone who had the misfortune or the fortune of needing his services. A great maestro he was, but an odious louse!

"*Je suis artiste jusqu'au bout des ongles,*" he would proclaim. Sexual payments were not unusual, Jean-Louis had been told candidly by one of his theatrical paramours. No wonder he had forced the old man to come to their home under lots of supervision when he could not be there himself. Gaby never asked why all these people were present while she worked her voice. All that arduous work had paid off. She had reached and was able to sustain clearly myriads of difficult arias, a feast in this day and age. Mozart, Rossini, Verdi and Puccini would love having her singing the lead in any of their opéras. Her high coloratura voice was a dream for opéra lovers—that is if Puccini ever made up his insecure mind and write the score of Tosca from the famed playwright Victorien Sardou.

When they arrived at the hotel particulier, he had not forgotten his fury. He climbed down the carriage, grabbed her waist, and lifted her out and down on the pavement.

"Stop this childish behavior. You are hurting me, my heel is caught in the stone," she exclaimed.

He abruptly let her go and did not bother to look back. He hastened up the marble steps. She ran to him and made a mad dash for his hand and gave it a tender squeeze. He kept it there for a while and then brusquely let it go.

Fernand caught the flying frock flung to him and quietly came to Gaby to help her out of her gray satin coat. Almost immediately Jean-Louis clasped her upper arm like a vise and he led her promptly in the library. For an instant she was left in the middle of the room as he walked to the sidebar to fix himself a whiskey. He downed the beverage and once more he became aware of her presence. He quickly pivoted on his heels and stared angrily.

"Why in God's name, Gaby, did you go to Barandi's without my knowledge," he bellowed ominously. There are pimps and prostitutes and Lilianne knows better than that. You walked to the mansard in Pigalle, unescorted, of all things, to practice with a theorist? Mon Dieu, Gaby, where is your sense of logic? You are young and very foolish. Did you even think of what could have happened, if only by pure chance I had not encountered Marie-Louise, who by the way, was more than pleased to share your escapade?" he finished incensed.

"But you took me there, Jean-Louis, just last week. There was nothing to fear, you know that." She had never seen this side of him and she began to feel threatened. He towered over her, his voice low and ominous. Maybe she should confess that her choice had been skewed and irresponsible. She started to walk closer to him to assuage his fears.

"Don't you ever, I repeat EVER go there without me." He cut her off.

"I hate you," she began, and turned her back to him. She strolled toward the sidebar for a cup of coffee. "How dare you—" before she could finish, she felt his breath on the back of her neck.

"You what?" he growled. He jerked her around forcefully. "I saved your life and you hate me?"

She continued to walk away. Damned if she'd admit her culpability now! Exasperated, she looked up to him. They had not been in enough altercations for her to sense how hard he tried to control his ire. Her green eyes filled with wrath focused on his stare. She drew even closer.

"Why do I need your permission about anything, Jean-Louis? I'm not a three-year-old child. I can manage my life quite well without a master. As a matter of fact, I did a pretty good job of it until recently. Remember, I lived on a plantation and survived the Civil War. I'm sure I can take care of myself in a sophisticated city without having you as my guardian angel."

"Gaby, the area you were in is seedy, dangerous and treacherous, even for a man alone. There are all sorts of unsavory characters who would like nothing better to rape, torment, and violate you in every conceivable ways or even kill you if they knew who you were and what you meant to me. The poor and downtrodden have been pushed to the outskirt of the city, exactly where you were—for the good of progress and modernity," he finished sarcastically. "The chance you took today cannot be repeated, Gaby, do you understand? I ask that you not go there without me."

At last, his voice had changed as he explained to her the dangerous nature of her decision. It was almost paternal. He wanted her to see the light. She shook her head as if his concern was overplayed. Stunned that she still displayed a recalcitrant glance, he placed his hands on her forearms.

"No, I don't ask, I forbid you to even go near Montmartre. Am I making myself clear?" he demanded, expecting acknowledgement of his command.

Gaby's pride was wounded. She was livid and wanted to regain her composure and equal status. "You are mad," she continued unwisely. "You are insecure and jealous of my love for music. It's your only competition, as you so proclaim. Why do you need to own me, Jean-Louis? Cease right now because you will fail. This whole ordeal is absurd, insane, and unthinkable. It's absurd, do you hear me?" she shouted. "I will go where I want to, when I want to, and how I want to, whenever I so desire. Is THAT understood?"

Because of her fury, the rage that returned to his face went unnoticed. He tightened his clasp on her forearms forcefully and forced her down on the leather chair next to the side bar. She looked up in horror. His face was now inches from hers.

"Don't you ever speak to me in these terms—ever again," he responded threateningly, "nor use that tone of voice—ever. You will regret it."

Flabbergasted, it took her several minutes to assess the situation and what had just transpired. She felt dizzy, but her frenzy mounted and exploded. His hands felt like steel clasps on her lacey sleeves. She freed one of her hands from his rigid grasp, stood up and reached for the cup of coffee on the sidebar. She wildly flung it at him.

Rage swelled. He pinned her wrists to the wall behind her.

"You are a beast, an animal, how dare you? Only a coward would lose control and immobilize someone smaller than them." She lifted her hand to strike him, but he caught her free wrist once more and this time his hand clamped down hard again on her forearm, tightening his grip like a vise.

"So, what's your point?" he asked sardonically.

She uttered a sharp shriek. "Let go of me, I'm numb. I cannot feel my wrists," she shouted.

He relented.

She inhaled deeply as she massaged her hands and swallowed hard. "My point? My point is that you are, *un lache*, a coward, a person who has no power and likes to prove that he has power over someone smaller and less powerful than he is. I hate you. I will never marry you—never, I'm leaving right now." She removed her engagement and flung it in his face, nearly missing his temple. She pushed him and stood up. "How could you?" She suddenly broke down, tears swelled in her expressive eyes. "Why, Jean-Louis?"

"You crazy little fool. Do you know what is happening in the streets these days? Kidnapping, rape, and murder—" His face brushed hers. She felt his breath on her cheek. "Look at me, damn it!" He pushed her harder against the wall.

She kicked him hard, bent down and slipped beneath his arms as she bolted toward the door. His long arm grabbed her and violently yanked her back to him. For a moment, she thought he would strike her. Instead, he lifted her up in his arms and carried her up the stairs, two at a time before he dropped her unceremoniously on the settee facing one of the fireplaces. He straightened up to his full height and slowly marched to the window, he parted the curtains and stared down the street.

"You little fool," he rasped. "Just yesterday, your lovely friend, Armande was attacked in her carriage. Her driver and footman were shot dead and they pulled her out and beat her savagely. She is still unconscious in Durand's clinic. Furthermore, late last night, Madame De LeFevre was beaten so severely that she was blinded and both her hips broken. She died early this morning."

"I can't live my life in constant fear, " she murmured. "I was not alone, for God's sake!"

"Go to your boudoir, Gabriella, before I completely lose my temper. I can assure you, you will not like the consequences." He glared down at his coffee-stained trousers.

"Go to my room? You are sending me to my room? You are dreaming, darling, but let me assure you of one certain flaw in you mighty character. You are a controlling dupe and a dreamer," she shouted. Your behavior is unaccepta—"

"I'm going to show how unacceptable my behavior really is," he sputtered. "I have to return back to the city, but all in my household have instructions to watch over you. You will be locked up in this room until I return tonight. Is that sufficiently curtailing your independence? Hopefully, it will inculcate some logic in your pretty but empty little head!" As he spun around, he threw his stained coat and vest on the floor and strode to his dressing room.

She watched his strong defined jaws tighten. Better not say anything now. She would pack up and leave him tomorrow.

"And don't try to leave," he shouted from the adjoining room. "Guards will be placed at our apartment door. You can manipulate the servants, I've noticed that, but these men have your safety in mind. Don't even try, you'll make a fool of yourself."

Gaby watched Christian, Jean-Louis' personal servant keep an eye on his dressing room. His eyes were glued to its half-open door while Charles entered the room with large wooden logs in his arms. He walked ever so softly and lowered the wood quietly into the fireplace.

Juliette, the dining room maid, stepped in as well with a tray that she quickly hid on the carpet behind the settee. Promptly, Christian nodded them out of the room and furtively closed the door behind them.

Dressed in full formal attire, he re-entered their bedroom and noticed the fire. A smile hung from his lips. Most of the servants had been in his service ever since he could remember, he paid the bills, he thought, but his servants' allegiance had quickly turned to the pretty brunette that was watching his every move, unperturbed.

"I will see you tonight," he murmured, his anger diminishing with every passing minute. "Don't try to climb out of your prison," he shot gazing at the windows. "As you can see, no trees were planted close to the balconies. There was a reason for that, Gaby."

She did not answer. Instead, she stared him down until he placed his hands behind his head and massaged the back of his neck. He gazed at her once more, turned on his heels, and spoke sharply to Fernand, who had been privy to the entire scene—his facial features unable to hide signs of reprobation.

"The door is to remain locked until I return." He called out to two of his men who were waiting downstairs and called out to the other men to send two of his recruits. Then he stared at Fernand. The devoted servant lowered his gaze; he understood that the Duke had caught on to his less than candid approach.

Gaby had not budged during the entire scene. She sat in the settee with scorn written all over her face. That was probably the way she stood up to her creditors during the war. A coward he was, he thought, towering over her. Disgust engulfed his whole being. How did he lose control? He adored her. Red imprints from his hands imprinted on her pretty alabaster forearms reminded him of his cruelty. He gazed at her face, her eyes and eyelashes still wet from the cascade of tears she'd shed. He came closer and tried to gather her to him as he tried to assuage the pain he had inflicted. Like a virulent storm that suddenly lost its tailing tumultuous wind, Gaby was now serene and silent. He preferred her shouting venom.

"Let go of me," she ordered in English. He obeyed.

She stood up and left the room proudly—her head high. He did not think a bouquet of flowers and a loving note would do the trick this time. She was going to make him pay. He could see it in her eyes as she turned around at the top of the short staircase that led to her boudoir.

"I hate you, don't ever come close to me again, never, ever again," she remarked in a low and grave voice.

He held her gaze. She turned away decidedly.

Before leaving the library, he poured himself a hefty amount of scotch.

* * *

The grand festivities from The Grande Exposition Universelle held on the Champ-de-Mars awaited him in the Imperial court. Queen Victoria and her court had just arrived and he and the Goncourt brothers had watched closely as the Emperor of Prussia, Wilhelm, and his mignon secretary of state, the arrogant and scheming Otto von Bismarck, seemed to overly enjoy the capital.

"This man should be watched and analyzed like a hawk," Goncourt murmured in between his teeth. Jean-Louis surveyed silently their every move and expression for a window on the conflicts that were sure to come up between the two countries.

There had been talks about placing a new King on the throne in Spain. Jean-Louis had already spoken to Louis Napoléon about that. It just would not be wise to have a Prussian or Austrian monarch in such close proximity. A hostile force would surround France, especially if a Hohenzollern was placed on the throne. The Emperor and Eugénie were in seventh heaven—a phrase Jean-Louis had picked up from his American fiancée. Yesterday, both the Tsar of Russia and the King of Prussia had saluted their host during the Grande Parade. Jean-Louis looked on suspiciously at the grand circus, as he liked to refer to it.

He arrived home later than usual. He would have liked to have her by his side tonight. She was observant and he liked to share his impressions with her. Great conversation would not be on the menu tonight. He smiled shaking his head. Inside his home, he nodded his security away and he opened the door. Lucky for him, the room was lit up like the 14th of July. Otherwise, he would have fallen over the packed suitcases that stood by the doors.

"Gaby, where do you think you're going?"

As he entered the room she was packing her things, everything that was hers was laid out on their bed. All of the jewels, clothing, and furs he lavished on her were still in the closet.

He stumbled in and flung his jacket and shirt on the canapé. He proceeded to their bed and chucked the coverlet along with her clothing to the foot of the bed. All her clothes slid onto the carpet. He unbuttoned his pants.

"Don't you dare, Jean-Louis!" she commanded, livid with anger. She was certain that he had come to bed her, against her will.

Oblivious to her babbles, he removed his pants fully and then his shirt and stark naked he continued to walk around the bed to grab an extra pillow. She did not move out of his way. He bent over her and touched his chest to hers while he reached for the pillow lying on the sofa.

Pushed to her limits of decency, she shoved him with all the strength she could summon.

Shocked, he straightened fully. It was his time to be at a loss for words.

"Gaby, have you lost your head?" he exclaimed, as he reached and clasped her to him. He pressed her arms behind her back and her body closed to him.

He kept her close to him until she slowly ceased to gesticulate, her small body exhausted. The tenseness and madness he had tried to control were no longer visible. She was calm and did not try to move. She turned her head towards his face, the only part of her body that was not constricted.

"I'm leaving you tomorrow," she said flatly.

"And where, may I ask, will you be going, Gaby?"

"To Philippe's apartment."

"You can't. Your cousin let the Austrian Cardinals use it for the duration of the Fair."

"Then the convent. They rent small apartments to many aristocratic ladies. I'll be well either way and able to lead my life as I damn well please, and by the way my first call will be to Maître Lauriot, I'm returning to the stage! " she responded in English furious.

Jean-Louis looked down at her. Her voluptuous body was pressing against his and now that his anger had quieted down, he was not about to argue with her—about anything. He wanted her badly, and he would deal with her demands tomorrow.

He lowered his hand from her spine to her buttocks and pressed her into his thighs. Instantly she recognized that look of lust in his brilliant blue eyes.

"Jean-Louis, don't violate me," she murmured. "If you have any respect for the relationship we had, please let me be." Her treacherous body always responded to his touch.

Deaf to her demands, he slid his arms under her knees, rolled her to him, and gently lowered her on the bed. He quickly positioned and molded his body over hers. She felt his manhood swell like a hard stone against her lower stomach and his mouth began to caress her mouth, cheeks, temples, the base of her neck as he playfully gravitated to the warm and soft mounds of flesh peeking out from her décolleté.

As always in these instances, controlling her body and mind was a lost battle. Highly sensual herself, she loved making love with Jean-Louis. He knew it and played all his cards way too perfectly. He reached for her lips again, applying more pressure on her full mouth, taunting her with his hands, pulling away the satin robe, feeling his way to her naked bottom, toying with her sensual femininity.

"Open your mouth, Gaby. Kiss me back," he whispered.

In a desperate last attempt, she turned her head away. He lowered his lips on her breast, kissed, and tucked at it hard, interrupting the kissing solely, to mouth and grasp her other breast.

"I love you, Gaby," he murmured, his lips on her stomach slowly gravitating toward her womanhood. "I want you."

He could turn on her sensual nature just by talking in the low, husky voice that would naturally deepen when he became aroused. She wanted him just as much now.

Taking his own sweet time, he tasted her to his heart's content as he swallowed her wetness and ravaged her moist lips. How long could she hold back? By now, she could no longer avert her own desire.

As if he knew her every thought, he patiently aroused all her womanly needs, applying all his vast knowledge. Well aware by now that he would not relent; he wanted her to return his passion. She felt herself drift into temptation. In vain, she attempted to shame herself into resisting. What type of a sick person was she? She pondered. He had treated her like a wanton child just hours ago. He was now taking her against her will! Well, as he often reminded her sex had nothing to do with love. A woman could play that game as well and—she wanted him. Yes, she wanted him more than anything else at that moment. To feel him inside her, awakening all her sensitive places, to absorb his flesh high in her own body and feel him stir inside her like a gigantic wave that overpowered her being. At the height of passion he lifted himself away from her, rolled on his side, and then on his back. Quickly he gathered her to him and lifted her on his stomach as he placed one hand at the nape of her head pressing her mouth closer to his and the other on her breast. The nearness of his lips and the firm caress on her breast removed the last of her objections.

"Open your mouth Gaby, kiss me," she heard a distant voice murmured. "I want you. I want you so much. I love you, chérie." Without much prying, he thrust himself in her warmth.

The slow and steady pressure he exerted mounted. Gaby gave up all pretense of resistance. She was just following Jean-Louis' advice, sex was just a need—that was all, and there was no reason why she as a woman should not let herself enjoy it as well. She fell into another world, one where there was no anger, just wonderful sensations that rocked her body. She surrendered—fully.

They stayed speechless for a very long time after the act. He could take her to such ecstasy, she mused helpless. This is how lords must have felt when a castle fell to the enemy. She fell to Jean-Louis and responded with all the sexuality she harbored in that treacherous little body of hers. He turned his head to her and she noticed the ironic smirk he so often sported when he knew he had won a battle or a card game for that matter. Oh, well, this was just a battle. She was going to win the war. Maybe. He had brought her to climax and then unable to hold himself back, he'd joined her in the thrill and rapture of the moment.

He stayed inside her for a long time and gently rolled her over, taking her with him on her side, placing his heavy muscular leg on top of her hips and thighs.

She did not fight him or try to pull away. There was nowhere else she would have wanted to be now but next to Jean-Louis, feeling safe and needed in his embrace. Tomorrow she would take some decisions. She fell quickly into a deep sleep and like a young child, tears that had shaken her hours before still raked her body in her sleep.

Jean-Louis was wide-awake. He bent over her, pulled her wet, curly dark brown curls from her forehead and kissed her eyelids.

"I love you, Gaby, no, I adore you, you came so close to death this afternoon, in Montmartre," he whispered, as he encircled her body and held her tighter. The carnage that could have occurred if his security had not called on him was too awful to face. A group of Republican women roamed the streets earlier that day. They had killed one Countess by pulling her out of her carriage and beat her so savagely that her lifeless body had been left on the pavement, unrecognizable, just hours prior to Gaby and Lilianne's escapades.

He lay motionless while he held Gaby in his arms. He wondered what consequences he'd have to pay in the morning. He evaluated the situation and considered all possibilities. Less than two months from now they'd be married. All arrangements were in motion, she was staying put and preparing for it—no compromises . . . possibly if she really wanted to make a point, he might allow her to go over his Grandmother's house. He could not see the two of them in the same room for more than two hours—never mind four weeks. Here again it might work he opined quietly. It would appease the gossips. If Gaby was going to have to live in this Grande Société, she might as well follow some rules of propriety. He knew she couldn't care less. No, this whole mess was absurd. She was going to stay here with him. That was that.

The little angel had thrown her engagement ring at his head! Strangle her, that's really what he had wanted to do. He would tell her his plans tomorrow morning. No he would not permit her to move out. He lay awake staring at the cherubs painted on the ceiling for a long time while an unsettling sensation churned in the pit of his stomach. Hours later he'd have to attend an early conference.

Before he left the room, he took one last look at the woman he loved resting comfortably in bed. He brushed a kiss on her cheek. The storm had passed. He marched content out of their apartment.

* * *

He returned in late morning, and he mounted upstairs. He noticed the suitcases by the door.

Where in the world was she going now? He felt morose and downright sad that he had lost his composure yesterday. She infuriated him. How can she not understand that she could have disappeared or been raped or worse? She waited for him upstairs ready to start her sermons all over again. She was well rested now and he was tired.

"Gaby, you are not going anywhere, so you might as well ask Pierre to bring your suitcase back up in your dressing room."

"You cannot stop me, Jean-Louis we are not married, remember? Thank God."

"Gaby, please I'm tired, let's continue this conversation tomorrow. We'll both be angry once more. Why?"

"Angry or not, I'm leaving and I will never, ever set foot in this house again," she enunciated with great clarity.

He walked in his dressing room. She followed in the room.

"I hope you have a lovely time in Italy and I sincerely wish that your ship will be attacked by pirates and sunk, well maybe not sunk, I love Cunnan ... but the crew would be better off without you," she ended.

He chuckled. "Where is all that meanness stored, Gaby? I would never have fathomed you'd say all these awful words to me."

She could not contain her fury. "How dare you, you left marks on my forearms, and you locked me in this bloody room and I hide meanness in me, you are just mad, just insane, I hate you, I hate myself for loving you, I hate the day we met and I hope you die!"

"Damn it, Gaby, you want your freedom very well, you won. You can experience your damn freedom until our wedding day—but not another minute! Get your clothing and whatever you need, I'll take you down to the convent tomorrow. You need to accompany me to the opéra this evening. After the four weeks, that will be it, I'll bring you back, like it or not, I will not play the game any longer than that. Do you understand? And I don't want to see you in Montmartre under any circumstances—none Gaby. Understood?"

"What are you going to do, surround me with security guards to know my every move Jean-Louis? Answer me."

He slammed the door and did not answer.

"Damn you, Jean-Louis, I don't need you. Leave me alone!" She grabbed her coverlet and walked to her dressing room.

Chapter Thirty-Seven

As they sat next to each other at the opéra, they waited for the performance of Hortense Schneider, a wonderful soprano who had taken many of Gaby's roles since her semi-resignation from the stage. Tonight's performance was *La Grande Duchesse de Gérolstein*, a comic opéra that described a bit too closely the situation between France and Prussia. Jean-Louis had mentioned that being disagreeable to the Prussian Emperor and Bismarck was not a brilliant idea. Instead, Louis Napoléon had listened to his hardened councilors. In his loge, with Gaby by his side, he evaluated the Prussians' reaction. They appeared to take the irony with good humor.

Gaby was always a bit torn when she watched an opéra. This particular one was not one that she would have liked to sing, but it reminded her what she had given up—the stage. Tears begun to stream down her cheeks as she felt a gentle pull on her sleeve—a handkerchief was passed on to her.

She could not understand how Jean-Louis revered control. What Jean-Louis-Pierre De Pleyssis said, everyone had to follow. She had willingly let him take her virginity and now the one gift, her music that had been given to her to relieve her anxieties had been forbidden. He was mad. Although he had retracted his words not to let her attend the Conservatory, she had the uncertain feeling that he had designs upon it. Why she had accepted to go out with him tonight was beyond her understanding. The arrangement at the convent had been completed earlier today.

"We are going to the Emperor's ball, tonight, " he had told her, "and you will have your temporary independence starting tomorrow morning."

It must have been the caffeine in the coffee, the charge, as they called it in France that had mollified her. She'd agreed. He had taken her to the opéra to sweeten her disposition before the Grand Ball. The thing that saddened her the most was that she could not stop the love mania that had weakened her resolve.

At the soirée in the Tuileries, the Emperor ambled by them and politely asked her to share a few of his favorite arias with his guests. She had seen Jean-Louis lean toward the Emperor. Quickly she'd immobilized him with a furious glare. Promptly she'd directed herself toward the orchestra.

Sitting in front of the room, two seats away from the Louis Napoléon, sat the Spanish Empress, the beautiful Eugénie. Gaby wondered if she experienced the same sadness when faced with her husband's Frenchness. By all accounts, the young Spaniard was worse off. The Emperor was a womanizer and it was said that he was in a passionate relationship with a nineteen-year-old Countess, La Castiglione, who drove him utterly mad and led him to dig deeply into France's public coffers.

As the aria begun its urgent climb from a soft caressing note to a voluptuous emotional high, she allowed the passion of music to flow through her veins. She was home and never wanted to leave this perfect world. Alas, she was reminded of her passion as her gaze fell on the influential Duke De Bourbonne.

She noticed his well-defined jaw flinch as words of love from the aria caressed the audience. She sensed his jealousy over her great musical gift and his resentment when she chose to jump at the opportunity to sing in this venue.

Why couldn't Gaby have been a great writer instead? He pondered annoyed. Her music was like another man to him. He adored her and did not want to share anything of hers with anyone else. It was as simple as that. He continued to listen to the mesmerizing voice coming from the diminutive raven-haired beauty while his mind drifted back to happier days.

He recalled the very first time he had seen her again in Paris at the opéra, the run to the marble staircase, the interminable kiss that they had shared and the fury that had reached a pinnacle when he'd realized that she had been in Paris. She was so beautiful with her long curly black hair framing her heart-shaped face and these gigantic emerald eyes that mirrored all the love in the world.

Louis Napoléon smiled at her and then glanced at Jean-Louis as he shook his head in disbelief. The audience was awestruck by the melody that emanated from the small angel with the expressive demeanor. Jean-Louis raised his eyebrows and acknowledged her gift. Nonetheless, his gaze did not underestimate the favorable impression that the adoring crowd showered upon her.

In reality, rather than make a scene, he'd better think of something else that pleased him akin to having her in his bed tonight. It's not as if she was begging to come home—the arrogant little brat. On account of her passion for music, she could have been killed had not her security alerted him. Going into Montmartre unescorted was pure folly he fumed.

To her credit, he pondered, in the absence of parental supervision, being frivolous and scared had not been an option for her. She had faced countless hardships with her fearless attitude and had developed a sense of confidence, non-existent in most women in her social strata. Gaby loved challenges and she just could not see a challenge that somehow she could not surmount. He recognized that easily in her, for he had it in him. But, for God's sake, his immense height and formidable stature alone weakened his opponents' resolve. Gaby was five feet tall. What was she thinking?

The Emperor, he knew, already had plans for her and he was not quite sure if he'd agree. Her matrilineal lineage was Italian and her father was mostly English. Her art was one thing to be enjoyed by both of them but in the long-term picture she could, like himself, become very influential in the talks if he decided to accept the role of chief negotiator. After all, she loved him and that should suffice.

He was brought back from his diatribe by the loud applause that followed her performance.

The Emperor had been watching his friend and saw the perfect opportunity to send his First Minister to learn a bit more about the pretty American soprano. Everyone surrounded her, asking millions of questions. Perfect timing, the Duke rarely left her side at parties.

"Jean-Louis-Pierre," Louis Napoléon called out. "Join us in the library." As the Duke began to follow the Emperor, his ministers trailed Gaby. Many asked, was she beautiful and stupid? Was this the reason he guarded her responses vehemently when in company? After all, his Grandmother was not too fond of his new paramour. Was she the temptress extraordinaire that arrested all in her passage? It certainly seemed that Jean-Louis-Pierre was fond of these women, even if the passion in his eyes lasted but for a short while. Actually the ministers find neither. Gaby answered the questions posed to her, cautiously and intelligently. Her knowledge of political grand standing was impressive, the ministers reported to the Emperor. She could be trusted. Another notch on her belt was her relationship with Cardinal Thornsen, one of the Pope's close advisors. She spoke fluent Italian. All was reported to Louis Napoléon to the Emperor's delight. France would have a great advantage. All returned to the salons where the ministers were assembled including Jean-Louis-Pierre De Pleyssis.

After the bizarre interviewing, Gaby followed the crowd back towards the ballroom. The orchestra blasted Libiamo, a drinking loving aria from the golden age of Grand Opéra. She obtained a flute of champagne from the butler and sang along, while lifting her glass along with the other guests.

"*À votre santé, À l'amour, À la France.* She would leave Jean-Louis forever if he forbade anything to her ever again. She would become independent once again. The life of an opéra singer would take her away from Paris to formidable capitals, she thought. Aristocrats in Paris looked at the colonials as lacking in the social graces and the European polish. Most were astounded when she revealed that the sisters at the Sacré Coeur in New Orleans had given her music and dancing instructions since she was a child. In effect, she had fine-tuned her education at the Convent of the Ursulines. She had learned from these wonderful women the art of theatrics and the demonstration of passion while singing the incantation at the morning prayers in the convent. Her capricious nature returned with new ideas of independence. Jean-Louis had been forgotten.

In stark contrast, Jean-Louis could not detach his heart from the woman who had stood defiant in front of him way too often. Frightened by his own emotions, he devoured her with his eyes. He wanted to hold her and forgive her stubbornness and bold comportment. Singing for Gaby was a wonderful release and perhaps, he mused, he should be less self-oriented, more tolerant. Let her enjoy her life, he reflected, although dictating other's lives was his duty. He had been given a great deal—great wealth, a fine education and cultural and political influence accorded to his social station. These advantages came at a cost—service to name and country, to render to humanity his services. To help a new generation to achieve the proper respect, income and education they so richly deserved. That was the reason why he needed to dictate, he reassured himself.

Why did he have to care so much for Gaby? She was the missing puzzle piece in his life. He felt lost without her. His only other option was to grovel. Gaby was not the kind who could be told what to do. Now he would court her all over again and grovel he would. His life would be a lot more enjoyable for it. Decidedly, he walked toward the group she was socializing with. He encircled her waist and complimented her on her performance.

"Mademoiselle Thornsen, the last time I saw such an expressive performance, you were on my ship in the middle of the afternoon drinking a much better brandy," he murmured in her ear, "I liked your outfit much better then, as well."

He refused to let anyone dance with her.

She hated to admit to herself how she loved being in his arms and how handsome she found him. Jean-Louis-Pierre De Pleyssis was in demand, in great demand and she hated it.

Now that she would no longer live under his roof, the Societée was about to find out that a rift existed between them, mothers would introduce their daughters and courtesans would return his avowing smile. *Un enfant de cœur, a choir boy,* he'd never been and everyone in Paris was well aware of it!

Melba and several women she had encountered in the Bois had shared that they would let him have his indiscretions whenever he wanted to. The revelation had been shocking. After all, the liaison was far from secret and yet no one appeared to even give it any credence. Although it often happened in New Orleans, affairs of any sort did not seem to be taken as blatantly blasé as it was on the European continent.

The Emperor needed his expertise and Jean-Louis had to stay behind as she climbed in their carriage alone on her return to the hotel particulier. She'd gathered her belongings and packed. She would spend the night in her boudoir, no need to have him close to her tonight. Why make things harder than they already were? Late in the night she felt warm hands touching her shoulders. She sleepily turned wanting to wish him away, instead he bent down and kissed the words coming out of her mouth.

"I just want to hold you, Gaby," he whispered as he picked her up and brought her back to their room.

He held her close to his chest all night.

She woke up much too late. Jean-Louis had departed for another meeting early, Maude told her. She lay in bed a while longer. Taking in the surroundings sadly, she forced her stubborn spirit to think about the return from Montmartre.

All these weeks of love and passion were a joke, a lie on his part. So what if he spent every day and every night by her for the rest of his life. She was never going to forgive him his fury. Why didn't she push him away last night? She did not have any pride left in her. She had drunk too much champagne at the ball. It must have thwarted her resolution. Realistically, she was not at fault. What could she have done? He was thrice her size. She had to look forward. He had promised her that he would give her a month of freedom to experience Parisian life. She had to figure a way to escape; perhaps the convent would forget her transgressions. After all, it was the core of the Catholic faith to forget trespasses. The Duke De Pleyssis was influential and his money flowed. To go against his will was unthinkable. Gaby thought that Parisian life was fun if one traveled in the right circles, but she now realized that she could find herself the mistress of someone she did not love just to achieve her goals. Jean-Louis could certainly cancel her contracts at the Académie de Musique if he chose to do so. She realized that now. Perhaps she should swallow her pride and return to New Orleans or perhaps follow Philippe to Rome.

Later that morning she walked down the winding marble staircase and wide and imposing balustrade. She'd waited a tad too long and thought that his carriage had left the courtyard. Regrettably, Jean-Louis was already downstairs, waiting quietly in the dining room.

He turned to her and flashed an amusing smile.

"Miss Independence, are you ready to go?"

"Yes, but I don't need you I can take care of myself, quite well. Leave."

He called out to Pierre to enter the room.

"Pack some extra blankets for Mademoiselle Thornsen, everyone is dying of pneumonia in Paris these days, and place Mademoiselle's luggage in the carriage."

The old servant followed the command obediently.

Gaby took one last look around at the beautiful surroundings she had called home for almost two years. She hugged Maude, her maid. Quickly she pivoted on her heels and pre-empted him into the courtyard and inside the carriage. The convent was less than two blocks away. Suddenly, a devastating sadness overwhelmed her. Minutes later, they were in the convent's courtyard and her trunks were brought upstairs. He must have made the arrangement earlier this morning. She passed him and shot a disdainful look.

"I can take care of myself, goodbye."

Jean-Louis reached for her and pulled her back to him as she crossed his path.

"A month from today, Gaby, not an hour more."

She did not answer but tried to pull away—to no avail. He pressed her to him and kissed her tenderly on her lips. "I love you. I miss you already, Gaby. I'll visit tomorrow morning." He tried to kiss her once more but this time, she pushed him away and as quickly as she could she ran out before he could change his mind and force her to return to his house.

He would not follow her in the courtyard of the convent not in front of the nuns. He would not dare. She was right. The sanctity of the convent stopped him. He looked at her, smiled, turned on his heels and entered his carriage.

From the top of the balcony she watched him. She almost ran after the carriage, but her pride held her back. Thank goodness, she thought to herself, better survive a broken heart than spent a lifetime being ordered about. She walked in and followed the nun to her Spartan room. Better leave soon and regain the conservatory, there she had good friends and her music to sustain her soul.

Chapter Thirty-Eight

Jean-Louis had left her at the convent Sunday, late in the morning. The first week had been more difficult that she'd suspected. She missed him terribly. When he'd ask to see her outside the convent for an end of the week date; she just could not refuse.

She knew quite well he expected her to relent and follow him home before the end of the month. She would not. That was the least she could do to save the last vestiges of pride.

The evenings in the convent were uneventful and like in the olden days in her native land on the plantation, she went to bed early. When one sleeps, the following day arrives much quicker. This had been her motto when her life became too complicated or too dull.

Jean-Louis had proclaimed haughtily that he would come and visit during the week. He had not. Well, she'd do quite well on her own, she repeated to herself.

She dressed quickly. She was in need of fresh air and exercise to clear her tormented thoughts.

She climbed down the marble staircase and walked out on the Pont d'Anjou to reach the Conservatoire. The day dragged on. Everything seemed to be going wrong. Even Marie-Louise was not there to keep her company.

By now the word spread that the couple *Lumière* had decided on a little of fresh air before the marriage. She was accosted by dozens of reporters. Better to keep out of sight and silent.

Jean-Louis did not show up the following day, either. She met Gérard and Marie-Louise at the theater.

They intended to go to the Saverin for a nightcap. The couple was very much in vogue these days in Paris; they gave fabulous parties if you had the chance to be invited. Naturally, Gaby and Jean-Louis always received invitations. Well, this time nothing had been addressed to her personally.

Gérard had told Gaby that Marie-Louise would attend as well as they had been asked to do a *pas de deux* together.

Maybe Jean-Louis had received an invitation at the house. Surely he'd forgotten to hand it to her. No, that did not make any sense, she thought. Marie Hélène Saverin knew it all. Gaby would have been most surprised if she was not cognizant of the separation. Furthermore they shared the same street with Jean-Louis and his Grandmother. Oh, well, that is exactly what should be expected. She would tell Jean-Louis and return the favor once they married!

Mon Dieu, where was Jean-Louis anyway? It was the third day and she had not seen any activities when she passed the house.

After the theatre, she decided to join a few friends at the Fouquets. Marie-Louise had already gone to the Sevarin. She always had a great time at the Fouquets. After most of the performances artists would congregate. It was most interesting to review the feelings and nuances that each artist who essentially played the same part on different days would bring to a scene.

Wednesday flew by and Gaby finally received an invitation to Marie-Josée-Mireille De la Gentiles, Jean-Louis Grandmother's best friend. The only one she had received since society had learned about their separate lives. Gaby adored Marie-Josée. The only person in Jean-Louis' super status level that was brilliant, kind, and considerate with everyone she came in contact with. An anomaly at best in the circle she lived in. It was a private dinner, rather than a grande soirée. Gaby liked small gatherings, it was easier to mingle and have a conversation.

Where was Jean-Louis? Her pride prevented her from asking. When questions arose about the relationship, she would smile as if she knew, but did not want to divulge his whereabouts. Who in heaven's name was she kidding? She would have to get accustomed to it, but where was he? He'd said he would come and visit before going to the Tuileries. That was over five days ago.

She had been less than pleasant or enticing on Sunday morning. She'd been self-conscious for appearing weak in spirit. Mon Dieu, what a charade, she played. Less than a week after the crisis, her obsessive nature began to develop and the same compulsive obsessive refrain she experienced for years mounted.

She asked Marie-Louise in passing if the party at the Saverin had been agreeable. Marie-Louise would have loved to convey to her Jean-Louis' presence, but nothing was said. Jean-Louis had not attended. She had been too proud to ask if Lorraine Du Bois, Madame Pelletier, or Sandrine Dufault had been there. She knew he had spent a significant amount of time before his departure for the Americas with the trio. Her obsessive manuscript did not stop there. She had him leaving for England with a few of these beautiful ladies devoid of self worth.

Thursday and Friday were just as torturous and Gaby was thrilled when Saturday evening finally arrived and she began to dress for the dinner at Marie-Josée.

She climbed in the carriage as they passed Jean-Louis' house. Timidly, she slightly raised the curtain with her reticule. All was quiet. The drapes were drawn shut in their rooms. She promptly let go of the fabric and sat with her hands crossed on her lap. She allowed her cruel thoughts to torment her.

* * *

Jean-Louis had returned earlier that afternoon. He'd been shocked that the little brat had not even set her delicate little feet in the townhouse.

He changed promptly, got back in his carriage, and arrived at La Countesse's magnificent estate on the outside of Paris within the hour.

As usual, the beautiful Mademoiselle De Conte Thornsen was one of the last to arrive. Beautiful aristocratic women, namely Madame Pelletier had surrounded Jean-Louis upon his arrival. He observed Gaby entered the salon. Her elegant presence was electrifying. All eyes were on her delicate allure and assertive demeanor. She was wearing a gold fourreau with gold payette in her hair. He smiled, recalling how much she loved fashion and how she felt great guilt over the amount of money she spent on her frivolous wardrobe. She would even assist to his own fitting with the tailor if he allowed it! She must be having the time of her life now for in retrospect she had not packed much. Politely she conversed with the guests and just prior to entering the salon she scanned the room. Momentarily she focused on his amused glance and would not let it go.

He adored that aspect of her personality. It set her apart from all the women he'd met. Playing games were not her forte. When it came to their love, her emotions always took first priority above all else. He saved her an embarrassing moment and excused himself. Promptly he walked to her and reached for her hand as if he had seen her minutes earlier. He led her to a more secluded area where Marie-Josée and his Grandmother gossiped.

"You look ravishing, chérie," he whispered.

"Thank you," she responded coolly, unable to hold her questioning spirit. "Where have you been?" She smiled sensuously in his eyes. What theatrics was she playing, she told herself. The truth was that she was devastated for God's sake and instead she was pretending that she was walking on stage devoid of all emotions.

"If you had been to the townhouse, as I falsely presume you would, you'd have been pleasantly surprised to find that Christian had decorated the house with your favorite roses. Furthermore, you would have been given an invitation to rejoin me in Deauville for a week of hunting and riding. The foxes were numerous and you would have had a grand time as well, Mademoiselle Thornsen."

"Good God, Jean-Louis what made you think that I would return to the house? Am I that predictable—that pathetic?" she whispered back.

"An obvious mistake on my part, my gorgeous American." He took her waist and pressed her body to him, molding her to him, expertly his hands descended on the curve below her waist. "I missed you, Gaby," he whispered, his lips caressed her temples. "You would have love the Assunian leather boots I picked up personally for you along with a brand new riding outfit I ordered from Madame Badoitte."

"Oh, could Maude bring all these goodies to my apartment at the convent?" she laughed.

"I think not," he retorted. "You want them, you come and get them."

"In other words, I'm being bought?" she asked.

"I wish it could be that simple," he said half-serious. "Shall we dine?" He pointed to the dining room, knowing quite well that he had pressed the magic button.

They were cleverly seated next to one another at a long rectangular table superbly dressed. She loved the French tables. Jean-Louis had Madame Pelletier on his left side. The beautiful widow proceeded to take every opportunity to sway Jean-Louis' interest away from Gaby. She was witty and smart and her sexual appetite brought on bold advances. She would not let a wife or *petite amie* stand in the way of her desire. Now her sight was set on Jean-Louis-Pierre De Pleyssis.

Gaby could not possibly show her anger and extreme jealousy.

Count Armand, Marie-Josée's long-time companion, saved Gaby. "Jean-Louis-Pierre," he started, "the word in Paris these days in the salons and cercles, is that you and Count Bismarck are becoming quite chummy?"

Gaby glanced towards the old aristocrat. She smiled. Madame Pelletier had no desire to engage in strategic political discourse, getting Jean-Louis in her bed was her sole goal at the present. Perfect timing, Gaby thought as she stretched her hand to reach for a flute of Champagne. Jean-Louis was now engaged in the dialogue and silence fell in the room.

"If anyone can wring a treaty from the fox himself, it certainly will be you, my friend," the Count concluded, appreciating full well that Bismarck and the political scene in Northern Europe were two key words that would keep the male population talking and Jean-Louis out of Madame Pelletier's claws.

Later that evening came the entertainment. The guests were led to the music room. Gaby reached for Jean-Louis' hand and held it tightly. He looked down and brushed a light kiss on her magnificent mane. They both walked hand in hand and came to sit in the back of the room. Entranced by the power of the musical performance, she came back to reality when she heard the Count's gruff voice.

"Gaby, do us the honor. It would delight us so to hear your magnificent voice. Anything you wish, ma chère," he agreeably requested.

She heard the Count's remarks and smiled back. She hated to deny the amiable Armand, but this setting certainly was neither the time nor the place. It would enrage Jean-Louis. Another altercation on the way, Gaby acquiesced to herself.

"Oh, Monsieur, you know how much I would like to accept your honorable request, but I have to respectfully decline, I have been forbidden by Maître Lauriot not to force my vocal chords, regretfully I need to decline." She flashed her beautiful dazzling smile, hoping that it would soften the denial.

"Our loss, Gabriella . . . our loss, my chère," the disappointed voice responded.

She smiled and nodded her pretty head.

Jean-Louis relaxed in the large comfortable sofa and Gaby reclined next to him, prepared to enjoy the rest of the entertainment and the artists. The soirée had been magnificent, the champagne, outstanding, all spoke about the grapes used by the Champagnards. Pinot Meuniet, Chardonnay, Pinot noir, the making of champagne was a culture in France and Gaby was vastly interested. She adored the yellowish bubbly.

"You mean to tell me, Gabriella, that Jean-Louis has not taken you to Champagne yet?" Arthur Duchamp said reproachfully.

"She loves champagne way too much. She would want to establish residence in the savory province." Jean-Louis replied sarcastically, taking Gaby in his arm and gently rolling her closer to him. Laughter rose in the room, she elegantly nodded to the butler, picked up a flute and toasted the room.

Duchamp was another friend of the Countess Marie-Josée. Not an aristocrat, probably the only other one besides Gaby, but very close to Jean-Louis' Grandmother. She had met him twice; his young wife seemed to endure with great boredom each one of the soirées she attended. Naturally, the age difference was apparent and he rarely stood by her side. Monsieur Duchamp was never too far from Jean-Louis' Grandmother even when her old friend, Monsieur De Lacquissence was present. Odd, Gaby thought, the dowager never gave this bourgeois her glacial stare. He made her laugh, something unusual. Gaby had asked Jean-Louis about their relationship.

"Gaby," he'd answered reproachfully, "you have been in France too long. Duchamp and my Grandmother? That would be the joke of the century." And yet, these two seemed awfully chummy.

Gaby had not pursued the subject. Besides she was pleased the French were beginning to accept her. "Candid, in a charming sort of way, *trés moderne*," she'd heard others describe her demeanor in one of the salons she religiously attended.

The early morning hours were upon them and Jean-Louis sent Gaby's carriage back to the convent.

"Get in beauty," he told her, following closely behind her and closing his own door. The footman took his cue and proceeded toward the Ile Saint Louis.

"Jean-Louis, I don't want to go to Saint Louis. We said a month. I don't want to return before then, you know how obsessive I can be," she admitted candidly, "I would excoriate my very existence if I fell in this endeavor. Please, let's go to the Faubourg."

Jean-Louis looked momentarily annoyed and then he knocked on the vignette and had the coachman take them to the apartment. Better not fight her now, he reflected. He wanted her in his arms tonight. With Gaby, he had to pick and choose his battles. They reached the Faubourg and the footman opened the door. They climbed down the fancy carriage and ran on the sidewalk to the entrance. The concierge let them in and Jean-Louis stopped just long enough to pick her up in his arms and strode quickly to the elevator.

Holding tightly to the lapel of his jacket, she stretched upward and kissed his chin and then his lips.

"I want you so much," she whispered lustily.

He smiled and kissed her back. Few words were needed as they entered the foyer of the apartment and tore off each other clothes to satisfy their passion.

"Spank me. Satisfy your anger toward me," she said inebriated.

"You don't know how much I would like the privilege," he laughed, "and I'll definitely take a rain check—soon when we don't have a riding appointment in Vincennes. I don't want to put you through a double punishment. I want you to ride with me tomorrow without the risk of angering you after the fait accompli." He laughed.

"Men are always concerned about their needs. Let me do the beating, then." She said tugging at his belt.

Laughing he quickly pulled away from her grip.

"You are a fun lover, Gaby," he muttered falling on their bed. He pulled her down with him, and placed his large stature on hers while firmly he urged her thighs to open and receive him.

The sun was well on its way to lighten the City of Lights when the couple finally fell asleep.

Hunger woke them up. They quickly got dress and chose a favorite place in Vincennes to have café and croissants and then continued riding west of Paris.

"I love our Sunday rides, Jean-Louis. It's such a special day for me."

He looked at her, amused. He had not chosen this arrangement. Especially now, she continued looking towards him with adoring eyes. He looked down at her in disbelief.

"Let me lessen your hardship and return you full time to Saint Louis then."

"She took the reins of the horse and pushed him to a fast gallop." He followed closely until they reached a clearing and a lively stream crossing their path. Gaby slowed the horse and came to a full stop. She dismounted and lifted the heavy saddle to provide the horse a well-deserved rest.

Jean-Louis followed and came to rest his back against an old tree trunk while Gaby started walking toward the stream.

What was it with this American girl that he could not quit? He looked seriously and intensely toward the pretty brunette descending the steep hill to the stream. He had thought about it seriously while in Normandy with his friends.

Ribaud adored Gaby but he had not been bashful about bringing three other beautiful blondes, definitely not averse to the idea of a lovely tryst with the Duke. He had no desire to satisfy his manly needs with anyone other than Gaby, he had told her countless times.

"Your needs?" she would say. "The things I fear most when business takes you away from me."

He smiled as he watched her roll up her riding pants and removed her boots as she stepped in the water. She turned around and waved at him to join her.

"It feels delicious. Come join me, darling," she shouted.

He did not move nor answer, just kept on looking at her. He really could not fathom ever not loving Gaby. She had been born for him to adore. There were no other answers and why did it happen?

He was still lost in his analysis of his love for her when she came upon him and wiggled her wet fingers at him, sprinkling water on his face and attire.

"You are now blessed my friend." She laughed.

"I should have taken you up on your kind invitation to whip you this morning." He grinned, grabbed her hips, and pulled her down hard on him.

"I'll take a rain check tonight." He continued.

Gaby blushed. Her face turned crimson. In fact, it had been a drunken moment of pure lust.

He forcefully placed his lips on hers, forcing her mouth open to receive his seeking tongue deep in her mouth. His rugged coat pressed against her thin blouse and her breasts in dire need of his caresses arched to him.

"I can visually attest of my extreme effect on you, my dearest darling." She peeped at him and shot him an ironic sideways smile.

"Absolutely correct, my chérie. Don't forget my voracious sexual appetite. How foolish of you to leave me to fend for myself," he said, knowing that it would turn on her obsessive-compulsive nature. Serves her right. She should be back in the house with him. He would tell her tonight that he expected her back in St. Louis full-time tomorrow.

The rest of the afternoon they spent loving, riding, stopping in a quaint small inn for dinner and returned late in the apartment in the Faubourg.

They started reading in front of the fireplace. Gaby reclined in his arms and quickly fell sound asleep. The following morning, he got up early, ready for his weekly routine. He came back to the room, slipped his hands under the satin blankets, and touched her burning body.

"Sleeping beauty, I'll be back late tonight. Do you want to meet for a déjeuner later? He frisked her curly mane and smiled. "I'll send word later." He bent down, kissed her, and left.

Flabbergasted, Gaby sat up in bed. As far as he was concerned, everything had been settled. He had not even apologized. In a fit of sudden anger, she jumped out of bed trying to intercept him before he reached the elevator. To no avail, he was gone. She returned to the apartment, angry with herself for taking so long to wake fully.

Well, he would just have to be surprised. To Saint Louis she would not return until he apologized. Not quite sure that it would ever happen, she went back in and stayed in the Faubourg until past midday. She adored this little apartment. It reflected their love and no one else's. He had no other memories but theirs.

Should she forget it all and return to their life? It had been a difficult two weeks, she pondered, and then she remembered the event of that awful afternoon. She just wished she had not thrown scalding coffee at him while she kicked his tibia like a wild bohemian. You are absolutely mad, a raving maniac Gaby, she told herself. What has happened to your spirit and self-esteem? No, he should suffer and now he was suffering perhaps more than she. Good, she told herself, and she prepared to return to the convent.

Jean-Louis was unpleasantly surprised when he returned home earlier than expected, finding that Mademoiselle Thornsen had not shown up. Gaby had not answered his billet. That was it. Now, even if she decided to return earlier, he would stick to the schedule he had delineated. One month—no more, no less.

The rest of the week dragged by. No one had ever told them that the separation would be that difficult.

Early Wednesday, Jean-Louis met Luke who was on his way to reassess a property east of Paris. Taking Luke's offer to accompany him, both men rode off. Jean-Louis had not shared his spontaneous destination with Gaby. In effect both were playing cat and mouse games. But this ordeal was getting out of hand—childish. He was tired of it!

Chapter Thirty-nine

Gaby had not seen Jean-Louis since last Sunday. He usually stopped daily by the convent before going to his meetings. Why had he not mentioned anything about a trip? Why had she not seen him? In view of the fact that since Tuesday night he had not attended any soirées, she wondered about his whereabouts? In spite of everything, he did not have to tell her about his absences. She had made that very clear from the onset, but he always made it a point to tell her anyway. He never failed to mention his meetings or travels.

After three weeks of living apart, she was happy that he had given her an ultimatum. She lay in bed with her hands behind her neck, staring at the white ceiling devoid of decoration. Freedom and independence was not as much fun as she had once believed. It would have been a lot easier had she not fallen madly in love. Possessiveness of someone's heart and the knowledge of belonging to someone—all heart and soul was an emotion that she had given away without a second thought on account of her annoyance with his overwhelming controlling personality.

Saturday and Sunday were the days that she had been living for these past three weeks. Their 'end of the week' as Jean-Louis coined it was always passionate and fun—just the two of them either in Paris or out in the suburbs. Riding hard on difficult terrains and tasting sensational cuisine in well-known inns in the evening was always great fun—never a dull moment. Their intellect intermingled on many subjects. She purchased books in pairs—both were voracious readers. She would always write her thoughts at the end of each chapter and quite often while riding in their carriage they would discuss the writings. He was amused by her choice of books. She loved writings that pursued knowledge. A month ago she had purchased the translation into French of Darwin's *The Origins Of Species* by Émilie Le Tonnelier Breteuil du Chatelet, Voltaire's cherished mistress. A few times Jean-Louis had balked at her choices, but in perspective she always tried to find an interesting turn on the content of the book. "A flop or not, you usually have a curious take on the content, Gaby," he'd shared with her. She'd hold on to the compliment for weeks.

She loved listening to his political and historical perspective. She had changed and matured so much since her arrival in France. She was now twenty-three years old. She had met fascinating people, mostly French and English, and surprisingly she had come to have a better understanding of her beloved country.

The western expansion was taking place in America and the spirit of Manifest Destiny was taking hold on the American psyche. Good or bad, only history would reveal its true influence on posterity. And why would it not be wonderful? After all, Americans were good, hard-working, practical people who embraced the spirit of the Enlightenment and its inherent goal to reform society through reason and the advancement of science.

It was six-thirty in the morning. Gaby rolled out of bed and listened to the hustle and bustle in the streets. If she did not run outside to breathe a bit of fresh air, she would surely perish. Quickly, she got dressed and walked outside. The guardian had just opened the gate. She walked out on the hard, cobbled stones wrapped in her black woolen cape draped with brown mink with a large mink hat that covered her magnificent hair and half of her pretty face.

She walked for a long time and then decided to walk over the Pont de la Concorde to Notre Dame. Her sadness had not lifted. In fact it coupled with her anxiety over Jean-Louis' whereabouts. It was getting worse. She stopped on the middle of the bridge as tears streamed down her face and sobs raked her body.

Servants who walked to their masters' houses were looking at her strangely. With her fine clothing, kid gloves, and leather boots, she did not fit the image of the typical working girl that wandered on the bridge at this ungodly hour. Aristocrats were either returning from soirées usually inebriated beyond words, or lovers had just left the warm beds of their mistresses returning home to their families or the privacy of their hotel particulier.

Gaby placed her elbows on the cold parapet that bordered the bridge and cried some more. Why had she not realized the immensity of her actions? Had he forgotten her that quickly or had he returned to one of his paramours, someone who would not dare shout or disagree with him; someone who would not even dream of kicking him and pouring scalding coffee on his dove grey suit no matter how obnoxious he behaved? At times she reacted like a wild boar. Her mother had been right when she'd said, "you let anger rule your intellect and emotions, defying logic—two highly unfeminine traits. No one will ever have you once they get to know you. You should have been a man; you certainly act like one." And unlikely as it was these horrific words coming from her mother had helped her. She had relied on that manly attitude and demeanor; without it, she would have sunk to nothingness when left all alone on the plantation.

But Jean-Louis had given her the confidence to be the woman that she was. His lovely, magnificent angel, he'd sometimes called her. He adored her as she was. He loved it all. In a sense, they completed one another to perfection. The perfect entity she thought, as cascading tears rolled down her fine features. That last episode, however, might have been too much. Awful doubts engulfed her. What if he'd come to the conclusion that life was just as fun without her? After all, thesed past years, he'd had time to assuage his needs. The very thought clouded her vision with more tears.

Meanwhile, Jean-Louis sat in his carriage staring at the Seine that meandered down stream as he returned home from Normandy where he had spent some time with friends. From afar he noticed a well-dressed woman standing on the bridge looking at the Seine towards Notre Dame. He focused hard and moved closer to the window . . . Gaby? What in God's name was Gaby doing on the bridge at seven o'clock in the morning with the bands of rowdies searching for easy targets to rob or violate or kill for a few gold coins? What was she thinking? He tapped the vignette and asked Matthew, the coachman, to halt the carriage.

"Monsieur, we think that Mademoiselle Thornsen is standing on the bridge." They'd realized as well. He jumped out of the carriage, crossed the busy street and began to walk in her direction. He should stabilize her hands first; she always kept her gun on her waistline or boot, an easy reach for her. Gaby was an excellent shot and could defend herself quite well. He had made sure of that, but in that helpless position she was now exposing herself to danger. He came behind her and quickly and firmly placed his hands on her waistline feeling for the small Wesson and Smith. Predictable, he thought, good. It was there. He relaxed his hold somewhat.

She turned frantically, her mouth shouting something in English he did not comprehend. When she recognized him, her first reaction was relief. "Thank God," she cried. Without shame she reached for his hands that still encircled her waist and she applied force so as to tighten his grasp.

"What in God's name are you doing outside at this ungodly hour, Gaby?" he questioned as he strived to stay calm.

She raised a face full of tears and sadness.

"Where have you been? I should be asking you the question. Coming home at seven in the morning. Who were you with, Jean-Louis? How could you? I've been crying because it is Saturday, our day, and you come —"

"If you let me talk, Gaby, I'll tell you—I was in Normandy."

"For pleasure or business?" she demanded.

"Both, if you must know."

She turned and stared; her eyes filled with unshed tears all over again.

"Gaby, stop darling, I came home to pick you up. Luke has just inherited a castle in Normandy that he has never visited. Ribaud was in Beaunne, he came to Paris and I met up with them. However I am here, I would not compromise our day." He bent down and kissed her mouth. "Although by coming out like that you could have ended it permanently. Are you aware how quickly a man could throw you over the bridge in the position you were in."

Jean-Louis looked around and was aware of four old men standing aimlessly nearby. At least security was strict. He nodded to the men. Gaby decidedly kept them on their feet—at an early hour. He pulled her to him and kissed her long and hard.

God, how he wanted her. "You feel good, Gaby. I missed you." After drying up her tears he led her back to the carriage.

Matthew wore a huge smile on his face. "Is Mademoiselle coming home?" he asked.

"Yes," Jean-Louis said. Upon hearing that, Gaby disengaged from his arms.

"I am not going in. It will be too hard to return to the convent when we come back."

She had hoped that Jean-Louis would apologize and ask her to return home, but he didn't.

Feeling downright angry with her now, he disengaged fully from her embrace and helped her into the carriage.

Sitting in the seat across from Gaby, he lifted and rested his long, muscular legs on the seat next to her then crossed them at the ankle. "Gaby, you are very difficult, at times, it's downright annoying. Woman of substance or not, I feel that sometimes you do things against your will and your own good judgment. In the process you hurt both of us for absolutely no other reason than to appease your absurd pride. What are you trying to prove anyway and for whom, Gaby?"

"Jean-Louis, you held me prisoner with your forceful hands on my forearms and locked me in my room like an unruly child. Need I remind you how I should feel about that? Well, let me tell you, control is something that I cannot stand."

"Cease, Gaby. Your behavior was not one that should be included in an etiquette's textbook. For such a tiny creature you pack a solid kick and I never quite liked coffee spots on my dress greys, you little tyrant," he replied tersely with no apologies.

"Well, maybe so, but you see, never in a million years would I have used physical force to make you heed to my wishes no matter how annoyed I might have been with you. Never," she said.

Looking down at the beautiful tigress facing him, he smirked. She wouldn't have lived to talk about it, he thought, and feeling just plain awful, he pulled her across the seat and pressed her close to him.

"All right, I have come to get you. We will go to Beaunne. I know you stayed there overnight on your way back to Paris. The food in Bourgogne is scrumptious. You'll love it, chérie. The nouveau Beaujolais has just come out. It will sweeten your disposition."

He tapped the vignette. "To the house."

"Yes!"

The two coachmen were delighted. The Duke had convinced Miss Thornsen to return. Everyone in the household would be thrilled. They missed her.

Gaby pushed her cold little body next to Jean-Louis'. Her head rested on his chest.

An apology, she would not get—no matter what she advanced. Her weekend was precious. Wasn't she crying over her behavior less than half an hour ago? She had to learn from her mistakes—to truly live, rather than to exist. Hold on to your pride, but work at being happy, she silently ordered her indomitable spirit. Finally, when two people were in love, happiness took hold of their being and an euphoric feeling impeled most to do the right thing. To do unto others as you would have them do unto you. The Golden Rule . . . she mused as she nesled even closer next to him.

Soon the carriage stopped in front of his home. He disentangled himself and without asking her to come in, he stepped out. Ten minutes later, he was back out with her dark mink coat on his arms. The servants were placing her bag in the luggage compartment.

"It's quite cold, Gaby. You'll need extra warm clothing. Maude packed a bag for you."

At the name of her former maid, a tinge of melancholy touched her soul. Gaby loved Maude and she knew that she was missed. Resting comfortably now, Jean-Louis took Gaby in his arms and kissed her. The lack of sleep suddenly caught up with her and the clanking of the wheels on the pavement provided a wonderful rhythm to lull her into a deep sleep.

Jean-Louis smiled. He tightened his grasp around her body and reached for the documents he had brought along with him. Four hours later, they had almost reached Le Chateau Parme, a charming old medieval castle turned in a splendid inn.

Chapter Forty

The following week, the troupe that auditioned for the Magic Flute met at the Fouquets to celebrate their hard work prior to having their dreams fulfilled or blown out to pieces. The Golden age of Grand Opéra had retrieved its popularity. The mixture of melodramas and great choruses along with the introduction of ballet performances between the second and third act brought an era of extravagant and dazzling spectacles that titillated the Parisian opéra scene.

The artistic connection between the tenors, sopranos, dancers and chorus worked splendidly well. Sadness overwhelmed Gaby at the last rehearsal. She had chosen to love Jean-Louis over her infinite love for opéra and performing. Eh bien, she consoled her morose spirit at the very least, she would always stay involved with all aspects of production, and would continue to share the rehearsal stage with the top tenors and divas in Europe. She set the bar for all—that was an infinite joy. No auditions for Mademoiselle De Conte Thornsen but she was a permanent pillar at the opéra at the tender age of twenty-three.

"Strut your stuff, Gabriella," the director would tell her in English. He liked the English idioms that she'd shared with him.

In a sense, she had it all, she repeated to herself. She never experienced rejection and she was always asked to practice with the new productions.

Gaby's real issue was that ninety-nine percent of the time, she was far better than the chosen sopranos. And these ladies were not second-rate singers. They were the best singers the world of opéra had to offer. If she was better than these women, then the art of opéra singing was not perfect. She could have raised the bar up a few more notches.

"Mon Dieu, we have the perfect singer for the perfect part, but we cannot use her. It's incomprehensible. How frustrating, perhaps, because of my deep and blind passion for the art, I cannot comprehend for the life of me the Duke's outright refusal to see her

447

perform on stage," the director repeated at each last rehearsal before the Grand Gala.

"Eh bien," Lauriot retorted devastated, "as an artist, I have come to realize that our passion for opéra is too great to identify with the delineation of the classes in everyday life. What is acceptable for the aristocrats versus the bourgeois? I just see talent. I can animate a conflict, decide who will play the role that displays integrity, and choose the actor that will show the evil ways of humanity. In essence, I am God on stage. To me, all conflicts on stage become real, but they can always be manipulated to fit the plot. My life is the stage." He proclaimed with an overly dramatic overture.

"Life is not a stage, Gabriella fits well in both of these worlds, although she is viewed as a free-spirited American, I understand her mother had an impeccable Italian aristocratic lineage," the director lamented.

"I am not quite certain, Lauriot, that the Duke's status in life is the reason behind his refusal. He has always gone against all rules of propriety. No, I believe that there are things that we may not be aware of," Barandi sadly replied. " I'm quite certain of it. He may have bedded every soprano and ballerina in every major production, but the little American possesses his heart and because of that, his aristocratic, possessive demeanor emerges."

"How dreadful. I would have thought more of him had he let Gabriella pursue her dream. Ah, being an artist, but it is the essence of a life well lived in my eyes. What could be better than to depict people's lives and their complexities, no matter who you are? After all, most men and women in our modern time are required to understand music and the intensity of great opéra. It is our human emotions that are being extracted. When we depict the life of a great woman or a great man, it should be a great honor. To all appearances, to depict the character of greatness, to deny artists to portray it, the best artist, that is, is like saying that the life is not worth revealing . . . is not worth exploring—not worth living. How absurd these aristocrats still are!"

"The Duke included!" the grand director retorted.

Eavesdropping in the *coulisses*, the wings behind the curtains of the stage, she'd been shocked at such frankness. Quickly she'd scurried to her dressing room reluctant to let on that she had overheard the conversation. She would never repeat this conversation to Jean-Louis. He would have had both blackballed from all the major European opéra houses.

Yet, she understood the Maestro's dismay. Lauriot could not understand why a man with such great lineage, such great integrity, would not want to have his Maîtresse depict on stage the human condition with the great gift that she had been blessed with. That was beyond understanding.

Lauriot had tried to convince Jean-Louis in a most inspirational argument why he should let Gabriella sing in his production. "In effect, Monsieur le Duke," he'd explained, "next to Mademoiselle Thornsen, the greatest sopranos of my stage become mediocre personalities. They are bland, no longer fascinating. Why should people be forced to listen to mediocrity? She has been given an outstanding gift, the—"

"No, my decision will not be revoked." Jean-Louis' retorted in a tone that did not allow further questioning. His look had shot down all hopes that the lover of music could change the Duke's position. And so it had had to be. In effect, she had chosen her bed and she had to sleep in it and most of the time she did not regret it.

A large table had been set out for them and many reporters were interviewing the performers. Lilianne, an accomplished ballerina was almost certain to get the part. La Gazette was interviewing her and talk that the Emperor would be in attendance at the first performance was thrilling.

"Gabriella," she heard her friend Gérard call out, "look who's walking outside. You are very lucky, my friend, why couldn't the Duke like men? What a beauty."

Gaby roared that crystal clear laughter that enchanted the world.

"Don't even dare look, Gérard, my jealousy is unpardonable." She turned fully backwards to admire him. God, how she loved him. Now she was the one who wished the next few days would fly by. She wanted to be home in his arms and retrieve their lives together.

Surprisingly enough he'd showed up at the oddest venues. She watched as friends recognized and engaged him in conversation. One was the culture minister, the same one who'd confided to friends that Jean-Louis' lovebird was completely devoid of common sense. To his credit, she had made a complete fool of herself, not on one but on two successive occasions. She smiled recalling the incidents. She had learned a lot about French culture these past years. Now she actually liked Jean Barraulte.

She continued to stare at Jean-Louis; he might notice her. Fat chance they were inside. Someone motioned in her direction. He looked up, smiled, and quickly took leave of the interlocutors as he entered the elegant restaurant.

Unable to tear her eyes away, she continued to stare. "Mr. Popular," she flippantly shared with Gérard. Jean-Louis was held back at every table. A distant association, a nod alone from the Duke was considered an honor. But the great one adored her. How did she ever pull that one off? Would she had let herself be seduced if she had known the great appeal that he had on people? Probably not, she thought. Her sense of self-survival would have kept her sane and logical. The first time he'd approach her closely on the ship, she'd suddenly lost her head . . . and balance while she pointed at the frolicking dolphins. His heady presence had perturbed her all day. He'd realized then that he had made an impact.

Jean-Louis had finally arrived at her table. Inadvertently, she must have been looking at him while she reminisced of the wonderful days spent at sea.

"Well, Mademoiselle Thornsen, I thought you were hard at work at the Conservatoire. Instead, I see you absorbed with your friends. The life of an artist!" His expression questioned the joyous gathering. He bent down and brushed her temple with a kiss.

"Tomorrow is the final audition. We decided to throw in the towel and come and enjoy the delicacies the Fouquets has to offer," she said sweetly, warmth emanated from her every pore. "What are you doing here? I was under the impression that diplomats were overworked souls that forgot *la table* and the common joys."

"Right again, ma chérie, except that most diplomats do not have the exquisite chance to be in love with a most extraordinary woman such as yourself." Surprise silenced the group and just as quickly he pulled her up, grabbed her reticule and nodded toward the exit doors.

"Eh bien extraordinary woman, come. I have a fun afternoon planned for the two of us." He grasped her elbows and led her outside.

They strolled on the Champs Elysée, hand and hand for a few moments but then she remarked his carriage was waiting at one of the intersections.

"Jean-Louis, you knew I was here?" she asked, not too pleased.

"Watch yourself carefully, my gorgeous stranger. All eyes are on you, especially when I found out that you are having a good time with people other than me. I have a real difficult time with that."

She laughed. "You scoundrel."

A few heads turned as two couples heard the irreverent American calling the Duke De Bourbonne a scoundrel.

He took her to lunch in a lovely little village where they had the most delicious pastries on earth. They went riding and stopped in an artistic small community where artists were painting diverse fall scenes, the lights and colors were magnificent. Berthe Morisot and her husband Eugène Manet, the brother of the celebrated Impressionist painter, were having a déjeuner outside of the inn. Both were watching their little girl play with another child. It was rare in these times to see family enjoying the outdoors. They did not disturb the couple. Frankly, Gaby wanted time alone with Jean-Louis. She was silent for a long time and so was he.

"You know, Jean-Louis, I adore everything that touches my artistic nature. I told you that I took painting lessons before the Civil War. I loved it, but I was asked to stop coming. The teacher had no patience with my style," she laughed. "I made horrible blunders when it came to blending colors and working the palette."

"They actually asked you not to return," he asked stupefied. "That bad?" He amused her when he came back with some ordinary American expression proclaimed with his haughty French accent.

She smiled and nodded. "Well, not that bluntly, but the artist gave me the name of the most awful teacher we had in our parish. You know how these things go, the reputation of a few teachers, I was sent to the one and only one that thought the un- teachable!"

"We will have a friend of Monet come to the house to teach you, if you wish to seriously pursue this interest," he said sweetly. "What do they know in Louisiana about an artistic nature. I'm certain that with the proper training, you'll excel in painting just like you do in everything else you place you heart and soul into."

She looked up at him with all the love she felt in her heart and she let herself be kissed tenderly. She was reminded of her spring vacation with her cousin Philippe.

"In late spring, Philippe and I would ride to Mississippi with his aunt. We had an old Aunt who lived in Biloxi. Did you know that Le vieux Biloxi was the first French capital of the Louisiana Purchase? A Mr. Bartam, a naturalist in the 1770s, had placed the picturesque little shrimp town on the Golf coast on the map. The French had also explored the area. The people are kind, hard working, and the seafood is outstanding. Both Philippe and I would wait on the pier, early in the morning, for the shrimpers to return to the docks and then we would run as quickly as our legs would let them toward the Beauvoir's house to grilled these poor little beasts that would instantly turn orange, from fear, Philippe would say, as they grilled on the coals. Religion did not play a great role in his life then."

"Your cousin, Philippe—will he come to our wedding?"

"Assuredly." He wrote a couple days ago. He adores me and would not miss it for the world. He'll like you too, Jean-Louis, you'll become inseparable, I know."

Jean-Louis was not too certain of it. Perhaps he could not quite understand a man of the cloth having such a close relationship with his cousin. Gaby was blabbering once again about Mississippi.

"Back to my unfulfilled dream," she was saying, "the one about learning how to apply pleasing colors to a canvas. I distinctly recall an artist, years ago, that told me in the *vieux* Biloxi that my inability to work with a palette, in effect to blend color . . ." she looked up at Jean-Louis before divulging this fearsome rencontre—he was listening intently now. She decided against revealing more. She laughed instead. "The fellow said I should give it up completely, forever."

Jean-Louis laughed as well and gathered her in his arms. Actually, the old man had said that it was her tumultuous inner self that was revealed in the painting. "You're trying to make sense of your world." The man asserted. "You must have huge sad secrets inside yourself, young lady," the old man continued. "The day you come to term with your fears, try painting again. Your black and white designs have pleasing proportions," he'd finished simply.

Flabbergasted and frightened by the man who'd looked inside her soul, she'd never tried her hand at painting again.

She nearly confided the episode to Jean-Louis, but stopped short instead. He'd ask questions about her past that she was neither willing nor able to answer. The past was history. She had acquired the tools to make herself happy. Now she was fulfilled and she would make sure that it would continue.

Jean-Louis made love to her upon returning to Paris.

"This interlude is driving me mad," he gasped as he gathered her tightly to his chest.

Today she was ready to return to the mansion. Game over!

Jean-Louis now had a different perspective. He told the carriage driver to drive around Paris for another hour or so; he wanted her again, but would not take her back to the house. If she moved back in before the wedding, rumors ran rampant in Paris, another embarrassment would occur. Gaby will need to come to term with the society after all, he analyzed—the return to St Louis was out of the question now.

The beautiful Gabriella De Conte Thornsen had imbibed too much champagne. Her sensuality showed no restraint. He cast a skeptical glance downward. She was hard to resist.

"I want to feel your chest on my back, you legs on my hips, your face in my hair and your strong arms surrounding me completely all night long, Jean-Louis," she whispered, kissing his throat. He smiled. His desire insurmountable, he let passion dictate the moment.

The coach stopped in front of the austere convent. The footman came round and lowered the steps.

"Why not your house?" she questioned candidly. "I'm ready."

He smiled. "Not tonight, darling," he chuckled.

"Why not Jean-Louis? Where are you going? Are you meeting someone tonight? More business preparations?"

"No, chérie, of course not." He stepped out and combed his hands through his hair. Quickly he reached into the carriage and helped her down onto the sidewalk. "I feel that it is more appropriate to continue this present living arrangement until after the wedding."

"Well, perhaps, there will not be a wedding!" she responded irate. "You practically begged me not to leave your home and now it's the best living arrangement until the wedding?" She argued spitefully. She was mortified. His needs had been assuaged and now he was out God knows where!

She crossed the street. He followed close behind. Heavy bronze wrought iron gates stood between the convent and the street. She pushed open the rungs on the entryway and walked inside the courtyard as she knowingly let the full force of the gate thrust him back in the street.

Gaby knocked at the door of the pristine white building, one of the young novices let her in. She immediately walked inside while Jean-Louis incensed stood outside the gate. She did not bother to look back.

For a moment, he was inclined to jump the gate, but his anger would take over and that would create another sordid separation. He would deal with her tomorrow. It downed on him that he should have explained the reasoning behind his refusal. Gaby was not the type to accept a prompt and logic response. A convoluted explanation was always de rigueur with her.

The American ambassador was giving a grand ball next week and she certainly would be in attendance. Her friends were performing and she would want to see them. He would explain then the reason behind his refusal—now was not a good time. He jerked his eyes away. He was inflamed and she was mortified. Gaby had a huge ego; now was definitely not a good time to try to mend their relationship.

Chapter Forty-One

The Gala at the American Ambassador was at hand. Gaby accompanied her friends to the Embassy—Marie-Louise, Liliane and her Count who was in Paris for a full month. She had been uncertain about attending. Ulysses Grant had been elected to the Presidency. Many believed that his true strength lay in fighting an enemy—not in conducting an administration of pencil pushers. As a Southerner, she hated him. She could not forget that Sherman himself had appointed Grant to scorch the South! The Vice-President would be in attendance and Michael Striker had asked her to be present.

She wore a splendid emerald gown that matched her eyes. The décolleté plunged to a new low. The nights were cool in Paris so she'd purchased the matching satin redingote. She was still wearing it when she entered the ballroom. She glanced at the mirrors and casted a last critical appraisal—magnifique was the word that came to mind!

After the episode last week, she had not attended any other parties and she ignored the notes he had sent to her private apartment in the convent. Jean-Louis watched her as she entered the foyer. He caught her glance and smiled. She did not acknowledge his presence by strolling to him.

"Gabriella, is that the way you entertain in Amerique?" Marie-Louise asked as she ambled toward her friend. "It has the touch of a Vatel, you recall Gabriella, the celebrated master of activities from another century, the director of entertainment under the superintendant of Louis XIV, Nicolas Fouquet in the chateau of Vaux le Vicomte" her friend lectured.

Gaby smiled. "I hope that Michael will not suffer the sort of the poor Fouquet," she smiled. But why does it surprise you so, Marie-Louise? In spite of everything, many of us uncultured colonials are rooted in the western European traditions. You see," she continued teasingly, "we often borrow the elegant traditions of the old continent and add to it our youthful, spontaneous, and practical customs."

"Touchée, mon amie," Marie-Louise offered, she reached for Gaby's hand and gave it an affectionate squeeze. "I see the Duke. He is watching you, go to him Gabriella. Don't ever waste a happy moment. They are always short-lived," she whispered as she glanced toward her lover.

"Have a wonderful evening, Marie-Louise." Gaby replied.

These past three days had been long and weary. Jean-Louis had not given her a sign of life and she missed him. She loved playing Miss Independence as long as he showed great interest in her whereabouts. Insecurity overwhelmed her whole being when he became distant.

It was a light-hearted society they lived in. Jean-Louis had lived this life. How difficult would it be for him to return to his heady nights in Paris? Not that difficult, she reluctantly sensed.

She had lots of admirers tonight. Everyone seemed to be stopping her. Michael, the ambassador walked over.

"Ma jolie compatriote," he said in French, "comment allez-vous? I hear that you will be joining Jean-Louis in his upcoming trip to Italy," he asked as he twirled her on the dance floor. She acquiesced. She had forgotten all about Italy.

The Ambassador wanted to know more. "Well, is Philippe still in Rome, or has he started his trip to Paris?"

"Michael, you seem to know so much more than I do. Let me ask you a few questions," she responded coyly. "I understand that his appointment as Cardinal of Paris will be effective within a month or two. The last time I heard from him, he was still in Rome. What did you hear?"

Everyone thought of her as well informed and it was natural for Michael to pry for information he hoped to gain because of their common nationalities. Jean-Louis had instructed her well on the subject. She knew very well how to distract the curious.

"Do not elaborate, Gaby. Everyone will know soon enough."

She had had to learn the hard way on less influential issues the first few months of their relationship in Paris. Her most intimate thoughts had been plastered on every newspaper imaginable. She even had to be aware of her surrounding while supping in restaurants and at the Conservatoire. Some unsavory remarks she had made to Marie-Louise about Jean-Louis' Grandmother, her haughtiness and lack of empathy for her servants had been repeated to every written source in Paris. The gathering in the salons had kept these observations alive longer than she could have dreamed of.

"Well, Michael, I hear that you will be returning to Washington next year. Is that correct?"

It was his turn to smile. She'd caught him playing the same game. Gabriella will be a great diplomat, the Ambassador reflected.

"I'm afraid so, Gabriella. I do not believe that Béatrice will accompany me if and when it comes to pass. The new administration will want to appoint one of their men and a new delegation. I'll cross the bridge when the time comes," he replied with a hint of sadness.

He brought her back to a small table away from the crowd and they spoke about their countries and their mutual friends for a long time. Finally, she noticed the men emerged from the library.

"I'm afraid, Michael, that we have been caught resting. I see Béatrice looking quite annoyed. You need to return to her and your guests." Noticing sadness on his face, she quickly added, "I love talking to you. You are such a fascinating man. I hope with all my heart that the President will extend your stay. You have done so much for Franco-American relations. I, for one, would miss you terribly."

They both stood up and he walked her back to her friends.

"A bientôt, the evening is formidable. Once more you have outperformed your prior dinners. It looks good for us." She laughed, pivoted on her heels, and waved her gloved hand. Michael stood, evaluating her strangely, but the moment was lost. Béatrice had just joined him.

"Chéri, you have other guests. Come." She spoke the words with her beautiful smile—but hate was present in her eyes.

Too bad Gaby reflected sadly, the woman feels no emotion for him but his status pleases her.

Where was Jean-Louis? Had he left without saying anything? What was wrong? He never held a grudge. All this talk about Italy was weighing on his normally spirited self, she thought.

The men had returned to the library to discuss the upcoming trip to Italy. She noticed Jean-Louis coming out, and now, everyone seemed to be in the ballroom except him. She was unwilling to leave before his return. Hours later, she noticed that he rested calmly in one of the adjoining smoking salons.

Friends encircled him, mostly ladies. By now few really knew the status of their relationship. Everyone talked about it and both were evasive. They needed time before the marriage, was the statement that Jean-Louis' Grandmother whispered to those who dared to ask.

Gabriella decided to wait until he returned to the ballroom.

She noticed Madame Pelletier, whose husband had just died in the Piedmont in Italy. She was now embroiled in what looked from far away, a serious conversation with Jean-Louis. He was looking down on her, apparently interested in her babbles. She knew that he had had an escapade with her years ago and that in Paris these days, there was no difference between love, sex, and affection. They all rolled perfectly and conveniently, in one small, tidy package.

Promptly, she asked Monsieur De Valle with whom she had been dancing to walk with her towards the group socializing with her fiancé.

She arrived, smiled at the assemblage, and she touched Jean-Louis' arm gently with her long and slender fingertips.

Recognizing her touch, he turned to her and momentarily lost control of his aloofness. He had not seen her without the redingote and the décolleté of the dress had him take a second, harder look at her. She would never wear that dress in public again. He'd toss it he fumed inwardly.

In contrast, Gaby felt delicious. She was beautiful and he desired her. She loved knowing that she could still arouse him with a touch and her smile.

Nonchalantly, he acknowledged her presence and continued his conversation while he kept his distance. She did not move away from him. Madame Pelletier was much too close and her smile, beauty and charm provoked insane jealousy.

As he watched the merry-go-round, Monsieur De Valle was wildly amused.

"Ah, eh bien you two, tell us what is your sentimental status? Is the wedding taking place or can we have the pleasure of asking Gabriella to accept an invitation?"

"Yes to the first and a resounding no to the second," Jean-Louis answered promptly.

More relaxed now, Jean-Louis looked at Gaby and gave her that long sensual smile.

"Never fall for an American girl, De Valle, way too difficult to handle. Since you asked, Gabriella has decided that she wants to experience freedom and independence in Paris before she loses it forever—in her own words, my friend." He shook his head in disbelief.

De Valle laughed heartily while Madame Pelletier did not miss a beat.

"Does that mean, my dear Duke, that you are free as well? What a lovely surprise." She wrapped her arm around Jean-Louis' and smiled a devastating beam.

Jean-Louis looked down at Gaby as if to say—your turn.

Not to be outdone, Gaby stepped closer to him and placed her arm gently on his back and forced him closer.

"Jean-Louis is in one of his amusing moods tonight. Women are quite possessive in my family. I'll have to return home and lock him in his room after what I have just heard—and seen," she replied glaring at Madame Pelletier's arm still wrapped up around Jean-Louis'.

Embroiled in rage she nevertheless smiled at him with adoring eyes.

"I would love to dance," she murmured sensuously.

He politely excused himself, a half smile hung down the side of his mouth. He took her elbow and led her toward the dance floor.

"Why such a rapid change of demeanor, Mademoiselle? Where have you been? I wrote at least a dozen notes, none merited an answer Gaby?" He demanded sarcastically. "Or do I detect that Madame Pelletier's advances annoyed you and jolted you back to reality?"

"No," she replied coyly. "I merely wanted to be in your arms once more."

He looked down at her innocent eyes. Her loved her candor and spontaneity. There was so little of it in his world. He slid his arms on her waist and held her closer to him as they whirled on the dance floor.

"Just to see if I still liked it as much," she could not help but to respond as she raised her expressive eyes to him.

Momentarily, he stopped in his steps. Had there not been hundred of eyes watching Paris' most talked about couple flirt with one another, he would have left her standing all by herself on the dance floor. But years of good breeding made him realize that she would be made a fool of and although he wanted to teach her a lesson, he recalled his Grandmother's assertive words to essentially put an end to the constant charade.

"She is but a child, Jean-Louis, she needs to be controlled. Surely, you know that," the dowager had said.

He did not, however, want the tout Paris to excoriate her every mood. He gently looked down at her smiling face and quickly led the little witch off the dance floor and down the staircase to the foyer. He picked up a flute of champagne from the roving butlers.

With ill-conceived annoyance, he looked down at her pretty face once more. He'd love to take her to bed just to question her 'liking it as much' reaction. Instead, he bent down, gave her a friendly kiss on her forehead, and said as she stood questioningly, watching the butler help him get into his coat, "Funny, ma chérie," he said thoughtfully, "telepathy played with our emotions tonight. I was just thinking that I'm not quite sure that I like it as much." He kissed her forehead amicably once more and departed.

Stunned, she stood motionless for a few moments, long enough to watch him walk out the door and down the stairs toward his waiting carriage. He gazed back at her angry and shaken face and for an instant watched from afar her reaction.

"Jean-Louis!" She ran after him.

Now again she was totally oblivious that she was bringing attention to herself and that many eyes were focused in her direction. That's what he loved about her. She displayed no pretension when her sentiments were at stake. Poor Gaby, she always wore her emotions on her sleeve, so spontaneous she never let gossip deter her from her sincere display of sentiment. Out of the blue he had an inkling of running back to her and taking her home. Instead, he decidedly walked toward his carriage and did not look back. The grooms were harnessing the last horse. No, he would let her marvel in her anger a bit more. He continued his descent and waved the butler to bring the carriage forward.

"Jean-Louis, wait, wait, I'm sorry, I did not mean—" she stood at the top of the marble staircase.

He had wanted to wait for the full four weeks and then return to the Loire promptly where their wedding ceremony would take place, but frankly now, he was not quite certain he could wait out the last days.

She flew down the stairs hoping to dissuade him from leaving—to no avail. She stared at the passing carriage with tears in her eyes and began to slowly turn back. A significant crowd of onlookers watched the charade. No longer sad but raving mad, shooting disdainful glances to the curious, she haughtily asked for her coat and carriage to be brought forward. To her pleasant surprise, the carriage showed up quickly. It always seemed to happen in that manner—as if someone was watching her every move.

Furiously she climbed in the carriage. Now she had to take hold of herself, she told herself. She hated him. She had to go on without him. She could not possibly let him make decisions for her life. She had been wrong in going to Montmartre, that was a given. She understood that now. It did not entail, however, the drama that followed. Granted, she had caused a lot of it, she begrudgingly acknowledged, but . . . she had to return to her other passion—singing. Sadly, her desire to perform, to share her voice with others was no longer a great need. Jean-Louis was her passion.

As she sat ensconced in the elegant carriage, her head resting on the deep velvet squabs, resentful discontent filled her spirit. Why this drastic change in her personality? Had she been in France too long? She never really cared about what people thought of her before. Why did she suddenly need to be loved and admired? Why was it primordial to her? Did she want Jean-Louis to be proud of her in front of his peers? Well she was, she mused. All in Paris adored her singing. Crowds in Milan or Venice would too! All couldn't wait to engage her. Marriage however to a man with Jean-Louis' lineage would be difficult. The great divide between the classes still existed. But why would she want to be married? She asked herself aloud raving mad. She had never wanted to be tethered before—why now?

The break-up was good. She had lost control of her being. Her thoughts reverted to Jean-Louis and his hurtful words as he left her behind on the staircase. Tears streamed down her face. To return to her former life might be too difficult. Not now. But when? She asked her defeated spirit. A decision was required otherwise before long she would be married and in his claws for life. Yet, she wanted more than anything to be his wife—to share his life.

Maybe she should wait out the month he had given her to come back to her senses and obediently follow his urging to return home.

Now she was too tired and too disappointed. She'd think of something tomorrow. Maybe she would wake up and the controlling soul would be forgotten.

Chapter Forty-Two

Gaby had received another invitation to another grand ball. The season had started once more and invitations were received on a continuous basis. She decided not to go. All naturally wanted her to sing. She was much in vogue for recitals. Instead she solicited Martine LaGourde, a radiant new mezzo-soprano to sing in her place. The De Valliers were introducing the new debutantes.

"I'll turn in early with a good book and forget about Parisian society for a while," she told Marie-Jane, Lilianne's younger sister who had come from the province. Visiting her sister in Paris was a treat the young girl dreamed of all year. Today, however, the fun was nowhere in sight. Lilianne was crying senselessly for the Count had returned to his family in Provence.

Gaby often accepted invitations to forget about her sadness. The first week she had done everything in her power to stay out of Jean-Louis' way. But her resolve had weakened at the reception given by Marie-Josée. They had spent a wonderful picture perfect end of the week in the Faubourg apartment. She knew quite well that unless she returned to New Orleans incognito, he would find her, bring her home, and marry her. He counted her days of independence and reminded her often that they were engaged. Sickly enough, it comforted her. After last week, she wasn't so sure anymore.

I have joined the ranks of stupid females that surrender heart and soul to their soul mate, she whispered to herself, disappointed.

At week's end, Jean-Louis would find lovely things to do and it certainly would not have taken much for her to return to the townhome had he asked her to. He would pick her up early and they would forget about all that had happened on that fateful day when she had returned from Montmartre with Lilianne.

Weekdays however were lonely. The convent was quiet and two of the pensioners were not too talkative. Another two demented souls had come willingly to the convent to do penance for their lustful sins.

Lately, Jean-Louis was everywhere and her jealousy mounted if she saw him speaking to other women. So why make herself so unhappy? She walked back to the convent from the Conservatoire. It was very cold in Paris. Last week a family of scrawny cats had set up camp outside the heavy bronze gate of the saintly dwelling. Twice a day she brought warm milk to the undernourished kittens.

Bundled up in a white mink coat and matching hat, a birthday gift from Jean-Louis, she ran inside the convent and came back out with two cups of warm milk. She marveled at the brightness of these young animals that recognized her readily—by her scent probably. She bowed down watching the animals lap up the warm liquid. She squatted down and reached out for one of the frightened kitten that had lost a significant amount of weight these past several days. She wanted to shelter the animal in the warm kitchen of the convent, "there are enough stray cats in Paris, let nature take its course," the Mother Superior terse reply shot forth. Consequently everyday she'd stop to give it food and keep it warm in her fur coat. One dead animal protecting another so went the laws of nature! She did not hear a carriage slow down in the near by street. It came to a halt. Jean-Louis was coming home. He noticed her immediately and begun marching toward the gilded gate. Her sweet presence gentled him. Little did these poor little chatons know about her wild temperament when pushed to the limit—the iron angel, he thought, amused.

He missed her so. She missed him too. They were both playing games and they were both miserable. He should never have allowed her to leave.

She noticed his boots and turned quickly.

"Go away, you annoy me. I have more important things to do than to talk to you."

"Like feeding stray cats?"

"Yes," she replied curtly.

"I presumed the Mother Superior said 'no cats inside, let nature take its course'."

"Yes." She looked up, surprised that he knew. "Do you have spies in there, too?" She nodded toward the convent.

He abruptly changed the subject. "I miss you Gaby, come back—please." He knelt down next to her on the snow that had started to blanket the sidewalk and noticed her eyes filled with tears.

"Well, that's too bad because I'm very happy. I do not miss you one bit," she said, in a vain attempt to control her sudden anger over the humiliation she endured in front of his peers."

He grabbed her chin and kissed the tears streaming down her cheeks.

"Please come back, Gaby," he implored.

She said nothing and the cat decided to add insult to injury and urinated on his boots. She grabbed the impertinent little beast quickly and furrowed it in her manchon, muff. Jean-Louis grinned and shook his head.

"They never did that to me!" She smiled back.

"Gaby, I'm willing to compromise. You seem quite enamored with these kittens, take these beasts and return with me. You could nurse them back to health in our house."

She tried to stand up. He placed a hand under her chin and forced her to look up at him.

Facing her, he knelt down and gently his hands cupped her face. He looked at the dark-green eyes filled with unshed tears ready to drench her beautiful face.

"I miss you so, darling. I am miserable. I hate my return to my house in the evening. It's lonely and unbearable without you, Gaby." He gently tried to pull her up with him—to no avail, she kept on looking down at the little kitten that was in no mood to scamper away from the warmth of the fur.

He knelt closer to her and placed his hand under her coat, feeling her waist and gently pulling her to him. He gently caressed her back.

"Come back, Gaby. His lips brushed her temples applying more pressure as he attempted to have her face him fully. "I love you darling. His lips sensually gravitated to hers.

She knew that she would capitulate if this *pas de deux* continued a while longer.

The humiliation she had had to endure in front of all of their friends, dear God, an apology was in order and it was not forthcoming, she pondered.

"Have you forgotten, Jean-Louis, your arrogant behavior, plus your pretentious refusal to take me back to your house less than a week ago after our crazy amorous afternoon at Chatou. I was ready then. I presume the champagne at the Fouquets had left me weak and way too malleable. No, I'm not going back—not now, anyway. That is for certain. I am no longer playing your little cat and mouse game. What are you thinking of? I am not a puppet on a string!" She shouted. "Do you go to the Park Manceau, to the Marionettes to fantasize all of your sordid demands?" She jerked quickly to her feet and brusquely walked away from him. "I want nothing to do with you, just go away and stay away from me."

She bolted towards the wrought iron fence of the convent and he followed close behind her. Jean-Louis-Pierre De Pleyssis never took no for an answer. He reached to her in an attempt to pull her back to him, but her agility got the best of him and the heavy wrought iron crashed back in his face. He was thrown backwards forcefully on the pavement. That was the second time in less than a month that the Duke de Bourbonne had been on the receiving hand of the clanking iron gates and forced out of the convent.

Gaby ran up the stairs and down the long and narrow hallway where her apartment was located. In her haste she had taken the little kitten in with her. In the hallway, she passed the young priest who had pleaded her case to the Mother Superior on her behalf, in lieu of her cousin. He adored her but she also recognized the influence Philippe could have on his career. Gaby pressed her finger to her lips; her eyes darted to the kitten. Silently the cleric's slim figure ambled through the narrow corridor. She mouthed silent thanks. She owed him a lot. After all, she had been living in sin since her arrival in France. The Mother Superior had balked at her presence in the convent.

She entered her room and dropped the animal on a satin hassock next to the hearth. Without much thought, she picked up the satin coverlet that Jean-Louis had given her when they'd returned from

Montmartre on their engagement day. The border of the comforter was embroidered with their initials. In the background a picture of the Tempète with both of their effigies were painted on the dark-green satin. He had placed a fabulous emerald ring in a flat pocket sewn just below the drawing. She softly caressed the smooth texture in her hand. Unexpectedly a racket blasted in the hallway. Within seconds, her locked door tumbled down in the middle of the room and Jean-Louis stood bigger than life incensed in the archway. He took in the room and begun to stride threateningly towards her.

Still clutching the satin coverlet, she zigzagged backwards in between the chairs facing the fireplace and quickly landed on a day bed recovered in gold velours with matching pillows.

His voice amplified in the calm and saintly community. Frightened she sat rigid. Facing her, he pulled her up and clasped her shoulders. Her face must have registered sheer terror.

"If you ever pull a trick like that, ever, ever again, Gaby," he compressed her arm so tightly that she felt it going numb. Her face must have lost some of its peachy color. He softened the clasp but continue the tirade.

She returned his glare.

"You will not win this battle, Gaby, I can assure you. So you might as well give up now. I will not concede, you will return to the house next week, there is no compromise on that, like it or not," he roared.

She stared and did not acknowledge the insinuations.

"You know what I mean, Gaby?" he hollered threateningly. "Is that understood?" he repeated, livid.

She did not respond but held his gaze.

Jean-Louis tried to surmount his fury. This is an exercise in self-control, he reminded himself. It will be helpful in Italy. He steadied her shoulders. "Have you lost you speech, Miss De Conte-Thornsen?" he demanded.

She looked up at him unwilling to concede anything.

The priest, thank God, came to her rescue inadvertently.

"Arrêtez, Monsieur le Duke. Mademoiselle is in a convent. You are invading her privacy and her right to peace and prayers along with everybody else's rights."

"Shut up," was the response as Jean-Louis let go of Gaby and turned his rage to the priest and the large number of nuns and novices--all out of their rooms watching the circus defile.

"Mademoiselle here," Jean-Louis continued, now facing the priest, has been living in my house for the past two years. I'm sure you don't believe for an instant, knowing my reputation, that I have given her a private apartment while I bring her champagne and chocolates, waiting duly and patiently for our wedding night," he shouted.

"This is a pure and saintly home, Monsieur. Mademoiselle ☐has every right to repent for her past behavior and live here—forgiven," the priest continued calmly. ☐

"Well, Monsieur le Curé, let me make it a little less holy as I take my fiancée right in front of your eyes and give you a few lessons in un-saintly behavior that she will not dislike or repent for. Of that I am certain. Perhaps you'll change your mind about this pure and saintly angel."

Gaby gestured to the priest to say no more. She placed her forefingers over her mouth. No need to aggravate the situation at this time and get the gentle priest in trouble.

The priest said no more, and Jean-Louis turned back to Gaby as she still held her fingers to her mouth. He stood ready to continue his tirade but stopped momentarily. He watched Gaby's defiant face on one side and the priest and the sisters on the other looking at him as if he was a wild beast. The situational picture suddenly turned hilarious. He stared at her a while longer, then back at the priest who stood in the door and at a half a dozen nuns who tried to steal a view of the action. He suddenly wanted to laugh. The innocent-looking woman in front of him, all five-foot of her was driving him mad. Why did he want her so? He had organized his life so well, done what he wanted to do all his life and now he was a prisoner of his emotions. She dictated every phase of his life.

He stayed still for a while longer and then sarcastically, but much more subdued, he turned toward the priest.

"Go back to your rooms, all of you, the show is over. I will send my administrator tomorrow first thing to pay for repairs and for the replacement of the door plus for whatever damage that I have incurred." He continued to look sternly at the sisters and the priest. They were still overwhelmed by the situation. He tried to sound less authoritarian.

"You will have guards tonight to keep Mademoiselle safe," he emphasized ironically. Now leave and give us some privacy. I will be gone shortly."

His stern voice was so overpowering that no one thought of disobeying his order. They looked at Gaby who showed no fear. Silently they all filed down the hall to their respective chambers.

Relieved, Gaby sat back down on her daybed. She expected him to leave, but he stood and stared down at her. She took note of the taut set of his jaws. He strode close to her, kneeled down, and slid his hands on her warm neck. He tipped her face to his.

"Tell me, Gaby, why do I become a beastly lunatic when you anger me? Women never angered me before, they pleased me— enormously."

He looked at her once more and knew that she knew the answer. He could not control her. True, he could bend her to his will through sheer strength, but emotionally she had full control of herself—and of him as well. He was well aware of that. He did not wait for an answer; instead he kissed her jaw, close to her ear, and then her cheek and then placed his lips hungrily on hers. He kissed her long and tenderly enjoying every fold and every tormenting texture of her sweet mouth. Plunging his tongue in her mouth, searching for hers, trying desperately to entangle her sweetness fully in his by rhythmically probing deep and hard, he waited for her quivering response before gently moving his body and coming to sit next to her. Passionately, he encircled her body and pressed her demandingly to his.

"I love you, Gaby." He murmured. His hands roved on her shapely body. He kissed her again, loosened her blouse and slipped his hand on her breast. His kiss demanded a passionate response. He received none.

"Kiss me!" he ordered.

She did not give him the pleasure of a victory.

After a long, frustrating moment, he reluctantly disentangled from her body and fully straightened to his full length. He stood gazing down at those green expressive eyes that drove him wild.

He heaved a long sigh and paused a moment, inclined to pick her up and take her back with him. Instead, he turned quickly and started towards the door. His peripheral vision spotted the cat. The animal had risen on its front paws to enjoy the show as well. As an afterthought he walked back toward the chair, picked up the kitten that looked dismal and he walked to the doorway.

"It too will be waiting for you at home. Three more days, Gaby, that's it. No more. This interlude was a huge mistake. I will not let you make another error when it comes to us." Within minutes he was gone.

She sat a while longer. His scent still here, his taste on her mouth, she was unwilling just yet to let go of the sensations she craved.

He was a total lunatic all right, but yet, she still thought of herself as the best partner he could ever have.

Yes, she could at time be less than malleable, capricious perhaps, accustomed of having her own way, but after all, she had had to endure hardship all of her young life. She had had to be obstinate. Things happened for some unknown reasons that usually unraveled later when no one suspected. Oh, well, she would let life play its tune.

She lay back down on her little cot. She heard men's voices outside the main entrance. The guards had arrived. Jean-Louis never forgot anything. She was safe. She fell soundly asleep.

The following morning, she woke up late. She dressed quickly and walked out of the convent promptly unwilling to elaborate on last night's explosive performance. What business of theirs was it? She grabbed her white mink and walked out in the freezing Paris air.

Of all people who should be out late as well, Jean-Louis stood right outside of his home large and open wooden doors. She watched him walk down the marble steps with a large group of people. Two appeared to be women. They spoke on the sidewalk for a few minutes and the blonde kissed him on both cheeks. Moments later the group got in their respective carriages.

Inflamed, her insane jealousy turned to anger. She froze on the sidewalk hoping that Jérome, the conductor would not notice her. No such luck, the young man stopped the carriage and jumped down to help her pass safely across the street. He stopped the constant flow of carriages. Many coachmen did not always care about the populace that crossed the streets at this time of day. Jean-Louis watched.

She'd charmed the servants to her will—so much so that they forgot who was paying their salaries, he pondered shaking his head. Sure enough, it showed this morning. Jérome helped miss De Conte-Thornsen across the street while he waited in his carriage. She looked devastatingly beautiful. He waited patiently with a smirk on his face. She ambled, regal, deigning not a glance. He continued to stare. In a split second, she broke her stature and glanced sideways without turning her head. She must have noticed Arianne and Plebe on his doorsteps a little earlier and was making certain he was alone. Playing with her, he bent forward, opened the door, and with a gesture showed her that no one was using her place in the carriage. The little witch pretended not to notice his enticing movement.

He kept his gaze on her as she crossed the street and walked elegantly and assertively on the bridge Louis Philippe with her carriage following close by.

He wished he could walk near her, her delicate and soft little hands in his, just to be in her precious inner personal circle. God, he was beginning to sound like the Emperor with the intriguing Castiglione! Beginning, he smiled, that was the understatement of the year. Gaby controlled his every cell! He remembered the pliable beauty on the Tempète. Although he should have realized from the very beginning that she was fearless. He had walked in raving mad one day, ordering her never to touch his things. Her first move had been to walk across the room and to sit in his chair. He had been amused at her impertinence and had pitied the poor fellow who would one day marry her!

Eh bien, he would see her tomorrow night and save her from the pointed remarks of the Beau Monde. He'd show up late at the De Valliers since his English friends were in Paris. He'd party first with them—he needed it—to retrieve a sense of self. Gaby had two engagements that night. She arrive late as well.

* * *

Tonight another grand ball had been given. This time it was in one of the magnificent hotels located very close to Jean-Louis' home. Lauriot had begged her to sing. At first she had baulked, but La Rochefoucault had asked her to sing a few arias. La Rochefoucault was one of the Emperor's close advisors and he was giving the ball in celebration of the Universal Fair. Jean-Louis would attend. In her beautiful carriage, Gaby contemplated the status of artists in a rare moment of sadness. Beethoven had advanced their independence when he'd suggested to the King of Prussia, that he had had to work hard at his God-given gift for he had not been born with a title that would have given him the world on a silver platter. Well, he was a composer, a ring up the ladder from a soprano. He composed the music. A singer was solely the interpreter, she mused. She parted the glass curtain on the window. Coaches' lamps flickered in the dark night. Her carriage bowled out on the cobblestones. Singing would lift her spirits. She would countenance no peers in her delivery. Her sad heart would infuse the heroine with a fire that would intensify her tragic destiny.

As usual Gaby was late and Hortense had begun the musical program. Jean-Louis stood near the library, none too happy about seeing his future bride sing her heart out in front of the many Europeans heads of State that were in attendance this evening, namely Queen Victoria of England, the Tsar of Russia, and King Wilhelm of Prussia. As a wedding present he'd begun the building of a fine theatre in his home. She would love it, he concurred, and furthermore he'd have more control over the invitations that she'd accept.

While he waited patiently for the little tyrant to arrive, Jean-Louis noticed one of his security guard striding anxiously toward him. A note exchanged hands. He quickly read it. "Miss Thornsen is in the library on the first floor, Monsieur," the man whispered. Pivoting on his heels with an impenetrable expression, Jean-Louis marched to the Emperor and murmured a few words. Louis Napoléon was visibly startled. Without waiting for an answer, Jean-Louis crossed the room. Rapidly, he climbed the large staircase with his security guards in tow and marched in the mahogany-walled library. Gaby, still wearing a long white satin cloak, sat on a sofa, her gloved hands restless on her knees as she surveyed the entrance anxiously—a terrified look on her face. She bolted out of her seat and ran into his arms. He gathered her tightly and pressed her to his chest.

Bands of Republicans roamed the city incensed by the Emperor's lavish and decadent life style while the poor of the city starved. Many took matter in their own hands. Sadly enough many in the National Guards armed and trained their leaders. Their intent was to create havoc and fear in the ruling class. He had told Louis Napoléon to deal swiftly with the guards. But all the forewarning had been placed on the back burner and the masked balls and the débaucherie continued extravagantly. This last incident came as a surprise to him. Gaby had an army of guards watching her every move. Perhaps there were traitors in his security detail. He would get to the bottom of it. Meanwhile Gaby needed encouragement. No need to place fears in her mind.

"Everything is fine, Gaby. Your attackers have been dealt with," he pronounced calmly and reassuringly.

"Their faces were pressed on both sides of the windows—two shoved long knives at the glass. I could not understand everything. I felt the depth of their hatred. Two brown Rottweiler dented the windows, barking incessantly and showing their fangs." She recoiled at the vision of the dogs. "They were ready to tear me apart Jean-Louis!"

"Your carriage was stopped by a band of Republicans intent on getting rid of the Empire and all aristocrats. They're the descendants of the Jacobin movement of '89, Gaby and they're enticing the populace. They are opposed to all reforms coming from the Empire. Their most ardent wish is to install a new administration—a Third Republic," he whispered, almost to himself.

"Why me?" she questioned. "I agree with Louis Napoléon," she continued angrily, "you do not do reforms well in France. Instead, you start revolutions!"

"You're safe, Gaby; you're safe, darling." Her trembling body began to relax as he caressed her cheeks. "Let's leave!" He suddenly interjected as several curious guests poked their heads in the library. Without a word, they passed by the snooping bystanders and quickly stepped in his waiting carriage.

"To the Faubourg!" he commanded.

During the short ride to the apartment, she recounted the full incident.

"On the way to the soirée, by the Tuileries, I noticed a crowd of Republicans shouting insults to guests riding inside their carriages on their way to the festivities."

"Why did you ask the driver to veer away from the crowd?"

"I was concerned . . . they were reluctant but I pressed on Jean-Louis. My carriage has no coat of arms, I surmised that I could pass unnoticed."

"You should have listened to Justin, for God's sake. Had he not been there, you'd be in a very dire state. I hope you've savored your independent phase. Are you more willing to be more dependent on my loving care?" he said with a smirk. She looked up. He winked back at her.

They entered the apartment. Jean-Louis walked to the fireplace and placed large logs in the chimney. She looked around nothing had been touched. Her satin slippers by the cream satin settee and her lounge gown on the frame of the bergère were exactly where she had left them. Standing against the marble of the mantle, he smiled as he studied her and watched her study every inch of the apartment.

"St. Louis and the Faubourg are sacred ground, Gaby." He turned and bent down to stoke the fire.

"I missed you so Jean-Louis," she said with emotion as she stood up and came to rest by him.

"Good." He smiled. "May I assume that our marriage plans are still standing?" he half-jokingly asked.

She nodded.

That very night their passion ignited. She fell asleep worriless in his arms. In contrast, his concern for her safety kept him awake and anxious. He would have to increase her security. The bastards almost had their way. Perhaps inculcating a bit of fear in his independent-minded fiancée might be a very good thing, he thought. Thank God that he had forbidden her the stage. To keep her safe in that venue would have been a much more difficult task. He looked down upon her. The little brat displayed not a care in the world. He shuddered at the thought. Tomorrow they would restart their life and return back to Saint Louis. He'd even get up and walk to Fauchon to purchase her favorite preserves and croissants.

Eh bien, all is well that ends well, he thought. He let himself relax next to her and he chased the anxieties that had plagued him since he'd heard the news this evening. He rolled in next to her and he let her heartbeat and sweet breath nurse him to sleep. Tomorrow, he would be on to another adventure with his lovely American mistress.

* * *

The following morning Gaby woke up to the sweet scent of warm buttery croissants and fresh-brewed coffee.

"Gaby," Jean-Louis solicited, "have you been awake since I last spent the night with you? It's almost one in the afternoon."

"Oh, dear God," she smiled. "I do admit that I rest quite nicely when I'm close to you, Jean-Louis. I leave you in charge of all my anxieties!"

"Eh bien, mademoiselle. Here is your petit déjeuner." He brought the silver tray to the bed.

"Well, if you ever loose your aristocratic standing, darling, I have just the right job for you. All is scrumptious and the service is impeccable."

He laughed back and kissed her on the forehead.

"You're right, Gaby, I do like your indomitable spirit." But still he continued half-heartened, "Just loving me and everything I stand for might be a nice change once in a while," he said, more serious that he had intended to be.

"Jean-Louis I have given up a lot already, namely what I came to France for—my career on stage. It is not a small sacrifice. Jean-Louis—"

He did not let her finish her sentence. Instead, he placed half a croissant in her mouth and waited with a cup of coffee in hand until she swallowed the entire morsel. He then forced a sip of coffee, replaced the tray on the table, and then came back to the bed and he placed his body upon hers, his arms framing her pretty face.

"Gaby," he began seriously, "our temperaments are such that we will have to travel through stormy weather for the rest of our lives. I have come to term with this phase of our relationship," he said, half resigned.

She smiled. She would try to prove him wrong, she promised herself. It was raining hard outside and the Faubourg was the perfect place to just be content in each other's company.

Later that night, the valet that lived downstairs brought her a note.

Oh, dear God, she thought. Renaud was to pick her up early tomorrow morning to take her to Deauville. His mother was turning sixty years old. She had given her word that she would sing for her. She had been working on her repertoire for quite some time now. How to approach the subject with Jean-Louis? He could not be angry about it, except that Jean-Louis hated Renaud.

"Jean-Louis, I have a singing engagement in Deauville," she began.

"Cancel it," he said, "we've been reunited for less than twenty-four hours and you're already missing your profession?" he said arrogantly.

"You could join us, you love Deauville . . ."

"Us?"

"I would if it was for another occasion, but Renaud's Grandmother will turn sixty on Wednesday and he's picking me up tomorrow morning to honor her. You know how much she loves my singing," she finished as she rolled out of bed.

"Your kisses are still warm on my lips and you're telling me that Renaud, the viper, will good-naturedly pick you up to spend two days with him in his Grandmother's castle!"

She pivoted quickly and watched his fury come alive.

"Cancel," he commanded. "I will not suffer this insolent behavior not now and certainly not when we marry!"

"Well . . . likewise, I do not know that I want that kind of entrapment!" she replied with blazing eyes.

Silence weighed heavily in the room. Both stood defiant, neither one willing to compromise. He stormed out of the room and got dressed.

With dismay, she stared, not knowing what to expect.

"Obviously, we have both been fools to think that our love for one another could surmount the challenge of our expectations. This is the last straw, Gaby. I'm giving you back your freedom. I'll ask my lawyers to draw the annulment of our engagement tomorrow. You'll get the papers in less than a week. We're done—you're free."

He put on his jacket, and threw the keys on the table next to the door.

"Have a good life, Gaby," were his last words as he walked past the door and slammed it behind him.

Flabbergasted she let herself fall back on the sofa. This was not really happening she thought. She pulled herself back up and ran to the window. She parted the curtains to watch his carriage pull away. That was it. She knew it. Slowly facing reality, she tried to make sense of what had just occurred. She fell apart in uncontrollable sobs that lasted throughout the day. She decided against returning to the convent. Perhaps Jean-Louis would change his mind. It did not happen. Later that evening she rolled in between the sheets, the sweet aroma of their passion lingered amidst her tears. Jean-Louis was gone. He would not return. Her mind drifted to the Civil War . . . to her Mother's trial . . . to Philippe's departure for Rome. Tomorrow Deauville . . . she summoned her sense of logic. How painful this separation might prove to be she'd power trough it and emerge the better for it.

Chapter Forty-Three

The following week she spoke to the Directeur of the Opéra de Paris and Maître Lauriot.

"I want to return to the stage." She assured them that a decision had been taken. At first the Directeur balked, well aware of the precarious situation he'd be placed in, but Lauriot convinced him otherwise.

Less than two weeks later, posters all over Paris announced her triumphant return to the opéra. Yes, Paris loved her, she thought. She still had not received any papers suggesting that her marriage plans to Jean-Louis had been formally cancelled—but all knew in the capital. Jean-Louis was ubiquitous with women that she had encountered at all her performances. He roamed the halls while she sang and spent a great deal of time speaking with his friends as if nothing Gaby could have done touched him. He had gone on with his life while he sported beautiful aristocratic women every night.

It was getting quite cold in Paris. She grasped two scarves that she wrapped very tightly around her throat to protect the jewels of an opéra singer—her vocal cords. She walked to the Conservatoire. She'd promised Marie-Louise she'd take a ballet lesson with Dame Margot. Walking would do her good. She needed to clear her spirits and deep breathing would improve her mood.

As she arrived at the Conservatoire, she failed to notice the carriage that had been following her. She met Marie-Louise in the foyer. Melba, the Australian opéra singer was the talk of the tout Paris. She'd arrived from the Scala in Milan a fortnight ago. Her maestro however was mesmerized by the young American soprano. He'd asked for a private meeting with Gaby. The man appeared whenever Gaby arrived. He'd meet her in her loge, at the theatre, at a soirée that had been given in her honor, and always he'd speak of the virtues of the Italian opéras in the new united Italy.

"You'd thrive in our famed opéra houses, Mademoiselle. I understand that your Mother was from Italian lineage, Mademoiselle De Conte. One always returns to the source. With your talent the sooner the better!

Marie-Louise and a few minor opéra singers had noticed the attentions. "He's mesmerized, Gabriella," Marie-Louise confided.

"I speak fluent Italian," Gaby retorted to her friends. "It is always wonderful to encounter someone who speaks your language." She knew however that the real goal was to have her accept a very lucrative contract in Milan. Finally she'd agree to have dinner with him. Why not? She questioned. The move would be beneficial to all. She'd forget Jean-Louis, she'd be close to Philippe and her career would flourish.

The girls continued the climb to the second floor. Gaby nodded. She really liked Marie-Louise. She was smart, vivacious, and a whole lot of fun. They had gotten friendly from their very first meeting a couple of years back and from that time on, they had become inseparable.

"I like the shorter tutu," Gaby expressed, "it is less cumbersome for practice, and the padding in the chaussons provides more support for the long-standing pointe. It causes fewer bloody toes. I love dancing and the lessons are invaluable in my trade, Marie-Louise, but I truly admire your diligence. My body is shot when I practice with Madame Margot."

Marie-Louise was a beautiful ballerina and her lover, the Count, was a wealthy, still very handsome landowner in the South of France. He never missed her practices when he was in Paris. Her lover thought it absolutely acceptable to see her on stage—why couldn't Jean-Louis have felt the same way? She pondered.

Marie-Louise had been close-mouthed about her upbringing, but she had shared that she had lost her virginity at the age of sixteen. She had fallen madly in love with a married man—the father of one of her ballet classmates. The scandalous affair had caused Marie-Louise's father to send her away to Paris. It seemed like every ballerina in Paris had the same story. Did they make it up? Gaby asked herself pensively. All of them seem to be of certain means, but all were in dismal relationships. Apparently her lover helped with the rent in her Rue Victor Hugo apartment. She did not have the means to rent in such an upscale neighborhood. Gaby surmised that the Count had set her up in the lovely apartment years ago.

"All this could end very quickly, Gabriella," she repeated often, very realistic about her situation and station in life. "I only know how to dance. It just cannot be a hobby for me, Gabriella. My father made it clear that I was no longer welcome in our home." She'd heave her usual long sigh. I want to become a first ballerina with the Ballet de Paris."

Gaby knew that she also posed for many of the new artists in Paris. Degas had used her many times in more than one of his dancing scenes. Marie-Louise and Lilianne were her best friends since Jane Victoria, rather than to return to her native Poland, had taken a boat to New York. She had met a wonderful man and had married.

"You appear so joyous, Marie-Louise. Your beautiful eyes reflect your inner happiness. Is the Count in town? The ballerina nodded. "Is he picking you up from practice today?"

"Yes, yes," she replied, "Madame Margot is letting me out a bit early."

Gaby always thought it odd that Marie-Louise could stand the arrangement. She had tried to empathize but could not. Although her own childhood was not a fairytale, she was in a very different situation, highly educated in both the arts and economics. She had the financial resources to return to New Orleans and expand her sugar business on River Road on the Mississippi if she had to. Weeks ago, she'd shared the story with Jean-Louis.

"I am not strapped down. Besides, I would never let love control my life and actions. I could not fathom the pain knowing that my lover would return to his other family. In my eyes it might be more painful than a full separation. In Marie-Louise's case it had happened several times a year for the past decade."

"Thanks, my chérie." Leaning back, Jean-Louis roared with laughter. "Elaborate, you would not let love control your life, I have an inkling that I do a pretty good job at controlling your assertive behavior."

"You do," she replied uneasily, "but with us we are solely talking about my professional life that has been superseded, and here again, I chose to let you control this aspect, but with Marie-Louise ..." She reminisced silently as she began to undress. Yes, she was fully independent now, but she missed Jean-Louis immensely. Perhaps it was that same independence that she so revered that had thwarted her chance at happiness. She wandered how long the pain would linger. No matter what happened in her life she would never forget Jean-Louis.

"You have to understand, Gaby," he'd explained, "that women in France and the rest of Europe for that matter, do not have the choices that American women enjoy." "Although the 1870's are seeing radical changes in the family and its relations, cultural habits are hard to change. Women without financial means in Paris have essentially three choices: to become courtesans, to join the nunnery, or suffer the hardship of a pretty hard life if they marry the simple butcher or plumber, chérie." He'd kissed her tenderly and she wished his arms enveloped her right now.

"Well, perhaps I am being a bit hypocritical. Love does control my life. You made it clear that you did not want me to perform on stage and like the perfect mistress, I obeyed," she'd retorted pensively.

Jean-Louis had taken her in his arms and pulled her to him more tightly this time. "I have my reasons, Gaby."

She'd let it go at that. His reason was his jealousy and possessiveness of everything that she loved. Sharing was not something that he did well.

Jean-Louis had become quite passionate about the subject of equality. He often stated that the establishment of a more equal society was one of his goals and the reason why he'd accepted to return to politics. She wondered if these same deliberations extended to womanhood. She doubted it.

"You know that I am an adamant believer in conservative nationalism. Before the division of classes can be eliminated, a strong government is needed to keep the parties from civil war, Gaby. I'm not quite sure that I will be able to avert the fall of the Empire if I travel for an extended period of time abroad. The Emperor has lost his luster." He'd state pensively.

She missed him. Their conversations were always lively and interesting. He treated her as an equal, in that area of her life, and she loved it. Perhaps the equality she longed for had destroyed her sentimental life. It would be so easy to swallow her pride and ask Jean-Louis to take her back. More than a few times she had been on the brink of walking to the house when she'd notice the light in his library late at night. She would apologize and obey his every wish while in return she'd enjoy his love and protection in his arms in their home. Her pride and self-esteem had forbidden it.

The thought alone launched repulsive spasms up and down her spine. A puppet on a string she was not. In effect, it was her decisive personality that had drawn him to her. She just wished she'd cancelled her outing at the castle in Deauville on that fateful day and kept her insecurities about marriage to herself. Jean-Louis had been pushed to the limit—there was no turning back. Her tormented relationship had come to an end.

Pensively she walked inside the mirrored salle de dance, she sat on the bench, and tied the ribbons of her chaussons around her long and shapely legs. Although short in stature, her body had perfect symmetry with large beautiful breasts. She often would tie bands of satin around her bosom when dancing to emphasize her lean and graceful torso. She remembered the look in Jean-Louis' eyes on that fateful day on the Tempète when he had caught her in his cabin dancing and singing Libiamo loosely wrapped up in his coverlet. It seemed like yesterday. His piercing glance had shot to her naked breasts. She could still smell his scent and sense his roving hands.

How could she have known that Jean-Louis would pay her a surprise visit in the middle of the day? As he had taken her in his strong arms, his hands had gently lifted the satin cover and found her warm body and soft skin obviously to his liking.

She smiled thinking back of that lustful look when he had gazed down upon her as his hand caressed her nipples. He had pushed away the coverlet to look for himself at the surprising assets.

"Were did you hid these beauties? He'd laughed in her mouth. Timidly she'd return the smile as she focused on the silk straps still thrown haphazardly on the bedpost. He had kissed her so passionately that very first time that she wished she could be in his arms right now doing the exact same thing, feeling the sensations that his body evoked.

"A la barre, Mesdemoiselles!" the lovely voice of Dame Margot brought her back sadly to reality. She and Marie-Louise walked elegantly to the mirror and the barre.

Still processing the information, Gaby continued her sad daydreaming. Why did she feel superior to Marie-Louise? After all, she was in love with a man who had at first seemed like her knight in shining armor. He had not asked her to marry him, but he had told her they would marry. They had been engaged, almost married. Jean-Louis had kept his word.

He never said anything he did not intend to pursue. Now, the separation was final and he had returned to his libertine life. Not a novel denouement for the time.

Although she hated to admit it, he had been right about Montmartre. Men had been killed in the area where she and her friend had walked. A barricade had been set up recently and she'd heard that rifles were being sold in the street to anyone who wished to have one. Furthermore, the price of the rifle would rise with the amount of bodies it had killed—a crazy, senseless world. The unrest in some part of the city was frightening. The problem with their relationship was simple. Jean-Louis did not compromise or apologize and she in return always had had difficulties with authority.

The stage drowned her sadness. Tonight she would meet with Maestro Luigi Garildo. If anything, their conversations would be lively—a common passion. After the season she would visit Rome and stay with Philippe, she thought. Who knows, maybe she would even accept an engagement in Milan. The engagement came sooner than later. The Maestro had presented her with a very lucrative contract and on a whim she'd accepted to sing for the next opéra season in Milan.

Chapter Forty-Four

Today would have been their wedding day. Their engagement had not been annulled. Papers had not been drawn up but for the past week the social gazette had not been complete without an article on their doomed romance. Editors and reporters had tried in vain to get a response—to no avail. His face was on the front page of all newspapers for political reasons or in the Gazette for the latest gossips on his amorous escapades. Twice she'd dethroned him in the social section. Her first return performance at the opéra had been a huge success and recently at the American ambassador's ball she had sung magnificently in concert with the Paris Orchestra.

Renaud, her very best friend, was often at her side. She'd begun to venture out with male friends as well. The Duke of the Rochefoucault, whose reputation as a rake competed with Jean-Louis', had proven to be a most gallant and charming escort. There was no shortage of men to take her out and show her Paris. Plus naturally Degas, Manet and Basille often included her in their weekend outings. Renoir and Monet were preparing to spend the summer in Chatou. She loved watching them prepare their palette side by side—naturally pigments in tubes were now available, it made it easy for plein air. In the evening, they'd compare what they had seen, how the light had been captured at a particular time of the day and what they should expect the following day at a slightly different time. Not unlike her when she prepared for a performance. Dance and theatrics were taken into consideration and played an important role in the rendition of the performance. It was also pleasant to forget about the ominous political unrest. Courbet was political and adamant about a Third Republic, Manet liked to talk about it but Degas, Monet, Renoir and Basille were more intent on an acceptance to the Salon.

Shockingly, with a different beauty in his loge Jean-Louis had attended most of her performances at the opéra. He never stayed as she walked out on stage; instead, he'd roamed the halls speaking to friends. The poor girls were left behind like old shoes. She'd peeked through the curtain to watch him. Jean-Louis showed no emotion. A half smile hung down his lips and his demeanor showed no sadness or regrets. Once more he was the man of the moment.

At first she had been shocked that she'd accepted to leave Paris, but she could no longer tolerate the situation with Jean-Louis. Thoughts of her annulled wedding day tortured her. Swiftly the resolution had been taken. To show the Grand Monde that her life was still *magnifique* and that independence from the Duke was quite splendid, she'd accepted the invitation to attend one of the most prestigious grand balls of the year. Renaud would be her escort. Jean-Louis was sure to be in attendance.

Her wedding day, she thought, as the carriage wheels stumbled along the cobblestone of the city. Eh bien, she would forget the world; she would be the most beautiful and talented woman in attendance and for support she counted on concentrating on the fun loving days she would experience in Milan. Princess Mathilde's soirée would be great fun. Sheepishly, the host had asked her to sing a few of her favorite arias. She'd accepted. It was a step in the right direction. The goal was to forget Jean-Louis.

Late as usual, she did not have to wait on the second floor of the foyer to be announced. A diva could, she smirked. With all her charm, she stepped down the pink Italian marble staircase with equanimity and great theatrics. The crowd loved it.

All looked up to her. Her first glance landed on Jean-Louis and his new paramour, a Russian Princess, a friend of Princess Mathilde, the Emperor's sister. This one was brand new on the scene and from what she'd heard; Jean-Louis seemed quite taken by her. It was unusual for him to escort someone more than a week. Her heart broke. She forced her thoughts to the stage in Milan. Her glance continued to sweep the room. As she descended, Renaud gallantly waited for her as well as the philanderer Emperor Louis Napoléon, with Empress Eugénie and Princess Mathilde.

"Thank you, Mademoiselle," the Emperor intoned. He kissed her hand and he glimpsed a bit too long at her décolleté. Her couturière, Madame Badoitte, had lowered the sweetheart opening and had also taken the scissors to the back of the dress that Gaby had chosen—a peachy furrow that hugged every curve of her curvaceous body. Her heavy mane was held up with golden and diamond studded barrettes that held back a loose chignon.

As she strolled amongst the guests, she liked listening to the words of praise lavished on her by the society. "The carrying power of her sound comes through as her voice opens up . . . her top notes soar over the orchestra . . . she sings with an entrancing deep expressivity . . . there is honesty in the portrayal of each roles she plays" and it did not end there, her looks, theatrics and of course murmurs of a passionate affair with Jean-Louis were the talk of every recital she attended. Tonight, the Queen of England, the Russian Tsar, and the Prussian King were getting an earful. She would be magnificent, she told herself. She swirled around approaching the Maestro and quickly glanced around the room. Jean-Louis was paying great attention to the Princess. She had all to do to hold back a cascade of tears. Her decision to leave the city had been a wise one, she mulled—devastated. He would never acknowledge the dénouement. Her last hope, that of a reunion was doomed. Jean-Louis had gone on with his life. She would do the same.

She sensually acknowledged her royal audience and spoke about the recital she had chosen this evening. Her charming American accent drew full attention. Even Jean-Louis, his profile in full view smiled at her amusing description of the role she was about to play.

The light deemed as all eyes focused on the beautiful soprano. Lustrous notes soared in textured richness and effortless carrying power. Her impulsive ardor matched her theatrical mood and her taste for sensual abandon. Affecting serenity, her voice dipped to chilling low notes, then promptly soared over the orchestra in a sumptuous, vibrant, splendid voice. The recital was one of her best, she happily conceded amongst the bravos from the frenzied audience. She nodded to the Beau Monde elegantly as many surrounded her to shower her with invitations to more balls and grand dinners. Formal thank-yous and requests covered the grand piano that had been set up for her accompaniment. She reveled in her beauty and great fame.

As she was escorted to a more private salon the first one to step out of the crowd was the Russian Princess. She sweetly advanced toward Gaby. Forced to follow her, Jean-Louis sighed and came close to her with his rendezvous. Silence fell across the room and all glances were fixed their way.

"Thank you, Mademoiselle, you take my breath away," the Princess exclaimed.

Gaby nodded with a grand smile directed at the couple facing her. Jean-Louis smirked but kept silent. He could not quite control his roving eyes aimed at her breasts.

"Mademoiselle," the Russian continued in heavily accented but good French. "I understand that you will be leaving Paris for Rome next season?"

"Milan," Gaby interrupted politely.

"Pardon. Nevertheless I hope perhaps that your travels will take you a bit further East to St. Petersburg, as I have never seen a greater opératic talent than yours Mademoiselle De Conte Thornsen," she finished sweetly. The crowd had surrounded the threesome. The Princess looked around wondering why the throng of onlookers surrounded them. Jean-Louis did not make things easier for the poor girl. Everyone knew that today would have been the wedding in the Loire.

"Eh bien, Gaby," he pronounced reproachfully, "isn't it a bit egotistical to leave France and the opéra at the height of your fame. Maître Lauriot should have been rewarded for his succinct artistic choice with a few more seasons."

She smiled in his eyes. "Well Jean-Louis, I have this magnificent gift that I have chosen to share with the world," she coyly retorted. "Surely, I will return to Paris, perhaps I'll grace the stage for a few performances next year." She directed her sight once more to the stunned Princess.

"Your majesty, au plaisir," she spoke without answering the Princess' invitation. Elegantly, she pivoted on her golden satin slippers and found herself surrounded by admirers. Renaud again saved the day. She felt his gentle hand reach for her elbows as he gathered her to him and whirled her on the dance floor.

Later that night, after too many flutes of champagne, she walked upstairs to the balcony that overlooked the grand Jardins Des Tuileries. The night was cold but beautiful. She'd handled herself exactly the way she'd desired. Renaud was gambling in the salon.

A door opened, she glanced back. Jean-Louis stood in the doorway and stared for a good long while. She did not lower her gaze.

He slowly began to march toward her. Shoulders squared, jaws set, and with flawless determination he took her in his arms as his mouth swooped down on hers with great passion. Amidst the orchestra blasting Mozart she gave in to his passion and met his ardor just as intensely.

"Jean-Louis," she gasped, "you're taking some liberties that are going to land us on the front page of all the papers tomorrow!"

"Gaby, on this night, our night, Gaby, I would have taken a whole lot more liberties." He gathered her more tightly to him and he let his head rest on her entangled mane. "I still love you Gaby," he murmured in the long curls that now streamed down her back because of the passionate embrace. "You can have it your way," he pronounced as he disentangled himself from the embrace and stared hard in her eyes. "Wife, mistress . . . I want you back." He sighed and straightened to his full length.

"There are rumors that you will marry the Princess," she whispered candidly, tears swelling in her eyes.

"There are always rumors, Gaby. The only ones that are truthful are the ones that tie us together. I will jump many hoops for name and country, but marriage is not one of them."

"But the Emperor, I understand is pressing hard for that union, an alliance with Russia is of primary importance—"

He did not let her finish the sentence; instead, he grasped her elbow and led her to a deserted area one floor below the large terrace. They opened a wrought iron gate. A high trellis of rosebushes bordered a clandestine verandah where marble tables and wide comfortable sofas lay hidden under the wide balcony where she had been standing a short while back. Their passion ignited again. "The truth is, Gaby, I can't leave without you," he murmured. "Life is not worth living unless you're by my side."

"It appears to me that you have been doing quite well. Have you read the gazette lately?" she responded sarcastically.

He paid no heed to her remark, but instead, he pressed her to him and continued, "I love you with every breath that I take." He took her face in his hands, their lips met and tears of joy filled her eyes as she heard the word that she had been yearning for. I'm willing to leave it all behind, Gaby, we could return to Boston, I have a great apartment in Louisburg square, lots of good friends, our lives would be much simpler." He stopped as he saw the horror on her beautiful face.

"I like Paris, Jean-Louis ... and I don't think that Boston would be a good fit. I am a Southerner darling and I have not forgotten the horrific acts the Yankees inflicted upon us. Many more years need to pass before I could extend any semblance of forgiveness." She replied candidly.

Later that evening, they slowly climbed up the short path to the terrace. He tried to fix her untangled hair and brushed a soft kiss on her forehead.

"I will see you next week," he spoke softly.

"Why not now or tomorrow?"

"The Princess is leaving by train tomorrow, back to St Petersburg. I am quite certain that the press has noticed our little escapade. I do not want to see our photos all over the front pages of every major newspaper. She will be made a fool of and the alliance may suffer because of it."

"Will you also bed her this evening to keep the dear Princess satiated so as to not unravel the political balance?" she fumed.

"I will not, Gaby, not tonight, not tomorrow, not ever—" He did not have the time to finish his sentence as a brouhaha echoed right outside the double doors. They both turned at precisely the right moment when twinkles of light flashed from every corner of the balcony. He had it right, the photographers and drafters had noticed the disappearance of the famed couple.

Jean-Louis quickly straightened up and marched toward the crowd. She watched him for a while and slowly begun to turn her back to the assembly, when she heard his parting last comment.

"Cancel Milan!" he exclaimed, before opening the door in front of a multitude of curious glances.

Instant later the crowd downstairs surrounded him. He walked past them and from that time on, the Duke was once again—for all the grand monde at any rate, the charming rake who took his place happily as the perfect escort to the lovely Russian Princess.

Stunned, Gaby stayed behind. She waited alone to make sense of what had just happened. Within minutes, Renaud broke through the crowd. He came close to her, caressed her shoulders and took her hand. "Come, Gabriella, let's return downstairs," he whispered sweetly. "Stay away from Jean-Louis-Pierre. He will only hurt you and do not, under any circumstances, marry him. He'll control every minute of your life, including using your powerful Italian connections to achieve his goals."

Astounded, she looked up to him.

"Certain things cannot be left unsaid, Gaby, especially when it comes to you," he smiled. He promptly took her waist and led her away on the dance floor. Her loose hair and reddened enticing lips told a story. She gave a radiant smile to the crowd. A diva needs a little drama she consoled herself. You're on stage, Gabriella, act like it. She danced the night away with Renaud. She owed him so much. After all this time, she ardently wished she could have developed feelings for him, but she knew that her heart belonged to Jean-Louis.

The scene was not lost on the Duke who watched the entire scene while leaning against a pillar as he seemingly appear interested in the conversation at hand with the Princess and her entourage.

Chapter Forty-Five

In the process of stretching her long lean legs against the barre, Gaby opened her eyes to check her form in the mirror. Jean-Louis sat in a large leather burgundy chair made available for known visitors of the *petit rats de l'opéra*. His long muscular leg crossed over his left knee as he stared at her breasts. She slowly brought her leg down from the barre and stretched her arms over her head in each direction prior to slowly coming into a standing position.

He nodded at her. She stood upright in the center of the salle and stared at him. Distinctly Renaud's words echoed in her mind.

Marie-Louise had seen him as well. She twirled her stunning blond hair and waved elongated fingers in his direction. It was difficult for men and women not to gaze out and dream about her fine attributes. Gaby stopped cold. Marie-Louise touched Gaby's elbow.

"Look who's here, Gabriella, go to him. I know you still love him. I hear that he has been in his loge listening to your singing all last week," she urged. "I'll continue alone."

Gaby opened the door that led to the salon and walked out toward Jean-Louis. The change of temperature outside the dancing room made her shiver, goose bumps covered her bare body and instantly a frisson shook her from head to toe.

"Hello, it's cold out here," she laughed as she wrapped her arms around her torso.

He did not answer and kept on staring at her.

"You came to see me, correct?" She spun around and looked through the looking glass. Her friend was practicing. Momentarily, jealousy fired. Had he started an affair with Marie-Louise? After all, she never practiced on these days and certainly not in this particular suite. She looked from Marie-Louise to him; her expressive eyes uncovered her thoughts.

He should play the game a while longer, Jean-Louis thought to himself, but he didn't have the heart to see her sad. Right now, he wanted her in his arms—better yet, in his bed. He reached for her arms and pulled her close to him leading her away from the visible area behind the wall into the interior salon. He parted his coat open and gathered her more tightly to him, his lips searched for hers.

"I miss you," he said. He grasped her body and gathered her in between his legs, holding on to her bottom tightly, and kissing her cheeks. His lips gravitated down the side of her neck. Her ability to make wise decisions quickly dissipated. In a quick instant of clarity, she pulled away.

"Jean-Louis, anyone could walk in on us," she said reproachfully. "Please let me get dressed. I'll meet you in the foyer shortly." She pulled away reluctantly from his arms and looked back questioningly.

"You came to see *me*, correct?"

He winked and frowned his eyebrows in a questioning regard.

"Hum ...I wonder?" He replied, trying to get her back in his arms. She shot him a severe look.

"You scoundrel, why do you like to see me suffer so?"

"To bring you back to your senses, Miss Independence."

"You are infuriating, I should be the one asking you to return to your senses, begging on your knees for forgiveness. I was not the one who left this time."

"It did not affect you so terribly that you gave up on the idea of spending quality time with Renaud De Beauvoir if I recall correctly," he pronounced sarcastically. "And continue to do so!"

She stared at him and raised her shoulders.

"He's a wonderful friend, one I can depend on and who has my happiness in sight—always." She responded fiercely.

"When he's not traveling the world, and spending fortunes in the casinos of the world!"

She began to pivot on her chaussons to return back to the grande salle, when he pulled her back in his arms, brushed a kiss on her temple, and turned her around swatting her behind.

"Go get dress. Let's have dinner?"

She was about to turn away.

493

"I just have a cover up and my cape, I'll need to return to my apartment."

He winced. He had forgotten now he had an apartment to contend with.

"Our home is closer we will stop there instead. All of your clothing is still in your closet."

She shot a suspicious look. Stop all altercations, her little voice murmured, go with him. Forgive and forget.

"Will we eat there as well," she questioned coyly.

"Proper French etiquette does not allow retorts to such improper allusions."

As she emerged from the dressing room, he draped his coat around her curvaceous body.

Gérard was walking up. She stopped and stared at Gérard's devastated face. He was madly in love with the premier dancer of the Ballet de Paris. They had been in a relationship for nine months now and while Serge took the relationship lightly and was less than the perfect lover, poor Gérard was madly in love with him.

He was very close to Marie-Louise, both had sensual conflicts in common and they candidly shared their frustrations.

Gaby was always the listener, she had learned from an early age to adapt to the ups and downs of life and look positively towards the future as long as she stayed in control. Well she had pretty much lost control and unlike the two others, her own sentimental affairs with Jean-Louis were the talk of the tout Paris.

Gérard smiled at Gaby as he noticed Jean-Louis standing behind her.

She pulled him aside.

"I am so terribly sorry, Gérard. I know how much you wanted that part."

Gérard had not gotten the part for the Pas de Deux in the ballet, *Gisèle*. Naturally, Gérard already distraught about his own life story was totally oblivious to Jean-Louis' presence. He started talking to Gaby about the new young dancer they had picked to dance.

Impatient and angry over the time Gaby spent with her friend, he squeezed her forearms and tried to lead her toward the door. She stalled him a bit more. She knew how vulnerable Gérard truly felt. She could not bring herself to leave him here alone facing the new chosen dancer. Maybe she could run up and get Marie-Louise to interrupt her practice to stay with Gérard awhile.

"Well, Gérard, you're a brilliant artist, you have to enter the stage and leave the luggage behind, put on a happy face and be prepare to dance. For the next fortnight, your life belongs to the public." She tried to place a light note on the ordeal.

"Are you going to the De Bugeotte this evening with Marie-Louise?"

Gaby nodded, unaware of the anger displayed on Jean-Louis' face, she turned to Jean-Louis.

"Darling, wait for me, for just a few minutes while I run upstairs to see if I can interrupt Marie-Louise's practice."

"Don't bother, Gaby, continue your practice." Anger emanated from his every pore.

"Wait, Jean-Louis please," she shouted after him. I'm coming, wait for me, please." While she tried to accommodate the world, her own world was falling apart. His long strides had already taken him past the vast and sumptuous foyer. In the blink of an eye, he shoved the revolving door and swiftly he crossed the short path that separated him from his waiting carriage. Without waiting for his groom to bring down the steps, he quickly climbed in the sedan.

Flying down the stairs toward the side entrance where the artists exited the opéra, Gaby tried in vain to catch up with him. Instead she heard the tapping of the vignette as the carriage begun to move forward.

"Damn you!" she shouted. On the sidewalk with her pink tights, tutu, ballet shoes and his open coat that covered most of her body, rage overwhelmed her.

The carriage slowed in front of the conservatoire to let pedestrians walk by. Jean-Louis was shocked at her choice of words in public. He looked at her with a smirk on his face.

A cold, angry stare met his. He had the urge to get out and take her in his arms and home, but instead he tapped the door of the carriage once more.

She turned back toward the building, aware by now that a large crowd of onlookers stared at her. Women shot disdainful glances. The language of the *précieuses* had long left the vocabulary of the French salons, however, the common, ordinary display of temper in public was outrageous and decidedly vulgar. To make matter worse, Claude Lotard of the Gazette de Paris, strode by with his wife and daughter. Tomorrow morning she could hear the rumble of the new headlines.

She decided not to attend the ball that evening—no need for more insolence. Besides Gérard needed a good listener. She walked back inside the revolving doors of the Petit Conservatoire. Gérard apologized profusely for provoking another dispute.

"Don't even think about it, Gérard. How about a lovely dinner after the gala, you and me at the restaurant St. Louis? We both need a rest from this insanity. What do you say?"

Gérard was always amazed at Gaby's strength of character. He obliged happily.

"I admire you so, Gaby. When I'm around you I always feel a sense of strength that emanates from you onto others. I'm so happy that we are friends." He hugged her and kissed her on both cheeks, "*à ce soir, ma chère*," he exclaimed theatrically as he waved back and headed to the elevator.

Once again Gaby questioned her indomitable spirit. Why did she think that she could fix everyone's problems? She couldn't even fix her own—her pride would not let her.

In the meantime, in his carriage, Jean-Louis' anger dissipated. He laughed as he recalled Gaby on the sidewalk swearing at him. The press was going to do a number on her behavior. He had noticed both Claude and Jean Le Rouche. Serves her right, he thought.

He had not intended to attend the ball this evening. He had planned on a fun dinner with Gaby and his friends, but after the incident, he'd show up late to save her from the crowd. They would make Gaby's life miserable otherwise. If she weren't such an angel, she'd do well to attend to his needs not the world around her. He decided to have dinner with his friends and join her later. No one would dare laugh at her if he was by her side. Now he wished he had been more patient with her. He'd be making love to her right now.

But to see her use blasphemous language and to tap her foot on the pavement had been a sight to see. The little tigress, oblivious of the European varnish, always placed herself in precarious positions for the sake of others.

Yes, definitely, he would meet her at the De Valliers' ball later tonight. Louis Napoléon and Queen Victoria and Albert would attend. He would be the guest of honor and he wanted her to be introduced formally to Queen Victoria as his future bride. Once again they would be the talk of the town. The diva and the Duke reunited. He reminisced on the simplicity of life in the United States. Perhaps he should forgo all his responsibilities to name and country and return with Gaby to a more peaceful and less complicated life. The Iron Angel would not hear of it! He smiled.

His British friends had arrived from London last evening. Long nights were de rigueur with this group. He looked forward to it—he needed it. The little American drove him mad.

Chapter Forty-Six

At around nine o'clock for a quiet dinner she'd told Gérard. To bask in the company of a man, who like her, had a passion for music was what the doctor advised, she sadly smiled. After all, she'd come to Paris to study music not to let her potential fall prey to lust and love.

As fate would have it, both Jean-Louis and Gaby arrived at their chosen restaurant at just about the same time.

In the ornate foyer facing the street, Gaby waited for the young flower girl to pin a rose onto the light turquoise frills that bordered her décolleté. Momentarily she recognized the loud and grave voice of Jean-Louis echoing through the windows. She turned and took a few steps toward the revolving door to scan the street. A large group of men and women were coming up the stairs. Mesmerized, she hugged the door as she rose up on her tiptoes to glance outside from the stained glass window. Mischance struck. The door opened and slapped her down on the thickly-weaved, burgundy carpet. Excruciating pain radiated up her spine. She could not stand up quickly enough to avoid an inebriated Jean-Louis' powerful thrust at the door. While he still spoke to his friends that trailed him, he stumbled over his lover's body. Simultaneously incredulous and annoyed he quickly took hold of the situation as he knelt down to survey the damage.

"Gaby," he exclaimed, what are you . . .? You are injured, chérie," he remarked, staring at her stunned and pained visage. The powerful force he'd used to open the resisting door must have sent her flying across the highly polished hardwood floors, he assumed.

Gaby did not budge, although the Maître d'hôtel and Gérard were now at her side. She looked distressed and vanquished.

The drunken friends suddenly saw a comical reprieve in this solemn moment and began intoning loudly, "Little Miss Gabriella sat on her tuffett, after rudely spying on her beau. Along came the Duke who knocked the helpless curious girl down and then sat beside her to assuage her insolent temper . . . tra.la.la.la.la.la." The disgraceful song kept on as curiosity inside the dining room was aroused.

Jean-Louis shot a glacial glance to Henry. The drunken Brit halted his lyrical poetry in its track. He quickly picked up Gaby in his arms and gently placed her down on the sofa as he knelt down in front of her and rested his hands on her laps. He looked around. Fortunately the accordion in the dancing room had drowned out Henry's drunken ballad. No one was in the foyer of the restaurant besides his friends.

"I'm sorry, Gaby but what were you doing behind the door?" He smiled and teasingly continued, "Spying on my friends and I?" He looked up toward Gérard, none to please to see him.

She wanted to let him know that she was here with a male escort intent on having a wonderful dinner. She needed to talk about a life she loved, her music, the people involved in the arts, the opératic world, but instead, at that moment she noticed the contrite look in his blue eyes. They seem to be telling her, let me take care of it all. Come back. Defeated, she only hoped that his present inebriated state would lessen his victory.

"Jean-Louis, take me home," she whispered. "I want to go home."

Thinking that she was talking about New Orleans, he stared at her stunned. Had she been drinking? Probably. It made no sense. These past months had been difficult for her. Life in Paris had not been a bowl of cherries, as she was fond of saying. No wonder she wanted to leave it all behind and return to the comfort of her country. However, there had been a small improvement, he thought. This time, he had been included.

"Not now, Gaby, we can't," he answered her sweetly. But I promise you that we will one day, perhaps when we return from Italy." He murmured sweetly.

She looked at him in complete disbelief.

"You are mad, cruel, manic—all of the above!" she shouted. How can you reject my advances after your loving words last week at the ball? I groveled tonight, literally asked to be taken back and—no, no, no, forget it all, forget me. I never want to speak to you again. Just leave."

She pushed his limp arms away from her thighs, stood up, and walked to Gérard, who stood nearby perplexed. She proceeded to wrap her arm under his and prodded him along in the restaurant.

Jean-Louis questioned his sober state. The episode went right over his head. Privy to the absurd scene, his friends surrounded him. Luke placed his arm around him and looked to Henry.

"Let's eat," he said. All strode in the restaurant.

From the corner of her eye, Gaby saw them enter the main dining room. Damn, she thought, they had not asked for a private room. No, they wanted to drive everyone insane, and naturally, the management would not rebuke the Duke De Bourbonne and his friends. A long table had a 'reserved' sign on it—only two tables in front of theirs. As Jean-Louis walked past her with his loud and drunken friends, he caressed her shoulders, bent down, kissed the back of her neck, and casually kept on walking to his reserved table.

Anything to make her feel plain absurd, she pondered, heartbroken. She pretended not to feel.

He sat down, his back to her with a tall shapely redhead sitting next him. Germaine Goulet, the artist, and Josephine De Bervege, the unfaithful wife of the celebrated cartoonist, were sitting across from Jean-Louis. On either side of Luke, three other men that she had never met nor seen conversed freely. The men appeared to be French— artists, maybe—they wore white open shirts, and beards à la Manet. All chatted happily with an absolutely dark goddess who starred curiously at her.

Gaby gawked so more; her jealous tendencies re-surfaced. The woman looked like the woman who had walked out of his house this morning, she'd kissed Jean-Louis on both cheeks.

Poor Gérard was having a one-man conversation. She forced herself to listen and to appear interested in the turmoil that was the young dancer's life. To no avail, she tried hard to pay attention, but her gaze wandered on the table across to the far side.

The goddess whispered to Jean-Louis and he suddenly stood up, walked around the table, and squeezed in between the two other women, forcing Luke to take his place. Now he faced her, smiling that sensuous smile of his. For an instant, their gazes met—his with a

500

smile in his now bloodshot blue eyes and hers with darts that could kill.

She tried to refocus her attention on her dining partner. The red-haired woman and the dark-haired goddess on each side of Jean-Louis appeared to be sharing a lengthy conversation with one another; one of them lay her opulent breast on Jean-Louis' back as she nonchalantly continued. Suddenly, the goddess turned to face Jean-Louis and unabashedly kissed him softly and reached for his hand under the table.

Gaby had sworn to be stoic and proud as she pretended to lend an interested ear to her friend. This spectacle however—she could not fathom. Unable to watch and to sit still, she replaced her napkin on the table and stood up.

"I am so terribly sorry, Gérard," she spoke softly, her beautiful eyes submerged with tears, "but I suddenly feel quite ill and feverish. Please continue without me. I see Alain Bernard and Arnaud sitting next to the window. Please go and finish the soirée with them. My carriage is waiting for me outside."

Gérard acquiesced. Gabriella was most private and rarely spoke about her sentiments. He had seen the Duke walk in with his friends. What was going on between these two, only God and the lovers knew.

"I hope you'll feel better soon. I'll see you tomorrow, Gabriella. Bonsoir," the young man said as he called the waiter to his table.

Gaby hoped to leave with as little fanfare as possible, but this was not meant to be. Jean-Louis disentangled himself immediately from the two women and walked briskly towards her table. He reached for her arm, as she was about to leave. Surprised and not willing to make another embarrassing blunder, she let him take control. "No more," he murmured in her ear, and he led her towards the foyer, not before his obnoxious English friends called out to him.

"Jean-Louis-Pierre, at two o'clock Chez Régine," they shouted. "Let's finish la *Tournée des Grands Ducs*, to go round all bars," one of them said with a thick English accent.

Gaby had heard the expression before. It was the rounding off of all the great bars in Paris.

"We are going back to our house, fini," Jean-Louis fumed, ignoring all of his friends' comments.

"What?" she responded, "are you mad? You rejected the idea less than an hour ago, to choose your drunken friends over me, I presume."

Not willing to get into another emotional upheaval, Jean-Louis grasped her arm and pulled her to him forcing her in the revolving doors.

"We need to work on our communication, Gaby. I need to learn more American phrases," as he led her forcefully outside. "This manège is over. I hope you enjoyed the ride while it lasted. As you so rightly stated, it drove me mad."

Luke and the goddess came running out. "Send your carriage back to get us, Jean-Louis-Pierre," they called out. "You're lost, my friend. You're smothered. Remember what her compatriots did to us during the Revolutionary War. I warned you," Luke laughed. "We've had firsthand experience with their kind."

Jean-Louis nodded. He picked up Gaby in his arms, placed her on the rich and comfortable velvet seats, and without ceremony slid in close to her as well. He drew her to him and kissed her.

"I hate you," she whispered, holding tightly to his back forcing him to her breasts.

"What a lovely thought," he murmured in her mouth as he continued to kiss her. "Do you want to start again?" He looked down, waiting for an answer.

"After you," she retorted smelling the strong scent of alcohol on his breath.

He graciously complied with a smirk on his face. Vigorously he grasped her full body and pressed it to him forcefully. He wanted her to be a part of him.

"I adore you, Miss Thornsen. You are my breath, my air, anything and everything that keeps me alive. I want nothing more than to stand next to you, to feel your warmth next to mine. I want nothing. I need nothing when you're with me. You are my reason d'être. I've stopped asking why. It just is."

Shocked at the level of emotion displayed by her usually cool, levelheaded former fiancé, when not in bed, she smiled up at him and winked.

"Keep it up," she replied coyly with a sideways smile.

"Insensitive insolent," he said.

"Now that I know how you feel, I will ask for my independence more often." Without waiting for an answer she held on to his face. Her hands splayed on his rugged skin and she kissed him back with all the love she felt in her passionate body and soul.

If someone had asked how they walked to their upstairs apartment, it would have been a mystery to both.

Back in their room passionately attached to one another, they enjoyed the ecstatic moments they so craved. They let their passion run over their weary bodies intertwined in each other. Suddenly they were jolted out of bed when loud voices downstairs brought them back to reality.

"We gave you ample time to reconnect your liaison Jean-Louis-Pierre, now come with us and celebrate. The little woman needs to learn that she is dealing with a man larger than life. I can't believe that you are envisaging a Grand-Père's life, Jean-Louis-Pierre," Luke shouted outside of the room.

Jean-Louis got up. He placed a towel around his waist and ambled toward the door. Gaby heard his husky voice.

"Go without me. I'll see you tomorrow."

"Gabriella, unchain him!" Luke shouted.

She got up as well, covering herself with a white satin peignoir as she walked out of the room behind her lover.

"Luke, why do you always assume that I'm this horrific boulder weighing on your friend's soul—a controlling force?" she demanded, irate.

"Because you are, my lovely," he responded flatly. "Not even I can bring Jean-Louis-Pierre back to his senses. I hope that he will not regret it."

"He won't, you pretentious British . . . invader," she retorted angrily for lack of finding a proper insult. She stormed back into the room and slammed the door violently behind her.

"Well, my friend, my point precisely," Luke roared with laughter as he stared at the now closed door that still vibrated from the fierce force Gaby had used.

Jean-Louis smiled. She was a force to be reckoned with, no doubt, but better than a supple, malleable doormat that stuck to tradition and feminine ideals, which at the time was less than palatable.

"We will see you tomorrow, Luke, at the stables in Vincennes at around four in the afternoon. I'm afraid that the little witch will displease you even more. In American English my friend, she will probably kick our derrieres."

Both men laughed.

"You're doomed, Jean-Louis-Pierre." Luke turned and walked downstairs back to the waiting friends who had followed him close behind. "The great Jean-Louis-Pierre De Pleyssis has met his match," he announced to his friends. Everyone had a good laugh and the drunken soirée continued.

Gaby was waiting in the room. As he entered, she smiled. He loved her. His lust for her was unequaled, no disputing that fact, but he liked her and that was almost as important.

"Where is your whip, mistress?" he teased. Before she could retort, he strode quickly to her, disrobed her, and kissed her while throwing her on the bed. He rolled in next to her and then on her.

The following morning, she slept very late and Jean-Louis was already downstairs, reading the paper in the day room overlooking the Seine.

"Good morning, Gaby," he said casually. "Did you sleep well?"

"Quite well, after you left my bed, Monsieur." she responded.

He smirked, amused at her ironic retort.

"I was under the false pretense, that you enjoyed my attentions immensely."

He looked up at her amused. "I did." She replied sweetly.

She laughed and came closer behind him. She wrapped her arms around his torso and let her head and long brown curls fall on his shoulders as she kissed his cheeks.

"Why did you come down to breakfast without me? I wanted to wake up with you next to me," she whispered softly.

"I needed to review a few documents. You have been the center of my undivided attention these past few weeks, ma chérie," he responded coolly.

Surprised by his offhand remark and chilly demeanor, she almost responded that the honeymoon had been short-lived but didn't. She would not willingly start an argument. What would be the use? He would win the battle again. She let go of her embrace and walked to the sidebar to pour a cup of coffee.

Earlier this morning, Maude had comforted her.

"The house was so dull and dreadful without you, Mademoiselle, Monsieur came in just to sleep. He must have felt the emptiness as well," Maude had confided.

But now, Gaby's insecure fears returned. Jean-Louis was mercurial. She never quite knew what to expect. Was the challenge over for him now that he had won the battle? After all, twice he'd refused to take her back to the house after he had had his pleasure satisfied. Was he going to counsel her to return to the convent next?

He must have seen the dark shadow on her pretty, expressive face for he stood up and came close to her. He took her hand.

"I'm famished," he said, "let's have breakfast." He led her out of the sunroom, into the library, past the foyer, and into the long hall leading to the dining room.

The Paris townhouse was beautiful, elegant but yet quite modern for the times. She felt surprisingly at home within these walls. She noticed that her portrait had replaced one of his in one of the halls leading to his office. She had completely forgotten about it. He had been adamant about this portrait. She had find a million excuses not to pause for the artist; he had cancelled a full weekend of activities and had Laramie, the artist, come at seven o'clock on a Sunday morning.

"You will not be bored, darling. I will gaze at your beautiful features and read your favorite story while Laramie, here, performs the intricate task of catching the expression of your infinite soul." She'd rolled her eyes to the heavens.

So she had sat for long hours while the painter worked on his canvas. She was now happy that she had it done it before the separation and that it was hung close to his study.

Shaking her gloomy sentiments, she gave his hand a gentle squeeze, raised his hand to her mouth, and kissed the inside of his palm. She followed Jean-Louis into the dining room.

"Why aren't you eating, Gaby?" he demanded noticing that she had not touched her plate.

"I'm not the least bit hungry." Watching Marie carry a large soufflé plate, she reconsidered. "But I'll join you now, I will not pass on Marie's chocolate soufflé."

He laughed huskily. She loved to hear him laugh so she continued to tell him amusing stories that she either had been told about the people they both knew or funny experiences that had happened to her.

They never seem to be bored with one another. There was a comfort zone in that relationship that was quite novel for the Parisian scene. Although fun and talkative, Gaby was surprised that his passionate nature had not resurfaced.

She decided to stand up and to walk to the fireplace. She wished that she would have been wearing one of her low décolleté dress, but it was cold. Oh well, she just wished he'd been there when she woke up.

I'm pathetic, she angrily told herself. Get on with your life, Gaby. Jean-Louis has. He has returned to his normal activities. She gazed at the burnished logs and placed her hand close to the fire. She looked back as she heard the servants removed the trays. Thinking that Jean-Louis would follow her to the fireplace to encircle her waist and press her to him, as was his tendency to do when they had a day to themselves, she was shocked when he casually got up, grabbed his coat, and strode to the door.

"Where are you going?" she demanded.

"I'll return later, chérie," he casually answered and walked out.

Momentarily flabbergasted, she ran after him. Madame Pelletier's remarks and his response to her banter just before leaving the American ambassador's house resonated. Had he really lost interest? But then why would he have taken her home? She was not about to be miserable. She called out to him as he descended the marble staircase to his carriage.

"Jean-Louis, can I come with you? Where are you going? I'm dressed."

There was no answer and she could no longer see him. Wherever his destination, she had not been invited.

She walked back to the library where she had left all of her music books and went up to her music room. When sad, singing and drowning in her musical world always lifted her mood. She would try to mend things up tomorrow. After all, he still loved her.

And then doubts set in. Had he returned to his libertine life? It's not as if he needed a wife who could not bear children. Why would he have brought her home? Would he adopt a Parisian life style once their marriage had been consummated? Renaud's deductions echoed in her mind.

Oh, God, she thought last evening that all her anxieties had been lifted forever. It was just a continuation. He had said at the ball of the ambassador that he was not quite sure whether he liked having her in his arms as well. She had taken it as a vengeful retort, but in actuality perhaps that is exactly what he was feeling. Had he gone to one of his former mistresses to see if the spark was still there? He had been inebriated last evening. In her compulsive obsessive behavior, she now was sure of it. She had been stupid to let him persuade her to return. In her immense chagrin, she felt tears streaming down her face.

Maude had said that Monsieur had just come in to sleep. Why had she not realized it this morning? He had returned to his former life. She was now certain of it. After all, his entire home was his domain, he had always told her. So why had he brought her back? He loved her personality. She would be an interesting person to live with. No, she couldn't, she wanted all of him or nothing at all.

Two hours later, she heard him walk in the library.

"Fernand, where is Mademoiselle Thornsen?"

The old butler replied that she had returned to her music room shortly after his departure. He walked up the stairs and nonchalantly walked in her room. He clasped her by the shoulder and pressed her forcefully to his length, then tenderly kissed her.

"Let's see whether I enjoy it as much? Was all that waiting worth it?" he stated amused.

She shot him a fiery look.

"I'm no guinea pig," she angrily responded, unable to pull away from his passionate embrace. "Are you trying to drive me mad?" She felt his arm slide behind her back.

"Why are you anxious, Gaby?

"When you left and you did not answer my pleas, I felt sad and I came here to find solace. I think that I will always be like that, Jean-Louis. Where did you go, anyway?"

He took her in his arms and started kissing her, a bruising kiss that sent her senses in dreamland.

"Yes, that is exactly as I remember it," he said teasingly. He lowered his hands to her breasts. "Yes, for sure, I like that." He winked at her, clasped her hips and moved her bottom toward his harden manhood. "Absolutely, I still love it," he laughed.

"Do you?" She placed her two hands on his chest and pushed him away. "You're making me suffer for no apparent reason." She pretended to appear angry, but instead she tightened her embrace and held him close. There was no denying their passion. He tore the dress away from her body and knelt down on the carpet to taste her. At the height of passion, he reached for her wrist, sensually flattened her fingers against his thigh and placed a huge diamond on her left hand. The weightiness of the ring forced her to look down at her finger, but she could not utter one word as he gently grabbed her bottom with one hand and her back with the other and then lifted her onto the bed.

"I had hoped for it to be ready yesterday?"

"Is that why you went out without me?" she asked, hopeful.

"Well, for what other reason would I leave the most beautiful girl in Paris?"

"I love you so much, Jean-Louis."

Not willing to divulge her anxieties, she took his face in her hands and began kissing him incessantly. "I was afraid you might have gone to Madame Pelletier's house," she said, not able to contain what was driving her mad.

He looked at her in disbelief.

"After what we have gone through this past month, it's lucky that I did not lose my lust for women in general!"

"I will make you happy, Jean-Louis. I love you more than life itself and always will," she pronounced solemnly. She turned in his arms and nestled her body into his. Their magnetism was great.

Chapter Forty-Seven

All arrangements had been made. Gaby and Jean-Louis had left early that day for the trip would be long. Jean-Louis knew well that Gaby was displeased with the idea of marrying in the Loire. His Grandmother had not even asked about the location of the wedding. The Loire was the home of the ancestral home, such was his pronouncement and there was no returning on that decision.

"Why not Villefranche?" Gaby had asked. "How difficult is it for your family and friends to ride down to the South of France? They vacation there at the drop of a hat to soak up the sun in the middle of winter, for goodness sake!"

"Gaby, that's an impossibility. I want us to be married in the Loire. It is important to me and to you as well. For society's sake, this will crown you as my equal, my wife, my Duchesse," he bent down and kissed her questioning pout. "Besides, you are well aware that my Grandmother would be devastated if we don't marry in the ancestral home. We will not be there for long. We will ride down to Villefranche for our honeymoon," he smiled, knowing that he'd hit the jackpot.

"We are going south after the ceremony, Jean-Louis, you're not joshing?"

He moved his head from side to side.

"Non, Mademoiselle, I am most serious," he answered.

She threw herself in his arms as she encircled his large frame.

"Jean-Louis, I adore you," she exclaimed, pulling on his lapel to force him down toward her lips.

Her wardrobe had already been sent down to the Loire.

"Should we sleep in different rooms tonight? One more night of freedom, darling, should I savor it all to myself before I become your chattel," she laughed, half-seriously. "What rights will you have upon me, Jean-Louis?" she demanded curiously. "As your wife, you know. Do you recall what you said in Paris? I was so enamored with the marriage idea, that truly I was not listening," she continued assertively.

"The right to torment you, to torture you, as you aptly proclaim, when you're angry with me. Financial rights, property rights—"

"Stop, stop, I don't want to be wed. It's too restrictive. I love my freedom way too much."

Laughing uproariously, he picked her up and placed her on his knees.

"All of the above and many more that I can't quite predict now. You see I gave you ample warning after our little talk almost two years ago. It's all downhill from now. You're all mine." He encircled her body tightly, stressing the word *mine* to emphasize the rhetoric he'd just pronounced.

She could not respond. The no-win situation that awaited stunned her. Fear enveloped her. Jean-Louis was absolutely correct. Oh, God, why had she even mentioned marriage? She had it all. The scene in Maître Lauriot's apartment and later in their home came to mind.

Mon Dieu, why did she want marriage? Had she lost her mind? They were perfectly happy. The set-up was perfect.

She pulled away from him and sat on the opposite side, frightened.

"Oh, you cannot be serious, Gaby. Are you truly afraid to marry? What is wrong there? You practically asked me to marry you two years ago. What has changed? I was just teasing, darling. Nothing will change between us," Jean-Louis replied as he detected terror on her face.

"You are powerful, darling, influential in every possible circle I can think of. Why in fact do we have to marry? It is no longer that important to me. I'm frightened, Jean-Louis."

He reached for her hand and brought her back next to him.

"Gaby, do not be foolish, darling. I want you to share my name— my illustrious name, darling. You should be ecstatic," he teasingly added, as he gathered her small body to his.

No words, no caresses reached her.

"Nothing will change between us, Gaby, just my world, the aristocracy will change, if you will. You will suddenly be seen under a different light, a part of them, my darling.

And when our trip to Italy is upon us, we'll be prepared. The wedding will be behind us, allowing us to enjoy our friends, our interests, our Parisian life fully until we are set to go. I really do no want anything to be hanging over our head. It is just a formality, darling, that will protect you if anything should happen to me as well. You will acquire some rights as well, as my wife, chérie," he smirked. "Look at me, Gaby. I'm not such a bad catch, darling. Don't look so saddened," he teased.

She relaxed in his arms and smiled.

"I presume," she remarked seriously, which brought another bout of glorious laughter from the Duke.

"Is that a presage of my future life?" he said, amused. "You promised to make me happy. Am I now to endure tortuous days at the hands of an increasingly angry and unfulfilled wife for the rest of my life? Is that it, Gaby?" he questioned ironically.

Seeing the absurdity of her insecurities in his smiling eyes, she placed her arms around his neck and kissed him passionately.

"I'm sorry, so sorry, darling," kissing him one more time. "Our union will be the paradise that I promised to you years ago."

The carriage continued on its bumpy road.

At four in the afternoon, the Duke's carriage entered the magnificent Chateau De Bourbonne. Everyone in livery attire waited. Anxious glances shot in their direction. In essence, few knew what to expect from the new mistress Mademoiselle De Conte-Thornsen. She was different from all the other friends the Duke had brought to the castle. The Duke was infinitely enamored with her. Everyone had heard about the love story. In just a short while it had become the love affair of the century. Young servants invoked the egalitarian future of France, and young aristocrats were beginning to envisage marrying for love rather than for financial security and lineage.

Jean-Louis-Pierre De Pleyssis, the Duke of Bourbonne, the most influential and certainly the richest man in Europe was marrying a commoner, even more astounding, an American artist.

Times were changing. Hope for humanity was in the air—for all stations of life. Young women in the villages and in the salons were mesmerized with the possibilities it could have on their lives. Until now, fathers or uncles or even brothers promised girls in marriage. The Duke had always done as he pleased and this last act was viewed as treason to tradition. Everyone in the village was talking about it. They had met the young American months after they had reconnected their dalliance. Who would have thought that the Duke would marry someone below his aristocratic class, and an American at that?

The Countess Guyslene De Farge had told her friend Lou Anne De Grangeais, one of Jean-Louis many adolescent amorous flames that Gabriella was perhaps not the purported great passion in Jean-Louis-Pierre's life.

"You know Lou Ann, Gabriella is well connected in the Vatican," Guyslene had said in passing.

"I'm well aware of it, and knowing intimately Jean-Louis-Pierre's analytical mind, he wants to use her connection to help him achieve his goals in Italy. Her cousin is a trusted advisor to the Pope. After their return, our cherished Duke will return to his gay and private life. I can assure you of that. Love is not an emotion that Jean-Louis-Pierre is captivated by. As a matter of fact, he is incapable of long-term intimacy. Mark my words, Guyslene."

"But, I understand that he is perfectly dedicated to her. In Paris, I heard that he is the one who forbids her to pursue her musical career on account of security."

Lou Ann looked at her friend with complacency.

"Precisely, he wants her to be of sound mind and body so as to accomplish his mission quickly and efficiently. Besides, Guyslene, what are you thinking of? Look at Jean-Louis-Pierre's position in life. How could he allow his *maîtresse attitrée* to perform on stage? Seriously, my dear friend."

"Lou Anne, it is the latest rage. Every aristocrat and their brothers and uncles these days, seem to install a young beautiful diva or ballerina in an elegant apartment in the city and go on with their merry activities while in our beautiful and most entertaining capital. Fame is an aphrodisiac if you already have power. If you have none, then fame becomes power and that is most certainly the most enticing sexual motive."

"I read none of your sentimental visions in their relationship," replied Lou Anne, a sad tone in her voice.

"I'm telling you that it is the new wave, but the difference with Jean-Louis-Pierre and Gabriella is that he took her to Saint Louis, in his home, immediately. Now that is telling, quite different from his other loving escapades. You should know that, Lou Anne," Guyslene said candidly as if she wanted to inculcate reality in her friend's mind.

"Whatever his feelings at the moment, I know Jean-Louis-Pierre well enough to be absolutely sure that he will not be faithful to the colonial," Lou Anne retorted louder than necessary, her voice quivering holding back tears.

Realizing that she had touched a soft spot, Guyslene deviously continued.

"Eh bien, ma chère, we need to rid our language of such words as *colonial* and *naturelle*. Gabriella will soon become the Grande Duchesse de Bourbonne—very soon, very soon, very, very soon. A small faux pas could cost us many invitations to his grand entertaining style. Frankly, I'll swallow everything as quickly as the union is legalized. I will become her best friend if it means being invited to her soirées and balls. The Count, after all, expects me to. That is the very least I can do for my cherished husband who is now quite content with the premier ballerina of the Paris Ballet, leaving me alone and terribly free to handle my life in the way I see fit for the contentment of my physical and emotional well-being," Guyslene laughed mischievously. "Don't you agree, my dear friend?"

Lou Anne had retrieved her sang-froid and replied quite happily, "I could not agree with you more, my dear friend. The wedding should be lots of fun."

The women continued strolling down the majestic alleys surrounding the Chateau de Bourbonne. Black swans glided on the murky waters.

Not too far away, Gaby and Jean-Louis had reached their rooms. Tomorrow would be busy. The wedding party would gather at the estate of Jean-Louis' Grandmother, seven kilometers down the Loire.

Cunnan had arrived late in the afternoon and Marie-Louise as well. Her Count had been unable to make the ceremony and Gaby was pleased. Well, good riddance, Gaby thought, Marie-Louise would perhaps meet someone interesting at the wedding.

Jean-Louis' Grandmother had taken care of the invitations for their friends in the Loire. The staff in the chateau was accustomed to large feasts and celebrations. Many had been present at Jean-Louis' birth. Service was a generational profession in the castles in Europe.

"Darling, I will be an *étrangère* at my own wedding!" Gaby murmured a tad of melancholy in her voice.

"Just as well, chérie. You will be exposed soon enough to all that refinery."

Dinner was served at nine o'clock. The scrumptious feast led them to an after-dinner drink in the library. Ensconced in a large brown velvet smoking chair in each other's arms, letting the warmth of the fire toast their bodies, Jean-Louis bent down and kissed her mouth passionately.

"I love you, Gaby. I'll always love you," he said simply, his voice filled with all the love he felt for her.

"Jean-Louis," she struggled to reply. Gently she pushed him away and stared in his eyes. "Will you always consider me your equal in most endeavors for the rest of your life, darling? Can you promise never to have a paramour on the side or hurt me?"

He looked surprised. "Hurt you?" he questioned.

"Physically, I mean." Her voice was so low and grave that if he had not learned to decipher her questions before she could utter the words, he wouldn't have heard her whispers.

"No, Gaby," he replied emphatically, without hesitation. "I would never hurt you, nor torment you with another woman. You should know that well, chérie. My analytical mind would prevent me from even thinking of marrying you if there was a millimeter of doubt in my soul."

She reclined safely in his arms. "I know that, Jean-Louis." She took his hand and kissed it.

"Gaby," his voice was now guttural and solemn. "The same conditions will affect your behavior, Gaby."

"I'd never think of abusing you. Do I sound like I'm mentally challenged?" she replied, stunned.

He exploded into a fit of laughter. "No, chérie. Well, perhaps I should specify, no kicking, and no spilling scalding hot beverage on my person," he retorted ironically, mimicking a stern, paternal reprimand.

"I will not venture along these lines, Monsieur le Duke!"

"You did say I should treat you as an equal in all areas of my life. Aren't these pre-conditions that need to truly come to life before our big day?"

"Cease. I promise never to cause you physical harm!" She laughed gloriously, flashing a radiant smile that quickly prompted a sensuous kiss on her sexy lips. Jean-Louis deepened the kiss.

"I love you very much, Miss De Conte-Thornsen and I can't wait to make you my wife." Instead of seeing ecstasy in her eyes, he noticed the dark cloud that overwhelmed her pretty features.

Gaby clasped his upper arm, as she placed her face on his muscular biceps, staring at an invisible scene that no one was privy to, not even the great Jean-Louis-Pierre De Pleyssis.

"Gaby," He pulled up and held her at arms length, as he faced her squarely. "Listen carefully. I do not know why you suddenly have these moods that appear to overwhelm you. It is not important. Whatever happened in your past has no impact now. What is reality is that I am here for you. Do not fright. I love you, chérie and I will always protect you—always for as long as I live and beyond through personal security and financial backing. Do you understand, Gaby?"

She nodded.

"Remember, the word *paradise* was intended for us, darling," he murmured. "We will have a wonderful life." He pressed her back in his arms and gathered her tightly to his chest.

Her tensions assuaged, she slowly eased in his wide comforting chest.

"I'll always be there for you," he repeated holding her securely sealed to him. "I'll adore you until the end of times," he whispered in her ear.

Tears streamed quietly down her cheeks. She held on to him as if her life depended on it. And it did.

The following morning started with his Grandmother's grand entrance in the dining room. Jean-Louis was having his morning coffee, reading the paper.

"This affair is greatly unnerving Jean-Louis-Pierre. Where is your secretary—Patrick, not Armand? I have tried to contact him. The only response I receive from him is that he has everything under control. I found his insubordination abhorrent. Where is Cunnan?"

"Good morning, Madame." The Duke smiled. "Would you care to sit and have le petit déjeuner with us? Cunnan was here earlier this morning. He will be down for breakfast momentarily and Gabriella is busy with the dressmaker upstairs. She would appreciate a few kind words. I know that she'd love your personal approval."

"I have no time, Jean-Louis-Pierre. You have placed a great imposition on my person and I intend to carry the festivities to perfection.

"Gaby has Madame Rouet, the best in all of the world's capitals. Where is Madame Perideot? Has she arrived, yet?"

Jean-Louis walked to his chair.

"Please, Madame, sit with me for a short while. Let's talk."

"Why is it that your future wife does not have a personal secretary?"

"Gaby does not need one; I have enough administrators to handle all our needs."

"Why do you truly enjoy going against all aspects of tradition and society's etiquette?"

"Because it is absurd, Madame. We need to look toward the future of society. All members of society and frankly the type of traditions you are focusing upon are meaningless and superfluous and I dislike form without substantial structure. Voila," he retorted unequivocally.

"What has become of you, Jean-Louis-Pierre?" she said pensively, taking a seat at the great long table next to her grandson. "Everything is over. You can't go back on your decision. I hope that once this passion is behind you, you will return to your senses, do what you must to rein her in, and go on with the life that you were born to lead."

She leaned back dejected and sad. Cunnan walked in the room.

"Madame, a great pleasure to meet you again on this grand occasion," Cunnan proclaimed with all the formality he could summon.

She nodded. He walked around Jean-Louis to kiss the dowager's hand. Jean-Louis looked at him and smirked. Before Cunnan could continue the conversation, Gaby breezed in the room.

"Voila, I'm done. I'm all yours now, darling. Let's go riding today before the soirée," she said. She had spoken too soon. Her future husband had guests. She first noticed Jean-Louis' Grandmother. Jean-Louis smiled at her. He raised his eyebrows as he greatly enjoyed the developing comedy.

The Duchesse did not give her the time to assess the situation so as to formulate the proper retort. "Gabriella, you are taking the formalities quite flippantly. This is the soirée before your wedding to the Duke De Bourbonne, Gabriella. Do not forget the status. I do not want a repeat engagement soirée, which turned out to be vulgar and terribly embarrassing, I might add. This will not happen this evening when my good and proper name is on the wedding invitations," the Duchesse exploded heinously.

The amused smirk on Jean-Louis-Pierre De Pleyssis fell from his face to be replaced by contained anger and annoyance.

"Madame, Gaby and I are grateful to you for posting our invitations but your anxious verbiage of which I am certain is related to the large number of guests invited, is not well taken. Gabriella is under great strain, as well. Gabriella will be a member of our family tomorrow. I intend to have everyone heed her words including member of my own family." He glared down at her with so much intensity that the old woman retracted her attack.

She had gone too far, she surmised silently.

Jean-Louis stood up, indicating that the audience was over. The dowager stood up as well, and with a great sigh, she prepared to take her leave.

"Yes, Jean-Louis, perhaps we are all under great duress."

"We don't have to be," he replied severely. "Good day. We will meet this evening." Jean-Louis saw her to the door. Luc, the butler, brought her to her carriage. It was clearly a cold shoulder from her grandson, who habitually helped her into her carriage.

Jean-Louis sat back down and both Gaby and Cunnan walked to the table. Gaby sat next to him.

"Well, I presume our riding promenade is out of the question," she said as she tried to humor the heaviness of the moment.

Cunnan walked to the young man and tapped his friend on the shoulder.

"Let it go, Jean-Louis-Pierre. I understand your pain, but there is absolutely nothing that you can do about it."

Gaby sat silently.

Moments later, Jean-Louis looked at Gaby and took her hand and kissed it.

"Regardless of it all, Gaby, we will be happy. I promise you that," Jean-Louis said solemnly.

Cunnan smiled and started eating.

Gabriella De Conte Thornsen would be the next Duchesse De Bourbonne, and that was the reality of the moment, the Duke reasoned. A reality the grand society would accept.

The night before the grand marriage, Gaby slept in the music room. She was obsessive about his former paramours, consequently the past months, carpenters, plumbers, architects had been busy adding and refurbishing a new private apartment in the old castle for the Duke and his future Duchesse. She could not stand the thought of sleeping in a room where her future husband had serenaded other women on her wedding night. To please her, he had had the second floor transformed into suites for their return as husband and wife.

Brightly illuminated, the music room had been the perfect place to reminisce on her life—what she had, what she would gain, and what she would lose from this formidable alliance she had dreamed of for almost four years now. She sat up in bed, frightened. The phrase that he had uttered years ago in favor of non-marriage resounded deeply in her mind. "Mistresses are usually adored, Gaby. It is the wife who needs to adapt to a new life. It can be difficult at times if the wife is in love with the man that she marries."

Well, Gaby was totally in love with Jean-Louis. Would he change? She would be his now, the challenge gone. Mon Dieu, Gaby, she told herself, holding her upper arms so as to warm her entire being. Run away, now! He will hurt you emotionally, maybe even worse. Remember when you went to Montmartre? She could not let go of her obsessive fears, knowing damn well that none of her fears were founded, but still reviewing in her mind the horrid images of a less than perfect union. Totally exhausted, she finally fell asleep in the wee hours of the morning.

She woke up early. Her obsessive fears returned. What was she getting into? An uncontrollable fear shook her. How could she maintain any control of her own life, marrying the most influential man in Europe? Was she mad? She trembled. Why didn't I evaluate these facts earlier? Leave, that was it, she should just leave. She would leave now. Everyone was so busy, her departure would not be missed. Why hadn't she talked to Cunnan yesterday?

Philippe had not been able to come. He had been detained in Avignon—important affairs for the Church. Well, that was the perfect excuse. No, but for God's sake, she mused thinking of Philippe's flippant demeanor at such an important moment in her life. What about me? I have no one to confide in, no parents, no friends that could understand my dilemma, she mulled over, devastated.

No Gabriella, she angrily chided herself, come what may, the decision has been taken. There is no turning back.

Chapter Forty-Eight

At exactly eight o'clock, everyone entered the room. She was no longer a human, she thought—a puppet that's what she was. Everyone pulled and poked at her from all sides. She let herself be pampered from head to toe and finally they slipped the magnificent wedding gown embroidered with satin and pearls.

For the very first time in her life she wished she had a doting mother who could give her the security and confidence needed to face a life of ownership. How could she have agreed to a marriage? How could she have longed for it?

Marie-Louise entered the room and looked at her with great teary eyes. The only friend she had in Paris to confide her fears and anxieties was wishing at this very moment to be in the same position of bondage. Women, our insecurities were our demise, she thought. Marriage—the end of all dreams. Frightened by the vision alone, she began trembling again.

Thinking that her friend's emotions were being tasked, Marie-Louise held her and kissed her tenderly.

"I am thrilled for you, Gabriella. You achieved everything that you deserve and much more. Jean-Louis-Pierre adores you. I know that your life will be wonderful and happy, Gabriella. I love you so, you look ravishing, my dear friend. I have never seen such a picture perfect couple."

"Thank you, Marie-Louise," Gaby answered simply, and without delay she was taken downstairs to the private chapel.

Gaby heard the rambling murmurs of the guests already seated in the pews. She closed her eyes, clasped her communion cross, prayed fervently to be granted a loving and fruitful life, and bravely took her first steps alone entering the foyer. Now, all eyes were upon her.

The trembling started once more. My dear God, she would faint, she knew it. Her face burned, her step were unsteady. She was told to stop. She stopped in the foyer of the chapel. She gazed at the crowd.

The orchestra and soprano took her appearance as a cue to begin the traditional, ceremonious ode.

Oh, thank God, Cunnan strode to her side—to her rescue. He took her in his arms and did not let her go until he felt her glacial little body retrieve some warmth and stability. She looked up to him grateful. Slowly, gently, he pushed her away from him and took her hands in his, as he looked down at her frightened features.

"The world will be yours, dear Gabriella. Jean-Louis-Pierre adores you. I can attest to that. Look down the aisle. He is anxiously waiting." He nodded behind him in Jean-Louis' direction. Gaby glanced down the aisle above all the onlookers and guests. Jean-Louis waited for her. He was both magnificent and frightening. She focused her gaze on her future husband who smiled at her, while Marie-Louise walked down the aisle and took her place on the opposite side of Jean-Louis' family.

Sheer dread plastered on her perfect visage, she started her long walk down the long center aisle with Cunnan. The old organ resonated gravely into the high arches of the glorious Cathedral into Richard Wagner's "Bridal Chorus." Gaby forced herself to take heart in the music. It was calming her—giving her hope.

Finally, they reached the altar. Jean-Louis was but an arm's length away.

Cunnan stared at Jean-Louis, raised his eyebrows and rolled his eyes down to Gaby. An air of understanding passed between the two men. Cunnan took Gaby's hand and firmly placed it into Jean-Louis'. She looked up from behind her veil. Her trembling hand nestled in his.

"You are so handsome, Jean-Louis." Gaby whispered candidly. "You look like a king."

He smiled kindly and caressed her fingers lovingly.

"I'm supposed to shower *you* with compliments, Gaby." He smirked, sensing her cold fingers.

"Well, what are you waiting for?" she replied, trying to inject some lightness in this momentous instant that terrified her. She forced a smile on her innocent face.

Jean-Louis stood silent for a moment, just gazing at her intensely, and gently he squeezed her small hand and led her to the altar.

"Of all the men in this whole wide world, I am the happiest and luckiest today," Jean-Louis murmured tenderly, as he walked her closer to the Cardinal who was waiting for them and who wondered what to make of all the conversation.

She was forgetting all of the steps that they'd practiced the day before.

The words of reassurance that she had just ingested frightened her even more so. Jean-Louis' intense look reminded her of the influence she was giving him over her person.

Obediently, she sailed through the repetition of the vows uttered by the Cardinal while all the while, ideas of running down the aisle the other way, all alone, repudiating all the vows she had just taken, thundered in her overloaded mind.

Jean-Louis looked down to her adoringly. He held her hands firmly while Cunnan came and handed him the rings.

The Cardinal pronounced the wedding vows.

She heard Jean-Louis say, "I do."

Then the prelate turned to her, as he once more pronounced the vows and waited for the acquiescence that was not forthcoming. Looking down at Gaby whose intent look was focused on the Duke, the Cardinal repeated the vows once more, deliberately this time around, as if she had not understood his words.

As the phrase 'obedience to your husband' was repeated not once but twice by the cleric, Gaby tried to pull her hand away.

Flabbergasted, Jean-Louis' reflexes responded simultaneously. He held on to her ever more securely.

The Cardinal waited a few extra moments and then once more said, "Will you, Gabriella Maria Caroline De Conte Thornsen take Jean-Louis-Pierre Auguste De Pleyssis, Duke De Bourbonne for your lawful wedded husband?"

Silence once more. Gabriella glacial glare focused into Jean-Louis' eyes trying to pull away from his grasp.

"Gaby," Jean-Louis said very calmly and gently in English. His voice was a caress. "Darling, the Cardinal is asking you if you wish to marry me," he said simply. "I want to share my life with you."

His voice had taken such a profound and loving texture that she took a step toward him wanting to be reassured and embraced. In the process she caught his Grandmother's inflamed stare. Quickly she surveyed the crowd. All eyes were upon her—awaiting her response. She swallowed hard, and held his hand ever more tightly.

"Yes I want to—yes, I do." She smiled up at him. Jean-Louis smiled back and relaxed his grasp.

"I love you, Gaby," he said before pulling her into his arms and kissing her long and hard—long before the Cardinal had time to give his blessing. The permission had been granted from above.

For the crowd, still incredulous about the Duke's motives, that last kiss did not leave much cinder for the gossips.

"Jean-Louis is madly in love with Gabriella," Jean-Louis-Pierre's uncle whispered to his wife. "Just now he reminded me of his father and mother on their wedding day. I hope that their lives together will be long and fruitful.

"These days, that kind of love is so rare," Jean-Louis' cousin whispered to the dowager who remained silent.

The Duke raised his head and stared intently in Gaby's eyes.

"I adore you, Duchesse."

Radiant, he took her hand, turned toward the crowd, and walked down the aisle, his new bride in tow.

It had taken thirty-three years to assuage one of the most ardent rakes of the French social circle, and lo and behold, a diminutive American had taken his heart forever.

They walked directly to the foyer of the chapel to receive their guests.

Gaby followed the protocol to the letter.

Everyone was settling in the grand ballroom and the butlers offered Champagne to the guests.

After all had been greeted, Jean-Louis reached for two flutes of Champagne and offered one to Gaby. He led her toward a secret door that uncovered a narrow stone staircase.

"Come Gaby, the view of the valley is magnificent from this vantage point. I spent many hours as a child listening to the call of the wild late at night, right here." He nodded to the very top of the tower. She began to climb behind him.

He picked her up in his arms and walked up the winding tower. He opened the small wooden door facing him and let Gaby walk outside. A large garden opened up on the roof of the castle. The magnificence of the Loire Valley mesmerized her senses. "Breathtaking Jean-Louis," she remarked. He took her hand and led her to a stone parapet where he sat. He pulled her down on his knees and reached for her lips.

"Tell me, Duchesse, I have the strange feeling that you were about to leave me at the altar if I hadn't had the presence to brace your wrists to mine. Am I correct, Gaby?"

"No, no, no, I was frightened, that's all. Everyone was pulling me in every possible direction. I—I felt I was loosing control. I was petrified. I'm sorry, I did not think it showed," she managed to respond.

Jean-Louis laughed. "I thought so. I should have sent my Grandmother to stay with you."

Gaby looked even more conflicted.

"That would not have been an enlightened idea, n'est-ce pas? I can see it on your face. You are not too fond of my Grandmother, are you Gaby?" He smiled.

"No, not really." She responded candidly. "But it's not important. I have you. I'll share everything with you. For whatever reason, extended family ties have never worked for me. That's all." She heaved a long sigh and gazed intensely in his eyes. Quickly she reached for his mouth with her lips. "Just hold and kiss me, darling, and everything will be fine," Gaby whispered into his mouth.

Jean-Louis did as he was told and took a bit more liberty.

An hour later the Duke and his Duchesse walked back down to the main castle and entered the ballroom where guests had been awaiting their presence politely.

Halfway through their first waltz, she realized the step that she had taken. Jean-Louis looked down at her and raised his eyebrows questioningly. She raised hers back as if to say, we did it. Laughing, he twirled her slender and graceful body on the dance floor.

After dinner, Jean-Louis broke with tradition when it came to the grand ball. Unwilling to share Gaby with other men and having no desire to twirl on the dance floor some of the attendees, he raised his arms to invite the crowd to join in the dancing. Catching his Grandmother's angry stare, he dismissed it quickly. He would assuage her rage later.

Jean-Louis was elated and certainly not above showing it. The party was a wonderful surprise to many of the inhabitants as well.

At around ten o'clock that evening, the couple slipped out of sight.

Taking Gaby in his arms, he returned her to the very top of his castle where the full moon illuminated the valley. They still could hear the guests dancing to the happy melodies the orchestra serenaded.

Reaching for her waist and then her body, crunching the heavy satin gown to him in the process, he pulled her backside into his chest and placed a kiss in her ears.

"Tell me, Gaby, I want the truth" he murmured, "were you ready to leave me at the altar?" Jean-Louis demanded with a hint of disbelief in his voice, or perhaps sadness, Gaby was not quite sure.

"No, of course not," she responded quickly. "I experienced great panic while walking down the aisle." She waited anxiously before continuing. "You know, darling, it was most difficult. I waited in the room all by myself. It got overwhelming."

"I understand," he replied pensively. "This arcane tradition weighs heavily on my character. Although I never wished it, I followed tradition, Gaby, I am sorry, indeed.

"We should have spent the night in our apartment last evening. Anyway, it was a beautiful day—our day, Gaby. I have never seen a bride as beautiful as you," he whispered in her ears. "I love you, Gaby. We will have a wonderful and exciting life," he proclaimed decidedly and just as quickly changed the subject. He would have to come to terms with what happened at the altar. Holding her possessively close to him he repeated, "I love you, Gaby."

The couple stayed a long time studying the stars and then he led her down to their new apartment. As they walked in the beautifully decorated sitting room, Jean-Louis strode to the sidebar and poured himself a glass of brandy.

"You prefer champagne, Gaby? Come here, darling."

"Yes," she replied timidly, not moving a centimeter.

"Come here, Gaby," he asked once more, a bit annoyed at her standoffish attitude.

Instead, she plopped down on the heavily tufted green-and-gold sofa, her wedding gown all around her small body.

"Have you forgotten your vow of obedience already, Madame?" he remarked sarcastically.

"Ouf, out the window already." She laughed.

He looked at her first and a great cavernous laughter exploded and resounded all around the room. Quickly he stood up and strode across the room decidedly. Lifting the small beauty close to him, he pressed her to his heart, took her hand, and placed it on his beating heart.

"I am happy, no, elated; I lay my entire life at your feet, Madame," he whispered eloquently in her ear.

Tears swelled up in her beautiful eyes. "What classic have you subtracted this profound exclamation from?" she laughed in between tears rolling down her cheeks.

"I presume I'll need to show more of my romantic side, Duchesse. Do you like it?"

"Immensely," she whispered sweetly.

He turned her in his arms, his lips on her naked décolleté. He started unbuttoning all the small buttons that kept the corset to the dress close to her torso.

"You looked magnificent today," His lips lowered to the peeking mounds staring at him. I love you so much, Gaby. Today is the second happiest day of my life," he quipped, recalling the words she had uttered years ago. "Perfection, Gaby; you are perfection."

She gave him a sideways smile.

"Well?" he asked waiting.

"Well, what?" she retorted.

"Your turn, Madame. You have read tons of classics, you should at least remember one or two romantic phrases, from an aria, at least!"

Half naked, her heavy bouffant dress weighing heavily on her hips, she walked to the rosewood secretary and took out a small jewelry box that she brought back to the place where he was standing.

"It's yours, Jean-Louis. It's my wedding present to you," she whispered tenderly, handing him the elongated burgundy-and-gold *coffret*.

Gently, Jean-Louis received the velvet box from her hands. He touched it and looked at Gaby, deeply troubled not knowing how to react to the present, his eyes were swelling up with tears.

"You did not have to chérie, tradition does not—"

"Hush," she responded, surprised at his reddened eyes, "just open it and shed a few tears," she responded sweetly. "Please, for our wedding."

He caught her by the waist and kissed her hungrily, long and hard, while all the while holding the box in his hand behind her head.

Regretfully, he pulled his lips slowly away from hers.

"You are very flippant, Madame," he murmured, kissing her forehead and pressing his eyelids on her bouncy mane. He stayed there for a long while, just holding her.

"Now, let's take a look at my present."

"It's your dog collar, Jean-Louis."

"What?" He looked down at her curiously.

"Just an American expression," she responded gaily, not willing to explain any further.

He opened the box slowly, visibly shaken. A gold medal of the angel Gabriel with the face of a woman hung on a long golden thick chain.

Jean-Louis pulled it out completely.

"Thank you, Gaby, it's beautiful," he pronounced solemnly. "I'll cherish it forever."

She took the chain from his hands, stepped on the satin hassock and proceeded to clasp it around his neck.

"It will always protect you, darling. Philippe had the jeweler at the Vatican mold it—the Pope has blessed it. Look, I have the same one, except that the angel is a woman—me." She smiled.

He lowered his head and kissed her naked breast, and continued to push her wedding gown off her hips. Finally, she was stark naked, and he pulled her up and out of the embroidered satin gown and placed her onto the yet untouched bed. He bent down upon her and covered her body with his, his elbows ensconced on the satin pillow that framed her face and her expressive eyes.

"Gaby, did you realize that our wedding day coincides with the day we first made love on the Tempête?"

"Yes, I do, Jean-Louis." She encircled his head with her arms, "I kept on remembering that day earlier while walking down the aisle. I was so frightened, darling. I really do not understand. There was a fear of the unknown—my fingers, my toes, my body, my mind were numb, my heart pounded. I could hardly take a breath of air. Important events in my life bring upon me onslaught of pure panic. I am terribly sorry if I embarrassed you in front of your friends." She paused, and looked up at him. "I could not really comprehend what I was doing. I couldn't be logical and I didn't know how to handle this delicate situation that would change my life forever. I was polarized, one part of me wanted you to hold me, to absorb me into you; the other part wanted to run away from all the staring eyes." She quivered, as she recalled all too vividly the frightening moments she'd suffered as she walked down the isle to meet the love of her life.

"Gaby, I adore you, you have lost nothing and gained a great deal—ME." He laughed holding on to her securely, and then most profoundly, "I promise to you, Gaby, that we will have a happy and exciting life and yes, I promise never to be unfaithful. I hold you to the same high standard, Gaby." Jean-Louis repeated once again as he finished solemnly. He waited and looked at her, watching how she internalized what he had just told her and then feeling his manhood come alive, he bent down, took her head in between his hands and kissed her passionately.

"After such a passionate kiss, Duchesse, it is your turn to show me the paradise you so often spoke of in our heathen days," he exclaimed, kissing her once more on her nose and pulling her with him on her side first and then on his chest, as he caressed the curvaceous hips.

"I'd be delighted, Monsieur. You are well aware that I've always loved playing the lead," she winked at him, and lowered her breasts to his taut stomach. "Eden is just beginning, Sire!"

* * *

Jean-Louis kept his promise, less than a week after the grand wedding; he had taken her back to Villefranche sur Mer.

After the County of Savoy had been given to Napoléon III in 1860, the Duke had built a castle overlooking the magnificent bay where their love affair had flourished in the picturesque village. Gaby called it her second home.

Back in the glorious French capital, she had been asked by the grand of the town to lend her expertise in charitable organizations. Although not adverse to the idea, she'd refused most appeals. She liked working at the convent and responding to the need of the orphans. Actually, the convent was the only place where she taught voice and sang at Grand Mass with the sisters. That is all she had consented to prior to her marriage, and that is all she would consent to now. Jean-Louis' Grandmother had requested her presence for tea a day later. The subject had resurfaced, not as a question but as a duty now that she was Jean-Louis' wife. The meeting had been a calamity with Gaby terminating the reunion and making an enemy out of the dowager. He'd heard about it that very same night and had infuriated his Grandmother even more so, when he'd stated that volunteering was not Gaby's choice at the moment.

He had not shared with Gaby the revolution that she'd instigated in the aristocratic Parisian salons. He loved having her nearby. Especially now, she was totally absorbed with the construction of her theater. He had been right. Of all the magnificent gifts they had received, the theater was her passion.

Tonight it would just be the two of them. They had entertained or been entertained since their return to the capital. After dinner they'd gone upstairs in their apartment and had continued the discussion started over dinner. Without pressure he had begun her political education. Unrest had started in Paris and it would get worst before it got better. Of that he was certain although the Emperor and his advisors were deaf to the cries of the descendants of the revolutionary Jacobins.

"Les Republicans, Gaby, are inciting the crowds against the Empire. You know how virulent these men and women can become when enticed against the Emperor. Remember 1789, it was the Absolute Crown they hated then. Now, with their great dislike of Louis Napoléon . . . let's hope that the National Guards will not join them. We are fortunate to have had a great architect such as Haussmann who was sufficiently clairvoyant to enlarge the Grandes Avenues. This splendid architectural feat alone squashed a lot of skirmishes. Instead of the crowded tenements that used to adorn our capital, it is difficult now to amass ammunitions and hide when there is so much clarity in the streets. You have seen many of the working poor sent packing in the suburbs. Did you know, Gaby that Pierre Renoir's parents lived in front of the Palais du Louvre?"

"Yes, Lise Trehot told me that Pierre actually worked in the Sèvres factory, painting lovely pastoral scenes on their cups, plates, and vases. I was not aware that his parents had been displaced. Wasn't his father a tailor? I heard that he sewed uniforms for the military. I assumed that these artisans would have been relocated in the upper floors of the new vertical buildings. Wasn't that one Louis Napoléon's grand cultural project?" she asked.

"Yes, chérie, the plan was to have Paris as the new center of commerce—which in effect he has accomplished with the Halles, the large market in the very center of the city. To finish his cultural dream, the new apartments buildings were to be populated with the new wealthy bourgeoisie—bankers, lawyers, doctors on the first floors, the state workers a few levels above—all the way to the boulangers and maids on the very top of the buildings? I believe that Louis Napoléon's dream to reform and to modernize France has been partly accomplished. I would never have accepted the assignment had I not seen a window of fundamental changes for the future. Unfortunately, he is now sickly and he is led at the highest level by a pompous group who rely on France's brilliant past."

"Are you in danger, Jean-Louis?" She asked anxiously.

"No, darling, and neither are you, but be aware of your surroundings, that's all." He left it at that.

In retrospect, their lives were heavenly. Her cousin, Cardinal Thornsen was to be sent to Paris. According to the Emperor, he would be the force that would coalesce the Pope and his Princes to the empire.

Early, right after Jean-Louis's departure, Gaby had gotten a *dépêche*, an official dispatch, that Philippe would be arriving in Paris earlier than noted in his previous letter. The note had been sent from Beaunne. The Cardinal would arrive in Paris and would say Mass in Notre Dame. Gaby was in a formidable mood. Finally, Jean-Louis and Philippe would meet.

Jean-Louis had told her months ago that he might work closely with an important representative of the Vatican. He had heard some rumors that the Cardinal had been appointed to work toward the full reunification of the Papal States with the French delegation. "Your cousin, Gaby, Cardinal Thornsen, may have a temporary assignment in Paris.

Her joy was uncontainable. Philippe was the perfect choice. She waltzed from one room to the next. Philippe would stay with them for his home was being refurbished. The men would get along so well, she knew. They were alike in many ways; they both shared a great sense of integrity and conscientiousness toward their chosen profession and calling. Furthermore, they both adored her.

In the sanctity of her home would be reunited the persons she held dearest to her heart. She was elated.

Both Philippe and herself had been born and raised in Louisiana on their respective plantations; both had suffered at the hands of their socially astute parents who did not give a damn whether they lived or died. Their servants, Tita and her husband Gustav, had provided great nurturing and a social education, which included skills such as fishing, cooking, shooting, and planting and they had infused in both of them the love of the land and its infinite power. Both had survived with each other's help and both had achieved their lives' passion. Not bad, she thought.

Ready, she called Maude and told her that she would walk to Notre Dame.

"Madame should be aware of her surroundings," the maid said. "These are not peaceful times, Madame. You've heard that a group of Republican women in the suburb have revived the beatings of the affluent. Just like during the years before the Revolution, Madame, aristocrats were stopped in the streets and beaten often so badly that these women were emotionally scarred for life. Madame, the same thing happened last night to Madame De Baudevant, she was pulled from her carriage—"

"Eh bien, Maude, I will not be intimidated by the sort," Gaby interrupted. "I suffered a great deal as well during the Civil War. It was not easy, Maude. I will be well, but, thank you." She marched to the door under the anxious gaze of her servants.

Out in the courtyard, she looked back and gave a tender look toward her theatre that was coming along rapidly. Last week, Maître Lauriot had been flabbergasted at the rapid advancement of the construction.

"I will help you in my spare time, Gabriella, we'll bring marvelous rendition of the great opéras to you, ma chère grande artiste." He'd proclaim with great gusto. She smiled at the repartie. Later that night she'd confided to Jean-Louis that lately the Maître spent more time in her theatre than at the opéra on the Boulevards.

Antoine, the gatekeeper and a few other men stood in attention by the porte-cochère, which faced the Quay De Bourbon. She noticed passersby staring. After all, only working girls would venture out without a chaperone. Nonchalantly, a group of men started following her more closely than necessary. She knew who they were. Jean-Louis always made sure that he knew her whereabouts every second of the day. Safe, she smiled and walked on. Before crossing the bridge to the Sainte Ile where the magnificent Notre Dame de Paris displayed its magnificent gothic architecture, the group of men that had been following closed in on her.

"Madame." A tall burly fellow came closer to her. "The bridge will be closed today. We would ask you to return home and take your carriage to the Pont Neuf. We are terribly sorry for the inconvenience," the man said curtly as if she should have known better.

"Very well, thank you," she responded just as curtly. She knew quite well that their jobs were on the line if perchance Jean-Louis found out that she had walked on over the bridge by herself.

She smiled as Antoine re-opened the wide gates once more. Her carriage was waiting and the footman had just lowered the steps. She stepped inside and sank in the red velvet banquette and laid her head on the tufted squabs. Her thoughts harked back to her youth with her cousin in Louisiana.

Philippe was an artistically endowed young man. They both loved singing and in the summer time they were sent to an opéra camp in the Old French Opéra House located in the French Quarter in New Orleans. The Cardinal's voice was angelic, she recalled. It filled the church where her uncle, Philippe's father, and his new family were parishioners. Jean-Christian Thornsen had developed an exceptional love for the arts, opéra, ballet, and the theatre. He was the largest contributor to the conservatory, providing large sum of money during the Opéra season. In New Orleans it was held from January to May because of the great heat and humidity that plagued the city in the fall. No great names would sign on if the timing of the season had not been changed to a more clement time.

Although emotionally, Philippe did not matter much to Jean Christian; he loved to show off his son every Sunday. He provided fabulous vocal coaches to the young Thornsen, whose voice was exceptional by nature. The old man accepted no slacking from his gentle son. He restricted his diet and beat him unmercifully if he showed any laziness towards his vocal duties. It came to pass that he wanted his son to go to Milan to study voice. Gossip had spread throughout the parish that the old Thornsen was contemplating having his youngest son castrated by the Vatican's surgeon who still performed the opération.

Jean Christian was in his last years and was convinced that his son had been granted a God-given gift. He should dedicate his life to music, he had told the local priest sternly—a castrato's voice does not change.

When he left for Milan, Philippe was only eleven years old. A few days before his twelfth birthday, he had been castrated—a late age by all standards, for if chosen by a maestro to pursue musical studies at some of the most prestigious conservatorios in Naples or in Rome, children as young as six would have the opération.

What had precipitated the father's decision was the realization that Philippe's mother Anne-Marie-Josephine, Gaby's aunt, had been sexually involved with the Archbishop of the parish whom she loved more than life itself. After too numerous to count sinful years, the cleric had decided to expiate his sins and had asked for a transfer to Africa. Anne-Marie-Josephine, devastated and unable to shake her grief, had admitted her escapades to her husband in a moment of weakness. Shortly thereafter, Philippe's mother had committed suicide. She had embarked on a riverboat on the Mississippi and dove in the murky water of the river, to her untimely death. This awful episode in the old man's life was the talk of all the salons in New Orleans. It had probably contributed to the old man's savage decision. Gossip ran rampant.

Philippe was sent back a year later. His vocal chords were not quite to the approval of the Italian maestros. "His recalcitrant personality made it impossible to submit to hours of assiduous musical instructions," had been the terse response from the director of the chorale.

Upon his return to New Orleans, Philippe had been banished to the plantation with the overseer as his closest ally.

Because of the proximity of their properties and the infinite love she possessed for her cousin, she had shown him the compassion he so dearly deserved. For the next seven years, they'd never left each other's sight for more than a few days. Their plantations were adjacent and since her mother greatly disliked her presence in the large home, she would stay with cousin Philippe to stay clear of her mother's cruel disposition.

Philippe had become very religious and both had started planning their lives outside of Louisiana.

He wanted to return to Rome and devote his life to his religious beliefs. She had decided to attend the Académie de Musique in Paris, France. Both had realized their well-kept secret dreams and within an hour, she'd be in his arms and Philippe in hers. She raised her eyes to the sky and thanked everyone in heaven for her grand chance in life.

* * *

Waiting patiently close to the parvis of Notre Dame, the Duke hoped to catch a glimpse of his wife before she went inside the Church.

He had news to discuss with her. The plans for their imminent trip to Italy had been pushed forward. He had spoken with Louis Napoléon earlier today, and had also been informed by the Emperor that her cousin Philippe, Cardinal Thornsen, the man he had heard so much about, was staying in Beaunne and was due to arrive tomorrow, late in the afternoon.

His residence was being prepared, Gabriella might want to send word to him to come and stay in their home. Finally, he would meet the 'super human', she so adored. Had he not been a priest, Jean-Louis pondered, he might have been terribly jealous of this giant of a man. He hated to question her about her past. For whatever odd reason, her life had started when she met him and he was quite pleased to leave it at that. Jealousy crept up along his spine when she spoke of another man. Gaby worshipped her cousin and was most protective of his every move. He would try to be pleasant on her account. The Adored One might be useful especially since the Emperor had told him he held a most powerful and influential position in the Vatican—a close confidant to the Pope on foreign affairs.

Something horrific had happened to him in his youth while in Rome. In any case, he was a very influential American religious figure in Rome, with close proximity to Pius the IX, the very Pope who had first approved of the Italian Nationalistic movement, until he had been banned from Rome and had to seek refuge in the castle of Gaëta. Pius the IX's own backlash against the movement, after his return to Rome in April 1850, was one that he and Philippe would have to mollify.

The Pontiff had taken an extreme conservative position and refused any alignment with the rich City States who had unified under the Italian flag in 1866. Although the Italian Southern States were poor, the emerging society in Northern Italy embraced modern trends and an economic revival. And why not? Jean-Louis thought. Very much aware of his diminishing political hold on Italian society, Pius the IX denounced the modern tendencies categorically in his 1864 Encyclical "Quanta Cura", which was closely followed by his Syllabys of Errors. In it he renounced paganism, rationalism, separation of Church and State, and socialism as non-Catholic. He placed all who believed in the latter under the threat of excommunication. Loud verbiage was common. Excommunication was still a threat that few considered irrelevant!

He and his French negotiators would have to pursue a very tight and cunning policy. In effect, the Pope no longer trusted the French Emperor although he enjoyed the security of the French troops that already protected Rome. Consequently to protect Louis Napoléon's new project, the Industrial Revolution and trade, the Pope and his Princes needed to come to an understanding. It was the French delegation's role to cajole the Pontiff to surrender Rome. It needed not be the calamity that the Pope invoked continually. Not a small task, he pondered.

No, in effect Philippe would be a most appropriate ally, the Duke concluded. He would just have to set ground rules. He would not permit Gabriella to overly dote on the cousin. That was all. The cleric would be well occupied. He would see to that.

While waiting patiently on the bank of the Seine for his wife, Jean-Louis evaluated the meeting he had had this morning with the Emperor and his advisors. Considering all that had unraveled politically in the past decade, he often wondered why he should even try to appease all sides. Yes, he had been bred for duty, but few listened to his concerns—which at this point were not the reunification of the Papal States to the kingdom of Italy, but rather the aggressive nature of the Prussian State smartly guided by Bismarck. Perhaps he and Gaby should embark once more on the *Tempète* and travel the world. They'd marvel in their love and good fortune. Gaby always emphasized how happy she had been during the heady days of the crossing. He smiled as he thought of his challenging wife with her resplendent smile and pert character. He loved her so. He was dreaming of course. To disregard the responsibilities that his nation and family heaped on his shoulders was tantamount to treason.

Nevertheless, he needed to increase security for her safety. Gabriella was closely monitored. Why frighten her? She loved her freedom and her spontaneity was always like a breath of fresh air to him. If he could control her safety without her knowledge—she would be the better for it.

And once and for all, he intended to cease his personal vendetta on anyone who befriended her. After all, Gaby adored him. She had already given up so much—her love for performing on stage and her independence—he would try to be more indulgent toward Philippe. Lest he forget, the Cardinal had not tried to dissuade her when her decision to return to Paris had been taken. They loved opéra and singing. The truth is that they only had had each other while growing up. Both had been neglected—perhaps even hated by their parents. No, he was going to be friend with Philippe. Gaby deserved the effort.

Hooves thumping heavily on the pavement brought him back to reality. Gaby's carriage had just arrived. By the by, following a tad too closely, he also noticed another black carriage with the Ecumenical Decal imprinted on its door. He began to walk over the short path between the Cathedral and the convent.

Earlier that day she had told him about little François who had been sick with a devastating flu. The boys and girls were in need of her ministrations and Gaby loved going to the orphanage, which was located inside the enclave of the Ursuline convent.

"There are many boarding ladies," she'd told him with a smirk, "some have come to purge a great love affair. Others come to acquire spirituality in their lives and then Jean-Louis," she'd give him a sideways glance, "I've met a few whose families or husbands have actually sent them there. Many appear to know you quite well, Jean-Louis. Were you the reason beyond some of these incarcerations, my love?" He had been flabbergasted at her frankness. Well perhaps, in his youth there had been times.

Unaware of her husband's presence, Gaby tapped on the window to let the coachman know that she wanted him to stop. Her carriage came to a halt very close to the location where Jean-Louis stood. He watched her climbed down from the carriage in front of the convent. The second carriage came to a complete halt as well in the narrow street perpendicular to the large place in front of Notre Dame.

He had a perfect view of the street and of the black heavy wrought iron gates of the orphanage.

Gaby climbed down gracefully and stood in front of the convent with smiling eyes directed at a tall, slim, dark, daunting young man in a long black robe with a miter on his head. With great anticipation, she waved and began to run toward the cleric who had just stepped down from the trailing carriage. Upon seeing Gaby, the cleric shouted her name. He ran to her with open arms as he reached and gathered her to him. He hugged her for a long time, kissed her tenderly on her neck and mouth, his hands roving over her shoulders and back. He gently pushed her away as if to admire all of her and quickly hugged her again tightly back in his arms, pressing her back to him, kissing her temple, her hair, her hands.

"Gabriella," he murmured, "I have been waiting years for this moment." She smiled back and lovingly returned his bear hug.

"Your fault Philippe," she responded. "I would have loved for you to attend our wedding." She replied with a bit of resentment in her voice.

The pretty Duchesse meant the world to Cardinal Philippe Thornsen. She had been the most important person throughout his life. He would refuse her nothing. Her delight was his bliss and its first prayers were always for her happiness. Philippe knew Gabriella was an angel. She was all love and intelligence and gave of herself freely to anyone who asked. Incomparable to any man or woman, he adored her with all his might and her appearance filled him with delight. He smiled and hugged her even closer.

The Duke stood, frozen in place while he stared intently at the affectionate display from afar. From his vintage point, it was a passionate encounter. So that was where she spent her days of *bienfaisance*—her volunteering work with the poor children of the city, he fumed? What a blatant lie! Instead, she flew in the arms of her love—a priest. There was no shame in that girl. The child she miscarried was probably not his, he pondered inflamed but from this fellow—a man of the cloth. No, he was wrong. She probably did not abort naturally. Durand had not seen anything unusual, now that he focused on it. How could he have been so taken by the story? He was not a choirboy after all. Her perfect, pure, naïve, little face that reflected confidence, warmth, passion, and consideration for the plight of those less fortunate than she was—all a ruse, a farce, a deceitful operetta where she reigned in real life as the deceitful, mean-spirited, conniving star!

Jean-Louis' fury mounted. He had been duped. Less and less lucid, incapable to observe any further, rage driven, he raced toward the interlaced couple. He came to a full halt in front of Gaby and the Cardinal. Beaming, she took a step toward her husband. His menacing demeanor flashed disaster. She perceived his inhuman glare. Self-survival and protection of her cousin were now primordial.

"Jean-Louis, non, don't, let me introduce you to . . ."

Instead, the Duke grabbed the Cardinal by his habit and with one blow to the stomach he sent the cleric flying on the cobblestones. Stunned, Philippe fell backwards and hit his head on the rim of the sidewalk as he rolled in the trash bins placed in front of the convent's gate. Jean-Louis turned his icy glare to Gaby.

"Get back in the carriage and go home. I'll deal with you later!"

"Philippe, run inside the Cathedral!" She warned her cousin as she bolted his way to intervene. Instead the Duke snatched her in flight walked a few steps back and threw her furiously in her carriage. He shouted orders to the footman and slammed the door on her face.

Gabriella managed to jump out of the carriage from the opposite door as Jean-Louis marched back to the fallen Cardinal. He was vicious when angered. He would kill poor, lovable, weak Philippe. She had always been the stronger of the two. She had always protected him as a child. Philippe's sweet, lovely, tender disposition, his sharp intellect and beautiful angelic voice. None of these virtues would hold against the wrath of Jean-Louis-Pierre De Pleyssis.

"Oh, dear God," she murmured.

Jean-Louis' fury intensified as she called out not to harm her cousin.

Not to harm him? Jean-Louis smoldered. What a noble and novel idea! He wanted to kill this pretentious, scandalous mouse of a man. He knew she was married, he seethed, and he came to Paris to hunt her down. Was he aware of the Ten Commandments? Thou should not covet another man's wife? If the man facing him was not such a coward, he would have married Gaby. The hypocrite!

Slowly the Cardinal began to rise. He was bent over the spot where Jean-Louis had pounced on him.

Relentless, the large French man came back to him, grabbed him by the arm, and gave him a right hook under the chin that send the poor cousin once more in the trash bins.

God must have been smiling upon them. Gaby intercepted a familiar carriage passing by. She forced the coach to a full stop by placing herself in front of it. Doctor Durand, Jean-Louis' family doctor, his wife and two brothers, were on their way to Grand Mass at ten o'clock in the Cathedral. They saw the drama develop and jumped out of their stagecoach. The young and spirited Gabriella needed to return to her carriage. One of the brothers escorted the pretty Duchesse in the doctor's coach. Stunned Durand asked a group of men mesmerized by the demonstration, to help in restraining the Duke.

"*C'est un Evêque, Jean-Louis-Pierre, allons, reviens à toi*. He's a Cardinal, Jean-Louis-Pierre, please take hold of your senses." The physician shouted.

Of all things, the Duke De Bourbonne fighting a Cardinal, he was going mad, the men were flabbergasted.

Although unaware of what had transpired, Durand was almost sure that Gabriella had something to do with it. He had just seen her carriage roll toward the Cathedrale from the Ile-Saint-Louis, the couple's residence while in Paris.

By now, le tout Paris was aware of the effects that the young American beauty had on one of the most desired French aristocratic man. It was going to be the subject of the day for weeks in all the salons. Jean-Louis had to be stopped.

From the corner of his eyes, Durand perceived Gabriella running toward the collapsed Cardinal as she looked with horror at the spectacle. Mon Dieu, the driver must not have realized that she had stepped down once more. She was taking great risks with her life as she pushed through the crowd to reach the mêlée.

Durand stepped behind her and grabbed her arm. He asked two of his escorts to help in restraining Jean-Louis-Pierre, while he managed to pull the young American out of the crowd and return her to his carriage with his wife as a chaperone.

"Please, Gabriella, do not stay, your sight will only aggravate the situation. I can handle it from now. I'll take the Cardinal to my clinic. Please climb back in. Do you want to return home or stay in our home until Jean- Louis-Pierre retrieves his senses?"

"No, I'll return home. Please, doctor, take care of my cousin. It's not his fault, just a misunderstanding that could turn deadly. Oh, mon Dieu, please, take Philippe away, please, doctor," she begged.

He accompanied her to his carriage although he was not aware of the full impact of the story. What was happening to the Duke? Had he lost his mind?

Quickly the old man returned to the site of the fight. There was a crowd holding on to Jean-Louis-Pierre and the Duke had retrieved his *sang-froid*. He starred icily at Philippe who was covered with blood and incapable of holding his head upright.

The doctor quickly placed the Cardinal back in his carriage and climbed in beside him. The driver was ordered to Durand's private clinic.

Jean-Louis gazed at the carriage. Suddenly aware that commoners were holding him back, he gave a brusque shoulder thrust that freed him as he marched back toward La Place de la Cathédrale. Parishioners, rich and poor waiting for High Mass ogled the Duke of Bourbonne. He straightened to its full height once more and sliced through the crowd.

His horse and carriage were waiting for him on the street along the Seine. He stopped, glanced at the new painters who had set up shops on the banks of the Seine. He stared aimlessly at their works. He remembered the real colors, the movement, the access of light, and the true to life characters and scene. How often he and Gabriella had walked along that stretch, hand in hand? She admired the new art, that had prompted him to take her to Montmartre for lunch, a popular meeting place for many Impressionists painters. She always wanted to stop by Notre Dame and light a candle in appreciation for all the good things God had granted her. She had in her own way re-ignited his faith in a Supreme Being. He had started praying again to a Prince of Peace and prosperity. It felt good, after so many years of doubt about his faith. He had retrieved some sense of spirituality. Where was it now? He could not believe what had just transpired. He took one last look at the scene and at the banks of the Seine, oblivious to the hundreds of people watching him. He decided to climb in the carriage rather than to ride his horse, which he had wanted to do at first to regain his home quickly to teach her who was going to have the last word in this ordeal. It was time to take a hold of his emotions and calm his temper. She was only twenty-three—just a child after all. He wanted this nightmare to be a great mistake but quickly logic returned. The little witch connived it all—the work of charity at the convent and everything she'd charmingly fed him. After all why not, he was well regarded in Paris. It made sense for her to reconnect their relationship, after the religious louse had left her in Grenoble. But how could she have been so amorous this morning? She clung to him. All theatrics, he told himself. She was good. He would let her explain. There might be a perfectly sound reason for the behavior he'd just observed. As he reached the boulevard Saint Louis and the residence, he saw her carriage parked in front of the gates. Was she planning a quick get away? He raged. The gates opened, the carriage stopped in front of the great marble steps, the Duke climbed out, slammed the door shut and stormed in his house.

"Where is Madame?" he shouted fiercely.

"Upstairs, Monsieur, in your apartment," declared Maude. She was alarmed that she'd revealed her mistress whereabouts, but even more frightened to lie openly to the Duke.

He flung his light coat on the floor. His loose white cotton shirt showed his immense muscular body. He ran upstairs, and walked in the library. Over to the sidebar he poured himself a glass of brandy first. Hopefully the warmth of the cognac would restrain his fury. He sat down on his large leather chair crossing one of his long muscular legs over his right knee.

All the while Jean-Louis forced himself to recall all facts prior to entering their apartments—anything that would bring to mind happier times. The brandy was working its warmth. His anger dissipated as he imagined her cute little face looking at him with adoring eyes. He felt her passionate body close to his as she gently woke him up this morning. How she pleased him. Perhaps it was harmless. After all, she had been a virgin when they made love on his ship—he was certain. After all these years, if there had been any relationship between Gaby and Philippe, the priest would have taken her much earlier. Yes, there was a reason behind this carnival. He was going to give her a chance to explain. What about her faith? That counted for something. She couldn't. She just wouldn't. Conflicted, he stood up and began to climb the long staircase to their apartment.

Then his mind refocused to the early afternoon. How he had caught her in her cousin's arms. What about if she really was in love with the priest? At this moment he could not fathom his life without her. Of course, on his ship maybe she'd thought she had to give in. Surely she might have thought that she'd be hurt or raped or perhaps given a room close to the mariners. She had told him on the ship to kill her first; he remembered that quite well now when teasingly in Villefranche she'd reiterated candidly that she would have been a fool not to give in to his sexual advances. Yes, it might have been easier to give in to the priest in Grenoble, for the two of them to consummate their sexual liaison. There was the reason for her late arrival in Paris, he concluded fiercely.

His anger re-ignited. He bolted upstairs to their room. He would give her a chance to explain, he told himself, and then rein her in and set rules. She was going to follow and obey willingly—or else.

Chapter Forty-Nine

As he walked from his private study upstairs to their apartment, he rationalized and compartmentalized their new lives. He loved her body and her sharp mind. He did not need her absolute love. He would get over her. This was the life of ninety-nine percent of Parisian couples. He would return to his leisurely and wandering life—and the priest was not coming to Rome with him. That was it. Louis Napoléon could take it or leave it.

Pleased at the self-control he displayed, he downed the last bit of scotch in the glass and left the empty vessel on a secretary. Somewhat appeased and rational he continued to stride to their room. Seconds later, he felt the sexual urge that tortured him every time he walked these halls. The scent of her perfume was everywhere like an aura who would not quit. Might as well start their new chapters now, he thought. He would take her—willingly or not. She was his wife and she would abide.

The door half ajar, he stopped and observed her.

Gaby walked back and forth from their bed to the fireplace. She kneaded her lovely hands and looked up to the ceiling as if she would find an inspiration written in between the painted roses and cherubim on the walls. Perhaps she'd dreamed of a miracle that would stop this horrid nightmare—except that it was not a dream.

She was frightened to death by now. Maude had not helped much. She'd heard Jean-Louis come in--over forty minutes ago. She had thought of going down to explain, but she had decided against it after Maude had expressed that Monsieur looked terrifying.

"*Madame, laissez les portes ouvertes*, leave the doors open, just in case you need to escape quickly," the maid had said.

"Why Maude, have you ever seen Monsieur in such a furious state?" she'd questioned.

"Non, Madame. Monsieur was always very calm and unresponsive. It's only been since your arrival that he gets into these massive furies." Realizing that she had said too much, the maid continued with compassion "oh, Madame, I am sorry. Monsieur must love you very much to enter into such states of madness when it comes to your relationship!"

A lot of help, thought Gaby. "Thank you Maude, I will be fine. You may go."

The maid left, knowing that she had made matters worse for her mistress. Why was it that she could never find the right words of comfort? She brooded over sorrowfully. She walked out and almost stepped on the Duke's toes. She saluted him.

Happen what may, Gaby finally told herself, she could not stand it any longer. She strode toward the half-open door. There he was, leaning on one of the pillars right outside of the double entrance doors. She stepped backwards as she wriggled her hands—terrified. She quickly retreated in the room.

Guilty as hell, he told himself, all doubts evaporated. She was the mistress of the priest. He let himself in and kicked both doors shut with his boots. He strode to the fireplace, and once more he stopped by one of the table to fix himself another brandy. Glass in hand, he stood in front of a large white and gold satin canapé and while he stared at her he crashed heavily on the sofa. His glare fixated on her. He stared at her so severely that she trembled.

Where should she start? She knew what he had seen looked horribly bad and now in hindsight, she wished she had had more time to think of words that would have mollified him. She wandered if he had given Philippe a fatal blow. No, he would not be here. Poor Philippe, so unaware of what he had so candidly started.

"Yes?" Jean-Louis started. He shot a venomous look in her direction. "I'm waiting Gaby, what do you have to say for yourself? What lies are you going to speak to try to cover up this abominable behavior? As you can see, I am quite calm now. I'll test your negotiating skills, my chère."

"Jean-Louis, please listen to me," she pleaded, "I swear to you this is not what it appears to be."

"Start by telling me—what does it appear to be like, Gaby?" he demanded.

Tortured, she tried to explain. "You know Jean-Louis, Philippe is my cousin, he loves me like a sister and he is the only true brother I have ever known. We took care of one another—always, but never in the way you are thinking of. Never."

"So let me ask you, Gaby—you would find it totally normal if I grabbed my very distant cousin Marie-Hélène-Murielle by her hips and kissed her tenderly on the mouth, the neck, pressed my body into hers, let my hands rove all over her back in a middle of a Parisian street?" He was shouting by the time he finished.

"No," she responded furiously, "of course not, that is sick!" The thought alone was repulsive. "It would be different with you, because you'd want to bed her and I could not bear that behavior. I could not come to terms with being a scorned wife!"

He shot her a contemptuous glare. She did not inculcate the comparison, too involved in her own safety and Philippe's.

"Jean-Louis, please tell me—did you hurt Philippe? Is he all right? I could not bear knowing that he was hurt because of me." She said it all in the same breath. As soon as it was pronounced, she realized the enormity of her demented questions.

That was too much for Jean-Louis to bear. All the talk of self-control he had been so proud of earlier went out the windows. He rose.

She swallowed hard and took a step backward.

"Let me answer your last question to put your mind at ease before I beat you." He paced steadily toward her. His voice was grave and low.

"Gaby, I would have gladly killed him if Durand and his entourage had not been on their way to attend mass. They stopped to help him and to hold me back. You are right, there is a God and his God protected him. It's you turn, now. I don't think you'll have his luck. Perhaps you should have become a nun after all!"

Relieved at first that her cousin had not been gravely injured, she stood still for an instant. He was with Doctor Durand, she sighed, appeased. She had had an instant of respite. Her foolishness blasted in her mind! She retreated backwards quickly and began running. In retrospect she should have galloped out of the room when he had told her that Durand had taken Philippe with him. Now he was marching upon her and she looked for words to assuage his anger. None were forthcoming.

"I adore you, Jean-Louis, you know that," she let her emotions pour out of her. "I know it looked bad, I know it now, but I have nothing to ask your forgiveness about. Except perhaps for the joy to be reunited with Philippe. Again I did not do anything wrong. I did not deceive you. Philippe, is my cousin," her voice possessed a commanding tone he had not heard from her before. "I have not done anything wrong, I wouldn't do anything that could hurt our love, our union. How can you even doubt my love? I have given up everything for you—my world, my musical dreams, my independence . . ." She looked intently in his eyes. She saw a flicker of hope in his glance. He stopped and bit his lip.

She had placed an ounce of doubt in his mind. Perhaps he had been wrong, he thought. After all, she had not returned Philippe's caresses—just his hugs and smiles. Maybe Philippe was secretly in love with his wife and her kind nature understood the pain the priest experienced as a child.

She pursued this fallibility. With all the love she could muster in her most tender voice, she spoke to the volume of passion that she knew resided in his heart. Her green eyes locked on his icy blues.

"I love you, Philippe—Jean-Louis. That slip of the tongue dispersed all his doubts. She bolted towards her maid's door that automatically had closed when he had kicked their bedroom doors shut. She desperately reached for the door handle. It resisted. He reacted viciously and grabbed one of her forearms and he held it so tightly that it became numb. He turned her around savagely and his enraged face stared down at her as he grabbed her other wrist. She thought he would make good on his threat. Instead, he squeezed harder, wild brutal icy blue eyes focused on her from head to toe. She screamed—her fierce shriek brought him back to the moment at hand. He released her. A violent pain in her lower abdomen forced her to loose her footing. She fell backward onto the rosewood carvings of her nightstand. The intricately carved vase de Sèvres he had offered to her on her birthday tipped. Shards of porcelain shattered on the carpet.

The table held her back and she retrieved her sense of stability for just an instant. That was the end. He would kill her, she thought. Another paralyzing cramp gravitated down her spine. She fell down to the floor. He had no intention on letting the ordeal go. Instead like a vulture he stood by the table waiting for her to stand back up. The humiliation was worse than the pain. She hated him. She would kill him if given a chance!

"So, Gaby, you have changed my name to Philippe?" He was not appeased by his brutality and her apparent confusion and lack of response. Your priest has never spoken to you about adultery? What a shame. You might have averted this little scene had you been more careful. Both of you did a pretty good job at hiding from my men in Grenoble. The world looked for you. Not even the ablest detectives in Europe could locate your amorous whereabouts!" he shouted venomously. "Is it this semblance of marital security that now gives you the courage to embrace in a public street? Well, ma chère let me set you straight—my name is Jean-Louis. The priest will be sent back to Rome and you, ma chérie, will be at my disposition whenever I deem to have you emotionally and physically. Is that understood?"

She nodded. By now, the pain in her middle was so violent that she would have nodded to her executioner.

Tears streamed down her face but her avenging green eyes looked up with repugnance.

She swallowed hard. "Stop the insanity. Move away. You're going to kill me."

He looked down at her for a second as if there was a moment of clarity in his blind fury. She pushed him away. The tenderness in her womb was excruciating, but it also gave rise to rage. She felt an intense strength emanating from her every pore and in a superhuman way, she kicked his shin swiftly and powerfully. Surprised, he stepped back. That was all that she needed. The lithe ballerina body was quickly out of his reach. She ran behind the table that had steadied her and picked the broken fallen vase. She threw it at him with the last of the remaining flowers but missed her target. He stood up ominously, flabbergasted at her strength of character. Well, she was going to learn to suppress her impulses, he thought.

Now, fear, madness and self-survival all wrapped up in one took hold of her. She reached for the small Baccarat crystal star with its razor-edge rays pointed to the heavens. This, as well, had been given to her to set her jewelry in as they returned home from their soirées. Two hearts were attached to one another on a rounded base shaped in a single heart. The rays on the stars had very sharp pointed edges and this time she used the focus she practiced while hunting ducks and hit him right below the heart, missing it by less than an inch. Much of the crystal glass shattered as it reached his gargantuan chest, but one of the edges pierced his shirt, punctured the skin, and inserted itself in his chest. Blood sipped on his snowy white shirt. He touched the area, surprised at the damage she had inflicted.

"Not bad, Gaby," he said admiringly, as he saw the blood on his shirt.

"I hope you bleed to death at my feet. I'll kick you while you're down . . . on your last breath," she shouted through tear-laden eyes.

He stared at the woman he adored. She had no other emotions left in her except for the hatred emanating from her curvaceous little body. She looked up at him impassively when he reached for her and pulled her to his chest. His blood stained her clothing. He tore the dress off her body as he picked her up and tossed her in their bed.

"No," she screamed. She had not expected this form of humiliation, "don't you dare!" she screeched as he covered her body with his large and powerful frame.

He undressed while still lying on her, and brutally spread her legs apart. She smelled and tasted his blood. She caught a glimpse of the area where the crystal had ruptured his skin, blood dripped on her, it also tinted their satin sheets.

Nothing affected him now. He had fought so many battles and been injured more often than he liked to remember. Free of his clothing, his hands grabbed her breasts while his manhood drove hard inside her.

Even at the time when she wished him dead; she felt her body respond to his touch, her nipples hardened, and her mouth longed to be invaded by his—how despicable. He kissed her hard and cruelly, and placed his mouth brutally on hers as she repeatedly turned her face sideways. Tired of her fighting him, he took his pleasure, meanly, brutally, possessively—and then it was done. She was left without an ounce of self-esteem. He had taken it all. He stayed inside her for a moment. She was crying openly now, sobs engulfed her soul and convulsed her body.

He fell back on his pillow and gave in to the urge of looking at her one more time. She saw pain in his eyes.

"Get out of our room," he said fiercely.

To be mortified in such a manner was more than she could stand. She slowly wiped her tears with the bloody sheets, grabbed the coverlet, wrapped herself inside it, and rolled out of bed.

This last gesture had not escaped his eyes. That day on the Tempête passed in front of his eyes. It always affected him.

He watched her walk painfully to his side of the bed. She looked fierce, blood on her cheeks, wrath in her eyes. Shamed to his core that he could have stooped so low as to take her like a harlot, he lowered his eyes. When she had called him Philippe with such passion in her voice, he had lost all reason. Still, a harlot she was. His response, however, was inadmissible.

Her wild brown mane hung perfectly over the top of her opulent breasts. He wondered what she would do next.

She got very close to his face, fury and hate mixed in the green eyes staring into his.

"You, inhumane snake! Can you truly look into your heart and believe that I would cheat on you in the arms of another man. You know," she emphasized, "my love for you held no boundaries. I gave up everything for you—my art, my independence, my friends, and my country. I know why you act like a wild beast; you cannot stand not having full control of my every movement, my every thought if they are not about you; you are jealous of everything and anything that gives an equal or superior timeframe to my attention. Deny it, you coward! Twice, you have destroyed my faith in you. There will not be a third one. I'm returning home to America. Time is a great healer."

She stopped for just an instant, her eyes filled with tears once more and without realizing it, she spoke her thoughts aloud. "We have so many wonderful memories . . . I only want to remember those and take them with me—forever." She lingered a bit too long on her past dreamy life, then her eyes refocused on the tyrant lying in her bed.

His gaze did not reveal what he was thinking but his words left no room for hope.

"Gaby, leave my room with your coverlet solely. If I see you leave with anything larger that your cup of coffee, I'll lock you up in this room when I take my leave in the morning and let you out at night when I return. Is that suitably curtailing your independence, my love? I have a full battalion of security guards under my command. Clear, Gaby?"

As he threatened to make her his prisoner, he rolled over and walked to his dressing room. He rung out to Maude and ordered a cleaning crew immediately. He turned to Gaby.

"Call Dr. Durand and ask him to come as soon as possible. Gaby, write a note to Durand, I'll dictate."

"Do it yourself, I'm not your personal secretary!"

He started toward her again threateningly. This time she stood still, fearless.

"So what, you decided that I was not sufficiently punished? You can beat me to death now I will not retreat? I hate you!"

He took in a big breath, sighed and pulled on the cord to call his secretary.

"Gaby you are not taking the easy way out. You're not making it easy on yourself."

"Keep your condescending comments to yourself. I have never taken the easy road, Jean-Louis. I was raised on a plantation with over two hundred people, although most had freedom papers, their freedom was limited. I understand what it feels like to be subdued and managed. I remember Tita and Gustaf telling Philippe and I." He was visibly shaken at the mention of Philippe's name. "Life was not always easy for me," she continued, "but I chose my battle and made decisions, and by and large I always won the war because I emotionally detach myself from it all. Now my only weakness is you, but it will not always be so. I will not forget today."

Shedding silent tears, she turned away from him, reached for her peignoir, and started toward the door. As she reached for the gold handle, a sharp pain ripped through her abdomen. Momentarily she was immobilized. She had all to do to keep from falling over but just as quickly the pain subsided.

Jean-Louis wondered another pregnancy? When did she last have the flow? Now that he thought about it, it seemed longer than the usual four weeks. With all the changes in her life this month it probably was fairly common to be late. Why did he feel so horrible? He had caught her kissing another man, for God's sake!

He looked in the mirror and was startled by the large pool of blood that covered his chest. His wife would have been a formidable adversary in the Civil War. The Yankees might have needed a couple of extra regiments to rein her in. A pretty bad cut he had there—inches away from his heart.

Durand arrived as the Duke was cleaning his wound. The maids were cleaning the room. Minutes ago it looked like a ravaged battlefield.

"Jean-Louis what has happened here? Where is the little angel? Is she fine?"

"Yes of course, I'm the one who called you, right? The little angel inflicted this wound. She missed first with the vase and then she had to finish the job with a many-faceted crystal star!"

Durand laughed as he gave Jean-Louis a shot.

"It does not seem too bad. You'll survive. These darn things are more painful than bullets—sometimes they splinter. It is close to a main artery, Jean-Louis-Pierre, so keep it clean and bandaged until the scab starts to cover the wound—one to two weeks, my friend. Where is Gabriella? I would like to talk to her. My patient, Cardinal Thornsen asked about her. What happened Jean-Louis-Pierre?" the doctor questioned.

"The Cardinal is fortunate that his lucky angel, Dr. Durant, came to his rescue," Jean-Louis responded sarcastically.

There was a knock at the door and the sound of a door opening.

"Doctor?"

"Oh, mon Dieu, what has happened to you, Gabriella? Let me see, let me fix that beautiful face, Gabriella, you have blood all over—oh, Mon Dieu, come here my poor child." He pulled her in his arm. She pushed him away and tried to continue to speak. To no avail, sobs prevented her to catch her breath to formulate the information she needed to know about Philippe. The old man kept her in his arms, as he tried to console this adorable young woman he had grown to feel such great affection for.

Shocked, he turned to Jean-Louis. The Duke was always so reserved. He would never have expected anything of the sort. These two always looked so in love.

"It may be impersonal, Jean-Louis-Pierre, but my father and I have been attached to your regal family for so long, I would like to understand this morning. Why, Jean-Louis-Pierre? The Cardinal is castrated for heaven's sake; surely it had nothing to do with jealously as everyone suspects?"

The doctor was checking Gaby's pulse as he spoke.

Stunned, the Duke stared at his physician and then Gabriella. Philippe castrated? He remembered now.

"Leave us!" he ordered suddenly.

"No, please, doctor, how is Philippe?" Gaby sighed. She held on to the doctor's hand.

Durand was placed in an impossible situation. He realized that he had unveiled something important. Whatever had transpired, he knew that being a third party in this altercation was not where he should be. He decided that he would wait outside.

"Your cousin is resting. He is fine, Gabriella." He whispered calmly to Gabriella, "but I . . . believe that both of you have something to say to one another. I'll be right outside, Gabriella," he responded kindly.

Gaby was not about to talk to her husband about anything. She just wanted to ask more questions of Durand about her cousin's health and where he was staying since his residence was in the process of being refurbished. She quickly let go of the rotund medical man and started back toward her music room where she had taken refuge. Jean-Louis stepped in front of her and posed his large hands on her shoulders.

"Why didn't you tell me?" he inquired venomously.

"I did on the ship, obviously another tarnished memory. I was under the impression then that you hung to each and every one of my words. Castration should be a big enough event for a man." She pulled away.

"Enough, Gaby, whose husband inflict such a horrific act on your beloved cousin?"

Shocked at the unending insults, she stepped forward and hit him with all her might at the exact location where the star had punctured his skin.

The giant facing her gasped and bent forward as he held the chair next to him for control.

"Gabriella," he murmured ominously. It was the first time he had called her Gabriella ever since he had nicknamed her Gaby on the ship. "You are stepping over the boundaries of intelligence and self-survival. You may choose your own battles and win most of the time, but I can assure you right now, you will not win this battle between you and I, the physical one, if you know what I mean."

She swallowed hard and looked up at him with disdain.

"I told you on the ship, his father was an aficionado of opéra. Philippe was sent to Rome at eleven to study his voice. He sang with the conservatorios in Milan. After a year, his father was asked by the maestro for the permission to have Philippe castrated so as to keep his angelic voice. The father agreed. Philippe became a castrato." She retorted bitterly.

"Tell him to never kiss you on the mouth again—ever." He walked out and rejoined his physician. She heard the two men talking outside in the sitting room.

Durand asked to see Gaby. Jean-Louis retorted that Maude was helping her with her toilette. The muffled sound of their boots descending the staircase spoke clearly to Gaby. What had happened hours earlier had reached its final denouement. She heard Dr. Durand and Jean-Louis speak about the Emperor's soirée this very evening. Jean-Louis told him that he would attend to face the music.

That easy, she thought, he had almost taken two lives and now he played the great martyr, and would 'face the music.' Why had she married? She should have run away at the altar. She swallowed bitterly.

She slowly returned to her closet and grabbed nightwear and her furs and asked Maude to fix her bed in the room across the hall—her music room. Tomorrow she'd move herself downstairs, closer to freedom.

Maude hurried close to her mistress and tenderly washed her. The poor woman was visibly distressed. She held Maude close to her heart for a long time and assured her that all was well and will continue to be well.

"Trés bien, Madame," the maid spoke, relieved.

Thank God, Philippe had been spared. Now she just wanted to be left alone. She would find a solution to the horrific ordeal that had just transpired. She walked down to the second floor—her music books were in the library. She stayed ensconced in her favorite chair for a long time, and then climbed back upstairs. She curled up on the sofa next to the fireplace, and sang herself to sleep.

Chapter Fifty

After his meeting with the Emperor, the Duke rode home. He followed her scent to their room and found it empty. Bitterly, he recalled his banishing orders.

In her music room, he found her curled up under the coverlet. A glacial shoulder wedged out from under the brown mink coat and her soft brown curls cascaded over her eyes. A music book had fallen on the carpet.

Naturally, lights illuminated the room and with it he could see firsthand, the pain he had inflicted. He recalled her cute little wink in the ocean near his castle in Loire. Instead the skin around her pretty eyes was swollen from all the tears she'd shed.

He looked at her for a long time. Thank God she had not been at the soirée tonight. Everyone gossiped about their fight and her beloved priest. The new American Ambassador of the United States had been the first to make allusion to the brawl earlier this morning.

"Jean-Louis-Pierre, I understand that the Cardinal you almost killed today will be traveling with you to Italy. I got it from the most reliable source, the Emperor himself. I presume you two don't get along well?" He'd questioned humorously.

With a half-smile on his face, Jean-Louis thought about the remark. Actually, he liked Eliju B Washburne. They had worked together in Boston and the diplomat had introduced him to the architect Bull Finch, who built his home in Louisburg Square in Beacon Hill. He was new in Paris and wanted to make a name for himself.

"I was not aware that it was the case," he responded, thinking that he was going to change the Emperor's plans. He was not about to see his wife and her cousin cavort in front of him. *Bien placé ou pas*! Well-heeled or not!

"Where is Gabriella, anyway?" One of the men in Washburne's entourage ventured.

Jean-Louis had not answered and had walked away from the group. He knew that he and Gabriella were the talk of the evening. Frankly, he did not care. The Emperor knew he was the one who would see through the negotiations—the most qualified, surely. But if he chose someone else, he would be delighted. Gaby and he would have plenty of adventures in a much safer venue. He only went through this exercise because of his responsibility to name and country. Therefore, everyone would abide by his rules—including the Emperor.

As he stood standing over his wife, shame overwhelmed him. Poor Gaby, he thought, she aimed to fix everyone, and more often than not, she was demonized for the good her selfless demeanor provided. It always worked against her. She was often misunderstood. Perhaps it was the great cultural divide, he pondered, and he was the product of that very traditional society he often excoriated. He had lost control today. It would never happen again. He gently picked her up and she rolled toward his chest, as she did every time she fell asleep before he returned home. Her weight against his wound hurt like hell. He deserved it. He should carry her around the whole house all night to expiate for the pain that he had inflicted upon her.

He carefully placed her in their bed, tucked her in, and curled up against her. Tomorrow, she would push him away and make his life pure hell—for a while anyway, and then she'd forget. He promised himself that this was the first and last time he would lose control. He gently turned her back against his chest. He curled up against her curvaceous body and fell asleep.

An urgent shriek woke him up in the middle of the night. Gaby twisted, grasped his torso, she gasped for air. Simultaneously, a wet sticky substance slid on her leg. Wide-awake, by now, he turned to the ashen and unresponsive body lying next to him.

"Oh, mon Dieu, Gaby, where are you bleeding from?"

He called the servants to summon Durand immediately.

Gaby was coming in and out of consciousness, doubled over. Half an hour later Durand was in the residence again.

"I have awful cramps, doctor. I feel like passing out every time it comes." She had a hard time speaking French.

"Speak English, darling, I'll translate." She pushed him away and continued to speak to the doctor.

"It feels like what I experienced in Grenoble when I lost the baby," she gasped.

"Jean-Louis, we should try to take her to my hospital. It's very private. She will have better care if she needs a procedure."

"Very well." The Duke prepared to lift her from the bed.

"Where am I going?" she managed to shout, frightened. "No, I'm not going. Please stop, I'm scared. Jean-Louis are you coming?" She asked terrified, before the new wave of spasms sapped her breath away.

He took her fully in his arms. Maude placed her black mink coat around her shoulder.

"I will not leave you for an instant, Gaby, everything will be fine, darling." He hurriedly descended the staircase and placed her gently in the carriage.

Inside the carriage, she regained a bit of self-control. She soon realized who was holding her in his arms. She recoiled from his embrace in horror.

"Take your murderous hands off me!" She tore his hands from her body and swung at him.

"Gaby—"

She continued with all the might she could muster to beat his arms away in uncontrolled anger.

"Don't touch me! Get away! I hate you with all my being!"

Afraid of convulsions, he held her arms behind her back. Immobilized into inaction she hurled her vocal fury at him.

"I wish you were dead—dead, you understand!"

He sensed her fever mounting. Now, more importantly, he needed to appease her. She had told him earlier in no uncertain terms she would like to see him bleed to death at her feet. He was also very confident that at that very moment—she meant it.

Her Italians roots resurfaced and her rage needed to be reined in for both of their sakes. She had retrieved some color and was now more alert, less frightened. He was still bleeding profusely.

He smiled down at her and wrapped his arms around her tighter. She pushed him away, squirming cleverly out of his embrace just to find herself restrained even more tightly. He was more forceful this time around, for the life of him she would stay put. He glanced down once again, bent down, and brushed his lips to her temple and down to her earlobe, her voluptuous breasts teased his gaze, they spoke to him as she breathed her venom at him. He let his gaze stayed there for a moment longer, while he took in the outraged insults that she felt no remorse at articulating.

His left side burned like hell. Remorse. How could he have retorted to such a sordid behavior against a woman of all things—a woman he adored more than life itself? He could not fathom such reaction—so terribly out of character for him. With Gaby, however, each thought, each action, was out of character. He felt like a stranger in his own skin when it came to her. Mercurial emotions flowed freely, stoking unknown chords that he could not comprehend. He had had to admit to himself after they had moved in together that his life revolved around her.

The squalid tribulation reinforced the already known facts. How could he have known that the imbecile kissing his wife fully on the mouth, in the middle of town, in front of the convent where she purported to do *des oeuvres de bienfaisance,* volunteer work, was her castrated cousin! He expected that her trust and belief in God would make her forget the dispute and forgive his repulsive demeanor.

Now, he had to resign himself to her coolness.

To complicate the circumstances even further, the trip to Italy on the Tempète would set hurdles to her daily routine. Yes, she would have more freedom than at the time of her last passage, however, submitting to his rule was a must on his ship. Gaby was accustomed to do whatever she wanted. To be in the precarious situation of near total submission to his law would be another source of contention between them. She was not going to like being under his command once more and yet it was primordial. Without discipline and total submission to his imperative on the ship, her very life could be in grave danger.

Mariners were hardened and often devious men. Some had committed murders, rape, and robberies and the slightest weakness on his part would place everyone at risk. He did travel with his ship and he always made sure that his security ran a background check on the mariners sailing for him. Nevertheless, a mariner's life was arduous and the men traveling the oceans were adventurers for the most part. Since the mid 1850's he had traveled the South China seas and he'd been involved in the first French invasion into Peking. The second opium war had forced China to open up more trading ports. It also allowed for the navigation of the Yangtze River. Sailors on these trips were hardened men who saw the least bit of kindness as weaknesses. From one war to the next—he had loved that life. Now however there was Gaby and he loved her more.

On this particular mission he would be traveling with the French delegation, more niceties were *de rigueur,* lessening the difficulties that usually arose during the long crossings. All the same, he would not change his ways of commanding to suit the lovely soul next to him.

He hated the stupid Cardinal. Why hadn't he stayed in Rome where he belonged? He now wished he had more time to make her forget his unimaginable behavior but they had just a few more months in Paris. He would have liked to leave before the holidays to avert the storms. It was unlikely, however. Either way, by the end of January, they would be on their way. The Pope needed support and the Emperor finality.

All of a sudden, looking at Gaby who was now quite serene. He longed for his adopted country. He had spent a few Christmases in Boston and for the first time in his life, Christmas had been meaningful. He had experienced family warmth, not what the French and English called 'colonial unpolished mannerism,' but real caring for others during the festive times.

Instead of Italy, he would have preferred to take her to New England, to share with her the savage beauty of this New World expanding its horizons westward—her country.

In the carriage, he'd zoned out, oblivious of the fury and frustration she showed at being restrained in his arms. She must have stopped at one point, realizing the futility of the effort. He looked down at her. Thank God, the storm had passed. She was still, quiet and serene. He might have killed her, for God's sake. Just the thought sent chills along his spine.

"I love you, Gaby," he murmured in her ears with all the passion he felt for her.

"What a novel idea. I always imagined that the word 'love' defined the pleasure that one can give to another human being, to respect morally and physically. You must have read a different version of the definition. Being violated by your own husband is not an act of love," she continued, leaving sarcasm behind and retrieving her furious and outraged tone of voice. "You do not know love, never have, and never will! You're just a beast and I hate you! You're just a mad man!"

He did not retort. He consoled himself with the thoughts that her words were the only weapons to inflict upon him—to retaliate somehow. She would come around. Patience was necessary now.

He brushed a gentle kiss on her forehead.

"Gaby, ever since I've met you, I have often questioned the distinction between a passionate love like ours and madness?"

He continued kissing her cheeks and neck and bent gently down to kiss her exposed breasts.

The loss of blood had weakened her strength and resolve. She meekly pushed him away. An immense tiredness engulfed her mind and body. She would leave him as soon as she felt better. She had a grand life to lead and being a controlled wife was not in her plans.

Finally, they arrived at the clinic. Durand's staff opened the large black and gilded iron gates. The carriage entered in the courtyard. Within minutes they closed the gates behind them. No need to have press coverage of the hospitalization, however distasteful the marital dispute had been. Tomorrow was going to be bad enough. All newspapers would cover the Duke beating the Papal envoy to Paris in front of Notre Dame. The Catholics were already upset with Louis Napoléon over his appointment of a lay minister of education and earlier of his secret dealings with Cavour, the prime minister of Victor

Emanuel II, first King of the reunited Italy. The Emperor treaded a fine line—he needed to appease the liberals but also the Catholics.

Chapter Fifty-One

The Duke and the Duchesse had spent the day in the same room. He was positioned on a long faint divan with his long legs and feet resting on top of her bed. She was pretending that he was not there. She would look through him if a nurse or Durand entered to check on both of the patients.

The doctors were perplexed with Gaby. The bleeding had subsided. She appeared to be just fine.

"It may just have been a heavy menstrual cycle," Durand said hesitantly. "We might need to take further steps when you emotions stabilize a bit, Gabriella."

In a strange turn of events, Jean-Louis had lost quite a bit of blood. The crystal heart had severed a large vein. It had just missed the large artery.

"Amazing aiming skills, Gabriella. You'll be in good hands Jean-Louis-Pierre." Both men laughed.

A nurse changed Jean-Louis' bandages several times that day. Jealous sentiments mounted inside her. I'm morally challenged, she repeated to herself, and looked away.

Durand made his rounds several times during the day. Naturally she asked about Philippe.

"How is he, doctor? Will he survive? Is he in massive pain?

"No," Durand said. "By now he feels better than both of you. Le Cardinal is recuperating quite well and he asked after you, Gabriella. He sends his love."

Jean-Louis was livid. She did not care if her husband lived or died. She had not been shy to throw it again in his face this very afternoon, but yet she felt sorrow for the person who had caused this horrific ordeal.

"I would not help you if you were bleeding to death, I'd kick you to activate your departure to the other world!" she'd reiterated this morning. But the little witch was concerned about the moronic cousin who had brought about this sordid episode. Kissing her the way he had when he was well aware that she was married.

He endured her coolness during the day. When night fell, however, he pretended to be tired. The nurses were at his beck and call. All were amazed that the man who truly needed their ministrations—he was still bleeding—would sit devoted by his wife's bedside when she seemed to be recovering quite nicely. They had seen the newspaper headlines and most probably heard the gossip. Naturally, the distinguished Jean-Louis-Pierre De Pleyssis must have had reason to act so rashly. He should be the one in bed and resting, the nurses opined in the hallways.

Jean-Louis nodded to the nurse to dim the lights.

"Jean-Louis, are you here?" Gaby called out momentarily.

"Yes, Gaby," he responded sweetly.

He stood up, walked to the side of her bed, and rolled in. Gently he took her little body in his arms. Immediately she reclined against his chest, reached for his hand and placed it across her breast. He would easily have given up years of his life to circumvent the incident yesterday.

"Why do they turn off the lights in a hospital? They don't in the United States," she stated flatly.

"You're in France, ma chérie. Remember the old adage, when in Rome—why and when were you in a hospital, Gaby?" he demanded suddenly curious.

She did not answer him but tapped his hand. Then secure in his embrace she fell asleep.

The next morning, Durand walked in smiling at the sleeping couple.

She quickly sat up upright and disentangled herself brusquely from Jean-Louis. He laughed at her pride, but duly rolled out of bed. The cover that she pretended to erect to hide her insecurities resurfaced. She had told him that something had happened in her childhood, a horrific nightmare that had left her with this uncertainty—the fear of the dark. She was not quite sure why, she'd shared.

All in all, it served him well. He never pursued it further than that. The past was the past and she had tools to handle this emotional setback. Edison had been born in the right time for Gaby, he thought. The light bulb had just been patented. He stood up and walked to the washbowl as he massaged the back of his head.

"Jean-Louis, you asked to return to your residence. I think that you can if you wish. I believe that Gabriella is ready to return home as well. I'll come and check on both of you tomorrow."

A nurse changed Jean-Louis' surgical dressing and once again, rage and jealousy mounted in Gaby's pretty little head. Why was it, she wondered, that every woman on earth showed Jean-Louis their charms and lovely dispositions?

He chuckled as the young nurse swabbed alcohol on his wound. While she, Gaby had been the martyr, he had a laughing session with his nurse. She hated him and then unable to control her jealousy, Gaby called out to Dr. Durand.

"Doctor, is there a minute shard of glass on the upper right quadrant of Jean-Louis' chest?" She faked concern.

The old clever physician smiled. He understood just by the look in her expressive green eyes the fury that she harbored inside. He asked the nurse to move away and personally inspected the area Gaby had pointed to.

"Eh bien, yes, maybe. I guess the Duke is in need of my ministrations." He winked at Jean-Louis, picked up the alcohol bottle and poured it straight on the scar.

Gaby smiled as Jean-Louis stared at her. She wished Durand had dumped the full bottle in the wound!

"I'll see you two tomorrow. By the way, your cousin is out walking and will say Mass tomorrow at the convent. He wants to see you, Gabriella." The old doc looked at Jean-Louis whose expression was impassible. Likewise, Gaby looked at her husband questioningly. He kept silent.

"Please tell him to come see me as soon as he feels up to it—as quickly as he wishes," she added, shooting a nasty look at Jean-Louis, "I miss him so."

Jean-Louis swallowed hard but did not utter a word.

The following day, an unmarked black coach brought the Duke and Duchesse De Bourbonne back to their mansion on the Ile Saint Louis.

To Gaby's surprise, Madame Perideot must have been summoned or, closer to the truth, she had just taken the liberty to come and nurse the Duke back to health. She accused Gaby for the bad press and the pain the ogre suffered. Gaby did not care anymore. Things she could change, she'd try hard at transforming, but that was impossible, so why even venture there.

Good, Gaby thought. None of the servants in his house would go beyond the call of duty. He might as well enjoy Hawkeye. Sure enough, Gaby was not too far from the truth.

Jean-Louis was nurtured back to health with his favorite dinners, his favorite drinks, and warm teas. Comfortable pillows would suddenly appear out of nowhere when he'd sit down in the library to read. His nurse would appear and coax him to lie down so as to retrieve his strength quickly. Most of the time, he would abide.

In any case, Jean-Louis did not leave Gaby's side. He followed her everywhere. If she was reading in her room—he would appear. If she'd go down for coffee, he'd follow close behind. If she was in bed resting, he'd rolled in next to her. At night was the only time she used him. She was scared. He might as well do something to comfort her, she rationalized.

After ten days of Madame Perideot's overbearing behavior, Gaby asked Jean-Louis to send her back and he complied. The nursemaid returned to Normandy a day later.

"Good riddance!" Gaby unapologetically exclaimed as the old lady's carriage left the courtyard. Happy with herself, she turned her back and walked back into the mansion.

Things were extremely cool between them.

A week later Jean-Louis attended a few meetings. In effect, she did not really want to leave him. So life would carry on like that a while later. Both were resigned to a few weeks of down time.

Chapter Fifty-Two

Everyone in Paris knew what had happened although the conversations centered on the reasons beyond the brawl. It had made front-page news for five days—the Duke beating a man of the cloth . . . the Duke held back by a group of commoners . . . Gabriella De Pleyssis with a sheer look of terror on her face guided by Dr. Durand back to her carriage. No one was missing, she thought sadly.

Philippe Thornsen still bruised from the past week's beating arrived late in the afternoon at the De Pleyssis' mansion. The Duke had not yet returned home.

When her cousin's carriage rolled in the residence, Gaby ran into the courtyard to meet her beloved Philippe

"Oh, my Philippe," she said as she gathered her cousin in her arms and kissed him tenderly on both cheeks.

In unison, Maude, Fernand and Pierre standing in attention glanced toward the entrance to the grand house. The Duchesse was fearless!

"Not too hard, Gabriella, the beast packed a mean punch there." He tapped his upper right cheekbone. "How are you?" he inquired tenderly, "I was not the one in the hospital."

"They kept me for observations, I think that I'm fine. Doctor Durand seems to think that the excessive bleeding was more of an emotional response to the trauma, rather than a spontaneous abortion. I have not gotten pregnant in three years. Frankly, I do not have much hope of carrying a child through a full pregnancy no matter what happens, Philippe." She reached for his hands and pulled him closer to her. They stayed interlaced for a long time while the servants ogling their mistress prayed fervently that the Duke's arrival would not rain on their parade.

"I missed you so, how I wish that you could be assigned here permanently." She took his arm and led him to the entrance of the foyer. Fernand, the butler, took his coat. She walked to the library. The Cardinal followed closely.

"Your wish might be granted, Gabriella. Although I'm not quite happy about it, save for the fact that I'd be close to you. But . . . " he paused for a short while, "I love working in the Vatican. Making policy, studying the Bible in our libraries with some of the greatest thinkers of our time is a veritable treasure, Gabriella. It's living with history, responding to the present and preparing for the future of the Church."

The following two hours they reminisced. They shared their lives and experiences abroad and with every sentence uttered, Philippe found a way to implore Gabriella to leave her husband.

"Gabriella, when it comes to you, I could not care less what my Church endorses. You're my lifeline, Gabriella. Your life will be endangered living with the beast. I am not extreme in my views, Gabriella, look at my face. Look at what he is capable of doing. I am a man of the cloth, have you seen anyone coming to my legal aid? No, no one will touch him or accuse him of anything. Instead, it is all a big joke. The Duke lost his *sang-froid, his cool,* over his pretty American wife. Ah Ah Ah! Have you heard about any repercussions that the Duke might suffer? Not even the Pope will touch that one!" He pursued impassioned.

Gaby sighed. Philippe was right. Anyone else would have been taken to the Court of Justice. With Jean-Louis, not even a rebuke from the most inconsequential clerk in Louis Napoléon's court dared remark on his horrific demeanor. In effect Jean-Louis had a Bourbon lineage, Catholics liked the Bourbon and so did the Pope!

"I am married, Philippe," Gaby calmly reminded him.

"I know people in high places, too, Gabriella. Your marriage can be annulled!"

"I'm not quite sure what I will do next, Philippe. Marriage is solemn."

He looked down, brushed down the pleat of his habit, and clasped the Christ hanging down from his waist.

Gaby heard the large wooden gates open and the sound of Jean-Louis' carriage rolled on the uneven cobblestones. At the door, Fernand bid good day to the Duke and both cousins became aware of the clinking of his boots in the foyer. Finally, his impressive stature stood still at the entrance of the library.

Jean-Louis stared at the couple that sat calmly next to the fireplace. Both stared back. He hated that glare. What did the priest plant in her smart little head now? He pondered. He did not move from his viewpoint. They did look alike. He noticed the resemblance with disdain. One could feel that there were extraordinary sentiments of comfort and trust between them. In his own house, he felt like a stranger, he silently raged. Less than a week and a half ago Gaby waited for him at the entrance of the foyer, happy and joyful as if God had entered the room. The incident had spoiled the trust and total bliss that they possessed for one another. How would she regain her faith in him? Certainly not while the cherished cleric was around. He had to find a way to send him back to Rome.

He walked to the sidebar, fixed himself a brandy and clutched the chair next to his wife. He needed to be in her sphere of personal energy. Jean-Louis did not mutter a sound. Silence reigned in the room.

"Philippe came this afternoon to visit. He'll have dinner with us. I invited him." Finally Gaby broke the stillness by stating the obvious.

Jean-Louis nodded. Silence again. He could not bring himself to say anything to the man adored by his wife. Not sensually he hoped, but a deep love nonetheless—one that had been nurtured throughout their years growing up with one another. Jean-Louis struggled to be a good host. The goal was to stay in Gaby's good graces, although he was furious with her still. She should have known better, used her good sense—her logic. She knew he was possessive of her, anything that she loved or dedicated herself to, he essentially resented. That should not have come as a big surprise to her. Why would the Cardinal be any different? He concluded glowering.

Nevertheless, he made an effort toward conversation. "I hear that you might be given the post of Archbishop of Notre Dame De Paris. *Est-ce vrai*, is it true, Philippe or just rumors?"

Philippe returned a despicable glare. He had no intention to respond to the beast, but he considered that it would pain Gabriella.

"There are talks on the subject." Philippe quietly stated without emotion.

Philippe was not too keen about taking the assignment in Paris—even if it meant being close to her, Gaby reflected. He loved doing research and writing, so this post was not the gift that everyone around him seemed to think it was.

Once more the silence became uncomfortable. The crackling sound of a wooden log engulfed by fire became audible. The wall of silence needed to fall. Philippe had asked her to leave Jean-Louis this afternoon, to return to Rome with him. Her response had been direct and prompt.

"No, I'll work through it, Philippe, you see in my own pathetic way, I cannot see myself without Jean-Louis, not now anyway; and I know quite well, he could not live without me. I do wish you had seen us in more auspicious time, Philippe. We do have a spiritual connection that I have never seen in other couples. No, no—we will pull through," she'd finally acquiesced with a sigh.

She remembered the night in the hospital when Jean-Louis had held her. Even then she had not wanted to be anywhere else but safe in his arms—and her love was returned. No, she just had to become more assertive, to take the reins once more and tell him what would happen next. She'd felt secure in her new decision until he'd walked in.

Dinner was served. All three stood up and silently ambled toward the dining room. The meal went along the same lines. Gaby tried to make conversation by finding topics of common interest, but she received only one-liner responses.

"What about cards?" she ventured after dinner.

The Duke was not about to leave them alone. The Cardinal took the lead. He did not want to be here. No need to pretend, he thought. His faith required him to love his enemy; he never had real trouble with anyone, except for his father, but he had come to terms with the hate he felt for him. God knew he had made many sacrifices at the Vatican, but with Gabriella their relationship was so complex that he was being tested again.

"Gabriella, I think I will take my leave now. I'm tired. I'll see you soon and I'll send word tomorrow. Meanwhile you are welcome in the apartment any time. Here is an extra pair of keys to the property," he said calmly, handing two bronze keys to his cousin. "Come and go as you wish, my dear Gabriella." He held her hands for a long time. Philippe's glare toward the Duke was a bomb ready to explode. He wanted to hug her, but knowing better he walked out of the dining room in the foyer.

The couple followed him. Jean-Louis stopped and stood by the banister, as Gaby continued toward the entrance doors. It was then, that the bomb exploded. Fury took hold of Philippe as he stood in front of the butler waiting for his cape. He stared at Jean-Louis who held on to the marble pillar—a panther ready to pounce on its prey any minute.

"Gaby, don't be a fool. Join me," the Cardinal implored.

Knowing that she was in the middle of another explosive situation, Gaby marched resolutely toward Jean-Louis and stood defiant. She lifted her eyes to his.

"If you only dare move or come close to Philippe while I go to him and embrace and reassure him, I swear to you, Jean-Louis, I'll leave you and I'll return back to New Orleans to my calm and decent world—my plantation. Understood?" She held on to the pleats of his thick velvet maroon jacket, and gave two sharp little pulls.

He smiled down at her. Damn the little Spartan warrior! His arms curled around her waist and pressed her even closer to him.

"Let me tell you one simple truth, Gaby—I will never release you from your vows—never. Is that understood?" he replied calmly.

She pulled back awkwardly at first and then confidently and ran back to her cousin who was livid by now.

"He's told you, Gabriella! He'll never release you. But you need to know that the all powerful Duke has enemies—including me the Cardinal," he shouted. "I wouldn't have any qualms about using these men and their contacts to pressure and bring down this giant of a man—both physically and figuratively!" he roared, incensed. For Gaby there were no limits. He had to make her understand and now was as good a moment as any.

"Come back," Philippe, declared, "Do not stay with the beast. His behavior will not change, Gabriella. It will happen again, Gaby, I assure you. Please return with me. You will like Rome. No, you will love Rome. My connections are extensive. We will annul your marriage. You may even want to try to enter La Scala in Milan; Monsieur De La Grada is at the Vatican constantly."

Jean-Louis kept silent. When the word annulment was mentioned, he grasped his fingers around the bronze globe placed artfully on top of the Italian marble pillar that lined the staircase.

Philippe continued his invective. He had good practice at sounding convincing—the pulpit.

"Come back, Gaby, I'll take care of you, the beast has nothing over you. He will release you. I'll make certain of that." Now he held her hands as he attempted to make her see the light. He had to preach to her, but at this very moment, he realized he was not even scratching at the gate. "Please, Gaby, trust me, it will happen again. What life do you have with him, a little bird in a cage? Think of your many talents, think, come home dearest." The Cardinal supplicated his dear cousin.

"I am home, Philippe," she said softly. "It may not look like it to you now, but I am using all of my talents and more. Jean-Louis lets me live my life as I see fit, within our cultural context naturally." She looked up at the Cardinal. "I have never been happier, Philippe. We will work through what has just occurred last week. I hope that you will find it in you to do the same, dear Philippe. You are the two most important people in my life." She held his hands even tighter and walked closer to him.

Jean-Louis squinted. He held on even more tightly to the golden globe attached securely to the top of the pillar, as if he wanted to glue his whole being to it. He willed himself still.

"No Philippe, I'm staying," Gaby continued. "I love Jean-Louis with all my being." She stared at her cousin, decisive and driven.

That look never failed her. Philippe understood there was nothing he could do but to stay close and provide her with the knowledge that no matter what, he would be there for her, come hell or fire. He resigned himself to the present fact and now pressed her to him. The beast could kill him he no longer cared.

Why had he not fought to attend their marriage or at least try to talk to her and dissuade her before the grand event? He had heard a lot of good about Jean-Louis, but all the good came from powerful men who had seen his gusto, passion and great intellect in combat and in political circles, but why had he not asked a woman? Everyone knew him as a womanizer, not having much respect for the weaker sex, but Gaby was invincible, he thought, everyone fell for her, why wouldn't the rake? After all, he was a man and every man, powerful or not, had a passion for a woman. A woman who brought them to their knees, who made them grovel and cry. Yes, he thought, Gaby could have been this woman in the Duke's life. She had that same effect on him. After reading her letters a hundred times, he'd acquiesce to her will and now his own lack of decisiveness had contributed to this grand woman being verbally abused and God knew what else?

"Gaby, think again, darling," he whispered in her ears, his long dark robe still, as if he had willed it. Nothing would rob him of this powerful moment.

She stayed in his arms and then ever so slowly disentangled herself from the embrace.

"I'm staying, Philippe. Do not worry, everything will be fine." She took his elbow, walked him to the door, and watched as his carriage left the courtyard.

As she turned back, tears rolled down her face. She noticed her husband still by the staircase. He had not moved an inch since she had told him to behave, and his unequivocal response had been that their life together would go on. He'd never release her from her vows, he had said. He would find her wherever she was. He knew her world. He had been there in combat and for pleasure.

Why worry? She had no intention of leaving him now. She adored him. She'd faced the dilemma if it ever came again. Worry was just a limiting force and she always detested limits.

She stopped, looked up at him before stepping on the marble staircase to reassure her tormented mind that she had made a wise decision. Yes, she had. She continued climbing up the stairs.

He placed his right hand on his neck and massaged away the tension. He waited a short while and followed close behind.

Chapter-Fifty Three

She walked into the room and threw herself on the bed. At any other time, he would have rolled in next to her and his ardent nature would have been sufficient to assuage her sadness and anxiety, but tonight he just wished they could forget about this whole damn week. He slowly walked to the bed and knelt beside her as he pressed his lips on her jaw.

"What have we done to your perfect life?"

She turned and looked at him with fury.

"We? You, Jean-Louis! Philippe was helpless in this whole sordid affair!"

Now it was his turn to be inflamed. "Me? Damn your Cardinal, Gaby, I would have liked to have seen your reaction if you'd had caught me kissing my cousin on the mouth, massaging her back, kissing her hands. Enough of this ridiculous situation, I overreacted I'll admit to that, but your dear cousin was inappropriate and I'm getting tired of holding the blame for the whole distasteful affair. Besides it's time that you fulfill your marital duties. I need to eat, I need to drink, and I need to make love," he fumed, rolling off the bed and heading toward the salon adjacent to their room.

"Eat, drink, and make love somewhere else! Your threats or actions do not hurt me any longer, not emotionally. Go, I have no doubt that you will find more than one willing female." She shouted back

Momentarily the enormity of what she had just said shocked her. She looked up at him, terrorized by what she had spoken. She recognized that she could never accept that he would actually make love to another woman. She adored making love to him and he knew it. As he stood by his dressing room, he looked at her, knowing exactly what she was thinking. Unwilling to embarrass her, he walked toward the bed once more.

"No, I did not mean that, I could not bear it," she murmured.

He looked at her for a long time, his lust for Gaby was great. Yet, he wanted her to come willingly. He took a deep breath and kissed her on her forehead.

"I'm going to the Devereaux's party. Let me face the music alone."

The following morning, Gaby was not in bed. He never knew from one moment to the next what she would come up with. Did she change her mind? Did she leave? Where would she go?

He hurried downstairs and found her by the sidebar, pouring a cup of coffee. Every woman he had ever known drank tea or hot chocolate, besides the usual champagne, the *boisson de rigueur,* the habitual drink, in their circles of friends, but not Gaby. Coffee was her fix, her charge she called it. She would whine and be downright miserable if coffee was not prepared as soon as she got out of bed. Jean-Louis was relieved when he saw her.

She gave him a stern look as if to say, "I'm not over it," and she continued to the far end of the table.

"Couldn't you choose a seat any further than mine, Gaby?" he chuckled amused.

"No my love, I have a strong sense of self-preservation," she replied sarcastically.

Breakfast had been served. He unfolded the white napkin embroidered with his initials and placed it on his lap. "Will you join me at the Tuileries *ce soir*?" he questioned sheepishly as he reached for a cup of coffee that had just been poured by the servant. The gilded soft-paste porcelain breakfast service from the Sèvres factory showed Hercules performing his twelve labors.

She did not return his smile.

"No! How can you even think about it?"

"To my eyes you're the prettiest woman in Paris, my love. My great love for you made me act foolishly. Parisians understand. I can assure you that you will not need to endure any impertinence from our friends. And off the record, I seem to have more physical damage than you have, ma chérie," he mocked.

Amused, she was not. She shot him a furious look and went to the sidebar again to pick up la Gazette. Pierre had just brought in the paper.

"Don't read this trash, Gaby. It will hurt you. I heard all about it last evening. You cannot be attentive to any of their silly writings," he stood up, came close to where she was standing and took the paper away from her. "Trust me everything will settle down quite quickly if we do not give fodder to the situation. We will need to return to our perfect life as quickly as possible. Even if you think our perfect life is hellish," he smirked and winked at her.

She remained silent, although, she pondered, he knew his world— he spoke the truth.

The silver baskets on the sidebars were filled with croissants and raisin brioches with small crystal containers of fresh homemade apricot jam, Gaby's favorites. He poured himself a cup of coffee, turned, and stared at her. She was beautiful. He adored her in light rose. This morning, she wore a pretty frilly, very sensual day dress that revealed her perfect anatomy.

He walked to his favorite chair and sat as he continued to stare. She ambled closer to him. She pulled up a dark green rococo armchair, and sat on his opposite side. She gazed intently at the fire.

"You came home late last night. Did you meet anyone of interest?" she ventured nonchalantly.

Jean-Louis heard the true question behind the transparent remark. He folded the documents he had picked up and walked to her. He reached for her hand and led her to the oversize sofa as he took his seat next to her. His lips brushed her temple and he kissed her softly.

"Yes, chérie, there were some persons of interest, but if you mean one or two particular females, no. You are my world."

She looked up at him. He kissed her lips again. She quickly turned away and stood up.

Smiling, he leaned toward his pretty wife as she moved away from the sofa and teasingly untied the organza bow. The ribbons fell gracefully on her bottom. He followed her with his eyes.

Over her shoulder, she shot him a disagreeable, annoyed glance as she strode gracefully to the sidebar for more coffee and sugar. She turned back to return to her seat and collided against his chest.

This time, his physical need for her was much too great to let her stray away. He took the coffee from her hands, replaced the cup on the sidebar, and gathered her in his arms. As he untied the organza bow slightly more, he slipped his hands on her bottom, cupped it, and forced it toward him. His mouth fell hard on hers, hungry, his tongue invaded her most private places. She did not shy away, instead she responded passionately to his touch.

"I love you, Gaby," he murmured, moving one of his hands away from her hips he let it ascend to her breast.

Gaby's desire was great.

Half naked, he brought her back to the extra long sofa and placed her gently on her back. He covered her body with his and sweetly kissed her lips.

At this most importune moment, a knock at the door interrupted their passion. Within moments, Fernand would knock and walk in to announce a guest. His ears perked up. He wanted to finish the act, but the arrogant voice of his Grandmother demanding to gain immediate entrance to the couple's dining area altered his passionate mood. Jean-Louis took a deep breath and covered Gaby's breasts with soft kisses once more. He pulled away, buttoned his pants, and helped Gaby up from the sofa.

"You're hearing the same voice that I'm hearing?" he asked. She nodded as she bent down to retrieve her skirt and blouse. Jean-Louis helped her back into her attire and rearranged her tousled hair as he sneaked a kiss on her jaw.

"I love you, darling," he said before he answered Fernand and allowed the entrance of his Grandmother.

"Madame La Duchesse is waiting to be shown in, Monsieur."

"Show her in, then," he pronounced, annoyed.

The Duke was back in his big overstuffed leather chair perusing through documents while Gaby retrieved her place standing by the sidebar. Both looked flushed. When the dowager walked in, the Duke stood up, stepped to her side and kissed her hand. He then walked back to his chair and stood there waiting for his Grandmother to sit down. She did not. He waited a few more minutes and then returned to his leather chair. Gaby came to sit next to him.

Her visit was not going to be pleasant. He'd go into damage control mode again after the old woman's departure. The Duke was very much aware of the old lady's tenacious temperament. His Grandmother would not leave them alone until she had delivered a long tirade. Might as well face the music now, he thought. She never had the tendency to repeat herself. He hoped it would hold true this time. He was still mad at the cleric for having messed up his life with his moronic demeanor.

"You look like two soldiers from the American Civil War," the old Duchesse started immediately.

"Were you there to assert such a vivid vision?" Gaby demanded insolently.

"I see, Gabriella, that you are defending your traditional roots. For heaven's sake, fighting in the privacy of your home is one thing, but you have social responsibilities, social and political obligations," she emphasized, daggers in her steely-blue eyes. "You went to St. Cyr, Jean-Louis-Pierre. Mon Dieu, to make an Emperor wait is unheard of! The Universelle Fair is almost over and they need you to fulfill your aristocratic obligations. The man is given to equality, but seriously, Jean-Louis-Pierre, his nationalist spirit is well known. You do not want to find yourself in prison like your hero, Voltaire, who visited the dungeon on numerous occasions," she concluded.

Jean-Louis lifted his head and stared at her for a short moment. Once more he lowered his head and continued to study his documents.

"Madame, they need us, therefore they will wait. Our trip will not take place until June so there is no need to activate our affairs. Besides, Gaby does not want to go out until . . . hence, it is her choice."

"Her choice? Her choice?" the old woman shouted. "Jean-Louis-Pierre, are you mad? Are you living in the 19th century? What choice do women have? You tell her to go and that is it. Voila—" the sophisticated white-haired woman concluded violently.

Gaby's fury mounted. She stopped short from taking her own defense.

Jean-Louis looked up. He hoped that Gaby would hold her rage in check. Silent, he continued his lecture knowing that the Duchesse would continue her outburst. Consequently he bowed his head and lowered the leather bound documents.

Seeing that no response was coming from her grandchild, the dowager turned toward Gaby.

"And you, my chère, what are you going to do? You know in Europe we women have our independent lives. God knows I amused myself grandly, although the Duke, my husband, never liked it much. We had our altercations, naturally. I never won the battles, but I made him expiate his sins in other ways. Nothing deterred me from continuing my modern life. Love is flighty, my dear, you have to take it when it presents itself to you. Do you understand? Marriage is formidable, but you must know that Jean-Louis-Pierre will have his paramours and that by jealousy or passion you will handle your life in your own personal way. This way of life will not change, Gabriella. Am I making myself clear?"

Gaby looked at Jean-Louis who did not seem perturbed about the atrocious commentary that one very close member of his family spewed in her face. His head hung over his papers and he pretended not to hear.

"Madame, I pray you, I do not care to hear such an outrageous discourse. I may be old-fashioned or avant-garde, but after all these years of slavery, we are living in an age where the advancement of the woman and of the family is making great strides. My marriage is sacred. If it were not, I would not be here today. I cannot fathom Jean-Louis with another woman other than myself. I would return home if it were the case. You see, Madame, this is the difference between my standing and the standing of married women of your aristocratic class. Their assets are given to their husbands in marriage. I may have been raised without much love, but I am financially independent, and Jean-Louis does not control my financial affairs. You see, your great fortune and your perfect social standing have married you well, but lasting love and passion have passed you by, Madame. You are poor and controlled when it comes to your own life; controlled by your social standing and everything that you feel the need to follow in order to be accepted. So in reality, all your wealth is not helping you in the least. Emotionally, you are not better off than the poor harlot in Montmartre," Gaby finished.

Jean-Louis lifted his head. The two women looked at each other like adversaries on a war field—neither would declare defeat.

"You are absurd and idiotic and my grandson would do well to leave you now," the old woman retorted.

Jean-Louis knew that his wife would not ask the old lady to leave their house. Consequently, he got up, reached for his Grandmother's arm and led her politely but firmly to the front door.

"Madame," he pronounced calmly, "Gaby does not want to go out tonight, or tomorrow, or the next day, consequently all of you words are wasted. I will be there this evening for a few hours. I'll make an appearance." He tried to soften the words that had just flown out of his mouth.

Suddenly, the old lady saw an opening. She had her grandson's ear now. Elegantly, she moved closer to him.

"Stop being so stubborn, Jean-Louis, you know when I'm right. Rein her in, for heaven's sake. Madame Pelletier is asking for you. A change of pace might do you well. Your wife is very different from us. Ah, if your grandfather was still alive. He would have taught you so much," she murmured in an almost non-audible whisper.

"Good day, Madame," he replied curtly. He stood up, slowly marched to his Grandmother, took hold of her elbow, and respectfully walked her back to the foyer while she waited for her carriage. As the coach rolled in front of the grand entrance, he walked her down the stairs, helped her in, and then tapped on the vignette to indicate to the driver that the Duchesse was ready to rejoin her residence.

Gaby waited in the morning salon close to the fireplace, perturbed as her husband approached and encircled her shoulders.

Had she heard the last comments, he wondered? He turned her around in his arms and kissed her tenderly. Slowly but surely, their lives would return to normal. She had shown him less than an hour ago that she was willing to resume.

"Don't be troubled, Gaby, my Grandmother's cultural ideas do not reflect mine. She's set in her aristocratic comportment. No one will change her opinions, and frankly, her comments have absolutely no bearing on the way I choose to conduct my life. I could not care less. You and me, Gaby, that's all that I care about." He walked upstairs.

Gaby was in absolute despair. What a crazy society she'd embarked in. She was caught sentimentally, emotionally, and culturally and the worst of it all was that he knew it. She slumped back in the sofa and forced herself to read the new translation of Darwin's *On the Origins of Species.* Clémence Royer, a woman had translated in French the sixth edition of the book. All in Paris had a peculiar idea on it except that after much evaluating Darwin's himself had called her a self-aggrandizing figure, who did not have a good knowledge of biology. Gaby had read the English version and the first translation. She wanted to connect the dots for herself.

She heard him come down. He entered the room where she was lost in her lecture.

He was beautiful, she thought, dressed in a black velour jacket and matching vest. Of course women wanted him. She began to consider what the Grande Duchesse had shared. Perhaps Jean-Louis might entertain the idea. He had not fought the old witch much! This morning was really the first time she'd realized that he perhaps would actuate a romance if she had not given in to him. Would he really have gone elsewhere?

"Will you stay at home this evening, or will your friends visit with you in the theatre Gaby?" he asked. All admired the magnificence of her personal theater. Upon her return to Paris, Lauriot had arranged for the very first rendition of a brand new Opéra written just for her. They'd practiced forever and Jean-Louis was almost always present. "He loves my singing as well as everyone else in Paris," she'd said, amused. Actually, her friends' take on the subject was significantly different—the Duke was there because of his extreme possessiveness.

"I feel that I'll never be able to show my face in public!" she fumed and then she recalled that one of his old paramours lived a block up the street.

"Jean-Louis, you know the other day, I took the Boulevard D'Anjou, and it's absolutely magnificent this time of the year. With the illuminations, the view is formidable."

He looked at her questioningly. "Gaby, I would like to know why after thirty years in Paris, I would, out of the blue, want to take le Quay d'Anjou and le Pont Alexandre III? Tell me, ma chérie, you understand my practical side."

"To change your perspective—not really, Jean-Louis," she replied mortified. "Do you remember what you told me this morning in the bathroom? Well, I am jealous and I'm wondering—"

He burst out laughing.

"Gaby, after this morning with you, I would be much too tired to even think of a romantic escapade. You are the best lover a man could ever dream of."

"Well, then your Grandmother's comments are correct. You are with me because of sexual attraction."

"Gaby, cease," he interrupted and walked away from her and toward his butler who was waiting with his overcoat.

Anxious, she was the first to reach the entrance doors. She tried to push the panel closed. With his shoulders he stopped it, took her in his arms, and kissed her first tenderly, and then his hunger for her not appeased, he took her mouth passionately. She let herself be kissed and gently pushed away as she stared in his eyes.

"Jean-Louis, in all truth you would not let yourself go with another woman?" she asked candidly.

He stopped a minute and looked at her gravely and kissed her on her forehead.

"Absolutely . . . not," he teased.

"Good," she replied. She sent him on his way and locked the doors behind him.

Chapter Fifty-Four

The crazy ideas that so many of his contemporaries placed in her pretty little head shook her confidence, he thought, as the carriage thumped on the cobblestones.

In hindsight, he felt guilty that he had not been more decisive with his Grandmother. He never paid much attention to her lectures, but Gaby had been upset and he had not come to her rescue. He often forgot that she was young, and impressionable. He should be more attuned to her emotional needs. They had had a difficult two weeks and now her emotions ruled her life.

It was of primary importance, however, that she kept her thinking cool and savvy. Gaby was about to play a significant role in European politics. He had to keep her above the sordid gossips fomented by his aristocratic world. When he'd returned tonight, he'd discuss the complex issues they were to face shortly. Ferdinand De Lesseps was the guest of honor this evening. It had taken ten years for the Companie Universelle Du Canal Maritime de Suez to finish the colossal architectural feast. They had been invited to attend the opening in Egypt. Gaby had been delighted when he'd shared with her their upcoming trip, but the absurd episode with the Cardinal had now taken center stage.

Upon his arrival at the Récamier's mansion, his sole appearance solicited the usual *grand hommes* of the Paris political scene to gather around him. He smiled. It had not been too difficult for him. Everyone had forgotten the affair Thornsen. An absurd scene *de jalousie,* it was said. And since the pretty Gaby was not by his side, women immediately began to chase him wildly.

The new group of debutantes appeared to have more charm, intelligence, and boldness than their older sisters, he thought. It might have been fun to work and play in this new environment without attachment. How easy it would have been had he not fallen in love with Gaby. He'd stopped asking why, but when she was in his arms, the entire universe could come to a halt and he dreamed for nothing else than to stay exactly where he was. Go figure. He leaned on a pillar surrounded by women waiting for nothing better than to be asked to dance. The Emperor and two of his ministers made their entrance. He excused himself and slowly began to amble in their direction.

He was taken to the grand library on the upper level along with many of Europe's leaders. Jean-Louis listened and evaluated the men who had absolute power over thousands of their countrymen, the power to send them to unnecessary wars, to satisfy their egos for in effect it was only a dozen aristocratic men who decided the fate of so many. Sadly, he realized he was one of them. He sighed and recalled the United States of America. That was a nation who defended itself, he thought. Its leaders would not think of starting preemptive wars on a whim.

Moreover, he could not forget Otto von Bismarck. The conservative Prussian Chancellor with the ironclad will had conquered the Germanic states. Once subjugated, he had been very lenient with their leaders. They'd suffered no war reparations, instead, the liberal Princes were asked to view themselves as full members of the aggrandized Prussian kingdom.

"Lets not treat them cruelly after their mortifying defeat," he'd proclaimed to his congregated generals. Lo and behold, the bourgeoisie had asked him for forgiveness in the Full Assembly. Of course, the populace needed to achieve equality in both financial and cultural acceptance, but the process needed time, he'd proclaimed. Good changes took time. Consequently, one needed patience and integrity to improve the situation. That man was a cunning conqueror. Louis Napoléon would surely have to deal with this man and certainly not with his usual arrogance and the narcissism of the generals he relied upon.

The situation he understood quite well. He 'got' Bismarck as Gaby flippantly remarked earlier. They were two aristocrats that not only loved their countries, but also had a very complex and more global perspective than the leaders of the time. Bismarck would not involve the new united Germany overseas in uncertain and costly colonial ventures. Louis Napoléon had not thought twice about sending troops to Mexico while he supported the crowning of his Austrian cousin, Maximillian, on the throne of the Mexican nation only to reverse his lofty goal in 1867 when the Mexican Republicans asked for his head! The same had happened with the American Civil War, for a certain period of time in 1861 and 1862, the Emperor had entertained the idea to intervene on the side of the Confederacy. He was pleased that He and Cunnan had been in Cochinchine then!

All right, he had had enough. He was going back to his wife. He bid his goodbyes and walked out. Many revelers were still outside at three o'clock in the morning, strolling, probably talking about the Duke and his Duchesse. Only in France, he reflected, would this sordid story have a life of its own. Of course, no one dared mention anything to him. The voices would come to a complete silence as he approached different groups of *connaissance,* acquaintance.

When he returned she was alone in the library still reading.

"Another major bore darling," he exclaimed loudly as he advanced toward her and pressed his lips on hers. "Without you, chérie, the soirée was drawn out and repetitive, "I did have the ear of Queen Victoria and Prince Albert. The Queen inquired about you, Gaby."

"My singing, I'm certain," she replied, uninterested.

"Yes, of course, you have a standing invitation at court," he smiled. "Naturally, Gaby, no one in her right mind would ask me about your absence," he replied calmly. She did not respond to his kisses, but he knew she was happy to see him. They had not slept much last night and now that she was willing to have him, well . . .

"The soirée was tied to all the festivities for the Exposition Universelle in Paris. The international heads of state were formally introduced to Louis Napoléon's magnificent new capital. It has taken nearly sixteen years to renovate, to modernize and beautify. The balls, the musical nights, the opéras, the theaters—all demonstrate the magnificence of the formidable Paris. I wished, Gaby, that you had been by my side this evening," he continued good-naturedly.

"I'm just not ready," she said.

He did not make light of her response. "That is the problem, politics and culture intertwine. The balls are a venue for politicians to meet, and there is always a salon where men can convene to discuss political and military intrigues. The world has not changed much since the Conference of Vienna in 1815."

She looked up, curious. "What do you mean, Jean-Louis?"

Good, he thought he could begin to expand on their upcoming roles in Italy.

"Then, Gaby, the five most important political heads of state and their ministers negotiated the treaty for a year, amidst balls, receptions, ballet, and much more. The ensuing treaty worked as no major wars between the great forces in Europe—namely England, France, Prussia, Russia, and Austria—erupted. Many revolutions and skirmishes were fought on many territories—but no major war. That is good, Gaby. So, essentially that is one of the reasons that I continue the 'ball scene'." He smiled. "Many influential politicians attend, including myself. All my life I've played in this aristocratic ballet."

"Philippe mentioned that the Emperor publicly aligned himself with the Vatican and that French troops protect Rome from Garibaldi and his Red Shirts compatriots? I don't quite understand, Jean-Louis wasn't the Emperor involved with the Carbonari movement in his youth?" she questioned. Jean-Louis swallowed hard and froze. He hated to even hear her cousin's name. He passed over the Emperor's youthful political inclination.

"While," Jean-Louis quickly responded, seeing a God-sent window to discuss their roles in Italy, "at the same time the Emperor chose a stealth plan with the Sardinian monarch, Victor Emmanuel II, to oust the Pope of his large principalities."

"But Victor Emmanuel II is Pope Puis the IX's archenemy. The Catholics in France will be inflamed and will not support the Emperor's efforts and resolutions. They were incensed by the very first union with the powerful Secretary of State, Benessimo Cavour, when France agreed to join forces with Victor Emmanuel to defeat Austria in 1859," she evaluated succinctly. "You know Villefranche and Nice were part of the regions along with the Duchy of Savoy that were given to France after Austria's defeat." She stared at him, afraid of what she was about to hear.

"Eh bien, Gaby, this will be one of our roles. Louis Napoléon is presently in the process to assuage the Pope's fears. The treaty that the French delegation and we are about to parley is important for it will reduce the power of the Church and it will bring about modernity and industrialism to the European states. The Pope will keep the Vatican, but his Princes will lose the rest of their lands, as they will automatically return to the Italian crown. Rome I'm certain will be the next capital of the Italian kingdom.

Speechless, Gaby shivered. "Philippe is aware of this development?" she questioned.

"I doubt it, Gaby, but I believe your cousin must have entertained the idea." Jean-Louis responded coolly.

"So our role will be to destroy everything my cousin stands for, Jean-Louis?"

"I don't believe so, Gaby, he has been spoken to and I believe that his neutral American point of view has been taken into consideration by some in the Vatican."

Chapter Fifty-Five

Two days later, Gaby was incensed. Jean-Louis had not cancelled the soirée they were to have—a gala in honor of the Exposition Universelle. Louis Napoléon and Eugénie were guests of honor.

Under no circumstances would she have all these aristocrats in her house. There were enough party lovers in Paris to hold such feast. It was out of the question. Besides she still hardly spoke to him. He'd convinced her to feed him sexually and she had. The fear of seeing him go elsewhere to assuage his needs was too great. But most of the time she still hated him. No, she was not about to play the ever-loving, subservient wife. Less than two weeks ago, he had almost killed Philippe for no other reason than a few friendly kisses she had placed on her cousin's cheeks. Incensed, she ran down to the library when she heard Pierre greeting Jean-Louis.

"Hello Ga—"

"Jean-Louis, what is it I hear? You did not cancel the gala? Lilianne called to say that the orchestra and the ballet would need to practice Saturday. She wanted me to choose the musical pieces. We are not entertaining. It is still too early. That's final."

"Gaby, there was never any talk of canceling our social obligations. I don't know where you got this absurd idea. Besides, we need to face the music now. We are going to have the soirée. Annulling it would be the toast of the tout Paris."

"Let the rumors feed themselves. Who really cares? For two weeks now, we have been the center of attraction. They can say what they wish. It's probably not far from the truth. You were not exactly discreet when you decided to act like a wild beast in front of Notre Dame. I will not see anyone," she stated with an iron-will.

"The ball will be held and you will be the hostess. No negotiations on this issue. Your theatre is ready. It will be a magnificent feast and the Paris Philharmonic Orchestra has agree to accompany you." He turned away from her and started upstairs. "Come chérie, it's been a long day. I need to rest before dinner."

591

"You're staying down here and you're hearing me out," she shouted, irate. "I will not—I repeat, not—be the hostess of this ball. You can ask your lovely Grandmother if you so desire, but count me out. I still feel too vulnerable to put on this huge act!"

The Duke was taken by surprise at her tone of voice and recalcitrant attitude. After all, he had been more than accommodating these past two weeks and had taken all responsibilities for the affair. He still thought that the beloved Cardinal had been a total moron and should truly bear the brunt of her discontent. At the thought of Philippe, his patience waned quickly.

"You will attend as my wife and hostess even if I have to drag you to the ballroom," he responded furiously. He turned back and looked at her sad and frustrated face. He remembered the incident. He did not care much about the cousin or the gossip, but he felt awful about the pain and embarrassment she still experienced. He walked back to her.

"Gaby, be reasonable, chérie. Why do we have to continue this strange pas de deux? You, my dear left your marks on me." He smiled that long sensuous smile, "I would not want to be your archenemy—"

"Because I have neither forgotten nor forgiven you, I do not want to have anything to do with you and your jealous world right now. You pretend that everything is sweet and wonderful between us. Well it's not."

She then turned away and started the long walk up the stairs toward her music room.

"Gaby," he snapped back, in his loud authoritarian voice, "get used to the idea. Sunday night we are going through with the soirée. There is no room for negotiation."

She did not stoop to his level and did not acknowledge his statement. Argument would not serve any purpose. He would not change his mind. She sighed. Might as well call Madame Hélène Coutreau, her *couturière*, seamstress. The servants had probably begun the preparions. She had seen them working their magic for both their engagement and her wedding receptions. They really did not need her to be the inspector of the finished work. She just went on her merry way, sent word to the dressmaker, hairdresser, the make-up artists and then her dear friends at the Conservatoire. The painters,

Édouard Manet and his wife, Suzanne Leenhoff, Claude Monet and Camille would attend, Berthe Morisot, her sister Edma, even Edgar Degas might make a cameo appearance. And, of course the Goncourt brothers—friends of Jean-Louis as well would attend. She would take charge of the entertainment. That night of all nights she wanted to be surrounded by friends.

Jean-Louis climbed up the stairs behind her. Gaby did not join him in their room. Instead, she strode in her music room and started the preparation for the musical spectacle. She was still lost in her work at dinnertime.

Relaxed and well rested, he followed the music, entered the room, paused to watch her practice, and quietly came behind her and brushed his lips to her jaw line. Better not say too much, he thought, Durand had told him that she was recuperating quite nicely and tonight he wanted her in his arms.

"Will you join me for dinner?"

She did not answer but got up and followed him in the dining room. They touched on simple uninteresting tidbits.

"*La Belle Sansone* is playing in the Faubourg, would you care to go?

"No, I will not go. I'm not emotionally ready to face your world."

"*Trés bien*, I just wanted to please you, I much rather spend the evening here with you, by ourselves." He smiled, and nodded. She knew exactly what he meant and frankly at this point she did not care.

"How much longer will I need to live in this inferno, Gaby?"

"Much longer, much longer, maybe forever," she answered promptly.

He smirked, got up, and walked to the fireplace where the chess game had been set up on a square rosewood, heavily ornamented game table.

"Punish me—here. " He pointed to the table where the large ivory pieces were placed. She loved playing the game. She strode quickly to the table and sat upright, very proper. They played chess most of the evening.

He was good at it and so was she. They'd usually have a perfect evening—just the two of them. He remembered happier days on the Tempête.

It was getting late and Gaby's eyes were closing. Besides he was going to wipe her out, she gave him the game, pushed her chair back, ready to bolt upstairs.

"Gaby, you can't," he proclaimed in a drunken tone, "I need closure when I play chess, you know that, get back down here, now."

"Well, I don't, goodnight," she replied, annoyed, as she made a dash toward the door.

He ran after her and lifted her in his arms before she could escape in the foyer.

"Why do I need to suffer so, emotionally and physically, chérie?" Dramatically he placed his hand on his right side where the crystal star had pierced his skin.

She slid down from his embrace and continued her walk upstairs.

"Gaby, you have me wrapped around your fingers, you know that, don't you?" He held on to the top rail of the banister as he trailed her curvaceous body up the stairs.

She did not even turn back to acknowledge his remark.

"The little witch," he uttered loud enough for her to hear. He then obediently followed her upstairs and into bed. He rolled on top of her and braced her head in his hands and kissed her long and hard.

"I love you so much, Gaby," he professed again. This time he did not let her go when she tried to roll away from him.

He knew that she adored him, too. He recalled the conviction in her voice when she'd told her cousin that she would not leave him. "I have never been so happy in my life, Philippe. I will not leave," she'd stated. He held her closer to him as if he wanted to absorb her small body into his as he kissed her shoulders, neck, ears, back. She would be responsive tonight.

Actually, she doubted he would have let her go and secretly she was happy about it. At the same time, she did not want to appear to be in his arm willingly—not yet, anyway. He knew quite well all her vulnerable points, so at night she could not push him away. She was always frightened when the lights turned off. Knowing it, he used it well as was the case during the two nights they had spent in the hospital. Tonight would not be different, she mused, except that madness, embarrassment, disgust with her weakness flashed out of nowhere.

"Don't touch me!"

"Very well, Gaby, have it your way." He rolled out of bed almost as quickly, stood up, and walked to his dressing room.

She heard him getting dressed.

"Where are you going?" I am pushing him to the limits she told herself, maybe to another woman. In turn, she jumped out of bed and followed him into his room.

"Jean-Louis—" she said as the door slammed on her. She pushed it back open angrily, and followed him inside his dressing room.

"Jean-Louis, answer me damn it, where are you going?"

He did not bother to answer. He passed by her in his sitting area, strode down the hallway, down the staircase, and directed himself towards the entrance door.

The butler, Fernand, had been awakened and sent to call the groom who was bringing the carriage in the courtyard of the property.

Gaby was stunned at this new demeanor. After all, she was the one who had been persecuted. She watched him—incredulous, and finally bolted down the stairs after him. She finally reached him. Sometimes he was no match to her agility. She clasped his arm.

"Where to, Jean-Louis, where?" She reached and held his sleeve.

"To the club, Gaby. I'm no two-year-old. This charade will have to stop." He walked out the door. She followed. Before getting in his carriage, he stopped and turned around. He looked at her. She stood outside, barefooted, freezing in her white satin robe coming undone at the breast and waist, uncovering her shapely body. Knowing exactly what she was thinking, he did not say a word but came back close to her.

"Or what?" she asked.

He looked down at her, pulled the robe over her breasts and hips, and tied the slippery satin ribbon snuggly.

"Get in, you'll catch pneumonia."

She did not move.

He picked her up, walked up the stairs and deposited her inside the warm foyer.

Astonished, she only heard words coming out of her mouth. "Jean-Louis, when will you return?" She demanded.

He simply ignored the demand and stepped in the waiting carriage.

The sound of the horses' hooves pounding the cobblestones and the smooth rolling of the carriage's wheels resonated in the courtyard as the monumental gates opened to let the Duke's carriage exit. Returning to her room, she illuminated her bedroom and dressing room and unable to sing to relieve her melancholy for fear of waking up the servants, she decided to write anything that would force her out of the excruciating, unceasing mental anguish she resented.

Jealously, madness, guilt, remorse, total confusion—writers often used these inadequacies within the self to express the complexities of emotions locked in one's soul, she thought. She wrote on Jean-Louis' desk, her husband's manly scent still all around her. Leaving reality behind, she entered her world of perfection—perfect love, perfect relationship, laughter, opéra singers, and singing in the world's best opéra houses. Tonight, she was in Venice at La Fenice, singing the lead role in Verdi's La Traviata. The famous composer wrote and played the first performance of his famous opéra in the magnificent opéra House.

Jean-Louis found her at five in the morning, slumped on his desk, inkwell and plume resting in her delicate hands. Her long hair had fallen out of the ribbon she must have used to tie up the curls so as to keep it from obstructing the paper.

He began reading some of the pages in full view. She described La Fenice with such beautiful words. He visualized their entrance in the famous opéra house in Venice. Her knowledge of opéra and her succinct sense of historical perspective showed through. He bent down and lingered his lips on the perfect profile.

What kind of monster had he become? Jean-Louis pondered. The one person, he adored, who adored him back . . . how could he hurt her so? He hated himself. He stayed close to her and kneeled down next to her.

A strong scent of alcohol emanated from his breath. She woke up.

"Hello, beauty, will you have me now?" he whispered in her ear.

Rubbing her fists over her puffy eyes, she tried to stand up. If he had been with a woman, he would have dropped in bed.

Jean-Louis picked her up in his arms and placed her gently in bed. He pushed her hair away from her face and quickly undressed and rolled in next to her as he maneuvered his hands under the blankets to her warm breasts.

She lay quietly letting him place his lips where his hands had wandered.

Filled with drunken passion, he let his full body fall on hers. No need to resist his love, she reached for his head and pressed it close to her body. She wanted him to please her and she let herself be made love to. The world ceased to be for long and passionate moments.

"Work for your pardon," she whispered almost out of breath from the warmth that radiated from her body. Her will and resistance had been subdued and she let herself be taken in a sensual world where she knew she could escape the realities of her often-tormented world.

A while later, while he held his wife possessively into him, he thought amusingly that he could live forever in that position—and never want for anything else.

Gaby had fallen into a deep sleep and Jean-Louis admired her perfect profile. He kissed her to his heart's content, and collected her into his side, while he anticipated that the ugly episode would vanish quickly. Hopefully, she would forgive him. He rolled her body next to his, placed his muscular legs over hers, his hands on her breasts and he finally fell asleep.

Chapter Fifty-five

On the day of the party, Jean-Louis came in earlier and took her upstairs. These soirées lasted until four or five o'clock in the morning. He had been working hard and he wanted to take a nap before the gala. They woke up later than they should have. The servants had the house and the gala under control. The help was like a fine-tuned orchestra. Each and everyone knew what to do, what to expect, they even prepared for blunders.

Gaby organized the musical distraction. Later that evening the first opéra in HER theatre would be sung. She'd chosen a five act grand opéra—Don Carlos by Verdi. She'd take on the role of Elizabeth De Valois in the complex opéra of the life of Prince Carlos. His father Philip II of Spain had been obliged to marry his son's betrothed as part of a peace treaty ending the Italian War between the Houses of the Habsburg and the Valois. It was modern and written in French and a perfect gift to the Emperor who had dedicated himself to the beautification of Paris. A capital he could be proud of, he had pronounced years ago! Well on this very point he had achieved his goal. It was going to be a sumptuous affair after all. Four hundred guests would attend. The momentous event was upon them.

She loved their home in Paris. It was grandiose. The grand ballroom was exquisite for grand affairs but yet their private apartment was quite inviting. It overlooked the Seine from their bedroom windows. She often walked across the Pont Sully to Notre Dame and to the Académie on the Grands Boulevards. On the left Quarter, the Institut De France, the impressive Académie Française safeguarded the pureness of the French culture and language and was the place where she often took her place to listen to Jean-Louis' conferences with the illustrious men of his world. It was close by and they would often walk home on the cays. She adored Paris, the beauty of the city, the works that Hauffman had started and now almost completed made it an exceptional capital. It was grandiose and most romantic, yet the political situation was unsettling. Jean-Louis was involved in so many twists and turns. She had to be more aware of her whereabouts, he constantly reminded her.

Preoccupied, Jean-Louis had left the room quickly after breakfast. He had been reading the paper, but at one point an article must have pointed to a weak point in the negotiation he was involved in, for he rolled the paper, walked to the library, picked up some documents, and walked back upstairs.

"I'll be back soon, darling." He strode to Gaby, bent down, and kissed her jaw. Sticking to her coolness, she let herself be kissed.

She trembled under his touch just enough to draw a smile on his sexy mouth. Not willing to show any further emotion, she walked away and let him depart without questioning his whereabouts.

An hour later, as she was getting ready, he surprised her in her dressing room. An elegant dinner had been set up for both of them. Walking behind her, he reached for her hand. "Since you will be the perfect hostess tonight and will dance with too many young men, I thought we'd spend an hour together, ma chérie." He smiled and pressed her toward him.

"Are we friends, yet?" he asked with a smile.

"No," came the resolute reply.

Although he tried to interest her in all types of conversation, her answers were curt and to the point.

"Eh bien, darling, I presume the cold war is still on. I hope you will have a nice time this evening. Save me a few waltzes." He quickly stood up, came behind her, pulled out a glittering *rivière* of pink diamonds and placed it on her neck. He then sweetly reached for her hand and left the matching bracelets and earrings in her palms.

"How did you know to purchase matching pink jewelry? It will be beautiful with my dress tonight."

"I stopped by Madame Coutreau's shop."

"Thank you, it's beautiful," she replied warmly—touched. She looked at herself in the mirror. She liked what she saw.

It was so wonderful getting presents. She always felt touched every time he came with gifts, not quite knowing what to say, just elated that he would think of her and go out of his way to please her. She resolved that she would do the same for him in the future. At this moment she felt loved and secure; she was about to throw herself in his arms and kiss him, but without pressing her any further he walked in his dressing room.

An hour later, they emerged at the top foyer, the Duke and Duchess De Bourbonne walked down the marble staircase to the grand ballroom to await their guests.

Gaby was breathtaking in a white Alençon lace ball gown that adorned her sensual body. The Carmelite nuns in Alençon had kept secret the sought after technique after the ravages of the French Revolution. The Second Empire had revived the art and it was the latest fashion in Paris. Her new pink diamonds necklace was the talk in the women's circle. They both welcomed their friends as if nothing had happened. Of course, le tout Paris by now knew what had transpired but no one would dare comment. *Les amoureux*, the lovers, as the couple was called, looked perfectly happy and at ease with one another.

She had spent a great deal of time these past few days to create a gay ambiance for her guests. Her friends included some of Europe's best entertainers. The ones that were available and in Paris had sent word that they would attend. Of course it was a great honor to entertain the Duke, his Duchesse and their friends.

The powerful couple danced the first waltz, apparently supremely in love. All the gossip might just have been a farce, many surmised. Although Jean-Louis-Pierre had almost killed her cousin, the Cardinal, but she must have explained the situation rationally—whispers wagged. All the talk about late nightly visits to Dr. Durand's hospital must just have been *des rumeurs,* spread about by many unscrupulous reporters. By all appearances they were as in love as ever . . . and so went the gossip. The women took their leave to the salons and the men directed themselves toward the library where gaming tables were in place.

An hour later, everyone mixed once more in the Grand ballroom. Gaby became apprehensive. She had not seen Jean-Louis for close to two hours. The men he had been gambling with were back in the ballroom. Coyly she stepped up to the second floor pretending to greet guests she had not spoken to as she scanned the room in search for Jean-Louis. Many of his former mistresses were in attendance.

Nonchalantly, the Duke stood behind a pillar involved in conversation while he observed his wife.

Looking arrestingly magnificent, she focused her attention on one of his former mistress. He knew what she was doing. A smirk tugged at the corner of his mouth. He moved forward in full view. Their eyes met. For an instant there was a look of relief on her gorgeous face. Then quickly she retrieved her arrogant gaze and walked back down.

The whole situation was maddening. The imbecile priest, Jean-Louis pondered, had dared to hold his wife in such a passionate embrace. She could evoke such anger and emotion in his character. How can his personality change so drastically?

He scanned the room. He had known most of the women under thirty in attendance, some quite intimately, but never had he paid much attention to any of his paramours. They were delightful company, but he always had been non-committal. Why Gaby? What was this connection that they both possessed toward one another? He needed to keep his anger in check. She would forgive him this time, he was sure of that, but he had hurt her pride although she had done much more physical damage to him, the little hellcat.

The orchestra played grandly. Playfully and breaking all rules of propriety and etiquette, the Duke walked to his wife. He curled his arm around his wife's waist, brought her back gently to him, and begun singing offbeat with the orchestra. Unaware that his great height allowed him to watch her reflection in the mirror facing them above the fireplace, she rolled her eyes from side to side at every false note he took, amusing the crowd with her expressive features. Not to be outdone, he suddenly reached for the fan she was holding in her left hand, fanned it out, and placed it in front of her face. Laughter erupted. She turned to him, wildly amused. He nodded toward the mirror and pressed her even tighter to him.

"Madame, can you match that?"

"Our dogs could match your cacophony," she laughed and gestured to the orchestra to entice them to choose an aria.

They proceeded amiably. Silence reigned.

Her perfect soprano voice rose in the formidable mansion. The crowd was brought to a level of emotion rarely seen in this type of gathering. Gaby's engaging smile and superb theatrics brought a loud ovation from the guests. Even Jean-Louis' Grandmother sitting at one of the front table facing the stage was entranced. It was a rare moment that left the crowd astounded at the performance they had just witnessed.

Gabriella De Pleyssis was an amazingly talented diva and actress. The guests were silent and dazed.

"Well," she asked, as she winked at the crowd who was still recovering from the splendid performance.

"Well, what? You won, fair and square," he said amiably and before anyone could ask for an encore, he nodded to the orchestra. He took his wife's waist assertively and twirled her away from the crowd to the dance floor. Again, the orchestra started *Libiamo from Verdi's La Traviata,* their signature aria.

"Encore, Gabriella, encore!" the director of the opéra De Paris proclaimed.

"Just one, just one more," the guests begged, forgetting their manners as they took on the flippant behavior of the De Pleyssis.

Jean-Louis continued to dance, nodding to his guests to join them, totally oblivious of the poor director left standing in the middle of the ballroom with his half empty flute of champagne.

Gaby was furious. How rude he had been toward the man who had accepted her in his program and had done so much for her. After a few dances, he would not let her go. She left him on the floor with the prettiest smile she could muster notwithstanding the fury that was mounting, and began socializing with the guests making sure to attend to the hurt feelings of the director of the Conservatoire.

Don Carlos had been a huge success. Now the guests were back in the ballroom but Jean-Louis had not resurfaced. Where was he? No doubt some young wife or single beauty charmed him in some corner of the mansion.

Unsane, she was! She had chosen to stay away and for the past few days had been just miserable to him. Demurely, she mounted the marble staircase again, peeking in the library where men usually gathered. Jean-Louis was not present.

Pretending to oversee the merrymaking and her guests—once more, she glanced into the private salons. Her husband was surrounded by not one, but five female vultures—two of them with their respective escorts. The others, she knew too well who they were. She did not want Jean-Louis less than a hundred miles apart from these women—never mind in his personal sphere!

He had bedded four of the five and had had a long-term fling with Madame Talleyrand. Her husband had not taken too well to the affair and she had been sent to the country for quite a few years. Why she was back in Paris was anyone's guess? However reading and enjoying the pastoral life was not in Leonie's realm of expertise.

Gaby's jealous green eyes met his for a split second.

How could she still adore this man? She asked herself. How could he invoke in her such fury? Twice already tonight, she had been caught being suspicious. Why did she forget and forgive so easily? It must be her Catholic background, she surmised. It prevented her from holding a grudge. Forgive and forget. She had always thought of herself ahead of her time. A man would never have any control over her, well certainly that bubble burst many moons ago. Obviously she would have to deal with her overbearing husband.

She promptly took the downstairs path once more and pretended that her heart was not broken. Theatrics came in handy. How easy it was for an actress to hide her sad heart behind a mask and then walk on stage. She looked for a waiter. As she was about to pick a glass of Cristal from the tray, two strong hands that she recognized immobilized her tiny waist. He pulled her back to him.

"Spying on me, Duchesse?"

"Yes," she replied candidly. "Were you with them all that time?"

"No, not all that time. I waited for you to come searching for me. It took you an awful long time, Gaby," he responded sarcastically. He swirled her on the dance floor to the beat of the sweeping music and quickly to the balcony and down the magnificent park that encircled the mansion. Off and away from curious onlookers, he took his wife in his arms in an embrace she could not get away from and kissed her.

"Kiss me, Gaby," he demanded. As she hesitated, he none too gently pressed her closer to his chest. "Now, Gaby."

"What kind of hosts are we, gallivanting in our own backyard, you know what the reporters will say to that, Jean-Louis, 'with private apartments in their luxurious town home, the Duke and his wife showed their *manqué de cire*, lack of polish, by fornicating in their gardens!'"

Jean-Louis laughed heartily.

"Well, my chère, judging from your choice of words, I can assure you that you'd be the one being granted the title of *femme ordinaire,* ordinary woman. Rightly so, chérie."

He picked her up in his arms and ran down one flight of stairs to a fragrant rose garden where he stood an instant and gently kissed her impertinent mouth.

She let herself be held closely as he sat with her on an ornate cement king's chair.

"Kiss me now, or I will drag you upstairs, past our guests, into our private apartments and love you so that you screams of pleasure will upstage the orchestra."

"A difficult choice, Mon Dieu, what should I do?" She played the *précieuses,* affected mannerism. He did not let her finish her thought. His lips came down hard on hers.

The champagne weakened her resolve and she felt good being in his arms. She felt his breath on her shoulders and his lips on her breasts. Life was just wonderful again. She let all her defenses down and kissed him back passionately.

"I'm sorry Gaby," she heard his grave voice murmured in her ear. "I'm truly sorry. What happened was inconceivable. I had walked over to surprise you and take you about for a fast déjeuner but mostly to catch a glimpse of you working with the young orphans. There had been new development concerning our trip to Italy that I wanted to discuss with you. Your kisses still warm on my lips from the morning, I missed you. Upon seeing the wild embrace between Philippe and yourself . . . I was blinded by pain and fury and extreme jealousy. Momentarily, I concocted that he was the reason behind your delay to Paris, the cause of your miscarriage. I am thankful that a crowd was there. He would be dead today had I not been restrained." He stopped abruptly.

Stunned at his candid revelation, she remained quiet.

"Gaby," he continued and simply stated, "I beg of you, beware of your friendly manners with men. I am possessive of you and I do not want another episode like the one we have just experienced, to be repeated—ever. Please watch your ways when in the company of other men. Don't ever try to make me jealous, ever, even unwillingly, watch your demeanor for I become irrational when it comes to you.

Shocked by his apology, candid revelation, and non-negotiable remarks, she reached for his face and kissed him with all the passion that emanated from her soul.

THE END

إلى جيـم

...

الأوسـط السعيـد

ليني تايلور

LAINI TAYLOR

أَحْلامُ

الملائِكَة والوُحُوش

نقلها إلى العربية

عقبة زيدان

كنان تومه

أحلام الملائكة والوحوش

ليني تيلور

عدد الصفحات: 620

الطبعة الأولى باللغة العربية: 2025

الناشر: الخيّاط

هـذا الكتـاب عمـلٌ أدبـي خيالي. الأسـماء والشـخصيات
والأماكـن والأحـداث هـي مـن وحـي خيـال المؤلف.
أي تشـابه مـع وقائـع أو أماكـن أو أشـخاص، سـواء كانوا
أحيـاءً أو أمواتـاً، هـو محـض صدفة غيـر مقصودة

ISBN: 978-1-96142-039-7

KHAYAT®
PUBLISHING HOUSE

Washington, DC
United States
+1 7712221001
info@khayatpublishing.com
www.khayapublishing.com

يحكى أن
ملاكاً وشيطاناً وضعا أيديهما على قلبَي بعضهما

فكانت نهاية العالم

1

آيس كريم الكوابيس

أعصاب مشدودة، دماء صراخ، توحُّش، تخبّط، مطاردة، افتراس، رعب، رعب... ورعب-

"إليزا. إليزا!".

صوت، ضوء ساطع، ثم سقطت إليزا نصف واعية. شعرت بقوة اصطدامها بالأرض. "كان مجرد حلم"، قالت هامسة. "كان مجرد حلم. أنا بخير".

كم مرة في حياتها نطقت بهذه الكلمات؟ أكثر مما تستطيع أن تحصيها. لكن هذه كانت المرة الأولى، التي تقولها لرجل اقتحم غرفتها ببسالة، وهو يحمل مطرقة ذات مخالب، لينقذها من القتل.

"لقد كنتِ... كنتِ تصرخين"، قال زميلها في الغرفة، غابرييل، وهو يتفحص الزوايا بحثاً عن أي أثر لوجود قتلة. كان شعره أشعث، وعيناه متيقظتين بشكل جنوني، ويداه ترفعان المطرقة عالياً بقوة متأهباً للانقضاض. "أعني... كنتِ تصرخين حقاً وبصوتٍ عالٍ".

"أعلم"، أجابت إليزا بصوت مبحوح، وقد جف حلقها. "يحدث ذلك أحياناً." حاولت أن تجلس في سريرها، بينما كان قلبها ينبض بقوة

كأنه نيران مدفع- مدمر وعميق يتردد صداه في جسدها كله. ومع أن فمها كان جافاً وأنفاسها متقطعة، إلا أنها حاولت أن تبدو لامبالية. "آسفة لإيقاظكَ".

رمش غابرييل وأخفض المطرقة."ليس هذا ما قصدته، يا إليزا. لم أسمع أي شخص يصرخ بهذا الشكل في الواقع. كان صراخاً من أفلام الرعب".

بدت عليه ملامح التعجب. أرادت إليزا أن تقول: اذهب بعيداً، من فضلك. يداها ترتجفان، و قريباً لن تتمكن من السيطرة على ذلك، ولم تكن تريد أن يراها أحد بهذه الحال. قد يكون انهيار الأدرينالين بعد الحلم سيئاً للغاية."أعدك أنني بخير. حسناً؟ أنا فقط...".

اللعنة.

الارتجاف. الضغط المتزايد اللاذع خلف جفونها وكل ذلك خارج عن سيطرتها.

اللعنة اللعنة اللعنة.

انحنت وأخفت وجهها في غطاء سريرها بينما تعالى النحيب واستولى عليها. وبقدر ما كان حلماً سيئاً—بل كابوساً—كانت العواقب أسوأ، فقد بقيت واعية ولكنها لا تزال عاجزة. ظل الخوف—الخوف، الخوف—يتصاعد وكان هناك شيء آخر. يأتي مع الحلم في كل مرة ولا يتلاشى معه، بل يبقى كشيء جلبته الأمواج على شاطئ عقلها. شيء مرعب—جثة مخلوق أسطوري نافق تركت لتتعفن على شاطئ عقلها. إنه شعور بالندم. لكن يا إلهي، كانت الكلمات باردة جداً لوصفه. هذا الشعور الذي يتركه الحلم معها مثل سكاكين من الذعر والرعب تستقر فوق جرح نازف من الذنب.

الذنب بسبب ماذا؟ هذا هو الجزء الأسوأ... يا إلهي، إنه غير قابل للوصف، وكان هائلاً، هائلاً جداً. يا له من ذنب. لم يحدث شيء أسوأ من ذلك في أي زمان ومكان، والذنب ذنبها. لكن مهما كان تفسير الحلم، إلا أن إليزا كانت ترفضه باعتباره سخيفاً.

لم تفعل، ولن تفعل ذلك أبداً.

لكن عندما تلبّسها الحلم، لم يعد شيئاً يهم—لا العقل ولا المنطق ولا حتى قوانين الفيزياء. لقد خنق الرعب والشعور بالذنب كل شيء.

كان الأمر سيئاً.

عندما توقف النحيب أخيراً ورفعت رأسها، كان غابرييل جالساً على حافة سريرها، مبدياً تعاطفه وقلقه. ثمة تهذيب ما في غابرييل إيدنغر يوحي بأن هناك فرصه كبيرة في علاقاته المستقبلية. كان خبير أعصاب، ربما أذكى شخص تعرفه إليزا، وأحد ألطفهم. كلاهما كان زميلين باحثين في المتحف الوطني للتاريخ الطبيعي في سميثسونيان—NMNH— وكانا ودودين ولكن لم يكونا صديقين حقاً طوال العام الماضي، إلى أن انتقلت صديقة غابرييل إلى نيويورك للحصول على درجة الدكتوراه الخاصة بها، وكان بحاجة إلى زميل في الغرفة لتغطية الإيجار. إليزا تعلم أن ذلك كان مخاطرة، حيث تتداخل الحياة الشخصية مع العمل لهذا السبب وبالتحديد هذا الصراخ والنحيب .

لن يستغرق الأمر الكثير من البحث بالنسبة إلى شخص مهتم لتحديد... عمق الغرابة التي بنت عليها حياتها. تبدو أحياناً وكأنها فوق ألواح على الرمال المتحركة. لكن الحلم لم يكن يزعجها منذ فترة، لذا استسلمت لإغراء التظاهر بأنها طبيعية، لا تشغلها سوى الاهتمامات العادية لأي طالبة دكتوراه تبلغ من العمر أربعة وعشرين عاماً بميزانية صغيرة. ضغط الأطروحة، الزميلة الشريرة في المختبر، مقترحات المنح، الإيجار.

الوحوش.

قالت لغابرييل:"آسفة. أعتقد أنني بخير الآن".

"جيد". بعد وقفة غير مريحة، سألها بغبطة:"كوب شاي؟".

شاي. كان هذا لمحة لطيفة أكثر من عادية. قالت إليزا:"نعم، من فضلك".

وعندما ذهب ليعد الشاي، تأهبت. لبست رداءها، غسلت وجهها، وتنشقت من أنفها، وتأملت نفسها في المرآة. كانت منتفخة وعيناها محمرتين. رائع. كانت عينان جميلتان في العادة. لقد اعتادت على تلقي الإطراء من الغرباء. عينان كبيرتان ومشرقتان طويلتا الرموش—على الأقل لم يكن بياضها ورديًا بسبب البكاء—بل كانت أفتح من بشرتها بعدة درجات لونية، مما جعلهما تبدوان وكأنهما تتوهجان. في الوقت الحالي، كان من المثير للاشمئزاز أن تلاحظ أنهما كانتا تبدوان... مجنونتين قليلًا.

"أنتِ لستِ مجنونة"، قالت لانعكاسها في المرآة، وكان لهذه العبارة رنين تأكيد غالبًا ما يقال—طمأنينة ضرورية وتكرار معتاد. أنتِ لستِ مجنونة، ولن تكوني كذلك.

في أعماقها لبثت فكرة أخرى أكثر يأسًا. لن يحدث لي ذلك. أنا أقوى من الآخرين. وعادة ما تصدق نفسها.

عندما انضمت إليزا إلى غابرييل في المطبخ، كانت ساعة الفرن تشير إلى الرابعة صباحًا. الشاي على الطاولة بجانب علبة من الآيس كريم مفتوحة مع ملعقة مغروسة فيها. أشار إليها."آيس كريم الكوابيس. تقليد عائلي". "حقًا؟ نعم فعلًا".

حاولت إليزا للحظة تخيل الآيس كريم كمواساة لها من قبل عائلتها بعد الكابوس، لكنها لم تفلح. فالتباين كبير جدًا. مدّت يدها إلى العلبة. قالت:"شكرًا". أكلت قليلًا في صمت، شربت رشفة من الشاي، بينما كانت متوترة في انتظار الأسئلة التي يجب أن تبدأ.

ما الذي تحلمين به يا إليزا؟

كيف لي أن أساعدكِ، إن لم تتحدثي معي يا إليزا؟ ما مشكلتك؟ سمعت كل ذلك من قبل.

سأل غابرييل:"كنتِ تحلمين بمورغان توث، أليس كذلك؟ مورغان توث بشفتيه المنتفختين؟".

حسناً، لم تسمع به من قبل. أجبرت إليزا نفسها على الضحك. كان مورغان توث خصمها، وكانت شفتاه موضوعاً جيداً لكابوس، لكن لا، لم يكن قريباً حتى. قالت:"لا أريد حقاً التحدث عن الأمر".

سأل غابرييل بكل براءة:"التحدث عن ماذا؟ ما هذا 'الأمرُ' الذي تتحدثين عنه؟".

"أنت لطيف. وأعني ذلك. أنا آسفة".

"حسناً".

لقمة أخرى من الآيس كريم، وصمت آخر قصير قطعه سؤال غير مباشر آخر. أوضح غابرييل:"كنت أعاني من الكوابيس عندما كنت طفلاً. لمدة عام تقريباً. كانت مكثفة جداً. حسب رواية والديّ، كانت حياتنا معلقة إلى حد كبير. كنت أخاف من النوم وكان لدي كل هذه الطقوس، والخرافات. حتى إنني حاولت تقديم قرابين، وهي ألعابي المفضلة، والطعام. وعلى ما يبدو سمعني أخي الأكبر وأنا أعرضه كقربان بدلاً مني. لا أتذكر شيئاً، لكنه يقسم على ذلك".

سألت إليزا:"تقديمه لمن؟".

"لهم. لمن كانوا في الحلم".

اعتراها بريق من الأفكار والأمل، ربما أمل أحمق،"لهم". كانت تدرك أنهم من بنات أفكارها ولا وجود لهم في أي مكان آخر، لكن بعد الحلم لم يكن بالإمكان التحلي بالمنطق. سألت:"من هم؟" لكنها استدركت. إذا لم تكن ستحدثه عن حلمها، فلا ينبغي عليها أن تتدخل في أحلامه. وتلك هي القاعدة في حفظ الأسرار، وهي ملمة بها: لا تسأل لئلا تُسأل.

"وحوش"، قال بلا مبالاة، وفوراً فقدت إليزا اهتمامها—ليس بسبب ذكر الوحوش، ولكن بسبب نبرته المرتجلة. أي شخص يمكن أن يقول"وحوش" بتلك الطريقة اللامبالية، فهو لم يلتقِ بالتأكيد بها."أنتِ تعلمين، أن تكوني مطاردة هي واحدة من الأحلام الأكثر شيوعاً"، قال غابرييل، وبدأ في

الحديث عن الأمر، واستمرت إليزا في احتساء الشاي وتناول القليل من آيس كريم الكوابيس بين الحين والآخر، وتهز رأسها، لكنها لم تكن تصغي له. لقد درست تحليل الأحلام بشكل شامل منذ وقت طويل. لم يساعدها ذلك من قبل، ولا الآن، وعندما اختتم غابرييل قائلاً:"إنها تجسيد لمخاوفنا أثناء اليقظة، والجميع يمتلكها"، كان صوته مهدئاً ومتعالياً في آن واحد، وكأنه قد حل لها المشكلة.

أرادت إليزا حقاً أن تقول: وأعتقد أن الجميع يحصلون على أجهزة تنظيم ضربات القلب عندما يبلغون السابعة من العمر لأن"تجسيد مخاوفهم أثناء اليقظة" تجعلهم يصابون بعدم انتظام ضربات القلب؟ لكنها لم تقل ذلك، لأنه كان حديث كليشيه يتكرر في الحفلات.

هل تعلمين أن إليزا جونز لديها جهاز تنظيم ضربات القلب مذ كانت في السابعة من عمرها بسبب كثرة كوابيسها التي سببت لها اضطراباً في ضربات القلب؟

حقاً؟ هذا جنوني.

سألته:"إذاً ماذا حصل معك؟ ماذا حدث لوحوشك؟".

"أوه، لقد حملوا أخي وتركوني. يجب أن أضحي لهم بماعز كل عيد القديس ميخائيل"، لكنه ثمن زهيد مقابل ليلة نوم هادئة".

ضحكت إليزا."من أين تحصل على ماعزك؟" سألت، متابعة المزاح.

"من مزرعة رائعة في ميريلاند. ماعز معتمد للتضحية. يمكنك أيضاً الحصول على حملان إذا كنت تفضلين".

"من لا يفضل؟ وما هو عيد القديس ميخائيل؟".

"لا أعرف. اخترعته للتو".

وأحست إليزا بلحظة من الامتنان، لأن غابرييل لم يحاول الاستفسار، وساعد الآيس كريم والشاي وحتى انزعاجها من حديثه الأكاديمي في تخفيف آثار الحلم. وقد جعلها تضحك على الأقل. وكان ذلك شيئاً رائعاً.

ثم اهتز هاتفها على الطاولة.

من يتصل بها في الرابعة صباحاً؟

مدت يدها إليه... وعندما رأت الرقم على الشاشة، رمته. أسقطته. وربما ألقته. ارتطم بالخزانة وارتد إلى الأرض. لثانية، تأملت أن يكون قد تعطل تماماً. بقي هناك، صامتاً، ميتاً. ثم—بززززززز—آه لا زال حياً.

متى شعرت بالندم لأنها لم تحطم هاتفها؟

مجرد أرقام ظهرت دون اسم، لأن إليزا لم تخزن اسم صاحب هذا الرقم في هاتفها. لم تتذكره ولكنها أدركت وكأنه كان موجوداً طوال الوقت، وفي كل لحظة من حياتها منذ... منذ أن هربت. لا زال كل شيء موجوداً. وهذه الصدمة الغريزية الفورية لم تتضاءل مع السنين.

سألها غابرييل، وهو يميل لالتقاط الهاتف:"هل أنتِ بخير؟".

أوشكت أن تقول له: لا تلمسه! لكنها أدركت أن هذا غير منطقي فاستدركت مباشرة، وبدلاً من ذلك، لم تمد يدها إليه عندما قدمه لها، لذلك اضطر إلى وضعه على الطاولة، وهو مستمر في الاهتزاز. متسائلة وهي تحدق فيه. كيف استطاعوا العثور عليها؟

كيف؟ حتى إنها غيرت اسمها. واختفت. هل كانوا يعرفون مكانها طوال الوقت، وكانوا يراقبونها طوال هذه المدة؟ فكرة أن سنوات الحرية كانت مجرد وهم... فكرة مرعبة.

توقف الاهتزاز. تحولت المكالمة إلى البريد الصوتي، وراح قلب إليزا يدق كمدفع مرة أخرى: انفجار بعد انفجار يهزها من الداخل. من كان؟ أختها؟ أحد"أعمامها"؟

أمها؟

تساءلت إليزا للحظة عما إذا كانوا سيتركون رسالة—وإذا كانت ستجرؤ على الاستماع إليها لو حصل—قبل أن يصدر الهاتف اهتزازاً آخر ينبه إلى وصول رسالة نصية.

يقول نص الرسالة: شغلي التلفاز. شغلي الـ...؟

نظرت إليزا من الهاتف، وهي مضطربة بعمق. لماذا؟ ماذا يريدون منها أن ترى على التلفاز؟ حتى إنه لم يكن لديها تلفاز.

غابرييل يراقبها بتمعن، تتلاقى عيونهما في اللحظة التي سمعا فيها الصرخة الأولى. كادت إليزا أن تقفز من كرسيها واقفة. ومن مكان ما في الخارج جاء صراخ طويل غير مفهوم. أو أنه من داخل المبنى؟ ارتفع الصوت عالياً.

إنه من داخل المبنى. انتظري. إنه شخص آخر. ما الذي يحدث بحق الجحيم؟ الناس يصرخون في... صدمة؟ فرح؟ رعب؟ ثم بدأ هاتف غابرييل بالاهتزاز أيضاً، وانطلقت سلسلة من الرسائل في هاتف إليزا—زززززززز. من الأصدقاء هذه المرة، بمن فيهم تاج في لندن، وكاثرين التي كانت تقوم بعمل ميداني في جنوب أفريقيا. تنوعت الصياغات، لكن جميعها كانت نسخة من نفس الأمر المقلق: شغلي التلفاز.

شغلي التلفاز.

هل تشاهدين هذا! استيقظي.. التلفاز.. الآن..

إلى أن وصلتها رسالة أخيرة - جعلتها تتمنى الانكماش كجنين في رحم يقاوم الخروج للحياة- تقول:

"تعالي إلى المنزل، لقد سامحناك".

2

الوصول

ظهروا يوم الجمعة في وضح النهار، في سماء أوزبكستان، وقد تمت مشاهدتهم لأول مرة من مدينة سمرقند القديمة على طريق الحرير، حيث سارع طاقم الأخبار لبث لقطات... لهؤلاء الزوار.

الملائكة في صفوف منظمة بشكل مثالي، كان من السهل عدهم. عشرون مجموعة مكونة من خمسين: ألف. نعم ألف ملاك. كانوا يندفعون غرباً، قريبين بما يكفي من الأرض إلى درجة أن الناس الواقفين على الأسطح والطرقات تمكنوا من رؤية أغطيتهم البيضاء الحريرية وهي ترفرف وسماع صوت القيثارات الرنانة وصداها.

القيثارات.

انتشرت اللقطات على نطاق واسع في جميع أنحاء العالم، وتم تعطيل البرامج الإذاعية والتلفزيونية؛ اندفع مقدمو الأخبار إلى مكاتبهم، يلهثون ومن دون نصوص. مزيج من الإثارة والرعب. عيون مفتوحة كنقود معدنية، أصوات عالية وغريبة. في كل مكان، بدأت الهواتف ترن، ثم انقطعت في صمت عالمي هائل مع تعطل أبراج الهاتف المحمول بسبب التحميل

الزائد. استيقظ الجزء النائم من الكوكب. تعثرت اتصالات الإنترنت. بدأ الناس في البحث عن بعضهم البعض. امتلأت الشوارع. ارتفعت الأصوات وتضاربت، تعالت واشتدت. كانت هناك مشاجرات. غناء. شغب. وفيات.

حيوات جديدة ولدت أيضاً. الأطفال الذين وُلدوا خلال وصول الملائكة أطلق عليهم لقب"الملائكة الصغار" من قبل أحد المذيعين، والذي كان أيضاً مسؤولاً عن الإشاعة التي تقول إن جميعهم لديهم وحمات ولادة على شكل ريشة في مكان ما على أجسادهم الصغيرة. لم يكن هذا صحيحاً، لكن الأطفال سيتم مراقبتهم عن كثب بحثاً عن أي إشارة إلى النعمة أو القوى السحرية في هذا اليوم من التاريخ—التاسع من أغسطس—انقسم الزمن فجأة إلى"ما قبل" و"ما بعد"، ولن ينسى أحد متى وعندما بدأ"ذلك".

كازيمير أندراسكو، ممثل، شبح، مصاص دماء، وأحمق، غط في نوم عميق في تلك الأثناء، لكنه ادعى فيما بعد أنه فقد الوعي أثناء قراءة نيتشه—في الوقت نفسه لوصول الملائكة كما أشار—وقاسى من رؤياه لنهاية العالم. بالرغم من أنها كانت ملامح لخطة كبرى ولكنها غير مكتملة، وسرعان ما تلاشت إلى نهاية مخيبة لآماله عندما أدرك مقدار الجهد اللازم الذي ينطوي عليه تأسيس عصبة عمل.

كانت زوزانا نوفاكوفا وميكولاس فافارا في قصر آيت بن حدو، أشهر قصر في المغرب. أما ميك فقد أنهى للتو المساومة على خاتم فضي قديم—ربما قديم، ربما فضي، لكن بالتأكيد خاتم—عندما جرفهم الضجيج المفاجئ؛ أخفاه عميقاً في جيبه، حيث سيظل سراً لبعض الوقت.

في أحد مطابخ القرية، تجمعوا خلف السكان المحليين وشاهدوا التغطية الإخبارية باللغة العربية. رغم أنهم لم يفهموا التعليقات ولا الهتافات اللاهثة من حولهم، إلا أنهم وحدهم كانوا يمتلكون السياق لما كانوا يرونه. كانوا يعرفون ما هي الملائكة، أو بالأحرى، ما ليست عليه. لم يقلل ذلك من صدمة رؤية السماء مليئة بهم. ما أكثرهم!

كانت فكرة زوزانا أن"تطلق العنان" حسب تعبيرها، للشاحنة المتوقفة أمام مطعم سياحي. أصبح الأمر الواقع اليومي مشوهاً إلى درجة أن سرقة السيارات صارت أمراً عادياً. بدا الأمر بسيطاً: إنها تعلم بأن كارو لا تستطيع الوصول إلى الأخبار العالمية؛ وكان لا بد لها من تحذيرها. ولو اضطرت لأن تسرق مروحية وتطير بها إليها.

إستير فان دي فلويت، تاجرة ألماس متقاعدة، شريكة قديمة لبريمستون، وجدّة بديلة من حين إلى آخر لطفلته البشرية، كانت تمشي مع كلابها من نوع ماستيف قرب منزلها في أنتويرب عندما بدأت أجراس كنيسة"سيدتنا" تدق بشكل غير منتظم. لم يكن الوقت المخصص لذلك، وحتى لو كان، فإن هذا الرنين الفوضوي كان مبالغاً فيه، ويكاد أن يكون هستيرياً. أما إستير، التي لم تكن أي من عظام جسدها منهكة وهستيرية، أخذت تنتظر شيئاً ما أن يحدث منذ أن ظهرت بصمة يد سوداء على باب في بروكسل وأحرقته حتى الرماد. بعدها استنتجت أن هذا هو ذلك الشيء، وعادت إلى المنزل مسرعة، وكلابها الضخمة التي بحجم اللبؤات تسير بجانبها.

شاهدت إليزا جونز الدقائق القليلة الأولى على بث مباشر على حاسوب محمول خاص بزميلها في السكن، لكن عندما انهار مخدم الانترنت، سارعا بارتداء ملابسهما، وقفزا في سيارة غابرييل، وقادا إلى المتحف. ورغم أن الوقت كان مبكراً، إلا أنهما لم يكونا أول الواصلين، واستمر زملاؤهما في التدفق خلفهما ليتجمعوا حول شاشة تلفزيون في مختبر في الطابق السفلي.

كانوا مصدومين وغارقين في عدم التصديق، وبقدر لا يستهان به من السخط المنطقي أن مثل هذا الحدث تجرأ على أن يحدث في سماء العالم الطبيعي. إنها خدعة، بالطبع. لو أن الملائكة حقيقية—وهو أمر مثير للسخرية—ألم يكن من المفترض أن تكون أقل شبهاً بالصور الموجودة في كتب التعليم المسيحي للأطفال؟

يبدو الأمر مثالياً جداً. لا بد أنه مدبر.

"كفى هراءً عن القيثارات"، قال عالم الحفريات."هذه مبالغة". لكن هذا اليقين الظاهري يقوضه التوتر الحقيقي بينهم، فهم ليسوا أغبياء، وهناك ثغرات واضحة في نظرية الخدعة التي أصبحت أكثر وضوحاً مع اقتراب المروحيات الإخبارية من تلك الكائنات الطائرة، وأصبحت اللقطات المذاعة أكثر وضوحاً وأقل لبساً. لم يرغب أحد في الاعتراف بذلك، ولكن الأمر بدا... حقيقياً أجنحتهم، على سبيل المثال. تمتد بسهولة لأكثر من اثني عشر قدماً، وكل ريشة كأنها لسان من لهب. الصعود والهبوط السلس لها، الرشاقة والقوة التي لا توصف في طيرانهم—كل ذلك يتجاوز أي تكنولوجيا يمكن تخيلها اقترح غابرييل:"قد يكون البث مزيفاً. قد يكون كل شيء محاكاة بالحاسوب. حرب العوالم للقرن الحادي والعشرين".

كثر الهمس، لكن لم يبدُ أن أحداً يقتنع بذلك حقاً.

ظلت إليزا تراقب بصمت. لخوفها طعم مختلف عن خوفهم، و... أكثر تطوراً بكثير. وهذا طبيعي. فخوفها نما معها طوال حياتها.

بعد الحادثة التي وقعت على جسر تشارلز في براغ قبل بضعة أشهر، كان قادرة على الاحتفاظ ببعض الشك، بما يكفي على الأقل لمنعها من الانهيار. ربما كان ذلك الحدث مزيفاً: ثلاثة ملائكة، ظهروا ثم اختفوا، من دون أن يتركوا أي دليل. شعرت الآن وكأن العالم كله ينتظر بأنفاس محبوسة، عرضاً لا مجال للشك فيه. حتى هي كذلك. وهذا ما حصلوا عليه الآن.

فكرت في هاتفها، الذي تركته عمداً في الشقة، وتساءلت عن الرسائل الجديدة التي قد يحتويها. كما فكرت في تلك القوة المظلمة الهائلة التي تدفقت منها في الليل، في الحلم. شعرت بتشنج في أمعائها مثل قبضة قد أحكمت بشدة، وهي تشعر تحت قدميها بحركة الألواح التي وضعتها فوق الرمال المتحركة لتلك الحياة الأخرى. هل اعتقدت بأنها قادرة على الهروب منها؟ كانت هناك، دائماً هناك، والحياة التي بنتها علاوة على ذلك بدت لها هشة مثل حي من الصفيح فوق فوهة بركان.

3

اختيار مهارات الحياة

"ملائكة! ملائكة! ملائكة!".

هذا ما صرخت به زوزانا وهي تقفز من الشاحنة التي انحرفت عن الطريق وتوقفت على المنحدر الترابي. كانت"قلعة الوحوش" تلوح أمامها: هذا المكان في صحراء المغرب حيث يختبئ جيش متمرد من عالم آخر لإحياء موتاه. ذلك الحصن الطيني بأفاعيه ورائحته الكريهة، وبجنوده المتوحشين الضخام، وحفرة الجثث. هذا الخراب الذي هربت منه هي وميك في ظلام الليل. خفية. بناءً على إصرار كارو.

وقد كانت على حق رغم ذعرها، ... فحياتهم عرضة للخطر. وها هما قد عادوا مجدداً، يطلقون الأبواق ويهتفون؟ لم تكن مجرد غريزة البقاء. ظهرت كارو ، وهي تحوم فوق سور القصر، رشيقة مثل راقصة باليه في حالة انعدام الجاذبية. هرعت زوزانا نحوها صعوداً بينما نزلت صديقتها لتلاقيها "الملائكة"، همست لها زوزانا، المحملة بالأخبار."يا للجحيم يا كارو. مئات ومئات منهم في السماء.. العالم ينهار". نطقت كلماتها، وبينما هي تتحدث رأت زوزانا صديقتها. تنظر إليها وتخطو إلى الوراء.

ما هذا بحق الجحيم...؟

باب السيارة، أقدام تجري، وكان ميك بجانبها، يرى كارو أيضاً. لم يتحدث أحد. لم يكن هناك صوت. الصمت كان كفقاعة فارغة: تشغل مساحة ولكن خالية من الكلمات.

كارو... كان نصف وجهها أرجوانياً ومنتفخاً، خدوش متقشرة وقروح متخثرة. شفتها مشقوقة ومنتفخة، وشحمة أذنها ممزقة و مخيطة. أما بقية جسدها، فلم تستطع زوزانا رؤيته. فقد سحبت أكمامها لأسفل حتى غطت يديها، وقد شبكت قبضتيها بطريقة طفولية غريبة. كأنها تحتضن نفسها بحنان.

بدا عليها وكأنها تعرضت لأذى وحشي واضح. ولا يمكن أن يكون هناك سوى مذنب واحد.

إنه الذئب الأبيض. ذاك النذل اللعين. اشتعل الغضب في زوزانا.

ثم رأته. كان نازلاً من التل نحوهم مختالاً، وقد تنبه الكيميرا لوصوله، فشدت زوزانا قبضتيها. بدأت تتقدم، مستعدة للوقوف بين ثياغو وكارو، لكن ميك أمسكها من ذراعها.

"ماذا تفعلين؟" همس وهو يسحبها نحوه."هل جننت؟ ليس لديك إبرة عقرب مثل الكيميرا المدعوة ميك-ميك."

وميك-ميك هي نوع من الفأر العقربي الشجاع في إريتز، وعلى الرغم من كره زوزانا للاعتراف بذلك، لكن ميك كان على حق. فهي فأرة أكثر منها عقرباً، وميك واحدة زيادة عليها.

وحينها قررت زوزانا أنها ستفعل شيئاً حيال ذلك. أممم. بعد أن نتجنب الموت هنا، بالطبع. لأن... يا للجحيم، هناك الكثير من الكيميرا، عندما تراهم جميعاً ينحدرون معاً من التل، تتلاشى شجاعتها داخل صدرها. لكنها اطمأنت لذراع ميك حولها—ولم يكن لديها أي شك في أن عازف الكمان اللطيف يمكن أن يحميها أفضل مما تستطيع هي حماية نفسها.

همست له:"بدأت أشك في قدرتنا على مهارات البقاء". وأردفت،"لماذا لم نصبح ساموراي؟ لنصبح ساموراي".

"لا بأس"، قالت كارو مع اقتراب الذئب منها، محاطاً بثلة من الضباط. التقت عينا زوزانا المتحديتان بعينيه. رأت علامات خدوش متخثرة على خديه، واشتعل غضبها من جديد. إنه إثبات، ودون أي شك الآن في هوية المعتدي على كارو.

انتظري. هل قلت للتو"لا بأس" يا كارو؟

كيف تقولين لا بأس؟

لكن لم يكن لدى زوزانا وقت للتفكير في الأمر وهي تلهث من الغضب. وسرعان ما بدا خلف كارو، شيء ما يتشكل في الهواء، ويملأ المكان بكل الروعة التي تتذكرها، إنه...

أكيفا!؟

ما الذي يفعله هنا؟

ظهر سيراف آخر بجانبه. نفس الشخص الذي بدا غاضباً جداً على الجسر في براغ. وهي الآن غاضبة أيضاً، وبمنتهى التركيز، وكأنها تقول"اقترب خطوة واحدة وسأقتلك". يدها على مقبض سيفها، وعيناها ثابتتان على الكيميرا المتجمعين.

لكن أكيفا لم ينظر إلا إلى كارو، التي... لم تبدُ منزعجة لرؤيته. كما لم يبدُ ذلك على الباقين.

حاولت زوزانا فهم المشهد. لماذا لم يهاجما بعضهما البعض؟ كانت تعتقد أن هذا ما يفعله الكيميرا والسيرافيم — خاصة هذان الكيميرا والسيرافيم.

ماذا حدث في قصر الوحوش أثناء غيابها وميك؟

كل جندي من الكيميرا كان حاضراً آنذاك، ورغم غياب المفاجأة، كان العداء حاضراً. تلك النظرات الوحشية المتبادلة. جلست زوزانا على الأرض

تضحك مع هؤلاء الجنود أنفسهم؛ وراحت ترقّص لهم دمى عظام الدجاج، مزحت معهم وتبادلوا المزاح. إنها تحبهم.. حسناً، ربما تحب بعضهم. لكن الآن، جميعهم مرعوبين بلا استثناء، وبدوا مستعدين تماماً لتمزيق الملائكة إرباً إرباً. عيونهم طفقت تتجه إلى ثياغو ثم تبتعد عنه، بينما كانوا ينتظرون الأمر لقتلهم، وكانوا على يقين بأن ذلك الأمر سيأتيهم حتماً.

لكنه لم يأتِ.

أدركت زوزانا أنها حبست أنفاسها، ثم أطلقتها ببطء، وجسدها بدأ يسترخي تدريجياً. لمحت إيسّا في الحشد ورمتها بنظرة استفهام واضحة، وكأنها تسألها:"ما الذي يجري بحق الجحيم؟". ردت عليها إيسّا في المقابل بنظرة مشوشة، وخلف ابتسامة قصيرة وغير مطمئنة، بدت متوترة ومستنفرة.

ما الذي يحدث؟

قالت كارو شيئاً بصوت ناعم وحزين لأكيفا—باللغة الكيميرية بالطبع. اللعنة. ماذا قالت؟ رد أكيفا أيضاً بنفس اللغة، قبل أن يوجه كلماته التالية إلى الذئب الأبيض.

ربما كان السبب في أنها لم تفهم لغتهما، وبالتالي كانت تراقب وجهيهما بحثاً عن أدلة، وربما لأن زوزانا رأتهما معاً من قبل، وعرفت المشاعر المتبادلة بينهما، لكنها فهمت هذا: بطريقة ما، في هذا الحشد من جنود الوحوش، مع ثياغو في المقدمة، هي لحظة تخص كارو وأكيفا.

الاثنان صبوران بوجهين صارمين وعلى بعد عشرة أقدام من بعضهما البعض، ولم ينظرا إلى بعضهما البعض في تلك اللحظة، لكن زوزانا شعرت وكأنهما زوج من المغناطيسات يتظاهران بعدم التجاذب.

ولكن كما تعلمون، إن كل ما يعمل، سيتعطل.

4

بداية

لم يعد الأمر مجرد عالمين وحياتين.

لقد اتخذت كارو قرارها. قالت لأكيفا:"أنا كيميرا". هل كان قبل ساعات فقط عندما"هرب" من القصبة مع أخته ليطيرا ويحرقا بوابة سمرقند؟ كان من المفترض أن يعودا ويحرقا هذه البوابة أيضاً، وليعزلا الأرض وإريتز عن بعضهما البعض إلى الأبد. تساءل أي عالم هي ستختار؟ وكأنه كان لديها خيار. قالت:"حياتي هناك".

لكن حياتها لم تكن هناك بالفعل. فهي محاطة بمخلوقات من صنع يديها، والتي غالباً ما احتقرت معظمهم كعاشقة للملائكة، وقد كانت تعلم أن ما ينتظرها في تلك إريتز ليست أي حياةً، بل واجب ومعاناة، وإرهاق وجوع. خوف واغتراب. موت، على الأرجح.

ألم! بالتأكيد. وماذا بعد؟

قال أكيفا:"يمكننا محاربتهم معاً. لدي جيش أيضاً".

تجمدت كارو في مكانها متأففة. لقد تأخر أكيفا. لقد اندفع جيش من السيرافيم عبر البوابة بالفعل — جيش الدومينيون التابع لجايل القاسي،

فيلق الإمبراطورية النخبوي—وهكذا كان العرض غير المعقول الذي قدمه أكيفا لعدوه، مما أثار دهشة الجميع، بمن فيهم أخته. محاربتهم معاً؟ رأت كارو نظرة لا تصدق من ليراز، وكأن تلك النظرة تقول شيئاً، شيئاً واحداً كان مؤكداً: إذا كان عرض أكيفا غير معقول، فإن قبول ثياغو له كان غير مفهوم أيضاً

الذئب الأبيض يفضل ألف ميتة قبل أن يتحالف مع الملائكة. كان سيمزق العالم حوله. سيعتبر ذلك نهاية كل شيء، قبل أن يفكر حتى في قبول مثل هذا العرض.

لذلك كانت كارو مندهشة مثل البقية—لكن لأسباب مختلفة— عندما... أومأ ثياغو برأسه.

همسة مفاجأة جاءت إما من نيسك أو ليسيث، نائباه من الناجا. وبغض النظر إلى بعض الحصى التي انزلقت أسفل التل نتيجة حركة ذيل، كان ذلك هو الصوت الوحيد من الجنود. في أذني كارو، كان الدم يضج. ماذا يفعل؟ كانت تأمل أن تكون لديه خطة، لأنها بالتأكيد لا تعرف.

ألقت نظرة خاطفة على أكيفا. لم يكن هناك أي أثر للحزن أو الاشمئزاز، أو القلق أو الحب الذي ظهر في وجهه في الليلة السابقة؛ كان خلف قناعه، وكذلك هي خلف قناعها. كان عليها أن تخفي كل اضطرابها الداخلي، لا سيما أن لديها الكثير لتخفيه.

عاد أكيفا إلى هنا. ألا يمكن لأحد أن يبقى هارباً من هذا القصر اللعين؟ لقد كان تصرفاً شجاعاً؛ أكيفا كان دائماً كذلك—شجاعاً ومتهوراً. لكن الأمر لم يعد يتعلق به وحده الآن. كل شيء حاولت هي تحقيقه أصبح في خطر. الموقف الذي يضع فيه الذئب الأبيض: أن يأتي لعذر مقنع آخر لعدم قتله؟

ثم هناك موقفها الخاص. ربما كان هذا ما أقلقها أكثر من أي شيء آخر ها هو أكيفا، العدو الذي وقعت في حبه مرتين، في حياتين مختلفتين، مع قوة بدت وكأنها تصميم الكون نفسه وربما كان كذلك فعلاً، ومع ذلك،

لم يكن ذلك مهماً. كانت تقف بجانب ثياغو. هذا هو المكان الذي صنعته لنفسها، من أجل شعبها: بجانب ثياغو.

وعلاوة على ذلك—رغم أن أكيڤا لم يكن يعلم ذلك—هذا هو ثياغو الذي صنعته لنفسها: واحد يمكنها أن تتحمل الوقوف بجانبه. الذئب الأبيض... لم يكن نفسه في هذه الأيام. لقد حبست روحاً أفضل داخل الجسد الذي تكرهه—أوه، زيري—وكانت تصلي لكل شيء في التشكيلة اللامتناهية لآلهة العالمين ألا يكتشف أحد السر. كان سراً مؤلماً، ويمكن في أي لحظة أن ينفجر كقنبلة في يدها. نبضات قلبها كانت تختل وتنزلق في إيقاع متقطع. كفّاها كانتا رطبتين بالعرق.

الخدعة عظيمة لكنها هشة، والمسؤولية على عاتق زيري لينفذها بعدما بثت فيه كارو هيئة الذئب الأبيض. هل سيخدع كل هؤلاء الجنود؟ معظمهم خدم لعقود مع الجنرال، وبعضهم لمئات السنين عبر تجسدات متعددة، وكانوا يعرفون كل حركة وكل نبرة منه. كان على زيري أن يكون الذئب في الأسلوب والإيقاع وفي القسوة الباردة المكبوتة—أن يكون هو، ليتمكن من توجيه شعبهم نحو التخلي عن الانتقام العقيم.

لا يمكن أن يحدث ذلك إلا بالتدريج. الذئب الأبيض لن يستيقظ هكذا ليتمدد ويقرر التحالف مع عدوه الدود.

لكن هذا بالضبط ما توجب على زيري أن يفعله الآن.

صرح ثياغو بصوت هادئ وبكل موضوعية:"يجب إيقاف جايل. إذا نجح في الحصول على أسلحة ودعم بشري، فلن يكون هناك أمل لنا جميعاً في هذا. نعم لدينا هدف مشترك". حافظ على نبرة صوت منخفضة تنقل سلطة مطلقة من دون أن يظهر أي قلق حول كيفية استقبال قراره. كانت هذه طريقة الذئب، وكان تقليد زيري له لا تشوبه شائبة."كم عددهم؟".

أجاب أكيڤا،"ألف في هذا الجانب من العالم. وبالتأكيد سيكون هناك تواجد عسكري كثيف على الجانب الآخر من البوابة".

سأل ثياغو:"هذه البوابة؟" وأومأ برأسه نحو جبال الأطلس.

قال أكيفا:"لقد دخلوا من البوابة الأخرى، لكن هذه البوابة يمكن اختراقها أيضاً. ولديهم الوسائل لاكتشافها".

لم ينظر إلى كارو عندما قال ذلك، لكنها شعرت بشيء من اللوم. فبسببها، كان رازغوت، ذلك المسخ، طليقاً، وقد يكون قد أظهر لدومينيون هذه البوابة كما أظهرها لها. يمكن أن يقع الكيميرا في مصيدة هنا، ويعزلون ويصعب عليهم تراجعهم إلى عالمهم بينما يطبق عليهم أعداؤهم من السيرافيم من كلا الجانبين. قد يتحول هذا الملاذ الآمن الذي قادهم إليه إلى قبر لهم.

تلقى ثياغو الأمر بأريحية."حسناً. دعونا نكتشف ذلك".

نظر إلى جنوده، وهم بدورهم نظروا إليه بحذر، محاولين تفسير كل حركة من حركاته. ماذا يخطط؟ كانوا يتساءلون، لأنه ببساطة لا يمكن أن يكون الأمر ما يبدو عليه. قريباً سيأمر بقتل الملائكة. لا بد أن هذا جزء من استراتيجية ما. بالتأكيد.

أمر،"أورا، سارساغون، اختارا فرقاً للسرعة والتخفي. أريد أن أعرف إذا كان هناك دومينيون على أبوابنا. إذا كانوا هناك، فامنعوهم. احموا البوابة. لا تدعوا ملاكاً يمر حياً." ابتسم ابتسامة ذئبية تعكس متعته بفكرة موت الملائكة، ورأت كارو بعض التوتر يغادر وجوه الجنود. هذا بدا منطقياً بالنسبة إليهم إن لم يكن كذلك بالنسبة إلى البقية: الذئب يتلذذ بفكرة إراقة دماء السيرافيم."أرسلوا رسولاً حالما تتأكدان. انطلقا"، قال، وفعلا. اختار أورا وسارساغون فرقهما بإيماءات سريعة وحاسمة وهما يتحركان بين الحشد. باست كيتا-إري، الغريفون، فازرا وأشترا، ليليفيت، هيلغيت، إميليون.

"ليعد الجميع إلى الساحة. كونوا مستعدين للمغادرة إذا كانت التقارير إيجابية". توقف الجنرال قليلاً."واستعدوا للقتال". ومرة أخرى، تمكن بظل ابتسامة أن يلمح إلى أنه كان يفضل النتيجة الأكثر دموية.

كان الأمر محكماً، وتسرب أمل قليل إلى قلق كارو. عمل جيد؛ أوامر تُعطى وتُنفذ. كانت الاستجابة فورية وغير مترددة. استدار الحشد وتحرك صعوداً نحو التل. إذا استطاع زيري الحفاظ على هذا السلوك القيادي المهيب، فإن حتى أكثر الجنود صلابة سيُسرعون لتحقيق رضاه.

ولكن، حسناً، لم يتحرك الجميع بالسرعة نفسها. وتحركت إيسّا بتحدٍّ، عكس تيار الجنود النازلين من التل، ثم كان هناك أمر نواب ثياغو. باستثناء سارساغون، الذي تلقى أمراً مباشراً، بقيت حاشية الذئب متجمعة حوله. نيسك، ليسيث، رارك، وڤيركو. هؤلاء هم نفس الكيميرا الذين تآمروا لجعل كارو وحيدة عند الحفرة مع ثياغو—باستثناء نيسك، الذي ارتكب خطأ مواجهة إيسّا والآن لم يعد كما كان—كم تكرههم. لم يكن لديها شك في أنهم كانوا سيساعدونه لو طلب ذلك، ولا يسعها إلا أن تكون سعيدة لأنه لم يرَ ذلك ضرورياً.

والآن، أصبح تباطؤهم مشؤوماً. لم يتبعوا أمر ثياغو لأنهم اعتقدوا أنهم معفيون منه، لأنهم توقعوا تلقي أوامر أخرى. والطريقة التي تعاملوا بها مع أكيڤا وليراز لم تترك شكاً فيما توقعوا أن تكون تلك الأوامر.

"كارو"، همست زوزانا عند كتف كارو."ما الذي يجري بحق الجحيم؟".

بل ما الذي لا يجري؟ كل التصادمات التي ظنت كارو أنها تجنبتها في الأيام الماضية قد ارتدت لتصطدم ببعضها البعض هنا. قالت وهي تشدّ على أسنانها:"كل شيء يدور".

استعد نيسك وليسيث الوحشيان بأيديهما نصف المرفوعة، لإشهار هامساتهما على أكيڤا وليراز، لإضعافهما والانقضاض عليهما لقتلهما—أو محاولة ذلك. أكيڤا وليراز واقفان بلا اكتراث في وجه التهديد، وزيري في المنتصف. زيري المسكين اللطيف، يرتدي لحم ثياغو ويحاول أن يمثل وحشيته أيضاً—لكن فقط بالشكل وليس القلب. كان هذا تحديه الآن. لم يكن مجرد تحدٍّ. كانت حياته وكل شيء يعتمد عليه.

لم يكن التحدي يقتصر فقط على حياة زيري، بل على مصير التمرد بأكمله ومستقبل—إن كان هناك مستقبل—الكيميرا الذين لا يزالون على قيد الحياة وكل الأرواح المدفونة في كاتدرائية بريمستون. كانت الخدعة هي أملهم الوحيد.

بدت الثواني العشر التالية ثقيلة كالحديد المطوي.

وصلت إيسّا إليهم في نفس اللحظة التي تحدثت فيها ليسيث."ما هي الأوامر، يا سيدي؟".

عانقت إيسّا ميك وزوزانا ورمقت كارو نظرة لامعة مشرقة. بدت متحمسة، كما رأت كارو. بدت بريئة.

قال ثياغو لليسيث ببرود:"لقد أصدرت أمري. ألم يكن هذا واضحاً؟".

قفزت أفكار كارو مباشرة إلى الليلة السابقة. بعد أن صرفت أكيفا ببرودة أعصاب لم تشعر بها حقاً، وأرسلته بعيداً لما اعتقدت أنها ستكون المرة الأخيرة، قالت لها إيسّا:"قلبك ليس مخطئاً. لا تشعري بالخجل".

إنها تقصد حبها لأكيفا. وماذا كان جواب كارو؟"لا يهم". حاولت أن تصدق ذلك: أن قلبها لا يهم، لا هي ولا أكيفا يهمان الآن، وأن هناك عوالم على المحك، وهذا هو ما يهم حقاً.

"سيدي"، اعترض نيسك، شريك ليسيث من الناجا."لا يمكن أن تكون جاداً في ترك هؤلاء الملائكة أحياء—"

ترك هؤلاء الملائكة أحياء. حتى إ، هذا يمكن أن يكون موضع تساؤل: حياة أكيفا، وحياة ليراز. لقد عادا إلى هنا لتحذيرهم. ثياغو الحقيقي لم يكن ليتردد لحظة واحدة في تمزيق أحشائهما بسبب مشاكلهما.

لم يكن أكيفا يعلم أن هذا ليس ثياغو الحقيقي، ومع ذلك عاد، من أجلها.

نظرت كارو إليه، ووجدت عينيه تنظران إلى عينيها، وتلاقت نظراتهما بوضوح مؤلم كان بمثابة الفناء النهائي للكذب.

المهم. وأياً كان الذي منعهم من قتل بعضهم البعض على شاطئ بولفينش قبل سنوات... فهو أمر هام.

لم يرد ثياغو على نيسك. ليس بالكلمات على الأقل. النظرة التي أرسلها إليه حولت كلام الجنود إلى صمت. كانت لدى الذئب دائماً تلك القدرة؛ وكان تقليد زيري لها صادماً.

قال بلهجة مهددة:"إلى الساحة. باستثناء تين. لدينا حديث حول... توقعاتي... عندما أنتهي من هذا، يمكنك الانصراف".

ذهبوا. ربما كانت كارو قد استمتعت بانسحابهم المخزي، لولا أن الذئب حول نظره إلى إيسّا بعد ذلك، ثم إليها وقال:"أنتِ أيضاً".

وكما كان الذئب ليفعل. حيث لم يكن يثق في كارو قط، بل يستغلها ويكذب عليها، وفي هذا الوضع كان بالتأكيد سيصرفها مع البقية. وكما كان لزيري دوراً يجب أن يلعبه، كان لها دورها. في الخفاء، قد تكون القوة الدافعة وراء هذا الهدف الجديد، الممسوحة ببركة بريمستون وبمباركة أمير الحرب، ولكنها في نظر جيش الكيميرا كانت لا تزال—على الأقل في الوقت الحالي—الفتاة التي عادت من الحفرة غارقة في الدماء. دمية ثياغو المحطمة.

لم يكن لديهم خيار سوى العمل من النقطة التي بدأوا منها، وتلك كانت الحفرة—الحصى، الدم، الموت والأكاذيب—ولم يكن لديها خيار في هذه اللحظة سوى التمسك بالخدعة.

أومأت بالطاعة للذئب، وكان من المؤلم أن ترى عيني أكيفا تظلمان. بجانب أكيفا، كانت ليراز أسوأ. كانت محتقرة.

كان ذلك صعباً بعض الشيء.

مات الذئب! أرادت أن تصرخ. لقد قتلته! لا تنظري إلي بهذه الطريقة! لكن بالطبع، لم يكن بإمكانها ذلك. في هذه اللحظة، كان عليها أن تكون قوية بما يكفي لتبدو ضعيفة.

قالت كارو:"هيا"، وهي تحث إيسّا وزوزانا وميك على المضي قدماً. لكن أكيڤا لم يترك الأمر بسهولة."انتظري". تحدث بالسيرافية التي لن يفهمها أحد غير كارو."لم آتِ هنا لأتحدث معه. كنت سأبحث عنكِ وحدك لأمنحكِ الخيار لو استطعت. أريد أن أعرف ما الذي تريدينه".

ما الذي أريده؟ أخمدت كارو موجة من الهستيريا شعرت وكأنها ضحكة خطيرة. وكأن هذه الحياة تحمل أي شبه مع ما أرادته! لكن في ظل هذه الظروف، هل كان هذا حقاً ما تريده؟ بالكاد فكرت فيما قد يعنيه ذلك. تحالف متمردو الكيميرا يتحد مع أبناء أكيڤا غير الشرعيين لمواجهة الإمبراطورية؟

ببساطة، كان ذلك جنوناً. قالت:"حتى وإن اتحدنا، سنكون أقل عدداً بكثير".

"التحالف لا يعني فقط كثرة عدد السيوف". أجاب أكيڤا، وكان صوته كظل من حياة أخرى، وأضاف برقة:"بل أكثر من هذا".

حدقت كارو فيه لثانية من دون حذر، ثم تذكرت نفسها وأخفضت بصرها قليلاً ثم أكثر. كان ذلك جواباً على سؤال ما إذا كان يمكن إقناع الآخرين بحلمهم بالسلام."هذه هي البداية"، قال أكيڤا قبل لحظات، واضعاً يده على قلبه قبل أن يتوجه إلى ثياغو. لم يلاحظ أحد ما يعنيه بذلك، لكن كارو فهمت وشعرت بحرارة الحلم تشتعل في قلبها.

نحن البداية.

كانت قد قالت هذا له منذ زمن طويل؛ وها هو ذا يقولها الآن. هذا ما كان يعنيه عرضه للتحالف: الماضي، المستقبل، التكفير عن الشرور، التجدد. الأمل.

هذا يعني كل شيء.

ولم تستطع كارو الاعتراف بذلك. على الأقل ليس هنا. نيسك وليسيث قد توقفا على التل لينظرا إليهم: كارو"عاشقة الملائكة" وأكيڤا الملاك

الذي يتحدث بهدوء بالسيرافية، بينما يقف ثياغو هناك ويتركهم؟ بدا كل شيء خطأ. الذئب الذي يعرفونه كان ليكون قد ملأ أنيابه بالدماء الآن.

كل لحظة كانت اختباراً للخداع؛ كل كلمة تقال كانت تجعل تسامح الذئب أقل تصديقاً. لذا أنزلت كارو بصرها نحو الأرض الصخرية المحترقة وحنت كتفيها مثل دمية مكسورة لتبدو مقنعة."الخيار خيار ثياغو"، قالت بلغة الكيميرا وحاولت أن تلعب دورها.

نعم حاولت.

لكنها لم تستطع ترك الأمر عند هذا الحد. بعد كل شيء، كان أكيفا لا يزال يطارد شبح الأمل. من وسط كل الدماء والرماد، كان يحاول استعادة الحلم إلى الحياة. ما الخيار الآخر المتاح؟ كان هذا ما تريده.

كان عليها أن تعطيه إشارة.

أمسكت إيسّا بمرفقها. مالت كارو نحوها، وهي تدير جسدها بحيث يتوسط جسد المرأة الأفعى بينها وبين الكيميرا الذين يراقبونها، ثم بسرعة خشيت أن يفوّت أكيفا الإشارة، رفعت يدها ولمست قلبها.

كان قلبها يخفق بشدة وهي تبتعد. نحن البداية، فكرت، وغمرتها ذكرى الإيمان. كان ذلك الإيمان يأتي من ذاتها الأعمق مادريغال، التي ماتت وهي مؤمنة، يا له من شعور جارح. انحنت نحو إيسّا، وهي تخفي وجهها كي لا يرى أحد احمرار وجنتيها.

كان صوت إيسّا خافتاً جداً، حتى بدا وكأنه فكرة في رأسها."هل ترين، يا صغيرة؟ قلبك ليس مخطئاً".

ولأول مرة منذ وقت من أمد طويل، أيقنت كارو بحقيقة"إن قلبها على صواب".

من وسط الخيانة واليأس، بين الوحوش الكاسرة والملائكة الغزاة، وخدع كبركان على وشك الانفجار، هنا، وبطريقة ما، كانت ثمة بداية.

5

لعبة التعارف

انتبه أكيفا إلى الإشارة، فقد رأى أطراف أصابع كارو تلامس قلبها عندما
استدارت. في تلك اللحظة، أصبح كل شيء بالنسبة إليه يستحق العناء.
الخطر الذي أحاط به، والتوتر الذي اجتاحه وهو يجبر نفسه على التحدث
إلى الذئب، بدت جميعها تافهة مقارنة بما شعر به حينها. حتى صمت ليراز
بجانبه، بدا وكأنه ينسجم مع عمق اللحظة.

قالت ليراز بنبرة جافة، مشوبة بالتحدي:"أنت مجنون... تقول إن لديك
جيشاً أيضاً؟ ليس لديك جيش يا أكيفا. لديك قطعة محاربة فقط. هناك
فرق".

"أعلم"، رد بهدوء. لم يكن القرار بيده. إخوتهم اللقطاء كانوا ينتظرونهم
في كهوف كيرين. أجل، هذا صحيح. لقد وُلِدوا ليكونوا أسلحةً، لا أبناءً أو
بنات، ولا حتى رجالاً أو نساء، بل مجرد أدوات حرب. ومع ذلك، الآن، كانوا
أسلحةً تُستخدم لخدمة هدفه. ورغم أنهم تجمعوا خلف أكيفا لمعارضة
الإمبراطورية، إلا أن التحالف مع عدوهم اللدود لم يكن أبداً جزءاً من الاتفاق

قال بثقة، وقد ارتسمت على شفتيه ابتسامة تحمل مزيجاً من الأمل والتحدي:"سأقنعهم".

وضعت كارو يدها على قلبها، وكأنها تستشعر وطأة كلماته. همست ليراز بصوت مشوب بالقلق، لكنه صارم:

"ابدأ بي. لقد جئنا هنا لنحذرهم، وليس لنتحد معهم".

كان أكيڤا يعلم أنه إذا استطاع إقناع ليراز، سيتبعهم الآخرون. لكنه لم يكن يعرف كيف، لكن اقتراب الذئب الأبيض عطّل محاولته.

كان الذئب يسير باتجاهه وبجانبه ملازمته المستذئبة، فتلاشت نشوة أكيڤا. عاد بذاكرته إلى أول مرة رأى فيها الذئب. كان ذلك في باث كول خلال هجوم الظل عندما كان مجرد غزّ طري العود خرج لتوه من معسكر التدريب. لقد رأى الجنرال الكيميري يقاتل، وأكثر من أي إشاعة روجت عنه، لقد شكّل ذلك كراهيته للوحوش. سيف في يد وفأس في الأخرى، و ثياغو يندفع عبر صفوف الملائكة، يمزق حناجرهم بأسنانه بشكل غريزي، وكأنه جائع.

تلك الذكرى أغضبت أكيڤا. كل شيء يتعلق بثياغو كان يثير اشمئزازه، وليس أقلها العلامات التي تركتها كارو على وجهه بالتأكيد في محاولة للدفاع عن نفسها. عندما وقف الجنرال أمامه، كان كل ما يمكن أن يفعله أكيڤا هو عدم دفع وجهه وإسقاطه على الأرض. سيف في قلبه كما كان مصير جورام، ثم يمكنهم أن يبدأوا بداية جديدة، جميعهم أحرار من أسياد الموت الذين قادوا شعوبهم ضد بعضهم البعض لفترة طويلة.

لكن هذا لم يكن ممكناً.

نظرت كارو مرة من السفح، وقد طغى القلق على وجهها الجميل—الذي ما زال مشوهاً بسبب العنف الذي رفضت الإفصاح عنه له—ثم ابتعدت، وبقي ثياغو وتين فقط في مواجهة أكيڤا وليراز، والشمس حارة وعالية، والسماء زرقاء، والأرض مملة.

قال ثياغو :"ربما، يمكننا التحدث بعيداً عن العيون".

"يبدو لي أنك تحب الظهور". قال أكيفا، مسترجعاً ذكريات التعذيب وكأنها حدثت للتو. كان تعذيب ثياغو له كاستعراض: الذئب الأبيض نجم العرض الدموي.

ظهرت لمحة من الحيرة واختفت على جبين ثياغو ."دعنا نترك الماضي، أليس كذلك؟ الحاضر يعطينا ما يكفي للحديث عنه، وبالطبع هناك المستقبل".

المستقبل لن يكون لك، فكر أكيفا. كان من السخرية أن يعتقد أنه إذا حدث هذا الحلم المستحيل، فإن الذئب الأبيض سيقوده إلى تحقيقه، وسيظل هناك، لا يزال أبيض، لا يزال مغروراً، ولا يزال يقف عند باب كارو بعد أن يتم كل شيء وينتصر.

لكن لا. كان ذلك خطأ. فكَّ أكيفا فكه وأحكمه مرة أخرى. لم تكن كارو عبارة عن جائزة ليفوز بها؛ لم يكن هذا سبب وجوده هنا. كانت امرأة وستختار حياتها بنفسها. كان هنا ليفعل ما يستطيع، مهما كلفه ذلك، لكي تكون لديها حياة تختارها يوماً ما. مهما كان فهذا شأنها الخاص. لذا كزّ على أسنانه. قال:"لنتحدث عن الحاضر".

قال الذئب:"لقد وضعتني في موقف صعب بقدومك إلى هنا. جنودي ينتظرون مني قتلك. ما أحتاجه هو سبب واحد لعدم القيام بذلك".

أثار هذا غضب ليراز. وعندها سألته:"هل تعتقد أنك تستطيع قتلنا؟ فلتجرب أيها الذئب".

نظر ثياغو إليها، غير مبالٍ تماماً. قال:"لم نتعرف بعد".

أجابته ليراز بحدة وبصراحتها المعتادة:"أنت تعرف من أنا، وأنا أعرف من أنت، وهذا يكفي".

قال ثياغو :"كما ترغبين".

علقت تِين بسخرية:"أنتم جميعاً تبدون متشابهين على أي حال".

ردت ليراز:"حسناً إذاً، قد يجعل ذلك لعبة التعارف على بعضنا البعض أكثر صعوبة من جانبكما".

سألت تين:"ما هي هذه اللعبة؟".

"لا يا لير". قال أكيڤا. ثم استطرد:"هذا بلا جدوى".

قالت ليراز:"تكمن اللعبة في محاولتنا التعرف على الذي قتل الأجساد السابقة. أنا متأكدة أن بعضكم يتذكرني". رفعت يديها لتظهر حصيلة القتلى لديها، وأكيڤا أمسك بيدها القريبة منه بقبضته المميزة ودفعها نحو الأسفل.

قال:"لا تتفاخر بهذا هنا". ما خطبها؟ هل كانت تريد حقاً أن يتحول هذا إلى حمام دم—مهما كان هذا"الشيء" الذي كان بمثابة وقفة غير مسبوقة في الأعمال العدائية؟

ضحكت تِين ضحكة متوحشة بينما كان أكيڤا يدفع يد أخته نحو الأسفل."لا تقلق يا قاتل الوحوش. هذا ليس سراً. أتذكر كل ملاك قتلني، ومع ذلك ها أنا أقف وأتحدث إليك. هل يمكن قول الشيء نفسه عن العديد من الملائكة الذين قتلتهم؟ أين هم جميعاً الآن؟ وأين أخوك؟".

ارتعشت ليراز. شعر أكيڤا بالكلمة كلكمة في جرح—شبح هازايل ارتفع ببساطة ووحشية—وعندما زادت الحرارة من حولهم، علم أنه لم يكن فقط بسبب غضب أخته، بل غضبه هو أيضاً.

ها قد عدنا إلى الوضع المعتاد: عداء. أو . . . ربما لا.

قال ثياغو:"لكن لم يكن الكيميرا هو الذي قتل أخاك. إنه جايل. وهذا يقودنا إلى النقطة الأساسية". وجد أكيڤا نفسه محط اهتمام عيني عدوه الباهتتين. لم يكن هناك أي سخرية في تلك النظرات، ولا حتى سخرية خفية، ولا أي استمتاع بارد كما كان ينظر إليه في غرفة التعذيب قبل سنوات، بإصرار غريب. قال بثقة:"ليس لدي شك في أننا جميعاً قتلة بارعون". وأضاف بصوت هادئ:"حسب معرفتي، فإننا نقف هنا لسبب آخر".

شعر أكيفا في بادئ الأمر بالإحراج—أن يتعلم الرزانة من ثياغو؟—ثم شعر بالغضب. قال:"نعم. ولم يكن ذلك للتفاوض على حياتنا. هل هي تحتاج سبباً لعدم قتلنا؟ ماذا عنك: هل لديك مكان آخر تذهب إليه؟".

قال ثياغو ببساطة وصدق:"لا، ليس لدينا". وأضاف:"لهذا السبب أستمع. وفق كل ذلك، إنها فكرتك". نعم، كانت فكرته المجنونة بتقديم السلام للذئب الأبيض. الآن، وهو يقف وجهاً لوجه معه، حيث لم تكن كارو موجودة بالقرب منه، رأى سخافة ذلك.

لقد أعمته رغبته الشديدة في البقاء بالقرب منها، ألا يفقدها في اتساع إريتز وأعدائها إلى الأبد. لذا قدم هذا العرض، وكان فقط الآن، متأخراً، يرى مدى غرابة أن الذئب كان يفكر فيه.

كان يبحث عن سبب لعدم قتله؟

بدا ذلك تجهماً، واستفزازاً. لكن هل يمكن أن يكون صادقاً؟ هل من الممكن أن تكون هذه الحقيقة، أنه يريد هذا السلام ولكنه يحتاج إلى تبرير لجنوده؟

قال أكيفا:"انسحب غير الشرعيين إلى مكان آمن. في أعين الإمبراطورية، نحن خونة. أنا قاتل أب وملك، وذنبي يلوثنا جميعاً". فكر في كلماته التالية."إذا كنت تعني بجدية أن تفكر في هذا—" قاطع ثياغو قائلاً:"هذه ليست خدعة من ناحيتي. أعدك".

ردت ليراز بسخرية:"تعدني؟ عليك أن تفعل أفضل من ذلك، أيها الذئب. ليس لدينا سبب لنثق بك".

قال ثياغو:"لن أذهب إلى هذا الحد. ما زلتم أحياء، أليس كذلك؟ لا أطلب شكراً على ذلك، لكنني آمل أن يكون واضحاً تماماً أنه ليس صدفة. جئتم إلينا نصف موتى. ولو أردت إنهاء الأمر، لفعلت".

لم يكن هناك جدال في ذلك. لا شك أن ثياغو قد تركهم يعيشون. وقد سمح لهم بالهروب.

لماذا؟ لأجل خاطر كارو؟ هل توسلت من أجل حياتهم؟ أم... هل ساومت لأجلهم؟

نظر أكيفا إلى المنحدر حيث ذهبت كارو. كانت تقف في مدخل قنطرة القصبة تراقبهم من بعيد، بعيدة بما يكفي لكيلا تُقرأ تعابيرها. التفت إلى ثياغو ورأى أن وجهه لا يزال خالياً من القسوة أو الخداع، بل وحتى من بروده المعتاد. كانت عيناه مفتوحتين، ليستا مثقلتين بالغرور أو الازدراء. كان ذلك تغييراً ملحوظاً فيه. ما الذي يمكن أن يفسره؟

خطرت فكرة على بال أكيفا، وأحس بالاشمئزاز منها. في غرفة التعذيب، لا بد أن غضب ثياغو كان غضباً شخصياً، مثل غضب منافس خاسر. وخلف كراهية الأعراق التي دامت لقرون، كانت هناك مشاعر شخصية؛ غضب المغرم بكارو، انتقام من حب مادريغال لأكيفا.

ولكن الآن، كل هذا الغضب كان غائباً—غائباً مثل الأسباب التي أثارته. أكيفا لم يعد منافساً، لم يعد تهديداً، لأن كارو اتخذت قراراً مختلفاً هذه المرة.

بمجرد أن خطرت هذه الفكرة في ذهن أكيفا، أصبح غياب العدائية لدى ثياغو دليلاً على صحتها. الذئب الأبيض كان متأكداً بما يكفي من مكانه إلى درجة أنه لم يعد بحاجة إلى قتل أكيفا. كارو... يا نجوم السماء. كارو!

لولا تاريخهم الدموي، لكان من السهل رؤية الأمر على حقيقته: الجنرال والباعثة من الموت، سيد وسيدة الأمل الأخير للكيميرا. ولكن أكيفا كان يعرف قلب ثياغو الحقيقي، وكارو تعرفه كذلك.

ذلك التاريخ ليس قديماً: عنف ثياغو، نظرة كارو المنكسرة، ترددها المرتعش، الكدمات، الجروح. ومع ذلك، بدا المخلوق الذي يقف أمام أكيفا الآن أفضل ما في ثياغو: ذكي، قوي، وعاقل، حليف قوي. وهو ينظر إليه، لم يعد أكيفا متأكداً بماذا يجب أن يأمل. إذا كان ثياغو بالفعل هكذا، فإن التحالف قد ينجح، وسيتمكن أكيفا من البقاء في حياة كارو ولو

بالقرب منها. سيتمكن من رؤيتها على الأقل ومعرفة أنها بخير. سيتمكن من التكفير عن خطاياه، وجعلها تعرف ذلك. كما أنه قد يكون لديهما فرصة لإيقاف جايل.

من جهة أخرى، إذا كان ثياغو حقاً كذلك—ذكياً، قوياً، وعاقلاً—وكان يقف جنباً إلى جنب مع كارو لتشكيل مصير شعبهما، فأي جانب سيأخذه أكيڤا؟ والأهم من ذلك، هل يمكنه أن يتحمل ما يراه؟

قال ثياغو:"وهناك شيء آخر، شيء أدين لك به. أعلم أنني مدين لك بشكر لأجل أرواح بعض جنودي".

ضيّق أكيڤا عينيه وقال:"لا أعرف عمَّ تتحدث".

قال ثياغو:"في الهينترموست. تدخلتَ في تعذيب جندي كيميرا. هرب وعاد إلينا بأرواح فريقه".

أه، الكيرين. لكن كيف يمكن لأي شخص أن يعرف أن أكيڤا فعل ذلك؟ لم يجعل أحداً يراه. لقد استدعى الطيور، كل الطيور لأميال حوله. والآن هز رأسه، مستعداً لإنكار ذلك.

لكن ليراز فاجأته بسؤالها لثياغو:"أين هو؟ لم أره مع الآخرين".

هل كانت تبحث عنه؟ رمقها أكيڤا بنظرة سريعة. كانت نظرة ثياغو أكثر حدة."لقد مات"، قال بعد لحظة.

مات الكيرين الشاب، آخر أبناء قبيلة مادريغال. لم تردّ ليراز بكلمة. قال أكيڤا:"أنا آسف لسماع ذلك".

حوّل ثياغو نظره مرة أخرى إلى أكيڤا. قال:"لكن بفضلك سيعيش فريقه مرة أخرى. ولنعد إلى حديثنا: ألم يكن معذب ذلك الجندي هو نفسه الملاك الذي يجب علينا الآن أن نواجهه؟".

أومأ أكيڤا برأسه."جايل. قائد دومينيون. هو الآن إمبراطور. نحن هنا بينما يجمع قوته، وبينما لا يعني وعدكَ شيئاً لي، سأثق بشيء واحد: أنك تريد إيقافه. لذا إذا كنت تعتقد أن جنودك يمكنهم تمييز ملاك عن آخر

لفترة كافية لمحاربة دومينيون بجانب غير الشرعيين، فانضم إلينا وسنرى ما سيحدث".

أضافت ليراز ببرود موجهة كلامها إلى تين:"نحن نرتدي الأسود وهم يرتدون الأبيض. إذا كان ذلك يساعد".

ردت تين بسخرية:"كلهم لهم نفس الطعم".

قال ثياغو محذراً:"تين، من فضلك"، ثم قال لأكيفا:"نعم، سنرى". أومأ بالموافقة، وهو يحدق في عيني أكيفا، وما زالت العقلانية حاضرة، والقسوة غائبة، ومع ذلك لم يستطع أكيفا إلا أن يتذكر ثياغو وهو يمزق الحناجر، وشعر أنه يقف على حافة قرار سيئ جداً.

جنود الموتى وغير الشرعيين معاً. في أحسن الأحوال، ستكون التجربة مريرة. وفي أسوأ الأحوال، ستكون كارثية.

لكن رغم شكوكه، كان هناك ضوء يجذبه نحو المستقبل، مستقبل مشرق يدعوه إليه. لا وعود تُقدّم، فقط هناك الأمل. ولم يكن هذا الأمل فقط بفضل إشارة كارو الخفية. على الأقل لم يكن يعتقد ذلك. لقد اعتقد أن هذا ما عليه فعله، وأنه لم يكن تصرفاً أحمق، بل كان جريئاً.

الزمن فقط هو الذي سيخبرنا.

6

خروج الوحوش

أشرفت كارو للتو على مهمة نقل ذلك الجيش الصغير من عالم إلى آخر، ولم تكن تجربتها تلك الأفضل على الإطلاق. فمع العدد الكبير من الجنود غير المجنحين ومع عدم توفر وسيلة لنقلهم من مواقعهم، اضطروا للقيام برحلات متقطعة. وجراء ذلك، اختار ثياغو"تحرير" العديد منهم، حيث قام بجمع أرواحهم ووضعها في المباخر. وصف الأجساد بأنها"عبء زائد"، مستثنياً بالطبع جسده وجسد تين وبعضاً من قادته الآخرين الذين امتطوا مخلوقات طائرة ضخمة.

هذه المرة، شعرت كارو بالارتياح عندما رتبت الجميع في الساحة وتأكدت من أن ما تبقى من"العبء الزائد" يمكن تحمله، ولن تكون هناك حاجة لتحرير أي شخص.

تم وضع الجثة الأخير في الحفرة..

ألقت النظرة الأخيرة على الحفرة من الجو، شعرت وكأن مغناطيساً يجذب نظرها نحو الحفرة. بدت أصغر كلما ارتفعت، حتى صارت مجرد

فجوة مظلمة في الأرض المغطاة بالغبار، في نهاية الطريق المتعرج الذي يمتد من القصر، مع وجود بعض التلال الصغيرة المحفرة والمجارف المغروسة فيها كأوتاد.

تخيلت رؤية آثار الهجوم الذي شنّه ثياغو عليها وحتى البقع الداكنة التي قد تكون دماً. وعلى الجانب الآخر من التلال، حيث لا يمكن لأحد غيرها أن يميز، كان هناك تلة أخرى في التراب: قبر زيري، الذي تسبب حفره في تقرح يديها. وكان عليها أن تنحني بعد ذلك على حافة تلك الظلمة المليئة بالحشرات الزاحفة لتجمع أرواح أمزالاغ والظلال الحية التي قتلها الذئب وأتباعه بسبب وقوفهم إلى جانبها.

تمنت لو كانوا حولها الآن بدلاً من أن يكونوا في المباخر، لكنهم سيبقون في تلك المباخر... لفترة لا تعلمها، حتى يحين الوقت الذي لا يمكن لأحد تخيله الآن: وقت أفضل بعد كل ما حدث، حيث لا يكون للخديعة ضرورة. هل يمكن أن يأتي ذلك الوقت؟ سيأتي إذا عملنا على تحقيقه، قالت لنفسها.

أفادت تقارير كشافة ثياغو بعدم وجود أي وجود للسيرافيم في نطاق عدة أميال من البوابة، وهو ما كان بمثابة ارتياح، ولكن ليس شيئاً يمكن لكارو أن تثق به. وبوجود رازغوت بين يدي جايل، لم يعد هناك شيء مؤكد. كان الشعور بالخروج – أو بالأحرى الهروب – مع ما كان يحدث، أمراً خاطئاً، ولكن ماذا يمكنهم أن يفعلوا؟ عددهم الآن لا يتجاوز سبعة وثمانين من الكيميرا – سبعة وثمانين وحشاً في نظر هذا العالم، وربما شياطين إذا نجح جايل في تسويق خدعته المقدسة.

كانوا قلة، غير قادرين على هزيمته أو دفعه للتراجع. إذا هاجموه الآن، لن يخسروا فقط، بل سيساعدونه في قضيته.

نظرة واحدة إلى هؤلاء الجنود الذين صنعتهم كارو، ستجعل البشر يضعون قاذفات الصواريخ بين يدي جايل.

لكن غير الشرعيين مع أكيڤا، لديهم على الأقل فرصة.

بالطبع، كان ذلك مصدر قلق بحد ذاته: التحالف. إقناع الكيميرا به. السير على حافة الخداع لإقناع جيش متمرد بالتصرف ضد غرائزه الأساسية. أدركت كارو أن كل خطوة إلى الأمام ستواجه مقاومة كبيرة من إحدى المجموعات.

ولصياغة المستقبل، سيتعين عليهم الفوز في كل خطوة. ومن يشمل"هم"؟ بالإضافة إلى ثياغو، كانت إيسّا وتين – التي هي في الواقع هاكسايا ،ولكنها تمتلك نفس القدر من حماسة تين الحقيقية – على علم بالسر. وكذلك الآن زوزانا وميك.

"ما الذي جرى لكِ؟" سألتها زوزانا بدهشة بمجرد أن غادر أكيڤا وثياغو لعقد مفاوضاتهما."هل أصبحت صديقة للذئب الأبيض؟".

ردت كارو:"هل تعلمين ما يعنيه الصيد بالشراك؟ إنه إلقاء الدم في الماء لجذب أسماك القرش".

تابعت زوزانا:"كنت أقصد ‹التودد›. ماذا فعل بكِ؟ هل أنتِ على ما يرام؟".

قالت كارو:"الآن أنا على ما يرام". ورغم أنها شعرت بالارتياح عندما أخبرتهما بالحقيقة حول زيري، فقد بكى كلاهما، مما دفعها للبكاء أيضاً، وعزز مظهرها الضعيف في أعين المجموعة.

يمكنها تقبّل هذا الأمر، لكن يا غبار السماء ونجومها، فقد كان أكيڤا شيئاً آخر. أن تجعله يظن أنها متوددة للذئب الأبيض؟ ولكن ما الذي يمكنها فعله تحت مراقبة صارمة من كامل قوات الكيميرا؟ بعض العيون كانت تراقب بفضول ولسان حالها يقول: – هل ما زالت تحبه؟ – بينما عيون أخرى مليئة بالشك، متلهفة لإدانتها ونسج المؤامرات حول كل حركة. لم تعطهم أي حجة لذلك، لذا ظلت بعيدة عن أكيڤا وليراز في القصر، وتحاول الآن ألا تنظر حتى في اتجاههما على الجهة البعيدة من التشكيل.

كان ثياغو في مقدمة الجيش، ممتطياً المحارب الطويل والرشيق يوثم الذي يمتلك مزيجاً من صفات الحصان والتنين. كان الأكبر والأكثر لفتاً للأنظار بين الكيميرا، وعلى ظهره، بدا ثياغو وكأنه أمير.

قريباً من"كارو، كانت إيسّا تمتطي المحارب رووا، وفي وسط المجموعة، وبشكل غير متناسق مع محيطهم، كان كل من زوزانا وميك، وكأنهما عصفوران صغيران يركبان على ظهري طيرين جارحين. كانت زوزانا على ظهر ڤيركو، و"ميك على ظهر إميليون، وكلاهما متشبث بحبال جلدية، بينما كان جسدا الكيميرا القويان يرتفعان تحتهما أثناء صعودهما في الجو.

قرون ڤيركو الحلزونية ذكّرت كارو ببريمستون، الذي يمتلك جسداً شبيهاً بالسنوريات ولكنه ضخم، عضلاته تشبه عضلات الأسد المحقونة بالمنشطات، ومن مؤخرة عنقه الثخين برزت مجموعة من الأشواك التي غطتها زوزانا ببطانية من الصوف، والتي اشتكت من رائحتها التي تشبه رائحة الأقدام."إذاً، خياري هو أن أتنفس رائحة الأقدام طوال الطريق أو أن أفقأ عينيّ بأشواك الرقبة؟ رائع".

صاحت الآن:"أنت تفعل ذلك عمداً!" بينما كان ڤيركو يقوم بالالتفاف الحاد إلى اليسار، ما جعلها تنزلق من على السرج المؤقت المصنوع من الأحزمة، إلى أن عاود الالتفاف في الاتجاه المعاكس ليعيد توازنها.

كان ڤيركو يضحك، لكن زوزانا لم تكن كذلك. كانت تدير رأسها بحثاً عن كارو وتصرخ:"أحتاج إلى حصان جديد. هذا يظن نفسه ظريفاً!".

"عليكِ أن تظلي معه!" صرخت كارو وهي تتجه نحوها. كانت تطير قريباً، مضطرة إلى الانعطاف حول زوج من الغريفون المثقلين. كانت تحمل على ظهرها حقيبة ثقيلة من العتاد وسلسلة طويلة من"المباخر"، التي تحتوي على عشرات الأرواح. كانت تصدر صوتاً مع كل حركة، ولم تشعر يوماً بأنها أقل رشاقة مما هي الآن."لقد تطوع بنفسه".

في الواقع، لو لم تكن زوزانا خفيفة الوزن، لما كان من الممكن إحضار هذه البشرية معهم. كان ڤيركو يحملها بالإضافة إلى حمولته الكاملة، أما بالنسبة إلى إميليون، فقد أخذ اثنان أو ثلاثة جنود بعضاً من عتاده بصمت حتى يتمكن من حمل ميك، الذي وإن لم يكن كبيراً، لم يكن خفيفاً كزهرة مثل زوزانا. ولم يكن هناك مجال لترك كمانه خلفه أيضاً. كان واضحاً أن صديقي كارو قد كسبا مودة حقيقية من هذه المجموعة، بطريقة لم تستطع هي نفسها أن تكسبها.

على الأقل من معظمهم. كان هناك زيري. قد لا يبدو مثل زيري الآن، لكنه زيري، وكارو تعرف...

تعرف أنه يحبها.

"لماذا لا يوجد لديكِ حصان مجنح في هذه المجموعة؟" تساءلت زوزانا، وهي تشحب بينما كانت تحدق في الأرض التي تبتعد أكثر فأكثر."حصان طائر لطيف برجلَين ناعمتين بدلاً من الأشواك، وكأنه يطفو على سحابة".

قال ميك:"لأنه لا شيء يرعب العدو أكثر من الحصان المجنح".

قالت زوزانا:"مهلاً، هناك أشياء في الحياة أكثر من إرعاب الأعداء. مثل عدم السقوط ألف قدم نحو حتفك – آآآه!" صرخت عندما غاص ڤيركو فجأة ليمر أسفل الحداد آيجير، الذي كان يجهد لحمل كيس من الأسلحة في الهواء. أمسكت كارو بطرف الكيس لتساعده، وارتفعا معاً ببطء بينما تقدم ڤيركو إلى الأمام.

صرخت كارو بعده باللغة الكيميرية:"من الأفضل أن تكون لطيفاً معها! وإلا سأدعها تحوّلك إلى حصان مجنح في جسدك القادم!".

زأر ڤيركو:"لا!. ليس هذا!!". استقام، ووجدت كارو نفسها في واحدة من تلك اللحظات التي لا يزال بإمكان حياتها أن تفاجئها فيها. فكرت في نفسها وفي زوزانا قبل بضعة أشهر، عندما كانتا في حصة الرسم الحي أو مسترخيتين بأقدامهما فوق طاولة التابوت في بويزون كيتشن. كان ميك

آنذاك مجرد"فتى الكمان"، إعجاب سري، وها هو الآن معهما، يحمل كمانه على ظهره، ويستعد للرحيل إلى عالم آخر بينما تهدد كارو الوحوش بالانتقام عبر إحيائهم بسبب سوء سلوكهم؟

للحظة، رغم عبء كيس الأسلحة و"المباخر" وحقيبتها – ناهيك عن عبء واجبها الثقيل والخداع ومستقبل عالمين – شعرت كارو بشيء من الخفة، بالأمل.

ثم سمعت ضحكة مليئة بالخبث العابر، ومن زاوية عينها رصدت حركة يد. كانت كيتا-إري، محاربة برأس ابن آوى، ورأت كارو على الفور ما كانت تفعله. كانت تلوح بعلامات الهامسا – عيني الشيطان الموشومة على راحتي يديها – باتجاه أكيفا وليراز. كان رارك بجانبها يفعل الشيء نفسه وهما يضحكان. أملت كارو أن يكون السيرافيم خارج النطاق، لكنها خاطرت بإلقاء نظرة في اتجاههما، لترى ليراز وهي تتوقف في منتصف حركة جناحيها وتلتف، والغضب واضح في وقفتها حتى من بعيد.

إذاً، لم يكونوا خارج النطاق. مد أكيفا يده ليوقف شقيقته ويمنعها من الالتفاف على من هاجماهما.

المزيد من الضحك من الكيميرا الذين كانوا يسخرون منهما، وأغلقت كارو يديها بقوة حول علاماتها. لم تستطع أن تكون هي من يضع حداً لهذا – فقد يصبح الأمر أسوأ. بأسنان مشدودة، راقبت أكيفا وليراز يبتعدان أكثر، وكان تزايد المسافة بينهما نذير سوء لهذه البداية الشجاعة.

"هل أنت بخير، يا كارو؟" جاءها همس بنبرة أفعى.

التفتت كارو. كانت ليسيث تقترب منها. قالت كارو:"أنا بخير".

"أوه؟ تبدين متوترة".

رغم أنها من عرق الناجا مثل إيسّا، إلا أن ليسيث ورفيقها نيسك كانا ضعف حجم إيسّا – ثعبانان ضخمان بجانب أفعى صغيرة، بعنقين سميكين وعضلات قوية ولكن سريعة، ومزودين بأنياب سامة بالإضافة إلى التناقض

الغريب في امتلاكهما أجنحة. كان ذلك من صنع كارو بالكامل. غباء، غباء قالت كارو لليسيث:"لا تقلقي عليّ".

"حسناً، هذا صعب، أليس كذلك؟ كيف لا أقلق على عاشقة الملائكة؟". منذ وقت قريب جداً كانت هذه الإهانة مؤلمة. لم تعد كذلك."لدينا العديد من الأعداء، يا ليسيث" قالت كارو بصوت خفيف."معظمهم من نصيبنا بالوراثة، مثل الواجب، لكن الأعداء الذين نختارهم بأنفسنا مميزون. يجب أن نختارهم بحذر".

تجعد جبين ليسيث، ثم سألت:"أتهددينني؟".

"أهددكِ؟ من أين أتيت بهذا؟ هل تفوهتُ بذلك؟ كنت أتحدث عن صنع الأعداء، ولا يمكنني تخيل أي جندي من جنود إعادة الإحياء يكون غبياً بما يكفي ليجعل من إعادة الإحياء نفسها عدوه".

هنا، فكرت كارو، خذي ذلك وفسريه كما تشائين.

تحركوا جميعاً في الجو، وفي تلك الأثناء تباعدت الكثافة أمامهم لتكشف عن ثياغو على ظهر يوثم وهو يعود إلى وسط الجيش. تجمعت القوات حولهم، وتباطأت حركتهم.

"سيدي"، حيّت ليسيث القائد، وكانت كارو تستطيع رؤية النميمة تتشكل في أفكارها. يا سيدي، عاشقة الملائكة هددتني. نحتاج إلى تشديد قبضتنا عليها.

حظاً سعيداً في ذلك، فكرت كارو، لكن الذئب لم يمنح ليسيث – أو أي شخص آخر – فرصة للتحدث. بصوت مرتفع بما فيه الكفاية ليكون مسموعاً من دون أن يبدو أنه يرفع صوته، قال:"هل تظنون أنه لأنني أركب في المقدمة، لا أعلم كيف يتصرف جيشي؟" توقف للحظة."أنتم كالدم في جسدي. أشعر بكل رعشة وزفرة. أعرف ألمكم وفرحكم، وبالتأكيد أسمع ضحكاتكم". مرّ بنظره على الجنود المحيطين، وتوقفت عيناه عند كيتا-إري التي لم تكن تضحك عندما استقر نظره عليها.

"إذا أردت منك استفزاز حلفائنا... سأخبركِ بذلك. وإذا كنت تشكين في أنني نسيت أن أعطيك أمراً، فتفضلي بإعلامي. وفي المقابل، سأقوم بإعلامكِ".

كانت الرسالة موجهة إلى الجميع، لكن كيتا-إري كانت الضحية غير المحظوظة لسخرية الجنرال المخيفة. "ما رأيك في هذا الترتيب، أيها الجندي؟ هل يلقى استحسانك؟".

بصوت خافت يملؤه الإحراج، همست كيتا-إري: "نعم، سيدي".

شعرت كارو بشيء من التعاطف تجاهها... تقريباً.

"أنا سعيد جداً". رفع الذئب صوته للتو. "معاً قاتلنا، ومعاً تحملنا فقدان شعبنا. نزفنا وصرخنا. تبعتموني إلى النار، وإلى الموت، وإلى عالم آخر، لكن ربما لم يكن أبداً شيء يبدو غريباً مثل هذا. اللجوء مع السيرافيم؟ قد يبدو غريباً، لكن سأكون شديد الخيبة إذا خنت ثقتكم. ليس هناك مجال للخلاف. أي شخص لا يستطيع التعايش مع مسارنا الحالي يمكنه مغادرتنا فور عبورنا البوابة، ويواجه مصيره بمفرده".

مسح الوجوه بنظره. كان وجهه صارماً، لكنه مضاء بنوع من البريق الداخلي. "فيما يتعلق بالملائكة، لا أطلب منكم شيئاً سوى الصبر".

"لا يمكننا محاربتهم كما فعلنا من قبل، معتمدين على أعدادنا حتى ونحن ننزف. أنا لا أطلب إذنكم لإيجاد طريقة جديدة. إذا بقيتم معي، فأتوقع منكم الثقة. المستقبل مظلم، ولا أعدكم بشيء سوى هذا: سنقاتل من أجل عالمنا حتى آخر صدى لأرواحنا، وإذا كنا أقوياء بما يكفي، ومحظوظين بما يكفي، وأذكياء بما يكفي، قد نتمكن من إعادة بناء بعض مما فقدناه".

ثم حدق في عيونهم الواحد تلو الآخر، مما جعلهم يشعرون بأنهم مرئيون، ويحسب لهم الحساب، ومهمون. كانت نظرته تعبر عن ثقته فيهم، وأكثر من ذلك، عن ثقتهم وإيمانهم به. تابع قائلاً: "هذا واضح جداً: إذا فشلنا في مواجهة هذا التهديد المحدق، فسننتهي. ستنتهي الكيميرا".

توقف للحظة. وبعدما عادت نظرته إلى كيتا-إري، قال بلطف مصطنع جعله يبدو أكثر قسوة:"هذا أمر لا يدعو إلى الضحك، أيتها الجندية". ثم دفع يوثم إلى الأمام وشق طريقه عبر القوات ليستعيد مكانه في مقدمة الجيش. راقبت كارو الجنود وهم يعودون بهدوء إلى تشكيلهم، وعرفت أن أحداً منهم لن يتركه، وأن أكيفا وليراز سيكونان بأمان من ضربات الهامسا العشوائية لبقية الرحلة.

بدا هذا جيداً. شعرت كارو بشيء من الفخر بزيري، وأيضاً بالرهبة.

كان الجندي الشاب هادئاً بطبيعته الأصلية، شبه خجول – على عكس هذا المتحدث البليغ المهووس الذي يحمل جسده الآن. بينما كانت تراقبه، تساءلت للمرة الأولى – وربما كان غباءً أنها لم تفكر في ذلك من قبل – كيف يمكن أن يؤثر عليه كونه في شخصية ثياغو.

لكن الفكرة تلاشت بأرضها. هذا كان زيري. من بين كل الأمور التي كانت كارو تقلق بشأنها، لم يكن إفساده بسبب السلطة هو أحدها.

غير أن ليسيث كانت كذلك. نظرت إليها كارو التي كانت لا تزال تحوم بالقرب منها في الهواء، ورأت الحسرة في عيني الناجا، وهي تراقب جنرالهم وهو يستعيد مكانه.

ما الذي كانت كارو تفكر فيه؟ وهي تعرف أنه ليس هناك أدنى فرصة أن يترك قادة ثياغو الجيش، لكنها تمنت لو فعلوا. لا أحد يعرفه أفضل منهم، ولا أحد سيراقبه عن كثب مثلهم. أما ما قالته لليسيث عن صناعة عدو من الأرواح المعدة للتجسد، فلم يكن مجرد مزحة أو خطراً عابراً. إذا كان هناك شيء مؤكد للجنود المبعوثين، فهو أنه إذا دخلوا المعركة حتى النهاية، فسوف يحتاجون إلى جسد جديد.

"بقرة مصابة بالجنون"، قالت كارو. لكن البقرة ضخمة وبطيئة بالنسبة إلى جسدك الجديد.

وما إن رمتها ليسيث بنظرة ثانية، حتى سارعت كارو بالسخرية،"مووو".

7

هبة الجموح

سرعان ما حلق الكيميرا فوق القمم العالية. أصبح القصر خلفهم،
والبوابة أمامهم مباشرة، رغم أن كارو كانت بالكاد تستطيع أن تتبينها. حتى
عن قرب، بدت متموجة، وعليهم العبور من خلالها اعتماداً على الإيمان فقط،
إلى درجة الشعور بحوافها بمجرد دخولها. وعلى الكائنات الكبيرة أن تطوي
أجنحتها والاندفاع بسرعة نحوها، كي لا تشعر بأي مقاومة وتتجاوزها. كانت
هذه المجموعة تعرف ما تفعله، واختفت عبر المعبر واحدة تلو الأخرى.

استغرق الأمر وقتاً، وكانت أجسادهم الهائلة تختفي في الأثير. وعندما
جاء دور ثيركو، نادت كارو على زوزانا:"تمسكي جيداً!"، وفعلت، واندفعوا
عبر الشق. ذهب إميليون وميك بعد ذلك، ولم تكن كارو تحب أن يبتعد
صديقاها عن نظرها، لذا أومأت للذئب، الذي كان يدور ليتأكد من مرور
الجميع، أخذت نفساً عميقاً أخيراً من هواء الأرض، وانطلقت.

لامست وجهها ريشة ناعمة، كأنها غشاء لا يمكن إدراكه يفصل بين
العوالم ليبقيها مميزة، ثم... صارت في الجانب الآخر.

وصلت إلى إريتز.

لا سماء زرقاء هنا؛ السماء مقعرة بيضاء فوق رؤوسهم وتتحول إلى اللون الرمادي المعدني في الأفق المرئي، وما تبقى ضائع في الضباب. تحتهم كان هناك فقط الماء الباهت يتماوج بدرجات الأسود. هذا خليج الوحوش. كان هناك شيء مرعب في سواده. شيء لا يرحم.

الرياح القوية، أجبرت الجنود إلى إعادة تنظيم صفوفهم. سحبت كارو سترتها لتغطي نفسها أكثر وارتجفت. في اللحظة التي اندفع فيها آخر الجنود عبر الشق، كان يوثم وثياغو آخر من عبرا. امتزجت تفاصيل يوثم الحصانية والتنينية بشكل لا يمكن تمييزه، خضراء ومتموجة، ويبدو أنها تتدفق إلى الوجود من العدم. وبما أن فيسبينغ ليست له أجنحة طبيعية، فإن كارو حين أعطته هذه الهيئة، كانت حريصة في الحفاظ على طوله: فجعلت له مجموعتان من الأجنحة، الزوج الرئيسي مثل الأشرعة وزوج أصغر مثبت بالقرب من رجليه الخلفيتين. بدا الأمر رائعاً في نظرها.

كان الذئب قد أحنى رأسه عند عبوره البوابة، وبمجرد أن مر، جلس ليقيّم قواته. استقرت عيناه بسرعة على كارو، ورغم أنه توقف عندها لفترة وجيزة فقط، شعرت بأنها – كانت تعلم أنها – هي أول من يهمه في هذا العالم أو أي عالم آخر. فقط عندما علم أين هي، وكان راضياً عن حالتها، التفت إلى المهمة التي بين يديه، وهي توجيه هذا الجيش بأمان فوق خليج الوحوش.

وجدت كارو صعوبة في الابتعاد عن البوابة وتركها هناك، حيث يمكن لأي شخص أن يجدها ويستخدمها. كان من المقرر أن يقوم أكيفا بإغلاقها بعدهم، لكن جايل غيّر خطتهم. الآن سيحتاجون إليها للعودة وبدء نهاية العالم.

أخذ الذئب القيادة مرة أخرى، متجهاً شرقاً، بعيداً عن الأفق المعدني وباتجاه جبال أديلفاس. في يوم صافٍ، كانت القمم ستكون مرئية من هنا. لكن اليوم لم يكن صافياً، ولم يكن بوسعهم رؤية شيء أمامهم سوى

الضباب المتكاثف، وهو ما كان له إيجابياته وسلبياته.

فمن الناحية الإيجابية، الضباب وفر لهم غطاء. لن يُرصدوا من مسافة بعيدة من قبل أي دوريات من السيرافيم.

ومن الناحية السلبية، فالضباب وفر غطاء لأي شخص آخر...- أو أي شيء - لن يُرصد من مسافة بعيدة من قِبلهم.

كانت كارو في مركز المجموعة، بعدما جاءت بجانب رووا لتفقد إيسّا، عندما حدث ما حدث.

فسألتها إيسّا:"يا فتاتي الجميلة، هل تتحملين الوضع؟".

أجابت كارو:"أنا بخير، لكنك بحاجة إلى المزيد من الملابس".

أجابت إيسّا:"لن أجادل في ذلك"، كانت ترتدي في الواقع ملابس – سترة من ملابس كارو، مشقوقة بشكل واسع عند العنق لتناسب غطاء رأسها الأفعوي – لكن شفتيها كانتا زرقاوين، و كتفاها مشدودتين إلى أذنيها وهي ترتجف. ينحدر عرق الناجا من مناخ حار. كان المغرب يناسبها تماماً. أما هذا الضباب البارد، فلم يكن يناسبها كثيراً، وكانت وجهتهم الباردة أقل، على الرغم من أنهم سيكونون هناك محميين من العوامل الجوية، وتذكرت كارو الغرف الحرارية الأرضية في المتاهة السفلية للكهوف، إذا بقي كل شيء كما كان عليه منذ سنوات.

كهوف الكيرين.

لم تعد كارو قط إلى مكان مولدها، موطن حياتها الأولى. كانت قد خططت للعودة يوماً ما. وها هو المكان الذي من المفترض أن تلتقي فيه هي وأكيڤا لبدء تمردهما، لولا أن الأقدار اختارت شيئاً آخر.

لكن، كلا. كارو لا تؤمن بالقدر. لم يكن القدر هو من قتل خطتهما، بل الخيانة. ولم يكن القدر هو من يعيد خلقها الآن—أو على الأقل هذه النسخة المشوهة منها، المليئة بالشك والعداء. بل كانت الإرادة.

"سأجد لكِ بطانية أو شيئاً ما"، قالت لإيسا—أو بدأت تقول. ولكن في

تلك اللحظة، حدث شيء ما.

أو بالأحرى، شيء ما هجم عليها.

أو عليهم جميعاً.

شعور بالضغط مع انخفاض الضباب، مصحوباً بنوبة من اليقين. انكمشت كارو وأرجعت رأسها إلى الخلف لتنظر إلى الأعلى. ولم تكن وحدها. كان الجنود في كل مكان حولها في الصفوف يتحركون، ينخفضون، يسحبون أسلحتهم، ويدورون بعيداً عن... شيء ما.

فوقهم، بدت السماء البيضاء قريبة بما يكفي للمسها. كانت فراغاً، وقد سرى اندفاع في دم كارو واهتزازات مثل موجات منخفضة لا يمكن سماعها، ثم فجأة، هبت عاصفة، وكأنها تغمر كل شيء، دافعة أمامها ريحاً تطيح بالجنود وكأنهم كانوا ألعاباً في وجه المد، يا له من شيء مهيب.

اندفع شيء من فوقهم وحجب السماء، وسرعان ما لامس رؤوس الجميع. كان ضخماً ومفاجئاً إلى درجة أن كارو لم تستطع أن تستوعب ما هو، وعندما اجتاحهم، لامسها، وجذبها التيار وراءه وأدارها حول نفسها. كان الأمر أشبه بسحب تحت الماء، وتطايرت مجموعات"المباخر" الخاصة هنا وهناك، وفي تلك الأوقات العصيبة فكرت في سطح الماء الأسود العميق تحتهم، وفي"المباخر" وهي تغطس فيه – ليبتلعها"خليج الوحوش"، ولكنها كافحت من أجل السيطرة على نفسها... ثم فجأة ساد هدوء غريب، هدوء ما بعد العاصفة. كانت مجموعة مباخرها معلقة في سلسلة محكمة، لكن لم يُفقد شيء، وكل ما تطلبه الأمر الآن هو نظرة سريعة لتفقدها.

صيادو العواصف.

المخلوقات الأكبر في هذا العالم، باستثناء ما يحمله البحر من أسرار في الأعماق. لها أجنحة يمكنها أن تذود عن منزل أو تدمره بخفقة واحدة. سرب من هذه الطيور الضخمة قد اندفع للتو فوق الفرقة، وكانت ضربة جناح واحدة من أقربها كافية لتفريق تشكيلات الكيميرا. قبل أن يكون هناك

أي مساحة في رأس كارو لتتعجب، قامت بجرد محموم للمجموعة.

وجدت إيسا متشبثة برقبة رووا، مرتجفة لكنها بخير. أسقط الحداد أيجر حزمة الأسلحة – جميعها ضاعت في البحر. أكيڤا وليراز كانا لا يزالان في مكانيهما في المقدمة البعيدة، وزوزانا وميك كانا أيضاً في المقدمة، ليس بعيداً، لكنهما في مأمن من قوة ضربة الجناح. لم يبدُ عليهما أكثر من خدوش طفيفة، لكنهما بقيا فاغري الفكين، مذهولين من المنظر المهول – وعادت الصفوف للتجمع من جديد، لم يبق هناك جندي واحد إلا وكان مذهولاً من المخلوقات الضخمة التي عادت واختفت في الضباب. الجميع بخير.

لقد تعرضوا للتو لهجوم من صيادي العواصف.

في عالمها الأول، كانت كارو طفلة من الأعالي، كانت مادريغال من الكيرين، آخر قبيلة في جبال أديلڤاس. كانت تلك المخلوقات الضخمة تجوب بين القمم، رغم أن الكيرين أو أي شخص آخر عرفته كارو لم ير صياد عواصف عن قرب. لم يكن بالإمكان صيدهم؛ فهم مراوغين للغاية، أسرع من أن تتم ملاحقتهم، وأذكى من أن تتم مفاجأتهم. كان يُعتقد أنهم يستطيعون الشعور بأدق التغييرات في الهواء والمناخ، وكطفلة – كمادريغال – كان لدى كارو سبب لتصديق ذلك. كانت تراهم من بعيد، ينجرفون مثل ذرات في خيوط الشمس، وكانت تطير خلفهم، متلهفة لرؤية أقرب، ولكن بمجرد أن تبدأ أجنحتها في ضرب الهواء بنية الوصول إليهم، كانت أجنحتهم تخفق وتحملهم بعيداً. لم يُعثر يوماً على عش، أو حتى قشرة بيضة، أو جثة؛ إذا كان صيادو العواصف يفقسون، أو يموتون، فلا أحد يعرف أين.

الآن حصلت كارو على رؤيتها الأقرب، وكان ذلك مثيراً.

كان الأدرينالين يتدفق في جسدها، ولم تستطع أن تمنع نفسها. ابتسمت. كانت النظرة قصيرة جداً، لكنها رأت أن جسم صيادي العواصف مغطى بفراء كثيف، وأن عيونهم سوداء، بحجم الأطباق ومغطاة بغشاء

داخلي، مثل طيور الأرض. كانت ريشاتهم تتألق بألوان قزحية، ليست بلون واحد بل بجميع الألوان، تتغير مع انعكاسات الضوء.

بدوا كأنهم هبة جامحة، وتذكير بأن ليس كل شيء في هذا العالم محصور بالحروب الأبدية. استجمعت نفسها في الجو، وحلّت سلسلة "المباخر" المعلقة حول رقبتها، وهبطت نحو زوزانا وميك.

ابتسمت لصديقيها، وهما لا يزالان في حالة ذهول، وقالت: "مرحباً بكم في المملكة". بغض النظر عن الحصان المجنح.. أعلنت زوزانا، بعينين متسعتين ومتحمستين: "أريد واحداً من هؤلاء!".

8

رضّ السماء

"صيادو العواصف مجدداً"، صاح المحارب ستيفان من النافذة، متراجعاً لإفساح المجال لميليل.

كانت النافذة الوحيدة لزنزانتهم. أربعة أيام قضوها في هذا السجن. كانت الشمس قد غربت ثلاث ليالٍ وأشرقت ثلاث ليالٍ أخرى لتضيء عالماً لم يعد له معنى. نظرت ميليل إلى الخارج وهي تستعد.

تشرق الشمس. ضوء كثيف مشع؛ سحب متوهجة، بحر ذهبي، والأفق خط من الإشعاع النقي الذي يصعب النظر إليه. كانت الجزر مثل ظلال متناثرة لوحوش نائمة، أما السماء... كما هي، فكانت غير طبيعية.

لو كانت من لحم، لكان يُقال إنها متورمة. هذا الفجر، مثل غيره، فجر ألوان جديدة وكثيفة ظهرت بين عشية وضحاها: أرجواني، نيلي، أصفر باهت، وأزرق ناصع رقيق. كزهور أو نزيف، لم تكن ميليل تعرف ماذا تسميها. كأنها تملأ السماء، وتنتشر مع مرور الساعات، تتعمق، تبهت، ثم تختفي لتحل محلها ألوان أخرى.

بدا المكان جميلاً، وعندما أُحضرت ميليل وفريقها إلى هنا لأول مرة من قبل آسريهم، افترضوا أن هذا كان مجرد طبيعة السماء الجنوبية. لم يكن هذا هو العالم الذي يعرفونه. كل شيء في الجزر البعيدة كان جميلاً وغريباً. كان الهواء غنياً وكان له كيان، ويحمل الروائح معه بسهولة: عطور، أصوات الطيور، كل نسيم كان حياً بالأغاني العائمة والروائح مثلما كان البحر مليئاً بالأسماك. أما البحر، فقد كان يحتوي على ألف لون جديد كل دقيقة، ولم تكن كلها من درجات الأزرق والأخضر. أما الأشجار فبدت أشبه برسوم خيالية لطفل منها بأشجار نصف الكرة الشمالي الباسقة المستقيمة. والسماء؟ حسناً، السماء هي وراء كل هذا.

أدركت ميليل الآن أن هذا لم يكن طبيعياً، وكذلك تجمع صيادي العواصف الذي يزداد يوماً بعد يوم.

هناك، فوق البحر، كانت المخلوقات مجتمعة في دوران لا ينتهي. جنود الدم من غير الشرعيين، ميليل، حاملة الاسم الثانية، لم تكن شابة، وخلال حياتها رأت العديد من صيادي العواصف، لكن لم تر أكثر من نصف دزينة في مكان واحد، ودائماً عند أطراف السماء، تتحرك في خط. لكن هنا كان العشرات. عشرات يتشابكون مع المزيد من العشرات.

بدا المشهد غير طبيعي، لكن رغم ذلك، ربما كانت ستعتبره ظاهرة طبيعية لولا وجوه الحراس. كان الستيليون متوترين، فهناك شيء ما يحدث، ولم يخبرهم أحد بما يجري. لا عن الخلل الذي أصاب السماء ولا عن الذي جذب صيادي العواصف، ولا حتى عن مصيرهم.

أمسكت ميليل بقضبان النافذة، ومدت رأسها لمشاهدة المنظر الكامل للبحر والسماء والجزر. كان ستيفان محقاً. خلال الليل، ارتفع عدد صيادي العواصف مرة أخرى، وكأن كل واحد منهم في"هذا البر" كان يستجيب لنداء ما. يدورون ويدورون، بينما السماء تنزف وتشفى وتتشوه من جديد.

أي قوة يمكنها أن تتسبب في تعطيل السماء؟

تركت ميليل القضبان واقتربت من باب الزنزانة. طرقته ونادت:"هييييي؟ أريد التحدث إلى أحد!".

بدأ فريقها يلاحظ ويتجمع. أولئك الذين ما زالوا نائمين في أسرتهم المعلقة استيقظوا ووضعوا أقدامهم على الأرض. كانوا اثني عشر في المجموع، وقد أُسروا جميعاً من دون أن يصابوا بأذى - وإن لم يخل الأمر من ارتباك في طريقة أسرهم: ذهول شديد، وتشتت تام حتى ليبدو الأمر وكأنه انهيار في وظائف المخ - ولم تكن الزنزانة زنزانة رطبة بل كانت مجرد غرفة طويلة نظيفة لها باب ثقيل مغلق.

كان هناك مرحاض، وماء للاغتسال. أراجيح للنوم، وأثواب من القماش الخفيف حتى يتمكنوا من خلع دروعهم السوداء وخوذاتهم الثقيلة إن أرادوا ذلك - وما لبثوا أن قاموا بذلك. الطعام كان وفيراً وأفضل بكثير مما اعتادوا عليه: سمك أبيض وخبز خفيف، وأي فواكه! بعضها كان بطعم العسل والزهور، ذو قشور سميكة ورقيقة ومتعددة الألوان. وتوت أصفر حامض وكريات أرجوانية منثورة لم يعرفوا كيف يأكلونها، بعد أن جردوا من سكاكينهم لأسباب مفهومة.

كان هناك نوع من الفاكهة يحتوي على أشواك حادة ويخفي في داخله قواماً كالكاسترد؛ فتناولوه أولاً، وكان هناك نوع لم يستطع أي منهم أن يستسيغه: ثمرة وردية لحمية غريبة، تكاد تكون بلا طعم وملطخة مثل الدم. تركوها دون لمس في السلة المركونة بجانب الباب.

لم تستطع ميليل إلا أن تتساءل عما إذا كانت هذه الفاكهة - أو أي فاكهة منها - هي التي أثارت غضب والدهم الإمبراطور عندما ظهرت بشكل غامض عند قدمي سريره.

لم يكن هناك رد على ندائها، فطرقت مرة أخرى."هييييي؟ هل هناك أحد!". هذه المرة فكرت في إضافة"من فضلكم" على مضض، وازداد انزعاجها عندما أدار أحدهم المفتاح على الفور. وكأن أيدولون - بالطبع

كانت أيدولون - كانت واقفة هناك فقط في انتظار كلمة"من فضلك".

كانت الفتاة الستيلية وحدها، كالمعتاد، ومن دون سلاح، مرتدية قطعة بسيطة من القماش الأبيض تتدلى من كتفها البني، مع شعرها الأسود المجدول بالأغصان والمتجمع على الكتف الآخر. وأساورها الذهبية المنقوشة موزعة بشكل متساوٍ على ذراعيها النحيلتين، وحافية القدمين، مما جعل ميليل تشعر بعدم الارتياح من شدة الحميمية. إلا أن تلك الحميمية مجرد وهم، بالطبع.

لم يكن هناك أي شيء في أيدولون يشير إلى أنها جندية – أو أن أياً من الستيليين كانوا كذلك، حتى إنهم لا يمتلكون جيشاً – ولكن هذه الشابة كانت، بلا شك، هي القائدة عندما تم... اعتراض فريق ميليل. وبسبب ما حدث في ذلك الوقت – ما زالت ميليل لا تستطيع استيعاب الأمر – وعلى الرغم من أنهم كانوا اثني عشر من غير الشرعيين المخضرمين ضد فتاة أنيقة واحدة، لم يفكر أي منهم في محاولة الهروب.

كان هناك المزيد في أيدولون- كما كان هناك المزيد في الجزر البعيدة - من الجمال.

"هل أنتم بخير؟" سألت تلك الفتاة الأنيقة بابتسامتها الدافئة وبلهجتها الستيلية التي يمكن أن تخفف من حدة أشد الكلمات؛ ورقصت عيناها المتألقان مثل النار عندما سلمت عليهم بإيماءة – برفع الكف بحركة انسيابية من ذراعها المغطاة بالذهب لتحيي الجميع.

همهم الجنود فيما بينهم، ذكوراً وإناثاً، مسحورين جميعاً بأيدولون الغامضة ذات العينين الراقصتين، لكن ميليل نظرت إلى الإيماءة بريبة. لقد رأت الستيلية تقوم بأشياء... بمثل هذه الإيماءات الرشيقة، أشياء لا يمكن تفسيرها، وكانت تتمنى لو أنها تبقي ذراعيها بجانبها."نحن بخير إلى حد ما"، قالت."بالنسبة إلى السجناء". بدت لهجتها تبدو فظة مقارنة بلهجة أيدولون، وصوتها خشن ومبحوح. شعرت بأنها كبيرة وغير رشيقة، مثل سيف

حديدي."ما الذي يحدث هناك في الخارج؟".

ردت أيدولون بخفة:"أشياء لا ينبغي أن تحدث".

كان هذا أكثر مما حصلت عليه ميليل منها من قبل."أي أشياء؟" أرادت جواباً."ما الذي يحدث للسماء؟".

"إنها متعبة"، قالت الفتاة بعينيها المتلألئتين وكأنها كانت شرارة في الكور. كعيني أكيفا، فكرت ميليل. كل الستيليين الذين رأوهم حتى الآن كان لديهم نفس العيون."إنها تتألم"، أضافت أيدولون."إنها كبيرة جداً، كما تعلمين".

السماء متعبة؟ إجابة سخيفة. كانت تعبث معهم."هل له علاقة بالريح؟" سألت ميليل، وهي تفكر في الكلمة المناسبة، لتمييزها عن أي ريح أخرى.

بالفعل، وصفها بالريح كان أشبه بوصف"صياد العواصف" بعصفور. كانت جماعة ميليل" تقترب من كاليفيس عندما ضربتهم الريح، وقبضت عليهم مثل ريش متطاير وجذبتهم إلى الخلف، إلى حيث جاؤوا، مع كل ما كان في طريقها في السماء - طيور، فراشات، سحب، ونعم، حتى صيادو العواصف - بالإضافة إلى أشياء كثيرة لم يكن سطح العالم يمسك بها بإحكام كما ينبغي، مثل زهور الأشجار، وحتى زبد البحر.

قوة جارفة بلا حول ولا قوة، على امتداد أميال. تم أسرهم والمضي بهم - أولاً باتجاه الشرق، وهم يضربون بأجنحتهم لاستعادة السيطرة على أنفسهم، ثم... عم السكون. كان قصيراً وصامتاً جداً، مما أتاح لهم بالكاد وقتاً لالتقاط أنفاسهم قبل أن تأتي القوة الكاملة مرة أخرى وترسلهم مجدداً، غرباً هذه المرة، عائدين إلى كاليفيس وما بعدها، حيث أُطلق سراحهم أخيراً. يا لها من قوة! لقد شعرت ميليل وكأن الأثير نفسه قد سحب نفساً عميقاً وزفره. كان لا بد أن تكون هذه الظواهر مرتبطة، فكرت ميليل. الريح، السماء الصاخبة، تجمع صيادي العواصف؟ لا شيء من هذا كان طبيعياً أو صحيحاً.

وتلاشت تعابير وجه أيدولون التي تتسم بالجمال المعتدل، ولم يعد

هناك بريق في عينيها الآن. قالت:"لم تكن تلك ريحاً".

"إذاً، ما كان ذلك؟" سألت ميليل، آملة في أن يستمر هذا الصدق المفاجئ.

"سرقة"، قالت، وبدا أنها على وشك الانسحاب."عذراً. هل هناك شيء آخر؟".

قالت ميليل:"نعم. أريد أن أعرف ما سيفعلونه بنا". وبحركة أفعوانية سريعة، أدارت أيدولون رأسها، مما أجفل ميليل.

"هل أنتِ متحمسة جداً لأن يفعلوا بكِ شيئاً؟"، أشارت ميليل بعينيها."أنا فقط أريد أن أعرف——".

"لم يُتخذ القرار بعد. لا نحضر الكثير من الغرباء هنا. أعتقد أن الأطفال سيحبون رؤية عيونكم الزرقاء العجيبة". قالت ذلك بإعجاب، بينما كانت تحدق في يافث، أصغر أفراد الفصيل، وهو ذو بشرة فاتحة جداً. احمر وجهه حتى حدود شعره الأشقر. التفتت أيدولون مرة أخرى إلى ميليل بنظرة متأملة."من ناحية أخرى، طلب راث أن نسلمكم للمبتدئين. للتدريب".

التدريب؟ على ماذا؟ لم تجرؤ ميليل على السؤال؛ منذ أن تواصلت مع هؤلاء الناس، رأت أشياء توحي بوجود سحر لا يمكن تخيله. تلك الفنون كانت مفقودة منذ زمن طويل في الإمبراطورية، وملأت قلبها بالرعب. لكن عيني أيدولون كانتا مليئتين بالمرح. هل كانت تمزح؟ لم تشعر ميليل بأي عزاء. قالت الستيلية إن الغرباء قليلون جداً. سألت ميليل:"أين الآخرون؟".

"الآخرون؟".

لم تكن ميليل متأكدة تماماً من رغبتها في الإلحاح، لكنها أجابت:"نعم"، وحاولت أن تبدو ثابتة. كان مهمتها، في النهاية، أن تكتشف. تم إرسال فريقها لتتبع مبعوثي الإمبراطور المفقودين. تم الرد على إعلان جورام للحرب ضد الستيليين – أن السلة مليئة بالفواكه – مما يعني أنه تم استلام الرسالة،

لكن السفراء لم يعودوا أبداً، والعديد من الوحدات العسكرية المرسلة في مهمة البحث عن الجزر البعيدة اختفوا أيضاً. خلال أيامها هنا، لم تر ميليل وفريقها أي أثر لأسرى آخرين، ولا حتى سمعوا عنهم. قالت:"رسل الإمبراطور. لم يعودوا".

"هل أنت متأكدة من ذلك؟" سألت الفتاة بنبرة محببة، مثل العسل الذي يخفي مرارة السم. ثم، وبشكل متعمد، لم تفارق عيناها ميليل، انحنت لتأخذ ثمرة من السلة بجانب الباب. كانت واحدة من تلك الكرات الوردية التي لم يستطع غير الشرعيين تحملها. قد تكون فاكهة، لكن الأشياء كانت أساساً أكياساً لحمية من العصير الأحمر، دافئة وتذوب في الفم بشكل مزعج.

قضمت الفتاة منها، وفي تلك اللحظة، كانت ميليل تقسم إن أسنانها كانت مدببة. كان الأمر أشبه بحجاب تم سحبه جانباً، ووراءه كانت أيدولون ذات العينين الراقصتين مجرد وحش. رقتها اختفت؛ صارت تراها... بشعة. انفجرت الثمرة وأمالت رأسها إلى الخلف، تمتص وتلعق لتلتقط العصير السميك في فمها. كان عمود عنقها مكشوفاً بينما فاض العصير الأحمر من شفتيها، مكوناً خطوطاً لزجة ومعتمة على فستانها الأبيض، حيث تفشت مثل زهور من الدم، لا شيء سوى الدم، وما زالت تمتص الفاكهة. تراجع الجنود عنها، وعندما أخفضت أيدولون رأسها مرة أخرى لتنظر إلى ميليل، كان وجهها ملطخاً بالأحمر.

مثل مفترس، فكرت ميليل، يرفع رأسه عن جثة ساخنة.

"لقد أحضرتم لنا لحمكم ودمكم مع أرواحكم"، قالت أيدولون بفمها الملطخ، وكان من المستحيل الآن حتى تذكر الفتاة الرشيقة التي بدت عليها منذ لحظات."ما الذي كنتم تعتزمون فعله بمجيئكم إلى هنا، إن لم يكن لتقديم أنفسكم إلينا؟ هل كنتم تظنون أننا سنحتفظ بكم كما أنتم، بعيونكم الزرقاء وأيديكم السوداء وكل شيء؟" رفعت قشر الفاكهة ورمته. سقط على

الأرضية المبلطة محدثاً صوتاً كالصفعة.

لا يمكن أنها تقصد... لا. ليس الفاكهة. لقد رأت ميليل أشياء، نعم، لكن عقلها رفض قبول تلك الاحتمالية. ببساطة، لا. كانت مجرد مزحة بشعة. اشمئزازها منحها جرأة."لم تكن أبداً أرواحنا. ليس لدينا ترف اختيار أعدائنا. نحن جنود"، قالتها وكأنها تعني عبيد.

قالت أيدولون بازدراء"جنود. نعم. الجنود والأطفال يفعلون ما يؤمرون به". ثم ثنت شفتيها وهي تتفحصهم جميعاً، وقالت:"الأطفال يكبرون ويكبرون، لكن الجنود فقط يموتون". فقط. يموتون. كل كلمة كانت طعنة، ثم انفتح الباب دون أن تلمسه، وعلى الجانب الآخر منه دون أن تتحرك، بدت واقفة في الممر. لقد فعلت ذلك من قبل: جعلت الزمن يبدو وكأنه يتشوش ويتقطع، خطوات وثوان ابتلعت من المشهد.

ابتلعته مثل ذلك العصير الأحمر الذي يتخثر في الفم، والذي لا يمكن أن يكون دماً.

أجبرت ميليل نفسها على القول:"إذاً سنموت؟".

"الملكة هي من ستقرر ما سنفعله بكم".

ملكة؟ كان هذا أول ذكر لملكة. هل هي التي أرسلت إلى جورام سلة الفاكهة التي أدت إلى تعليق أربعة عشر من"السيوف المكسورة" على مشنقة ويستواي وجارية تتدحرج من باب المزراب في كفن؟

سألت ميليل:"متى؟ متى ستقرر؟".

قالت الفتاة:"عندما تعود إلى البيت. استمتعوا بلحمكم ودمائكم ما دام بإمكانكم ذلك، أيها الجنود الأعزاء. سكاراب ذهبت إلى الصيد". ترنمت بالكلمة."صَيد، صَيد". وابتسمت ابتسامة شريرة، ومرة أخرى رأت ميليل أسنانها المدببة... ومرة أخرى رأت أنها ليست كذلك.

تذبذب في الزمن، تذبذب في الواقع. ما الذي كان حقيقياً؟ ومضة

وتقطع، وأُغلق الباب، واختفت أيدولون، و...

... وعمّ الظلامُ الغرفةَ.

رمشت ميليل بعينيها، وهزت نفسها لتتخلص من الثقل المفاجئ ونظرت حولها. ظلام؟ كانت كلمات أيدولون لا تزال تتردد في الزنزانة –"صَيد، صَيد" – لذا لا يمكن أن تكون قد مرت سوى ثانية، لكن الغرفة ظلت مظلمة. كان ستيفان قد أغمض أيضاً، والبقية. أما ياف الشاب، الذي بالكاد تخرج من معسكر التدريب بوجهه المستدير كوجه طفل، فقد بدأت دموع الرعب تلمع في عينيه الزرقاوين.

صَيد، صَيد، صَيد.

اندفعت ميليل نحو النافذة بحركة من جناحيها ونظرت إلى الخارج. النهار لم يعد نهاراً. الظلام الدامس للّيل كان يخفي ألوان السماء، باستثناء القمرين الخافتين؛"نيتيد" في شكل هلال و"إيلاي" مجرد شبه باهت، ولكنهما يبعثان معاً ما يكفي من الضوء ليضيء أطراف أجنحة صيادي العواصف بالفضة بينما كانوا يتحركون في دوائر لا تنتهي.

صيد، جاء صوت أيدولون - صدى أو ذكرى أو شبحاً - فاستندت ميليل على الحائط، بينما كان يوم كامل ضائع يمر من خلالها ويختفي في كل دقيقة مسروقة، شعرت برعشة تقربها من نهايتها. هل سيموتون هنا، جميعهم؟ لم تستطع - أو لم ترد - أن تصدق أيدولون بشأن الفاكهة، لكن ذكرى رقائقها الكثيفة بين أسنانها لا تزال تجعلها ترغب في التقيؤ.

قد يكون هؤلاء الناس سيرافيم، وبدأت صورة ملكتهم الغامضة تدور في رأس ميليل – سكاراب؟ – ثم تتحول إلى شيء مرعب.

صَيد، صَيد، صَيد.

ماذا تصطاد؟

9

الهبوط

في الساعة 15:12 بتوقيت غرينتش، وتحت أنظار العالم أجمع، نزلت الملائكة على الأرض. لعدة ساعات، بينما كان مسار رحلتهم يتجه مباشرة غرباً من سمرقند، مروراً ببحر قزوين وأذربيجان، في حين بقيت وجهتهم لغزاً. عبر تركيا، حافظوا على المسار في الاتجاه الغربي، عبروا الأراضي المقدسة بعد تجاوز خط الطول 36 دون التوجه جنوباً. بعد ذلك، كان من المتوقع مرورهم بمدينة الفاتيكان، وهذا ما حدث.

السرب الذي كانوا يطيرون فيه، مؤلف من عشرين رفاً مثالياً يضم كل رفّ خمسين ملاكاً، هبطوا في الساحة الكبرى لكاتدرائية القديس بطرس في روما.

تابع العلماء والطلاب المتخرجون والمتدربون الذين تجمعوا في الطابق السفلي من المتحف الوطني للتاريخ الطبيعي في واشنطن العاصمة، الحدث على الشاشة بصمت، بينما كان في زي باروكي يليق بلقبه - قداسة أسقف روما، نائب يسوع المسيح، خليفة أمير الرسل، الحبر

الأعظم للكنيسة الجامعة، رئيس أساقفة إيطاليا ورئيس أساقفة ومطران المقاطعة الرومانية، صاحب السيادة على دولة الفاتيكان، خادم خدام الله - تقدم البابا لتحية ضيوفه الرائعين.

في تلك اللحظة، حدث تغيير في وسط الحشد. وصار من الصعب تمييز التفاصيل. الكاميرات، طائرات الهليكوبتر مع كاميراتها تحوم في الجو، ومن هذا الموقع المرتفع، بدت الملائكة مثل شبكة حية من النار والحرير الأبيض.

رائع. الآن، تقدم واحد منهم—يبدو أنه كان يرتدي خوذة فضية مزينة بالريش—وفي حركة انسيابية جماعية، ركع الباقون على ركبة واحدة.

اقترب البابا، مرتجفاً، ويده مرفوعة في تحية المباركة، ومال قائد الملائكة برأسه في انحناءة خفيفة جداً. وقف الاثنان مواجهين لبعضهما البعض. بدا أنهما يتحدثان.

سأل عالم الحيوان المذهول:"هل... أصبح البابا للتو المتحدث باسم الإنسانية؟".

"وما الخطأ بذلك؟" رد عالم الأنثروبولوجيا بحالة من الذهول.

شكل زملاء إليزا مركزاً إعلامياً مؤقتاً عبر تجميع عدد من أجهزة التلفزيون وأجهزة الكمبيوتر في إحدى القاعات الدراسية الفارغة. على مدار عدة ساعات، تحولت طبيعة تعليقاتهم تقريباً بالكامل بعيداً عن نظرية الخدعة نحو المجالات الأكثر إزعاجاً من التساؤلات مثل... إذا كان هذا حقيقياً، كيف يكون حقيقياً، وماذا يعني، وكيف يمكننا تفسيره؟

أما بالنسبة إلى التعليقات التلفزيونية، فقد كانت تافهة. لقد كانوا يرددون المصطلحات التوراتية كما لو لم يكن هناك غد، وربما لن يكون هناك غد!

ا-دوم-بوم-بوم.

نهاية العالم. هرمجدون. نشوة الطرب[1].

كان خصم إليزا، مورغان توث—صاحب الشفتين الممتلئتين—يستخدم مفردات مختلفة تماماً. قال:"يجب أن يتعاملوا معها كغزو فضائي." وأضاف:"هناك بروتوكولات لذلك".

"البروتوكولات". كانت إليزا تعرف بالضبط ما كان يقصده.

"سيكون ذلك جيداً بالنسبة إلى الجماهير"، قالت إيفون تشين، أخصائية الأحياء الدقيقة، وهي تضحك."إنه المجيء الثاني! استعدوا لإطلاق الطائرات المقاتلة!".

أطلق مورغان تنهيدة مبالغاً فيها تعبر عن الصبر. قال بتعالٍ شديد:"نعم، مهما كان هذا، أود أن يكون هناك بعض الطائرات المقاتلة بيني وبينهم. هل أنا الوحيد غير الغبي على هذا الكوكب؟".

"نعم، مورغان توث، أنت كذلك"، قال غابرييل بنبرة ساخرة."هل ستكون ملكنا؟".

"بكل سرور"، قال مورغان وهو يرسم انحناءة خفيفة ويقلب غرة شعره الطويلة المدللة أثناء النهوض. كان شخصاً صغيراً ذا وجه وسيم على كتفين نحيلتين ومنحدرتين، وعنق بحجم إصبع إليزا الصغير. أما بالنسبة إلى شفتيه الممتلئتين، فكانتا دائماً في حالة ابتسامة ساخرة، وكانت إليزا تعاني دائماً من الرغبة في رمي الأشياء على تلك الشفتين. عملات معدنية. دبابيب جيلاتينية. لكمات.

كان كلاهما طالبين في مرحلة الدراسات العليا في مختبر الدكتور أنوج شودهاري، وحصلا على زمالات بحثية تنافسية للغاية مع واحد من أبرز علماء الأحياء التطورية في العالم، لكن منذ اليوم الذي التقيا فيه، كانت العداوة

---

1. حالة أو تجربة الانجراف في انفعال غامر. تجربة صوفية تسمو فيها الروح إلى معرفة الأمور الإلهية. الصعود النهائي للمسيحيين إلى السماء في آخر الزمان بحسب اللاهوت المسيحي

التي شعرت بها إليزا تجاه هذا الفتى الأبيض المغرور أشبه بالغثيان. لقد ضحك بالفعل عندما أخبرته باسم الجامعة العامة المتواضعة التي جاءت منها، مدعياً أنه كان يعتقد أنها تمزح، وتلك مجرد البداية. كانت تعرف أنه لا يعتقد أنها قد حصلت على مكانها هنا بجدارتها، وأنه لا بد أن نوعاً من"التفضيل الإيجابي" هو السبب – أو ربما أسوأ من ذلك. أحياناً، عندما يضحك الدكتور شودهاري على شيء قالته إليزا، أو ينحني فوق كتفها لقراءة بعض النتائج، كانت ترى افتراضات مورغان الخبيثة في ابتسامته، وهذا كان يثير غضبها. إنه يلوثها بهذا– ويشوه صورة الدكتور شودهاري أيضاً، الذي كان رجلاً محترماً، متزوجاً، وأيضاً بعمر والدها. اعتادت إليزا على أن يتم التقليل من شأنها، لأنها سوداء ولأنها امرأة، لكن لم يكن قد أظهر أحد هذا القدر من البذاءة حيال ذلك كما فعل مورغان. كانت ترغب في هزّه بعنف، وهذا أقصى ما فكرت فيه. إليزا هادئة بطبيعتها، حتى بعد كل شيء، وكان هذا الغضب نفسه يثير غضبها – أن مورغان توث يمكن أن يؤثر عليها، ويثنيها مثل سلك رفيع بفضل بشاعة شخصيته فقط.

"أعني، عن جد"، قال وهو يشير إلى شاشات التلفاز، حيث الملاك ذو الخوذة والبابا ما زالا يتحدثان. استطاع أحدهم الحصول على كاميرا أقرب إلى الحدث، الآن على الأرض معهما، رغم أنها لم تكن قريبة بما يكفي للحصول على صوت."ما هذه الأشياء؟" تساءل مورغان."نحن نعلم أنهم ليسوا كائنات سماوية-".

"نحن لا نعلم أي شيء بعد"، سمعت إليزا نفسها تقول، رغم أن آخر شيء كانت تريده – يا إلهي، ما هذه السخرية – هو الجدال لصالح الملائكة فقط مورغان كان قادراً على استفزازها بهذه الطريقة. كان صوته – المشحون بالعدائية والمليء بالإزعاج – يثير في نفسها رغبة تلقائية في الجدال. كل ما عليه فعله هو اتخاذ موقف معين لتشعر فوراً بالحاجة إلى معارضته. ولو أعلن أن اللبن أبيض، لصرحت إليزا بأن اللبن أسود. ورغم

ذلك، كانت إليزا حقاً، لا تحب اللبن حتى الملون منه.

سألته:"هل أنتِ عالم فعلاً؟ منذ متى بدأنا نقرر ما نعرفه من دون أن تكون لدينا أي بيانات؟".

"أنتِ تجعلين وجهة نظري أكثر وضوحاً، يا إليزا. البيانات. نحتاج إليها. أشك في أن البابا سيحصل عليها، ولا أسمع الرئيس يطالب بها".

"هذا لا يعني أنه لا يطالب بها. لقد قال إنه يتم النظر في كل السيناريوهات".

"كلام فارغ. أفترض أنه إذا نزل صحن طائر على الفاتيكان، فسوف يخصصون له مدرجاً في وسط ساحة القديس بطرس!".

"لكنه ليس صحناً طائراً، أليس كذلك يا مورغان؟ هل حقاً لا تستطيع أن ترى أن هذا الوضع مختلف؟". كانت تعلم أنه لا جدوى من الجدال معه، لكنه كان يثير جنونها. كان يتظاهر بعدم فهم الحساسية الشديدة لهذا الموقف وكأنه فوق كل ذلك—بعيد عن اهتمامات العامة إلى درجة أن قلقهم يبدو له سخيفاً."يا لبدائية تقاليدكم! ما هذا الشيء الذي تسمونه ‹الدين›؟" لكن إليزا كانت تعرف أن هذا تهديد مختلف تماماً عن صحن طائر. لو كانت هناك عملية هبوط لكائنات فضائية، لكان ذلك قد وحّد العالم، تماماً كما يحدث في أفلام الخيال العلمي. لكن"الملائكة" لديها القدرة على تقسيم البشرية إلى ألف شظية.

وكانت إليزا تعرف ذلك جيداً. فقد كانت إحدى تلك الشظايا لسنوات. قالت:"لا توجد أشياء كثيرة يُقتل الناس ويموتون من أجلها عن طيب خاطر، لكن هذا الشيء مختلف. هل تفهم؟ لا يهم ما تؤمن به، أو ما تعتقد أنه سخيف. إذا استخدمت السلطات أياً من البروتوكولات، فلن يكون الوضع جميلاً في الخارج".

أطلق مورغان تنهيدة أخرى، وضغط أطراف أصابعه إلى صدغيه في تعبير يشير إلى:"لماذا يجب أن أتحمل مثل هذا الضعف العقلي؟ لا يوجد سيناريو

يكون فيه الوضع جميلاً. نحن بحاجة إلى السيطرة على الوضع، لا أن نسقط على ركبنا مثل مجموعة من البسطاء المبهورين". وهنا كانت إليزا مجبرة على عضّ لسانها، لأنها كانت تكره أن تتفق مع مورغان توث، لكنها اتفقت مع ما يقوله هذه المرة. وقد كانت تخوض القتال لسنوات—كي لا تسقط على ركبتيها مجدداً، ألا تُجبر على الركوع، ألا تُطرح أرضاً وتُجبر على البقاء هناك، ألا تُجبر أبداً.

والآن، السماء تنفتح وتنسكب منها الملائكة؟

كان الأمر مضحكاً بطريقة ما. ترغب أحياناً في الضحك وفي أحيان أخرى ترغب في ضرب قبضتيها على شيء ما، على جدار أو ابتسامة مورغان توث المصطنعة.

تتخيل كيف سينظر إليها إذا عرف من أين أتت. ممّ أتت. ممّ هربت. بالطبع سيمقتها إلى درجة الازدراء الذي لم يُسبق له مثيل. وربما إلى درجة الابتهاج الممزوج بالاشمئزاز. كان ذلك سيفرحه لعام بأكمله. قررت أن تصمت، وهو ما اعتبره مورغان انتصاراً، لكنها شعرت، من نظرة عينيه المتلألئتين كعيني سمكة، أنه كان ينبغي لها أن تصمت في وقت أبكر. وذكرت نفسها: إن الأشخاص الذين لديهم أسرار لا ينبغي لهم أن يصنعوا أعداءً ومن طبقة عميقة من ذاكرتها، انبثق صوت والدتها بشكل واضح وغير متوقّع، وكأنه كان رداً على ذلك. قالت:"الناس الذين لديهم أقدار، لا يجب أن يضعوا الخطط".

"يا إلهي!" صوت مليء بالبهجة من أحد المذيعين المحرجين، مما لفت انتباه إليزا إلى صف أجهزة التلفاز. حدث جديد. كان البابا قد التفت جانباً ليصدر أوامر لأتباعه، وفي هذه اللحظة اقترب فريق إخباري يجر الكاميرات والميكروفونات بسرعة فائقة.

"يبدو أن الزوار سيدلون ببيان!".

10

الجنوح إلى الذعر

تقدم ملاك يرتدي خوذة من الفضة المنقوشة يعلوها الريش الأبيض. كانت تشبه خوذة جندي روماني، بالإضافة إلى واقي الأنف – شريط ضيق من الفضة يمتد من حاجب الخوذة إلى ذقنه، مما يقسم وجهه فعلياً إلى نصفين. هذا التصميم أخفى أنفه وكل شيء باستثناء زوايا فمه، بينما ترك عينيه، وعظام وجنتيه، وخط الفك مكشوفة.

يا له من اختيار غريب، خاصة إذ أخذنا بعين الاعتبار إلى أن بقية الفرقة الذين كانوا حاسري الرأس، ووجوههم الجميلة مكشوفة. هناك أشياء أخرى غريبة في هذا الملاك لكنه من الصعب تحديدها، وسرعان ما طغى بيانه على الجميع.

لاحقاً، ستطلق التحليلات حول غرابته، وظله الواسع غير المألوف، وصوته الرخو تتخلله الهمسات بين الجمل، وكأن شخصاً ما كان يلقنه الكلمات. ستنشر التفاصيل مع الشعور العام بالغرابة الذي خلّفه – كبقايا لزجة على أصابعك، لكن هذه المرة على عقلك.

لكن ليس بعد. أولاً، بيانه، والتوجه الفوري العالمي الذي حذر به: توجه مباشر نحو الذعر.

قال:"يا أبناء وبنات الإله الواحد الحق" – لكن... قالها باللاتينية، لذا لم يفهمه إلا قلة قليلة بالفعل. عبر الكرة الأرضية بأسرها، وسط صلوات ولعنات وتساؤلات نطق بها المليارات بمئات اللغات، هرع الجميع للبحث عن ترجمة.

ماذا يقول؟؟؟

في الوقت الذي استغرقه نشر الترجمات، شهدت أغلبية البشرية رسالة الملاك أولاً من خلال رد فعل البابا عليها.

لم يكن ذلك مطمئناً.

شحبت ملامح الحبر الأعظم. تراجع خطوة إلى الخلف متعثراً. حاول أن يتكلم في لحظة ما، لكن الملاك قاطعه من دون أن يلقي نظرة جانبية.

هذه كانت رسالته إلى البشرية:

"يا أبناء وبنات الإله الواحد الحق، لقد مرّت أجيال كثيرة مذ جئنا إليكم آخر مرة، رغم أنكم لم تغيبوا يوماً عن نظرنا. ولقرونٍ عديدة، خضنا حرباً تتجاوز قدرة البشر على الفهم. لقد خميناكم طويلاً جسداً وروحاً بينما حجبنا عنكم حتى المعرفة بالتهديد الذي يترصد بكم. العدو الذي يتعطش إلى دمائكم.

بعيداً عن أراضيكم، خيضت معارك عظيمة. أُريق الدم، والتُهم اللحم. لكن مع تزايد الكفر والشر بينكم، نمت قوة العدو. والآن قد جاء اليوم الذي تتساوى فيه قوتهم مع قوتنا، وقريباً ستتفوق عليها. لم نعد نستطيع أن نترككم بريئين من هذا الضلال. لم نعد قادرين على حمايتكم دون مساعدتكم".

أخذ الملاك نفساً عميقاً وأطال التوقف قبل أن ينهي بصعوبة:"الوحوش... قادمة لتنال منكم".

وبالتزامن مع ذلك، بدأت أعمال الشغب.

11

تناسل الصمت

وقف أكيفا متماسكاً. بدت الكلمات التي قالها للتو معلقة في الهواء.
كان الجو في أعقاب نطقه، كما اعتقد، أشبه بالضغط في مسار صيادي
العواصف - كل الهواء كان يتدفق نحو كارثة مقبلة. كان المصطفون حوله
في كهوف كيرين مائتين وستة وتسعين من ذوي المتجهمين غير الشرعيين،
هم كل من تبقى من فيلق الإمبراطور اللقيط، الذين قدم لهم للتو اقتراحه
الذي لا يمكن تصوره. كان الضغط يتزايد، وثقل الهواء يتحدّى الارتفاع
الشاهق. وفجأة... علا ضحك، هستيري ومضطرب.

"وهل سننام جميعاً جنباً إلى جنب، وحش-سيراف، وحش-سيراف؟"
سأل زاثانيل، أحد إخوة أكيفا من أبيه، ولم يكن يعرفه جيداً.

لم يكن هالك الوحوش معروفاً بروح الدعابة، لكن لا بدّ أن هذه مزحة:
اللجوء إلى الأعداء؟ الانضمام إليهم؟

"ونمشط شعر بعضنا البعض قبل النوم؟" أضاف سوراث.

"أو بالأحرى ننقي القمل من رؤوسهم"، قال زاثانيل مجدداً وسط المزيد
من الضحك.

عانى أكيفا من ذكرى جسدية حادة عن مادريغال وهو نائم إلى جانبها، ولم تكن النكتة مضحكة بالنسبة إليه. لقد كان الأمر أقل إضحاكاً هنا، في الكهوف التي يتردد فيها صدى شعبها المذبوح، حيث لا يزال بإمكانك إذا نظرت عن كثب أن ترى آثار دماء الجثث المسحوبة على الأرض. كيف سيكون شعور كارو عندما ترى هذا الدليل؟ كم كانت تتذكر اليوم الذي تيتمت فيه؟ لقد ذكّر نفسه بأن اليتم الأول كان منذ وقت قريب، وكان خطأه، وكانت غلطته. فأجاب:"أعتقد أنه سيكون من الأفضل أن نبقى في مكانين منفصلين". تلاشى الضحك تدريجياً، وبدأ الجميع يحدّقون فيه، بوجوه تأرجحت بين الاستهزاء والغضب. لم يكن أي من هذين الموقفين يناسب أكيفا، وكان عليه نقلهم إلى مكان آخر تماماً: ودفعهم إلى القبول، ولو على مضض.

ولو بدا هذا الأمر بعيد المنال. ترك أكيفا جماعة الكيميرا في وادٍ جبلي حتى يتمكن من العودة لاحقاً ليأخذهم إلى بر الأمان. تواقاً لتأمين سلامة كارو—وبقية الكيميرا أيضاً. هذه الفرصة المستحيلة لن تتكرر. إذا فشل في إقناع إخوته وأخواته بالمحاولة، فقد فشل في تحقيق الحلم.

قال لهم مخاطباً:"الاختيار لكم. يمكنكم الرفض. لقد تحررنا من خدمة الإمبراطورية؛ نحن نختار معركتنا الآن، ويمكننا اختيار حلفائنا أيضاً. الحقيقة أننا دمرنا الكيميرا. وهؤلاء القلة الناجون هم أعداء حرب الأمس. الآن نواجه تهديداً جديداً، ليس فقط لنا، بل لكل الإريتز: إن وعود حقبة جديدة من الطغيان والحرب ستجعل حكم والدنا يبدو ليّناً بالمقارنة. يجب أن نوقف جايل. هذا هو الأهم".

"لسنا بحاجة إلى الوحوش لتحقيق ذلك"، قال إليون، وهو يتقدم إلى الأمام. على عكس زاثانيل، كان أكيفا يعرف إليون جيداً ويحترمه. فهو من كبار اللقطاء الباقين على قيد الحياة، ولم يكن كبيراً في السن، بالكاد بدأ شعره يشيب. كان مفكراً، ومخططاً، غير متباه، ولا يؤيد العنف من دون ضرورة.

"حقاً؟" واجهه أكيفا."الدومينيون عددهم خمسة آلاف، وجايل الآن

إمبراطور، وبالتالي يتحكم في الفيلق الثاني أيضاً".

"وكم عدد هؤلاء الوحوش؟".

"هؤلاء الكيميرا،" أجاب أكيثا،"عددهم حالياً سبعة وثمانون".

"سبعة وثمانون" ضحك إليون. لم يكن ساخراً، بل كان حزيناً تقريباً."هذا عدد قليل. كيف سيساعدنا ذلك؟".

"سيساعدنا بقدر سبعة وثمانين جندياً"، قال أكيثا. كبداية، فكر دون أن ينطق. لم يخبرهم بعد أن الكيميرا لديهم الآن سحر إحياء أرواح جديد."سبعة وثمانون بجانب الهامسا ضد الدومينيون".

"أو ضدنا"، أشار إليون.

تمنى أكيثا لو يستطيع نفي احتمال أن تُستخدم الهامسا ضدهم؛ ما زال يشعر بالغثيان من وميض راحات أيديهم الشاحبة كالرماد، كألم خافت في معدته. قال:"ليس لديهم سبب ليحبونا أكثر مما نحبهم. أو أقل. انظروا إلى بلادهم. لكن مصالحنا، على الأقل في الوقت الحالي، متوافقة. لقد أعطى الذئب الأبيض وعده—".

عند ذكر الذئب الأبيض، فقد الجمع رباطة جأشه."الذئب الأبيض حي؟" صرخ العديد من الجنود."ولم تقتله؟" صرخ الآخرون، وملأت أصواتهم الكهف، تتردد وتنعكس من جدرانه العالية وتبدو وكأنها تتكاثر لتتحول إلى جوقة من صيحات شبحية.

"الجنرال حي، نعم"، أكد أكيثا. كان عليه أن يصرخ ليُسكتهم."ولا، لم أقتله". لو تعلمون كم كان ذلك صعباً."ولم يقتلني هو أيضاً، رغم أنه كان بإمكانه بسهولة". هدأت صيحاتهم، ثم هدأت أصداؤها، لكن أكيثا شعر وكأن الكلمات قد نفدت منه. عندما يتعلق الأمر بثياغو، تتلاشى قدرته على الإقناع."لو كان الذئب الأبيض ميتاً، هل سيكون الحال أفضل؟ لا تشغلوا بالكم فيه"، قال لنفسه،"فكر فيها، فكر في كارو". وقال بعد تفكير:"هناك الماضي، وهناك المستقبل. الحاضر ليس سوى ثانية واحدة تفصل بين

الاثنين. نحن نعيش معلّقين في تلك الثانية وهي تتسارع—إلى أين؟ طوال حياتنا، كانت الإمبراطورية تدفعنا—نحو إبادة الوحوش—وقد حدث ذلك وانتهى. صار ماضياً، لكننا ما زلنا على قيد الحياة، أقل من ثلاثمائة منا، وما زلنا نندفع إلى الأمام نحو شيء ما، لكن لم تعد الإمبراطورية هي التي تقودنا من الآن فصاعداً. وبالنسبة إلي، هذا ما سيكون". كان يمكن أن يقول: هدفنا القضاء على جايل. ربما سيبدو أنه يقول الحقيقة. لكنها تبقى حقيقة صغيرة تطغى عليها حقيقة أكبر. في ذاكرته كان يسكن صوت أعمق من أي صوت سمعه على الإطلاق، يقول:"إما أن تكون عبداً للحياة، أو للموت".

وتلك كانت آخر كلمات بريمستون.

"الحياة"، قال لإخوته وأخواته الآن."أريد أن يكون المستقبل للحياة. الكيميرا ليسوا هم من يقف في الطريق. لم يكونوا أبداً. كان ذلك جورام، والآن جايل".

عندما يتعلق الأمر بالكراهية الكبرى والصغرى، كان أكيفا يعلم أن الكراهية في صميم الفرد ستفوز، وقد حرص جايل أن يفوز بهذا الشرف.

لم يكن غير الشرعيين يعلمون بعد... إلى أي مدى وصلت الأمور. احتفظ أكيفا بالخبر لنفسه للحظة، غير راغب في النطق به. يشعر، أكثر من أي وقت مضى، بأنه مذنب، وكأن الذنب كله يقع على عاتقه. وأخيراً، ألقى الخبر فوق صمتهم الثقيل كما يُلقى بجثة.

"هازايل مات".

هناك أنواع من الصمت، تماماً كما توجد أنواع من الكيميرا. كلمة"كيميرا" لا تعني شيئاً محدداً سوى"مخلوق ذو مظهر مختلط، مخلوق ليس سيرافاً". إنه مصطلح يشمل كل الأنواع التي تمتلك لغة وقدرات عالية وتعيش في هذه الأراضي، ولم يكن مصطلح"ملاك" ليُوجد لولا عدوان السيرافيم، الذي وحّد القبائل ضدهم. والصمت الذي سبق إعلان أكيفا، والصمت الذي تلاه، كانا مختلفين تماماً، كاختلاف كيرين عن هيث.

في العام الأخير، تقلص عدد غير الشرعيين إلى جزء ضئيل مما كانوا عليه. فقدوا الكثير من الإخوة والأخوات إلى درجة أن من بقي منهم يمكنهم أن يغرقوا في رماد من رحلوا. كانوا مُبرمجين على توقع ما حدث، لكن هذا لم يُسهّل الأمر عليهم، ففي الأشهر الأخيرة من الحرب، عندما بلغت أعداد القتلى مستويات من العبث، حدث تحوّل. تزايد غضبهم—ليس فقط بسبب الخسائر، بل بسبب إدراكهم بأنهم كانوا مجرد أسلحة، لم يشعروا بالحزن. لكنه لامس قلوبهم. وبكل المعايير، كان هازايل مفضّلاً بينهم.

"قُتل بكمين على يد الدومينيون في برج الفتح". بينما كان يتحدث، عاد أكيفا في مخيلته إلى تلك اللحظة، وكأنه يرى الحدث مجدداً، وكيف أنه، في وهج سيريثار الذي جاء إليه متأخراً، شاهد أخاه وهو يموت. لم يُخبرهم بالبقية: أن هازايل مات دفاعاً عن ليراز أمام جايل وخطته المروّعة. كان ذلك سبباً كافياً لمعاناتها.

"صحيح أنني قتلتُ والدنا. هذا ما ذهبت لأجله، وفعلته. مهما كان ما سمعتموه، لم أقتل ولي العهد، ولم أكن لأفعل ذلك. ولا المجلس، ولا الحرس، ولا السيوف الفضية، ولا خدم الحمام. كل ذلك الدم. كل هذا كان من فعل جايل، وكان جزءاً من خطته. بغض النظر عما حدث في ذلك اليوم، كان سيُلصق التهمة بي، ويستخدمها كذريعة لإبادتنا جميعاً".

طوال حديثه، أخذ الصمت بالتحول، وشعر أكيفا بأن ارتخاء تدريجياً بدأ يعم، كالأيدي التي تراخت قبضاتها على مقابض السيوف. ربما هذا الأمر جديد عليهم، حيث إن حياتهم ستكون محكومة بالفناء بغض النظر عما فعله أكيفا في ذلك اليوم، وربما لم يكن ذلك هو ما يهم. هذان الاسمان— هازايل وجايل—يمكن أن يكونا قطبي الحب والكراهية لديهم، ومعاً يمكن أن يجعلا الأمر برمته حقيقياً. صعود عمهم، نفيهم، وحتى حقيقة حريتهم— التي ما زالت غريبة عنهم، لغة لم تتح لهم الفرصة لتعلّمها.

يمكنهم فعل أي شيء الآن. حتى... التحالف مع الوحوش؟

قال أكيفا:"لن يتوقع جايل ذلك. سوف يغضبه ذلك في البداية. بالإضافة إلى أنه سيُربكه. لن يعرف ما الذي يتوقعه في عالم تتحالف فيه الكيميرا مع غير الشرعيين".

"ولا نحن، على الأرجح"، قال إليون مستغرقاً، وكأن المجهول يثير فضوله بقدر ما يخيفه.

قال أكيفا:"هناك شيء آخر. الكيميرا لديهم مجسدة أرواح جديدة. ويجب أن تعلموا، قبل أن تقرروا أي شيء، أنها كانت مستعدة لإنقاذ هازايل". انحبس صوته للحظة. لكن الأوان كان قد فات.

استوعبوا ذلك."ماذا عن ليراز؟" سأل إليون، وثار لغط بين الجنود. ليراز ستكون هي المحك. قال أحدهم،"بالتأكيد لم توافق على هذا".

وتلا أكيفا دعاءً من أجل أخته، لأنه عرف أنه قد كسب رضاهم الآن."إنها معهم، في المخيم وتنتظر كلمتي. ويمكنكم أن تتخيلوا——" سمح لنفسه لأول مرة منذ وصوله واستدعائهم بأن يبتسم."إنها تفضل أن تكون هنا معكم. لكن جايل لن ينتظر".

نظر إلى إليون أولاً."هل كل شيء على ما يرام؟"؟

رمش الجندي عدة مرات بسرعة، وكأنه يستيقظ. عقد حاجبيه."الهدنة"، قال بتحذير،"يمكن أن تكون هشة بسبب طرف غير موثوق به".

"إذاً لا يجب أن نكون نحن هذا الطرف"، قال أكيفا."هذا أفضل ما يمكننا فعله". النظرة في عيني إليون اقترحت أنه يستطيع التفكير في حلول أفضل، تبدأ وتنتهي بالسيوف، لكنه أومأ برأسه. شعر أكيفا بالارتياح، وكأن صيّادي العواصف مروا أمامه وأعادوا تشكيل الهواء.

إليون أعطى وعده، والبقية كذلك. بدا الأمر بسيطاً، وسلساً، وهذا أقصى ما يمكن إنجازه في الوقت الحالي: أنهم عندما تأتيهم الرياح بالأعداء، لن يبادروا بالقتال. لقد أعطى ثياغو الوعد نيابةً عن جنوده.

قريباً سيعرف الجميع قيمة الوعود.

12

فكرة حميمة

سألت زوزانا وهي ترتعش:"هل تعلم ما قد أفعله؟".

"ماذا الذي قد تفعلينه؟" استفسر ميك، وهو جالس خلفها، وذراعاه ملتقّتان حولها بالكامل ووجهه مدفون في انحناءة رقبتها. هذا العنق هو الأكثر دفئاً في جسدها الآن، حيث كان نفس ميك يخلق مناخاً استوائياً صغيراً، بضع بوصات مربعة جميلة من الدفء.

"هل تتذكر المشهد في حرب النجوم، حينما شقّ"هان سولو" بطن التونتون وأدخل لوك داخله حتى لا يتجمد حتى الموت؟".

"آه، يا للطفك. هل ستضعينني في جثة طازجة ودافئة لتحافظي علي دافئاً؟".

"ليس أنت. بل أنا".

"أوه. حسناً. جيد. إن الشيء الذي أفكر فيه بعد هذا المشهد هو أن الأمعاء ستبرد بسرعة، وبصراحة، أفضل أن أكون باردة من أن أكون مغطاة بأحشاء التونتون الرطبة".

قالت زوزانا:"حسناً، كفى. لا داعي لذكر التفاصيل".

"إنه يُسمى كيس نوم سكاي ووكر. امرأة في أمريكا جرّبتها مع حصان".

أصدرت زوزانا صوت اختناق."توقف الآن".

"كانت عارية".

"يا إلهي". سحبت نفسها إلى الأمام لتتمكن من الالتفات للنظر إليه. على الفور بدأت حرارة رقبتها في الانخفاض. وداعاً أيها البقعة الاستوائية الصغيرة."لم أكن بحاجة إلى هذا المشهد في ذهني".

قال ميك متأسفاً."لدي فكرة أفضل، على أي حال".

"فكرة دافئة؟".

"نعم. كنت أحاول جمع شجاعتي عندما شتّتِني بحديثك عن حرب النجوم".

كانت جيش الكيميرا، بالإضافة إليهم وليراز—وقد سبقهم أكيفا ليحصل على الإشارة من جيشه—يخيمون في وادٍ محمي في الجبال. كلمة"محمي" كانت نسبية، وكذلك"وادٍ". عند التفكير في الوديان، تتخيل المروج والأزهار البرية والبحيرات المتلألئة، لكن هذا المكان كان أشبه بحفرة قمرية. على الأقل كانوا بعيدين عن أسوأ الرياح؛ كان الهدوء كافياً لإشعال النار، رغم أنه لم يكن لديهم الكثير من الوقود، والحطب الذي قام أحدهم بقطعه— ربما رارك؟ أو آيجير؟—بفأس حربية، والذي بالكاد اشتعل، ثم أطلق شرارات خضراء وتصاعدت منه رائحة كريهة تشبه الكرنب المهمل منذ عقود في شقة عمة زوزانا في براغ.

حقاً، ذلك العطر لم يكن من المفترض أن يوجد في عالمين.

تساءلت زوزانا عن الفكرة التي قد تكون لدى ميك والتي تتطلب هذا القدر من الجرأة.

تساءلت زوزانا:"هل ستثير هذه الفكرة إعجابي؟".

"إن نجحت؟ نعم. وإن فشلت، وعدت إلى هنا بمظهر محرج أو...

ربما مطعون، لا تسخري مني، حسناً؟".

مطعون؟"لن أسخر منك أبداً"، قالت زوزانا، وكانت تعني ذلك في تلك اللحظة."خصوصاً عندما يكون هناك حالة طعن. لا يوجد حقاً طعن، أليس كذلك؟".

"لا أعتقد أن هناك طعناً، لكن بالتأكيد هناك إحراج". أخذ نفساً عميقاً."ها أنا ذاهب". ثم غادر مكانه من خلفها وأخذ الدفء معه تاركاً إياها مكشوفة تماماً لما يحيطها، وسرعان ما أدركت بأنها لم تشعر بالبرد من قبل، لكنها الآن شعرت به. وكأنها خرجت مبللة من أحشاء التونتون—يا إلهي

"ماذا يفعل ميك؟" سألت كارو وهي تقفز من على الحاجز الحجري الذي كان يحميهم—من الرياح. كانت قد قضت وقتها هناك، تراقب وصول أكيفا. بعد غروب الشمس، لم تتوقع زوزانا عودة السيراف القريبة، لكنها لم تكلف نفسها إخبار صديقتها.

"لا أعرف"، ردّت زوزانا."شيء شجاع، فقط لكي يمنعنا من التجمد حتى الموت". وعلى الفور، ندمت على شكواها تلك.

تألمت كارو."آسفة لأننا لسنا مستعدين بشكل أفضل، يا زوزي"، قالت بصوت يغمره الندم."كان يجب أن تبقي هناك. إنه غباء مني أني سمحت لك بالمجيء".

"اصمتي. أنا لست آسفة، ولست في الحقيقة متجمدة حتى الموت، وإلا كنت تسلقت كومة البطانيات مع إيسا".

كان هناك تجمع حول بعض أعضاء المجموعة ذوي الدم البارد، حيث تم تخصيص جميع البطانيات المتوفرة—بما في ذلك وسادة دبابيس[2] زوزانا ذات الرائحة الكريهة—لهذا الغرض.

---

2.   وسادة الدبابيس أو وسادة الخياطة: هي وسادة صغيرة محشوة بعرض 3-5 سم، تُستخدم في الخياطة لتخزين الدبابيس أو الإبر برؤوسها البارزة للإمساك بها بسهولة وجمعها والحفاظ عليها منظمة

على الأقل، كانت زوزانا ترتدي سترة صوفية، وميك كانت لديه كنزة. لقد كانا محظوظين لأنهما تركا كل أغراضهما في القصر عندما هربا، وإلا لما كان لديهما حتى هذا.

"إلى أين هو ذاهب؟" سألت كارو. كان ميك قد اتجه في الاتجاه المعاكس لمكان استراحة الكيميرا."إنه لا... لا يمكن أن... أوه. إنه يفعلها". كانت نبرتها مليئة بالخوف والإعجاب في آنٍ واحد.

شاركتها زوزانا كلا الشعورين."ماذا يفكر؟" همست."توقف. توقف فوراً". لكن الأوان كان قد فات.

يداه مغروستان عميقاً في جيوب بنطاله الجينز، وقدماه تتحركان بخجل مثل متشرد مذعور، تقدم ميك نحو... ليراز.

نهضت زوزانا للاستطلاع. وقفت بمفردها في أبعد نقطة من هذا الخندق الصخري عن الكيميرا، تبدو غاضبة كما كانت في القصبة، وعلى جسر تشارلز أيضاً. ربما أكثر غضباً. أم إن هذا هو وجهها الطبيعي؟ لم تشهد زوزانا حتى الآن أي دليل على أنها كملاك يمكن أن تظهر بوجه آخر.

تذكرت حين كانت هي وميك يتسليان أثناء التحليق بتأليف إعلانات شخصية لأعضاء المجموعة، وكان إعلان ليراز شيء مثل:"ملاك متحمس غاضب دائماً تبحث عن وسادة دبابيس للتدرب على العبوس والسوداوية، وليس على القبلات".

لكن ميك كما علق؛ لم يرد أن يكون معها على تلك الوسادة. أدركت زوزانا أنه كان يفكر بالجزء"الحميمي"—من المشهد. لكن أفكاره المجنونة تلك محكومة بالفشل. لا يمكن بأي حال أن توافق ليراز على المجيء إلى هنا لتدفئة الجموع المجتمعة بجناحيها، جناحيها المشتعلين، الجميلين، والدافئين.

كان ميك يتحدث إليها في هذه اللحظة. يؤشر بيديه وكأنه يتكلم عن البرد، ثم بعد ذلك مباشرة، فتح ذراعيه مثل جناحين، وأشار إلى مكان ما، ثم

أطبق كفيه وكأنه يناشدها أو يرجوها. نظرت ليراز إلى زوزانا وكارو وانتبهت إلى أنهما تراقبان. ضاقت عيناها. عادت إلى التركيز على ميك، لكن لفترة وجيزة فقط، ونظرت إليه—من أعلى، لأنها كانت طويلة—بلامبالاة تامة. لم تقل شيئاً، حتى إنها لم تهز رأسها، فقط أدارت ظهرها له وكأنه لم يكن موجوداً.

كيف تجرؤ؟ "أيتها التونتون"، تمتمت زوزانا.

التفتت كارو إليها:"ماذا؟".

"لا شيء".

عاد ميك، خائباً لكنه غير مطعون، ورغم أن مهمته قد فشلت—ماذا كان يفكر؟ هل يمكن أن تهتم ليراز براحتهم؟—إلا أن جرأته كانت مذهلة. الكيميرا، رغم وحشيتهم، كانوا أكثر تقبلاً منها.

"بطلي"، قالت زوزانا دون أي تلميح للسخرية، وأمسكت بيد ميك لتعيده إلى النار الهزيلة، لتبدأ في خلق المزيد من المناطق الاستوائية حول رقبتها

13

معاً

غرُبت الشمس. نهضت نيتيد، وتبعتها إيلاي، واستمتعت كارو بدهشة صديقيها وهما يريا القمرين الشقيقتين لأول مرة، حتى لو كانتا مجرد شريحتين الليلة. لقد حصلا على لمحة أخرى من صائدي العواصف أيضاً، على الرغم من أن هذه المرة من مسافة أقرب من المعتادة. انخفضت درجة الحرارة أكثر فأكثر، وضاقت تجمعات المخلوقات الباردة. طبخوا وأكلوا. حكت أورا قصة ذات لازمة إيقاعية مؤرقة.

وقفت ليراز بعيدة، قدر الإمكان عن تجمعات الوحوش، وبينما وضعت كارو يديها تحت إبطيها لتحصل على بعض الدفء، بدت حرارة أجنحة ليراز وكأنها دفء مهدور، يشبه سكب الماء في الصحراء. ومع ذلك، لم تستطع لوم ليراز، بعد ومضات الهامسا التي عانت منها خلال الرحلة. حسناً، يمكن أن تلومها على وقاحتها تجاه ميك الذي لم يكن لديه سحر الهامسا، وبصراحة: من يمكنه أن يكون لئيماً مع ميك؟ حتى أسوأ الكيميرا لم يتمكنوا من فعل ذلك. وانظروا إلى زوزانا! لم يكن لقبها"مك-مك" بين الكيميرا بلا سبب،

ورغم ذلك، حول ميك شراستها إلى عسل. حتى الآن، كانت ليراز الوحيدة التي أثبتت أنها محصنة ضد تأثير ميك.

كانت ليراز مميزة في انعزالها، بشكل مذهل حتى.

لكن كارو شعرت بمسؤولية تجاهها، إذ تُركت هناك كنوع من... ماذا؟ سفيرة من نوع ما؟ لا أحد كان أكثر ملاءمة لهذا الدور منها. كانت هناك تلك اللحظة قبل أن يغادر أكيفا، عندما وقع نظره على كارو من بعيد.

لا أحد يستطيع أن يفعل ذلك مثل أكيفا، يحرق طريقاً عبر الفضاء، يجعلك تشعر أنك مرئي، مميز. لم يتحدثا منذ مغادرتهما القصبة، ولا حتى اقتربا من بعضهما البعض، وكانت كارو حذرة في الاتجاه الذي توجه نظراتها إليه، لكن تلك النظرة وحدها كانت مليئة بالعديد من الرسائل، وأحدها كان رجاءً بأن تهتم بأخته.

لم تستخف بالأمر. كما أنها كانت قادرة على القول بأنه لا أحد يمكن أن يلوّع ليراز، وتأمل ألا يكونوا أغبياء لفعل ذلك، وخاصة بغياب أكيفا كي يدعمها.

متى سيصل؟

في الأسفل، كانت النيران تقذف شراراتها الخضراء وتطلق روائح الملفوف المزعجة، لكنها تبعث القليل من الدفء، ومضت كارو تذرع الجرف، تراقب الكيميرا من جهة، وتبحث عن أكيفا من جهة أخرى. ولم تر أي إشارة لوميض أجنحته في الظلام.

كيف حاله؟ ماذا لو عاد بأخبار سيئة؟ إلى أين ستذهب الكيميرا إن لم يكن إلى كهوف الكيرين؟ هل سيعودون إلى أنفاق المناجم حيث اختبأوا قبل اللجوء إلى عالم البشر؟ ارتجفت كارو من هذه الفكرة.

ومن فكرة المواجهة الكبرى لغزو الملائكة. ومن فقدان الفرص.

أدركت كم اعتمدت حينها على فكرة هذا التحالف، مهما كان مجنوناً، وكل ما يعنيه لهذه الشراكة للمساعدة في تلبية احتياجاتهم

الأساسية وإعطائهم الحجة. الكيميرا بحاجة إلى هذا. هي بحاجة إلى هذا. وفوق ذلك، كانت تتجمد في العراء بينما يستمتع غير الشرعيين بمنزلها القديم وينابيعه الساخنة؟

لا، مستحيل.

سمعت من بعيد صوت خدش مخالب على الحجر، إنها الإشارة الوحيدة على اقتراب الذئب الأبيض، فالتفتت نحوه. كان يحمل لها الشاي، الذي قبلته بامتنان، ولفت أصابعها حول الكوب المعدني الساخن ورفعته إلى وجهها لتتنفس البخار.

"ليس عليكِ أن تبقي هنا في العاصفة. كاسغار وكيتا-إري يتوليان الحراسة".

"أعلم. لا أستطيع البقاء ساكنة. شكراً على الشاي".

"بكل سرور".

"إلى أين أرسلتَ الآخرين؟".

من هنا، رأت كيف تحدث مع نوابه ثم أرسل أربع فرق يتألف كل منها من عنصرين، لتعود في الاتجاه الذي جاءت منه.

"لينتشروا حول المناطق الشرقية من الخليج. يراقبون الأفق. سيعود أحد إلى هنا خلال أربع وعشرين ساعة، ثم بفواصل زمنية قدرها اثنتا عشرة ساعة بعد ذلك، حتى نضمن أن الطريق آمن قبل مغادرتنا الجبال".

أومأت برأسها. كان ذلك قراراً ذكياً. خليج الوحوش كان منطقة تخضع لسيطرة السيرافيم.

في الواقع، كل مكان الآن كان تحت سيطرة السيرافيم، ولم تكن لديهم أي فكرة عما كانت تفعله بقية قوات الإمبراطورية، أو أين كانت تفعل ذلك الجبال وفرت بعض الحماية، لكن للعودة إلى العالم البشري، عليهم أن يبقوا في العراء طوال الوقت الذي سيستغرقه عبور أعدادهم الكبيرة من البوابة، واحداً تلو الآخر.

سأل، بصوت منخفض جداً:"كيف تعتقدين أن الأمر سيسير؟".

نظرت كارو إلى الأسفل نحو أفراد المجموعة المبعثرين على حواف الجوف الصخري الواسع. كانت أعصابها في حالة تأهب قصوى، لكن لم يكن أحد ينظر إليهم، وعلى أي حال، لا بد أن المسافة والظلام جعلاهم مجرد ظلال، والرياح تنقل أصواتهم بعيداً."أعتقد أن الأمر جيد"، قالت."أنت تقوم بعمل جيد". كانت تعني تقمص شخصية ثياغو."إنه أمر غريب قليلاً".

"غريب"، كرر خلفها.

"مقنع. في بعض الأوقات.. كدت أنسى".

لم يدعها تكمل."لا تنسي. أبداً. ولا للحظة". تنفس بعمق."أرجوكِ". كان هناك الكثير وراء هذه الكلمة."أرجوكِ، لا تنسي أنني لست وحشاً. من فضلك، لا تنسي ما تخلّيت عنه. من فضلك، لا تنسي من أنا".

شعرت كارو بالخجل لأنها عبّرت عن تلك الفكرة. هل كانت تعنيها كمديح؟ كيف يمكنها أن تتخيل أنه سيفهمها كذلك؟"أنت تتقن دور المجنون الذي قتلتَه". بدا له وكأنه اتهام.

"لن أنسى"، قالت كارو لزيري. تذكرت لحظة قلقها القصيرة من أن ارتداء جلد الذئب قد يغيره، لكنها عندما أجبرت نفسها على النظر إليه الآن، أدركت أنه لا يوجد خطر من ذلك.

عيناه لم تكونا عينا ثياغو، ليس الآن. كانتا دافئتين للغاية. بالطبع، ما زالتا عيني الذئب الشاحبتين، لكن الاختلاف كان أكبر مما كانت تعتقد أنه يمكن أن يكون. كان من غير الواقعي كيف يمكن لروحين أن تنظرا من خلال نفس العينين بأسلوب مختلف تماماً، بحيث تبدوان وكأنهما تعيدان تشكيلهما بالكامل. بدون كبرياء الذئب، يمكن لهذا الوجه أن يبدو طيباً في الواقع. بالطبع، يبدو ذلك خطيراً. لم يكن الذئب يبدو طيباً أبداً. كان مهذباً، نعم، ومؤدباً. يبدو لطيفاً في تقليد الطيبة؟ ربما. لكن الطيبة الحقيقية؟ لا، والفرق كان هائلاً.

"أعدكَ"، قالت، خافضة صوتها حتى أصبح بالكاد مسموعاً وسط صخب الرياح."لا يمكنني أن أنسى من أنت".

اضطر زيري إلى الاقتراب ليسمع كلماتها، ولم يبتعد عنها بعد ذلك، بل رد بنفس النبرة الغامضة، قريباً بما يكفي لتشعر أذنها بتيار أنفاسه،"شكراً." كانت نبرته دافئة كنبرة أكيفا، لكن ليس كعيني أكيفا، المليئتين بالتوق.

استدارت كارو فجأة نحو العتمة، لتمنح نفسها بعض المسافة. لم يكن بإمكان روح زيري أن تغيّر وجود الذئب جسداً بما يكفي بحيث لا يجعلها قربه منها ترتجف. كانت جراحها لا تزال تؤلمها. أذنها لا تزال تخفق حيث مزقتها أسنانه. ولم تكن بحاجة حتى لإغماض عينيها لتتذكر كيف شعرت حين كانت محاصرة تحت ثقل جسده.

"كيف حالكِ؟" سأل ميك بعد لحظة صمت.

أجابت:"أنا بخير. سأكون أفضل عندما نعرف". وأومأت باتجاه الليل، وكأن السماء تحمل المستقبل—وهو ما افترضت أنه إذا كان أكيفا عائداً إليهم، فقد فعل، بطريقة أو بأخرى.

فجأة، شعرت بانقباض في قلبها. ما مدى عمق المستقبل؟ إلى أي مدى يمتد؟ ومن سيكون معها فيه؟

قال زيري:"أنا أيضاً. على الأقل، سأكون أفضل إذا كانت الأخبار جيدة. لا أعرف ماذا أفعل إن فشلت هذه الخطة".

"ولا أنا". حاولت كارو أن تظهر شجاعة."لكننا سنفكر في شيء إذا اضطررنا لذلك".

أومأ برأسه متردداً."أتمنى أن أرى... المكان الذي وُلدت فيه". لقد كان طفلاً عندما فقدوا قبيلتهم، ولا يملك ذكريات عن الحياة قبل لوراميندي."يمكنك تسميته موطنك"، قالت كارو."بالنسبة إلي يمكنك ذلك".

"هل تتذكرينه؟".

"أتذكر الكهوف. يصعب تذكر الوجوه. أرى والديّ كظل".

كان مؤلماً لها أن تعترف بذلك. زيري كان طفلاً، لكنها كانت في السابعة عندما حدث الأمر، ولم يكن هناك أحد آخر يتذكر. ستبقى قبيلة الكيرين موجودة طالما أنها تحمل ذكراها، لكن معظمها قد تلاشى بالفعل.

انحنت مع وخزة الضمير. هل ستنسى وجه زيري أيضاً؟ كانت فكرة جسده في قبره الضحل تطاردها. كيف علقت الأتربة في رموشه، ثم آخر لمحة من عينيه البنيتين قبل أن تغطيهما. كانت البثور على يديها لا تزال تؤلمها بسبب دفنه على عجل؛ لم تستطع أن تشعر بذلك الألم دون أن ترى وجهه وهو مرتخٍ في الموت. لكنها كانت تعلم أن ذلك سيفقد وضوحه قريباً بما يكفي. كان يجب أن ترسمه—لطالما أرادت ذلك— بينما كان لا يزال حياً. لكنها لم تكن لتُظهر له. كانت لديه طريقته في قراءة الإشارات الصغيرة، ولم تكن تريد أن تمنحه الأمل. ليس الأمل الذي كان يرغب فيه على أي حال.

"هل ستريني المكان عندما نصل إلى هناك —إذا وصلنا—؟" سألها.

"لن يكون لدينا الكثير من الوقت".

"أعلم. لكنني آمل أن يكون هناك بعض الوقت لأكون وحدي، حتى ولو لفترة قصيرة".

وحده؟ تجمدت كارو. ماذا كان يظن، أنهم سيختلون بأنفسهم؟

لكنه تجمد أيضاً عندما رأى ملامحها."لا أعني وحدي معك. أعني، ليس أنني لن أرغب... لكن لم أقصد ذلك. فقط—" أخذ نفساً عميقاً وأخرجه بصعوبة."أنا فقط متعب، يا كارو. ألا أكون مراقباً، وألا أقلق من ارتكاب خطأ، حتى ولو لفترة قصيرة. هذا كل ما قصدته".

يا إلهي، كم كانت أنانية، تفكر فقط في نفسها؟ الضغط عليه كان كبيراً، ساحقاً، ولم تستطع حتى تحمل فكرة أن تكون وحدها معه؟ لم تستطع حتى أن تتظاهر بذلك؟"أنا آسفة جداً"، قالت بأسى."عن كل هذا".

"لا داعي للأسف. من فضلك. لن أقول إن الأمر سهل، لكنه يستحق العناء".

بدا صوته مليئاً بالإخلاص.

مرة أخرى، كان التعبير غريباً تماماً على وجهه الذئبي وصوته، ويضفي لمسة من الحلاوة على جماله الجنرالي الذي كان بعيداً عن متناول الآخرين. آه، يا زيري. "من أجل ما قد ننجزه". وأكمل جملتها، "معاً".

"معاً".

تمرد قلب كارو، وإذا كان هناك ظل للشك المتبقي، فلم يكن ليتحمل هذا الوضوح المفاجئ. كان قلبها نصفاً مختلفاً عن الـ"معاً"—حلم بدأ في جسد آخر، وعلى عكس الكذبة التي كانت تخبر نفسها بها لشهور، لم ينتهِ فيه على ما يبدو.

أجبرت نفسها على الابتسام، لأنه لم يكن خطأ زيري، وكان يستحق منها أفضل من ذلك، لكنها لم تستطع أن تجعل نفسها تقول الكلمة—"معاً". ليس له، على أي حال.

. . .

رأى زيري التوتر في ابتسامة كارو. أراد أن يصدق أن ذلك بسبب اضطرارها لرؤيته من خلال هذا الجسد، لكن... كان يعلم. هكذا فقط. إذا لم يكن يعلم يقيناً قبل هذه اللحظة، فذلك خطؤه هو، وليس خطأها، وها هو الآن يستقر بداخله.

لا أمل هنا. لا حظ.

تمنى لها ليلة سعيدة وتركها هناك تذرع الجرف—ترقب عودة الملاك—وشعر، وهو يبتعد، بأن ملامح وجهه تعود تدريجياً إلى تعبيرها المعتاد. مع انحناء طفيف عند زوايا الشفتين يوحي بشيء من السخرية—السخرية القاسية. لكنها لم تكن تلك من تعبيرات زيري.

لم يكن يشعر بالسخرية. كارو ما زالت تحب أكيفا؟ فئياغو الحقيقي سيشعر بالاشمئزاز والغضب في ذلك الموقف. أما ثياغو المزيف، فيشعر

فقط بقلبه محطماً.

و يشعر أيضاً بالغيرة، وذلك ما سبب له الغثيان.

شعر بفقدان جسده أكثر من أي وقت مضى، ليس لأن ذلك كان سيحدث فرقاً بالنسبة إلى كارو، وإنما لأنه أراد أن يطير—أن يتحرر ولو لفترة قصيرة، أن يُنهك جناحيه ورئتيه، أن يصطدم بنفسه مع الليل ويظهر حزنه على هذا الوجه الذي لم يكن حتى له—لكنه لم يكن يستطيع حتى فعل ذلك. لم يكن لديه جناحان، بل أنياب فقط، ومجرد مخالب.

كان بإمكاني أن أعوي على القمرين، فكر وهو يغوص في هوة من اليأس، وفي ذلك الفراغ البارد الجديد حيث كانت الأمل يسكن يوماً، وضع أملاً آخر، لكنه بالكاد أضاف أي دفء إلى ذلك البرد.

لم تكن له علاقة بالحب؛ لا فائدة من إضاعة الأمل على الحب. كان ذلك مسألة حظ، والسبب الوحيد الذي جعله يوماً يعتبر نفسه محظوظاً، كان أنه تُرك ليتحلل في قبر ضحل في عالم البشر."زيري المحظوظ"—يا لها من نكتة.

أمله الجديد كان ببساطة أن يكون كيرين مجدداً، يوماً ما. أن ينجو من هذا—وألا يُكتشف، وألا يُحرق كخائن، وألا يُترك ليزول.

لا يزال يعتبر ما قاله لكارو الآن صحيحاً: أنه يستحق التضحية، إذا كان ذلك قد يساعد في قيادة الكيميرا نحو مستقبل خالٍ من وحشية الذئب الأبيض.

لكن بعيداً عن ذلك، كان أمل زيري متواضعاً. أراد أن يطير مجدداً، وأن يتخلص من هذا الجسد البغيض بفمه المليء بالأنياب، ومخالبه الحادة.

إذا أحبّته أحداهن يوماً ما، فسيفكر بمرارة، كم جميل لو يستطيع لمسها دون أن يجرحها بمخالبه.

14

أطول خمس دقائق في التاريخ

شعرت ليراز... بالذنب.

ولطالما مقتت هذا الإحساس وتمنت لو غاب هذا الشعور عنها تماماً؛ أي شعور آخر حتى ولو قاد إلى الفوضى. على سبيل المثال الآن، كانت تشعر بالغضب تجاه مصدر شعورها بالذنب، ورغم أنها كانت تدرك أن هذه استجابة عاطفية غير ملائمة، لم تستطع التخلص منها. كانت غاضبة لأنها كانت تعلم أنها مضطرة لفعل شيء ما لتخفيف هذا الشعور بالذنب.

تباً.

كل هذا بسبب ذلك الإنسان وعينيه المتوسلتين وارتجافه بسبب البرد. ولماذا طلب منها أن تدفئه هو وفتاته؟ هل كانت مسؤوليتها؟ لماذا هما هنا أصلاً، يسافران مع الوحوش؟ هذا ليس عالمهما، وهما ليسا مشكلتها. هذا الشعور بالذنب كان سخيفاً بما يكفي، لكن الأسوأ قادم.

أصبح الأمر أكثر غباءً.

كانت ليراز غاضبة أيضاً من الكيميرا، وليس للسبب الذي كان سيبدو منطقياً. لم يكونوا يصوبون هامساتهم نحوها ليسحروها. لم تكن قد شعرت

بسحرهم يحفر في أعماقها طوال الوقت الذي كانوا يعسكرون فيه هنا. ولهذا السبب كانت غاضبة. لأنهم لم يعطوها سبباً لغضبها.

المشاعر كانت غبية.

أسرِع يا أكيفا، فكرت في سماء الليل، كما لو أن أخاها قد ينقذها من نفسها. هناك فرصة ضئيلة لذلك. لقد كان حطاماً من المشاعر، وكان ذلك سبباً آخر للغضب. كانت كارو قد فعلت ذلك به. كان بإمكان ليراز أن تتخيل أصابعها حول عنق الفتاة. لا، كانت ستلف شعرها السخيف في حبل وتخنقها به.

لكن بالطبع، لن تفعل ذلك.

قررت أنها ستمنح أكيفا خمس دقائق أخرى للوصول، وإذا لم يأتِ، ستفعل ما عليها فعله لتوقف مهزلة المشاعر هذه.

كانت هذه المرة الثالثة التي تمنح فيها"خمس دقائق". وكل"خمس دقائق" كانت أقرب إلى خمس عشرة دقيقة.

أخيراً، بدأت ليراز تسير بخطوات ثقيلة، تلعن أكيفا داخلياً مع كل خطوة. لقد منحته أطول"خمس دقائق" في التاريخ، ومع ذلك لم يصل لإنهاء هذا. كان المعسكر نائماً، باستثناء كلب الغريفون الذي يحرس على قمة أحد الصخور. لم يكن بوسعه حتى معرفة ما يجري من هذا الارتفاع.

توقف الذئب عن التسكع على الحافة منذ نصف ساعة تقريباً، وعاد إلى أحد مواقد النيران البعيدة – لحسن الحظ. والجميع نيام.

لن يعرف أحد ما كانت على وشك فعله.

اقتربت ليراز بهدوء وكأنها تترصد. وصلت إلى التجمع... حيث تحلق الوحوش... ونظرت إليه باشمئزاز للحظة قبل أن تقترب.

النار خافتة وبالكاد تصدر أي دفء. وهناك، البشريان—ميك وزوزانا— نائمان متلاصقين كالتوأمين في رحم. جنينان. حدّقت فيهما بعطف لوقت طويل. كانا يرتجفان.

ألقت نظرة واحدة وسريعة حولها.

ثم جلست بجانبهما وفتحت جناحيها. كان من ضمن قدرات السيراف الأساسية التحكم في الحرارة؛ ببساطة أخذت الحرارة بالارتفاع خلال ثوانٍ، وانتشر الدفء في المكان، لكن استغرق الأمر وقتاً أطول حتى يتوقفا عن الارتجاف. لم تعرف ليراز يوماً ما هو الشعور بالبرد. بدا أنه شعور غير مريح. ضعيفان، فكرت وهي تراقبهما، ولكن كان هناك شيء آخر، كلمة أخرى تتحدى تلك الفكرة: شجاعان.

كانا ينامان بوجهيهما ملتصقين.

لم تستطع ليراز أن تستوعب ذلك. لم تكن أبداً قريبة إلى هذا الحد من أي روح حية. أمها؟ ربما. لكنها لا تتذكر. رأت في هذا المنظر ما جعلها ترغب في البكاء، لذلك، فكرت أنه يجب أن تكرههما، لكنها لم تفعل، وتساءلت عن السبب، وهي تراقبهما وتحافظ على دفئهما. بعد فترة، رفعت عينيها لتبحث حول النار. كانت تتساءل حول شيء آخر: هل شارك أكيفا وكارو... هذا؟ هذا التقارب الشجاع؟ ولكن أين كانت كارو؟ كان هناك إيسا، الناجا، تستريح بسلام على ما يبدو، لكن كارو لم تكن بين هؤلاء النائمين.

إذاً، أين هي؟

اضطرب قلبها، وعرفت الجواب. كيف كنت بهذه الغفلة؟ مع تسلل الخوف—والخوف جعلها غاضبة—رفعت رأسها إلى الأعلى، وهناك، بالطبع، كانت كارو، جالسة على الجرف الصخري.

منذ متى وهي هنا؟—ركبتاها مضمومتان إلى صدرها وذراعاها ملفوفتان حولهما بقوة. مستيقظة؟ نعم، بالتأكيد. باردة، بوضوح. تراقب. مفتونة.

تلك اللحظة التي فيها التقت نظراتهما، مالت كارو برأسها جانباً بحركة مفاجئة تشبه الطائر. لم تبتسم، لكن كان في نظرتها دفء مفتوح بدا وكأنه يمتد نحو ليراز.

التي كانت ترغب في إرسال ذلك الدفء مباشرة إليها عبر سهم.

ثم، بكل بساطة، أخفت كارو وجهها بين ركبتيها وعادت إلى النوم. لم تكن ليراز تعرف ما تفعل بنفسها، وقد تم كشفها. تتراجع؟ تحرق الجميع؟ حسناً، ربما ليس هذا. في النهاية، بقيت حيث هي.

لكن عندما استيقظ معسكر الكيميرا، وأعلن عن عودة أكيڤا بخبر جيد: تم الوفاء بوعد غير الشرعيين—كانت ليراز قد نهضت، ولم يعرف أحد ما فعلته إلا كارو. فكرت ليراز في تحذيرها من إخبار أحد، لكنها خافت من أن إظهار هذا القدر من الاهتمام سيجعلها أكثر ضعفاً ويمنح كارو المزيد من القوة عليها، لذلك لم تفعل. لكنها فعلت شيئاً آخر؛ نظرت إليها نظرة حادة

"شكراً"، قال أكيڤا بهدوء عندما كانت لديهما لحظة لوحدهما.

"على ماذا؟" سألت ليراز، ضيقت عينيها وكأنه قد يعرف كيف قضت الساعات الأخيرة.

هز كتفيه."للبقاء هنا. الحفاظ على السلام. لم يكن ذلك ممتعاً".

"لم يكن ممتعاً"، قالت،"ولا تشكرني. قد أكون أول من يسحب سيفه إذا حصلت على دعم".

لم ينخدع أكيڤا. قال وهو يكتم ابتسامة:"ممم هم م".

"الهامسات؟".

"لا"، اعترفت على مضض."لم يمسني أحد".

رفع حاجبيه في دهشة."رائع".

كان ذلك مذهلاً. عبست ليراز، وهي تتذكر غضبها السخيف بسبب ذلك— ماذا كان يعني تركها بسلام هكذا؟ كان الأمر غريباً. لكنه كان أيضاً سخيفاً. لكن قول ذلك سيبدو غبياً، وربما هو كذلك. بدا أكيڤا متفائلاً. لم تره ليراز يبدو هكذا... قط. شعرت بقلبها ينقبض - شعور سيئ وجيد في آن واحد.

كيف يمكن أن يكون الشعور سيئاً وجيداً؟ أكيڤا كان سعيداً؛ وهذا الجيد. هازايل يجب أن يكون هنا؛ وهذا هو السيء.

"هل أخبرتهم عن هازايل؟"، سألت أكيڤا محاولة طمس الألم السيئ بالألم الجيد.

أومأ أكيڤا برأسه، ورأت ليراز بمزيج من الذنب والانتصار الصغير – لكن في الأساس الذنب – أن الأمل قد اختفى من ملامحه، وحل محله الألم."هل يمكنك تخيل كم كان هذا كله ليكون أسهل لو كان هنا؟".

بدلاً مني، فكرت ليراز، رغم أنها تعلم أن هذا ليس ما قصده أكيڤا. لكنها كانت تعنيه. ربما كانت تتصرف نيابة عن هازايل في الليل، بمشاركة دفئها، لكن ما فعلته كان ضئيلاً مقارنة بما كان يمكن أن يجلبه هازايل لهذا التجمع الغريب من الوحوش والملائكة. كان يمكنه أن يجلب الضحك والابتسامات العفوية، وتكسير الحواجز بسرعة. لا أحد كان يمكن أن يقاوم هازايل لفترة طويلة. أما موهبتها، فكرت ليراز بشعور من الاشمئزاز، فكانت مختلفة جداً، وغير مرغوب فيها في المستقبل الذي يحاولون بناءه.

كل ما كانت تجيده هو القتل. لقد كانت تتباهى بذلك لوقت طويل، وتتفاخر به، ورغم أن التباهي قد زال، إلا أن تفاخرها سيظل إلى الأبد. كانت أكمامها مرفوعة طوال الوقت الآن، تخفي الحقيقة المروعة لعدد الضحايا— الحقيقة الفظيعة التي لم تكن تقتصر فقط على يديها.

كانت وشوم معسكر النار، صفوف العد—كل صف يتكون من أربع خطوط دقيقة يتوسطها خط—لم تكن مقتصرة على يديها. كانت تصعد على ذراعيها، تعطي جلدها مظهر الدانتيل الأسود. لم يكن أحد يملك عدداً مثل عددها. لا أحد.

كان ينتهي عند مرفقيها، وينقطع عند عد ناقص: خطين دقيقين هما آخر عمليتي قتل استطاعت تسجيلهما. قبل لوراميندي. لوراميندي.

كانت تحلم حلماً متكرراً منذ ذلك الحين، وقد اقتنعت في ذلك الحلم، بأن ذراعيها ستعودان وتنموان من جديد، بعد قطعهما. لكن كيف فعلت

ذلك تحديداً، لم يكن الحلم واضحاً. آه، الذراع الأولى يمكن قطعها، بالطبع. أما قطع الثانية! هذا اللغز الذي تخطاه عقلها وتجاهله. كيف يمكن لشخص ما أن يقطع كلتا ذراعيه؟

لكن النقطة هي أنهما لن ينموا مجدداً. أو على الأقل، كانت تستيقظ دائماً قبل أن يحدث ذلك. كانت تبقى مستيقظة تحدق، ولا تستطيع العودة إلى النوم حتى تتخيل نهاية، نهاية ينفجر فيها الدم من جذوع ذراعيها ليتشكل إلى عظام ولحم وأصابع—تتصلب حتى تصبح كاملة مرة أخرى. كاملة من دون ندب.

بداية نظيفة. كالخيال.

لم تخبر أحداً بذلك إلا هازايل، الذي حاول أن يلهيها لمدة نصف ساعة بحل لغز قطع الذراعين، وانتهى به الأمر ممدداً على ظهره معلناً أنه مستحيل. لم تخبر أكيفا لأن، حسناً، لم يكن موجوداً. بعد لوراميندي، تركهم، ورغم أنه عاد، كان في عالمه الخاص. مثل الآن. كان ينظر من فوقها، ولم تكن بحاجة لتتبّع نظراته لتعرف إلى من كان ينظر. كان يحدق؛ فقامت ليراز بالنقر بأصابعها أمام عينيه.

"قليل من الرصانة يا أخي؟ الكيميرا سيجعلونها تدفع الثمن إذا ظنوا أن هناك شيئاً بينكما. ألم تسمع ما يطلقونه عليها؟".

"ماذا؟" بدا أكيفا متفاجئاً حقاً."لا. ماذا يطلقون عليها؟".

"عاشقة الملائكة".

رأت عينيه تتوهجان، ودورت عينيها."لا تظهر سعادتك. هذا لا يعني أنها تحبك. هذا يعني فقط أنهم لا يثقون بها". كانت توبخه وكأنها هي التي تفهم هذه الأمور—أو تهتم. ما كانت تعرفه ليراز عن المشاعر كان أكثر مما يكفي، شكراً، لكن... حسناً، لم تكن ستتحدث عن الأمر أو شيء من هذا القبيل، لكن كان هناك شيء في النصف الجيد من هذا الألم في قلبها يجعلها ترغب في أن تلتف حوله بجناحيها وتحميه من البرد.

15

رعب معتاد

لم تنم إليزا في ليلة وصولهم. شعرت بالكابوس جاثماً على كتفها، وتعرف تماماً ما سيحدث إن غلبها النوم، لكن هذا لم يكن السبب الرئيسي. لم يكن أحد لينام. العالم بأسره كان مضطرباً كمن لسعته جمرة متوهجة، وكانت شرارات الجنون تتطاير. الأخبار بعد خطاب الملاك كانت تستعرض الفوضى المرعبة: أعمال شغب وعنف طائفي، انتشار طوائف الخطف المقدس والتعميد الجماعي، نهب ومواثيق انتحار، بل وحتى—يا للمصيبة— تضحيات بالحيوانات. وطبعاً، كانت هناك أيضاً حفلات الأبوكاليبس التي استمرت طوال الليل، وشباب الثمالة في أزياء الشياطين يتبولون من فوق الأسطح، والنساء اللواتي يقدمن أنفسهن ليحملن بأطفال الملائكة.

غباء بشري معتاد.

هوس وغضب، ونداءات يائسة لسبب ما، وكانت هناك الكثير من النيران. جنون، نشوة، شَماتة، ذعر، ضجيج. المتحف الوطني للتاريخ الطبيعي كان يقع في ناشيونال مول، وعلى بُعد خطوات، كان آلاف الناس

يتدفقون نحو البيت الأبيض، ليس برسالة موحدة للرئيس، بل رغبةً في المشاركة بشيء ما في هذه الليلة التاريخية. أي شيء، لكن ماذا سيكون؟ البعض حمل الشموع، والبعض الآخر مكبرات صوت؛ وقلة ارتدت تيجاناً من الشوك وسحبت صلباناً ضخمة، بينما كانت الأسلحة تخفى في الجيوب والأحزمة.

إليزا بقيت في الداخل.

لم تذهب إلى منزلها، خشية أن يكون أحد بانتظارها هناك. ولا شك أنهم يعرفون أيضاً أين تعيش. ويعرفون مكان عملها أيضاً، لكن المتحف على الأقل محميّ بالأمن بشكل جيد.

قالت لغابرييل:"سأبقى هنا. لدي بعض العمل الذي يجب أن أنجزه". في الواقع لم تكن تكذب، فعليها استخراج الحمض النووي من عدة عينات فراشات مُعارة من متحف علم الحيوان المقارن في هارفارد. كانت الساعة تشير إلى موعد تسليم أطروحتها، لكنها لم تتوقع أن يلومها أحد على أخذ إجازة ليوم في ظل هذه الظروف.

تساءلت إن كان هناك أي شخص في العالم أنجز شيئاً اليوم—باستثناء مورغان توث بالطبع. لقد غادر إلى المختبر غاضباً بعد أن ألقى الملاك رسالته، وقضى بقية بعد الظهر هناك، وكأنه أراد أن يثبت بهدوئه كم هم البشر الآخرون على هذا الكوكب حمقى. لكنه رحل أخيراً، وأصبح المختبر لها. أغلقت الباب بالمفتاح، خلعت حذاءها، وحاولت أن تركز أفكارها.

ما معنى كل هذا؟ ما الذي يعنيه حقاً؟

ارتفع صوت طنين في قاعدة جمجمتها، أشبه بفزع مكبوت وبداية صداع. تناولت قرصين من التايلينول وجلست على الأريكة مع حاسوبها المحمول لتشاهد الخطاب مرة أخرى.

شعرت بالقشعريرة تسري في جسدها قبل حتى أن يفتح الملاك فمه

ويلقي كلماته اللزجة المشوشة. لم يكن من الممكن رؤية فمه لارتدائه تلك الخوذة الغريبة التي تغطي محور وجهه وكأنها تقسمه نصفين، مما أضفى عليه مظهراً مزعجاً—خاصة مع حقيقة أن عينيه لم تكونا دافئتين أبداً. زرقاوين بشكل صادم، لا عمق فيهما وقاسيتين.

ثم كانت هناك طريقته في الانحناء إلى الأمام قليلاً، وتحويل وزنه بين الحين والآخر وكأنه يعدل شيئاً على ظهره، رغم أنه لم يكن هناك شيء. أم هل كان هناك؟

لا شيء يمكنها رؤيته على أي حال. رفعت إليزا مستوى الصوت. كان هناك ذلك الهمس، يملأ فترات صمته، لكنها لم تستطع أن تميز سوى الصوت الغريب كصوت الورق. من أين كان يأتي؟

شاهدت الخطاب عدة مرات، تستمع إلى اللاتينية دون الرجوع إلى الترجمة، فقط تركز على الملاك محاولة أن تلتقط عناصر الغرابة التي لم تستطع تحديدها بدقة. لكنها كانت تدرك طوال الوقت أن تتجنب رسالته.

كانت CNN أول من أعاد بث الخطاب مع ترجمة نصية، وعندما قرأت إليزا الترجمة لأول مرة، تسلل البرد إلى أعماقها وبدأ يحولها إلى جليد.

... العدو الذي يتضور جوعاً ... اللحم المفترس ... الظلال ... الوحوش.

أجبرت نفسها على مشاهدة النسخة المترجمة مرة أخرى، بينما كانت أصابعها تتلمس ندبة صغيرة عند عظمة الترقوة. لم يعد لديها جهاز تنظيم ضربات القلب بعد الآن، كانوا قد أزالوه عندما كانت في السادسة عشرة- ليس لأن الرعب قد خف، بل لأن جسدها أصبح قوياً بما يكفي لتحمله. الوحوش قادمة من أجلك.

اخترقها البرد من الداخل إلى الخارج. قشعريرة الرعب. الوحوش قادمة كان رعباً معتاداً.

لأنه مجرد حلم.

16

كم تساوي تلك الوعود

"في كهوف الكيرين".

سيلتقي اليوم جيشان. جنودهما تربوا على كراهية بعضهم البعض، لم ينظر أحدهم إلى الآخر إلا بنية القتل، ولم يحاول معظمهم على الإطلاق كبح هذا الدافع. لكن لدى الكيميرا بعض الوقت للتدرب. لديهم أكيڤا وليراز للتدرب على الامتناع عن القتل، وحتى الآن، سار الأمر على ما يرام

لم يتم اختبار غير الشرعيين بعد، لكن أكيڤا كان يؤمن أن إخوته وأخواته سيڤوا بوعدهم بعدم المبادرة بالهجوم. ورغم أن كهوف الكيرين والجبل الذي يضمها كانا لا يزالان بعيدين، فقد تخيل أنه يستطيع أن يشعر بزئير مائتين وستة وتسعين فكاً وهم يكرون بكل غرائزهم، وبكل نبضة من عمرهم.

"الهدنة لا يمكن أن تكون أقوى من أضعف الأطراف على أي من الجانبين"، حذّره إليون، وكان أكيڤا يعرف أن هذا صحيح. أما بالنسبة إلى غير الشرعيين، فقد كان يؤمن بعدم ضعف الرابط بينهم. رمزهم، في الواقع، عبارة عن سلسلة، مما يدل على أن كل جندي جزء من الكل وأن قوتهم تكمن في وحدتهم. لم يكن غير الشرعيون يقدمون وعوداً باستخفاف.

وماذا عن الكيميرا؟ راقبهم أثناء الطيران، واعتبر أنه من الجيد أنهم توقفوا عن التلويح المستفز بهامساتهم التي بدؤوا بها الرحلة. لكن الثقة، لا تزال بعيدة المنال؛ كان عليه أن يكتفي بالأمل في الوقت الحالي. الأمل. ثم ابتسم من غير قصد عندما تذكر اسم كارو.

كارو، واحدة من بين الكثيرين في التشكيل، وأصغر من معظمهم، لكنها ملأت عين أكيفا. مسحة من الأزرق الفاتح، وبريق من الفضة. حتى وهي مثقلة بالغضب، كانت مرنة في الطيران كعنصر هوائي. حولها طافت تنانين وأشياء تشبه الخيول المجنحة، وناجا وداشناغ وساب، غريفون وهارتكيند، وكانت تتألق في وسطهم كجوهرة.

مثل نجمة بين راحتي الليل.

ماذا سيكون شعورها هنا؟ وآثار قبيلتها في كل مكان في الكهوف: أسلحتهم وأدواتهم، أنابيبهم وأطباقهم وأساورهم. كانت هناك أدوات موسيقية بأوتار صدئة، ومرآة لا بد أنها عندما نظرت فيها كانت ترتدي جسداً آخر. كانت في السابعة من عمرها عندما حدث ذلك. كانت كبيرة بما يكفي لتتذكر اليوم الذي فقدت فيه قبيلتها كلها على يد الملائكة—ومع ذلك أنقذت حياته في بولفينش. ومع ذلك سمحت لنفسها أن تحبه.

"نحن البداية"، سمع صوتاً داخل رأسه، وكان يبدو كترتيلة. "كنا دائماً كذلك. هذه المرة، لنجعلها أكثر من مجرد بداية".

...

رأت كارو الهلال المظلل فوق الجبل أمامها، وشعرت بألم يقبض على قلبها. الوطن. هل هو حقاً كذلك؟ لقد قالتها لزيري: "موطني". والآن تختبر هذا الإحساس، وتشعر أنه حقيقي. لم تعد هناك أي شكوك حول هذه الكلمة. من بين كل الأماكن التي عاشت فيها خلال حياتها، هنا فقط كانت تنتمي بلا شك—لا كلاجئة ولا كمغتربة، بل ابنة بالدم، جذورها عميقة في هذا الصخر، وجناحاها ملتصقين بهذه السماء.

ربما كانت قد نشأت هنا حرة. ربما لم تشهد أبداً كيف كان قفص لوراميندي العظيم يمزق الضوء كله إلى فتات، ويلقي ببخل شديد، قليل منه على الأسطح —لم تكن هناك إشراقات كاملة من الشمس أو القمر على وجهك، بل فقط ضوء خافت مع ظلال القضبان الحديدية عليه. ربما قد كانت ستعيش حياتها في هذا البهاء من ضوء الجبال.

لكن حينها، لم تكن لتتعرف على بريمستون، أو إيسا، أو ياسري، أو تويغا والداها ربما بقيا على قيد الحياة. ويعيشان هنا.

ما كان لها أن تكون بشرية أبداً، أو أن تتذوق سلام ذلك العالم الغني الباذخ، وتزدهر في فنونه وصداقاته. ستنجب أطفالها الآن —أطفالاً من قبيلة الكيرين، متوحشين في الرياح كما كانت هي يوماً. زوج من الكيرين. ولم تكن لتتعرف على أكيڤا. وفي اللحظة التي انبثق هذا الخاطر في عقلها دون استئذان، رأته. كان يطير مع ليراز، على الجناح الأيمن للتشكيل. حتى على هذه المسافة، شعرت بالصعقة عندما التقت عيناها بعينيه، وانبثقت مجموعة جديدة من الاحتمالات التي لم تتحقق في ذهنها.

ربما كانت لتقوم بهذه الرحلة منذ ثمانية عشر عاماً، بدلاً من أن تموت كم من الأمور التي يمكن الندم عليها، ولكن ما الفائدة؟ جميع الحيوات التي لم تعشها تلغي بعضها البعض. ليس لديها سوى الآن. الملابس التي ترتديها، الدم في عروقها، والوعد الذي قطعه رفاقها. لو فقط يوفون به.

مستذكّرة خبث كيتا-إري العفوي، البعيدة كل البعد عن الشعور بالثقة. لكن ليس هناك وقت للقلق.

ها قد وصلوا. وكما هو مخطط، دخل أكيڤا وليراز أولاً. كان المدخل على شكل هلال قمري، وكان ارتفاعه يعادل عدة أطوال من قامة الكيرين، لكنه لا يمكن سوى لعدد قليل من الأجساد الدخول في وقت واحد. وهناك فجوات عالية ومنخفضة مخصصة للرماة، لكنها الآن خالية. عرف عن الكيرين أنهم رماة مشهورين. أما غير الشرعيين فقد دُربوا على جميع الأسلحة، لكنهم لم

يكونوا مسلحين عادةً بالأقواس. لماذا يفعلون ذلك؟ كانوا هم الجنود الذين يُرسلون أولاً لتحطيم الفولاذ الذي على الوحوش. دع الجسد الثمين ينحني إلى الخلف ويرمي السهام.

كان ما يهم أكيفا هو الفولاذ أثناء تفقده لتجمّع الجنود، فرأى التالي: أيدي إخوته وأخواته مسترخية بشكل غريب، لأنها حُرمت من مكانها المعتاد فوق مقابض السيوف. هذا هو المكان الذي تستريح فيه يد المبارز، لكن لإظهار التزامهم، امتنع غير الشرعيين —جميعهم، وعددهم مائتان وستة وتسعون—عن ذلك، حتى لا يبدون في وضعية التهديد. بعضهم وضع إبهامه في حزامه، والبعض الآخر عقد يديه خلف ظهره أو شبك ذراعيه على صدره. كلها أوضاع غير مريحة وغير طبيعية لهم.

لقد حانت اللحظة، وكانت عظيمة. جيش من الموتى يتقدم نحوهم— مشهد يعرفونه جيداً، وقد نجوا منه في السابق فقط بالصراخ والفولاذ. الفولاذ بلا تردد. عدم سحب أسلحتهم الآن كان يبدو ضرباً من الجنون".

لكن لم يسحب أحد سيفه. شعر أكيفا بفخر شديد بهم في تلك اللحظة، فخر يجعله يشعر بالقوة، وكأنه مشحون بالطاقة، وتمنى لو أنه يستطيع أن يذهب إلى كل واحد منهم ليحتضنه. لكن لا وقت لذلك الآن.

وقف إليون أمام الباقين، فتقدم أكيفا وليراز نحوه.

ضوء الهلال، كشف -بعض الشيء- المدخل إلى كهوف الكيرين كسلسلة من الكهوف المترابطة التي تنحدر تدريجياً إلى عمق الجبل. منذ زمن بعيد، فُتحت فيها الجدران وشُكّلت لتكوين مساحات متصلة، لكنها لا تزال بكل تفاصيلها خشنة وصخرية، إضافة إلى الصواعد التي تشبه الأنياب وهي تخفي المزيد من فجوات الرماة؛ كان هذا حصناً، رغم أنه لم ينقذ الكيرين. أرضيته من صخور غير مستوية، تتجمع فيها الثلوج والأمطار المتدفقة وتتحول إلى برك صغيرة متجمدة. رغم أن السماء كانت صافية اليوم، إلا أن الجليد قد غطى الأرض، وجعل الهواء يتجمد عند خروجه مع أنفاس الجنود.

السيرافيم صامتون، مستعدون. الضجيج المتصاعد يستحث الصدى.

استدار أكيفا مع البقية وشاهدوا جيش الكيميرا وهو يدخل.

أول الواصلين كانت سنورة نحيلة ورشيقة، ترافقها اثنتان من الغريفونات. كان هبوطهم سلساً، رغم أنهم مثقلون بالمعدات. أما تين، نائبة ثياغو في هيئتها الذئبية، تمتطي ظهر إحدى الغريفونات، وانزلقت على قدميها وتقدمت بخطوات رشيقة، وعيناها الجريئتان تحدقان بالملائكة قبل أن تتخذ موقعاً مواجهاً لهم. تبعها الآخرون، وشكلوا بداية صف. جيش في مواجهة جيش. جعل هذا أكيفا متوتراً؛ لكنه لم يكن يتوقع من الكيميرا أن يديروا ظهورهم لأعدائهم.

استمر الوافدون بالظهور، وبدأ يظهر له نمط التشكيلة القتالية: الأقل رعباً أولاً، ثم الأقل غرابة، مع فسحة بين المجموعات حتى يتمكن السيرافيم من التعود تدريجياً على وجود عدوهم اللدود. مع كل هبوط لاثنين أو ثلاثة من المخلوقات، أخذت التشكيلات تكتمل. في منتصف المجموعة تقريباً، وصل البشر، ونساء المطبخ، إيسّا التي انسلت بنعومة عن ظهر داشناغها لتخفض رأسها وتنحني بنعومة تحية للملائكة. يا لجمالها، وتبدو أقرب إلى حسناء غاوية لا مقاتلة. وانتبه أكيفا إلى إليون وهو يحدق فيها.

أما بالنسبة إلى كارو، فلا يمكن لدى الملائكة أدنى فكرة عما قد يفعلونه بها—تنساب بلا أجنحة، وبلا مظهر الوحش، وشعرها الأزرق كجوهرة يتدلى خلفها. لم يكن أحد ليميز حقيقتها: كيرين عادت إلى موطنها. وقد لفت انتباه أكيفا وجهها المضطرب وعرف أنها تعيش في خضم موجة من الحنين.

راح يراقب عينيها وهي تتفحص الكهف، وتمنى لو كان بجانبها. وراح يراقبها بدل مراقبة الوضع من كلا الجانبين وقد فوت ما حصل.

سبعة وثمانون مقاتلاً ليس عدداً كبيراً، كما لاحظ إليون سابقاً، وهم أقل من هذا العدد الآن بعد أن أرسل ثياغو الكشافة، لكن سرعان ما هبط معظم الكيميرا على الأرض. كان غير الشرعيين قد سمعوا بالطبع أن هؤلاء

المتمردين من الكيميرا مختلفون عن المعتاد. عندها استهدفوا قوافل العبيد في الجنوب، سمعوا بأنهم أشباح، وأن لعنة كلمات بريمستون الأخيرة عادت لتطاردهم. لكنهم الآن يرونهم بوضوح. إن هذه الوحوش المجنحة—معظمها—كبيرة الحجم، ويتمتع أكبرهم بجسد رمادي يجعلهم يبدون كأنهم نصف حجر أو حديد.

كان هناك زوج من الناجا لا يشبهان إيسا إلا تشابهاً عابراً؛ وإذا كان إليون قد رمش بعينيه نحوهما فذلك لسبب مختلف تماماً، وأقل سروراً بكثير. وكان هناك قناطير ثيران بحوافر عريضة كالأطباق، وهارتكيند لديه قرنان ضخمان أكبر من مقتنيات غرفة جورام كلها.

خطر على بال أكيفا أن مقتنيات والده الهمجية—رؤوس الكيميرا المثبتة على الجدران—لا بد أن الحرب ابتلعتها وتلاشت مع كل شيء آخر، وكان سعيداً لذلك. بل أمل أن تكون قد تبخرت. لم يكن يفهم حتى الآن ما الذي فعله ذلك اليوم، وكان يشك أحياناً في أنه هو من قام به. مهما كان، فقد كان عملاً ملحمياً وفاشلاً—أتى متأخراً لإنقاذ هازايل، بينما سمح لجايل بالفرار. طاقة غير مركزة، عنف بلا هدف. أفكار قاتمة جداً بالنسبة إلى لحظة كهذه. هزّ أكيفا رأسه لطردها. رأى في السماء مخلوق الفيسبنغ الذي يمتطيه ثياغو، ينخفض باتجاه الهلال. سيكونون آخر الواصلين. كل الكيميرا الأخرى قد وصلت؛ والجيشان الآن يقفان في مواجهة بعضهما، متوترين ومتيقظين، وكل منهما يقبض على وعده بين أسنانه.

أو على وعده الكاذب.

أدرك أكيفا أنه لطالما توقع هذا النجاح، فعدم مفاجأته به يدل على ذلك. شعر بالسرور—أو شيء أقوى من السرور. والتأثر، وامتنان في صميمه يمتد إلى روحه.

لقد صمدت الهدنة.

ومن يعلم إلى متى.

17

الأمل ويقين الاحتضار

من وسط حشد الكيميرا، وقفت كارو، وقد كان من الصعب عليها رؤية
الكَهف بسبب العدد الكبير من الجنود الذين أحاطوا بها، لكنها استطاعت
رؤية أكيفا وليراز بوضوح، واقفين بعيداً عن البقية مع أحد إخوتهما.

ها نحن هنا، كانت كارو تفكر. ليس بالوطن؛ بل بشيء آخر. نعم، هذا
كان الوطن، والذكريات الحية، ولكن ذلك قد مضى. هذا... الآن، هو عتبة
المستقبل. كان الذئب لا يزال في الهواء؛ كانت تشعر باقترابه من خلفها،
لكنها بقيت تراقب أكيفا. لقد فعل هذا، وشعرت بالعجب يتصاعد داخلها،
مثل رفرفة الفراشات أو الطائر الطنان أو... مثل صيادي العواصف. يا للروعة
هل يمكن أن يحدث فعلاً؟ إنه يحدث. عندما تهامسا هي وأكيفا حول
هذا الحلم لبعضهما البعض، تساءلا عما إذا كان بإمكان أي من أهلهما
ورفاقهما أن ينضم إليهما. ليس الجميع ولكن البعض. وها هم الآن في هذا
الكهف... وهنا كانت بدايات أولئك البعض.

كانت عينا كارو على الملائكة—وعلى أكيفا— عندئذ... شهدت اللحظة
الحرجة التي انهار فيها كل شيء.

تراجع أكيفا. بلا سبب ظاهر، ارتد وكأنه تلقى ضربة. كذلك ليراز والأخ الذي بجانبها، وعلى الرغم من أن كارو لم تكن تنظر مباشرة إلى الحشد الكبير من غير الشرعيين، إلا أنها رأت موجة الحركة تجتاحهم أيضاً. ماتت الفرحة داخلها. وعرفت أن هذا التحالف محكوم عليه بالفشل منذ أن حلم بريمستون بتلك العلامات. الهامسات.

من؟ اللعنة، من؟

لم يكن يهم إذا كان أحد الكيميرا أو كلهم. أحدهم ضغط على الزناد فعلاً. في لمحة من الثانية، تغير كل شيء. هكذا، تحررت شحنة التوتر في الكهف— وانفجرت الأعصاب والصدور—ثم التخلي الذي قاد إلى هذا الجنون الذي نزل عليهم والعودة إلى الطريقة التي تعاملوا بها دائماً.

ستُسفك الدماء. صرخت كارو مذعورة. لا. لا! وفي حركة لولبية مخترقة الهواء، حلقت فوق رؤوس الجيش، وراحت تبحث لتعرف: من فعل ذلك؟ من بدأ هذا؟ لم يكن أحد يقف ويعترف بيدين مرفوعتين. كيتا-إري؟ الساب بدت متنبهة، متوترة، قبضتاها مشدودتان؛ إذا كانت هي من فعلت هذا، فقد فعلته كجبانة شريرة، أطلقت شرارة معركة ستقتل الكثيرين.

زوزانا وميك!

توقف قلب كارو لبرهة... عليها إخراج صديقيها. ألقت نظرة خاطفة إلى الخلف، مع انحناءة الاستعداد للهجوم، وظهور الأنياب، تلك اللحظات البدائية التي يستسلم فيها الجنود لغرائزهم.

ورأت ثياغو، في الهواء.. "يوثم"، ذلك المخلوق برأسه الذي يزين عنقه الطويل، ويتفرع عنه جمال من بين جناحيه. وبطرف عينها لمحت خطأ في الهواء. بعد ثانية، أدركت مصدر الصوت الذي سبق ذلك... حيث اخترق سهم عنق "يوثم".

منذ أول مس جنون لذلك السحر، ترددت كلمة واحدة في ذهن أكيفا:"لا، لا، لا، لا، لا!".

ثم جاء السهم—صرخت الفيسبينغ. كان صراخها كصهيل خيل تحتضر،
فملأ الصوت الكهف واخترقهم جميعاً، انهار ذلك المخلوق في الهواء،
وتجمعت حشود الكيميرا بينما كان يهوي بشدة ليسقط على الصخور. كان
الاصطدام عنيفاً. عيناه الوحشيتان زائغتان، العنق ملتو، السهم محطم،
الجسد متوهج من شدة الدوران، لتلقي بفارسها بعيداً قبل أن تبحر أخيراً
في سكون مروع. وهكذا قُذف الذئب الأبيض حيث يقف غير الشرعيين، على
الأرض الملساء الجليدية، بينما ارتفع خلفه صياح جيشه.

رأى أكيفا كل ذلك من خلال حجاب من الرعب. هل خططت الكيميرا
لهذه الخيانة؟ كان متأكداً من أن الهامسا جاءت أولاً.

ولكن السهم. من أين جاء؟ من فوق. التقطت عين أكيفا حركات خفية
بين الهابطين، ورافق رعبه غضب على إخوته وأخواته. الفخر الشديد الذي شعر
به تجاههم اختفى. كل تلك الأيدي التي كانت تتجنب مقبض السيوف—بدا
وكأنه عرض فارغ بينما يختبئ الرماة في الأعلى بأوتار أقواسهم المشدودة.
ولم تكن الأيدي لتنتظر طويلاً.

الذئب الأبيض راكع. ابتسامات مشؤومة تكشف عن أنيابه. وفي وسط
تشكيل السيراف، امتدت يد. وتحركت البقية تباعاً. صار الأمر أشبه برقص
منظم. في لحظة تحولت اليد الواحدة إلى ثلاث، إلى عشر، إلى خمسين،
وكانت ردّة فعل أكيفا بطيئة ويائسة. رفع يديه الفارغتين في استغاثة، سمع
ليراز تصرخ بصوت مبحوح:"لا!".

لم تكن هناك سوى تلك اللحظة. لحظة. أيدٍ على مقابض السيوف. في
لحظة واحدة يتغير مجرى الأمور، ولا يمكن السيطرة على مسارها بعد ذلك.
بمجرد أن تُستل تلك السيوف من أغمادها، وبمجرد أن تتحرر عضلات
الوحوش المشدودة، سيكون هذا اليوم أحمر كدماء الكيرين الأخير، وسيملأ
الكهف مرة أخرى بالحزن على الجميع.

برق أزرق. عينا أكيفا التقتا بعيني كارو، وكانت نظراتها لا تحتمل.

ذلك الأمل، ويقين الاحتضار.

وللمرة الثالثة في حياته، شعر أكيفا في صميمه بكتلة من الغضب واليقين—مجرد لحظة، ثم ينقلب العالم. وكأن طبقة كتيمة انزاحت، فانكشف كل شيء أمامه: ثابت، مصقول، لامع وساكن. كان هذا هو السيريثار، أكيفا على أهبة الاستعداد لتلك اللحظة.

هل أخبر إخوته وأخواته أن الحاضر هو اللحظة الوحيدة التي تفصل بين الماضي والمستقبل؟ في هذه الحالة من الهدوء والصفاء البلوري—حيث كل هذا العنف قد تحول ببطء إلى حلم—لم يكن هناك انفصال. كان الحاضر والمستقبل شيئاً واحداً. كل نية لكل جندي رسمت أمامه بنور، ورأى أكيفا كل شيء قبل أن يحدث. في تلك الخطوط من الضوء، كانت السيوف مسلولة.

أيدٍ مقطوعة، متجمعة في أكوام، الهامسات وجثث القتلى المختلطة، أيدي السيراف والكيميرا، متناثرة.

كما تنبأ به الضوء، البداية ميتة، تماماً مثلما سبقها، وحلت بداية جديد مكانها: سيعود جايل إلى الوطن ولن يجد قوة متمردة ليحاربها—لا كيميرا ولا غير شرعيين ليواجهوه، بل فقط دماؤهم وقد تحولت إلى جليد أحمر على أرضية هذا الكهف، لأنهم لطفاء بما يكفي ليقتلوا بعضهم البعض من أجله. الطريق سيكون مفتوحاً، وستعاني الأرض. رأى أكيفا كل هذا، العار الكبير الذي سيهز العالم ويتردد صداه، ورأى... الميل نحو الفوضى... في الثواني القادمة، كيف ستسحب كارو سيوفها الهلالية.

ستُقتل اليوم، وربما تُقتل. إذا سُمح للموقف بأن ينقلب. ولا يجب السماح بذلك.

في أسترا، انطلقت من ذهن أكيفا موجة من الغضب والإحباط والحزن العميق، إلى درجة أنها فجرت برج الفتح العظيم، رمز إمبراطورية السيرافيم. لم يستوعب ما كان ذلك، أو كيف قام بفعله.

18

شمعة أطفأتها صرخة

كل هؤلاء السيرافيم، كانت أيديهم على مقابض السيوف، والكيميرا في اللحظة المشحونة قبل الانقضاض. كان ثياغو راكعاً في الميدان بين الجيشين—سيكون أول من يموت. امتدت يدا كارو نحو سيوفها، وفي داخلها لا يزال هناك صدى الصرخة المدوية:"لا!" لو كان هناك وقت للتفكير في تلك اللحظة—تلك اللحظة التي كانت مليئة بالنوايا كما لم تكن أي لحظة من قبل، مليئة بوعد الدم—لما صدقت أن أي قوة يمكن أن توقفها. كان أملها قد مات مع الردة الأولى للملائكة. مات أملها. فكرت. لم تكن لتصدق أن هناك قاعاً من اليأس أعمق من هذا. لكن الأوان قد فات. ضربة مفاجئة ومدمرة. سحبتها إلى الأسفل.

اليقين بالنهاية. رؤية شفرات الملائكة على وشك الانسلال والبتر، وسماع زمجرة الكيميرا وهي تستعد لتمزيق المستقبل بأسنانها، كما لو أن كل ذرة من الفكر أو الشعور التي كانت موجودة أو ستوجد يوماً قد شحقت واستُبدلت بهذه... بهذه... بهذه البقعة المريرة من العبثية. نهاية يائسة، صرخت، ولأجل ماذا؟

كان اليأس شاملاً، كاملاً كحالة من المس، لكنه عابر. ذهب، واختفى، بعد أن ترك كارو مدمرة، محطمة، تشعر وكأنها كانت... شعلة شمعة أُطفأتها صرخة. وفي أعقاب هذا الهول، ربما لم تكن أكثر من لولب من الدخان ترك ليطوف ويتلاشى في نهاية كل شيء—في زوال العالم نفسه.

نهاية يائسة، ولأجل ماذا؟ نهاية يائسة. نهاية يائسة.

وتوقفت يداها عن إكمال ما بدأته. لم تسحب سيوفها. لم تستطع. بقيت في غمدها على وركيها وكأنها مغمدة في أنفاسها، متفاجئة بشعورها—أن هناك حياة ما زالت بداخلها، وهواء لتتنفسه. لحظة واحدة.

نفس آخر، وثانية أخرى.

كانت في الجو، ثم تركت نفسها تهبط بوضعية قرفصاء مسترخية لتحط على ركبتيها، وعقلها لا يزال صدى لـ"لا!" بينما بدأت تدرك أن من حولها... لا شيء كان يحدث. لا شيء كان يحدث. الأعصاب المتوترة للوحوش ارتخت.

الأيدي السوداء بأعداد القتلى كانت مجمدة على مقابض السيوف؛ شفرات السيراف كانت تلمع في الضوء، كثير منها نصف مسلولة. الجيوش المتعطشة للدماء توقفت ببساطة...

كيف؟

بدا أن اللحظة طويلة جداً. كارو، المثقلة بصميم يأسها، لم تكن تدرك ما الذي يحدث. لقد شعرت أن اللحظة كانت تميل وتدفعهم نحو الكارثة.

كيف توقفوا جميعاً بهذه البساطة؟ هل أساءت قراءة الكارثة؟ هل كان كل شيء مجرد تظاهر من كلا الجانبين، مجرد استعراض بالسيوف؟ هل يمكن أن يكون الأمر بهذه البساطة؟ لا. لا، كان يفوتها شيء ما. كان من حولها صمت مشوش، ووميض بطيء، وأنفاس مجهدة خشنة كأنفاسها. حاولت أن تتخلص من الضبابية.

ثم رأت، في حرم الميدان بين الجيوش المتقابلة، الذئب الأبيض ينهض على قدميه. كل العيون ثبتت عليه، وعيناها أيضاً، وسرعان ما بدأ الضباب بالتلاشي.

هل من الممكن... هل كل هذا من فعلِه؟

نهضت. كان من الصعب أن تتحرك. ربما ذهب يأسها، لكنه ترك ثقله على كاهلها، كثيفاً وكئيباً.

رأت أن ركبتي الذئب تنزفان من أثر هبوطه؛ كان يوئم ميتاً، في بركة دمه. كان ثياغو قد نهض في الوقت الذي كان الدم قد أحاط به، وتجمع الدم الآن حول قدمي الذئب وهو يلطخ فراءه الأبيض وينتشر باتجاه الصف الأول من الملائكة. كان يوئم كبيراً، وكان الدم كثيراً، وكان الذئب يبدو في صورة درامية وهو واقف فيه، وكله أبيض اللون باستثناء دمه الذي كان يتدفق من ركبتيه وجبينه وكفيه.

أطبق كفيه المغطاتين بالدماء بإحكام. بدا وكأنه في حالة صلاة، لكن من الواضح ما يعنيه ذلك. بدلاً من الهجوم، وضم يديه اللتين تحملان الهامسا إلى بعضهما. تمالك نفسه. جندي ميت على الأرض، ولا انتقام من الذئب الأبيض الصنديد؟ كانت إشارة قوية، لكن كارو لم تفهمها بعد. كيف أوقف ثلاثمائة من غير الشرعيين قبل أن يستلوا سيوفهم؟

تحدث ثياغو:"أتعهد ورماد لوراميندي أنني ومن معي جئنا إليكم من أجل التحالف، وليس من أجل الدم. وتلك البداية سيئة، لم تكن جزءاً من الخطة. سأكتشف مَن مِن بيننا رفع يده مخالفاً لأمري الصريح. ذلك الجندي، مهما يكن، قد خالف كلمتي". قال هذا بغصة في حلقه، وبحدة مصحوبة بالاشمئزاز، وذلك وتّر كارو من الخوف.

استدار ثياغو، ومرّر نظره على جنوده، محدقاً بعينين ضيقتين."ذلك الجندي"، قال وهو ينظر إلى قلب جيشه،"خاطر بحياة هذه المجموعة بأكملها اليوم، وسيُعاقب".

كان الوعد صريحاً؛ والجميع فهموا ما يعنيه بذلك. كانت نظرته حادة وثاقبة، وتوقف عدة مرات عند بعض الجنود، الذين ذابوا تحت وقع نظراته ثم عاد ليخاطب غير الشرعيين:"هناك سبب للمخاطرة بحياتنا، لكننا لن نسببه لبعضنا البعض. بداية سيئة وتبقى بداية". وبإصرار بحث عن أكيفا بعد ذلك؛ شعرت به كارو ينتظر أن يتدخل الملاك ويساعده في جمع شتات هذه الهدنة. انتظرت هي أيضاً، واثقة من أن أكيفا سيقول شيئاً لإصلاح هذا الموقف—لكن الصمت امتد وجعل اللحظة قصيرة ومتوترة.

هنالك خطأ ما. حتى ليراز كانت تنظر إلى أكيفا بترقب. شعرت كارو بقلق يطعنها. وحين ظهر، بدا غير مستقر، أو مريض، كتفاه العريضان منحنيان تحت وطأة شيء ما.

ما خطبه؟ لقد رأته يبدو هكذا من قبل؛ وقد كانت هي السبب، لكن الآن، هل يمكن أن تأثير الهامسا هو السبب؟ ولماذا تؤثر عليه أكثر من البقية؟

بجهد واضح، قال أخيراً:"نعم. بداية"، لكن رافق صوته خواء بالمقارنة مع نبرة الذئب الرنانة وكلماته القوية، وتابع قائلاً:"بداية سيئة جداً. آسف على فقداننا، و... أندم بشدة على التسبب فيها. آمل أن نستطيع إصلاح هذا".

"ذلك ممكن وسيتحقق"، رد الذئب."كارو؟ لو سمحتِ".

هذا استدعاء. شعرت كارو وكأن الأضواء مسلطة عليها؛ سرى الخوف في عروقها بطريقة نابضة، لكنها جمعت إرادتها وتحركت. تحول كل التركيز نحوها بينما كانت تشق طريقها عبر الحشد، مباشرة إلى جانب يوثم.

توقفت وسط دمائه. بإيماءة من ثياغو، جثت على ركبتيها، وأزاحت عدتها من على ظهرها وأنزلتها، تأرجحت إحدى المباخر المعلقة على سلسالها. قام مفتاح بجانب السلسلة بتفعيل قفل عجلة يشبه آلية عجلة الاحتكاك في مسدس عتيق؛ أشعلت حجرة البخور في الزنبرك مع صوت يشبه فرقعة الأصابع المعدنية. وبعد لحظة، انبعثت منها رائحة كبريتية.

شعرت كارو باستجابة روح يوثم. كانت كسماء رمادية وإشارات من نار، وتحطم الأمواج. أومضت بالظهور ثم تلاشت روحه وهي تنسل إلى المبخرة. الآن أصبحت في أمان. نصف دورة لقفلها، ونقرة لإطفاء فتيلها، ثم استقامت من ركوعها، حريصة على أن تبقي الهامسا بعيدة عن إطلاق أي سحر تجاه الملائكة.

كانت كل العيون عليها. نظرت إلى ثياغو. لم يتحدثا، لكنه شعر بأنه التصرف الصحيح. قالت:"لم أقم قط بإعادة إحياء سيراف، لكن طالما أننا نقاتل في نفس الجانب، فسأفعل. إذا أردتم ذلك، مع أنه قد لا ترغبون. فكروا في الأمر؛ القرار لكم. هذا عرضي، ووعدي. وهناك شيء آخر". التقت عيناها بعيني الملائكة المصطفين أمامها مباشرة."ربما لا أبدو كذلك"، قالت،"لكنني كيرين، وهذا هو بيتي. لذا من فضلكم، افسحوا الطريق ودعونا ندخل".

ففعلوا، من دون اندفاع، ثم تفرقوا، مفسحين الطريق لها. نظرت إلى الخلف، فوجدت إيسّا بين الحشد. زوزانا وميك بعيون مفتوحة. أما حضور أكيفا كان كالشعلة في المحيط، يناديها، لكنها لم تنظر إليه. تقدمت خطوة إلى الأمام. لحق بها ثياغو. تبعهم الحشد، وسمح لهم غير الشرعيين بالمرور. ومع الدم على أحذيتهم، قادت كارو وثياغو جيشهم إلى الداخل.

تمتمت ليراز:"كيف فعل ذلك؟".

أيقظ السؤال أكيفا أخيراً من سباته بعد السيريثار.

"من الذي فعل ماذا؟"

"الذئب". بدت مذهولة."كنت متأكدة من أننا انتهينا. شعرت بذلك. ثم...". هزت رأسها وكأنها كانت تحاول تصفية ذهنها."كيف أوقف ذلك؟".

حدق فيها أكيفا. هل اعتقدت أن ثياغو هو من أوقفه؟

ضحك بشدة. ماذا يمكنه أن يفعل غير ذلك؟ كان يعلم أن نبضة خرجت منه—ليست متفجرة هذه المرة—ومهما كانت تحمل معها، فقد

شعر بالتحكم بنوايا الجنود جميعهم. هو من فعلها. هو من أوقف هذه المذبحة من الحدوث، و... لم يكن لأحد أي فكرة، لا حتى ليراز، وبالتأكيد ليس كارو.

بينما كان يتعافى من رد فعل سحره، كان بالكاد قادراً على ربط جملتين معاً، نهض الذئب واستغل اللحظة ونجح في كسب الإعجاب حتى من ليراز؟ إذاً، ما الذي يجب أن تشعر به كارو تجاهه؟ شاهدها أكيفا وهي تختفي في الممر على رأس جيشها، الذئب الأبيض بجانبها—كانا يشكلان ثنائياً لافتاً—وكل ما كان يمكنه فعله هو الضحك. ضحك وكأن زجاجاً يطحن في صدره.

ممتاز، فكر. يا لها من صفعة مثالية من... ماذا؟ القدر، نجوم الآلهة؟ الصدفة؟

سألته ليراز:"ماذا؟ لماذا تضحك؟".

"لأن الحياة حقيرة"، وهذا كل ما استطاع أكيفا قوله.

"حسناً إذاً"، ردت أخته ببرود."أعتقد أننا نستحق ذلك".

19

الصيد

في جميع أرجاء إريتز، اندفعت موجة من السحر. لم تكن ريح تنبئ بها هذه المرة، ولا صوت ولا حركة، لذلك كل من شعر به—وقد شعر به الجميع—اعتقد أنه شعور شخصي ما. كانت موجة من المشاعر الخام القوية إلى درجة أنها في لحظة، اجتاحت كل المشاعر الأخرى وحلت محلها، مع مرورها السريع اجتاحت كل كائن يؤمن—ويشعر—باليقين المطلق للنهاية.

كان مرورها سريعاً وقاتماً؛ من خلال انطلاقة عبر الأرض والسماء والبحر، ولم يكن أي كائن محصناً منها، ولا أي حاجز مادي أو معدني قادر على صدها. أسرع بكثير من أجنحة قد تطير بها، اجتاحت أسترا، عاصمة إمبراطورية السيرافيم، وبسرعة مماثلة اختفت. وفي أعقاب صمتها، لم يخطر لأي مواطن بأن يربط بينها وبين تحطم برج الفتح العظيم.

ولكن عند أطلال البرج، داخل الهيكل المعدني الضخم والدمار الذي تبقى منه، وقف خمسة ملائكة من السيرافيم، لكن ليسوا من مواطني

الإمبراطورية. لقد أتوا من بعيد، في رحلة صيد—صيد وصيد —والآن، في انسجام تام، مثل إبر البوصلة التي يديرها نفس المغناطيس، استداروا جنوباً وشرقاً.

هذا الشعور الطاغي كان بمثابة انتهاك صارخ؛ يعلمون أنه ليس من صنعهم، وتوقف كل منهم لفترة قصيرة لاختبار أقصى حدود قوته المروعة قبل أن يندفعوا بعيداً. كان لهذا طعم آخر من ساحر مجهول راح يعزف على أوتار العالم.

"قاتل الوحوش"، كما سمعوا أنه يُدعى في جلسات الشائعات في هذه المدينة الجبانة بأن هذا قاتل وخائن، قاتل الكيميرا، ابن سفاح وقاتل أبيه. هو من فعل هذا.

والآن، بأعين تستشيط غضباً، ثبت الخمسة من الستيليين أنظارهم على جبال أديلفاس البعيدة.

ملكتهم سكاراب، أفردت جناحيها وقالت بغضب شديد نفثته من بين أسنانها الحادة:"تابعوا الصيد".

20

تشوّه

في الجزر البعيدة، كان الليل قد حل، والكدمة السماوية الجديدة التي ازدهرت لن تكون مرئية حتى ساعة الفجر. لم تكن كغيرها. في الواقع، سرعان ما ابتلعت الأخريات—جميع الكدمات ذبن في امتدادها المظلم. انتشرت من الأفق إلى الأفق، بلون نيلي قاتم، تقارب السواد مثل سماء الليل. ولكن هذه الكدمة أكثر من مجرد لون. كانت طاغية، مبتلعة. كانت انكساراً وتشوهاً. قالت أيدولون ذات العينين المتراقصتين إن السماء متعبة، وتتألم. وكأنها تقلل من شأن الأمر.

السماء كانت تهوي. صيادو العواصف لا يحتاجون إلى رؤيتها تسودّ؛ يكفي أنهم شعروا بها. وبدأوا بالصراخ.

21

يدا نيتيد

لم تكن كهوف الكيرين قرية داخل جبل، بقدر ما كانت سلسلة من القرى المتصلة بشبكة من الممرات التي تنبثق من مساحة مشتركة ضخمة. المكان عبارة عن مزيج من فعل الطبيعة والزمن والأيدي، وكان الفضاء طبيعياً ومتدفقاً وغير مخطط له وغير محتمل. كان أعجوبة. وعموماً، كان الانطباع العام هو أنه حدث جيولوجي عجيب، لكنه في الحقيقة كان قد تشكل على مدى مئات السنين على يد أجيال من الكيرين المتمسكين بجمالية بسيطة:"أيدي نيتيد". لقد كانت هذه الأيدي أدوات الآلهة، ولم يكن من واجبهم، كما رأوا ذلك، أن يبرزوا أو يعظموا أنفسهم، بل أن يقلدوا – بطريقة أو بأخرى - أسلوبها.

نادراً ما كانت هناك أي تفاصيل تشير إلى أن شيئاً ما"صنع" بأيدي البشر. لم تكن هناك زوايا، حتى الدرجات بدت وكأنها تكونت طبيعياً، غير متماثلة وغير دقيقة.

كان المكان مظلماً، لكنه لم يكن غارقاً في الظلام التام. هناك فتحات ضوء تسمح بدخول أشعة الشمس وضوء القمر، معززة بمرايا مخفية من الهيماتيت والعدسات الكريستالية. ولم يكن المكان صامتاً قط. فقد كانت هناك قنوات دقيقة تمرر الرياح في أنحاء الكهوف، حاملةً الهواء النقي ومحدثةً صوتاً رخيما غريباً، خليطاً من ليلة عاصفة وصفير الحيتان.

أثناء سيرها داخل الكهوف، شعرت كارو بكل شيء يتدفق في داخلها من تجارب قديمة وجديدة، وكأن نهرين سريعين التقيا: ذكرى مادريغال ودهشة كارو، ممزوجتين في كل خطوة. عندما دخلت الكهف المركزي الكبير، تذكّرته على الفور، لكن المنظر خطف أنفاسها، فتسمرت في مكانها، رافعة رأسها وهي تنظر بانبهار.

تذكرت كارو خفقات أجنحة الكيرين فوق رأسها، أصوات النداء والضحك والموسيقى، ضجيج المهرجانات وأيضاً بساطة الحياة اليومية. هنا تعلمت الطيران في هذا الكهف.

كان الكهف شاهقاً، يصل ارتفاعه إلى عدة مئات من الأقدام، واسعاً إلى درجة أن الأصداء تضيع فيه ولا تعود. ارتفعت الصواعد المنبثقة من الأرضية، مكونة جداراناً متموجة بارتفاع عشرات الأقدام، وقد تشكلت على مدى مئات الآلاف من السنين، لكن سيحتاج الأمر إلى ملايين أخرى من السنين حتى تتصل مع نظيراتها النوازل من السقف العالي.

كانت الجدران مليئة بعروق من المعادن الثمينة اللامعة،، وفي أماكن أخرى هناك مصطبة بشكل تجاويف ذكرتها بخلية النحل، أو بشرفات دار الأوبرا. المكان حيث عسكر جنود السيرافيم، يطلون من فوق على الساحة المركزية، حيث أظهرت حلقات النار المنتظمة علامات على الاستخدام الحديث.

"واو"، سمعت زوزانا تهمس خلفها، وعندما استدارت باتجاهها، لترى وجه الذئب وهو يبتلع ريقه بصعوبة، يكافح مشاعر قوية اجتاحته. لم يكن

هناك أحد ليشهد تلك اللحظة؛ كل رفاقها كانوا في الخلف، لذلك لم يروا لمحة الحنين والفقدان التي اجتاحت ملامحه لبرهة.

"هيا"، قالت وهي تعبر الكهف.

كان عدد الكيميرا وغير الشرعيين مجتمعين يقارب الأربعمئة، وربما كان هذا العدد أكثر من عدد الكيرين الذين عاشوا في هذا الجبل في ذروة عصر قبيلتهم، لكن المكان يتسع للجميع، ولو كانوا متفرقين. يمكن للسيرافيم أن يحتلوا الكهف الكبير؛ كان بارداً هنا، حيث خرجت أنفاسها على هيئة سحب صغيرة. أما في الأسفل، فإن القرى أكثر دفئاً بسبب حرارة الأرض الجوفية. اتجهت نحو ممر يؤدي إلى واحدة من تلك القرى. أرادت أن تزورها لكن لوحدها، وفي وقت لاحق.

"من هنا".

22

جنون الهاوية

"كعكة شوكولا كاملة، حمام دافئ، وسرير، بهذا الترتيب". زوزانا عدّت ثلاث من أمنياتها على أصابعها.

ميك قال مع بعض التقدير:"هذا ليس سيئاً". ثم أضاف،"لكن لا كعكة. سأختار غولاش من بويزون كيتشن، مع فطيرة تفاح وشاي. ثم: حمام وسرير".

"لا، لا، هذه خمس أمنيات. أنت أهدرت كل أمنياتك على الطعام".

"وجبة كاملة هي أمنيتي الأولى: غولاش، فطيرة، وشاي".

"لا تغش. لقد فشلت أمنيتك. أنا الفائزة. وأنت وبطنك الممتلئ ستضطران لمشاهدتي وأنا آخذ حمامي الرائع الساخن وأستلقي في سريري الناعم الدافئ".

فكرة الحمام الساخن والسرير الناعم بدت وكأنها حلم بعيد. جسم زوزانا المتعب يتوسل الرحمة، لكنها كانت تعلم أن الأمر مجرد لعبة، ولا سبيل لتحقيق هذه الأمنيات.

رفع ميك حاجبيه وقال:"أوه، يجب أن أشاهدك تستحمين، أليس كذلك؟ يا لحظي العاثر".

"نعم، يا لحظكَ العاثر. ألا تودّ أن تستحم معي؟".

"بالتأكيد". كان جاداً."بالتأكيد أودّ ذلك. وسيكون من الصعب على شرطة الأمنيات أن تمنعني".

"شرطة الأمنيات!" ضحكت زوزانا ساخرة.

"شرطة الأمنيات؟" قالت كارو عند دخولها.

كانوا في سلسلة من الكهوف الصغيرة التي علمت زوزانا أنها كانت تشكل منزلاً لعائلة من الكيرين في الأيام الماضية. تحتوي على أربع غرف، تشكلت بانسيابية مع تضاريس الصخور، وكأنها شقة داخل الجبل. المكان يحتوي على بعض وسائل الراحة—نوع من الحرارة الطبيعية، وحتى خزانة حجرية فيها فتحة مائلة تشبه المرحاض (على زوزانا أن تتأكد من ذلك قبل الاستخدام)—لكن لم يكن هناك حمام ظاهر أو أسِرّة. فقط هناك بعض الفراء المتراكم في الزاوية، لكنه متسخ وقديم، وزوزانا شبه متأكدة من أن قبائلَ من القمل والعثّ الغريب يعيش فيها وينسج قصصاً عبر أجيال كثيرة.

هناك أيضاً مجمع كامل من المساكن المشابهة، مرتبة حول ما يشبه"ساحة" قرية صغيرة—نسخة مصغرة من الكهف الهائل الذي مروا به في طريقهم إلى هنا. لم يتطلب الكثير حتى استقر الجنود في مواقعهم.

حسناً، كان لدى الحداد أيجير عمل لينجزه، أما ثياغو فقد ذهب مع ضباطه للقيام بالأعمال التدريبية الاعتيادية تحضيراً للمعركة الملحمية. زوزانا لم تستطع ولم ترغب حتى باستيعاب شيء حول المعركة، ولا حقيقة ثياغو، ولا تلك المعركة الملحمية. كلما حاولت التفكير في الأمر، تبدأ بالارتجاف، ويتغير عقلها وكأنه يبحث عن برامج الأطفال أو—قناة الطبخ.

بالحديث عن الطعام، بينما كان ميك يستكشف أفضل موقع لمقر"إعادة

الإحياء"، استغلت زوزانا بضع دقائق لمساعدة نساء الكيميرا الصغيرات المضحكات، قوفي وأوار، في إعداد مطبخ مؤقت وتنظيم الإمدادات التي جلبوها من المغرب. لم يكن هناك ضرر في أن تكون لطيفة مع من يقدمون الطعام، وربما حصلت على بعض المشمش المجفف الإضافي.

قبل بضعة أشهر، لو أخبرها أحد أنها ستفرح يوماً بالحصول على بعض المشمش المجفف، لكانت رفعت حاجبها باستهزاء. أما الآن، فهي تعتقد أنها قد تستخدمه كعملة، مثل السجائر في السجن.

"نحن نلعب لعبة ثلاث أمنيات" قالت زوزانا لكارو. "كعكة، حمام ساخن، سرير ناعم. ماذا عنك؟".

قالت كارو: "السلام العالمي".

قلبت زوزانا عينيها. "نعم، أيتها القديسة كارو".

"علاج للسرطان" تابعت كارو. "ووحيد القرن لكل واحد منكم".

"عجباً. لا شيء يفسد لعبة ثلاث أمنيات مثل إيثار كارو. يجب أن تكون أمنيات لنفسك، وإذا لم تتضمن طعاماً، فلا معنى لها".

"لقد تضمنت طعاماً. قلت وحيد القرن، أليس كذلك؟".

"ممم. إذاً أنت تشتهين لحم وحيد القرن؟" تجعد جبين زوزانا. "انتظري. هل لديهم وحيد القرن هنا؟".

"للأسف، لا".

"كان لديهم" قال ميك. "لكن كارو أكلتهم جميعاً".

"أنا صيادة وحيد القرن".

قالت زوزانا: "سنضيف ذلك إلى إعلانك الشخصي".

ارتفع حاجبا كارو. "إعلاني الشخصي؟".

"ربما نكون قد كتبنا إعلانات شخصية في طريقنا إلى هنا" اعترفت زوزانا. "لتضييع الوقت".

"بالطبع فعلتم. إذاً، ماذا كان إعلاني؟".

. "حسناً، لم نستطع كتابته بالطبع، لكنني أعتقد أنه كان شيئاً مثل: محاربة مذهلة بين الأنواع تبحث عن،

اممم... عدو غير مميت لعلاقة غير معقدة، ومشي طويل على الشاطئ، ونهاية سعيدة؟".

لم ترد كارو مباشرة، ولاحظت زوزانا أن ميك كان ينظر إليها نظرة غير راضية. ماذا؟ ردت عليه بحركة حاجبها المعهودة. لقد تركت الجزء المتعلق بـ"الملائكة المبيدين غير مرحب بهم" خارج الموضوع، أليس كذلك؟ ولكن بعد ذلك، أسندت كارو وجهها بين يديها. بدأت كتفاها تهتزان، ولم تستطع زوزانا أن تميز إن كان ذلك بسبب الضحك أو البكاء. لا بد أنه ضحك، أليس كذلك؟"كارو؟" سألتها بقلق.

رفعت كارو وجهها، ولم تكن هناك دموع، لكن لم يكن هناك الكثير من الفرح أيضاً. قالت بهدوء:"غير معقد. كيف يكون ذلك؟".

نظرت زوزانا إلى ميك. هذا هو ما يعنيه أن يكون الأمر غير معقد. وكان الأمر رائعاً. لاحظت كارو تلك النظرة وابتسمت لهما، ابتسامة تحمل شيئاً من الحنين."فقط اعلموا كم أنتم محظوظون".

"أعلم"، قال ميك.

"بالتأكيد أعلم"، وافقت زوزانا بسرعة، وبحماس أكبر مما هو معتاد منها. كانت لا تزال تشعر بشيء غير مريح. آه، نعم، كانت جائعة، متسخة، ومتعبة، بلا شك—ولهذا السبب كانت أمنياتها الثلاث—لكن هذا الشعور تجاوز كل ذلك بكثير. للحظة هناك، في الكهف عند المدخل، شعرت وكأنها كانت تنظر إلى نهاية العالم.

ما هذا، بحق الجحيم.

عندما كانت طفلة، كانت لديها دمية مفضلة—كانت بطة في الواقع—ويبدو أنها قد جعلتها مقرفة بفعل عاداتها الطفولية، كما كان شقيقها توماس يحب تذكيرها بعاداتها في مص عيني الدمية. وقد وجدت

في ذلك نوعاً من الراحة، الشعور الصلب الأملس للعينين وهي تضغط عليهما بأسنانها الصغيرة.

وما كان يزعجها هو محاولات والديها في إقناعها بأن هذا قد يتسبب بقتلها."يمكن أن تختنقي، يا حبيبتي".

لكن ماذا تعني فكرة الموت لطفلة صغيرة؟ توماس هو الذي أفهمها بشكل مباشر. عن طريق... تجربة خنقها. الإخوة الكبار دائماً ما يكونون"مفيدين" في توضيح الأمور المزعجة. قال لها بمرح، بينما كانت يداه تحيطان بعنقها:"يمكنك أن تموتي، هكذا".

وقد نجح الأمر. لقد فهمت. الأشياء التي بإمكانها القتل. الكثير من الأشياء، مثل الألعاب... أو الأشقاء الأكبر سناً. ومع مرور السنوات، راحت تلك القائمة تطول وتطول.

لكنها لم تشعر بحجم الخوف هكذا من قبل. ماذا كان ذلك الاقتباس الذي يحب الشعراء القوطيون استخدامه؟"عندما تنظر إلى الهاوية، تنظر الهاوية إليك أيضاً؟" حسناً، لقد نظرت الهاوية إليها. لا، بل حدقت فيها، بقوة، وكأنها كانت تنظر مباشرة إلى أعماقها. والآن فإن زوزانا متأكدة من أن الهاوية قد تركت ندوباً في روحها، ومن الصعب تخيل أنها ستشعر بشكل طبيعي مرة أخرى.

لكنها لم تريد أن تشتكي لكارو من كل خوف أو هلع يراودها. لقد أرادت المجيء إلى هنا. كارو حذرتها أن الأمر سيكون خطيراً—وطبعاً، كان التحذير يشبه قليلاً تحذير تلك الطفلة من خطر الاختناق،... لكنها هنا الآن، ولا تريد أن تكون الطفلة المدللة بين أفراد هذه المجموعة.

وماذا بخصوص موضوع الحظ؟ قالت زوزانا بنبرة مسرحية:"أنا محظوظة لأنني ما زلت على قيد الحياة. عندما كنت صغيرة، كنت ألعق عيني البطة".

وجه كل من ميك وكارو نظراتهما نحوها، وبدت زوزانا سعيدة لأنها رأت حينها تلاشي الأسى من وجه كارو، ليحل محله قلق مشوب بالدهشة.

قالت كارو بحذر:"هذا... مثير للاهتمام يا زوز".

"أعلم. ولا أحاول حتى أن أكون مثيرة للاهتمام. بعض الأشخاص هكذا بالفطرة. أما أنت، بحياتك المملة العادية... يجب أن تخرجي أكثر وتجربي أشياء جديدة".

"أوه نعم،" قالت كارو، وضحكت."أنتِ على حق. كم هي حياتي مملة. سأبدأ بجمع الطوابع. هذا مثير، أليس كذلك؟".

"لا. إلا إذا كنتِ ستلصقينها على جسدك".

"يبدو وكأنه مشروع فني".

"بالتأكيد!" وافقتها زوزانا بحماس."هيلين بالتأكيد ستفعلها. وستحولها إلى عرض أدائي. تبدأ عارية مع وعاء كبير من الطوابع حتى يتمكن الناس من لعقها ولصقها عليها".

ضحكت كارو أخيراً بصوت عالٍ، وشعرت زوزانا بفخر كبير. لقد حققت الهدف: الضحك. ربما لا تستطيع أن تجعل حياة كارو—أو حبها—أقل تعقيداً، وربما ليس لديها أي نصائح مفيدة فيما يتعلق بغزو الملائكة أو خدعتهم الحربية أو الجيوش التي تبدو وكأنها على وشك أن تبدأ بقتل بعضها البعض، لكنها تستطيع فعل شيء واحد على الأقل. يمكنها أن تجعل صديقتها تضحك.

سألت زوزانا:"إذاً، ما الذي سيحدث الآن؟ هل سيقيم الملائكة مأدبة فاخرة على شرفنا؟".

ضحكت كارو مجدداً، لكنها كانت ضحكة قاتمة."ليس تماماً. التالي هو مجلس الحرب".

"مجلس الحرب"، كرر ميك، وقد بدا مذهولاً، مثل زوزانا أيضاً. مذهولة وغير مدركة لعمق الأمر. شعرت وكأن كل شعرة في جسد كارو ما زالت منتصبة من الرعب الغريب والمشحون بالتوتر منذ الساعة الماضية. رؤية يوثم وهو يموت؟ تلك كانت أول مرة لها. ومرورها فوق دمه، رغم أن ذلك

لم يعنِ للجنود كثيراً (وكأنهم يسيرون فوق الدم كل صباح في طريقهم إلى الإفطار)، إلا أن الأمر أزعجها، على الرغم من أنها بالكاد وجدت الوقت لاستيعابه. لقد تشوشت تماماً بسبب رعبها الرابض فوق صدرها، وماذا تطلق عليه الآن"حماقة النظر إلى الهاوية".

تنهدت كارو بقوة."لهذا نحن هنا". ثم نظرت بسرعة حولها في الغرفة وأضافت:"يبدو هذا غريباً".

شعرت زوزانا بأن العالم يفلت منها أكثر، وهي تحاول أن تتخيل ما يعنيه هذا المكان لصديقتها، أن تكون عائدة إلى هنا. لكنها لم تستطع بالطبع. هذا المكان كان يوماً موقعاً لمجزرة. ربما كان صدى الهاوية هو ما جعلها تتخيل، لكنها فكرت كيف سيكون الشعور لو عادت إلى بيت عائلتها ووجدته مهجوراً، الأسرّة متعفنة، ولا أحد هناك ليستقبلها—أبداً—فأخذت نفساً صغيراً.

سألتها كارو:"هل أنت بخير؟".

"أنا بخير. والأهم، هل أنتِ بخير؟".

أومأت كارو وابتسمت قليلاً."نعم، في الواقع أنا بخير". رفعت مشعلها ونظرت حولها."إنه شعور غريب. عندما كنت أعيش هنا، كان هذا المكان هو العالم بأسره. لم أكن أعلم أن هناك من يعيش خارج الجبال".

قالت زوزانا:"إنه مذهل حقاً".

"هو كذلك. ولم تري الجزء الأفضل بعد". نظرت كارو بمكر.

"أوه، ما هو؟ أرجوكِ قولي لي إن الحلوى تنمو هنا مثل الفطر".

وسجلت زوزانا ضحكة أخرى في رصيدها.

"لا"، قالت كارو."وليس لدي حلوى أيضاً، وأخشى أن مشكلة السرير أيضاً لا يمكن حلها، لكن..." توقفت لحظة، منتظرة أن تفهم زوزانا قصدها. هل يمكن أن يكون؟"بلا مزاح".

ارتسمت ابتسامة صافية على وجه كارو؛ كانت سعيدة لأنها تعرف كيف تسعد الآخرين."هيا. أعتقد أن لدينا بضع دقائق أخرى".

23

الغاية الكبرى

كانت حمامات السباحة الحرارية كما تتذكرها كارو، ولكن أيضاً لم تكن كما تتذكرها على الإطلاق، لأنه في ذكرياتها، كان هناك كيرين هنا. عائلات بأكملها تستحم معاً. نساء مسنات يثرثرن. وأطفال يتراشقون بالماء. كانت تشعر بيدي والدتها وهي تفرك رأسها بجذور السيلين لتشكل رغوة، حتى إنها تذكرت رائحتها العشبية التي تمتزج برائحة الينابيع الكبريتية.

"هذا جميل"، قال ميك، وكان كذلك بالفعل: الماء أخضر باهت حواري، والصخور تشبه رسومات الباستيل، مزيج من الوردي وزبد البحر.

المكان حميمياً لكنه ليس صغيراً، ولم تكن بركة واحدة بل مجموعة من الأحواض المتصلة، تتغذى من شلال رقراق، وبدا السقف وكأنه يتموج، متلألئاً بناميات من الكريستال وستائر من الطحالب الوردية الشاحبة، التي سميت "طحالب الظلام" لأنها تنمو في الظلام، وليس بسبب لونها.

"انظري هنا"، قالت كارو وهي ترفع المشعل، وتقودهما في الطريق إلى المكان الذي كانت فيه جدران الكهف مصقولة بالهيماتيت النقي. كالمرآة.

"واو"، تنهدت زوزانا، ونظر ثلاثتهم إلى انعكاساتهم جنباً إلى جنب. بدو مرهقين ووقورين. السطح المنحني للمرآة شوّه أشكالهم، واضطرت كارو إلى التحرك قليلاً لتتأكد ما إذا كان التشوه في وجهها ناتجاً عن تأثير مرآة بيت المرح، أم بسبب الضرب الذي تعرضت له.

بدا وكأن الهجوم قد حدث منذ زمن طويل، لكن جسدها وحده من يعرف الحقيقة. مر يومان، ولم يتعافَ وجهها بعد. وكذلك حالتها النفسية. في الواقع، كان التشوه في المرآة مناسباً لحالتها؛ كأنه انعكاس خارجي للتشوه الداخلي الذي كانت تحاول إخفاءه.

خلعوا ملابسهم وانزلقوا في الماء الحار اللطيف إلى درجة أنه في غضون ثوانٍ شعروا بأطرافهم وكأنها مصنوعة من خزف الدمى، وشعرهم كزغب البجع. أما شعر كارو وزوزانا فقد انساب مثل خصلات حوريات البحر على سطح الماء المتموج.

أغمضت كارو عينيها وغاصت بجسدها تحت الماء، وتركت الماء الجاري يسحب توترها بعيداً. ولو طلب منها لعب ثلاث أمنيات بصدق، ربما ستتمنى أن تنجرف بعيداً وكأن هذا هو نهر ليثي، نهر النسيان، وتأخذ استراحة طويلة من الجيوش والهلاك. لكنها بدلاً من ذلك، اغتسلت وخرجت من الماء. غض ميك نظره بأدب بينما ارتدت كارو ملابس نظيفة. "نظيفة" بمعنى أنها غُسلت في نهر مغربي وجُففت على سطح مغبر، إن كان هذا يُعتبر نظيفاً.

"لديكم على الأرجح ساعة من ضوء المشعل قبل أن ينطفئ"، قالت لصديقيها، وتركت لهما واحداً وأخذت الآخر. "هل تستطيعان العودة؟". أجاباها بأنهما يستطيعان، لذا تركتهما كارو ليستمتعا بلحظتهم المثالية وغير المعقدة معاً، وحاولت ألا تشعر بالكثير من الغيرة بينما كانت قدماها تقودانها عائدة نحو الصراع الصامت في صدرها بين الجيوش.

"ها أنتِ هنا".

استدارت حول منعطف نحو مركز القرية الذي يشبه خلية النحل، ووجدت ثياغو، أو بالأحرى زيري. عندما رأى كل منهما الآخر، ارتسمت مشاعر عابرة على وجهه، أخفاها بسرعة، لكنها لمحتها. مشاعر حب مختلط بالحزن، مما جعل قلبها يؤلم من أجله."أنا معك"، كانت قد قالت له في القصر، حتى لا يشعر بالوحدة في جسده المسروق. لكنه كان وحيداً. لم تكن معه حقاً، حتى عندما وقفت إلى جانبه. وكان هو يعرف ذلك.

أجبرت نفسها على الابتسام."كنت قادمة لأبحث عنك" كانت تعني ذلك على الأقل."هل اتُّخذ أي قرار؟".

تنهد وهز رأسه. كأنه مهمل، وهو ما لم يكن عليه الذئب أبداً، إلا ربما بعد المعارك مباشرة. بشعره الأشعث، وجبينه المغطى بدماء جافة جراء هبوطه العنيف، وركبتاه ويداه المليئتان بالجروح تبدوان وكأنهما قطع من اللحم المتضرر. ألقى نظرة حوله وأشار إلى كارو كي تتبعه عبر بوابة.

تصلبت لثانية واحدة فقط ورغبت في التراجع. هو ليس الذئب، ذكّرت نفسها، وهي تسبقه إلى الغرفة الصغيرة. كانت مظلمة، ذات رائحة عتيقة. أغلقت كارو الباب وأحدثت قوساً بمشعلها المتقطع لتتأكد من أنهما كانا وحدهما.

وحدهما.

هل كان هذا ما تمناه زيري في تلك الليلة؟ مجرد هذه اللحظة الصغيرة والحزينة ليدع شخصية الذئب تتلاشى؟ انهار متكئاً على الحائط بسبب الإرهاق. قال:"اقترحت ليسيث أن نختار كبش فداء لتنفيذ المذبحة".

"ماذا؟" صرخت كارو."هذا مروع!".

"لهذا السبب قلت لها لا، إلا إذا كانت ترغب في أن تقدم نفسها كمتطوعة".

"أتمنى ذلك".

"لقد رفضتْ". ابتسم زيري بابتسامة مريرة ومنهكة، ثم خفض صوته.

"لا يزالون ينتظرون لتحقيق ذلك. أن أكشف عن الخطة الحقيقية، التي يجب بالطبع أن تشمل المذبحة".

"هل تعتقد أنهم يشكون في شيء؟" سألت كارو بقلق، صوتها أصبح همساً سرياً كما كان صوته. كانت تتمنى لو تستطيع التحدث معه بالتشيكية، كما كانت تفعل مع زوزانا وميك، دون أن يسمعها أحد.

"نعم، هناك شيء ما. لكنني لا أعتقد أنهم قريبون من الحقيقة".

"لا يجب أن يقتربوا منها".

"أتصرف وكأن لدي خطة نهائية لأشاركها معهم، لكنني لا أعرف إلى متى يمكن أن أصمد. لم أكن يوماً جزءاً من تلك الدائرة. ماذا لو كان قد أخبرهم بخططه، وهذا التكتم يبدو خاطئاً بالنسبة إليهم؟ يا لهذه المشكلة..." رفع يديه إلى رأسه، وتأوه عندما لمس جرحه. "ماذا كان سيفعل الذئب؟ لن يفعل شيئاً. لن يعطي السيرافيم أي شيء، وسينظر إليهم بازدراء لأنهم تجرأوا على السؤال".

"أنت على حق". تخيلت كارو بسهولة تلك النظرة المليئة بالاحتقار التي كان الذئب يحملها في عينيه، وهو يواجه أعداءه. "بالطبع، هو كان سيخطط بالفعل لمذبحة".

"نعم. لكن هذه هي استراتيجيتنا في كل هذا: أن نبدأ بما يبدو معقولاً، حيث كان هو سيبدأ، ولكن لا نتبع ما كان سيفعله. لن أعطي الملائكة أحداً، ولن أقدم اعتذاراً. هذه مسألة تخص الكيميرا. إنه كلام نهائي".

سألت كارو: "وماذا إذا حدث ذلك مرة أخرى؟".

"سأضمن ألا يحدث". كانت كلماته بسيطة، ثقيلة، مليئة بالتهديد والأسف. لكن كارو تعرف في قرارة نفسها أن زيري لم يكن يريد هذه المسؤولية، لكنها تذكرت كلماته عندما كان محلقاً في الهواء—"سنقاتل من أجل عالمنا حتى آخر صدى لأرواحنا"—والطريقة التي وقف بها بين جيشين مضرجين بالدماء وفصل بينهما.

لم يكن لديها شك في أنه يستطيع أن يواجه أي تحدٍ."حسناً"، قالت، وكانت نهاية الأمر.

ساد الصمت بينهما، واستقرت النفوس، تغيرت طبيعة"الوحدة" التي شعرا بها حيث طغى التعب عليهما في الظلام المتذبذب الممزوج بمشاعر من الحب والثقة والتردد والحزن.

"علينا أن نعود"، قالت كارو، رغم أنها كانت تتمنى لو تستطيع منح زيري مزيداً من السلام."الملائكة ينتظرون".

وافق زيري وتبعها إلى الباب. ثم قال لها"شعرك مبلل".

"كنا في الحمام"، أخبرته وهي تفتح الباب، متذكرة أنه لم يكن يعلم ذلك.

"أستطيع القول إن هذا يبدو مغرياً". وأشار زيري إلى الفراء المتصلب بالدم على قدميه، وإلى يديه اللتين بدتا كقطع من اللحم النيئ. بالإضافة إلى الجرح في رأسه، حيث اصطدم بالأرضية الصخرية للكهف.

تقدمت كارو نحوه، ورفعت يدها لتلمسه؛ فانتفض، بسبب التورم الكبير تحت الدم المتخثر.

"أوه، هل تشعر بأي دوار؟".

"لا. مجرد ألم بسيط. أنا بخير". وبنفس الوقت كان يتملى وجهها." تبدين الآن أفضل بكثير".

لمست خدها، وأدركت أن الألم قد اختفى. كذلك التورم. وضعت يدها على شحمة أذنها الممزقة، ووجدت أن الجلد قد التحم. ماذا؟ شهقت قائلة."إنه الماء!". وقد تذكرت ذلك وكأنه جزء من حلم."لأن لديه بعض الخصائص العلاجية".

"حقاً؟" نظر زيري إلى يديه المتهالكتين مرة أخرى."هل تستطيعين إرشادي إلى هناك؟".

"أمم..." توقفت كارو بحرج."بالتأكيد، لكن زوزانا وميك هناك".

احمرّ وجهها. ربما كانت زوزانا وميك متعبين بما يكفي ليقضيا بعض الوقت في المياه المنعشة. كان من المحتمل جداً أن يستغل أصدقاؤها ساعتهما من العزلة بطريقة... مممم... على نمط زوزانا وميك.

فهم زيري ما عنته. احمرّ وجهه هو الآخر، وغمرت الحرارة ملامحه الباردة المثالية. زيري تقمص هذا الجسد بطريقة أكثر جمالاً مما فعل ثياغو.

قال بخجل وضحكة مكتومة، محاولاً تجنب عينيها:"سأنتظر"، وضحكت كارو معه.

وهكذا، كانا هناك، عند مدخل الغرفة، يتورد وجهيهما، ويضحكان بخجل، ويقفا قريبين جداً من بعضهما البعض—ومع أنها أبعدت يدها عن جبهته، إلا أن جسدها ما زال ينجذب نحوه—عندها مرّ شخص قريباً منهما وتوقف فجأة.

يا للآلهة ونجوم السماء، أرادت كارو أن تصرخ."هل تمزحون معي؟". بالطبع، بالطبع، إنه أكيڤا. موسيقى الرياح غطت على صوت خطواته. لم يكن يبعد سوى عشرة أقدام، وبالرغم من مهارته في إخفاء مشاعر المفاجأة، إلا أنه لم يستطع هذه المرة.

تجمد في مكانه مذهولاً، وارتسم الذهول على وجنتيه. أدركت كارو من أنه حتى زفيره اللاإرادي قد وشى بمشاعره. بالنسبة إلى أكيڤا الصبور الصلب، اعتبر هذه الإشارات الصغيرة كتلقّي صفعة مدوّية.

تراجعت كاروو خطوة مبتعدة عن الذئب الأبيض، لكنها لم تستطع محو الصورة التي شكّلاها في تلك اللحظة. شعرت بوميض مشاعرها عند رؤية أكيڤا، لكنها شكّت في قدرته على ملاحظتها في خضم ضحكتها ووجهها المحمّر، والآن، ما زاد الأمر سوءاً، كان إحساسها بالذنب، وكأنها كُشفت في موقف شائن. تضحك وتحمرّ مع الذئب الأبيض؟ بالنسبة إليه، كان هذا خيانة بكل تأكيد.

الجاذبية التي تدفعها للطيران نحو أكيفا هي نوع خاص من الجاذبية، ولكن قلبها وحده هو الذي رفرف. إلا أن قدماها بقيتا ثابتتين، متسمرتين ومثقَلتين بالذنب.

صوته جاء بارداً وسريعاً:"لقد اخترنا مجلس النوّاب. ربما عليكم أن تفعلوا ذلك أيضاً". توقف قليلاً، وبدت ملامحه وكأنها تسير في الاتجاه المعاكس بسبب ملامح وجه الذئب. بينما كان واقفاً ينظر إليهما، تلاشت إنسانيته تدريجياً، وعاد إلى ما كانت عليه هيئته حين رأته كارو أول مرة في مراكش: ميت الروح."نحن جاهزون عندما تكونون أنتم كذلك". ثم أردف بصوت داخلي ساخر:"عندما تنتهين من التورد والمرح مع الذئب الأبيض". ثم استدار وغادر قبل أن يتمكنا من الرد.

"انتظر"، نادت كارو، لكن صوتها خرج مخنوقاً، وحتى إن سمعها وسط همسات الرياح، لم يستدر."كان بإمكاننا إخباره"، فكرت."أن نخبره الحقيقة"، لكن الفرصة ضاعت، وكأنه أخذ الهواء معه. لوهلة طويلة، انقطعت أنفاسها، وحين التقطتها، حاولت جاهدة أن تبدو طبيعية.

قال زيري:"أنا آسف".

"على ماذا؟" أجابت محاوِلة أن تتحدث بنبرة خفيفة زائفة، وكأنه لم يرَ كل شيء ولم يفهم. ولكن بالطبع، لقد فهم.

"أنا آسف لأن الأمور لا يمكن أن تكون مختلفة معك".

كارو فهمت ما يقصده. يقصدها هي وأكيفا، المسكين زيري، مع أنه كان صادقاً ومتعاطفاً تماماً."يمكن أن تكون مختلفة"، قالت، متفاجئة من نفسها، وفي مكان الشعور بالذنب والعذاب الذي كان يتآكلها، وجدت نفسها تشعر بالعزم. بريمستون آمن بذلك، وكذلك أكيفا، و... أسعد لحظات حياتها، عندما كانت هي نفسها تؤمن بذلك."الأمور يمكن أن تكون مختلفة"، قالت لزيري. وليس بالنسبة إليها هي وأكيفا فقط."بالنسبة إلى الجميع"، أضافت، محاولة استدعاء ابتسامة."هذه هي الغاية الكبرى".

24

استعدوا لنهاية العالم

بعد عدة ساعات، كانت كارو قد نسيت تماماً الشعور الذي خلفته تلك الابتسامة.

نعم، الأمور قد تكون مختلفة. لكن أولاً، عليك قتل الكثير من الملائكة وربما تدمير الحضارة الإنسانية إلى الأبد. وأوه، من المحتمل أيضاً أن تخسر في النهاية. قد نموت جميعاً. لكن لا بأس، هذا غير مهم.

لم يكن الأمر مفاجئاً للجميع. ولم يتأمل أحد أن يكون هذا الاجتماع هو"مجلس للسلام".

كان اجتماعاً سيُكتب عنه في كتب التاريخ بلا شك. على قمم جبال أديلفاس، التي لطالما كانت الحصن الرئيسي بين الإمبراطورية ومناطق المشاع، اجتمع ممثلو جيشين ثائرين وجهاً لوجه."السيرافيم والكيميرا"،"غير الشرعيين والمتقمصون"، قاتل الوحوش والذئب الأبيض، ليسوا أعداء اليوم، بل حلفاء.

وكانت الأمور تسير كما هو متوقع.

"أنا أؤيد المسار الواضح". قال إليون، الأخ الذي أخذ مكان هازايل بجانب أكيفا. كان هو واثنان آخران—برياثوس وأوريت—يمثلون غير الشرعيين بجانب أكيفا وليراز. بينما كان مع ثياغو وكارو كل من تين وليسيث.

"وما هو المسار الواضح؟" سأل الذئب.

أجاب إليون، وكأن الأمر بديهي،"نغلق البوابات. ندع البشر يتعاملون مع جايل".

ماذا؟

لم يكن هذا ما توقعته كارو."لا"، قالت فجأة، رغم أن الرد لم يكن من حقها.

اعترضت ليراز في اللحظة ذاتها، واصطدمت كلماتهما في الهواء. لا. كانتا تجلسان قبالة بعضهما تماماً عبر الطاولة، وتلاقت أعينهما، عينا ليراز الضيقتان، وعينا كارو الحذرتان.

لا، لن يغلقوا البوابات بين العوالم، ويحاصروا جايل وجنوده الألف من الدومينيون في الجانب الآخر ليتولى البشر"التعامل" معهم. قد يتفقان على هذا، لكن لأسباب مختلفة.

قالت ليراز بصوت هادئ وخالٍ من النبرة:"سأتولى أمر جايل بنفسي". بدت نبرتها حاسمة، وأعطت شعوراً وكأنه حقيقة مبرمة منذ زمن، وغير قابلة للنقاش."بغض النظر عمّا سيجري، هذا أمر محسوم".

دافِع ليراز كان الانتقام، ولم تلُمها كارو على ذلك. لقد رأت جسد هازايل، كما رأت ليراز محطمة بالحزن، وأكيفا إلى جانبها يعاني من الألم ذاته. حتى من داخل بئر أحزان كارو العميق تلك الليلة، كان المشهد قد مزّق قلبها. أرادت موت جايل هي الأخرى، لكن هذا لم يكن هاجسها الوحيد.

قالت كارو بحزم:"لا يمكننا تحميل هذا للبشر. جايل هو مشكلتنا نحن".

كان إليون مستعداً للرد."إذا كان ما تخبرينا به عن البشر وأسلحتهم صحيحاً، فيجب أن يكون القضاء عليهم أمراً سهلاً بالنسبة إليهم".

ردت كارو:"سيكون الأمر كذلك إذا رأوهم كأعداء". كان استعراض جايل بمثابة ضربة بارعة من المكر."سيعبدوننا كآلهة"، هذا ما قاله جايل لأكيفا، ولم تكن كارو تشك في صحة كلامه. قالت لإليون:"تخيّل لو أن نجومك المقدسة انفصلت عن السماء ونزلت لتقف أمامك، حية تتنفس. كيف بالضبط ستتعامل معها؟".

أجاب إليون بلا تردد، وبمنطق لا تشوبه شائبة:"أتخيّل أنني سأمنحهم كل ما يطلبونه". ثم أضاف:"ولهذا السبب يجب أن نغلق البوابات. أولويتنا يجب أن تكون مملكتنا. لدينا ما يكفي للتعامل معه هنا ولسنا مضطرين أن نخوض معركة في عالم ليس عالمنا".

هزت كارو رأسها، لكن كلماته أزعجت أفكارها، وللحظة لم تجد أي رد. كان محقاً. من الضروري أن يفشل جايل في جلب أسلحة البشر إلى المملكة، والطريقة الأسهل لوقفه هي إغلاق البوابات.

ولكن هذا كان غير مقبول.

لم تستطع كارو ببساطة أن تزيح البشرية من طريقها وتدير ظهرها لعالم بأكمله، خاصةً وأن عرض جايل كان يعنيها مباشرة. لقد جلبت المخلوق المشوه رازغوت إلى المملكة وأطلقت سراحه حاملاً المعرفة الخطيرة التي يمتلكها—عن فنون الحرب، الدين، الجغرافيا—وقد قدّمها إلى جايل على طبق من ذهب.

لقد جلبت هذا الدمار إلى العالم البشري كما لو أنها هي التي جمعت بين هذين الملاكَين الشريرين بنفسها.

وفي اللحظة التي كانت تبحث فيها عن الكلمات، التفتت تبحث عمن يدعمها حول الطاولة الحجرية، والتقت عيناها بعيني أكيفا. أحست تلك النظرة كصفعة على قلبها، شعاع محترق. وجهه خالٍ من التعابير؛ أياً كان ما يشعر به نحوها—فهو يشبه الاشمئزاز. الخيبة؟ ألم عميق محير؟— كان مخفياً في مكان عميق.

"إغلاق الباب هو طريقة الوحيدة لحل المشكلة"، قال أكيثا، بينما كانت عيناه موجهتين مباشرة نحو ثياغو. "لكنها ليست طريقة جيدة جداً. أعداؤنا لا يبقون دائماً حيث نضعهم، وغالباً ما يعودون إلينا في لحظات غير متوقعة، وأكثر فتكاً".

لم يكن هناك شك في أن أكيثا كان يشير إلى هروبه السابق وعواقبه. الذئب الأبيض لم يفوّت مغزى الكلام. "بالفعل"، قال. "دع الماضي يكون معلمنا. القتل هو الحل النهائي الوحيد". ثم ألقى نظرة نحو كارو وأضاف بابتسامة صغيرة: "وأحياناً، حتى القتل لا يكون نهائياً".

احتاج الباقون لحظة لاستيعاب أن قاتل الوحوش والذئب الأبيض قد توصلا إلى اتفاق، رغم برودة ذلك الاتفاق.

"الأمر سيكون محفوفاً بالغموض"، قالت ليراز مخاطبة إليون. "وغير مُرضٍ أيضاً." بدت كلماتها بسيطة، لكنها باردة كالثلج. فلديها من تنوي قتله والاستمتاع بذلك.

سأل إليون: "إذاً، ما الذي تقترحونه؟".

قالت ليراز: "نفعل ما تعودنا أن نفعله. نقاتل. أكيثا سيدمر بوابة جايل كي لا يتمكن من استدعاء تعزيزات. نأخذ الألف الموجودين هناك، ثم نعود عبر البوابة الأخرى، نغلقها خلفنا، ومن ثم نتعامل مع البقية هنا في المملكة".

فكر إليون في الأمر. "مع تجاهل الاقتراحات للحظة والاحتمالات المستحيلة هناك، الألف في العالم البشري يشكلون نسبة ثلاثة إلى واحد، وهذا لصالحهم".

ابتسمت ليراز بخبث: "سآخذ هذه النسبة بكل سرور. ولا تنسَ، لدينا شيء هم لا يملكونه".

سأل إليون: "وما هو؟".

نظرت ليراز أولاً إلى أكيثا، ثم التفتت لتحدق بالكيميرا.

لم تتكلم؛ لكن نظرتها كانت ممتلئة بالاستياء والتردد، ولكن كان معناها واضحاً:"لدينا الوحوش". ربما أرادت قولها مع حركة ساخرة من شفتيها.

"لا"، قال إليون على الفور. نظر إلى بريائوس وأوريت بحثاً عن الدعم."لقد اتفقنا على عدم قتلهم، هذا كل ما في الأمر، رغم أننا كنا في كامل حقنا لفعل ذلك بعد أن خرقوا الهدنة——" قاطعت تِين الحديث، أو بالأحرى"هاكسايا"، التي بدت وكأنها تستمتع بالالتفاف، بالطريقة التي تتقنها مذ أن عرفت كارو حقيقتها الثعلبية عندما كانتا صديقتين منذ زمن بعيد، وهي الآن ليست أكثر اختلافاً وإنما أكثر حدة ووحشية. كانت هاكسايا قد ادعت ذات مرة أنها مجرد"مجموعة من الأنياب يحملها جسد"، والطريقة التي كانت تبتسم بها باستخدام فكَّي تِين الذئبيين بدت وكأنها نوع من التحدي."قد آكلكم يوماً"، بدا أنها فكرت بذلك سابقاً، وربما الآن الآن.

"إذاً نحن الذين خرقنا الهدنة؟" تساءلت بسخرية، قبل أن تكمل:"إذا كان الأمر كذلك، فلماذا إذاً دماؤنا هي التي تلطخ أرضية الكهف؟".

"لأننا أسرع منكم، وكأنك بحاجة إلى مزيد من الإثبات"، قالت أوريت بازدراء.

مع هذه الكلمات، كادت تِين أن تقفز فوق الطاولة وتقضمها بأسنانها المكشرة، غير مبالية بالهدنة."رماتكم هم من يجب أن يثبتوا كلامك".

"كان ذلك دفاعاً. منذ أن أطلقتم الهامسا، كنا أحراراً من وعودنا".

حقاً؟ كارو أرادت أن تصرخ. كأنهم لم يتعلموا شيئاً؟ كانوا كالأطفال. لكن أطفال من القتلة.

"كفى". مزقت زمجرة ثياغو الباردة والحادة كأمر عسكري، التوتر بين الجنود، مما جعل كلا الجانبين يتراجعان قليلاً. أخفضت تِين رأسها احتراماً لقائدها.

أما أوريت، فقد حدّقت بعينين مملوءتين بالغضب. لم تكن جميلة مثل ليراز، مثل الكثير من الملائكة. ملامح وجهها كانت غير محددة،

ووجهها ممتلئ، وأنفها قد تعرض للكسر منذ وقت طويل، مضغوطاً بشكل مسطح عند وسطه بسبب ضربة قوية."أنت من يقرر متى يكفي؟" سألت ثياغو بتحدٍ."لا أعتقد ذلك". ثم التفتت إلى زملائها وقالت:"كنت أظن أننا متفقون على أننا لن نمضي قدماً إلا إذا أثبتوا حسن نيتهم. لا أرى حسن نية. أرى وحوشاً تضحك في وجوهنا".

"لا"، قال ثياغو بهدوء."أنت لا ترين ذلك".

وأضافت ليسيث بنبرة ساخرة:"صلّي ألا تري ذلك أبداً".

تابع ثياغو حديثه وكأن ليسيث لم تتحدث:"قلت إنني سأعاقب أي جندي أو جنود يخالفون أوامري، وسأفعل. ليس لإرضائكم، لأنكم لن تكونوا شهوداً على ذلك".

سألت أوريت بتحدٍ:"وكيف سنعرف؟".

أجاب الذئب:"ستعرفون"، وكان صوته مليئاً بالتهديد، كما كانت كلماته لكارو سابقاً، لكن بدون نبرة الندم التي رافقتها في تلك المرة.

إليون لم يكن مقتنعاً. توجه إلى الباقين وقال:"لا يمكننا الوثوق بهم بجانبنا في المعركة. يمكننا قتال جايل دون أن نخلط الكتائب. هم يتبعون قائدهم، ونحن نتبع قائدنا. نبقى منفصلين".

لكن ليراز كانت تمعن النظر في الكيميرا، وقالت:"حتى وجود زوج واحد من الهامسا في كتيبة يمكن أن يضعف الدومينيون ويمنحنا التفوق".

"أو تُضعفنا"، جادلت أوريت."وتفقدنا تفوقنا".

ألقت كارو نظرة سريعة على أكيفا، فرأت شرارة تضيء عينيه—لمعة مفاجئة لفكرة ما—وعندما تكلم، قطع الحديث فجأة، توقعت منه أن يعبّر عن تلك الفكرة، مهما كانت. لكنه قال ببساطة:"ليراز على حق، وكذلك أوريت. ربما من المبكر الحديث عن خلط الكتائب. دعونا نترك هذا الموضوع الآن". ومع انتقال الحديث إلى خطة الهجوم بشكل أعمق، بقيت كارو تتساءل: ما تلك الشرارة؟ ما تلك الفكرة التي لم يتحدث عنها؟

استمرت كارو في التحديق فيه، متسائلة، وكان عليها أن تعترف أنها كانت تأمل أن تكون تلك الفكرة طريقاً للخروج من كل هذا، لأنه كان يتضح لها مع كل لحظة تمر أن السيرافيم والكيميرا متحدون في شيء واحد على الأقل. وهو عدم اكتراثهم المتبادل، وسط خططهم، بالتأثير الذي سيتركه هذا الهجوم على البشر.

حاولت كارو أن تعبر عن مخاوفها مع استمرار مجلس الحرب، لكنها لم تستطع أن تُسمع صوتها. بدا لها أن ليراز كانت تتعمد الصياح في كل مرة تحاول فيها الكلام، وإذا كانت مصالحهما قد التقت سابقاً في تلك الـ"لا" المشتركة، فقد تباعدت الآن بشكل جذري. ليراز أرادت دم جايل. لم يهمها أي يد ستتلطخ به.

قالت كارو ملحة، عندما شعرت أن التوافق بينهم بدأ يتحقق وكأنه أمر واقع:"اسمعوني". وكان من العجيب أن هذا المجلس استطاع الوصول إلى توافق، لكن يبدو أنه معجزة سيئة."في اللحظة التي نبدأ فيها الهجوم، نصبح جزءاً من مخطط جايل. ملائكة بيض تهاجمهم ملائكة سود؟ دعكم مما سيفكر فيه البشر عن الكيميرا. لديهم روايتهم الخاصة، فبالنسبة إليهم، الشيطان هو ملاك——".

"لا يهمنا ما سيعتقده البشر عنا"، قالت ليراز."هذا ليس حفلاً. إنه كمين. ندخل ونخرج بسرعة. إذا حاولوا مساعدته، يصبحون أعداءنا أيضاً". ووضعت يديها على الطاولة الحجرية وكأنها جاهزة للانقضاض في أي لحظة. واه، إنها مستعدة لحمام دم.

"هذا العدو المحتمل الذي تستخفين به"، قالت كارو،"يملك..." أرادت أن تقول إنهم يمتلكون بنادق هجومية وقاذفات صواريخ وطائرات عسكرية. تفاصيل كثيرة لا يمكن للغاتهم التعبير عنها بشكل كافٍ. فقالت بدلاً من ذلك:"أسلحة دمار شامل".

"وكذلك نحن"، ردت ليراز ببرود."لدينا النار".

كانت نبرتها باردة إلى حد جعل كارو تتوقف فجأة.

"ماذا تعنين بذلك؟" سألت كارو بصوت مرتفع ملؤه الغضب. كانت تعرف تماماً ما تقصده ليراز، وهذا أذهلها. حين وقفت فوق رماد لوراميندي، عرفت ما يمكن أن تفعله نار السيرافيم. ولم تكن تصدق أن هذه هي نفس ليراز التي استخدمت حرارتها لتدفئة زوزانا وميك أثناء نومهما، وهي الآن تهدد بحرق عالم كامل؟

تدخل أكيفا قائلاً:"لن يصل الأمر إلى ذلك. البشر ليسوا أعداءنا. يجب أن يكون هدفنا التسبب بأقل قدر ممكن من الأضرار الجانبية. إذا أصبح البشر دمى لجايل، فذلك بسبب جهلهم".

كانت هذه المواساة باردة."أقل قدر ممكن من الأضرار الجانبية". كافحت كارو لتبقي وجهها خالياً من التعابير بينما كان عقلها يتمرد. سواء كان ذلك مجازياً أو حرفياً، فإن العالم البشري يصبح كالحطب الجاف أمام لهب مثل هذا."نهاية العالم". وهذه بالطبع كارثة بالنسبة إلى سجلها الحافل بالكوارث، والذي أصبح مليئاً بها في الأشهر الأخيرة."من الجيد أن هناك عالمين فقط لأقلق بشأن تدميرهما"، تابعت"إلا أنه... يا للجحيم، ربما هناك المزيد. ولمَ لا؟". لكن إذا كان هناك عالمان، فما هو احتمال أن يكونا الوحيدين؟

"تفضلوا، يا عوالم، احصلوا على كارثتكم هنا!" فكرت كارو بسخرية مريرة. نظرت مرة أخرى حول الطاولة، لكنها كانت محاطة بمحاربين في خضم مجلس الحرب، وكل ما تم الاتفاق عليه هنا يمكن أن يُدرج تحت عنوان:"بالطبع، يا غبية. ماذا كنتِ تظنين سيحدث؟" ومع ذلك، حاولت مرة أخرى.

قالت:"لا يمكن قبول أي مستوى من الأضرار الجانبية".

ظنت أنها رأت نوعاً من المواساة في عيني أكيفا، لكن لم يكن صوته هو الذي أجابها. إنما صوت ليسيث، من خلفها مباشرة، تقول بصوت حاقد:"لمَ

كل هذا القلق؟ هل أنتِ كيميرا أم بشرية؟".

ليسيث. أو كما أصبحت كارو تحب أن تفكر فيها: محبة المستقبل لمضغ العشب.

احتاجت إلى كل ذرة من ضبط النفس لديها كي لا تلتفت، وتحدق في وجه الناجا وتقول:"موو". بدلاً من ذلك، ردت بنبرة تقريرية، مع لمحة طفيفة فقط من الترفع:"أنا كيميرا في جسد بشري، يا ليسيث. كنت أظن أنكِ تفهمين ذلك الآن".

"إنها تفهم تماماً. أليس كذلك، أيتها الجندية؟" قال ثياغو، ملتفتاً نصف التفاتة نحو الناجا، بعينين تحملان تحذيراً واضحاً. ستتلقى توبيخاً لاحقاً، فكرت كارو. لقد كان الذئب واضحاً جداً قبل هذا المجلس بأن عليهم أن يظهروا جبهة موحدة مهما كان الأمر. بدا لها ذلك دليلاً على أن ليسيث لم تستطع الالتزام بذلك الأمر.

"نعم، يا سيدي"، قالت ليسيث، بنبرة بدت مقبولة إلى حد ما من الاحترام.

تابعت كارو:"وبعيداً عن البشر، ماذا عنّا؟ كم واحد منا سيموت؟".

"بقدر ما يلزم"، أجابت ليراز من الطرف الآخر للطاولة. وكانت كارو تود أن تهز تلك الملاك الجليدية الجميلة، ملكة الموت.

"وماذا لو لم يكن أي من ذلك ضرورياً؟" سألت كارو بتحدٍ."ماذا لو كان هناك طريق آخر؟".

"بالتأكيد"، قالت ليراز بملل ظاهر."لماذا لا نذهب فقط ونطلب من جايل الرحيل؟ أنا متأكدة من أنه سيغادر إذا طلبنا منه بلطف—".

قاطعتها كارو بسرعة:"هذا ليس ما أعنيه".

"إذاً ماذا؟ هل لديكِ فكرة أخرى؟".

وبالطبع، لم تكن لدى كارو أي فكرة. وردت بمرارة:"ليس بعد".

"إذا فكرتِ في أي شيء، أنا متأكدة أنكِ ستخبريننا".

آه، تلك النظرة الحادة، وذلك الصوت الساخر والمستفز.

شعرت كارو بالكراهية التي تكنها لها ليراز وكأنها صفعة. هل تستحق ذلك؟ ألقت نظرة سريعة نحو أكيفا، لكنه لم يكن ينظر إليها.

أعلن ثياغو:"لقد انتهينا هنا. جنودي بحاجة إلى الراحة والطعام، ولدينا مهمات لإتمامها".

قالت ليراز:"نطير عند الفجر".

لم يعترض أحد.

وهكذا انتهى الأمر. فكرت كارو وهي ترى المجلس يتفرق: استعدوا لنهاية العالم.

أو... ربما لا. وهي تراقب أكيفا يغادر دون أن يلقي باتجاهها نظرة واحدة، وقد علقت في ذهنها تلك الشرارة التي قفزت في عينيه، لكنها لم تكن تعتزم الاعتماد عليه أو على أي شخص آخر للوقوف من أجل العالم البشري. أما بالنسبة إليها، فهي لن تستسلم بهذه السهولة. ما زال لديها بعض الوقت.

ليس الكثير، ولكن بعض الوقت. وهو ما يجب أن يكون كافياً، صحيح؟ كل ما عليها فعله هو ابتكار خطة لمنع نهاية العالم وإقناع هؤلاء الجنود القساة المعاندين بتبنيها. وربما عليها في... حوالي اثنتي عشرة ساعة. إنجاز أكبر عدد ممكن من عمليات إعادة الإحياء.

ليست مشكلة؟

25

أنتم، جمعاً

بعد انتهاء أعمال المجلس، انسحب أكيفا إلى الغرفة المخصصة له وأغلق الباب خلفه.

وقفت ليراز على بابه بصمت. رفعت يدها لتطرق الباب، لكنها تراجعت. شردت لدقيقة تقريباً، وملامح وجهها تتأرجح بين الشوق والغضب. شوقٌ إلى الزمن الذي كانت فيه محاطة بأخويها، وغضبٌ من غيابهما وحاجتها إليهما شعرت... بالضعف.

هازايل على جانب، وأكيفا على الجانب الآخر؛ لقد كانا دائماً درعيها، في المعركة بالطبع، فقد تدربوا معاً منذ سن الخامسة. في أفضل حالاتهم، كانوا يقاتلون كجسد واحد بستة أذرع، بعقل واحد مشترك، ولم يكن ظهر أي منهم مكشوفاً أمام عدو. لكنها تدرك الآن أنه لم يكن الأمر مقتصراً على المعركة فحسب؛ بل على أمور الحياة كهذه اللحظة. مع غياب هازايل وانعزال أكيفا في عالمه الخاص، شعرت وكأن الرياح تضربها من كل الجهات، وكأنها قادرة على تمزيقها.

ليست أمام بابه لطلب المواساة. لكن ما كان يؤلمها أن احتياجات أكيفا، على الأرجح في مكان آخر. أن ينغلق على نفسه مع حزنه وبؤسه، ويتركها هنا بالخارج؟

لم تطرق بابه. بدلاً من ذلك، حنت كتفيها وسارت بعيداً. لم تكن تعرف إلى أين تذهب، ولم تهتم بذلك. اعتبرت كل شيء مجرد ملء للوقت—لكل ثانية حتى تصل إلى تلك اللحظة التي توجه فيها سيفها إلى قلب عمها وتغرزه ببطء، ببطء شديد.

لن يمنعها أي شيء من تنفيذ ذلك، لا البشر وأسلحتهم، ولا مخاوف كارو المحمومة، ولا الدعوات إلى السلام.

ولا أي شيء.

...

لم يكن أكيفا في حالة حداد. الصور التي كانت تطارده—جثة أخيه، كارو وهي تضحك مع الذئب—تشبثت بإحكام عميقاً في عقله. عيناه مغمضتان ووجهه هادئ وخالٍ من الأحلام، لكنه لم يكن نائماً، ولا مستيقظاً. إنما في مكانٍ لجأ إليه منذ سنوات، بعد معركة بولفينش، أثناء تعافيه من الإصابة التي كادت أن تقتله. ورغم أنه لم يمت، واستعاد استخدام ذراعه بشكل كامل، إلا أن الجرح في كتفه لم يتوقف عن الألم ولو لثانية واحدة، هو هناك الآن.

يقبع وسط الألم، حيث قام بالسحر.

ليس السيريثار، فذلك شيء مختلف تماماً. أي سحر صنعه عمداً، صنعه—أو ربما وجده—في هذا المكان. في البداية، كان الأمر أشبه بالمرور عبر باب سري إلى مستويات مظلمة في عقله، لكن مع مرور الوقت، ومع تزايد قوته ودخوله في أعماق أكثر، أصبح الإحساس بالمكان يتسع أكثر فأكثر، وبدأ يستيقظ بعد ذلك بشعور غامض وغير متزن، وكأنه عاد من مكان بعيد جداً.

هل صنع ذلك السحر أم عثر عليه؟ هل لا يزال يعيش داخل نفسه أم خارجها؟ لم يكن يعرف.

من دون أي تدريب، اعتمد أكيفا على الغريزة والأمل، وفي تلك الليلة، راح يسأل نفسه في كل دقيقة عن كليهما.

عندما أتته الفكرة كوحي وسط المجلس، كانت عن الهامسا.

ورغم يقينه حول إمكانية تحقيق اتفاق كامل بين الجيشين في وقت قصير، ومع علمه أن الأمر سيكون مليئاً بالتوتر، لكنه أيضاً يعلم أن أفضل طريقة لاستغلال قوتهم الجماعية هي في تحالف حقيقي، وليس مجرد هدنة مؤقتة. التكامل. سواء هاجموا الدومينيون في كتائب متحدة أو موزعة. لكن ليراز كانت محقة: وجود الهامسا- في كل وحدة، سيضعف العدو ويساعد في موازنة الكفة وتحقيق النصر.

لكن كيف سيقنع إخوته وأخواته بأن يثقوا بالكيميرا، خاصة بعد البداية السيئة بينهم. والهامسا سلاح لا يملكون ضده أي دفاع.

ولكن ماذا لو وجدوا طريقة للدفاع؟

هذه هي فكرة أكيفا.

ماذا لو تمكن من العمل على إيجاد تعويذة مضادة قادرة على حماية غير الشرعيين من تأثير الهامسا؟ لم يكن يعرف إن كان بإمكانه إنجاز ذلك—أو حتى ما يجب عليه فعله. إذا نجح، هل سيتسبب ذلك في إثارة المزيد من الصراع بدلاً من حله؟ بالتأكيد لن يكون الكيميرا سعداء بفقدانهم لتلك الميزة.

وماذا عن... كارو؟

هنا حيث فقد أكيفا المنظور. كيف يمكنك أن تميز بين الغريزة والأمل المتخفي في زيها، وبين الأمل واليأس الذي يتنكر في حضورك؟ لأنه إذا نجح في ذلك، فإن الفرصة لتحالف حقيقي بين جيوشهم ستأتي مع فرصة أخرى، أكثر شخصية.

ستكون كارو قادرة حينها على التقرب منه، وعلى أن تضغط يديها على جسده دون قصد الألم. لم يكن متأكداً من رغبتها في ذلك، يبقى أمله قائماً بتلك الفرصة، وبرغبتها.

...

جيشا السيرافيم والكيميرا، وضعا حراساً عند مدخل الممر الذي يربط القرية بالكهف الكبير، بهدف إبقاء الجنود بعيدين عن بعضهم البعض، لتفادي خطر المتربصين، الذين قد يكونون مختبئين خلف أي زاوية. لا مجال للتهاون. معظم الجنود من كلا الجانبين شعروا بأنهم محاصرون تحت السقوف الصخرية والجدران التي لا نوافذ لها في هذا المكان. لا سماء، لا مجال للهروب—خصوصاً بالنسبة إلى الكيميرا، الذين يعرفون أن غير الشرعيين قد أقاموا معسكرهم بينهم وبين المخرج.

استراحوا وأكلوا واستصلحوا ما تبقى من أسلحة من مخازن الكيرين التي نهبها العبيد منذ زمن بعيد. كان آيجير يذيب القدور والأدوات المعدنية ليصنع منها الشفرات، تداخل صوت طرقاته مع ضجيج الجبال. تم تكليف بعض الجنود لإشغالهم بإعادة تجهيز السهام القديمة، لكن لم يكن هناك نشاط يشغل غالبية القوات، وكان عدم انشغالهم أمراً خطيراً. ولم يلاحظ أي نشاطات لغاية الآن من قبل الملائكة الغاضبين لأن أي وحش لم يُعاقب بعد على خرق العهد، زعموا أنهم شعروا بالمرض الذي تسببه"الهامسات" ينبض عبر الجدران نحوهم.

أما الكيميرا، ورغم التزامهم بأوامر قائدهم الواضحة، فقد انتهزوا الفرصة لإراحة أجسادهم من الوقوف، بالاتكاء بوضع أيديهم على أقرب جدار. من المستبعد تماماً أن تكون قوة الهامسا في كفوفهم تمر عبر الجدران الحجرية، وتؤثر على الملائكة الذين اشتكوا أن قواهم تخور بسبب القدرات السحرية للهامسا، وصاروا يطلقون عليهم"جزارو الأيدي السوداء"، وتهامسوا عن رغبة قطع أيديهم الموسومة وحرقها.

وفوق كل هذا الارتباك والتوتر المتزايد، أخذ اليأس ينحت طريقه في داخل كل واحد منهم، وما زال يتردد صداه فيهم مثل نبضات طبل خافتة، سواء أكانوا وحوشاً أم ملائكة. لم يتحدث أحد عن ذلك، كل واحد منهم يحتفظ بهذا الضعف لنفسه. ربما لم يشعر هؤلاء الجنود بيأس أعمق من الذي مر بهم سابقاً، لكنهم بالتأكيد عرفوا معنى اليأس، والخوف من خلال معاناتهم الصامتة.

...

"حسناً؟" سألت إيسّا كارو حول عودتها وحدها إلى القرية خلف ثياغو وتين وليسيث، وبعد أن تملصت من صحبتهم، وجاءت لملاقاتها عند منعطف الطريق."كيف سار الأمر؟".

ردت كارو:"متوقعاً. عطش للدماء واستعراض شجاعة".

سألت إيسّا بفضول:"من الجميع؟".

حاولت كارو جاهدة تجنب نظرات إيسا، لعدم إخبارها بالحقيقة. لم يظهر أكيثا أو ثياغو أياً من تلك الأمور، لكن النتيجة كانت نفسها وكأنهما فعلا. فركت كارو عينيها. يا إلهي، كم هي متعبة."استعدي لهجوم شامل".

"إذاً سيكون الهجوم قريباً؟ حسناً. علينا أن نبدأ العمل".

زفرت كارو زفرة حادة. لديهم فقط حتى الفجر. كم وحشاً يستطيعون إعادة إحيائهم في هذا الوقت القصير؟"ما فائدة عدد قليل إضافي من الجنود في مواجهة معركة مثل هذه؟".

قالت إيسا:"نفعل ما بوسعنا".

"هذا كل ما يمكننا فعله؟ ذلك لأن المحاربين هم من يضعون خططنا".

صمتت إيسّا للحظة. كانتا لا تزالان على أطراف القرية، عند منعطف حاد في الممر الصخري الذي تبدأ خلفه المساكن، ويستمر الطريق نحو"الميدان".

سألت إيسّا بلطف:"وماذا لو وضع فنان ما الخطط؟".

شدّت كارو على أسنانها لأنها تعلم أنها لم تقدم للمجلس أي بديل للنظر فيه. تذكرت السخرية في كلام ليراز:"لماذا لا نذهب ونطلب من جايل أن يرحل؟" يا ليت. ويعود الملائكة جميعهم إلى منازلهم بسلام دون أن يموت أحد. ثم النهاية.

"حدوث ذلك مستبعد تماماً".

"لا أعرف"، قالت لإيسا بمرارة، وهي تبدأ في السير ببطء على الطريق."هل تتذكرين ذلك الرسم الذي رسمته مرةً، لمهمة؟ كان علي أن أوضح مفهوم الحرب؟".

أومأت إيسا."أذكره جيداً. تحدثنا عنه طويلاً بعد أن تغيبتِ".

رسمت كارو حينها رجلين وحشيين يواجهان بعضهما البعض على طاولة، وأمام كل واحد منهما وعاء ضخم مليء... بالبشر.

أطراف صغيرة تتلوى، تعبيرات بائسة على وجوههم. وبدا كل منهما يغرس شوكته في وجبة الآخر—بجوع شديد—يرمون بالقطعة تلو الأخرى من البشر في أفواههم المفتوحة.

"أردت من خلال الرسم أن أبين فكرة أن من يفرغ وعاء الآخر أولاً يفوز بالحرب. ورسمت ذلك قبل أن أعرف حتى عن المملكة، أو الحرب هنا، أو دور بريمستون فيها".

قالت إيسا:"روحكِ علمت مسبقاً، قبل عقلكِ".

أجابت كارو:"ربما. كنت أفكر في ذلك الرسم أثناء مجلس الحرب، وبدورنا في كل هذا. نحن نخدع أنفسنا. نستمر في ملء الوعاء من جديد، والوحوش تستمر في غرز شوكاتها العملاقة فيه، وبسببنا، هناك دائماً المزيد ليأكلوه. لا نخسر أبداً، لكننا لا ننتصر أيضاً. نستمر فقط في الموت. هل هذا ما نفعله؟".

"هذا ما فعلته أيدينا"، صححت إيسا، واضعة يدها الباردة على ذراع كارو."يا فتاتي العزيزة"، قالت لها برقة. بدت حينها جميلة جداً، لطيفة

الوجه كوجه العذراء في لوحات عصر النهضة. ثم تابعت"أنتِ تعرفين أن بريمستون كان يحمل آمالاً كبيرة لكما، أنتِ وأكيفا".

تذكرت كارو حديث بريمستون معها—أي"مادريغال" الساكنة فيها، حين كانت في زنزانتها قبل إعدامها—وقد قال لها إنه قادر على الاستمرار في عمله قرناً بعد قرن فقط لأنه يؤمن بأنه يحافظ على حياة الكيميرا"إلا أن يُعاد بناء العالم". قالت كارو بهدوء، مرددة ما أخبرها به حينها.

"لا يمكنه القيام بذلك"، قالت إيسّا بنفس الهدوء."ولا حتى أمير الحرب. ولا ثياغو بالطبع. لكن ربما أنتِ تستطيعين".

"لا أعرف كيف أصل إلى تلك المرحلة"، اعترفت كارو لإيسا، وكأنها تشاركها سراً مرعباً."نحن هنا، الكيميرا والسيرافيم، معاً ولكن ليس قلباً واحداً. لا يزالون يرغبون بقتل بعضهم البعض، وربما سيفعلون. وجودهما معاً لا يعني عالماً جديداً".

"انصتي إلى غرائزكِ، يا عزيزتي".

ضحكت كارو، ضحكة تعب تملؤها السخرية."ماذا لو كانت غرائزي تقول لي أن أنام، وأستيقظ عندما ينتهي كل شيء؟ العالم قد أُصلح، البوابات أُغلقت، الجميع عاد إلى عالمه الصحيح، وسيكون جايل فيه مهزوماً، ولا مزيد من الحروب".

ابتسمت إيسّا فقط وقالت:"لن ترغبي في النوم خلال كل هذا، يا حبيبتي. هذه أوقات غير عادية". ابتسامة غريزية ملائكية إلى درجة المكر."أو ستكون كذلك، بمجرد أن تكتشفي كيف تجعلينها كذلك".

ربتت كارو على كتفها بلطف."رائع. شكراً. أنا غير مستعجلة".

جذبتها إيسّا إلى حضنها الدافئ، وكان أشبه بآلاف الاحتضانات السابقة من إيسا، تلك التي دائماً ما تمنحها القوة—قوة إيمان الآخرين بها. حتى إيمان بريمستون بها أيضاً.

السؤال، هل ما زال أكيفا يؤمن بها؟

اعتدلت كارو في وقفتها مجدداً. وقد أوشكا على الوصول إلى"مقر إحياء الوحوش"، الغرف التي اختارتها زوزانا وميك. رأت بريق المشاعل الخضراء من خلال الباب المفتوح. ومن بعيد، على طول الطريق، كانت تسمع أصوات المجموعة وتصلها رائحة الطعام. خضار الأرض، الكُسكسي، خبز مرقوق، وآخر ما تبقى من دجاجهم المغربي الهزيل. إن الرائحة شهية، ولم تظن كارو أن ذلك فقط بسبب تضورها جوعاً. بل أوحى لها الأمر بفكرة.

الاستماع إلى غرائزكِ؟ ماذا عن الاستماع إلى معدتها بدلاً من ذلك؟ لم يكن ذلك خطة ولا حلاً؛ مجرد فكرة بسيطة. خطوة أولى."أخبري زوزي وميك أنني سأكون هناك قريباً"، قالت لإيسا، وانطلقت تبحث عن الذئب.

26

نزيف وتفتح

في حوالي الساعة السابعة صباحاً، وبعد أكثر من أربع وعشرين ساعة من الاستيقاظ، استسلمت إليزا أخيراً للإرهاق، وسقطت مباشرة في الحلم ككل مرة، بدأ الحلم بالسماء. سماء عادية، ليست أكثر من مساحة زرقاء مترامية، تتناثر فيها بعض السحب، لا شيء مميز. ولكن في الحلم، إليزا تشعر بالسماء وتدركها بطريقتها، من دون تفكير أو شك. ولا يكون هذا خيالاً أو وهماً طالما هي فيه. ويصبح أشبه بالسير خارج حدود عقلها المعروف إلى مكان أعمق وأغرب، لكنه شديد الواقعية.

أول ما أدركته إليزا هو أن هذه السماء مميزة، وبعيدة، بعيدة جداً. ليست بعيدة كـ"تاهيتي" أو"الصين"، بل نوع من البعد الذي يتحدى ما تعرفه عن الكون. وظلت تراقبها، حابسة أنفاسها، تنتظر حدوث شيء ما.

على أمل ألا يحدث شيء تخشاه في الوقت نفسه.

مثل الشعور بالندم، كانت كلمتا"الأمل" و"الخوف" قاصرتين تماماً عن وصف حدة المشاعر في الحلم. كان الأمل والخوف العاديان أشبه بظلال

لهذه المشاعر—مجرد تمثيلات قابلة لاستيعاب عواطف نقية ومرعبة، إلى درجة أنها قد تدمرنا في الحياة الواقعية، تمزق عقولنا وتجعلنا نُجَنُّ. حتى في الحلم، كان الشعور كافياً لتمزيق إليزا إلى أشلاء—الضغط الكبير، غير المحتمل، لهذه اللحظة المشحونة بالتوتر.

راقبي السماء. هل سيحدث شيئاً؟

لا يمكن. لا يمكن أن يحدث.

لا لا ..

يموت النحيب في حلقها. وصلاة تغلغلت عبر مزيج الأمل واليأس، حادة كنغمة كمان، كلمة واحدة ممدودة—"أرجوك"—نطقتها طويلة ونقية، وتكاد تستمر إلى الأبد—الذي قد لا يكون بعيداً على الإطلاق. لأن العالم كان على وشك أن ينتهي.

مرات لا تحصى، استسلمت فيها إليزا لهذا الحلم، مجبرة على مشاهدته يحدث ويحدث. كانت المرة الأولى وهي في السابعة من عمرها، ومنذ ذلك الحين يتكرر ويتكرر، ورغم معرفتها بما سيحدث، إلا أنها كانت تقع في كل مرة في نفس لحظة الرعب، حتى عندما يكون لا يزال متاحاً—ثم يُنتزع منها بعيداً.

تتفتح في السماء. يبدأ الأمر صغيراً: بالكاد يمكن رؤيته، مجرد تشويش في الأفق، مثل قطرة ماء في بحر من الحبر. سرعان ما تنمو بسرعة، وتنضم إليها أخرى.

السماء... تتدفق وتزدهر. دوامات من الألوان تشع من الأفق إلى الأفق، تتداخل وتتحد كأنها فسيفساء من البقع الملونة. يبدو المنظر جميلاً ومروعاً في آن معاً. ثم مروع، ومروع ومروع إلى الأبد، آمين.

هكذا سينتهي العالم. بسببي. بسببي أنا. لم أرتكب شيئاً أسوأ من هذا قط، في أي وقت مضى، وفي أي فضاء. لا أستحق أن أعيش—السماء ستنهار، وسيدخلون بسببها. هم. المطاردون، الهائجون، الملتهمون.

الوحوش قادمة من أجلك. الوحوش.

هربت إليزا منهم، في الحلم. استدارت وهربت، وكان شعورها بالتوتر والذنب كغول جائع يطاردها. بطريقة ما، كل هذا بسببها.. هي من سمح لهم بالدخول.

مستحيل. لن أسمح—

"ما الذي يحدث؟ هل نمتِ هنا؟".

شهقت إليزا واستيقظت، لتجد مورغان أمامها، يقف عند الباب، وشعره مبلل بالشامبو، متدلياً على جبهته على طريقة أعضاء فرق الشباب. مط شفتيه معبراً عن اشمئزازه. يا إلهي، من يرى هذه الأحلام لا يقيم اعتباراً لنظراته الساخرة. بالرغم من أنه بدا و كأنه ضبطها وهي تفعل أمراً مشيناً، مع أنها كانت تغفو فقط على الأريكة في المختبر أثناء مناوبتها وهي بكامل ملابسها.

جلست إليزا مستقيمة. كانت شاشة الحاسوب المحمول قد انطفأت. كم من الوقت كانت نائمة؟ أغلقت الحاسوب، ومسحت فمها بظهر يدها.

كل شيء على ما يرام، لم يسل لعابها ولم تصرخ أثناء نومها، لكن ظل شيء يضغط على صدرها، هي تعرف أنها صرخة على وشك الخروج لولا أن مورغان أيقظها -ليبارك الله وجوده المزعج- لكانت فجرت المختبر.

سألت وهي تهم بالنهوض:"كم الساعة الآن؟".

"أنا لست منبهكِ"، قال مورغان واتجه نحو جهاز لتحليل الـDNA. كان هناك جهازان ضخمان لتحليل الحمض النووي في المختبر، ولم تستطع إليزا أبداً تحديد الفارق بينهما، لكن مورغان يفضل الجهاز الموجود على اليسار، لذلك طالما حاولت الوصول قبله لتستخدمه. تلك الانتصارات الصغيرة هي ما تجعل اليوم أقل إرهاقاً. أما هذا اليوم فقد بدأ بالحلم، واستمر بالإرهاق، والعالم ينهار من حولها، وهي عالقة بملابس الأمس. لم تتوقع إليزا أن يحمل اليوم أي نوع من الحلاوة.

لكنها مخطئة؛ حمل اليوم شيئاً حلواً بالفعل. كما حمل أيضاً الكثير من الأمور الأخرى، وسرعان ما خرج عن أي توقعات ممكن أن تخطر على بالها.

بعد ساعتين تقريباً، سُمِع طرق على الباب جعل إليزا ترفع نظرها عن العمل وقد واجهت صعوبة في التركيز، والبيانات تتمايل أمام عينيها، وكانت ممتنة بسبب هذا التشتيت. أجاب الدكتور شودهاري على طرق الباب.

كان قد وصل إلى المختبر بعد مورغان بوقت قصير، واختصر تعليقاته على الأحداث الجارية بكلمتين فقط:"هذه أيام غريبة"، قال هذا وقد رفع حاجبيه قبل أن يتوجه إلى مكتبه. أنوج شودهاري ليس شخصاً ثرثاراً. إنه رجل هندي طويل القامة، في الخمسينيات من عمره، بأنف بارز وشعر كثيف بدأ يشيب عند الصدغين، يتحدث بلكنة إنجليزية مهذبة ويمتلك أسلوب رجل نبيل من العصر الفيكتوري.

"كيف يمكنني مساعدتكما؟" سأل الرجلين عند الباب.

بنظرة واحدة إليهما، شعرت إليزا وكأنها انتقلت إلى مشهد من مسلسل تلفزيوني. بدلتان داكنتان، قصتا شعر نظاميتان، ملامح باردة لا تعبير فيها. عميلان حكوميان."الدكتور أنوج شودهاري؟" سأل الأطول بينهما، وهو يبرز شارة. أومأ الدكتور شودهاري برأسه."نود منك أن تأتي معنا".

"الآن؟" سأل الدكتور شودهاري، بنفس الهدوء الذي قد يتحدث به زميل وهو يعرض عليه شرب كوب من الشاي.

"نعم". لم يقدموا أي تفسير، ولا كلمة واحدة لتخفيف صدمة مطلبهم. تساءلت إليزا إن كان العملاء الحكوميون يخضعون لدورة في كيفية أن يكونوا غامضين. ما الذي يجري؟ هل كان الدكتور شودهاري في مشكلة؟ بالطبع لا. عندما يدخل عملاء حكوميون إلى المختبرات ويقولون"نود أن تأتي معنا"، فإنهم يحتاجون عادة إلى خبرة أحد العلماء.

وكان تخصص الدكتور شودهاري هو علم الوراثة الجزيئية التطوري. لذا، السؤال... أي حمض نووي يريدون تحليله؟

التفتت إليزا نحو مورغان، ووجدته يراقب الموقف بشغف غريب ومريب، كأنه يشاهد سيناريو غزو فضائي."بروتوكول غزو الكائنات الفضائية"، فكرت إليزا. وبمجرد أن شعر بنظراتها عليه، استدار بابتسامة ساخرة وقال:"ربما لستِ الشخص الوحيد الفهيم على هذا الكوكب"، بطريقة أوضحت أنها في رأيه تتصدر قائمة الحمقى.

وهذا ما جعل الأمر أحلى بكثير—ها هي، لحظتها العتيدة في يوم مظلم كان على وشك أن تزداد ظلاماً—عندما سأل الدكتور شودهاري العملاء:"هل يمكنني إحضار مساعدة؟" وبعد إيماءة مقتضبة بالموافقة، التفت... نحوها.

نحوها هي. كانت اللحظة ثمينة، مليئة بالانتصار، حلاوتها تكاد تكون لا تُصدق."إليزا، هل تمانعين في مرافقتي؟".

من الصوت الذي أصدره مورغان، كادت إليزا تصدق أن الهواء خرج من رئتيه عبر كل فتحة في رأسه، وليس فقط من فمه وأنفه. لا بد أن أذنيه وعينيه شاركتا أيضاً في ذلك، على طريقة الرسوم المتحركة. ذلك الصوت معبّر للغاية، كفحيح ساخر مفعم بعدم التصديق والظلم، والاحتقار.

"لكن دكتور شودهاري—" حاول مورغان الاعتراض، قاطعه الدكتور شودهاري بنبرة جافة وعملية.

"ليس الآن، يا سيد توث".

ونهضت إليزا عن على كرسيها، متوقفة للحظة أمامه لتقول بصوت خافت وساخر:"تقبّل ذلك، يا سيد توث".

ردّ مورغان، وقد امتلأ صوته بالمرارة والغضب:"هذا ما يجب أن أقوله لكِ"، ورافق كلماته نظرة مليئة بالتلميح نحو الدكتور شودهاري. توقفت إليزا، وهي تشعر بشعور غريب أن كفّها قد أصبح ساخناً وصلباً بشدة ومتحمس لصفعه على وجهه. كانت واعية لوجود العميلين ومعلمها، لذا سيطرت على رغبتها تلك في الصفع، لكن يدها ظلت تشعر بتك الرغبة.

جمعت المعدات بناءً على طلب الدكتور شودهاري، وخرجت مع العميلين تاركةً مورغان ليغرق في غضبه الطفولي العنيف.

كانت هناك سيارة حكومية تنتظر في الخارج. سوداء، أنيقة. تساءلت إليزا إلى أي جهة ينتمي هذين الرجلين. لم تتمكن من قراءة شارتيهما. هل هما من مكتب التحقيقات الفيدرالي؟ وكالة المخابرات المركزية؟ وكالة الأمن القومي؟ من يملك الصلاحية على... الملائكة؟

أشار الدكتور شودهاري لإليزا أن تدخل السيارة أولاً، ثم ركب بجانبها. انغلق الباب بصوت ناعم، وصعد العميلين إلى المقعدين الأماميين، وانطلقت السيارة وسط حركة المرور. ومع ابتعادهم عن المتحف، بدأت نشوة الانتصار التي شعرت بها إليزا تتلاشى، وبدأ القلق يحل محلها. "لحظة، فكّري في هذا قليلاً".

سألت: "آه، عذراً، إلى أين نحن ذاهبون؟".

جاء الرد من المقعد الأمامي: "ستُعلمين حال وصولنا".

حسناً.

الوصول إلى أين؟

لا بد أنه إلى روما. أليس كذلك؟

ألقت إليزا نظرة خاطفة نحو الدكتور شودهاري، الذي ضم كتفيه قليلاً ورفع حاجبيه. "سيكون هذا مثيراً للاهتمام"، قال بهدوء.

وها هي تتساءل؟ هل سيكون كذلك؟ هل سيُتاح لهما حقاً الوصول إلى الزوار؟

رسمت في مخيلتها صورة سريعة لنفسها وهي تقترب لأخذ مسحة خد من أحدهم، وشعرت بوخزة من الهستيريا تجتاحها. من كان يظن، بعد كل ما تخلت عنه، أن العلم هو الذي سيجعلها تواجه الملائكة وجهاً لوجه؟ كادت تضحك بصوت عالٍ. "انظري إلي، يا أمي!" يا إلهي. كان الأمر مضحكاً فقط لأنه كان سخيفاً للغاية.

لقد اختارت مساراً لحياتها بعيداً عن ماضيها قدر الإمكان، فأين قادها؟ إلى واحدة من أكبر الأحداث في تاريخ البشرية، وهي ستكون هناك... تضع مسحة قطنية في فم ملاك؟"افتح فمك" شعرت بوخزة أخرى من الهستيريا، لكنها كتمتها وغلفتها بسعال خفيف.

إليزا ستقوم بتحليل الحمض النووي للملائكة. إذا كان لديهم حمض نووي. وهي تظن أنهم يمتلكونه. لديهم أجساد مادية؛ فلا بد أن تكون مكونة من شيء.

لكن ما الذي سيبدو عليه؟ أي شبه سيحمله مع الحمض النووي البشري؟ لم تستطع حتى أن تتخيل، لكنها كانت واثقة من أن حل هذا اللغز سيكون على المستوى الجزيئي.

ستعرفهم على حقيقتهم.

في خضم دوران أفكارها، وإرهاقها، وقلقها، وثقل الحلم الذي لا يزال جاثماً على كتفها—مثل طائر جارح ينتظر اللحظة المناسبة—استمرت أفكارها في الالتفاف. أصبح الأمر أشبه بمطاردة شخص بكل طاقتك، وعندما تمد يدك لتمسك به، يستدير عليك فجأة، وبطريقة وحشية، ينقض على عنقك.

ستكتشفين حقيقة الملائكة، هكذا حاولت إليزا التحكم في أفكارها. ستكتشف ذلك بالطريقة التي تدربت عليها. تتابع النوكليوتيدات، وتبدأ الأشياء، من العالم إلى الكون وحتى المستقبل، في أن تتخذ معنى منطقياً. كـ"علم تطور السلالات" النظم. العقلانية.

ثم دارت الفكرة من جديد، وأمسكت بها، وأجبرتها على النظر فيها، ولم تكن تلك الفكرة التي اعتقدت أنها تطاردها، بل عيناها تنبضان بالجنون. لم تكن كذلك. سأعرف حتماً حقيقة الملائكة.

الفكرة الحقيقية التي ترددت في عقل إليزا كانت: هل سأعرف حقيقتي؟

27

مجرد مخلوقات في عالم

عندما انضمت كارو إلى زوزانا وميك وإيسا، اكتشفت أنهم كانوا منشغلين أثناء وجودها في مجلس الحرب، حيث يعدّون المكان، ويفرغون الصناديق، وينظفون الأسنان ويصنفونها. حتى إن زوزانا ساهمت في ترتيب بعض العقود—التي لم تكن مشدودة بعد، في انتظار موافقة كارو.

"هذه جيدة"، قالت كارو بعد فحص دقيق.

"هل ستنجح؟" سألت زوزانا.

نظرت كارو إلى العقود بتمعن أكبر. "هل هذا عقد يوثم؟" سألت وهي تشير إلى الأول. صف من أسنان الخيول والإغوانا مع أنابيب من عظام الخفافيش—مزدوجة، لتناسب الأجنحة الثنائية—إلى جانب الحديد واليشم لتحقيق الحجم والجمال.

قالت زوزانا: "فكرت أنه من البديهي وضعه".

أومأت كارو برأسها. ثياغو سيحتاج يوثم ليقود المعركة. "لديك موهبة في هذا"، قالت لصديقتها. العقد لم يكن مثالياً، لكنه كان قريباً جداً من ذلك—ومذهلاً بالنظر إلى قلة خبرة زوزانا.

"بالتأكيد". قالت زوزانا بتواضع."الآن عليكِ فقط أن تعلّميني السحر لتحويلها إلى لحم حي".

"لا تغريني"، قالت كارو بضحكة داكنة."ماذا؟".

"هناك قصة عن رجل محكوم عليه أن يخدم كعبّار على نهر الموتى إلى الأبد. ولكن هناك تفصيل واحد، وهو أنه لا يعلم ذلك. كل ما عليه فعله هو أن يسلم عصاه لشخص آخر، فيسلمهم مصيره أيضاً".

سألت زوزانا:"وهل ستسلمينني عصاك؟".

"لا. لن أسلمك عصاي".

"ماذا لو تقاسمناها؟".

هزت كارو رأسها بامتعاض وتعجب."زوزي، لا. فلديك حياة لتعيشيها، وأفترض أنني سأعيشها بينما أساعدكِ؟".

"نعم، ولكن...".

"إذاً دعينا نرَ هنا. يمكنني إما أن أقوم بأعظم وأروع وأدهش شيء سحري سمع عنه أحد على الإطلاق—وبعد انتهاء أمور الحرب، أساعدكِ في إحياء شعب بأكمله من النساء والأطفال، وبناء جيل جديد من المخلوقات في بداية عصر جديد لعالم جديد لا يعرف بوجوده أحد. أو... يمكنني العودة إلى المنزل وأداء عروض دمى للسياح".

شعرت كارو بابتسامة ترتسم على شفتيها."حسناً، عندما تضعين الأمر بهذا الشكل"، ثم التفتت إلى ميك."هل لديك شيء تقوله بشأن هذا؟".

"نعم"، قال بجدية، جدّية حقيقية."أقول، لنناقش المستقبل لاحقاً، بعد أن تنتهي 'هذه الحرب' كما قالت زوزي، عندما نعلم أنه سيكون هناك مستقبل".

"وجهة نظر جيدة"، قالت كارو، ثم توجهت نحو مباخر الأرواح.

أفضل سيناريو كان إحياء عشرات الأرواح، وهذا يدعو للتفاؤل. السؤال كان: من؟ من هم الأرواح المحظوظة اليوم؟ تأملت كارو، وبينما كانت تفرز

مباخر الأرواح، بدأت في تكوين مجموعة"نعم"، ومجموعة أخرى "لا". اممم... هذه المجموعة ابقوا أمواتاً، لا نحتاج مزيد من ليسيث السامة في هذه الأزمة، ولا مزيد من رازور ووسخه. أرادت جنوداً ذوي شرف رفيع، يمكنهم الإيمان بالهدف الجديد بدلاً من عرقلته في كل خطوة. لا شك أن الخيارات الواضحة قليلة، جعلتها تتردد بشأنهم، وفكرت أيضاً كيف سيتم استقبالهم باليروس، إكساندر، ميناس، ڤيا، وأزاي. الجنود الذين تحدوا أمر الذئب الحقيقي بقتل المدنيين السيرافيم، وبدلاً من ذلك طاروا إلى الخطوط الخلفية ليموتوا وهم يدافعون عن شعبهم. كانوا أقوياء، أكفاء، ومحترمين، لكنهم عصوا أمر الذئب. هل سيكون في إحيائهم حكمة؟ هل تضيف علامة جديدة في قائمة"الأمور التي لن يفعلها ثياغو أبداً"؟

ربما، لكن كارو أرادتهم؛ وكانت مستعدة لتحمل اللوم. كانت تريد أيضاً الأمزلاغ والظلال الحية أحياء، وهي على ثقة أن ذلك سيكون دفعاً بعيداً جداً. احتفظت بمباخر أرواحهم جانباً، كنوع من التميمة ليوم أكثر إشراقاً. وسيأتي الوقت المناسب لتلبسهم ثوب الأحياء من جديد.

وضعت فريق باليروس في مجموعة"نعم". وكان هناك روح سادسة معهم. شعرت بها تلامس حواسها، كأنها سكين من الضوء يخترق الأشجار، ورغم أنها لم تكن مألوفة لكارو، تذكرت حديث زيري عن الفتى الداشناغ الشاب الذي انضم إلى قتالهم ومات إلى جانبهم.

لم يكن هناك أي منطق في اختيار فتى غير مدرّب كواحد من الأرواح التي سيتم إحياؤها، خاصة وأنهم لم يحيوا سوى عشرة أرواح قبل المعركة الضخمة المقبلة، لكن كارو فعلت ذلك على أي حال، بنوع من التحدي.

"خيار مجسدة الأرواح".

تخيلت نفسها وهي تقول ذلك لليسيث، أو كما صارت تسميها الآن،"بقرة المستقبل"، تلك المرأة الأفعى السامة."هل لديكِ مشكلة مع هذا؟" على أي حال، الفتى الداشناغ لن يكون فتى بعد الآن. لم يكن في حيازة كارو أسنان

فتيان، وحتى لو كانت لديها، فهذا ليس مخصصاً لهم. إذاً، سوف يستيقظ ليجد نفسه حياً، بالغاً، ومجنحاً، في كهف بعيد مع كائنات القائمين من الموت والسيرافيم. سيكون يوماً مثيراً له بلا شك.

جزء من عقل كارو ظل يخبرها أن هذه فكرة سيئة، لكن شيء ما بدا صحيحاً بالنسبة إليها بشأنه. الداشناغ مخلوقات كيميرا هائلة، قلة قليلة منها مخيف، لكنها اعتقدت أن الأمر يتعلق بنقاء روحه، كخنجر من ضوء، شرف وهدف جديد لوجوده. قالت لمساعديها:"حسناً. لنبدأ".

مرت الساعات. دخل ثياغو في منتصف العمل ليتولى مهامه، وقد بدا خالياً من الجروح المتخثرة التي سرعان ما التأمت—وقد تعاون هو وكارو في إضافة كدمات جديدة إلى أذرع وأيدي الأجساد.

لم يتمكنوا من إحياء عشرة أجساد كما خططوا، في غضون ست ساعات، لكنهم نجحوا في إحياء تسعة جنود فقط، واضطروا إلى التوقف. أولاً، لم تكن هناك مساحة كافية إضافية لهم. هذه التسعة قد ملأت الغرفة تماماً. ثانياً، سيطر الإرهاق على كارو، مما جعلها غير قادرة على التركيز. بدأت تشعر بالدوار والتشتت، لم تعد قادرة على العمل. انتهينا.

ويبدو أن زوزانا شعرت بنفس الشيء."أقايض ما أملك مقابل جرعة من القهوة"، تمتمت، وهي ترفع يديها كأنها تصلي باتجاه السقف. في الوقت الذي دخلت فيه إيسّا حاملة الشاي، لم تتحمس زوزانا للشاي."أعني قهوة، قلت قهوة"، مخاطبة السقف، وكأن الكون نادل أخطأ في إحضار طلبها.

على كلٍ، شربوا الشاي بصمت، وهم يتأملون عملهم. تسعة أجساد، وكل ما تبقى الآن هو نقل الأرواح إليها من المباخر. تركت كارو ميك وزوزانا يتوليان هذه المهمة، إذ كانت ذراعاها ترتعشان، وتؤلمانها. أسندت ظهرها إلى الحائط بجانب ثياغو، وهي تراقب زوزانا تمر على صف الأجساد الجديدة، وتضع مخروطاً من البخور على جبين كل رأس جديد.

سألت ثياغو الذئب:"هل سجلتهم في قائمة الدعوة للمجلس؟".

أومأ برأسه."تشاوروا فيما بينهم، وفي النهاية قبلوا حضورهم. جعلوا الأمر يبدو وكأنهم يقدمون لنا معروفاً، بالطبع. قالوا على مضض: 'نوافق على ذلك، لكن لا تتوقعوا منا أن نستمتع بحضورهم'".

"هل قالوا ذلك حقاً؟".

"ليس حرفياً".

قالت كارو:"حسناً. إنه الكبرياء. قد يتظاهرون بعدم الاستمتاع، لكنهم سيفعلون".

كانت هذه فكرتها الصغيرة، خطوتها الأولى: إطعام السيرافيم. خلال مجلس الحرب، قال أحدهم وربما يكون إليون أو بريائوس، بكلمات كشفت على أن غير الشرعيين، بعد فرارهم على عجالة من مواقعهم على حدود الإمبراطورية، قد استنفدوا بالفعل مخزونهم القليل من الطعام الذي تمكنوا من حمله معهم. والآن إطعامهم—وعددهم يقارب الثلاثمائة—سيستنزف مخازن الكيميرا أيضاً، لكنه كان لفتة تضامن من أجل التحالف.

نحن نأكل معاً ونجوع معاً. نحن في هذا معاً.

وربما يوماً ما سنعيش معاً. مجرد مخلوقات في عالم واحد. لمَ لا؟ صوت قدح—لولاعة صغيرة حمراء من البلاستيك عليها وجه شخصية كرتونية، لا تتناسب مع جدية الموقف—أشعلت زوزانا أقماع البخور، واحداً تلو الآخر على طول الصف. بدأت رائحة بخور بريمستون الخاص بالأرواح المبعوثة تملأ الكهف الصخري، واستيقظ يوثم أولاً، ثم تبعه الآخرون.

اختلطت مشاعر كارو. شعرت بالفخر: بنفسها، وبزوزانا أيضاً. الأجساد التي أُعيد إحياؤها بدت جيدة الصنع، قوية ومهيبة، غير مشوهة أو مبالغاً فيها كما في المرة السابقة. هذه المرة أشبه بأسلوب بريمستون، مما جعلها تشعر بالحنين والاشتياق إليه. وبالغصة أيضاً.

والآن إعادة ملء القوارير. لمزيد من اللحم لإطعام طواحين الحرب التي لا تتوقف.

28

عاشقة الملاك، عاشق الوَحشة

كما قادا المضيف عبر الممر المتعرج إلى القرية المعزولة، ها هما كارو وثياغو يقودانهم الآن عائدين إلى الأعلى.

كان"غير الشرعيين" قد سبقوهم بالفعل إلى الكهف المركزي الواسع الذي يستخدم كمكان للتجمع. وقد أخذوا بوضوح النصف البعيد من الكهف، تاركين النصف الآخر للكيميرا، وكأن خطاً غير مرئي يفصل بين الطرفين، يجمعهما المكان ولكن يفصلهما الوجود.

دخل الطعام، في أوعية ضخمة مليئة بالكسكس، مع الخضار والمشمش واللوز. كمية الدجاج القليلة موزعة بشكل خفيف فوق الطعام، وكان من الصعب حصول الجميع على قطعة منها، لكن طعمه كان واضحاً في الطبق. كما قُدّمت الأرغفة المخبوزة على صخرة ساخنة—كمية الخبز كانت أكثر مما رأت كارو في حياتها كلها في مكان واحد. ومع أن الكمية بدت هائلة، إلا أنها استُهلكت بسرعة.

همست زوزانا، بعد أن هدأ صوت الملاعق على الصحون:"أتعلمين ما الذي سيكون رائعاً الآن؟ الشوكولاتة. لا تحاولي أبداً عقد تحالف بدون شوكولاتة".

لم تستطع كارو تخيل أن"غير الشرعيين"، الذين عانوا طيلة حياتهم من الحرمان، قد عرفوا شيئاً عن الحلويات.

أضاف ميك مقترحاً:"ما رأيك ببعض الموسيقى؟".

ابتسمت كارو وقالت:"أظن أن هذه فكرة رائعة".

أخرج كمانه وبدأ بدوزنة أوتاره.

منذ دخولهم إلى الكهف، كانت كارو تترقب وصول أكيفا، محاولة عدم إظهار قلقها لعدم حضوره بعد.

لم تَرَ ليراز أيضاً؛ رأت فقط مئات من الملائكة غير المعروفين، بوجوههم الخاوية والمتجهمة. بالطبع—فهذه عشية نهاية العالم، وكل يدعو لعدم الراحة. شعرت كارو أن الهدنة هشة منذ لحظة وصولهم، وأن هؤلاء الجنود قد يقتلون بعضهم البعض بالسكاكين بنفس الروح التي قد يتقاسمون فيها الخبز.

بدأ ميك بالعزف، وراحت كارو تراقب السيرافيم وتتفحص تلك الوجوه الشرسة الجميلة واحداً تلو الآخر، متسائلة عن أرواحهم. وتدريجياً، بدأت تشعر بأثر الموسيقى عليهم. لم يختفِ العبوس تماماً من وجوههم، إلا أن الأجواء بدأت تلين. حتى إنها شعرت تقريباً بذلك الزفير الطويل البطيء الذي خرج معه بعض التوتر من بين مئات الأكتاف.

عند الفجر سيعودون إلى عالم البشر. وقد تساءلت كارو: عما يحدث هناك؟ كيف قدم جايل نفسه لهم، وكيف استُقبل؟ هل سارعوا لتزويده بالأسلحة؟ هل كانوا يدربونه الآن على استخدامها؟ أم كانوا يشكون في نواياه؟ بعضهم بالتأكيد كان يشك، لكن من كان الأعلى صوتاً؟ من دائماً يكون الأعلى صوتاً؟

المتدينون.

الخائفون.

همست زوزانا:" كارو، أحتاج ترجمة".

التفتت كارو إلى صديقتها التي اعتادت تعلم مفردات الكيميرا من ڤيركو أثناء تناول الطعام في القصر. سألت:"ما الذي يقوله؟ لا أستطيع فهمه".

أعاد ڤيركو تكرار الكلمة التي تساءلت عنها، فترجمت كارو:"السحر".

"آه"، قالت زوزانا. ثم بعينين متجهمتين:"حقاً؟ اسأليه كيف عرف ذلك؟".

نقلت كارو السؤال له.

"كلنا شعرنا به"، أجاب ڤيركو."أخبريها. الآن."

رمشت كارو بعينيها في حيرة. وبدلاً من الترجمة، سألت:"شعرتم بماذا في نفس اللحظة؟".

قابلها ڤيركو بنظرة ثابتة وقال ببساطة:"النهاية".

شعرت كارو بقشعريرة تسري في جسدها. كانت تعرف تماماً ما كان يقصده، لكنها سألت على أي حال:"ماذا تعني بـ 'النهاية'؟".

"ماذا قال؟" أرادت زوزانا أن تعرف، لكن كارو كانت متسمرة أمام ڤيركو. كان هناك فهم يغمرها تدريجياً، كشيء كان يحوم حولها ويبتعد عنها لفترة طويلة، لكنه أخيراً استسلم وتوقف عن المراوغة.

نظر ڤيركو حوله إلى الحضور المتجمعين في مجموعات متفاوتة، بعضهم مغمض العينين ويترنح مع الموسيقى، وبعضهم الآخر يحدق في النار. قال:"بعد كل ما حدث، فكرت في نفسي: الملائكة محظوظون فعلاً. ولا بد أنني بدأت أفقد عقلي. نسيت نصف سيفي داخل غمده. وقفت هناك بفم مفتوح، وشعرت وكأن قلبي شحب من مكانه. اعتقدت أنني وصلت إلى نهاية حياتي الطويلة، هكذا فكرت". تركها تستوعب كلماته، وشعرت ببرودة ثم دفء يكتنفانها في موجات متتابعة.

قال ڤيركو:"لكن الجميع شعروا بالأمر ذاته. لم يكن الأمر متعلقاً بي فقط، وهذا فيه نوع من الراحة. حدث لنا جميعنا شيء ما. أحدهم قام بأمر..".، توقف قليلاً."لا أعلم ما هو، لكنه هو السبب في أننا ما زلنا أحياء".

تراجعت كارو إلى الوراء، مذهولة. كيف لم تتوقع ذلك على الفور؟ لم تشعر أبداً بذلك اليأس من قبل، حتى عندما وقفت وغبار رماد لوراميندي يغطي قدميها. وكان هذا الشعور قد أتى ورحل كشيء عابر. كموجة صوتية، أو جسيمات من الضوء. أو... انفجار من السحر.

موجة من السحر في لحظة مفصلية من الكارثة، أبعدتهم عن حافة الهلاك. وإذا كان الذئب الأبيض قد قام وقال كلمته، فإنه قد تحدث بصمت تلك اللحظة، مساعداً على إعادة تجميع أنفسهم بينما كانت أرواحهم تترنح. لكنه لم يوقفهم عن قتل بعضهم البعض.

أكيڤا هو من فعل ذلك.

انتشر الادراك في عروق كارو كحرارة متدفقة، وقبل أن تسأل نفسها ما إذا كانت محقة، شعرت بأنها متيقنة.

دخل أكيڤا أخيراً إلى الكهف، ميزته كارو بطرف عينها. قفز قلبها. وعندما التفتت سريعاً لتتأكد - أنه هو- لم ينظر نحوها. شعرت بالهمهمة التي دبت في المجموعة حولها، سمعت رغم أن الكلمات المبهمة لم تتضح إلا بعد لحظة "لقد كان هو، هو من أنقذنا." هل هناك شخص آخر قد اكتشف ما اكتشفته هي؟

التفتت لترى من تحدث، وفوجئت برؤية الصبي الداشناغ، الذي لم يعد صبياً بعد الآن. وصار اسمه راث، ولم يكن بإمكانه معرفة شيء عن نبض اليأس؛ فقد كانت روحه في مبخرة حينها. إذاً عمَّ كان يتحدث؟

استمعت كارو باهتمام.

قال:"لم أكن لأعيش حتى أصل إلى هينترموست"، متوجهاً بالكلام إلى باليروس والبقية الذين عادوا معه إلى الحياة.

"كنت أتجه جنوباً مع بعض الآخرين. الملائكة كانوا يحرقون الغابة خلفنا. قرية كاملة من شعب الكابرين، وبعض فتيات الداما اللواتي حررن من تجار العبيد معي. حوصرنا ونحن مختبئون في وادٍ، ووجدونا. اثنان من غيــ—.." ثم صحح لنفسه."اثنان من غير الشرعيين. كانا أمامنا مباشرة. سمعنا صرخات الأريز وهي تُذبح، لكنهما نظرا إلينا، و... تظاهرا بعدم رؤيتنا. تركانا نذهب".

قال باليروس:"ربما لم يرياكم".

رد راث باحترام مؤكداً:"رأيانا. وكان أحدهما هو". أشار بذقنه نحو أكيفا."عينان برتقاليتان مثل عيني الداشناغ. لا يمكنني أن أخطئهما".

سمعت كارو كل هذا وهي تشعر بنفس الإحساس الذي كان يتردد داخلها طوال الوقت، ذلك الفهم الذي يقترب، ينتظر فقط أن تتوقف عن مقاومته. بالطبع لم يكن زيري فقط من أنقذه أكيفا في هينترموست، بل أيضاً أنقذ العبيد والقرويين، أولئك الفارون الذين تركهم الذئب ليلاقوا حتفهم عندما اختار قتل عدوه بدلاً من مساعدة قومه.

تأمل باليروس وقال بابتسامة صغيرة وهو ينظر عبر الكهف:"هالك الوحوش، يُدافع عن الوحوش؟" وأضاف مقتبساً بتأمل:"وتنطوي الساعات بغرابة مع اقتراب النهاية".

"تنطوي الساعات بغرابة". كانت جملة من أغنية، يعرفها جميع الجنود. لم تكن تحمل الأمل، لكنها ملائمة في سياق تلك الصرخة السحرية. مع اقتراب النهاية. النهاية.

لم تستطع كارو منع نفسها من النظر مرة أخرى إلى أكيفا. ما زال يتجاهلها، وهذا ما جعلها تعتقد أنه لن يفعل ذلك أبداً.

ها هما هنا في كهوف الكيرين. إنها ليلة المعركة. لقد جمعا جيوشهما، وهذا في حد ذاته يعتبر إنجازاً لا يمكن تصوره، لكن لم يكن كما تخيله. لم يكونا جنباً إلى جنب. ولم يتمكنا حتى من النظر إلى بعضهما البعض.

نبض كارو يصر على خداعها، يتسارع ثم يهدأ، وكأنه مخلوق محبوس داخلها. أكيفا هناك محاط بقومه، وهي هنا، مع قومها، وبدا أن كل ما يربطهما معاً الآن هو عدو مشترك وتلك الخيوط العذبة والنقية من الموسيقى

جلس ميك على حجر، ورأسه منحنٍ فوق كمانه، وأنغام عزفه كانت مختلفة عما كانت عليه في القصر. هناك حيث انسجمت مع السماء. أما هنا، فكانت مجرد صدى يتردد.

هنا، بدت الأنغام حبيسة، كنبضات قلب كارو.

شعرت برأس زوزانا وقد اتكأ على كتفها. إيسَّا على الجانب الآخر، هادئة ويقظة، والذئب اضطجع أمامها، مرتكزاً على مرفقيه قرب النار مسترخياً. أنيق كعادته، ورائع، من دون قسوة، من دون توحش، وكأن الملامح التي تميز جسده المستعار بدأت تتغير ببطء من الداخل. وقد استطاعت كارو رؤية بوادر جمال أكبر بدأ في الظهور، عندها فكرت في فن بريمستون الممتزج مع روح زيري. لم يكن لذلك أي علاقة بثياغو الآن. ذلك الوحش قد اختفى إلى الأبد، وإن كان هناك من يستطيع تطهير العيوب، فهو زيري حتماً

لكن عليه أن يكون حذراً، ولا يسترخي كثيراً. قامت كارو بمسح سريع للحشد المحيط، متيقظة بشكل خاص لمراقبة ليسيث حيث تراقبها عن كثب. غير أنها لم تكن موجودة. رأت نيسك وحيداً، دون شريكته المعتادة، جالساً بجوار النار وعيناه مثبتتان على اللهب.

شعرت كارو بنظرات الذئب نحوها، وقد تجاهلته، فبصرها ينجذب بقوة مغناطيسية عبر الكهف إلى أكيفا. أكيفا، أكيفا.

هذه المرة، سمحت لنفسها أن تنظر. حبست أنفاسها، ويبدو أن نبضها قد توقف أيضاً، أجبرت نفسها على التريث. وكأنها تلعب لعبة طفولية قديمة ملؤها الخرافات، فتنهدت وأخذت قرارها: إذا لم ينظر هذه المرة، فقد فقدته. وفكرة فقدانه أعادت إليها صدى اليأس السابق، كشمعة تصرخ أثناء انطفائها.

رفعت عينيها ونظرت عبر الكهف. و...

... نار ملتهبة. كما عيناه، تحييان عينيها: فتيل يحرق الهواء بينهما. ها هو ينظر إليها. وبالرغم من وقوفه بعيداً، ومع كل ما بينهما—الكيميرا، السيرافيم، الأحياء جميعهم، الأموات جميعهم—شعرت وكأن تلك النظرة لمسة منه. كخيوط الشمس. نظراتهما إلى بعضهما البعض. أي مخلوق يستطيع ملاحظة ذلك. عاشقة الملاك. عاشق الوحشية.

فلير من يرى.

يا لهذا الجنون وهذا التخلي، لكن بعد كل ما حدث، لم تستطع كارو أن تجعل نفسها تهتم بما يكفي لتصرف نظرها. فعينا أكيڤا ناراً وضوءاً، وأرادت أن تبقى فيهما إلى الأبد. غداً، نهاية العالم. الليلة، أشعة الشمس.

وأخيراً، كسر أكيڤا نظره. وقف وتحدث بهدوء إلى الملائكة حوله، وعندما غادر الكهف متسللاً بين الآخرين، توقف لحظة عند المدخل الطويل المقوس، ولم ينظر نحوها مرة أخرى. لا بأس، فقد أرادها أن تتبعه.

لم تستطع، بالطبع. سيُكشف أمرها. فالكهوف الأمامية مليئة بغير الشرعيين، وحتى لو لم تكن ليسيث موجودة—أين هي؟— وهناك العديد من الكيميرا الآخرين يراقبون تحركاتها. لكن عليها المحاولة. لم تتحمل فكرة أن ينتظرها أكيڤا. شعرت أن هذه آخر فرصها.

"سأذهب لأخذ قسط من النوم"، قالت كارو وهي تنهض، متثائبة— تظاهرت بالنعس وسرعان ما أصبح حقيقياً—ثم غادرت الكهف من الباب المقابل للباب الذي خرج منه أكيڤا، الباب الذي يؤدي إلى القرية وليس الباب الذي يؤدي إلى أكيڤا.

ولكن بمجرد أن أصبحت في الخارج وبعيداً عن مرأى الجميع، استخدمت السحر لتخفي نفسها، ثم عادت مجدداً إلى الكهف، عابرة دون أن تُرى، تنساب بهدوء فوق رؤوس الجيشين المجتمعين، وقلبها يقرع كالطبل، لملاقاة أكيڤا.

29

حلم تحقق

"يمكن للأمور أن تكون مختلفة".

هكذا قالت كارو لزيري قبل اجتماع مجلس الحرب."هذا هو المغزى".

هل كان هذا هو المغزى حقاً؟ أن تبني عالماً لتعيش فيه مع عشيقها؟ زيري بالطبع لاحظ النظرات المتبادلة بين كارو وأكيفا عبر الكهف، تساءل إن كان هذا هو السبب الذي ضحى من أجله بحياته.

"من أجلنا جميعاً".

هل كان ذلك من أجله أيضاً؟ ما الذي يمكن أن يتغير بالنسبة إليه؟ سيصبح حراً من هذا الجسد يوماً ما، سواء من خلال إعادة إحيائه أو التلاشي، بطريقة أو بأخرى. كان دائماً هناك شيء ينتظره.

راقب زيري أكيفا وهو يغادر، ولم يُفاجأ عندما غادرت كارو بعد فترة وجيزة أيضاً ومن باب آخر، لكنه لم يشك في أنهما سيلتقيان. عاد بأفكاره إلى حفلات أمراء الحرب، وما شاهده وأحس به، وهو مجرد صبي آنذاك، من مكائد البالغين وتعقيداتهم. لكن الأمور الآن قد توضحت له كعين الشمس.

الطريقة التي انحنى بها جسد مادريغال الراقص بعيداً عن الذئب، باتجاه الغريب. وحتى إن لم يكن قد فهم التعقيد الكامل لتلك المكائد الخاصة بالبالغين في ذلك الوقت، إلا أنه شعر بنوع منها—أول إحساس، كأنها رائحة عطر غريبة، مسكرة... ومخيفة.

لم تعد تلك المكائد غامضة بالنسبة إليه، وما زالت رائحتها السامة والمخيفة تفوح، وما إن رأى كارو وأكيفا يغادران، حتى شعر وكأنه عاد إلى طفولته. مستبعداً. متروكاً. ربما سيظل يشعر بهذا الإقصاء معها دائماً، بغض النظر عن عمر الأجساد التي يتقمصانها.

ظهر شخص عند الباب—الذي خرجت منه كارو—وفي لحظةٍ ظن أنها قد عادت، لكنها كانت ليسيث.

لم يدرك زيري أن تلك الأفعى لم تكن هنا مع البقية، وقد لام نفسه لعدم انتباهه لغيابها، فالذئب الحقيقي كان ليعرف إذا كان أي من جنوده مفقوداً. لكن تلاشى لومه بعد أن لاحظ ملامح ليسيث. بدا من تقاسيم وجهها عدم الارتياح والذهول، وبدا جافاً ومليئاً بتعابير قاسية تتراوح بين المكر والوحشية. لكن الآن... بدت مذهولة.

لقد اتسع منخاراها بشكل ملحوظ، ضاغطة على شفتيها بشدة حتى بدتا بلا لون. عيناها، على غير المتوقع، أظهرتا ضعفاً واضحاً رغم بروز كتفيها وحدة ذقنها اللذين يظهران عنفواناً كبيراً. ألقت إليه إيماءة مقتضبة، فنهض، بدافع الفضول، وتوجه نحوها.

الأفعواني الآخر نيسك، رأى كل شيء، فانضم إليهما عند الباب.

سأل زيري:"ما الأمر؟".

خرجت كلماتها مشحونة... وكأنها مستاءة."سيدي، هل فعلت شيئاً ليجعلك غير راضٍ عني؟".

أراد زيري أن يجيب بنعم وأنها فعلت الكثير، لشكه القوي بأنها كانت الخائنة التي كشفت الهامسا لغير الشرعيين، إلا أنها أنكرت ذلك سابقاً،

ولم يكن لديه أي دليل على ذلك. أجاب بهدوء:"ليس على حد علمي. لمَ هذا القلق؟".

ردت ليسيث، بحدة:"هذا المنصب من حقي. لقد انتظرت هذا طويلاً، ولدي خبرة تكتيكية أكبر وأنا أقوى، وعندما يتعلق الأمر بالتسلل، فلا مجال للمقارنة. لكن لم يتم إخباري حتى بما كنت تخطط له".

قاطعها زيري بحيرة:"بما كنت أخطط له؟ عمّ تتحدثين؟".

رمشت ليسيث بعينيها، ثم نظرت إلى نيسك، وعادت بعينيها إليه."مهاجمة السيراف، سيدي. إنه يحدث الآن".

هل شحب وجهه؟ هل لاحظوا تغير لونه؟ ردة فعله هذه ليست في محلها. كان يجب عليه أن يشتعل غضباً ويكشر عن أنيابه في اللحظة التي أدرك فيها أن جنوده لا يتبعون أوامره."لم أخطط لشيء من هذا".

سرعان ما اختفى استياؤها بعد قوله هذا، وفهمت أنه لم يكن يتجاهلها عمداً، عادت إلى طبيعتها الوحشية.

أمرها:"خذيني إلى هناك".

"حاضر، يا سيدي"، ثم استدارت بنعومة أفعى، لتقود الطريق.

تبعها زيري، وخلفه نيسك.

من يكون خلف ما حدث؟ أيمكن أن تكون هي؟ تساءل زيري. أول ظنٍ له أن ليسيث، بسبب حذرها اللاذع، ستكون أول من يشك به في التمرد. هل هي..؟ هل هذا فخ؟ ربما. ومع ذلك، لم يكن لديه خيار سوى أن يتبعها. ربما كان عليه أن يستدعي تين، وخاصة أن الذئبة لم تتبعه من تلقاء نفسها نزلوا عبر الممرات المتعرجة العديدة في الكهوف، بعيداً عن الممرات التي يعرفها. في كل مرة يدورون حول زاوية بمشاعلهم، تقفز أمامهم حشرات كبيرة شاحبة اللون وتهرب فزعاً، ثم تدس نفسها بطريقة تلقائية في شقوق الجدران. رائحة ثقيلة كالمعادن الرطبة تغمر الكهوف، وتضغط على الصدور كأنها رداء ضيق، مثلما كان لحن الرياح. لكن مع تقدمهم، بدأت

روائح جديدة تتسلل من بين الظلال، أضافت جو الغموض إلى جوف العتمة. روائح حيوانات، نفاذة وثقيلة.

مجموعة من الكيميرا مشبعون برائحة اللحم المتفحم ورائحة الشعر المحروق، مما أضاف ضغطاً على معدة زيري إضافة إلى الشعور بضغط الترقب المقلق. أي كيميرا خاض معركة ضد السيراف يعرف تماماً رائحة الجسد المحترق.

حاسة الشم لدى زيري في جسده الجديد أقوى بكثير مما كانت عليه في جسده البشري، وما زال يتعلم كيف يفكك المعلومات التي تقدمها له وكيف يميز بين الروائح المتعددة في العالم. بين العطور أيضاً. خلال أيامه القليلة في هذا الجسد، اكتشف أن الروائح السيئة أكثر من الجيدة، لكن الروائح الجيدة كانت أفضل مما تخيل.

ثمة رائحة الآن، تنساب من بين الروائح الأخرى كخيط ذهبي في نسيج معقد، رقيقة ولكن مشرقة كصوت جرس. "هل هي بهار" تساءل. إنها من النوع الذي يحرق اللسان ويترك خلفه إحساساً بالنقاء.

من كان هناك يا ترى؟ لم يكن زيري متأكداً، لكنه واثق أنه كان سيرافاً. ومع ذلك، طغى على كل شيء حتى على رائحة الكيميرا الواخزة. شعر بتوتر يضغط على قاعدة جمجمته. الخوف. نعم، إنه الخوف.

ماذا يكون – ومن – سيجد أمامه؟

...

تحركت كارو غير مرئية عبر ممرات منزلها القديم. عبرت من مجال الكيميرا إلى مجال السيرافيم. لم تكن تعرف أين تبحث عن أكيفا، لكنها افترضت أنه سيجعل ملاقاته سهلة. على أي حال، تأملت أن تكون محقّة.

كلما اقتربت من مدخل القاعة الرئيسية، ازداد الكهف برودة، وسرعان ما رأت أنفاسها تتشكل كالبخار أمامها. بقي هناك سيراف واحد أخير لتتجاوزه – إنه إليون، حيث بدا مرهقاً ويائساً في حين ظن ألا أحد يراه – حبست

أنفاسها إلى أن أصبح بعيداً عن الأنظار، حتى لا تكشفها سحابة بخار أنفاسها

لم يكن هناك سيرافيم آخرون؛ صاروا كلهم خلفها الآن.

لم يبق سوى أكيفا. باب مفتوح، وها هو أمامها. ينتظر.

للحظة، تجمدت كارو في مكانها. هذه كانت أقرب مسافة لها إليه –
وأول مرة يكونان فيها بمفردهما – منذ... متى؟ منذ اليوم الذي جاء إليها
متنكراً بجانب النهر في المغرب، وأعطاها الوعاء الذي يحتوي على روح إيشا.
لقد قالت له أشياء قاسية في ذلك اليوم – بإنها لم تثق به، يا لها من كذبة
– ولم تتراجع عنها بعد.

لا تزال تحت تأثير التخفي، عبرت من الباب ورأته يرفع رأسه، شاعراً
بوجودها. ارتفعت حرارة في عنقها وهو يتفحصها بنظراته، حتى وإن لم
يستطع رؤيتها. ظهر بغاية الجمال، وغاية التركيز. فشعرت بحرارته تتسلل
إليها، شعرت بشوقه.

سأل، بهدوء شديد:"كازّو؟".

أغلقت الباب خلفها، وتحررت من التخفي.

...

أن تجد مبرراً لغضبها، أعطاها شعوراً ببعض الراحة. حتى وهي
راكعة، وقد أرهقتها الهجمات المستمرة من تعويذات الهامسا المباشرة،
استطاعت ليراز أن تفكر بهدوء، دون عواطف، بأن العالم صار منطقياً ثانيةً.
وهذا ما جعل الوحوش يتركونها بحالها تلك الليلة في العراء، في حين
بقيت بكامل إرادتها.

ينتظرون اللحظة المناسبة.

أربعة جنود. ثلاثة منهم يقفون بأذرع مرفوعة، يهاجمونها بالسحر. أما
الرابع، فقد أمسك بفأس كبير ذي شفرتين.

وطبعاً، هذا لا يشمل الثلاثة الذين سقطوا من بينهم موتى حديثاً، إلى
درجة أن قلوبهم ما زالت تنبض.

"ما كان يجب أن تفعلي ذلك"، قالت قائدة هذه المجموعة الصغيرة من القتلة، وهي تخطو فوق جثث رفاقها، وتبتسم ابتسامة مفترسة. "تين".

لم تكن ليراز تعرف لماذا شعرت بالدهشة عندما أدركت أن مهاجمتها كانت نائبة الذئب الأبيض، الذئبة التابعة لثياغو، لكنها شعرت بالدهشة على أي حال. هل كانت قد بدأت بالفعل تصدق أن الذئب الأبيض قد نال الشرف؟ يا لها من حماقة. تساءلت عن مكانه الآن، ولماذا كان يفوّت "المتعة".

"صدقي أو لا تصدقي"، قالت تِين بلهجة متكاسلة، "لم نكن ننوي قتلك".

"سأختار ألا أصدقك". لقد طاردوها في الظلام، ولم يكن لديها أدنى شك في أن حياتها كانت على المحك.

"آه، لكنه صحيح. أردنا فقط أن نلعب لعبتك".

للحظة، لم تفهم ليراز عمّ تتحدث. كان من الصعب التفكير وسط الصخب والضجيج الناتجين عن السحر، لكن بعد ذلك تذكرت. لعبتها بهدف التعارف. أي منا قتل أياً منكم في الأجساد السابقة.

تعمّق الشعور بالغثيان في أحشائها، ولم يكن بسبب الهامسا وحدها. بالطبع، فكرت. أليس هذا بالضبط ما تخيلت أنه سيحدث؟ كان هذا هو الهدف من اللعبة التي تخيلتها، والتي لم تجد فيها أي ذرة من الفكاهة.

قالت ليراز: "لا تقولي لي. لقد قتلتك مرة. أم كانت أكثر من مرة؟".

قالت تين: "هذا يكفي".

"وماذا الآن؟ هل من المفترض أن أعتذر؟".

ضحكت تين، وتلألأت ابتسامتها.

"نعم عليك الاعتذار. ورغم أنني لا أستطيع تخيلك تقدمين الاعتذارات، فسأكتفي بأخذ أسلحتك بدلاً من ذلك. قد تعيشين حياة طويلة وسعيدة بدونها. ربما لا، لكن هذا شأنك الخاص".

كانت تعني قطع يديها.

"هيا إذاً، افعليها"، قالت ليراز وهي تلفظ كلماتها بازدراء.

ردت تين:"لا داعي للعجلة".

راحت ليراز تضعف مع كل ثانية يوجهون فيها هامساتهم باتجاهها. تلك التعويذات الملعونة. يا لهم من جبناء: أرادوا إضعافها قبل أن يمزقوها.

لم يكن هذا مخططهم، إلا أن مقتل ثلاثة منهم في أقل من دقيقة أجبرهم على الانتقام.

ثلاث جثث. خسارة غاية في الغباء. مجرد رؤيتهم جعلت ليراز تشعر برغبة في الصراخ. لماذا جعلتموني أفعل هذا؟

اقتربت تين، تحيط بها اثنتان من الدراكيند، كائنات بجلد متقشر وأطواق ضخمة من اللحم المغطى بالقشور، تمتد من أعناقهم مثل أطواق نبلاء مشوهة. كانت أيديهم مرفوعة، والتعويذات تدك البؤس في جمجمة ليراز. كل تركيزها انصب على التماسك مع أنها تعرف عدم قدرتها على الصمود طويلاً. قريباً، ستجعلها تلك التعويذات ترتعش عاجزة.

عجز مستفز ومهين، وقاتل.

"الآن"، قالت لنفسها. إذا كان لها أي فرصة للنجاة من هذا، فعليها أن تتحرك.

تساقطت تعويذات الهامسا الثلاث على جسدها كالمطارق الثقيلة.

لكن وسط كل الألم، تسربت إليها فكرة واحدة واضحة: يداي أسلحتي.

اندفعت.

اعترضت تين ليراز وأمسكتها من معصمها. وفي لحظة التلامس، انفجرت التعويذات في جسد ليراز، ناشرة الوهن في أوتارها، ولحمها، وعظامها، وعقلها. موجات عنيفة متتالية اجتاحتها، حرارة بيضاء تحرقها من الداخل، وعجز كامل وكأنه عاصفة تجرف كل شيء في طريقها.

"يا نجوم الآلهة." شعرت ليراز وكأن هذا السحر سيأكلها حية، سيلتهمها حتى تتحول إلى رماد أو إلى لا شيء.

وحين أمسكت تين بمعصمها، كانت يد ليراز الأخرى قد وصلت إلى هدفها. وضعت كفها على صدر تين، وأطلقت صرخة مدوية، مباشرة في وجه الكيميرا، فاشتعلت النار والتهبت.

الشعر الرمادي المتلبد على صدر ذئبة الكيميرا اشتعل بالنيران، وصدرت منه رائحة نفاذة. أعادت ليراز في لحظة إلى مشاهد جثث المحارق في لوراميندي. كادت تفقد تركيزها للحظة، لكنها تشبثت به، ويدها تواصل حرق الفراء وصولاً إلى اللحم.

اتسعت تكشيرة تين، وأطلقت زئيراً هائلاً متوازياً مع زئير ليراز. متواجهتان، والأيدي متشابكة على الأجساد، تصرخان بغضب وألم متبادل، حتى تدخلت أيادٍ أخرى، لتنتزع ليراز وتلقي بها بعنف نحو جدار حجري. الاصطدام كان عنيفاً إلى درجة أن عينيها زاغتا، ووجدت نفسها مستلقية على ظهرها، تكافح لالتقاط أنفاسها.

كانت هذه نهاية فرصتها.

شعرت بأيدٍ تمسك ذراعيها، ثم لمحت وجوه—الدراكيند الاثنين فوقها. فاهاهما فاغران، محمران مرعبان، يصدران صوت هسيسٍ، وتفوح منهما رائحة كريهة. رفعاها بقوة، وأكمامها الطويلة التي علقت بين راحاتهم وجسدها، لم تمنع أيديهم من الإمساك بلحمها.

جلدها الموشوم، مصيرها المريع.

مرة أخرى، وجدت نفسها وجهاً لوجه مع تِين، الذئبة، وعلى وجهها ملامح كراهية مذهلة—خطمها الذئبي مجعد في تكشيرة لا يمكن لأي إنسان أو سيرافيم أن يجاريها في وحشيتها. "لم ننتهِ من اللعبة بعد،" قالت. "أتذكرِك، أيتها الملاك، لكن هل تتذكرينني؟".

ليراز لم تتذكر كل القتلى الذين شمتهم على ذراعيها من رماد نيران المعسكر وسكين ساخن—كانوا في ذاكرتها مجرد ضباب، فكيف ستتذكرهم الآن. كم من الكيميرا الذئبيين قتلتهم ليراز خلال عقود حياتها؟ لا يعلم

ذلك سوى نجوم السماء."لم أقل أبداً إنني سأكون جيدة في هذه اللعبة".

اختنقت الكلمات من حلقها.

"سأعطيكِ تلميحاً"، قالت تِين. كلمة واحدة، خرجت مع زمجرة مفعمة بالكراهية. كانت اسم مكان.

"سافات".

الكلمة شقت ذاكرة ليراز، وسال منها الدم. سافات. كان ذلك منذ زمن طويل، لكنها لم تنسَ—لا القرية، ولا ما حدث خارجها مباشرة. كانت قد دفنت تلك الذكرى بعيداً، وكأنها صفحة ممزقة قد أحرقتها.

لكن لا يمكنك حرق الذكريات.

كانت هناك ذكرى لما فعلته لعدوٍ كان يحتضر منذ زمن بعيد، وذكرى كيف نظر إليها أخواها بعدها لفترة طويلة.

"أهذه أنتِ؟" سمعت نفسها تقول بصوت أجش. لم تكن تنوي التحدث. بسبب قدراتها المنهارة. و... سافاث واحدة من المئات التي روعتهم وقتلتهم من الكيميرا في حياتها، بدا هذا مجرد ضباب، لكن ذلك الحدث لم يكن كغيره. مجرد كلمة سافات، كفيلة بأن تعيد كل شيء.

لكن كان هناك شيء لا يشبهك."لم تكوني أنتِ"، قالت ليراز، وهي تهز رأسها محاولةً أن تستعيد تركيزها."ذلك الجندي كان—".

كانت ستقول بمكر ثعلب، لكن تِين قاطعتها:"ذلك الجندي الذي مات لأول مرة على يديك. لقد دنستِ جسدي البشري، أيتها الملاك. لا يمكنكِ معرفة من نحن بمجرد النظر؟ ليس لديكِ أي فرصة".

"أنتِ محقة"، قالت ليراز، وشعرت أن رأسها مثل دوامة من الزجاج المطحون—تدور، تدور.

"لعبة جديدة"، قالت تِين، وهي تسخر منها."إذا فزتِ، تحتفظين بيديكِ. كل ما عليكِ فعله هو أن تخبريني وظيفة كل واحدة من علاماتكِ".

وتخيلت ليراز نفسها وهي تخبر هازايل بأنها حلت لغز حلمها

المتكرر."كيف قطعت ذراعيها بنفسها؟".

الأمر بسيط. قدّمي الفأس إلى الكيميرا.

لأنه ليس هناك أي احتمال للفوز بهذه اللعبة.

نظرت تِين إلى الوحش الضخم الحامل للفأس وأشارت إليه بالتقدم وهي تقول للدراكيند،"ارفعوا أكمامها".

أطاعوا، وشعرت ليراز فقط بتصلب أحشائها عند رؤيتهم لنقوش جسدها—تِين نفسها ارتبكت عند رؤية العلامات الكاملة التي كانت مخفية—ثم اختفى كل شيء في ظلام مدوٍّ، مثل انهيار جَليدي من الرماد، عندما أمسك الدراكيند بذراعيها العاريتين. أربع أيد من الهامسا تغرس قوتها في لحمها. كان ذلك يعني الموت الرحيم. رأت ليراز التلاشي الذي كانت ستصبحه. مالت نحوه. لا يمكن لأي سيراف أن يتحمل هذا. ستموت دون أن تشعر بموتها. لم تكن تلك نهاية سيئة.

لا رحمة، إذاً. لا بد أن تِين أمرت الدراكيند بأن يبقوها واعية، لأن الانهيار توقف، ووجدت ليراز نفسها تحدق عن قرب في الجلد المشوه حيث طبعت يدها الملتهبة حرقاً على صدر الذئبة. بدا متفحماً، أسود ينزف، والحروق بدأت تتقشر كاشفة عن اللحم الأحمر المتقرح تحتها. مشهد بشع.

"تفضلي"، أمرت تِين بصوت يقطر بالخبث."سأجعل الأمر أسهل عليكِ. ابدئي من النهاية وارجعي إلى الوراء. بالتأكيد تتذكرين الأحدث بينهما".

كان الرد الذي خرج من ليراز همساً ضعيفاً، بالكاد يستحق الرد."لا أريد أن ألعب لعبتكِ"، قالت. شيء ما بداخلها كان ينهار. خفقات قلبها كانت أشبه بقبضات طفل عاجزة. أرادت أن تُنقذ. أرادت أن تكون في أمان.

"لا يهمني ما تريدينه. والرهانات تغيّرت. إذا فزتِ، سأجعل رارك يقوم بقطع نظيف. وإذا خسرتِ..." كشرت بفكّها لتكشف عن أنيابها الصفراء الطويلة، وعضّت بأسلوب مبالغ فيه، مما لم يترك أي شك حول نيتها. قالت:"أقل نظافة. وأكثر متعة".

ثم أمسكت تِين بيدي ليراز وسحبت ذراعيها لتصبحا مشدودتين."لنبدأ بي. أي واحدة، أيتها الملاك الجميلة؟ أي علامة هي لي؟".

"ولا واحدة منها"، شهقت ليراز.

"كاذبة!".

لكنها كانت صادقة. لو كانت ضربة سافاث محفورة كوشم على جسدها، لكانت على أصابعها، لأنها كانت منذ زمن بعيد. لكن في نهاية ذلك اليوم، كان هازايل قد حرص على أن يضع عدة الوشم في يده وينظر إليها—نظرة طويلة وهادئة أكثر مما اعتادت من هاز، وكأن ما فعلته في ذلك اليوم لم يغيرها وحدها، بل غيّره هو أيضاً—ثم دفعها إلى حقيبته قبل أن يدير ظهره لها.

كانت ليراز قد سمعت ذات مرة أن هناك شعوراً واحداً فقط يمكنه، في الذكرى، استعادة القوة الفورية للأصل بالكامل—شعور واحد لا يتلاشى مع الزمن، ويجرك إلى الوراء لعدد من السنوات لتعيش ذلك الإحساس النقي وغير المُخفف، وكأنك تختبره مجدداً.

لم يكن الحب—ليس لديها خبرة في ذلك—ولم يكن الكراهية، أو الغضب، أو السعادة، أو حتى الحزن. ذكريات تلك المشاعر ليست سوى أصداء للشعور الحقيقي. الشعور بالخزي. الخزي لا يتلاشى أبداً، وأدركت ليراز للتو أن هذا هو أساس عواطفها—حالتها المريرة والمتكدرة"الطبيعية"— وأن روحها كانت تربة مسمومة لا يمكن أن ينمو فيها أي شيء جيد.

لا أستطيع أن أتخيل أنك تقدمين الاعتذارات، كانت تِين قد قالت سابقاً، وكانت محقة. لكن ليراز فكرت أنها ستقدم اعتذاراً الآن. كانت ستعتذر عن سافات. إذا كان صوتها لا يزال يخصها. إذا لم يكن يتسرب منها، يرتفع وينخفض وكأنه قد يكون ضحكاً، وقد يكون—لو لم تكن ليراز ولو لم يكن ذلك غير وارد—بكاءً.

كانت ستفقد ذراعيها، سواء بالطريقة النظيفة أو الأقل نظافة، وهنا جاء الضحك: كان ذلك مروعاً، وسادياً، وكان أيضاً، حرفياً، حلماً يتحقق.

30

الاقتراب والملامسة

في البداية، لم يكن هناك أحد.

إلا أنه شعر بوجودها—لم يستطع أكيڤا تأكيد ذلك. لكنه أدرك بأنه ليس وحيداً في القاعة.

بعدها أُغلِق الباب مصدراً صريراً، وسرعان ما امتلأ الهواء بها. ووقفت كارو أمامه كشعاع من الضوء وكأنها تجسيد لأمنية طال انتظارها.

قال لنفسه: لا تتأمل بشيء. أنت لا تعرف لماذا جاءت. اقتربت قليلاً، إلى درجة أن جلده نبض بالحياة، ويداه، اللتان تحملان ذكرياتٍ خاصةً— الحرير، النبض، الخفقان—وكأن لهما إرادة مستقلة. وضع يديه خلف ظهره ليشغلهما بأي شيء آخر غير الامتداد نحوها، وهو أمر غير مقدور عليه بالطبع. فقط لأنها نظرت إليه—تلك النظرة تحديداً، راح يجادل نفسه، وكأنها تخلت عن محاولتها لتجنب النظر—ذلك لا يعني أنها تريد منه شيئاً أكثر من هذا التحالف المؤقت.

"مرحباً"، قالت بصوت خافت وخفضت نظرها، احمرّت وجنتاها خجلاً، وفي تلك اللحظة خسر أكيڤا رهانه ضد الأمل.

لقد احمرت خجلاً... يا إلهي، كم هي جميلة.

"مرحباً"، رد بصوت خافت، خشن، والآن تجاوز أمله حدوده. تمنى لو تقولها مرة أخرى. فربما تلك الـ"مرحبا الخجولة" تذكرها بمعبد إيلاي، حين خلعا أقنعة المهرجان ورأيا بعضهما البعض لأول مرة منذ معركة بولفينش.

مرحباً، كانا قد قالاها حينها، وكأنهما يتلوان تعويذة همساً. مرحباً، نُطقت مثل وعد. مرحباً، نفساً مقابل نفس. النفس الأخير قبل قبلتهما الأولى.

"اممم"، ملقية نظرة سريعة على عينيه قبل أن تُبعدها بسرعة مرة أخرى، ويزداد احمرار وجهها."مرحباً".

اقتربت أكثر، ما جعل منسوب الحذر يرتفع. راقبها تخطو خطوة، ثم أخرى، وأخيرا ها هما وحدهما. يمكنهما الحديث الآن، بعيداً عن أعين المتربصين. مجرد وجودها هنا، كان يعني شيئاً. ومع وهج نظراتهما، لم يستطع أكيفا كبح أمله بأن شيئاً ما... يعني كل شيء.

أن تمتلك الأمل، كان كأن تلقي بنفسك من فوق هاوية، وتضع الحبل في يدها. ولها القرار في تركه إن أرادت.

راحت تتلفت حولها، رغم أن المكان خالٍ إلا من طاولة حجرية طويلة في الوسط وعدد قليل من الرفوف التي تحمل شموعاً قديمة جداً. كان اللوح، كما افترض أكيفا، غير اعتيادي. كان مقطوعاً بدقة أكبر من بقية الأسطح الصخرية هنا. أملس، زواياه الحادة نادرة في جوٍ مليءٍ بالمنحنيات.

"أتذكر هذه الغرفة"، قالت كارو بحنين، وكأنها تتحدث عن ذكريات بعيدة."هنا كان يتم تجهيز الموتى للدفن".

شعر أكيفا ببعض القلق، فقد قضى ساعات مستلقياً فوقها غارقاً في أحلامه. استلقى عليها ككثير من الجثث قبله."لم أكن أعلم. أرجو ألا يكون هذا نذير شؤم". مررت أطراف أصابعها برفق على اللوح الحجري للطاولة. أدارت ظهرها له. راقب أكيفا كتفيها وهما يرتفعان وينخفضان مع تنفسها

وشعرها الأزرق المضفور كلهب في قلب شعلة. لم يكن مرتباً؛ خصلات ناعمة خرجت عن نسقها، لتتناثر كالزغب على عنقها. خصل من الأزرق مدسوسة خلف أذنيها، خصلة شاردة تتدلى برفق على خدها.

شعرت أصابعه برغبة عارمة في إزاحة هذه الخصلة بلطف والشعور بدفء بشرتها.

"كنا نتحدى بعضنا للدخول إلى هنا والاستلقاء". ثم أضافت بنبرة هادئة:"عندما كنا صغاراً".

دارت ببطء حول الطاولة ثم وقفت أمامه من الطرف المقابل، وكأن الطاولة تقف حاجزاً بينهما. رفعت نظرها إلى السقف المرتفع، الذي اتصلت ذروته في المنتصف بفتحة أشبه بمدخنة.

"هذا من أجل الأرواح كي تنطلق إلى السماء ولا تبقى حبيسة داخل الجبل. كنا نقول إنه إذا نمت هنا، ستظن روحك أنك متّ، وستصعد إلى السماء". سمع أكيفا نبضة ابتسامة في صوتها قبل أن يراها تومض على وجهها، نبرة خفيفة وسريعة، لكنها حنونة.

"مرة تظاهرتُ أنني نمت وفقدت روحي، وأجبرت كل الأطفال الآخرين على مساعدتي في البحث عنها. بحثنا عنها طوال اليوم، في كل مكان، عبر القمم". تحدثت مع ابتسامة هذه المرة."أمسكت بأحد العناصر الهوائية وتظاهرت بأنها روحي. يا له من مسكين. كم كنت شقية صغيرة".

أدرك أكيفا أن هذا الوجه ما زال أرضاً غامضة بالنسبة إليه، وتلك الابتسامة جعلتها تبدو أكثر غرابة. إذا كانت معرفته بمادريغال لشهر، فهو بالكاد عرف كارو لليلتين؟ أو ربما ليلة واحدة قد قضى معظمها نائماً. أما في لقاءاتهما القليلة الباقية، فكل ما رآه منها هو غضبها، ودمارها، وخوفها الأمر مختلفاً تماماً الآن. بابتسامتها هذه، كانت مشرقة مثل ضوء القمر. ولا يتعلق الأمر فقط بوجهها الجديد. حيث ظل يعاملها وكأنها مادريغال لكن في جسد آخر، لكنها الآن أكثر من ذلك. لقد عاشت حياة أخرى منذ أن

عرفها - وفي عالم آخر تماماً. كيف يمكن أن تكون قد تغيرت؟ لا علم له. لكنه سيعلم يوماً. شعر بألم الاشتياق وكأنه ثقب انفتح في صدره. وكل ما أراده من تلك العوالم أن يبدأ من جديد ويقع في حب كارو.

قالت، وهي لا تزال غارقة في ذكرياتها البعيدة:"لقد كانت أياماً حلوة".

سألها أكيفا، محاولاً ممازحتها:"كيف تظاهرتِ بأنك فقدت روحك؟" يقصد حين كانت طفلة تلعب، لكنه استدرك بينه وبين نفسه: من يعلم؟ فهي تخون كل ما تؤمن به. تقتل وتستمر في القتل حتى لا يبقى أحد.

تلاشت ابتسامة كارو بعد أن لمحت تعابير وجهه. ظلّت صامتة للحظات تنظر في عينيه. أدرك أكيفا في تلك الأثناء أن عليه تعلم الكثير عن عينيها أيضاً. عينا مادريغال كانتا بنيتين دافئتين، أشبه بالصيف والأرض. أما عينا كارو فهما سوداوين متلألئتين، كنجوم في سماء ليل حالك. وبالطريقة التي نظرت بها إليه، اخترقت عيناها عمق روحه، ولم تكونا مجرد حدقتين واسعتين، بل ليلتان حالكتان، مربكتان.

قالت بصوت هادئ:"أستطيع أن أخبرك كيف تتظاهر بفقدان روحك لكن عليك استعادتها أولاً"، وعرف أكيفا أنها لا تتحدث عن لعبة. "أن تنقذ أرواحاً"، قالت."وتدع لنفسك بأن تحلم مرة أخرى". انخفض صوتها ليصبح همساً خفيفاً:"لا بد أن تغفر".

ساد الصمت. الأنفاس محبوسة. القلوب تخفق. شعر أكيفا وكأن العالم يدور به، محاولاً دفعه إلى الأمام: ليقترب منها ويلمسها، ليحقق السكينة، أو أي حركة يمكن أن تقوده إلى تحقيق ذلك. نظرت إلى الأرض مرة أخرى، وقد عادت إليها لمحة من الخجل."أنت أعلم مني. أنا مبتدئة".

قال لها:"أنت؟ لا، لم تفقدي روحك أبداً".

"لقد فقدتُ شيئاً ما. بينما كنتُ تنفذ الكيميرا، حين كنتُ أصنع الوحوش لثياغو. وهي نفس الأفعال التي كنت أكرهك بسببها، لكنني لم أتمكن من رؤيتها...".

قال أكيفا:"إنه الحزن. الغضب. يحولنا إلى الشيء الذي نحتقره".
وأضاف:"أنا الشيء الذي كنتِ تحتقرينه. هل ما زلت كذلك؟". هو الوقود
لكل ما فعله شعبانا ببعضهما البعض منذ البداية. هذا ما يجعل السلام
يبدو مستحيلاً. كيف يمكنك أن تلوم أحداً على رغبته في قتل من قتل
أحبائه؟ كيف يمكنك أن تلوم الناس على ما يفعلونه في حزنهم؟".

بمجرد أن نطق هذه الكلمات، أدرك أكيفا أنها بدت وكأنه يبرر دائرة حزنه
المدمرة وما ألحقه بشعبها. استولى عليه شعور بالخجل."لم أقصد... لم
أقصد نفسي. ما فعلته، يا كارو، أعلم أنني لن أتمكن أبداً من التكفير عنه".
سألته بحدة، وكأنها تبحث في عينيه عن الحقيقة خلف خجله:"هل تؤمن
بذلك حقاً؟".

هل كان يؤمن بذلك حقاً؟ أم إنه كان غارقاً في الشعور بالذنب إلى
درجة أنه لم يستطع الاعتراف بأنه كان يأمل في أنه، في يوم ما، بطريقة ما،
يستطيع التكفير؟ هل كان يأمل أنه في يوم ما سيشعر بأنه قد فعل من
الخير أكثر مما فعل من الشر، وأنه بوجوده في هذا العالم لم يكن سبباً في
انحداره نحو الأسوأ؟ هل التكفير، ميزان الحياة؟

إن كان كذلك، فقد يكون الأمر ممكناً. ربما، لو عاش أكيفا سنوات طويلة،
محاولاً التكفير، قد يتمكن من إنقاذ أرواح أكثر مما هدر. أدرك أنه لا يؤمن
بذلك، وهو يواجه حدة سؤال كارو. قال:"نعم، أؤمن بذلك. لا يمكنك التكفير
عن إزهاق روح بإنقاذ روح أخرى. أي فائدة يمكن أن يجنيها الموتى من ذلك؟".

قالت كارو:"الموتى." وتابعت بنبرة متأملة:"لدينا الكثير من الموتى
بيننا، لكن من سوء أفعالنا، قد يظن المرء أنهم جثث تتشبث بأرجلنا، بدلاً
من أن تكون أرواحاً تحررت إلى العلى". رفعت بصرها نحو المدخنة التي
تعلوهما، وكأنها تتخيل الأرواح التي عبرت من خلالها في زمن مضى.

تابعت:"لقد رحلوا، لم يعودوا يشعرون بالألم، لكننا نحمل ذكراهم
معنا، نرتكب أسوأ الأفعال باسمهم، وكأن هذا ما يريدونه، أن ننتقم لهم؟

لا أستطيع التحدث باسم جميع الموتى، لكنني أعلم أن هذا ليس ما أردته لكَ عندما متَّ. وأعلم أن هذا ليس ما أراده بريمستون لي". نظرتها لا تزال حادة، ثاقبة، داكنة كليل حالك. شعر أكيفا وكأنها تتهمه، بالطبع كانت تريده أن يحمل حلمهما إلى الأمام، لا أن يجد طريقاً لتدمير شعبها. لذلك، عندما قالت:"أكيفا، لم أشكرك يوماً على جلبك روح إيثا لي. أنا... أنا آسفة على ما قلته لك حينها—" أصابه الذعر.

فكرة أن تعتذر له كانت مرعبة.

"لا". ابتلع ريقه بصعوبة."لم يكن هناك شيء قلته لي لم أستحقه، بل أكثر من ذلك". هل كان يرى الشفقة في عينيها؟ أم الاستياء؟"هل أنت مصمم على ألا أغفر لكَ؟".

هز رأسه وقال:"لا أفعل شيئاً لأجلي يا كارو أو لأجل الأمل في الغفران أو أي شيء آخر".

تحت وطأة نظرتها السوداوية العميقة، كان عليه أن يسأل نفسه: هل هذا حقاً صحيح؟ ربما نعم، وربما... لا. مهما حاول ألا يتمسك بالأمل، كان الأمل يطفو على السطح، بإصرار. لم تكن لديه سيطرة على ذلك أكثر من سيطرته على همس الرياح. لكن هل هذا هو السبب وراء أفعاله؟ هل كان من أجل رضاها؟ لا. حتى لو كان يعلم تماماً أن كارو لن تغفر له أبداً، ولن تحبه مرة أخرى، فإنه سيظل يفعل كل ما في وسعه — ما يتجاوز قدرته لإعادة بناء العالم من أجلها.

حتى لو شاهدها برفقة الذئب الأبيض؟

لكن... لم يكن يعلم تماماً أن الأمل قد انتهى. ليس بعد.

أنا أسامحكَ. أحبك. أريدك في نهاية كل هذا. الحلم، السلام، وأنت.

هذا ما كانت كارو ترغب في قوله، أو سماعه. لم ترد أن تسمع أنه قد تخلى عن الأمل فيها، وليس مجرد السلام، بل أن يكونا معاً في هذا السلام. هل تقطع الحلم على يديه إلى أجزاء ليتحول إلى حطب؟ أم هي فعلت ذلك؟

هل انتهى أمر الحلم في النيران بالفعل؟ قالت أخيراً:"أنا أصدقك".

لم يكن هناك أمل لنفسه. كان ذلك نبيلاً، ولكنه كان قاتماً أيضاً، ولم يكن القناة التي تحتاجها كلماتها غير المنطوقة. كانت تلك الكلمات ثقيلة بداخلها، وتتشبث بها بشدة.

كيف يمكن للمرء أن يلقي بعبارة"أحبك" في الهواء هكذا؟ إنها بحاجة إلى ذراعين تتهيآن شوقاً لالتقاطها. على الأقل كلمة"أحبك" التي لم تنطقها كارو ولم تضطر إلى ذلك. بعد شهور من سحقها لهذه الكلمة في لجة غضبها والتحايل عليها حتى فقدت شكلها الطبيعي، لم تكن قادرة على أن تفجرها هكذا، كما لم تكن قادرة على لمس وجه أكيفا وتقبيله.

تقبيله. بدا ذلك وكأنه أمر بعيد المنال بملايين الأميال.

عيناها تؤديان تلك الرقصة المترددة مرة أخرى، ترميان نظرات خاطفة، كأنها تأخذ لقطات مصورة لوجهه، ثم تكسر نظرها مرة أخرى على الأرض أو على يديها. تحاول أن تحتفظ بكل اللمحة في عقلها. لون بشرته الذهبية، شفتاه الممتلئتان، تعابيره المثيرة، و... التقهقر في عينيه. كانت عيناه تتجهان نحوها مثل أشعة الشمس، قبل أن تنسحبا عنها مترددة وحذرة. كانت كارو ترغب في أن تشعر بدفء الشمس مرة أخرى. ولكن عندما رفعت عينيها عن يديها المضطربتين، كان أكيفا ينظر إلى اللوح الحجري.

وما بينهما، قد يظن المرء أن هذه الطاولة كانت تحفة أثرية مذهلة.

حسناً. لم تكن عبارة"أحبك" الشيء الوحيد الذي جاءت لتقوله. أخذت نفساً عميقاً، وقررت المتابعة.

"أحتاج إلى أن أخبركَ بشيء".

رفع أكيفا رأسه مرة أخرى. فوراً، لسماع نبرة جديدة في صوت كارو جعلته يشعر بالتوتر. ترددها، الاهتزاز في صوتها. لم يعد بحاجة إلى النضال لإبقاء الأمل بعيداً. الأمل قد تخلى عنه.

ماذا ستقول؟ أنها مع الذئب الآن. أن التحالف كان خطأ.

أن الكيميرا سيرحلون. وأنه لن يراها مرة أخرى أبداً.

أراد أن يقاطعها ويقول، لدي ما أخبرك به أيضاً، كي يمنعها من قول ما تريد قوله. أراد أن يخبرها عن قوته السحرية الجديدة، التي لم يختبرها بعد، ويطلب مساعدتها. وهذا ما يأمله، إذا وقفت معه فعلاً. أراد أن يخبرها بما جعله ممكناً—لجيوشهما، حتى وإن لم يكن لهما. الأشياء تتغير. يمكن تغييرها، من قبل أولئك الذين لديهم الإرادة. حتى العوالم، ربما.

قالت كارو :"الأمر يتعلق بثياغو"، شعر أكيڤا بقشعريرة النهاية. بالطبع إنه الذئب. عندما رآهما متقاربين، يضحكان، أحس بذلك، لكن جزءاً من عقله أصر على إنكار ذلك—حتى التفكير فيه لا يُحتمل—ثم، عندما نظرت إلى ثياغو بتلك الطريقة، كان قد أمل أن...

قاطعت كارو شروده:"ما تظنه غير صحيح"، وشعر أكيڤا بما سيأتي بعد ذلك. واستعد للألم.

همست:"لقد قتلتُه".

"مهلاً... ماذا؟".

"قتلتُ ثياغو. إنه ليس هو. أعني، ليست روحه". أخذت نفساً عميقاً، وكأنها تسحب الهواء بصعوبة، ثم تابعت بسرعة:"روحه رحلت. لقد انتهى. لقد كرهتُ أن أتركك تظن أنني... وهو ... لم أكن لأستطيع أن أسامحه أبداً، أو..." نظرت إليه بسرعة، وكأنها قرأت أفكاره:"أو أضحك معه. ألم يكن من الممكن أن يكون هناك سلام أو تحالف لو بقي حياً؟ أبداً. كان سيقتلك أنت وليراز في القصر".

"انتظري"، قال أكيڤا محاولاً استيعاب ما تقوله."انتظري". ما الذي تقولينه؟ كلماتها لم تستقر في ذهنه بشكل منطقي. الذئب مات؟ الذئب مات، ومن كان يتجول الآن مدعياً هذا اللقب... لم يكن هو. حدّق أكيڤا في كارو. الفكرة كانت تدور في رأسه. لم يكن يعرف حتى ما هي الأسئلة التي يجب أن يطرحها.

قالت:"أردت إخبارك، لكن كان عليّ أن أكون حذرة. فكل شيء هش جداً. لا أحد يعلم. فقط إيسّا وتين... إذا اكتشف بقية الكيميرا هذا الأمر، سنفقدهم هكذا". وفرقعت بأصابعها.

أكيفا لا يزال يحاول استيعاب الفكرة.

قالت:"لم يكونوا ليتبعوا أحداً سوى ثياغو. كنا بحاجة إليه. هذا الجيش بحاجة إليه، وشعبنا أيضاً، لكن... كنا بحاجة إلى نسخة أفضل منه".

وتذكر أكيفا انطباعه عن الذئب الذي تفاوض معه حول هذا التحالف. ذكي، وقوي، وعاقل. ظن شيئاً في ذلك الوقت، ولكن لم يكن ليتخيل هذا. أخيراً، بدأت التفاصيل تتجمّع في رأسه. بطريقة ما، قامت كارو بوضع روح أخرى في جسد الذئب.

سألها:"من؟ من هو؟".

موجة من الحزن لفحت وجهها."إنه زيري.. الكيرين الذي أنقذتَ حياته". الكيرين الشاب، آخر أفراد قبيلته. إذاً لم يمت."لكن... كيف؟" سألها أكيفا، وهو يحاول تخيّل سلسلة الأحداث التي أدت إلى هذا الوضع.

صمتت كارو للحظة، وعيناها شاردتين. ثم قالت:"ثياغو هاجمني". رفعت يدها لتلمس خدها الذي كان منتفخاً ومتورماً عندما طار إليها أكيفا في المغرب، هو وليراز يحملان جثة هازايل بينهما. كانت قد شُفيت تقريباً الآن. بدا وكأنها على وشك أن تقول المزيد، لكنها توقفت. ضمت شفتيها لتكتم ارتجافة، وتذكر أكيفا غضبه الشديد عندما رآها مصابة بسبب تلك الوحشية. قبضته تذكرت ذلك، وقلبه وأحشاؤه أيضاً تذكرا، ذلك المزيج الغريب بين الحنان والرعب الذي رآه بين كارو والذئب في تلك الليلة في القصر، وأخيراً، بدأ كل شيء يتضح.

لكن ذلك لم يواسه.

تابعت:"لقد هاجمني وقتلته. ولم أكن أعرف ماذا أفعل. كنت أعلم أن الآخرين سيجبرونني على إعادته إلى الحياة لو عرفوا، ولم أستطع تحمل ذلك.

فالأمور كانت سيئة، تصور كيف ستكون بعد ذلك؟ لم أعرف ماذا سأفعل... توقفت عن الكلام.

ثم اتسعت عيناها فجأة، مركزة عليه بحدة. ثم ابتسمت. لم تكن ابتسامة مشرقة كابتساماتها تلك، بل من نوع آخر تماماً، قالت:"بقدر ما فكرت في ذلك، لم أدرك حتى هذه اللحظة أن كل شيء يصب عندك".

"أنا؟" سأل بدهشة.

"أنتَ من جلب لي إيسّا وزيري. لولا فضلك، لما كان لدي أي حلفاء، ولا أي فرصة".

مرة أخرى، أثقلت كلماتها—وامتنانها—روح أكيڤا بإحساس عميق بالخجل."لو لم أكن أنا يا كارو، لكان لديك الكثير من الحلفاء". الكثير. كم عدد الجثث التي أثقلت هذه الكلمات؟ لوراميندي. الآلاف والآلاف.

قالت:"توقف عن قول ذلك". ثم أضافت:"أكيڤا. ما أقصده هو الغفران. إنه السبيل الوحيد للمضي قدماً. عندما كان ثياغو لا يزال الذئب، حاولت إقناعه أن طريقه يقود إلى الموت. لكنه لم يكن يسمعني. لم يستطع. لقد ذهب بعيداً جداً. وكان لساني يتعثر بكلماتك وأنا أجادله، وكنت أعرف أنك، مهما ذهبت بعيداً، ستعود. وكان ذلك سبباً في عودتي أنا أيضاً".

كلماته؟ أكيڤا لم يكن لديه أي كلمات الآن. كل هذا كان بعيداً جداً عما كان يخشى أن تخبره به، إلى درجة أنه لم يستطع استيعاب الأمر.

قالت:"أنتَ قلت إن الأمر يعتمد علينا، إذا كان المستقبل سيضم الكيميرا أم لا". وتابعت:"ولم تكن تلك مجرد كلمات. لقد أنقذت حياة زيري. لو لم تفعل، لما كنا هنا الآن. كنت ستكون ميتاً، وأنا... كنت سأكون للذئب...". لم تكمل جملتها. مرة أخرى، ظلت نظرتها مظللة بظل من الرعب، تاركة لأكيڤا تخيل كلمتي—ثياغو هاجمني—وما تعنيانه.

اشتعلت نيران غضبه بشدة حتى كادت تعميه. اضطر إلى دفعها جانباً. ثياغو لم يعد موجوداً ليتم عقابه. وهذا ما زاد غضبه.

قال:"لم أكن هناك لأحميك. ما كان يجب أن أتركك معه أبداً".

قاطعت كارو كلامه قائلة:"أنا حميت نفسي. لكن بعد ذلك احتجت إلى المساعدة، وكان زيري هناك، والآن نحن هنا، جميعنا. هذا ما أحاول أن أقوله".

غادرها الرعب؛ صار اللمعان في عينيها دموعاً، والابتسامة على شفتيها امتناناً، وشعر أكيفا بموجة من الكراهية لذاته عندما وجد نفسه يتساءل لمن كل تلك الدموع والامتنان.

استذكر مرة أخرى نظرة الحنان التي مرت بينها وبين الذئب في القصر، وتذكر كيف كانا يقفان معاً ويضحكان في اليوم السابق.

يا نجوم السماء. كان من الممكن أن يكون ميتاً الآن لو كان الذئب هو ثياغو الحقيقي، ومع ذلك ظل قلقاً بشأن من قد تحب كارو؟ هذا"ثياغو العاقل، القوي، الذكي"، هذا الكيرين البطولي وأقرب حليف لكارو. إنه تهديداً أكبر لآماله من ذلك المجنون القاتل؟

هناك جيوش على أهبة الاستعداد للطيران، وهو هنا قلق بشأن من قد تحب كارو؟ تابعت:"لكن حتى هذا ليس كل شيء. لقد جلبت لي إيشا، ولا يمكنك أن تتخيل ما جلبته معها... يا أكيفا، لقد أحدث هذا فرقاً كبيراً". أشرقت عيناها، ولمعان سوادهما عكس وهج نيران جناحيه. "إنه... ليس الخلاص بالكامل، لكنه بداية. أو سيكون كذلك، عندما نتمكن من الوصول إلى هناك".

ثم أخبرته عن الكاتدرائية.

حجم الأخبار... جعله عاجزاً عن الكلام، فتبددت كل مخاوفه الصغيرة.

كان لدى بريمستون كاتدرائية تحت المدينة—لم يعثر عليها أكيفا عندما كان يتجول في ذهول بين الأنقاض، فقد كانت مدفونة، ومداخلها منهارة ومختفية. وفيها تسكن الأرواح. أرواح لا تُعد ولا تُحصى. أطفال، نساء.

أرواح الآلاف من الكيميرا الذين لم يفقدوا الأمل بعد في العودة. أكيفا كان قد أخبر كارو في المغرب، أنه سيفعل أي شيء—أنه سيموت لأجل

كل كيميرا إذا كان ذلك سيعيدهم. قال ذلك في يأس وهو يعتقد أن كلماته فارغة، وأنه لا يوجد شيء يمكن أن يفعله ليثبت أنه يعنيها.

قال على الفور:"دعيني أساعدك".

ثم أضاف بصوت مفعم بالإلحاح:"كارو... أرجوك. هناك الكثير من الأرواح، لا يمكنك القيام بذلك وحدك".

هل قالت إن هذا ليس تكفيراً؟ لكنه الآن أقرب بكثير مما تصور. ويرتبط بما يريده أكثر من أي شيء في حياته؟

لم تكن مشاعر العار التي كانت تلاحق أكيفا هذه المرة قادرة على الوصول إليه. كان يريد ما أراده دائماً، وكان عليه أن يعترف بذلك، بغض النظر عن مخاوفه وهواجسه. سواء كانت تحبّه، أو تحب الذئب، أو لم تحب أحداً، سيعرف الحقيقة. قال لها:"كل ما أريده هو أن أكون بجانبك، أساعدك. وإذا استمر الأمر إلى الأبد، فليكن، طالما أن الأبدية معك".

الطاولة الحجرية تفصل بينهما، حاجز مادي، لكن لم يكن هناك حاجز أمام ابتسامتها التي ردت عليه بها. ابتسامة جديدة تماماً، وأكيفا أدرك أنه يستطيع أن يقضي ألف سنة معها، يكتشف أنواعاً جديدة من الابتسامات. هذه الابتسامة لم يستطع مقاومتها، حلوة مثل الموسيقى وثقيلة مثل الدموع. هي كلها، كل توترها، وكل حذرها وترددها، يذوب نحو الضوء. هذه الابتسامة هي قلبها، إنها له.

قالت بصوت خافت:"حسناً". يا لها من كلمة بسيطة، لكنها ساطعة وممتلئة، وكأنها شيء ما، باستطاعته أن يمد يده إليه ويمسكه.

حسناً. أيمكنه مساعدتها؟ إنها"حسناً" إلى الأبد؟ إذاً حسناً.

أهذه النهاية. أم البداية؟ لو أن بإمكانهما التحليق معاً الآن إلى لوراميندي. ولتكن الأبدية هذه اللحظة. لكن بالطبع، الأمر ليس بهذه البساطة. لكن كارو تابعت كلامها، وهذه المرة كانت كلماتها مليئة بالأشواك.

"إن عشنا إلى ذلك الحين".

31

نقيض البقاء

وقف زيري في المدخل، وبنظرة خاطفة أدرك الوضع كاملاً.

ثلاثة من جنوده كانوا ممددين عند قدميه: أورا، سهيد، وفيس. أجسادٌ مهدورة، ألمٌ ضائع، ودماءٌ مسفوحة تخضب الأرض. أما من بين من بقي على قيد الحياة، بدا رارك، الأضخم بينهم، بفأسه الكبير الذي يلمع بخفوت في الظلام، عينا زيري ركزتا على ليراز مباشرةً. نيران جناحيها راحت تخبو—تخبو إلى درجة الموت—لكنها بقيت أكثر الأشياء بريقاً في الغرفة. كانت ترتجف بشدة، ووجهها شاحب كالشمع، وعيناها فارغتان، وقد انحسرت الحياة منهما، لكنها ظلت... تضحك؟ ربما تبكي؟ صوت رهيب، مشوش، غير مفهوم.

محاطة بالكيميرا، مكبلة بأيديهم، شدة قبضاتهم أبقتها واقفة، تُبقيها واقفة لكنها تقتلها في آن معاً.

هل يمكن للسيرافيم أن يموت من لمسة الهامسا؟ بنظرة واحدة على ليراز، أدرك زيري أن الجواب نعم. لكن لم تكن تلك الطريقة التي يعتزمون

فيها قتلها. أمسكوا بذراعيها ممدودتين أمامها، وفي تلك اللحظة، ظن زيري أنه فهم ما كانوا ينوون فعله.

رارك. الفأس. يريدون قطع ذراعيها.

الفأس على كتف رارك العريض، و... الحقيقة بدأت تتضح من بقايا الأصوات والصور والروائح. الزمجرة. اللعاب المتساقط من الأنياب الصفراء، ورائحة النصر العفنة."تِين".

الحقيقة التي صعقت زيري كلكمة هي تلك الكلمة، التي كادت أن تفقده أنفاسه."تِين".

من بين كل الجنود الذين تحت إمرته... شريكته في الخطايا، شريكته في المؤامرة. الوحيدة التي تعرف أسراره.

كانت على وشك الانقضاض. ورغم أن جسدها بدا بشرياً أكثر من الآخرين، فقد بدا ظهرها محدباً، فوق رأسها المنخفض، والفرو يكسو كتفيها المنتصبين كالذئب، وصوت زمجرتها وحشياً، وغرائزياً، يشعر به من يسمعه. في الغرفة تفوح رائحة الدماء والأمعاء المحترقة، وآخرة، خانقةً، أقرب إلى الموت. جثث وانتقام لا رجعة عنه.

وزيري أدرك ما كانت"تِين"—"هاكسايا"—تخطط لفعله.

"توقفي". أتى صوت الذئب الأبيض، سلساً وبارداً كالحديد، لكنه يخفي رعباً موجهاً لزيري وحده. هذا المشهد لم يكن ليرعب الذئب الأبيض، الذي مزق الملائكة بأسنانه الحادة من قبل. وبعد أن التفتت تِين باتجاهه، لم يفهم زيري مصدر رعبه العميق الذي شعر به في تلك اللحظة.

زيري لم يقتل بأسنانه، بل قاتل جنباً إلى جنب مع الكيميرا، قتلوا بمناقيرهم ومخالبهم وقرونهم وذيولهم الحادة، وبأي سلاح آخر استطاعوا استخدامه.

أمام قوة السيرافيم الساحقة، كل ما يهم هو البقاء على قيد الحياة. لكن الأمر معهم ليس أكثر من نقيض البقاء.

هذا يضع كل شيء على المحك، ما عدا مكر تين.

لأنه كان مكر تين، تجمد زيري في مكانه، بينما استدار كل من رارك وأتباع الدراكيند نحوه، والتفّ حوله نيسك وليسيث. لأنه كان مكر تين، لم يكن يعرف ماذا يقول. شعر بنظرات هاكسايا ترصده من خلف عيني الذئبة الصفراء، ولم تكن في تلك النظرات أيّ رهبة، بل نظرات تفيض بالاحتقار الماكر والمتمرّد.

تحدّته بنظراتها، وكأنها تقول:"تجرأ على معاقبتي، وسترى".

محتال.

خفق قلبه بعنف. حاول أن يُبطئ نبضاته. كان الناجا قادرين على قراءة حرارة الجسد، كالثعابين؛ لذا استطاع نيسك وليسيث استشعار اضطرابه، وثياغو"الذئب" لم يكن ليقع ضحية الاضطراب أبداً. أجبر زيري على التزام تعبير الذئب الافتراضي: الهدوء البارد، والتقييم الغامض بنصف عينيه المفتوحتين.

سأل بهدوء قاتل:"ما معنى هذا، يا ملازم؟".

ظهر على وجه رارك علامة من الدهشة الخفيفة، واستدار أتباع الدراكيند، ويول وأغويلال، بنظرات ملثمة إلى تين. من الواضح أنها أخبرتهم أن هذه كانت أوامر قائدهم، ولم يكن لديهم سبب للشك في كلامها. فهي كانت نائبته، الملازم الأكثر ثقة لديه.

ليس بعد الآن.

"هذا انتقام". قالت تين من دون أن تضيف"سيدي". واعتبر ذلك استخفافاً صارخاً، بل رسالة تحذير.

"هذه الملاك شريرة. انظر إلى ذراعيها".

نظر إليهما، وشعر بالغثيان—من حصيلتها المذهلة، لكن أيضاً من معاناتها. لم يكن يعرف ليراز بالطبع. إنها جميلة، ولمَ لا؟ معظم السيرافيم كانوا كذلك.

إلا أنها أيضاً عدوانية وسريعة الغضب، وبكامل قوتها تضاهي تين في شراستها. لكنه رآها محطمة ومفجوعة من قبل، تحمل شقيقها الميت بين ذراعيها، من دون كل تلك الشراسة، بدت فتاة هشة، منكسرة. كما رأى فيها أشياء أخرى أيضاً.

بالعودة إلى القصبة، لدهشته، كانت تين قد سألت عنه—عنه هو، "زيري"—بطريقةٍ أظهرت بوضوح أنها... لاحظت غيابه. مجرد معرفتها بوجوده أصلاً كان مفاجأة له، وعندما أخبرها أن الجندي الكيرين قد مات، رأى—وكان واثقاً مما رآه—وميضاً من الحزن في عينيها، ظهر واختفى بسرعة، كشيء أفلت للحظة ثم أُعيد احتجازه.

بالطبع، هذا لم يكن السبب الذي جعله يمنع جنوده من قتلها أو تشويهها في هذا الكهف النائي—بل أسباب أكبر وأقل شخصنة من ذلك بكثير. لكن السبب وراء شعور الغضب الذي تصاعد في داخله، بارداً كالبرودة التي تخيلها لغضب الذئب الحقيقي، وسريعاً في إخماد اضطرابه تحت طبقة من العزم الثابت الذي لا يلين. عاد نبض قلبه إلى وتيرة هادئة وثقيلة كضربات مطرقة.

"أطلقوا سراحها". قال بلامبالاة وبنظرة باردة تجاهها. ابيضت عيناها كلياً، تقلبتا إلى الأعلى تحت رموشها المرتجفة ما بين الموت والحياة-"وإلا سبق السيف العذل".

أطلق ويول وأغويلال قبضتيهما عنها على الفور، وانهارت متكئةً على الجدار، لم تسقط لأن تين كانت لا تزال تمسك برسغيها وكأنها تتحداه بتجاهل أوامره أمام الجميع.

"العذل؟" سألت ببراءة مصطنعة مع مسحة من السخرية اللاذعة. "وما العذل يا... سيدي؟".

نطقها لكلمة "سيدي" كان أسوأ من عدم قولها، إهانة صريحة لم يكن الذئب ليسمح بها أبداً. "هل ترغب في تبرير نفسك؟".

سمع شهقة نيسك أو ليسيث من خلفه لدهشتهما من تمردها. كان رارك يحدّق بفكين مفتوحين على اتساعهما، ولم يكن زيري بحاجة إلى التفكير فيما سيفعله الذئب. كان كمن ينزلق على دماء لزجة. خطوة واحدة خاطئة وتتزحلق، وتلطخك الدماء، فتصبح هي كل حياتك. لكن أي خيار لديه؟

ازداد حذره—بكل ما في جسده المستعار من قوة غير طبيعية، بالشر والمكر في عيني تين، وبثقل المستقبل الذي كان يخيم على الجميع إن هي أحرجته.

كيف يمكن أن تكون بهذا الغباء؟

شعر وكأن الزمن قد توقف، لحظة خاطفة كالصفعة، هو الوقت الذي استغرقه للوصول إليها، ليضع يديه على رأسها، واحدة خلفه، وأخرى على خطمها.. ثم حطم رقبتها.

لا وقت حتى للدهشة.

ذلك الصوت—لم يكن مجرد طقطقة، بل صوت طحن وتفكك تخللته سلسلة من فرقعات متتابعة كالألعاب النارية—خَلت عيناها من الحياة. لا حقد، لا مكر، لا تهديد بعد الآن، وبرغم أن اللحظة قبل أن ترتخي عضلاتها بدت طويلة، إلا أنها لم تدم أكثر من ثانية واحدة. سقطت، وفي سقوطها أفلتت أخيراً رسغي ليراز، التي سقطت بدورها، بوجهها أولاً نحو الأرض، كأنها فقدت الإحساس بالاتجاه.

كتم زيري هلعه عند اصطدامها بالأرض، وأجبر نفسه على تجاهلها وهي مستلقية هناك، مع خفوت النيران المتبقية في جناحيها، ورعشتها البسيطة، هي الدليل الوحيد على أنها ما زالت حية.

واجه جنوده وقال، وكأن شيئاً لم يكن،"لا يهمني تبربر نفسي".

بدت نظرته تحدياً مفتوحاً لأي واحد منهم يجرؤ على طلب تفسير.

رارك أول من تكلم."سيدي، نحن... قالت تِين إن هذه أوامرك. لم نكن لنفعل".

"أصدقك، أيها الجندي"، قاطعه. بدا على رارك الارتياح، لكنه ارتياح سابق لأوانه.

"أصدق أنك بالفعل تعتقد أنني أعتقد بهذا الغباء". نفث زيري الكلمات الأخيرة من بين أسنانه المطبقة. "بضع ساعات فقط قبل أن نحلق، ونحن أقل عدداً بشكل يائس، إلى المعركة، وتعتقد أنني سأحرم جيشي من قوته في لحظة أشد احتياجنا إليها". أشار بيده إلى الجثث التي تخطاها عند المدخل.

"أتعتقد أني سأهدر هذه الأجساد التي دفع الآخرون حياتهم ثمناً لها. أو أنني سأجازف بكل خطة وضعتها، ومن أجل ماذا؟ من أجل تلك الملاك؟ هل تعتقد أنني غبيٌّ إلى درجة أن أرمي كل شيء بعيداً، بدلاً من أن أنتظر... بضع ساعات فقط... لمواجهة ألف ملاك، وهم التهديد الحقيقي؟ هل من المفترض أن يبعث ذلك في نفسي شعوراً أفضل؟".

لم يجبه أحد، وهز رأسه، وقد ارتسم الاشمئزاز على وجهه.

"الأمر الذي أوشكتم على تنفيذه، يناقض كل أمر سمعتموه من فمي، ولو كنتم قادرين على التفكير أبعد من أنوفكم، لكنتم شككتم فيه. فعلتم هذا لأنكم أردتم فعله. ربما كلنا نرغب في ذلك، لكن بعضنا أسياد رغباتهم، وبعضنا عبيد لها، وكنت أظن أنكم أذكى من هذا".

وكي لا تعتقد ليسيث أنها بمنأى عن توبيخه، التفت نحوها.

"من حسن الحظ أن تين لم تر فيكِ أهلاً لتضمكِ إلى عصبتها، إذ إنكِ لم تتركي لدي أدنى شك أنك كنتِ ستنضمين بحماسة. لقد نجوتِ من حكم زملائك، لكننا نعرف أن ما أنقذكِ مجرد صدفة، لا الحكمة".

عند ذكر العقوبة، تصلب كل من رارك، ويول، وأغويلال، وتعمّق الصمت المربك الذي فرضه زيري قبل أن ينهي معاناتهم. قال: "لقد فقدتم ثقتي، وأنتم الآن منزوعو الرتبة. ستقاتلون في المعركة القادمة، وإذا نجوتم، فستقدمون الألم قرباناً لإحياء رفاقكم حتى أقرر أن ذنوبكم قد تطهرت. هل تقبلون بذلك؟".

"نعم، يا سيدي"، قالوا جميعاً، حتى نيسك وليسيث، انصهرت أصواتهم الخمسة في صوت واحد.

"إذاً، اغربوا عن وجهي، وخذوا هؤلاء الثلاثة معكم. أورا، سهيد، قيس. اجمعوا أرواحهم وتخلصوا من جثثهم، ثم انتظروني في غرفة الأرواح. لا تخبروا أحداً بما حدث هنا. هل هذا واضح؟".

كررت الأصوات مجدداً:"نعم، يا سيدي".

أخذ زيري يرتب ملامحه لتظهر تعبيراً من الاستسلام، مع ارتجافة خفيفة لشفتيه تُوحي بالقرف.

"سأتولى أمر هذين الاثنين بنفسي".

تين وليراز، واحدة حية والأخرى ميتة. قالها بنبرة مظلمة، وترك لهم حرية تخيّل ما سيحدث. أمسك تين من فراء رقبتها، وليراز من ذراعها، بخشونة—— مع الحرص على فصل قبضته عن علامة الهامسا بكم ردائها—وكأن كليهما كانتا جثتين تُسحبان عبر الممر مثل البضاعة. لم يتمكن من حمل مشعل، لكن بوهج النيران الخافتة في جناحي ليراز، استغنى عنه. إذا ماتت، سيكون مصيره في الظلام.

الظلام آخر همه.

"اغربوا!" زمجر، فانطلق الجنود مسرعين، يسحبون الجثث معهم، تاركين خلفهم خطوطاً من الدماء.

وبعد أن رحلوا، عدّل زيري قبضته على ليراز، رافعاً إياها بسهولة——وبرفق—بذراع واحدة. شعر بشيء ما وبقدرٍ كبير من الحميمية. أن يحمل جسدها—بعث فيه شيء من القشعريرة—لذا أبقى مسافةً بينهما، رغم أن ذلك زاد من صعوبة تحركاته نحو الباب، وخاصةً محاولته تجنب إيذائها له بتعويذات وشوم الهامسا في كفيها.

وعندما غيّر قبضته على تين ليتجاوز منعطفاً في الممر، انحنى رأس ليراز وسقط بقوة على رأسه، وجبينها استقر على فكه. شعر زيري بحرارة الحمى

المنبعثة من بشرة السيرافيم لأول مرة، قبل أن يُبعد رأسها بلطف. استنشق من بعيد رائحة بنكهة التوابل، كأنها موجة حرارة شقت مساراً لرائحة أخرى، أكثر رقةً، وغير مألوفة—عطرٌ سريٌّ، طبيعي من دون شك، وخافتٌ إلى درجة أن أنفه الكيريني ما كان ليكتشفه لولا هذا القرب.

رائحة... بالكاد موجودة، لكن مجرد تلميح لوجودها الهش كرائحة أزهار الليل—لا حلاوة مفرطة فيها، بل مجرد همسة مثل الندى على براعم الوداع في أبهة ساعات الفجر.

تابع زيري سيره، لم يلتفت ليستنشق تلك الرائحة، لكن حتى وهو يسير في الظلام، يجر جثة ويحمل ملاكاً يمكنها أن تشق بطنه إن استعادت وعيها—إن استعادته.

ذلك العطر الخفي جعله ينتبه إلى المخالب في أصابعه، والأنياب في فمه، وكل الأشياء التي تؤكد أنه ليس هو"نفسه"، الذي يلبس هيئة وحش. شعر وكأن استنشاقه لعبير امرأة من خلال حواس هذا الجسد ولمسها بيديه يعد شذوذاً عن الطبيعة.

ورغم ذلك، استمر في حملها، واستمر في التنفس والاستنشاق، وشكر ليسيث، رغم أن نواياها أبعد ما تكون عن البراءة—فهي قادته إليها في الوقت المناسب. كان يتمنى فقط لو وصل أبكر بقليل، ليجنبها من الضرر الذي ألحقته قوة تعاويذ الهامسا في جسدها. هل يمكن أن تستعيد عافيتها بما يكفي لتتمكن من الطيران مع الآخرين؟ هذا مستبعد.

ماذا لو كان هناك شيء يمكنه فعله من أجلها؟...

تشكلت هذه الفكرة، بعد وصوله إلى أحد فروع الممرات حيث هناك تبلور قراره. إذا كان هناك شيء يستطيع أن يفعله من أجلها، فسوف يفعله هناك شيء يمكن فعله، وسيفعله.

استدار وسلك ممراً ثانوياً، وألقى جثة الذئبة عند مدخل البرك الحرارية، قبل أن يحمل ليراز إلى حافة المياه.

مياه الحياة—هل هي فعالة في معالجة الجروح والكدمات؟ لم يكن زيري متأكداً.

اضطر إلى تغيير وضعية حمله لها ليتمكن من نقلها بكلتا ذراعيه إلى داخل البركة، وعندما أنزلها إلى المياه، غرق في الظلام، واعتراه الذعر للحظة، معتقداً أن نيران جناحيها قد انطفأت.

لكن لا. ظهر بعض الوهج من تحت سطح الماء؛ نيرانها لا تزال مشتعلة، باهتة كجمر خافت.

فتح قبضته حتى انفلتت من بين أصابعه—فقط ذراعه تحت مؤخرة عنقها، وجهها فوق السطح—راح ينتظر ويراقب شفتيها وجفنيها بحثاً عن أي علامة على الحياة.

و... بشكل تدريجي لم ينتبه إليه في البداية، بدأت توهجات المياه تحتها تتزايد، للحظة تحركت فيها ليراز أخيراً، متوهجةً قليلاً، ليتمكن زيري من تمييز احمرار وجنتي الملاك، في خضم الأخضر الحواري للماء، وعروق الطحالب. شاهد لون الرموش الذهبية الداكنة ترمش ببطء قبل أن تفتح عينيها، وتنظر إليه مباشرة.

تذكر كلماتها له في القصر بعد أن قال لها"لم نتعرّف بعد"، لترد عليه بغضب:"أنت تعرف من أكون، وأنا أعرف من أنت، وهذا يكفي".

لكنها في الواقع لم تكن تعرف.

قال مجدداً، بينما كانت ليراز تحاول التوازن تحت سطح المياه الهادئة والمظلمة:"لم نتعرّف بعد، أليس كذلك".

32

كعكة مؤجلة

"إذا عشنا إلى ذلك الحين".

ليس هذا ما قصدته كارو. ولا شيء منه حتى. في الواقع، لم ترد أن تقول أي شيء. حين وقف أكيڤا أمامها على الجانب الآخر من الطاولة الحجرية، وعيناه مليئتان بالأبدية، فكل ما أرادته هو أن تصعد فوق الطاولة معه. لكن منذ متى أمنياتها تتحقق؟

أكيڤا أراد أن يقضي الأبدية معها؟... هذا أضاء سماءها بالشهب، كالرعود الصاعقة، كقطعة حلوى مؤجلة لوقت لاحق. "حسناً تناولي عشاءك أولاً. لن تموتي قبل الحصول على الحلوى".

"سنعيش إلى ذلك الحين"، قالها بحرارة وثقة. "سننجو من كل هذا. سننتصر".

"أتمنى لو أن ثقتي مثل ثقتك". أجابت مستغرقة: جيوش، ملائكة، بوابات، أسلحة، حرب.

"كوني واثقة، يا كارو، لن أسمح بحدوث أي مكروه لكِ. بعد كل ما مررنا به... لن أدعكِ تبتعدين عن ناظري".

توقف قليلاً، وقد اعتلى وجهه احمرار خفيف، خجول، وكأنه ما زال غير متأكد من فهمه لها، أو إن كانت كلمته الآن تعني ما كان يأمله، ثم أضاف أكيفا:"طالما أنكِ تريدينني معكِ".

"أريدني معك"، قالت دون تردد.

سمعت خطأ ترتيب كلماتها—أن أكون معك—لكنها لم تُصلح كلامها. كان ذلك ما تعنيه بالضبط."لكن لا يمكنني أن أكون معك دائماً. ليس بعد، فكتائبنا منفصلة، هل تتذكر؟".

"أتذكر. ولدي شيء أريد أن أخبركِ به. أو بالأحرى، أن أُريكِ إياه. أعتقد أنه قد يساعد". رفع ساقه ليصعد إلى الطاولة، ثم أشار إليها لتنضم إليه قبل أن يجلس في منتصفها. صعدت فوق الطاولة وشعرت بدرجة الحرارة ترتفع مع اقترابه منها. لم يعد هناك حاجز بينهما. ثنت ساقيها تحتها—كانت برودة الحجر تسري في جسدها—وتساءلت عما سيحدث الآن.

لم يكن الأمر مجرد انعكاس لرغبتها. لم يمد يده نحوها، فقط أخذ ينظر إليها بشغف - وقد باحت عيناه ببعض التردد - الذي يحمل في طياته شيئاً من العنفوان. "كارو، هل تعتقدين أن الكيميرا سيوافقون على ضم الكتائب معاً؟".

"ماذا؟ لو طلب ثياغو ذلك، فلن يمانعوا. لكن ما أهمية هذا؟ فإخوتك وأخواتك لن يوافقوا. كانوا واضحين جداً بهذا الشأن".

قال بنبرة هادئة:"أعلم، وذلك لأن لديكم سلاحاً لا نملك سبيلاً لمواجهته". أومأت برأسها. وأطبقت كفيها على سطح الطاولة الحجرية لإخفاء عيني الهامسا؛ حيث أصبحت لديها عادةً أن تخفي عيني كفيها في وجود السيرافيم، لتتجنب انطلاق نار منها غير مقصود. لكنها في وضع محفوف بالمخاطر. قالت بنبرة لطيفة:"اعتادت أيدينا قتالكم مع أننا تصالحنا"، لكن قلبها لم يكن عدواً ولم ترد أن يكون أي جزء منها عدواً لأكيفا.

"لكن، ماذا لو لم تكن أيدينا تريد العداء؟" قالها بإصرار."أعتقد أن بإمكاني إقناع غير الشرعيين بالاندماج وبالمنطق. المواجهات الفردية معنا

ليست في صالح الدومينيون، لكن الأمر ليس المواجهات الفردية، مع أن أعدادنا محدودة. إن وجود الكيميرا في صفوفنا لن يزيد قوتنا فحسب، بل سيضعف العدو. بالإضافة إلى التأثير النفسي؛ فرؤيتنا معاً ستربكهم".

توقف لبرهة، ثم أضاف:"هذا هو أفضل استغلال لقوانا".

"أين يقود هذا الحديث؟ ربما كان يجب أن تقول هذا لإليون وأوريت".

رد قائلاً:"سأفعل. إذا وافقتِ، وإذا... نجح الأمر".

"إذا ماذا؟ إذا نجح؟".

ظل ينظر إليها بتلك النظرة التي تجمع بين التردد والإصرار، ثم مدّ يده ببطء، وبرؤوس أصابعه لامس خدّها برفق، مبعداً خصلة من شعرها خلف أذنها. تلك اللمسة الصغيرة كانت شرارة أضرمت ناراً في داخلها، سرعان ما تلاشت في ألسنة لهب أعمق عندما بسط كفّه بالكامل على خدّها.

كانت عيناه مشعتين، يملأهما الأمل والبحث، وكانت اللمسة خفيفة كهمسة، لكنها كانت... طعماً من الكعكة التي لا تستطيع كارو أن تتذوقها. لم تكن مجرد إغواء.

بل كانت عذاباً. أرادت أن تدير وجهها وتقبّل كفّ أكيفا، ثم معصمه، لتتبع نبضه إلى مصدره.

إلى قلبه. إلى صدره وصلابته. إلى ذراعيه اللتين يحيطان بها—هذا ما أرادته. أرادت حركةً تحاكي حركة، جلداً يناور جلداً، وعرقاً يتحول إلى لهيب، وأنفاساً تسمعها النجوم. يا إلهي. لمسة منه جعلتها حمقاء. سلبتها تماماً من واقعها، ذلك الواقع الذي تقرع فيه طبول الحرب، وجيش الملائكة على الأبواب وأسلحة وصراع، لمسة نقلتها إلى ذلك الفردوس الذي تخيّلاه منذ زمن طويل—كعلبة مجوهرات تنتظرهما ليجداها ويملآها بالسعادة.

مجرد خيال. حتى لو وصلا إلى"العالم الأبدي"، فلن يكون فردوساً، بل عالماً مزقته الحروب، عالماً عليهما أن يتعلما فيه ويتخليا فيه عن كثير مما

عرفاه. عالم مليء بالعمل والألم... و... و...

و"كعكة"، فكّرت كارو بعناد. قد تكون هناك حياة، على الأطراف، هنا وهناك. أكيثا كل يوم، في العمل والألم، نعم، لكن أيضاً في الحب. كعكة كطريقة حياة.

عندها، أدارت وجهها فعلاً، وطبعت شفتيها على كف أكيثا، وشعرت برجفةٍ تسري في جسده. هي تعلم أن المسافة بينهما أقل بكثير من البعد الجسدي وذراعيهما. يا لسهولة الغرق في تلك المسافة الصغيرة والضياع في فردوسٍ صغير مؤقت...

سأل، بصوت أجشَّ:"أتذكرين؟ هذه هي البداية". ثم راحت أنامله تتتبع مساراً ناعماً من خدها إلى أسفل عنقها، تترك لمسته خلفها ناراً وسحراً، تشعل كل ذرةٍ فيها. توقفت أطراف أصابعه عند عظم الترقوة، وانسابت كفّه كوشاحٍ من أسراب الطائر الطنان، وحطت برفقٍ على قلبها.

قالت بصوت خافت:"بالطبع أتذكر".

"أعطني يدكِ". مدّ يده، فمدّت يدها إليه. جذبها نحوه، وعين كارو معلّقة على ياقة قميصه المثلثة، وفي ذهنها كانت قد أدخلت يدها بالفعل تحت القماش لتضع كفّها على قلبه متناسية عيني الهامسا.

توقفي.

في أعماقها، أدركت الخطر وتراجعت، ضامة قبضتها."لا أريد أن أؤذيكَ".

"ثقي بي"، قال، وقد انصهر تردده عندما لامست شفتيها كفه، ولم يتبق سوى شدة العاطفة والجاذبية—وكأن مغناطيسيهما قد تلامسا من هذه المسافة، ولا يمكن فصلهما بسهولة. لم تكن مقاومة كارو قوية بما يكفي. أرادت أن تلمس أكيثا بقدر ما تريد الهواء لتتنفسه. لذا، تركته يوجّه يدها، و...

حين لامست مفاصل أناملها ياقته، تسلل الارتياح إليها وتابعت بها إلى أبعد. قالت له:"نحن البداية". ثم بسطت أصابعها، وأدخلتها برفق تحت

حافة القماش لتصل إلى صدره. جلد أكيفا حيّ تحت أطراف أصابعها، وبعد تلك اللمسة أرادت أن تنهال عليه بشفتيها. رغبة جارفة، ساحقة، لذا استغرق الأمر معها بعض الوقت -محمومة، وكف يدها ذو الهامسا- ملتصقة بجلده – كي تستوعب الأمر.

لم تؤذه لمستها.

بدهشة في صوتها، همست:"أكيفا... كيف؟".

غطّى يدها بيده، ضاغطاً كفّها على صدره، وشعرت بلهيب الهامسا، كما تشعر دائماً عند وجود السيرافيم، إحساساً بالوخز، لكن أكيفا لم يرتعد أو يتراجع أو يتهرب. بل ابتسم. المسافة بينهما تقلّصت، ثم اختصرها أكثر، وهو يميل نحوها، منحني الرأس، ويدور قليلاً وهو يهمس، "إنه السحر"، ثم أراها ما يقصد.

على الجزء الخلفي من عنقه، كان هناك رمز تعرف كارو أنه لم يكن موجوداً من قبل. أسفل رقبته، نصفه مخفي تحت ياقته، استطاعت أن تراه بوضوح: عين. عين مغمضة. هذا وشمه الخاص لمواجهة سحر بريمستون. لم يكن لونه أزرق نيلياً مثل وشم الهامسا، ولم يكن وشماً بالأساس، بل ندبة."متى فعلتَ هذا؟" سألته.

"الليلة".

تتبّعت الخطوط الدقيقة البارزة للندبة بطرف إصبعها."يبدو أنها قد شُفيت تماماً".

أومأ برأسه، مستوياً بكتفيه ورافعاً رأسه من جديد. ورغم أن كارو بدأت تدرك ما قد يكون أكيفا قادراً عليه، إلا أن ذلك ما زال يدهشها. أن يقوم بجرح وشفاء نفسه في بضع ساعات، هذا مذهل، لكنّ ذلك لا يعتبر لا شيء أمام السحر الذي يحتويه. إنه يتفادى تأثير أقوى سلاح للكيميرا— إنه سلاح العودة إلى الحياة، وهذا ربما يُحتسب سلاحاً. ربما هذا الأمر كان سيخيفها سابقاً، لكن الآن، ليس الخوف ما تشعر به كارو.

"يمكنني أن ألمسكَ بحرية"، همست بدهشة. لم تستطع—أو ربما لم تُرد—مقاومة الرغبة في إثبات ذلك أكثر، فبدأت بتحريك كفّها فوق بشرة جلده الدافئة الناعمة، حتى شعرت كأنها تحتضن نبض قلبه بيدها.

"كما تريدين"، قالها وهو يرتعش، لا من الألم.

الجلد والأبدية كوّنا معاً مزيجاً حسياً خارقا، وسرعان ما تلاشت المخاوف التي كانت وراء حاجته إلى هذا السحر، تلاشت وكذلك كل شيء خارج إيقاع نبض قلبيهما...

... إلى أن جاء طرق على الباب.

كان المشهد مستحيل التصور: كتف أحدهما إلى كتف الآخر، مبللان تماماً، يسيران عبر الممرات بخطوات صامتة وعزيمة صارمة، عابرين من نطاق الكيميرا إلى مكان السيرافيم بخط مستقيم عبر الكهف الرئيسي حيث تجمّع تقريباً كل من كان هناك... ثياغو وليراز، يجرّان جثة تين خلفهما.

صمتت كل الأصوات. كان ميك قد وضع كمانه للتو جانباً ونهض. تمدّد ورأسه في حضن زوزانا، حتى شهقتها التي قطعت الهدوء جعلته ينهض بسرعة.

انتصبت إيسّا بكامل قامتها، لتبدو أكثر من أي وقت مضى بصورة أفعى من أحد المعابد القديمة، ومن حولها، نهضت جماعة الكيميرا في حالة تأهّب واستعداد للقتال إن دعا الأمر. لكنهم لم يدعوا الأمر. تابع الاثنان سيرهما، وعيونهما مثبتة إلى الأمام بتعبير صارم، واختفيا في صمت، عابرين أمام حراس السيرافيم عند الباب البعيد دون توقف أو كلمة تفسير عندما وصلا إلى باب قاعة أكيڤا، وجداه مغلقاً. تأفّفت ليراز بسخرية ولم تطرق الباب، بل دفعته بقوة، فُتح على إثرها مصطدماً بالجدار. ثم حدّقت في المشهد الذي استقبلها: أكيڤا وكارو، بعيون نصف مغلقة من شدة الرغبة، متقابلان على اللوح الصخري، يتلامسان والأيدي على القلوب

قد يقول البعض إن إيلاي—إلهة القتلة والعشاق السريين—كانت

تتجول في تلك الليلة عبر الممرات، تقوم بإثارة الفوضى. في تلك الأثناء التي يمكن أن يكون فيها أحد المتحالفين أو حتى ليراز ميتة، أو أن يُقبض على كارو وأكيفا في وضع أكثر حساسية من حالة الهيام تلك وأيديهما على قلبي بعضها البعض. لو تأخرا قليلاً، كانا سيتبادلان القبلة.

إلا أن إيلاي راعية مزاجية، وقد خذلتهما—بشكل مذهل—من قبل. كارو لم تعد تؤمن بها بعد الآن، ولن تلومها لأنه عندما اقتحم الباب، لم يكن هناك سوى ليراز والذئب وهما من يلامان.

"حسناً"، قالت ليراز، بصوت جاف في الوقت الذي كان جسدها مبتلاً،"على الأقل ما زلتما مرتديين ملابسكما".

وحمداً لله على ذلك، قالت كارو لنفسها، وهي تسحب يدها بسرعة من داخل قميص أكيفا. شعرت فوراً ببرودة الغرفة. كأن جسدها اعتاد حرارة أكيفا، مما جعل كل شيء حولها يبدو بارداً. احتاجت بضع رفات من عينها لتتخلص من دوار الرغبة وتستوعب موضوع ملابسهما المبللة الملتصقة بأجسادهما، وصوت تنقيط الماء، ناهيك عن الرائحة المنبعثة من الكبريت.

هل أخذ زيري ليراز لتستحم في برك المياه الكبريتية الحارة؟ حسناً، هذا... غريب. بالكامل وهي ترتدي ملابسها؟ حسناً، هذا أقل غرابة مما نحن عليه، لكنه ما زال غريباً جداً، ثم دفع الذئب شيئاً ما عبر العتبة، وعندها توضحت لها الصورة بالكامل.

"هذه جثة تِين – هاكسايا .خائنة العهد". قال الذئب.

ماذا؟ غيرت كارو جلستها على الطاولة الحجرية ثم قفزت بسرعة لتقف بجانب الجثة. رأت فوراً بصمة اليد الحارقة على صدر الذئبة، ونظرت نحو ليراز التي ردّت عليها بنظرة باردة خالية من الشفقة.

انضم أكيفا إليها بجانب الجثة، وفي غضون ثوانٍ امتلأ الممر بالسيرافيم، وأيضاً بعض الكيميرا الذين اجتازوا قطاعاتهم ليروا ما الذي يحدث.

كان من المضحك تقريباً أن يكون هذا الفعل العنيف هو ما حرّك جيوشاً لتختلط بحرية أكبر. مضحك تقريباً، لكن الموت ليس كذلك على الإطلاق.

بدا الوضع برمته أشبه ببرميل بارود، وبقربه عود ثقاب مشتعل على وشك السقوط عليه. في اللحظات التالية، اختلطت الأسئلة والأجوبة في هرج ومرج. شرح الذئب ما حدث، مع حرصه على ذكر التفاصيل الدقيقة للإقناع. تِين هي من فعلت هذا. وتين ماتت.

أما هاكسايا، التي حاولت كارو أن تستوعب دورها في كل هذا، ولا سيما أنها تعرفها جيداً، كمادريغال، كانت تقاتل إلى جانبها وتثق بها، فهي شرسة، لكن يمكن توقع تصرفاتها. كما أنها ليست غبية. عندما جعلتها جزءاً من هذه الخدعة، كانت كارو قد وضعت حياتهم جميعاً بين يديها.

"لماذا قد تفعل ذلك؟" سألت، ولم تكن تتوقع إجابة. كأنها تحاكي الهواء، لكن ليراز هي من أجابها. "كان الأمر شخصيًّا"، قالت الملاك. توجهت إلى أكيڤا، وشيء ما في نظرتها الباردة تبدّل فجأة. شعرت كارو أن التغيير الذي حدث في تلك اللحظة أشبه بالتغيير الذي أحدثه زيري في وجه الذئب، ورغم أن السبب بالطبع لم يكن نفسه. لم يكن هناك شخص آخر ينظر من خلف عيني ليراز. الأمر أشبه بانزلاق القناع عن وجهها لتظهر تلك الملامح الأكثر لطفاً للوجه الطفولي الذي كانت عليه يوماً. ثم قالت:"سافاث". فأومأ أكيڤا برأسه مع نفس عميق، متفهماً.

كارو تعرف هذا الاسم، من: معركة سافاث. قريةً على الشواطئ الغربية لخليج الوحوش، أو هكذا كانت يوماً ما قبل مجيئها.

وجهت ليراز كلامها إلى ثياغو، مُديرة وجهها نحوه، لكن عينيها بقيتا منخفضتين:"ما تفعله بروحها هو شأنك، لكن يجب أن تعلم، أنني لا ألومها. كنت أستحق انتقامها".

ردّ عليها ثياغو بشيء ما، لكن كارو بالكاد سمعته، إذ كان فكرها مشغول بأمر عالق في ذهنها. نقلت نظرها من جسد تِين إلى ليراز، من بصمة اليد

المحترقة على صدر الذئبة إلى العلامات المحفورة على جسد الملاك، المخفية تقريباً تحت أكمامها الممتدة حتى كعب يديها.

"اعتادت أيدينا قتالكم مع أننا تصالحنا"، تذكرت كارو تلك الجملة.

عاد الملائكة إلى منازلهم بهدوء ولم يمت أحد. وكانت هذه هي النهاية.

راح قلبها ينبض بشدة. فكرة بدأت تتشكل في عقلها. لم تعلن عنها، لكنها تركت خيوطها تتفرع، لتتبعها، وتبحث عن أي عيوب فيها، وتتصور الحجج التي قد تُثار ضدها. هل يمكن أن يكون الأمر بهذه البساطة؟

الأصوات حولها تلاشت إلى همهمات خافتة بعيداً خلف طبقات أفكارها.

نعم، من الممكن أن تكون بهذه البساطة. الخطة على ما هي عليه الآن، أسوأ من معقدة.

يا للفوضى. نظرت كارو إلى الوجوه المتجمعة: أكيڤا، ليراز، والذئب في الغرفة معها، إليون وإيسّا عند الباب، والمخلوقات التي تتحرك خلفهم جنباً إلى جنب، تظهر كوميض من ريش ناري وجذوع مكسوة بالفرو، دروع سوداء حمراء، بشرة ناعمة وخشنة.

جميعهم مستعدون للطيران إلى أرض المعركة، لتجسيد نهاية العالم للإنسانية، كما رأت في أحلامها وكوابيسها.

أو ربما لا.

لم يكن أكيڤا ولا الذئب من لاحظ أولاً التغير في طريقة وقوف كارو، ولا الإشراقة التي ملأت ملامحها. بل ليراز التي سألتها بنبرة امتزج فيها الفضول بالحذر:"ما الذي طرأ عليك؟".

من الجيد أن تكون ليراز هي من لاحظت كارو."إذا خطرت لك فكرة أفضل، أنا واثقة أنكِ ستخبريننا بها"، قالت لها عند انتهاء مجلس الحرب، بازدراء ونبرة استهزاء. حينها، ثبّتت كارو عينيها عليها ، ومن صميم قناعتها تحول يأسها إلى يقين، وشعرت به في داخلها كالفولاذ.

"خطرت لي فكرة أفضل، أعيدوا تجمّع المجلس... الآن".

في قديم الزمان،
ذهبت فتاة لزيارة معرض الوحوش...

حيث كانت جميع المعروضات ميتة.

33

مثل غزوٍ فضائي

"عليهم التعامل مع الأمر مثل غزو فضائي".

جلست إليزا في الطائرة، وصدى كلمات مورغان لا يزال يتردد في ذهنها. خلف النافذة، امتدت أمامها لوحة غامضة من الليل—غيوم متناثرة تكشف بين الحين والآخر لمحات متقطعة من... العتمة. هل كانت تحلّق فوق المحيط الأطلسي؟ كم بدا الأمر غريباً، ألا تعرف حتى موقعك على الخريطة. تُرى، كم مرة يحدث هذا مع الآخرين؟ أن يجدوا أنفسهم تائهين، لا يدركون أين هم في هذا العالم؟

ارتجفت قليلاً وسحبت جبينها مبتعدة عن زجاج النافذة البارد. لم يكن ثمة شيء يُرى سوى بقايا سحب متناثرة وليل كثيف. فكّرت: لو كانت هذه قصة في كتاب أو فيلم، لكانت قادرة على قراءة النجوم لتحدد اتجاهها. الأبطال دائماً يمتلكون المهارات العشوائية المناسبة للتعامل مع المواقف المستحيلة. شيء من قبيل: يا للحظ! ذلك الصيف الذي قضيته على متن قارب التهريب مع عمي والبحّار الوسيم الذي علّمني فن الملاحة السماوية، ها هو ينقذني الآن!

أها.

لكن إليزا لم تكن تملك أيّاً من تلك المهارات العشوائية. حسناً، كانت تستطيع إطلاق صرخة أفلام رعب مميزة، وهذا شيء يستحق الذكر، أليس كذلك؟ أوه، وكانت أيضاً ماهرة في استخدام المشرط. ذات مرة، أثناء تدريسها لطلاب مختبر التشريح، مازحها أحدهم قائلاً إنها تعرف تماماً الأماكن المثالية لطعن شخص ما. ضحكت حينها ووافقت على كلامه، رغم أن تلك لم تكن مهارةً اضطرت لاستخدامها قط.

إذاً، يمكن تلخيص مهاراتها الخارقة في: الطعن بدقة عالية مع الصراخ كأبطال أفلام الرعب. يا لها من بطلة!

تنهدت إليزا. كان الإرهاق يتملكها بالكامل. قدّرت أنها لا تزال يقظة من ست وثلاثين ساعة—إذا استثنت الغفوة القصيرة التي أخذتها في مختبر التشريح—ولم يكن الأمر سهلاً أبداً. من الجهة المقابلة، كانت أصوات شخير د. تشاودهاري الرقيقة تتسلل كتعذيب بطيء. تُرى، كيف سيكون النوم دون أن يلاحقك الخوف؟

من ستكون هي لو لم يكن هناك كابوس يطاردها في كل لحظة؟ من تكون حقاً؟ هل هي"إليزا جونز" التي صنعتها بيديها، أم تلك النسخة المهزوزة التي صُقلت وشحقت بيد الآخرين؟

لا ينبغي للمؤمن أن يخطط لقدرِه.

تلك كانت آخر أفكارها قبل أن تشعر بالطائرة تميل قليلاً، إيذاناً بالهبوط. أعادت وجهها نحو النافذة الباردة، لترى أن الظلام في الخارج لم يعد مطلقاً. خيوط رفيعة من نور الفجر بدأت تتسلل ببطء، مرسومة كخطوط باهتة تتبع ملامح العالم في الأسفل. رفعت حاجبيها في حيرة، وانحنت إلى الأمام محاولةً تعديل زاويتها للحصول على رؤية أوضح. لم تزر إيطاليا من قبل، لكنها كانت متأكدة من أن هذا المكان ليس إيطاليا.

إيطاليا لا تحتوي على... صحراء، أليس كذلك؟

ألقت نظرة خاطفة على المسافرين الآخرين الجالسين على بُعد عدة صفوف، لكن ملامحهم لم تُظهر أي شيء غير مألوف. الجميع كان غارقاً في صمته، ولا أثر لأي علامات توتر أو دهشة.

مع اهتزاز الطائرة بفعل الاضطرابات الجوية، استيقظ د. تشاودهاري أخيراً. التفت إليها وهو يتمطّى قائلاً:"هل وصلنا؟".

أجابت إليزا وهي تراقب الظلام من جديد:"لقد وصلنا... إلى مكانٍ ما". ثم مال د. تشاودهاري نحو نافذته لينظر هو الآخر إلى الخارج. حدّق طويلاً، رفع حاجبيه بدهشة، ثم عاد إلى وضعه في المقعد وكأنه لم يرَ شيئاً.

"هممم"، كانت تلك طريقته المعتادة في التعبير عن:"أمر غريب للغاية".

شعرت إليزا وكأن ضلوعها تضغط على قلبها.

إلى أين يأخذوننا؟

عندما لامست عجلات الطائرة مدرجاً صحراوياً مقفراً، كان قرص الشمس قد بدأ بالظهور خلف سلسلة من الجبال البعيدة، كاشفاً عن أرض شاحبة بلون الغبار. بدا المبنى الوحيد الذي يعمل كصالة استقبال للطائرات منخفضاً ومترباً، مغطئ بطبقة كثيفة من الرمال العالقة.

الشرق الأوسط؟ تساءلت إليزا في نفسها، ثم أردفت بسخرية: أو ربما كوكب تاتوين؟ لفتت انتباهها لافتة مرسومة يدوياً، كانت الكلمات المكتوبة عليها غير واضحة، أشكالها متداخلة وغريبة. ربما كانت باللغة العربية. هذا بالتأكيد يستبعد كوكب تاتوين.

كان هناك رجل بزي عسكري يقف بجانب المدرج. تقدّم نحوه أحد العملاء، تبادل معه بضع كلمات سريعة قبل أن يسلمه مجموعة من الأوراق. وفي ظل المبنى المترب، كان هناك رجلان يستندان إلى سيارة دفع رباعي. الأول كان يرتدي بدلة داكنة كالمعتاد، أما الآخر فكان ذا بشرة داكنة ويرتدي عباءة، وعمامة زرقاء لامعة ملتفة حول رأسه.

قال د. تشاودهاري، بنبرة تأملية:"طوارق. رجال الصحراء الزرق".

الصحراء الكبرى؟ فكرت إليزا وهي تحدّق إلى الخارج بعينين جديدتين، محاولةً استيعاب ما حولها. أفريقيا؟

لم يتحدث العملاء بكلمة واحدة، بل اكتفوا بقيادتهم نحو المركبة.

كانت الرحلة طويلة وغريبة، عبر امتدادات شاسعة من الفراغ القاحل، تتخللها أحياناً مدن خربة مذهلة، وومضات عابرة من حياة؛ حبال غسيل معلّقة على أسطح المنازل الطينية، أو خيوط دخان رقيقة توحي بأن هذه الأماكن لا تزال مأهولة. مرّوا بأطفال يركبون الجمال، وبقطيع من النساء يمشين بخطى ثابتة، يرتدين أوشحة رأس وفساتين طويلة بالية، ألوانها بهتت بفعل الشمس الحارقة.

عند نقطة بدت مشابهة لغيرها، انحرفت المركبة عن الطريق، وبدأت تهتز وتتأرجح في صعودها إلى تلة، تتزحلق أحياناً فوق الحصى الناعم. قبضت إليزا بإحكام على المقبض المثبت فوق الباب، وشعرت أن أفكارها المتناثرة عن الملائكة والطمأنينة قد بقيت بعيدةً هناك، مع الطائرة المتروكة خلفهم.

كان هذا الشعور مختلفاً تماماً، أدركت ذلك فجأة، بإحساس غريزي خام، شعور ظنّت أنها تخلّت عنه منذ زمن بعيد. تسلل إليها شعور قاتم، كأنه انبثق من زوايا ذاكرتها، من طفولتها، حين كانت تؤمن ببراءة بما قيل لها: بأن الشر حقيقي، وأنه يراقبها، وأن الشيطان يختبئ في ظل سياج السرو، ينتظر ليرتشف روحها.

لا وجود للشيطان، همست في داخلها بلهجة غاضبة. لكن مهما حاولت إقناع نفسها بما اعتقدت به منذ أن غادرت منزلها، كان من الصعب تصديق ذلك الآن، وسط كل ما يحدث.

الوحوش قادمة من أجلك.

"انظري". أشار د. تشاودهاري بيده.

رفعت إليزا نظرها إلى الأعلى، نحو ظلال الجبال البعيدة، حيث ظهرت قلعة بُنيّة من الطين الأحمر، تقف شامخة وسط الصحراء كأنها حارس قديم. ومع اقترابهم، ومع كل ارتطام لعجلات السيارة بالصخور المتناثرة، لاحظت إليزا المزيد من التفاصيل: مركبات أخرى مصطفة خارج أسوار القلعة، تتنوع بين سيارات جيب وشاحنات نقل عسكرية ثقيلة، ومروحية يبدو أنها متوقفة عن العمل. جنود يتجولون حول المكان، يرتدون أزياء مموهة بألوان الصحراء، لكن ما أثار انتباهها أكثر كان هؤلاء...

حبست أنفاسها، واستدارت نحو د. تشاودهاري. لقد رآهم هو أيضاً.

بروتوكول غزو فضائي، فكرت إليزا. يا للهول.

أجرى أحد العملاء مكالمة هاتفية، وبحلول الوقت الذي توقفت فيه مركبتهم بجانب المركبات الأخرى، كان رجل ذو شارب عريض، أسود ومهندم، ينتظرهم للترحيب. كان يرتدي ملابس مدنية أنيقة، ويبدو أن حديثه ينم عن سلطة واضحة."مرحباً بكم في المملكة المغربية، دكتور. أنا د. يوسف أمهالي".

تبادل الرجال التحية بالمصافحة، بينما اكتفى بإيماءة احترام نحو إليزا تحدث د. تشاودهاري:"د. أمهالي".

فقاطعه الرجل بسرعة:"من فضلك، ناديني يوسف".

"يوسف، هل يمكنك إخبارنا لماذا نحن هنا؟".

"بالتأكيد يا دكتور. أنتم هنا لأنني طلبت حضوركم. لدينا... حالة تتجاوز نطاق خبرتي".

"وما هو مجال خبرتك؟" سأل د. تشاودهاري.

"أنا متخصص في علم الأنثروبولوجيا الجنائية".

قالت إليزا، بسرعة ودون تروٍّ:"ما نوع الحالة؟".

رفع يوسف حاجبيه ونظر إليها بتقييم سريع. للحظة شعرت أنها أخطأت في طرح السؤال، وأنه كان من الأفضل لها أن تلتزم بدورها المعتاد:

المساعدة الصامتة، أيتها المطيعة. لكنها تابعت، فقد كان الشعور بالخوف يعصف بها، وكانت تحتاج إلى معرفة ما الذي ينتظرهم.

عندما رفع رأسه قليلاً وهو يشمّ الهواء، شد أنفه باشمئزاز، شعرت إليزا به أيضاً: رائحة نتنة تملأ الجو. إنها رائحة تحلل.

قال يوسف:"هذا النوع من الحالات يا آنسة، تزيد رائحته سوءاً في يوم حار".

جثث.

تابع د. يوسف أمهالي:"نوع الحالة الذي قد يشعل حرباً".

التفتت إليزا إلى د. تشاودهاري بنظرة قلقة، محاولة استيعاب المعنى الخفي لكلام يوسف. مقبرة جماعية، فكّرت. لكن لماذا يحتاجون إليهم هنا؟ لماذا جُلبوا إلى مكان معزول كهذا؟

سأل د. تشاودهاري أخيراً السؤال الذي كان يتردد في ذهنها، قائلاً:"أنت المتخصص هنا". وأضاف مُلمحاً:"ما الذي تحتاجني من أجله؟".

ردّ د. يوسف:"لا يوجد متخصصون في هذا الأمر". توقف للحظة، ثم ارتسمت على شفتيه ابتسامة مشوبة بالسوداوية، كأنها خليط بين السخرية واليأس. لكن خلف تلك الابتسامة، استطاعت إليزا أن تلمح شيئاً آخر: الخوف. شعرت به يتسلل إليها، ويزيد من قلقها.

ما الذي يحدث هنا؟

قال يوسف، مشيراً بيده ليتقدموا أمامه:"من الأفضل أن تروا بأنفسكم. الحفرة في هذا الاتجاه".

34

أشياء معروفة ومدفونة

استغرق الأمر منهم عشرين دقيقة على الأقل لإنهاء الأوراق؛ توقيع سلسلة من الاتفاقيات السرية التي زادت من توتر إليزا مع كل صفحة توقعها. تلا ذلك ربع ساعة أخرى من الارتباك في ارتداء بدلات الوقاية من المواد الخطرة، مما رفع مستوى قلقها إلى حدود جديدة. وأخيراً، انضموا إلى موكب طويل كأشباح بيضاء، تتحرك بنسق منظم على امتداد الطريق.

توقف الدكتور أمهالي عند قمة المنحدر. خرج صوته مكتوماً، متأثراً بجهاز التنفس في بدلته الواقية:"قبل أن نتابع، أود أن أذكركما بأن ما ستشاهدانه الآن مصنف وسري للغاية. الحفاظ على السرية أمر جوهري. العالم ليس مستعداً لرؤية هذا، ونحن بالتأكيد لسنا مستعدين ليتم اكتشافه. هل هذا واضح؟".

أومأت إليزا برأسها. ضيق مجال رؤيتها بسبب البدلة أجبرها على إدارة رأسها بالكامل لترى إيماءة الدكتور تشاودهاري. خلفه، لمحت عدة كائنات بيضاء تتحرك في انسجام؛ لا شيء يميز أياً منهم عن الآخر.

إذا رمشت بعينيها، فقد تفقد أثر الدكتور تشاودهاري نفسه. شعرت وكأنها تخطو إلى نوع من المطهر.

ازدادت غرابة المشهد عندما ظهر الموقع المحظور أمامهم. أسفل القصبة، كانت مجموعة من الخيام الصفراء الحادة اللون تحيط بها حبال متشابكة. مولدات ضخمة تصدر أزيزاً منخفضاً تمد الخيام بالكهرباء عبر أسلاك تبدو كأنها أنسجة من شبكة عنكبوتية سرية. الموظفون يتحركون بتثاقل، أشبه باليرقات، أجسادهم مغطاة بالبلاستيك الأبيض.

في الخلفية، كان الجنود يقفون على أهبة الاستعداد، بينما تحوم المزيد من المروحيات في السماء. كانت الشمس حادة، والهواء يندفع بقوة إلى قناعها من خلال أنبوب ضيق، مما جعل التنفس أشبه بشفط الهواء من فتحة ضيقة. تحركت بتثاقل نحو الأسفل، ملابسها الواقية تعيق كل خطوة. شعرت بأن الخوف أمامها يمتد كظل طويل، يطاردها بلا هوادة.

ما الذي يوجد في الحفرة؟ ما الذي تخبئه تلك الخيام؟

قادهم الدكتور أمهالي إلى أقرب خيمة، ثم توقف فجأة. قال مقتبساً:"الوحوش قادمة إليكم". كانت تلك كلمات الملاك. في تلك اللحظة، شعرت إليزا بأنها مجرد نبضات قلب محتجزة داخل كيس بلاستيكي. وحوش؟ هنا؟

قال الدكتور:"يبدو أنهم بالفعل بيننا".

بحركة حاسمة، رفع الدكتور أمهالي باب الخيمة ليكشف عن...

... وحوش.

لكن، أدركت إليزا ببطء أن كلمة وحش قد تشمل طيفاً واسعاً من الكائنات. شياطين، كوابيس مروعة قد تُوقف قلب فتاة صغيرة من شدة الفزع. لكن ما تراه الآن أمامها لم يكن من هذا النوع، لا من قريب ولا من بعيد. هذه ليست وحوشها. وسرعان ما عاد نبض قلبها إلى وتيرته الطبيعية، شعرت بالخجل من نفسها. بالطبع، ليست وحوشها.

ماذا كانت تظن؟ أو بالأحرى، لماذا لم تفكر؟ وحوشها تعيش في عالم مختلف، في مستوى آخر من الوجود، في عوالم الأحلام المتسعة.

"هل تسمي هذه وحوشاً، يا يوسف؟" ربما كانت ستقولها وهي تضحك، بارتياح مشوب بالدهشة."أنت لا تعرف شيئاً عن الوحوش".

لكنها لم تضحك. همست بدلاً من ذلك:"أبو الهول".

"عذراً؟" سألها الدكتور أمهالي.

"يبدون كأبي الهول"، وضحت بصوت أعلى دون أن ترفع عينيها عنهم. الخوف اختفى تماماً، وكأن يداً خفية نزعته منها واستبدلته بشعور غامر بالافتتان."كائنات أسطورية".

امرأتان على هيئة قطط.

اثنتان متطابقتان. فهود برؤوس بشرية. خطت إليزا إلى داخل الخيمة، لتشعر على الفور بتراجع حرارة الجو حولها.

كانت الخيمة باردة بسبب جهاز تكييف يطلق أزيزاً، فيما كان الكائنان مسجيين على طاولات معدنية موضوعة فوق براميل من الجليد الجاف. جسداهما القططيان مغطيان بفراء أسود ناعم، وأجنحتهما—أجنحة حقيقية—مكسوة بريش داكن.

كانت حناجرهما منحورة، وصدراهما ملطخان بدماء متخثرة.

تقدم الدكتور تشاودهاري بخطى حذرة، وأزال خوذته من بدلة الوقاية.

قال الدكتور أمهالي على الفور:"دكتور، لا بد أن أعارض هذا".

لكن الدكتور تشاودهاري لم يُعره انتباهاً. اقترب من أحد الكائنين. بدا رأسه صغيراً، منفصلاً عن جسده المغطى بالبزة البيضاء، بينما ارتسم على ملامحه تعبير يتأرجح بين الشك والدهشة.

خلعت إليزا خوذتها أيضاً، فاجتاحتها رائحة خانقة على الفور—نسخة أنقى بكثير من الرائحة التي كانت تتسرب عبر المنحدر—لكنها استطاعت الآن أن ترى الكائنين بوضوح أكبر.

اقتربت من الدكتور تشاودهاري لتقف بجانبه أمام الجثة. كان المرافقون يوبخونهم محذرين من المخاطر واللوائح، لكن من السهل تجاهلهم أمام هذا المشهد المذهل.

قال الدكتور تشاودهاري بلهجة عملية:"أخبرني بما تعرفه".

"دكتور——".

روى الدكتور أمهالي ما يعرفه، ولم يكن الكثير. لقد عُثر على الجثث، أكثر من عشرين منها، في حفرة مكشوفة. هذا هو لبّ الموضوع.

قال العالم المغربي:"كنت آمل أن أتمكن من رفض الأمر بسهولة باعتباره خدعة، لكني لم أستطع. الآن، أملي أن تستطيعوا أنتم ذلك".

رفع الدكتور تشاودهاري حاجبيه دون تعليق.

سألت إليزا:"هل كلها تبدو هكذا؟".

"ليس تماماً". أجاب الدكتور أمهالي، وأشار برأسه الجامد نحو قطعة قماش بيضاء مرتفعة فوق جسم أكبر بكثير من حجم أبو الهول.

ما الذي يوجد تحتها؟ تساءلت إليزا، لكن الدكتور تشاودهاري لم يهتم بالنظر، بل أعاد تركيزه على أبي الهول. لحقت به، ومررت إصبعاً مغطى بالقفاز على ساق القطط الأمامية، ثم انحنت فوق أحد الأجنحة الداكنة. رفعت ريشة بإصبعها وتأملتها.

قالت بدهشة:"بومة. هل ترى هذه الحواف؟".

وأشارت إلى الحافة الأمامية للريشة:"هذه الحواف المضلعة فريدة من نوعها في ريش البوم. هي التي تجعلها تطير بصمت. هذه تبدو كأنها ريش بومة".

"لا أعتقد أن هذه بومات" قال الدكتور أمهالي.

هل أنت متأكد؟ تساءلت إليزا في عقلها بسخرية، لأنني سمعت أن بومات أفريقيا تكون برؤوس بشرية. شعرت بشيء أشبه بالنشوة. كان الخوف يسير معها أسفل المنحدر، وفي اللحظة التي ذُكرت فيها كلمة

الوحوش، التف حولها وضغط عليها—الحلم، الكابوس، المطاردة، الاتهام—
والآن رحل، تاركاً خلفه ارتياحاً وتعباً ودهشة. والدهشة هي التي طغت على
كل شيء، مثل الطبقة العلوية من الآيس كريم. آيس كريم الكوابيس،
فكرت وهي تكاد تضحك بجنون.

لعقة.

"أنت محق. إنهم ليسوا بومات". وافق الدكتور تشاودهاري، وبالطبع،
ربما وحدها إليزا، التي تألف نبراته، كانت تستطيع التقاط الجفاف الخفي
في سخرية كلماته."على الأقل، ليست بالكامل".

ما تلا ذلك كان فحصاً سطحياً من الرأس إلى القدمين بهدف التأكد من
عدم كونها مجرد خدعة.

"ابحثي عن أي آثار لعمليات جراحية"، طلب منها الدكتور تشاودهاري،
فامتثلت له، وبدأت تفحص الأماكن التي تتصل فيها الأجزاء المتباينة من
أجساد هذه المخلوقات: عند الرقبة ومفاصل الأجنحة بشكل رئيسي.

لم تستطع أن تشارك الدكتور أمهالي آماله؛ لم تكن تريد أن تجد أي دليل
على عمليات جراحية. فإذا وجدتها... فمن أين، أو بالأحرى، مِمّن جاءت تلك
الرؤوس؟ سيكون الأمر أقرب إلى فيلم رعب منه إلى اكتشاف علمي مهيب
وفي كل الأحوال، كان هذا الفحص بلا جدوى. كانت تعرف في قرارة
نفسها أن هذه المخلوقات حقيقية. كما تعرف أن الملائكة حقيقية.
هذه أشياء تعرفها.

كلا، أنتِ لا تعرفين ذلك، قالت لنفسها. هذه ليست طريقة عمل الأمور.
أنتِ تتساءلين، ثم تجمعين البيانات وتدرسينها، وأخيراً تطرحين فرضية
وتختبرينها. عندها فقط قد تبدئين بفهم شيء ما.

لكنها كانت تعرف، ومحاولة الإيحاء لنفسها بعكس ذلك كانت كالصراخ
في وجه إعصار.

أنا أعرف أشياء أخرى أيضاً.

ومع هذا التفكير، ظهر أحد تلك الأشياء فجأة. كأن قارئة طالع قد قلبت ورقة تاروت في عقلها لتكشف لها هذه المعرفة، هذه الحقيقة التي كانت مخبأة في مكان ما داخلها طوال حياتها... أو حتى منذ زمن أبعد من ذلك بكثير. كانت موجودة، وكانت حقيقة ضخمة يصعب على العقل استيعابها فجأة. حقيقة كبيرة جداً.

أخذت إليزا نفساً عميقاً، وهو ما لم يكن قراراً حكيماً وهي واقفة بجوار جثث، واضطرت إلى التراجع بخطوات متعثرة، محاولة طرد رائحة الموت من رئتيها بأخذ أنفاس قصيرة وسريعة، متعمدة لتنقية رئتيها من غشاوة الموت الخانقة.

"هل أنت بخير؟" سألها الدكتور تشاودهاري.

"أنا بخير"، أجابت وهي تحاول أن تخفي اضطرابها. لم تكن تريد أن يظن أنها ضعيفة ولا تتحمل الموقف، وبالتأكيد لم تكن تريد أن يتمنى لو أنه أحضر مورغان توث بدلاً منها، لذا عادت إلى العمل على الفور، متجاهلة تماماً ورقة التاروت التي انقلبت في عقلها وكشفت الحقيقة...

هناك كون آخر.

هذا ما كانت تعرفه. في المدرسة، كانت إليزا تتجنب الفيزياء بشكل واضح، مفضّلةً دراسة علم الأحياء، لذا لم تكن تملك سوى فهم سطحي للغاية لنظرية الأوتار، لكنها كانت تدرك أن هناك ما يُثبت علمياً احتمالية وجود أكوان موازية. لم تكن تعرف تفاصيل هذا الإثبات، ولم يكن الأمر مهماً. هناك كون آخر.

لم يكن عليها أن تثبت ذلك.

اللّعنة. الإثبات موجود هنا، ميت عند قدميها. والإثبات موجود في روما، على قيد الحياة. انتابتها موجة من الضحك الجنوني. "يجب أن يتعاملوا مع الأمر كأنه غزو فضائي"، كان مورغان قد قالها، وكان محقاً تماماً، ذلك المتحذلق الصغير.

لقد كان بالفعل غزواً فضائياً. كل ما في الأمر أن الفضائيين بدوا كالملائكة والوحوش، ولم يأتوا من الفضاء الخارجي، بل من عالم موازٍ.

تخيلت، والضحك يتصاعد إلى حافة الهستيريا، أن تطرح هذه النظرية على الطبيبين الواقفين بجانبها—"مرحباً، هل تعلمون ما الذي أفكر فيه؟"— لكن في تلك اللحظة أدركت أن هذا الضحك لم يكن ضحكاً على الإطلاق، بل كان هلعاً.

لم يكن الأمر متعلقاً بالوحوش أو الرائحة أو الحرارة أو حتى بالإرهاق الشديد، ولم يكن أيضاً بفكرة وجود كون آخر. كان الأمر متعلقاً بالمعرفة. كان الشعور بهذه الحقيقة متغلغلاً في أعماقها—حقيقة ثقيلة كوحوش مدفونة في حفرة. ولكن الوحوش كانت ميتة ولا يمكنها إيذاء أحد. في حين أن المعرفة هذه يمكنها أن تمزقها إرباً.

يمكنها أن تمزق سلامتها العقلية.

لقد حدث هذا من قبل، في عائلتها."لديكِ الموهبة"، كانت والدتها قد قالت لها عندما كانت صغيرة، وهي راقدة على سرير المستشفى، محاطة بالأنابيب والآلات التي تئن بأصوات التنبيه. كان ذلك أول مرة يخرج فيها قلبها عن السيطرة ويتحول إلى كتلة من العضلات المرتعشة، على وشك أن يقتلها. لم تحتضنها والدتها حينها، حتى في تلك اللحظة. كل ما فعلته أنها ركعت بجوارها ويداها متشابكتان في الصلاة، وعيناها مشتعلتان بالحماسة—وبالحسد.

دائماً، بعد ذلك، كان هناك الحسد."ستكونين عيوننا. ستهديننا جميعاً".

لكن إليزا لم تكن تهدي أحداً إلى أي مكان."الموهبة" كانت لعنة. أدركت ذلك حتى في سن صغيرة. كانت سجلات عائلتها حافلة بنوبات الجنون، ولم تكن تنوي أن تكون الحلقة الأخيرة في سلسلة"الأنبياء" الذين ينتهي بهم المطاف في المصحات، يهذون بنبوءات نهاية العالم ويلعقون البقع على الجدران. عملت بجد كبير على قمع"موهبتها" لتصبح الشخص الذي أرادت

أن تكونه، ونجحت في ذلك. من مراهقة هاربة إلى زميلة في مؤسسة العلوم الوطنية، وإلى طبيبة في القريب العاجل؟ لقد حققت نجاحاً مدهشاً في كل شيء... عدا أمر واحد: الحلم. كان يأتي متى شاء، أكبر من أن يُدفن، وأقوى منها. أقوى من أي شيء آخر.

لكن الآن، بدأت أمور أخرى تتحرك في داخلها، حقائق ليست من صنعها، وذلك بثّ الرعب في كيانها. عدة مرات شعرت وكأن الأرض تتأرجح من تحتها. كان الدوار يشتد عليها، وبدأت تشتبه في أن حرمان نفسها من النوم لتفادي الحلم قد أضعف شيئاً آخر بداخلها. تنفست بعمق، وأخبرت نفسها بأنها قادرة على التحكم بعقلها كما تتحكم بعضلاتها.

"إليزا، هل أنتِ متأكدة أنكِ بخير؟ إذا كنتِ بحاجة إلى بعض الهواء النقي، من فضلكِ-".

"لا. لا، أنا بخير". أجبرت نفسها على الابتسام، ثم انحنت مجدداً فوق كائن أبو الهول أمامها.

توصلوا في النهاية إلى أنهم لن يتمكنوا من تحقيق أمل الدكتور أمهالي. لم يجدوا أي آثار لخياطة جراحية، ولا أي رقعة مكتوب عليها"صُنع بواسطة فرانكشتاين" مخيطة على الجزء الخلفي من الرقبة.

لكن كان هناك شيء آخر.

أمسكت إليزا إحدى الأيدي الميتة لكائنات أبو الهول بيدها المغطاة بالقفاز، واستغرقت في النظر إلى العلامة لفترة طويلة قبل أن تتحدث.

"هل رأيت هذا؟".

من وقفة الدكتور أمهالي الصامتة، خمنت أنه قد رآها، وربما كان ينتظر منهم أن يكتشفوها بأنفسهم.

رمش الدكتور تشاودهاري عدة مرات وهو ينظر إلى العلامة، محاولاً استيعاب ما تعنيه، حتى قال أخيراً:"الفتاة على الجسر".

الفتاة على الجسر: الجمال ذو الشعر الأزرق التي قاتلت الملائكة في

براغ، ويداها ممدودتان أمامها مغطاتان بوشم العيون النيلية. لقد ظهرت على غلاف مجلة تايم، ومنذ ذلك الحين، أصبحت هذه العيون رمزاً مرتبطاً بالشياطين. كان الأطفال يرسمونها بالحبر على أيديهم ليتصرفوا كالأشرار. أصبح هذا الوشم بمثابة الرقم 666 الجديد.

قال الدكتور أمهالي بصوت مكثف:"هل بدأت تفهم ما يعنيه هذا؟ هل ترى كيف سيفسر العالم الأمر؛ الملائكة طارت إلى روما؛ هذا أمر يبعث على الارتياح للمسيحيين، أليس كذلك؟ الملائكة في روما، تحذّر من الوحوش والحروب، بينما هنا، في بلد مسلم، نقوم نحن باستخراج... شياطين. ماذا تتوقع أن تكون ردة الفعل؟".

أدركت إليزا قصده وشعرت بخوفه. كان العالم بحاجة إلى استفزاز أقل بكثير من"شياطين" حقيقية من لحم ودم حتى يفقد صوابه. ومع ذلك، كانت هذه الكائنات تشعل فيها شعوراً بالدهشة، ولم تستطع أن تتمنى لو كانت مجرد خدعة.

في جميع الأحوال، كانت هذه المخاوف تخص الحكومات والدبلوماسيين، والشرطة والجيش، وليس العلماء. كان عملهم يقتصر على الأجساد أمامهم—دراسة المادة الفيزيائية فقط، لا غير. كان هناك الكثير من العمل بانتظارهم: جمع عينات الأنسجة وتخزينها، بالإضافة إلى القياسات التفصيلية والتصوير لكل جثة كمرجع. لكنهم اختاروا أولاً أن يقوموا بنظرة عامة على المهمة التي أمامهم.

"هل كل الأجساد تحمل هذه العلامات؟" سأل الدكتور تشاودهاري.

"كلها باستثناء واحدة"، أجاب الدكتور أمهالي.

تساءلت إليزا عن تلك الجثة المستثناة، لكن المخلوق التالي الذي رأوه—الكائن الضخم الذي كان تحت القماش الأبيض—كانت لديه العلامات، وكذلك الأجساد في الخيمة التالية، والتي تليها، حتى نسيت إليزا أمر تلك الجثة الوحيدة.

كان من الصعب عليها أن تعي تماماً ما تراه—وما تشمه—جسداً بعد الآخر. كانت تشعر بالغثيان، والإرهاق، وشبح الهلع الذي لم يبتعد كثيراً— ذلك الإحساس بأشياء معروفة ومطوية في أعماقها. كما كانت فريسة لحزن غريب. الانتقال من خيمة إلى أخرى، والنظر إلى هذا التشكيل من الكائنات غير الأرضية، كان كأنه استعراض كرنفالي، حيث كل المعروضات ميتة

كانت جميع الأجساد مزيجاً عجيباً من أجزاء حيوانات يمكن التعرف عليها، وكل جثة في مراحل متقدمة من التحلل بشكل متتابع. كلما كانت الجثة أعمق في الحفرة، فهذا يعني أنها قد ماتت منذ وقت أطول، مما يشير إلى أنهم لم يُقتلوا دفعة واحدة، بل تم قتلهم على فترات متقطعة، الواحد تلو الآخر. أياً كان ما حدث هنا، لم يكن مجرد مذبحة.

ثم وصلوا إلى آخر خيمة مخصصة لعزل الكائنات، موضوعة على جانب وحدها في أقصى طرف الحفرة. قال الدكتور أمهالي وهو يرفع غطاء الخيمة:"هذه الجثة دُفنت وحيدة، في قبر ضحل".

دخلت إليزا، وعند رؤيتها لهذا"العرض" الأخير في هذه الحديقة الميتة من الكائنات، شعرت بالحزن يتوهج داخلها بقوة لم تشعر بها من قبل. هذا هو الكائن الوحيد الذي لم تكن لديه العلامات على راحتيه. لقد دُفن وكأن شخصاً ما اهتم به—لم يُلقَ في الحفرة المتعفنة، بل وُضع في مكانه ثم غُطي بالتراب والحصى. غطت جسده طبقة من الغبار الرمادي، مما جعله يبدو كتمثال من منحوتات الفن.

ربما لهذا السبب استطاعت أن تفكر فوراً بأنه كان... جميلاً. لأنه لم يكن يبدو حقيقياً. كان أشبه بفن. شعرت وكأنها قد تبكي لأجله، رغم أن ذلك لم يكن منطقياً. إذا كانت الأجساد الأخرى"مسخية" إلى حد ما، فهذا الكائن بدا"شيطانياً" بامتياز:

بنية جسده بشرية في أغلبها، مع قرنين أسودين طويلين، وحوافر مشقوقة، وجناحين خفاشيين منتشرين على الأرض على كلا الجانبين، يمتدان

لأكثر من ثلاثة أمتار، وطرفاهما منحنيان قليلاً ليلامسا جوانب الخيمة لكن، لم تشعر بأنه شيطاني، تماماً كما لم تشعر أن الملائكة كانت ملائكية حقاً.

ما الذي حدث هنا؟ تساءلت بصمت. لم يكن من ضمن مهامها أن تعرف الإجابة، لكنها لم تستطع منع نفسها من التفكير. تساؤلات تهاجمها، كأسراب من الطيور المذعورة: من قتل هذه الكائنات؟ ولماذا؟ وماذا كانوا يفعلون في برية المغرب؟ و... ما أسماؤهم؟ جزء من عقلها أخبرها أن هذا ليس رد الفعل المناسب عند رؤية"وحوش" ميتة—أن تتساءل عن أسمائهم—لكن هذه الجثة الأخيرة تحديداً، بملامحها الدقيقة، جعلتها تشعر برغبة شديدة في المعرفة.

كان طرف أحد قرنيه مكسوراً، مجرد تفصيل بسيط، لكنها تساءلت كيف حدث ذلك. ومن هذا التساؤل البسيط، وجدت نفسها تنجرف إلى كل التساؤلات الأخرى.

كيف كانت حياته؟ ولماذا انتهى به الحال ميتاً هنا؟

كان الرجلان يتحدثان، وسمعت إليزا الدكتور أمهالي يخبر الدكتور تشاودهاري أن هذه الكائنات يبدو أنها عاشت في القصبة لبعض الوقت، وغادرتها منذ يومين فقط.

قال الدكتور أمهالي:"شاهد بعض البدو رحيلهم".

قالت إليزا بسرعة:"انتظر، رأى البعض منهم أحياء؟ كم عددهم؟".

"لا نعرف. الشهود كانوا في حالة هستيرية. قالوا: العشرات".

العشرات. شعرت إليزا برغبة شديدة في رؤيتهم. كانت تريد أن تراهم وهم أحياء، يتنفسون.

سألت بنبرة ملحة:"وأين ذهبوا؟ هل عثرتم عليهم؟".

رد الدكتور أمهالي بنبرة تحمل سخرية خفيفة:"لقد ذهبوا... هناك"، قال مشيراً بيده نحو السماء."وكلا، لم نعثر عليهم".

وفقاً للشهود، فإن"الشياطين" قد طاروا باتجاه جبال الأطلس، على الرغم من عدم العثور على أي دليل يدعم هذه الرواية. لولا الجثث المتحللة التي تؤكد صحة القصة، لكان من السهل رفض الأمر باعتباره مجرد جنون. ومع ذلك، استمرت المروحيات في تمشيط الجبال، وانطلق العملاء عبر سيارات الجيب والجمال لتتبع أي قبائل بربرية أو رعاة قد يكونون قد شاهدوا شيئاً خرجت إليزا من الخيمة مع الطبيبين.

لن يعثروا عليهم، فكرت وهي تنظر إلى الجبال، إلى القمم المغطاة بالثلوج التي بدت غير منسجمة تماماً مع هذا الجو الحار.

هناك كون آخر، وقد ذهبوا إليه.

35

ثلاثية السقوط

"ابتعد عني".

ما إن أغلق الباب خلفه، حتى التفَّ الإمبراطور جايل، حاكم السيرافيم، بحركة عنيفة، محاولاً التخلّص من المخلوق الخفي الذي كان يمتطي ظهره. لو كان رازغوت قد أراد البقاء، لما تمت إزاحته. قبضته كانت قوية، وإرادته أقوى، وبعد حياة طويلة من العذاب الذي يفوق الوصف، بات تحمله للألم هائلاً.

عادةً ما كان رازغوت يجد لذةً في إلحاق الأذى بالآخرين، لكن بشاعة جايل تجاوزت حتى متعته في التعذيب، فقرر إرخاء قبضته. سقط على الأرضية الرخامية بصوت مكتوم وارتطام خفيف، وصار مرئياً في اللحظة التي لامست فيها أطرافه الأرض. حاول الاعتدال، ساقاه الضامرتان ممدودتان جانباً. قال بلهجة متهكمة، ممزوجة بمسحة من التفاخر:"أعتذر منك".

ردّ جايل وهو ينزع خوذته ويسلّمها لأحد الحراس بجانبه:"وتعتقد أنني يجب أن أشكرك؟". في لحظات الخلوة فقط يمكن رؤية ما أفسده الزمن في وجهه: ندبة بشعة تمتد من خط شعره إلى ذقنه، محت أنفه، تاركةً فمه

في حالة من التشوه تجعل كلماته تخرج متلعثمة ومشوّشة. سأل بصوت متوتر، والبصاق يتطاير من شفتيه:"على ماذا؟".

ارتسمت شبه ابتسامة على وجه رازغوت المشوّه، جلده المتورم الأرجواني اللون مشدود فوق لحمٍ منتفخ. ردّ بامتعاض، متحدثاً باللاتينية—وهي لغة لا يفهمها الإمبراطور بالطبع:"لأنني لم أكسر عنقك حين سنحت لي الفرصة. كان سيكون أمراً بالغ السهولة".

قال جايل بلهجة آمرة وقد ضاق صبره:"كفى التكلم بلغات البشر. ماذا تقول؟".

كانا في جناح فاخر داخل قصر البابا، الملاصق لكنيسة القديس بطرس، وقد عادا للتو من اجتماع مع قادة العالم، حيث قدّم جايل طلباته... أو بالأحرى، ردد كل كلمة همس بها رازغوت في أذنه.

أجاب رازغوت بلغة السيرافيم، وبنبرة عذبة:"الكلمات، يا مولاي. لولا كلماتي، ماذا تكون سوى وجهٍ جميل؟" أطلق ضحكة خافتة، فركله جايل.

لم تكن الركلة استعراضية؛ لم يقصد بها إظهار القوة، بل كانت وحشيةً في بساطتها. ركلة سريعة وحادة، طرف حذائه المدعّم بالفولاذ اخترق جانب رازغوت عميقاً في كتلته اللحمية المشوهة. صرخ رازغوت، كان الألم لاذعاً وساطعاً، كأنه خنجر حاد يغرز في جسده، فتكور على نفسه.

ضحك.

كان هناك شرخ في قشرة عقل رازغوت. عقله الذي كان يوماً ما راقياً ومتوهجاً، أصبح هذا الشرخ بمثابة عيب في جوهرة ثمينة، أو تصدّع في كرة كريستالية. أخذ هذا الشرخ يمتد ويتشعب، يحوّل كل شعور طبيعي إلى نسخة مشوهة وغريبة من ذاته: شعور يمكن التعرف عليه، ولكنه منحرف بشكل خطير. عندما رفع بصره إلى جايل، امتزج الحقد بالسخرية في عينيه كانت عيناه وحدهما تكشفان عن حقيقته. فمن يقف وينظر إليه بين أبناء جنسه، لن يصدّق أن هذا المخلوق ينتمي إلى ذات السلالة. السيرافيم،

بكل ما فيهم من تناغم ورشاقة، قوة وجلال—حتى جايل، ما دام النصف المشوّه من وجهه مغطى—فيما بدا رازغوت ككائن زاحف، مخلوق مشوّه من اللحم، أقرب إلى كائن شيطاني منه إلى ملاك. كان جميلاً في زمنٍ مضى، نعم، لكن الآن لم يبق إلا عيناه لترويا تلك القصة. شكلهما اللوزي كان بديعاً وسط وجهه المتورم المتلوّن بكدمات قاتمة.

كانت هناك علامة أخرى أشد رعباً تدل على أصله: أشواك عظمية مكسورة تبرز من لوحي كتفيه. أجنحته اقتُلعت من جسده. لم تُقطع، بل انتُزعت انتزاعاً. الألم عمره ألف عام، لكنه لن ينساه أبداً.

قال جايل وهو يحدّق به من علٍ، بنظرة لا تخلو من الاستعلاء:"عندما تصبح الأسلحة في أيدي جنودي، وعندما أرى البشرية راكعة أمامي، حينها ربما سأقدّر كلماتك".

كان رازغوت يعرف أفضل من ذلك. ويعلم أنه مقدّر له أن يصبح وصمة عار في اللحظة التي يحصل فيها جايل على أسلحته، مما وضعه في موقف مثير للاهتمام، كونه الشخص المكلف بجلب تلك الأسلحة له.

إذا كان مصيره أن يصبح وصمة عار سواء فشل أو نجح، فإن السؤال هو: هل يفضل أن يكون وصمة عار ضعيفة ومطيعة، أم وصمة عار عنيدة ومستفزة تُسقط طموحات الإمبراطور حوله كأنها قلعة من الرمال؟

بدت الإجابة سهلة ظاهرياً. كم سيكون بسيطاً أن يُذلّ ويدمر جايل. لقد أضحك رازغوت نفسه أثناء الاجتماع الذي كانوا فيه للتو، اجتماع بالغ الجدية والأهمية، بمجرد التفكير في الخطوط السخيفة التي قد يدشّها لجايل ليكررها. الأحمق كان واثقاً جداً من عبودية رازغوت المتذللة إلى درجة أنه كان سيكرر أي شيء يُقال له.

يا له من إغراء عظيم. وقد ضحك رازغوت عدة مرات وهو يتخيل الأمر تصوّر نفسه وهو يضحك بخبث، متخيلاً الإمبراطور يصرخ أمام قادة العالم:"لا يوجد إله، أيها الحمقى! ليس هناك سوى الوحوش، وأنا الأسوأ بينها!".

كان الأمر ممتعاً أن يمسك رازغوت بالأوراق الرابحة. بالنسبة إليه، هو يفهم تماماً أنه لو جاء جايل إلى هنا بدونه، وتحدث إلى الأرض بلغته الأصلية، لكان مضيفوهم قد وضعوا كل براعتهم البشرية في العمل، يرمزون برنامج ترجمة، وعلى الأرجح كانوا سيتمكنون من فهمهم تماماً خلال أسبوع، بل وحتى الرد عليهم بصوت مولّد بواسطة الكمبيوتر.

كما قد يتخيل المرء، لم يشرح رازغوت هذا لجايل. كان من الأفضل اعتراض كل مقطع لفظي والسيطرة على كل عبارة.

إلى السفير الروسي: هل لدى أحدكم علكة؟ نفَسي لا يُحتمل.

أو ربما، إلى وزير الخارجية الأمريكي: لنوثق اتحادنا بقبلة. تعال إليّ، عزيزي، وانزع خوذتي.

ألن يكون ذلك ممتعاً؟

لكنه كبح نفسه، لأن القرار—إما تدمير جايل أو مساعدته—كانت له عواقب عميقة وبعيدة المدى، تتجاوز بكثير ما يمكن للإمبراطور نفسه أن يتصوره.

أوه. تجاوزه تماماً. "ستحصل على أسلحتك"، قال رازغوت له. "لكن يجب أن نمضي بحذر، يا سيدي. هذا عالم حر، وليس جيشك لتأمره. يجب أن نجعلهم راغبين في أن يعطونا ما نحتاج إليه".

"يعطوني ما أحتاج إليه"، صحح جايل.

"أوه نعم، أنت"، عدّل رازغوت كلامه. "كل شيء لك، يا سيدي. أسلحتك، حربك، والستيليين الذين لا يمشّون، يتوسلون أمامك".

الستيليون، كانوا الهدف الأول لجايل، وكان هذا غنياً بالتفاصيل.

لم يكن رازغوت يعرف ما الذي أثار كراهية الإمبراطور الخاصة تجاههم، لكن السبب لم يكن يهم، بل النتيجة فقط. "كم سيكون اليوم حلواً". تظاهر بالتملق، وتصنع الانحناء، وأخفى ضحكته، وكان ذلك شعوراً رائعاً في داخله، لأن، أوه، كان يعلم أشياءً، نعم، وكان من الجيد أن يكون هو الوحيد الذي يعرف

كان رازغوت قد أفشى أسراره مرة واحدة فقط، وإلى شخص واحد فقط، إلى ذاك الذي كانت رغبته في المعرفة قد جعلته بغلاً لملاك محطم، إيزيل دهش رازغوت من مقدار افتقاده لذلك المتسول العجوز. كان ذكياً وخيّراً، وقد دمره رازغوت. حسناً، وماذا كان الإنسان يتوقع؟ أيتوقع شيئاً مقابل لا شيء؟ من باحث إلى مجنون، ومن طبيب إلى نابش قبور، كان ذلك مصيره. لكنه حصل على ما أراده، أليس كذلك؟

حصل على معرفة تتجاوز حتى ما كان يمكن لبريمستون نفسه أن يخبره به، لأن حتى ذاك الشيطان العجوز لم يكن يعلم هذا السر. رازغوت تذكّر ما لم يعد أحدٌ سواه يتذكره.

"الكارثة".

رهيبة، رهيبة، رهيبة إلى الأبد.

لم تُنسَ الكارثة صدفةً. لقد عُدّلت العقول، أُفرِغت، امتدت الأيدي إلى الداخل وكشطت الماضي بعيداً. لكن ليس عقل رازغوت. لم يتمكن أحد من محوه.

لقد حاول إيزيل، ذلك الأحمق العجوز، أن يخبر الملاك ذا العينين الناريتين الذي جاء إليهما في المغرب. اسمه كان أكيفا، وكان يحمل دماء الستيلييين، لكن دون معرفة الستيلييين. لم يستمع إليه."يمكنني أن أخبرك بأشياء!" أخذ إيزيل يصرخ، محاولاً لفت انتباه الملاك الغاضب."أسرار! عن قومك. رازغوت لديه قصص".

لكن أكيفا قاطعه، رافضاً أن يسمع كلمة واحدة من ملاك ساقط. كما لو كان يعرف ما يعنيه ذلك حقاً!"ساقط". نطقها وكأنها لعنة، لكنه لم يكن لديه أدنى فكرة."كما ينمو العفن على الكتب، تنمو الأساطير على التاريخ"، قال إيزيل، بنبرة حكيم انهار عقله."ربما عليك أن تسأل شخصاً كان هناك، قبل كل تلك القرون. ربما عليك أن تسأل رازغوت".

لكن أكيفا لم يسأل. لم يسأل أحد رازغوت قط."ماذا حدث لك؟

لماذا فعلوا هذا بك؟".

"من تكون حقاً؟".

آه، آه، وآه. كم كان عليهم أن يسألوا.

التفت رازغوت إلى جايل، متخلياً عن ذكرياته، ليعود إلى واقعه. قال بلهجة مطمئنة:"سنقنع البشر، لا تقلق. إنهم دائماً هكذا، جدال وجدال مستمر. هذا طعامهم وشرابهم. أما هؤلاء المتغطرسون من رؤساء الدول؟ فهم ليسوا هدفنا الحقيقي. هذا مجرد استعراض. بينما هم يهزون رؤوسهم الذابلة في وجه بعضهم البعض، فإن الناس يعملون لمصلحتك، في الخفاء".

"تذكر كلماتي.

بالفعل هناك مجموعات ستبدأ في بناء ترساناتها، جاهزة لتسليمها لك. لن يكون الأمر سوى مسألة اختيار، يا مولاي، ممن ترغب في أخذها".

"أين كل هذه العروض إذاً؟" بصق جايل بغضب، واللعاب يتطاير من فمه."أين؟".

"الصبر، الصبر—".

"لقد قلت إنني سأعبد كإله!".

"نعم، حسناً، أنت إله قبيح"، قذف رازغوت الكلام بحنق، غير قادر هو نفسه على تجسيد الصبر الذي كان يعظ به."تجعلهم يشعرون بالتوتر. تبصق عندما تتحدث، تختبئ خلف قناعك، وتنظر إليهم وكأنك ستذبحهم جميعاً في أسِرّتهم. هل فكرت في تجربة شيء من السحر الشخصي؟ قد يجعل عملي أسهل".

مرة أخرى، ركل جايل رازغوت. كانت طعنة الألم أكثر حدة هذه المرة، وسعل رازغوت دماً على الأرضية الرخامية الفاخرة. غمس طرف إصبعه في الدم وبدأ بخربشة كلمة بذيئة.

هزّ جايل رأسه باشمئزاز، واتجه بخطوات غاضبة نحو الطاولة حيث كانت المشروبات مُعدة. صب لنفسه كأساً من النبيذ وبدأ يذرع الغرفة جيئة

وذهاباً."الأمر يستغرق وقتاً طويلاً جداً"، قال بصوت حاد يقطر بالازدراء."لم آتِ إلى هنا من أجل طقوس وتراتيل. أتيت من أجل الأسلحة".

تظاهر رازغوت بالتنهد وبدأ يجرّ نفسه ببطء، بشق النفس، باتجاه الباب."حسناً. سأذهب وأتحدث إليهم بنفسي. سيكون أسرع على أي حال. نطقك للاتينية مريع".

أشار جايل إلى اثنين من جنود الدومينيون الذين يحرسون الباب، وكان رازغوت يضحك بينما أمسكوا به من تحت إبطيه وسحبوه إلى الخلف، ليلقوه بقوة عند قدمي جايل. انفجر رازغوت بالضحك على نكتته."تخيّل وجوههم!" صرخ، وهو يمسح دمعة من عينه الداكنة اللامعة."أوه، تخيل لو دخل البابا إلى هنا الآن ورآنا نحن الاثنين في كل عظمتنا! 'هل هؤلاء هم الملائكة؟' سيصرخ، ممسكاً قلبه. 'إذاً ماذا يكون الوحوش باسم الرب؟'".

انحنى رازغوت، وهو يهتز من شدة الضحك.

لكن جايل لم يشاركه هذا المرح."نحن لسنا زوجاً"، قال بصوت بارد وناعم جداً."واعلم هذا، أيها الشيء. إذا اعتبرتني يوماً-".

قاطعه رازغوت."ماذا؟ ماذا ستفعل لي، أيها الإمبراطور العزيز؟" رفع بصره نحو جايل وثبّت نظره عليه، بثبات تام، وهدوء شديد."انظر إليّ. انظر إلى داخلي واعرف. أنا رازغوت، ساقط ثلاث مرات، أتعس الملائكة. لا يوجد شيء يمكنك أن تأخذه مني لم يُؤخذ بالفعل، ولا شيء يمكنك أن تفعله لم يُفعل بالفعل".

"لم تُقتل بعد"، قال جايل، دون أن يتزحزح.

عند ذلك، ابتسم رازغوت. كانت أسنانه مثالية وسط وجهه البشع، وكان الشرخ في عقله واضحاً في عينيه المجنونتين. بتهكم واضح، شبك يديه معاً وتظاهر بالتوسل،"ليس ذلك، يا مولاي. أوه، آذني، عذبني، ولكن مهما فعلت، أرجوك، أرجوك، لا تمنحني السلام!".

وتحركت نوبات من الغضب عبر وجه جايل المشقوق إلى نصفين، وفكه

مشدود بإحكام إلى درجة أن ندبته أصبحت بيضاء احمرّ باقي وجهه حتى بات قرمزياً. كان ينبغي عليه أن يفهم، حينها. هذا ما كان رازغوت يفكر فيه، وهو لا يزال يضحك، بينما انقضّ عليه جايل بأطراف حذائه المدعمة بالحديد، مولّداً ألماً بعد ألم، عائلة كاملة من الآلام، سلالة من العذاب. تلك كانت اللحظة التي كان على جايل أن يدرك فيها، أخيراً، أنه ليس المسيطر.

لم يكن بإمكانه قتل رازغوت؛ كان بحاجة إليه. ليس فقط لترجمة اللغات البشرية، بل أكثر من ذلك: لفهم البشر أنفسهم، لفهم تاريخهم وسياساتهم ونفسياتهم، ولصياغة استراتيجية وخطاب يناسبهم.

بإمكانه أن يركله، أوه نعم، ورازغوت سيهمس للألم طوال الليل، يواسيه كأنه يحتضن مجموعة من الأطفال الرّضّع، وفي الصباح سيحصي كدماته، ويرقم أحقاده وأوجاعه، ثم يستمر في الابتسام، ويستمر في معرفة كل الأشياء التي لا أحد يتذكرها، الأشياء التي ما كان ينبغي نسيانها أبداً، والسبب—أوه، نجوم الآلهة، السبب الأروع والأكثر رعباً—الذي يجب أن يترك جايل الستيليين بسببه وشأنهم.

"أنا رازغوت، ساقط ثلاث مرات، أتعس الملائكة!" غنى رازغوت بخليط من اللغات البشرية، من اللاتينية إلى العربية إلى العبرية ثم عاد من جديد، يكسر الجمل بتأوهات مع كل ركلة تصيبه."وأنا أعرف ما هو الخوف! أوه نعم، وأعرف ما هي الوحوش أيضاً. أنت تظن أنك تعرف، لكنك لا تعرف. ولكنك ستعرف، أوه نعم، ستعرف. سأحصل لك على أسلحتك، وسأفعل ذلك بسرعة، وسأضحك عندما تقتلني كما أضحك الآن بينما تركلني، وستسمع صدى ضحكتي في نهاية كل شيء وتعرف أنني كنت أستطيع إيقافك. كنت أستطيع أن أخبرك".

لا تفعل هذا، أوه لا، ليس هذا. كان بإمكانه أن يقول. وإلا سيموت الجميع. "وربما كنت سأخبرك"، أضاف رازغوت بلغة السيرافيم،"لو كنت ألطف مع هذا الشيء المسكين المكسور".

36

الشخص الوحيد غير الغبي على هذا الكوكب

"مرحباً، أيها الملك مورغان". قال غابرييل وهو يُطلّ برأسه داخل المختبر."كيف حال الشخص الوحيد غير الغبي على هذا الكوكب في هذا اليوم الجميل؟".

"اذهب إلى الجحيم"، ردّ مورغان دون أن يرفع عينيه عن شاشة حاسوبه ابتسم غابرييل ابتسامة عريضة وقال:"آه، رائع، يبدو أن صباحي جميلٌ أيضاً". ثم خطا إلى داخل المختبر وأخذ ينظر حوله."هل رأيت إليزا؟ لم تعد إلى المنزل".

أصدر مورغان صوتاً من أنفه أشبه بالـ"سِئزش"."نعم، رأيتها. منظر إليزا جونز نائمة وفمها مفتوح أفسد يومي تماماً".

قال غابرييل بنبرة لطيفة مفعمة بالحيوية:"أوه. لا أظن أن هذا هو السبب. ربما كان يومك قد بدأ بالخراب منذ لحظة استيقاظك من حلمٍ كنتَ فيه محبوباً، ثم تذكرت أنك ما زلت أنت".

التفت مورغان أخيراً ونظر إلى غابرييل بملامح متجهمة.

"ماذا تريد، يا إدينجر؟".

"أعتقد أنني أخبرتك مسبقاً. أبحث عن إليزا".

"كما ترى، هي ليست هنا"، قال مورغان وهو يعود إلى شاشة حاسوبه. وكاد أن يضيف، بنبرة لاذعة تغمرها السخرية، أنها ربما لم تعد حتى إلى البلاد، ثم يُتبع ذلك بتعليق لاذع مفاده أن غيابها هو السبب في الصفاء غير المعتاد للجو، عندما قطع غابرييل حبل أفكاره.

قال غابرييل:"لدي هاتفها. لم تعد إلى المنزل، وهناك قرابة المليون رسالة جديدة. لم أكن أظن أنه من الممكن أن يعيش أحد بدون هاتفه كل هذه المدة. هل أنت متأكد أنها بخير؟".

تغيّرت ملامح وجه مورغان قليلاً. ظل ملتفتاً بعيداً، وكان يمكن لغابرييل أن يلمح انعكاس تعابيره على شاشة الحاسوب لو أنه أولى مزيداً من الانتباه، لكنه لم يكن يوماً من هؤلاء الذين ينتبهون كثيراً لمورغان توث.

"ذهبت إلى مكان ما مع الدكتور شودهاري". قال مورغان، ونبرته لم تتغير، ما زالت لاذعة، لكن في عينيه الآن بريق دهاء وبرود لئيم."سيعودون قريباً، إذا أردت ترك الهاتف".

تردد غابرييل قليلاً. قلب الهاتف في يده، ثم ألقى نظرة سريعة حوله في الغرفة. لمح سترة إليزا ملقاة على كرسي بجوار أحد أجهزة التسلسل الجيني."حسناً"، قال أخيراً، ثم تقدم بضع خطوات ووضع الهاتف بجوار السترة."هلّا أخبرتها أن ترسل لي رسالة حين تأخذه؟".

"بالطبع"، ردّ مورغان، وفي تلك اللحظة، تردد غابرييل عند عتبة الباب، مرتاباً من هذا التعاون المفاجئ. لكن سرعان ما أضاف مورغان:"بالمناسبة، لدي اقتراح... حاول أن تحبس أنفاسك حتى يحدث ذلك".

ابتسم غابرييل وهز رأسه قبل أن يغادر.

وانتظر مورغان خمس دقائق، خمس دقائق كاملة—ثلاثمائة نبضة صغيرة لعقرب الثواني—قبل أن يغلق الباب، ويتناول الهاتف من مكانه.

37

مستغرق في نشوته

"هل أنتِ متأكدة من أنكِ قادرة على فعل ذلك؟" سأل أكيفا شقيقته، وتجاعيد القلق ترتسم على جبينه. كانا يقفان عند مدخل الكهف، حيث كادت جيوشهما أن تفني بعضها البعض في اليوم السابق. أما المشهد أمامهما الآن... فكان مختلفاً تماماً.

"ماذا؟ قضاء بضعة أيام برفقة عشيقتك؟" ردّت ليراز وهي تعدّل حزام سيفها دون أن تنظر إليه. "الأمر ليس بهذه السهولة. إذا حاولتَ إجباري على ارتداء ملابس بشرية، فلن أكون مسؤولة عمّا قد يحدث".

ابتسم أكيفا، لكنها ابتسامة باردة خالية من أي تعبير مرح. لم يكن هناك شيء يرغب فيه أكثر الآن من قضاء بعض الأيام مع كارو، محاولاً إقناع عمّه السادي، المتعطش للحروب، والذي كان نقيضه في كل شيء، بالعودة إلى دياره.

قال لأخته بنبرة أرادها أن تكون خفيفة:"سأحمّلكِ مسؤولية إضافية على تصرفاتكِ، يا ليراز".

لم يكن يريد أن تبدو كلماته جارحة، لكنها التقطت نبرته بسرعة. اشتعل الغضب في عينيها وهي تقول:"ماذا؟ ألا تثق بي مع حبيبتك الثمينة؟ ربما يجدر بك أن ترسل كتيبة كاملة لحراستها".

أو أذهب بنفسي، فكّر في أن يقول. لقد وعد كارو بألّا يدعها تغيب عن ناظريه، لكنه اكتشف الآن أنه سيفعل ذلك، للمرة الأخيرة. كانوا قد اتفقوا جميعاً على خطتها، رغم جرأتها ومكرها، وكان دوره في هذه الخطة جوهرياً، إلا أن الخطة ستبقيه في إريتز، بينما ترافق ليراز كارو إلى عالم البشر.

قال:"أنتِ تعلمين أنني أثق بكِ"، وصوته ينقل شبه الحقيقة. كان يثق بها لحماية كارو. لكن عندما سألها إن كانت واثقة من قدرتها على القيام بذلك، كان يقصد شيئاً آخر."عندما يحين الوقت، هل ستتمكّنين من كبح رغبتك في قتل جايل؟".

ردت بحدة:"قلتُ إنني سأفعل، أليس كذلك؟".

أجابها أكيفا:"لم يكن ذلك مقنعاً".

في مجلس الحرب الذي انعقد من جديد، استقبلت ليراز فكرة كارو بضحكة قصيرة تنمّ عن عدم التصديق، ثم أخذت تنقل نظراتها بين الحاضرين حول الطاولة، واحداً تلو الآخر، وهي تزداد استياءً كلما فكّرت في الأمر.

التفكير في عدم قتل جايل... على الأقل، ليس الآن.

وعندما اتفق الجميع بعد نقاش طويل، غرقت ليراز في صمت مشبوه، أدرك أكيفا من خلاله أنها، مهما قالت الآن، عندما تقف أمام عمّهما الشرير، ستفعل ما تراه مناسباً، وفق هواها.

قالت مجدداً، بنبرة قاطعة:"قلتُ إنني سأفعل"، ونظراتها تتحدّاه أن يشكك في كلامها.

تخيل نفسه يقول: لنكن واضحين، يا لير. هل تخططين لتدمير كل شيء؟

لكنه قرر أن يتخلى عن الأمر.

"سنثأر لهازايل"، قالها دون أن تكون مجرد مواساة أو نصف حقيقة. كان يريد ذلك بقدر ما تريده هي.

قهقهت ليراز بضحكة ساخرة:"حسناً، المستغرق بالنشوة ربما يفعل".

شعر أكيڤا بوخزة. مستغرقاً بالنشوة. قالتها وكأن الحب تافه، بل أسوأ من ذلك، وكأنه إهمال للواجب. هل الوقوع في الحب خيانة لذكرى هازايل؟ تذكر ما قالته له كارو سابقاً عن الظلام الذي نغرق فيه باسم الأموات، وإن كان هذا ما سيريدونه حقاً لنا. لم يكن بحاجة للتفكير في الأمر؛ كان يعلم أن هازايل لن يعترض على سعادته، لكن ليراز كانت تفعل ذلك بوضوح.

لم يردّ على تعليقها اللاذع. ماذا يمكنه أن يقول؟ كان يكفيه النظر حوله ليدرك أن الحب لم يكن تافهاً. في هذا الكهف، كان الامتزاج غير المريح بين السيرافيم والكيميرا أقرب ما يكون إلى المعجزة. ومع ذلك، كانت معجزتهما، هو وكارو. لم يكن ليُعلن ذلك، لكنه كان يعرف في قلبه أنه كذلك.

بالطبع، كان لليراز دورها في الأمر أيضاً، هي وثياغو. كان مشهداً مذهلاً أن يراهما يقفان كتفاً بكتف، ينسجان وحداتهما العسكرية معاً بمثابة قدوة للجميع. لقد تفاوضا على خطة الكتائب المختلطة وقاما بتوزيع المهام بنفسيهما. أكيڤا وضع علامة الهامسا الجديدة، الوشم المضاد، على جميع إخوته وأخواته البالغ عددهم مئتين وستة وتسعين فرداً. والآن، أمام عينيه تحديداً، كانت الجيوش تختبر تلك العلامات على بعضها البعض.

بعض الجنود من كلا الجانبين بقوا في أماكنهم مترددين، لكن الغالبية بدت منهمكة في نوع من... حسناً، لنسمّها لعبة التعارف، لعبة أقل عدائية بكثير مما كانت ليراز قد واجهته في السابق.

راقب أكيڤا شقيقه زائانيل وهو يحثّ ساب، برأسها الشبيه برأس ابن آوى، أن تُريه كفيها. ترددت، ثم نظرت إلى الذئب الذي أومأ لها مشجعاً، فرفعت يديها أخيراً، عيناها الحادتان موجهتان مباشرة نحو زائانيل. ولم يحدث شيء.

كانا يقفان على بقعة الدم الداكنة ليوثيم، في ذات المكان الذي كاد كل شيء أن يتهاوى فيه بالأمس، ولم يحدث شيء. ارتخت عضلات زائانيل، وابتسم ضاحكاً، ثم ضرب ساب على كتفها بقوة بدت كأنها هجوم، لكن ضحكته كانت أكثر دفئاً، ولم تُظهر ساب أي انزعاج.

على بُعد خطوات قليلة منهما، رأى أكيڤا إيسّا تقبل دعوة إليون. مدّت يدها برشاقة ووضعتها فوق يده الموشومة والمليئة بالندوب. كانت في هذه الصورة قوةٌ تمنّى أكيڤا لو يستطيع تحويلها إلى إكسير. القليل... والمزيد، فكّر، وكأنها صلاة.

ثم بحث عن الوميض الأزرق الذي اعتاد أن يتتبعه دوماً، فوجدت عيناه كارو في اللحظة ذاتها التي نظرت فيها إليه. شرارة. توهج. مجرد نظرة واحدة منهما جعلته يشعر وكأنه ثمل بالنور. يا نجوم السماء، لماذا لم تكن قريبة؟ لقد سئم أكيڤا من تلك المساحات الهائلة من الهواء التي تستمر في التمدد بينهما. وقريباً، ستحلّ محلّها أميالٌ وأجواء تفصل بينهما

"آسفة"، قالت ليراز بهدوء، مقاطعة أفكاره."لم يكن ذلك منصفاً".

شعر أكيڤا بدفء يتدفق في داخله، وموجة من الحنان تجتاحه تجاه شقيقته الهشة، التي كانت الاعتذارات بالنسبة إليها مهمة صعبة وليست باليسيرة. قال، محاولاً التخفيف:"لا، لم يكن كذلك. وبالمناسبة، كان من الإنصاف أن تنتظري بضع دقائق قبل اقتحام المكان في وقتٍ سابق. أراهن أننا كنا على وشك التقبيل في تلك اللحظة".

ضحكت ليراز ضحكة مكتومة، بدت وكأنها فوجئت، وسرعان ما انحسرت التوترات بينهما."أعتذر إن كان موتي الوشيك قد عكّر صفو تقبيلكما".

قال أكيڤا مبتسماً:"أسامحك". كان من الصعب المزاح بشأن الرعب الذي كاد أن يصيبها، لكنه شعر أن هذا ما كان هازايل سيفعله، وهذا ما أصبح مبدأً توجيهياً له—التفكير بما كان سيفعله هازايل—الذي غالباً ما يُفضي إلى التصرف الصحيح."سامحتكِ هذه المرة"، شدد على قوله."في

المرة القادمة، رجاءً حاولي أن تختاري توقيت موتك الوشيك بتفكيرٍ أكثر. والأفضل ألا تفعلي ذلك مجدداً".

فكر في إضافة"جرّبي، على وشك التقبيل" أو"تقبيلاً حقيقياً"، لكنه لم يقلها، جزئياً لأنه من الصعب تخيّلها، وجزئياً لأنه كان يعلم أن الأمر سيُزعجها. لكنه كان يتمنى ذلك لها—أن تجد ليراز يوماً ما نفسها منشغلة بالنشوة.

"سأذهب للاستحمام قبل أن نغادر"، قال لها وهو يدفع بجسده بعيداً عن الجدار الحجري الذي يستند إليه. ساعات من استخدام السحر المتواصل جعلت جسده يشعر وكأنه ثقيل مثل الرصاص. حرّك كتفيه ومدّ رقبته، متنهداً من الإرهاق.

قالت ليراز، محاولةً استجماع نبرتها الطبيعية:"عليك الذهاب إلى برك المياه الحارّة. إنها... رائعة للغاية".

توقف في منتصف خطوته وحدّق فيها."رائعة للغاية؟" كررها متعجباً. لم يذكر أنه سمع ليراز تستخدم كلمة"رائعة" من قبل، و... هل كان ذلك احمراراً يتصاعد على وجنتيها؟

هذا مثير للاهتمام.

قالت:"الماء العلاجي، بالطبع". بدت نظرتها ثابتة ومباشرة أكثر من اللازم؛ كانت تحاول التغطية على شعور آخر باّدعاء البرود، وكانت تبالغ في ذلك. إضافةً إلى ذلك، كان هناك ذلك الاحمرار.

أمر مثير جداً للاهتمام.

قال أكيڤا:"حسناً. لا وقت لذلك الآن". كان هناك ماء في مكان قريب على طول الممر."سأكون هناك"، قال لها وهو يغادر. كان يود الذهاب إلى برك المياه الحارّة—كان يود الذهاب إلى هناك مع كارو —لكن ذلك كان مجرد بند آخر يُضاف إلى قائمة أمنياته التي سيفعلها عندما يحصل على حيز من الحرية.

الاستحمام مع كارو.

أحس بحرارة تتبعه لهذه الفكرة، ويا للعجب، لم يصادفها الحاجز المعتاد من الذنب أو الإنكار. لقد اعتاد على الاصطدام بهذا الحاجز إلى حدّ أن غيابه بدا وكأنه أمر غير واقعي، تماماً كأنها تدور حول نفسها وقد ألفتَ ذلك الدوران، لتجد بدلاً من الجدار الذي ألفته جيداً، امتداداً مفتوحاً نحو السماء.

حرية.

وإن لم يكونا قد بلغاها بعد، فقد أصبح أكيفا حراً على الأقل ليتجرأ ويحلم، وهذا بحد ذاته كان أمراً عظيماً.

كازو سامحته. كارو تحبه.

ورغم ذلك، افترقا مجدداً، ولم يقبّلها، وكلا الأمرين لم يكونا على ما يُرام. حتى لو لم يكن عليهما إخفاء مشاعرهما أمام جيوش بأكملها، وحتى لو استطاعا سرقة لحظةٍ خاصة، كان لدى أكيفا مقولة يكررها الجنود حول الوداع: لا تقل وداعاً. إنه نذير شؤم، وتقبيل الوداع ليس سوى شكل آخر من أشكال الوداع. قبلة البداية لا ينبغي أن تشبه قبلة الفراق.

ينفتح الممر المنحني في نهايته على زاوية، حيث قناة من الماء المتجمّد تنبثق من الجدار الصخري الخشن، وتنساب بارتفاع الخصر لعدة أمتار في مجرى ضيّق قبل أن تختفي مجدداً في عمق الصخر. وكغيرها من عجائب هذه الكهوف، بدت طبيعية، لكنها على الأرجح لم تكن كذلك. خلع أكيفا حزام سيفه وعلّقه على نتوء صخري، ثم نزع قميصه.

جمع الماء البارد في كفيه، ثم رفعه إلى وجهه. حفنة تلو الأخرى، إلى وجهه، وعنقه، وصدره، وكتفيه. غطس برأسه في الماء، ثم اعتدل واقفاً، وهو يشعر بالماء يتبخر على الفور بسبب حرارة جسده، متدفقاً في قنواتٍ ضيقة بين مفاصل جناحيه.

كان قد وافق على خطة كارو لأنها منطقية وذكية، ومخاطرها أقل بكثير من الخطة السابقة، وإن نجحت، فسيقل تهديد جايل لعالم البشر بشكل

كبير، كإعصارٍ يُخفِض تصنيفه إلى مجرّد عاصفة عابرة. صحيح أن مملكة الأرض ستظل قائمةً كمصدر للقلق، لكنها كانت كذلك دائماً.

المهم أنهم سيمنعون عدوهم من الحصول على ما أسمته كارو"أسلحة الدمار الشامل".

لقد سخرت ليراز من كارو في مجلس الحرب الأول، مقترحةً أن يطلبوا بكل بساطة من جايل أن يغادر، لكن في جوهرها، كانت هذه هي الخطة: أن يطلبوا منه بأدب أن يأخذ جيشه ويرجع إلى وطنه، دون الحصول على ما جاء من أجله. شكراً لكم، وليلة سعيدة.

بالطبع، كانت نقطة القوة في الخطة هي الإغراء الذي سيقدّمونه له. كانت الخطة بسيطة وعبقرية—لم تكن لطفاً—ولم يشكّ أكيفا لحظة في أن كارو وليراز يمكنهما تنفيذها. كلتاهما كانتا قويتين، لكنهما كانتا أيضاً أكثر شخصين يعنيان له شيئاً في العالم—العالمين—وكل ما أراده هو أن يحمل كلاً منهما بأمان إلى المستقبل الذي يحلم به، المستقبل الذي لا تكون فيه حياة أحد مهددة، وتصبح أصعب القرارات فيه هي: ماذا نأكل على الفطور؟

ليراز كانت محقّة، فكّر أكيفا وهو مستغرق في نشوته. لم يكن يتوقع أن يحصل على لحظة أخرى خاصة مع كارو لوقت طويل، لذلك عندما سمع صوتاً خلفه—أشبه بشهيقٍ خفيف—استدار بسرعة، ونبضات قلبه تتسارع، متوقعاً أن يراها.

لكنّه لم يجد أحداً.

ابتسم. كان يشعر بوجودٍ أمامه بوضوح، كما لو أنه سمع شهيقاً. لقد جاءت مجدداً، بكل بهائها، وهذا يعني أنها استطاعت الحضور دون أن يلاحظها أحد. مهما كانت المبررات التي حاول إقناع نفسه بها قبل دقائق—بأن"قبلة البداية لا ينبغي أن تكون في لحظة الافتراق"—لم تصمد عزيمته أمام اندفاع الأمل الذي اجتاحه. كان بحاجة إلى ذلك،

بحاجة إليها.

بدا له أن التفاهم الذي مرّ بينهما، اليدان على القلبين، كان غير مكتمل. لم يتوقع أنه سيكون واثقاً من سعادته، أو يستطيع التنفس بعمقٍ كامل مرةً أخرى، حتى... ومرّة أخرى، وللمفاجأة، لم يكن هناك أي حاجز من الذنب يعترض الأمل، بل كان فقط امتداداً مفتوحاً من الاحتمالات أمامهما... حتى يُقبّلها.

قال مبتسماً:"كاؤو؟ هل أنتِ هنا؟" وانتظر أن تتجسد أمامه، مستعداً لاحتضانها في اللحظة التي تظهر فيها. يمكنه فعل ذلك الآن. على الأقل، عندما لا يكون أحدٌ في الجوار.

لكنها لم تتجسد.

كان هناك شيء آخر أيضاً، إحساس اجتاحه، أو بالأحرى اقتحمه، وجعله يُدرك... حياته بوعي جديد ككيان منفصل، ككتلة متألقة ووحيدة في نسيجٍ كثيف من الكائنات، حقيقية و... ضعيفة. اجتاحته قشعريرة.

سأل مجدداً، بتردد:"كاؤو؟ هل هذه أنتِ؟" رغم أنه كان يعلم في قرارة نفسه أن الإجابة هي لا.

ثم سمع خطوات في الممر، وفي لحظة، دخلت كارو. لم تكن متنكرة، بل ظهرت أمامه بوضوح—مشرقة تماماً—وحين توقفت فجأة، وقد احمرّت خجلاً لرؤيته نصف عارٍ، أدرك من خلال ابتسامتها أنها جاءت حقاً مدفوعةً بالأمل ذاته الذي كان قد تفتّح بداخله منذ لحظة.

قالت بصوت ناعم وعينين واسعتين:"مرحباً."

كان أملها يمتد نحو أمله، ليلتقيا معاً بحيث لا يمكن للكلمات وصفها. لكن أكيفا شعر بشيءٍ آخر يمتد نحوه أيضاً، شيءٌ بارد، وخطير، ويمتد نحو حياته. كان تهديداً. خطراً خفياً يتسلل عبر الظلال.

وكان قابعاً هناك، في الزاوية، معهما.

38

مصادفة مميزة من غبار النجوم

في المغرب، استيقظت إليزا على بداية جديدة. لم تكن تصرخ، ولم تكن حتى على وشك الصراخ. في الواقع، لم تشعر بالخوف على الإطلاق، وكان هذا في حد ذاته مفاجأة لطيفة. لقد استسلمت للنوم مدركةً أن عليها أن تغفو— فالحرمان من النوم قد يكون قاتلاً في نهاية المطاف—وقد عقدت أملها على أحد أمرين، إما (أ) أن تدعها الأحلام بسلام، وهو ما سيكون معجزة، أو (ب) أن تكون جدران هذا المكان سميكة بما يكفي لكتم صرخاتها.

يبدو أن الاحتمال (أ) قد تحقق، وهذا ما منحها شعوراً بالراحة، إذ إن الاحتمال (ب) كان سيخفق حتماً. كان بإمكانها سماع نباح الكلاب في الخارج، مما يعني أن الجدران، رغم سماكتها، لم تكن قادرة على كتم الأصوات إذاً، ما الذي أيقظها إن لم يكن حلماً؟ الكلاب، ربما؟

كلا. هناك شيءٌ آخر...

لم يكن حلماً، بل شيءٌ أشبه بحلم، ظلَّ يتراقص بعيداً عن وعيها، كطيفٍ يتلاشى أمام ضوء ساطع. بقيت مستلقية في مكانها، شاعرةً لوهلة بأنها

كانت قادرة على الإمساك به لو حاولت. كان عقلها لا يزال يتلمس أطراف اليقظة، عالقاً في تلك الحالة الغائمة بين الاستيقاظ والنوم، حيث تتشابك خيوط الحلم والواقع. وفي لحظةٍ ما، شعرت وكأنها طفلة تخرج من غرفتها لتواجه الظلام الهائل بمصباحٍ صغير.

فكرة مجنونة تماماً، لذا نهضت بسرعة وهزّت رأسها، محاولةً طرد تلك الأفكار بعيداً. "اذهبي، أيتها الأحلام. لا مكان لكِ هنا". كما توضع الأسلاك الحادة على حواف النوافذ لمنع الحمام من الوقوف عليها، كانت بحاجة إلى ما يشبهها في عقلها ليبعد الأحلام. ربما أسلاكٌ شائكة ذهنية. فكرة رائعة.

لقد ساعدت هذه الأسلاك الشائكة الذهنية ونالت قسطاً كافياً من النوم ليبعدها مؤقتاً عن شبح الموت الذي قد يسبب الحرمان من الراحة. أزاحت قدميها عن السرير وجلست. كان حاسوبها المحمول بجوارها. في وقت سابق، حمّلت الدفعة الأولى من الصور، ثم شفّرتها وأرسلتها إلى بريدها الإلكتروني الخاص بالمتحف، قبل أن تحذفها من الكاميرا.

كانت هي والدكتور شودهاري قد شرعا في جمع عينات الأنسجة من الجثث بعد ظهر ذلك اليوم، وسيتابعان العمل في الصباح. توقعت أن يستغرق الأمر بضعة أيام. نظراً للتكوين الغريب لتلك الجثث، كان عليهما جمع عينات من كل جزء: لحم، فرو، ريش، حراشف، ومخالب. أما بقية العمل، فسيتم في المختبر، وسيبدو هذا الترحال القصير وكأنه حلم. حلم سريع وعجيب.

ولكن، ماذا ستكشف نتائج تلك العينات؟ لم تستطع حتى البدء في التخمين. هل ستظهر تراكيب من حمض نووي مختلف؟ نمر هنا، بومة هنا، وإنسان فيما بينهما؟ أم إن الحمض النووي سيكون متجانساً، مع فروق تعبيرية فقط، كما يفعل الجين البشري حين يعبر عن تنوع الأشكال، كالعين أو الأظافر، وكل ما يكوّن الجسد؟

أو... ربما سيكتشفان شيئاً أكثر غرابة، شيئاً لا مثيل له في هذا العالم؟ ارتجف جسدها بقشعريرة باردة. كان الأمر كبيراً للغاية، إلى درجة أنها لم تكن تعلم أين تضعه في عقلها. لو كان مسموحاً لها التحدث عنه، لو استطاعت الاتصال بتاج الآن، أو بكائرين—لو أن هاتفها كان بحوزتها— ماذا كانت ستقول؟

نهضت واقتربت من النافذة لتلقي نظرة. كانت تطل على ساحة داخلية، فلم يكن هناك ما يُرى. ارتدت إليزا بنطالها الجينز وحذاءها، ثم تسللت إلى الخارج عبر الباب.

التسلل، بالطبع، لم يكن ضرورياً. لو كانت في فندق ضخم وعصري، لربما شعرت بهالة من التشويق، وانطلقت حيثما شاءت. لكن هذا المكان لم يكن فندقاً عصرياً. كان عبارة عن"قصبة"، ليست القصبة الشهيرة، بل قصبة قديمة تحولت إلى فندق، غير بعيدة كثيراً عن موقع العمل. حسناً، في الواقع كانت تبعد بضع ساعات بالسيارة، لكن في هذه التضاريس، تبدو هذه المسافة كأنها لا شيء. لو واصلت القيادة عبر هذا الطريق، لوصلت إلى صحراء"الصحارى الكبرى"، التي تعادل مساحتها مساحة الولايات المتحدة بأكملها. في هذا السياق، تُعتبر بضع ساعات بالسيارة مسافة"غير بعيدة".

القصبة تُدعى"تمنوغالت". على الرغم من استقبالها عند البوابة من قبل أطفال عابسين يشيرون بعصي خشبة إليها كأنهم يوجهون إليها الطعنات، إلا أن إليزا أحبت هذا المكان.

كانت تمنوغالت مدينة طينية في قلب واحة من النخيل، معظمها أطلال مهجورة، باستثناء الجزء المركزي الذي تم ترميمه، لكن ليس إلى مستوى الفخامة. كان لا يزال يبدو كأنه منحوت من الطين—وإن كان منحوتاً بعناية—أما الغرف فكانت مريحة بما يكفي، بأسقف عالية من العوارض الخشبية وسجاد صوفي يغطي الأرضيات. كان هناك أيضاً تراس

على السطح، يطل على قمم أشجار النخيل المتمايلة. في الليلة الماضية، عندما تناولت العشاء هناك مع الدكتور شودهاري، رأت عدداً من النجوم أكثر من أي وقت مضى في حياتها.

"لقد رأيتُ من النجوم أكثر مما رآه أي شخص طوال حياته".

توقفت إليزا عن المشي وأغمضت عينيها، ضاغطة بأطراف أصابعها عليهما، وكأنها بذلك تستطيع تهدئة الاضطراب الذي كان يجتاحها. كانت بحاجة لاستحضار"أسلاكها الذهنية" لطرد أسراب حمام الأحلام المزعج.

"لقد قتلتُ من النجوم أكثر مما سيراه أي شخص يوماً".

هزت إليزا رأسها. بدأت خيوط الذعر والشعور بالذنب تتسلل إلى عقلها الواعي، كما تتسلل الجذور الشاحبة اليائسة عبر ثقوب أوعية النبات. كانت تُفكر في أشياء لا يمكن احتواؤها، ولم يعجبها ذلك."تجاهلي الأمر"، قالت لنفسها."لم تقتلي شيئاً. أنتِ تعلمين ذلك".

لكنها لم تكن واثقة. فجأة، بدأت تشعر بقناعات قوية وغير مبررة حول أسئلة كونية كبيرة، مثل وجود أكوان أخرى. لكنها لم تكن متيقنة من عدم وجودها—على الأقل، ليس بذلك اليقين العميق والمطمئن. بدا صوت العقل هشاً وغير مقنع، وهذا لم يكن مؤشراً جيداً.

خطوة ثقيلة بعد أخرى، صعدت إليزا الدرج عائدة إلى الشرفة، مكررة لنفسها أن ما تشعر به هو مجرد ضغط، وليس جنوناً."ما زلتُ عاقلة، ولن أفقد عقلي. لقد كافحت كثيراً لأجل ذلك". وعندما خرجت إلى الهواء الليلي، شعرت ببرودة مفاجئة وسمعت نباح الكلاب بشكل أوضح، آتياً من الأرض القاحلة في الأسفل. رأت الدكتور شودهاري لا يزال جالساً في المكان نفسه الذي تركته فيه قبل ساعات. لوّح لها بإيماءة صغيرة.

سألته وهي تقترب:"هل كنت هنا طوال هذا الوقت؟".

ضحك بخفّة وقال:"لا، حاولت النوم. لم أستطع. عقلي... لا يتوقف عن التفكير في تداعيات ما رأيناه".

"وأنا كذلك".

أومأ برأسه."اجلسي، من فضلك"، قال، ففعلت. ساد صمت بينهما للحظات، محاطين بسكون الليل، ثم تحدث الدكتور شودهاري قائلاً:"من أين جاؤوا؟" بدا السؤال بلاغياً، كما ظنت إليزا، لكن التوقف الطويل الذي تلاه أوحى لها بأنه ينتظر منها محاولةً للإجابة، لو تجرأت.

أجابت ببساطة،"من كون آخر. صدقني. إنها معلومة أعرفها؛ وكأنها كانت موجودة في عقلي مثل القمامة المتناثرة".

رفع الدكتور شودهاري حاجبيه."بهذه السرعة؟ كنت أظن، يا إليزا، أنك ربما تؤمنين بالله".

"ماذا؟ لا. لماذا تظن ذلك؟".

"حسناً، لم أقصد الأمر كإهانة. أنا أؤمن بالله".

"أنت؟" كانت تعرف أن هناك العديد من العلماء الذين يؤمنون بالله، لكنها لم تشعر من قبل أنه متديّن. علاوة على ذلك، تخصصه—استخدام الحمض النووي لإعادة بناء التاريخ التطوري—يبدو مناقضاً تماماً لفكرة الخلق."ألا تجد صعوبة في التوفيق بينهما؟".

هزّ كتفيه قائلاً:"لطالما زوجتي كانت تقول إن العقل قصرٌ فيه مكان لكثير من الضيوف. ربما يتكفّل كبير الخدم بوضع وفود العلم في جناح مختلف عن مبعوثي الإيمان، حتى لا يتجادلوا في الممرات".

كان هذا التشبيه غير متوقع على الإطلاق منه، مما أذهل إليزا. فقالت، مترددة:"حسناً، إذا حدث صداماً بينهم، من تعتقد سيفوز؟".

"تقصدين، من أين أعتقد أن الزوار قد جاؤوا؟". أومأت برأسها.

"عليّ أن أقول أولاً إنه من الممكن أنهم جاؤوا من مختبر ما. كما أعتقد أنه يمكننا استبعاد فكرة التلاعب الطبي، لكن ألا يمكن أن يكون أحدهم قد نجح في صناعتهم؟".

"تقصد، مثل مخبأ شرير داخل بركان؟".

ضحك."بالضبط. ولو كانت المسألة تتعلق فقط بالأجساد—ما يمكن تسميتها بـ 'الوحوش'—فقد يكون لهذه النظرية وجهة نظر. لكن الملائكة... إنهم أكثر تعقيداً". نعم. النار، والتحليق. سألت إليزا:"هل سمعت أن قواعد بيانات التعرف على الوجوه لم تتعرف على أيٍّ منهم؟".

أومأ برأسه."نعم، سمعت. وإذا أخذنا بعين الاعتبار، ولو قبل الأوان، أن يكونوا قد جاؤوا من... مكان آخر، فمن هم المنافسون لهم لدينا؟".

أجابت إليزا:"كون آخر، أو... الجنة والجحيم".

"نعم. لكن ما أجد نفسي أفكر فيه، هنا، وأنا أحدّق في النجوم... 'التحديق' كلمة لطيفة، أليس كذلك، مقارنة بنجوم كهذه؟".

هذا التفكير غريب حقاً، فكرت إليزا، وأومأت موافقة. تابع:"وربما، هو تداخل بين الضيوف في القصر—" أشار إلى رأسه ليدل على ما يعنيه بكلمة"قصر"—"لكني أجد نفسي أفكر: ماذا يعني ذلك؟ ألا يمكن أن تكونا مجرد طريقتين مختلفتين لوصف نفس الشيء؟ افترضي أن 'الجنة' و'الجحيم' ليسا سوى كونين آخرين".

"سوى كونين آخرين" كررت إليزا بابتسامة."وكأن الانفجار العظيم كان مجرد انفجار".

قهقه الدكتور شودهاري."هل الكون الآخر لا يتسع لتلك الملائكة؟ وهل يهم ذلك؟ إذا كان هناك مجالٌ تعيش فيه 'الملائكة'، فهل يصبح الأمر مجرد مسألة إشارات، إذا اخترنا أن نسميه 'السماء'؟".

"لا"، أجابت إليزا بسرعة وبحزم، مما أدهشها قليلاً."الأمر ليس مسألة دلالات. إنه مسألة دافع".

"عذراً؟" قال الدكتور شودهاري، ناظراً إليها باستغراب.

كان هناك شيء في نبرة إليزا قد تغيّر، وأصبح أكثر حدة.

سألت:"ما الذي يريدونه؟ أعتقد أن هذا هو السؤال الأهم. لقد جاؤوا من مكان ما. هناك كون آخر. هم يتصرفون حسب رغبتهم. وهذا أمر مخيف".

لم يقل الدكتور شودهاري شيئاً، بل أعاد بصره إلى النجوم. بقي صامتاً لفترة كافية حتى ظنت إليزا أنها ربما قد أوقفت تدفق حديثه الجديد، لكنه قال في النهاية:"هل أخبرك بشيء غريب؟ أود أن أعرف رأيك فيه".

بدأ الأفق في التلاشي، وقريباً ستشرق الشمس. رؤية الأفق من هذا المكان، وتحت هذه السماء الممتدة بلا نهاية، يجعلك تشعر حقاً بأنك ملتصق بالجاذبية بصخرة عملاقة تندفع بسرعة عبر الفضاء. ومن هذا المنظور، يمكنك أن تتخيل مدى ضخامة ما يحيط بها: الكون، الذي يتجاوز حدود الفهم البشري، وهذا مجرد كون واحد.

ربما يفوق الإدراك البشري، لكنه لا يفوق إدراك العقول الأخرى."بالطبع سمعتِ عن إنسان بلتداون"، قال الدكتور شودهاري."نعم". ربما تكون تلك الجمجمة المزيّفة أشهر خدعة علمية في التاريخ—كانت تُعرض على أنها لإنسان بدائي تم العثور عليه في إنجلترا منذ حوالي مئة عام.

قال الدكتور شودهاري:"حسناً. في عام 1953، تم إثبات أنها كانت مزيفة، وهذه السنة مهمة. في خضم الاندفاع لمحو هذا العار، أزيلت من المتحف البريطاني، حيث ظلت لأربعين عاماً تُعرض كدليل خاطئ على نظرية خاطئة حول تطور الإنسان. بعد ذلك بضع سنوات فقط، في عام 1956، تم اكتشاف آخر في جبال الأنديز الباتاغونية. عالم حفريات ألماني هاوٍ عثر على مخزون من..." وتوقف هنا لإضافة بعض الدراما على حديثه."هياكل عظمية للوحوش".

ثم... بدأت الأمور تتداخل في ذهن إليزا بطريقة غريبة. وكأن الحلم قد تسلل إلى وعيها، وفشلت"أسلاكها الذهنية" في إبعاده. قال الدكتور شودهاري إنه سيخبرها بشيء غريب، وحتى وهي تغوص في هذه الحالة المتغيرة، كان لديها ما يكفي من الوعي لتدرك أن الهياكل العظمية للوحوش هي النقطة المحورية هنا، وليس الموقع الذي اكتُشفت فيه. لكن عقلها قفز بها إلى هناك.

إلى جبال الأنديز الباتاغونية.

بمجرد أن ذكرها، رأتها بوضوح: جبال شاهقة، حادة كالأسنان، صُقلت على العظم. بحيرات زرقاء نقيّة بطريقة لا تصدّق. جليد يكسو المنحدرات، ووديان مغطاة بالضباب، وغابات تختبئ تحت سحب ثقيلة.

برية قاتلة—قاتلة بالفعل—لكنها لم تقتلها.

لم تكن سهلة الكسر، لأنها نجت من أهوال أسوأ بكثير. شعرت إليزا بأنها تنقلب إلى داخلها، كما يُقلَب الثوب من الداخل إلى الخارج، ومع ذلك ما زالت جالسة هناك بجوار الدكتور شودهاري، تستمع إلى حديثه—عن الهياكل العظمية للوحوش، وكيف أنها، في أيام الاستهزاء التي تلت فضيحة بلتداون، لم تكن سوى مزحة، مزحة تتحدى التفسير—لكن كلماته كانت كصوت الماء المتدفق فوق قاع مغطى بآلاف الحجارة المصقولة، آلاف الحجارة التي تلمع تحت السطح، وكانت هي تلك الحجارة، وكانت أكثر من ذلك. كانت"أكثر" من نفسها، ولم تكن تعرف ما يعنيه ذلك، لكنها شعرت به.

كانت أكثر من ذاتها، واستطاعت رؤية المكان الذي كان يتحدث عنه الدكتور شودهاري—ليس الهياكل العظمية للوحوش التي اكتُشفت هناك، بل الأرض نفسها والسماء التي تعلوها. مالت برأسها تنظر إلى الأعلى، فرأت السماء فوقها الآن، والسماء فوقها حينها—لكن متى؟ متى كان ذلك؟—ثم أدركت، بمرارة الحزن، أنها لا تستطيع الوصول إلى السماء.

لقد حُرمت من السماء، الآن، وإلى الأبد.

شعرت بالدموع تنساب على وجنتيها في اللحظة التي لاحظها فيها الدكتور شودهاري. كان لا يزال يتحدث. قال:"متحف علم الحفريات في بيركلي يحتفظ بالبقايا الآن. ربما بدافع الفضول أكثر من القيمة العلمية، لكن لدي شعور أن هذا الأمر سيتغير. إليزا، هل أنتِ بخير؟".

مسحت دموعها، لكنها استمرت في الانهمار، ولم تستطع أن تنطق بكلمة.

للحظة، شعرت بدوار وهي تحدق إلى النجوم—لم تكن مجرد نظرة، بل تحديقاً حقيقياً—شعرت باتساع الكون من حولها، مترامي الأطراف، مليئاً بالأسرار، وبوجود شيء أكبر بكثير وراء ذلك، وأكبر من كل ما تستطيع تخيّله، وأبعد من كل أفق قد تبلغه.

وفي تلك اللحظة، بدا أن أعماقها المجهولة تتطابق مع اتساع الكون اللامتناهي في الخارج. لم يكن هناك كون آخر فقط.

بل كان هناك الكثير.

الكثير، أكثر من أن يُحصى، أكثر من أن يُدرك، وبطريقة تتجاوز كل معرفة.

"لقد رأيتُها"، فكرت إليزا. "لقد عرفتها". والدموع كانت تنهمر على وجهها الآن، وفجأة فهمت طبيعة الحلم، وكان أسوأ، أسوأ بكثير مما كانت تخشاه. لم تكن تلك نبوءة. لم تكن ترى نهاية هذا العالم.

على الأقل، لم تكن نهاية هذا العالم.

الحلم لم يكن عن المستقبل، بل عن الماضي. كان "ذكرى"، وسؤال عن كيف يمكن لإليزا أن تمتلك مثل هذه الذكرى الطاغية على كيانها.

هذا يعني أن الأمر لا يمكن إيقافه. لقد حدث بالفعل.

"لقد رأيتُ بالفعل أكواناً أخرى. لقد زُرتُها".

"ودمّرتُها".

39

سليل

جذبها إليه كما العنبر، عبر ممرات متعرجة محفورة في صخور الجبل الحصين لشعب مندثر، وبهذا وجدت سكاراب، ملكة الستيليبيين، الساحر الذي أتت لقتله.

لقد تعقبته عبر نصف العالم، وها هو أمامها الآن، وحيداً في مكان مغلق وصامت. ظهره إليها، عارٍ حتى الخصر، يغرف الماء من قناة على جدار الكهف، ويرشه على وجهه وعنقه وصدره. كانت المياه باردة، وجسده متوهجاً بالحرارة، فتصاعد منه بخار كأنه ضباب.

انحنى ليغمر رأسه في الماء، ويدعك شعره بأصابعه الموشومة. شعره كثيف، أسود، قصير. وعندما اعتدل، انسكب الماء على مؤخرة عنقه، وحينها لاحظت سكاراب علامة الندبة، التي تتخذ شكل عين مغمضة.

على الرغم من شعورها بقوة تكمن في تلك العلامة، لكنها لم تكن مألوفة لديها، ولم تسمع بها حتى.

كالعاصفة الهوجاء اليائسة، ظنت أن هذه العلامة هي من صنعه الخاص، لكنها لم تسلب من السيريثار، وإلا لكانت شعرت بنبضات صاحبها. مع أن موجاتها الكهربائية كالأوزون، لكن أعمق. يُسكر العقل.

كعنصر الأوزون، لكن أكثر ثراءً.

أمامها يقف الساحر المجهول الذي يعزف على أوتار العالم، والذي، وإن لم يوقفوه، سيقودهم إلى الخراب. كانت تظن أنها ستشعر بنجاسة كيانه حين تراه، وأن روحها ستتوق إلى قتله كما يندفع البرق نحو الصاعقة، لكن لا شيء هنا كان كما توقعت. ولا اختلاطها مع السيرافيم والكيميرا، ولا هو

"هل ستفعلينها، يا سيدتي، أم أتكفل الأمر بنفسي؟".

صوت كارناسيال تسلل إلى عقلها بألفة أشبه بالهمس. كان يقف على بُعد خطوات قليلة خلفها—متخفياً مثلها—لكن ذهنه لامس ذهنها كنسمة دافئة تلامس أذنها، مع طيف من رائحته. بدا لها الأمر شديد الواقعية.

ردت عليه، وشعرت به ينكمش بعيداً.

—"ماذا تظن؟" أجابت، وكانت هذه كلماتها الوحيدة، لكنها حملت في طياتها أكثر بكثير.

التواصل الذهني، أو ما يُعرف بـ"تيلسثيجيا"، أشبه بفن الأحلام أكثر منه بالكلام. ينسج المرسل خيوطاً محسوسة، من الكلمات أو من دونها، لتشكيل رسالة تُبث إلى المتلقي على جميع المستويات: صوت وصورة، طعم، لمس، رائحة، وذاكرة. وحتى—إن كان متقناً للغاية—عاطفة. سكاراب لم تكن متقنة لهذا الفن بأي حال، لكنها كانت قادرة على ربط عدة خيوط معاً في رسالتها، وهذا ما فعلته الآن. انطوت رسالتها على بث إحساس بمخالب قطة تخدش، ولسع نبات القراص ودفعت بها إلى كارناسيال، حتى تراجع.

هل اعتقد أنه لمجرد أنها منحته جسدها خلال أول موسم أحلام لها، يحق له أن يقتحم عقلها دون دعوة؟

يا للرجال.

موسم أحلام واحد كان موسماً واحداً لا أكثر. إن اختارته مرة أخرى في العام المقبل، فقد يبدأ الأمر باكتساب معنى، لكنها لا تظن أنها ستفعل. ليس لأنه لم يُرضِها، بل ببساطة: كيف لها أن تعرف قيمته إن لم تقارنه بأحد آخر؟

"اغفري لي، يا ملكتي".

وصلت رسالته هذه المرة من مسافة ملائمة، تشبه المسافة الجسدية بينهما، وكانت خالية من رائحة أو ملمس، كما ينبغي أن تكون. شعرت بلمحة من الندم، وكانت تلك لمسة جميلة منه. كارناسيال لم يكن يجيد هذا النوع من التواصل مثلها، وسيطول الوقت قبل أن يتمكن أي منهما من إتقان هذا الفن؛ فكلاهما ما زالا صغيرين—لكن كان لديه المقومات لذلك. لم تختره سكاراب لحرسها الشخصي عبثاً—وليس لأنامله الموسيقية التي عزفت على أوتار رغباتها في الربيع بشغف، ولا لضحكته العميقة كالرنين، ولا لجوعه الذي كان يتناغم مع جوعها، وكأنها كانت رسائل عقلية يتم تبادلها على جميع المستويات.

كان ساحراً ماهراً، كغيره من حرسها، لكن لا أحد منهم ينبض بقوة جوهرية مثلما ينبض بها هذا السيراف أمامها. جالت عيناها على ظهره العاري، وشعرت بلمحة من الدهشة. كان ظهر محارب، مشدود العضلات ومليئاً بالندوب، وزوج من السيوف يتقاطعان في حزام معلق على صخرة بجانبه. إنه جندي. استخلصت هذا عندما كانت في أستراي، حيث تحدث الناس عنه بذعر ورهبة، لكنها لم تصدق الأمر تماماً حتى رأته. لم يشبه الصورة التي كونتها عنه. السحرة أمثالها لا يستخدمون الفولاذ؛ لا يحتاجون إليه. عندما يقتل الساحر، لا يسيل الدم. وعندما تقتله هي، كما جاءت هنا لتفعل، سيتوقف ببساطة... عن الحياة.

الحياة ليست سوى خيط رفيع يربط الروح بالجسد، وبمجرد معرفة مكانه، يمكن اجتثاثه بسهولة كما تُقطف الزهرة.

"افعليها"، أمرت نفسها، ومدّت يدها لتلتقط خيط حياته، مدركةً وجود كارناسيال خلفها، يترقب. "هل ستفعلينها، أم أفعلها أنا؟" سألها، وكانت إجابته تلك بمثابة إهانة. لقد شك في قدرتها، لأنها لم تفعلها من قبل قط.

خلال التدريبات، كانت تلمس خيوط الحياة وتدعها تعزف بين أصابعها—أصابع ذاتها اللامادية. كان الأمر بمثابة وضع شفرة على حنجرة الخصم في مباراة مبارزة. لكنها لم تقطع خيطاً أبداً، وكان القيام بذلك هو الفارق بين وضع الشفرة على حنجرة الخصم وبين شق حنجرته فعلياً. وكان ذلك فارقاً هائلاً.

لكنها قادرة على فعله. لإثبات نفسها أمام كارناسيال، خطر لها أن تنفذ حركة البتر النظيف. لحظة واحدة وينتهي كل شيء. لن تشعر بخيط ذلك الغريب، ولن تقرأ ماهيته، بل ستقصّه بنبضة مباشرة، وسيموت من دون أن ترى وجهه أو تلمس حياته.

تذكرت أوتار اليورايا في تلك اللحظة، وشعرت بقوة متهورة تجتاحها.

كانت مجرد أسطورة. "على الأرجح". في العصر الأول لشعبها، الذي كان أطول بكثير من هذا العصر الثاني وانتهى بوحشية لا توصف، كان الستيليون مختلفين جداً عما هم عليه الآن. كانوا محاطين بأعداء أقوياء، يعيشون في حروب مستمرة، مما جعل جزءاً كبيراً من سحرهم مخصصاً لفنون الحرب.

كانت تُروى حكايات عن اليورايا، القيثارة السحرية التي تشد أوتارها من خيوط الحياة لأعداء قُتلوا. واعتبرت سلاحاً للأنيمات الذين لا وجود لهم في العالم المادي؛ لا يمكن العثور على أثر لهم، ولا حتى إرث.

يقال إنه كان على الساحر أن يصنع تلك القيثارة بنفسه، وتموت معه. قيل أيضاً إن تلك القيثارة مستودع لأعمق القوى، لكنها مظلمة أيضاً، ولا يمكن إكمالها إلا بقتل أعداد هائلة، وعزفها قد يدفع بصانعها إلى الجنون بنفس القدر الذي قد يمنحه قوة.

عندما كانت صغيرة، كانت سكاراب تُرعب مربياتها بالتخطيط لصنع يورايا خاصة بها."ستكونين أنتِ أول وتر في قيثارتي"، قالت ذات مرة، بخبث، لمربية تجرأت على إجبارها على الاستحمام رغماً عنها.

ترددت الكلمات نفسها في ذهنها الآن."ستكونين أول وتر في قيثارتي"، فكرت مخاطبةً ظهر الغريب الموشوم بالسحر. مدت يدها بأنيمتها لتنفيذ الاغتيال، واجتاحها شعور بالذعر، لأنها بالفعل، لوهلة قصيرة، كانت تعني ذلك.

"احذري ما الذي تصوغين حياتك وأفكارك على أساسه، أيتها الأميرة"، قالت لها المربية يومها بجانب حوض الاستحمام."حتى لو كانت اليورايا حقيقية، لا يمكن تحقيقها إلا لمن لديه أعداء كُثر، ونحن لم نعد كذلك. لدينا عمل أكثر أهمية من القتال".

العمل، نعم. العمل الذي شكّل حياتهم—وسلبها منهم في الوقت نفسه."ليس كأن أحداً يشكرنا عليه"، ردت سكاراب حينها. كانت طفلة صغيرة آنذاك، أكثر افتتاناً بحكايات الحروب من واجبات الستيليبين المقدسة والمملة.

"لا نفعل ذلك من أجل الشكر، ولا من أجل البشر على الأرض، على الرغم من أنهم سيستفيدون منه أيضاً. نفعل ذلك من أجل بقائنا، ولأنه لا أحد سوانا يستطيع القيام به."

ربما كانت قد مدت لسانها لمربيتها في ذلك اليوم، لكنها حين كبرت، أخذت تلك الكلمات بجدية. بل إنها، مؤخراً، رفضت دعوة مغرية للعداوة من الإمبراطور الأحمق جورام. كان بإمكانها أن تُضيف وتراً من خيط حياته إلى قيثارتها، لكنها بدلاً من ذلك، أرسلت له سلة من الفاكهة، وللسخرية فقد مات على يد هذا الساحر.

لم تكن تريد أعداء. لم تكن تريد قيثارة يورايا، أو حرباً. على الأقل، هذا ما حاولت سكاراب إقناع نفسها به، رغم أنه في الحقيقة—وفي السر—كان

هناك صوت بداخلها يرغب بتلك الأمور. ملأها ذلك الصوت بالخوف، لكنه أيضاً ألهبها بالإثارة، وكانت تلك الإثارة المظلمة هي أكثر ما أخافها.

لم تنفذ سكاراب"النبضة القاتلة". عندما أدركت أنها كانت تحاول إثبات نفسها لكارناسيال، تمردت على الفكرة——"هو" من يجب أن يثبت نفسه لها——وبالإضافة إلى ذلك، كانت ترغب في رؤية وجه هذا الساحر، وفي لمس حياته، لتعرف من هو قبل أن تقتله. لم يكن من السهل سحب الـ"سيريثار". لم يكن بالأمر الجيد، لكنه كان، دون شك، عملاً عظيماً. أرادت أن تعرف كيف استطاع تحقيق ذلك عندما ضاع بعدما كل علم السحر في ما يُعرف بإمبراطورية السيرافيم.

بدلاً من قطع خيط حياته، مدت سكاراب موجة أنيمتها لاستشعاره. ثم انتفضت.

كانت انتفاضة صغيرة، لكنها كانت كافية لجعله يستدير.

"سكاراب". جاء إرسال كارناسيال مشحوناً بالإلحاح:"افعليها".

لكنها لم تفعل، لأنها الآن أدركت الحقيقة. لقد لامست حياته، وعرفت ما هو حتى قبل أن ترى وجهه. وعندما فعلت، رأت وجهه، ورآه كارناسيال أيضاً. ورغم أنه لم ينتفض، إلا أن سكاراب شعرت بارتجافات صدمته تتداخل مع صدمتها هي. هذا الساحر المعروف بلقب"هالك الوحوش"، لا يمكن السماح له بالبقاء حياً، والذي كان غير شرعي ومحارباً وقاتل أبيه.

عيناه المتوهجتان بالنار——تبحثان في الهواء الخاوي حيث كانت سكاراب تقف غير مرئية——وكان ذلك كافياً لتعرف اليقين، لكنها عرفت شيئاً آخر عنه، وبثته لكارناسيال بلغة بسيطة——خالية من إحساس أو شعور، مجرد كلمات بثتها أيضاً إلى الآخرين، أولئك الذين كانوا منتشرين في الكهوف والممرات يحاولون فهم ما يحدث في هذا المكان. أرسلتها إلى سبيكترال وريف، لكنها ترددت قبل أن تطلق، بشكل مفاجئ وغير كافٍ، هذه الأخبار إلى نايتنغال، التي كانت ستعني لها... الكثير.

حبست سكاراب أنفاسها، منتظرة، بينما كان الساحر يتفحص بنظره المكان حيث وقفت. وعلى الرغم من أنها كانت تعرف أنه لا يمكنه رؤيتها، إلا أنها قرأت يقينه بوجودها في ثبات نظرته، وكانت ردة فعله مفاجأة أخرى في سلسلة المفاجآت التي تتراكم فوق بعضها.

عندما شعر الساحر بحقيقة وجود شخص غير مرئي أمامه، لم يُظهر أي ذعر. لم تتصلب ملامحه، بل تراخت... ثم ابتسم، تاركاً سكاراب في حيرة عميقة. ابتسامة نقية من السرور والسعادة، ابتسامة خالصة، مشرقة، وبريئة، إلى درجة أن سكاراب، التي كانت ملكةً، شابةً وجميلةً، والتي ابتسم لها كثير من الرجال من قبل، شعرت بالخجل لأنها كانت محور هذه الابتسامة.

إلا أنها بالطبع، لم تكن كذلك.

عندما تحدث، كان صوته منخفضاً وعذباً وممزوجاً بخشونة الحنين. "كارو؟ هل أنتِ هنا؟".

اشتعلت وجنتا سكاراب حمرةً أكثر، وشكرت السماء على كونها غير مرئية، كما شكرتها لأنها دفعت كارناسيال بعيداً عن عقلها في اللحظة السابقة حتى لا يشعر بالوهج الذي أشعلته فيها ابتسامة هذا الغريب. كان جماله من ذلك النوع الذي يجعلك تسكن تماماً، تحبس دهشتك كأنك تحبس أنفاسك. قوته كانت جزءاً من هذا الجمال—ذلك العبير الخام، الوحشي، والمسكر من السيريثار، الممنوع والملعون؛ مجرد استنشاق وجوده كان لذةً محرّمة—لكن سعادته هي التي اخترقتها بعمق، شديدة إلى درجة أنها شعرت بها في قلبها بقدر ما شعرت بها في عينيها.

"يا للهول". لم تشعر سكاراب بسعادة كتلك التي رأتها عليه في تلك اللحظة، وكانت متأكدة أنها لم تلهم أحداً بها من قبل.

تذكرت أول ليلة لها مع كارناسيال في الربيع، عندما انتهت الطقوس والرقصات وتركوهما أخيراً بمفردهما، شعرت حينها بجوعه وبهجته قبل

أن يلمسها حتى. بدا الأمر حقيقياً في ذلك الوقت، لكن فجأة، لم يعد كذلك الآن.

كانت هذه النظرة أكثر بكثير من ذلك، وأصبحت الطعنة ألماً لها وتساءلت:"لمن كانت هذه النظرة؟".

تدفقت إليها الإرسالات من ريف وسبيكترال، ومن كارناسيال أيضاً— لكن ليس من نايتنغال، التي لم تخبرها بعد—ولوهلة غمرتها الرسائل. كان ريف وسبيكترال أكبر سناً وأكثر خبرةً من سكاراب وكارناسيال في فنون السحر والتواصل الذهني، وكانت إحدى إرسالاتهما—تلك التي وصلت متشابكة إلى درجة أن سكاراب لم تستطع تمييز أيهما أرسلها—تحمل ردة فعل من الصدمة الساحقة، إلى حد أنها جعلت سكاراب ترمش وتتراجع خطوة إلى الخلف.

تحدث الساحر مرة أخرى، وقطب جبينه بحيرة بينما تلاشت ابتسامته."كارو؟ هل أنتِ هنا؟".

"هناك من يقترب".

سمعت سكاراب خطوات تتردد في الممر، فتحركت بسرعة إلى جانب الحائط، مما جعلها تلتصق بكارناسيال في زاوية الغرفة. شعرت بجسده يتوتر فوراً عند ملامستها، ثم ابتعد على الفور—خائفاً من إغضابها بسبب لمسة غير مقصودة، وشعرت بالأسف لسقوطه من عينها، وسط هذه الفوضى المذهلة.

ثم ظهر أحدهم في المشهد.

كانت فتاة في مثل عمر سكاراب تقريباً. لم تكن سيرافيم، ولا من الكيميرا الذين يتجمعون مع السيرافيم في هذا المكان.

كانت... غريبة. ليست من هذا العالم. لم تَر سكاراب إنساناً من قبل، وعلى الرغم من أنها كانت تعرف ما هم عليه، إلا أن رؤيتهم الفعلية كانت مثيرة للفضول. لم يكن للفتاة أجنحة ولا سمات حيوانية، بدت بساطة

هيئتها كنوع من الأناقة المجردة. كانت رشيقة، تتحرك بخفة غزال عند المساء وهو يتشكل في ظلال منتصف الصيف، وجمالها كان من نوع عجيب إلى درجة أن سكاراب لم تستطع أن تحدد ما إذا كان أكثر إرضاءً للنفس أم أكثر إثارة للدهشة. كانت بشرتها بلون الكريمة، وعيناها سوداوين كعيني طائر، وشعرها يلمع بوهج أزرق. وكان وجهها، مثل وجه حبيبها الساحر، متورداً بالفرح، مشوباً بنفس الحياء العذب والمرتعش، وكأن هذه اللحظة كانت شيئاً جديداً بينهما.

"مرحباً"، قالت الفتاة، وكانت الكلمة أشبه بهمس خفيف، رقيق مثل رفرفة جناح فراشة.

لكنه لم يُجب بنفس اللطف."هل كنتِ هنا منذ قليل؟" سأل، وهو ينظر من حولها.

عندها أدركت سكاراب حقيقة أن هذه الفتاة، قادرة على التخفي، مما يعني أن هذه البشرية تستطيع استخدام السحر.

"لا"، أجابت الفتاة، وقد بدت مترددة الآن."لماذا؟".

حركته التالية كانت مفاجئة للغاية. أمسك ذراع فتاته وسحبها نحوه، وضعها خلفه محاولاً حمايتها من شيء مجهول، ينظر إلى الفراغ في الغرفة الذي، بالطبع، لم يكن فارغاً على الإطلاق."هل هناك أحد ما؟" قالها بلهجة السيرافيم هذه المرة، وعندما اجتاحت عيناه سكاراب الآن، لم تكن تحمل إلا ما توقعته أن تراه من قبل: الشك، ولهيب الغضب المكتوم. الحماية، أيضاً—لأجل تلك الغريبة الجميلة ذات الشعر الأزرق التي كان يحميها بجسده.

بجسده العاري، لاحظت سكاراب وبفضول، كيف وقف كالدرع، قوياً وشرساً، وكأن ذلك يحدث فارقاً. وكأن خيط حياته وخيط حياة حبيبته ليسا هشين كخيوط العنكبوت المتلألئة في الأثير، يسهل قطعهما كما يُقطع خيط الحرير.

"هل سنقتله؟" جاء إرسال كارناسيال، خالياً من أي نغمة أو خيوط حسية قد تعكس موقفه في هذا الحدث.

"بالطبع لا"، ردّت سكاراب، وشعرت بغضب غير مبرر تجاهه، وكأنه فعل شيئاً خاطئاً."إلا إذا كنت تود أن تشرح لـنايتنغال أننا وجدنا وريثاً من سلالة فيستيڤال وقطعنا خيط حياته".

كما كادت أن تفعل. ارتجفت. لأجل إثبات أنها قادرة على القتل، كادت أن تقتله.

"وريث من سلالة فيستيڤال". كانت هذه الكلمات التي بثتها إلى كارناسيال وريف وسبيكترال، لكنها لم ترسلها بعد إلى نايتنغال، التي كانت الساحرة الأولى لجدة سكاراب، الملكة السابقة، والتي جلست مرتين في طقوس الـ"ڤيانا" حزينة، ونجت. لم ينجُ أحد آخر في العصر الثاني من طقوس الـ"ڤيانا" مرتين، وكانت جلستها الأولى من أجل فيستيڤال. ابنتها.

ربما كانت سكاراب ملكة، لكنها كانت في الثامنة عشرة من عمرها، لا خبرة لديها، وفي أعماقها كانت تشعر أنها في مواجهة شيء أكبر منها بكثير. جاءت لتصطاد ساحراً متمرداً، تأمل في تنفيذ أول عملية قتل لها، لكن ما وجدته هنا كان أعظم من ذلك بكثير، وستحتاج إلى مشورة جميع سحرتها،"وخاصة نايتنغال"، قبل أن تقرر أي شيء.

"إذاً، علينا أن نغادر"، قال كارناسيال، متجاهلاً تعليقها الجارح الأخير."قبل أن يقتلنا".

إنه اقتراح جيد.

في الحقيقة، لم يكن لديهم أي فكرة عن هذا السيرافيم وعما هو قادر عليه. لذا، أخذت سكاراب نفساً عميقاً أخيراً من عبق قوته المسكرة، ثم انسحبت.

40

توقُّع الأسوأ

راقب الستيليون، بإعجاب، ما يحدث في الكهوف على مدى الساعة
التالية، وتعلموا الكثير، لكن بقيت العديد من الأمور محيرة.

أما الذي يُدعى أكيثا، فقد ازدرَت نايتنغال استخدامه لهذا الاسم
الإمبراطوري، وهو ليس سوى ابن غير شرعي. لذا، كانت تناديه فقط بـ"ابن
الحفل"، كانت واحدة من أفضل فناني التخاطر والتواصل في الجزر البعيدة،
ورسائلها عادةً ما تنطوي على طبقات متقنة من الجمال والمعاني والتفاصيل
والفكاهة. غياب كل ذلك الآن كان كافياً ليخبر سكاراب بأن نايتنغال غارقة
في مشاعرها وتحاول أن تحتفظ بها لنفسها. ولم يكن لسكاراب أن تلومها،
إذ لم يكن باستطاعتها رؤيتها — فهم حافظوا جميعاً على أقنعتهم السحرية
بالطبع — ولم يكن بإمكانها أن تعرف كيف تتعامل المرأة الأكبر سناً مع
الظهور المفاجئ لهذا الحفيد. أو ما يشير إليه ظهوره عن مصير"الاحتفال"،
الذي ظل لغزاً لسنوات طويلة.

ورغم أن من حق سكاراب، بصفتها ملكة، أن تلامس عقول رعاياها، إلا أنها لم ترغب في التدخل في أمر كهذا. اكتفت بإرسال شعور بسيط من الدفء إلى نايتنغال — صورة ليد ممسكة بيد أخرى — وأبقت تركيزها على نشاط من حولها.

استعدادات للحرب؟ ما هذا؟ تمرد.

بدا الأمر غريباً للغاية بالنسبة إلى سكاراب، أن تنجرف وسط هؤلاء الجنود الذين طالما كانوا مجرد شخصيات خيالية في القصص التي ترعرعت عليها. كانوا، في حقيقة الأمر، قصص لمخلوقات من الجانب الآخر من العالم، محصورون في حروب متواصلة قرناً بعد قرن، وقد فقدوا كل سحرهم. وهم الآن بمثابة قصة توجيهية تُروى لتحذير الآخرين. "نحن لسنا كذلك"، هكذا كان فحوى تعليم سكاراب، مع استخدام هؤلاء المخلوقات ذوي البشرة الفاتحة كأمثلة.

لقد ظل الستيليون دائماً منعزلين، رافضين كل اتصال بالإمبراطورية، رافضين الانخراط في فوضاهم، تاركين إياهم يحترقون في حروبهم المتهورة على الجانب الآخر من العالم.

وإذا كان الكيميرا قد احترقوا ونزفوا؟ وإذا كانت قارة بأكملها قد تحولت إلى مقبرة جماعية؟ وإذا كانت حياة أبناء وبنات نصف العالم — بمن فيهم السيرافيم — قد اقتصرت على الحرب، دون أمل في حياة أفضل؟ لا شأن لنا بذلك.

تحمل الستيليون واجباتهم الجليلة بشق الأنفس، ولم يكن بمقدورهم تحمّل أكثر من ذلك. وحده ذلك السحب العميق والمرعب للسيريثار، الذي جرف سماء العالم، هو ما دفع سكاراب للابتعاد إلى هذا الحد؛ لأن الأمر، هذه المرة، بدأ يمسّهم ويفتك بهم.

المهمة بسيطة: العثور على الساحر وقتله، استعادة التوازن والعودة إلى الديار. لكن الآن؟ لم يتمكنوا من قتله، وأصبح هو جزءاً من شيء غريب

بالفعل، لذا اكتفوا بمراقبته. وحينما تجمّعت الجيوش المتمردة في كتائب وغادرت الكهوف، تبعهم الستيليون المخفيون الخمسة. طاروا جنوباً، متجاوزين الجبال، ومن ثم انحرفوا غرباً، وظلوا في السماء لثلاث ساعات قبل أن يحطوا عند سفح قمة تشبه زعنفة سمكة قرش.

كان هناك ثلاثة من الكيميرا في انتظارهم—كشافة، كما حدّدت سكاراب بعد برهة وهي تتسلل بصمت حول الجموع لتقف في ظل الجنرال الذئبي، المسمى ثياغو.

"أين الباقون؟" سأل الجنرال الكشافة، الذين اكتفوا بهز رؤوسهم بوجوم "لم يأتوا"، قال أحدهم. وعند جانب الجنرال وقفت جندية من السيرافيم ذات مظهر مهيب يفوق المعتاد، وهي من التفت إليها أولاً ليقول،"علينا أن نفترض الأسوأ حتى نتيقن".

أي أسوأ؟ تساءلت سكاراب بفضول تشوبه اللامبالاة، لأن كل هذا كان مجرد مفهوم مجرد بالنسبة إليها. كانت صيّادة وساحرة وملكة، وحارسة الدمار. ربما حلمت في طفولتها بقطع أوتار حياة الأعداء لتنسج قيثارتها الـ"يورايا"، لكنها لم تخض حرباً قط. ذات يوم، كان أبناء شعبها مقاتلين، لكن ذلك كان في زمن آخر. وعندما كانت سكاراب، أثناء عزلتها في الجزر البعيدة، تتجاهل مصائر الملايين بازدراء لحماقات دعاة الحرب، كانت تفعل ذلك دون أن تشهد موتاً في المعركة.

لكن هذا على وشك أن يتغير.

...

"لكن لماذا ستأتي ليراز معنا؟ لماذا ليس أكيڤا؟" سألت زوزانا مرة أخرى.

"أنت تعرفين السبب"، ردّت كارو مجدداً." نعم، لكني لا أكترث لأي من تلك الأسباب. كل ما يعنيني هو أني سأضطر إلى قضاء وقت معها. تنظر إليّ وكأنها تخطط لانتزاع روحي من أذني."

"ليراز لا تستطيع انتزاع روحك، يا حمقاء"، قالت كارو، محاولة تهدئة مخاوف صديقتها."ربما دماغك، لكن روحك؟ مستحيل".

"آه، حسناً إذاً."

كادت كارو أن تخبر زوزانا كيف أن ليراز أبقتها هي وميك دافئين في تلك الليلة أثناء نومهما، لكنها فكّرت أنه إذا وصل ذلك إلى ليراز، فقد تفقد صوابها. لذا، بدلاً من ذلك قالت:"أتظنين أنني لا أفضّل أن أكون مع أكيفا أيضاً؟" وربما، للمرة الأولى، تسلل القليل من الإحباط إلى صوتها.

قالت زوزانا:"حسناً، من الجيد أنك اعترفتِ بذلك أخيراً. لكن بعض الشقاوة لن تضرك هنا."

"عذراً؟" ردّت كارو، وكأن أي تقليل من دهائها يعدّ إهانة لا تُغتفر."لقد استوليثُ على تمردٍ بأكمله، ألا يكفي ذلك؟".

"معكِ حق." وافقت زوزانا."أنتِ داهية، ماكرة، وشقية. أقف إجلالاً لك".

"لا زلت جالسة."

"أجل، أجلس إجلالاً."

وهكذا كانتا عائدتين إلى الحفرة التي قضتا فيها ليلتهما الباردة. لقد وصلوا للتو، وقريباً سيواصلون رحلتهم مرة أخرى، باتجاه"خليج الوحوش" والبوابة. على الأقل، بعضهم سيذهب، لكن أكيفا لم يكن من ضمنهم. كانت كارو تحاول أن تتماسك، لكن الأمر كان صعباً. عندما أوضحت لها خطتها— عندما كانت في غرفة أكيفا وجثة تين ملقاة عند قدميها، وبدأ عقلها يرسم السيناريوهات بسرعة—كان أكيفا هو من تخيّلته بجانبها، وليس ليراز.

لكن بعد أن عرضت الفكرة على المجلس، بدأت تدرك أن خطتها لم تكن سوى جزء صغير في إطار استراتيجي أكبر بكثير، وأنه في حال المضي قدماً بها، سيُطلب من أكيفا، بصفته"هالك الوحوش"، البقاء هنا..

وهذا ما كان: سترافقها ليراز بدلاً من أكيفا، ولعل هذا هو الأفضل. كان الكيميرا سيشككون في قرار ثياغو بإرسال كارو عبر البوابة مع أكيفا. ولا

تزال هناك خطة التضليل التي يجب المحافظة عليها. هناك الكثير جداً مما ينبغي التحكم به، وهذا أمر يثير الغضب.

على الأقل، ما إن تعبر البوابة، كما أخبرت نفسها، لن يكون لديها جيش الكيميرا بأكمله يراقب كل خطوة تقوم بها.

بالطبع، في غياب أكيفا، لن تكون هناك خطوات تستحق المراقبة على أي حال.

"لدينا جميعاً أدوارنا التي علينا أن نؤديها"، قالت لزوزانا وميك، وكأنها تذكّر نفسها بذلك. "إخراج جايل هو مجرد البداية. سريع ودون أي دمار... نأمل ذلك. وبمجرد أن يعود إلى إريتز، لا يزال علينا أن نهزمه. وكما تعلمين، الاحتمالات ليست في صالحنا تماماً."

وهذا كان تقليلاً من شأن الأمر.

"هل تظنين أنهم قادرون على فعلها؟" سأل ميك، وهو ينظر إلى الجنود الذين بدأوا بالهبوط في الحفرة، الكيميرا والسيرافيم معاً. كانوا يشكلون مشهداً مذهلاً في السماء، أجنحة الخفافيش تختلط بأجنحة اللهب، وجميعهم يتحركون بتناغم سلس.

صحّحت له كارو:"نحن. وأجل، أظن أننا قادرون على ذلك. علينا أن نكون".

"سنفعلها."

"سنهزم جايل". ومع ذلك، كان هذا أيضاً مجرد بداية. كم عدد البدايات اللعينة التي يتعين عليهم تجاوزها قبل أن يصلوا إلى الحلم؟ حياة مختلفة تماماً. وئام بين الأجناس. سلام.

"يا حلوتي"، قالت لها إيسّا عندما كانوا لا يزالون في الكهوف. باستثناء القلة القادرين على الطيران مثل ثياغو، بقي معظم الكيميرا غير المجنّحين هناك. وعند وداعها، كرّرت إيسّا الرسالة الأخيرة التي تركها بريمستون لكارو:"ابنتي وكل سعادتي. حلمك هو حلمي، واسمك هو حقيقتك.

أنتِ أملنا جميعاً".

"حلمك هو حلمي".

نعم، حسناً. تخيلت كارو أن رؤية بريمستون لـ"الوئام بين الأجناس" ربما لم تتضمن ذلك العدد من القُبلات كما في رؤيتها.

"توقفي عن الهذيان حول القُبلات. هناك عوالم بأكملها على المحك. القُبلات لاحقاً؛ التركيز الآن".

كان من المفترض أن يحدث ذلك عندما تبعت أكيفا إلى الزاوية المنعزلة—يا آلهة النجوم والغبار، رؤية صدره العاري أعادت إلى ذهنها ذكرياتٍ دافئة جداً—لكن لم يحدث شيء. فقد شعر أكيفا بقلق مفاجئ، مصمماً على أن هناك شخصاً أو شيئاً ما معهما في المكان، وغير مرئي، وشرع في البحث عنه والسيف في يده.

لم تشك كارو في كلامه، لكنها لم تشعر بوجود أي شيء هي الأخرى، ولم تستطع تخيّل ما قد يكون هناك. أرواح عناصر الهواء؟ أشباح القتلى من الكيرين؟ الإلهة إيلاي في مزاج سيئ؟ مهما كان، انتهت لحظتهم القصيرة سوياً، ولم يتمكنا من وداع بعضهما بشكل لائق. فكرت أنه ربما كان سيجعل الفراق أسهل لو تمكنا من ذلك. لكنها تذكّرت وداعهما الأخير عند فجر أحد الأيام في"بستان القداس" قبل سنوات، وكيف كان الأمر صعباً، كل مرة، في أن تبتعد عنه بالطيران، واضطرت للاعتراف بأن قُبلة الوداع لا تجعل الأمور أسهل بأي شكل.

لذلك ركّزت عقلها على المهمة، وحاولت ألّا تبحث عن أكيفا، الذي كان في مكان ما على الجانب الآخر من مجموعة الجنود الذين بدأوا بالهبوط.

هذه هي الخطة:

بدلاً من عبور البوابة لمهاجمة جايل في أرض غير مألوفة، سيأخذ ثياغو وإليون القوة الرئيسية لجيوشهم المتحالفة شمالاً إلى البوابة الثانية ليكونوا هناك في استقبال جايل حيث ترافقه كارو وليراز عائداً إلى موطنه.

وهنا تصبح الأمور مثيرة للاهتمام. لم يكن لديهم عِلم بعد بموقع جنود جايل، ولا يمكنهم توقع ما سيواجهونه عند البوابة الثانية. سيتعاملون مع الأمور كما هي، لكنهم توقعوا، بالطبع، قوةً هائلة. نسبة عشرة إلى واحد إذا كانوا محظوظين، وأسوأ إذا لم يكونوا كذلك.

إذاً، أعطتهم كارو سلاحاً سرياً. زوجاً منه، في الواقع.

ها هما، جالسان بهدوء، بعيداً عن الجنود ومُرتفعين عنهم، عند حافة الحفرة، ينظران إلى الأسفل. بينما كانت كارو تراقب، رفعت"تانغريس" مخلبها السنوري الرشيق ولعقته، كحركة القطة، على الرغم من أن الوجه— واللسان—كانا حيين أيضاً.

لقد منحت كارو للتمرد"الظلال الحية". أحسّت بمشاعر متضاربة حيال ذلك. لقد كان هذا ذريعة لإعادة إحياء أبو الهول، تانغريس وباشيز—وأيضاً أمزالاغ معهما، بما أن روحه كانت في نفس المبخرة، وتحدّت أي شخص أن يجادلها في ذلك—وهذا كان أمراً جيداً. لكنها لطالما شعرت برعب من تخصصهم الفريد، وهو التسلل دون أثر، بصمتٍ تام، وذبح الأعداء وهم نائمون.

مهما كانت هِبتهما أو سحرهما، فقد كانا يتجاوزان الصمت والخداع. بدا الأمر وكأنّ أبو الهول يفرز مادة مُنوّمة لضمان أن الفريسة لا تستيقظ، بغض النظر عمّا يُفعل بها. لن يستيقظوا حتى يموتوا. ربما يكون من السذاجة أن تتأمل في تجنّب مجزرة في هذه المرحلة، لكن كارو كانت ساذجة، ولم تكن تريد أن تكون مسؤولة عن أي مجازر إضافية.

"جنود الدومينيون لا يمكن إصلاحهم"، قال لها إليون."قتلهم وهم نائمون هو رحمة أكبر مما يستحقونه."

لا أحد يتعلم أي شيء، أبداً، فكرت. سيُقال نفس الشيء عن غير الشرعيين من قبل أي شخص في الإمبراطورية. علينا أن نبدأ بأن نكون أفضل من ذلك. لا يمكننا قتل الجميع.

"إذاً تُبقيهم أحياء"، قالت ليراز، وكانت كارو تنتظر المزيد من سخريتها الباردة، لكن، لدهشتها، لم يصدر منها شيء. قالت، وهي تحدّق في يدها، تقلبها وتنظر إليها مجدداً. "أقطع الأصابع الثلاثة الوسطى لهم فهي الأهم للمحاربين، ليكون عاجزاً عن القتال. على الأقل، حتى يتعلم استخدام يده الأخرى، ولكن هذا سيكون مشكلة في المستقبل". ثم نظرت مباشرة إلى عيني كارو ورفعت حاجبيها وكأنها تقول:"حسناً؟ هل يكفي ذلك؟".

كان... يكفي.

لقد وافقوا جميعاً على ذلك، وكان لدى كارو الوقت الكافي أثناء الطيران لاستيعاب غرابة فكرة الرحمة—للدومينيون، على وجه التحديد—الصادرة من ليراز. وجاء هذا في أعقاب رد فعلها الغامض على هجوم تين."لقد استحققتُ انتقامها"، قالت، دون أي أثر للغضب.

لم ترغب كارو في معرفة ما الذي استحقت ليراز الانتقام من أجله؛ كان يكفي كارو أن تنتهي دورة الانتقام هذه. رغم صعوبة تحقق ذلك بعد حرب طويلة الأمد تغذيها الكراهية، أن يقرر أحد الطرفين:"كفى. لقد استحققتُ ذلك. دعونا ننهِ الأمرَ هنا". لكن هذا، في الواقع، ما قالته ليراز."ما تفعلينه بروحها شأنك الخاص"، أضافت، تاركةً لكارو حرية استعادة روح هاكسايا من الجسد الذي كان ينبغي ألّا يحتفظ بها منذ البداية.

لم تكن كارو تعرف ما الذي ستفعله بروح هاكسايا، لكنها احتفظت بها. والآن، لم تكتفِ ليراز باقتراح إبقاء جنود الدومينيون على قيد الحياة، بل اقترحت حتى إبقاء جزء صالح للاستخدام من أيديهم. قد لا يتمكنون من شد أوتار الأقواس أو التلويح بالسيوف بسرعة، لكنهم سيكونون في حال أفضل بكثير مما لو قُطعت أيديهم بالكامل عند المعصم. كان هذا أكثر من مجرد رحمة؛ كان نوعاً من اللطف. يا للغرابة.

وهكذا، تم الاتفاق. ستقوم الظلال الحية، إن استطاعت، بشلّ حركة الجنود الذين يحرسون بوابة جايل، أو أكبر عدد ممكن منهم.

أما أكيڤا، فسيطير باتجاه الغرب مباشرةً حيث توجد أكبر حامية للإمبراطورية في الأراضي الحرة السابقة. دوره—وهو الدور الذي قد يُحدث فرقاً كبيراً—كان زرع بذور التمرد في الفيلق الثاني، ومحاولة تحويل جزء من قوات الإمبراطورية على الأقل ضد جايل. في حين أن قوات الدومينيون كانت نخبوية وأرستقراطية، وستقاتل للحفاظ على الامتيازات التي وُلدت بها، كان جنود الفيلق الثاني في معظمهم مجنّدين إجبارياً، وهناك سبب للاعتقاد بأنهم لم يرغبوا في خوض حرب أخرى—وخاصة حرب ضد الستيليين، الذين ليسوا وحوشاً. اعتقد إليون أن سمعة أكيڤا كـ"قاتل الوحوش" ستؤثر على صفوف الجنود، خاصة أنه أثبت جدارته في التأثير على إخوته وأخواته.

كانت كارو أيضاً بحاجة إلى نوع من الإقناع، لإجبار جايل على المغادرة، لكن ذلك كان نوعاً خاصاً من"الإقناع" الذي تستطيع ليراز إدارته بنفس كفاءة أكيڤا، وهكذا تم الترتيب.

"سأذهب لأستطلع ما لدى الكشافة من أخبار"، قالت لميك وزوزانا، وهي تضع معداتها أرضاً من دون إحداث ضجيج، ثم تقوم بالتنفس لتخفيف التوتر. كان يقلقها بشكل عابر أن الكشافة الذين كانوا في انتظارهم لم يتجاوز عددهم ثلاثة"ليلڤيت، هيلغت، وفازارا". إلا أن زيري أرسل أربعة من الكشافة.

أقنعت كارو نفسها بأن الجندي الرابع تأخر فحسب، لكن بعد ذلك سمعت"الذئب" يقول لليراز:"علينا أن نفترض الأسوأ."

وهكذا فعلت.

و... هذا ما حدث.

41

أمور مجهولة

كان هناك الكثير من الأمور المجهولة. من موقعهم في جبال أديلفاس،
كان المتمردون أشبه بالعميان. لم يروا سوى بلورات الجليد وعناصر
الهواء، بينما امتد خلف القمم عالم مليء بجنود الأعداء والعبيد المقيدين
بالسلاسل، والقُبور الضحلة، ورماد المدن المحترقة المتطاير في الهواء. كل
هذا كان بمثابة مشهد مسرحي خلف ستارة مغلقة بالنسبة إليهم.

لم يعرفوا إن كان جايل قد أرسل قواته لمطاردتهم. كما لم يعرفوا إن
كان قد وجد بوابة الأطلس وسيطر عليها منذ أن عبروها. لم يجدها بعد، لكن
حتى في تلك الأوقات أرسل دورياته الاستكشافية تمشط"خليج الوحوش"
بحثاً عنهم.

لم يعرفوا أيضاً إن كان قد عاد إلى إريتز منتصراً أم لا. ولم يكن لديهم
أي وسيلة لمعرفة أن باست وسارساغون، الكشافين اللذين لم يعودا، قد
قُبض عليهما وتعرضا للتعذيب بعد ساعات من مغادرتهما فوهة البركان
قبل يوم ونصف.

ولم يكن في وسع المتمردين أن يتخيلوا حتى، أن في الجانب الآخر من العالم، كانت السماء قد ظلّت مظلمة كغسقٍ لنهار كامل—ظلمة غريبة وقاسية، رغم سطوع الشمس، إلا أنها متوارية خلف سحب الرماد، وقد بدت كعين ملتهبة تنظر من خلف عباءة سميكة. تسلل بعض من ضوئها على البحر والجُزر الخضراء المتناثرة مما جعل الألوان تبدو زاهية كما في المناطق الاستوائية.

السماء مسوّدة، والهواء خانق، وما زال صيادو العواصف يدورون في الأصقاع، ينعقون وقد بحت أصواتهم من شدّة الهول. أما الأسرى في زنازينهم التي لا تشبه زنازين السجون، يتأملون السماء من نافذتهم وهم يرتجفون من رعب لا اسم له، يخافون من جلاديهم الذين لم يروهم بعد. لا أيدولون ذات العينين الشريرتين، ولا غيرها. لم يُجلب لهم طعام أو شراب. لم يتبقَّ سوى سلة من البلح الأحمر، ولم يصل بهم الجوع بعد للتفكير في تناولها.

ميليل، حاملة الاسم الثانية، وإخوتها وأخواتها من جماعة غير الشرعيين، بدوا وكأنهم في طي النسيان، وبالنظر من بين القضبان الحديدية لنافذة السجن، لم يشاهدوا أو يتخيّلوا أكثر من ظلمة حالكة تشير إلى نهاية العالم

كانت سكاراب والسحرة الأربعة التابعون لها على علم بحالة سمائهم. وصلتهم رسائل، حتى إلى هذا المكان النائي، وشعروا بالكوارث وكأنما ثقلٌ يتسلل إلى أرواحهم، كأنما تقلّصت نفوسهم تحت ظل الفناء.

كانت سكاراب والسحرة الأربعة التابعون لها قد أحسّوا بقرب الدمار— القريب جداً— ولم يحاولوا تنبيه الجنود الذين اختلطوا بهم خفية. ربما كانت لامبالاتهم نتاج قرونٍ من العزلة. فقد تعلموا أن هؤلاء القوم حمقى، وأنهم يستحقون حروبهم. بل، وفي الجزر البعيدة، كان هناك اعتقاد بأن تلك الحروب تتسبب باليأس: أنها تشغل الإمبراطورية بحروبها العبثية بدل التفكير في مهاجمة الستيليين والاشتباك معهم.

ورغم ما قد يبدو من غرورٍ في قناعة الستيليين بأن عليهم قبل كل شيء ألا يُزعِجوا، إلا أن هذا الغرور كان له ما يبرره. نعم، يجب بأي ثمن أن يُترَك الستيليون وشأنهم، أن يُترَكوا بسلام.

سكاراب كانت تعلم، من منتصف العالم البعيد، ما لم تكن تعرفه ميليل والآخرون المتروكون في زنزانتهم تحت ذلك تحت جنح الظلام الدامس: أن أيدولون، ذات العينين الشريرتين، كانت واحدة من كثيرين يجاهدون لأجل السماء الكئيبة، ويمسكون بأطراف هذا العالم لئلا يتفكك. ليس لديها وقت للأسرى الآن، ولا لأي شيء آخر.

وبالطبع، من الممكن أن المتسللين الخمسة ذوي العيون النارية لم يشعروا بالفخ الذي كان يُنسج على مقربة منهم—مع أنهم يتمتعون بحساسية فائقة وقادرون على تمييز الأنفاس المنبعثة من آلاف صدور الأعداء المتربصين. لكنهم اكتفوا بالمراقبة، ولم يقوموا بتحذير المتمردين اكتفوا بالمراقبة.

أوامر سكاراب إلى الآخرين واضحة ومجردة من الأحاسيس والمشاعر: "هذا لا يعنينا".

لقد كان هذا القول حقيقةً ثابتةً دائماً. لم يكن لديها طريقة لمعرفة مدى زيفه في هذا اليوم تحديداً، أو ما الذي تواجهه تلك الفرقة الهجينة والممزقة من الجنود، أو ما الذي سيحدث إن فشلوا.

كانت هناك الكثير من الأمور المجهولة.

42

الأسوأ

بدأ الأمر مع شعور أحست به كارو يتسلل إلى عمودها الفقري. نظرت نحو أكيفا عبر حشد الجنود. في ذات اللحظة التي نظر هو أيضاً نحوها. تقطب حاجباه قلقاً.

هناك شيء ما——

وفجأةً وكأن الشماء خانتهم. أطبقت عليهم وأضاءت——بضباب شفاف مشبع بالنور، تماماً كما بدت حين عبورهم من البوابة. لكن هذه المرة لم يكن صيادو العواصف هم من يهبطون من السماء.

بل جيش كبير.

نار الملائكة، جحافل منهم، الجناح يلامس الجناح، أضاؤوا السماء، أشعلوها. أغرقوا ضوء النهار بسطوعهم——كثيرون جداً. نيرانهم تعقبت الظلال بلمح البصر. سيوفهم مسلولة ولا مجال للفرار منهم ولا المناورة. ظلال، تطاردها النار. بسرعة فائقة. كل شيء يحدث بسرعة، بسرعة رهيبة.

لقد بدأ الأمر.

الفوهة التي قدموا منها بدت كوعاء مشروخ الحواف، الدومينيون كغطاء من النار، هم كثيرون جداً، جناحاً إلى جناح وسيوفهم مسلولة، وعندما يهبطون في نفس واحد، لا مجال للهرب، ولا مجال لتجاوزهم.

ولم يعد هناك أي وقت للتردد في الأسفل. كل ما حدث في كهوف الكيرين سابقاً، يحدث الآن وبسرعة تقطع الأنفاس. السيوف: تسحب من أغمادها؛ الأيدي: منتصبة نحو السماء. عيون الهامسا: انطلقت فوراً مثل عشبٍ ركب ريحاً عاتية. ترنحت صفوف المهاجمين، وفي لحظة تراجعهم اندفع المتمردون يزأرون لمواجهة الهجوم. لم يرضوا بأن يُسحقوا بين نيران المهاجمين وحجارة الكهوف، بل انطلقوا ليواجهوا قوات الإمبراطور، ورغم قلة عددهم إلا أنهم يملكون قوة السحر.

مع أول تماسٍ، مد أكيفا يده لاستحضار الـ"سيريثار"—لكنه سرعان ما سقط على ركبتيه وكأن رعداً قد صعق رأسه فبدأ يترنح، وهناك من أخذ بيده. إنه راث، ذلك الداشناغ الذي لم يعد مجرد صبي وضع راث يده الضخمة على كتف أكيفا. الكتف ذاته الذي مزقته وحشية أحد الكيمرا من قبل، والآن كيمرا آخر يسنده، وعلى وقع ضجيج السيوف، انطلق الفتى راث إلى المعركة. انتفض أكيفا واقفاً وسحب سيفيه، محاولاً رؤية كارو... وكارو في المقابل تحاول رؤيته والوصول إليه. هناك زوزانا وميك، وملاك يندفع نحوهما، ولن تستطيع الوصول إليهما في الوقت المناسب. بدأت تفتح فمها لتصرخ حين رأت ڤيركو. لقد انقضّ عليه.

تمزّق. تحول الملاك إلى أشلاء، وفي يدها سيوفها الهلالية، كمن يرقص وهي تشقّ طريقها عبر الأعداء للوصول إلى أصدقائها.

أكيفا يحاول مجدداً استحضار"سيريثار"، لكن الرعد يصعق رأسه مجدداً، فيجثو على ركبتيه. لبرهة، أحسّ بيد باردة لطيفة تلامس جبينه، ثم اختفت. محاط ببريق، وصليل، وهدير، وطعن، وأنياب، وصيحات، وترنح. ولا زال السحر محجوباً عنه. كل ما يستطيع فعله الآن هو الوقوف والمواجهة.

زوزانا التي لم تعتد رؤية هذه المشاهد الوحشية، تمزيق وتقطيع وكل هذا الهراء، لم يكن أمامها سوى المتابعة بعد إدراكها بأن عدم رؤية ما يحدث هو أسوأ من رؤيته. كان ميك الجميل بجانبها مباشرة، وڤيركو جاثياً أمامها هناك، وقد بدا مخيفاً وجميلاً أيضاً.

الأشواك في عنقه التي كانت تبدو كأشواك قنفذ طرية ومسترخية، قد تفتحت بالكامل. ها هي الآن أكبر، وأكثر حدة، وذات حواف مسننة، تضاعف حجمها، وصارت أشبه بلبدة أسد من السكاكين.

وصلت كارو، وسيوفها ملطخة بالدماء، في الوقت التي بدأ فيه ڤيركو بإعادة أشواكه إلى طبيعتها—بانسجام تام في حركته—مما جعل زوزانا تفتن بذلك... الجمال المثالي. لعل هذا المشهد ينسيها فظاعة وهول ما شاهدت أثناء المعركة. وبالطبع لم تعد ترى لبدة ڤيركو ذات الأشواك الطرية – التي تساعدها في التمسك بها أثناء امتطاء صهوته - ذات رائحة كريهة، بل هي سعيدة أكثر بوجود صديق له لبدة من السكاكين.

يقفز ميك ويركب خلفها، تتهيأ عضلات ڤيركو تحتهما. يأخذ شهيقاً عميقاً، قوياً، ثم... يحلق، وبعدها... يختفون.

رأى زيري ڤيركو يختفي—يتلاشى من الوجود—وكارو تستدير، تبحث. ليس عنه، زيري يعلم ذلك، ولم يعد هذا يؤلمه كما في السابق. عاصفة قوية، تيارات الهواء التي أحدثتها ضربات أجنحة ڤيركو، تعصف بشعر كارو ويخفق إلى الخلف كعلم في ساحة معركة، حريرياً أزرق يرفرف في خضمّ الصراخ وصخب القتال. تحيطها هالة من السكون الغريب في الوقت الذي كان زيري فيه يقوم بحمايتها، ليس زيري فقط بل كل من الكيميرا وغير الشرعيين، فهي حارسة الأرواح، وبانتظارها مهمة أخرى أكثر إلحاحاً؛ تنفيذ مخططها ضد جايل.

يبحث زيري عن ليراز، فيراها هناك، وكذلك أكيڤا. يقاتلان جنباً إلى جنب، بكل بسالة. أكيڤا يستخدم سيفين متشابهين، وليراز تحمل سيفاً وفأساً،

وابتسامتها تبدو كسلاح ثالث، تقريباً. إنها الابتسامة نفسها التي أظهرتها في اجتماع مجلس الحرب، حينما سخرت من احتمالات المعركة. قالت بلهفة:"واحد منا وثلاثة منهم؟" وزيري يرى الآن ما كانت تقصده: واحد لثلاثة وأكثر بكثير. نيسك وليسيث يقفان بشكل مذهل إلى جانب أكيفا وليراز. كل منهما يحمل سيفاً بيد واليد الأخرى مرفوعة تطلق سحر الهامسا، فتتراجع قوة الدومينيون تحت تأثير الهامسا، فهم لا يستطيعون مجاراة سرعة وقوة هذين الاثنين من غير الشرعيين.

يملأ الأمل قلب زيري للحظة. إنه الأمل الذي يعرفه جيداً ويكرهه: الأمل القبيح، الأسود، الذي ينبع من فكرة القتل، اقتل أكثر، تبقى على قيد الحياة لفترة أطول.

اقتل أو مُت. لا خيار آخر.

الجثث في كل مكان، والمزيد يسقط. تلمع في ذهن زيري صورة سريعة للكهف وقد امتلأ بالجثث، كأن الجبال قد ضمّت أيديها لتقدم القتلى قرباناً لنيتيد، إلهة الدموع والحياة، وللنجوم، وللعدم.

جثث لأبناء الكيميرا، ولغير الشرعيين، ثم—سقوط ظلام آخر.

فوقهم، سماء أخرى من النار تهوي، أجنحة تحجب الشمس، وحتى ذلك الأمل الأسود القبيح لزيري لا يمكنه الصمود أمام هذا المشهد. موجة أخرى من جيوش الدومينيون بنفس ضخامة الأولى، واليوم تبدو إلهة نيتيد للدموع وليس الأمل.

"كارو!" تنادي زيري، صوت الذئب يخرج من بين شفتيه—يخترق ضوضاء المعركة ويحثّ الجنود المتعبين على الاستمرار، الاستمرار وكأن الحياة جائزة تُنال بسفك الدماء. اقتل واقتل واقتل كي تبقى حياً. كم عدد القتلى، وكم من الوقت يمكن الاستمرار؟ في النهاية، الأمر مجرد عملية حسابية، ومع أن ثياغو حقق انتصارات في معارك كان النصر فيها مستحيلاً، لكن أياً منها ليس بهذا القدر من الاستحالة.

ثم إن هناك حقيقة أخرى... هذا ليس ثياغو.

يصدر الأوامر، ويستجيب له كل من الكيميرا وغير الشرعيين. بحلول الوقت الذي يصل فيه إلى كارو، كان حاجز من الجنود قد تشكّل، وفي مركزه تقف كارو، أكيفا، ليراز، وثياغو.

"عليكم المغادرة"، قال الذئب. كان صوته أعلى من الفوضى من حوله، وعيناه حازمتان. هذا الذئب الأبيض لن يمزق حناجر أحد اليوم. "اخرجوا من هنا. استخدموا سحركم. لديكما مهمة يجب إنجازها."

كانت كارو أول من اعترض. "لا يمكننا تركّكم الآن-".

"يجب عليكم المغادرة. من أجل المملكة". من أجل إريتز. من المفهوم أن هذا يعني: إذا لم يكن من أجلنا.

لأننا سنكون قد متنا.

"لن أذهب إلا إذا حددت أحداً يكون في مأمن"، قالت كارو بصوت مخنوق. "شخصاً... أي شخص."

شخص ينتظر انتهاء القتل بأمان، ثم يعود لجمع الأرواح بعد انتهاء كل شيء. فكرة بلا جدوى. فالسيرافيم بعد أن عرفوا أمر الإحياء، بدأوا يتخذون احتياطات لمنعه. يحرقون الموتى، ويحرسون الرماد حتى يتلاشى بالكامل. ومع ذلك، أومأ زيري برأسه. حان وقت الفراق. شعروا بترددهم كشبكة معقدة—من الحب والرغبات و... حتى بدايات لم تكتب لها الحياة. إلى درجة أن التفكير فيها يبدو ضرباً من السخرية.

ينظر زيري إلى ليراز، فتبادله النظرة، ثم يشيح كل منهما بوجهه سريعاً: زيري يتجه بنظره إلى كارو، وليراز إلى أكيفا. مجرد ثانية—وكأنها أبدية— سمحوا لأنفسهم فيها بوداع صامت. يتمنون أمنيات لا طائل منها، ويتركون احتمالاتهم لتسقط على الأرض مع الجثث.

في الأساطير، قيل إن الكيميرا وُلدوا من الدموع، والسيرافيم من الدماء، لكن في هذه اللحظة هم جميعاً أبناء الندم.

عندها بدأ كل من كارو وأكيفا بالالتفات نحو بعضهما البعض من أجل نظرة أخيرة، وملامحهما قد علاها الفراغ، مشحونة بخسارة لا يمكن إدراكها

قال أكيفا:"خذهم. أوصلهم إلى البوابة. تأكد من ذلك."

رمش أكيفا مرتين بسرعة. لم يكن يريد الرفض، لكنه كان على وشك فعله. ينبغي أن يكون هنا، يقاتل—

"قد تكون البوابة محروسة"، قال الذئب، متوقعاً ما سيقوله أكيفا."قد يحتاجون إلى المساعدة". كانت المعركة من حولهم تصل إلى ذروتها."اذهب!". هزّ أكيفا رأسه موافقاً، وغادروا.

ظلّت نظرة ليراز معلّقة في عيني زيري بينما يختفون. لا يوجد تلاشٍ تدريجي، فقط قفزة مفاجئة من الوجود إلى العدم، وعند تلك الحافة، لم تكن هناك ابتسامة ليراز القاتلة أو نظرة التحدي أو رغبتها في الانتقام. فقط ملامح مشوبة بالحزن، وجمال يخطف أنفاسه.

ثم اختفت. في قلب دائرة الجنود، بقي الذئب الأبيض وحيداً."يا لك من محظوظ يا زيري"، فكر، والشعور بالفراغ يملؤه.

رفع نظره. عبور الجيوش قد بدّد الضباب، ورأى صفوفاً من الجنود. جنود، وجنود، وجنود.

يضحك. يستجمع قوة جسده المستعار، يكشف عن أنيابه، ويقفز. إنهم كثيرون للغاية، مما سهل عليه الأمر. كل ما عليه هو القفز والإمساك بأحدهم في الهواء، وعند الإمساك به، يقتله. ثم يقفز إلى التالي، بينما يسقط الجسد. إلى التالي، والتالي، حتى تصبح الأرض بعيدةً في الأسفل، وأجنحتهم تتشابك في تدافع يائسٍ للهرب منه. المزيد منهم يحاصرونه من الخلف. لا فرائس تتناقص ولا الدم الذي يسفكه أيضاً، ثم تخبو ضحكاته.

إنه الذئب الأبيض.

أما ليراز، فتطير بسرعة نحو البوابة. المعركة تدوي من خلفها، ثم تتلاشى مع صخب الهواء، ذلك الهواء الذي يلسع عينيها.

"لم نتعرف بعد".

هذا ما قاله لها عند الينابيع الساخنة، قبل أن يمنحها سره وكأنه يضع مقتله في يدها."يمكنك قتلي بهذا. لكنني أثق بأنك لن تفعلي".

ثقة. هل وثقت به لأنه أنقذ حياتها، أم لأنه منحها سرّه، أم كلاهما؟ وهي تراه يقاتل، كانت طريقته مزيجاً من الكفاءة والجرأة؛ كان وحشياً ورشيقاً في آن، لكن لم يكن ذلك شيئاً مقارنة بالرقة والجمال اللذين رأتهما فيه حين كان في جسده الحقيقي ويرقص بأسلوب الكيرين بالشفرات الهلالية بدت تلك الشفرات جزءاً منه. أما هذه السيوف، فلا. هذا الجسد لا يبدو كذلك أيضاً. منذ أن أخبرها بحقيقته، بدا لها جسد الذئب الأبيض أشبه بزيّ تنكري في نظرها، وكأن بإمكانه خلعه والخروج منه، طويلاً، نحيلاً، داكناً، ذا قرنين وجناحين. في عين خيالها، لا يزال مجرد ظل. لم تره إلا من بعيد، وكم تمنت لو أنها عرفته حينها عن قرب.

بعد لحظة بدا لها هذا التمني سخيفاً وتافهاً. ما أهمية ذلك الآن؟ وقد تركته خلفها وربما هو الآن في طريقه إلى الموت—مرة أخرى وربما إلى الأبد إن أحرق السيراف جسده. لا معنى لشيء حقيقي عندما يتعلق الأمر بالوجوه؟ الأرواح فقط هي الحقيقية، وعندما تتطاير في الهواء، تذوب وتتلاشى، كما حدث مع روح هازايل، وعدد لا يحصى من الأرواح الأخرى... يا للخسارة.

تضع ليراز يدها على بطنها. تتلاشى النيران، ويخفت العالم.

كيف استغرقت كل هذه السنوات لتشعر بقيمة الحياة؟

واصلوا الطيران، وقد مر الوقت بسرعةٍ هائلة مذ غادروا الجبال حتى وصلوا فوق مياه الخليج المظلمة. بدا لهم من فوق كبحرٍ يغشاه الضباب الذي يغطي الأفق والأرض التي تحيط به. أخيراً، تلمح كارو ميك وزوزانا فوق ڤيركو أمامهم. يحاول البشر الحفاظ على السحر الخادع، لكنه يتذبذب، غير مستقر، وقد رصدتهم دورية دومينيون. إنهم يقتربون.

ينعطف ڤيركو ويهبط، فيتجاوز الممر ويختفي شيئاً فشيئاً. ثم تصل كارو، أكيڤا، ولیراز إلى حافة الممر المتذبذب للشق في السماء، وبدلاً من أن تندفع كارو مباشرةً عبره، تستدير نحو أكيڤا، تنظر إليه، يغمرها شعور الإرهاق من استحالة الفراق في هذا الجو المشحون بالخطر. كيف يمكنها أن تتركه هكذا؟

تصرخ لیراز عليها:"اذهبي! اذهبي الآن!".

تقبض كارو على يد أكيڤا. عاجزة، تحاول أن تصنع لحظة أخيرة معه. نظرة على الأقل، إن لم تكن كلمات، بل أكثر منها كشيء لتتذكره. يده دافئة جداً، وعيناه مشرقتان—لكن يسكنهما طيفٌ من أشباح مفعمة بالحزن، مجروحة القلب، غاضبة، تلعن النجوم. يضغط على يدها."سنكون بخير"، لكن اليأس يتسرب من صوته. غير مصدق ما يقول، وكارو أيضاً.

يا إلهي، يا إلهي. إنها ترغب في جره معها عبر البوابة.

لیراز تواصل الصراخ عليها، وصوتها يملأ رأس كارو بالهلع والغضب. يلمس أكيڤا كوعها، يدفعها برفق نحو البوابة. تشعر بتمزقات السماء تلفح وجهها. صرخات لیراز—"اذهبي! اذهبي!"—ترن في رأسها، تغذي رعبها. تشعر بالغضب يتصاعد في عروقها، إلى درجة كرهها، حتى لو للحظة أرادت أن تقول لها أن تصمت، في الوقت ذاته، يدير أكيڤا ظهره لها، ثم استدار محدقاً في عيني شقيقته للمرة الأخيرة ولجزء من الثانية كأنه يقول لها؛ اعتني بها، يريد أن يقول لكنه لم يفعل."واعتني بنفسك، أرجوك، يا لير".

"المباخر ممتلئة، يا أخي".

المباخر؟ برمشة عين تذكر حين أخبره هازایيل بذات الشيء. أكيڤا هو السابع الذي يحمل هذا الجسد؛ ستة أكيڤات ماتوا قبله، مما يعني أن مباخر الأرواح ممتلئة."عليك أن تعيش"، قال له هازایيل حينها.

هازایيل هو من مات، بينما أكيڤا بقي حياً.

أفكاره مبعثرة. جنود الدومينيون سيكونون فوقهم في ثوانٍ. رآهم يتوافدون خلف ليراز. علقت تلك المشاعر المحمومة داخل جسده، نابعة من صرخات شقيقته—"اذهب! اذهب! اذهب!"— لم يرَ ليراز سابقاً أكثر حياةً مما بدت عليه تلك اللحظة. رأى في تعابيرها هدفاً، وطاقة، وعزيمة وتركيزاً جعلها متوهجة.

ثم، فجأة، ترتطم قدماها بصدره.

قوة خارقة، صدمت أضلاعه، سحبت أنفاسه. وكأن أنفاسه وأفكاره قذفت إلى خارجه، راح يترنح وقد قُذف بعيداً، حتى فقد توازنه. عاجز عن التنفس، ولا يرى.

وعندما استعاد توازنه، وجد نفسه قد عبر البوابة.

يغمر اللهب البوابة، وقد ظلت ليراز على الجانب الآخر توصدها بالنار حتى انقطع الاتصال بين العالمين.

أُغلق الشق في السماء كجرح كوي بالنار ليلتئم. ليراز بقيت هناك، وأكيفا هنا مكانها، مع كارو.

43

نار في السماء

وساد صمت.

لكنه لم يكن صمتاً حقيقياً. كانت هناك نارٌ ورياح، وفرقعة، وهمس، وصوت لهاثهم الصعب. لكن من صدمتهم، استسلموا بالصمت، وهم يحدقون في ألسنة اللهب المتوهجة. اضطرمت فجأة، ثم انطفأت بسرعة، دون أن تترك خلفها دخاناً أو رائحة. انتهى كل شيء، وكل ما احترق—كل ما كان يفصل بين العالمين—لم يترك وراءه بقايا من رماد أو دخان. اختفت البوابة تماماً.

جالت كارو بنظرها بحثاً عن أي أثر يدل على أنها كانت هناك. ندبة، تموّج، صورة باهتة للشق الذي كان، لكن لم يكن هناك شيء على الإطلاق. ثم استدارت نحو أكيفا.

أكيفا كان هنا. كان هنا، وليس ليراز. ماذا حدث للتو؟ لم ينظر إليها حتى؛ عيناه مفتوحتان على اتساعهما، يملؤهما الفزع، وهو يحدق في الفراغ الجديد في السماء. "ليراز!" ناداها بصوت مبحوح، لكن الطريق كان مغلقاً،

بل مختفياً. السماء أصبحت مجرد سماء الآن، الغلاف الجوي الرقيق فوق هذه الجبال الأفريقية، وتلك الظاهرة التي جعلت إريتز تبدو كأنها... كأنها بلدٌ مجاور، في الجهة الأخرى من حاجز دوّار... انتهت. الآن أصبحت إريتز بعيدة جداً، بعيدة بشكل مستحيل وخيالي، كأنها مكان أسطوري، والدماء التي تُراق هناك—يا إلهي. تلك الدماء ليست أسطورية. الدماء، الموت.

وهنا، كان كل شيء هادئاً جداً، لا شيء سوى صوت الرياح الآن، وأصدقائهم، ورفاقهم، و... وعائلتهم، كل جندي متبقٍ من غير الشرعيين، إخوة أكيڤا وأخواته بالدم، يقاتلون في سماء أخرى، ولا يمكنهم فعل شيء حيال ذلك لقد تركوهما هناك. وحين استدار أكيڤا أخيراً نحوها، بدا عليه الذهول. كان شاحباً، غير مصدق لما حدث.

"ما... ما الذي حدث؟" سألت كاروه وهي تتجه نحوه محلقة في الهواء

قال بصوت مشوب بالحيرة، وكأنه كان يحاول فهم ما جرى:"ليراز... دفعتني عبر البوابة. لقد قررت...". ابتلع ريقه بصعوبة."قررت أن أعيش. أرادتني أنا... أن أكون من يبقى حياً."

ظل يحدق في الهواء وكأنه يمكنه الرؤية عبره إلى العالم الآخر، وكأن ليراز ما زالت هناك، على الجانب الآخر من ستار رقيق. لكن مع اختفاء البوابة، بات من المستحيل فجأة استيعاب أنها كانت موجودة أصلاً. أين تقع إريتز؟ وأي سحر هو الذي جعلها قريبة إلى هذا الحد؟ من الذي صنع تلك البوابات؟ ومتى؟ وكيف؟

ذهبت أفكار كاروه مباشرة إلى تصورها المعتاد عن الكون المعروف: كواكب تدور حول شمس، عظمة لا يحدها الإدراك، محاطة بفراغ شاسع غير مفهوم. لم تستطع تخيل كيف يمكن لإريتز أن تتناسب مع هذه الصورة. كان الأمر أشبه بمحاولة تجميع قطعتين من أحجية مختلفة في لوحة واحدة.

قالت محاولة طمأنة أكيڤا :"ليراز تستطيع التعامل مع تلك الدورية. أو على الأقل، يمكنها أن تختبئ بسحر التمويه وتهرب."

رد بصوت مشحون بالألم:"وإلى أين؟ إلى المجزرة؟".

المجزرة. كلمة واحدة، لكنها أحدثت في داخلها صرخة مكتومة، شعرت بها في أعماق قلبها وأحشائها. وكأن كل كيانها الداخلي يصرخ. خنقت تلك الكلمة روحها، وجعلتها تفكر في لوراميندي. هزت رأسها بعنف. لا يمكنها أن تعيش تلك المأساة مرة أخرى. لا يمكنها العودة إلى إريتز فقط لتجد الموت في انتظارها. مجرد التفكير في ذلك كان يفوق طاقتها.

قالت بإصرار:"يمكنهم الفوز."

أرادت من أكيفا أن يهز رأسه موافقاً، أن يشاركها في الأمل."الكتائب المختلطة. الكيميرا سيضعفون المهاجمين، وأنت قلت..." توقفت لتبتلع غصة في حلقها."قلت إن جنود الدومينيون ليسوا نِدّاً لغير الشرعيين".

بالطبع، لم يكن ذلك ما قاله. ما قاله هو أن المواجهة الفردية بين جندي من الدومينيون وأحد غير الشرعيين ليست في صالح الدومينيون. لكن هذا لم يكن قتالاً فردياً على الإطلاق.

لم يصحح أكيفا كلماتها. لكنه أيضاً لم يهز رأسه، ولم يطمئنها بأن كل شيء سيكون بخير. قال فقط:"حاولت الوصول إلى السيريثار... مصدر القوة. ولم أستطع. أولاً مات هازايل لأنني فشلت، والآن سيموت الجميع-".

قاطعته كاروه كلماته، وهي تهز رأسها بقوة."لن يحدث ذلك."

تابع وكأنما لا يسمعها:"أنا من بدأ كل هذا. أقنعتهم. وأنا من بقي حياً؟".

كانت كاروه لا تزال تهز رأسها. قبضتا يديها مشدودتان بقوة. تطوي جسدها في الهواء، وقبضتاها تضغطان على صدرها، في تلك المساحة الضيقة أسفل القفص الصدري، حيث شعرت بفراغ مخيف ينهشها من الداخل. لم يكن هذا مجرد جوع جسدي، على الرغم من كونها ضعيفة وهزيلة من قلة الأكل، شعرت أن جسدها قد تقلص ليصبح هيكلاً هشاً، وكأنها لم تعد سوى ظل لما كانت عليه. لكن هذا الجوع لم يكن للطعام وحده. كان حزناً وخوفاً وعجزاً يغلي في داخلها.

منذ زمن، توقفت عن تصديق أنها وأكيفا مجرد أداتين في يد القدر، أو أن حلمهما كان جزءاً من خطة محكمة أو مصير محتوم. لكنها اكتشفت الآن أن لديها في أعماقها طاقة غاضبة تجاه الكون ذاته. كيف يمكنه ألا يكترث؟ كيف يمكنه ألا يساعد؟ بل كيف يمكنه أن يبدو وكأنه يعمل ضدّهم؟ ربما هذا هو المكتوب. ربما هذا هو المصير. وربما يكرههم.

كان الصمت مطبقاً من حولهما، أما الآخرين فبعيدون جداً... بعيدون جداً.

تذكرت فتى الداشناغ من المناطق النائية، وتذكرت الظلال الحية وأمزالاغ، الذي أعادته إلى الحياة لتوها—أمزالاغ الذي لطالما أمل أن يجمع أرواح أطفاله من أنقاض لوراميندي—وتذكرت كل الآخرين، لكن أكثر من ذلك كله، فكرت في زيري. زيري الذي كان يتحمل العبء وحده الآن، الذي كان يواجه الخداع وحده في غياب إيسا وتين وهي نفسها. زيري الذي كان يموت كما الذئب.

يتلاشى.

لقد أعطى كل شيء، أو سيفعل قريباً، بينما هي هنا، بأمان... مع أكيفا. ومشاعرها كانت خليطاً ساماً يغلي في حفرة معدتها الفارغة، لأنه في أعماقها، دون أن تستطيع الاعتراف بذلك، تحت كل هذا الرعب والفوضى، أحست بشيء... يا إلهي، لا يمكن أن يكون فرحاً. ربما هو شعور بالراحة لأنها ما زالت على قيد الحياة. لا يمكن اعتباره خطأ أن تشعر بالراحة كونها على قيد الحياة، ربما يكون خاطئاً. وخاطئاً جداً، وجباناً أيضاً.

ظل جناحا أكيفا يرفرفان ببطء ليحافظا على تحليقه، بينما بقيت كارو تحوم بسكون. خلفهما، يطير ڤيركو ذهاباً وإياباً بحركات قصيرة، وهو يحمل ميك وزوزانا على ظهره. فجأة. كارو انتبهت فجأة.

ڤيركو. ليس من المفترض أن يبقى هنا؛ فهو لا يمكنه التظاهر بهيئة بشرية إطلاقاً. عليه أن يُنزل ميك وزوزانا ثم يعود إلى البوابة. لكن أفكار

كارو قفزت عن هذه النقطة الآن. ينظر أكيڤا إليها، وبدت متأكدة من أنه يشعر بنفس المزيج القاتل من الراحة والرعب الذي شعرت به هي. بل ربما أسوأ، بسبب تضحية ليراز. "أخذتِ القرار"، هو من قال. "أنني أنا من يجب أن يعيش."

هزت كارو رأسها مرة أخرى، كأنها تحاول طرد كل الأفكار السوداء. نظرت إليه مباشرة وقالت: "لو كنت أنت، لو كنت أنت على الجانب الآخر الآن، كما كدت أن تكون، كنت سأصدق أنك بخير. سأضطر إلى تصديق ذلك، وعلي أن أصدقه الآن. لا يوجد شيء يمكننا فعله."

" قال أكيڤا: "يمكننا العودة. يمكننا الطيران مباشرة إلى البوابة الأخرى."
لم تكن لديها إجابة لذلك. لم تُرِد أن تقول لا. قلبها خفق بفكرة العودة، حتى حين كان عقلها يحذرها من أن الفكرة مستحيلة. بعد صمت، سألت: "كم من الوقت سيستغرق ذلك؟" من هنا إلى أوزبكستان، ومن ثم، على الجانب الآخر، من سلسلة فيسكال إلى أديلفاس.

شد أكيڤا فكه ثم أرخاه، وقال بصوت مشدود: "نصف يوم. على الأقل."
لم ينطق أي منهما بالحقيقة بصوت عالٍ، لكنهما عرفاها: بحلول الوقت الذي يمكنهما فيه العودة، ستكون المعركة قد انتهت، سواء انتصروا أم هُزموا، وسيكونان قد فشلا في مهمتهما هنا، بالإضافة إلى كل شيء آخر. وكان ذلك فشلاً لا يمكنهما تحمله.

كرهاً لدورها كصوت العقل في وجه الحزن، سألت كارو بحذر: "لو كانت ليراز هنا معي، وأنت هناك، ماذا كنت ستريدنا أن نفعل؟".

تأمل أكيڤا كلماتها، وعيناه تشتعلان من تحت ظلال الغم، ولم تستطع كارو أن تخمن ما يدور في ذهنه. أرادت أن تمد يدها لتلامس يده كما فعلت على الجانب الآخر للعالم، لكنها شعرت بأن ذلك سيكون خاطئاً بطريقة ما، وكأنها تستغل عواطفه لإقناعه بالتخلي عن شيء بالغ الأهمية بالنسبة إليه. لم تكن تريد ذلك. لم تستطع أن تتخذ هذا القرار بدلاً عنه. لذا،

انتظرت بصمت، وجاء جوابه ثقيلاً، محملاً بالألم:"كنت سأريدك أن تفعلي ما جئتِ لأجله."

وهكذا، لم يكن الأمر خياراً حقيقياً. وليس بوسعهما الوصول إلى الآخرين في الوقت المناسب لإحداث فرق، وحتى لو تمكنا من الوصول، فما الفارق الذي يمكن أن يصنعاه؟ ومع ذلك، شعرت كارو بأن الأمر يشبه خياراً، يشبه الابتعاد عن شيء عزيز، وبدأ بداخلها يتفتح، مثل بقعة دم على قماش أبيض، أول إدراك للذنب الذي سيطاردها لاحقاً.

هل فعلتُ ما يكفي؟ هل بذلتُ كل ما أستطيع؟ لا.

حتى الآن، بالكاد تقف على حافة الكارثة والمعركة لا تزال مستعرة في العالم الآخر، كانت تستطيع أن تتذوق بالفعل كيف سيلوث هذا الذنب أي سعادة قد تحاول أن تجدها أو تبنيها مع أكيفا. سيبدو الأمر أشبه بالرقص فوق ساحة معركة، بخطوات متأنية حول الجثث، في محاولة لبناء حياة من هذا الخراب.

انتبه، لا تخظ هناك، واحد اثنان ثلاثة، لا تتعثر بجثة أختك.

"اممم، يا جماعة؟" كان ذلك صوت ميك. استدارت كارو نحو صديقيها، وهي تحاول أن تخفي دموعها.

قال ميك بصوت متردد، يبدو عليه الذهول مثل وجهه الشاحب:"لست متأكداً من الخطة الآن..." بدا مصدوماً، مثل زوزانا، التي كانت تتشبث بفيركو، بينما ميك يتشبث بها بدوره."لكن يجب أن نغادر. المروحيات؟" كان ذلك بمثابة صدمة لكارو. مروحيات؟ ها قد رأتهم الآن، وسمعت الصوت الذي كان ينبغي أن تلاحظه من قبل:"وومب وومب ووومب..."

قال ميك:"إنهم يأتون إلى هنا. بسرعة." وبالفعل كانوا كذلك—عدة مروحيات اقتربت من اتجاهات مختلفة، كأنما تتوافد نحوهم من كل اتجاه. ما الذي يجري بحق الجحيم؟ هذه أرض لا تخضع لسلطة أحد. ما الذي تفعله المروحيات هنا؟ وسرعان ما انتابها شعور سيء جداً.

قالت وهي تحس برعب جديد ينبثق في داخلها:"القصبة... اللعنة على تلك الحفرة."

...

إليزا... ليست على طبيعتها اليوم. لكنها تجيد التظاهر بغير ذلك، أو هكذا اعتقدت وهي تأخذ رشفة من شاي النعناع البارد. يجب أن تشكر عائلتها على هذه القدرة، فكرت وهي تستحضر مشاعر مريرة خاصة موجهة إليهم. شكراً لكم - فكرت بسخرية مغموسة بالغضب- على تعليمكم لي فن الانفصال التام بين عواطفي وملامح وجهي. إنها مهارة مفيدة جداً حين أحتاج إلى التظاهر بأنني لا أفقد صوابي.

بعد سنوات من إخفاء البؤس، والعار، والارتباك، والإذلال، والخوف، بات بإمكانها أن تمر عبر الحياة كفراغ متحرك، واجهتها بهدوء لا يمكن زعزعته، بالكاد تظهر أي حياة حقيقية.

إلا عندما يسيطر عليها الحلم، بالطبع. في تلك اللحظات، كانت تبدو حية بكل معنى الكلمة. تماماً. ويا لها من حياة مشوشة. ليلة أمس، على سطح القصبة... أو ربما صباح هذا اليوم؟ الأرجح كلاهما. استمر الأمر طويلاً بما يكفي ليشمل طلوع الفجر. لم تستطع التوقف عن البكاء. لم تكن نائمة حتى، ومع ذلك وجدها الحلم. حلم الذكرى.

مرت عاصفة من خلالها، تماماً كما تفعل دائماً، محصنة ضد إرادتها. وكانت تلك العاصفة مزيجاً من الحزن، والفقدان الذي لا يمكن إدراكه، وشدة الندم التي أصبحت مألوفة لها أكثر مما ينبغي.

مع اختفاء النجوم وبزوغ الفجر، هدأت العاصفة التي اجتاحتها. أما اليوم، فها هي الأرض المدمرة التي خلفتها العاصفة وراءها: مياه تنحسر، وخراب ممتد. و... كشف. أو على الأقل بداية الكشف، زاوية ما تبرز من بين الركام. هكذا شعرت: جُرف الحطام بعيداً، وعقلها أشبه بسهل فيضانٍ نظيف ومهيب. وعند قدميها، شيء بالكاد مرئي، زاوية ما تبرز من الأرض.

ربما كانت زاوية صندوق—كنز قراصنة أو صندوق باندورا—أو ربما زاوية... سطح.. سطح معبد مدفون. أو مدينة بأكملها. أو عالم.

كل ما عليها فعله هو أن تنفخ الغبار بعيداً، وستعرف، أو على الأقل ستبدأ بمعرفة ما هو مدفون بداخلها. يمكنها أن تشعر به هناك. ينمو، متسعاً، رهيباً ومذهلاً -موهبتها الملعونة- يتحرك في داخلها. لقد بذلت الكثير من نفسها لإبقائه مدفوناً، حتى إنها شعرت أحياناً أن أي طاقة قد تملكها للفرح أو الحب أو النور ذهبت كلها إلى هذا الجهد. لديك مقدار محدد فقط مما يمكنك تقديمه.

إذاً... ماذا لو توقفت عن المقاومة واستسلمت له؟

هنا العقدة. لأن إليزا لم تكن الأولى التي يراودها هذا الحلم. هذه"الهبة". إنها مجرد مبتدئة مقارنة بسلسلة المخضرمين الطويلة. بعض التقدم وسيؤدي بها إلى المصحة. ذلك هو الجنون. فقد أحست بروح شكسبير تسكنها اليوم. لكن بالطبع روح التراجيديات، لا الكوميديات. ولم يغب عنها أنه عندما قال الملك لير تلك العبارة، كان قد قطع شوطاً كبيراً في طريقه إلى الجنون. وربما هي على نفس المنوال.

ربما كانت تفقد عقلها. أو ربما...

... ربما في طريقها لإيجاده.

على الأقل، في الوقت الحالي، كانت تمتلك سيطرة على نفسها. حيث تجلس تحتسي شاي النعناع البارد على سطح القصبة—ليس في الفندق، بل في"مقبرة الوحوش"—وتأخذ استراحة من العمل في الحفرة.

الدكتور شودهاري صامت اليوم، وقد وجه إليزا عندما تذكرت الطريقة الخرقاء التي ربت بها على ذراعها الليلة الماضية، عاجزاً عن التعامل مع انهيارها التام.

اللعنة. لم يكن هناك الكثير من الناس الذين تهتم فعلاً برأيهم فيها، لكنه كان أحدهم. والآن... هذا. عقلها استمر في العودة إلى تلك اللحظة،

دورة أخرى في دوامة العار، إلى أن لاحظت حركة غريبة تنتشر بين العمال المتجمعين.

كان هناك ما يشبه محطة مؤقتة للتزود بالطعام والشراب أقيمت أمام البوابات الضخمة والعتيقة للحصن: شاحنة تقدم الشاي وأطباق الطعام، مع عدد قليل من الكراسي البلاستيكية للجلوس عليها. أما القصبة نفسها، فقد طُوِّقت بحبال، حيث كان فريق من علماء الأنثروبولوجيا الجنائية يفحصها بدقة بالغة، حرفياً وكأنهم يستخدمون أمشاطاً دقيقة.

لقد عثروا في إحدى الغرف على شعر أزرق طويل، كما يبدو—نفس الغرفة التي وجدوا فيها، متناثرة على الأرض، مجموعة غريبة من الأسنان التي أدت إلى تكهنات بأن"الفتاة على الجسر" و"شبح الأسنان"—الظل الذي التقطته كاميرات المراقبة في متحف الحقل بشيكاغو—ربما تكونا نفس الشخص.

ازدادت القصة غموضاً. والآن، هناك شيء جديد. لم تـَر إليزا بداية ما حدث، هذا الاضطراب الذي اندلع بين العمال، لكنها رأت كيف انتقل من مجموعة إلى أخرى من خلال الإيماءات والحديث السريع والعالي باللغة العربية. شخص ما أشار إلى الجبال. نحو الأعلى، إلى السماء فوق القمم، في نفس الاتجاه الذي أشار إليه الدكتور أمهالي قبل ذلك ساخراً عندما قال:"لقد ذهبوا من ذلك الاتجاه."

إنهم الكائنات الحية، الوحوش.

أخذت إليزا نفساً حاداً. هل وجدوهم؟

تمكنت من رؤية لمعان الطائرات وهي تتحرك في البعيد، ثم، على يمينها، انفصل رجلان عن الحشد العام من الناس—أشخاص لم تستطع تحديد وظائفهم، حيث تجمع هناك عدد كبير من الرجال، ومعظمهم لا يبدو أنهم يفعلون شيئاً—واتجها نحو المروحية التي كانت جائمة على قطعة من الأرض المستوية.

ظلت تراقب، وقد نسيت تماماً كوب الشاي في يدها، بينما بدأت شفرات المروحية بالدوران، تزداد سرعتها حتى انطلقت سحب من الغبار باتجاهها، وارتفعت المروحية عن الأرض لتطير. ضجيج صوتها مرتفع جداً—وومب وومب وومب—وقلبها ينبض بقوة بينما تفحصت وجوه الناس من حولها. شعرت بالعجز بسبب حاجز اللغة، وبغرابة كبيرة كونها شخصاً دخيلاً هنا.

لا بد أن هناك من يتحدث الإنجليزية، واعتبرته اختباراً صغيراً لشجاعتها. أخذت نفساً عميقاً، ألقت كوبها الورقي في سلة المهملات، وتوجهت نحو إحدى العاملات القليلات في الموقع.

لم يتطلب الأمر سوى بضع أسئلة لتفهم سبب الاضطراب. نار في السماء، قيل لها.

أخبروها أن النار تشغل السماء. سألت:"نار؟ مزيد من الملائكة؟". أجابت المرأة، وهي تحدق في البعيد:"إن شاء الله."

تذكرت إليزا ما قاله الدكتور أمهالي في اليوم السابق:"إنه أمر لطيف جداً بالنسبة إلى المسيحيين، أليس كذلك؟""الملائكة" في روما،"الشياطين" هنا. يا لها من كليشيه للنظرة الغربية، ويا له من خطأ فادح. المسلمون أيضاً يؤمنون بالملائكة، كما استنتجت إليزا، ويبدو أنهم لن يمانعوا أن يحظوا ببعضهم.

أما بالنسبة إليها، فكان لديها شعور داخلي بأنهم أفضل حالاً من دونهم. واضطرت للتساؤل—خاصة في ضوء ما بدأت تصدقه—لماذا كان احتمال وجود الملائكة يخيفها أكثر من احتمال وجود الوحوش؟

44

خبر عاجل

كان وصول السيرافيم إلى الأرض حدثاً مخططاً بدقة، استغلوا فيه كل فرصة لإبهار البشرية. جلبوا معهم أدوات موسيقية مصممة خصيصاً لهذه المناسبة، وارتدوا أزياء معدة بعناية، واختاروا مواقع ظهورهم بعناية لتحقيق التأثير الأعظم. وحتى لو لم يقوموا بكل ذلك، فإن جمالهم ورشاقتهم كانا كافيين. سبقتهم سمعتهم وقرون من الأساطير ساهمت في استقبالهم. لذا من شبه المستحيل أن يخطئوا.

أما "الوحوش"، فقد كان ظهورهم الأول أقل جاذبية بكثير. ملابسهم متجعدة ومشبعة بدماء جافة، وموسيقاها اختارها لهم منتجو برامج تلفزيونية متلهفون للإثارة، كما أن جمالهم ورشاقتهم كانا... معدومين إلى حد كبير.

لأنهم موتى بالأصل.

بعد يومين فقط من التصريح المذهل الذي أدلى به قائد الملائكة قائلاً:"الوحوش قادمون من أجلكم" - يومان من الشغب، ومواثيق الانتحار

الجماعي، والعمادات الطارئة في كنائس مكتظة، ويومان من اجتماعات متوترة ومداولات خافتة بين مجلس مغلق من قادة العالم—ظهر خبر عاجل فجأة، قاطعاً برامج أخرى، لينفجر في وعي البشرية الجماعي بقوة لا تقل عن قوة الوصول الأول، إن لم تكن أكبر.

"إنه خبر عاجل."

كانت وسائل الإعلام تعمل بوتيرة جنونية—صحافة أشبه بخلية طيور طنانة، بسرعة هائلة، لا وقت لالتقاط الأنفاس. الخوف في تلك الأيام كان يتلون بكل النكهات الممكنة، بالإضافة إلى قدر كبير من الإثارة. ومثل هذه الأوقات بمثابة حلم يتحقق لمذيعي الأخبار.

في هذا السياق، جاء الإعلان عن الخبر العاجل الأخير بأسلوب مختلف، متميز بجدية ورزانة لافتتين.

انفرد بالخبر أهم مذيع أخبار في العالم، رجل اعتاد المشاهدون أن يعتبروه قريباً للقلب وللعقل، يظهر كل ليلة في غرف المعيشة الأمريكية بوجه شاب لا يتغير، باستثناء أثر طفيف لطول إضافي في جبينه بفعل تراجع الشعر عن جبهته ببطء عبر السنوات. يتمتع بالكرامة—وليس من أصحاب المظاهر ذوي مسحة الشيب (الحقيقية أو المصطنعة) في شعرهم.

والحق يقال، لولا أخلاقياته الإعلامية كصحفي في مكانته، لجعل الوضع أسوأ بكثير مما هو عليه الآن.

"أيها المواطنون الأمريكيون، يا مواطنو الأرض..." يا لها من جملة، مواطنو الأرض! جملة يتمنى جميع المذيعين الأقل شأناً أن يكونوا هم من قالوها، وهم يرتجفون غيرةً وحسداً."لقد حصلت محطتنا للتو على أدلة يبدو أنها تثبت صحة مزاعم الزوار. أنتم تعرفون ما أقصد. التحقيقات الأولية المستقلة تشير إلى أن هذه الصور حقيقية، على الرغم من أنه، كما سترون، هناك العديد من الأسئلة التي لم نجد لها إجابات بعد. أحذركم. هذه الصور ليست مناسبة للأطفال."

تجمد ملايين المشاهدين في أماكنهم وحبسوا أنفاسهم. بعضهم أرسل أطفاله إلى غرفهم، بينما عرض المذيع الصور بصمت ودون أي مقدمات إضافية.

في غرف المعيشة بأنحاء البلاد، وفي الحانات، والمكاتب، وأماكن السكن الجامعية، ومحطات الإطفاء، وحتى مختبرات الأقبية في المتحف الوطني للتاريخ الطبيعي، وفي كل مكان آخر، حين ظهرت الصورة الأولى، انعقدت الحواجب من الدهشة.

كانت فترة حساسة، تلك اللحظة القصيرة التي تمتزج فيها الحواجب المعقودة بصدمة عدم التصديق التلقائية. لكن هذه الفترة لم تدم طويلاً. فخلال الثمان والأربعين ساعة الماضية، بدأت البشرية تتعلم كيف تصدق ما يحدث، حيث دفعت الأحداث غير المسبوقة الكثيرين إلى التصديق التام وبسرعة جنونية انتقلت العقول من حالة"ما هذا بحق الجحيم؟" إلى"يا إلهي!"، وبلغ الذعر على الأرض مستوى غير مسبوق.

إنه زيري ذلك الشيطان. بالطبع، لم يكن هناك أحد يعلم اسمه، أو يتساءل عنه كما فعلت إليزا.

الإعلان الشخصي الذي ألفته زوزانا وميك للكيرين أثناء طيرانهم كان شيئاً على شاكلة:"بطل نبيل في جسد محارب مهووس مثير للهيبة، يضحي بكل شيء لإنقاذ العالم. وقد يضحي بكل شيء من أجل الحب، لكنه يأمل ألا يضطر إلى ذلك. أنا حقاً أستحق نهاية سعيدة."

في حكاية خرافية قدمتها زوزانا، كان زيري سيحصل بالتأكيد على نهاية سعيدة. لأن من يحملون القلوب النقية ينتصرون دائماً. كما أن هناك وعداً بين زوزانا وميك أشبه بوعد في الحكايات الخرافية: عندما يكمل ثلاث مهام بطولية، يمكنه أن يطلب يدها. قالت ذلك مازحة، لكنه أخذ الأمر بجدية، فقد أتم واحدة فقط من المهام الثلاث—حيث إن زوزانا، في سرها، اعتبرت أن إصلاحه لجهاز التكييف في غرفتها عملاً بطولياً قد احتسبته له.

تضحية زيري بجسده الذي وُلد به كانت بلا شك عملاً بطولياً. لكنها، ككل الأشياء في الحياة، لم تكن حكاية خرافية. في الواقع، الحياة أحياناً تبدو مصممة على إثبات مدى بعدها عن تلك الحكايات.

وكما هو الحال الآن، وفي مكان بعيد جداً، حدث شيء ما. كان هناك اتصال لا أحد يمكنه أو سيمكنه ربطه بأي شيء آخر، سواء في هذا العالم أو في"المملكة". ما يحدث في المملكة يبقى فيها، وما يحدث على الأرض يبقى على الأرض. لم يكن هناك من يتتبع مسارات الزمن بحثاً عن الصدف ولكن هذا... يبدو وكأنه تلميح إلى عالمين متوازيين.

في اللحظة ذاتها التي بدت فيها صورة جسد زيري الكيريني على هيئة جسد بشري—تلك اللحظة—في"المملكة"، اخترق نصل أحد جنود الدومينيون قلبه.

إذاً هناك عوالم أخرى أبعد من هذين العالمين، ربما تكون مترابطة، وربما تكررت أصداء قصته في كلا الجانبين، ظلال فوق ظلال فوق ظلال. أو ربما هي مجرد صدفة. صدفة قاسية. غريبة. وبينما كانت صورة جسد زيري المحترق تُنقش في وعي البشرية—كشيطان !— فقد مات مرة أخرى.

لكن الألم هو أسوأ بكثير هذه المرة. لم يكن بجانبه أحد ليمسك به، ولا حتى نجوم لينظر إليها بينما حياته تتلاشى. سرعان ما مات وحيداً، ولم يكن بجواره أي شخص يحمل مبخرة للاحتفاظ بروحه. كان قد وعد كاروه بأنه سيعين شخصاً"للأمان"، لكنه لم يفعل. فلم يكن لديه وقت لذلك.

والآن لن يكون بيننا أبداً.

عندما شعرت كاروه بروح زيري تنفصل عنه في الحفرة، وتلامس روحه حواسها، شعرت بنقاء نادر فيها—رياح جبال أديلفاس العاتية والصافية؛ الوطن—إنه المكان المناسب الذي تخلى فيه عن جسد الذئب الأبيض المقيت، لينطلق بعيداً عن السيوف المتناحرة، والصراخ الذي كان يحيط به. لم يأبه لأي صوت حينها. فقط الضوء.

لقد عادت روح زيري إلى وطنها.

"سيداتي وسادتي"، قال المذيع من مكتبه في نيويورك، بصوت غاية في الجدية، خالٍ تماماً من متعة مبطنة بالمآسي."هذا الجسد تم اكتشافه فقط يوم أمس في قبر جماعي على حدود الصحراء الكبرى. إنها واحدة من جثث كثيرة وُجدت هناك، لا توجد جثتان متشابهتان، ولا أي منها على قيد الحياة. لا يُعرف من قتلهم، لكن التقديرات الأولية تشير إلى أن الوفيات وقعت منذ ما لا يزيد عن ثلاثة أيام."

ظهرت المزيد من الصور، ومن بين الكم الكبير من الصور التي الثُقطت في الموقع—على يد إليزا—بدا أن هذا الاختيار من الصور تم انتقاؤه لرفع منسوب الرعب إلى أقصى حد: حناجر مقطوعة بوحشية، لقطات قريبة لأبشع صور الفكوك المشوهة، حالات من التحلل والوجوه المتيبسة، عيون غائرة في محاجرها، ألسنة منتفخة.

في الواقع، فإن مورغان توث هو من أرسل تلك الصور الأكثر كآبة إلى شبكة الأخبار—مباشرة من حساب البريد الإلكتروني الخاص بإليزا، بالطبع. بالرغم من وجود بعض الصور الشاعرية والمؤثرة للوحوش القتلى؛ أظهرت فيهم الكرامة والعنفوان. لكنه ترك تلك الصور جانباً.

والآن، وهو متكئ على إطار باب في طابق القبو بالمتحف، راح يراقب ردود أفعال زملائه بابتسامة متعجرفة ومستمتعاً بذلك أشد الاستمتاع؛ أنا من فعل هذا. وبالطبع، الجزء الأفضل لم يأتِ بعد. إذ لم يثق بالحمقى في شبكة الأخبار وبقدرتهم بأن يربطوا النقاط بشأن تحديد هويتهم، لذا أرفق رسالة تفيدهم بهذا الأمر. نعم هذا هو الجزء الأجمل. معتقداً أنه بذلك سيضفي تأثيرا علنياً على عذابات إليزا.

"السادة والسيدات المحترمين"، كتب مورغان، متقمصاً شخصية إليزا يا لإليزا. لا بد أنه يشعر بشيء يشبه التعاطف أو الشفقة تجاهها الآن. حقاً، كل شيء بات منطقياً بعد أن عرف من تكون. بالطبع، نوع الشفقة

الوحيد الذي يمكن أن يشعر به مورغان توث، هو النوع الذي قد يشعر به قِط تجاه فأر بين مخالبه."آه، أيها المسكين، لم تكن لديك فرصة معها منذ البداية". أحياناً تشعر القطط بالملل فتترك فريستها تهرب منهكة نحو الأمان، بالطبع لا تفعل ذلك أبداً بدافع الرحمة. بالنسبة إلى مورغان فهو لم يكن يشعر بالملل تلك اللحظة، ولا يبدو أنه سيفعل قريباً.

"السادة والسيدات المحترمين"، وأضاف على لسانها."ربما تتذكرونني. سبع سنوات قضيتها تائهة، بينما في الظاهر كان المسار الذي قد سلكته في ذلك الوقت مفاجئاً، أؤكد لكم الآن أن كل ذلك إنما هو جزء من خطة أعظم. خطة الله."

قبل يومين فقط، قالت له إليزا، بنبرة ملؤها الغطرسة التي لا تُحتمل:"هناك أشياء قليلة فقط قد يقتل الناس ويموتون من أجلها وهم مسرورون، لكن هذا الأمر عظيم".

"لا يا إليزا،" أجاب مورغان بعد تفكير،"هذا الأمر أكثر من عظيم. استمتعي."

"في سبيل الله"، تابع مورغان في رسالته إلى المحطة،"أود بكل سرور أن أُقتل وأموت، وبكل سرور أيضاً، أتحدى محاولات حكومتنا وغيرها لإخفاء الحقيقة عن الناس بشأن هذا العار غير المقدس."

كلمة"العار" كانت اختياراً ممتازاً. شعر مورغان بالقلق من أنه ربما جعل إليزا تبدو ذكية أكثر مما ينبغي، لكنه طمأن نفسه بأن ذلك لا مفر منه.

"لا أستطيع أن أبدو غبياً حتى لو حاولتُ".

كان زملاؤه متجمعين حول شاشات التلفاز قريبين جداً إلى درجة أنه لم يتمكن من رؤية الصور.

لكن لم يكن ذلك مهماً، فقد أُتيحت له الفرصة للتمعن فيها عن قرب سابقاً - فشكراً غابرييل إيدنغر، وشكراً، إليزا الساذجة، لعدم وضع كلمة مرور على هاتفك— ولم يكن لديه أدنى شك في أنه بعد اليوم، سيكون هو

وليس هـي مـن سيواصل هذا العمل المهم مع الدكتور شودهاري. بمجرد أن اكتشاف اسم إليزا، سينهي أمرها. "إذاً، لنبدأ"، فكر بهدوء وهو يراقب البث."كفى صوراً عن الوحوش المتحللة."

كان يعلم أن كل ذلك مجرد مقدمة، وأن أخبار"الشياطين" هـي مـا يهم الجمهور حقاً. أما بشأن من قام بتسريب الصور للصحافة، فلن يهتم العالم كثيراً. لكن مورغان كان يحتاج إلى أن تكتمل هذه القطعة الأخيرة من الأحجية.

وأخيراً، حين سمع المذيع الشهير يقول، بنبرة المندهش:"أما السؤال عن مصدر هذه الصور الصادمة، فهو يقدم الإجابة على لغز آخر كنا قد فقدنا الأمل في حله. لقد مرت سبع سنوات، لكنكم ستتذكرون القصة وستتذكرون هذه الشابة". شعر مورغان توث بحماس شديد وهو يشق طريقه بكوعه إلى داخل حشد العلماء. لم يكن ليفوّت هذه اللحظة. وهناك، على شاشة التلفاز، ظهرت صورة كانت قد حصلت على نصيبها من الأضواء. قبل سبع سنوات، ظهرت هذه القصة، وظلت عالقة دون حل حتى انتهى بها الأمر إلى أن تُنسى ضمن قضايا"الملفات الباردة". شعر مورغان برغبة في ركل نفسه لعدم ربطه الأمور منذ اللحظة الأولى التي قابل فيها إليزا جونز.

لكن كيف كان له أن يتعرف عليها كفتاة في تلك الصورة؟ كانت قطة مريعة. عيناها تنظران نحو الأرض، وحركتها جعلت من صورتها ضبابية. وعلى أي حال، فقد شطبها من ذاكرته باعتبارها ميتة. كما اعتبرها الجميع.

العنوان الإخباري لخّص كل شيء:"طفلة نبيّة مفقودة، يُعتقد أنها قُتلت على يد طائفة ما".

إليزا جونز، نبيّتهم؟ كانت الفكرة الأولى التي خطرت في بال مورغان—أو على الأقل أول فكرة منطقية بعد أن تبددت صدمته الأولى ليغرق في موجات متلاحقة من السخرية والضحك—هي أن يطبع لها بطاقات عمل ويوزعها في مكان ما لتجدها.

إليزا جونز المدعوة نبيّة. وبالطبع، لن يفوت الجزء المفضل. يا إلهي، الجزء الذي جعل هذه القصة تصل إلى قمة الجنون، تلك القمة التي تطل على مدينة المجانين. لا، ليس الأمر مجرد جنون عادي؛ إنه نوع من الجنون الذي يتفوق على أي جنون آخر، جنون يسير معصوب العينين وبيدين مقيدتين خلف الظهر.

يا إلهي. مورغان سقط حرفياً عن كرسيه من شدة الضحك. طائفة عائلتها اللطيفة؟ لم تكن مجرد طائفة عادية تتحدث عن"المختارين" بل هم مختلفون بشكل مذهل. يدّعون بأنهم انحدروا من ملاك.

منحدرون من ملاك.

كان هذا أفضل شيء سمعه مورغان توث في حياته.

القديسة إليزا جونز.512/1 الملاك (أو نحو ذلك). هذا ما كان سيكتبه على بطاقة العمل الخاصة بها. لكنه حين رأى ما أرسلته إليزا إلى نفسها بالبريد الإلكتروني من المغرب، حصل على فكرة أفضل. الفكرة نفسها تُعرض الآن

"لقد صلينا جميعاً من أجلها قبل سبع سنوات"، قال أشهر مذيع إخباري في العالم، والذي يتقاضى أعلى أجر."كنا نعرفها حينها فقط باسم إلازيل. كان يُعتقد من قِبل كنيستها... أنها تجسيد لملاك يحمل الاسم نفسه، سقط إلى الأرض منذ ألف عام. إنها قصة مذهلة، ولم تنتهِ بعد. في تطور غير متوقع، سيداتي وسادتي، الفتاة الشابة لم تكن فقط على قيد الحياة وتعيش تحت اسم مستعار، بل إنها عالمة في العاصمة الوطنية، وقريباً ستحصل على درجة الدكتوراه..."

لكن مورغان لم يسمع باقي الخبر، لأن أحدهم شهق قائلاً:"إنها إليزا!!"، ثم اندلعت الفوضى بين الحضور. وكان ذلك عادياً بالنسبة إليه. افعلوا كل ما تريدون، أيها الحمقى الرائعون. جنّوا كما تشاؤون.

فكر مورغان توث، وهو يسير عائداً إلى مختبره بابتسامة متعجرفة: من الرائع أن تكون الملك.

45

كشف الحقائق

بدا الاضطراب التالي الذي اجتاح القصبة مختلفاً في طبيعته منذ البداية. لم تكن هناك أي"إن شاء الله" أو نظرات موجهة نحو السماء هذه المرة. بدلاً من ذلك، كانت هناك علامات الاستهجان، والحنق بشكل جلي، و... يبدو أنهم ينظرون إلى... إليزا.

لقد عانت إليزا معظم حياتها من مشكلة جنون الارتياب. لم يكن ذلك بالفعل جنون ارتياب، بل كان مجرد توقع مألوف للاضطهاد الروتيني: بسيط وقاسٍ ومؤكد. أخذ الناس ينظرون إليها، وكانوا يحكمون عليها. في بلدتها الصغيرة في فلوريدا، بالقرب من غابة أبالاتشيكولا الوطنية، كان الجميع يعرفون من تكون. وبعد أن هربت... حسناً. أصبح الأمر شعوراً دائماً بالبرد يسري في مؤخرة عنقها، وخوفاً من أن تُكتشف أو يتم التعرف عليها، كانت تتلفت يمنة ويسرى طوال الوقت.

مع الوقت، خفّ هذا الإحساس تدريجياً—لم يختفِ أبداً، لكنه تراجع إلى ما تحت السطح. فعندما تعيش وأنت تحمل سراً، يبقى جنون الارتياب

قريباً دائماً. حتى إذا لم تفعل شيئاً خاطئاً (وهو أمر ممكن في حالتها)، فستشعر بالذنب فقط لأنك تملك ذلك السر. وكل نظرة فاحصة تُوجه نحوك تأخذ معنى مقلقاً.

إنهم يعرفون.

يعرفون من أنا. هل يعرفون؟ لكنهم لم يعرفوا. ولن يعرفوا أبداً. على الأقل، لم يحدث ذلك من قبل. ولأجل ذلك، كان عليها أن تشكر إحدى الغرائب الخاصة بكنيستها. فقد كانوا يرفضون تماماً"المنحوتات" ليس فقط صور الإله أو"الأسلاف"، بل حتى صور الأنبياء. وعند رؤيتها لأول مرة، لم تُلتقط لها أي صور على الإطلاق. ولم يكن هناك أساساً الكثير منها قبل ذلك، فعائلتها لم تكن من النوع الذي يحرص على"حفظ الذكريات للأجيال القادمة"، بل كانوا أشبه بأولئك الذين يستعدون لنهاية العالم، مخبئين أسلحة في قبو ما.

الصورة التي استخدمت في الأخبار كانت قد التقطت بواسطة سائح مرّ عبر بلدة سوبشوبّي—هذا بالفعل هو اسم البلدة القريبة من مجمع كنيستهم—الذي وبعد أن نُبه من قبل أحد السكان المحليين، التقط صورة لأولئك"غريبي الأطوار من طائفة الملائكة" عندما دخلوا للتزود بالإمدادات.

"غريبو الأطوار من طائفة الملائكة" ستبقى قصة محلية متداولة لعقود، لكنها انفجرت على المستوى الوطني بمجرد اختفاء إليزا. والدتها—"الكاهنة الكبرى"—لم تبلغ عن اختفائها إلا بعد أسابيع من الواقعة، عندها يئست تماماً وقررت الذهاب إلى المسؤولين الذين تزدريهم باعتبارهم مشركين وكفاراً، طلباً للمساعدة في العثور على نبيّتهم المفقودة. بالطبع، بدا الأمر مشبوهاً. وظل العنوان الإخباري مثل شوكة علقت في خيال المواطنين:"طفلة نبيّة مفقودة، يُعتقد أنها قُتلت على يد طائفتها."

وهذا كان كافياً.

كان بإمكان إليزا أن تُبرئهم في أي وقت. فقط عليها أن تظهر—في نورث كارولينا حيث ترعرعت ذلك الوقت—وتقول:"ها أنا هنا، ما زلت حية." لكنها لم تفعل ولم تشعر بأي شفقة تجاههم. لا حينها، ولا الآن، ولا أبداً. ومع أنه لم يُعثر على أي جثة—رغم البحث المضني لعدة أشهر—فقد اضطرت الشرطة في نهاية المطاف إلى تركهم وشأنهم."عدم كفاية الأدلة"، كحجة رسمية، لكن ذلك لم يُغير شيئاً في رأي العامة، ولا في قناعة المحققين.

يا له من حدث بغيض، وليس عليك سوى النظر في عيني الأم، كما قالوا، لتعرف أسوأ ما يمكن تخيله. أحد المحققين ذهب إلى حد التصريح، على الكاميرا، بأنه قد استجوب في مسيرته قاتل غينزفيل، كما استجوب ماريون سكيلينغ—اسمها الذي، لم يكن خافياً على الصحافة الصفراء، يمكن أن يُقرأ كـ"جريمة قتل ماريون"—، وقال إن كليهما منحاه نفس الشعور:"كالسقوط في حفرة عميقة مظلمة، وأجد صعوبة في النوم، وأنا أعلم أن تلك المرأة لا تزال حرة في العالم." بالطبع إليزا تتفق معه تماماً في هذا الشعور.

وكانت النتيجة هي قناعة راسخة بأن الفتاة إلازيل مدفونة بالتأكيد في مكان ما في غابة أبالاتشيكولا الشاسعة. لم يكن هناك أدنى شك.

على الأقل... ليس حتى اليوم."إليزا، تعالي معي، من فضلك." تحدث الدكتور شودهاري بصوت حاد ومتوتر.

خلفه، كان الدكتور أمهالي... أسوأ من أن يوصف بالتمنع. بدا غاضباً للغاية، وكأن بخاراً يخرج من أنفه مثل ثور في أفلام الرسوم المتحركة. فكرت إليزا في هذا، محاولة العثور على ملاذ من تفاهة الفكرة، حتى ولو فهمت بعد سبع سنوات من الخوف، حول ما الذي يحدث.

يا إلهي، يا إلهي.

يا نجوم السماء. عبارة أخرى، مثل ورق التنجيم تُقلب في عقلها وترمى أمامها دون سابق إنذار. "يا نجوم السماء" أثارت شيئاً ما في ذاكرتها، لكنها لم تستطع التوقف للتفكير في الأمر الآن.

"ما الأمر؟" سألت الدكتور شودهاري، لكنه استدار مباشرة وابتعد، متوقعاً أن تتبعه.

وكأنهم في منتصف اللامكان، في أرض ساخنة وقاسية، وسط محيط عسكري. ماذا يمكنها أن تفعل غير أن تتبعه؟

...

الحقائق كُشفت، والجثث خرجت. كاروه لم تفكر حتى في هذه الاحتمالية. شعرت وكأن هذا انتهاك، وكأن منزلها قد تعرض للاقتحام.

"أي منزل؟" تساءلت بيأس عميق. كان هذا فصلاً من حياتها لا رغبة لها أبداً في استعادته، ومع ذلك لم تستطع مقاومة الانجذاب نحو الأسفل، وهي تنظر إلى الشخصيات التي تتحرك تحتها.

وهي تمشي تحت الشمس، ترى ظلها—صغيراً بسبب المسافة—يحوم ويتراقص كفراشة مظلمة بين الناس في الأسفل. كان بإمكانها التخفي، لكن لا يمكنها إخفاء ظلها، وقد التفتت امرأة شابة سوداء البشرة عند رؤيته، فرفعت رأسها إلى الأعلى.

عادت كاروه إلى الخلف، وسحبت معها ظل الفراشة بعيداً.

باستطاعة كاروه أن تشم الرائحة الكريهة لجثث الكيميرا حتى من مكانها في الأعلى. يا للقرف. إلا أن خطتها لتجنب الصراع والمواجهة بين"الشياطين والملائكة" قد تلاشت مع الريح. أو بالأحرى، بشكل ما، لم تذهب مع الرياح

"كان عليّ أن أحرقهم"، قالت لأكيفا، الذي شعرت بحضوره بجانبها من خلال الحرارة وحفيف أجنحته."بماذا كنت أفكر؟".

عرض أكيفا عليها:"يمكنني أن أحرقهم الآن".

توقفت لبرهة قبل أن ترد:"لا"، ثم أضافت:"سيكون ذلك أسوأ."

إذا اشتعلت كل الجثث فجأة، بغض النظر عن كون السيرافيم هم من أضرموا النار لفعل ذلك، فسيبدو المشهد... جهنمياً."لا يمكن إصلاح هذا. علينا فقط المضي قدماً." لم يرد على الفور، وأطبق عليه صمت ثقيل.

لحسن الحظ أنهما لم يتمكنا من الالتقاء، لأن كارو لطالما خشيت الألم الذي قد تجده في عيني أكيڤا، وهما يواصلان تنفيذ مهمتهما هنا، مطيعين عقليهما وليس قلبيهما. سيعودان إلى المملكة عندما ينهيان مهمتهما هنا، ليس قبل ذلك. ولكن ماذا سيجدان عندما يعودان؟

شعرت وكأن نصف موت يحوم فوقها مع إدراكها أن أفضل ما يمكنهم أن يأملوا فيه الآن لم يكن بالكثير على الإطلاق. حتى لو نجحوا هنا ودفعوا جايل إلى التقهقر والعودة إلى المملكة، فما الذي ينتظرهم بعد ذلك؟ لم يكن هناك حتى مستقبل من"التضحية" ومخلفاتها، عيشة التوتر على حواف الحياة مع مذاقات سعادة مزيفة لتلطيف قسوتها. كعكة السعادة المؤجلة للمستقبل، الكعكة كطريقة للعيش. كل ذلك ذهب، خنقته سماء تسقط وظلال تطاردها النار: والعدو ببساطة، كما أدركت كارو منذ البداية، أكبر من أن يُهزم.

لكن كيف استطاعت أن تتأمل غير ذلك؟ لأن أكيڤا قد أقنعها. نظرة واحدة منه، ووجدت نفسها مستعدة لتصديق المستحيل. بالرغم من أنها لا تستطيع رؤيته الآن. إذ إن ثقته قد أضرمت إيمانها بهذا الكمال، فما الذي يمكن أن يفعله مشهد يأسه بها؟ أو يأسها به؟ فكرت في اليأس الذي اجتاحهم جميعاً في الكهف، وتساءلت: هل هذا يأس أكيڤا نفسه؟ هل يمكن أن توجد مثل هذه الظلمة داخله؟

سأل:"كيف نجد جايل؟".

كيف؟ هذا الجزء السهل. الحمد لله على التكنولوجيا الحديثة. كل ما يحتاجونه هو الوصول إلى الإنترنت ومقبس شحن لهواتفهم لتتصل ببعض المعارف. ربما يريد ميك وزوزانا أيضاً طمأنة عائلتيهما أنهما بخير.

الاثنان الآن على الأرض مع ڤيركو، على بعد بضعة أميال، مختبئين في ظل تكوين صخري. حتى في الظل، فإن درجة الحرارة قاتلة، حرارة مميتة، في الواقع، وهم بأمس الحاجة إلى الماء، والطعام أيضاً، والأسرة.

شعرت كاروه بانقباض في قلبها.

مجرد التفكير في احتياجات الحياة الأساسية، بدا وكأنه رفاهية لا توصف. ولكن من الأسهل أن تهتم باحتياجات أحبائك من أن تهتم باحتياجاتك الخاصة، ولهذا السبب فكرت في البحث عن الطعام والراحة. زوزانا لم تنطق بكلمة واحدة منذ أن عبروا البوابة. لا سيما أنها أول مواجهة قريبة لها مع"كل هذا الهراء الحربي" وقد تركت أثرها عليها، كما البقية الذين لم يكونوا بحال أفضل بكثير.

قالت كارو لأكيڤا:"هناك مكان يمكننا الذهاب إليه. لنذهب ولنأخذ الآخرين".

46

فطيرة وزهور الهندباء

"كيف... كيف يمكنك التفكير بأنني قد أفعل هذا؟". صُدمت إليزا. ولكن الأمر أسوأ بكثير مما كانت تخشاه. لقد خمنت أن الدكتور شودهاري قد اكتشف من تكون، وبالفعل اكتشف ذلك، لكن ذلك ليس كل شيء.

لا يمكن إلا أن يكون ذلك الوغد من فعل ذلك، توث. حتى كلمة "وغد" لم تعد وصفاً دقيقاً يمكن أن يعبر عن مدى انحطاط مورغان توث في تلك اللحظة.

إنه ضبع ربما، آكل جيف، أراه يبتسم بأسنانه البارزة فوق الدمار الذي تسبب لي فيه.

لم تعرف كيف اكتشف سرها. تذكرت وهي ترتعش بأن الأشخاص الذين يملكون أسراراً، لا ينبغي أن يصنعوا أعداء. لكنها أصبحت متأكدة من أنه الوحيد الذي يمكنه الوصول إلى صورها المحمية بكلمة سر. هل يدرك ما قد فعله من خلال نبش هذا القبر أمام العالم؟ السؤال الأصح: هل كان يهتم أصلاً؟

لقد كان ذكياً بما يكفي ليبقى خلف الكواليس. ويمكنها تخيله الآن، وهو يزيح غرّته بعيداً عن جبينه العالي جداً بينما يفتعل كارثة بدم بارد.

خلع الدكتور شودهاري نظارته وفرك جسر أنفه. كانت تلك مناورة لكسب الوقت، وإليزا عرفت ذلك. كانوا قد دخلوا إلى أقرب خيمة أسفل التل، وكانت رائحة الموت تحيط بهم، حتى في برودة الهواء المبرد.

كان الدكتور أمهالي قد أراها البث على جهاز لابتوب، ولا تزال تحاول استيعاب ما شاهدته. مع شعورها بالغثيان. الصور صورها، وقد عُرضت هكذا دون سياق مناسب. كانت مرعبة.

ماذا كانت ردة فعل العالم؟ تذكرت الفوضى التي اندلعت في الناشيونال مول قبل ليلتين. كيف هو الوضع الآن؟

عندما أنزل الدكتور شودهاري يده، نظر إليها بشكل مباشر، حتى وإن بدت عيناه غير مركّزتين بعض الشيء من دون نظارته. "هل تقولين إنك لم تفعليها؟".

"بالطبع لم أفعل. لن أفعل هذا أبداً".

قاطعها الدكتور أمهالي بحدة: "هل تنكرين أن هذه صورك؟".

استدارت نحو الدكتور أمهالي بحدة، وقالت: "أنا من التقط الصور، لكن هذا لا يعني أنني-".

"ويبدو أنه تم إرسالها من بريدك الإلكتروني" قاطعها بحدة.

"إذاً لقد تم اختراقه"، ردت بنبرة تنبئ بنفاد صبرها. بالنسبة إليها، كان الأمر واضحاً تماماً، لكن كل ما يراه الطبيب المغربي هو غضبه... وشعوره بالذنب، لأنه هو من جلبهم إلى هنا، مما أدى إلى جر بلاده إلى هذه الفضيحة.

"تلك الرسالة لم تكن مني" أجابت إليزا بإصرار. ثم استدارت نحو الدكتور شودهاري: "هل بدت وكأنها مني؟ يا للعار والخزي؟ هذا ليس... أنا لا-". كانت تغرق في كلماتها، عاجزة عن التعبير. نظرت إلى جثتي أبو

الهول الميتين خلف معلمها. لم تكن تراهما مقدسين، كما لم تَرَ القداسة في الملائكة أيضاً.

"قلت لك الليلة الماضية، أنا حتى لا أؤمن بوجود الله."

لكنها رأت التحول في عينيه—الشك—وأدركت مؤخراً أن تذكيره لها بما حدث الليلة الماضية ربما لم يكن استراتيجية موفقة. كان ينظر إليها وكأنه لا يعرفها. ارتفع الإحباط داخلها. لو كانت مجرد ضحية مكيدة لتوريطها في تسريب الصور إلى الصحافة، ربما كان بإمكانه تصديق براءتها ودعمها. لكن لا، لقد حدثت أمور كثيرة. انهيارها العاطفي على سطح القصبة. بكاؤها الذي بدا وكأنه سيغرق الصحراء. لو أنها لم تكتشف كطفلة نبية ميتة. لو... لو... لو سألها الدكتور شودهاري بصوت بطيء ومشحون:"هل ما يقولونه صحيح؟ هل أنتِ... هي؟".

أرادت أن تهز رأسها نفياً. لم تكن تلك الفتاة الضبابية ذات العينين المنخفضتين. لم تكن إلازيل. ربما كان ينبغي لها أن تغيّر اسمها بشكل أكثر حسماً عندما هربت وتخلت عن حياتها السابقة، لكن بطريقة ما، شعرت أن اسم"إليزا" أكثر من مناسب لها. أما اسمها السري أثناء الاحتجاجات عندما كانت طفلة، فهو ذلك الاسم"العادي" الذي تتشبث به في داخلها أثناء ألعاب الخيال والهروب العقلي.

إلازيل قد تُجبر على الركوع في الصلاة حتى تصبح ركبتاها ملتهبتين، أو تردد الترانيم حتى يصبح صوتها خشناً مثل لسان قطة. إلازيل قد تُجبر على القيام بالكثير من الأشياء—الكثير والكثير—التي لم تكن تريد القيام بها.

كانت في الخارج تلعب. عادية مثل فطيرة، وحرة مثل أزهار الهندباء. يا له من حلم.

ولهذا السبب احتفظت بالاسم، وعاشت به بأفضل طريقة استطاعت: فطيرة وزهور الهندباء. عادية وحرة. رغم أن الحقيقة بينت أن ذلك الشعور دائماً ما بدا وكأنه مجرد تمثيل. ومع ذلك، منذ سن السابعة عشرة، كانت

إلازيل هي الذات السرية المغلقة داخلها، بينما الآن إنما تعيش في العلن—مثل الأمير والفقير اللذين تبادلا الأماكن: أحدهما ارتفع، والآخر جُرد من كل شيء. بالطبع، الأمير والفقير، كما تذكرت الآن، قد عادا في النهاية إلى مكانهما الأصلي. لكن ذلك لن يحدث معها. لن تكون إلازيل تلك مرة أخرى. لكنها عرفت أن ذلك ليس ما يقصده الدكتور شودهاري. ولهذا السبب، بتردد، أومأت برأسها.

صححت كلامه:"كنت هي. تركتهم. هربت. كرهت ذلك. كرهتهم." أخذت نفساً عميقاً. لم تكن كلمة"كره" الكلمة الصحيحة. لم يكن هناك كلمة مناسبة؛ لم تكن هناك كلمة معبرة بما يكفي لوصف الخيانة التي شعرت بها إليزا، وهي تنظر إلى طفولتها بعين شخص بالغ يفهم الآن مدى الجدية التي استُغلت بها وتعرضها للإيذاء.

منذ أن كانت في السابعة من عمرها. عادت إلى المنزل من المستشفى ومعها جهاز تنظيم ضربات القلب ورعب جديد هائل طغى حتى على خوفها من والدتها. منذ اللحظة الأولى التي أعلنت فيها"هبتها" عن نفسها، أصبحت محور طاقة الطائفة وآمالها كلها.

لمس الناس المستمر لها. الكثير من الأيدي. لم يكن لها أي سيادة على نفسها. يعترفون بخطاياهم لها، يتوسلون الغفران، ويخبرونها بأشياء لا ينبغي لأي طفلة في السابعة أن تسمعها، ناهيك عن فكرة العقاب. كانت دموعها تُجمع في قوارير، وقصاصات أظافرها تُطحن إلى مسحوق وتُخلط في خبز القربان. وأما دمها الأول، دم الحيض؟ لطالما حاولت أن تبعد أفكارها عن تلك اللحظة. ذكرى لا تزال قاسية جداً، رغم أن ذلك حدث منذ أن كانت بنصف هذا العمر. إنها الآن في الرابعة والعشرين من عمرها، ولم تقضِ ليلة واحدة مع عاشق. لم تكن تستطيع استقبال أي شخص معها في الغرفة أثناء نومها. لمدة عشر سنوات أُجبرت على النوم فوق منصة في وسط المعبد، حيث كانت الجماعة تحتشد حول قاعدتها. يا إلهي. صوت الشهيق والزفير،

والنحيب، والشخير، والسعال. الهمسات. وأحياناً، في قلب الليل: أصوات أنفاس متزامنة، إيقاعية، لم تفهم معناها إلا بعد سنوات طويلة.

لن تتمكن أبداً من محو ذاكرة التنفس الجماعي غير المرغوب فيه لعشرات الأشخاص المحيطين بها أثناء الليل.

كانوا ينتظرون أن يزورها الحلم. كانوا يأملون ذلك. يصلّون. نسور جائعة تبحث عن فتات بسبب رعبها. إذا لم يتمكنوا من أن يحظوا بالحلم بأنفسهم، أرادوا أن يكونوا قريبين منه. وكأن صرخاتها قد تمنحهم الخلاص. أو، والأسوأ، كأن الحلم، الوحوش، ذلك الرعب المروع الأبدي، قد ينفجر منها—تلك الرؤى المدمرة، لتسحق الخطاة في كل مكان وتُعلي من شأن المختارين: هم.

وكأن إليزا قد تكون هي نفسها منبع نهاية العالم. غابرييل إدينجر حصل على"آيس كريم الكوابيس"، أما هي؟ فقد حصلت على ما هي عليه.

"ما زلت أكرههم" ما زلت أكرههم قالت الآن، ربما بانفعال أكثر نوعاً ما. كان الدكتور شودهاري قد وضع نظارته مرة أخرى، وعيناه تنظران إليها بحذر من خلف العدسات. عندما تحدث، كان صوته يحمل الحذر المرهف الذي يُستخدم عند الحديث مع من يُعتقد أنهم في حالة عقلية غير مستقرة

"كان عليك أن تخبريني"، قال لها وألقى نظرة نحو الدكتور أمهالي. تنحنح، واتضح أنه غير مرتاح."يمكن اعتبار هذا... نوعاً من تضارب مصالح، يا إليزا."

"ماذا؟ لا يوجد أي تضارب. أنا عالمة."

"وأنتِ ملاك"، قال الطبيب المغربي بسخرية واضحة.

من يسخر بهذا الشكل؟ تساءلت إليزا، وقد بدأت تشعر بالوهن. ظنت أن السخرية من هذا النوع مجرد شيء تفعله شخصيات الكتب.

"نحن لسنا... أعني، هم ليسوا، هم لا يدّعون أنهم ملائكة"، قالت وهي غير متأكدة من سبب شعورها بالحاجة إلى تقديم أي تبرير نيابة عن أحد

"عذراً، بالطبع لا"، قال الدكتور أمهالي بسخرية باردة."أحفاد الملائكة. أوه، وتجسدات الملائكة أيضاً، لا تنسي ذلك". حدّق بها نظرة حادة كأنه يطعنها."أهي رؤى نهاية العالم، يا عزيزتي؟ أخبريني، هل ما زلتِ ترينها؟، قالها وكأن الأمر يتجاوز مجرد كونه سخيفاً، وكأن الفكرة بحد ذاتها تُدنّس أي دين محترم ويجب معاقبتها.

شعرت إليزا بأنها تتضاءل، تتقلص أمام اتهامين مزدوجين وسخرية جارحة. شعرت بأنها تختفي. لم تكن"إليزا" الآن، ليست في هذه الخيمة، ولا في أعين هؤلاء الرجال. كانت إليزا الطفلة.

"لستُ هي. أنا أنا." كم كانت تتوق يائسة إلى تصديق ذلك."تركت كل هذا خلفي، لقد هربت." قالت الكلمة الأخيرة مشددة، لأنها لا تزال تبدو لها بسيطة للغاية."هربتُ. ألا يعني ذلك شيئاً؟".

قال الدكتور شودهاري:"لا بد أن الأمر كان صعباً عليكِ للغاية".

لم يكن ذلك بالضرورة، فالكلام الخطأ يُقال. في ظروف أخرى، ربما كانت هذه المحادثة ستؤدي إلى ذلك: إلى شعور بالشفقة المشروعة من جانبه أمام قصتها المليئة بالمشقة."بالطبع كان صعباً عليّ." لم يكن لديها شيء: لا مال، ولا أصدقاء، ولا أي دراية بالعالم. لا شيء سوى عقلها وإرادتها، الأول كان يعاني من الإهمال الشديد—فقد حُرمت من التعليم—والثانية قد عُوقبت مراراً إلى درجة أنها كادت أن تُشل. و ربما كانت لتقول لوالدتها"العقي إرادتي، لكنك لن تحطميها أبداً."

لكن في ظل هذه الظروف، ومع النبرة التي قال بها ذلك—تلك الدقة المتصنّعة، ذلك التنازل الأبوي—لم يكن ذلك التعليق هو الشيء الصحيح ليقال.

ردت عليه:"صعب؟"، وكأن الانفجار العظيم مقارنة بشعورها، مجرد انفجار عادي. هذا ما قالته له الليلة الماضية، على سبيل المزاح. ابتسمت بسخرية، وهو ضحك قليلاً. أما الآن فتقصده بنفس الروح... حسناً، إلى حد

ما... لكن الدكتور شودهاري رفع يديه بإيماءة مهدئة. لا داعي للانفعال.

"لا داعي للانفعال؟" ماذا يعني ذلك حتى؟"لا سبب للانفعال؟". بدا لها أن لديها الكثير من الأسباب. لقد تم اتهامها زوراً، وتم الكشف عن هويتها. تم انتزاع هويتها المكتسبة بفجاجة منها، ومن هذه اللحظة فصاعداً، ستظل مصداقيتها المهنية متقاطعة مع تاريخها الذي كافحت بكل جهد لإخفائه. ناهيك عن هذا الاتهام الخبيث وما قد يسببه من أضرار لها، والتبعات القانونية لخرقها اتفاقيات عدم الإفصاح، و... حسناً، التداعيات السلبية على العالم. لكن السبب الأكثر إلحاحاً كان يتشكل هنا في هذه الخيمة المليئة بأدوات الحماية من المواد الخطرة، في صحبة رجلين متعجرفين يصرّان على معاملتها كأنها مجرد ضحية ضائعة مصنوعة من الورق المقوى.

بغريزة، نظرت إلى شاشة الكمبيوتر المحمول التي أظهرت لها لحظة سقوطها. كانت الشاشة متجمدة على تلك الصورة القديمة لها، مع نفس التعليق القديم:"طفلة نبية مفقودة، يُعتقد أنها قُتلت على يد طائفتها".

"أنا لست غاضبة"، قالت إليزا، وهي تحاول ضبط أنفاسها بعناية.

"أنا لا ألومكِ على من تكونين، يا إليزا"، قال الدكتور شودهاري."لا يمكننا تغيير أصولنا."

"حسناً، هذه نبالة منك."

"لكن ربما حان الوقت الآن لطلب المساعدة. لقد مررتِ بالكثير."

وهنا بدأت الأمور تخرج عن السيطرة، وهو لا يزال يرفع يديه بتلك الطريقة التي توحي بـ"دعونا لا نفعل شيئاً متهوراً"، بينما إليزا كانت تحدق فيه. ما هذا كله؟

كان يتصرف وكأنها شخص هستيري، ولثانية واحدة، جعلها ذلك تشك في نفسها.

هل رفعت صوتها؟ هل كانت عيناها متسعتين وفتحات أنفها متوهجة، كالمجنونة؟ لا. كانت تقف هناك فقط، وذراعاها إلى جانبها، وكانت لتقسم على

أي شيء يستحق القسم—لو أن هناك شيئاً يستحق القسم عليه— إنها لم تبدُ مجنونة. لم تعرف كيف ترد. شعرت بإحساس غريب بالعجز أمام استجابة مبالغ فيها كهذه."ما أحتاج المساعدة فيه هو إثبات أنني لم أفعل هذا."

"إليزا. إليزا. لا يهم الآن. دعينا فقط نعيدكِ إلى المنزل، ونقلق بشأن ذلك لاحقاً."

بدأت دقات قلبها تضرب في أذنيها. إنه الغضب والإحباط وأشياء أخرى إنها حرة مثل أزهار الهندباء. عادية مثل فطيرة. حسناً، ربما ليست عادية. ربما لم تكن كذلك أبداً، لكنها كانت حرة.

نظرت إلى معلمها، هذا الرجل الوقور ذو العقلانية النادرة، الذي كانت تراه مثالاً للإنسان المستنير. شعرت بوزن نفاقه أمام حقيقتها—معرفتها الجديدة— والكفة تميل لصالحها بلا منازع.

"لا"، قالت، وسمعت نبرتها تتغير، تتحرر من كل ضعف."دعنا نقلق بشأن ذلك الآن."

"لا أعتقد".

"أوه، أنت تفكر كثيراً. لكنك مخطئ." أشارت بإيماءة إلى جهاز الكمبيوتر المحمول، وكل ما يمثله مع نشرات الأخبار الظاهرة على شاشته."مورغان توث هو من فعل هذا. تحقق من الأمر. الحقيقة تتجاوز فهمه بكثير، لا أتوقع منه أن يدركها. قد يكون ذكياً، لكنه سطحي كبركة مياه ضحلة. أما أنت."

مرة أخرى حاول التدخل، لكن إليزا أوقفته مرة أخرى."توقعت المزيد منك. لديك آلهة تتجول في ممرات قصر عقلك." وضعت علامات اقتباس جوية كبيرة وساخرة حول"قصر العقل." وهم يحاولون ألا يصطدموا بـ... ماذا كان؟ ممثلي العلم، كي يبقوا الأمور ودية هناك. أليس هذا هو مدى انفتاح عقلك؟ ثم أضافت، بنبرة أكثر حدة:"والآن رأيتَ ملائكة. ولمستَ الكيميرا". كلمة"كيميرا" خطرت في ذهنها بنفس الطريقة التي ظهرت بها كلمة"نجوم السماء" من قبل، كأنها بطاقة انقلبت فجأة."تعرف أنهم

حقيقيون. وتعرف—بالتأكيد تعرف—أنهم، مهما كان مصدرهم، كانوا هنا من قبل. كل أساطيرنا وقصصنا لها أصل حقيقي ومادي. أبو الهول. الشياطين. الملائكة."

ظل وجهه متجهّماً، لكنه كان يستمع.

"لكن فكرة أنني قد أكون منحدرة من واحد منهم؟ الآن هذا هو الجنون! أرسلوا إليزا إلى المنزل، أعطوها بعض المساعدة، ولأجل السماء، ابقوها بعيدة عن قصر عقلي". تابعت بمرارة:"أنت لا تخدم أمثالي هناك، أليس كذلك؟ من سمع يوماً عن ملاك أسود، على أي حال؟ وامرأة فوق ذلك. لا بد أن هذا صعب جداً عليك، أيها الدكتور."

هزّ رأسه، وبدا عليه الألم."إليزا، ليس هذا هو السبب".

"سأخبرك ما هو السبب" ردت، لكنها توقفت للحظة، تتساءل إذا كانت ستفعلها حقاً. أن تقول الحقيقة. هنا. لهذين الرجلين المشككين والمنافقين

نقلت نظرها بين أحدهما والآخر: من الاستياء المحبط في وجه الدكتور شودهاري—وإحساسه بإحراجها، على وهمها وهمها، عرضها المحزن—إلى الاحتقار المرتعش في وجه الدكتور أمهالي. لم يكن هذا الجمهور المثالي للإفصاح عن الحقيقة، لكن في النهاية لم يكن ذلك مهماً. كانت يقينيات إليزا الجديدة قد نمت إلى درجة لم تعد تحتمل الإخفاء.

تابعت:"عائلتي، هم أناس بائسون، قساة لا يرحمون ولن أسامحهم أبداً على ما فعلوه بي، لكن... كانوا على حق". رفعت حاجبيها واستدارت نحو الدكتور أمهالي."ونعم، ما زلت أرى الرؤى، مع أني أكرهها. لم أعد أرغب أبداً في تصديق أي من هذا ولا أريد أن أكون جزءاً منه. حاولتُ الهروب منه، لكنه لا يهم ما أريده، لأنني أنا. أليس هذا مضحكاً؟ قدري، هو حمضي النووي".

عادت إلى الدكتور شودهاري."هذا سيبقي ممثلي العلم والإيمان مشغولين وهم يتجادلون في الممرات. أنا منحدرة من ملاك. هذا قدري الجيني، اللعين".

47

كتاب إلازيل

لا مفر بعد الآن.

بعد أن اقتادوها عبر الموقع، راحت نظرات الاتهام تخرقها كرماح—
مسمومة. وبعد أن وضعوها في السيارة، وأغلقوا الباب بعنف، أمروا
بإعادتها إلى تمنوغالت لتنتظر مرافقتها إلى الوطن. استغرقت الرحلة بضع
ساعات، تحيط بها المناظر القاحلة لأرض وادي درعة، تمتد بلا نهاية في
جميع الاتجاهات. لم يكن لديها ما يشغلها سوى ذلك المزيج الغريب من
النشوة العارمة والغضب المتأجج.

حسناً، هذا كل ما لديها... بالإضافة للأمور المعروفة والمخفية. كل
الأشياء التي تتحرك في أعماقها. جسم بارز في سهل مغمور بالماء—ربما
برميل، وربما عالَم كامل. كل ما كان عليها فعله هو أن تنفض الغبار عنه.

بدأت إليزا تضحك. هناك، في المقعد الخلفي للسيارة، تفجّرت
الضحكات من داخلها وكأنها لغة جديدة تولد في تلك اللحظة. لاحقاً، جاء
موظفو الحكومة ليأخذوها، وطبعاً السائق سيقدم تقريره في هذه الواقعة،
كتمهيد لشرح ما حدث بعدها.

عندها توقفت عن الضحك.

في"الأيام الخوالي"—عندما لم يكن لديها ما يشغلها سوى بناء جيش من الوحوش في قلعة رملية في البرية—كانت كارو تقود شاحنة صدئة بشكل دوري فوق الأرض الوعرة والطرق الطويلة المستقيمة للوصول إلى أقرب بلدة هناك تدعى أغدز، متنكرة بارتداء حجاب يُخفي شعرها، وتتحرك دون أن تثير الانتباه بينما تشتري المؤن: أكياس ضخمة من الكسكسي، صناديق وصناديق من الخضروات وخبز ودجاج وكمية ضخمة من التمور والمشمش المجفف.

نظرت إلى بلدة أغدز من السماء. لم تبدُ مميزة حين مرت من فوقها، شعرت بالذين مرت بهم وكأنهم يسحبونها نحوهم، لكنها استمرت في المضي قُدماً إلى وجهتهم التي تبعد بعض الشيء والتي تعتبر أكثر تميزاً وسرعان ما رأت بستان النخيل. تفاجأت بتلك الواحة الخضراء التي بدت مثل بقعة طلاء مسكوبة على أرض جرداء. وهناك، في وسطها جدران طينية متداعية، شبيهة بالجدران الطينية المتداعية التي غادروها للتو.

قصبة أخرى هي تمنوغالت. في تلك الأماكن النائية الممتدة التي قد تتيح لهم فرصة لهدوء قصير تحتاجه مجموعتهم الصغيرة، تذكرت كارو أنها تضم فندقاً، وهو غير بعيد كي لا يجدوا صعوبة في العثور على ما يحتاجونه قالت كارو:"يمكننا أن نستريح هنا. لا بد أن لديهم إنترنت ومقابس كهرباء. حمّامات، أسرّة، ماء... وطعام".

أخذت ظلال الفراشات التي تُحيط بهم تتضخم شيئاً فشيئاً بينما تنخفض لتلاقيهم. وحين حطّوا رحالهم على الأرض، في ظل أشجار النخيل، بدؤوا بتعطيل سحر التخفي عن أنفسهم. التفتت كارو أولاً إلى أصدقائها لتتأكد من أحوالهم. بدا على زوزانا وميك الضعف والانهاك، يغطيهما العرق مع علامات حروق شمس واضحة—نعم يمكن للشمس أن تحرقك حتى لو كنتَ غير مرئياً—لكن الأسوأ كان ملامح الارهاق المحفورة على وجهيهما،

والارتخاء المريب الذي طغى على نظرات أعينهما، وكأنهما فقدا الاتصال بالعالم، كمن واجه صدمة صاعقة.

ماذا فعلتُ بهم؟ كيف لها أن تسحبهم إلى أتون الحرب؟

أجبرت نفسها على تحويل نظرها إلى ڤيركو بعد ذلك، متجنبة مواجهة عيني أكيڤا التي كانت تخشى النظر فيهما. ڤيركو... الذي كان سابقاً ملازماً للذئب، وأحد أولئك الذين تركوها وحيدة في الحفرة معه. الوحيد الذي نظر خلفه، صحيح، لكنه مع ذلك تركها في النهاية. ومع ذلك، كان هو أيضاً من أنقذ حياة ميك وزوزانا. بدا قوياً ومعتاداً على مشقة الطيران والقتال—لا حروق شمس عليه، ولا إرهاق، لكنّ التعب كان حاضراً في قسمات وجهه، وكذلك الصدمة. وما زال الشعور بالذنب واضحاً، لاحظت كارو. كان ذلك الشعور يلاحقه منذ حادثة الحفرة، يتجلى في كل نظرة يلقيها نحوها.

رمقته بنظرة أرادت لها أن تكون ثابتة وواضحة، ثم أومأت له برأسها. تسامح؟ امتنان؟ تضامن؟ لم تكن متأكدة. لكنه رد الإيماءة بجدية بدت أقرب إلى طقس رسمي. وأخيراً، التفتت كارو إلى أكيڤا.

لم تكن قد نظرت إليه فعلياً مذ عبروا البوابة. نعم، لقد رمته بنظرات خاطفة، دون تخفٍّ، وكانت مدركة لحضوره في كل ثانية، لكنها لم تنظر إليه، لا إلى وجهه، ولا إلى عينيه. كانت خائفة... وهي محقة في خوفها.

يبدو ألمه جلياً بلا جدال، ألم خالص إلى درجة أيقظت ألمها الخاص، طافت به إلى السطح كجرح جديد، واضحاً ومؤلماً بما يكفي ليكون قرباناً. لكن هذا لم يكن الأسوأ. لو أن الأمر مجرد ألم، لربما استطاعت الاقتراب منه، ربما تمسك بيده كما فعلت على الجانب الآخر من البوابة، أو حتى تصل إلى قلبه، كما فعلت في الكهف وتقول له ما زلنا في البداية.

لكن... بداية ماذا؟ تساءلت كارو بأسى، لأن ما رأته في عيني أكيڤا لم يكن مجرد ألم، بل غضب أيضاً، وتصميم لا يقبل المساومة، وهذا لا يحتمل التأويل.

كان كراهية. كان انتقاماً. وكان ذلك مخيفاً، جمدها في مكانها. حين رأت أكيفا للمرة الأولى في جامع الفنا في مراكش، كان بارداً تماماً بلا رحمة. ما رأته عليه حينها كان الانتقام الذي أصبح عادة، والغضب الذي تجمّد بفعل سنوات من الخدر. لكن لاحقاً، حين التقته في براغ، رأت إنسانيته تعود إليه، وكأن ذوباناً قد حرّر قلبه من جليده. لم تستطع أن تدرك ذلك تماماً في تلك اللحظة، لأنها لم تكن تعرف ما الذي يعنيه، أو ما الذي كان يعود منه. لكنها تعرف الآن. لقد أحيا نفسه من جديد—ذلك الأكيفا الذي عرفته منذ زمن بعيد، مليئاً بالحياة والأمل—أو على الأقل، بدأ بذلك. لكنها لم ترَ منه تلك الابتسامة بعد، تلك الابتسامة التي عرفتها في الماضي، ابتسامة كانت مشرقة كأشعة الشمس، تجعلها تشعر وكأنها مخمورة بالحب، خفيفة كنسمة، وفي الوقت ذاته متجذرة تماماً في العالم—الأرض والسماء والفرح... وهو.

بهت كل شيء أمام مشاعرها تلك. العِرق لم يعد يعني شيئاً، والخيانة أمست مجرد كلمة عابرة حين بدأت كارو تشعر بإمكانية الفرح مرة أخرى مع ذلك الإحساس الطبيعي بالسير في الطريق الصحيح، إلا أنها الآن، وهي تنظر إلى أكيفا، بدا ذلك الإحساس بالجفاء قد عاد مجدداً، وهو بدوره قاسمها نفس الشعور.

كما فهمت، أنه كان هناك آلاف الجنود غير الشرعيين في الآونة الأخيرة من العام المنصرم، لكن الاندلاع الجنوني للحرب الأخيرة قلّص عددهم إلى ما تبقى ممن تعرفهم من كهوف الكيرين. تحمّل أكيفا كل مشقاتها ونجا. ثم تحمّل موت هازايل وتعافى. وها هو الآن هنا، آمن بينما—وربما—قد خسر كل من تبقى.

ما رأته كارو في عينيه كان انتقاماً لا يزال ملتهباً ومنصهراً في أعماقه. وذلك ليس صواباً. ليس بالمكان الذي كان من المفترض أن يصلوا إليه. لكنه بدا... محتوماً.

قال لها بريمستون، قبل إعدامه مباشرة:"الصدق في وجه الشر هو أعظم أنواع القوة". لكنها ربما شعرت بحسرة ثقيلة في قلبها، كان ذلك مجرد طلب أكثر مما يمكن لأي شخص احتماله. ربما تلك القوة أكبر مما يمكن لأحد أن يمنحها.

الإحساس بالموت الجزئي ما زال يعشعش فيها.

شعرت وكأنها مسطّحة، فارغة، مجوفة. مرة أخرى. التفتت إلى صديقيها وبعد جهد خاطبتهما بنبرة شبه متماسكة:"هل يمكنكما الدخول والحصول على ملاذ لكما؟ ونحن ربما من الأفضل ألا يرونا هنا". تمتّت—أو لعلها كانت تأمل—أن تُلقي زوزانا تعليقاً ساخراً على ذلك، أو تقترح ڤيركو حتى البوابة مباشرة أو شيئاً من هذا القبيل، لكنها لم تفعل. فقط أومأت.

سأل ميك، في محاولة واضحة لاستعادة لمسة من روح زوزانا المعتادة:"هل تدركين أن أمنياتنا الثلاث على وشك أن تتحقق؟ لا أعلم إذا كانوا يملكون كعكة شوكولاتة هنا، لكن-". قاطعت زوزانا حديثه:"غيرت أمنياتي على أي حال"، وقالت وهي تعدّها على أصابعها:"الأولى، أن يكون أصدقاؤنا في أمان. الثانية، أن يسقط جايل ميتاً. الثالثة-".

مهما كان ما أرادت قوله، لم تتمكن من إكماله. لم يسبق لكارو أن رأت صديقتها تبدو بهذا الضياع والهشاشة من قبل. فقاطعتها برفق:"إذا لم تتضمن طعاماً، فهي كذبة. على الأقل، هذا ما قيل لي". تنهدت زوزانا بعمق، محاولة أن تستجمع قواها:"حسناً. إذاً يمكنني أن أطلب شيئاً بسيطاً... مثل السلام العالمي على العشاء." بدت عيناها مظلمتين، تنضحان بحدة غير مألوفة، وكأن شيئاً قد انكسر فيها. رأته كارو ونعته في داخلها. الحرب تفعل هذا بالناس، ولا سبيل للفرار منها. الواقع يقتحم حياتك كحصار لا مفر منه. صورتك المثالية عن الحياة تُحطم، وتفرض عليك صورة جديدة قبيحة. لا ترغب حتى بالنظر إليها، ناهيك حتى عن تعليقها على الجدار. لكنك ستفقد الخيارات بمجرد أن تعرف. أن تعرف ذلك حقاً.

لكن إلى أين تسير زوزانا الآن، بعد أن صار الذي رأته وعرفته جزءاً منها؟

وجبة السلام العالمي على العشاء، إذاً، تمتم ميك وهو يحك ذقنه المتغضنة. هل يأتي ذلك مع البطاطس المقلية؟

قالت زوزانا بصوت مبحوح يحمل بقايا من روحها السابقة:"أرجو ذلك، وإلا سأعيده وأرميه في وجوههم".

...

كان اسمها كنيسة القديسة إلازيل. تلك الكنيسة التي أسسها أتباعها —والذين فضلوا مصطلح"الكنيسة" على مصطلح"الطائفة"، بطبيعة الحال— كانت تُدعى"كنيسة عهد القديسة إلازيل". وكانت كل فتاة تُولد من نفس سلالتها تُطلق عليها اسم إلازيل عند التعميد. ثم، إذا لم تُظهر الفتاة"هبة القداسة" بحلول سن البلوغ، فتعاد تسميتها باسم آخر.

كانت إليزا هي الوحيدة خلال السنوات الخمس والسبعين الماضية التي احتفظت بهذا الاسم. وغالباً ما كانت تعتقد أن أسوأ ما في طفولتها الرهيبة —حبة الكرز على قمة كعكة طفولتها المريعة— التي جلبت لها حسد الأخريات.

لا شيء يشبه لمعة الحسد في العيون. وقلة من يعرفن ذلك كما تعرفه هي. كان الأمر بالنسبة إليها أشبه بتجربة خاصة؛ أن تكبر وأنت تعلم أن أي فرد من أفراد عائلتك الكبيرة قد يكون مستعداً لقتلك وأكلك، بأسلوب رينفيلد، إن كان ذلك يضمن له الحصول على"هبتك" لنفسه.

كنيسة عهد القديسة إلازيل، أمومية السلطة، ووالدة إليزا هي الكاهنة الكبرى الحالية. أطلق على المؤمنين الجدد المنتمين إلى الطائفة لقب"أبناء العمومة"، بينما كان أولئك الذين ينتمون إلى نفس سلالتها —يُبجَّلون حتى إن لم تكن لديهم"الهبة"—ويدعون"الإليود." وهذا المصطلح كان مستخدماً في النصوص القديمة للإشارة إلى نسل"النيفيليم"، الذين كانوا ثمرة اللقاء الأول بين الملائكة والبشر.

48

جياع

لم يكن للبطاطا المقلية أي أثر في تمنوغالت، وفيما اعتبرته زوزانا انتهاكاً صارخاً لقوانين الضيافة، لم تكن هناك شوكولاتة أيضاً—إلا في شكلها السائل: مشروب الشوكولاتة الساخن، وهو ما لم يكن كافياً لإرضائها في تلك اللحظة. ولكن إذا كانت قد استعادت جزءاً من ذاتها القديمة إلى درجة أن تشتاق إلى هذه الأشياء، فإنها لم تستعد بعد ما يكفي من تلك الذات لتشكو بشأنها.

"لن أعود من حيث أتيت"، فكّرت بكآبة وهي جالسة في الظل على شرفة سطح هذه القصبة الجديدة. جديدة بالنسبة إليها بالطبع، وإن لم تكن كذلك في جوهرها. كان من الغريب أن ترى الناس يتجولون في المكان بأحذيتهم الجلدية البالية، وكأنهم في موطنهم الطبيعي هنا. لكن هذا المكان كان يذكرها كثيراً بـ"قلعة الوحوش."

مع بعض اللمسات المحلية بالطبع: الطبول البربرية، الوسائد الكبيرة المنسوجة الموضوعة على السجاد المغبر، والشمعدانات الضخمة التي

تحمل بقايا سنوات من الشمع المذاب. ثم هناك الكهرباء والمياه الجارية؛ شيء أشبه بالحضارة، إذا جاز القول.

ومع ذلك، لم تستطع زوزانا أن تتخيل أي مياه جارية تضاهي برك المياه الحرارية في كهوف الكيرين بعظمتها. تلك الكهوف التي، بعد أن تركتهما كارو وحيدين فيها، ألهمتهما حلمَ يقظة: جلب الناس من الأرض إلى تلك الكهوف. ليس السياح الأثرياء، بل أولئك الذين يحتاجون إلى هذه التجربة ويستحقونها، للاستشفاء بالمياه.

تصوّراهم محمولين على ظهور صيادي العواصف، ينامون على فراء طازج في المساكن القديمة للعائلة. ضوء الشموع وموسيقى الرياح، وليمة تُقام تحت النوازل في الكهف الكبير. مجرد تخيل منح شخصٍ ما هذه التجربة كان أشبه بحلم.

والأغرب أن زوزانا، التي لم تكن يوماً محبة للناس، انغمست في هذا الحلم! لابد أن طبيعة ميك الطيبة بدأت تؤثر عليها، سواء أرادت ذلك أم لا على شرفة السطح، كانا يستمتعان بلحظة هدوء. الآخرون في الغرفة بالأسفل، إما مختبئين، أو نائمين، أو منشغلين بالبحث.

تولّى ميك وزوزانا مهمة جلب الطعام، وهكذا وجدا نفسيهما هنا، يتصفحان قوائم الطعام الموضوعة على طاولات مغلفة بمفارش.

لم يتحدثا عن المعركة على الإطلاق. ماذا يمكن قوله؟ "واو، ڤيركو مزّق ذلك الملاك وكأنه كان دجاجاً مطهواً ببطء، يتفتت بسهولة!" لا، لم تكن زوزانا تريد التحدث عن ذلك، ولم تكن تريد الخوض في الأشياء الأخرى التي شاهدتها أثناء هروبهما، ولا مقارنة ملاحظاتها مع ميك لتعرف ما إذا كان قد رآها هو الآخر. فإن كان قد رآها، فهذا سيجعلها أكثر واقعية. مثل رؤيتها يوثم، الذي قامت هي بنفسها بتعليق عقده المخصص للأرواح، يهاجمه نصف دزينة من قوات الدومينيون. أو رؤية روا، الداشناغ الذي حمل إيسّا عبر البوابة. كم واحداً آخر؟

قالت زوزانا فجأة:"هل تعلم؟". رفع ميك رأسه متسائلاً. تابعت""سأشتكي رغم كل شيء. ما الفائدة من العيش إن لم أستطع الشكوى من غياب الشوكولاتة؟ أي نوع من الحياة تلك؟".

رد ميك بابتسامة:"حياة باهتة". ثم أشار إلى القائمة وقال:"لكن أي غياب للشوكولاتة؟ ماذا عن هذا؟".

نظرت حيث أشار وقالت بحذر:"لا تعبث معي."

قال بلهجة جادة، واضعاً يده على قلبه:"أبداً. لا أمزح بشأن الشوكولاتة. انظري، أنتِ تفتقدين صفحة."

وبالفعل، كانت تفتقد صفحة، وهناك كانت واضحة على قائمة ميك، مكتوبة بالأبيض والأسود، وموضحة بخمس لغات، وكأن الشوكولاتة غير مفهومة بالنسبة إلى العالم:

Gâteau au chocolat

Torta di cioccolato

Pastel de chocolate

Schokoladenkuchen

Chocolate cake

لكن حين جاء النادل ليأخذ طلبهما، وقالت له زوزانا:"سنبدأ بكعكة الشوكولاتة. أحضرها أولاً، سنأكلها بينما تُعدّ باقي الطعام، حسناً؟"، أخبرهما—وبأسف بدا لها غير كافٍ على الإطلاق—أن الكعكة قد نفدت. ضجيج صافٍ.

تلك اللحظة التي شعرت فيها زوزانا بالتغير الذي حدث بداخلها بيقين تام، لأنه لم يكن شيئاً عظيماً. لقد أعيد رسم خطوط سياقها الداخلي، وتراجعت فكرة"أمر عظيم" إلى مكان بعيد جداً."حسناً، هذا مزعج"، قالت."لكنني أعتقد أنني سأبقى على قيد الحياة."

ارتفع حاجبا ميك بدهشة. طلبا أن يُحضر الطعام مباشرة إلى غرفتهما—وتأكد النادل ثلاث مرات من كمية الكباب والطاجن والخبز المرقوق والأومليت والفواكه والزبادي."لكن هذا يكفي لعشرين شخصاً!" كرر النادل بدهشة.

نظرت إليه زوزانا بثبات وقالت:"أنا جائعة جداً."

...

لم تعد إليزا تضحك بعد الآن. كانت... تتكلم نوعاً ما.

كان السائق ممسكاً بهاتفه، يصرخ وسط ضوضاء صوتها بينما يسرع على الطريق الطويل المستقيم."هناك شيء خاطئ بها!" صرخ."لا أعرف! ألا تسمعها؟" وأثناء محاولته تقريب الهاتف من صوتها الهائج، أفلتت يده من عجلة القيادة للحظة، فانحرفت السيارة عن الطريق نحو حافة الطريق الترابي ثم عادت مع صرير إطارات.

كانت الفتاة في المقعد الخلفي جالسة ومتيبسة تماماً، عيناها زائغتان وتحدقان، تتحدث دون توقف. لم يتعرف السائق على اللغة التي كانت تتحدث بها. لم تكن العربية، ولا الفرنسية، ولا الإنجليزية، وكان ليعرف الألمانية أو الإسبانية أو الإيطالية لو سمعها. لكن هذه اللغة التي سمعها شيء آخر تماماً، غريب على نحو لا يوصف. كان صوتها أشبه بزقزقة مرتفعة وهدير كصوت الرياح، وبدت الفتاة الشابة وكأنها ممسوسة، تنطق هذا الكلام وكأنها مغيبة، ويداها تتحركان بحركات بطيئة كأنها تسبح في الماء.

"هل تسمع ذلك؟" صرخ السائق."ماذا أفعل بها؟". راح ينقل بصره بجنون بين الطريق وصورتها في المرآة الخلفية، واحتاج إلى ثلاث، أربع، خمس مرات من هذه النظرات السريعة قبل أن يدير رأسه أخيراً، غير مصدق، ليتأكد ما إذا كان ما يراه في المرآة حقيقة أم لا.

كانت يدا إليزا تتحركان برشاقة في الهواء وكأنها كانت تطفو. لأنها بالفعل كانت كذلك.

ضغط السائق على الفرامل بقوة. اندفعت إليزا بعنف نحو المقاعد الأمامية ثم سقطت على أرضية السيارة. انقطع صوتها فجأة، وانحرفت السيارة بشدة إلى الحافة الترابية، ارتجّت بقوة بينما جسدها يرتطم كجثة بين المقاعد، للحظات عنيفة وصاخبة، بينما كان السائق يحاول استعادة السيطرة على السيارة. أخيراً توقف، وخرج من السيارة وسط سحابة من الغبار، ليفتح بابها بجزع.

كانت فاقدة للوعي. هز ساقها بذعر."آنسة! يا آنسة!".

إنه مجرد سائق، لا يعرف كيف يتعامل مع حالات الجنون هذه. الأمر أكبر منه بكثير، والآن ربما قتلها... لكنها تحركت.

"الحمد لله"، تنهد بارتياح. لكن ارتياحه لم يدم طويلاً. فما إن جلست إليزا واستقامت، حتى بدأ الدم يتدفق من أنفها، لزجاً وبراقاً، فوق فمها وأسفل ذقنها—إلى أن عادت مباشرة إلى ذلك الهذيان الغريب، ذلك الصوت الذي جعل السائق يشعر بتمزق روحه كلياً.

...

بمجرد أن عادت زوزانا وميك إلى الغرفة، قالت كارو: روما. الملائكة في الفاتيكان.

"حسناً، هذا منطقي"، أجابت زوزانا، متجنّبة أن تمنح أول فكرة خطرت ببالها صوتاً، والتي كانت تتمحور حول الوفرة السعيدة للشوكولاتة في إيطاليا."هل تمكنوا من الحصول على أسلحة بعد؟".

"لا"، قالت كارو، ولكن القلق بدا واضحاً عليها. حسناً ليس القلق فقط، أضيفي إلى القائمة: الإرهاق، الإنهاك، الإحباط، و... الوحدة. كان لديها تلك الوقفة"التائهة" مجدداً، كتفاها منحنيان إلى الأمام، ورأسها منخفض. ولم يفت زوزانا أن تلاحظ أنها تدير ظهرها لأكيفا.

"السفراء ووزراء الخارجية وأمثالهم يقضون الوقت في الحديث إلى أن يموتوا"، تابعت كارو."بعضهم يؤيد تسليح الملائكة، والبعض الآخر يعارض.

يبدو أنه لم يترك أعظم انطباع. مع ذلك، مجموعات خاصة تصطف لتعلن عن دعمها وأساطيل أسلحتها. يحاولون الوصول إليه لتقديم عروضهم، لكنهم حتى الآن مُنعوا - على الأقل رسمياً. من يعلم من قدّم رشوة إلى أحد المطلعين في الفاتيكان لنقل رسالة إلى جايل. إحدى هذه المجموعات هي طائفة ملائكية في فلوريدا، لديها على ما يبدو مستودع أسلحة جاهز". توقفت لحظة لتفكر في كلماتها."وهذا لا يبدو مرعباً على الإطلاق."

تساءل ميك بدهشة:"كيف عرفتِ كل هذا؟".

"جدّتي المزيفة"، أجابت كارو، مشيرة إلى هاتفها الموصول بالحائط."لديها شبكة علاقات واسعة جداً."

كانت زوزانا على علم بـ"جدّة" كارو المزيفة، وهي سيدة بلجيكية مرموقة حازت على ثقة بريمستون لسنوات عديدة، وكانت الوحيدة من بين معاونيه التي كانت لكارو علاقة فعلية بها. كانت هذه السيدة فاحشة الثراء، ورغم أن زوزانا لم تقابلها قط، إلا أنها لم تكن تشعر بأي دفء تجاهها. كانت قد رأت بطاقات عيد الميلاد التي ترسلها إلى كارو، وكانت شخصية بقدر تلك التي يرسلها البنك - وهو أمر يمكن التغاضي عنه، إلا أن زوزانا كانت تعرف أن صديقتها تشتاق إلى شيء أعمق، وهذا وحده جعلها ترغب في أن تسدد لكمة نحو عنق أي شخص يخيب أمل كارو.

استمعت زوزانا بنصف اهتمام بينما كانت كارو تخبر ميك عن إستير. بدلاً من ذلك، ركّزت انتباهها على أكيفا، وهو جالس على حافة النافذة البعيدة، بمصاريعها المغلقة خلفه، وجناحاه ظاهرين، مترهلين وباهتين.

التقت عيناه بعينيها للحظة، وبعد أن تجاوزت الصدمة الأولى التي اعتادت أن تشعر بها كلما نظرت إلى أكيفا - إذ كان عليك أن تقنع عقلك بأنه حقيقي؛ حقاً، هذا هو الشعور الذي يعتريك عندما تنظر إليه؛ عقلك يريد أن يقول:"هراء، بالتأكيد هو مجرد فوتوشوب"، حتى عندما يكون أمامك مباشرة - اجتاحتها كآبة ساحقة.

لم يكن أي شـيء يبدو سهلاً على الإطلاق بالنسبة إلى هذين الاثنين. علاقتهما، إذا كان يمكن تسميتها بذلك، كانت أشبه بمحاولة الرقص تحت وابل من الرصاص. والآن، بعدما وصلا أخيراً إلى حافة التفاهم، أسدل الحزن ستارة جديدة بينهما.

لا يمكن رفع الستارة مجدداً، فالأسى سيبقى. لكن يمكنك اختراقه، أليس كذلك؟ إذا كان لا بد لهما أن يعانيا، تساءلت زوزانا، أليس من الأفضل أن يعانيا معاً على الأقل؟

وفي اللحظة التي سمعت فيها طرقاً على الباب – الطعام الذي طلبوه – خطرت لها فكرة. ربما يمكنها المساعدة، على الأقل في مسألة التقارب الجسدي.

"لحظة واحدة!" قالت الطارق."أنتم الثلاثة، إلى الحمام. تذكّروا أنكم غير موجودين!".

تبع ذلك نقاش هامس قصير حول إمكانية أن يغظّوا أنفسهم بالسحر، لكن زوزانا لم تكن على استعداد لسماع ذلك. أين سيضعون الطعام بوجود كيميرا ضخمة تشغل نصف الغرفة، وملاك جالس على حافة النافذة، وفتاة ممددة على السرير؟"حتى لو كنتم غير مرئيين، فإنكم ما زلتم موجودين، وتشغلون حيزاً كبيراً، في الواقع."

وهكذا، توجهوا إلى الحمام. وإذا كانت الغرفة صغيرة، فإن الحمام كان أصغر بكثير، ورأت زوزانا أنه من المناسب أن ترتّبهم داخله بنفسها. دفعت كارو من أسفل ظهرها لتدفعها إلى الداخل، ثم ألقت نظرة متسلطة على أكيفا مع إشارة حاسمة برأسها تقول:"أنت التالي". دفعتهما معاً داخل الدش وأغلقت الباب عليهما. كان ذلك هو الحل الوحيد ليتمكن ڤيركو من دخول الغرفة أيضاً. بدا كل شيء معقولاً تماماً.

أغلقت زوزانا باب الحمام، ثم تراجعت. عليهما أن يتدبرا الأمر من هناك. لا يمكنها أن تفعل كل شيء من أجلهما.

49

عرض رعاية

"الصبر، ثم الصبر".

هذا ما نصح به رازغوت جايل قبل نصف يوم. الصبر. حتى وهو ينطق بهذه الكلمة، كان هو نفسه يشعر بلسعة نفاد الصبر. أما الآن، بعد انقضاء يومين كاملين منذ وصولهما، فقد بات الأمر أشبه بطعنة. لقد سخر من توقعات جايل حينها، لكنه في أعماقه بدأ يقلق.

أين عروض الولاء التي كان يتوقعها؟ هل أخطأ الحساب؟ هذه الخطة كانت فكرته بالكامل."ما عليك إلا أن تصل في مجدك". قالها لهم بثقة،"وسيتسابقون لإعطائك ما تريد." لكن ليس الرؤساء، ولا رؤساء الوزراء، ولا حتى البابا نفسه. صحيح أنهم سيفرشون لهم السجاد الأحمر، ولن يترددوا في الانحناء والمجاملات، لكن أصحاب القرار الحقيقيين سيكونون أكثر حذراً عندما يتعلق الموضوع بتزويد الأسلحة لمجموعات غير موثوقة. سيكون هناك تدقيق ومراقبة ولجان.

"آه، أعطني نصف مجنون، جزاراً متعطشاً للدماء!". قال رازغوت بعدما استجمع أفكاره."لكن خلصني من تلك اللجان!".

ومع أن الرؤساء ورؤساء الوزراء والبابا أظهروا كرم الضيافة، كان رازغوت يتوقع أن القوى الخفية والعنيفة في العالم قد بدأت تتحرك. الجماعات الخاصة، المجانين المتطرفون، أولئك الذين يطاردون الجحيم بنشوة، والمتفاخرون بيوم القيامة. هؤلاء كان ينبغي أن يصطفوا، ويقدموا العروض، ويدفعوا الرشاوى، ويحاولوا بأي وسيلة الوصول إلى الملائكة مهما كانت التكلفة."خذونا! خذونا أولاً! أحرقوا العالم، مزقوا الخطاة، فقط خذونا معكم!".

العالم مليء بمثل هؤلاء حتى في الأيام العادية، فكيف غابوا الآن؟ هل أخطأ رازغوت في تقدير افتتان البشرية بنهاية العالم؟ هل يمكن أن هذا المشهد المسرحي لن يتكشف بسهولة كما كان يظن؟

كان جايل في مزاج سيئ، يتجول في جناح الغرف الفاخرة بين شتائم منخفضة وصمت بارد. ولإنصافه، كان يحرص على إبقاء شتائمه خافتة، فلا يرتكب شيئاً"غير ملائكي" قد يزعج مضيفيه المتدينين. كان يؤدي دوره ببراعة عندما يُطلب منه ذلك: التظاهر الدبلوماسي، الولائم، السحر المبهر

وبالنسبة إلى الكنيسة الكاثوليكية، بدا أنها مصممة على مجاراتهم في استعراض الهيبة، ولا شك أن خزانة أزيائهم كانت الفائزة بالاستعراض بامتياز. أما رازغوت، فقد كاد يفقد عقله. إذا اضطر لتحمل مزيد من هذه المراسم، وهو متشبث على ظهر جايل يستمع إلى كاهن عجوز في ثوب فاخر يردد عبارات لاتينية، فقد يصرخ.

"سأصرخ وأكشف عن نفسي، فقط لأضيف بعض الإثارة إلى المشهد." هكذا كانت الأفكار تراود رازغوت بينما صدره يعصف بمزيج غريب من... الأمل. كان يراقب من بعيد بحذر واضح ذلك"الرقص المتردد" الغريب الذي أداه أحد خدم القصر البابوي عند عتبة الباب. خطوة إلى الأمام، خطوة إلى الخلف، وذراعان تتحركان كجناحي دجاجة مضطربة.

كان هذا الرجل واحداً من القلة المصرح لهم بدخول غرفهم والاهتمام باحتياجاتهم، وحتى الآن لم يكن يرفع عينيه عن الأرض أمام"قداستهم". فكر

رازغوت، أكثر من مرة، أنه ربما يستطيع إطلاق العنان لنفسه بالكامل دون أن يلاحظه هذا الرجل. هذا المستوى من التحفظ كان لدى الخدم، حتى إنهم كانوا أقرب إلى الأشباح. ومع ذلك، فإن فكرة حياة ما بعد الموت على هيئة شبح، كانت كافية لجعل رازغوت يشعر بالغثيان.

أو ربما السبب كان في تلك الولائم الباذخة التي تخرجها مطابخ القصر البابوي. لم يتلذذ البابا بمثل هذا الطعام الفاخر منذ قرون طويلة، لكنه وجد أنه، رغم توعك معدته المليئة، لم يقرر بعد التوقف عن التهام الطعام. ربما بعد قليل. وربما لا.

تنحنح الخادم بخفة. وكادت ضربات قلبه الخائفة تسمع من الجهة الأخرى للغرفة. حرّاس "الدومينيون" ظلوا بلا حركة، أشبه بالتماثيل، وجايل كان في حجرته الخاصة يستريح. فكّر رازغوت للحظة في التحدث. هل يمكن أن تكون فكرة سماع صوت من متحدث خفيّ هي أغرب ما يواجهه هذا الرجل اليوم؟ لكن لم يكن هناك ضرورة لذلك.

الرجل، بطريقة ما، استطاع أن يستجمع شجاعته وتقدم ببطء، وأخرج مغلفاً من جيب سترته المكوية بدقة ووضعه بعناية على الأرض.

تركّز نظر رازغوت بالكامل على المغلف. كان يعرف جيداً ما يمكن أن يكون. وأصبح الأمل في داخله أكثر وضوحاً

أخيراً. قفزت ساعة الزمن: اختفى الخادم، استُدعي جايل، وصار رازغوت مرئياً، مستلقياً على طاولة الضيافة، وفي يده المغلف. لم يُظهر أي علامة على الارتياح العميق أو الفضول الذي كان يعتمل بداخله. بدلاً من ذلك، كان ينزع شريحة رقيقة من اللحم المقدد عن رفيقاتها، وتأكد من إصدار صوت واضح يعبر عن استمتاعه.

"إذاً، ماذا يقول؟".

كان جايل نافد الصبر، متعجرفاً كعادته. راودت رازغوت ابتسامة صغيرة: "إنه تحت رحمتي."

"لا أدري"، أجاب رازغوت ببرود وبصراحة أيضاً. لم يفتح المغلف بعد."ربما رسالة إعجاب. أو دعوة إلى معمودية. أو ربما طلب زواج."

"اقرأها لي"، أمره جايل.

توقف رازغوت لوهلة وكأنه يفكر في رد، ثم... أطلق ريحاً مصحوبة بتعبير وجه مشدود يوحي بالجهد الكبير. لم تكن النتيجة مثيرة من حيث الصوت، لكنها كانت عظيمة من حيث الرائحة. لم يرق الأمر للإمبراطور، وعلى الفور تحول أثر ندبته إلى اللون الأبيض، تلك العلامة التي تظهر عندما يصل غضبه إلى حدوده القصوى. تكلم جايل وأسنانه مطبقة، وهذا ما ساعد على منع تطاير اللعاب من فمه.

"اقرأها لي"، كرر جايل بصوته الهادئ المخيف، وتيقن رازغوت أنه لم يعد يفصله عن التعرض للضرب سوى خطوة واحدة. ولو أطاع الآن، ربما يجنب نفسه بعض الألم.

"سهل الأمور عليّ"، كان جايل قد قال له سابقاً،"وسأجعل الأمور سهلة عليك."

لكن أين المتعة في السهولة؟ حشر رازغوت أكبر قدر ممكن من شرائح اللحم المقدد في فمه بينما ما زالت لديه الفرصة، أما جايل، بعد أن رأى ما ينوي عليه رازغوت، قام بضربه بحركة بسيطة من رأسه.

كلاهما كان يعرف أن هذا لن يُفضي إلى أي نتيجة. لقد أصبح هذا جزءاً من روتينهما اليومي.

وهكذا، تم القيام بضربه، ثم ظهور بعض الإصابات الجديدة على جسد رازغوت ترشح سائلاً ليس تماماً كالدم فوق وسائد حريرية تعود إلى خمسمئة عام، حاول جايل مجدداً.

قال جايل:"عندما نصل إلى الجزر البعيدة، بعد أن أحطم الستيليين في الشوارع، وقبل أن أسحقهم تماماً، سأجعلهم يتمنون الموت ويتوسلون لإنهاء حياتهم."

ابتسم رازغوت ابتسامة شيطانية وقال في نفسه: إلى أن تواجه الستيليين هناك حديث آخر. لكنه لم يرد أن يُفسد على الإمبراطور أوهامه.

تابع جايل وهو يحاول بشكل واضح الحفاظ على مظهر الكياسة—قناع لم يكن يناسبه أبداً—"إذا بذل... شخص ما... قصارى جهده ليكون متعاوناً من الآن وحتى ذلك الحين، ربما يمكنك إقناعي أن أمنحهم تلك الأمنية. وأراهن أن تكون الفنون الستيلية قادرة على... إصلاحك."

"ماذا؟"، اعتدل رازغوت فجأة، ورفع يديه إلى وجنتيه في محاكاة مبالغ فيها لملكة جمال تسمع إعلان فوزها:"أنا؟ حقاً؟".

لم يكن جايل أحمق بما يكفي ليفوته أن رازغوت يسخر منه، لكنه أيضاً لم يكن غبياً إلى درجة أن يُظهر إحباطه أمام هذا الكائن الساقط."آه، هذا خطئي وقد ظننت أن هذا سيهمك".

من الممكن أن رازغوت كان سيهتم بالأمر، لولا نقطة هامة، بل نقطتان، لكن الأولى هي الأهم: جايل يكذب. حتى لو لم يكن كذلك، فإن الستيليين لن يحققوا لعدوهم أي أمنية. رازغوت تذكرهم من الزمن الذي كان فيه بينهم، وعرفهم أعداء لا يمكن الاستهانة بهم. حتى لو وقعوا تحت رحمة أعدائهم، فإن هذا أمراً يصعب تخيله لأنه لم يحدث قط. إن وُضعوا تحت رحمة أعدائهم، فإنهم سيحرقون أنفسهم بالكامل قبل أن يستسلموا.

"هذا ليس ما أتمناه"، قال رازغوت."إذاً، ماذا تتمنى؟".

عندما ساوم رازغوت الفتاة الزرقاء الجميلة للحصول على طريقة للعودة إلى"المملكة"، كانت أمنيته بسيطة. الطيران؟ نعم، كان ذلك جزءاً منها. أن يصبح كاملاً مرة أخرى؟ لم يكن ذلك بهذه البساطة، فقد كان الأمر أكثر من مجرد جناحيه وساقيه اللذين تمزقا. كان يعرف أنه، بأهم الطرق، لا يمكن إصلاحها. لكن أمنيته الحقيقية، تلك التي استقرت في أعماق روحه، كانت بسيطة للغاية."أريد أن أعود إلى الوطن"، قالها بصوت خالٍ من السخرية ومن لذته المعتادة الخبيثة. بدا صوته وكأنه صوت طفل.

حدق جايل فيه بصمت. "أمر بسيط"، قال، وبسبب تلك العبارة، أكثر من أي شيء آخر قاله جايل أو فعله، أراد رازغوت أن يكسر عنقه. الفراغ بداخله كان هائلاً إلى درجة ساحقة، والوزن الناتج عنه مدمراً إلى حد أنه بات يخطف أنفاسه أحياناً عندما يتذكر أن جايل ليس لديه أي علم به على الإطلاق. لا أحد يعلم.

"ليس بهذه البساطة"، أجاب رازغوت. إذا كان هناك شيء واحد يعرفه رازغوت الساقط ثلاث مرات بكل يقين، فهو هذا: لن يستطيع العودة إلى وطنه أبداً.

وبسبب رغبته في إخفاء اضطرابه أكثر من رغبته في التوقف عن تعذيب الإمبراطور، فتح الرسالة. ماذا تقول؟ قال لنفسه. من أرسلها؟ ما نوع العرض؟ هل حان الوقت تقريباً؟

كانت الفكرة حلوة ومرة في آنٍ معاً. فرازغوت يعلم أن جايل سيقتله بمجرد أن ينتهي من حاجته إليه. حتى الحياة بأبشع صورها، قادرة على جعلك متمسكاً بها. بأقصى درجات البطء ودقة مملة ومع أصابعه المرتجفة، بدأ الملاك المنفي يفرد الصفحات. إنه نص أنيق، وما رآه حبر على ورق فاخر مكتوب باللاتينية. وأخيراً، قرأ على جايل أول عرض رعاية يتلقاه.

50

على السعادة أن تذهب إلى مكان ما

باتا قريبين جداً، وبدا الوضع برمّته عبثياً، بل سخيفاً إلى حد لا يُصدق. مقبض الدش يضغط على ظهر كازّو، بينما ريشات جناحي أكيفا عالقة في الباب. وكانت حيلة زوزانا التي بدت مكشوفة، لطيفة ولكن محرجة لكليهما إلى أقصى حد. وإذا كان هدفها إشعال أي شرارة بينهما، فقد نجحت فقط في إشعال حمرة خدي كارو خجلاً. المساحة ضيقة جداً، مع ضخامة جناحي أكيفا اللذين أجبراه على الانحناء نحوها، وكأن غريزة غامضة قد دفعت كليهما إلى الحفاظ على ذلك الفاصل الضئيل من المسافة بينهما.

كأنهما غريبان في مصعد.

ألم يكونا غريبين في الحقيقة؟ لأن الانجذاب بينهما كان قوياً إلى درجة تجعل من السهل أن يتوهم المرء أنهما يعرفان بعضهما جيداً. كارو، التي لم تؤمن بمثل هذه الأمور من قبل، كانت مستعدة الآن لتقبل فكرة أن روحيهما، بطريقة ما، تعرفان بعضهما البعض. "روحك تغني لروحي"، قال لها ذات مرة، وكانت لتقسم إنها شعرت بذلك فعلاً. لكن، بالرغم من كل

ذلك، فهما لا يعرفان. هناك الكثير مما يحتاجان إلى معرفته. إنها تتوق بشدة إلى اكتشاف كل شيء، لكن كيف يمكن تحقيق ذلك في أوقات كهذه؟ ليس بإمكانهما الجلوس على سطح كاتدرائية، يأكلان خبزاً ساخناً ويشاهدان شروق الشمس.

هذه لم تكن لحظة للوقوع في الحب.

"هل أنتما بخير هناك؟" سأل فيركو بصوت خافت أشبه بالهمس. تخيلت كارو لو أن موظف الفندق يسمع الصوت ويتساءل عمّن يختبئ في الحمام. عند هذه النقطة، بلغت غرابة الموقف مستوى جديداً. وسط كل ما كان يجري، وثقل المهمة المنوطة بهما، ها هما محشوران في حمام صغير، يختبئان من موظف الفندق.

"نعم، بخير"، قالت، بصوت مبحوح -يا لها من كذبة-. كان عليها أن تقول أي شيء ما عدا "بخير". أدركت حينها أن مجرد قول ذلك بهذه الطريقة العرضية يعد... تهاوناً. رعونة. نظرت إلى أكيفا بحذر، خائفة من أن يظن أنها تعني ما قالته فعلاً. "بالتأكيد، بخير، والجو جميل اليوم."

ما الذي استجد معك؟ إنها رؤية الألم مجدداً في عينيه، والغضب الذي يرافقه، كأنه جرح جديد يخدش قلبها. شعرت بالضعف وهي تضطر لتحويل نظرها بعيداً. أكيفا... أكيفا.

عندما التقيا مؤخراً في الكهوف، وتلاقت أعينهما عبر اتساع الكهف العظيم—عبر كل الجنود الواقفين بينهما، من كلا الجانبين، وعبر حجم العداوة المقيتة التي تفصلهما، وهمّ الأسرار التي يحملانها، وثقل الأعباء، حتى من تلك المسافة الشاسعة، بدت نظراتهما أشبه بلمسة حقيقية.

لكن الآن، مجرد خيط رفيع في الفراغ يفصل بينهما، ورغم ذلك، بدا لقاء أعينهما وكأنه... ندم.

"أبناء الندم"، قالتها بصوت مسموع. ثم همست: حسناً. سرقت نظرة أخرى نحوه. "أتذكر؟".

كيف لي أن أنسى؟" رد عليها أكيفا مع ألم يعتصر قلبه، وصوت مشوب بخشونة قد أحدثها الوجع.

روت له القصة—وهي مادريغال—في الليلة التي وقعا فيها في الحب. راح يتذكر كل كلمة وكل لمسة من تلك الليلة، كل ابتسامة وكل شهقة. استرجاع تلك الذكرى كان أشبه بالنظر عبر نفق مظلم، حيث كل حياته منذ ذلك الحين صارت ضبابية، ما عدا ذلك الضوء الساطع في نهايته. تلك الليلة بدت له كأنها مكان ما خبأ فيه كل سعادته، المطوية بعناية، وكأنها أمتعة لن يحتاجها مجدداً.

قالت كارو:"أخبرتني أنها قصة مروعة".

كانت تلك أسطورة الكيميرا حول كيفية نشأتهم، ولم تكن أقل من أسطورة اغتصاب. تقول الحكاية إن الكيميرا وُلدوا من دموع القمر، بينما جاء السيرافيم من دم الشمس القاسية."إنها حقاً مروعة"، أجاب أكيفا، وهو يكره هذه الأسطورة الآن أكثر مما كرهها من قبل، خاصة في ضوء ما عانته كارو على يد ثياغو.

وافقت كارو:"هي كذلك، وكذلك قصتكم."

في أسطورة السيرافيم، الكيميرا كانوا ظلالاً تحولت إلى حياة، وصنعتها وحوش هائلة تسبح في الظلام وتلتهم العوالم."لكن بنفس النغمة"، أضافت بصوت مليء بالتأمل."أشعر الآن أنني كلاهما: دموع وظل."

"وإن أردنا أن نحتكم إلى الأساطير، فأنا إذاً شيء من دماء..."، وأضافت بصوت أشبه بالهمس:"...ومن نور". كانا يتحدثان بهدوء خشية أن يسمعهما فيركو، الذي كان يقف على الجانب الآخر من الحاجز الزجاجي.

تابعت كارو:"في أسطورتكم كنتم أرحم بأنفسكم منا. لقد صنعنا أنفسنا من الحزن. أما أنتم، فقد صنعتم أنفسكم على صورة آلهتكم، ولهدف نبيل: أن تجلبوا النور إلى العوالم".

قال أكيفا بمرارة:"لقد أحسّنا خرابها بالفعل".

ابتسمت كارو قليلاً، وخرجت منها ضحكة تحمل طيفاً من الأسى."لن أجادلكَ في ذلك."

ذكّرها أكيفا:"الأسطورة تقول أيضاً إننا سنظل أعداء حتى نهاية العالم".

حين حكى لها تلك القصة، كانا متعانقين، عاريين ومرنين بعد أول تجربة حب بينهما—أول مرة يجتمعان فيها—وكانت نهاية العالم تبدو آنذاك بعيدة مثل أسطورة لقمر ينوح.

لكن أكيفا كاد يشعر بها الآن، تضغط عليهما بثقلها. بدت أشبه باليأس المتسلل. وقد تساءل في نفسه: عند أي نقطة يصبح كل شيء بلا جدوى، ولا يبقى شيء يستحق الإنقاذ؟

قالت كارو:"لهذا اخترعنا أسطورتنا الخاصة".

ثم تذكّر."ثمة جنة تنتظرنا لنجدها ونملأها بسعادتنا. هل ما زلتِ تؤمنين بذلك؟".

لم يقصد أن يبدو كلامه قاسياً كما نطقه، وكأنها مجرد أوهام حمقاء لحبيبين جديدين يحتضنان بعضهما البعض. أراد أن يوبخ نفسه، لأنه كان يؤمن بذلك. فقط بالأمس، عندما اتهمته ليراز بأنه"مفتون بالسعادة"، وهي على حق بذلك، كان يتخيل نفسه يستحم مع كارو، أليس كذلك؟ يحتضنها بين ذراعيه، ظهرها ملتصق بصدره، فقط يحتضنها ويراقب خصلات شعرها تتماوج على سطح الماء.

ظن حينها، أن هذا سيحدث قريباً.

حينما حلّق بعيداً عن الكهوف صباحاً، ورأى جيوشهم المختلطة تنساب في السماء بتناغم، تخيل أكثر من ذلك بكثير. تخيل مكاناً يخصهما. بيتاً... منزلاً. مع أنه لم يعرف يوماً معنى المنزل. لم يجربه قط. كانت حياته مجرد ثكنات، خيام وحملات عسكرية، وقبل ذلك قضى طفولته القصيرة في الحرملك. ومع ذلك، سمح لنفسه أن يتصور هذا الشيء البسيط، وكأنه ليس أكبر خيال يمكن أن يحلم به. منزل. سجادة، طاولة يجلسان عليها لتناول

الطعام معاً، كرسيان فقط لهما، وشموع متلألئة ليتمكن من الإمساك بيدها عبر الطاولة، فقط ليلمسها ويتحدثان ويكتشفان بعضهما البعض طبقة بعد طبقة. ويكون هناك باب يمكنهما إغلاقه ليبقى العالم في الخارج، وأماكن يضعان فيها أشياء تخصهما.

بالكاد استطاع أكيفا أن يتخيل ماهية تلك الأشياء، إذ لم يملك يوماً أي شيء سوى السيوف. وهذا وحده كان كافياً ليكشف كم كان حلمه هشاً، إذ إن عليه أن يستعير صوراً من البقايا المتعفنة في كهوف الكيرين، تلك الأماكن التي دمر فيها قومه ذات يوم حياة قومها.

صحون وغليون ومشط وإبريق و... سرير. سرير وبطانية تغطيهما معاً، بطانية تخصهما. شيء ما في هذه الفكرة الشديدة البساطة، ما بلور أمل أكيفا وهشاشته، وجعله يصدق، حقاً، أنه يمكن أن يكون... إنساناً، بعد الحرب. بدا له صباحاً، وهو محلق في الجو، أن كل ذلك يكاد سيكون في متناول يده.

لم يكلف نفسه عناء الحلم بموقع هذا المنزل، أو ماذا سيرى إذا فتح بابه، لكن الآن، عندما تخيل الأمر، لم يرَ إلا ما رآه في الخارج: ما يكمن خلف حدود"الجنة" الصغيرة الهادئة في أحلام يقظته.

الجثث متناثرة في كل مكان.

"ليست جنة"، قالت كارو متلعثمة، واحمر وجهها وأغلقت عينيها للحظة وجيزة. نظر أكيفا إليها، وقد أسرته رؤية رموشها الداكنة والمرتعشة فوق الجلد الأزرق الشاحب حول عينيها. وعندما فتحت عينيها، حدث ذلك الاصطدام المفاجئ بين نظراتهما، عمق عينيها السوداوين الخاليتين من البؤبؤ، ذلك السواد الذي لا قاع له. رأى فيهما كل قلقها، وكل الألم الذي يعادل ألمه، لكنه رأى أيضاً فيهما القوة.

قالت كارو:"أعلم أنه لا توجد جنة تنتظرنا. لكن على السعادة أن تجد مكانها، أليس كذلك؟ أعتقد أن المملكة تستحق بعضاً منها، ولهذا...". قالت

كلماتها بخجل، فالمسافة بينهما لا تزال قائمة."أعتقد أننا يجب أن نضع سعادتنا هنا، في هذا العالم، وليس في جنة عشوائية لا تحتاجها حقاً". توقفت، ثم رفعت عينيها إليه. نظرت ونظرت، كأنها تصب كل ما في داخلها من خلال عينيها الاستثنائيتين إلى عينيه ولأجله."ألا تظن ذلك؟".

"السعادة"، قالها بصوت رقيق، وكأنها شيء هش لا يمكن تصديقه، وكأن السعادة نفسها مجرد أسطورة، مثل آلهتهم ووحوشهم.

"لا تستسلم"، همست كارو."ليس من الخطأ أن تكون سعيداً لأنك على قيد الحياة."

ساد صمت، وكان بإمكانها أن تشعر بصراعه الداخلي وهو يبحث عن الكلمات. استمر في الحصول على فرص ثانية، ثم قال بصوت متردد:"ذلك ليس من حقي."

لم تجب على الفور.

كانت تعلم حجم الذنب الذي يحمله فوق كتفيه. خاصة تضحية ليراز التي هزتها حتى أعماقها. أخذت نفساً عميقاً آخر، ثم همست له، وهي تأمل ألا تكون مخطئة:"لقد وهبت نفسها"، مع إحساسها بأن ما قدمته ليراز لم يكن هدية لأكيفا وحده، بل لها أيضاً.

وإن كان بريمستون محقاً في قوله بأن الأمل هو الأمل الوحيد، وإن كانا هما الاثنان بطريقة ما تجسيداً لهذا الأمل، فقد كانت تلك هدية للمملكة أيضاً.

قال بعفوية:"ربما. لقد قلتِ سابقاً إن الموتى لا يريدون الانتقام، وربما يكون هذا صحيحاً أحياناً، ولكن عندما تكوني الشخص الذي بقي حياً-".

قاطعته كارو:"لا نعلم بأنهم-"، لكنها لم تستطع حتى إنهاء الجملة."الحياة تبدو مسروقة."

قال:"ممنوحة. والاستجابة الوحيدة التي تبدو منطقية للقلب هي الانتقام".

"أعلم ذلك. صدقني. لكني أختبئ معك في الحمام بدلاً من محاولة قتلك، لذا يبدو أن القلب يمكنه تغيير رأيه."

ارتسم على وجهه ظل ابتسامة. كان ذلك إنجازاً. بادلته كارو الابتسامة، ابتسامة حقيقية لا لبس فيها، مستذكرة كل ابتسامة جميلة منه، كل تلك الابتسامات المشرقة الضائعة، ومجبرة نفسها على تصديق أنها لم تُمحَ إلى الأبد. البشر يتحطمون. ولا يمكن دائماً إصلاحهم. لكن ليس هذه المرة، أبداً.

"إنها ليست نهاية الأمل"، قالت بجدية وبصوت ممتلئ بالإيمان، وكأنها محاولة منها لدفعه للتصديق،"لا نعلم شيئاً عن الآخرين، لكن حتى لو عرفنا، وحتى لو كان أسوأ مما نتصوره... إلا أننا لا نزال هنا يا أكيفا. ولن أستسلم طالما أن هذه هي الحقيقة". جدية مفعمة بالحماسة، وكأنها تحاول إرغامه على تصديقها وربما نجحت.

منذ البداية—في بولفينش، وسط الدخان والضباب—كانت هناك دهشة كبيرة في نظرة أكيفا إليها، عيناه جاحظتان وكأنه يحاول احتواء كل تفاصيلها، خائفاً من أن يرمش، أو حتى يتنفس. عاد إليه شيء من تلك الدهشة الآن، وعاد إليه صموده وصلابته، وغضبه الذي بدا لا يمكن زحزحته، واستسلموا لها. كم هو عجيب أن كثيراً من التعبير يكمن في العضلات المحيطة بالعينين، ورأت كارو كيف ذهب التوتر عنها، وانطلق فيها شعوراً بالارتياح ربما كان مبالغاً فيه مقارنة بالتغير الصغير الذي أحدثه، والذي ربما كان متناسباً جداً، وهذا ليس بالأمر البسيط. ليت التخلي عن الكراهية يكون بنفس البساطة. كأن تدع وجهك يسترخي فقط قال أكيفا:"أنتِ على حق، أنا آسف".

"لا أريدكَ أن تكون آسفاً. أريد لك أن تكون... حياً."

حياً. قلب ينبض، دم يجري في العروق، نعم، لكنها كانت تريد أكثر من ذلك.

أرادته أن يكون حياً، بعينين تتوهجان بالحياة، بروح تقول: "نحن البداية."

"أنا حي"، قالها، وفي صوته حياة، ووعد.

كانت كارو لا تزال أسيرة ومضة من الذكريات التي رأته فيها من خلال عيني مادريغال. في ذلك الجسد، كانت أطول، لذا كان خط النظر مختلفاً، لكن هذه اللحظة نسجت صلة مباشرة مع الذكرى: بستان القداس لأول مرة، قبل القبلة الأولى بقليل. وهج نظرته، وانحناءة جسده نحوها. هذا ما ربط بين الماضي والحاضر، وصنع دائرة من الزمن أعادت قلبها إلى حالته الأبسط

بعض الأمور تظل بسيطة دائماً، مثل مغناطيسين مثلاً، حيث لا يتطلب الأمر سوى حركة صغيرة للغاية. ليس الأمر بتلك الصعوبة ولا بسيطاً كقبلة. بمجرد أن كان خد كارو على مستوى صدر أكيڤا، التصقت به ثم تبع بقية جسدها خدها. تلك المسافة اللعينة بينهما اختفت. أخذ قلب أكيڤا ينبض بمحاذاة صدغها، وذراعاه التفّتا حولها ليحتضنها. كان دافئاً كالصيف، وشعرت بالزفير الذي تحرك داخله، يحرره ليقترب منها أكثر، وصدر منها زفيرها الخاص، زفير التحرر، لتلتقي به في هذا القرب. يا له من شعور جميل. لا هواء بيننا، فكرت كارو، ولا مزيد من العار. لا شيء آخر بيننا.

بدا ذلك جميلاً جداً. سافرت يداها حوله لتحتضنه بقوة أكبر، ثم تشده. كل نفس أخذته كان يحمل دفء رائحته، ذلك الدفء المألوف الذي استذكرته وعادت لاكتشافه مجدداً وكأنها تتحقق من ثباته وواقعيته التي لطالما أدهشتها، رغم أن تأثيره كان يبدو... غير أرضي بكل عناصره.

الحب عنصر، تذكرت كارو ذلك منذ زمن بعيد جداً، وشعرت وكأنها تطفو. وبدا أكيڤا للناظر ناراً وهواء. لكن حسياً كان حاضراً جداً، حقيقياً بما يكفي لتتشبث به إلى الأبد.

أخذت يد أكيڤا تتحرك على طول شعرها، مرة بعد مرة، بينما شعرت بضغط شفتيه على قمة رأسها. ما ملأها لم يكن الرغبة، بل الحنان، والامتنان

العميق لأنه حيّاً، ولأنها حية مثله. لأنه وجدها مرة، ولأنه وجدها مرة أخرى. و... يا لنجوم السماء المتناثرة... نحن مرة أخرى. لتكن تلك آخر مرة يضطر فيها للبحث عني.

سأجعل الأمر سهلاً عليك. قالت في نفسها وهي تضغط وجهها على نبض قلبه. سأكون هنا. وكأنه سمعها ووافقها، فشدّ ذراعيه حولها أكثر.

عندما فتحت زوزانا باب الحمام ونادت، "الحساء جاهز!"، انفصلا ببطء، وتبادلا نظرة مليئة بالامتنان والوعد والتواصل. حاجز قد كُسر. ليس بقبلة—ليس بعد، ليس الآن—ولكن بلمسة، على الأقل. لقد أصبح كل منهما ينتمي إلى الآخر ليحتضنه. شعرت كارو بحرارة أكيفا تملأ جسدها وهي تخطو خارج الحمام. وحين لمحت انعكاسهما معاً في المرآة، محاطين بإطار واحد، قالت لنفسها: هذا هو الصح.

نظرة أخيرة مرت بينهما في زجاج المرآة—ناعمة، مفعمة بالفرح والنقاء، رغم أنها لم تكن خالية تماماً من الحزن والألم—ثم تبعا فيركو إلى غرفة النوم، حيث كان هناك أنواع مذهلة من الطعام مبسوطة على الأرض مثل وليمة سلطان.

بدأوا في تناول الطعام. كارو وأكيفا بقيا قريبين بما يكفي ليكونا على مسافة لمسة، وهو ما لاحظته زوزانا مع رفع حاجبها وبتعبير يحمل شيئاً من الرضا الماكر. كانوا بالكاد قد بدؤوا في التهام المجموعة الهائلة من الأطباق، عندما سمعوا أصواتاً تتعالى في الخارج. أبواب سيارات تُغلق بعنف، وصوتان ذكوريان يتنافسان بغضب. كان يمكن أن يكون أي شيء—خلافاً خاصاً لا أكثر—ولم يكن ليدفع الخمسة جميعاً للوقوف على أقدامهم—وأولهم أكيفا—ثم تحركهم جميعاً نحو النافذة.

الصوت الثالث هو ما دفعهم إلى ذلك.كان صوتاً أنثوياً، ذا شجئٍ أليم وعالق في خضم الصوتين الآخرين المتشابكين، مثل طائر في شبكة.

وكان يتكلم السيرافية.

51

فرار

لم يستطيعوا الرؤيا بشكل واضح من خلال نافذتهم، لذا قامت كارو وأكيفا بخدعة سحر التخفي وخرجا لاستكشاف الأمر. تبعهما ميك وزوزانا، دون تخفٍ، تاركين ڤيركو في الغرفة.

كان الشجار قائماً في الساحة الأمامية حيث الردهة الترابية التي اعتاد أطفال القصر اللعب فيها، يدفعون بعضهم البعض بعربة يدوية ويحدقون بغضب في نزلاء الفندق. لم يكن هناك مجال للشك حول مصدر الشجار.

ظهرت شابة، نصفها داخل السيارة ونصفها الآخر خارجها، وباب السيارة مفتوح، ويبدو أنها بالكاد مدركة لنفسها أو لما حولها. بدا وجهها خالياً من التعبير، لكنه ملطخ بالدماء. شفتاها ممتلئتان، وبشرتها داكنة وناعمة، لكن عينيها... كانتا مثيرتين للاضطراب: جميلتين جداً، ولونهما فاتح أكثر مما ينبغي، ومتسعتين بشكل مبالغ فيه، والبياض فيهما نقي إلى درجة مرعبة. ذراعاها كانتا مرتخيتين على حجرها، وجلست على حافة المقعد، رأسها مائل إلى الخلف، في حين تدفق من فمها المدمى سيل من لغة ما.

استغرق العقل لحظة لترتيب الأمور: دم، امرأة، لغتان مختلفتان، كل منهما صاخبة ومتناقضة. رجلان يتجادلان بالعربية. أحدهما، كما يبدو، هو من أحضر المرأة إلى هنا وكان حريصاً على التخلص منها. أما الآخر، فكان موظفاً في الفندق، وكان من الواضح أنه يرفض تحمل المسؤولية.

"لا يمكنك أن تتركها هنا فقط. ماذا حدث لها؟ ماذا تقول؟".

"وكيف لي أن أعرف؟ بعض الأمريكيين سيأتون لأخذها قريباً. دعهم يقلقون هم على أمرها."

"حسناً، وفي هذه الأثناء؟ إنها بحاجة إلى رعاية. انظر إليها. ما الذي حدث لها؟".

"لا أعرف". بدا السائق متجهماً وخائفاً."هذه ليست مسؤوليتي."

"وهل هي مسؤوليتي أنا؟".

استمر الجدال على هذا النحو، بينما استمرت المرأة... على نفس المنوال الغريب"يفترسون... يفترسون بشراهة، ضخام، وصيّادون!" صاحت باللغة السيرافية، صوتها كان حزيناً وعذباً ومشبعاً بالألم، أشبه بضجيج نحيب أغنية خارجة من هذا العالم. حمل صوتها لحناً عميقاً كأنه ينبعث من روحها، مرثية حياتية لما فُقد ولن يعود أبداً.

"الوحوش... الوحوش! كارثة كبرى! أزهرت السماء ثم اسودت، ولم يعد هناك شيء يستطيع احتواءهم. كانوا ينسلخون ولم يكن ذلك خطأنا. كنا نحن من فتح الأبواب، النور في الظلام. لم يكن من المفترض أن يحدث هذا! لقد تم اختياري لأكون واحدة من الاثني عشر، لكنني سقطت... وحيدة تماماً. هناك خرائط في داخلي، لكنني ضائعة، وهناك سماء في داخلي لكنها ميتة. ميتة، ميتة، وستظل ميتة إلى الأبد... يا نجوم السماء!".

شعرت كارو بقشعريرة تسري في عنقها. وأكيفا بجانبها. سألته:"ما الذي يحدث لها؟ هل تعرف عمّ تتحدث؟".

"لا".

"هل هي سيرافيم؟".

تردد للحظة قبل أن يجيب مرة أخرى بالنفي. "إنها بشرية. ليس لديها هالة. ولكن هناك شيء-".

شعرت كارو بذلك أيضاً، لكنها لم تستطع تسميته. من تكون هذه المرأة؟ وكيف تتحدث السيرافية؟

"ميليز ضاعت!" صرخت المرأة، وشعرت كارو بأن شعر ذراعيها ينتصب "حتى ميليز، الأولى والأخيرة، ميليز الأبدية، ميليز التهمت."

سألت كارو أكيفا:"هل تعرف من تكون ميليز؟".

"لا.".

"ما الذي يجري هنا؟".

استدارت كاروه بسرعة عند سماع صوت زوزانا، ورأت صديقتها المذهلة، الجنية الشرسة، وهي تقطع الطريق نحو الرجلين بخطوات واثقة. راحا يحدقان بها لبرهة، ربما يحاولان استيعاب تناقض نبرتها الحادة مع قوامها النحيل حتى يتملّيا منظرها الجذاب. توقف الرجلان عن الجدال.

"إنها تنزف!" قالت زوزانا بالفرنسية، التي كانت اللغة الأوروبية الأكثر تداولاً بسبب الماضي الاستعماري للمغرب. "هل فعلتما هذا بها؟".

امتزجت في صوتها مسحة من الغضب، كحد سكين لم يُشهر بالكامل بعد، فسارعا كلاهما إلى إعلان براءتهما.

لكن زوزانا لم تأبه. "ما خطبكما، تقفان هنا فقط؟ ألا تريان أنها تحتاج إلى مساعدة؟".

لم تكن لديهما إجابة مقنعة، ولم يكن لديهما تفكير بجواب، لأن زوزانا—بمساعدة ميك—كانت قد بدأت بالفعل في تولّي مسؤولية المرأة الشابة. أمسك كل منهما بمرفقها، وساعداها على الوقوف. أما الرجلان فاكتفيا بالمشاهدة، وقد خيم عليهما الصمت والحرج، بينما كانت زوزانا وميك يأخذانها بعيداً.

لم يكن هناك توقف في تدفق كلماتها السيرافية—"أنا ساقطة، وحيدة تماماً، لو نطحت الصخر لن أكون كاملة مرة أخرى..."—"ليس هناك أدنى إشارة للتركيز في عينيها المضطربتين. لكن قدميها تحركتا من دون أي مقاومة منها، لذا تولى زوزانا وميك اصطحابها.

وبعد بضع ساعات، عندما جاء الأمريكيون في بدلاتهم الداكنة للمطالبة بها، قادهم موظف الفندق أولاً إلى غرفة"إليزا". لكنهم وجدوا الغرفة خالية، خالية تماماً من أي شخص أو ممتلكات. عندها، اصطحبوهم إلى غرفة"الفتاة الصغيرة الشرسة" زوزانا وصديقها، اللذين طلبا لنفسيهما نصف طعام المطبخ.

طرقوا الباب، لكن لم يتلقوا أي إجابة، ولم يسمعوا أي حركة من الداخل. وعندما فتحوا الباب ودخلوا، لم تكن المفاجأة كبيرة عند العثور على الغرفة خالية.

لم يرَ أحد خروجهم، حتى أطفال القصر الذين كانوا يلعبون في الساحة التي تشكل المعبر الوحيد المؤدي إلى الشارع.

وفي الواقع... لم يرَ أحد وصولهم أيضاً.

لم يتركوا وراءهم سوى أطباق فارغة تماماً—ولمحبي نظريات المؤامرة، فقد تركوا شيئاً آخر—بضع شعرات زرقاء طويلة في الحمام، حيث داعبت يد ملاك رأس شيطانة، محتضنين في عناق طويل... وطويل جداً، طال انتظاره.

في قديم الزمان...
أنطلقت رحلة

من شأنها أن تخيط كل العوالم معاً بخيوط من نور

52

بارود وتفسخ

بالنسبة إلى مورغان توث، كان الأمر أشبه بعيد الميلاد—بمعناه المرتبط بالجشع والهدايا، وليس بمعناه المرتبط بميلاد المسيح بالطبع. لأنه، بصراحة، من يهتم بذلك؟

الرسائل النصية التي تصل إلى هاتف إليزا تزداد جنوناً ويأساً مع مرور الساعات. وصار الأمر أشبه بمهرجان جنون مجاني يُسلّم إليه مباشرة، وكاد يتمنى لو كان لديه شريك في الجريمة—شخص يشاركه دهشته بأن هناك أناساً بهذه الغرابة حقاً في العالم! لكن لم يكن هناك شخص واحد يعرفه، يمكنه أن يخبره بما فعله دون أن يرتعب بخوف مملوء بالاستقامة الزائفة، وربما يتصل بالشرطة.

أغبياء.

اعتقد أنه بحاجة إلى معجبة، أو ربما إلى صديقة، إلى عينين مفعمتين بالإعجاب وصوت يهمس:"مورغان، أنت سيئ جداً"، لكن سيئ بمعنى جيد. سيئ بطريقة جيدة جداً جداً.

رن الهاتف. في هذه المرحلة، أصبحت استجابته شرطية، كأنها تجربة بافلوف. رنين هاتف إليزا كان كافياً لجعل لعاب مورغان يكاد يسيل شوقاً إلى جرعة جديدة من الجنون الذي لا يُصدق. ولم تخيّب الرسالة أمله.

"أين أنتِ، إلازيل؟ لقد ولّى زمن المشاحنات الصغيرة. الآن عليك أن تدركي أنك لا تستطيعين الهرب من حقيقتك. لقد جاء أهلنا إلى الأرض، كما كنا نعلم دائماً أنهم سيفعلون. لقد قدّمنا لهم العروض. عرضنا أنفسنا عليهم كمساعدين وخادمات، في النشوة والخضوع. فيوم الحساب يقترب. دعي بقية هذا العالم الملعون يُقدم كعلف للوحوش بينما نحن نركع عند قدمي الله. لأننا بحاجة إليكِ أيتها المبجلة".

ذهب خالص. ذهب خالص.

"النشوة والخضوع." ضحك مورغان، لأن ذلك يلخص تقريباً ما يريده في صديقة.

تحمس جداً لأن يرد. حتى الآن قاوم هذا الإغراء، لكن اللعبة بدأت تفقد إثارتها. أعاد قراءة الرسالة. كيف يمكنك التعامل مع هذا الجنون؟ قالوا إنهم قدّموا"عروضاً". ماذا يعني ذلك؟ كيف تمكنوا من تقديم أنفسهم للملائكة؟ أدرك مورغان من الرسائل السابقة أن المرسلة—هي والدة إليزا حسب ما استنتج، فقد كانت قطعة فنية بحد ذاتها—كانت في روما. لكن حسب معرفته، فإن الفاتيكان فعلياً يحتجز"الزائرين" كأسرى، وهو ما وجده أمراً مضحكاً للغاية. تخيل البابا واقفاً على قبة كاتدرائية القديس بطرس بشبكة فراشات عملاقة، يلوّح بها قائلاً:"أمسكت ببعض الملائكة!".

بعد تفكير طويل، كتب رده.

"مرحباً، أمي! لقد أتتني رؤية جديدة. في هذه الرؤية، كنا راكعين عند قدمي الله، وهذا أمر جيد. الحمد لله! ولكن... كنا نقدم له جلسة عناية بالقدمين؟ لست متأكداً مما يعنيه ذلك. مع الحب، إليزا."

إنه يعلم أن ذلك تجاوز للحدود، لكنه لم يستطع أن يمنع نفسه. ضغط

زر الإرسال. في الصمت الذي تلا ذلك، بدأ يخشى أن هذا الفعل ليس بمزحة. لكنه ليس بحاجة إلى القلق. الجنون الذي يتعامل معه ليس من النوع الهش، بل متين.

"شعورك بالمرارة إهانة لله، يا إلازيل. لقد أُعطيتِ نعمة عظيمة. كم من أسلافنا ماتوا دون أن يروا وجوهاً مقدسة لذريتنا، ومع ذلك تجدين في نفسك الجرأة لتضحكي؟ هل ستختارين البقاء لتذوبي مع الخطاة بينما البقية منا يتسامون ليأخذوا مكانتهم في-".

لم يتمكن مورغان من إنهاء قراءة الرسالة، ناهيك عن التفكير في الرد عليها.

"هل هذا هاتف إليزا؟" إنه غابرييل. استدار مورغان بسرعة. كيف تمكّن عالم الأعصاب من التسلل إليه دون أن يلاحظه؟ هل نسي إقفال الباب؟

"يا إلهي، إنه هاتفها فعلاً"، قال غابرييل، وهو ينظر إليه بدهشة واشمئزاز. ومورغان، في خضم ارتباكه، تساءل عن مصدر الدهشة. إدينجر يحتقره بالفعل، فلماذا يبدو مصدوماً؟ وما الذي يمكنه قوله الآن؟ لقد تم القبض عليه متلبساً. لم يكن هناك ما يمكنه فعله سوى الكذب.

"إنها تتلقى رسالة نصية جديدة كل ثلاثين ثانية. من الواضح أن هناك من يحاول الوصول إليها بشدة. كنت سأرد فقط لأخبرهم أنها ليست هنا".

"أعطني الهاتف."

"لا."

لم يكرر غابرييل طلبه. بل ركل ساق المقعد الذي كان مورغان يجلس عليه بقوة كافية لإسقاطه على الفور. طار مورغان وسقط بقوة. وبينما كان يحاول معالجة الألم والغضب، لم يدرك أنه أسقط الهاتف إلا عندما وقف مجدداً، وهو يبعد خصلات شعره عن عينيه.

تباً. صار الهاتف في يد إدينجر الآن. وبدت ملامح الاشمئزاز والدهشة على وجهه أكثر عمقاً.

"إذاً، هذا أنت، أليس كذلك؟" قال غابرييل، محاولاً استيعاب الأمر."إذاً كل هذا من تدبيرك. يا إلهي، وأنا من أعطاك الوسيلة. أنا من أعطاك هاتفها."

تحول غضب مورغان إلى خوف. كان الأمر أشبه بوضع الملح في جرح عميق: ألم، وهيجان، وحرقة."عمَّ تتحدث؟" سأل مورغان، محاولاً التظاهر بالجهل، لكنه فشل في إخفاء ارتباكه.

هز إدينجر رأسه ببطء."يبدو إنها مجرد لعبة بالنسبة إليك، وربما دمرت حياتها."

"لم أفعل شيئاً"، قال مورغان، لكنه لم يكن مستعداً للدفاع عن نفسه. لم يفكر... لم يتوقع مطلقاً في احتمالية أن يتم القبض عليه.

كيف لم يخطر له ذلك؟

رد غابرييل ببرود:"حسناً. لا أستطيع أن أعدكَ بعدم تدمير حياتك. وبصراحة هذا الالتزام صعب. لكن يمكنني أن أعدكَ بهذا: سأتأكد من أن الجميع سيعلمون بما فعلت". رفع الهاتف عالياً."وإن أدى ذلك إلى تدمير حياتِك، فلن أشعر بالأسف على الإطلاق."

...

رسالة أخرى.

الثالثة. أحضرها الخادم نفسه، وعرف رازغوت من الظرف أنها من نفس المرسِل الذي أرسل الرسالتين السابقتين. هذه المرة، لم يكلّف نفسه عناء لعب أي ألعاب مع جايل. فور مغادرة الخادم سبيئيتي، أمسك بها ومزقها على الفور.

لقد بذل رازغوت جهداً خاصاً في صياغة رديه على الرسالتين السابقتين. بدا الأمر تقريباً وكأنه يكتب رسائل حب.

لقد سبق لرازغوت أن كتب رسالة حب... بالطبع. حسناً، لا، هذا ليس صحيحاً تماماً. لقد كتب واحدة. ولكن ذلك كان منذ زمن بعيد جداً، وكأن كائناً مختلفاً تماماً هو من كتب وداعاً عذباً لفتاة بلون العسل.

لقد بدا آنذاك ككائن مختلف بالفعل، وهذا مؤكد. حينها كان لا يزال يبدو كالسيرافيم، وكان عقله آنذاك لا يزال أشبه بالماس الخالي من العيوب، غير متصدع—والضغط اللازم لتصدع الماس!—وغير مغطى بالعفن والقاذورات التي تملأه الآن.

كان ذلك منذ زمن بعيد جداً، لكنه يتذكر كتابته لتلك الرسالة. اسم الفتاة ضاع منه، ووجهها كذلك. لم تبقَ منها سوى لمحة باهتة، ضبابية، بلون الذهب، لا أهمية لها—إنها إشارة إلى حياة ربما لم يرد اختيارها.

كتب بخط جميل ولكن متحمس، مائل إلى الأمام، قبل أن يغادر إلى العاصمة،"إن لم أعد، اعلمي أن ذكراكِ سترافقني عبر كل مجهول، إلى ظلمات كل غدٍ، وما وراء ظل كل أفق."

شيء كهذا. رازغوت يتذكر الشعور الذي وضعه في تلك الكلمات، حتى وإن لم يتذكر الكلمات نفسها بدقة. ولم يكن ذلك حباً، أو حتى أدنى درجات الصدق. كان مجرد تأمين لفرصه. لو لم يتم اختياره—وما هي احتمالات أن يتم اختياره من بين هذا العدد الكبير؟—لكان قد عاد إلى قريته متظاهراً بالارتياح، وكانت تلك الفتاة بلون العسل ستواسيه بنعومتها، وربما تزوجا وأنجبا أطفالاً وعاشا نوعاً من حياة رتيبة-سعيدة في ظل إخفاقه.

ولكنه تم اختياره. يا له من يوم مجيد. رازغوت كان واحداً من الاثني عشر منذ زمن بعيد جداً، والمجد كان له. يوم التسمية: يا له من مجد. الكثير من النور في المدينة إلى درجة أبهرت سماء الليل، ولم يعد بإمكانهم رؤية نجوم الآلهة، ولكن نجوم الآلهة كانت تراهم، وهذا هو المهم—أن تراهم الآلهة وتعرف: لقد تم اختيارهم.

فاتحو الأبواب، ذوو الأنوار في الظلام.

لم يعد رازغوت أبداً إلى موطنه، ولم يرَ تلك الفتاة مرة أخرى. ولكن انظر، هل كذب عليها حقاً؟ ها هو الآن يتذكرها، ما وراء ظل الأفق، في ظلمة غدٍ لم يكن ليتخيله أبداً.

"ماذا قالت؟"

صوت جايل اقتحم شرود رازغوت. هذه الرسالة لم تكن من فتاة ناعمة، بل من امرأة لم يرها قط—رغم أن اسمها لم يكن مجهولاً بالنسبة إليه— ولم يكن فيها أي حلاوة على الإطلاق. لكن ذلك كان لا بأس به. حواس رازغوت نضجت منذ زمنٍ بعيد. الحلاوة أصبحت تافهة بالنسبة إليه. دَع الفراشات والطائر الطنان يستمتعان بها. أما هو، مثل خنفساء الجيف، فقد كانت تجذبه روائح أكثر حدّة.

مثل البارود والتفسخ.

"أسلحة، متفجرات، ذخائر"، ترجم رازغوت لجايل. "تقول إنها يمكنها أن تحصل لك على أي شيء تحتاجه، وكل شيء تريده، بشرط أن توافق على شرطها."

"شرط!" زمجر جايل وهسهس كأنه يبصق الكلمة. "من تكون هي لتضع شروطاً؟".

لقد كان على هذه الحال منذ الرسالة الأولى. جايل لم يكن يقدّر المرأة القوية، عدا أنها شيء ليكسره ويواصل كسره. فكرة أن تجرؤ امرأة على تقديم مطالب؟ امرأة لا يمكنه أن يذلها؟ كانت تلك الفكرة تثير غضبه إلى حد الجنون.

"إنها أفضل خيار لديك، هذا ما هي عليه" أجاب رازغوت. كان ذلك واحداً من العديد من الأجوبة الممكنة، والوحيد الذي يحتاج جايل إلى سماعه. إنها كاسرة. لحمها مرّ. إنها بارود أسود ينتظر شرارة.

"لا أحد غيرها تمكن من شق طريقه إليك، لذا إليك خيارك اليوم: استمر في مناورتك لتلك الرؤوس المتجهمة، وراقبهم وهم يتعثرون في حقل ألغام الرأي العام، يخافون شعوبهم أكثر مما يخافونك، أو قدّم وعداً بسيطاً لتلك السيدة ذات المكانة، وانتهِ من كل هذا. أسلحتك بانتظارك، أيها الإمبراطور. وما هو هذا الشرط الصغير، مقارنة بذلك؟".

53

خبيرة حواجب

عندما دخل ميك وزوزانا بهو فندق سانت ريجيس الفاخر في روما،
توقفت عدة أحاديث فجأة، بينما رمقهما حامل حقائب بنظرة ثانية مليئة
بالدهشة، ورفعت سيدة أنيقة ذات شعر فضي وعظام وجنتين مشدودة
بجراحة تجميلية يدها إلى قلادة اللؤلؤ حول عنقها، ثم أخذت تمسح البهو
بعينيها بحثاً عن رجال الأمن.

لم يكن من المعتاد أبداً أن يستضيف فندق سانت ريجيس رحّالة
يحملون حقائب ظهر.

أما هذان الرحّالتان، فقد كان مظهرهما... حسناً، من الصعب وصفه
بدقة. ربما يمكن لشخص ذي بصيرة حادة القول إنهما يبدوان وكأنهما كانا
يعيشان في كهوف، وخاضا معركة طاحنة، وربما وصلا إلى هنا ممتطيين
وحشاً.

في الواقع، كانا قد وصلا للتو على متن طائرة خاصة من مراكش، ولكن
يمكن للمرء أن يُعذر إذا لم يخمن ذلك. فقد غادرا تمنوغالت على عجل، ولم

تتح لهما الفرصة لاستخدام دش، ولم تكن لديهما ملابس نظيفة تُذكر. وربما لم يسبق لأي منهما أن بدا بمثل هذا المظهر البائس في حياتهما.

اعتقد الزبائن والموظفون أن هذين المسافرين جاءا يطلبان استخدام الحمام فقط—ففي بعض الأحيان، يحدث ذلك، إذ لا يدرك العامة قواعد مثل هذه الأماكن الراقية—ثم سيتركانه متسخاً بعد أن يحاولا الاغتسال في الحوض. أليس هذا ما يفعله أمثال هؤلاء.

حارس الباب الذي سمح لهما بالدخول لم يجرؤ على رفع عينيه عن الأرض، مدركاً تماماً أنه ارتكب خطأً لا يُغتفر بسماحه لهؤلاء الدخلاء بتجاوز عتبة الفندق. لا شك أنه في أيام مضت كان الحراس يُعدمون على مثل هذا التقصير. ولكن، ما الذي بإمكانه فعله؟ لقد زعما أنهما ضيفان.

خلف مكتب الاستقبال، تبادل الموظفون نظرات أشبه بمبارزة في حلبة مصارعة."هل تتعامل معهم أنت، أم أفعل أنا؟".

ظهر البطل أخيراً."كيف يمكنني مساعدتكما؟".

كانت الكلمات التي قالها:"كيف يمكنني مساعدتكما؟"، لكن نبرة الصوت أوضحت أنها تعني شيئاً أقرب إلى:"إنه واجبي المؤلم أن أتعامل معك، وسأجعلكم تندمون على هذا".

استدارت زوزانا لمواجهة خصمها. رأت أمامها امرأة إيطالية شابة، في منتصف العشرينيات، أنيقة بشكل مبهر، وترتدي ملابس تنم عن ذوق رفيع. نظرة عينيها خالية تماماً من الطراوة، أو بالأحرى جافة.

أجرت المرأة مسحاً سريعاً من رأس زوزانا حتى قدميها بنظرة ناقدة، لتتوقف عند حذائها العالي المغطى بالغبار —فتوهجت عيناها بشيء يشبه الامتعاض، وارتسمت على شفتيها عقدة صغيرة من الاشمئزاز. بدا وكأنها على وشك إزالة بزاقة حية من فوق طبق جرجيرها.

"أتعلمين"، قالت زوزانا بالإنجليزية،"ربما كنت ستبدين أجمل بكثير لو لم تقومي بهذا التعبير على وجهك."

تجمدت على وجهها ملامح التساؤل. مع اتساع خفيف في إحدى فتحتي الأنف كان كافياً للإشارة إلى أن الإهانة قد أُخذت على محمل الجد. ثم، وكأن الزمن يتحرك ببطء شديد، ارتفع حاجب المرأة الرفيع، المشذّب بعناية، نحو غرّتها في حركة بطيئة ومشحونة بالتحدي.

المبارزة بدأت.

زوزانا نوفاكوفا فتاة جميلة.

لطالما شُبّهت بدمية أو بجنية، ليس فقط بسبب قامتها الصغيرة، ولكن أيضاً بسبب ملامح وجهها الرقيقة: مزيج متناغم من الزوايا والانحناءات تحت بشرة صافية كالبورسلين. ذقن صغير، خدان مستديران، عينان واسعتان ولامعتان، وفم مرسوم كقوس كيوبيد، رغم أنها كانت ستُبيد أي شخص يجرؤ على وصفها بهذا الشكل. كل هذه"الجاذبية"، كانت واحدة من أعظم الحيل التي لعبتها الطبيعة، لأنها... ببساطة، لم تكن كل ما في زوزانا نوفاكوفا. ولا حتى القليل.

مواجهة زوزانا كانت أشبه بسمكة تقرر، بدافع الفضول، التهام الضوء اللامع الذي يتراقص في الظلال، لتكتشف فجأة—يا للهول، تلك الأسنان، ذلك الرعب!—السمكة المفترسة خلفه.

لم تكن زوزانا تأكل الناس. كانت تذيبهم، تجردهم من كيانهم، تتركهم مجردين من أي كبرياء. وهناك، في بهو الفندق الفخم، المتلألئ بالرخام والكريستال والمذهبات، وفي أقل من ثانيتين، أعطت زوزانا حاجبها درساً مدهشاً في التعبير. ارتفع حاجبها في مشهد جدير بالمشاهدة. تلك الانحناءة، ذلك القوس. احتقار، سخرية، احتقار ممتزج بالسخرية، ثقة، حكم، استهزاء، وحتى شفقة. كل ذلك وأكثر كان مرسوماً بوضوح في حاجبها.

وكان حاجبها يخاطب حاجب المرأة الإيطالية مباشرة، موصلاً رسالة واضحة: لم ندخل هذا المكان لنستخدم مغسلتك. لقد أخطأتِ في تقديرنا. احذري العواقب.

وقد وصلت الرسالة إلى صاحبة الحاجب، التي سرعان ما فقدت عقدة الاشمئزاز التي كانت تلوّث فمها. وحتى قبل أن يتدخل ميك قائلاً بلطف، وبنبرة شبه معتذرة، "نحن نقيم في الجناح الملكي؟"، بدأت تذوق أول نكهات الإحراج المريرة.

"الجناح... الملكي؟".

الجناح الملكي في فندق سانت ريجيس استضاف ملوكاً وأيقونات موسيقى الروك، شيوخ نفط، ومغنية الأوبرا ديفا. تكلفة الليلة الواحدة فيه تقارب العشرين ألف دولار في الأيام العادية، وهذه لم تكن أياماً عادية.

كانت روما في تلك اللحظة مركز اهتمام العالم، تعج بالحجاج والصحفيين والوفود الأجنبية والسياح الفضوليين وحتى المجانين. لم تكن هناك أي غرف شاغرة على الإطلاق. كانت العائلات تؤجر شرفاتها وأقبية منازلها—حتى أسطحها—بأسعار باهظة. أما الشرطة، المثقلة بالعمل أصلاً، فكانت بالكاد قادرة على تفريق معسكرات الحجاج في الحدائق العامة.

لم يكن لدى زوزانا وميك أدنى فكرة عن التكلفة التي ستدفعها كارو—أو جدتها المزيفة، إستير، أو أياً كان من يدفع الفاتورة. في الظروف العادية، كان هذا البذخ سيشعرهما بالحرج والتواضع، وكأنهما كانا فلاحين وسط النبلاء. وبالفعل، هذا بالضبط ما كانت تلك المرأة تتمنى أن تجعلهما يشعران به. لكن ليس اليوم.

في ضوء تجاربهما الأخيرة، كان هؤلاء الأشخاص المرفهون والمعزولون عن الواقع يذكرون زوزانا بالأحذية الفاخرة التي تبقى محفوظة في صندوقها طوال أيام السنة الثلاثمائة والاثنين والستين التي لا تُلبس فيها. مغلفة بورق حريري، آمنة من الأذى، وكل ما يعرفونه عن الحياة هو حفلات السهرة وجدران ذلك الصندوق. يا لها من حياة مملة. ويا له من غباء.

في المقابل، كان الوحل والغبار الذي غطى جسدها، وحالة فوضاها الواضحة، أشبه بدرع واقٍ بالنسبة إليها.

لقد استحققتُ هذا الوحل. احترموا الوحل.

قالت بنبرة واثقة:"بالضبط. الجناح الملكي. من المفترض أنكم كنتم تنتظروننا."

خلعت حقيبة ظهرها وألقتها على الأرض، حيث أطلقت عند ارتطامها سحابة لا بأس بها من الغبار. أضافت بتململ: "سيكون رائعاً إذا أمكنكم الاعتناء بهذا."

رفعت ذراعيها عالياً في الهواء لتُريح كتفيها، ليس لأنها كانت بحاجة إلى ذلك فعلاً، بل لأنها كانت تعرف أن هذا سيكشف عن بقع العرق التي زينت قميصها بشكل مثير للذهول. كانت هناك دوائر متداخلة مرسومة بفعل العرق المتكرر، بدت وكأنها حلقات شجر، وكانت تعني لها شيئاً عميقاً وغريباً. تلك البقع كانت شاهدة على رحلتها عبر قصة خيالية مظلمة... قصة قد لا ينجو الآخرون من مثلها.

هذا القميص لن يُغسل أبداً.

"بالطبع"، قالت المرأة، لكن صوتها كان الآن مجرد صدى باهت لصوتها السابق. كان من المضحك رؤية صراعها الداخلي وهي تحاول كبح تعابير وجهها التي أرادت بشدة أن تزم شفتيها أو تعقد حاجبيها، أو حتى أن تمنح تلك النظرة الباردة، نصف المغلقة، التي تُبدع فيها النساء الإيطاليات.

لكنها كانت مهزومة. حاجبها النازل، الذي حاول قبل دقائق الصمود في المعركة، قد عاد إلى مكانه الطبيعي، واستقر هناك، متحولاً من علامة تعجب متعجرفة إلى فاصلة متواضعة.

في غضون لحظات، كان ميك وزوزانا يرافقان إلى المصعد. صعدا إلى الأعلى. ثم شمح لهما بالسير في ممر مترف إلى حد العبث، ممر بدا وكأنه مصنوع للمبالغة في استعراض الفخامة. وأخيراً، إلى أن اجتمعا مجدداً ببقية أفراد مجموعتهما.

54

الجدّة المزيفة

لأغراض عملية، افترقوا عند مطار تشامبينو على أطراف روما، حيث هبطت الطائرة النفائة التي استأجرتها إستير.

كانت زوزانا وميك قد نزلا من الرحلة—الراكبان الوحيدان من المجموعة المُسجلان على القائمة—وعبرا خطوط الجمارك والهجرة كالبشر العاديين، بينما قام الآخرون بحيلة الاختفاء عند باب الطائرة. توجهوا مباشرة إلى الفندق وكأنهم طيور تسير على خط مستقيم، بينما استقل ميك وزوزي سيارة أجرة للّحاق بهم إلى هناك.

في غرفة المعيشة في الجناح، كانت كارو تجلس متكئة على أريكة من الحرير المطرز بنقوش زهرية بلون الليمون. أمامها، على طاولة مذهبة، خريطة لمدينة الفاتيكان، وحاسوب محمول مفتوح، ونحت شاهق من الفاكهة الطبيعية، بما في ذلك أناناس—وكأنك تستطيع ببساطة أن تلتقطه وتأخذ قضمة منه. كانت كارو تحدق في العنب بشيء من التردد، لكنها خشيت أن تلمسه كي لا تخرب ذلك العمل الفني برمته.

"خذيها إن أردتِ ذلك"، قالت جدتها المزيفة، إستير فان دي فلو، التي جلست بجانبها، تمسد بإحدى قدميها العاريتين ظهر الكلب الضخم الممدد أمامها.

لم تكن إستير، رغم ثرائها الفاحش، من ذلك النوع من النساء المسنات الثريات اللواتي يسعين للحفاظ على شبابهنّ عبر مبضع جراح، أو يلتزمن بحميات صارمة من أجل الحصول على رشاقة عظيمة ولكن بلا روح، أو يرتدين ملابس -لمصممين صارمين- أشبه بتماثيل العرض.

كانت إستير ترتدي بنطال جينز وفوقه قميص طويل حصلت عليه من سوق شعبي، وكان شعرها الأبيض مربوطاً بعقدة غير مرتبة بعض الشيء. لم تكن زاهدة، كما يبدو من مظهرها وهي تحمل في يدها الفطائر، وانحناءات جسدها تنم عن حياة لم تُحرم من متعها. شبابها—أو، بالأحرى، مظهرها الذي يوحي بسبعين عاماً، رغم أنها تجاوزت القرن الثالث عشر من عمرها— لم يكن نتيجة جراحة أو حمية، بل بفضل أمنية سحرية.

بروكسيس، تلك الأمنية الأقوى على الإطلاق، والتي تكلف ثمناً باهظاً، ولا تُمنح سوى مرة واحدة في الحياة. ومعظم تجار بريمستون كانوا ينفقون أمنيتهم تلك على شيء واحد: العمر الطويل. لم يكن معروفاً بدقة ما مدى طول ذلك العمر. كانت كارو تعرف صياداً ماليزياً قد تجاوز المئتين عندما رأته آخر مرة، ولا يزال يحتفظ بنشاطه. ويبدو أن المسألة تتعلق بالإرادة أكثر من أي شيء آخر.

غالبية الناس يسأمون من فكرة أن يعيشوا أكثر ممن حولهم. أما بالنسبة إلى إستير، فقد قالت إنها لم تعد واثقة من قدرتها على تحمل دفن المزيد من كلابها.

الجيل الحالي لا يزال فتياً وفي أوج صحته. الكلبان كانا يدعيان ترافلر ومائوسيلا، نسبة إلى اسمي حصاني الجنرالين لي وغرانت. جميع كلاب إستير الضخمة كانت تُسمى على أسماء خيول حربية. كان هذان الكلبان

الزوج السادس الذي تقتنيه، وأخيراً قررت تكريم الأمريكيين بتلك الأسماء حدّقت كارو في برج الفاكهة. "أظن أن بناء هذا الشيء استغرق ساعات."

"وقد دفعنا لهم مبلغاً جيداً مقابل مجهودهم. كُلي كُلي."

أخذت كارو بعض العنب، وشعرت بالارتياح لأن البرج لم يسقط.

"عليك أن تتعلمي الاستمتاع بالمال الآن، يا عزيزتي"، قالت إستير، وكأنها تُعدُّ كارو لتدخل هذا العالم الفاخر، وهي بمثابة دليلها فيه. إلى جانب الخدمات الأخرى التي قدمتها إستير لصالح بريمستون فيما يخص كارو عبر السنين—مثل تسجيلها في المدارس وتزوير وثائق الهوية لها وما إلى ذلك—لعبت دوراً محورياً في إنشاء العديد من حساباتها البنكية، ومن المؤكد أنها تعرف صافي ثروة كارو أكثر مما تعرفه كارو نفسها الدرس الأول: نحن لا نقلق بشأن كيفية بناء منحوتات الفاكهة. نحن فقط نأكلها.

قالت كارو: "في الواقع، لن أضطر إلى التعلم، لأنني لن أبقى هنا".

نظرت إستير حولها في الغرفة. "ألا يعجبك فندق سانت ريجيس؟".

تبعت كارو نظرتها. المكان كان هجوماً على الحواس، وكأن المصمم تلقى تعليمات بتجسيد مفهوم "البذخ" في مساحة من أربعمئة أو خمسمئة قدم مربعة. سقف عالٍ مع قوالب ذهبية منقوشة. ستائر مخملية حمراء، مكانها الطبيعي ربما غرفة نوم مصاص دماء. كل شيء مذهّب. بيانو كبير مع أطباق فضية مكدسة بالبسكويت فوق غطائه اللامع. وعلى الحائط، علّقت لوحة جدارية ضخمة لملك راكع يتم تتويجه "في الواقع، لا. وأعترف بذلك، ولكنني أقصد الأرض. لن أبقى هنا."

قامت إستير بإغماض عينيها ببطء. ربما لتأخذ لحظة وتتخيل كيف يمكن أن يترك المرء ثروة بحجم ثروة كارو. "حقاً؟ حسناً. بالنظر إلى قطعة الجنة الموجودة هناك"—وأومأت برأسها نحو الغرفة المجاورة—"لا ألومك."

كانت إستير... مُعجبة بأكيفا. "يا إلهي"، همست عندما قدّمته كارو إليها.

والآن قالت:"لا أعرف بالضبط، ولكن أعتقد أن المرء قد يتخلى عن أشياء كثيرة من أجل الحب."

لم تقل كارو شيئاً عن الحب، لكنها لم تُفاجأ من كونه واضحاً."لا أشعر أنني أتخلى عن شيء"، قالت بصدق. حياتها في براغ باتت بعيدة كأنها حلم. كانت تعلم أن هناك أياماً ستفتقد فيها للأرض، لكن في الوقت الحالي، كان عقلها وقلبها مكرّسين بالكامل لشؤون المملكة، حاضرها الغامض— يا نيتيد، ويا نجوم السماء، أو أي أحد منكما، أرجوكم احموا أصدقاءنا— ومستقبلها الهش. نعم، كما أشارت إستير، كان أكيفا جزءاً كبيراً من كل ذلك

قالت إستير:"حسناً. يمكنكِ الاستمتاع بالثراء الآن على الأقل. أخبريني، ألم يكن الحمام رائعاً؟".

وافقتها كارو الرأي. الحمام كان أكبر من شقتها بأكملها في براغ، وكل شبر فيه كان من الرخام. كانت قد خرجت للتوّ، وشعرها الرطب والمعطر ينسدل على كتفيها.

تناولت الخريطة، وفردتها على الأريكة بينهما."إذاً، أين يقيم الملائكة؟".

كانت خطة كارو في النهاية بسيطة جداً، لذا لم تكن بحاجة إلى الكثير من المعلومات سوى تحديد مكان جايل. مدينة الفاتيكان قد تكون صغيرة مقارنة بالدول ذات السيادة، لكنها قد تتحول إلى كابوس من البحث العشوائي إذا بدأت تتنقل بين الغرف بلا خطة.

أشارت إستير بظفرها المقضوم نحو القصر البابوي."هنا، إنه بقمة الترف". كانت تعرف أي النوافذ تمنح أقرب وصول إلى قاعة كليمنتينا، قاعة الاستقبال الفاخرة التي مُنحت لجايل لاستخدامه الشخصي، كما كانت تعرف مواقع الحراس المحتملة، سواء حرس الفاتيكان السويسري أو فرقة الملائكة الخاصة.

سحبت إصبعها بعد ذلك نحو متحف الفاتيكان، حيث كان الجزء الأكبر من الجنود يقيمون في جناح مخصص للتماثيل القديمة، المكان نفسه الذي

أمضت فيه كارو ذات يوم حياةً عادية، بعد ظهرٍ كاملٍ في رسم الاسكتشات قالت كارو:"شكراً، هذا مفيد جداً".

بالطبع، قالت إستير وهي تسترخي على الأريكة المذهبة المزعجة."أي شيء لأجل حفيدتي المفضلة، حتى لو كانت مزيفة. والآن أخبريني، كيف حال بريمستون؟ ومتى سعيد فتح البوابات؟ حقاً أفتقد ذلك الوحش العجوز."

وأنا أيضاً، سرحت كارو بفكرها، وشعرت ببرودة تجتاح قلبها. كانت تهاب هذه اللحظة منذ بداية الرحلة إلى هنا. على الهاتف، لم تستطع أن تخبرها بالحقيقة. كانت طريقة استقبال إستير لها غير متوقعة تماماً—"شكراً للسماء! أين كنتِ يا طفلة؟ كنت قلقة عليكِ جداً. شهور كاملة بدون أي خبر منكِ. كيف لم تفكري في الاتصال بي؟" مما أربك كارو. بدت وكأنها جدة حقيقية، أو على الأقل كما تخيلت كارو أن تكون الجدة الحقيقية: عاطفة تتدفق دون حساب. بينما كانت إستير سابقاً دائماً تُبدي مشاعرها كأنها تصرف مصروفاً، بجدول زمني وبتردد.

قررت كارو أن تخبرها بالحقيقة الصعبة وجهاً لوجه، لكن الآن وقد حان الوقت، لم تجد الكلمات المناسبة طريقها إلى لسانها. لقد.. مات.

كانت هناك مذبحة. وقد... مات.

كان الطرق على الباب في تلك اللحظة أشبه بتدخل العناية الإلهية. قفزت كارو على قدميها."ميك وزوزي"، قالت وهرعت نحو الباب. كان الجناح كبيراً جداً إلى درجة أنه عليك فعلاً الركض لتصل إلى الباب في الوقت المناسب. وحين وصلت، فتحته على الفور.

"ما الذي أخركما؟" سألت وهي تضم صديقيها في عناق دافئ لكنه ممزوج ببعض الرائحة الكريهة. رائحتهما، وليس رائحتها.

ساعتان للوصول من المطار إلى هنا! قال ميك وهو يهز رأسه:"هذه المدينة مجنونة."

كانت كارو تعرف ذلك جيداً. فقد أُتيحت لها رؤية منظر المدينة من الجو، حيث شاهدت الدائرة الضخمة والنابضة بالبشر الذين احتشدوا حول محيط الفاتيكان المغلق. حتى من الجو، تمكنت من سماع هتافاتهم، لكنها لم تستطع تمييز الكلمات. من الأعلى، بدا لها المشهد مقلقاً، يشبه إلى حد بعيد الطريقة التي يحاصر بها الزومبي في الأفلام حدود تجمعات البشر، محاولين اقتحامها. أما بقية المدينة، فعلى الرغم من أنها لم تكن"زومبية" تماماً، لكنها أوشكت أن تكون.

قالت:"آمل على الأقل أن تكونا قد أخذتما غفوة في سيارة الأجرة".

الجميع قد نالوا بضع ساعات من النوم أثناء الرحلة الجوية فقد كانوا بحاجة ماسة إليه. استندت كارو برأسها على كتف أكيفا، وانجرفت في ذكريات جسده العاري وهو بجانبها. بدت أحلامها... أكثر إنعاشاً من أن تكون مهدئة.

ردّت زوزانا:"نمنا قليلاً. لكن ما أريده حقاً الآن هو حمام."

تراجعت خطوة إلى الوراء وألقت نظرة سريعة على كارو."انظري إلى نفسكِ! ساعتان فقط في إيطاليا وأصبحتِ أيقونة للموضة. كيف حصلتِ على ملابس جديدة بهذه السرعة؟".

"هذا ما يحدث هنا" ثم قادتهم كارو إلى الداخل."عندما تصلين إلى هاواي، يقدمون أطواق الزهور. أما في إيطاليا، فيقدمون الملابس المثالية والأحذية الجلدية."

"حسناً، يبدو أن الذين يقدمون الملابس كانوا في استراحة عندما وصلنا"، ردت زوزانا، مشيرة إلى نفسها."أرعبنا بهيئتنا كل من كانوا في البهو."

"يا إلهي." شعرت كارو بالحرج بمجرد تخيل الموقف."هل كان الأمر سيئاً؟".

لم تمر كارو بهذا الموقف بفضل وصولها متخفية عن طريق السماء والشرفة، وليس عبر الشارع والبهو.

قال ميك:"زوزي كانت تخوض معركة مع نظراتهم."

رفعت زوزانا حاجبها بتحدٍّ."عليكِ أن تري هذا الآخر."

"ليس لدي أي شك"، قالت كارو بابتسامة."إستير اشترت لنا جميعاً ملابس جديدة."

وأثناء كلامها، دخلوا إلى غرفة المعيشة.

"في الواقع، لقد أرسلت من يتسوق لنا"، قالت إستير بلكنتها الفلمنكية الموسيقية."آمل أن تناسبكم الملابس جميعاً."

نهضت وتقدمت إلى الأمام."سمعت الكثير عنكِ، يا عزيزتي"، قالت بحرارة، وهي تمد يديها لتحتضن يدي زوزانا بين يديها. في تلك اللحظة، بدت الجدة تماماً كما تخيلتها.

لكن إستير فان دي ڤلو لم تكن جدة أحد. لم يكن لديها أطفال، كما أنها تفتقر إلى أي غريزة أمومة تقريباً. إنما لعبت دور"الجدة" أكثر كحليف سياسي لكارو منه كعلاقة عاطفية.

في حياتها، ساعدت هذه المرأة العجوز في نقل عدد لا يحصى من الألماس إلى أيدي الأثرياء الفاحشين، وكذلك إلى يدي بريمستون، دون أن تخشى التعامل مع البشر وغير البشر على حد سواء—بل وحتى مع"تحت البشر"، كما كانت تسمي أكثر تجار بريمستون خبثاً، والذين حافظت معهم على شبكة معلومات عالمية.

كانت تسافر بين الدوائر النخبوية وكذلك العالم السفلي—وقد أخبرت كارو في مكالمة هاتفية أنها تملك كاردينالاً في جيبها وتاجر أسلحة في الجيب الآخر، ولا شك أن لديها جيوباً أخرى.

وكانت مقدّرة كشخصية شبه أسطورية، أولاً بسبب حفاظها الغامض على شبابها—وكان يسعدها سماع شائعة أنها باعت روحها للخلود— وكذلك بفضل بعض الخدمات المستحيلة التي زُعم أنها أدتها لأشخاص في مناصب عليا.

"هذا مستحيل، إلا إذا كنتِ تمتلكين القدرة على الوصول إلى السحر."

قالت زوزانا:"سمعتُ الكثير عنكِ أيضاً"، ورأت كارو اللمعان في عيني صديقتها، ذلك اللمعان الذي قد يكون إما نظرة مصارع ثيران يُقيّم الثور أو نظرة ثور يُقيّم المصارع. لم تكن متأكدة أيهما، لكن إستير كانت تمتلك نفس اللمعان أيضاً. النظرة التي تبادلتها المرأتان كانت مليئة بالاحترام المتبادل بين خصمين جديرين. كارو شعرت بالامتنان لأنهما لم تكونا خصمين بمعنى الكلمة، بل كانتا في صفها.

تبادل الجميع بضع كلمات صغيرة. حجم الكلاب. خدمة الغرف. حال مدينة روما. والملائكة.

لكن عندما قالت إستير:"أنا فقط سعيدة لأن كارو كانت ذكية بما يكفي لتأتي إليّ"، تغيّرت ملامح زوزانا قليلاً، حيث ظهر في وجهها غضب مكتوم جعلها تبدو كثور أمام المصارع.

قالت زوزانا، بنبرة عادية تخفي تحتها بعض اللوم:"لقد جاءت إليكِ من قبل."

عرفت كارو ما كانت زوزانا تحاول الإشارة إليه، فحاولت التدخل:"زوزي—" وقبل أن تكمل قاطعتها صديقتها."ودائماً كنتُ أتساءل منذ ذلك الحين. عندما جاءت كارو إليكِ للحصول على الأمنيات..." أمالت زوزانا رأسها ورمقت المرأة الأكبر سناً بنظرة تقول:"لنكن صريحين. أنتِ أخفيتِ عنها شيئاً، أليس كذلك؟".

تلاشت ابتسامة إستير على الفور، وأصبحت ملامحها سلسة، وكأنها ترتدي قناعاً من الحذر، ولا تبدو كجدّة ودودة الآن.

"لا يا زوزي"، قالت كارو وهي تضع يدها على ظهر صديقتها. وقد خاضتا هذا النقاش من قبل."لم تفعل ذلك. لن تفعل ذلك."

عندما أُحرقت البوابات الشتاء الماضي، وكانت كارو يائسة للعثور على عائلتها من الكيميرا—ويائسة للحصول على أمنيات غافرييل التي يمكن أن

تحملها هي ورازغوت عبر بوابة السماء إلى إريتز—ذهبت إلى إستير أولاً. وقالت إستير إنها لا تملك أمنيات أقوى من لاكناو، وصدقتها كارو، لأنه لا داعي لتكذب عليها؟

لكن إستير قالت الآن، بصوت جاد ومليء بشيء من الندم:"لقد فعلت." حدّقت كارو فيها متسائلة، إن كانت تعني أنها أخفت شيئاً عنها؟"ماذا؟" سألت بارتباك.

"حسناً، آسفة لأن أقول ذلك، يا عزيزتي، بالطبع. لكنني لم أعتقد حقاً أنكِ ستكتشفين ذلك. أنا امرأة عجوز جشعة. إذا كانت تلك آخر الأمنيات التي سأحصل عليها في حياتي، كان عليّ أن أحافظ عليها، أليس كذلك؟ لا أستطيع أن أشرح لكِ كم أنا سعيدة لأنني كنت مخطئة."

شعرت كارو بمعدتها تنقلب وقالت لها"لا لم تكوني مخطئة".

أمالت إستير رأسها، غير مستوعبة."لم أكن ماذا؟".

"لم تكوني مخطئة. أعني أنني لم أجد بريمستون. لأنه قد مات." قالت كارو هذه الكلمات بأريحية، بدون أي عاطفة في صوتها، وراقبت وجه إستير وهو يفقد لونه تماماً.

"لا. أوه، لا. لا." تمتمت إستير، ويدها ترتفع إلى فمها. "أوه، كارو. لم أكن أريد تصديق ذلك. "ثم امتلأت عيناها بالدموع.

سألت زوزانا:"ألم تخبريها بعد؟".

هزت كارو رأسها. وهكذا تخلصت من فكرة أن تخبرها بلطف فقد كذبت إستير عليها. عندما أُحرقت البوابات ولم تكن تعرف شيئاً، عندما كانت منهكة ومصابة بعد مواجهات كادت تودي بحياتها مع أكيفا وثياغو، ومعاملة بريمستون القاسية التي لم تخفف عنها، لجأت إلى إستير طلباً للمساعدة. وقد كانت في أسوأ حالاتها تلك اللحظة، رغم أنها لم تكن تعلم آنذاك أن الأمور ستزداد سوءاً بشكل لا يمكن تصوره خلال الأشهر التالية. وثقت بإستير، لتكتشف الآن أنها كذبت عليها وجهاً لوجه.

ومع ذلك، بدت إستير متأثرة حقاً، وشعرت كارو بوخزة صغيرة من الندم لأنها أبلغتها الخبر بتلك القسوة.

"إيسّا بخير"، قالت كارو، محاولة تخفيف الصدمة، وأتبعت كلامها بدعاء صامت أن يكون ذلك صحيحاً.

"أنا سعيدة لسماع ذلك."

كان صوت إستير يرتجف. "وماذا عن ياسري؟ وتويغا؟".

بعد سؤالها هذا، لا يمكن التخفيف عنها. فتويغا مات، وياسري أيضاً، رغم أن مصير روحها مثل روح إيسّا، فقد تم الاحتفاظ بها حتى تجدها كارو—أمل آخر محفوظ داخل مبخرة، كرسالة بالغة الأهمية من بريمستون. لم تكن كارو قادرة بعد على استعادة مبخرة ياسري، لكنها كانت تعرف مكانها: في أنقاض معبد إيلاي، حيث قضت هي وأكيفا شهراً من الليالي الحلوة، في حياة سابقة وكأنها من زمن آخر.

اكتفت بهزة رأس صغيرة نحو إستير. لم تكن مستعدة للخوض في موضوع إحياء الأرواح. فإستير لم تكن تعرف عن عظمة الأمنيات وعن استخدام بريمستون للأسنان—والأحجار الكريمة التي كانت جزءاً من تجارتها معه—ولم تكن كارو مستعدة للإفصاح عن أي شيء الآن.

"الكثيرون ماتوا"، قالت كارو، في محاولة فاشلة لكتم العاطفة التي ارتفعت في صوتها. "والكثيرون سيموتون إذا لم نوقف هؤلاء الملائكة ونغلق البوابة."

سألت إستير: "وهل تعتقدين أنكِ قادرة على ذلك؟".

آمل ذلك، فكرت كارو، لكنها قالت ببساطة: نعم.

تحدثت زوزانا مرة أخرى، وبغض النظر عمّا إذا كانت تشعر كمصارع ثيران أم ثوراً، إلا أن نظرتها ثابتة، مركزة ومليئة بالعزم. "بعض تلك الأمنيات سيكون مرحباً بها الآن."

"أوه، حسناً"، قالت إستير بارتباك. "الآن لم يتبق لدي أي أمنيات على

الإطلاق. أنا آسفة جداً. لو كنت أعلم فقط، لكنت قد احتفظت بها بشكل أفضل. أوه، يا عزيزتي المسكينة"، أضافت وهي تمسك بيد كارو بحنان.

"آه-هاه"، كان هذا كل ما قالته وهي تمط شفتيها.

ربما قليلاً من اللباقة الاجتماعية كما شعر ميك، كانت ضرورية لكبح تصرف زوزانا الواضح بهذا الشكل، فقال بارتباك:"حسناً، شكراً على، اممم... الطائرة النفاثة. والفندق وكل شيء."

"على الرحب والسعة"، ردت إستر، وشعرت كارو أن الوقت قد حان لإنهاء مراسم التعارف والمجاملات—وحتى التعليقات غير المرحب بها. فهناك عمل ينبغي إنجازه. التفتت إلى أصدقائها وقالت:"الحمام في آخر الرواق. ليس سيئاً جداً. الملابس في غرفة النوم الكبيرة. استمتعوا باللعب في تبديل الأزياء."

عبست زوزانا، وتجعد جبينها."والآخرون؟" ترددت قبل أن تضيف:"إليزا؟ هل أصبحت... أفضل حالاً؟".

تسلل توتر جديد إلى ذهن كارو. ماذا يمكنها أن تقول عن إليزا؟ إليزا جونز. يا لها من قصة غريبة. لم يعرفوا اسمها إلا بسبب بطاقة الهوية التي كانت بحوزتها، وليس لأنها أرادت الإفصاح عنه. ومن هناك، قادهم بحث سريع على غوغل إلى نتائج مذهلة: إلازيل، من نسل ملاك.

رغم أن الأمر بدا جنونياً—النوع من الأشياء التي كانت زوزانا ستصنع له يوماً قميصاً ساخراً في الماضي—إلا أن حقيقة تحدثها بطلاقة بلغة السيرافيم أضفت مصداقية لا يمكن إنكارها على القصة.

أما الكلمات التي تفوهت بها بلغة السيرافيم، فكانت مثيرة للقشعريرة، وانسابت منها وكأنها في حالة انسلاخ عن الواقع. وبالنسبة إلى سؤال زوزانا: هل أصبحت أفضل حالاً؟ لم تكن كارو تعرف كيف تجيب. كانت قد حاولت، وهي في المغرب، أن تستخدم موهبتها الخاصة في الشفاء لمساعدتها، ولكن كيف يمكنها ذلك وهي حتى لا تستطيع أن تلمح ما هو مكسور؟

كان أكيفا يحاول الآن بطريقته الخاصة، ما بعث في كارو بعض الأمل وهي تقود أصدقائها نحو باب غرفة الجلوس، متمنية أن تفتحه، فتجد أكيفا وإليزا جالسين معاً، غارقين في حديث عميق.

قالت وهي تمسك بمقبض الباب:"إنهما هنا". ثم التفتت إلى إستر وبذلت جهداً لتبتسم. كانت تكره التوتر، وتمنت، ليس للمرة الأولى، لو أن إستر كانت أكثر دفئاً. لكنها كانت تعلم، كما كانت تعلم دائماً، أن كل مرة تصرفت فيها إستر لمصلحتها—بما في ذلك السنة التي اصطحبتها فيها إلى منزلها في أنتويرب لقضاء عيد الميلاد، وصنعت غرفة معيشة تبدو كأنها من مجلة مليئة بالهدايا، بما في ذلك حصان خشبي خيالي منحوت يدوياً— عوضها عما مرت به.

لم تكن علاقة صداقة، أو شؤون عائلية، إنما عمل، ولا مكان فيه للابتسامات لكنها ابتسمت على أي حال، وردت على إستر بابتسامة أيضاً. كان في عينيها حزن، ربما ندم، وربما حتى توبة، ولاحقاً ستتذكر كارو أنها اعتبرت ذلك: حسناً، شيء ما على الأقل.

وكان كذلك.

لكن ليس كما ظنت.

55

شاعري مجنون

انحدر أكيڤا، مراراً وتكراراً، إلى مستويات مظلمة في عقله، إلى ذلك المكان حيث مصدر السحر. ومع ذلك، لم يقترب أكثر من فهم ماهيته— هل هو داخلي أم خارجي؟ أهو عميق؟ أو هو بعيد؟

حواسه تلك ليست كافية، لكنه قريب نسبياً من المرور عبر باب سري إلى عالم آخر. ومع كل مرة دفع فيها نفسه أبعد فأبعد، دون أن يلتقي بأي حدود، بدأ يتخيل امتداداً أشبه بالمحيط اللامتناهي، ثم أدرك أن حتى ذلك لم يكن مرضياً. الفضاء واللامحدود.

كان يؤمن بأنها ملكه، بأنها تشكل ذاته، لكنه بدا وكأنه يمتد إلى الأبد— كون خاص به، بُعد لانهائي يتجاوز فكرة "العقل" التي طالما حملها في ذهنه، تلك الفكرة عن الأفكار التي توجد ضمن نطاق رأسه، كنتيجة لوظائف دماغه ما مدى عظمة العقل؟ الروح؟ النفس؟ وإذا لم يكن لها ارتباط فعلي بالحجم الفيزيائي الذي يشغله جسده، فأين تكون؟

شعر بدوران رأسه من هذا التفكير. في كل مرة يخرج من ذلك المكان، يشعر بالتوهان والتعب، وكان الإحباط من جهله ينهشه.

وكان ذلك قبل أن يحاول الدخول إلى عقل شخص آخر.

عندما وقف عند عتبات عقل إليزا، أحس بوجود باب سري آخر، وعالم آخر واسع بامتداد عالمه الخاص، ولكنه مغاير تماماً.

الأبعاد اللامتناهية ليست مكاناً للعبث أو الاستكشاف العابر. بإمكانك أن تسقط وتستمر في السقوط. بإمكانك أن تضيع. وقد ضاعت هي. فهل يمكنه أن يسحبها للخروج؟ أراد المحاولة. من أجلها، لأن فكرة العجز المطلق كانت تثير اشمئزازه، وأراد أن ينقذها منه. ومن أجله أيضاً، بسبب تيار اللغة المستمر الذي لم ينقطع منها، والمليء بالرجاء والحزن. كانت لغته، غريبة وأليفة في آنٍ واحد—السيرافيمية، لكنها منطوقة بنغمات وأنماط لم يسمع بها من قبل.

و... يا نجوم السماء، تلك الأشياء التي كانت تقولها...

وحوش وسماء تسودّ، فاتحو الأبواب والأنوار في الظلام.

مختارون. ساقطون.

أمامي خرائط، لكنني تائه. في سماوات ميتة.

يا لها من كارثة.

ميليز."الشاعرية المجنونة" هكذا لقبتها زوزانا، وبالفعل هي كذلك: شاعرية وجنونية. لكن هذا لامس وتراً داخلياً في أعماق أكيفا، وكأن إيقاعه قد ضبط على نفس التردد الخاص به. كان يعني شيئاً، شيئاً مهماً، ولهذا عبر من لانهائيته إلى لانهائيتها. لم يكن يعرف ما إذا كان هذا ممكناً—أو، إن كان ممكناً، وإن كان يجب عليه القيام به. شعر وكأنه يعبر حدوداً محرمة.

كانت هناك مقاومة، لكنه اخترقها. بحث عنها، لكنه لم يجدها. ناداها، لكنها لم تجب. الفراغ من حوله كان مختلفاً عن عالمه الخاص. كان كثيفاً ومعتماً. متحركاً، مؤلماً، قلقاً، وخائفاً.

شعر بخطأ ومعاناة في ذلك المكان، وقد تجاوز الأمر حدود فهمه. فلم يجرؤ على الذهاب أعمق. لم يستطع العثور عليها. لم يستطع إخراجها. لم

يستطع. لكنه حاول، وقدم ألمَه قرباناً، على أمل أن يهدئ فوضاها ولو قليلاً وعندما عاد وفتح عينيه، شعر كأنه يستعيد نفسه. رأى أن كارو موجودة، ومعها زوزانا وميك. فيركو أيضاً، رغم أن الكيميرا كان موجوداً طوال الوقت. وأمامهم مباشرة، إليزا التي بدت أكثر هدوءاً، لكن أكيڤا رأى بعينيه ما أدركه بالفعل في قلبه: بأنه لم يتمكن من إصلاحها.

أطلق زفرة خيبة عميقة وكأنها شعور بالخسارة.

اقتربت كارو منه. وهي تحمل قارورة ماء، وسكبت له كوباً. وأثناء شربه، وضعت يدها الباردة على جبينه واتكأت على ذراع كرسيه، ولامس وركها كتفه. وكان هذا مستوى جديداً رائعاً وأكثر من العادي—أن تميل كارو عليه بهذه العفوية—وقد رفع ذلك من معنوياته.

لقد تحدثت من قبل عن السعادة وكأنها حقيقة لا يمكن إنكارها، بغض النظر عما يحدث—شيء منفصل عن كل شيء آخر وغير مرتبط به. كانت فكرة جديدة بالنسبة إليه، أن السعادة ليست مكاناً سحرياً للوصول إليه أو الفوز به—أرض مشرقة وراء حدود البؤس، جنة تنتظر العثور عليها— بل شيئاً نحمله بإصرار معنا عبر كل شيء، بسيطاً وعادياً مثل معداتنا وإمداداتنا: طعام، أسلحة، وسعادة.

مع أمل أن تختفي الأسلحة من الصورة في وقت ما.

طريقة جديدة للعيش. قالت كارو، وهي تتأمل إليزا: "تبدو أكثر هدوءاً على الأقل، لكن هذا ليس كافياً."

لم تقل له: "يمكنك المحاولة لاحقاً"، لأن كليهما كان يعرف أنه ليس هناك لاحقاً. فالليل يقترب، وسيرحلون—هو وكارو وفيركو—قريباً جداً، ولن يعودوا إلى هنا.

إليزا جونز، إذاً، ستظل تائهة، ومعها الـ"كارثة" وكل أسرارها. لكن المشكلة أن أكيڤا شعر بخطر في ترك الأمر يمضي هكذا.

قال: "أريد أن أفهم ما تقوله. ما الذي حدث لها".

"هل تمكنتَ من معرفة أي شيء؟".

"فوضى. خوف". هزّ رأسه. لا أعرف شيئاً عن السحر يا كارو، حتى مبادئه الأساسية غائبة عني. لدي إحساس بأن لكل واحد منا-". توقف باحثاً عن الكلمات." خريطة من الطاقات. لا أعلم كيف أصفها. إنها أبعد من العقل، وأعمق من الروح. أبعادها-" فكر قليلاً"جغرافيا. لكنني لا أعرف تضاريسها، ولا كيفية التنقل عبرها، أو حتى رؤيتها. الأمر أشبه بالسير في عتمة حالكة."

ابتسمت ابتسامة خفيفة، وامتزج صوتها بخفة مصطنعة وهي تسأله:"كيف لك أن تعرف ما العتمة؟". مرّرت يدها على ريشه، فانبثقت منه شرارات عند ملامستها،"أنت نورك الخاص."

كاد أكيفا أن يقول: أعرف ما هي العتمة، لأنه بالفعل يعرفها بأسوأ معانيها، لكنه لم يرد أن تظن كارو أنه عاد إلى حالة اليأس التي كانت قد انتشلته منها في المغرب. لذا كتم كلماته، وحمد الله أنه فعل، لأن كارو أضافت، بصوت خافت يكاد لا يُسمع:"وأنت نوري أيضاً."

نظر إليها، وغمره حضورها، كما كان يحدث له دائماً حين يكون بقربها— مع ماضيها كمادريغال وحاضرها ككارو—شعور بالحياة الجديدة، والنمو الذي ينبثق من الداخل. مشاعر وأحاسيس لم يعرفها قبلها، ولم يكن ليعرفها أبداً بدونها. كانت هذه المشاعر حقيقية، أشبه بجذور تتفرع وتمتد، متجاوزة كل الأبواب السرية، ومتسللة عبر كل مستويات الظلام. وما أسماه بـ"خريطة الطاقات" التي ذكرها، تلك الأبعاد والجغرافيا الغامضة للذات، تغيّرت بوجودها. كأن ركناً مظلماً في الفضاء انبثق فيه نجم جديد. أكيفا أصبح أكثر إشراقاً وأكثر اكتمالاً.

وحده الحب يمكنه فعل ذلك. أمسك يد كارو الصغيرة والباردة، بيده، وتمسك بها كما تمسك بنظرة عينيها. كانت السعادة هناك، شعوراً عادياً لكنه متأصل، متداخل مع القلق والحزن والعزيمة. لم يكن الحب يحل أي مشكلة، لكنه جعلها أخف وطأة.

سألها:"هل أنت جاهزة؟".

لقد حان الوقت للذهاب لرؤية عمّه.

...

ودّعوا بعضهم دون أن يقولوا كلمة"وداعاً"، لأن أكيفا أخبرهم أنها كلمة تجلب الحظ السيئ، كأنها تستفز القدر. مهما كانت الكلمات التي استخدموها، فقد خيّم ظل من الحزن يخيم عليهم جميعاً، لأن هذه لن تكون فراقاً قصيراً.

في آخر دروس اللغة التي سيقدمها ڤيركو لبعض الوقت، علّم زوزانا كيف تقول:"أُقبّل عينيك وأترك قلبي بين يديك"، وهي جملة وداع قديمة عند الكيميرا، بالطبع انتهى الأمر بزوزانا وهي تقلّد رد فعل مبالغ فيه وكأن قلباً نابضاً وُضع بين يديها. حرصت إستر على تجهيزهم، عادت إلى دور الجدّة الحنون، وكان هناك شيء أشبه بالاعتذار في تصرفاتها. تأكدت من أن الخريطة بحوزتهم، وأنهم يعرفون الطريق. سألتهم بقلق عمّا ينوون فعله أمام هذا العدد الكبير من الأعداء، لكن كارو لم تخبرها شيئاً. كانت إجابتها:"ليس الكثير، فقط إقناعهم بالعودة إلى ديارهم."

بدا القلق على وجه إستر، لكنها لم تُلح. قالت بحذر:"سأطلب زجاجة شمبانيا". ثم أردفت: للاحتفال بانتصاركم. أتمنى فقط أن تكونوا هنا لتشربوه معنا".

طوال ذلك الوقت، كانت إليزا جالسة تحدق بصمت. سألت كارو ميك وزوزانا:"هل ستتأكدان من حصولها على المساعدة؟ بعد رحيلنا؟".

تصلّبت ملامح زوزانا فجأة، وابتعدت نظرتها عن عيني كارو، لكن ميك أومأ برأسه. قائلاً:"لا تقلقي، فلديك ما يكفي لتقلقي بشأنه."

أدرك أنه حتى لو لم تفهم زوزانا سبب ضرورة الأمور أن تكون على هذا النحو، فقد ذكّرها بنفسه بذلك، مرات عدة، في الطريق إلى هنا."تذكري كيف أننا لسنا ساموراي، بكل بساطة، ولا يمكننا المساعدة في هذا.

سنكون عبئاً على ڤيركو فقط وسنعوّقه. وإذا حدث المزيد من القتال...".
لم يكمل جملته.

"شكراً". قالت كارو مع نظرة أخيرة يائسة ألقتها على إليزا."أعلم أنني
أترك الكثير بين أيديكما، لكنني أريتكما كيفية الوصول إلى المال. أرجوكما،
استخدماه. لأجلها، لأجلكما. لأي شيء تحتاجانه".

"المال"، تمتمت زوزانا وكأن الفكرة نفسها، إهانة.

استدارت إليها كارو."إذا كان هناك أي شيء يُمكن العودة إليه..." -إنها
تكره كلمة"إذا" وكأنها عدوها اللدود-"...سأجد طريقة لأعود وأحضركما".

"وكيف ستفعلين ذلك؟ ستغلقين البوابة".

"علينا ذلك، لكن هناك بوابات أخرى. سأجدها".

"وما الذي يجعلك تظنين أنك ستجدين الوقت للبحث عن بوابات؟".

"لا أعلم"، كان هذا هو الجواب المعتاد."لا أعلم ماذا سنجد عند عودتنا.
لا أعلم إن كان هناك أملٌ متبقٍ يمكننا العمل معه في هذا العالم. لا أعلم
كيف سأجد بوابة أخرى. لا أعلم إن كنت سأبقى على قيد الحياة. لا أعلم".

ظلت ملامح زوزانا القاسية بلا تغيير، ثم مالت برأسها إلى الأمام في حركة
بطيئة أشبه بصدام خفيف، لم تدركه كارو على أنه عناق حتى اللحظة الأخيرة،
حينما أحاطتها ذراعا صديقتها."كوني بخير"، همست زوزانا."لا بطولات. إذا
اضطررتِ لإنقاذ نفسك، افعليها وعودي إلينا. أنتِ وأكيڤا وڤيركو. يمكننا أن
نصنع لجسده جسداً بشرياً أو أي شيء. فقط عديني، إذا وصلتِ إلى هناك
ووجدتِ الجميع..."، لم تكمل الجملة."أمواتاً. فقط ابقي بعيدة عن الأنظار،
وعودي إلينا هنا حيّة".

لم تستطع كارو أن تقدم هذا الوعد، كما كانت زوزانا تعلم، لأنها لم
تمنحها الفرصة لتجيب، بل تابعت كلامها قائلة:"جيد. شكراً. هذا كل ما
أردت سماعه"، وكأنها سمعت وعداً بالفعل. بادلتها كارو العناق. ولطالما
كرهت الوداع كما كرهت كلمة"إذا". ولم يتبقَّ سوى الرحيل.

56

حبيبتي البربرية

حان وقت النظافة. تداور ميك وزوزانا على استخدام الحمام، حيث بقي أحدهما دائماً إلى جانب إليزا، بينما يراقب أي أخبار تتعلق بالملائكة. كان صوت التلفاز منخفضاً، بينما ظل جهاز اللابتوب الخاص بإستير مفتوحاً على عدة مواقع يتم تحديثها باستمرار. لكن حتى الآن، لم يحدث شيء، ولن يكون هناك جديد على الأرجح لبعض الوقت.

علمت زوزانا أن كارو تنوي القيام بتوقف قصير قبل التوجه إلى الفاتيكان: متحف التاريخ الطبيعي"متحف الحيوانات في روما". كان لديها إصرار هادئ يشع من عينيها عندما أعلنت نيتها للذهاب إلى هناك. لقد انكسر قلب زوزانا نصفين عندما أدركت السبب وراء هذا القرار—لتجديد مخزونها من الأسنان، تحسباً لوجود أرواح تم إنقاذها على الأقل خلال المعركة. ومع ذلك، ظل شعور العجز ينهشها، وهي تدرك أنها لن تكون هناك لتساعد كارو فيما قد يعثرون عليه عندما عودتهم إلى المملكة. ذلك الشعور المقيت بالعجز. أحست زوزانا بأن فكرة تصميم جديد لقميص قد بدأت تتبلور. فليكن ساموراي.

لأنك ببساطة لن تعرف أبداً ما ينتظرك خلف هذه السماء اللعينة.

لم يكن أحد يفهم تلك الفكرة، لكن من يهتم؟ اكتفت زوزانا بالتحديق فيهم حتى يشعروا بالإحراج ويبتعدوا. لا. قالت موبخةً نفسها. هذا ليس صحيحاً. لأنه لو كان كذلك، لما كان هناك حاجة لأن تكون ساموراي.

نظرت إلى إليزا الجالسة بجانبها وتنهدت. لم تكن إليزا تبدو وكأنها تحتاج إلى صحبة، أو حتى تدرك وجودها، لكن فكرة تركها وحدها في الزاوية كقطعة أثاث لم توضع بعناية، وتتمتم وبالكاد تسمع. لم تكن زوزانا ممرضة، ولا تملك هذه الغريزة، لكنها تدرك تماماً بأن إليزا تحتاج إلى من يعتني بأبسط احتياجاتها الإنسانية—طعام، ماء، وبداية جديدة على الأقل. لكنها أكثر هدوءاً الآن، بالرغم من كل ما فعله أكيڤا. أقل توتراً الآن، وهذا جعل الأمور أسهل قليلاً.

أما ما سيفعلونه بها بعد هذا اليوم، فلم تكن زوزانا مستعدة للتفكير فيه. يمكن تأجيله إلى الغد، حين تكون كل توترات اليوم جزءاً من الماضي، وبعد أن يحصلوا على نوم عميق في سرير حقيقي ووجبة لم تكن حتى قريبة من الكسكسي المغربية.

أما الآن، فقد كانت النظافة بحد ذاتها إنجازاً. شعور أشبه بولادة جديدة— فينوس تنهض من طبقة من القذارة. الملابس التي اختارتها متسوقة إستير كانت أنيقة وبسيطة، مصنوعة من مواد فاخرة وبقياس يكاد يكون مثالياً. أما ملابس زوزانا المتسخة، بما في ذلك حذاء الحمار الوحشي، فقد طوتها بعناية ووضعتها في عدة طبقات من أكياس البلاستيك. شعرت بأنها خيانة، خصوصاً عندما وضعت الحذاء القديم بجانب الجديد على الأرض، وخطر لها أن الأحذية القديمة تبدو وكأنها تُجبر على تدريب بديلها.

لماذا تخطو بخفة؟ سيقول الحذاء القديم المترهل للحذاء الجلدي الجديد، ودموعه الحذائية تتساقط. كما أنها ستقف كثيراً على أطراف أصابعها، لذا استعد لذلك.

يا لكِ من عاطفية، علّق ميك عندما عادت إلى غرفة الجلوس ودسّت الحزمة داخل حقيبة ظهرها.

"أبداً" ردت زوزانا بلامبالاة،"أنا أحتفظ بها من أجل متحف مغامرات العالم الآخر الذي سأؤسسه. وسيكون عنوان المعرض: الأشياء التي عليك ألا ترتديها أثناء التخييم في جبال متجمدة بينما تبني تحالفاً مع جيوش معادية".

أما ميك، الذي كان قد دخل الآن الحمام بدوره، فلم يكن يشعر بنفس القدر من الحنين تجاه ملابسه المتسخة. لقد كان سعيداً تماماً بالتخلص منها، لكن قبل أن يرميها في سلة المهملات، بحث بحذر في جيب بنطاله القديم وأخرج... الخاتم الذي قد يكون فضياً، وقد يكون أثرياً، والذي كان على وشك شرائه عندما انقلب العالم رأساً على عقب. وقلبه بين أصابعه، تفحص الخاتم عن قرب للمرة الأولى منذ ذلك الحين. زوزانا كانت دائماً قريبة (والحمد لله على ذلك)، لذا لم تسنح له فرصة لإخراجه من قبل. بدا له الآن وكأنه شيء بسيط، خصوصاً في هذا الفندق السخيف. في آيت بن حدو، كان يبدو مناسباً تماماً: بدائياً، باهتاً، وربما مائلاً قليلاً. أما هنا، فقد بدا أشبه بشيء سقط من إصبع أحد القوط أثناء غزو روما.

مجوهرات البرابرة.

رائع.

"من أجل حبيبتي البربرية"، فكر ميك وهو يحاول وضع الخاتم في جيب سرواله الإيطالي الأنيق الجديد، ولكنه انزلق من بين أصابعه. ارتطم الخاتم بأرضية الرخام مُصدِراً رنيناً خفيفاً، ثم بدأ يتدحرج وكأنه يحاول الهرب. تبعه ميك بخطوات سريعة، معتقداً أنه ربما خاتم فضي حقيقي بعد كل شيء، لأنهم يقولون إن الفضة الحقيقية تصدر ذلك الرنين الموسيقي. لكنه بغباء انزلق في فجوة صغيرة بقدر ثلاثة أصابع أسفل منضدة الزينة الرخامية. همس ميك:"عد إلى هنا. لدي خطط من أجلك."

ركع على ركبتيه محاولاً التقاطه، بينما في غرفة الجلوس، كانت حبيبته البربرية تسند كوب الماء إلى شفتي إليزا جونز المتململة، محاولة إقناعها بالشرب. وفي الغرفة الصغيرة في مؤخرة الجناح، كان الباب مغلقاً والموسيقى تصدح لتغطي على صوتها، في الحين الذي تجري فيه إستر ڤان دي مكالمة هاتفية.

لم تكن مكالمة سهلة بالنسبة إليها، ولكن يمكن القول إن أكثر ما يُمكن أن يبرر موقفها هو أنها كانت تأمل ألا تضطر إلى إجرائها. ترددت للحظة صغيرة جداً، رغم أن ظلاً لعمرها الحقيقي بدا وكأنه قد بدأ يلقي بلونه على ملامح وجهها، ولكن ذلك التردد لم يكن بسبب ذلك الظل.

زفرت بقوة، دفعت الهواء من صدرها بعنف، وقررت المضي قدماً. وعلى العموم، القوة لا تشحذ نفسها بنفسها.

اجتازت كارو ورفاقها أسطح روما، وقد تركوا خلفهم مهمتهم في متحف التاريخ الطبيعي، ولم يبقَ أمامهم سوى جايل. كان هواء الليل مشبعاً برطوبة الصيف الإيطالي، والمنظر من تحتهم لوحة باهتة من أسطح المنازل والآثار، أضواء وقباب، يتخللها شريط مظلم يشق المدينة: نهر التيبر. وصلت أصوات أبواق السيارات وصفارات المرور إليهم أثناء تحليقهم، ممزوجة بمقاطع من الموسيقى، ومع اقترابهم من الفاتيكان، بدأت أصوات التراتيل ترتفع أكثر وأكثر. لم تكن الكلمات مفهومة، لكنها حملت نغمات دينية مألوفة.

كانت هناك أيضاً رائحة كريهة—الرائحة التي لا تخطئها الأنوف: رائحة تجمع بشري مكتظ لوقت أطول مما ينبغي.

ومن الحدة اللاذعة للرائحة، خمّنت كارو أن الحجاج الذين تمكنوا من الوصول إلى مواقع قريبة من الحواجز، لم يكونوا على استعداد للتخلي عن أماكنهم في الصف من أجل أمر عابر كقضاء حاجاتهم.

رائع. فقد تحدثت الأخبار عن أزمة صحية عامة، حيث كان الناس يجلبون أحبّاءهم من المرضى وكبار السن إلى محيط الحواجز، على أمل أن مجرد

قربهم من الملائكة قد يشفيهم من أمراضهم—أو، وإن كان ذلك نادراً، أن الملائكة قد يخرجون ليباركوهم شخصياً. وقد زُعم حدوث معجزات، ورغم عدم وجود أدلة تثبتها، إلا أنها طغت على عدد الوفيات الموثق الناتج عن هذه الممارسات.

المعجزات تفعل ذلك. بدا الفاتيكان من السماء أشبه بإسفين—وإن كان إسفيناً متعرجاً، كأنه شريحة من فطيرة آخذة في الانهيار. داخل حدوده، كانت الساحة الدائرية الضخمة أبرز معلم فيه، محاطة بالأروقة المنحنية الشهيرة التي صممها مايكل أنجلو. غير أن الساحة كانت ممتلئة بشكل غير متناسق بالمركبات العسكرية، دبابات راقدة مثل خنافس قبيحة، وسيارات جيب تتحرك جيئة وذهاباً، وحتى مركبات نقل الجنود. وعلى الجانب الشمالي من الأروقة، كان هدفهم: القصر البابوي. قادتهم كارو في الاتجاه الصحيح.

كانت إستير، بفضل ما أسمته"الكاردينال الخاص بها"، قد تمكنت من تزويدهم بموقع دقيق للغرف التي مُنحت لجايل لاستخداماته. حلّق الثلاثة في دائرة واسعة فوق المباني—فالقصر لم يكن بناءً واحداً، بل مجموعة من المباني المتلاصقة—بينما كانوا يمسحون الأسطح بحثاً عن أي إشارات تدل على وجود ملائكة السيرافيم. توقعوا وجود حراس. رأوا الجنود البشر وهم متمركزين على الأرض—يتجولون مع كلابهم—وبالتأكيد عند مداخل المبنى، من الداخل والخارج. لكنهم توقعوا أيضاً أن يجدوا جنود الدومينيون منتشرين على السطح، لأن هذا كان الإجراء القياسي في"المملكة"، حيث هناك احتمال هجمات من السماء بقدر ما هي محتملة على الأرض. وها هم هناك. اثنان فقط. ببساطة.

"لا تؤذوهما" ذكّرت كارو أكيفا وفيركو—بشكل ربما لم يكن ضرورياً، كما أملت—ثم شعرت بحركتهما بعيداً. راقبت الحراس، ورأت ظلال أكيفا وفيركو التي ألقى القمر نوره عليهما وهما يهبطان نحوهم. عادت إلى ذاكرتها موجة الظلال التي اجتاحتهم في أديلفاس، تلك التي تبعتها النيران، ولم

تشعر بأي شفقة وهي ترى الجنود، في حركة واحدة متزامنة، يتيبّسون ثم يسقطون. ضربات سريعة على الرأس. تراخى جسدا الحارسين، لكنهما لم ينهارا. بدا وكأنهما ينزلقان في حركة بطيئة نحو السطح، حيث التقطهما أكيفا وڤيركو ووضعاهما برفق على الأرض. سيكون لديهما بعض الانتفاخات والصداع لاحقاً، لكن لن يعانيا أكثر من ذلك. لم يكن الأمر متعلقاً بما إذا كانا يستحقان الرحمة، بل بمعايير هذه المهمة: لا دماء. سرعة ونظافة، هذا هو المطلوب. لا مذبحة، لا مسرح جريمة، مجرد إقناع. كان عليهم أن ينهوا المهمة ويخرجوا قبل أن يستيقظ هذان الجنديان ويمسحا رأسيهما المتألمين.

هبطت كاروه بخفة على السطح، وألقت نظرة سريعة على أحدهما. وهو فاقد الوعي، بدا مثل أي واحد من غير الشرعيين الذين كانوا في كهوف الكيرين: وسيم، شاب، بشرة فاتحة."شرير وضحية في آن واحد"، فكرت، وتذكرت اقتراح ليراز بأخذ أصابع الجنود بدلاً من أرواحهم. تساءلت: هل يمكن لجنود الدومينيون أن يتعلموا العيش في عالم جديد—إذا كان هناك يوماً ما عالم جديد؟ هل يستحقون الخيار؟ وهي تنظر إليه الآن، نائماً بريئاً على ما يبدو، لكن من السهل التفكير بـ"نعم".

ربما حين يستيقظ، ستمتلئ عيناه بالكراهية، وسيكون فاقد الأمل.

لكن هذا أمرٌ ليوم آخر. الآن، هم هنا. نوافذ جايل صارت أمامهم في مرمى البصر. الهتاف عند محيط الفاتيكان أحاط بهم كأنه هدير البحر، لكنه خلق داخله فقاعة هادئة، وكأنهم في قلب عالم معزول عن الضوضاء.

"عندي فكرة أفضل"، كانت كارو قد أعلنت ذلك في كهوف الكيرين، واثقة أن هذا هو الطريق لتجنب كارثة وشيكة. نهاية سريعة وهادئة لهذه الدراما. لا صدام، لا أسلحة، ولا"وحوش". الملائكة ببساطة يختفون. هذا سهل..

"حسناً"، قالت وهي تتوقف لتكتب رسالة نصية سريعة إلى زوزانا قبل أن تغلق هاتفها وتضعه بعيداً."لننهِ الأمر."

57

إطعام الأسود

شمع طرق على باب الجناح الملكي، ولم يكن طرقاً عادياً. انتصب الكلبان، تراڤيلر وماثوسيلا، على أقدامهما فوراً متأهبين.

أما زوزانا وميك، فلم يستنفرا، لكنهما كانا أيضاً في حالة تأهب. كانا يقفان بجانب نافذة غرفة المعيشة، بعد أن انتقلا إليها من غرفة الجلوس لأن النوافذ في هذا الجانب تطلُّ نحو الفاتيكان. كانت أعينهما تتنقل بين شاشة التلفاز وبين طبقة السماء التي كشفت عنها الستائر المخملية الحمراء بعد أن أزاحاها قليلاً، وكأنهما يتوقعان أن يحدث شيء ما في أي من المكانين.

وقد يحدث ذلك فعلاً، فور أن تنجح كارو وأكيڤا في مهمتهما: الجوقة السماوية ستنطلق نحو السماء وتعود بسرعة البرق إلى أوزبكستان، حيث البوابة هناك. لا تدعوا... امممم، مصراع السماء... يغلق عليكم أثناء خروجكم السماء أم التلفاز؟ أيهما سيُظهر الحدث أولاً؟

وضعت زوزانا هاتفها على ذراع كرسيها ليكون في متناول يدها وتجيب فوراً إذا اتصلت كارو أو أرسلت رسالة نصية.

حتى الآن، وصلتها رسالة واحدة فقط:

"وصلنا. والآن ندخل. قُبلة/ لكمة."

وهكذا، كان الأمر قد بدأ. لم تستطع زوزانا أن تبقى ساكنة. كانت نظراتها تدور في دائرة لا تنتهي: السماء، التلفاز، الهاتف، ميك، ثم تتوقف أحياناً عند إليزا أيضاً.

ظلت الفتاة شاردة ومتقوقعة، عيناها براقتان ولكن ليستا ثابتتين. تستقران لوهلة، ثم تتحركان جيئة وذهاباً، بؤبؤاها يتسعان وينقبضان، حتى مع ثبات الضوء. بدا وكأن عقلها يعيش في واقع مختلف تماماً عن جسدها. عيناها تريان مشاهد أخرى، وشفتاها تتمتمان بكلمات شعرية مجنونة ناعمة، وقد كانت زوزانا سعيدة لعدم فهمها لما تقول. عندما ترجمت لها كارو بعضاً منها، كانت غريبة إلى درجة مرعبة، أشبه بفيلم رعب مليء بالمشاهد التي تتحدث عن الافتراس.

ليس النوع المألوف من افتراس زوزانا للصحن المليء بالبسكويت المغطى بالشوكولاتة الذي"حررته" من فوق البيانو. حسناً، هو بالضبط نفس شعور الافتراس، ولكن من وجهة نظر البسكويت.

دق دق دق. كان الأمر مقلقاً، بل مخيفاً، تلك القوة التي ترافقت مع الطرق. طرقٌ أشبه بطرق رجال الأمن، أو البوليس السري، أو حتى الغستابو. اختر أي جهاز شرطة سرية تريد، فهذا الطرق حمل معه وزن"لقد جاؤوا ليأخذوك تحت جنح الليل". ولا أحد ينطلق بحيوية لفتح باب يُطرق هكذا.

إلا أن إستر فعلت ذلك. كانت في الغرفة الخلفية، بالكاد رأوها منذ أن غادر الآخرون. خرجت الآن، حافية القدمين، تسير بهدوء عبر غرفة المعيشة دون أن تلقي نظرة جانبية واحدة. بينما كانت تختفي في الممر باتجاه الباب، والكلبان يحيطان بها، قالت بلهجة ثابتة:"ينبغي أن تحزموا أشياءكم الآن، يا أولاد."

ارتفعت نظرة زوزانا نحو ميك، ونظر هو إليها. بدا وكأن قلبها قد قفز على قدميه بنفس السرعة التي قفز بها الكلبان، ولم تمض لحظات حتى لحقت به هي أيضاً، تقفز من مكانها. "ماذا؟" سألت بنفس اللحظة التي قال فيها ميك: "يا إلهي!".

"يا إلهي ماذا؟".

قال: "اجمعي أشياءكِ. احزمي حقيبتكِ." ما زالت زوزانا لا تفهم ما الذي يحدث، ولكن بعد ذلك دخل رجلان، طويلان، عريضا الكتفين، يرتديان بدلتين فاخرتين. كانت لديهما أجهزة لاسلكية مثبتة على آذانهما الكبيرة الغبية. فكرت زوزانا لأول وهلة "يا إلهي، إنهم حقاً البوليس السري". لكنها رأت بعد ذلك الشعار المطرز على جيوب ستراتهم، وتحولت مخاوفها فوراً إلى أولى بوادر الغضب المكتوم.

أمن الفندق. فقامت إستر بطردهم.

"حسناً،" قال أحد الرجلين. "هيا. حان وقت مغادرتكم."

"ماذا تعني؟" واجهته زوزانا بثبات. "نحن ضيوف."

"لستم كذلك بعد الآن،" قالت إستر من عند الباب. "تحملتكم فقط لأجل كارو. أما الآن، بما أن كارو... حسناً".

التفتت زوزانا نحوها بغضب. كانت المرأة العجوز تتكئ على إطار الباب وذراعاها متقاطعتان، والكلبان يدوران حولها بقلق. كانت في عينيها نظرة تجمع بين المكر والافتراس، وأول انطباع شعرت به زوزانا هو أن أفعى قد ابتلعت الجدة ذات الشعر الناعم وتحولت إلى نسخة منها.

لم يخطُ رجال الفندق خطوة واحدة داخل الغرفة قبل أن يدرك عقل زوزانا تماماً ما يعنيه هذا.

كارو. ما الذي فعلتِه؟ صاحت، لأنها عرفت أنه إذا طردتهم إستر، فهذا يعني أنها لم تعد قادرة على تلقي أي اتصال من كارو—ليس لهذه الليلة فقط، بل دائماً.

"فعلتَ؟" ردت إستر ببرود، "كل ما فعلتُه هو أنني أبلغتُ الإدارة بأنني أجد نفسي محاطة بشباب عديمي الذوق. وفهموا فوراً من أعني. يبدو أنكم تركتم انطباعاً قوياً في الطابق السفلي."

"أعني، ما الذي فعلتِه لكارو؟" صرخت، وكادت أن تلقي بنفسها نحوها. في تلك اللحظة، شعرت بأنها قد تكون عقرباً (ميك-ميك) حقيقياً، مع إبرة وكل شيء، وويلٌ للكلبين حتى لو كانا بحجم الأسود أو الحمقى المتغطرسين الذين يقفون في طريقها.

كانت أشبه بفرخ صغير يسهل الإمساك به في الهواء، وقد فعل ذلك المتنمر القريب منها ببراعة، إذ أمسك معصمها بإحكام بحركة مدروسة. صرخت فيه بغض: "اتركني!"، وحاولت أن تفلت ذراعها من قبضته.

لكن لا جدوى. قبضته كانت أشبه بماكينة، وكأنه يقضي أوقاته في عصر تلك الكرات المطاطية السخيفة لتقوية قبضته. لكن عندها اندفع ميك، أمسك اليد التي كانت تضغط على معصمها وقال بصوت حازم: "اترك يدها." وفي مواجهة غير متكافئة بين عازف كمان وعضلات متنمر، حاول ميك بكل قوته أن يفتح أصابع المتنمر السميكة والقبيحة عن معصم زوزانا.

لكن لم يسعفه الحظ. كانت زوزانا بالكاد تدرك، وسط غضبها المتصاعد، مدى الإهانة التي تعيشها في تلك اللحظة؛ كم كانا بعيدين عن صورة الساموراي الشجاع.

دفع الحارس بيده الأخرى ميك بسهولة في ممر ضيق باتجاه الباب الأمامي، دون أن يكترث بحاجياتهم المتروكة. دفع بعدها زوزانا لتتبعه. كانت يدها تنبض بالألم حيث أمسكها، لكنه بدا ألماً ضئيلاً مقارنة بالإعصار الذي يدور داخل عقلها: غضب كاسح، وقلق لا يهدأ.

رفضت أن تكون مطيعة كخروف يُقاد. اندفعت جانباً، متهربة من الحارس، لتجد نفسها وجهاً لوجه أمام ترافيل وميثوسيلا، الكلبين اللذين كانا يحجبان الطريق نحو سيدتهما. نظر إليها الكلبان. أحدهما رفع شفته

كاشفاً عن أنيابه في زمجرة معهودة، وكأنما يقول:"انظري إلى هذه الأنياب، هل ترين؟".

كانت تريد أن ترد عليه بفخر:"رأيت ما هو أخطر منك". سحقاً فقد أرادت أن تكشف عن أسنانها هي الأخرى في تحدٍّ، لكنها بدلاً من ذلك تماسكت وثبتت في مكانها. رفعت نظرها لتلاقي عيني إستر. ظلت ملامح إستر جامدة، أشبه بقناع من الحجر. بدت أقل إنسانية في تلك اللحظة. فكرت زوزانا:"هذه ليست بشراً. هذه الجشع نفسه، مرتدياً جلداً."

"ما الذي فعلته؟ ما الذي فعلته يا إستر؟ ما. الذي. فعلته."

تنهدت إستر بإحباط، كأنما تخاطب طفلاً بليداً."هل أنتِ غبية؟ ماذا تظنين أني فعلت؟".

ردت زوزانا، غاضبة، والاشمئزاز يملأ نبرتها:"أظن أنكِ خائنة مريضة، هذا ما أظنه".

هزت إستر رأسها، وابتسامة احتقار خبيثة حلت مكان قناعها الجامد."أتعتقدين أنني أردت الأمور أن تصل إلى هنا؟ كنت سعيدة بالطريقة التي كانت عليها. ليس خطئي أن بريمستون مات."

صرخت زوزانا:"وما علاقة ذلك بكل شيء؟".

ردت إستر، وهي ترفع حاجبيها باستخفاف:"أوه، هيا. أعلم أنك لست الدمية الصغيرة التي تبدين عليها. الحياة خيارات، ولا يختار الحلفاء بقلبهم إلا الأغبياء."

استشاطت زوزانا غضباً:"حلفاء؟ ما هذا، يا أبدية؟". في تلك اللحظة، كان اشمئزازها من إستر يفيض على كل شيء. من الواضح أن إستر قد"اختارت" أن تتحالف مع الملائكة. لأن بريمستون قد مات، ولم تكن إستر تفكر إلا في مصلحتها الشخصية. وفي تلك اللحظة، مع معرفتها الحقيقية لعمر إستر، برق في ذهن زوزانا إدراك عميق عنها. قالت لها، والكلمة مغلفة بطبقة كثيفة من الاشمئزاز،"أنتِ... أراهن أنكِ كنتِ متعاونة مع النازيين، أليس كذلك؟".

لدهشتها، ضحكت إستر. قالت بسخرية:"تقولين ذلك وكأنه أمر سيئ. أي شخص بعقل سليم سيختار البقاء على قيد الحياة. هل تعرفين ما هو الغباء الحقيقي؟ أن تموتي من أجل معتقد. انظري أين نحن. في روما. فكّري في المسيحيين الذين أُطعموا للأسود لأنهم رفضوا التخلي عن إيمانهم. وكأن إلههم لم يكن ليغفر لهم رغبتهم في العيش؟ إذا كنتِ لا تملكين غريزة الحفاظ على النفس أكثر من ذلك، فربما لا تستحقين الحياة."

حدقت زوزانا في وجهها بذهول ممزوج بالغضب، ثم قالت بصوت حاد:"هل تمزحين معي؟ تريدين أن تلومي المسيحيين بدلاً من الرومان؟ ماذا عن فكرة بسيطة: ألا يقومون برميهم للأسود اللعينة من الأساس؟ لا تخدعي نفسك. الوحش هنا هو أنتِ".

بدت إستر وقد وصلت إلى حدود صبرها:"حان وقت مغادرتكما الآن". ثم أضافت بنبرة أكثر جفافاً:"وينبغي أن تعلمي أنه عند وفاتها، ستؤول جميع ممتلكات كارو إلى أقرب أقاربها". وارتسمت على شفتيها ابتسامة رفيعة بلا أي أثر للسعادة."جدتها المخلصة، بالطبع. لذا، لا تزعجي نفسك بمحاولة الوصول إلى تلك الحسابات".

عند وفاتها. عند وفاتها.. رفضت زوزانا استيعاب ذلك. كما دفع عقلها تلك الكلمات المؤلمة جانباً.

أشارت إستر نحو الممر، وقام الحراس بأيديهم القاسية الشبيهة بالمخالب بدفعهما باتجاهه. ثم قالت بنبرة مليئة بالازدراء:"يمكنكما الاحتفاظ بالملابس. على الرحب والسعة. أوه، ولا تنسيا الخضروات."

كانت تقصد إليزا بالخضروات. تلك التي ظلت طوال الوقت صامتة، فاقدة تماماً لإرادتها، كأنها غارقة في غيبوبة. إستر كانت تنوي رميها إلى الشارع، هي وزوزانا وميك، بثيابهم فقط.

عند وفاتها!.. تلاشى الإعصار الذي اجتاح عقل زوزانا، لكنه ترك خلفه همسات سوداء ملتصقة بجدران ذهنها. ماذا حدث؟ هل يمكن أن تكون...؟

اصمتي.

"دعيني أُحضر حقائبنا، على الأقل"، قال ميك بنبرة بدت هادئة وعقلانية إلى درجة جعلت زوزانا تغلي من الغضب. كيف يتجرأ على أن يكون هادئاً وعقلانياً في مثل هذا الموقف؟

"أعطيتك فرصة"، ردّت إستير ببرود."لكنّك اخترتِ أن تقفي هنا وتُهينيني بدلاً من ذلك. كما قلت سابقاً، الحياة هي سلسلة من الخيارات."

توسّل ميك:"على الأقل دعيني أحضر كماني. نحن بلا أي شيء الآن، ولا نملك وسيلة للعودة إلى المنزل. على الأقل أستطيع العزف في إحدى الساحات العامة لأجمع مال تذكرة القطار."

يبدو أن فكرة رؤيتهما يتسوّلان أثارت بداخلها شعوراً بالتفوق الطبقي، وربما أيضاً شيئاً من الاستمتاع بمذلّتهما. فقالت بلهجة متعالية وهي تلوّح بيدها باستخفاف:"حسناً." أسرع ميك في الانطلاق إلى آخر الممر، وعندما عاد، كان يحتضن حقيبة الكمان بين ذراعيه كأنها طفل صغير، بدلاً من حملها من مقبضها كالمعتاد. قال بصوت خافت:"شكراً لك". بدا وكأنه يعتقد أن إستر أظهرت لهما نوعاً من اللطف. فرمقته زوزانا بنظرة حادة.

هل فقد عقله؟

قال لها ميك بهدوء:"اذهبي وأحضري إليزا." فامتثلت لكلماته وأحضرت إليزا، التي بدت وكأنها تسير وهي غارقة في غيبوبة. توقّفت زوزانا مرة واحدة فقط وهي في طريقها إلى الخارج، لتواجه إستير عبر غرفة المعيشة.

"طالما قلت هذا من قبل، لكن كنت أمزح حينها"." لكن الآن لم تكن تمزح. لم تكن أبداً أكثر جديّة من هذه اللحظة."سأجعلك تدفعين ثمن هذا. أعدك."

ضحكت إستير بسخرية."ليس هكذا تسير الأمور في العالم، يا عزيزتي. لكن يمكنك المحاولة، إن كان هذا يسعدك. افعلي أسوأ ما لديك."

"انتظري فقط"، تمتمت زوزانا وهي تكزّ على أسنانها، بينما دفعها حارس

الأمن بقوة، مما جعلها تتقدم رغماً عنها عبر الممر، وإليزا بجانبها، حتى وصلتا إلى القاعة الكبرى ومنها إلى المصعد. ومن هناك، تم إنزالهما إلى الطابق الأرضي، حيث انتهى بهما الحال إلى السير مكرهين عبر البهو الفخم اللامع. كانوا محط أنظار الحاضرين وهم يهمسون، في حين كان أكثر ما أثار سخطها النظرات الساخرة الموجّهة إليها من المرأة ذات الحاجب المستفزّ—التي تجرأت مرة أخرى، في ظل هذا التحول في الظروف، على رفع أحد حاجبيها النحيلين كأنها تقول:"ألم أقل لكم؟".

الشعور بالمهانة كان كالسير عبر حقل من القراص؛ آلاف من الآلام الصغيرة التي اندمجت معاً لتصبح كالحريق الخافت. ولكن كل ذلك لم يكن شيئاً مقارنة بوجع قلب زوزانا وذعرها وهي تفكر في أصدقائهم، الذين، حتى في هذه اللحظة، باتوا تحت رحمة أعدائهم.

ماذا الذي يحدث لهم؟

بلا شك، إستير قد حذّرت الملائكة. ولكن ماذا وعدوها في المقابل؟ تساءلت زوزانا، والأهم من ذلك، كيف يمكن لها وميك أن يمنعاها من الحصول عليه؟ كيف؟ لم يكن لديهما أي شيء. لا شيء سوى كمان.

"لا أصدق أنكَ شكرتها"، تمتمت بغضب وهي تُدفع خارج الأبواب إلى الشارع. اصطدمت روما بحواسهم دفعة واحدة، بحيويتها وهوائها الدافئ الثقيل، وهو تناقض صارخ مع البرودة المصطنعة والهدوء الخادع الذي تركوه خلفهم." ولقد سمحت لي بأخذ كماني"، أجاب ميك بلامبالاة، وهو لا يزال يحتضن الحقيبة كأنها طفل صغير أو جرو. بدا عليه الرضا، وحتى نوع من السرور. كان ذلك أكثر مما يمكن أن تتحمله. توقفت زوزانا عن السير فجأة ثم استدارت لمواجهته. لم يبدُ عليه فقط أنه مسرور. بدا... كوتر مشدود. كأنه مشحون بالطاقة. كان يهتز من فرط الترقب.

"ما بكَ؟" سألته بحيرة، بينما كانت على وشك الجلوس على الرصيف والبكاء.

"سأخبرك بعد دقيقة. هيا. لا يمكننا البقاء هنا." فأجابته:"نعم، أعتقد أن ذلك أصبح واضحاً جداً".

"لا. أعني أننا لا يمكننا البقاء في أي مكان يمكن لكارو العثور علينا فيه. وستبحث عنّا. هيا". ظهرت نبرة من الإلحاح في صوته الآن، مما زاد من حيرتها. وضع ذراعه حولها ليدفعها إلى الأمام، وسحبت هي إليزا معها، التي بدت وكأنها تسير في حلم، كشخص يطفو في عالم آخر. ثم غمرهم الحشد الكثيف كأنه تيار لا يمكن مقاومته، ووجدوا فيه ملاذهم، حيث أصبح من السهل الاختباء وسط الزحام.

وهكذا، أصبحت الكثافة البشرية التي لعنوا وجودها في وقت سابق، هي ما وفّر لهم الحماية، وتمكنوا أخيراً من الهرب.

58

قبح غير مناسب

كل شيء كان كما يجب. النافذة الثقيلة غير موصدة، كما وُعدت،
والآن لم يتبقَّ على كارو سوى فتحها بصمت. لكنها ستصدر صريراً؛ مقاومةُ
الخشب تحدتها لأن تدفعها بقوة، مما قد يسبب الصرير.

منذ زمن طويل لم تشعر بندم على افتقارها لما أسمته يوماً"الأماني
عديمة الفائدة" التي اعتادت على اعتبارها حقاً مكتسباً — تلك الحبات
الصغيرة التي سرقتها من فنجان الشاي في متجر بريمستون وارتدتها
قلادة. الآن، شعرت بالرغبة في واحدة منها، خرزة بين أصابعها، لتتمنى بها
إسكات صرير هذه النافذة العنيدة.

لكنها لم تكن بحاجة إليها. احتاج الأمر إلى صبر مذهل لفتح النافذة
ببطء شديد، بينما قلبها ينبض كطبول حرب، لكنها فعلتها. أصبحت الغرفة
جاهزة لاستقبالهم، مظلمة باستثناء مستطيل ضوء القمر الممدود على
الأرض كأنه بساط ترحيب.

دخلوا واحداً تلو الآخر، أشكالهم تقطع خيوط الضوء إلى شظايا قبل أن تتوحد مجدداً بعد مرورهم. تسمروا للحظة. شعور غريب اجتاحهم، كأن الظلام يحتاج إلى الاستقرار، كماء غارق تحت الزيت.

نَفَسٌ أخير قبل الاقتراب.

السرير بدا غريباً في مكانه. هذه كانت قاعة الاستقبال، الأشهر في القصر بأكمله. لكن السرير وُضع هنا خصيصاً، ولا بد من الاعتراف بأنهم أبدعوا في العثور على قطعة باروكية بشعة، لكنها، بطريقة ما، استطاعت أن تحافظ على حضورها وسط الغرفة المتخمة بالزخارف.

كان سريراً ضخماً ذا أربعة أعمدة، نُحت عليه قديسون وملائكة في تفاصيل معقدة. الأغطية الملتوية كانت ترسم هيئة تحتها. الهيئة كانت تتنفس.

وعلى الطاولة المجاورة للسرير، وُضعت الخوذة التي اعتاد جايل ارتداءها لإخفاء بشاعته عن أعين البشر. تحرك قليلاً أثناء مراقبتهم له، متقلباً ببطء. أنفاسه كانت عميقة ومتزنة، كأنما كان غارقاً في نوم هادئ.

قدما كارو لم تكونا تلامسان الأرض. لم يكن ذلك قراراً واعياً؛ الطفو أصبح طبيعياً لها، جزءاً لا يتجزأ من قدرتها على التسلل بخفة. فلماذا تلمس الأرض إن لم تكن مضطرة؟

تحركت إلى الأمام تطوف بانسيابية، بينما أكيڤا يشق طريقه إلى الجانب الآخر من السرير، مستعداً.

كانت هذه اللحظة هي الأكثر خطورة: إيقاظ جايل وإبقاؤه صامتاً إن استفاق ومحاولة إقناعه التي كانت جوهر خطة كارو. إذا سار كل شيء كما خططوا له، سيكونون خارج النافذة وخارج المكان في غضون دقيقتين.

في يدها قطعة من الخيش، جاهزة لإسكات أي صوت قد يصدره قبل أن تتاح لهم الفرصة لإقناعه بأن الأفضل له أن يظل صامتاً. وبعد ذلك، بالطبع، لكتم أي أنين قد يصدر عنه أثناء الألم.

فعدم سفك الدماء لا يعني غياب الألم.

لم يسبق لكارو أن رأت جايل، لكنها ظنت أنها تستطيع تخيل نوع بشاعته الفريدة، بناءً على كل ما سمعته عنه من تقارير، وقد استعدت لذلك. وعندما تحرك الملاك النائم مرة أخرى، مزحزحاً وسادته، شحذت أعصابها لتواجه قبحه.

وبالفعل، واجهت القبح. لكنّه لم يكن القبح الذي توقعته.

فتح عينيه فجأة، عينان جميلتان على وجه مدمّر. لم تكن هناك ندبة طويلة تمتد من الحاجب إلى الذقن كما قيل، بل تورّم بلون الكدمات، وملامح انحطاط تتجاوز حتى انحطاط الإمبراطور نفسه."يا للأزرق الجميل"، قالها هذا الكائن بصوت أجش، أشبه بخرخرة مريضة.

لم تتح لكارو الفرصة لاستخدام قطعة الخيش. تحركت بسرعة، لكنها لم تكن بالسرعة الكافية؛ فقد كان يتوقع مجيئها متأهباً ومستعداً، بينما لم تكن هي قريبة بما يكفي لتكتم صرخته.

صرخ رازغوت بصوت حاد"لقد وصل ضيوفنا"، قبل أن تتمكن من إسكات وجهه القذر بقطعة الخيش الخشنة، كان قد أطلق إنذاره بالفعل. ثم اختنق صوته تدريجياً تحت القماش، لكنه لم يعد يهم. الخطر قد بدأ. انفتحت الأبواب بعنف، واندفع الجنود إلى الداخل.

59

نبوءة تحقق ذاتها

في الجناح الملكي لفندق سانت ريجيس، وقفت إستر ڤان دي ڤلو عند مدخل الحمام، متجمدة في منتصف خطوتها، وقد توقفت فجأة بسبب ما رأته."كمان"، كمان مستلقٍ في حوض الاستحمام.

إنه كمان...

كان صراخها غريزياً، أقرب إلى نعيق ضفدع يائس. أسرع كلباها نحوها، مذعورين من صوتها، لكنها دفعتهما بعنف بعيداً عنها، وألقت بنفسها على ركبتيها، ثم مدت يدها، تبحث بتوتر شديد في الفراغ أسفل منضدة الرخام وهي في حالة إنكار تام لما تراه، راحت تعبث وتبحث بجنون، حتى إنها لم تجد الوقت لتلعن. وعندما صرخت مجدداً، منهارة على الأرض الرخامية، كان صراخها سيلاً غير مفهوم من المشاعر، صرخة لم تعرفها من قبل.

كانت تلك المشاعر غريبة عليها. مشاعر الهزيمة.

في أقل من ساعة، أتقنت زوزانا فنَّ الزفير الغاضب. السماء بقيت فارغة بشكل قاطع، ولم يكن ذلك علامة جيدة. الوقت الذي مرّ منذ مغادرة

كارو وأكيفا وفيركو لفندق سانت ريجيس كان كافياً لتوقع هزيمة جايل، لكن لم يظهر أي دليل على ذلك، كما أن شاشة هاتف زوزانا بقيت فارغة مثل السماء.

بالطبع، أرسلت إليهم تحذيرات عبر الرسائل النصية، بل حاولت الاتصال، لكن المكالمات كانت تتحول مباشرة إلى البريد الصوتي. وكان ذلك يذكّرها بالأيام المريعة بعد مغادرة كارو لبراغ—وللأرض كلها—حين لم تكن تعلم إن كانت كارو حية أم ميتة.

"ماذا سنفعل الآن؟".

تواروا في زقاق ضيق، وراح ميك يتصرف بغرابة، كأنه خائف من شيء ما. أجلست زوزانا إليزا، على عتبة قبل أن تجلس بجانبها.

كان هذا الزقاق أحد تلك الزوايا الإيطالية التي بدت وكأنها خرجت من حلم قديم—صغيرة جداً، وكأن كل البشر في الماضي كانوا بحجم زوزانا— حيث يتحاور الطراز المعماري القروسطي مع عصر النهضة، كل هذا فوق عظام التاريخ القديم. وفوق كل ذلك، أضاف شخصٌ مجهول من القرن الحادي والعشرين لمسته الخاصة على الجدران برسوم غرافيتي فوضوية، تحمل رسالة تقول:

"افتح عينيك! هناك تمرد!".

تساءلت زوزانا في نفسها: لماذا يمتلك الأناركيون دوماً خطاً سيئاً إلى هذا الحد!

ركع ميك أمامها ووضع حقيبة كمانه على حجرها. وبمجرد أن رفع يديه عنها، شعرت بثقلها يغرق في حضنها.

"لماذا هي ثقيلة؟ لماذا تزن حقيبة كمانك خمسين رطلاً؟".

تجاهل ميك الإجابة المباشرة: وأضاف متسائلاً:"في الحكايات الخرافية، أيمكن أن يكون الأبطال أحياناً... لصوصاً؟".

"لصوص؟". زمّت زوزانا عينيها بشك."لا أعلم. ربما. روبن هود؟".

"ليست حكاية خرافية، لكن أوافق على، لص نبيل. جاك وشجرة الفاصولياء. سرق كل تلك الأشياء من العملاق. نعم، لكن ليس نبلاً كما يجب. كنت أشعر بالأسف تجاه العملاق دائماً". فتح ميك قفل الحقيبة بحركة سريعة، ثم أضاف:"لكنني لا أشعر بأي أسف بخصوص هذا". توقف للحظة وقال مبتسماً:"آمل أن نستطيع اعتبار ما قمت به واحدة من مهامي المعتادة".

ثم رفع الغطاء، لتكشف الحقيبة عن... ميداليات. كانت الحقيبة ممتلئة تماماً بها. تفاوتت أحجام الميداليات، من حجم عملة صغيرة إلى حجم صحن، وكانت بألوان برونزية متدرجة، من الساطع الذي يشبه النحاس إلى البني الداكن الباهت. بعضها كان مغطى بالكامل بطبقة من الزنجار الأخضر، وكلها كانت تحمل نقشاً خشناً لصورة واحدة: رأس كبش بقرنين ضخمين ملتفين وعينين مليئتين بالمعرفة، بحدقتين طويلتين ضيقتين.

بريمستون.

قال ميك، متصنعاً نبرة الكسل:"إذاً، عندما قالت الجدة المزيفة إنها لم تعد تملك أي أمنيات؟ لقد كذبت. لكن انظري، إنها نبوءة حققت ذاتها. والآن لم يعد لديها شيء".

60

لن يموت أحد اليوم

تحطمت الأبواب وفتحت، وتدفق الدومينيون إلى الداخل.

أول ما خطر لكارو أن تبحث عن ألم لتقدمه كضريبة لتفعيل الوهم، ولم يكن الألم صعب المنال، لأن رازغوت أمسك بمعصمها بقبضته الساحقة وثبّتها في مكانها.

سواء كانت مرئية أم لا، فقد وقعت في قبضته.

راحت تتلاشى وتتماسك، وهي تصارع هذا المنحط. ضحكاته الشبيهة بالخرخرة، وقبضته التي لا فكاك منها. كانت الشفرات الهلالية بحوزتها كملاذ أخير، لكنهم اتفقوا منذ البداية ألا تُسفك الدماء إلا كخيار أخير. لذا، توقفت يدها على مقبض سيفها بينما تراقب الجنود يدخلون الغرفة، لا يرحمون، كثيرون، سيوفهم مسلولة ووجوههم خاوية من أي تعبير.

مرة أخرى، كما حدث مراراً وتكراراً في الأيام الماضية، بدا الزمن وكأنه يتباطأ، كثيفاً مثل الراتينج. لزجاً وبطيء الحركة. كم يمكن أن يحدث خلال ثانية؟ ثلاث ثوانٍ؟ عشر؟ كم ثانية تحتاج لتخسر كل ما يعنيك؟

فكرت في إستر، وفي خضم صراعها المحموم، شعرت بالمرارة، لكنها لم تتفاجأ. لقد توقعوا قدومهم. لم يكن هؤلاء الحرس الشخصي الصغير المكون من ستة رجال يحرسون غرفة جايل. بل ثلاثين جندياً على الأقل أو أربعين؟

وهناك، عبر الأبواب المفتوحة، رأته. أخذ يتقدم بخطى هادئة، بلا استعجال، ليأخذ مكانه خلف صف متمترس من الجنود. رأته كارو قبل أن يراها، حيث كان ينظر إلى الأمام مباشرة، دون أن يلتفت.

كانت بشاعته كما سمعت عنها وأكثر. ندوب مجعدة كالحبال المعقودة، وأجنحة أنفه بدت وكأنها تتسلل من أسفل تلك التشوهات كما لو أنها محاصرة هناك، مثل فطر مسحوق أخذ بالتعفن البطيء. أما فمه، فهو كارثة أخرى وكأنه يتهاوى على بقايا أسنان متناثرة، وأنفاسه أثناء زفيرها، تصدر صوتاً كصوت الأقدام الغارقة في الوحل. لكن هذا لم يكن أسوأ ما في إمبراطور السيرافيم، وإنما تعابير وجهه المعجونة بالكراهية، حتى ابتسامته كانت تحمل جزءاً منها: خبيثة بقدر ما فيها من بهجة.

"ابن أخي"، قال جايل، وكانت تلك العبارة، مشبّعة بالعداء وزهوة الانتصار. تسلل نظر جايل من بين أكتاف جنوده، محدقاً نحو أكيفا. "قاتل الوحوش"، كما يُدعى، ذلك الفتى الذي نصح بقتله عندما كان مجرد طفلٍ صغير يبكي قبل النوم في معسكر التدريب. "اقتلوه"، هكذا نصح شقيقه جورام في ذلك الوقت. لا يزال يتذكر طعم تلك الكلمات في فمه— بوضوح، لأنها من أوائل الكلمات التي نطق بها بعد إزالة الضمادات عن وجهه حينها. وكانت تلك المرة الأولى التي حاول فيها التحدث، وسط ألم لا يوصف، وفم مليء بخراب أحمر رطب، وكانت النظرة التي رآها في عيني أخيه—وفي أعين الجميع—لا تزال قادرة على إشعاره بالعار.

لقد سمح لامرأة بجرحه. لا يهم أنه بقي حياً وهي لم تعش، وسيظل يحمل علامتها إلى الأبد.

"إن كنت ذكياً، عليك قتله الآن"، قد قال لأخيه آنذاك. لكن بالعودة إلى الوراء، كان من الواضح الخاطئ الذي قدم به النصيحة. فجورام إمبراطور، ولا يستجيب للأوامر.

"ماذا؟ ما زلت تحاول معاقبتها؟" كان جورام قد سخر منه، مستحضراً شبح فيستيڤال بينهما. كلاهما كان قد حاول وفشل في إذلال تلك الخليلة الستيلية؛ ربما ماتت، لكنها لم تنكسر أبداً."قتلها لم يطفئ غليانك؟ الآن تريد أن تأخذ الولد أيضاً؟ ماذا؟ هل تعتقد أنها ستعلم بذلك وتعاني أكثر؟".

"إنه ذريتها"، أجاب جايل مصراً. هي جرثومة ستنتقل إلى هنا. إنها عدوى، ولا يمكن لشيء آمن أن ينمو من نسلها.

"آمن؟" رد جورام بازدراء."ما حاجتي إلى محارب آمن؟ إنه بذرتي، يا أخي. هل تقصد أن تقترح أن دمي ليس أقوى من دم عاهرة فاجرة؟".

هنا كان جورام أعمى وجارح. فالسيدة فيستيڤال من الجزر البعيدة، يمكن وصفها بأشياء كثيرة، لكن"عاهرة" لم تكن واحدة منها.

ولا حتى أسيرة.

على أي حال فقد انتهى بها الأمر مع حريم الإمبراطور، وأياً كان السبب الذي جعلها تختار البقاء، فمن غير الممكن أن يكون ذلك ضد إرادتها. لقد كانت ستيلية، وبالرغم من أنها لم تُظهر قوتها يوماً، كان جايل متأكداً من أنها كانت تمتلكها. كما اعتقد دائماً أن اختيارها أخذته بتصميم شخصي منها. إذاً... لماذا قد تضع ابنة تلك القبيلة الغامضة نفسها في فراش جورام؟

ببطء، رمش جايل وهو يتأمل أكيڤا. لماذا حقاً؟ يكفي أن تنظر إلى ذلك الوغد لترى الحقيقة واضحة: أي دم كان أقوى من الآخر. الشعر الأسود، البشرة البرونزية—ليست داكنة تماماً كما كانت بشرة فيستيڤال، لكنها أقرب إليها من بشرة جورام الفاتحة. أما العينان؟ فكانتا بالكامل لها، وتلك الألفة مع السحر؟ إذا كان لا يزال هناك أي شك، فقد تبدد الآن تماماً.

كان يجب على جورام أن يستمع إلى أخيه. كان عليه أن يتركه يفرغ غضبه بالطريقة التي يراها مناسبة، ولكنه بدلاً من ذلك، سخر منه وأمر بنفيه، وألزمه بتناول وجباته وحيداً، قائلاً إنه لا يستطيع تحمل الأصوات المزعجة التي يصدرها أثناء الأكل.

أما الآن، فبإمكان جايل أن يضحك كما يشاء، أليس كذلك؟ ويصدر كل الأصوات المزعجة التي يرغب بها أثناء ذلك.

"قاتل الوحوش"، قالها جايل وهو يتقدم خطوة إلى الأمام رويداً، إذ أبقى حاجزاً كثيفاً من جنوده بينه وبين الدخلاء. كان الحاجز من أربعين جندياً من الدومينيون يفصلون بينه وبينهم، وعشرة منهم يحملون أسلحة خاصة جداً، تلك التي أسقطت أكيفا سابقاً بفعالية مذهلة بأيادٍ عارية.

لكنها لم تكن أياديهم بالطبع.

كانت أيادي موتى، جافة كجلود محنطة، بنيّة قاتمة، بعضها ذو مخالب، وكلها موسومة بعيون الشياطين. رفعوها أمامهم، كانت أيدي مقاتلي الكيميرا المقطوعة.

عند رؤيتها، أصدر الوحش الذي بجانب أكيفا زمجرة خافتة عميقة من حنجرته. انتصبت الأشواك التي تحيط بعنقه، مشكّلة ما يشبه زهرة قاتلة تتفتح. بدا وكأنه يتضاعف حجماً في تلك اللحظة، فتحول إلى كابوس معركة حيّ، وأكثر رعباً بسبب التناقض الحاد بين مظهره وبين الغرفة المزخرفة التي بدا وكأنه يملأها بأكملها فجأة.

أحس جايل بقشعريرة تسري في جسده. حتى وهو يقف بأمان خلف جدار من اللحم والنار الحية، وحتى وهو يتوقع هذا المشهد — بفضل تحذير تلك المرأة المرعبة التي من المفترض أن تكون حليفته البشرية — أصابه المنظر بالقشعريرة. ليس الكيميرا نفسه، بل الرؤية التي جمعت بين سيراف وكيميرا معاً! كانت الوحوش هاجس أخيه وقضيته الكبرى، أما جايل فقد كانت عينه على عدو جديد. ومع ذلك، فإن التحالف الذي رآه الآن أمامه

قلب ألف سنة من العداء رأساً على عقب — سرطان لا يمكن السماح له بالانتشار في"المملكة".

وحين يعود، سيقضي على أي أثر له. كان مطمئناً بفكرة أن بقية التمرد لا بد وأنها قد شحقت بالفعل. فلماذا يأتي هؤلاء الثلاثة إليه وحدهم، بلا جيش وراءهم؟ أراد أن يسخر منهم لغبائهم، لكنه تذكر كم كان قريباً من الهلاك، فشعر بقشعريرة أوقفت ضحكته في مهدها. لولا تحذير تلك المرأة، لكان نائماً في فراشه عندما تسللوا عبر النافذة.

كان قريباً جداً. الحظ وحده هو ما منحه اليد العليا هذه المرة. لن يكون مستهتراً مجدداً.

"أمير الأوغاد"، تابع جايل، وهو يشعر وكأنه يؤدي طقساً تأخر عن موعده لسنوات طويلة: تطهير عدوى الستيليين، واجتثاث آخر أثر لفيستيغال، وما كانت تسعى إلى تحقيقه. إنه الحامل السابع للاسم الملعون أكيفا.

هنا توقف لبرهة، متأملاً.

"لم يحمل أحد من أبناء الوصمة هذا الاسم وبلغ الرجولة قبلك. هل كنت تعلم ذلك؟ ذلك العجوز، بايون، خادم القصر، أعطاك هذا الاسم بدافع الحقد. أراد أن تتوسل أمك إليه لتغييره. أي امرأة أخرى في الحريم كانت ستفعل، لكن ليس فيستيغال. قالت له: داكتب ما شئت في قائمتك، أيها العجوز. لن يتورط ابني في مصيرك الواهن"

راقب جايل تعابير أكيفا عن كثب، باحثاً عن أي رد فعل يظهر على وجهه. ثم قال بلهجة ملؤها التحدي: "كلمات جريئة، أليس كذلك؟ ولكن، كم مرة أفلتَّ من الموت؟ اللعنة التي يحملها اسمك، وتلك الميتات التي سببتها لك بنفسي. كم مرة نجوت؟".

بدا له أن نقمته على الوحوش قد شحذته. شم جايل رائحة جرحه المخفي، واستطرد:"الآخرون يموتون وأنت تبقى؟ ربما نقلت اللعنة إلى غيرك. لم تعد تموت، لكن كل من حولك يسقط صريعاً بدلاً منك."

تصلّب فك أكيڤا حتى كاد يتكسر. أما جايل، فلم يُضِع الفرصة وواصل الضغط بنبرة مشفقة زائفة، ملوّحاً برأسه كما لو كان يتأسف له حقاً:"لا بد من أنه عبء ثقيل، أليس كذلك؟ الموت يبحث عنك ويبحث، لكنه لا يجدك. فأنت غير مرئي للموت، يا له من مصير! وأخيراً، يسأم من البحث ويأخذ من يصادفه بالقرب منك."

توقف جايل للحظة، ثم ابتسم ابتسامة زائفة وحاول أن يبدو صادقاً وهو يقول:"يا ابن أخي، لديّ أخبار جيدة لك. اليوم سنكسر اللعنة. اليوم، وأخيراً ستموت."

...

حتى مع استعداده النفسي لمواجهة عمه، لم يكن أكيڤا مهيأً لصدمة المشاعر العميقة التي اجتاحته عند إحياء هذه اللحظة. أصابته الذكرى كلكمة مباشرة إلى قلبه، صدى لما حدث في حملة برج الفتح. هناك، تماماً كما الآن، كان جايل وجنوده يسيطرون على الغرفة بالقوة. حينها قال جايل"اقتلوا الجميع"، ببرود مقيت، بينما امتثل جنوده بلا تعبير، يذبحون المستشارين، ويقطعون أوصال الحراس الأقوياء"السيوف الفضية" الذين تكبّد هازايل ووليراز عناء تجريدهم من أسلحتهم دون إلحاق الأذى بهم. حتى خدم الحمام لم يُعفَوا من القتل.

لقد كان حمام دم حرفياً: الإمبراطور وولي العهد مطروحان وسط بركة حمراء، الدم على الجدران، الدم يغمر الأرضية، الدم في كل مكان.

الصوت نفسه. الوجه نفسه. وحتى عدد الجنود. استطاع أكيڤا أن يخمّن، من الجروح التي بالكاد التأمت على وجوههم، أن بعض هؤلاء الرجال كانوا في البرج يوم انفجاره ونجوا بأعجوبة. كانوا يحملون السيوف ذاتها، والأسلحة الخسيسة التي باغتوه بها في ذلك اليوم الدامي.

وكانت تحية جايل كما هي أيضاً. آه، ذلك الصوت المتسلل كصفير زاحف: مع قوله"ابن أخي."

قالها حينها للأمير التافه يافث، قبل أن يقتله بدم بارد. والآن هو يوجهها إلى أكيڤا، متبوعة بلائحة طويلة من ألقابه التي ألقاها عليه بصوت متلذذ:"قاتل الوحوش. أمير الأوغاد. الجسد السابع الذي يحمل الاسم الملعون: أكيڤا."

أكيڤا، الذي كان يستمع بصمت، سمعها كلها، متسائلاً في أعماقه: هل أي من هذه الأسماء يعبر عني حقاً؟

ما الذي قصدته أمه حين قالت إنه لن يكون امتداداً لمصائرهم البائسة؟ شعر للحظة وكأن حتى اسم"أكيڤا" نفسه ليس اسمه الحقيقي، بل مجرد شيء آخر فرض عليه، كما فرض عليه درعه وسيفه. كان اسمه، مثل تدريبه، مجرد أداة أخرى من أدوات غير الشرعيين. وعند سماع رد فعل فيستيڤال على اسمه، بدأ يتساءل: من أكون غير ذلك؟ ماذا أيضاً؟

والإجابة الأولى التي خطرت في ذهنه كانت بسيطة للغاية، بقدر بساطة ما جاء إلى هنا لفعله، وبقدر بساطة رغباته.

أنا حي. تذكر تلك اللحظة—وقد بدت بعيدة جداً رغم أنها لم تكن كذلك—حين كان مستلقياً على ظهره في مسرح التدريب في كيب أرميسين، وفأس—فأس ليراز—منغرسة في الأرض الصلبة على بعد بوصات من خده. حينها كان يعتقد أن كارو قد ماتت، وهناك، وهو يلهث محدقاً في النجوم، تقبل أن الحياة ليست سوى وسيلة لعمل ما، أداة تُستخدم لتغيير العالم. حياته الخاصة: أداة لتشكيل المصير.

وتذكر استغاثة كارو قبل يوم واحد فقط، حين كانا محشورَين معاً في تلك المساحة الضيقة من الحمام.

"لا أريدك أن تشعر بالأسف،" قالت له."أريدك أن تكون... حياً."

كانت تعني شيئاً أعمق من مجرد البقاء على قيد الحياة كأداة. كان هناك شيء في طريقتها وهي تقولها، جعل أكيڤا يدرك أن الحياة بالنسبة إليها، في تلك اللحظة، كانت جوعاً.

ومهما كان اسمه أو ماضيه أو نسبه، كان أكيڤا حياً... وجائعاً أيضاً. جائعاً للحلم، للسلام، للشعور بجسد كارو ملتصقاً بجسده، للمنزل الذي قد يتشاركانه يوماً ما، في مكان ما، وللتغييرات التي سيريانها—وسيحدثانها— في المملكة لعقود قادمة.

كان حياً، ومصمماً على أن يبقى كذلك. لذلك، بينما كان عمه يهينه، مستقصياً عن نقطة ضعف—لم يكن القتل وحده كافياً، بل كان عليه أن يعذب أيضاً—ظل أكيڤا يسمع كلماته، لكنها لم تلامسه. كل تلك التهديدات كانت كظلٍّ يتلاشى مع بزوغ الفجر.

قال جايل: "اليوم سنكسر اللعنة. اليوم، أخيراً، ستموت."

هزّ أكيڤا رأسه. وفي ذهنه مرّ خاطر سريع: هل عليه أن يتظاهر بالضعف الذي لا يشعر به؟ في حمّام جورام، كانت تلك "التذكارات" البشعة المتمثلة بالأيدي المشوهة قد أعطت الدومينيون التفوق الذي احتاجوه لإخضاعه هو وهازايل وليراز. لكن الليلة كانت مختلفة. لم تداهمه موجة ضعف كما حدث من قبل. لم يشعر سوى بوعيٍ حاد بالندبة الجديدة في مؤخرة عنقه، حيث التقى سحره باللعنة وأزاحها جانباً.

تذكر الشعور بأطراف أصابع كارو وهي تتلمّس العلامة بخفة حين أراها لها. وتذكر ضغط كفها على قلبه، بلا أي صراخ للسحر في عروقه، بلا أي مرض، فقط النية التي حملها لمسة يدها.

كان مدركاً لمعاناتها مع وهجها المتلاشي ومواجهتها مع الكائن رازغوت. أراد أن يندفع نحوها، أن يحطم وجهه المتورم القبيح، ويحررها منه، وحتى أن يقتلع ذراعه المشوهة إن استلزم الأمر. وأراد كذلك أن يحشر ذلك المخلوق في زاوية ويُمطره بالأسئلة.

"المنحط". ماذا يعني هذا؟ لقد أتيحت له فرصة سؤاله من قبل، لكنه أضاعها، ولم يكن الآن هو الوقت المناسب أيضاً. كان يعرف أن كارو قادرة على التعامل مع هذا المخلوق.

كان خصمه الحقيقي يقف أمامه."ليس اليوم"، قال أكيفا لجايل، وكانت تلك أول الكلمات التي نطق بها منذ أن دخل هذا المكان."لن يموت أحد اليوم."

ضحكة جايل كريهة للغاية كما عهدها أكيفا."يا ابن أخي، انظر حولك. أياً كان ما قصدته بالتسلل إلى جانب سريري في الليل—وهنا، ولأول مرة"، حوّل جايل انتباهه بعيداً عن أكيفا ليلقي نظرة على كارو، وومضت في عينيه نظرة إعجاب—"...وكما أتوقع أن تفسيرها لا يمت إلى أي تفسير لطيف." توقف. ابتسم."أتوقع أنه يتعارض مع أهدافي تماماً."

كان مستمتعاً بنفسه. بالنسبة إليه، كان هذا امتداداً لصدى ما حدث في برج الفتح، إلى درجة أنه فشل في ملاحظة الاختلاف الجوهري: أكيفا لم يكن يرتجف تحت وطأة هجماته السحرية.

"هذا صحيح،" اعترف أكيفا."رغم أنني أشك في أنك تتوقع ما هو."

"ما هو؟" قالها بسخرية، واضعاً يده على صدره."تقصد أنك لم تأتِ لقتلي؟".

قالها وكأنها نكتة جيدة. ما السبب الآخر الذي قد يدفعهم للمجيء؟ لكن رد أكيفا جاء هادئاً: "لا. لم نفعل. لقد جئنا لنطلب منك الرحيل. أن تغادر كما أتيت، دون أن تراق دماء، ودون أن تأخذ أي شيء من هذا العالم معك. عد إلى وطنك. كلكم. هذا كل شيء."

"هذا كل شيء، أليس كذلك؟" قالها جايل متهكماً، متابعاً ضحكه بصوت مرتفع، وشيء من البصاق تطاير مع كلماته."تُقدّم الطلبات، إذاً؟".

قال أكيفا بنبرة ثابتة:"لقد كان طلباً. ولكنني مستعد لتحويله إلى مطلب."

ضيّق جايل عينيه، ورأى أكيفا كيف تحولت سخريته تدريجياً إلى حالة من الشك وعدم التصديق. هل بدأ يشعر أن هناك خطباً ما؟

"أيمكنك العدّ، أيها النغل؟" حاول جايل التمسك بنبرته الساخرة، لكنه لم يتمكن من إخفاء الحدة التي تسربت إلى صوته. وعندما دار بعينيه فجأة،

وكأنهما مثبتتان على عجلات، أدرك أكيفا أنه كان يعيد الحسابات في رأسه، محاولاً أن يستمد القوة من وضعه الحالي.

"أنتم اثنان فقط أمام أربعين" قال جايل. قال اثنان متجاهلاً وجود كارو تماماً. حسناً، لم يكن أكيفا ليصحح له. لم تكن تلك غلطته الوحيدة، لكنها الأكثر وضوحاً.

تابع جايل بنبرة زائفة من الثقة:"بغض النظر عن قوتكما أو دهائكما، فإن الأعداد هي التي تحسم الأمور في النهاية."

أجاب أكيفا دون تردد:"الأعداد لها أهمية". كان يفكر في الظلال التي طاردتها النيران، وفي الظلمة المتشابكة للكمين في أديلفاس."لكن أحياناً هناك عوامل أخرى تُغيّر مسار المعركة."

لم ينتظر أكيفا أن يسأله جايل عن تلك العوامل الأخرى.

فقط الأحمق من قد يسأل—لأنه يعلم أن الإجابة ستكون عرضاً عملياً—وجايل لم يكن أحمق. وقبل أن يتمكن الإمبراطور الوحشي من إصدار أوامره لجنوده بالهجوم أولاً، نطق أكيفا:"هل ظننت يوماً أن بإمكانك أن تفاجئني مجدداً؟".

وبعد ذلك نطق بكلمة واحدة فقط. كانت اسماً، في الحقيقة، رغم أن جايل لم يكن يعرفه. وفي لحظة واحدة، ارتسمت الحيرة على جبينه. لحظة واحدة فقط.

ثم تغيرت موازين المعركة.

61

القوة الخارقة اللازمة

"حسناً، لنترّو قليلاً"، قال ميك وهو يمسك بيده إحدى الأمنيات التي بدت كالصحن."ما هو الساموراي تحديدَ، برأيك؟ ألا تعتقدين أنه يجب علينا أن نعرف ذلك قبل أن نتمنى أن نصبح ساموراي؟".

"نقطة جيدة"، أمسكت زوزانا أمنية مشابهة في كفها. كانت أكبر بكثير من حجم يدها، وأثقل مما تبدو عليه."قد نحول أنفسنا إلى رجلين يابانيين". ضيقت عينيها وهي تحدق فيه."هل ستظل تحبني إذا أصبحت رجلاً يابانياً؟".

أجاب ميك دون تردد:"بالطبع. ولكن، رغم أن كلمة ساموراي كلمة رائعة، لا أعتقد أنها ما نعنيه حقاً. نحن فقط نريد أن نصبح قادرين على سحق الأعداء، أليس كذلك؟".

ردت زوزانا محذّرة:"حسناً، لا تصغها بهذه الطريقة. قد ينتهي بنا الأمر بأن نصبح ماهرين جداً في ركل مؤخرات الناس. لا تدر ظهرك لهم" أضافت بنبرة مهيبة."فهم لا يخطئون أبداً."

كانت صياغة التمني أمراً بالغ الأهمية. القصص الخيالية تعلّمك ذلك، حتى لو لم تكن كارو قد كررته مراراً.

رغم أن زوزانا استخدمت أمنيات سكوبي صغيرة من قبل، إلا أنها لم تمسك أبداً أمنية حقيقية بيدها. الآن، وهي تحمل واحدة، شعرت بثقلها يُرهِبها. ماذا لو أخطأت؟ هذه أمنية غافرييل. أي خطأ قد تكون عواقبه جسيمة.

لحظة. تراجعت بفكرها خطوة إلى الوراء. هذه أمنية غافرييل.

وكان هناك أربع منها في حقيبة كمان ميك.

الحقيبة الآن عند قدمي زوزانا. وما زالت تشعر بالذهول من جرأة ميك، وهو يسرق كنوز الأمنيات هذه مباشرةً من تحت أنف إستير الشريرة. يا له من إنجاز! تُرى، هل لاحظت إستير ذلك بعد؟ كيف ستكون حالتها الآن؟ وهل يمكن للانتقام أن يكون مرضياً عندما لا تشاهد غريمك وهو يعاني؟

في رأيها، نعم، بالطبع كان ذلك يُعد انتقاماً. وعلى أي حال، كانت هذه بالتأكيد إحدى المهام الثلاث التي أوكلتها إلى ميك. لكنهما كانا يختلفان حول أي مهمة كانت.

زوزانا أصرت أنها المهمة الثالثة والأخيرة، لأنها لا تزال تحتسب نجاحه في تشغيل مكيف الهواء في أوارزازات ضمن المهام. أما ميك، فقال إن ذلك لم يُحتسب—ولا بأي حال من الأحوال—لأنه كان في مصلحته الشخصية فقط، ليتمكن من الانقضاض عليها! ولذا كان يصر على أن هناك مهمة واحدة متبقية لينفذها.

لم تستطع زوزانا أن تتابع الجدال إلى حدٍّ بعيد دون أن يبدو وكأنها تتوسل لميك أن يطلب يدها للزواج فوراً، لذا قررت أن تترك له الأمر على طريقته. إلى جانب ذلك، كانت أيديهما مشغولة في الوقت الحالي: السماء ما زالت فارغة بشكل ينذر بالسوء، وهاتفها صامت تماماً

كالصمت الذي يحيط بهما. لم يكونا متأكدين مما يجب عليهما فعله أو محاولة فعله.

مهارات الطيران والقتال، أو هل يمكنهما المساعدة؟ ماذا يمكنهما فعله مما يعجز عنه أكيثا وفيركو وكارو؟ لم تظن زوزانا أن بإمكانك التمني للحصول على خبرة قتالية وحس استراتيجي. هل يمكن ذلك حقاً؟

وكانت هناك أيضاً إليزا لتفكر فيها. حتى لو استنفدا كل الأمنيات وملآ نفسيهما بالقوى الخارقة اللازمة، وانطلقا في السماء لإنقاذ الموقف، لا يمكنهما ببساطة أن يتركاها هنا جالسة بمفردها، أليس كذلك؟

لكن، لحظة.

نظرت زوزانا إلى إليزا، ثم إلى ميك. رفعت حاجبها. التفت ميك لينظر إلى إليزا هو الآخر. "أجل، بالطبع"، قال مباشرة، وكأن الفكرة راودته في نفس اللحظة.

وبسرعة، وسط ضغط الوقت والحاجة الملحّة، صاغا معاً أفضل صيغة يمكنهما التفكير فيها لمعالجة امرأة شابة كان مرضها لغزاً بالنسبة إليهما. في صمت مهيب، نطقت زوزانا الكلمات إلى الغافرييل بين يديها. بدا وكأنها كانت تخاطب بريمستون نفسه.

"أتمنى أن تُمنح إليزا جونز، المولودة كإلازيل المبجلة، السيطرة الكاملة على نفسها في العقل والجسد، وأن تكون بخير."

ثم، وكأن شيئاً ما تملّكها، أضافت في النهاية: أتمنى أن تصبح أفضل نسخة ممكنة من نفسها.

لأن هذا بدا لها، في تلك اللحظة، أصدق ما يمكن أن يتمناه أحد. ليس خيانة للذات من خلال الحسد أو الرغبة في أن تكون شخصاً آخر، بل تعميقاً للذات، ونضوجاً حقيقياً.

عندما يتجاوز التمني طاقة الميدالية السحرية التي تحتويها، لا يحدث شيء. كأنك تحمل سكوبي وتتمنى مليون دولار—لن يتحرك السكوبي، ولن يحدث شيء. لم يكن ميك وزوزانا يعرفان إن كان ما طلباه يقع ضمن حدود قوة الغافرييل. لذا راقبا إليزا عن كثب، بحثاً عن أي إشارة صغيرة تُظهر أن الأمنية قد بدأت تأخذ مفعولها.

لكن لم تكن هناك إشارة ما.

أو بالأحرى... لم تكن أي إشارة صغيرة على الإطلاق.

ولا حتى لمحة.

62

عصر الحروب

الكلمة التي نطق بها أكيفا كانت:"هاكسايا". لم يكن لدى جايل أي فكرة عما تعنيه هذه الكلمة، أو حتى إنها اسم، لكن النتيجة كانت واضحة بما يكفي.

ثانية واحدة. كان الهواء بجانب جايل فارغاً... ثم لم يعد كذلك. الشكل الذي ملأه—شريط من الفراء والأسنان—راح يتحرك. رأى جايل ذلك، لكن قبل أن يدرك تماماً ما كان يحدث، ارتطم به بقوة. نصفان من نفس الثانية: مشهد الفريسة والصيّاد، والهجوم الذي لم يترك له وقتاً للتفكير. شحب إلى الخلف بسرعة كبيرة.

ثانيتان. كان جنوده جميعهم أمامه. لم يلتفت أحد منهم إلا عندما شعر بالفولاذ البارد على جلده وأطلق شهقة لاإرادية. وبحلول الوقت الذي استداروا فيه، كان جايل قد وقع على ركبتيه عند عتبة الباب، وسكين موجهة إلى عنقه، ومهاجمه مختبئ خلفه، بعيداً عن متناولهم. انطلقت صرخة حادة، ملأت الغرفة غضباً.

كانت تشبه الفوضى التي تدور في رأس جايل، لكنها لم تصدر من فمه. لم يجرؤ على الصراخ، والشفرة الباردة تضغط على رقبته. كانت تلك الصرخات تأتي من المنحط، ذلك المخلوق الملتف والمتلوّي على السرير، لا يزال يصارع مع الفتاة.

ثلاث ثوانٍ.

وخزته السكين. للحظة، اعتقد جايل أن حنجرته قد شُقت، وداهمه الذعر. لكنه أدرك أنه لا يزال قادراً على التنفس. الجرح كان بسيطاً—مجرد خدش، لكن الألم كان حاداً.

"آسفة جداً"، جاء صوت—همسة أنثوية قريبة من أذنه. كانت النبرة مشبعة بالسخرية، والسكين حادة، لكنها لم تكن مترددة في استخدامها. خدش آخر، جرح آخر، ثم ضحكة خافتة من خلف كتفه. ضحكة عميقة، ساخرة، مستمتعة.

لم يكن لدى رجاله الوقت الكافي لفعل أي شيء سوى إدارة رؤوسهم نحو المشهد المربك. الوقت بين الثواني كان مشحوناً بصدمة صامتة، وعجّ بالصراخ المتواصل لهذه المخلوق المنحط رازغوت، الذي بدا وكأنه فقد عقله تماماً.

"لا، لا، لا!" صرخ بصوت مضمخ بالغضب الأسود."اقتلوهم! اقتلوهم!".

وكأن أحد الجنود تلقى الأمر مباشرة من رازغوت، تحرك نحو جايل، رافعاً سيفه باتجاه الكيميرا التي تمسك به. لكنها لم تنتظر. شدّت ذراعها حول جايل بإحكام أكبر، ومخالبها انغرست في جنبه، مخترقة ثيابه إلى لحمه. السكين ضغطت أعمق في رقبته أيضاً.

"توقفوا!" صرخ جايل، مخاطباً الجميع—هي ورجاله معاً. كان صوت صرخته أشبه بنباح مذعور، ولم يعجبه ذلك أبداً."تراجعوا!".

كان جايل يحاول التفكير فيما يمكن أن يفعله—خمس ثوانٍ—لكنه ارتكب خطأه الفادح عندما أرسل كل جنوده أمامه كدرع، ولم يبقِ أحداً

خلفه لحمايته. والآن، بسحب مهاجمته له إلى العتبة، أعطت نفسها كامل الحائط كحاجز... وجعلت جسده حاجزاً أيضاً. وخلفها لم يكن هناك شيء سوى غرفة فارغة. لم يتمكن أحد من الوصول إليها، وكان هذا خطأ جايل نفسه، إذ اختبأ خلف جدار من الجنود.

"ما أسرع نزف الدم". قالت بصوتها الوحشي العميق، وكأنها تحدّثه من قاع الغريزة. أظن أن الدم يريد أن يتحرر. حتى دمك يكرهك."هاكسايا" جاء صوت أكيفا تحذيرياً —والآن فهم جايل أخيراً أن الكلمة كانت اسماً. مهمتنا كانت: لا دماء. لكن الأوان قد فات لذلك. فعنق جايل قد تلطخ بالدم. وها هو يتلوى.

في تلك الأثناء، كان رازغوت لا يزال يصرخ. لكن الفتاة الآن تحررت منه، وتقف بجانب أكيفا. الثلاثة الآن بجانب بعضهم: بشرية وسيراف ووحش. الثلاثة الذين كان جايل قد تلقى التحذيرات بشأنهم. ولكن ماذا عن هذه الرابعة؟ هذه الكيميرا التي لم يكن يتوقعها؟ كيف حدث ذلك؟ كيف؟

عندما تحدث أكيفا مجدداً، كان يخاطب جايل بنبرة هادئة وكأنه يعيد خيطاً مقطوعاً في حديث غير منتهٍ."عوامل أخرى"، قال، بصوت سلس وهادئ على نحو مُهلك للأعصاب. ثم أعاد ما قاله منذ لحظات"عوامل أخرى قد تغير مسار المعركة. مثل إعطاء قيمة خاصة لحياة واحدة فوق حياة الآخرين. حياتك، على سبيل المثال. لو كانت الأعداد هي العامل الوحيد المهم، لكان بإمكانك الفوز هنا. وهذا بعيد عنك. أنت ستموت. ستموت أولاً، لكن قد ينتصر رجالك، إذا قرروا أن حياتك لا تعنيهم". توقف أكيفا للحظة، ثم حرّك نظراته نحو الجنود الواقفين هناك، وكأنهم كائنات قادرة على اتخاذ القرار، وليسوا مجرد جنود يُنفذون الأوامر."هل هذا ما تريده؟".

من كان يخاطب؟ جايل أم جنوده؟ فكرة أن بإمكانهم الإجابة، أن بإمكانهم اختيار مصيره، كانت صادمة ومروعة لجايل.

"لا"، وجد نفسه يتفوه بالكلمة بسرعة، قبل أن يجرؤ أي من جنوده على تقديم إجابة مختلفة.

أوضح أكيفا بهدوء:"أنت تريد أن تعيش".

نعم، أراد جايل أن يعيش. لكن فكرة أن عدوه قد يسمح له بذلك كانت غير قابلة للتصديق بالنسبة إليه.

"لا تلعب معي ألعاباً، يا قاتل الوحوش. ماذا تريد؟".

قال أكيفا:"أولاً، أريد من رجالك أن يُلقوا سيوفهم".

...

أما كارو فقد كانت تعاني من خرخرة رازغوت المزعجة ويده المتعرقة التي كانت تطبق على معصمها كالكماشة، ولهذا، في اللحظة التي نطق فيها أكيفا اسم هاكسايا، سحبت مرفقها بقوة، ثم استدارت بسرعة على كعبها لتضرب محجر عين ذلك المخلوق، مستغلةً لحظة المفاجأة التي ألمت به للإفلات منه.

ومع ذلك، بالكاد استطاعت الإفلات. رغم انزلاق قبضته المبتلّة بالعرق لكنها مزقت بشرتها بسبب قوتها الساحقة ذات المخالب. دفعت كارو قدمها بقوة على إطار السرير وسحبت بكل طاقتها، حتى انفصلت يدها أخيراً، لكن جلدها خرج ممزقاً ونازفاً. ومع ذلك، تحررت منه.

كان رازغوت ممسكاً بعينه ويصرخ:"لا، لا، لا!"، حين كانت عينه الأخرى مفتوحة، جامحة وشريرة، تدور في محجرها، تنظر بكراهية غريزية. أما كارو، فكانت تتراجع إلى الخلف، مبتعدة عنه، بينما كانت تسحب شفراتها الهلالية، وتتخذ مكانها بجانب أكيفا. كانت على أحد جانبيه، وڤيركو على الجانب الآخر، كلاهما يراقبان هاكسايا وهي تسيطر على الوحش جايل.

هاكسايا، التي عادت إلى الحياة، والتي استعادت شكلها الثعلبي الأصلي—نحيلة وسريعة جداً—بفضل الأسنان التي سرقوها من متحف التاريخ الطبيعي.

لم تكن جزءاً من الخطة منذ البداية. عندما تبلورت الفكرة لأول مرة في ذهن كارو في الكهوف، كان مصدر إلهامها هو جثة هاكسايا—أو بالأحرى، جثة تين التي كانت آخر جسد سكنت فيه روح هاكسايا. لكن كارو لم تكن تنوي أبداً أن تلعب هاكسايا أي دور في تنفيذ الخطة. جمعت حينها روح الجندي مع فكرة أن تقرر لاحقاً ما يجب فعله بها. وضعت المبخرة الصغيرة، التي احتوت على روح هاكسايا، في حزامها، ونسيت أن تضعها مع الأرواح الأخرى قبل مغادرة الكهوف.

مصادفة؟ قَدَر؟ من يدري.

أياً كان السبب، فقد كان ذلك ما دفع كارو، في وقت سابق من تلك الليلة، وبعد شعورها بشيء مقلق من إستير، إلى التفكير في منح ثعلبة الكيميرا هاكسايا فرصة لاستعادة شرفها.

كانوا يأملون ألا تكون هناك حاجة لجندي ظل في هذا المكان. كانوا يأملون، حتى عندما تسللوا عبر النافذة، مخترقين ضوء القمر المتشقق ليس ثلاث مرات بل أربع مرات، أن الخطة ستسير وفق أبسط صورها. لكنها لم تفعل.

ومع ذلك، لم يكونوا أغبياء ليأتوا دون استعداد.

هل يمكننا الوثوق بها؟، كان هذا السؤال الذي طرحه الثلاثة على أنفسهم. كانت روح هاكسايا الوحيدة بحوزتهم، مما جعلها المرشحة الوحيدة لهذه المهمة.

"لقد كان الأمر شخصياً"، كرر أكيفا كلمات ليراز. كان يشير إلى معركة ساقّاث، وإلى ما حدث هناك وجعل ليراز تتقبل الانتقام الوحشي كجزء من حياتها. في النهاية، اعتقدوا أن هاكسايا ستتمكن من تقدير خطورة المهمة التي كانوا بصددها، ومدى أهمية الرهان، وأن تلعب دورها. وبالفعل، يبدو أنها فعلت ذلك—مع استثناء صغير هو تجاهلها للقانون بعدم سفك الدماء. لكن ربما كان ذلك قراراً صائباً بالنظر إلى الموقف.

كان جايل شاحباً، وكانت عيناه جاحظتين بالذعر، وصوته يرتجف وهو يصدر الأمر لجنوده بإلقاء سيوفهم.

"تراجعوا"، أمرهم أكيڤا، فتراجعوا بحذر، متفرقين حتى التصقوا بجدران الغرفة.

كان من الصعب التفكير فيهم كأفراد، ككائنات عاقلة لها أرواح. حاولت كارو أن تنظر إلى وجوههم واحداً تلو الآخر، محاولةً أن تراهم كحقيقة واقعة: مواطنون من عالمها، صنعهم التدريب وشكلتهم الظروف ليصبحوا ما هم عليه الآن. ربما—إذا استطاع أكيڤا، وإذا استطاعت ليراز—يمكنهم فك هذه السلاسل، وتفكيك ما أصبحوا عليه، وإعادة تشكيل أنفسهم من جديد.

لكنها لم تستطع رؤية ذلك بعد. ليس الآن. لكنها استطاعت أن تأمل. ليس من أجل جايل. لا يمكن له أن يكون جزءاً من المستقبل الذي كانوا يبنونه. تقدم أكيڤا نحوه، بينما كانت شفرات كارو المسلولة تحرس جانبه الأيمن، وڤيركو يحرس جانبه الأيسر. كانوا على وشك إنهاء الأمر هنا

قال أكيڤا موجّهاً حديثه إلى الجنود:"استمعوا إلي. إن عصر الحروب قد انتهى. للذين تراجعوا عن سفك الدماء، سيكون هناك عفو." تحدث وكأن لديه القدرة على إصدار مثل هذه الوعود. وبالرغم من إدراكها الكامل للشكوك الثقيلة التي تغيم فوق مستقبلهم، صدقته كارو. لكن ماذا عن السيادة؟ هل صدقوه؟ لم تستطع أن تصرح بذلك. ظلوا صامتين، فقد دربوا على ذلك. أما جايل فقد كان صامتاً تحت سكين هاكسايا الملتصق برقبته، وصمت رعبه لم يكن فيه شك. أما رازغوت... فقد كان الوحيد الذي كسر هذا الصمت.

"عصر الحروب؟"، كرر ما قاله أكيڤا بتهكّم، وهو جالس عند حافة السرير، إحدى ساقيه تتدلّى بجانب السرير مثل شريط بالٍ لا قيمة له. كانت عينه التي غرست كارو مرفقها فيها مغلقة بسبب الورم، أما الأخرى

فقد بدت جميلة على نحو مقلق وغير منسجمة مع بقية ملامحه، لكنها مسكونة بالجنون مع ذلك السواد الخالص والقاتم.

دمدم بصوت غاضب:"ومن تكون لتُنهي عصراً؟ أأنت المختار من بين قومك؟ هل ركعت أمام السحرة وشرّعت روحك لأناملهم الحادة؟ هل عمّدت النجوم كما تعمد الأطفال في حوض ماء؟ أنا من أنهى العصر الأول، وسأنهي الثاني أيضاً". وبهذه الكلمات، رفع فجأة خنجراً لم يره أحد من قبل، وقذف به نحو أكيڤا. لم يتحرك أحد. الوقت قد فات لذلك.

حتى كارو، التي امتدت يدها متأخرة جداً، وكأنها تستطيع أن تمسك بالخنجر في الهواء أو على الأقل تصدّه، لكنه كان قد تجاوزها بالفعل. لم يتحرك ڤيركو، الواقف على الجانب الآخر من أكيڤا. ولا أكيڤا نفسه ولا حتى بمقدار شعرة.

وكانت يد رازغوت ثابتة، وتسديدته لا تخيب.

الخنجر، هو ما رأته كارو على حدود زاوية رؤيتها، مجرد لمحة في طرف عينيها. لم تستطع يدها الإمساك بالخنجر، ولم تكن رأسها لتدور بالسرعة الكافية لترى لحظة دخوله قلب أكيڤا.

قلبه. ذلك القلب الذي كانت قد وضعت كفها عليه، وخدّها أيضاً، لكنها لم تضع قلبها عليه بعد. ولم تضغط صدرها إلى صدره. ولم تضم حياتها إلى حياته. ليس بعد.

ذلك القلب الذي يُحرّك دمه، والذي كان نصفها الآخر. رأته بطرف عينها، وكان ذلك كافياً لأن ترى.

الخنجر اخترق قلب أكيڤا.

63

حدّ السكين

جليد ونهاية. تجمّدت اللحظة، بصورة مستحيلة، لا تُصدق. لكنها حقيقية.

يمكن لوجودك بأكمله أن يتحوّل إلى صرخة، عند حد سكين مقذوف، بهذه السرعة. وهذا ما حدث لكارو.

في تلك اللحظة، لم تكن كياناً من لحم ودم، بل كانت مجرد هواء يندفع ليتجمع في صرخة قد لا تنتهي أبداً.

64

إقناع

في أحد الأيام، كان هناك ملاك يحتضر وسط الضباب.

وكان ينبغي على الشيطانة أن تنهي أمره دون أدنى تردد. لكنها لم تفعل. وماذا لو فعلت؟

لقد سألت كارو نفسها هذا السؤال مئات المرات، بصيغ مختلفة، بل إنها تمنت ذلك في لحظات حزنها الحالكة في القصر المغربي، حينما لم تكن ترى سوى الموت الذي انبثق من رحمتها.

لو كانت قد قتلت أكيفا في ذلك اليوم، أو حتى تركته يموت، لاستمرت الحرب بلا توقف. وربما لمدة ألف عام أخرى؟

لكنها لم تفعل، ولم يحدث ذلك.

"عصر الحروب قد انتهى"، هذا ما قاله أكيفا للتو، وحتى في تلك اللحظة التي رأت فيها كارو ما رأته دون أدنى شك، وبينما كان كيانها بأكمله يستعد للصراخ، رفض قلبها أن يصدق أن عصر الحروب قد انتهى، ولن يموت أكيفا بهذه الطريقة. لكن السيف اخترق قلبه.

ومع ذلك، لم تتفجر صرخة كارو. بل حلت محلها صرخة أخرى، لكن قبلها كان هناك صوت. هو جزء من ثانية بعد أن غاص السكين في صدر أكيفا... الصلد. لم يكن صوت لحم ممزق.

استدار رأس كارو، وعيناها تتجولان في حالة من الذهول، تنسجان نمطاً عشوائياً وهي تحاول استيعاب ما رأته.

هناك وقف أكيفا، بلا حراك.

لا خطوة مترنحة، ولا دم، ولا مقبض سكين غرز في قلبه. وفي يأس شديد التفتت كارو بعينيها بسرعة. لم تكن الوحيدة التي فعلت ذلك، لكن لا أحد في القاعة استطاع أن يشعر بنفس الهاوية التي شعرت بها تلك اللحظة، أو بنفس البهجة التي اجتاحتها الآن عندما رأت السكين مغروساً في الجدار خلف أكيفا.

لا أحد عرف طعم العجب الذي اجتاحها وهي تدرك الحقيقة التي بدأت تتجسد أمامها، لكن الجميع في القاعة تذوقوا طعم تلك اللحظة.

كانت هاكسايا أول من تحدثت:"إنه غير مرئي للموت"، تمتمت، لأنه لم يكن هناك مجال للشك فيما حدث للتو. أكيفا لم يتحرك، والمسار لم يكن خدعة. لقد عبر السكين من خلاله.

كارو هي من استولى على عينيه في تلك اللحظة، ونظرت إليه لتراه نصف مذهول ونصف مطارد بأشباح من ماضٍ ثقيل. أرادت أن تسأله: هل فعلتَ هذا؟ لا بد أنه فعل. لم يكن أحد يعرف، حتى هو نفسه، ما الذي كان قادراً عليه حقاً. أما رازغوت، فقد انهار على الأرض، يصرخ ويلطم جبينه بقبضتيه. بخطوتين فقط وصلت إليه كارو، أمسكت به وأسقطته أرضاً وهي تبحث في طيات ثيابه عن أي أسلحة أخرى. المنحط لم يكن حتى واعياً لحضورها، وكأنه قد انفصل عن الواقع تماماً.

أما الدومينيون، فقد بدوا حذرين، لكن مبهورين أيضاً، بحضور أكيفا. شعرت كارو أنهم لن يقدموا على أي هجوم الآن، ومع ذلك، لم تشعر

بالاسترخاء. حياة أكيفا التي لطالما كانت على المحك، والمشهد الذي شاهدته بطرف عينها ما زال يوترها. أرادت أن تغادر هذا المكان سريعاً، وكل ما تبقى الآن هو إقناعهم بخطتها، البسيطة رغم كل شيء. وأخيراً، حانت تلك اللحظة.

مرة أخرى، واجه أكيفا عمه جايل الذي التزم الصمت، وجهه مشدود وشاحب، وارتجاف فمه المشوه فضح انهياره. في مواجهة مثل هذه القوة، حتى الشجاعة ستسخر منه.

لم يسحب أكيفا سيفيه، وبقيت يداه طليقتين. مد إحداهما نحو صدر عمه ووضعها مسطحة عليه. كانت الحركة تبدو ودية بشكل ما، لكن عيني جايل كانتا تدوران في محجريهما بجنون، يحاول أن يفهم ما الذي يحدث له. ولم يستغرق الأمر وقتاً طويلاً ليعرف.

راقبت كارو يد أكيفا، وقد ذكّرتها تلك اللحظة بأخرى مضت؛ عندما وصلت إلى باب بريمستون في باريس، مرهقة من جرّ أنياب الفيلة عبر المدينة. رأت حينها، لأول مرة، بصمة يد وسمت بالنار على الخشب. عندما لمستها بأصابعها، تناثر الرماد وسقط. ثم تذكرت كيشميش، محترقاً وينازع بين يديها، قلبه كان ينبض بالذعر قبل أن يخفت تدريجياً حتى توقف تماماً. وتذكرت أزيز الحرائق وهي تمزقها من الحزن—ذلك الحزن الذي أغرقها بالكامل ثم دفعها إلى حزن أعظم، عندما ركضت من شقتها عبر الشوارع لتجد باب بريمستون مشتعلاً. نار زرقاء جهنمية، وفي وهجها، بدت ظلال أجنحة.

في اللحظة ذاتها حول العالم، عشرات الأبواب التي كانت تحمل بصمات أيد متفحمة وسمت بنار غير طبيعية. أكيفا هو من فعل ذلك. كل السيرافيم مخلوقات نارية، لكن وسم العلامات تلك عن بُعد كان قدرة خاصة به، مكنته من تدمير كل مداخل بريمستون دفعة واحدة، قاطعاً عدوه عن العالم دون أدنى تحذير.

وعندما رأت كارو الجلد المتقرح على جثة تِين في كهوف الكيرين، حيث بدا وسم يد ليراز المحروقة واضحة على صدرها، راودها نفس التفكير.

تسرّب الدخان من تحت راحة أكيفا. ربما شمّ جايل الرائحة قبل أن يشعر بالحرارة التي بدأت تلتهم ثيابه، أو ربما لم يفعل، إذ لم يكن يرتدي درعاً يحميه، بل اكتفى بثياب العرض المهيبة التي اخترعها ليبهر البشرية. أياً كان السبب، الحرارة أو الدخان، فقد جعلت كارو تدرك التوهج في عينيه، ثم الذعر الذي استولى عليه بينما حاول جاهداً الإفلات من قبضة تلك اليد الضاغطة. لوهلة، تمنّت كارو ألا تقوم هاكسايا بقتله عن طريق الخطأ.

صرخة جايل كانت أشبه بعويل متذبذب، وراقبته كارو بينما تراجع أكيفا خطوة إلى الوراء. وها هو هناك: وسم يدٍ سوداء محترقة محفورة في صدر جايل، متفحمة وتفوح برائحة اللحم المحترق، بينما بدأ السواد يتقشر ليكشف اللحم النيئ تحتها. بصمة يد في اللحم. إقناع.

"عد إلى موطنك"، قال أكيفا بصوت ثابت."أو سأشعل الوسم فيك أينما كنت، وأينما كنتُ أنا، لا فرق. إن لم تفعل ما أقول، سأحرقك حتى لا يبقى منك حتى الرماد، ولن يكون هناك أثر يدل على المكان الذي كنت تقف فيه."

أفلتت هاكسايا جايل وتراجعت جانباً. لم تعد سكينها ضرورية الآن، فمسحت النصل على كم الإمبراطور الأبيض نفسه. هوى جايل أرضاً وكأن ساقيه لم تعودا قادرتين على حمله، وجهه مشبع بالألم والغضب والعجز الذي تجمد على ملامحه. بدا وكأنه يحاول استيعاب الوضع، يحاول فهم كل ما خسره. وأخيراً، انفجر قائلاً:"وماذا بعد؟ عندما أعود إلى المملكة حاملاً علامتك؟ ستحرقني حينها، أليس كذلك؟ لماذا عليّ أن أطيعك الآن؟".

صوت أكيفا ظلّ هادئً."أعطيك وعداً. عد إلى موطنك الآن. خذ

جيشك معك ولا شيء آخر. لا تُحدث فوضى. فقط عد، ولن أشعل الوسم. أعدك بهذا."

ضحك جايل بسخريةٍ مترددة، وكأنما لم يصدق."أنت تعدني؟ ستتركني أعيش، بكل بساطة؟".

راقبت كارو أكيڤا وهو يرد. منذ اللحظة التي اقتحم فيها جايل الغرفة، حافظ أكيڤا على هدوئه، وتمكن من إخفاء الكراهية العميقة التي أشعلها هذا الرجل داخله. قال بصوت متزن، لكن بشيء من القسوة:"هذا ليس ما قلته."

هل كان يفكر في هازايل؟ في ڤيستيڤال؟ أو في المستقبل الذي يحاولون تغييره الآن، حيث الأسلحة كانت على وشك إعادة تشكيل المملكة وتحويلها إلى شيء أكثر وحشية مما عرفته سابقاً؟

"لن أحرقك"، قال أكيڤا، وصوت احتقاره لعمه بدا واضحاً في نبرته."هذا وعدي الوحيد، لكنه لا يعني أنك ستعيش". ثم ترك لعقل جايل الشرير أن يملأ الفراغ بما هو أسوأ."ربما تكون لديك فرصة". ابتسامة رقيقة ارتسمت على وجهه."ربما ستراني قادماً". ثم غرق في صمتٍ عميق وطويل، قبل أن يتلاشى فجأة."لكن على الأرجح... لن تفعل."

لحقت كارو به واختفت هي الأخرى. ثم لحقهما ڤيركو وهاكسايا بعد لحظة، بينما ألقى أكيڤا وهمه السحري على كليهما. رأى جايل والدومينيون ظلالاً تتحرك نحو النافذة، ثم تلاشت تماماً، ولم يبقَ في المكان سوى أنفاس إمبراطور مكسور تتقطع بشدة، ونشيج وحش مجنون، وأربعون جندياً صامتون، لا يعرفون ماذا يفعلون بأنفسهم.

65

المختارون

هو واحد من بين اثني عشر في زمن بعيد، وكان المجد له.

أما هي، فقد اختيرت كواحدة من الاثني عشر. أوه، يا له من مجد.

برزوا من بين الآلاف. مرشحون جاؤوا من كل أرجاء المملكة، شباب يملؤهم الأمل، يملؤهم الفخر، وتغمرهم الأحلام. يا له من جمال. جميعهم رائعون وأقوياء، جلودهم من كل لون، من لون أفتح لؤلؤة إلى أغمق من الكهرمان الأسود. أحمر وأسمر وكريمي وبني، وحتى من قبائل أوسكو ريماروث، حيث الأفق أبدي الغروب، وكان بينهم زُرق.

هكذا كان السيرافيم في ذلك الحين: أعظم عطايا العالم، وكأنهم جواهر تناثرت على بساط غني الزركشة.

بعضهم جاء يرتدي الريش، وآخرون الحرير. بعضهم زينته المعادن الداكنة، وآخرون ارتدوا الجلود. لبسوا الذهب، وزيّنوا أجسادهم بالحبر، وكان شعرهم مجدولاً أو متموجاً. ذهبياً أو أسود أو أخضر، أو ربما كانوا حليقي الرأس في أنماط أشبه باللهب.

أما رازغوت، فلم يكن ليلفت النظر وسط هذا الجمع. لا بملبسه، الذي كان أنيقاً وبسيطاً، ولا بلونه، الذي لم يكن قد بدا باهتاً له من قبل حتى ذلك اليوم. كان لون بشرته حنطياً، وشعره وعينيه بنيين. كان جميلاً أيضاً حينها، لكنهم جميعاً كانوا كذلك، ولم يكن هناك من يفوقهم جمالاً أكثر من إلازيل

لقد جاءت من تشافيسيري، أرض القبائل الأشد ظلاماً بين السيرافيم. بشرتها سوداء كلون جناح الغراب في وقت الكسوفٍ، وشعرها ناعم مثل الريش، بلون وردة الفجر، يتهادى في شلالات باهتة على كتفيها الداكنين. كان على كل خد خط أبيض مرسوم، ونقطة فوق كل عين، أما عيناها، فكانتا بنيتين وليس سوداوين، وأفتح من بقية لونها، ومثيرتين للدهشة. ثم هناك بياض عينيها. لم تسقط ثلوج يوماً أنقى من بياض عيني إلازيل.

كل قبيلة أرسلت أفضل ما لديها. كلهم... ما عدا واحدة. كان لونها غائباً عن هذا الحشد: لم تكن هناك عيون النار بين تلك الجموع من نخبة شباب العالم. وحدهم الستيليون عارضوا هذا الاختيار وكل ما يمثّله، ولكن لم يبالِ أحدٌ، في ذلك الحين. في ذلك اليوم، نُسوا، وأُهملوا، بل حتى نُبذوا. لكن ذلك سيتغير لاحقاً.

يا لنجوم السماء... كيف سيتغير هذا.

وحدهم السحرة العارفون، كانوا يعلمون ما الذي يبحثون عنه، ولم يخبروا أحداً. كانوا يختبرون، وكانت اختباراتهم غامضة وعميقة. ومع كل يوم، كان عدد المرشحين يتناقص—المتأملون، والفخورون، والحالمون يعودون إلى حيث أتوا، بلا مجد لهم—لكن البعض صمد. يوماً بعد يوم، برز البعض بينما سقط آخرون، حتى بقوا في النهاية اثني عشر فقط أمام السحرة، وعندها فقط، ابتسم السحرة.

في ذلك اليوم، ودّع الاثنا عشر الحياة التي عرفوها ليصبحوا الفيريرا، الأوائل والوحيدين. انقسموا إلى فريقين من ستة أفراد لكل منهما، فريقان لرحلتين مختلفتين. دخلوا في تدريبات شاقة لتحضيرهم لما ينتظرهم، لكن

من أصبحوا عليه في النهاية لم يكن كما كانوا في البداية. لقد... حدث شيء لهم. حدث شيء لأرواحهم، أو ما يُعرف بالأنيميا—ذواتهم غير المادية، التي هي كليتهم الحقيقية، بينما كانت أجسادهم مجرد رموز ثابتة في الفضاء.

كان السحرة دائماً يسعون ويتعمقون، ومن هؤلاء الفيريرا قد صنعوا شيئاً جديداً. وهذا أسعدهم لأن عملهم كان جديداً، وكان عظيماً.

تم اختيار الفيريرا ليكونوا مستكشفين، حاملي النور لشعبهم، ليسافروا عبر جميع طبقات الكونتينيوم، وهو الكل الأعظم. شرحه لهم ماغوس ريغينت، عميد كلية الكوزمولوجيا، قائلاً:"الأكوان تتراصّ واحداً فوق الآخر كصفحات كتاب. ولكن في الكونتينيوم، كل صفحة لانهائية، والكتاب نفسه لا نهاية له."

كان ذلك يعني أن كل"صفحة" تمتد بلا حدود على مستواها الخاص. لا يمكن لأحد أن يأمل في الوصول إلى حافة الكون؛ لأنه ببساطة لا حدود له. إذا سافر مستكشف عبر المستوى، فإنه سيحلّق إلى الأبد ولن يجد شيئاً يصطدم به. كواكب ونجوم؟ نعم. عوالم وفراغ؟ كذلك. لكن حدود؟ لا وجود لها. لا شيء يمكن تجاوزه.

لذلك كان من الضروري الدفع عبر المستوى نفسه، لا على طوله، بل مباشرةً إلى داخله. كأن تكون رأس قلمٍ تُغرس في الصفحة لتخترقها وتكتب نفسها على الصفحة التالية. لقد تعلّم السحرة كيفية القيام بذلك، بعد آلاف السنين من الدراسة. وكان هذا هو عمل الفيريرا: أن يخترقوا، ويكتبوا أنفسهم وعرقهم على كل عالم جديد يلتقون به.

فريقٌ من الستة يتجه في اتجاهٍ واحد، والفريق الآخر في الاتجاه المعاكس. ولما تبقى من حياتهم، ستتسع المسافة بينهم باستمرار— لتصبح أعظم مسافة تم تحقيقها بين أفراد عرقهم أو أي عرق آخر.

كان هذا هو القمة بالنسبة إلى عالمٍ قديم جداً: لا أقل من رسم خريطة الكلية العظمى للكل الأعظم، وربط اكتمال الكونتينيوم بنورهم.

أن تفتح الأبواب... وتمضي، ثم تمضي، من كون إلى كون إلى كون. أن تعرفهم، وبمعرفتهم، بطريقة ما، تمتلكهم.

كان كل فريقٍ من الستة كلَّ شيءٍ لبعضهم البعض—رفاقاً، وعائلة، وحماة، وأصدقاء، وأحباء أيضاً. لقد كُلّفوا، بالإضافة إلى مهمتهم العظمى، أن ينجبوا ورثةً لمعرفةٍ لا أطفالاً. كانوا ثلاثة رجال وثلاث نساء، وهكذا رسم السحرة ذلك التكليف: ليس لإنجاب"أطفال"، بل "ورثة للمعرفة".

كانوا ليصبحوا بداية قبيلة جديدة، شيئاً أعظم مما كان عليه شعبهم يوماً. كانت إلازيل ورازغوت من الفريق ذاته، مع إياوث ودفيرا، وكلوس وأريث. وُجهتهم قد حُددت، وكانت ليلة أخرى من الضوء المتوهج، تجذب أعين نجوم الآلهة إليهم. من أجل مجد جميع السيرافيم، هذا الإنجاز العظيم أمامهم، امتدادٌ لأجنحة لن يُنسى أبداً، انطلاقة ستتردد أصداؤها عبر الزمن. وفي يومٍ بعيدٍ، بعيدٍ جداً إلى حد لا يُتصوّر، سيعودون إلى موطنهم... هم أو ذريتهم.

إلى ميليز. ميليز، البداية والنهاية، ميليز الأبدية. عالم السيرافيم الأم.

كان مقدراً أن يُذكروا إلى الأبد. أن يُبجَّلوا. أبطال شعبهم، فاتحو الأبواب، الأنوار في الظلام. كان كل شيء سيصبح مجداً.

أوه، يا للأسف. أوه، يا للشقاء. ضحكٌ يمزّق، وكأن البطن مليء بأسنان تلتهم الأحشاء.

هذا لم يكن ما حدث. لا. لا، ثم لا، ثم لا إلى الأبد.

حدثت النكبة.

كان الحلم بسيطاً ونقياً ومرعباً.

راقبوا السماء. هل سيحدث؟

لا يمكن أن يحدث.

لا يجب أن يحدث.

لكنه حدث.

لم يكن كل مستوى من مستويات الكونتينيوم ملائماً ليُفتح، ولم يكن كل عالم من العوالم اللانهائية المضاعفة مضيافاً للنور، كما تعلم الفيريرا، بأسىً لا يُوصف. كان هناك ظلامٌ لا يمكن الكلام عنه، ووحوشٌ بحجم العوالم نفسها تسبح فيه. لقد سمحوا لهم بالدخول. رازغوت وإلازيل، إياوث ودفيرا، كلوس وأريث. لم يكونوا يقصدون ذلك. لم تكن غلطتهم.

إلا أنها كانت غلطتهم، بالطبع. فقد تجاوزوا البوابة، وذهبوا أكثر مما ينبغي. لكن كيف كان لهم أن يعرفوا؟ لقد حذّرهم الستيليون. ولكن كيف كان لهم أن يعرفوا أن عليهم أن يصغوا للستيليين؟ كانوا مشغولين جداً بكونهم المختارين. أوه، يا له من مجد. أوه، ويا للشقاء.

وبحلول ذلك الوقت، كم من البوابات كانوا قد قطعوها؟ كم من العوالم "خاطوها بنورهم"؟ وكم من العوالم تُركت مفتوحة للوحوش بلا حماية، بينما كانوا يدورون ويهربون، مرة تلو الأخرى؟

كانوا يغلقون البوابات خلفهم، واحدة تلو الأخرى، وهم يندفعون عائدين نحو ميليز في حالة من الهلع واليأس. كانوا يغلقون كل بوابة، ثم يشاهدون الوحوش تمزقها وتواصل القدوم.

لم يستطيعوا إيقافهم. لم يُعلَّموا كيف يفعلون ذلك. وهكذا، كان هناك عالم تلو الآخر، صفحة تلو الأخرى في الكتاب الذي كان أعظم من أي شيء: ألا وهو الظلام.

الالتهام.

الأسوأ لم يحدث بعد، سواء كان ذلك عن طريق الصدفة أو بنية مقصودة، في كل الأزمنة، في رحاب الفضاء الشاسع، بالإضافة إلى الذنب الذي ارتكبوه وأخيراً، لم يتبقَّ أي عالم بين النكبة وميليز.

ميليز البداية والنهاية، ميليز الأبدية. عاد الفيريرا إلى وطنهم، وأتت الوحوش خلفهم. ثم التهمتهم.

66

أكثر بكثير من آمنة

استيقظت إليزا من الحلم لتجد نفسها ما زالت تحلم. لتدرك أنها كانت في حلم شديد العمق، وافترضت أنها الآن تغوص عبر طبقات الأحلام، وكأنها كانت تتسلقها وهي خارجة من الأرض، من أحد تلك المناجم المفتوحة التي تشبه الجحيم الذي بدا واقعياً. وكل مستوى تجتازه كان يقربها أكثر من اليقظة.

لكن لا بد أنه حلم، لمجرد أنه يتجاوز الواقع.

كانت جالسة على درجة سلم. أمر يبدو واقعياً بما يكفي حتى الآن. بجانبها فتاة: صغيرة، لكنها ليست طفلة بل مراهقة، جميلة كدمية، وعيناها واسعتان تحملقان فيها.

ابتلعت الفتاة ريقها بصوت مسموع، ثم قالت بإنجليزية مترددة، ذات لكنة غريبة:"اممم... أنا آسفة؟ أو... على الرحب؟ أياً كان ما يبدو... مناسباً لكِ؟".

"عفواً؟" قالت إليزا وكأنها تسأل: ماذا؟ ماذا تعني الفتاة بكلامها؟ لكن الفتاة بدت وكأنها اعتبرتها إجابة على سؤالها.

"عفواً إذاً"، قالت الفتاة وقد بدت وكأنها انكمشت قليلاً، بينما ظلت عيناها مفتوحتين من دون أن ترمشا. التفتت إليزا بنظرة جانبية نحو الشاب الذي كان بجانب الفتاة. رأت في عينيه دهشة مطابقة.

"لم نقصد ذلك"، قال الشاب. "لم نكن نعلم... أن... هذا سيحدث. أنهما فقط... نميا".

كان يعني الجناحين: جناحا الحلم اللذين نميا من كتفي إليزا أثناء الحلم. عندما استيقظت —إذا كان يمكن اعتبار الانتقال من حلم إلى آخر نوعاً من الاستيقاظ، وهو ما شعرت به لكنها لم تكن متأكدة تماماً من صحته—كانت مدركةً للتغيير الذي حدث لها، دون أن تحتاج إلى تأكيد بصري أو حتى شعور بالمفاجأة، كما يحدث في الأحلام. أدارت رأسها في تلك اللحظة لترى ما كانت على علم به. جناحان من نار حيّة. حرّكت كتفيها، شاعرةً بلعب العضلات الجديدة هناك، بينما استجاب الجناحان، ينثنيان وتتساقط منها زخّات جميلة من الشرر. كانا أجمل شيء رأته إليزا في حياتها، مما زاد الرهبة في داخلها.

بدا هذا الحلم أفضل بكثير مما اعتادت أن تراه.

"آسفة بشأن قميصك"، قالت الفتاة. لم تفهم إليزا في البداية ما قصدته، لكنها سرعان ما أدركت أن قميصها كان متراخياً وممزقاً، بسبب الجناحين اللذين مزقا قميصها أثناء نموهما. بدا الأمر غير مهم على الإطلاق، باستثناء شيء واحد: كان ذلك تفصيلاً غير متوقع... بالنسبة إلى حلم.

"كيف تشعرين؟" سأل الشاب بحذر، وعيناه مفعمتان بالقلق. "هل... عدتِ؟".

عدتُ؟ عدت إلى أين، أو... من أين؟ أدركت إليزا أنها لا تعرف أين هي. ما آخر شيء تتذكره؟ كانت في سيارة بالمغرب، يغمرها الخزي.

نظرت حولها الآن لترى زقاقاً ضيقاً يبدو وكأنه جزء من مسرحية معدة بعناية. طرق مرصوفة بالحصى ورخام، وأصص زهور الجيرانيوم الحمراء

مصطفة على حافة نافذة. حبال غسيل ممتدة فوق الرؤوس. كل شيء يشير إلى إيطاليا بوضوح، لكن عندما استذكرت النظر من نافذة الطائرة وقد لمحت منها الصحراء قالت:"ليست إيطاليا". كان هناك رجل عجوز، يرتدي حمالات سروال، يتكئ بثقل على عصاه، متجمداً في مكانه كأنه طبق من الورق المقوّى، يحدق فيها.

بدأ الأمر وكأنه وخز خفيف، إحساس داخلي يوحي بأن هذا ليس حلماً. كان على عصا الرجل العجوز شريط لاصق ملفوف حول المقبض. إحدى نباتات الجيرانيوم كانت ميتة. هناك قمامة، وضوضاء. أبواق معدنية مدوية من مكان ما خارج مجال الرؤية، شجار قصير بين كلاب، وضجيج خافت كأنه طنين خلايا نحل يطفو فوق كل شيء—ضوضاء بعيدة لأصوات كثيرة مختلطة. هل يمكن لهذه الأصوات والنغمات، أن تقتحم حلماً؟

في تلك اللحظة، بدأت إليزا تفهم.

ولكن لتفهم ما يحدث معها حقاً، كان عليها أن تصغي إلى داخلها. الإحساس بالتحرك داخلها، الذي كان يثور دائماً، هدأ الآن. الأشياء المدفونة التي لطالما حاولت الحفر للخروج منها، لم تعد تفعل ذلك. استغرقت لحظة لفهم السبب، وكان بسيطاً جداً: لم تعد مدفونة في داخلها لقد تأكدت من ذلك.

أدركت إليزا ما هي. هذا الإدراك كان أشبه بمشهد بطيء يعاد عرضه بشكل عكسي: فوضى عظيمة ترفع نفسها عن الأرض وتطير إلى الأعلى لتعيد ترتيب نفسها على طاولة. الشاي ينسحب من بقع صغيرة على الأرض ويصعد في الهواء ليصب نفسه في أكواب تستقر بدقة على صينية. الكتب، التي كانت في كومة غير منظمة، تقفز وكأنها ترفرف بأغلفتها كالأجنحة، ثم تستقر في مجموعات مرتبة فوق بعضها البعض.

إحساس ينبثق من الجنون. كل شيء هناك، كان لا يزال رهيباً— رهيباً جداً جداً—لكنه الآن هادئ، وأصبح ملكاً لها. هي الآن آمنة.

سألت إليزا:"ماذا فعلتما بي؟".

"لا نعرف"، أجابت الفتاة بقلق."لم نكن نعرف ما هي مشكلتك، لذلك تمنينا أمنية واسعة، على أمل أن السحر يقوم بما يجب فعله."

سحر؟ أمنية؟

"أنا أعرف ما كان خطبي"، قالت إليزا، مدركة أنها تقول الحقيقة. كان هناك تفسير لتلك الأشياء المعروفة والمدفونة. والتفسير لم يكن بسبب تجسدها كملاك.

تمازجت النشوة بشعور الانهيار لتولد شعوراً جديداً، بلا اسم، ولم تعرف إليزا كيف تتفاعل معه. وقد أدركت أخيراً ما خطبها، ولم يكن هو الشيء الذي كانت تخشاه أكثر من أي شيء آخر."لم أكن أنا"، قالت بصوت عالٍ، وكان هذا هو الشعور بالنشوة. الذنب الذي شعرت به في الحلم، لم يكن يوماً، ولن يكون أبداً ذنبها.

لكن الكارثة كانت حقيقية. أدركت ذلك الآن تماماً، وكان هذا هو الانهيار.

رفعت يديها لتتلمس رأسها، وقد شعرت أنه مألوف تحت أصابعها—أنا أنا، إليزا—لكن في الداخل، كانت هي ورأسها يحيطان الآن بأرضٍ جديدة شاسعة.

ظل الشاب والفتاة يراقبانها بحواجب معقودة، ربما يتساءلان إن كانت أصبحت الآن أكثر جنوناً مما كانت عليه. لكن لا لم تكن كذلك. هي تعرف ذلك تماماً. شعرت بعقلها، وجسدها، وأجنحتها، وكأنهم مضبوطون بدقة، مثل واحدة من إبداعات الطبيعة المثالية. حلزون مزدوج. مجرة. خلية نحل. كائنات غير مألوفة وغامضة إلى درجة أنها تجعلك تحلم بأن الخلق له إرادة وذكاء جامح.

لكنه ليس كذلك.

لم يكن الأمر أنها فهمت كل شيء. لا أحد يمكنه ذلك. ولكن...

عرفت مصدر كل شيء.

كان هذا ضمن الأشياء التي أصبحت معروفة ولم تعد مدفونة، كل شيء جزء منها الآن، منظم ومتشابك. وكان هذا الجمال عظيماً إلى درجة أنها كادت أن تعبده، على الرغم من أنها تعرف أن هذا بلا وعي. فالعبادة ستبدو بلا أيّ معنى وكأنها تعبد الرياح. كما رأت أن السحر والعلم ليسا سوى وجهين لعملة لامعة واحدة.

ورأت أن الزمن نفسه صار مكشوفاً أمامها، ممدوداً كأنه خيط من الـDNA. يمكن معرفته وحتى تعقبه.

ارتجف عقلها عند حافة هذا الاتساع الجديد. منذ لحظات فقط، ظنت أنها آمنة. لكنها رأت الآن أنها أكثر من مجرد ناجية، بل أكثر بكثير من مجرد ناجية.

"إذاً"، قالت، محاولةً ألا تبكي بينما ثبتت عينيها على منقذيها الشابين بكل دفء استطاعت أن تمنحه."من أنتما؟".

67

شرار متطاير

تبعت كارو أكيفا بعيداً عن القصر البابوي. كانا متخفّيين بالسحر، لذا عندما وصلت إليه، واقتربت منه، ارتبك في البداية. لكن ذلك استمر فقط لبضع ثوانٍ بسبب المفاجأة.

لم تكن تقصد فعل ذلك. حسناً، الأمر ليس صدفة أيضاً. لم يعثر أحدهما على الآخر لتلتقي وجوههما فجأة. الأمر فقط أن جسدها تصرف دون أن يستشير عقلها أولاً.

كانت تعرف مكانه من دفء الهواء وتدفقه حولها، وفي نيتها أن تتبعه إلى قبة كنيسة القديس بطرس. من هناك، خطّط الأربعة—كارو، أكيفا، فيركو، وهاكسايا—لرصد خروج جايل ومرافقة جيش الدومينيون خلسة طوال الطريق إلى أوزبكستان، ومن هناك إلى المملكة.

لكن جزءاً من كارو ظل عالقاً على حافة تلك اللحظة التي رُمي فيها السكين باتجاهه، تميزه الصرخة التي كادت أن تتجسد. لم تستطع رؤية أكيفا للتأكد من أنه بخير، ولذلك لم تستطع التقاط أنفاسها. لم يكن لديهم

أي انتصار ليحتفلوا به بعد، باستثناء أنهم ما زالوا أحياء، وكان ذلك كل ما استطاعت أن تهتم به في اللحظة التي استغرقتها للحاق به.

توقفا فوق الساحة الكبرى، وأعمدة مايكل أنجلو تتقوس تحتهما مثل ذراعين ممدودتين.

مدت كارو يدها حيث توقعت أن تجد كتف أكيفا، لكنها وجدت جناحه بدلاً من ذلك. رذاذ من الشرر تطاير، واستدار نحو لمستها وقد بدا متفاجئاً، فتعثرت واصطدمت به، لكنه أمسك بها وأبقاها قريبة منه، ولم يحتج الأمر إلى أكثر من ذلك.

مثل مغناطيسين يتصادمان... ويلتحمان مباشرة.

وجدت يدها وجهه، ثم تبعتها شفتاها. كانت حركاتها متخبطة، تمطر وجهه غير المرئي بقبلات شكر. غارقة تماماً في اللحظة، وقد حطت شفتاها حيثما اتفق—على جبينه، ثم عظم وجنته، ثم جسر أنفه. وفي عمق ارتياحها، بالكاد أدركت إحساس بشرته على بشرتها: دفء وملمس أكيفا، أخيراً، تحت شفتيها.

أنزلت يداً إلى صدره لتتأكد أن كل هذا لم يكن وهماً، أنه بخير حقاً ولم يصب بأذى. وعندما تأكدت أن قلبه ينبض، صعدت يدها مجدداً لتنضم إلى الأخرى حيث رقبته تلتقي بفكه، لتثبت وجهه بين يديها وتحدد موقع شفتيه لكنه لم ينتظرها لتجدها.

بضربة واحدة من جناحيه، اندفع في الهواء بقوة جرفتهما معاً. التصقت به كارو تماماً، أكثر حتى مما كانت عليه عند اختبائهما في الحمام. لكنها هذه المرة لم تكن تستند بوجهها إلى صدره، ولم تكن قدماها ثابتتين على الأرض.

تداخلت ساقاها مع ساقيه. حرّكت يديها على رقبته، صاعدة إلى شعره، وأمسكت رأسه بينما أخذها معه في دوامة حلزونية، جرفها بعيداً، تماماً، بعيداً.

وأخيراً. وأخيراً، قبّلا بعضهما.

كان فم أكيڤا جائعاً وحلواً وغنياً وبطيئاً وساخناً، قبلة طويلة وعميقة بكل المقاييس إلا اللانهائية. لكن لا، فالقبلة يجب أن تنتهي لتبدأ غيرها، وهكذا كان. انتهت، ثم بدأت من جديد.

قبلة أعقبت قبلة، وفي عالمٍ مغلق العينين، مغمور بالكامل في حضنهما، شعرت كارو وكأن كل قبلة تحتوي القبلة التي سبقتها. كان الأمر أشبه بالهلوسة: قبلة داخل قبلة داخل قبلة، تغوص أعمق وأعمق، أحلى وأشد حرارة وأكثر قوة، حتى إنها تمنت أن يكون اتزان أكيڤا هو ما يوجّههما، لأنها فقدت تماماً أي إحساس بتوازنها الخاص. لم يعد هناك"أعلى" أو"أسفل"، لم يعد هناك سوى شفاه، ووركين، وأيدِ. والآن بدأت تدرك دفء جسده وملمسه. النعومة، والخشونة، والحقيقة.

قبلة أثناء التحليق. غير مرئيين، فوق ساحة القديس بطرس. بدا الأمر وكأنه خيال، لكنه كان حقيقياً للغاية.

ثم، بدأت الابتسامات تتسلل إلى شفاههما المنسجمة، وتخللت ضحكات خافتة بينهما. راحا يلهثان، ليس فقط من الارتياح، ولكن أيضاً من نقص الأكسجين. ومن لديه وقت ليتنفس في خضم العشق؟ أسندا جبينهما إلى بعضهما البعض، وأطراف أنفيهما، وتوقفا للحظة ليتركا كل ذلك يغمرهما—القبلة، أنفاسهما، وكل ما فعلاه للتو.

تحتهما، كان الجنود البشريون يجوبون الساحة، متعجبين من دفقة مفاجئة من الشرر، بينما كانت كارو وأكيڤا يدوران في الهواء، يرتفعان بالسحر وبضربات أجنحة منسابة، وممسكين ببعضهما بقوة ذلك الجذب الذي شعرا به منذ لحظة لقائهما الأولى، في ساحة المعركة منذ زمن بعيد. لمست كارو قلب أكيڤا مرة أخرى، لتطمئن نفسها."كيف فعلت ذلك؟" سألت بهدوء، بينما كان رأسها لا يزال يدور من تأثير القبلة."ماذا حدث هناك؟".

"لا أعرف. لا أعرف أبداً. لكنه... حدث."

"لقد مر السكين عبرك. هل شعرت به؟" تمنّت لو كانت تستطيع رؤيته، لكنها، بما أنها لم تستطع، أبقت يدها على وجهه وجبينها ملتصقاً بجبينه.

شعرت بإيماءته، ثم مسّت أنفاسه شفتيها عندما تحدث."لقد شعرثُ به ولم أشعر. لا أستطيع أن أشرح. كنت هناك ولم أكن. رأيته يخترقني ويمرّ من خلالي."

صمتت كارو للحظة، محاولة استيعاب ذلك:"هل ما قاله جايل صحيح إذاً؟ أنك... غير مرئي للموت؟ ولا داعي للقلق أبداً بشأن موتك؟".

"لا أعتقد أن هذا صحيح"، كان يمرر شفتيه على ملامح وجهها كما لو أنه يراها بتلك الطريقة."ولكن كنتِ ستعيدينني في كل الأحوال."

هل كان هذا ما سيحدث لو مات أكيڤا؟ أم كانوا سيفقدون السيطرة على الموقف، ويتم الإطاحة بهم جميعاً؟ كارو لم ترغب حتى في التفكير في ذلك."بالتأكيد"، قالت بخفة مصطنعة."لكن دعنا لا نتعامل مع هذا الجسد بخفة، حسناً؟" اقتربت منه أكثر بحركة ناعمة."قد تكون روحك ما أحب، لكنني مغرمة إلى حد كبير بجسد تلك الروح."

انخفض صوتها مع كلماتها الأخيرة، وجاء ردّ أكيڤا بصوت خافت أجش، متوافق مع نبرتها."لا أستطيع أن أقول إنني غير سعيد لسماع ذلك". ثم مرّ وجهه بجانب وجهها ليطبع قبلة تحت أذنها، مما أرسل موجات كهربائية فورية عبر جسدها.

أصدرت همهمة خافتة من المفاجأة، بدت وكأنها"أوه"، لكنها بدون"يا إلهي". ثم رأت، فوق كتف أكيڤا، صعود الصفوف الأولى من جيش الدومينيون من القصر البابوي، بينما كانت جيوش جايل تعود إلى السماء.

68

سقوط

"لم يكن ذنبنا!" صرخ رازغوت عندما صدر الحكم على الفيريرا، لكنها كانت كذبة. إنّه خطؤهم، وهذه المعرفة خلقت بُعداً من الحزن والذنب في أجسادهم وعقولهم، طغى على كل ما كانوا يوماً عليه أو ما احتووه.

عادوا إلى ميليز، عاجزين عن التفكير بسبب الهلع. ما أطلق إنذاراً. لم يبق من الستة سوى أربعة الآن. إياوث ودڤيرا استدارا لمواجهة الكاتاكليزم، وتم هزيمتهما. عادوا إلى العاصمة وهم يصرخون: الوحوش قادمة! اهربوا! الوحوش قادمة!

نجح البعض في الهروب، عبر"الباب الخلفي"، إن صح التعبير. كانت العوالم مكدسة، مثل صفحات كتاب. جاءت الوحوش من اتجاه واحد، تدمر كل ما في طريقها. أما من استطاع، فقد هرب في الاتجاه الآخر، إلى العالم المجاور، في الجانب الآخر للمملكة.

لم يكن هناك وقت لتنظيم عملية إخلاء. تمكن بضعة آلاف من أصل ملايين من الفرار. لم يصل العدد حتى إلى عشرة آلاف، ولا حتى قريباً من ذلك. كل البقية تُركوا خلفهم.

الكثير منهم، الألوان، الجواهر التي تناثرت على الأرضيات المزخرفة. أعظم عطايا العالم. ضاعت.

الكثيرون وصلوا إلى البوابة، ولكن رُفضوا بسبب صغر المخرج. اثنان أو ثلاثة فقط يمكن أن يمروا في كل مرة، وكان ذلك ببطء، بينما كانت الوحوش تقترب. الصرخات من الجهة الأخرى ما زالت تتردد في أذني رازغوت إلى يومنا هذا، كأنها صرخة عالم كامل يحتضر. يتذكر كيف انقطعت تلك الصرخات فجأة ليحل محلها الصمت، وكيف كان بعض آخر من نجحوا في العبور ما زالوا يمدون أيديهم نحو أحبائهم العالقين في الجانب الآخر.

تم إغلاق البوابة، لكن هذا ما فعله الفيريرا مراراً وتكراراً أثناء انسحابهم، ولم يمنع الوحوش يوماً. بمجرد أن يُخدش الغلاف بين العوالم، لا تلتئم أبداً بالكامل. البوابة ستفشل مجدداً، وكانت الكاتاكليزم ستأخذ المملكة أيضاً، ثم الأرض، وكل العوالم بعدها، عبر كل بوابة قطعها الفريق الثاني من الستة، مهما كانت المسافة التي قطعوها. لكن الـستلييون كانوا مـن بين الذين نجحوا في الهروب من ميليز، وكانوا مستعدين. لقد عارضوا مشروع الفيرينغ منذ البداية، وفي السنوات التي أعقبت رحيل الفيريرا، كانوا يجهزون أنفسهم لفعل ما لم يكن أحد غيرهم قادراً عليه أو راغباً فيه: إصلاح الغلاف، الحجاب، الغشاء، الطاقة، طبقات الكل الأعظم.

أغلقوا البوابة وأبقوها مغلقة. تم إنقاذ المملكة، وتم إنقاذ الأرض، وكل العوالم الأخرى.

كان الستلييون هم من أنقذوا الجميع. أما الفيريرا، فقد نالوا نصيبهم: اللعنة، والعار، والإبادة.

مـن زنزانتهم، سمعوا ما فعله السحرة بذكريات الناجين. لم يتعلم السحرة قط الابتعاد عن التدخل. سرقوا من كل سيرافيم الماضي، ليس فقط كاتاكليزم، بل ميليز أيضاً، كي يتمكن شعبهم من بدء حياة جديدة. كي لا يستيقظ أحدهم في صباح ما ويدرك الحقيقة: على مـن يقع اللوم حقاً؟

على السحرة الذين حلموا بمشروع الـفـيـرينغ منذ البداية، واختاروا أفضل شبابهم لتنفيذه. كان السحرة شركاء في الذنب، لكن ليس في العقاب. أوه، لا، ليس هم.

كان إياوث ودڤيرا هما المحظوظان: التهما سريعاً، وماتا سريعاً.

أما الباقون، فقد كان أول ما عانوه هو اقتلاع أجنحتهم. نعم، اقتلاعها. ليس قطعاً. ليس تمزيقاً بشفرات حادة. بل سحباً، ببطء وقسوة. عظام تتشظى، أوه الألم، أوه الألم الذي لم يكن في أسوأ كوابيسهم. رأى رازغوت الثلاثة الآخرين يُشوّهون بجانبه. أيادٍ ثقيلة وُضعت على مفاصل أجنحتهم الجميلة، تدور وتلتوي، ووجوههم تلتوي معها، بألم لا يُطاق. وشعر بكل ذلك، كما شعروا هم بكل شيء. لأنهم متصلين ببعضهم البعض، ومهما تم فعله بهم، فقد كان الألم مشتركاً، ما يشعر به أحدهم، يشعر به الجميع. أوه، يا نجوم السماء. كان مجموع آلامهم معاً... أكثر من أن يتحمله أي كائن.

ولم يكن هذا حتى أسوأ ما حدث. تخيل. كل ذلك لم يكن سوى الملح على جرح عقابهم الحقيقي: النفي.

وحتى النفي، ربما كان بإمكانهم تحمله وصنع حياة ما ولو مشوهة في عالم سجنهم على الأرض. لكن، أوه، الحنق والبؤس.

لقد فرقوهم. أربعة كانوا، وكانت هناك أربعة بوابات أيضاً لسوء الحظ أو لقساوة القدر. جروهم إلى زوايا نائية، وألقوا بهم بعيداً. كل واحد بمفرده. بلا أجنحة. أرجلهم محطمة إلى لبّ العظام. ألقوا بهم في عالم آخر، أربع كائنات منكسرة، تتساقط من السماء لتحطم نفسها على تضاريس غريبة هناك، وليسوا حتى معاً.

أما رازغوت، فقد حملوه فوق خليج الوحوش. كان يوماً جميلاً والسماء صافية والماء أخضر كأنه زمرد. يا له من يوم جميل للألم. حملوه من إبطيه إلى حافة تلك البوابة الممزقة التي كانت ترفرف في السماء، ثم قذفوه من خلالها، و... سقط.

وسقط.

وسقط.

لم يمت، لأن ما أثبتته الممارسات في ذلك اليوم البعيد من المجد، وما صنعوه به بعد ذلك، أثبتت أنه كان فيريراً قوياً إلى درجة تتجاوز القوة نفسها. قوي جداً بحيث لا يمكن أن يموت من السقوط. وهكذا عاش، إذا كان يمكن تسميتها حياة، ولم يجد الآخرين حيث تم نفيهم، رغم أنه شعر بآلامهم—وبحزنهم وذنبهم، مضاعفاً أربع مرات—حتى بدأت تلك المشاعر تتلاشى عبر السنين.

على مر القرون، عرف متى ماتوا، كل منهم بدوره. لم يعرف كيف، أو أين، لكنه عرف. واحداً تلو الآخر، أخذوا منه جزءاً جزءاً، حتى لم يبقَ أحد. كلوس، أريث، إلازيل. رحلوا جميعاً.

وفي النهاية، أصبح رازغوت حقاً وحيداً.

أصبح شيئاً صغيراً تائهاً في فراغٍ عظيم. عاش بعقلٍ مشروخ، ألف عام في المنفى.

وأوه، الحنق. أوه، البؤس.

ما زال حياً.

...

قد تكون إستر فان دي فلو قد فقدت أمنياتها—مؤقتاً—لكن أموالها ونفوذها بقيا غير متأثرين. ولم تتمدد على أرضية الحمام يائسة. سرعان ما استجمعت نفسها، وأجرت مكالمات هاتفية، ودخلت الإنترنت لتبحث عن صور المذنبين—جعلوا الأمر يبدو سهلاً للغاية، شباب أغبياء بلا أي إحساس بالخصوصية—ثم نشرت تلك الصور عبر البريد الإلكتروني ولم يرسلوها إلى الشرطة التي كانت مشغولة هذه الأيام بمحاولة السيطرة على الجحيم من الانفلات، بل إلى شركة خاصة ذات سمعة جيدة إلى درجة جعلتها في الوقت ذاته سعيدة ومذعورة عندما سمعت منها.

قالت:"إنهم في روما. ابحثوا عنهم. وسيكون الدفع على مرحلتين. أولاً، مليون يورو. أعتقد أن ذلك سيكون كافياً؟" بالطبع سيكون كافياً، كما أكدوا لها، لم يشعروا بالسعادة بمقدار هذا المبلغ الفاحش، بل بالخوف منه، مدركين بلا شك ما قد يتبعه. "ثانياً"، أضافت إستر،"إذا نجحتم، فلن أدمركم."

بعد ذلك، بدأت تمشي ذهاباً وإياباً. الانتظار ينتمي لزوجات الجنود، وكانت إستر تمقت الانتظار بشدة. بقي كل من تراڤيلر وميثوسالا بعيدين عنها، حائرين وبائسين. ستائر الغرفة كانت لا تزال مفتوحة بالكامل، ليس لأن إستر كانت تهتم لرؤية ولكن لأنهم تركوها هكذا.

سارت جيئةً وذهاباً أمام النوافذ، لكنها لم تدِر رأسها نحوها. شعرت كأنها تتوهج غضباً. لقد شلبت، ودُنِّست. لم يكن لديها أي إحساس بتقبل مصيرها أو أنها تستحق هذا الجزاء. فقط غضب مدمر، ضيق الأفق، يملؤها كأنها على طريق حرب.

لا يعلم أحد كم من المرات مرت بجانب النافذة، تمشي وتستشيط غضباً، قبل أن تلاحظ أخيراً التغيير في السماء، وقد تحولت ليلتها من سيئة... إلى أسوأ بكثير.

ارتفع الملائكة.

انتشرت الصرخات في الشوارع في الأسفل. فتحت إستر أبواب الزجاج بقوة واندفعت إلى الشرفة.

"لا." شعرت بصوتها يخرج من أحشائها، أشبه بأنين عميق، وسحبته إلى أعلى، وأخرجته شرائط متتالية من الأنين، كل واحد يحمل الكلمة نفسها—"لا. لا. لا."—كأنها تُقتلع منها كقطع لحم حي.

الملائكة كانوا يغادرون؟

وماذا عنها؟ ماذا عن الصفقة؟ لقد أعطتهم كارو، ووعدتهم بالمزيد— كل شيء قد يحتاجونه لغزو العالم الآخر خلف ذلك الحجاب السماوي. أسلحة، ذخيرة، تكنولوجيا، وحتى طاقم عمل. وماذا طلبت في المقابل؟

ليس الكثير. فقط حقوق التعدين، لعالم بأكمله. عالم كامل لم يلمس بعد، مع سكان عبيد جاهزين للعمل، وجيش لحماية مصالحها.

كانت إستر قد تأكدت من عدم وجود أي منافسة، إذ لا عروض أخرى تصل إلى الملائكة، ولا رشاوى تتجاوز ما قدمته هي. كانت هذه أعظم صفقة تفاوضية في كل العصور.

أو، على الأقل، كانت كذلك.

وها هي إستر فان دي فلو تقف مرتجفة وصامتة، تشاهد أجنحة الملائكة وهي تحمل هذه الصفقة بعيداً.

"ليس الكثير"، قالت كارو بتهرب. "فقط أقنعهم بالعودة إلى ديارهم." وهكذا، يبدو أنهم قد عادوا بالفعل.

رحلوا، والسماء عادت خاوية مرة أخرى. عبثت إستر بجهاز التلفاز، تشاهد المنظر الذي يُبث من كاميرا على مروحية مع بقية العالم، حيث كان"الجيش السماوي" يعيد تتبع رحلته التي بدأها من أوزبكستان قبل ثلاثة أيام.

"يبدو أن الزوار يغادرون"، أعلن المعلقون الأكثر هدوءاً، رغم أنه لم يكن بالإمكان القول إن الأصوات الهادئة سادت في هذا اليوم. "إنهم يتخلون عنا!" كان هذا هو الصدى الأكثر شيوعاً. تطورٌ كهذا كان يحتاج إلى إلقاء اللوم. عند ظهور الملائكة لأول مرة في السماء، تحوّلت هتافات الحشود عند محيط الفاتيكان إلى صيحات وصرخات نشوة، لكن عندما أعادوا تشكيل صفوفهم وبدأوا في المغادرة، تحولت الهتافات إلى عويلٍ وبكاء.

لم يكن من الممكن الوصول إلى البابا للحصول على تعليق.

بحلول الوقت الذي رن فيه هاتف إستر، كانت قد تجاوزت الغضب بكثير إلى درجة الانفجار والسطوع الذي حول غرفة الانتظار للجنون نفسه. أن تكون قريبة جداً من العظمة ثم تُسلب منها... لكن صوت الرنين كان مثل أصابع تُقرع أمام عينيها.

"نعم؟ ماذا؟ مرحباً؟" أجابت وهي شبه ضائعة. لم تكن تعلم حتى من

كانت تتوقعه. ربما وكالة التحريات التي وظفتها لتعقب سارقي الأمنيات، ذلك كان أفضل تخمين لها وأعظم أملها. الملائكة قد رحلوا. بطريقة ما، خسرت إستر، ولم تكن غبية إلى درجة أن تتوهم أنها ستحصل على فرصة أخرى مماثلة لصفقة قوى كهذه. عندما تبين أنه سبيفيتي على الخط— الخادم الذي كان ينفذ أوامرها من داخل القصر البابوي بطلبٍ من الكاردينال شوت—اندلعت بداخلها شعلة من الأمل، شعلة نجاة.

"ماذا هناك؟" قالت بإلحاح."ماذا حدث، سبيفيتي؟ لماذا رحلوا؟".

"لا أعلم، سيدتي"، قال، وصوته يرتجف."لكنهم تركوا شيئاً خلفهم."

"حسناً؟" زفرت بنفاد صبر."ما هو؟".

"أنا... لا أعلم"، قال سبيفيتي. بدا الرجل مذهولاً تماماً، وربما كان ليقدم لها وصفاً أولياً لو أنها طالبته به. لكنها لم تفعل. في طمعها، كانت قد اندفعت بالفعل، مسرعةً نحو الممر الطويل.

استغرقت ساعات لتدخل إلى الفاتيكان، عبر الحشود النابضة، الكريهة الرائحة، والعويل المستمر، وعبر الحواجز العسكرية. ساعات وعشرات المكالمات الهاتفية، ووعود مفضوحة بتقديم خدمات مقابل أخرى. وعندما وصلت أخيراً، في حالة يُرثى لها، بشعرها المتطاير وعينيها المشتعلتين غضباً، أساءت فهم نظرة الرعب على وجه سبيفيتي، معتقدة أنها كانت ردة فعل لرؤيتها. بينما الحقيقة أن تلك النظرة قد سبقتها بساعات، وستبقى طويلاً بعد مغادرتها.

صرخت بقوة:"خذني إلى هناك".

وهكذا دخلت إستر أخيراً إلى غرفة جايل، وتقدمت نحو السرير الكبير المنحوت. كان المكان خافت الإضاءة. أخذت عيناها تبحثان عن صندوق كنز ربما، أو عن شيء ذا قيمة. ربما رسالة أو خريطة. لم تشعر بوجود الشيء حتى كانت على وشك الاصطدام به، وبحلول ذلك الوقت... كان الأوان قد فات.

امتدت الظلال نحوها، وكانت أذرعاً، هزيلة، قوية كأنها جلد غير مدبوغ، تحركت حولها ببطء، تكاد تكون كلمسة حانية. وكأن عاشقاً يسدل شالاً على كتفيها. جاءها ذلك الخاطر ومضى. الأذرع انقبضت حولها، وتحولت من ظل إلى لحم، حتى رأت إستر، لأول مرة، الشيء الذي سيكون رفيقها حتى آخر أيامها.

كان كلامه وعداً وتهديداً في آنٍ واحد، عندما قال لها بصوتٍ خشن، وضحكة متحشرجة: "لن تشعري بالوحدة أبداً بعد الآن."

69

لا تصطدم بشيء أثناء خروجك

في الثاني عشر من آب/ أغسطس، في الساعة 9:12 بتوقيت غرينتش، اختفى ألف ملاك عبر شقّ في السماء. لم يشهد أحد وصولهم. تخيّل الناس مشاهد سماوية: شُحُب كومولوس تملأ الأفق، وأشعة نور مائلة تنفذ عبرها كما في صور كُتيبات دروس الأحد الدينية. لكن الحقيقة كانت أقل روعة. واحداً تلو الآخر، عبروا شقّاً في السماء. بدت العملية أشبه برعي الماشية: خراف في طريقهم إلى جزّ صوفهم، أبقار إلى الذبح، واصلوا القدوم. بمعدل ست ثوانٍ تقريباً لكل جندي، استغرقت العملية أكثر من ساعتين، وكان هذا وقتاً كافياً لتجمّع أسراب من المروحيات خلفهم.

وكما هو متوقع، عجز زعماء العالم عن الاتفاق على اتخاذ أي إجراء بخصوص الملائكة. إرسال بعثة خلفهم؟ ماذا سيكون تأثير هذا القرار؟ ما الرسالة التي سيبعث بها؟ وما العواقب الدبلوماسية؟ والأهم، من سيكون مسؤولاً إن حدث خطأ ما؟

في النهاية، تطلب الأمر ملياردير مغامراً مستقلاً ليحاول ذلك. قاد مروحيته المتطورة بنفسه، وتردد للحظات فقط ليُحاذي شق السماء بدقة، مُحافظاً على رؤيته ثابتة طوال الوقت. بدأ بالاندفاع نحو الشق، لكن عندها، اشتعلت النيران.

نيران في السماء.

أدار المروحية في الوقت المناسب وشاهد الحريق من مقعده الأمامي: انتشر بسرعة، وانتهى فجأة. ومعه ضاعت فرصته في تحقيق رقمه القياسي العالمي الرابع. أول مهمة مأهولة إلى... الجنة؟ من كان ليعرف؟ لا أحد. والآن لن يعرفوا أبداً.

...

في أحد البارات الصغيرة في روما، شاهدت زوزانا وميك وإليزا النيران في السماء على شاشة التلفاز، ورفعوا كؤوس الـ"بروسيكو" احتفالاً بالنجاح.

"هل تراهنين على أن إستر لم تشرب تلك الشمبانيا التي طلبتها أبداً؟" تباهى ميك وهو يأخذ جرعة كبيرة من مشروبه الفوار.

بعد كل مخاوفهم ومؤامرات إستر الشريرة، نجحت كارو وأكيڤا وڤيركو في مهمتهم. رحل الملائكة، وبالتأكيد لم يحملوا معهم أسلحة

"في وجهك، أيتها الجدة المزيفة!" هتفت زوزانا منتصرة، لكن انتصارها تبعه شعور بالحزن. لقد أُغلق المدخل، وحقيبة الكمان المليئة بالأمنيات لن تُعيدها إلى إريتز، حيث كان يمكن أن يحدث أي شيء. لم يكن هناك ما يمكنها فعله الآن سوى مواصلة القلق... وربما الغرق في كآبتها.

سألت ميك: "ماذا تريد أن نفعل؟ هل نعود إلى المنزل؟".

زفر ميك بحسرة. "أعتقد ذلك. نرى عائلاتنا. ثم هناك ماريونيت عملاق وشرير يشعر بالوحدة الشديدة على الأرجح".

قالت زوزانا بسخرية:"ليبقَ وحيداً. أيامي كراقصة باليه انتهت."

"حسناً. يمكنكِ صنع زوجة له على الأقل، كي يستمتع بتقاعده."

عندما نوه ميك على كلمة"زوجة"، شعرت زوزانا بشيء يفور بداخلها. قطبت وجهها وكتمته.

نظرت إليهما إليزا وهي مرتبكة."هل ستعودان إلى براغ؟" هزت زوزانا كتفيها، وكأنها مستعدة للغرق في نوبة جديدة من الشفقة على الذات. وقالت في نفسها:"ربما سأبكي أيضاً. ماذا ستفعلين أنتِ؟".

"أستطيع أن أخبركما بما لن أفعله" -كان جناحاها متخفيين بواسطة السحر، وقد أتقنت ذلك بنفسها بطريقة ما، ولم يعد قميصها الممزق يبدو غريباً أبداً؛ إنما أشبه بصيحة موضة -"لن أنهي أطروحة الدكتوراه خاصتي. آسفة يا فراشات دانوس بليكسيبوس".

سأل ميك:"من؟".

ابتسمت إليزا."إنها فراشة المَلَك. هذا ما كنت أدرسه". توقفت، وصححت:"درستُها. لا أستطيع العودة إلى تلك الحياة الآن، رغم أنني أتوق بشدة إلى تحطيم جبهة مورغان توث بصفعة تاريخية. لكن ما أريده حقاً؟" نظرت إليهما بتمعن، وبعينين متوهجتين."هو الذهاب إلى إريتز."

زوزانا وميك حدقا فيها. ألقت زوزانا نظرة ذات معنى إلى شاشة التلفاز، حيث كانوا قد شاهدوا للتو البوابة تحترق.

رفعت إليزا حاجبيها وكتفيها في حركة واضحة:"وماذا في ذلك؟".

تنهد ميك بإحباط واضح. بالكاد تجرأت زوزانا على الأمل، لكن عندما بدأت إليزا تتحدث مجدداً، لم يكن حديثها عن إريتز.

"هل تعرفان أن فراشات الملك تهاجر لمسافة خمسة آلاف ميل ذهاباً وإياباً كل عام؟ لا توجد حشرة أخرى تفعل ذلك. والأكثر إدهاشاً أن الهجرة تتم عبر أجيال متعددة. الفراشات التي تعود إلى الشمال ليست هي نفسها التي ذهبت إلى الجنوب.

إنها أجيال عديدة متعاقبة، ومع ذلك تعيد تتبع الطريق بدقة."

صمتت إليزا للحظة، وارتسمت ابتسامة غريبة على شفتيها، وكأنها كانت غير متأكدة مما إذا كان ما تشعر به مضحكاً أم لا. وبصراحة، لم تستطع زوزانا أن تعرف ما يجب أن تفكر فيه بشأن إليزا الآن، بعد أن لم تعد"نباتية". لم يكن الأمر فقط أنها أصبحت منطقية، بل كانت... أكثر من بشرية، بطريقة ما. لم يكن بسبب الجناحين فحسب، إنما طاقة تشع منها، طاقة غامضة ومشبعة بشرارات غير مفهومة. ماذا بحق الجحيم فعلوا بها، بأمنية غافرييل واحد فقط؟

"لا أذكر حقاً كيف بدأتُ اهتمامي بها. لكن كان الأمر يتعلق بالهجرة، بالتأكيد، والآن يبدو كل شيء منطقياً. أعتقد أنني كنت أعرف أكثر مما توقعت أنني أعرفه، إن كان هذا منطقياً."

قالت زوزانا ببرود:"ليس حقاً".

"أنا فراشة"، قالت إليزا، وكأن ذلك يفسر كل شيء."بعد عدة دورات حياة. حسناً، ربما أكثر من عدة. ألف عام. لا أعلم كم جيلاً مضى."

تجهمت زوزانا، منتظرة أن تقول إليزا جملة مفيدة. لكن ميك، بنفس الطريقة الهادئة وغير المكترثة التي تقبّل بها ذات مرة حقيقة أن كارو كيميرا، قال ببساطة:"رائع."

ضحكت إليزا، ثم بدأت تروي قصتها: كإلازيل الحقيقية، وما كانت عليه، وما فعلته.

أخبرتهما عن الحلم الذي طاردها طوال حياتها، وما يعنيه. زوزانا، التي اعتقدت أنها فقدت قدرتها على الشعور بالدهشة، اكتشفت أنها كانت مخطئة—في زاوية بار صغير في روما.

لا، لم يكن ذلك مجرد دهشة. كان أكبر من ذلك. وجدت زوزانا نفسها مصعوقة، هناك، في زاوية بار في روما. عوالِم. عوالِم كثيرة. وانقسامات في بطانة الزمن والفضاء. أو شيء من هذا القبيل. وملائكة كانوا مثل

مستكشفي الفضاء لكن بلا سفن، وكأنهم خيال علمي، لكن بالسحر بدلاً من العلم.

أوضحت إليزا:"فعل السحرة شيئاً لعقول الفيريرا. لأرواحهم في الواقع. إنها أكثر من مجرد عقول؛ إنها الذات. كان جزءاً من واجبهم أن ينجبوا أطفالاً في رحلتهم، أولئك الذين سيولدون محمّلين بخرائطهم وذكرياتهم... مشفرة بداخلهم، كأنها معرفة أجداد مشقّرة وراثياً. جنون. لكي يتمكنوا يوماً ما من إيجاد طريق العودة."

قال ميك:"وأنتِ واحدة من هؤلاء الأطفال. بل عدد كبير منهم، أو شيء كهذا." أضاف بحماس:"ولديك الخرائط، والذكريات."

أومأت إليزا برأسها. كان حماس ميك وحده كافياً ليُشعر زوزانا بأن ما يحدث هنا أكبر من مجرد"وقت الحكايات".

خرائط. ذكريات.

"هناك الكثير من المعلومات هنا"، قالت إليزا وهي تطرق برأسها."لم أستوعبها بعد. عبر تاريخ عائلتي، كان هناك دائماً شيء من الجنون. أعتقد أن العقل البشري لا يتحمل كل هذا. مثل مخدم بيانات مثقل بالتحميل، وينهار ببساطة. كنتُ منهارة. أنتم من أعادني، ولن أستطيع أبداً أن أشكركم بما يكفي."

انتهت حالة الشفقة على الذات لدى زوزانا على الفور. جلست منتصبة بحماس."إذا كنتِ تقولين ما أظن أنك تقولينه، فأنتِ تستطيعين شكرنا بما يكفي."

أمالت إليزا شفتيها بتفكير متصنع، عيناها تتلألآن بمكر واضح."هذا يعتمد. ماذا تظنين أنني أقول؟".

أحاطت زوزانا يديها في حركة محاكية للخنق."تكلمي. الآن."

ابتسمت إليزا ابتسامة عريضة وقالت بكل بساطة:

"أعرف بوابة أخرى. طبعاً."

70

لم يعد الأبيض موجوداً

صفق جناحا جايل بالغضب وهو عائد إلى إريتز، وبشكل متقطع وغير سلس على الإطلاق. لقد مزّق طريقه عبر البوابة تقريباً، متمنياً لو كان بإمكانه تدميرها، أو تدمير أي شيء. أكيفا. نعم. تخيّله مثقوباً بالسهام كدمية تدريب على الرماية، متدلياً من مشنقة ويستواي ليتجمع الناس حوله ويحدقوا بفضول.

نظر حوله بقلق. اللعنة على ذلك الوغد، كان يمكن أن يكون في أي مكان. هل سبقه أكيفا عبر البوابة؟ أم سيتبعه؟ وفقاً لشروط اتفاقهما، ما إن يعبر جايل إلى إريتز، يصبح أكيفا حراً في قتله بأي طريقة يشاء—ما عدا إشعال النار في وسم بصمة اليد على صدر جايل. وهذا يترك له الكثير من الخيارات لكن جايل أيضاً كان لديه العديد من الخيارات. بل أكثر، لأنه لم يكن مقيّداً بالشرف، والشرف يجعل قائمة الطرق المتاحة لقتل عدوك أقصر.

كان يدرك تماماً أن نجاته تعتمد على كون عدوه شريفاً، لكن ذلك لم يجبره بأي شكل على اللعب بنفس القواعد. على العكس، كان من الضروري

أن يوجه الضربة الأولى. ولن يستريح حتى يرى ذلك الوغد ميتاً.

بمجرد عبوره البوابة، لم يتوقف جايل كي يشرف على العودة المملة والبطيئة لجيشه، بل طار مباشرة إلى المعسكر، مُحاطاً بفيلق من الحرس، مع رماة سهام متمركزين على الجوانب تحسّباً لأي ظهور محتمل لأكيفا.

كانت المناظر الطبيعية هنا مشابهة لتلك التي تركوها خلفهم: جبال بلون الغبار، ولا شيء يُرى. المعسكر يقع عند سفوح الجبال، على مسافة نصف ساعة تقريباً. في حقل من الحشائش سويت بالأرض بفعل الرياح، انتصبت صفوف الخيام مرتبة على شكل مستطيل تقريبي، مع أبراج مراقبة عند زواياه، يشغلها الرماة تحسّباً لأي هجوم جوي. كانت عبارة عن دفاعات رمزية؛ فلا شيء هنا ليواجهوه.

كان معظم جيش جايل مُنتشراً في الجنوب والشرق، لمطاردة الثوار. وكيف كان أداؤهم؟ سيعرف قريباً بما فيه الكفاية. وأقرب مما هو متوقع.

المعسكر بالكاد قد ظهر في الأفق حين رأى ما كان ينتظره على السياج الشائك.

...

رأت كارو ذلك أيضاً، وإن كان من مسافة أبعد، ولم تستطع أن تكتم شهقتها التي أفلتت منها. هناك، على السور، ترفرف في مهب الريح، راية قديمة ملوثة بالدم والرماد.

عرفتها على الفور. كانت الراية واضحة، مع أن شعار رأس الذئب في مركزها... غير واضح.

"النصر والانتقام"، كان مكتوباً بلغة الكيميرا. إنها راية الذئب الأبيض— ليست النسخة التي غُلقت في القصبة، بل الأصلية، المنهوبة بلا شك من لوراميندي بعد سقوطها.

لكن ما جعل كارو تشهق، لم يكن الراية بحد ذاتها. لو كانت الراية وحدها

معلقة هناك، لكان من الممكن تفسيرها كعلامة على أن الذئب الأبيض قد احتل هذا المعسكر. لكن مع ما كان يتدلّى أمامها، حاجباً رمز الذئب، لم يترك أي فرصة لسوء الفهم.

اعتقدت كارو أنها قد نجحت في السيطرة على أملها. لأنها آمنت وهي عائدة عبر الشق، بأنها مستعدة لاحتمال—بل احتمال كبير— أن الأخبار ستكون سيئة.

لكنها واهمة.

منذ أن تركوا رفاقهم خلفهم، كانت قد بدأت تؤمن، دون أن تعترف لنفسها، بأن كل شيء سيكون على ما يرام. لأنه يجب أن يكون كذلك. أليس كذلك؟

لكنه لم يكن كذلك. لم يكن كل شيء على ما يرام.

لم يعد أبيض كما كان ذات يوم، إنه جسد ثياغو الملطخ والمنكسر، يتأرجح هناك معلّقاً بحبل حول عنقه.

وهنا أتتها الإجابة أسرع مما توقعت، على السؤال الذي ظل يطاردها مذ تركوا المعركة مشتعلة في أديلفاس، واتخذوا القرار الصعب بإكمال مهمتهم الجوهرية قبل العودة.

هل فعلتُ ما يكفي؟ سألت نفسها حينها، وهي تعرف الإجابة مسبقاً. هل فعلتُ كل ما كان بإمكاني فعله؟

لا.

لقد خسروا رفاقهم. وماتوا.

أمسك بها أكيفا واحتواها بذراعيه. لم يتكلما، بل ظلا يراقبان في صمت، عاجزين، بينما كانا يحومان في الهواء على وقع ضربات جناحي أكيفا الثابتة. رأيا جايل يهبط أمام جثة الذئب الأبيض... ثم يضحك.

71

غياب

تقدمت كارو نحو الجسد بعد رحيل جايل. فقط للحظة، فقط لاحتمال ضئيل. وهي تقترب، تذكّرت آخر مرة نزف فيها هذا الجسد. حينها، كان سكينها الصغير هو الذي قتله، والجرح النظيف الذي تسببت به أُعيدت خياطته بسهولة ليُجهّز هذا الوعاء لاستقبال روح زيري.

أما هذا الجرح... فلم يكن نظيفاً.

انظري بعيداً.

لم تكن هذه الميتة سهلة، وعقل كارو صرخ لأجل ذلك اليتيم ذي العينين البنيتين، الذي اعتاد أن يتبعها في لوراميندي، خجولاً ومرتبكاً كغزال صغير. لقد قبّلته يوماً على جبينه، ولم تتذكر ذلك إلا لأنه أخبرها— وهو محمرّ الوجه خجلاً.

زيري. عرفت شعور روحه حين ألبستها هذا الجسد ذات مرة، والأمل... الأمل لا يتعلم أبداً.

بالطبع، كان لا بد أن تكون روحه قد تلاشت.

لم يكن من الممكن أن تبقى صامدة كل هذا الوقت، في العراء، أو عبر مثل تلك الرحلة. بالطبع، لقد اختفت. لكن مع ذلك، فتحت كارو حواسها باحثة عنها، لأنها لم تستطع إلّا أن تحاول.

هل فعلتُ كل ما بوسعي؟

حبست أنفاسها، والدموع غير المرئية تتساقط على خديها غير المرئيين. ومع ذلك، كانت تأمل.

الغياب له حضور أحياناً. وهذا ما شعرت به: غياب مثل عشب ميت مسحوق، حيث كان هناك شيء موجود واختفى. غياب مثل خيط انتُزع بوحشية من نسيج مُحكم، تاركاً فجوة لا يمكن رتقها أبداً.

كان هذا كل ما شعرت به.

72

إمبراطور لعدة أيام

تحسَّن مزاج جايل تدريجياً بينما كان يشق طريقه نحو خيمته، تتبعه حاشيته من الحراس. حيّاه الجنود في أبراج المراقبة عند اقترابه، ونزل أحدهم منزلقاً ليهبط قربه ويسير إلى جانبه.

"التقرير"، زمجر جايل، بينما كان يخلع خوذته ويلقيها باتجاهه.

"المتمردون؟".

"لقد حاصرناهم في أديلفاس، يا سيدي".

استدار جايل نحوه بحدة. "سيدي؟" كررها. لم يتعرف على الجندي. "أولستُ إمبراطورك كما أنني جنرالُك؟".

انحنى الجندي برأسه مرتبكاً. "شمُوّك؟" تلعثم، ثم أضاف: "مولاي الإمبراطور؟ لقد حاصرنا المتمردين في أديلفاس. غير الشرعيين والعائدون معاً، هل تصدق ذلك؟".

أوه، جايل يُصدّق ذلك. أطلق ضحكةً خافتة أشبه بالصفير.

"لستُ أكذب، سيدي"، قال الجندي، ظناً منه أن جايل يستهزئ به.

"سيدي" مرة أخرى. أطبق جايل عينيه حتى أصبحتا شقين دقيقين "وماذا بعد؟".

"لقد أبدوا دفاعاً مستميتاً"، قال الجندي، وقرأ جايل الباقي في ابتسامته الساخرة. الدفاع المستميت هو دفاعٌ محكوم عليه بالهزيمة. هذا ما كان يتوقعه، خاصة بعد رؤية جثة الذئب الأبيض، وكان هذا كل ما يحتاج إلى معرفته في الوقت الحالي. كانت دماء جايل تغلي بالإحباط المكبوت، وعضلاته متوترة بالغضب. لقد كان وديعاً كالأرنب—أرنب مخصي—لأيام في ذلك القصر اللعين، خائفاً من أن يضر سمعته إن هو استجاب لرغباته. وكل ذلك من أجل ماذا؟ من أجل أن يُطرد بعيداً مثل كلبٍ جبان؟ حتى إنه لم يجرؤ على قتل المنحط خوفاً من مخالفة أمر أكيفا اللعين بعدم سفك الدماء.

أخذ يبحث حوله عن خادمه."أين ميتشيل؟".

"لا أعلم، مولاي الإمبراطور. هل يمكنني مساعدتك؟".

تمتم جايل متذمراً:"أرسل إلي امرأة"، قال، واستدار ليغادر.

"لا حاجة، يا سيدي. هناك واحدة بالفعل في خيمتك، تنتظرك" -لا تزال تلك الابتسامة الماكرة على وجهه -"إنه احتفال بالنصر".

صفع جايل الجندي بقوة، إلى درجة أن رأسه استدار من الشرق إلى الغرب. ظهر خيط من الدم على شفته، لكنه لم يحاول حتى إيقاف النزف.

"هل أبدو لك منتصراً؟" زمجر جايل فيه."هل ترى كل أسلحتي الجديدة؟ بالكاد أستطيع حملها جميعاً! هذا هو انتصاري!" شعر بلون وجهه يتحول إلى الأرجواني، فتذكر شقيقه، الذي عرف بنوباته الغاضبة والدامية. كان جايل يفتخر بأنه مخلوق ماكر، لا يستسلم للغضب، لأن المكر يعني القتل ببرود وليس من منطلق الشغف.

لذلك، دفع الجندي بعيداً عنه—ثبّت ابتسامته في ذاكرته لعقوبة لاحقة—وشق طريقه إلى داخل خيمته، وهو يمزق ملابسه البيضاء السخيفة،

ويطلق شهقة ألم عندما نزع القماش المحترق الذي التصق باللحم النازف لجُرحه، مما أعاد فتحه.

أطلق لعنة. فقد ذكّره الألم بفشله وضعفه. كان بحاجة إلى أن يتذكر قوته، وإلى أن يُشعر دمه بالنبض وأنفاسه بالتدفق، ليُثبت من يكون— وتوقف فجأة.

رأى السرير فارغاً.

ضيّق عينيه وهو يتساءل: أين المرأة إذاً؟ مختبئة؟ مرتعبة؟ حسناً. شعر بالحرارة تتصاعد في جسده. ستكون تلك بداية رائعة.

"اخرجي، اخرجي، أينما كنتِ"، قال بصوت خشن بينما استدار في دائرة بطيئة. كانت الخيمة معتمة، وجدرانها القماشية مبطنة بالفرو لتحجب الرياح والضوء. لم تكن هناك فوانيس للإضاءة، إنما المصدر الوحيد للضوء هو أجنحة جايل...

...والمرأة. هناك.

لم تكن المرأة مختبئة، ولا خائفة. بل جالسة أمام مكتبه.

وقف جايل متصلباً. تلك الوقحة جالسة في كرسيه الوثير، أمام خرائط حملته الميدانية المنتشرة على مكتبه، تُدحرج ثقّال ورق تحت راحة يدها بلامبالاة. يدها الأخرى كما لاحظ جيداً، مستقرة على مقبض سيف.

زمجر بصوت أجش:"ما الذي تفعلينه؟".

"أنتظرك". لم يكن في صوتها أي أثر للخوف، ولا حتى التودد أو التواضع. بدت مضاءة بوهج أجنحتها الخاص، وبالإضافة إلى ذلك، بدا وكأن سكوناً مظلماً غريباً يحيط بها، إلى درجة أن جايل بالكاد استطاع أن يرى ظلها وهي جالسة هناك. اندفع إلى الأمام، مُستعداً لانتزاعها من الكرسي من شعرها. فضلت ذلك على أن تكون مختبئة أو مرتعبة. وربما ستبدي بعض المقاومة—

ثم رأى وجهها، وتوقف في مكانه.

إذا كان قد استغرق بعض الوقت لاستيعاب ما تعنيه هذه الزيارة، فذلك فقط لأن الفكرة نفسها كانت لا تُصدّق. لقد أرسل أربعة آلاف جندي من الدومينيون لسحق المتمردين الذين كانوا أقل من خمسمائة. وقد نجحوا، وأحضروا جثة الذئب الأبيض كدليل، بالإضافة إلى أن الحراس——

من خلفه، تحدث الجندي الذي لم يتعرف عليه، من مدخل الخيمة، وقد دخل دون دعوة أو إذن. "آه، ربما ينبغي أن أوضح شيئاً"، قال بابتسامة ساخرة. "لم أقصد الاحتفال بانتصارك، سيدي. بل بانتصارنا."

تلعثم جايل وهو يحاول الرد.

بخطوة واحدة، وبسحب سلس لسيفها من غمده، نهضت ليراز من على الكرسي.

...

"كارو"، قال أكيفا بينما كانا يتحركان بصمت عبر المخيم.

"نعم؟" همست. أشعرها المخيم المهجور بالرهبة، لكنها كانت تعلم أنه لن يبقى كذلك طويلاً. سيصل الجنود قريباً، وعندها سيكون البقاء هنا خطيراً. وإذا كانوا سيواجهون جايل، فعليهم أن يفعلوا ذلك الآن.

لكنها فوجئت عندما أسقط أكيفا فجأة سحره الواقي. "ماذا تفعل؟" همست بذعر. إنهم في مرأى من برج الحراسة، وحرس جايل الشخصي بالكاد قد تفرقوا. قد يكونون في أي مكان. فلماذا بدا أكيفا غير قلق؟ وغير... مندهش؟

"ذلك الجندي"، قال، مشيراً إلى خيمة الإمبراطور، والحارس الذي انزلق للتو إلى الداخل خلف جايل. "كان ذلك زئانيل."

إنها ليراز. اضطر جايل إلى أن يُرمش عندما بدا أن الرداء المظلم الغريب قد تحرك معها بينما خرجت من خلف المكتب. ساقان طويلتان، خطوات طويلة، دون أي استعجال. تقدمت ليراز من غير الشرعيين بخطوات ثابتة، يُحيط بها مرافقة من الظلام، وكانت يداها سوداوين بالحبر الذي يرمز إلى

الأرواح التي أزهقتها. الظلام الذي أحاط بها بدا وكأنه يتحرك معها، قبل أن يتكاثف ويتخذ شكلين بجانبها.

كانا اثنين: كائنين مجنحين بأجساد قططية، برأسي وعنقي نساء كأبو الهول. وكانا يبتسمان. قال الجندي من خلفه:"غير الشرعيين والعائدون معاً، إن كنت تصدق ذلك".

قالت ليراز بهدوء، وكأنها مضيفة تُجري تعريفات مهذبة:"أخي زثانيل". ثم أضافت، وهي تشير إلى الكائنين:"وهل تعرف تانغريس وباشيس؟ لا؟ ربما تعرفهما باسمهما الشائع. الظلال الحية."

لم يستطع جايل تصديق ذلك، على الرغم من رؤيته بأم عينيه. ليراز، تلك القاتلة الرائعة والمرعبة، تقف بين الظلال الحية. في معسكر مثل هذا، خلال حملات الكيميرا، لم يكن هناك رعب أعظم من هؤلاء القتلة الغامضين. قشعريرة باردة اجتاحت جسده. أراد أن ينادي على حراسه، لكن الفكرة جاءت متأخرة. أدرك الحقيقة الكاملة كقفص يُطبق عليه. لقد سقط المخيم، وكذلك هو.

ربما سقط حراسه، لكن جيشه لا يزال موجوداً. تجدد أمل جايل فجأة. لأن جيشه خلاصه، قادماً نحو المخيم بأعداد كافية لسحق هذه القوة التافهة العدد. حتى أكيفا لن يستطيع الصمود أمام مثل هذه الأعداد. لن يقع جايل في نفس الفخ مرة أخرى، ولن يسمح بأن يُؤخذ كوسيلة للمساومة. نظر إلى كائنات أبو الهول. إحداهما غمزت له، فشعر برعشة تسري في جسده.

"خطة رائعة"، قال، محاولاً كسب الوقت."الأعداء يتحدون."

ردت ليراز بابتسامة باردة:"إنها هديتك الخاصة لإريتز، وسأتأكد من أن يتذكرك الجميع من أجلها، (كإمبراطور لعدة أيام)، وسيكون هذا لقبك، لأن هذا هو كل الوقت الذي لديك. ومع ذلك، وخلاله، لم تكتفِ فقط بحلّ الإمبراطورية، بل حققت إنجازاً استثنائياً بتوحيد أعداء مميتين في سلامٍ دائم."

"دائم؟" سخر جايل. "بمجرد موتي، سيعودون إلى الاقتتال فيما بينهم."

اختيار سيئ للكلمات.

"موتك؟" نظرت إليه ليراز بدهشة مصطنعة. "لماذا، يا عمي، هل تشعر بوعكة؟ هل تخطط للموت قريباً؟".

لقد تغيّرت. لم تكن تلك القطة الهائجة والمتوحشة التي حاول أن يستولي عليها في برج الفتح. حينها، كان قد قال مستهزئاً: "لا توجد رحلة في العالم تضاهي العاصفة في غضبها". لكن من تقف الآن أمامه ليست عاصفة، ولا غضباً. بل هناك هدوء جديد فيها، لكنه لم يُقلل من شأنها. على العكس، بدا أنه يُعززها. لم تعد مجرد سلاح كما زُيِّت لتكون، بل امرأة تسيطر بالكامل على قوتها، لا تُقهر ولا تنكسر، وهذا ما كان خطيراً حقاً.

استمع جايل بقلق، مترقباً أي إشارة تدل على اقتراب جيشه. لا بد أنها لاحظت ذلك. هزت رأسها بأسف مصطنع، وكأنها كانت تشعر بالشفقة عليه، ثم نظرت إلى الجندي المبتسم، الذي أومأ برأسه تأكيداً.

"جيد." التفتت إلى جايل وقالت: "تعال. هناك شيء يجب أن تراه."

لم يكن جايل يرغب في رؤية أي شيء تُريده أن يراه. فكر في سحب سيفه، لكن كائن أبو الهول الذي غمز له تحركت نحوه كدخان نصف قطي، نصف بشرية، ولقّته كالإعصار. اجتاحه دوار لذيذ، نوع من الخدر اللطيف، وفقد فرصته. انتزعت ليراز سيفه بسهولة وكأنه طفل أو سكير وألقته بعيداً. ثم دفعته نحو الباب لتخرجه من الخيمة.

بمجرد خروجه، كان أول ما رآه "قاتل الوحوش" ينتصب أمامه مباشرة. ارتبك غريزياً، وكأنه يتوقع أن يأتي أكيفا ليقتله كما وعد، وحرّاسه قد تفرقوا واختفوا.

لكن أكيفا لم يكن ينظر حتى إلى جايل.

"ليراز!" صرخ أكيفا، وكانت في صوته فرحة كان ينبغي أن تحرق جايل، لكنه بالكاد لاحظ ذلك، إذ كان مشغولاً لما أخرجته ليراز ليراه.

ظلال جيش كعاصفة يحلق في السماء فوقه. بدا هائلاً، يمتد عبر الأفق بأكمله.

إلا أنه لم يكن جيشه.

تجمد في مكانه، رافعاً رأسه وحدّق إلى الأعلى، محاولاً أن يُحصي في ذهنه العدد الذي تمثله هذه الصفوف الهائلة. كانوا قد قالوا إن المولودين غير الشرعيين لا يزيد عددهم على ثلاثمائة، حتى لو نجوا جميعاً من الهجوم في أديلفاس. حتى لو...

لقد قال الجندي"لقد أبدوا دفاعاً مستميتاً". ويبدو أن ذلك صحيح. فإن جزءاً كبيراً من القوات الطائرة يرتدي الأسود الخاص بغير الشرعيين. أما البقية؟

نعم، الكيميرا كانوا بينهم أيضاً. لم يحافظوا على نفس التشكيلات الثابتة التي ميزت السيرافيم. لكن كما هو متوقع منهم تماماً: وحوش جامحة، بلا نظام موحد في الشكل أو الحجم أو الزي. بدوا كأنهم موسوعة من الوحوش قد فُتحت صفحاتها، ولتحفظ نجوم السماء أولئك الملائكة الذين تجرؤوا على التحالف معهم.

لتحفظ النجوم الفيلق الثاني، لأن جايل رأى، من خلال ضباب غضبه، أن قواته كانت تتألف من الكتلة الأساسية لهذه القوة. كانوا مسلحين بالسيوف والدروع، بدون ألوان أو رايات أو شعارات. مجرد سيوف ودروع... كثيرة جداً ومن بعيد، فوق الجبال، كانت قوات الدومينيون الخاصة بجايل تقترب، ولم يكن أمام جايل خيار سوى الوقوف على الأرض ومشاهدة القوتين وهما تتواجهان في السماء.

وبينما كان جايل يحدّق، خرج مبعوثون من كلا الجانبين ليجتمعوا في المنتصف. بصق جايل على العشب، ساخراً في وجه الأعداء الذين تحالفوا ضدّه."الدومينيون لا يستسلمون أبداً! هذا هو ميثاقنا! لقد كتبته بنفسي!".

كان يُصلّي في داخله، بكل ما أوتي من حماسة: دعهم يقاتلون. دعهم

يموتون. سواء انتصروا أم لا، فليأخذوا معهم الخونة والمتمردين إلى قبورهم

لم يكن قريباً بما يكفي ليرى من كان يتحدث نيابة عن الجانبين، ولا حتى أن يتخيل ما كان يُقال، لكن النتيجة أصبحت واضحة عندما انخفضت قوات الدومينيون في السماء—خلف تلة مغطاة بالعشب المتموج، بعيداً عن نظره—وهبطوا على الأرض بطريقة تشبه الاستسلام.

"ربما لا يستسلمون"، قال الجندي المبتسم بلهجة تعزية زائفة."ربما فقط جميعهم يحتاجون للتبول بشدة."

لم يكن جايل بحاجة إلى رؤية الدومينيون وهم يلقون سيوفهم أرضاً. كان يعلم أنه خسر.

لقد خسر صاحب السمو جايل الثاني، جايل، الإمبراطور لعدة أيام فقد جيشه وإمبراطوريته. وبلا شك، على وشك أن يخسر حياته.

"ماذا تنتظرين؟" صرخ وهو يندفع نحو ليراز. بخطوة بسيطة ومناورة سريعة، دفعته برشاقة ليسقط بوجهه على الأرض. ثم بركلة متقنة في مكانها، قلبته على ظهره، وهو يلهث طلباً للهواء.

"اقتليني!" صرخ وهو مستلقٍ على الأرض."أعرف أنك تريدين ذلك!".

لكنها فقط هزّت رأسها وابتسمت. أراد جايل أن يصرخ، لأن ابتسامتها لم تحمل الرحمة بل خططاً، ومن خلال تلك الخطط، رأى أن موته لن يكون سهلاً.

73

فراشة في قارورة

التقت كارو وليراز دون سابق ترتيب لإزالة جثة ثياغو من أعلى السور الخشبي. لم يُتح لهم التعامل مع هذا الأمر في الأيام السابقة، حيث كان المخيم يعج بالنشاط منذ استسلام الدومينيون. اجتماعات ونقاشات وهتافات وتحليلات، وحوارات حول الخطط والاستراتيجيات، وحتى الاحتفالات التي كانت ممتزجة بنصيب لا بأس به من الحزن بسبب الخسائر في صفوف أديلفاس، خسائر كثيرة، وبعضها لا يمكن تعويضه.

ما زالت كارو تحتفظ ببعض مباخر الأرواح، وفتحت كل واحدة منها على أمل العثور على ما تبحث عنه. وراحت تستشعر أثر الأرواح التي في داخلها، لكنها لم تجد في أيٍ منها ما كانت تأمله.

تقدمت بخطوات ثقيلة نحو الجثة التي لطالما كرهتها، لكنها في تلك اللحظة وجدت نفسها عاجزة عن الكره. هل كان ذلك كله من أجل زيري؟ أم بسبب حزنها؟ أو ربما هناك جزء صغير من هذا الكره بسبب ما فعله مع الذئب الحقيقي؟ ذلك الذي، رغم كل عيوبه العظيمة، قدّم الكثير—سنوات طويلة، موت متكرر، وألم بلا نهاية—من أجل شعبه.

لدهشتها، وجدت ليراز هناك بالفعل، واقفة أمام السور والجثة المتدلية منه."آه"، قالت كارو متفاجئة."مرحباً."

لم ترد عليها التحية. قالت ليراز دون أن تدير رأسها، وبصوت مشدود:"أنا من وضعه هنا." فهمت كارو أنها حزينة على زيري، رغم أنها لم تعرف كيف حدث ذلك، أو كيف وجدوا الوقت لتبادل المشاعر بينهما. لم يفاجئها ذلك، وتحديداً ليراز. ليس بعد الآن.

"كل ذلك من أجل جايل، تحسباً لأي شكوك قد تراوده عندما يأتي إلى المخيم — رمقتها ليراز بنظرة متوترة وأضافت:"لم يكن ذلك... قلة احترام." وردت كارو بهدوء:"أعلم."

بدت كلماتها غير كافية، فأضافت برقة:"إنه ليس هو، على أي حال."

"أعلم." ردت ليراز بصوت أجش. وخيم الصمت حتى قطعتا الحبال وأسقطتا الجثة على الأرض. كما أنزلتا الراية أيضاً. تلك الكلمات التي على الراية —النصر والانتقام— إنما تنتمي إلى زمن آخر. فتحت كارو الراية فوق الجثة، كالكفن، لتُخفي ما تبقى من آثار الموت العنيف.

"هل ستحرقينها؟". لم تقل"ستحرقينه" لأنها قصدت الجثة وهي شيء، وما بقي منه كان مجرد شيء. مجرد شيء فارغ، كصدفة تركتها أمواج البحر على الشاطئ.

أومأت ليراز برأسها، ثم جثت بجواره لتشعل النار في صدره العريض الميت. خيوط رفيعة من الدخان التفت حول يدها، و—"انتظري"، قالت كارو وهي تتذكر شيئاً. جثت هي الأخرى بجانبه، ومدّت يدها إلى جيب الجنرال. أخرجت شيئاً صغيراً بحجم إصبعها الصغير. كان أسوداً وأملس، ينتهي بطرف حاد."من جسده الحقيقي"، قالت وهي تسلّمه إلى ليراز. طرف قرنه."هذا كل شيء"، ثم اشتعل. ارتفعت النيران، نظيفة وباهرة وذات حرارة خارقة للطبيعة، لم تترك خلفها سوى رماد حملته الرياح بعيداً قبل أن تخمد ألسنة اللهب.

عندها فقط لاحظت كارو الصمت الذي خيّم على المخيم. التفتت نحو البوابة لترى الحشد متجمّعاً هناك، يراقب. يقف أكيڤا في المقدمة، وكذلك هاكسايا. نظرت الأخيرة إلى ليراز، ونظرت ليراز إليها. لم يعد بينهما أي عداء

"هيا"، قال أكيڤا، وأفسح الطريق للحشد ليبتعد، وترك كارو وليراز وحدهما مجدداً. لا جثة. ولا حتى رماد.

تلكأت كارو، وفي رأسها سؤال يتملّكها بشدة، لكنها قاومته ولم تسأله.

"لم أره يموت"، قالت ليراز. قبضت على طرف القرن في يدها المشدودة إلى صدرها. التزمت كارو الصمت، وحافظت على ثباتها، شاعرةً بأن الإجابة التي تتوق إلى سماعها على وشك أن تأتي.

"عند عودتنا من البوابة، كان الوضع فوضوياً. رأيته مرة، لكنني لم أتمكن من الوصول إليه، وعندما نظرت مرة أخرى، لم يكن هناك. بعد ذلك..." بدا عليها الاضطراب، ثم ألقت نظرة جانبية على كارو، وقالت ببساطة:"لا أعرف كيف حدث الأمر. كيف انتصرنا. لا يوجد تفسير." هزت رأسها كأنها تحاول تصفية ذهنها."رأيت جنوداً يسقطون من السماء، بلا سهام، بلا إصابات، ولم يكن هناك أحد يقاتلهم. الآخرون فرّوا. أعتقد أن الفارين أكثر من الذين سقطوا. لا أعرف."

سمعت كارو هذه الرواية من قبل، من تقرير إليون الأول إلى أكيڤا، مؤكداً من قبل باليروس. انتصار غامض—وانتصار مستحيل. ما الذي يعنيه ذلك؟

"وجدتُ جثته أخيراً. يبدو أنها سقطت في وادٍ. في مجرى ماء". ألقت ليراز نظرة على كارو، وكل ما فيها بدا متوتراً وحذراً. وكأنها تنتظر من كارو أن تقول شيئاً. هل اعتقدتْ أن كارو ستلومها؟

قالت كارو:"هذا ليس خطأك". مهما كان ذلك الشيء الذي أرادت ليراز سماعه، لم يُقل. أطلقت نفخة قصيرة من نفاد الصبر. "الماء"، قالت."هل الماء الجارية... تسرع في التلاشي؟".

نظرت كارو إلى ليراز بينما تسللت كلماتها إلى وعيها. تعمّق ثباتها. حبست أنفاسها. هل كانت تعني...؟

تذكرت كارو بوضوح تلك النظرة المحطّمة على وجه ليراز عندما اضطرت إلى إخبارها بكل لطف ممكن في ظل هذه الظروف، أن روح هازايل قد فُقدت. وكيف، دون جدوى، حملت جثته عبر سماءين، وفي سعيها لإحضاره لإحياء روحه، لكنها ألقت بروحه إلى العدم.

بالطبع لم يكن هذا هو السبب الذي جعل ليراز تحمل جثة ثياغو كل هذه المسافة، أليس كذلك؟

نظرة خاطفة من كارو إلى حيث كانت الجثة قد استقرت، لم تفلت من انتباه ليراز. "هل تظنين أنني لم أتعلم؟" سألت الملاك بنبرة غير مصدقة. ومع ذلك، تجرأت كارو على الأمل. "هل فعلتِ؟" سألت بصوت منخفض جداً بالكاد يُسمع.

"هل تعلمتِ؟ هل التقطتِ روح زيري؟ يا نجوم السماء وغبار الكون، هل فعلتِ؟".

بدأت ليراز ترتجف. "لا أعرف"، قالت بصوت مكسور. "لا أعرف". ثم انهار صوتها فجأة، وبدأت تبكي. راحت تتلمس حزامها بارتباك، ثم مدت شيئاً نحو كارو بيدين ترتجفان بشكل جنوني. رفعت مطرة الماء الخاصة بها.

"إنها ليست كمباخر الأرواح، لكنها تنغلق بإحكام. لم تكن لدي مبخرة، ولم أجد أحداً قريباً مني ليساعدني. فكرت أن الانتظار قد يجعل الأمر أسوأ، لكنني لم أستطع أن أجزم إن كان حدث شيء. لم أشعر بشيء، ولم أرَ شيئاً. لذلك أنا خائفة... خائفة من أنه قد رحل بالفعل."

أخذ صوتها يتسارع بشكل محموم، ثم يتوقف فجأة في فترات صمت متوترة. وفي عينيها كأن هناك حرباً دائرة بين أمل حذر وخوف جلي. همست بصوت يكاد لا يُسمع: "لقد... لقد غنّيت، لعل ذلك ينفع". شعرت كارو بقلبها يتمزق من الألم.

هذه المحاربة من غير الشرعيين، الأشرس بينهم جميعاً، جلست في مجرى ماء متجمد لتغني لروح كيميرا حتى تأوي إلى قارورتها، فقط لأنها لم تعرف ما الذي يمكن فعله غير ذلك.

الغناء لم يكن سيُحدث فرقاً، لكن كارو لن تخبر ليراز بذلك. إذا كانت روح زيري في تلك القارورة، فإنها ستتقبل أغنية ليراز عن طيب خاطر وتجعلها جزءاً من طقوس الإحياء إلى الأبد، فقط كي لا تشعر الملاك يوماً بأنها كانت ساذجة أو أنها أخطأت.

ومن يدري؟ فكرت كارو وهي تمد يدها نحو القربة. من يدري حقاً؟ لأنني بكل تأكيد لا أعرف.

وكانت يداها ترتجفان هي الأخرى بينما تدير الغطاء ببطء. حاولت أن تثبتها عند عنق القربة المعدني، الذي كان من المفترض أن يكون بارداً في هواء الجبل، لكنه كان دافئاً من احتكاكه بجسد ليراز.

ثم، بكل حذر ممكن مع أصابعها المرتعشة، رفعت الغطاء.

حبست أنفاسها، مستشعرة بحواسها، متمددة، متمنية. بدا الأمر أشبه بالتقدم إلى الأمام واستنشاق الهواء بعمق—ولكن دون حركة أو تنفس. جزء مجهول من ذاتها امتد، انفتح، ووصل.

ثم شعرت... بالوطن.

هذا ما لاقته. وطنها ووطن زيري. ربما وطنهم جميعاً الآن. وستشاركه بكل سرور. يمكن أن يصبحوا قبيلة كبيرة مجنونة، يأتون جميعاً، الملائكة والشياطين في راحة وفي حب، أو يتجادلون، أو يتدربون، أو يتعلمون عزف الكمان من ميك، أو يعلّمون أطفالهم الهجينين الطيران بأجنحة ليست كيرين ولا سيراف، بل مزيج من الريش والنار والجلد. أو ربما سيكون الأمر مثل لون العينين؛ سيرثون إما هذه أو تلك.

هل كانت تفكر في الأطفال؟ راحت كارو تضحك وتهز رأسها بالموافقة، بينما راحت ليراز تبكي وتضحك في آن واحد. سقطتا في أحضان بعضهما،

والقربة بينهما، وغطاؤها الثمين الذي أعيد إلى مكانه، والارتياح الذي صار أرضاً مشتركة بينهما.

لأن كارو، بحواسها، شعرت باضطراب أجنحة صيادي العواصف، والريح العالية التي تتجول فوق جبال أديلفاس، والأغاني الجميلة، الحزينة، والأبدية لمزامير الرياح التي تغمر كهوفهم بالموسيقى.

وأيضاً: نغمة لم تتذكرها من قبل. حيث النار محتضنة بين كفين، وقد اعتقدت أنها قد فهمت ما تعنيه.

ربما التقطت ليراز روح زيري كفراشة في قارورة، أو مطرة ذلك لا يهم. المهم أن الروح ملكها.

وبالنظر إلى حالتها، بدا جلياً من خلال بكائها وضحكها بين ذراعي كارو، بأن روحها ملكاً له أيضاً.

74

الفصل الأول

إذاً، فقد تمت الإطاحة بجايل، وأُغلقت البوابات دون أن يمر عبرها أي أسلحة جديدة يمكن أن تخلق فوضى أخرى. هُزمت جيوش الدومينيون، وأصبحت الفرقة الثانية، أو ما يُعرف بالجيش"الشعبي"، القوة المهيمنة في الأرض. كانت هذه الفرقة الأكبر عدداً دائماً تمثل أرضية وسطى بين الدومينيون ذوي النسب العالي وغير الشرعيين. وعندما وجدوا أنفسهم في وضع لا يُصدق يفرض عليهم الاختيار، انحازوا إلى غير الشرعيين.

تحت قيادة القائد أورميرود، الذي عرفه أكيفا واحترمه، أعلن الجيش الثاني وقوفه إلى جانب غير الشرعيين، مما ألغى فعلياً حكم الإعدام الصادر بحقهم وأعلن نهاية الأعمال العدائية.

لكن إعلان نهاية الحرب وتحقيقها أمران مختلفان تماماً. فرغم انتهاء القتال بين جيوش السيرافيم، كان الجيش الثاني بعيداً كل البعد عن اعتبار أعدائهم الكيميرا رفقاء سلاح. في الوقت الحالي، قطعوا على أنفسهم نفس الوعد الذي قطعه غير الشرعيين قبل أيام، ووعد كارو بألا يضربوا أولاً. الهدنة ليست تحالفاً، لكنها بداية.

تبيّن أن إليون، بعد الانتصار المذهل في أديلفاس، أنه هو من ذهب إلى كيب أرَمسين نيابة عن أكيفا ليلتمس دعم القضية الثورية، وقد نجح بوضوح في ذلك. الآن، سيُرافق إليون وأورميرود جايل إلى أستراي ليبدأ فصلاً جديداً في حياته. من قائد، إلى إمبراطور، إلى... فرجة. فالإمبراطور الذي دام لأيام معدودة كان على وشك أن يصبح نجم استعراض في حديقة حيواناته الخاصة. لم يكن أحدٌ يلوم ليراز لو قتلت جايل، ولم يكن أحدٌ ليتفجع عليه. لكنها، وهي واقفة فوق كتلة جسده المتلوّي الصارخ، اكتشفت أنها لا تملك الإرادة لفعل ذلك. ليس فقط لأنها سئمت القتل ورغبت في وضع حد لحصيلتها الدموية، بل أيضاً لسبب بسيط: لأن جايل أراد ذلك.

في برج الفتح، كانت هي من اختارت مواجهة الموت بدلاً من الاستسلام للمصير الذي رسمه لها جايل."اقتلني مع إخوتي، أو ستندم على أنك لم تفعل"، بصقت كلماتها في وجهه آنذاك، لكنه تظاهر بالإهانة.

"ستموتين معهم، بأسرع مما تتوقعين".

أجابت بصوت مختنق:"أسرع بألف مرة".

أما هو، فقد وضع يده على قلبه متظاهراً بالعاطفة:"عزيزتي. ألا تدركين؟ إن معرفتي بذلك هو ما يجعل الأمر ممتعاً." والآن، هي من تدرك حلاوة إنكار الموت بدلاً من تسبيبه. "كنت أفكر"، قالت بتأمل، وهي تقف فوقه،"أنه سيكون من الجيد للناس أن يروا بأعينهم الطغيان الذي تحرروا منه. أن تسمع عن فظائعه شيء، وأن تجربه شيء آخر".

توقف عن التلوي لينظر إليها بدهشة، وجهه يتجمد في حالة من الذهول "تعالوا وانظروا، هذا ما يبدو عليه الإمبراطور"، أضافت، وقد بدأت فكرتها تروق لها أكثر فأكثر. بعد أن تذكرت ما شهدته في الهينترموست، عندما غرس جايل السيوف في كفي زيري وأجبره على ابتلاع رماد رفاقه.

"تعالوا وألقوا نظرة، لتروا ما أنقذناكم منه، وستسجدون شكراً لنا. وربما تتقيؤون أيضاً".

أما رده الوحشي—سيل من الشتائم الممزوجة بالبصاق وسلسلة من تعابير وجه وصلت به إلى مستويات جديدة من القبح—فلم يكن منها إلا مواجهته ببرود قائلة:"نعم، افعل هذا بالضبط عندما يأتون لرؤيتك. رائع".

أما بالنسبة إلى العدالة الحقيقية، فالإمبراطورية لم يكن فيها نظام، ولم يكن أحد يعرف كيف يمكن البدء ببناء نظام فقط. ناهيك عن الحاجة إلى نظام حكم جديد يحل محل النظام البائس الذي تم إسقاطه للتو. ثم كانت هناك مهمة تحرير العبيد، بالإضافة إلى إيجاد عمل لعدد لا يحصى من الرجال والنساء الذين لم يعرفوا في حياتهم مهنة سوى الحرب.

ما كانوا يعرفونه في تلك الليلة عند سفوح جبال فيسكال، هو مدى جهلهم بما سيأتي. باختصار، كتبوا"الفصل الأول" على الصفحة الأولى من كتاب جديد، وكل شيء—كل شيء—ما زال ينتظر أن يُكتب.

تأملت كارو أن يكون الكتاب طويلاً... ومملاً.

"هذا ممل؟" كرر أكيفا، متشككاً، وهما يجلسان معاً عند أطراف الضوء المنبعث من النار، يتناولان حصص الدومينيون الغذائية. أما كارو فقد أخذت تراقب من بعيد ليراز تجلس بين تانغريس وباشيس، وتعتقد أن وجودهما مؤنس لها.

"هذا ممل"، أدركت كارو أن التاريخ يؤقلمنا مع الكوارث ذات البعد الملحمي. مرة، أثناء دراستها لعدد القتلى في معارك الحرب العالمية الأولى، وجدت نفسها تفكر: فقط ثمانية آلاف ماتوا هنا؟ هذا ليس رقماً كبيراً. لأنه بالمقارنة مع المليون الذين لقوا حتفهم في السوم، بدا الرقم ضئيلاً. الأرقام الهائلة كانت تُفقدك الشعور بالمآسي الصغيرة، والتاريخ لا يساوي أيام الدمار بأيام السلام.

في هذا اليوم، لم يُقتل أحد في العالم. وضعت اللبؤة صغيرها. تغذت الدعسوقات على المنّ. فتاة عاشقة أمضت الصباح كله سارحةً في أحلامها، متجاهلة واجباتها المنزلية، ولم يوبخها أحد.

ما الذي قد يكون أكثر سحراً من يوم هادئ؟

"هادئ... بشكل جميل"، أوضحت كارو."لا حروب لتضفي عليه طابع الإثارة. لا غزوات ولا غارات عبيد، فقط إصلاح وبناء".

ابتسم أكيفا بسخرية وسأل:"وكيف يكون ذلك مملاً؟".

أجابت كارو، مقلدةً صوتاً رتيباً بنبرة مصطنعة، وكأنها تتحدث باسم التاريخ:"الحادي عشر من يناير، عام... العقرب. يتم تفكيك حامية كيب أرمسين للحصول على الأخشاب. يُخطط لبناء بلدة في الموقع. هناك تردد بشأن ارتفاع برج الساعة المقترح. يجتمع المجلس، يتجادل...". توقفت عن الحديث وكأنها تضيف لمسة درامية، محركة عينيها من جانب إلى آخر."ثم يتوصلون إلى حل وسط. يُبنى برج الساعة. تُزرع الخضروات وتُؤكل. تُعجب الجماهير كثيراً بغروب الشمس".

ضحك أكيفا. قال مبتسماً:"هذا فشل متعمد في التخيل. أنا واثق من أن أشياء مثيرة تحدث في هذه البلدة الخيالية التي اخترعتِها".

"حسناً". توقف قليلاً ليفكر. ثم تكلم مقلداً نفس نبرة كارو الرتيبة."الحادي عشر من يناير، عام العقرب. تُفكك حامية كيب أرمسين للحصول على الأخشاب. البلدة التي يُخطط لبنائها هناك تصبح أول مدينة مختلطة الأعراق في إريتز. يعيش الكيميرا والسيرافيم جنباً إلى جنب كأنداد. بل... بعضهم...". توقف صوته عند تلك النقطة. وعندما استأنف الحديث، بنبرته الحقيقية، لكن بتأنٍ وحنان ملحوظين."بل بعضهم يعيشون معاً".

يعيشون معاً؟ هل كان يقصد...؟

نعم، هذا ما قصده. نظر إليها بثبات ودفء. لقد تخيلت ذلك، أو حاولت. أن يعيشوا معاً. دائماً ما كان يبدو الأمر كحلم ذهبي غامض بلا كلمات.

"بعضهم"، تابع أكيفا بصوت خافت الآن، "يستلقون تحت غطاء مشترك، يتنفسون عطر بعضهم البعض أثناء النوم. ويحلمون بمعبد مفقود وسط بستان من الذكرى، وبالأماني التي تمنوا تحقيقها هناك... وقد تحققت".

تذكرت كارو ذلك البستان—كل ليلة، كل لحظة، كل أمنية. تذكرت انجذابه إليها، كمدّ جارف. حرارته. ثقله. لكن ليس مع جسده الحالي. بالنسبة إلى هذا الجسد، ستكون كل تلك الأحاسيس جديدة تماماً. شعرت بالحرارة تسري في وجهها، لكنها لم تصرف نظرها عنه.

أضاف بصوت رقيق:"البعض، لن ينتظروا طويلاً بعد الآن".

بلعت ريقها، وعثرت على صوتها."أنت محق"، قالت بصوت يكاد يكون همساً."لا، هذا ليس مملاً".

...

"لم يعد هناك الكثير من الانتظار" لكن حتى الكثير، كان يعني مزيداً من الانتظار، ومعظم الوقت كان الانتظار محتملاً.

من غير المحتمل: ليلتان قضوهما في معسكر دومينيون، حيث أبقى إليون، وأورميرود، ومجموعة أخرى من بينهم الثور القنطور باليروس—الذي تولى قيادة ثياغو—كارو وأكيفا منشغلين بالتخطيط حتى الفجر. كانت كارو قد عقدت العزم على تهريب أكيفا إلى إحدى الخيام الفارغة المخصصة للحملات، لكن الفرصة لم تأتِ أبداً.

المحتمل: صباح اليوم الثالث، حين غادروا—أخيراً—ولأنهما غادرا معاً، كان هناك بعض الاعتراضات على الأمر. أصر أورميرود على أن أكيفا سيكون مطلوباً في العاصمة، التي لم يتم إدخالها بعد، بهدوء أو بالقوة، إلى هذا العصر الجديد ما بعد الإمبراطورية. لكن أكيفا رد قائلاً إنهم سيكونون أفضل حالاً من دون حالة الهلع التي قد يثيرها وجوده. وأضاف:"إضافةً إلى ذلك، لدي التزام مسبق".

بعدما لطّف تعبيره وألقى نظرة على كارو، كان من السهل إساءة فهم طبيعة"التزامه".

"بالتأكيد، يمكن الانتظار"، قال أورميرود، مذهولاً. احمر وجه كارو، وهي تدرك ما ظنوه جميعاً، ولم يكونوا مخطئين في ذلك.

"دعيني أساعدك"، توسّل إليها في الكهوف، عندما أخبرته كارو عن العمل الذي ينتظرها."كل ما أريده هو أن أكون بجانبك، أساعدك. وإن استغرق الأمر الأبد، فليكن. طالما أن الأبد سيكون معك".

بدت تلك اللحظة بعيدة جداً آنذاك، لكن ها هما هنا الآن. أمامهما عمل يجب إنجازه، وألم يجب دفع ثمنه، وعسل في نهاية المطاف. وقد وعدت كارو نفسها بأن تكون"نهاية المطاف" زاخرة. ألا يستحقان ذلك؟

أنهت ليراز النقاش بقرارها أن الكيميرا يحتاجون إلى مرافقة من سيرافيم على أي حال في هذا الوقت الحرج، حيث لا يزال السلام بعيداً عن أن يكون سهلاً، ومهمتهم ذات أهمية كبيرة. تحدثت بنفس الهدوء والطريقة المربكة التي اعتمدتها في مجلس الحرب. وكان التأثير نفسه: عندما تتحدث ليراز، تُولد الحقيقة. كان ذلك أشبه بقوة، فكرت كارو، وهي تنظر إلى ليراز بإعجاب متزايد. قوة لم تبدأ الملاك بعد في استكشافها. وأعجبتها أكثر بكثير عندما تُستخدم لصالحها، وليس ضدها. ولم يكن تأثير ليراز وحده هو السبب، بالطبع. فعندما أدرك السيرافيم ما هي المهمة الحساسة التي بدأت الكيميرا بتنفيذها، حاولوا التطوع للمشاركة فيها.

في تلك اللحظة، بينما كانت تنظر إلى وجوههم، شعرت كارو بأول رشفة من الأمل السهل لمستقبل إريتز. كما حدث من قبل، عندما اعترفت ليراز بأنها غنّت لروح زيري لتوجيهها إلى قارورتها، شعرت وكأن قلبها يتمزّق.

كل واحد غير الشرعيين الذين سمعوا النقاش، تطوع للذهاب إلى لوراميندي والمساعدة في استخراج الأرواح. كانوا جميعهم مقاتلين، يحمل كل منهم ذكريات تطارده، ومعظمهم يحمل آثاماً تلاحقه. لكن لم تتح لأيِّ منهم من قبل فرصة أن يقوموا بشيء أشبه بـ"عكس المذبحة"—وهو ما كانوا على وشك فعله الآن، باستخراج الأرواح المدفونة في كاتدرائية بريمستون. أولئك الآلاف المخفيون الذين اختاروا موتهم في ذلك اليوم على أمل أن يولدوا من جديد. أمل بريمستون، وأمل أمير الحرب: أن تجد فتاة

نشأت بين البشر، بلا ذاكرة عن هويتها الحقيقية أو معرفة بالسحر الكامن داخلها، طريقها إليهم يوماً ما، وأن تعيدهم إلى الحياة.

لكن الأمل الثقيل كان: هل يمكن أن يوجد عالم يستحق إعادتهم إليه؟

كان من الجنون الآن بعد كل شيء أن ذلك قد تحقق. وبينما وقفت كارو وسط مئات الجنود من كلا الجانبين، الذين كان لكل منهم دور في هذا الإنجاز، شعرت وكأن بريقاً غير مرئي يجذب عينيها إلى أكيفا، ذلك الشخص الذي من دونه ما كان لأي شيء أن يتحقق. عظمة الأمنيات. حياة زيري. مبخرة روح إيسّا. عرض التحالف. كل شيء. في كل خطوة على الطريق، كان هناك. لكن قبل ذلك كله، منذ وقت طويل، كان هناك الحلم. "أمنية حياة"، كما قال أكيفا ذات مرة. أمنية لحياة مختلفة تماماً.

كانت كارو، في حياتها السابقة كفنانة بشرية، تختبر أحياناً لحظة إبداعية نادرة. يحدث أن ترسم لوحة أفضل بكثير مما رسمته من قبل، إلى حد مبهر. وعندما تصنع شيئاً كهذا، لم تكن تستطيع التوقف عن النظر إليه.

كانت تعود إليه طوال اليوم، حتى إنها تستيقظ في منتصف الليل فقط لتتأمل فيه، مليئة بالدهشة والفخر. كان النظر إلى أكيفا يشبه ذلك. هو أيضاً يثبت أنظاره عليها كما هي، وهناك جوع يشتعل في نقطة التقاء أعينهما.

لم يكن شغفاً فحسب، ولا رغبة فقط، بل شيئاً أكبر يحتوي على كل تلك المشاعر وأكثر.

إنه جوع وشبع في نفس الوقت—"الرغبة" و"الامتلاك" يتلاقيان، دون أن يطفئ أحدهما الآخر. وسواء كان ذلك بسبب تدخل ليراز، أو بسبب القوة الكامنة في تلك النظرات، فلم يحاول أحدٌ أن يعترض بعد ذلك. ثم تحت أي سلطة عسكرية يمكن إلزام أكيفا بأي شيء؟

من يمكنه أن يملي على أكيفا ما يفعله؟

بالطبع، سيرافق كارو.

في قديم الزمان
لم يكن هناك سوى الظلام

وكانت هناك وحوش بحجم العوالم تسبح فيه

75

حاجة

كانوا أربعين من غير الشرعيين ومثلهم من الكيميرا. أما البقية – تلك القوة التي أسدلت ظلالها القاتمة على سماء سلسلة جبال فيسكال – فكانت ستحلق جنوباً لتقديم نفسها إلى أستراي.

قال أمزالاغ، الذي سيقود عملية التنقيب في كاتدرائية بريمستون:"سنحتاج إلى مبخرة أرواح وبخور". لقد فقد عائلته في لوراميندي، وكان متلهفاً للمغادرة والبدء. المجارف والمعاول، والخيام والطعام، كلها استولوا عليها من معسكر الدومينيون، لكن تلك الإمدادات المخصصة مثل المباخر سيكون من الصعب العثور عليها. ولهذا السبب، ولأسباب أخرى، تقرر أن يطيروا أولاً إلى كهوف الكيرين، والتي كانت، في كل الأحوال، تقريباً على طريقهم.

كانت كارو متحمسة لرؤية إيسّا، مدركة أن من بقوا في الكهوف لم يكن لديهم طعام يكفيهم لفترة طويلة، وليس لدى معظمهم أجنحة تمكنهم من مغادرة المكان والبحث عن الطعام. إضافة إلى ذلك، وبينما احتفظت

كارو وليراز وأكيفا بهذا الخبر سراً فيما بينهم في الوقت الراهن، ظل أيضاً السؤال المتعلق بزيري معلقاً.

لم يعلم، باستثنائهم وهاكسايا، بأن روحاً قد انتُزعت من جسد الذئب الأبيض، ولذلك مازالت كارو تأمل أن تُنسى هذه الحادثة برمتها وتدفن تحت سجادة التاريخ. لقد كان ثياغو، الابن البكر لزعيم الحرب، وألد أعداء السيرافيم، هو من غيّر قلبه وتحالف مع منبوذي الإمبراطورية ليشق طريقاً جديداً نحو المستقبل. ولكن، هل انتقص ذلك من المجد الذي يستحقه زيري لدوره العظيم في انتصارهم؟

ربما. لكن كارو كانت تعتقد أن ذلك لن يزعج زيري على الإطلاق. وربما، مع مرور الوقت، يمكنها رواية الحقيقة. أما بالنسبة إلى آخر أبناء الكيرين، فقد أدركت كارو أنهم سيحتاجون إلى اختلاق قصة جيدة لتفسير عودته المفاجئة، دون أي ارتباط بمقتل الذئب الأبيض. ولكن بما أن نهايته كانت غامضة –ولم يعد قط من مهمة المذبحة الأخيرة التي كلفه بها ثياغو، ولم يشاهد أحد جسده سوى كارو – شعرت بأنه يمكنها معالجة الأمر. بدا من الصواب أن يظهر مجدداً بينهم في موطن أسلافه... وموطنها هي أيضاً.

وربما تجد كارو الوقت الآن للعودة إلى قريتها التي نشأت فيها، عميقاً في قلب الجبال.

وبالطبع، لديها هناك سبب آخر لحرصها على العودة إلى الكهوف، وهو سبب لا يقل أهمية عن بقية الأسباب: تلك الممرات المظلمة المتشعبة، حيث يمكن لمن أراد أن يختفي لبضع ساعات... أو ثلاث... أو سبع. بالتأكيد تمتلك كارو الإرادة لذلك.

...

أما ليراز، فكان لديها أمل خاص بها، أمل حاد يغرس نفسه في قلبها كشوكة، لكنها لم تتحدث عنه بصوت عالٍ. كانت تخفي رأس القرن في جيبها العميق، لكن القارورة الآن مع كارو، وليراز تفتقد لمطرتها التي اعتادت

عليها على خاصرتها. لم تجرؤ على سؤال كارو، متى ستعيد إحياؤه؟ لم تتحدثا بوضوح حول هذا الأمر قط.

في ذلك الوقت، خارج السور، لم يكن الأمر يبدو مهماً أو ملحاً بأي شكل. الدموع والضحك! لو حاول أحدهم إخبارها بأنها ستبكي يوماً في ذلك الشعر الأزرق... حسناً. كانت ستمنحه نظرة باردة قاسية لا أكثر، لأن أي ردة فعل أخرى منها ستكون تصرفاً همجياً.

"لا تريدين التصرف بهمجية، أليس كذلك؟". تخيلت صوت هازايل في رأسها، بنبرته الكسلانة المليئة بالضحك."ستجفلين كل خاطبيك."

وهذا موضوع لا يجرؤ على طرحه سوى هاز. لم تنظر ليراز يوماً إلى رجل – أو امرأة – بتلك الطريقة..."تلك" الطريقة. ولو كان يعلم أن مجرد الفكرة نفسها تخيفها، لما أظهر ذلك قط. كان دائماً يعزز قوتها.

قال مرة، متظاهراً بالبطولة:"أي شخص يجرؤ على الاقتراب من أختي، سيضطر إلى التعامل مع... أختي". ثم قفز خلفها مختبئاً بخوف مصطنع.

هاز... ماذا كان سيقول عنها الآن، وهي تشتاق... إلى الهواء المحبوس داخل مبخرة؟ أكان هذا شوقاً حقاً؟ لقد شاهدت شغف أخويها – وكيف كانا مختلفين تماماً في هذا. شغف هاز متقلب، متكرر، ومفعم بالمرح. ورغم أن أرواح المتجسدين ممنوعة من لذائذ الجسد، إلا أن ذلك لم يمنعه قط. وقد كان يقع في الحب وكأنه كان هواية – ويخرج منه بالطريقة ذاتها. وربما، فكرت ليراز، أيعني هذا أنه لم يكن حباً حقيقياً.

أكيفا... فقط وإلى الأبد.

أكيفا ذلك الصامت المتألم. وليراز التي لم تشعر من قبل بقرب روحي منه كما شعرت الآن. وقد أدركت أن الأمر ليس لأنه قد تغيّر، بل لأنها هي التي تغيّرت. بدا ذلك غريباً.

أن تشعر بهذا الشوق، مصحوباً بكل هذا الخوف الذي يصاحبه. من المفترض أن تكره هذا الإحساس. وجزء منها فعل ذلك حقاً. تلك المشاعر

الغبية. سمعت صوت داخلها لا يزال يصرّ على ذلك، لكن ذلك الصوت أخذ يخفت شيئاً فشيئاً. أما الصوت الآخر، الذي بالكاد تعرّفت عليه على أنه صوتها، فقد أصبح أعلى وأوضح.

"أنا أريد"، قال ذلك الصوت المتدفق من أعماقها، من مكان ربما توقعت فيه أشياء كثيرة لتُكتشف. الضحك الحقيقي، مثلاً. ضحك هازايل: المنساب، السهل، المتحرر، والمريح. اللمس، أيضاً، على الرغم من أن مجرد التفكير في ذلك كان يجعل قلبها يخفق بسرعة.

كانت تعرف تماماً ما سيقوله هاز. نعم سيرميها بنظرة متفاخرة ويقول، "أرأيتِ؟ هناك طريقة أفضل بكثير لتحريك جسدك من القتال". ثم سيضيف، بلا شك ما كرره من قبل: "أرجو أن تفكي ضفائر شعرك. يعذبني مجرد النظر إليها. ماذا فعلت تلك الضفائر بكِ لتستحق هذا العقاب؟".

ضحكت ليراز قليلاً، وهي تستعيد حديثه، وربما بكت قليلاً أيضاً، وهي تفتقده، لكن أحداً لم يرَ ذلك. وتجمّدت دموعها قبل أن تصل إلى الجبال، لأنهم الآن قد وصلوا أعالي سلسلة أديلفاس. ألقت نظرة سريعة على كارو، ولمحة صغيرة على وميض الفضة على خاصرتها حيث تتأرجح القارورة.

متى؟ قالت متسائلة.

وماذا بعد؟

...

أما أكيفا، فقد شعر طوال الرحلة بأنه منقسم إلى نصفين.

هناك ذكرى قبلة كارو، وكل ما قاله لها، وكل ما فكر فيه ولم يقله – وهو الجزء الأكبر – وكل إثارة تعتمل داخله، عندما تتبع عينيه خطوط جسدها أثناء الطيران، فيما يداه تتوقان لتتبع تلك الخطوط أيضاً... هي كل ما يشغل ذهنه.

سيمضون ليلة في كهوف الكيرين للاستراحة، وكان يعلم أنهم لن يقضوا ليلة أخرى بعيدين عن بعضهم. لقد وصلوا أخيراً إلى نهاية تلك الليالي، وشعر

وكأن شيئاً كبيراً ينمو داخل صدره، ضغطاً عظيماً: فرحاً، جوعاً، وصيحةً متأهبة، صرخة بلا كلمات على وشك الانفجار من داخله لتتردد أصداؤها في كل مكان.

لم يرد سوى أن يهبط في الكهف عند المدخل، يلقي تحية سريعة على أولئك الذين ينتظرونهم، يرمي أمتعته على الأرض المغطاة بطبقة رقيقة من الجليد ويتركها هناك. يمسك بيد كارو، ويسحبها معه، يركض، إلى الداخل، ثم أعمق فأعمق، ليأخذها، ليضمها إليه، ليضحك بخفة قرب رقبتها، غير مصدق أنها أخيراً أصبحت له، وأن العالم أخيراً أصبح ملكهما، وهذا كل ما أراده. أو بالأحرى، هذا كل ما أراد أن يريده.

ولكن... كان هناك ما يقتحم أفكاره. شيء رافقه منذ وقت. مؤخراً: عندما استمع إلى روايات النصر في أديلفاس، ورأى الحيرة الغامضة في وجوه من يروونها. تلك المنطقية الغريبة التي يتقبلها الجميع فقط لأنها حدثت. بنفس الطريقة التي قبلوا بها ما حدث في الكهوف عندما واجهوا بعضهم لأول مرة، غارقين بالدماء، مستعدين للقتل والموت – ولم يفعلوا.

لكن ذلك الاقتحام كان قد حدث بالفعل. عندما حاول استحضار الـ"سيريثار" في معركة أديلفاس وحصل على الرعد بدلاً من ذلك. وقبل ذلك، عندما أحس بوجوده في الكهف معه، أو هكذا ظن. وحتى قبل ذلك، منذ لحظة أول وصول له إلى حالة الـ"سيريثار" الحقيقية، حالة من القوة عجز عقله عن فهمها، وجعلته يشعر بعدها وكأنه مجرد كائن ضئيل، يجره تيار كارثي. فيضان، أو إعصار. لم يستطع التحكم بها، لكنه بشكل ما استطاع استحضارها، لكن ذلك ليس ما أراده.

لقد تحدث مع كارو عن"شبكة الطاقات"، وبأن ذلك حقيقي – مكان راح يتنقل فيه، كالأعمى، منذ محاولاته الأولى مع السحر. كان يشعر بالاتساع الهائل اللامتناهي الذي بداخله، وقد شعر بالتواضع أمامه.

لكن... هذا لم يكن هو.

ما أقلقه أكثر من أي شيء آخر هو شكه بأن ما كان يبلغه عندما يصل إلى الـ"سيريثار" – أو بالأحرى، ما قرر أن يسميه الـ"سيريثار"، لأنه الكلمة الوحيدة التي يعرفها لوصف حالة من الوضوح الاستثنائي – لم يكن شيئاً ينبع من داخله، بل من خارج نفسه.

وأياً كانت هذه الاستجابة– مصدر القوة هذه – لم تكن منه، ولم تكن ملكه.

إذاً... ما هي؟

76

في انتظار السحر

هناك من يقوم بالمراقبة.

أولئك الذين بقوا في الكهوف لا بد أنهم أبقوا حارساً دائماً عند المدخل، يترقب عودتهم. فعندما اقتربوا – بحذر، خشية أن يكون شيء ما قد حدث أثناء غيابهم – كانوا جميعاً قد تجمعوا في الكهف عند المدخل لاستقبالهم، وكان الشعور رائعاً. شعور أشبه بالعودة إلى المنزل.

طارت كارو مباشرة إلى حضن إيسّا، وغمرتها طويلاً بما يكفي ليزحف سرب من الأفاعي – تلك التي نادتها أفعى الناجا لتؤنس وحدتها، أفاعٍ عمياء تسكن الممرات الرطبة أسفل الكهف – لتلتف حولها شاحبة ومتألقة لتوحّد ما بينهما.

همست إيسّا برقة:"يا حلوتي، هل كل شيء على ما يرام؟".

أجابت كارو، وقد غمرتها المشاعر حتى احمر وجهها:"على ما يرام وأكثر".

كانت تعلم في أعماقها أن هذه هي أقرب لحظة ستصل فيها إلى إخبار بِريمستون بأن الحلم قد بدأ: الحلم الأكثر استحالة، والأشد حلاوة.

بعد الترحيب الحار، بدأوا في تبادل الأخبار، وكانت كثيرة، لكنهم حاولوا إبقاءها مختصرة قدر الإمكان. ومع ذلك، لم يكن هناك نهاية طبيعية للتكهنات التي تلت ذلك، لولا أن إيسّا التقطت نظرات خاطفة بين كارو وأكيفا.

كانت تلك النظرات أشبه بفتيل مشتعل، المسافة بينهما تكاد تتوهج بحرارة خفية. رسمت إيسّا ابتسامة صغيرة على شفتيها، لم يلحظها أحد – بل لم يلحظا شيئاً سوى بعضهما البعض – وعندما قالت:"أعتقد أن مسافرينا منهكون"، وبدأت في تفريق الجمع بلطف، لم يخطر ببال أحد أنها فعلت ذلك من أجلهما..

كان الجميع يشعرون بنفس إحساس العودة إلى الوطن، حتى غير الشرعيين، وانطلقت المجموعة كلها معاً، يرافقهم أولئك الذين خرجوا لاستقبالهم. وعندما وصلوا إلى الكهف الكبير، حيث كان من الممكن أن تتجه الكاميرا إلى الأسفل نحو القرية التي كانوا يقطنونها سابقاً، لم يفعلوا ذلك. بل بقوا مع الملائكة ليعدوا وجبة مشتركة تحت سقف الكهف المرصع بالنوازل المتدلية.

لم تكن كارو جائعة. على الأقل ليس جوعاً من شأنه أن يدفعها لتناول حصص الغذاء المسروقة من دومينيون. لقد اجتاحها شعور أشبه بصباح عيد الميلاد. حسناً، لم تعرف الكثير من أعياد الميلاد في حياتها. العيد الذي أمضته مع إستر بدا أشبه بمسرحية – لامعاً ومميزاً، لكنه شعور أقرب إلى المشاهدة منه إلى المشاركة. أما العيدان اللذان قضتهما مع عائلة زوزانا، فقد كانا أفضل بكثير. لم يكونوا أطفالاً حينذاك، ولكنهم تصرفوا كالأطفال قدر الإمكان. طقوس العيد في منزل نوفاك هي نفسها ثابتة لا تتغير، حتى شقيق زوزانا الأكبر – الذي كان يحاول جاهداً أن يبهر كارو برجولته المزعومة – كان يهرع إلى الدرج فجر عيد الميلاد، متلهفاً لمعرفة ما إذا كانت ليلة العيد قد حملت معها سحراً جديداً.

الشعور الذي يسيطر عليها الآن هو شعور انتظارٍ يوشك على الانتهاء. ليس انتظاراً يملؤه الخوف، بل ذلك النوع المبهج من الترقب: انتظار السحر. والسحر الذي كانت كارو تنتظره الآن – تنتظره وتلمسه في ذات الوقت – بدا وكأنه يبادلها الشعور، كسطح مرآة تنتظر اللحظة التي تلتقي فيها أطراف أصابعك مع انعكاسها على الزجاج. لكنه كان سحراً من النوع الذي لا يخص سوى البالغين.

لم تستطع أن تتوقف عن النظر إلى أكيفا. وفي كل مرة تفعل ذلك، كانت تجد نظرته في انتظارها، أو سرعان ما تدور عيناه لتلتقي بعينيها. كل نظرة بينهما كانت حية، نابضة بالحياة ومشبعة بالعاطفة. كان هناك ضحك في انحناءة شفتيه، ضحك أصبح ممكناً أخيراً، بعد أن وصل انتظارهم الطويل إلى نهايته. لقد أصبحت هذه الحالة الطفولية بينهما مضحكة، فقط لأن النهاية كانت وشيكة، وكل ما هو"ليس هما" بدا وكأنه عقبة. الآن أصبح هذا الانتظار لعبة، مزاحاً بينهما، سباقاً لمعرفة من يمكنه الصمود لدقيقة أخرى، ورقصاً غير معلن. جسداهما – وسط جمعٍ من الناس – يتحركان كأنهما خاضعان لنفس الجاذبية المغناطيسية، بغض النظر عمّن يقف بينهما.

شعرت كارو وكأن جلدها قد استيقظ من سباته. لم تكن تدرك أنه كان خامداً، لكن منذ تلك القبلة في السماء – تحديداً منذ أن لامست شفتا أكيفا النقطة أسفل أذنها – بدا وكأن مفتاحاً قد أُدير بداخلها.

تيارات صغيرة، متناهية الدقة من الكهرباء، كانت تسري في جسدها، ترفع القشعريرة على بشرتها، وتجلب ارتعاشات ووَهَجاً من الدفء. لم تستطع أن تُهدّئ يديها. كانت تعرف هذه المشاعر جيداً من أيام دراستها: الدوبامين، النورإبينفرين. تذكرت قراءةً عن عالم وصف هذه المواد الكيميائية بأنها"كوكتيل نشوة الحب"، وكيف لم تتوقف هي وزوزانا عن الضحك وقتها. حسناً، الآن هي غارقة تماماً في هذا الكوكتيل. وجنتاها مشتعلتان، يداها ترتجفان، ومعدتها تمتلئ بفوضى من الفراشات.

فراشات صدرها الرقيقة، قلبها الذي يرقص بصخب على خشبة المسرح، وأنفاسها القصيرة المتلاحقة. حاولت أن تأخذ نفساً عميقاً لتهدأ، لكن كل نفس كان أشبه بعوّامة تقاوم الغرق في لجّة فرط التنفس، لكنه شعور جيد – بالرغم من أن الوصف يبدو سخيفاً. لكنه كان يجسد طيفاً كاملاً من المشاعر: من نغمات الفرح المفعمة بالخفة، إلى اللحن العميق والثقيل للمتعة المرتقبة، بطيئة وحلوة كشراب العسل.

كل هذا يعني شيئاً واحداً: كارو كانت تشتعل.

التقت عيناها بعيني أكيفا مجدداً. شرارة، ثم وميض. ضوء وحرارة يسابقان الانصهار. لا مزيد من الضحك الآن. رأت يديه المتشنجتين على جانبيه، تبحثان بلا جدوى عن السكون. جمعهما على شكل قبضتين، ثم أرخاهما، لكنهما لن تهدآ حتى يُسمح لهما بلمسها. جسده كله كان مشدوداً. وكذلك كان جسدها. كلاهما كان أشبه بوتر كمان مشدود، ينتظر اللحظة التي يطلق فيها لحنه.

سؤال ارتسم في عينيه، في انحناءة رأسه، في وقفته. كل كيانه شكّل سؤالاً واحداً. وكان الجواب سهلاً للغاية. أومأت كارو برأسها، وكأن المفتاح الغامض في داخلها يملك إعدادات متقدمة، لأنها أدارته فوراً. شعرت وكأن جلدها يغني تقريباً.

أخيراً. أخيراً.

استدارت لتنسل عبر الممر المؤدي إلى الحمامات – الحمامات؟ من أين جاءتها هذه الفكرة؟ احمرت وجنتاها بحرارة. فكرة رائعة جداً، بلا شك. لكنها حين استدارت، وقع بصرها على ليراز.

حيث كانت تقف بعيداً، طويلة ومستقيمة كالعادة، دائماً مستقيمة أكثر من اللازم، وكأن شخصاً ما – ربما إيلّاي نفسها – قد ربطت خيطاً بقمة جمجمتها ولم تسمح لها بالاسترخاء. هناك ظهرت صلابتها المعتادة والنظرة المليئة بالترقب المؤلم على وجهها. عندها، ارتجف المفتاح

المكتشف حديثاً داخل كارو، وكأن تيار الطاقة قد انقطع فجأة. اختفت كل التيارات الكهربائية، عادت حرارة جلدها إلى طبيعتها، وخمد"كوكتيل نشوة الحب" في داخلها. لا مزيد من الارتعاشات، وعادت نفسها إلى الهبوط داخلها كمرساة تغوص في البحر.

"يا إلهي، ما الذي يحدث معي؟" رمشت بعينيها، مبهوتة. روح زيري معلقة عند خصرها، وكانت على وشك أن...؟

هزت رأسها بعنف، بسرعة، لتستعيد السيطرة على نفسها. عبر الكهف، عقد أكيڤا حاجبيه، مشوشاً. ألقت عليه نظرة عاجزة، ولمست القارورة عند خصرها. فهم على الفور. تحركت نظرته نحو ليراز، التي كانت تتابع كل شيء بينهما، وكان يبدو على وجهها الانزعاج.

اجتمعوا عند الباب نفسه الذي كانت كارو متجهة إليه، ولكن لغرض مختلف الآن، ووجهة أخرى.

قالت كارو:"لن يستغرق الأمر وقتاً طويلاً."

فأجاب أكيڤا:"سأساعدك". أومأت برأسها، ممتنة.

كانت مستعدة لهذا منذ وقت طويل، قبل أن يقطع زيري عنقه ليصبح الذئب. عندما اختفى، وحين عادت جميع الدوريات ما عدا دوريته، جمعت كل ما ستحتاجه لتحضير جسد كيرين يكون قوياً وصادقاً قدر المستطاع.

أسنان بشرية وأخرى غزلانية، أنابيب من عظام الخفافيش، الحديد واليشم. حتى الألماس، الذي حفظته بعناية خصيصاً له. كل هذه المكونات كانت مخبأة معاً في كيس صغير من المخمل، مع أدواتها الخاصة بالبعث، محفوظة في أعماق الكهف مع مباخر الأرواح والبخور.

مكونات لأجل زيري.

حسناً، العنصر الأساسي لإعادة زيري كان في المطرة. لكنها أرادت أن تجعل الجسد الجديد قريباً قدر الإمكان من جسده الحقيقي كـِكِيرين. فجأة، ارتفع رأسها بسرعة مع فكرة خاطفة.

"انتظري لحظة"، قالت، وعبرت الكهف متجهة إلى حيث تقف ليراز وحيدة.

بدأت ليراز بالقول:"لا حاجة لأن تفعلي ذلك الآن".

لكن كارو لوّحت بيدها لتسكتها."هل ما زالت لديك قطعة القرن التي أعطيتك إياها؟". ترددت ليراز للحظة، كما لو أنها تأسف لتفريطها فيها، لكنها سلمتها إياها في النهاية. وبينما أخذت كارو قطعة القرن، وجدت نفسها تأمل، بصمت وعمق، أن تكون مشاعر هذه الملاك متبادلة. ليس فقط من أجلها، بل من أجل زيري أيضاً، الذي كان شعور الوحدة لديه أعمق حتى من ذلك الذي عانته كارو ذات يوم. هي، على الأقل، كان لديها بريمشتون، وذكريات والديها وقبيلتها. أما زيري... فمن كان لديه على الإطلاق؟

ليكن ما نقوم به بداية أخرى غير متوقعة ومجيدة. فكرت.

سألت كارو، وهي تنظر إلى ليراز:"هل ترغبين في الانضمام؟". لكن ليراز هزت رأسها نفياً، وهكذا تركتها هناك، واقفة خارج دائرة الجنود، وذهبت لتنجز هذا العمل الأخير.

77

لم نتعارف بعد

لم تستطع ليراز البقاء في الكهف الكبير.

شعرت بأنها شفافة للغاية، فأخذت تتجول بلا هدف، حتى وجدت نفسها في النهاية تعود إلى الكهف عند المدخل. كان أحد الكيميرا الذين لا يستطيعون الطيران يقف للحراسة، فتقدمت لتأخذ مكانه، وجلست على حافة صخرية.

غابت الشمس في وقتها المعتاد، وفتحة الهلال في سقف الكهف كانت في التوقيت المثالي لالتقاط كل شعاع من غروبها. راحت ليراز تراقب المشهد، ورأت الشمس وكأنها تذوب عند ملامستها للقمم البعيدة، منتشرة كالذهب المصهور على امتداد الأفق. انعكس الضوء البرتقالي على كل شيء أمامها، من هناك إلى حيث تجلس، ووصل إلى أعماق الكهف خلفها، حيث أضاء أطراف طبقات الجليد بانعكاسات باهرة.

ثم بدأ اللون الذهبي يبهت، ويبرد تدريجياً، ليتحول إلى رمادي. وفي اللحظة التي بلغ فيها لون السماء أعمق درجات الأزرق، تلك الثواني الأخيرة

قبل أن يغرق الأفق في سواد الليل وتبدأ النجوم بالظهور، سمعت صوت خطوات خلفها. ترددت في الالتفات، وخافت أن تنظر.

كانت الخطوات بطيئة، واضحة. "طقطق. طقطق". رنين حوافر. كان هذا أول ما أدركته: الحوافر. ولم تستطع منع نفسها. كان ذلك شعوراً مغروساً فيها، متأصلاً منذ زمن طويل، إحساساً عميقاً من الشك، وربما النفور. إنه كيميرا. ما الذي أصابها؟ فقط لأن أحدهم أنقذ حياتها، لا يعني أنها يجب أن تقع في حبه.

حب؟ يا نجوم السماء. كانت هذه أول مرة تجرؤ فيها الكلمة على التشكل في عقلها، لكنها جاءت على هيئة نفي، نافيةً الفكرة. ومع ذلك، أصابتها في أعماقها: خوف وإنكار ورغبة في الهروب.

كان البقاء في مكانها صراعاً بحد ذاته. ذكّرت نفسها بأنها لم تفعل شيئاً. لم تقل شيئاً، ولم تشجع شيئاً. لا قبل أن يموت زيري في جسد الذئب، ولا في أي وقت آخر. لم يكن هناك شيء بينهما لتندم عليه أو تهرب منه، ولا سبب يدعوها للفرار. هو مجرد رفيق سلاح. مجرد... لم نتعارف بعد.

توقف قلب ليراز للحظة. وهي التي قد اعتادت على صوت الذئب، لكن ذلك لم يكن يعني أنها أحبته أبداً. حتى عندما تحدث زيري إليها بنفسه – مرة واحدة فقط، عندما كانا في الحمامات، كلاهما مغمور في الماء الغريب والناعم حتى الصدر – كان في صوته خشونة، وكأن أنفاسه تحمل همهمة كامنة، يمكن أن تتحول إلى زئير في أي لحظة. كان صوته متطابقاً مع يديه ذات المخالب، وفمه ذي الأنياب. وحشية كامنة.

لكن هذا الصوت... كان عميقاً كأنغام مزامير الريح الكيرينية، ثرياً وسلساً بلا مجهود.

لطالما عرفت دورها في هذا الحوار. استجمعت صوتها، رغم أنها شعرت به يرتجف، وقالت: "أنت تعرف من أنا، وأنا أعرف من أنت، و.. هذا لا يكفي."

امتزج صوته بصوتها، مغيراً النص. وفي الصمت الذي تلا ذلك، شعرت

به ينتظر. كيف يمكن للمرء أن يسمع الانتظار؟ لم تكن تعرف، لكنها فعلت. كان ينتظر أن تستدير. ولم يعد بإمكانها تأجيل ذلك أكثر.

استدارت، وكان زيري الكيريني أمامها.

بالكاد استطاعت ليراز أن تتنفس. بدا طويلاً. لقد عرفت ذلك مسبقاً، كانت قد رأته يقاتل وسط مجموعة من جنود دومينيون الذين بدوا قصار القامة بجانبه. لكن رؤية طوله من بعيد شيء، ومواجهته أمامك، حيث عليك أن ترفع رأسك لتراه، شيء آخر تماماً. رفعت ليراز رأسها، متتبعة طول قرنيه اللذين أضافا المزيد إلى ارتفاعه المهيب. قرنان طويلان ومستقيمان، أسودان لامعان. سليمين، لاحظت بسرعة – أنه لا يوجد أي كسر فيهما – وتساءلت عما حلّ بذلك الجزء الذي كان يناسب راحة يدها تماماً.

جسده نحيف، مشدود العضلات، أقل عرضاً من أكيفا أو معظم غير الشرعيين، لكن هذا جعله يبدو أكثر طولاً. ومع ذلك، لم تكن كتفاه ضيقتين أبداً. خلفهما جناحاه المطويان الداكنان. استنتجت ليراز من طوله مدى امتداد جناحيه. يرتدي الأبيض، وهذا بدا غريباً، ولا بد أنه لاحظ العبوس العابر على جبينها، لأنه التقط طرف قميصه وقال:"إنها أشياء الذئب. لم يكن لديّ شيء... خاص بي، عدا" —ابتسم مشيراً إلى نفسه بكلتا يديه—"كل الباقي على ما أعتقد".

كانت تلك الابتسامة. ابتسم زيري، ورأت ليراز إنه هو.

لم تعد تراه كحوافر أو قرون، التي كانت تلاحظها قطعة قطعة. بل رأت كيانه. كان كما ينبغي أن يكون تماماً، وفي كل جانب فيه آسر ومبهر. جماله الكيريني كان من النوع الوحشي، المليء بالزوايا الحادة والجوانب البرية. قرون حادة، حوافر حادة، وحتى حواف جناحيه كانت حادة. إنه تجسيد للظلال والظلمة، على عكسها تماماً – كائن قمر يقابل كائنة شمس. ظلال تقطع وهجها.

لكن كل هذا كان مجرد صورة خارجية.

في ابتسامته، في عينيه، وفي انتظاره – ما زال ينتظر – رأت جوهره. رأت القوة، والنعمة، والوحدة، والشوق، والأمل. ورأت التردد.

كان يقف في مكانه، يسمح لنفسه أن يُحكم عليه. وشعرت بالخجل. رأت ذلك في سكونه. كان خائفاً من أن تراه وحشاً، وكيف يمكنها أن تطمئنه على شيء هي كانت قبل ثوانٍ غير واثقة منه؟ كيف يمكنها أن تخبره بأنه مهيب، وأنها تشعر بالصغر أمامه – عاجزة عن الكلام ليس من النفور، بل من الانبهار؟

حاولت. "أنا... أنت... هذا... إنه..."

لم تقل المزيد. لا كلمات. كانت تفشل في هذا، فذلك خارج حدود مهارتها. ماذا تعتقد؟ أنها ستكون قادرة على استحضار دفء من داخلها، بينما قضت حياتها كلها تكبحه؟

هل سيعتقد أنها تشعر بالاشمئزاز منه، بسبب الطريقة التي تتصرف بها – متصلبة كلوح خشبي، وصامتة كالصواعد التي تحيط بها.

عليها أن تحاول أكثر.

...أومأت برأسها.

رائع. على الأقل هذا أفضل قليلاً من صمت الصواعد. وضعت ذراعاً واحدة عبر صدرها، تشدها بقوة، وباليد الأخرى رفعتها كما لو أنها تريد منع نفسها من الإيماء مرة أخرى، لكنها انتهت بوضع يدها على فمها، وكأنها تمنع نفسها حتى من الكلام.

حقاً؟ هل هذا أفضل ما عندك؟

نظر زيري إليها وهي مربوطة كعقدة، يدها على فمها في إيماءة يمكن تفسيرها بسهولة بشكل خاطئ، وظهر في عينيه البنيتين – اللطيفتين والساحرتين – بريق من عدم اليقين.

هذا البريق دفعها لمحاولة أخيرة، ضخمة.

همست له: "أعجبني هذا". لم تكن بيدها القدرة على منع رأسها

من الإيماء كالحمقاء، لكنها خففت كلماتها إلى درجة أن زيري لم يفهم أمال رأسه مستفسراً:"ماذا؟".

أبعدت يدها وقالت، بأوضح صوت تمكنت من جمعه – لكنه ليس واضحاً:"أعجبني هذا. أقصد أنت". ثم أعادت يدها نحو فمها فوراً، واحمرت خجلاً. كانت مستعدة لأن تطلب من تلك الإلهة الكيميرا القاتلة أن تأتي لتنهي عذابها، عندما اختفى بريق عدم اليقين من عيني زيري.

الطريقة التي ابتسم فيها في تلك اللحظة كان يجب أن تثير انزعاجها، فقد بدت أنها تميل إلى السخرية، وكأنه يتهكم منها ومن ارتباكها الشديد. وليراز لم تكن الشخص الذي يتحمل الاستهتار به. لكن الابتسامة لم تتوقف هناك. بل تحولت من مسلية إلى سعيدة تماماً ثم إلى مطمئنة بعمق. كانت جميلة جداً إلى درجة أنها شعرت بها في قلبها.

قال:"جيّد. وأنا أيضاً أستلطفكِ".

زاد احمرار خديها، لكنه الآن يحمر خجلاً أيضاً، لذلك لم يبدُ الوضع سيئاً جداً.

لا، ما زال سيئاً.

وماذا بعد الآن؟ هل من المفترض أن تواصل حياكة جمل غير مترابطة؟ ربما كان عليها أن تبدأ بتعداد أشياء أخرى تعجبها، كما قد يفعل طفل، باستثناء أنها – أوه، حسناً، لا تحب الكثير من الأشياء، لذا ستكون القائمة قصيرة ولن تشغله سوى لحظة. لكنها لم تكن تريد قتل لحظة. بل أرادت أن تعيشها. تعيش لحظات كثيرة.

إذاً، كيف بحق النجوم يمكن فعل ذلك؟ هل فات الأوان لتتعلم؟

"آه" قال زيري، محركاً كتفيه ومرخياً جناحيه اللذين فتحا فجأة وظهرا في هذا الفضاء الضيق مهيبين كعاصفة.

تنحنح قائلاً وهو يحرك يديه مشيراً إلى الفتحة الهلالية في السقف حيث تحولت السماء إلى سواد والنجوم انتشرت بكثافة كالسكّر: أحد أسوأ الأشياء

حين كنت الذئب، هو عدم قدرتي على الطيران. أما الآن فأنا قادر على ذلك.

بدا مترددًا، وصوته متقطع، وهو يشير إلى الخارج.

أوه. حسنًا.

شعرت ليراز تقريبًا – تقريبًا – بالراحة لانتهاء هذا الموقف، حتى تتمكن من الاختفاء والذوبان. وأن تلعن نفسها. وأن تموت قليلًا.

لكن زيري تنحنح ونظر إليها. كان صادقًا للغاية. مليئًا بالأمل."هل... تريدين المجيء؟".

الطيران؟ ذلك شيء تجيد فعله. لم تكن مضطرة حتى إلى المخاطرة بالكلام وقول"نعم". فقط احتاجت إلى هزة رأس.

78

تنفس

مشطت كارو شعرها بهدوء، وكأنها تتمرن على التنفس. ثم وضعت المشط جانباً. ذلك المشط الذي وجدته سابقاً وقررت الاحتفاظ به. كان قطعة أثرية كيرينية مصنوعة من عظم محفور، مع صورة بدائية لصياد العواصف محفورة على مقبضه.

تنفسي.

تحت ضوء شعلة سكوهل المتراقصة، نظرت إلى نفسها، وهي لا تزال مرتدية الملابس التي أخذتها من إستر، والتي ما زالت بحالة جيدة، رغم أنها لم تحب فكرة أن هناك لعاب رازغوت ما زال على كمها. لقد تركت بعض حاجياتها هنا في الكهوف عندما غادرت، لكنها كانت أكثر اتساخاً من ملابسها الحالية. تساءلت إن كانت ستعيش بساطة الأيام الماضية وتكون لديها خزانة مليئة بالملابس، ومتعة اختيار زي نظيف ترتديه للقاء... من؟ ماذا يمكنها أن تسمي أكيفا؟

"صاحب؟" بدا وكأنه مصطلح من الأرض، لا يليق بما بينهما.

"عاشق؟" شعرت بأنه مصطلح متكلف وصادم.

"هل قابلت عاشقي؟ أليس رائعاً؟". "لا.. أقصد نعم، هو رائع بالفعل. لكنها بالتأكيد لن تناديه بذلك، حتى لو كانت تشعر بدوار من شدة رغبتها في ذلك.

"شريك؟" هذا جاف جداً."توأم الروح؟" وها قد اجتاح الدفء قلبها. متى بدت هذه الكلمة أصدق مما هي عليه الآن بالنسبة إليها وإلى أكيفا؟ ومع ذلك، كلمة، بدت لها مشبعة بدلالات باهتة. "أتحب فرقة بيكسيز؟ أقسم، وكأننا توأم روح!".

حسناً، ليس عليها أن تسميه بأي شيء الآن. كل ما عليها فعله هو الذهاب إليه، وهي متأكدة تماماً أنه لن يهتم بما كانت ترتديه.

أخذت نفساً أخيراً. نبضات قلبها تسارعت درجة، وكأنها أدركت أن الوقت قد حان – الوقت الحقيقي، الفعلي، أخيراً.

أصر أكيفا على مساعدتها في إحياء جسد زيري، ومن الجيد أنه لم يحتج إلى أدوات لتثبيته، في الوقت الذي لم تكن تظن أنها قادرة على ملامسة بشرة أكيفا العارية وهما يثبتانه، دون أن تنهار مرة أخرى في حالة الشغف الشديد الذي تملكها في الكهف الكبير.

غرقت في حالتها التأملية وهي تعرف أنه كان هناك. ثم، عندما انتهى الأمر – عندما اكتمل الجسد الجديد وتمدد على الأرض، لا يزال بلا حياة – عادت من حالتها تلك لتجده يراقبها. كأنه مصدوم بالسعادة، وبمجرد أن رأت ذلك الشعور في عينيه، تفتح نفس الشعور داخلها.

قال أكيفا:"هذه أطول مرة استطعت أن أنظر فيها إليكِ".

"ظننت أنكَ ستراقب عملية البعث"، أشارت كارو إلى الجسد الجديد، مستمتعة برؤيته بكل فخر. كان يبدو شبه مطابق لجسد زيري الحقيقي وبشرته، واعتقدت أنه سيتقبله بسهولة كشكله الطبيعي. حتى إنها لم تضف إليه علامات الهامسا، لأن زيري الحقيقي لم يكن لديه أي منها، وأيضاً لأنها أرادت أن تصبح تلك العلامات بلا جدوى يوماً ما.

"كنت أنوي المشاهدة"، قال أكيڤا، محرجاً، وهو يمرر أصابعه في شعره القصير الكثيف بتلك الطريقة التي كان يفعلها دائماً، "لكنني تشتتت."

"هذا ليس عدلاً. لم أحظَ بفرصة النظر إليك في المقابل".

"أعدكِ بأن أبقى ثابتاً لتفعلي ذلك لاحقاً." لاحقاً؟ كان يقصد بعد أن يشبعا رغبة البقاء في حالة الهيام.

تنفسي.

"أقبل."

ثم، وأخيراً، يا إلهي، حدث الأمر: الابتسامة.

الابتسامة التي لم ترها كارو بعينيها هاتين من قبل، بل كانت تتذكرها فقط من خلال عيني ماضٍ بعيد – من خلال مادريغال. ابتسامة دافئة مدهشة، ابتسامة جميلة إلى درجة مؤلمة. جعلت عينيه تتجعدان عند الزوايا، وشكّلت جماله إلى نوع آخر من الروعة، نوع بروعة السعادة، والسعادة تعيد تشكيل كل شيء. إنها تجعل القلوب كاملة، والحياة تستحق أن تُعاش. شعرت كارو بتلك السعادة تملؤها، تشعرها بالدوار والانبهار، وسقطت أكثر عمقاً في حبها له.

عرض عليها أكيڤا أن يتركها لتنهي عملية الإحياء وحدها، وقبلت، لأنها أرادت أن تحظى بلحظة مع زيري، كما خمّن أنه يجب عليها ذلك. وعندما رأت عيني زيري الجديدتين تفتحان – بنيتين، وليستا زرقاوين كالجليد، وبدون أي من غرور ثياغو الذي كان عليه أن يتجاوزه لئظهر شخصيته الحقيقية – كانت تلك اللحظة أحلى لحظة مرت بها في مسيرتها كمجسدة للأرواح. عانقته، واحتضنته، وأخبرته أن كل شيء قد انتهى، لم يعد عليه أن يختبئ بعد الآن. وكان ارتياحه عميقاً جداً إلى درجة أنه زاد من تقديرها، الذي كان بالفعل عميقاً للغاية، لكل ما تحمله من أجلهم جميعاً.

معاً، توصلا إلى تفسير بسيط قدر الإمكان لغيابه وعودته. ثم رحيله. اعتقدت كارو أنه كان سعيداً جداً بكونه في هيئة الكيرين مجدداً إلى درجة

أنه أراد فقط أن يطير، إلا أنه ربما شعر بتشتيتها. أو ربما كان بسبب معرفته بمن كان يحمل روحه في قِربة طوال ذلك الوقت، وهي الآن تنتظره هناك في الكهوف.

لسبب ما، غادر زيري على وجه السرعة، وها هي الآن بعد أن أتمّت واجبها الأخير، أصبحت حرّة. توقفت، وأخذت نفساً عميقاً. ومن جيب حقيبتها أخرجت بلهفة شيئاً صغيراً كانت تحمله منذ نزهة السلطان على أرضية الفندق الصحراوي في المغرب قبل أيام قليلة.

عظمة أمنيات. ابتسمت ثم أطبقت يدها. منذ الليلة الأولى، كان هذا طقسهما الوداعي في معبد إيلّاي: أن يتمنيا أمنية. وهي الآن مستعدة للطقوس من جديد، لكن ليس طقوس الوداع، فقد ودعت ما يكفيهما لعمر بأكمله.

ثم غادرت، وأخذت تسير ممسكة بعظمة الأمنيات قرب قلبها. أو هكذا بدأت، لكن سرعان ما كانت تنساب، تحلق بخفة من دون أن تلمس الأرض. فكرت: قد يصبح المرء متكاسلاً. لكنها لم تكن قلقة حيال ذلك كثيراً. عبرت الممرات الملتوية. الشعلة في يدها تومض بلون أخضر، تتمايل ألسنتها وكأنها ستنطفئ إذا زادت من سرعتها. لقد شارفت الشعلة على الانطفاء لكنها لم تكن بحاجة إليها بمجرد أن تكون مع أكيفا.

وها قد وصلت إلى مدخل كهف الشلال.

كانت هناك ضحكة مكتومة في حلقها بينما كانت تستدير عند الزاوية، مستعدة أن تهمس، وهي تضحك:"أخيراً، أخيراً، كدت أموت من الانتظار"، وهي تضغط شفتيها على شفتيه، على عنقه، جائعة، ضاحكة، متلهفة، و... توقفت فجأة. أكيفا لم يكن هنا. بالطبع، همس صوت صغير وبارد في قلبها. قمعت ذلك الصوت. اهدئي. أكيفا لم يصل بعد.

لكن هذا كان غريباً، لأنه قال إنه سيأتي مباشرة. حسناً، لا داعي للقلق. ربما ضلّ الطريق؟ لا.. إن كارو تحترم قدرات أكيفا أكثر من أن تصدق أنه

ضلّ. ربما ذهب ليقوم بشيء ما، معتقداً أنه يمكنه الوصل على الوقت. أو أنا قد وصلت بسرعة؛ زيري لم يتأخر.

كان لون الماء أخضر باهتاً، يتصاعد منه البخار، وتوهجت التكوينات البلورية من حوله، بينما كانت ستائر الطحلب الداكن تتمايل حيث غمرت أطرافها الأطول في التيار. فكرت كارو في أن تخلع ملابسها وتغمر نفسها في الماء، لكن ذلك لم يستغرق سوى لحظة، ولم يكن جاداً. كان شعور غامض بالتوجس يعقّد كتفيها كقبضة مشدودة.

إحساس بالتوجس أكثر بكثير مما كانت مستعدة له، وأدركت فجأة بعدما عصف بها هذا الشعور، أنها كانت تنتظر سقوط شيء آخر منذ اللحظة التي عادوا فيها عبر بوابة ڤيسكال.

أي شيء آخر؟.. لم تكن تعرف. ذلك الصوت الصغير البارد لم يكن يعرف أيضاً. لكنه فقط علم—هي فقط علمت، على مستوى ما—أن كل شيء سار بسلاسة.

أخذ ذلك الشعور يتسلل إلى عمودها الفقري، مثل الذي شعرت به قبل كمين الدومينيون مباشرة. هناك حلقة ما مفقودة. نعم. أكيڤا. هو المفقود من المفترض أن يكون هنا.

حاولت أن تكون عقلانية. رغم أنه لم يمر عليها سوى خمس ثوانٍ؛ سيظهر في أي لحظة. لكنه لم يفعل.

بالطبع، بالطبع. هل اعتقدتِ حقاً أنكِ ستنالين السعادة؟

تسارعت دقات قلب كارو وأصبحت أنفاسها خافتة. لكنها هذه المرة لم تكن رغبة مكبوتة، بل كان ذعراً بالكاد تمكنت من السيطرة عليه. أكيڤا لم يأتِ.

شعلتها لفظت أنفاسها وانطفأت. وهي لا تملك نار السيرافيم لتضيء طريقها. كان عليها أن تتحسس طريقها في الظلام، ممسكة بعظمة الأمنيات غير المكسورة، تضغطها بقوة إلى قلبها.

79

أسطورتان

"انظري."

رأى زيري صياد العواصف قبل أن تلمحه ليراز. لم يُشر إليه، بل اكتفى بتمتمة الكلمة، محاولاً ألا يُربكه أو يجعله يغير مساره. فتلك المخلوقات قادرة على التقاط أصغر الحركات من مسافات خيالية. وهذه أعجوبة أن تحلق على هذا القرب منهما.

ولكنها كانت تحلق باتجاههما.

نظرت ليراز، ووجد زيري نفسه مأخوذاً، ليس فقط بمنظر صياد العواصف الذي بدا وكأنه يتجه مباشرة نحوهما، بل بالانعكاسات المتلألئة للنجوم على ملامح وجه ليراز الرقيقة وانحناءاته الساحرة. بل أكثر من ذلك في الحقيقة، حيث راح يراقبها وهي تراقبه، مستمتعاً بالدهشة التي انعكست على ملامحها.

إلى أن قالت، وعيناها تضيقان:"هناك شيء غير طبيعي."

التفت زيري، ورأى أنه في اللحظة التي انشغل فيها بتأمل ليراز، انحرف صياد العواصف عن مساره ولم يتجه نحوهما. ورغم أنه لا يزال بعيداً، لم

يدرك على الفور ما الذي أقلق ليراز. ثم أخذ يحلق في الهواء منساباً مع تيار صاعد. بدا المشهد بديعاً.

ضيق زيري عينيه:"هل هو—؟".

"نعم". قالت ليراز بنبرة حادة، ولسبب وجيه. كان هذا المشهد أشبه بشيء لا يُصدّق... كأنه يشبه رؤية كيرين وأحد غير الشرعيين يطيران معاً في ضوء النجوم. شيء غريب، فكّر زيري، أن عليه التركيز أكثر في المرة القادمة. ومع ذلك، رأى الأمر مدهشاً.

ذلك البريق المميز كان لجناحي سيراف. أول ما خطر في ذهن زيري أن ملاكاً كان يطارد الصياد، بطريقة ما ويلاحقه. لكن لا شيء في طريقة طيرانه أظهر أي علامة على الاضطراب. كان فقط يطير، وهناك ملاك يطير بجواره.

سألها:"هل سمعتِ بشيء كهذا من قبل؟".

ضحكت ليراز بصمت، بالكاد كانت أنفاسها مسموعة."لا.. لكن أعلم أن جورام سيرغب بأحد منهم ليضعه في غرفة التذكارات الخاصة به. هذه هوايته منذ بعض الوقت. كل سيد أو سيدة متملقة في الإمبراطورية كانوا يأملون أن يحضروا له واحداً، لكن دون جدوى. وبعضهم ماتوا وهم يحاولون، وأخيراً اضطر إلى استدعاء صيادين محترفين. الأفضل بينهم. وتعرف كم عدد ما أمسكوه؟". كانت هذه أطول جملة تنطقها ليراز منذ أن وجدها زيري في مدخل الكهف، يوم بدت عاجزة عن التعبير. ومرة أخرى، وجد زيري نفسه مأخوذاً بالنظر إليها، حتى كاد أن ينسى أمر صياد العواصف وسر الملاك الذي يطير بجواره."كم عددهم؟" سألها.

"ولا واحد."

"أنا سعيد بذلك."

"وأنا كذلك."

مع شعور موجع بالحزن العميق، أدرك أنه على الرغم من أن ليراز تقف أمامه تماماً في اتجاه الريح، ورائحة التوابل المنبعثة منها كانت واضحة

لحواسه كما الألوان الزاهية، إلا أنه لم يعد قادراً على التقاط تلك الرائحة الأخرى—ذلك العطر السري، الهش، الذي كان مختبئاً فيه. الذي استنشقه حين حملها بين ذراعيه، لكن حواسه كبيرين لم تكن حادة مثلما كانت حواس الذئب، وقد ضاعت منه الآن. على كل، سيظل يتذكر دائماً أنها كانت هناك. على الأقل كونه كان ذئباً، هذا قد منحه ذكرى تلك الرائحة.

تسمرا في مكانيهما صامتين، يراقبان الصياد وهو يواصل طيرانه، متمايلاً ومنعطفاً، والملاك يحافظ على إيقاع طيرانه معه، أحياناً يتقدم، وأحياناً يتأخر.

"هيا بنا"، قالت ليراز عندما بدأ الصياد يبتعد عنهما متجهاً شمالاً. "لنلحق بهما."

قاما بذلك، وشاهدا كيف كان مسارهما متعرجاً، يقودهما قريباً من واجهات الجرف حيث الرياح تنطلق مندفعًة عبر الممرات الضيقة، ثم ترتفع بهما للتحليق حول قمة صغيرة، مخترقًة تضاريس السحب. وأخيراً، انعطفا وعادا نحو ليراز وزيري. شاهدا صياد العواصف يقترب، ولم يدرك زيري إلا عندما صار قريباً جداً أن الشيء الذي كان يطير بجانبه لم يكن وحده. بل هناك أشخاص آخرون يركبون فوق الصياد نفسه. لم يستطع ملاحظتهم من قبل، فهم على عكس السيرافيم، لا ينبعث منهم أي ضوء.

"هل هذا—؟" قال زيري، مصدوماً.

"أعتقد ذلك،" همست ليراز بدهشة.

إنه كذلك. وعندما لمحهم أولئك الأشخاص، أطلقوا صيحات حادة بلغتهم البشرية الغريبة. بالطبع، لم يتمكن زيري من فهم كلماتهم، لكن نبرة الانتصار بدت واضحة، وكذلك الفرح الخالص والهستيري.

ومن ذا الذي يلومهم على ذلك؟

لقد روّض ميك وزوزانا صياد عواصف.

وسيصبحان أسطورتين.

80

خَيار

لم يكن أكيڤا يعلم ما الذي يحدث له. ها هو في كهف الشلال، قلبه ينبض بعنف، منتظراً كارو. ثم فجأة، لم يعد هناك. وتعثر الزمن.

"هناك الماضي، وهناك المستقبل، والحاضر ليس سوى ثانية واحدة تفصل بينهما." هكذا قال لإخوته وأخواته قبل وقت.

لقد كان مخطئاً. لم يكن هناك سوى الحاضر، والحاضر لانهائي في حقيقته. الماضي والمستقبل ليسا سوى غشاوة نضعها على أعيننا كي لا تقودنا تلك اللانهائية إلى الجنون.

ما الذي يحدث له؟

فقد إدراكه لجسده. وعلق داخل ذلك العالم العقلي، الكون الخاص به، الكرة اللانهائية لذاته حيث اعتاد ممارسة السحر. لكنه لم يأتِ إلى هنا بإرادته، ولم يستطع إيجاد سبيل للخروج.

هل وُضع هنا قسراً؟

رغم إحساسه بالحاضر. إحساس بأن أصواتاً تمر على أطراف وعيه، لكنه لا يستطيع سماعها. إنما شعر بها فقط كموجات تتراقص على سطح إدراكه،

كأصابع تتلمس الحرير الناعم من الجانب الآخر. كانت الأصوات متنافرة. طاقات تتصارع. لكنها ليست طاقته.

طاقته متشابكة، متشنجة. هذا الشيء الوحيد الذي يعرفه: لم يكن حيث ينبغي أن يكون. ستأتي كارو ولن تجده. ربما حدث ذلك بالفعل. خرج الزمن عن مساره. هل مرت عشر دقائق؟ ساعات؟ ليس مهماً. عليه أن يركز. فليس هناك سوى الحاضر. عليك فقط أن تفتح عينيك في الاتجاه الصحيح لتكون حيث ترغب في أي وقت. لكن هناك عدداً لانهائياً من الاتجاهات ولا بوصلة لديه. ليس مهماً، لأن أكيڤا لم يستطع فتح عينيه. كان مدفوعاً إلى العمق، محاصراً. كل ذلك يُفرض عليه.

لم يكن حيث ينبغي أن يكون. ما زال مأخوذاً. العجز عن الفعل في لحظة كان أمله فيها ممتلئاً إلى حد أنه لا يستطيع احتواءه فحطمه. أن يتم سحقه الآن، وسلب إرادته، بينما كارو تنتظره، بينما وصل بعد كل شيء إلى لحظة قد تكون لهما فقط، كان أمراً لا يُحتمل. لذا لم يعد أكيڤا يحتمله. فدفع بكل قوته.

وفجأة، جاء الرعد. سلاح الرعد داخل رأسه. تراجع، لكنه لم يستسلم طويلاً. الرعد مجرد صوت لن يعيقه. وإذا كان كل هذا يعيقه، إذاً لا شيء يقيده. استجمع قوته في زئير صامت ودفع. انفجر داخله بلا رحمة. إنه جاهزٌ للانفجار، ومن دون متردد. واندفع من خلال ذلك الصمت، إلى ما وراءه، إلى صمت ما بعد العاصفة، وأطياف ما بعد الصدمة العنيفة، و... ذاته. شعر بنفسه. بثناياه الضاغطة على الصخر وهو مستلق على الأرض في سكون بين أصوات وهواء متوتر بسبب تنافرهما.

"الاتجاه خطأ." "كان صوت امرأة لا يعرفها، لكنه صوت ذو مخارج أنعم من السيرافيمية التي يعرفها، وإن لم تكن غريبة تماماً.

"أضعنا وقتاً كافياً هنا"، قالت بنبرة أكثر حدة وأكثر شباباً. ونضجاً أيضاً."هل كان يجب أن أتركه يحضر لقاؤها؟ هل تعتقدين أن تركه يلتقي

بها سيجعله أكثر استعداداً للرحيل بعدها؟".

"لقاؤها؟ إنه في حالة عشق، يا سكاراب. عليك أن تتركيه يختار."

"لا يوجد خيار."

"هناك خيار. أنتِ من يصنعه."

"بتركه يعيش؟ أظن أنكِ يجب أن تكوني ممتنة لذلك."

"أنا ممتنة". قالتها مع تنهيدة. "لكن يجب أن يكون قراره، ألا تفهمين ذلك؟ وإلا سيظل دائماً عدوكِ."

"لا تغريني، أيتها العجوز. هل تعرفين ما الذي يمكنني فعله بعدو كهذا؟".

خيّم صمت جديد، لكنه كان مشبعاً بالصدمة. فهم أكيفا أنهما كانتا تتحدثان عنه، لكنه لم يفهم أكثر من ذلك. أي خيار؟ أي عدو؟ سكاراب، كما تسمى. كان هناك شيء ما... شيء ينبغي أن يتذكره.

عندما تكلمت الأخرى، ارتفع صوتها من صدمة عميقة: "هل تقصدين أن تصنعي منه وتراً لقيثارة؟ أهذا ما ستفعلينه بحفيدي".

حفيد!.. للحظة فقط، عندما سمع ذلك، قال أكيفا لنفسه: إذاً ليس أنا من يتحدثون عنه. إنه ليس حفيداً لأحد. فهو غير شرعي. وكان.. فقط إذا اضطررت إلى القول.

"كيف لك أن تضطري؟"، جاء هذا كردة فعل أقرب إلى صرخة. "إنه شيء مظلم بدأتِه يا سكاراب. عليكِ أن تنهيه. نحن لسنا كذلك. نحن لسنا محاربين".

"يجب أن نكون."

صدمات الدهشة.

"لقد كنا.." تابعت سكاراب مع نغمة عناد في صوتها، وإرادة الشباب تتصادم مع حكمة العمر. "وسنكون كذلك مرة أخرى."

ما الذي تقولينه؟ قالت جدته المدافعة عن أكيفا وهي مصدومة ومرتبكة. شعر أكيفا باضطرابها يتغلغل فيه، وفهمه. دخل إلى صميمه وأصبح جزءاً منه،

كما دفع هو يأسه يوماً إلى كل جندي في كهوف الكيرين. هذه المرأة دعته حفيداً. وكان هناك قطعة أخرى أساسية في هذا اللغز تدعى سكاراب. مع سلة الفاكهة التي أرسلها الستيليون بوقاحة رداً على إعلان الحرب من جورام، كان هناك مذكرة غير موقعة مختومة بشمع يحمل رسم خنفساء. الستيليون

فتح أكيڤا عينيه وهرع على الفور. كانوا في كهف يشبه كهوف الكيرين، وهم يبدون مثلهم وأصواتهم مألوفة أيضاً، وقد امتزجت بألحان الرياح. لم يكن بعيداً إذاً؟ وكارو ليست بعيدة. سيتمكن من العثور عليها وتصحيح الأمور.

وقفت المرأتان أمامه، وارتعشتا قليلاً عندما اندفع بحركة مفاجئة. وهذا يعني شيئاً ما؛ إذ لم تتراجعا خطوة إلى الوراء، بل لم تتحركا حتى. أما عينا سكاراب، فلم تتسعا من الدهشة فقط بل ركزتا عليه. عندها توقّف مجدداً، كأنه تجمد أثناء نهوضه وتجمد الزمن معه، حتى اجتاحه فجأة شعور حاد بالوعي، ذلك الإدراك العميق الذي اختبره من قبل، حين شعر بوجود خفي ما داخل الكهف. الآن، بدا وكأنه يرى بوضوح الكيان الذي يمثل حياته. وهشاشته.

حدقتا فيه. لم يكن قادراً على الحركة، والشيء الوحيد الذي أراد فعله حينئذ، هو أن يحدق فيهما في المقابل.

لم يرَ أكيڤا ستيلياً منذ أن كان في الخامسة من عمره. حين نظر نظرة أخيرة يائسة إلى والدته وهو يُسحب بعيداً عنها. الآن، هنا، أمامه، امرأتان. المرأة الأكبر سناً... وقد عجز أكيڤا عن تحديد شبهها بفيستيڤال، فوجه أمه كان قد تلاشى من ذاكرته، لكن النظر إلى هذه المرأة جعله يشعر وكأنه يتذكر وجهها.

سكاراب وصفتها بـ"العجوز"، لكنها لم تكن كذلك. لم تكن شابة أيضاً. حملت ملامحها بصمات الزمن: تجاعيد طفيفة حول عينيها، زوايا فمها محفورة بقسوة خفيفة. شعرها كان مضفوراً بإحكام كالتاج، وخيوط فضية مع

بارزة فيه كانت لامعة كأنها زينة متعمدة. في عينيها، بقايا ارتجافات من صدمة حديثة، وألم عميق، عميق جداً. ومن النظرة الأولى، شعر أكيڤا بانتماء إليها.

أما الأخرى... فشعرها الأسود حرّاً، متوحشاً. ارتدت ثوباً رمادياً كالعاصفة، طياته مائلة ومربوطة عند كتفها، تاركاً ذراعيها البنيتين مكشوفتين، مغطاتين بأساور ذهبية متقاربة من المعصم إلى الكتف. وجهها كان قاسياً. ليس كقساوة تعبير ليراز أو زوزانا، بل قساوة منحوتة، وكأن ملامحها صُنعت للصيد. حاجباها منحنيان، يظللان عينيها بحدة كالخط. عظام وجنتيها وفكها كانت كالحواف المنحوتة بإزميل، لكن فمها الممتلئ الداكن هو الوحيد الذي يحمل أثراً من النعومة. إلى أن ابتسمت.

عندما ابتسمت، رأى أكيڤا أن أسنانها كانت مشذبة ومروّسة.

تراجع إلى الخلف.

وللمرة الأولى، لاحظ أن هناك أكثر من المرأتين. بل هناك امرأة أخرى ورجلان، خمسة في المجمل. لم يتحدثوا، لكن عيونهم كانت مشتعلة بالنظر إليه.

"أيها الذكي"، قالت سكاراب، لتعيد انتباه أكيڤا إليها. والآن، رأى أن أسنانها طبيعية، بيضاء ومستقيمة. "يجب ألا نقلل من شأنك، أليس كذلك؟" ثم التفتت إلى المرأة الأخرى. "أم إنكِ من أطلقت سراحه، يا نايتنغال؟".

نايتنغال.

هزت رأسها، دون أن تُبعد عينيها عن أكيڤا ولو للحظة. "لم أفعل، أيتها الملكة".

ملكة؟

"لكنني لن أقيده مجدداً. هذا هو المكان الذي نمنحه فيه الكرامة التي يستحقها بميلاده ونتحدث معه."

سأل أكيڤا: "نتحدث عن ماذا؟ ما الذي تريدونه مني؟".

كانت سكاراب هي من أجابته، بنظرة جانبية مظلمة نحو نايتنغال، المتغطرسة المتعالية، إلى درجة أن أكيفا أدرك الآن، لو لم يكن قد سمع بالفعل، أنها ملكة. "لقد تم اتخاذ قرار نيابة عنك. من قِبلي".

"وما هو؟".

"ألا نقتلكَ".

لم تكن مفاجأة تامة، بالنظر إلى ما سمعه، لكن الطريقة التي قالتها بها، بصراحة وقوة، أثارت وقعاً ثقيلاً.

"وماذا فعلتُ لِئطرح موتي كخيار؟"، كان أكيفا متأكداً من براءته، لذلك لم يتوقع العنف في ردها.

"الكثير"، قالت، وكأنها تقطع كلماتها كما تقتطع الهواء بأسنانها."لا تشكك في ذلك، يا سليل فيستيڤال. بحق السماء، كان ينبغي أن تكون ميتاً بالفعل."

حاول أن ينهض، لكنه وجد نفسه ما زال مثبتاً. "هل بإمكانكِ إطلاق سراحي؟" سألها، وسرعان ما اندهش لقيامها بذلك.

قالت له:"حررتك لأنني لا أخافك".

وقف أكيفا."ولماذا ستخافينني؟ هل هددتك أصلاً؟ لطالما تساءلت عن عائلتي من جهة أمي؟ ولم أفكر لمرة واحدة في إيذائهم."

"ومع ذلك، لم يقترب أحد من تدميرنا خلال ألف عام كما فعلت أنت."

"عمّ تتحدثين؟"، صرخ، غاضباً. لم يقترب أبداً من الجزر البعيدة، ولم يرَ ستيلياً في حياته. ماذا كان يقصدون؟

قاطعت نايتنغال:"سكاراب، لا تستفزيه. إنه لا يعلم. كيف له أن يعلم؟".

"أعلم ماذا؟" سأل أكيفا، بصوت أكثر هدوءاً، لأن كلماتها امتزجت بحزن، وليس بغضب، وجعلت الاتهامات تبدو أقل سخافة.

سرى التطفل في ذهنه كقوة عاصفة تجتاحه. ذلك الشعور بعدم السيطرة، كأنه صار أداة لشيء آخر. ثم سأل متردداً:"ماذا فعلت؟".

81

شرطة الأمنيات

قالت زوزانا، وهي تصرخ من على ظهر صيّاد العواصف:"يا إلهي! كل الجبال تبدو متشابهة!".

لقد كانوا تائهين، رغم أن وصولهم إلى هذا الحد يعتبر مذهلاً حقاً، ناهيك عن أسلوب الرحلة الذي كان لا يقل إدهاشاً.

الفضل الأول لذلك يعود أساساً إلى الخرائط المحفوظة في ذهن إليزا، والثاني إلى الموسيقى، إذ نجح ميك في سحر مخلوق طائر بحجم سفينة صغيرة بكمانه—كمان جديد وأفضل من الذي تركه خلفه في حوض إستر— كي يحملهم. أما زوزانا، فلم تكن تجد أي مشكلة في نسب الفضل إلى نفسها أيضاً. كانت واثقة بأن حماسها طوال الوقت كان القوة الحقيقية الدافعة لهذا المسعى.

منذ اللحظة التي كشفت فيها إليزا أنها تعرف بوابة أخرى—البوابة التي نُفيت من خلالها جدتها الكبرى قبل ألف عام—كانت زوزانا مستعدة للانطلاق. لم يهمها أنها في باتاغونيا (أينما كانت باتاغونيا هذه... آه، بحق

الجحيم. أهي بعيدة جداً. جداً، حقاً؟)، لكن لديهم الوسائل للوصول إليها.

لكن الأمنيات كانت ممتعة، ونادرة أيضاً، ولا تُقدّر بثمن، ومقدسة؛ فقد صنعها بريمستون بنفسه، ولم يكن من اللائق أن تُنفق كما تنفق النقود على السكاكر. بالإضافة إلى ذلك، كان من المحتمل أن تكون كارو بحاجة ماسة إلى الغافرييل أكثر مما قد يحتاجون هم، وهذا إن استطاعوا إيصالها إليها أصلاً. لذا، فإن الاتفاق الذي توصلوا إليه بينهم كان بسيطاً: أن يوصلوها إليها. وهذا دون اللجوء إلى استخدام الغافرييلات إن أمكن.

مزح ميك مرة بشأن"شرطة الأمنيات"، بينما كانوا يلعبون لعبة الأمنيات الثلاث في الكهوف، والآن أخذ يمازح زوزانا بأنها أصبحت"شرطة الأمنيات" بالفعل.

قال بعينين متوسلتين:"لا مهارات ساموراي؟ أو ربما طلب قوة خارقة بصياغة أكثر حذراً؟".

قالت:"يمكننا أن نطلب من ثيركو أو أي شخص آخر أن يعلمنا القتال. إنها أمنية غير ضرورية."

قال عازف الكمان للفنانة:"إنها أمنية كسولة. وهذا هو جمالها. تعلم الأشياء صعب. صحيح. صحيح. نحن بالفعل نعرف كيف نتعلم تلك الأمور" قال مبتسماً. ثم استدار إلى إليزا متابعاً."عالمة وزميلة ذكية في تعلم الأشياء، هل تريدين الانضمام إلينا في تدريب وحوش الساموراي؟ ننوي أن نصبح خطرين."

"أنا معكم"، ببساطة قالت إليزا جونز التي عرفت بلقب الخوخة.

حقاً. حتى لو لم يكن القدر قد جمعهم معاً في هذا المسعى الجنوني، كانت زوزانا ستختار أن تكون صديقة لها. وهذا لم يحدث، مما جعل زوزانا ممتنة لذلك. لو أن إليزا كانت من النوع الذي يشتكي، أو يتصرف كالأميرة المدللة، أو من الذين يصدرون أصواتاً مزعجة أثناء الأكل، لكانت هذه الرحلة كابوساً.

لكن ما كانت عليه الرَحلة، بدلاً من ذلك، هو شيء مذهل.

أولاً، الوصول إلى باتاغونيا (التي تبين أنها في الأرجنتين في الأساس، مع شريحة صغيرة من تشيلي؛ من كان يعرف؟). كل ما احتاجوه لذلك كان المال، ولم يكن لديهم نقص فيه بفضل حسابات كارو التي بدت مرتبة تماماً ولم تمسها تصرفات إستر الشريرة.

لو أني أرى وجهك أيتها الجدّة الزائفة. هذا ما فكرت به زوزانا بأسف لعدم تمكنها من التباهي أمام إستر أو إغاظتها بشكل فعلي، لكن ميك، من جانبه، كان أكثر هدوءاً بشأن الموضوع."العيش مع نفسها لبقية حياتها هو عقاب كافٍ"، قال لها.

تخيلوا قليلاً.

أن إليزا، لا زالت تحمل في داخلها شغفاً عارماً للانتقام، وهذا جعل زوزانا تحبها أكثر.

مظهرها البريء، بعينيها الكبيرتين الجميلتين، كان خادعاً؛ فهي تعرف تماماً كيف تضمر الضغائن. مع ذلك، امتنعت عن إهدار أمنية على خصمها الحقير الذي وصفته وكأنه مجرد شخص تافه، حتى أقنعتها زوزانا أن أمنية بسيطة من نوع شينغ—وهي من الأمنيات المتواضعة التي لديهم منها العشرات، ولا تحمل مجداً حقيقياً لكارو—يمكن أن تحقق انتقاماً مرضياً للغاية.

حدثتها زوزانا عن انتقام كارو الرائع من كاز، وأضحكتها هي وميك بلا توقف وهي تصف كيف كان جسده العاري المثالي يؤدي رقصة الحكة المتشنجة فوق منصة العرض. لكن ما ألهم إليزا أكثر كان الجزء الثاني من الانتقام: الحاجبان اللذان نما بشكل غير طبيعي على وجه سفيتلا.

قبل أن تنطق بأمنيتها، قبّلت إليزا قطعة شينغ وكأنها كانت نرد الحظ وقالت:"أتمنى أن ينمو شاربان لمورغان توث بمعدل بوصة في الساعة، ابتداءً من الآن، ولمدة شهر كامل."

تلك اللحظة القصيرة من التساؤل عمّ إذا كانت الأمنية تفوق قدرات الميدالية. اختفى الشينغ فور انتهائها من لفظ الكلمة الأخيرة.

قال ميك بابتسامة ساخرة:"أتدركين أنكِ للتو وصفتِ شارب هتلر؟".

من البريق في عينيها، أدركا أنها كانت تعرف تماماً ما فعلته. لكن الانتقام لم يكن مكتملاً إذا لم يعرف الهدف من كان وراءه، لذلك أرسلت إلى بريده الإلكتروني في العمل صورة لها وهي ترفع إصبعها إلى شفتها وكأنه شارب، مع عنوان الرسالة:"استمتع".

أعلنت زوزانا بحماس:"علينا أن نفعل الشيء نفسه مع استير أيضاً".

"الآن".

ها قد فعلواها، وبدأوا رحلتهم بأفضل الطرق الممكنة: تخيلوا، بروح من التضامن، الرعب والحيرة التي ستجتاح أعداءهم.

رحلة طويلة بالطائرة، ثم تسوق للحصول على معدات وأدوات لمواجهة الطقس البارد، رحلة طويلة بالسيارة، ثم مسيرة شاقة في الثلج؛ اللعنة، كان الشتاء في نصف الكرة الجنوبي—لكنهم وصلوا أخيراً وصاروا قريبين بما يكفي من البوابة للتفكير في استخدام الغافرييلات للطيران. كادوا يفعلونها، لكن الأمر أصبح مسألة شرف للحفاظ عليها، فقال ميك:"لنرَ ما على الجانب الآخر أولاً قبل أن نقرر. يمكن لإليزا أن تحملنا".

وهذا ما فعلته. وهكذا اكتشفوا ما لا يعرفه أحد في كل إريتز: أين يعشش صائدو العواصف. وما لم يكن أحد يتخيله على الإطلاق: أنها تحب الموسيقى.

وكان هذا رسمياً: حيث أنجز ميك مهامه الثلاث الخيالية. أما الخاتم الذي كان يحترق في جيبه؟ ذلك الذي بدا بسيطاً مقارنة بأضواء حمام الجناح الملكي الرخامي اللامع؟

بدا المشهد مثالياً تماماً الآن، وهم فوق ظهر صيّاد العواصف، بينما البحر الشمالي يمتد أسفلهم، تتناثر فيه الجبال الجليدية والمخلوقات

البحرية التي لم تكن بأي حال من الأحوال حيتاناً.

لم يكن بإمكانه أن يحط على ركبة واحدة دون المخاطرة بالسقوط، لكن هذا كان أمراً ثانوياً في ظل هذه الظروف.

سألها:"هل تتزوجينني؟".

وكان الجواب: نعم.

...

"يا إلهي، كم أنا سعيدة برؤيتكما!" صاحت زوزانا الآن، وهي تكاد تطير من الفرح عند رؤية ليراز وزيري. زيري! ليس الذئب الأبيض، بل زيري الحقيقي! أوه. هذا يعني أنه لا بد أنه قد... ولكن الأمر كان على ما يرام، أليس كذلك؟ لأنه هنا الآن بجسده الكيريني مرة أخرى، ويبدو تقريباً كما كان في شكله الطبيعي.

كان يبتسم ابتسامة عريضة، وسيماً للغاية، وليراز بجانبه تبتسم بدورها، جميلة، وتضحك بذهول من صميمها، تضحك. تضحك مثل شخص يعرف كيف يضحك. ليراز.

بدا ذلك أكثر إثارة للدهشة من الركوب على ظهر صيّاد العواصف نفسه. لكنه لم يكن كذلك.

لأن لا شيء يوازي تلك الروعة.

"هل يمكنك أن تخبريهم، أننا لا نستطيع العثور على الكهوف؟"، سألت زوزانا إليزا بعد أن هدأت موجة الضحك والصيحات بلغات غير مفهومة تماماً.

تتحدث إليزا لغة السيرافيم، وهو أمر مفيد لكنه كان مزعجاً بعض الشيء بالنسبة إلى زوزانا، لأنها لم تعد تملك حجة قوية لاستخدام أمنية لتعلم إحدى لغات إريتز بنفسها. مع ذلك، لو أرادت أن تتعلم لغة أخرى، لكانت لغة الكيميرا، لأنها بكل تأكيد، أكثر إثارة.

"سنضطر لتعلم الإحياء، والتخفي، والقتال أيضاً، والآن لغات غير بشرية؟

ما هذا أنحن في مدرسة؟". قالها ميك بتنهيدة مُبالغ فيها لم تنطلِ عليها. لكن إليزا لم تترجم، وأدركت زوزانا أنها كانت تحدق في زيري بدهشة. آه! صحيح. جسده. لقد رأت جسده في الحفرة. كان عليها أن تشرح ذلك لاحقاً

"إنه هو"، أكدت زوزانا."سنخبرك لاحقاً."

وهكذا بدأت الترجمات—من إليزا إلى ليراز، التي بدورها ترجمت إلى زيري بلغة الكيميرا—ومن ثم قاداهم الاثنان عائدين جنوباً، وسألوهم أسئلة مثل من أين جاؤوا، وما إذا كان لصيّاد العواصف اسم. وعندما لاحظت زوزانا القنطرة، أدركت وجود عيب في تصورها المبالغ فيه حول الدخول المهيب بجناحين يخفقان كإعصار يذهل الجميع ويبهرهم.

صيّاد العواصف—الذي لم يكن لديه اسم—لن يتمكن من الدخول عبر القنطرة الهلالية. حسناً، اللعنة.

كان عليها أن توقف الأحاديث الجانبية كي تستطيع الفهم:"نحتاج إلى جمهور. يجب أن يتم مشاهدة هذا، والحديث عنه في كل مكان. أريد أن تُكتب أغانٍ حول هذا الأمر. هل تمانعون؟ هل يمكنكم الذهاب لإحضار الجميع؟ وكارو؟".

عند هذه النقطة، بدا زيري وليراز محرجين وغريبين بعض الشيء، واقترح ميك، بلطف، أن كارو وأكيفا ربما كانا... مشغولين.

تصادمت المشاعر! بعد إثارة فكرة أن كارو وأكيفا كانا"مشغولين" أخيراً!. هذا ليس عدلاً، أن يثار هذا كله في لحظات مجدها الخاصة.

"يمكننا مقاطعتهما لأجل هذا، صحيح؟" قالت متوسلة."إنهم يحلقون في دوائرهم الآن، يحاولون تفادي اللحظة التي سيضطرون فيها للنزول ودخول الكهوف سيراً على الأقدام".

"لا"، قال ميك بصوت الحكمة.

"لكن".

"لا".

"حسناً. لكنني أريد أن يرانا أحد".

رآهم الجميع.

ذهبت ليراز لإحضارهم، واحتشدوا تحت الهلال، وارتفعت صيحات الإعجاب والذهول.

سمعت زوزانا صيحة فيركو المليئة بالود،"ميك ميك!"، وأخيراً شعرت أنه لا بأس بأن تنهي هذه الرحلة الرائعة.

وضعوا المخلوق الضخم قدر الإمكان بالقرب من الواجهة الصخرية، وقفزوا من على ظهره بخفة، وأخذوا يحتضنون عنقه الضخم بعناق مليء بالشكر والوداع. حيث من المفترض أنه سيرحل الآن ويتركهم، رغم أنهم تمنوا في داخلهم أن يبقى."إذا لم يرحل، سنطلق عليه اسماً". وقفوا يراقبونه بحنين وهو يرتفع أعلى وأعلى حتى أصبح مجرد شكل مقطوع من القبة السماوية المتلألئة.

حينها فقط، وعندما استداروا نحو الكيميرا والسيرافيم الذين تجمّعوا أدركوا أن هناك خطباً ما، وقد خيّم جو من الكآبة على الحشد... بالإضافة إلى كارو التي وقفت بعيداً. لماذا؟ ولماذا لا تفعل شيئاً؟ وأين أكيفا؟

لوّحت لهم كارو بيدها، وابتسمت ابتسامة خاطفة تنم عن دهشة، وهزت رأسها بخفة، واتسعت عيناها لرؤية أجنحة إليزا بالطبع، لكن حتى ذلك لم يدفعها للتقدم والترحيب بهم. كانت تتحدث إلى ليراز، التي لم تعد تضحك مثل شخص يحترف الضحك. بل عادت إلى حالتها المزرية: شفتان مشدودتان، ومنخران أبيضان من الغضب، أكثر شراسة من أي وقت بدت فيه الذئبة البيضاء.

نسيت زوزانا كل مجدها واندفعت نحو صديقتها."ماذا؟ ماذا؟ ماذا؟ بحق الله، كارو، ماذا؟".

"إنه أكيفا". بدت كارو في غاية الضياع. لم يكن من المفترض أن تبدو كذلك."لقد رحل."

82

ضلال

"هناك سبب".

"لكن ما الذي فعلته؟".

"هناك سبب وجيه لدفع الجزية".

هذه الكلمات التي خاطبت نايتنغال فيها أكيفا، لم يكن حديثاً منطوقاً، بل كان عبر الأثير، وهي ليست مجرد كلمات. لقد كانت ذكريات انفتحت أمامه، بالصوت والصورة، والعاطفة وانكشفت له على شكل رعب وصداع. وكان من المستحيل ألا يفهمها.

وقف أكيفا أمام نايتنغال وسكاراب، وقد شاهدهما ظاهرياً، ومعهما الثلاثة الآخرون خلفهما. لكن في عمقه كان يمر بتجربة مختلفة تماماً جعلته ينكمش مما رآه.

"اهدأ. أنت ابن طفلي".

هذه فيستيفال. قدّمتها نايتنغال إلى أكيفا عن طريق التخاطر، بشكل ذكرى مشبعة بالحنين، حتى إنه، خلال تلك اللحظة، فهم شعوراً لم يعشه من قبل ولا يمتلك سياقاً له: حب الوالد لابنه الضائع.

"أريد أن أعرفك. أن أساعدك، لا أن أؤذيك. لذا عليك أن تصغي إلي. أنت طفل طفلي، لكنني لم أعرف عنك أبداً. لقد ضاعت فيستيڤال منا. اختفت. فقط لأنك موجود، أعلم الآن ما حدث لها. أعلم أن ابنتي الحبيبة كانت محظية في حريم طاغية دمّر نصف عالم".

لم تحاول أن تنكر اليأس الذي سببته لها هذه الحقيقة. شعر أكيڤا وكأنه الجذر الذي تسبب في ذلك الألم، وكأن الزمن يعمل بالعكس، وكأنه كان السبب في اختيار والدته الذي أدى إلى وجوده.

"وأعلم أيضاً أن هذا لم يكن ليحدث لها... رغماً عنها. إنها ستيلية، إنها ابنتي القوية. لذا، لا بد أنها اختارت هذا".

تدفقت الذكريات بشكل متسق كأنها ذكريات أكيڤا نفسه. وتحت سطح كلمات نايتنغال، ثمة تجسيد نقي للمرأة التي كانت فيستيڤال عليها، جميلة ومضطربة. مضطربة؟ بحسّ عميق يتبع خيوط القدر بإلحاح، حتى لو قادتها إلى الظلام.

"لذا، لا بد أن لديها أسبابها".

من عقل نايتنغال إلى أكيڤا مرّرت الرسائل فهماً عميقاً بأن الكثير من الستيليين كانوا يعتبرون القدر شيئاً حقيقياً، كالحب أو الخوف—بعداً من أبعاد حياتهم له من الثقل ما يكفي لتشكيلها. وكانوا يسمّونه أنانكي، هذا الحسّ الذي يشعر بجاذبية المصير. إذا كان أنانكي قوياً، يمكنك إما اتباعه أو مقاومته، لكن المقاومة كانت تحمل معها شعوراً ساحقاً بالغلط يطارد كل خياراتك. والسبب... عليك أن تكون أنت.

تلاشت الذكريات، تاركةً فراغاً، ليتوه فيه أكيڤا.

"أنت..." ترددت في الفراغ، لتتبعها كلمات أخرى:"أنت. ابني لن يكون عالقاً في مصائركم الضعيفة. "لكن قبل أن يتمكن أكيڤا من استيعاب ذلك، أُرسلت رؤية جديدة، وازدهرت في المكان الذي كانت فيه فيستيڤال. كانت مختلفة تماماً: باردة، وبعيدة، وهائلة.

"الاستمرارية التي هي الكل الأعظم مرتبطة ومقيدة بالطاقة. نحن نسميها"الحُجُب". لديها أسماء أخرى، عديدة، لكن هذا أبسطها. إنها تتجاوز إدراكنا. هي البداية ومرتع كل الأشياء، وهذا ما نعرفه: الحُجب تحافظ على تماسك العوالم، وعلى تميزها. تلامس بعضها، لكنها تبقى منفصلة، كما قُدر لها أن تكون. عندما تمر عبر بوابة، فأنت تخترق جرحاً في الحجب."

الحُجب، الاستمرارية، عظمة الكل. لم تكن هذه مصطلحات قد سمع بها أكيڤا من قبل، لكنه مُنح فكرة عنها، وكان في الفكرة نوع من التبجيل يقترب من العبادة. لم تكن صورة أو ذكرى، لأن ذلك مستحيل. لا أحد يمكنه رؤية الاستمرارية. لقد كانت كل شيء. العوالم بكليتها.

حتى الآن، كان أكيڤا يعرف عالمين: إريتز والأرض. لكن في إرسال نايتنغال، فهم... أن هناك الكثير.

كان الأمر مذهلاً ومربكاً. ما لمحه في فكرة الاستمرارية، كافياً لجعله يرغب في السقوط على ركبتيه. رأى الفضاء من حوله وهو يتفتح، ويفتح، ويفتح، بلا نهاية، بلا حدود لأبعاده. كإله يرفع رؤوسه الألف بعد الألف، واحدة تلو الأخرى، ويفتح أفواهه الألف بعد الألف ليطلق زئيراً هائلاً، يهزّ صداه أركان العوالم.

"نستمد الطاقة من الحُجب لصنع السحر. إنها المصدر. مصدر كل شيء. لكن الأمر ليس بسيطاً. لا يمكن للطاقة أن تُؤخذ بلا مقابل. هناك ثمن للمقايضة على الطاقة. وهذه هي الجزية."

"جزية الألم"، نطقها بصوت مسموع، لعدم معرفته بكيفية التواصل بنفس الطريقة التي يتحدثون بها أثيرياً. رأى جبين"سكاراب" ينعقد، بينما جبين نايتنغال أخذ يسترخي. نظرت إليه بفضول، وقد حمل ردّها له شفقة لطيفة.

"للألم طريقة واحدة. الأسهل والأكثر بدائية. جزية الألم... هي كاستخدام محراث لقطف زهرة. أهذا كل ما تعرفه؟".

أومأ برأسه. كان هذا النوع من الحديث الأثيري يثير قلقه.

"هذا ليس كل شيء، وإلا لما كنا هنا!". اعترضت سكاراب بصوت عالٍ الطريقة التي نظرت فيها إليه، محملة باللوم. يبدو أن أكيڤا فهم ما تقول وأجاب بصوت مبحوح:"السيريثار".

نظرة سكاراب أصبحت أكثر حدة."إذاً، أنت تعرف."

"أنا لا أعرف شيئاً". قالها بمرارة حزّت بنفسه أكثر من أي وقت مضى. مدركةً اضطرابه، تقدمت نايتنغال نحوه. لم تمد يدها إليه، لكنه شعر بلمستها، كما شعر مرة من قبل بتلك اللمسة الباردة على جبينه، وقد منعته حينها من استدعاء القوة في معركة أديلفاس، والتي هدّأته لفترة وجيزة بعدها. وفي اللحظة التالية، عرف شيئاً آخر، وكان ذلك صاعقاً له: لغز الانتصار في أديلفاس. كان ذلك بفضلهن، بالطبع.

هؤلاء الملائكة الخمسة بطريقة ما قلبوا الموازين ضد أربعة آلاف من الدومينيون. على مدى السنوات الماضية، حاول أكيڤا مراراً أن يتخيل سحر بني جنسه، لكنه لم يتخيل أبداً قوة كهذه.

ثم تحدثت نايتنغال بصوت عالٍ، دون أن تلامس عقله هذه المرة، وكان أكيڤا سعيداً بذلك، خصوصاً عندما سمع المزيد مما كان عليها قوله. ولا يمكن لأي لمسة طيبة أن تخفف من وطأة هذا.

"السيريثار هو الطاقة بذاتها، المادة الخام للحُجب. إنه... قشرة البيضة وصفارها أيضاً. يحمي ويغذي. يمنح الشكل للزمان والمكان، وبدونه لن يكون هناك سوى الفوضى. لقد سألتَ عمّا فعلته! لقد أخذتَ السيريثار."

كان صوتها مفعماً بالحزن."لقد أخذت الكثير منه دفعة واحدة إلى درجة أن دفع الجزية مقابله سيكلفك حياتك مئات المرات، لكنك لم تمت، لأنك لم تدفع الجزية. يا طفل طفلي، أنت لم تعطِ شيئاً، فقط أخذت. هذا أمر لا ينبغي أن يكون ممكناً، وهو أمر خطير للغاية. ما قالته سكاراب صحيح. لقد تبعناك إلى هنا لنقتلك".

"قبل أن تتمكن من قتل الجميع"، قالت سكاراب، دون أي مسحة من الرقة في كلماتها. لم يكن لذلك أهمية. كان أكيثا يهز رأسه، ليس إنكاراً، بل تصديقاً. لقد صدّقهم. شعر بحقيقة ما يقولونه، وقد كان هذا الجواب على السؤال الذي لطالما نهشه من الداخل طوال هذا الوقت. لكنه لا يزال لا يفهم. قال مجدداً:"أنا لا أعرف شيئاً. كيف لي أن أقتل...؟ الجميع."

أصبح صوت نايتنغال مبحوحاً."لا أفهم لماذا قادت الأنانكي ابنتي إلى خلقكِ. لماذا يجب أن تلد الحُجب دمارها بنفسها؟".

أنانكي. أصداء ورنين المصير.

"دمار؟" رد أكيثا بصوت أجوف. وهو الذي كان واضحاً له طوال حياته بأنه لم يكن ملكاً لنفسه، بل مجرد أداة للإمبراطورية، حلقة في سلسلة؛ حتى اسمه، مجرد اسم مستعار. لكنه كسر تلك السلاسل، وادعى لنفسه حريته، واعتقد أنه أخيراً أصبح حراً.

لم يفهم بعد ما تحاول نايتنغال إخباره به، أو لماذا شككت سكاراب في حياته، لكنه فهم هذا: طوال هذا الوقت، كان عالقاً في شبكة مصير أعظم بكثير مما تخيله يوماً.

خفق قلبه بعنف، وأدرك أكيثا أنه ليس حراً.

"ليس ممكناً أن تأخذ دون دفع المقابل"، كررت نايتنغال. قالتها بحدة ووضوح، كأنها تريد أن تتأكد من أنه يفهم. كانت نظرتها مليئة بالارتباك والحذر، ومع ذلك بدت فيها ومضات أخرى—لوم؟ ربما رهبة؟

"لا يمكن لأحد آخر أن يفعل ذلك"، أضافت، وعيناها مثبتتان عليه بلا انحراف. كلمة واحدة تراءت له—سواء من الأثير أو من عقله، لم يكن متأكداً.

الضلال.

"لكنك فعلتها ثلاث مرات. أكيثا، أن تأخذ دون مقابل، هذا يُضعف الحجب". تحركت نظرتها نحو سكاراب للحظة. بلعت ريقها

بصعوبة."وبإضعاف الحجب..." ثم ترددت. إذاً هذا هو الأمر، وأكيفا على علم بهذا. هنا تكمن الحقيقة. تربصت الكلمات خلف عينيها، عميقة ومظلمة كأي قصة سبق ورؤيت.

لكنه التقط أصداءها، شظاياها: مختار. منحط. خرائط. سماوات. كارثة. ميليز.

وحوش.

حاولت نايتنغال أن تتهرب من الإفصاح، لكن سكاراب لم تسمح لها بذلك.

"أردتِ التحدث إليه، أليس كذلك؟ إذاً تحدثي. أخبريه بما نفعل على مدار الساعة في جزرنا الخضراء البعيدة، وما عليه أن يشكرنا عليه. أخبريه لماذا جئنا من أجله، وما الذي كاد أن يجلبه علينا. أخبريه عن الكارثة."

83

معظم الأشياء ذات الأهمية

حملت غافرييل في راحتها. وتجمع الكل حولها في الكهف الكبير. الكيميرا، غير الشرعيين، البشر. وحتى إليزا، بغض النظر عما أصبحت عليه. نظرت كارو إلى حيث كانت الفتاة تقف بجانب ڤيركو، ولم تكن تعرف إليزا، لكنها كانت تعلم أن هناك شيئاً مشتركاً بينهما: لم تكن أيٌّ منهما بشرية بالكامل، بل وأكثر، وكل واحدة منهما كانت الوحيدة من نوعها.

سألت زوزانا:"ما الأمنية التي ستطلبينها؟".

نظرت كارو إلى الميدالية الثقيلة في يدها. بدت وكأن بريمستون ينظر إليها من خلالها. بدت صناعتها بسيطة وغير متقنة، لكنها لا تزال تستحضر عينيه إلى ذهنها، وصوته العميق الذي كان أشبه بظل للصوت نفسه.

"أنا أحلم بها أيضاً، يا صغيرتي،" هذا ما قاله لها في الزنزانة بينما كانت تنتظر الإعدام، وتمنت لو أنها تستطيع أن تُريه ما هو أمامها الآن—رغم أن أي أمنية ليست قادرة على تحقيق ذلك."انظر إلى ما فعلناه. انظر كيف تقف ليراز وزيري جنباً إلى جنب". كانت مستعدة للمراهنة بكل شيء على أن بشرتيهما اللتين توشكان على التلامس مشحونتان بالكهرباء، تماماً كما

شعرت ببشرتها المشحونة بالكهرباء حين وقف أكيفا قريباً منها. وهناك كيتا-إري، الذي كان قبل بضعة أيام فقط يرفع راحتيه المنقوشتين بالهامسا في وجه أكيفا وليراز وهو يضحك.

الآن، يقف بجانب أوريت، الملاك الذي يتفاوض على طاولة المجلس الحربي، يجادل الذئب حول انضباط جنوده. وأمزالاغ، الذي كان مستعداً، في الجسد الذي صنعته كارو له—ليس هائلاً ورمادياً كجسده الأخير، ولا مرعباً—للذهاب واستعادة أرواح أطفاله من رماد لوراميندي.

كانوا وقورين ومتحدين، رفاقاً قاتلوا معاً ونجوا من معركة مستحيلة، يحملون معهم لغزها، وأكثر من ذلك، إحساساً بالتضامن. بعد معركة أديلفاس، بدأ يتسلل شعور بالقدر المحتوم.

القدر. مرة أخرى، لم تستطع كارو التخلص من الإحساس بأن القدر، إن كان موجوداً، فإنه يكرهها. أما عن سؤال زوزانا—ما الأمنية التي ستطلبها على هذا الغافرييل؟ ما الأمنية التي يمكن أن تعيد أكيفا إليها، التي يمكن أن تقضي على هذا الشعور القاسي الذي بدأ يغزوها، بأنهم قد ينجزون كل ما كانوا يعتقدون أنهم بحاجة إلى إنجازه، ومع ذلك لن يُسمح لهما بأن يكونا معاً؟ كان بريمستون دائماً واضحاً جداً بشأن حدود الأمنيات.

"هناك أشياء أكبر من أي أمنية"، قال لها عندما كانت طفلة صغيرة.

"مثل ماذا؟" سألته، ولا زالت إجابته تطاردها إلى لآن، مع ثقل الغافرييل في يدها، وكل ما تريده هو أن تصدق أنه يمكن أن يحل مشاكلها."معظم الأشياء ذات الأهمية"، هذا ما قاله بريمستون، وكانت تعلم أنه كان على حق. لكنها لم تستطيع أن تتمنى الحلم، أو السعادة، أو أن يتركهم العالم وشأنهم. لقد علمت ما سيحدث. لا شيء. الغافرييل سيظل هناك، وصورة بريمستون ستبدو وكأنها تلومها على سخافاتها. لكن الأمنيات لم تكن عديمة الفائدة أيضاً، طالما أنك تحترم حدود قدراتها.

"أتمنى أن أعرف مكان أكيفا"، قالت، ثم اختفى الغافرييل من كفها.

84

الكارثة

بدأت نايتنغال بسرد القصة، لكن سكاراب تولت المتابعة. أخذت المرأة
الأكبر سناً تتحدث بلطف زائد، محاولةً التقليل من هول قصة هي جوهر
الرعب نفسه—وكأنها تخشى ألا يكون المحارب الذي أمامها قادراً على
تحمّلها. لكنه تحمّلها. شحب وجهه. وتصلب فكّه بقوة إلى درجة أن سكاراب
تمكنت من سماع صوت عظامه تصطك ببعضها، لكنه تحمّل.

أخبرته عن غرور السحرة الذين اعتقدوا أنهم قادرون على امتلاك عنان
الاستمرارية، وأخبرته عن الفيريرا، وكيف أن الستيليبيين وحدهم وقفوا ضد
رحلتهم. أخبرته عن اختراق الحُجب، وكيف تم تعليم الاثني عشر المختارين
طريقة اختراق نسيج الوجود نفسه، مادة تتجاوز فهمهم إلى درجة أنهم كانوا
كطيور الجيف التي تنقر أعين الإله.

ثم أخبرته عمّا وجدوه على الجانب الآخر من حجاب بعيد جداً. أطلقوا
عليهم اسم نيثيلام، لأن تلك الوحوش لم يكن لديها لغة لتسمّي نفسها.
نيثيلام كانت الكلمة القديمة للفوضى، وهذا ما كانوا عليه.

لا يمكن وصفهم.

لم يرَ أحد على قيد الحياة تلك المخلوقات، لكن سكاراب شعرت بوجودهم، أقل هنا مما شعرت به في موطنها، لكنهم موجودون دائماً. لم يتوقفوا أبداً عن الوجود. يضغطون، يمتصون، يقضمون.

أن تكون ستيلياً يعني أن تذهب إلى النوم كل ليلة في بيت حيث الوحوش كغربان فوق السطح، في محاولة لاقتحامه. لكن السطح هو السماء. وهكذا الأمر مع السماء في الجزر البعيدة، حيث كل شيء إما بحر أو سماء، لذا تحدثوا عنه ببساطة هكذا: السماء تنزف، السماء تزهر. السماء تمرض، السماء تضعف، السماء تفشل. والسماء أحد الحجب، المكوّنة من طاقات لا يمكن حسابها—السيريثار—هو ما كان الستيليون يرعونه، ويحرسونه، ويغذونه، كل ثانية من كل يوم، بحيواتهم نفسها.

هذا كان واجبهم. هذا هو ما جعلهم يحافظون على البوابة مغلقة عندما فشل الفيريرا أنفسهم. وهذا هو السبب في أن حياتهم كانت أقصر من حياة أقاربهم الفاجرين في الشمال، الذين لم يعطوا شيئاً، بل أخذوا فقط من هذا العالم الذي لجؤوا إليه بحثاً عن ملاذ، ثم استولوا عليه بالقوة.

استنزف الستيليون طاقتهم على الحجب التي أفسدها الحمقى، ليحافظوا عليها في مواجهة القوة العمياء والضاربة للنيثيلام، الوحوش. لكنها كانت أكثر من مجرد وحوش. إنها هائلة ومدمرة إلى درجة أن سكاراب لم تجد كلمة تعبّر عنها سوى كلمة واحدة: آلهة.

لماذا توجد كلمة كهذه أصلاً، إن لم تكن للتعبير عن عظمة غير مرئية مثل هذه؟ أما بالنسبة إلى نجوم الآلهة، التي طالما عبدها قومها، فلم تكن بالنسبة إلى سكاراب أكثر من قصة تُروى قبل النوم. وما الفائدة من آلهة مشرقة تراقب من بعيد، بينما تسعى آلهة مظلمة في كل لحظة لالتهامك؟

تخيلت النيثيلام كجذور سوداء هائلة، وأفواهها الضخمة—تمتص بنهم، مغطاة بأنسجة غضروفية نابضة—ملتصقة بالحجاب مثل ثعابين البحر التي تتغذى على لحم أفعى بحرية جرفتها الأمواج إلى الشاطئ، بطنها

الشاحب مكشوف للشمس، تلفظ أنفاسها الأخيرة بينما الطفيليات حية عليها. مسعورة تمتص بجنون في لحظاتها الأخيرة لتنهب كل ما تبقى.

لم تخبر أكيفا بذلك. كان هذا كابوسها الخاص، ما تراه عندما تغلق عينيها في الظلام وتشعر بحركة تلك الكائنات وهي تتلوى على الحجب. فقط أخبرته بما قالته الأسطورة، لأن الحقيقة كانت في الأسطورة: كان هناك ظلام، ووحوش هائلة بحجم العوالم تسبح فيه.

وعندما أخبرته عن مِليز، رأت الفهم يجتاحه، ومن ثم الفقدان. كان انعكاساً لما رأته قبل وقت قصير، عندما أرسلت نايتنغال له عن فيستيڤال. ربما كانت المرأة الأكبر سناً تقصد أن تكون طيبة. أو ربما كانت عمياء بفعل حزنها على خسارتها الخاصة. لقد فوجئت سكاراب بأنها كانت الوحيدة التي رأت تأثير ذلك على أكيفا، أن يوهَب والدته من خلال الأثير—أول أثير له، وعقله بالتأكيد كان يحاول أن يضع مسافة بينه وبين الواقع—ثم تُسلب منه مرة أخرى وبشكل مفاجئ للغاية.

والآن مِليز. مِليز، تاج الاستمرارية، بستان العظمة. عالم موطن السيرافيم، وكل عظمة مائة ألف عام من الحضارة. راقبت وجه أكيفا وهي تمنحه، في الوقت ذاته، أعماق لا تُصدّق من تاريخه الخاص، عظمة أجداده، مجد السيرافيم في العصر الأول، ثم تسلبها منه.

مِليز، هي البداية والنهاية. مِليز التي ضاعت.

ذكّرت نفسها بحال أكيفا، وقسّت قلبها على موجات الفقد والحزن التي تجتاحه، كل واحدة منها تبدو وكأنها تنتزع منه شيئاً حيوياً، تاركة إياه... أقل مما وجدته. هل كان هذا ما أرادته؟ أن تقلل من خطره؟ ماذا كانت تريد منه حقاً؟ لم تكن متأكدة تماماً. كانت قد صادته لتقتله، لكن الإجابة، كما عرفت الآن، لم تكن بهذه البساطة.

بعد معركة أديلفاس، عندما كانت تقطع خيوط الحياة لجنود مهاجمين، تجمعها لتكون بداية لـ"يورايا"—ذلك السلاح الأسطوري لأجدادها—ترسخت

في ذهنها فكرة أن خيط حياته سيكون مجدها. حياته توتر أوتار قيثارتها. قوته، تحت سيطرتها.

وربما كان هذا هو الجواب. ربما كان ذلك هو النهاية التي دفعتها أنانكي فيستيثال نحوها طوال الوقت.

سكاراب كانت تتمنى لو كانت أنانكي الخاصة بها أوضح في هذا الشأن. لكن في أمر واحد، كانت واضحة تماماً: النيثيلام هم قدرها.

وهي كانت قدرهم.

كانت دائماً تشعر بوجودهم، لكن ذلك عندما تستلقي للنوم، وتظلم السماء فوقها، حيث تشعر بأنها تقف في مواجهتهم في رقعة شاسعة من خلال حاجز لطالما كان موجوداً —حتى قبل أن يكون هناك أي أمل معقول يعزز موقفها— ...زاد الشعور بالتحدي. مواجهة، قوة ضد قوة، وحاجز لم يعد موجوداً. هي عدوّتهم، كما كانوا أعداءها.

هي كابوسهم، كما كانوا كابوسها.

سكاراب، سوط آلهة الوحوش. المطالِبة بكل العوالم التي تم التهامها. لم يكن هناك أي شرارة أمل حتى الآن.

رأت سكاراب أن نايتنغال شعرت بما ينمو داخلها—ليس فقط اليورايا الذي بدأ للتو، بل معرفة الغرض منه—وكيف أرعبها. ومن ذا الذي لن يفعل؟ بنى الستيليون حياتهم في هذا العصر الجديد على الاعتقاد بأن الكارثة لا يمكن هزيمتها، إلا بالتراجع فقط. لذا قاموا بالتراجع. قاموا بذلك، وماتوا صغاراً ودون مجد. لقد قبلوا بواجبٍ، سيحتقرهم أسلافهم عليه.

سيعيشون في خوف، ينزفون طاقتهم، دون حتى التفكير في مواجهة العدو في معركة، لأن العدو هو ملتهم العوالم. لم يعد الستيليون من المحاربين. ولأن ما كانوا يخاطرون به، إذا فشلوا، هو... كل ما تبقى.

كانت إريتز السد أمام طوفان من الظلام الذي لا نهاية له. إذا فشل الستيليون، ستسقط كل العوالم الأخرى.

لم تقل شيئاً من هذا لأكيفا. بحلول ذلك الوقت، كانت قد أخبرته بكل شيء ما عدا دوره الخاص في هذه القصة. كان يجب أن يكون الأمر سهلاً بالنسبة إليها لتُكمل. انظر إلى ما فعله. لكن صوتها خانها.

بغرابة، وفي مواجهة الحزن العميق الذي تسببت فيه له، تذكرت ابتسامته—ابتسامة لها وليست لها —وتذكرت الإشراق الذي كان فيه آنذاك، والفرح، وكيف جعلها ذلك تشعر بالذهول وكأنها مبتدئة تتعرّف لأول مرة على لغة سرية متلألئة ومليئة بالاكتشافات. كانت قد رأت ذلك مجدداً في كهف الشلال، حيث كان ينتظر... ينتظر ما وصفته لنايتنغال بـ"موعده"، متجنبة استخدام الكلمة الحقيقية لما كان ينتظره. لما أشعلته تلك الغريبة ذات الشعر الأزرق الجميل في داخله، والإشراق الذي ولد من ذلك.

إن أكيفا في حالة حب. يا للأسف، لكنه لم يكن مشكلتها. مقارنة بالنيثيلام، فالحب كأثر قدم في الرماد، عابر وسهل الإزالة بلمسة واحدة.

طالت وقفتها أكثر مما ينبغي، وحاولت نايتنغال، بمنتهى الرقي، أن تأخذ عنها عناء رواية القصة، كأنها تسحب رأس الخيط من كبة خيطان، لتغزل منها القطعة الأخيرة بنفسها. لكن سكاراب هزت رأسها، وجدت صوتها، وأخبرت أكيفا بنفسها بقية القصة. وشعرت بمرارتها في صدرها، عندما سقط على ركبتيه. فكرت في فيستيڤال، التي لم تعرفها قط، والتي قادها مصيرها البشع إلى نصف عالم بعيد: أن تتخلى عن قداستها لطاغية ملك من أجل أن تجلب هذا الرجل إلى الوجود: أكيفا الذي صار لسبب لا يمكن تفسيره، أقوى من الجميع. ومع ذلك، كان مصير سكاراب البشع الخاص أن تجعله يسقط على ركبتيه، لكنها فكرت أن فيستيڤال ستفهم.

الأنانكي تحفر أخاديد عميقة إلى درجة أنه عليك مجاراتها أو قضاء حياتك محاولاً تسلق الجروف للهروب منها.

لم تكن سكاراب تنوي الهروب. لطالما كانت تسير نحو هذا المصير، منذ اللحظة التي سمعت فيها عن قيثارة مشدودة أوتارها بأرواح مسلوبة،

وقبل ذلك، منذ اللحظة الأولى التي تجمعت فيها الطاقات لتخلق منها ما هي عليه، اختارت مسارها، وعلق أكيڤا في تبعاته.

قامت بهذه الرحلة لتصطاد ساحراً وتقتله. وستعود من هذه المهمة بكامل عتادها لتصطاد الآلهة وتقتلها.

...

كان يا ما كان، كان هناك ظلام فقط، ووحوش هائلة كالعوالم التي تسبح فيها. كانوا يحبون الظلام لأنه يخفي بشاعتهم. كلما ابتكر مخلوق آخر ضوءاً، كانوا يطفئونه. عندما وُلدت النجوم، ابتلعوها، وبدا أن الظلام سيكون أبدياً لكن جنساً من المحاربين النيّرين سمع عنهم وسافر في عالمهم البعيد ليقاتلهم. كانت الحرب طويلة، نور ضد ظلام، وقُتل العديد من المحاربين. في النهاية، عندما هزموا تلك الوحوش، بقي مئة فقط على قيد الحياة، وهؤلاء المئة صاروا نجوم الآلهة، الذين جلبوا النور إلى الكون.

حاول أكيڤا أن يتذكر أول مرة سمع فيها تلك الأسطورة، حيث الوحوش تلتهم العوالم وتسبح في الظلام. أعداء النور، ملتهمي النجوم. هل سمع ذلك من والدته؟ لم يستطع أن يتذكر.

خمسة أعوام فقط قضاها معها، وأعوام طويلة بعدها لمحاولة محوها من ذاكرته. ربما كانت الحكاية قد وصلت إليه من معسكر التدريب، كجزء من دعاية تهدف إلى بناء كراهيتهم للكيميرا، لأن تلك كانت الطريقة التي حُرفت بها القصة في الإمبراطورية: إلى أسطورة خام قبيحة وسخيفة.

كان قد رواها لمادريغال في ليلتهما الأولى معاً، وهما مستلقيان فوق ثيابهما على ضفاف طحالب ناعمة، مثقلان بالمتعة والكسل. ثم ضحكا عليها قالت مادريغال:"والعم القبيح زامزومين، الذي صنعني من ظل! ...سخافة". أو ربما ليست سخافة. سكاراب أطلقت عليهم اسماً آخر غير الذي عرفه أكيڤا، لكنه كان منطقياً بالنسبة إليه. كما أن السيريثار أصبح يعني في الإمبراطورية حالة السكينة التي يعمل فيها نجوم الآلهة من خلال

السيف، كان النيثيلام نقيضها: الجنون العارم في ساحة المعركة، الدافع للقتل بدلاً من الموت. هذه الأسماء حملت يوماً ما دلالات عميقة حول طبيعة عالمهم. لكن الحقيقة ضاعت بطريقة ما.

الآن عرف أكيڤا أن الوحوش حقيقية. أنهم، كل ثانية من كل يوم، كانوا يضربون على حجب العالم. أولئك الشعوب الذين كانوا يحملون نصف دمه بالانتماء، عاشوا حياتهم في تفانٍ لتعزيز ذلك الحاجب بحياتهم.

وأنه هو... هو... من كاد يمزقه بالكامل.

راكعاً على ركبتيه. بالكاد يدرك كيف وصل إلى هناك. ما فعله الڤيريرا كان نصف كارثة فقط. ومن جهله كاد يجهز على ما تبقى.

جلست نايتنغال على ركبتيها أمامه، وخاطبته أثيرياً، بينما بقيت سكاراب واقفة في مكانها، غير متأثرة. "ليس الجهل فقط. إنما الجهل والقوة. إنهما مزيج سيئ. القوة غامضة كالحُجب نفسها. أنت أقوى من أي شخص آخر. لا يمكننا أن ننزعها منك إلا بقتلك، ولا نرغب في ذلك. كما لا يمكننا تركك، ونأمل أن تتمكن من احتوائها بمفردك."

أدرك أكيڤا خياره الذي لم يكن خياراً على الإطلاق. "ماذا تريدون مني؟" سأل، بصوت مبحوح، رغم أنه كان يعرف الجواب بالفعل.

"تعال معنا"، قالت نايتنغال بنبرة عالية فيها حزن ورقّة. لكن أكيڤا نظر إلى سكاراب، ولم يرَ أي حزن فيها، ولا أي رحمة. أضافت جدته، بصوت خافت جداً: "تعال إلى البيت."

البيت. شعر بالخيانة وهو يسمع هذه الكلمة، خاصةً وأنه كان ينظر إلى سكاراب. البيت بالنسبة إليه هو ما سيبنيه مع كارو. البيت هو كارو.

شعر أكيڤا بمستقبله يتفكك بين يديه. فكر في البطانية التي لم توجد بعد، ذلك الرمز لأبسط وأعمق آماله: مكان للحب والأحلام. هل سيتعين عليه هو وكارو أن يمزقا تلك البطانية إلى نصفين، ويحمل كل منهما نصفه الممزق حيثما تأخذهما أقدارهما؟

"لا أستطيع"، قال، بيأس، دون أن يفكر فيما يعنيه ذلك، أو في أن يُفسر خياره هذا. نظرت إليه نايتنغال، وظهرت عند زوايا فمها لمحة خفيفة من خيبة الأمل. أما سكاراب، فلم يظهر على وجهها أي شيء، ومع ذلك أوضحت طبيعة خياره بشكل جليّ، في حال كان لديه أي التباس.

مرتان من قبل، اجتاح أكيفا ذلك الوعي المفاجئ والعميق بحقيقة حياته. هذه كانت المرة الثالثة، ومعها جاء رسالة أثيريّة، أقل دقة مما أرسلته نايتنغال، لكنه كان واضحاً تماماً أنه من سكاراب. لم يكن ما أرسلته قاسياً، لكنه كان خالياً من الرحمة. وفهم أكيفا أنه لم يكن هناك مكان للشفقة في عالمها، ليس بالنسبة إليها. إنها ملكة شعب مستعبد تحت عبء ثقيل إلى درجة أن استمرارية الكون بأكملها تعتمد عليهم. لم تستطع أن تتردد، ولم تفعل ذلك أبداً.

إن في هذا قوة، لا قسوة. رسالتها الأثيرية كان صورة: خيط متألق يُمسك بين إصبعين، ومعها جاء الفهم أن هذا الخيط كان حياة أكيفا، وأن الأصابع كانت أصابعها، وأنها تستطيع إنهاءه بسهولة كما يمكنها أن تكسره.

ولن تتردد بفعل هذا. لكنه شعر بشيء آخر في الإرسال وأثار دهشته. إنه من الأسهل للجميع، والأكثر أماناً لها، أن تقتله الآن. وإنما لم يكن الأمر فقط أكثر سهولة أو أماناً. بل هناك شيء آخر، غامض، لم يستطع أكيفا أن يفهمه تماماً، يكمن هناك في صورة الخيط اللامع. وتر قيثارة.

كانت سكاراب ونايتنغال قد تناقشتا بشأنه في وقت سابق، وشعر أكيفا أن الملكة ستكسب شيئاً بطريقة ما إذا قتلته. لكنها لم تكن تريد ذلك."إذاً؟" سألت. والخيار بدا واضحاً. الحياة أولاً. عليك أن تكون حياً، في النهاية، لتتمكن من فهم كل شيء آخر.

قال أكيفا:"حسناً. سآتي معكما. "وبالطبع، لأن إيلاي كانت تسير هنا—— الإلهة الشبح التي طعنت الشمس، والتي خانت عشاقاً أكثر مما ساعدت—— خطت كارو إلى الكهف في تلك اللحظة بالضبط، وسمعته.

85

نهاية

"أكيفا؟".

لم تفهم كارو ما الذي يدور أمامها. أمنيتها البسيطة في إيجاد أكيفا قد تحققت. بمجرد أن اختفى الغاڤرييل في كفها، عرفت مكانه: قريب لكنه مخبأ في زاوية عميقة وغير معروفة من كهوف الكيرين. قادتهم أمنية الغاڤرييل إلى هناك، عبر العديد من المنعطفات، حتى وصلوا أخيراً إلى هذا الركن ليجدوا... أكيفا على ركبتيه.

كان هناك خمسة آخرون، غرباء ذوو شعر أسود، وسمعت ما قاله لهم، لكنه لم يكن منطقياً. لم تركض نحوه. لم تركض ولم تلمس قدماها الحجر، لكنها صارت بقربه في ثانية واحدة، تسحبه من أجل الوقوف بجانبها وتنظر إليه، إلى داخله. تغمره بحضورها، وتعرف. على الفور.

هذه هي النهاية.

بدا لها كنار خمدت، وكل شيء قد ضاع وأصبح فارغاً.

"أنا آسف"، قال، ولم تستطع أن تدرك ما الذي حدث خلال ساعات قليلة ليصل إلى هذه الحالة.

أين تلك النظرة المليئة بالحياة، وأين الضحك، وأين المزاح، وأين الرقص، وأين الجوع؟ ما الذي فعلوه به؟

استدارت نحو الغرباء، وهناك رأت أعينهم.

أوه.

"ما هذا؟" سألت، وشعرت على الفور بالخوف من سماع الإجابة. لكنها انتظرتها، رغم ذلك. الإجابة جاءت بطيئة، أو ربما كانت تدرك الزمن بشكل خاطئ مرة أخرى، وعندها أخذها أكيڤا بين ذراعيه وقبّل قمة رأسها قبلة طويلة، متأنية.

بالنسبة إلى القبلات، ربما كانت تلك القبلة جيدة، لو أنها وقعت على شفتيها. أما بالنسبة إلى الإجابات، فإنها سيئة للغاية. إنها وداع، بكل ما تحمله الكلمة من معنى. شعرت بذلك في صلابة ذراعيه، في ارتجاف فكه، وفي الهزيمة التي استقرت على كتفيه.

ابتعدت عنه، خارجة من تحت ضغط شفتيه التي حملت طعم الوداع. سألته:"ما الذي تفعله؟". ثم تذكرت متأخرة ما كانت قد سمعته منه في البداية."إلى أين ستذهب؟".

"عليّ أن أذهب معهم".

تراجعت كارو خطوة إلى الخلف، وألقت نظرة أخرى على هؤلاء الذين قصدهم بـ"هم". شعب أكيڤا، الستيليون.

كانت تعلم أنه لم يلتقِ بأحد منهم من قبل، ولم تستطع أن تخمن ما الذي يعنيه وجودهم هنا الآن. تلك المرأة الأكبر سناً بالقرب منه، وهي جميلة للغاية، أما المرأة الأصغر هي التي لم تستطع كارو أن تبعد عينيها عنها.

ربما كان ذلك لأن في داخلها فنانة. أحياناً، ونادراً، ترى شخصاً لا يشبه أي أحد آخر، حتى ولو قليلاً، شخصاً لا يمكن أن يُخطئه أحد أو ينساه. وهذا ما كانت عليه هذه السيرافيم.

لم يكن الأمر حتى متعلقاً بالجمال—ليس لأنها لم تكن جميلة، بل لأن جمالها حاد ومظلم. لكنها فريدة. زواياها الحادة، صرامتها، وقفتها الملكية التي عبرت عنها أكثر من الكلام.

ها هي، فكرت كارو، بشيء من الحسد، إنها امرأة تعرف تماماً نفسها منذ يوم ولادتها. وها هي على وشك أن تأخذ أكيفا معها.

ومع ذلك، ومهما يكن، لم تتساءل كارو أو تخشَ للحظة أن أكيفا سيتركها بإرادته. شعرت بحضور أصدقائها ورفاقها يملؤون الفراغ خلفها. كانوا جميعاً هنا: إيسا، ليراز، زيري، زوزانا، ميك، حتى إليزا. بالإضافة إلى عشرين من غير الشرعيين وأكثر من أربعين كيميرا، جميعهم مستعدون للقتال من أجل أكيفا عندما وجدوه.

فقط لأنهم وجدوه عاجزاً عن القتال.

قال لهم:"عليّ أن أذهب".

لكن ليراز هي من ردّت."لا"، قالت، بأسلوبها الذي يشبه إلقاء الحقيقة كأمر واقع والوقوف فوقها كلبؤة تحرس فريستها." لا لن تفعل."

ثم سحبت سيفها وواجهت الستيليين."لير، لا". رفع أكيفا يديه، متوسلاً."رجاءً. أعيدي السيف. لا يمكنكِ هزيمتهم."

نظرت إليه وكأنها لم تعد تعرفه.

قال أكيفا:"أنتم لا تفهمون. كانوا هم في المعركة".

نظر إلى الستيليين، مركّزاً على المرأة الأكبر سنّا."أليس كذلك؟ أنتم قاتلتم أعداءنا عوضاً عنّا".

هزّت المرأة رأسها."لا. لم نفعل"، قالت، فارتسمت الحيرة على وجه أكيفا. ثم أضافت، مشيرةً إلى الشابة الشرسة التي تقف بجانبها "سكاراب فعلت".

والتزم الجميع الصمت، بعد أن تذكروا الطريقة التي سقط بها أعداؤهم كأنهم فارقوا الحياة فجأة، يهؤون من السماء بلا حول أو قوة. امرأة واحدة!

امرأة واحدة فعلت ذلك!

أعادت ليراز سيفها إلى غمده ببطء.

همست كارو:"أرجوك أخبرني ما الذي يحدث".

وعندما التفت أكيڤا مرة أخرى إلى المرأة الأكبر سناً، شعرت لوهلة قصيرة وكأنه يتجاهل طلبها. لكنه كان في الواقع يوجه طلباً خاصاً.

سأل:"هل يمكنكِ، رجاءً؟".

لم تكن كارو تعرف ما الذي يعنيه بذلك، لكنها شعرت بشيء صامت يحدث بين المرأتين: جدال بلا كلمات. لاحقاً، ستفهم أنهما تناقشتا حول ما إذا كان ينبغي عليهما أن تخبراهم—أن ترسلا إليهم الإجابة على سؤالها—وأن نايتنغال قد انتصرت في هذا الجدال. لأن كارو، بعد ذلك، ستفهم كل شيء.

داخل عقلها—داخل عقولهم جميعاً—طفت تجربة من الإحساس والشعور صارت مكتملة إلى درجة أنها أشبه بالعيش فيها. تجرية لا ترغب كارو في أن تعيشها أبداً.

فهمت لماذا طلب أكيڤا من جدته أن تجيبهم أثيرياً، لأنه لا حقيقة تُروى بالكلمات يمكن أن تضاهي هذا.

لقد أحاطتها ودخلت إلى أعماقها: تاريخ من المآسي والرعب الذي لا يوصف، قاسٍ ومعقد ومع ذلك مُسلم إليهم ببساطة فائقة. تم نقله إلى عقلها، مضغوطاً ودقيقاً، ككون محصور في لؤلؤة. أو مثل ذكريات مضغوطة في عظمة أمنيات، فكرت كارو. لكن هذا التاريخ كان أعمق وأكثر رعباً بكثير من تاريخها الخاص. إنه أشبه بحلم... كابوسي.

وأخيراً، فهمت ما حدث لأكيڤا منذ أن رأته آخر مرة، لأنها الآن أصبحت مثله: ناراً خامدة، وكل شيء فيها مفقود وفارغ.

كيف يمكن للمرء أن يستوعب شيئاً بهذا الحجم وبهذا القبح؟ لقد وجدت كارو الجواب.

تقفين هناك، تلهثين، وتتساءلين كيف سمحت لنفسك يوماً أن تتخيلي نهاية سعيدة.

لحظة طويلة مرت دون أن يتحدث أحد. بدا رعبهم ملموساً، وأنفاسهم أعلى مما ينبغي. كان هناك، للحظات قصيرة في إرسال نايتنغال، شعور بوزن هائل وجوع وحشي مرتجف. والآن، بعدما عرفوه، لن يستطيع أي منهم أن ينسى أبداً: ضغط النيثيلام على غلاف عالمهم.

كانت كارو تقف على بعد خطوة واحدة فقط من أكيڤا، لكن شعرت وكأن بينهما هوّة، بالفعل. كان دوره في القصة قد تجلى بوضوح خلال الرسائل الأثيرية، ولم يكن هناك مجال للشك: عليه أن يذهب.

إعادة تشكيل إمبراطورية كانت تبدو لهم يوماً أمراً ضخماً للغاية، لكنها الآن مجرد ملاحظة جانبية أمام سؤال بقاء إريتز. وأخذت كارو تترنح تحت وطأة الحقيقة.

نظر أكيڤا في عينيها، ورأت ما كان يود أن يسألها عنه لكنه لم يفعل، لأن مصيرها لم يكن مجرد تفصيل يُضاف إلى قصته. لا ليس بإمكانها الذهاب معه، فبدونها، لا يمكن أن يكون هناك إعادة إحياء لشعب الكيميرا.

كان هو من يفترض أن يبقى بجانبها ــ"كالتزام سابق"، كما قال لأورميرود ــ لكن الآن لم يعد يستطيع. وقصتهما، في النهاية، لن تكون قصة إريتز بأكملها: السيرافيم والكيميرا معاً، و"طريقة حياة مختلفة". بل كانت مجرد رفة جناح واحدة بين ملايين الرفرفات في عالم محاصر، ومرة أخرى، تفرقا بعيداً عن بعضهما.

قطعت ليراز الصمت أخيراً. "وماذا عن نجوم الآلهة؟" سألت، وكأنها تتوسل."في القصة، يحاربون الوحوش وينتصرون".

"لا توجد نجوم آلهة"، قالت سكاراب، ومع كلماتها جاء إرسال موجز وقاتم: سماء مشقوقة، وإدراك عميق بأنه لا يوجد شيء هناك في شاسع الكون يراقبهم، ولا مساعدة قادمة.

لآلاف الآلهة التي شُمّيت وعُبدت في ثلاثة عوالم وأكثر، هل جاءتهم المساعدة يوماً؟ قالت سكاراب بصوت يعكس قتامتها: "لم تكن هناك أبداً".

كانت تلك اللحظة الأسوأ، الأشد ظلمة على الإطلاق، وكارو ستتذكرها دائماً كأحلك الظلال—ذلك النوع من السواد الذي لا تستطيع الظلال أن تصل إليه إلا عندما تكون بجانب أكثر الأضواء سطوعاً.

لأن إرسالاً آخر جاءهم حينها.

شَقَّ طريقه عبر الإرسال السابق، كان مشرقاً وباهراً. مثل ضوء، متدفق وغامر. جيشٌ من الضوء. وكانت هناك أشكال محاطة به، ذهبية وكثيرة، وعرفت كارو من هم وما كانوا. عرفوا جميعاً، على الرغم من أن الظلال لم تتطابق مع الأسطورة. هذا هو منطق الأحلام، والمعرفة العميقة في القلب. هؤلاء، هم المحاربون المضيئون.

نجوم الآلهة.

رأت كارو رأس كاراب ينتفض إلى الأعلى، وكذلك رأس نايتنغال، وقرأت في ملامحهما الصدمة، وعرفت أن هذا الإرسال لم يكن من صنعهما، ولا من صنع بقية الستيليين أيضاً، الذين بدوا مذهولين تماماً مثل الآخرين.

إذاً، من أين جاء هذا؟

وفي هذا الوقت؟

كلمة واحدة، من خلف كارو، من داخل مجموعتها الخاصة، وصوت مألوف، لكنه كان غير متوقع إلى درجة أنها لم تستطع تحديده في البداية. اضطرت إلى الالتفاف لترى بعينيها، وأغمضت عينيها ثم فتحتهما مرة أخرى قبل أن تصدق ما رأته.

"الأشخاص المؤمنون بقدرهم لا يجب أن يضعوا خططاً"، هذا ما كانت ستقوله إليزا لاحقاً وهي تضحك. لكنها الآن قالت:"ليس هناك نجوم آلهة... بعد."

ولأنها كانت هي إليزا. تقدمت، مبتهجة وتكاد تشع. لقد نُسيت تقريباً وسط مخلوقات هذا العالم المتشابكة، وليس من المستغرب، أن أحداً لا يعرف ما هي حقاً.

كانت قد أخبرت ميك وزوزانا أنها فراشة، لكنهما لم يستطيعا استيعاب ما يعنيه ذلك—ولا تبعاته—ومع ذلك، كانت أكثر من ذلك بكثير. إنها صدى وأكثر من ذلك أيضاً. إنها الجواب.

الغموض يغني تحت جلدها؛ وهي مشبعة به مثل لؤلؤة سوداء. ليس هناك أي سيرافيم سوداء في هذا العصر الثاني؛ أولئك من تشافيسيري قد هلكوا مع ميليز، ولهذا كان الستيليون ينظرون إليها، مذهولين.

كانت نظراتها مثبتة على سكاراب، وسكاراب كانت تحدق بها بالمثل.

"من أنتِ؟" سألت الملكة، وقد بدأت صرامتها تتلاشى لتتحول إلى دهشة.

بعينين تلمعان بدعوة صامتة، أومأت إليزا برأسها، كأنها تدعو سكاراب لتعرفها—لتلمس خيط حياتها—وفعلت سكاراب، بإصبع واحدة من أنيمتها، لمسة خفيفة كالريشة، تتبعت مسار الخيط.

ارتجفت إليزا.

كان الإحساس جديداً عليها، وجعل القشعريرة تغطي جسدها. استطاعت أن تفكر أن الأمر بدا مضحكاً: أن يستجيب جسدها بطريقة عادية جداً مثل القشعريرة للمسة ملكة سيرافيم ذهبية تتبع خيط حياتها ذاته.

مهما كان ما قرأته سكاراب هناك، فقد رأى الجميع النار ترقص في عينيها، ثم أصبحت هي أيضاً مرحة.

لم يفهم أيٌّ منهم ما حدث حينها، باستثناء إليزا وسكاراب. حتى نايتنغال لم تفهم. لكن كل من كان حاضراً في كهوف الكيرين تلك الليلة—سواء كانوا سيرافيم، كيميرا، أو بشراً—قالوا بعد ذلك إنهم شعروا في تلك اللحظة بعصر مظلم يتلاشى بهدوء، وعصر مشرق يولد.

صارت النهاية تتداخل مع البداية، وصار الأمر مثيراً ومربكاً، بدائياً ومخيفاً، كهربائياً ولذيذاً.

كان الأمر أشبه بالوقوع في الحب.

خطت سكاراب خطوة إلى الأمام. طوال حياتها وهي تطاردها أنانكي، ذلك الإلحاح الذي لا يهدأ لقدرها. كان ذلك شعوراً خانقاً، وغامضاً في الوقت نفسه. سبب لها شكوكاً ومخاوف. لكن لم يسبق لها أن شعرت بذلك الإشباع المثالي، كقطعة أحجية وجدت مكانها الصحيح، هكذا تشعر الآن. لقد اكتملت. وأكثر من ذلك فقد تحققت.

الأنانكي. في حالة سكون. تحررها سكاراب منها أشبه بالصمت المفاجئ الذي يعقب صراخ طفل يصبح لا يُحتمل، ثم يتوقف فجأة.

وقفت أمام هذه المرأة—هذه السيرافيم التي جاءت من العدم، من السلالة الضائعة لتشافيسيري، أولئك الذين كانوا جميعاً مقدسين في أعين ميليز بوصفهم المختارين— وكل شكوك ومخاوف سكاراب قد تلاشت.

سألت:"كيف؟". كيف كان ممكناً؟ من أين جاءت إليزا؟ من أين جاء إرسالها، وماذا يعني؟

نظرت إليزا إلى كارو وأكيفا، ثم إلى زوزانا وميك، ثم إلى ڤيركو، الذي عرفت الآن أنه حملها على ظهره بعيداً عن القصبة، بعيداً عن العملاء الحكوميين ومن يدري ماذا أيضاً.

هؤلاء الخمسة أنقذوها. أنقذوها من العار والجنون، ومن حياة بلا مستقبل. بسببهم، هي الآن هنا، حيث كان ينبغي لها أن تكون، وأوه، أصبح لديها مستقبل الآن. أصبح لديهم جميعاً مستقبل، يا له من مستقبل.

ألقت نظرة على بقية المجموعة أيضاً، وشعرت بنفس الاكتمال الذي شعرت به سكاراب.

كان هذا صحيحاً. ومقدراً. وفي الوقت نفسه مستحيلاً وحتمياً، كما هو الحال مع جميع المعجزات.

"أعتقد أن الوقت قد حان"، كانت هذه إجابتها. قالتها بدهشة وكلماتها مشبعة بوزن القدر. حتى لو لم تفهم المجموعة ما الذي تعنيه، فقد شعروا بجلال اللحظة، وصمتوا.

حسناً، باستثناء زوزانا. كانت هي وميك متشبثين ببعضهما البعض، يشربان كل ما يجري بعيونهما وآذانهما، ويحاولان فهمه أيضاً—على الأقل الكلمات—لأن زوزانا قد دسّت أمانياً في جيبها في وقت سابق، عبارة عن لعنة على شرطة الأمنيات. وما إن وجدت نفسها في حضور الغرباء، حتى تلاشت على الفور اثنين من اللوكناوز، واحدة لنفسها والأخرى لميك، تمنح كلاهما لغة الملائكة.

لم تكن الأماني التي استعملتها زوزانا ذات فائدة كبيرة في تفسير ما يجري، لذا تجرأت وسألت:"اممم، وقت ماذا بالضبط؟".

تحركت موجة من المرح بينهم جميعاً—ومعها شعور بالارتياح، لأن أحداً قد تجرأ على التعبير عن السؤال الذي كان الجميع يريدون إجابته.

"حقاً، وقت ماذا؟".

قالت إليزا:"وقت التحرير. وقت الخلاص. وقت نجوم الآلهة."

"إنها مجرد أسطورة"، قالت سكاراب، مترددة لكنها مستعدة للاقتناع. مثل البقية، حيث تحتفظ في ذهنها بالرؤية التي جاءتها من إرسال إليزا، ولم تكن تعرف كيف تفهمها. لكنها تعلم فقط أنها تريد أن تصدقها.

"إنهم كذلك"، وافقت إليزا بابتسامة، والجميع يراقبها. الجميع يصغي إليها. كم كان غريباً أن تصبح هي مركز تلك اللحظة—هذه اللحظة العظيمة في قصة جميع عوالمهم.

قالت لهم:"فهم شعبي أن الزمن محيط، وليس نهراً. إنه لا يتدفق بعيداً ليفرغ نفسه وينتهي. إنه ببساطة موجود—أبدي وكامل. البشر قد يتحركون خلاله في اتجاه واحد، لكن ذلك ليس انعكاساً لطبيعته الحقيقية—بل فقط حدودنا نحن. الماضي والمستقبل هما من صُنعنا نحن."

"أما بالنسبة إلى الأساطير، فبعضها مختلق، مجرد خيال. لكن بعضها حقيقي. بعضها قد عاشه آخرون بالفعل. وفي جريان الزمن، الأبدي والكامل، بعضها لم يُعش بعد."

توقفت للحظة، تجمع الكلمات التي ستجعلهم يفهمون.

"بعض الأساطير هي نبوءة."

عرق من المحاربين المضيئين سمع عن النيثيلام، وسافر إلى عالمهم البعيد ليقاتلوهم. هؤلاء هم نجوم الآلهة، الذين جلبوا الضوء إلى الكون.

في خضم هذا كله، كانت كارو وأكيفا قد تجاوزا المسافة بينهما. وانتهيا متشبثين ببعضهما، ودهشتهما جعلت الكهف يدور حولهما.

لم يُنسَ وداعهما ولم يتم تجاهله. اختفى الخوف، لكن الحزن لم يختفِ. مهما حدث هنا الليلة، كان الفراق لا يزال بانتظارهما.

كانت لوراميندي تنتظر، كل تلك الأرواح الصامتة تحت الرماد. وكارو لا تزال الأمل الأخير للكيميرا، وأكيفا هو ما هو عليه—شيئاً لا يمكن قياسه وخطير. لكن كليهما قد رأى شيئاً في ذلك الإرسال الذهبي، والمستقبل الجديد الذي فتح أمامهما كان مهيباً بقدر ما كان مرعباً.

كان الأمر أيضاً، وبطريقة ما، مؤكداً على الفور. وكأن إرسال إليزا قد نسج نفسه في خيوط حياة الجميع وأصبح جزءاً منهم. لم يكن هناك مجال للتراجع عن هذا.

أمسك زيري بيد ليراز عندما اجتاحهم الإرسال الأول القاتم، وما زال يمسك بها. وكانت تلك هي المرة الأولى التي يمسك فيها أي منهما يد شخص آخر، وبالنسبة إليهما وحدهما، فإن عظمة ما تكشّف تلك الليلة طغى عليها جمال لا يُصدق: روعة الأصابع المتشابكة. وهذا هو ما خُلقت الأيدي من أجله دائماً، وليس لحمل الأسلحة.

لكن هذه الروعة ظلت مشوبة بالحزن، مع ازدياد فهمهما أنهما لم ينتهيا بعد من حمل الأسلحة.

ليس قريباً حتى.

إليزا كانت قديسة مبجلة، وكانت أيضاً من الفيريرا. الأمر الأول كان عظيماً، لأنها منحتهم هذا الإرسال الأثيري وكل ما يحمل من نبوءات، لكن الأمر الثاني أعظم، أنها قد حققت نبوءتها الخاصة.

الخرائط والذكريات حُفظت فيها. إلازيل من تشافيسيري، منذ زمن بعيد جداً، قد سافرت إلى ما وراء الحُجُب ورسمت خرائط العوالم هناك، وبسبب ما صنعه السحرة المغرورون من الاثني عشر، أصبحت تلك الخرائط الآن ملكاً لإليزا، وكذلك ذكريات أسلافها عن تلك الوحوش.

لا أحد على قيد الحياة قد رأى النيئيلام أو سافر في الأراضي التي دمرتها، لكن إليزا حملت كل ذلك بداخلها.

إذا كانت سكاراب ستواجه الكارثة، فإنها ستحتاج إلى دليل. وقد أصبحت كذلك الآن، وأصبح لديها واحد.

وأكثر من مجرد دليل. فالجميع شهد عليه. سكاراب وإليزا هما مصيراً محققاً، نصفان أصبحا كاملين منذ اللحظة التي وقع فيها بصر كل منهما على الآخر. حتى كارناسيال، ظل صامتاً طوال الوقت، تنازل عن آماله بهدوء كما احتفظ بها دائماً. أما بالنسبة إلى البقية، فقد رأوا جميعاً الظلال في الإرسال، وصدقوها بالطريقة التي تصدق بها الأحلام، دون تفكير أو شك.

قالت إليزا:"بعض الأساطير حقيقية. بعضها قد عشناه بالفعل. وبعضها لم يُعَش بعد في جريان الزمن، الأبدي والكامل."

وأدرك الباقون شيئين في آنٍ واحد: هوية المحاربين المضيئين، وما كانوا عليه.

كانت الـ"ماذا" بسيطة، لكنها لم تكن أقل عمقاً بسبب بساطتها. إنهم هم نجوم الآلهة، الذين لم يأتِ دورهم بعد في تدفق الزمن.

أما الـ"من"؟ فهي ظلال غارقة في الضوء، مهيبة، و... مألوفة.

رأوا أنفسهم، كل واحد منهم، من رأث، فتى الداشناغ الذي لم يعد فتى،

إلى ميك عازف الكمان القادم من العالم الآخر، وزوزانا صانعة الدمى. إلى أكيفا وليراز اللذين لن يتوقفا أبداً عن الحنين إلى وجود هازايل بينهم. إلى زيري من الكيرين، المحظوظ في النهاية، وحتى إلى إيسّا التي لم تكن يوماً محاربة. وإلى كارو.

كارو، التي بدأت هذه القصة في حياة سابقة على ساحة معركة، عندما ركعت بجانب ملاك يحتضر وابتسمت.

يمكنك تتبع خطٍ يبدأ من شاطئ بولفينش، مروراً بكل ما حدث منذ ذلك الحين—حيوات انتهت وبدأت، حروب كُسبت وخُسرت، حب وعظام أمنيات وغضب وندم وخداع ويأس، ودائماً، بطريقة ما، أمل—لينتهي هنا، في هذا الكهف في جبال أديلفاس، في هذه الصحبة.

القدر انحنى محيياً، كل هذا كان أنيقاً ومنظماً، لكنه لا يزال يسلب أنفاسهم وهم يسمعون سكاراب، ملكة الستيلييين وحافظة الكارثة، تقول، بحماس اهتزت له كل الأعمدة الفقرية، بما في ذلك عمودها هي:

"ستكون هناك نجوم آلهة، وسنكون نحن تلك النجوم".

86

خاتمة

كانت كارو تستيقظ في معظم الصباحات على صوت مطارق الحدادين، لتجد نفسها وحيدة في خيمتها. إيتّا وياسري تغادران بهدوء قبل بزوغ أول خيوط الضوء لمساعدة ڤوڤي وأوار في إعداد كميات هائلة من وجبات الإفطار التي تبدأ بها أيام المعسكر. أما هاكسايا، فقد كانت ترافق فريق الصيد، تختفي لأيام أثناء تتبع قطعان سكِلت على طول نهر إرلينغ، أما أين يقضي تانغريس وباشيز ليالِيهما، فلا أحد يعلم.

مع أول ضربة مطرقة على سندان آيجير—المنبّه اليومي لكارو—كانت فرقة التنقيب التي يقودها أمزالاغ قد انتهت من تناول إفطارها وانطلقت إلى الموقع، بينما تبدأ الفرق الأخرى بالتوجه نحو خيمة الطعام الجماعية.

إلى جانب الحدادين—الذين باتوا الآن يصنعون القوارير بدلاً من الأسلحة—كان هناك صيادون، وحمّالون للمياه، ومزارعون. تم بناء القوارب وتحضيرها، ونسجت الشباك. وحتى بعض المحاصيل الصيفية المتأخرة قد زُرعت في أراضٍ خصبة على بُعد أميال قليلة، رغم أن الجميع توقعوا شتاءً قاسياً يفترسه الجوع، بعد عام من تدمير الصوامع وحرق الحقول.

لكن الأفواه الجائعة أصبحت أقل. إنها حقيقة مؤلمة، وليست بشارة. هذه الحقيقة، رغم قسوتها، ستساعدهم على الاستمرار.

أما البقية، فقد انشغلوا بالمدينة.

ما تبقى من العظام بعد الحرق تم دفنه أولاً، ولم يكن هناك شيء يُمكن إنقاذه من الرماد. في النهاية، ستبدأ عملية البناء، لكن الآن عليهم تطهير الأنقاض وسحب القضبان الحديدية المدمرة التي كانت تشكل القفص العظيم. كانوا لا يزالون يبحثون عن عدد كافٍ من الحيوانات القوية لإنجاز هذه المهمة، ولم يكن لديهم فكرة عما سيفعلونه بكل الحديد بعد إيجاد الوسائل اللازمة لنقله.

بعضهم رأى أن لوراميندي الجديدة يجب أن تُبنى تحت قفص كما كانت القديمة، وفهمت كارو أن الوقت ما زال مبكر جداً على الكيميرا ليشعروا بالأمان تحت سماء مكشوفة. لكنها كانت تأمل أنه بحلول الوقت الذي سيُتخذ فيه هذا القرار، قد يختارون بناء مدينة تستحق مستقبلاً المزيد من الإشراق.

قد تصبح لوراميندي جميلة يوماً ما.

"أحضِرا معكما مهندساً معمارياً عند عودتكما"، قالت كارو لميك وزوزانا، بنبرة نصف مازحة، عندما انطلقا إلى الأرض على ظهر صياد العواصف، الذي أطلقا عليه اسم ساموراي. كانت رحلتهما أساساً من أجل الأسنان، إلى جانب الشوكولاتة—بحسب زوزانا—وأيضاً للاطلاع على حال عالمهما بعد تشريف جايل. كارو لا زالت تفتقدهما.

لكن بدون زوزانا التي تشتت أفكارها، فكارو كانت دائماً على بعد خطوة واحدة من الغرق في مستنقع الشفقة على الذات أو مرارة الذكريات. رغم أنها لم تكن وحيدة تماماً—وعلى بعد مليون ميل من أوقات الوحدة التي عانتها في الأيام الأولى للتمرد، عندما قادهم الذئب نحو الدماء، وقضت أيامها تحيي الجنود لبدء حرب—إلا أن الوحدة التي تعرفها الآن أشبه بغطاء

من الضباب: لا شمس، لا أفق، مجرد برودة زاحفة مستمرة، لا فكاك منها إلا في الأحلام.

في بعض الصباحات، عند استيقاظ كارو على صوت أول ضربة مطرقة، كانت تشعر وكأنها تهوي من عالم ذهبي حلو، يفقد كل تفاصيله مع تدفق الوعي—مثل رؤية تغشاها الدموع. لم يكن يتبقى لها سوى إحساس فقط؛ إحساس بدا وكأنه انطباع روح، كما يحدث لها عندما تفتح مبخرة أرواح أو عندما تحفظ الأرواح من الموتى.

ورغم أنها لم تشعر بروحه أبداً—لأنه لحسن الحظ لم يمت أبداً—ظل الإحساس يغمرها بالدفء، كأنها تقف تحت الشمس: دفء ونور، وشعور بحضور أكيفا قوي جداً إلى درجة أنها تكاد تشعر بيده تلامس قلبها، ويدها تلامس قلبه.

هذا الصباح بدا إحساسها أقوى من المعتاد. بقيت مستلقية، ودفء خفي لا يزال عالقاً على صدرها وكفها. لم ترغب في فتح عينيها، بل في أن ترتفع مجدداً إلى ذلك العالم الذهبي وتجد أكيفا هناك، وتبقى معه.

تنهدت وهي تتذكر أغنية سخيفة من الأرض تقول إنه إذا أردت أن تتذكر أحلامك، فعليك فور استيقاظك أن تناديها وكأنها هررة صغيرة. الأغنية بأكملها كانت تقريباً تردد:"تعالوا هنا بيس بيس بيس بيس بيس..."، ولطالما جعلتها هذه الأغنية تبتسم. لكن الآن، أصبحت الابتسامة أقرب إلى الالتفاف مرير، لأنها كانت تتمنى حقاً أن تنجح الطريقة، لكنها لم تكن تعمل

ثم، عند مدخل خيمتها، جاء صوتٌ ناعم يزيل الحرج:"كارو؟".

كان الصوت منخفضاً بما يكفي كي لا يوقظها إن كانت لا تزال نائمة. وعندما رأت الشخص الذي وقف عند فتحة الخيمة، وخيوط الفجر تلقي بنفسها على طول ذراعه القوية كأنها ورق ذهبي على لوحة مذبح، انتفضت فجأة وكأنها زنبرك تحرر من مكانه. ألقت الغطاء جانباً، ونهضت على ركبتيها قبل أن تدرك خطأها.

لقد كان كارناسيال.

لم تستطع إخفاء ألمها. وقد رفعت يديها لتغطي وجهها. "أنا آسفة"، قالت بعد لحظة، وهي تدفع كل ما تشعر به إلى أعماقها، كما تفعل كل صباح، لتتمكن من مواصلة يومها.

أنزلت يديها، وابتسمت لساحر ستيلي قائلة: "ليس سيئاً أن أراك حقاً".

"لا بأس". دخل كارناسيال إلى الخيمة. لاحظت كارو أنه جلب معه الشاي وحصتها الصباحية من الخبز، كي يتمكنا من الانطلاق فوراً إلى موقع العمل. قال وهو يبتسم: "من الجيد أن أعرف كيف يبدو الأمر عندما يكون أحدهم سعيداً برؤيتك. رغم أنني لا أظن أن معظم الناس يحصلون على رد فعل كهذا. أنا لم أحظ به أبداً، لكن الآن، سأبقى متأملاً في ذلك طوال حياتي."

"ربما تكون لعنة، على أية حال"، قالت كارو وهي تأخذ الشاي منه.

كانت تعرف أن كارناسيال قد شارك الملكة شيئاً ما في الماضي، وأن ذلك انتهى الآن. كانت تظن أن هذا هو السبب الذي دفعه للتطوع للقدوم إلى لوراميندي بدلاً من العودة إلى الجزر البعيدة مع الآخرين. أضافت، "أو ربما يكون مثل السكوهل"؛ ذلك النبات الجبلي الذي كانوا يحرقون صمغه ذو الرائحة الكريهة على مشاعلهم عند الكهوف. "ولا ينمو إلا في أسوأ الظروف". لن تجد السكوهل في مرج مشمس مبهج، بل فقط على جرف صخري متجمد، مغطى بالجليد. ربما كان الحب الذي يحطم القلوب مشابهاً له، ولا ينمو إلا في بيئة غير ودية.

هز كارناسيال رأسه. لم يكن يشبه أكيڤا كثيراً حقاً، لأن أكيڤا كان الستيلي الوحيد المعروف في هذا الجزء من العالم.

"لقد فعل الشيء نفسه، كما تعلمين"، قال لها بنبرة تجمع بين الذكرى والتأمل. "أول مرة رأيناه فيها حين جئنا لنقتله. وكان ذلك على وشك الحدوث، لو لم نتبين من يكون". توقف لحظة، وكأنما استعاد تفاصيل تلك اللحظة

في ذهنه، ثم أضاف:"أطلقت سكاراب صوتاً خافتاً، فاستدار وحدّق باتجاه المكان الذي كانت تختبئ فيه تحت تأثير السحر. وابتسم... كأن الفرح ذاته قد غمره فجأة وسط الظلام. لأنه ظن أنها أنتِ".

ارتعشت يد كارو وهي تحمل كوب الشاي، فثبتته باليد الأخرى، ولكن دون جدوى تُذكر."متى عدت؟" سألت لتغير الموضوع. كان قد ذهب إلى أستراي ممثلاً لمحكمة الستيليبين. ليراز وزيري ذهبا أيضاً للقاء إليون وباليروس ومناقشة خطط الشتاء القادم.

قال كارناسيال:"البارحة ليلاً. بعض من جماعتكم عادوا معنا. إكساندر غاضب جداً لأنه، حسب كلماته، فاتته الفرصة ليصبح مقدساً."

مقدساً. أو نجم مقدس.

كان هناك الكثير من النقاش حول ما يعنيه ذلك منذ ليلة رسالة إليزا، لكنهم، في الغالب، اتفقوا على أنهم لن يصبحوا"آلهة" بأي تفسير معقول. ومع ذلك، كانت هناك وحدة غير عادية وجدية بينهم في تقبل مصيرهم. كانوا سيلعبون دوراً في تحقيق الأسطورة. ربما كانت أسطورة للسيرافيم من قبل، لكنها الآن أصبحت ملكاً للجميع. الفاني وغير الفاني لم يعد ذا أهمية. كانت الحرب تلوح في الأفق، حرب ذات نطاق ملحمي يجعل الركب ترتجف والعقول تذبل، وحدهم المحاربون المشرقون هم من سيبددون الظلام.

قالت زوزانا:"سأفترض أنني مقدسة بكل بساطة. يمكنكم أن تصدقوا ما تريدون".

كانت كارو تستمتع بفكرة أنك"يمكنك أن تصدق ما تريد"، وكأن الواقع مجرد بوفيه مفتوح. يا ليت الأمر كان كذلك.

ثلاثة أضعاف الحصص من الكعكة، لو سمحت.

واصل كارناسيال الحديث عن إكساندر."يقول إنه من حقه أن يكون أحد النجوم المقدسة، لأنه أراد العودة إلى كهوف الكيرين معكِ، لكن تم إرساله

إلى أستراي بدلاً من ذلك. كنت أخشى أن يتحداني ليأخذ مكاني". ابتسم وهو يتحدث.

وجدت الابتسامة طريقها إلى شفتي كارو، وهي تتخيل الجندي الضخم، الشبيه بالدبة، يجادل القدر بحثاً عن ثغرات. قالت:"من يدري. ليس وكأننا تمكنا من تجميد إرسالات إليزا وعمل قائمة بالأسماء". لم يكن بإمكانهم مشاهدة الرسالة مرة أخرى، لأن إليزا كانت قد ذهبت إلى الجزر البعيدة مع الستيليين وأكيڤا."ربما رأى كلٌّ منا ما أراد أن يراه."

"ربما"، قال كارناسيال موافقاً."لكنني رأيتكِ."

لم تستطع كارو الرد بالمثل. لم تره في تلك الرؤية. ما رأته كان نفسها، متوهجة وسط إشعاع ذلك المشهد، ورأت أكيڤا إلى جانبها. المشهد بالنسبة إليها أشبه بعوامة الإنقاذ، وظلت متمسكة به.

كانت تؤمن بأن الوقت سيأتي حين تتحرر من واجباتها لتكون معه—أو على الأقل وقت يتمكنان فيه من تطويع التزاماتهما وتنسيقها معاً. إذا كانا محكومين بأن يظلا عبدين للقدر إلى الأبد، ألا يمكنهما على الأقل أن يكونا عبدين للقدر على نفس القارة؟ وربما تحت نفس السقف؟ يوماً ما.

وتأمل أن يتم ذلك قبل أن تستدعيهم حرب سكاراب جميعاً لمواجهة النيثيلام. ومتى سيكون ذلك؟ ليس في القريب المنظور. فهذه ليست مواجهة يمكن اختصارها. الفكرة نفسها قوبلت بمعارضة عنيفة عندما عاد الستيليون إلى موطنهم، وفقاً لما نقله كارناسيال، الذي كان يتلقى رسائل من قومه.

المعارضة لم تكن شاملة. وعلى ما يبدو هناك الكثيرون ممن وقفوا مع ملكتهم، يأملون في مستقبل خالٍ من واجبات تجاه الحجب.

"هل سمعت أخباراً من الوطن؟" سمحت كارو لنفسها أن تسأل. كانت هناك بعض الرسائل من أكيڤا، وكانت تأمل أن يجلب اليوم لها رسالة أخرى أوماً كارناسيال."وصلتني رسالة قبل ليلتين. الجميع بخير."

"الجميع بخير؟" كررت، متمنية لو كانت تمتلك مهارة زوزانا في رفع حاجبها لتُظهر بالضبط ما تعنيه بهذا الرد."هل هذا كل شيء فعلاً؟".

"أكثر من بخير، إذاً"، قال وهو يتراجع قليلاً."الملكة في المنزل، غلاف الحجب يلتئم، واقترب موسم الأحلام."

كانت كارو تدرك أن الحجب تلتئم لأن أكيفا لم يعد يستنزفها، وأن الاستقرار الطبيعي بدأ يعود تدريجياً، لكنها لم تكن تعرف ما هو موسم الأحلام. فسألت.

"إنه... وقت جميل من السنة"، أجاب كارناسيال بصوت خشن، وأشاح بنظره بعيداً.

"آه"، قالت كارو، ولم تكن تفهم بعد."ما الجميل فيه؟".

ظل صوته خشناً وهو يجيب:"هذا يعتمد بالكامل على من تشاركينه". وهذه المرة، كانت كارو هي من أشاحت بنظرها بعيداً.

آه.

ارتدت حذاءها وربطت شعرها بشريط قماشي مزقته من إحدى قمصانها الاثنتين. فخامة. أحضري لي أربطة مطاطية، فكرت، متمنية لو كانت تملك قدرة التخاطر مثل زوزانا.

كانت قد ارتدت ملابسها بالفعل. هذه الحياة لا تصلح لملابس النوم، رغم أنها لا تملك ملابس نوم. كانت تتناوب بين طقمين من الملابس، تنام وتستيقظ في نفس الطقم حتى يفشل في اجتياز"اختبار الشم"—رغم أنه، بصراحة تجاوز بعض الاختبارات هذه الأيام. يبدو الأمر مضحكاً قليلاً أن تتخيل المتجر في روما الذي اشترت منه مساعدة التسوق لدى إستر هذه الملابس، وتحت أي ظروف وجد القميص طريقه إلى يوم عادي.

ربما كانت فتاة ترتديه فتاة إيطالية بينما تقود دراجة نارية صغيرة، وذراعا شاب تلفان خصرها بخفة. امنحيها قصة شعر على طراز أودري هيبورن، لمَ لا؟ أحلام اليقظة في روما تستحق قصات أودري هيبورن. شيء واحد كان

مؤكداً: قد يكون قميص تلك الفتاة المتخيلة شبيهاً تماماً بقميص كارو، لكنه الآن لم يعد يشبه بأي حال القطعة التي ترتديها كارو: ذلك القميص الملطخ برماد الأيام، والخشن بفعل مياه الأنهار، والباهت تحت وهج الشمس، والمتيبّس من كثرة العرق. "حسناً"، قالت وهي تنهي شايها وتأخذ الخبز من كارناسيال لتأكله في الطريق. "أخبرني بما يحدث في أستراي." وقد أخبرها بالفعل.

الهواء الصباحي منعش حولهما، وأصوات الضحك تنبعث من المعسكر الذي بدأ يستيقظ—حتى ضحكات الأطفال، لأن اللاجئين بدأوا يجدون طريقهم إلى هنا. وفي هذا الوقت من اليوم، عندما كانت الأرض مغمورة بتلك الألوان الخفيفة التي تشبه الحلوى عند الفجر، لم يكن بإمكانك أن ترى بوضوح أن التلال البعيدة شاحبة وميتة.

تمكنت كارو من رؤية كل شيء وصولاً إلى التلال حيث كان معبد إيلاي ينتصب، وقد أصبح الآن أطلالاً سوداء، رغم أنها لم تستطع رؤية تفاصيل الخراب بوضوح.

كانت هناك لتستعيد المبخرة الخاصة بروح ياسري. ذهبت بمفردها، متأهبة لمواجهة ألم الذكريات التي تنهشها حتى العظم، ذكريات ذلك الشهر المليء بأعذب الليالي. لكنها، حين وصلت، وجدت المكان بالكاد يشبه ما كان عليه. بستان الريكويم، الذي قد استعاد شيئاً من حيويته بعد أن أضرم فيه ثياغو النيران قبل ثمانية عشر عاماً، قد التهمته ألسنة اللهب مرة أخرى العام الماضي، كما حدث مع كل شيء آخر.

لا ظلال لأشجار عتيقة، ولا أثر لطيور الأفانجيلين—تلك الطيور-الأفاعي التي كان صوت هسيسها يرافق شهر الحب ذاك، وصراخها المحترق يشير إلى نهايته.

لكن، لم تكن هذه هي النهاية، أليس كذلك؟ كُتبت فصول أخرى منذ ذلك الحين، وستُكتب فصول جديدة. وكارو لم تعد تعتقد، في نهاية المطاف،

أن هذه الفصول ستكون مملة، كما تمنت ذات ليلة في معسكر الدومينيون مع أكيفا. ليس مع وجود النيثيلام في الخارج، وملكة جريئة تمسك بمصير العالم من عنقه.

صعدت كارو وكارناسيال التلة التي كانت تخفي المدينة المدمرة عن أنظار المعسكر. وهناك، ظهرت أمامهما. لم تكن كما كانت عندما جاءت كارو من الأرض قبل شهور، لتجدها جرداء، خالية من أي حياة، بلا أرواح تحس بوجودها، وبلا أمل. كانت قضبان القفص لا تزال كما تركتها حينها، وكأنها عظام وحش هائل ميت. لكن هذه المرة، كانت هناك حركة أسفلها. فرق من الثيران-الحشرية متعددة الأرجل، المعروفة بالميريا-أوكس، تجر الكتل الحجرية السوداء التي كانت ذات يوم أسواراً وأبراجاً لقلعة سوداء ضخمة.

لكن تحت كل هذا، عرفت كارو أن هناك جمالاً مدفوناً.

كاتدرائية بريمستون تلك، أعجوبة من عجائب العالم، كهف من الروعة والجلال، إلى درجة أنه كان نصف السبب الذي دفعه هو وسيد الحرب لاختيار هذا المكان لبناء مدينتهما قبل ألف عام. الآن، أصبحت مقبرة جماعية. لكن، منذ اللحظة التي اكتشفت فيها كارو ما فعله شعب لوراميندي في نهاية الحصار، لم تفكر فيها كمقبرة. بل كما أرادها بريمستون وسيد الحرب: حاوية أرواح... وحلم.

كانت تقضي أيامها هنا، تساهم في التنقيب، ولكن في الغالب تجوب الأرض الميتة، تترقب بأحاسيسها الدقيقة أي لمسة خفيفة تشير إلى وجود أرواح دفينة، منتظرة اللحظة التي يتحرك فيها الركام ليكشف عن شق يؤدي إلى ما تحت أقدامهم. لم يكن أحد غيرها يشعر بالأرواح؛ فقط هي. لم تشعر بها بعد، لكنها كانت واثقة أنها ستشعر بها قريباً، وستجمعها كلها، ولن تدع واحدة تفلت من بين أصابعها. وماذا بعد؟

ماذا بعد؟

تنفست كارو بعمق ورفعت نظرها. ستكون السماء زرقاء اليوم. الكيميرا والسيرافيم سيعملون تحتها جنباً إلى جنب. الأخبار تنتشر في الجنوب بأن لوراميندي تُبنى من جديد، وكل يوم يصل المزيد من اللاجئين إليهم. قريباً، سيأتي العبيد المحررون من الشمال، معظمهم وُلد هناك، وعاش في العبودية. في أسترا أيضاً، كان الكيميرا والسيرافيم يعملون معاً، ولكن عملهم أصعب من مجرد حمل الحجارة. كانوا يُعيدون بناء إمبراطورية.

يا له من مشهد. في الجهة الأخرى من العالم، حيث تنتشر مئات الجزر الخضراء عبر البحر بتكوينات غريبة، تبدو أشبه بقمم ثعابين البحر أكثر من كونها أرضاً مأهولة، كان شعب ذو عيون متوهجة يستعد لموسم أكثر عذوبة.

حسناً، افترضت كارو أنهم يستحقون ذلك. باتت الآن تفهم طبيعة العمل الذي يشكّل حياتهم، وما الذي يقدّمونه من أنفسهم للحجاب الذي يُبقي إريتز متماسكة. لم تكن تعلم لماذا يُطلقون على ذلك الموسم اسم"موسم الحلم"، لكنها أغمضت عينيها وتخيلت للحظة أنها تستطيع لقاء أكيفا هناك، إن لم يكن في أي مكان آخر، في ذلك المكان الذهبي داخل أحلامها، لتشاركه إياه.

…

لم يكن أكيفا يعلم إذا كانت رسائله تصل إلى كارو أم لا، لكنه استمر في المحاولة مع مرور الأسابيع التي تحوّلت إلى شهور. كانت نايتنغال قد حذرته من أن المسافة الشاسعة تتطلب مستوى من الدقة لن يصل إليه إلا بعد سنوات. كانت هي ترسل بعض الرسائل نيابة عنه، لكنه كان يجد صعوبة في صياغة ما يود قوله بالكلمات. ما كان يرغب حقاً في إرساله هو المشاعر، على الرغم من أنه قيل له إن إرسال المشاعر مهارة تتطلب مستوى متقدماً جداً من التخاطر، ولا ينبغي أن يتوقع النجاح فيها بعد.

كانت الجزر البعيدة متناثرة حول خط الاستواء، لذا فإن الشمس تغرب فيها في وقت مبكر من المساء، وفي نفس الساعة على مدار العام. وأكيفا في ذاك الوقت من الشفق يأخذ بعض اللحظات لنفسه يومياً في محاولة لإرسال رسالة إلى كارو. بالنسبة إليها، في الجهة الأخرى من العالم، كان ذلك التوقيت قبيل الفجر مباشرة، وأحبّ فكرة أنه، بطريقة ما، يستيقظ معها، حتى لو لم يكن بإمكانه أن يختبر ذلك بنفسه.

يوماً ما.

"ظننتُ أنني سأجدكَ هنا".

استدار أكيفا. كان قد صعد إلى المعبد الموجود أعلى الجزيرة، كما يفعل في معظم الأمسيات، بحثاً عن العزلة. مائة وأربعة وثلاثون يوماً مضت، ولم يصادف أحداً في هذا المكان سوى الشيوخ المسنين الذين يعتنون باللهب الأبدي. كان هذا اللهب يكرّم نجوم الآلهة، ورفض الشيوخ الاعتراف بأن آلهتهم لم تكن موجودة. لم تحاول سكاراب إثارة الأمر، واستمر اللهب في الاشتعال.

لكن هذه المرة، كانت أخته ميليل هي من وجدها هنا. كانت تلك التي عثر عليها مسجونة في الجزيرة عندما وصل إليها. تم تحريرها هي وبقية فريقها في ذلك اليوم، إلى جانب عدد من جنود ومبعوثي جورام الذين كانوا محتجزين في حبس منفصل. أُتيحت للجميع فرصة البقاء أو المغادرة، لكن غير الشرعيين، الذين لم تكن لديهم عائلات يعودون إليها، فقد اختاروا البقاء... على الأقل في الوقت الحالي.

بعضهم، ومن بينهم ياف، الأصغر سناً، كان لديهم دافع قوي للبقاء بسبب"موسم الحلم"، الذي كان على وشك الانتهاء، وربما سيشهد إدخال العيون الزرقاء إلى سلالة الدم الستيلية. أما ميليل، فقد زعمت أن سبب بقائها كان النيثيلام، وأنها أرادت أن تكون حيث ستبدأ الحرب القادمة. لكن أكيفا لاحظ أن مظهر ميليل بدا أقل عدائية مع مرور الأيام، ولاحظ

أنها أصبحت تقضي وقتاً أطول في الغناء بدلاً من التدريب. لطالما امتلكت صوتاً جميلاً، والآن بدأت لكنتها تلين لتقترب من طريقة حديث الستيلييين، وكانت تتعلم أغاني قديمة من ميليز، تلك الأغاني التي تحمل سحراً في طياتها.

حيّاها من دون أن يسألها عن سبب بحثها عنه. كان من المقرر أن يلتقيا على العشاء بعد ساعة، لذا افترض أنها جاءت إليه الآن لأنها أرادت التحدث على انفراد. ومع ذلك، لم تشرع في الحديث مباشرة، وكأنها كانت تنتظر اللحظة المناسبة.

"أي جزيرة هي؟" سألته وهي تقف بجانبه، تنظر معه إلى المشهد الممتد أمامهما. في الأيام الصافية، يمكن رؤية ما يقارب مائتي جزيرة من هذا الارتفاع. حوالي تسعين بالمائة منها كانت غير مأهولة، وربما بالكاد صالحة للسكن. كان أكيڤا قد اختار واحدة منها لنفسه. ولكارو أيضاً، على الرغم من أنه لم ينطق بذلك أبداً. أشار إلى مجموعة من الجزر غرباً، حيث كانت الشمس تغرب خلفها.

قال:"الجزيرة الصغيرة التي تبدو كأنها سلحفاة"، فأصدرت ميليل صوتاً وكأنها تعرفت عليها، رغم أنه شك في ذلك. لم تكن واحدة من الجزر ذات التضاريس الحادة الناتئة من الحمم القديمة، ولم تكن واحدة من الكالديرات ذات البحيرات الخفية المثالية.

سألته ميليل:"هل توجد فيها مياه عذبة؟".

أجاب:"حين تمطر"، فضحكت. كان المطر في هذا الموسم غزيراً— يتساقط كل بضع ساعات على شكل زخات قصيرة لكنها غزيرة بشكل لا يصدق، لم يسبق لها مثيل في الشمال.

يرتفع منسوب الشلالات التي تنحدر من هذا الجبل بسرعة، وتتحول من زرقاء إلى بنية خلال دقائق معدودة، ثم تعود إلى طبيعتها تقريباً بنفس السرعة. كان الهواء ثقيلاً، وكانت السحب تتحرك ببطء وعلى مستوى

منخفض، محملة بأثقال ضخمة من المطر. واحدة من أكثر الأشياء غرابة التي رآها أكيفا على الإطلاق كانت ظلال تلك السحب وهي تطارد سطح البحر، حيث يبدو شكلها أشبه بظلال مخلوقات بحرية عملاقة. في البداية، لم يصدق أنها ليست كذلك، وما زال يطلق المزاح بسبب ذلك.

"انظر، حوت روركوال!"، أشارت أيدولون إلى ظل سحابة أكبر من نصف الجزر، ثم ضحكت على فكرة وجود وحش بحري بهذا الحجم.

كان ذلك يذكّر أكيفا بالنيثيلام. لم تكن تلك الفكرة بعيدة عن ذهنه أبداً سألت ميليل:"وماذا عن المنزل؟".

نظر إليها بطرف عينه وقال:"من المبالغة أن نسميه منزلاً".

لكنه كان شيئاً على أي حال. الأمل هو ما كان يبقي أكيفا متماسكاً، وكانت فكرة كارو هي ما يدفعه للاستمرار يوماً بعد يوم في دروسه التأسيسية في أنيميا، التي كانت الاسم الصحيح لـ"نظام الطاقات" خاصته، والتي تمثل الجذر ليس فقط للسحر، بل للعقل والروح والحياة نفسها. فقط عندما يُصبح متأكداً من سيطرته الكاملة على نفسه وعلى قدرته المدمرة في استنزاف سيريثار، سيكون حراً ليذهب إلى حيث يشاء.

أما بالنسبة إلى كارو، وإن كانت قد تأتي يوماً ما إلى هنا لترى ما يشغل به أكيفا أوقات فراغه، فقد كان يعلم أن واجبها سيبقيها بعيدة لفترة طويلة قادمة. ومع ذلك، وجد عزاءً بسيطاً في معرفة أن زيري، وليراز، وزوزانا، وميك كانوا معها، لضمان أنها تعتني بنفسها. وأيضاً كارناسيال، الذي وعد بتدريبها على طريقة أدق لدفع الغُشر، طريقة لا تعتمد على الألم.

مع ذلك، فإن فكرة كارو وهي تمضي أيامها في دروس يومية مع ساحر من الستيليين لم تكن تماماً مصدر راحة صرفة لأكيفا.

سألت ميليل:"لكن الأمور تسير على ما يرام، صحيح؟".

هز كتفيه بلامبالاة، متردداً في إخبارها بأن المنزل كان جاهزاً بالفعل. كان جاهزاً منذ فترة. كل صباح، عندما يستيقظ في البيت الطويل الذي

يتشاركه مع إخوته وأخواته من غير الشرعيين، كان يستلقي لوهلة وعيناه مغمضتان، متخيلاً الصباح كما قد يكون، لا كما هو في الحقيقة.

سألت:"هل تحتاج شيئاً لهذا الأمر؟ سيلف أعطتني إبريقاً جميلاً، ولم أستخدمه أبداً. يمكنك أن تأخذه".

كان عرضاً بسيطاً، لكن أكيفا ألقى على ميليل نظرة شك. لم يكن لديه إبريق، ولا الكثير من الأشياء الأخرى، لكنه لم يعرف كيف يمكن لها أن تعرف ذلك. "حسناً، شكراً لك"، قال، محاولاً أن يكون مهذباً. على الرغم من لطف العرض، شعر بأنه تدخل في شؤونه.

منذ قدومه إلى هنا، كانت حياة أكيفا معظم الوقت أشبه بكتاب مفتوح. روتينه، تدريباته، تقدمه، وحتى مزاجه، كانت كلها موضوعات مفتوحة للنقاش العام في أي لحظة. إحدى الساحرات—وغالباً ما كانت نايتنغال— تبقي تواصلاً مستمراً مع أنيميا خاصته، وهي عملية مراقبة شُبّهت بوضع الإبهام على نبضه.

أكدت له جدته أن لا أحد يقرأ أفكاره، وكان يأمل أن يكون ذلك صحيحاً، كما كان يأمل ألا تتناثر محاولاته غير المتمرسة لإرسال الرسائل مثل قصاصات الورق على كامل السكان.

لأن ذلك سيكون محرجاً جداً.

على أي حال، وبالنظر إلى شعوره بأنه أشبه بمشروع جماعي للستيليين، أراد الاحتفاظ بهذا الأمر لنفسه. لم يتحدث عنه قط—عن الجزيرة، المنزل، آماله—على الرغم من أنهم، كما يبدو، يعرفون كل شيء على أي حال. وبالطبع، لم يأخذ أحداً إلى هناك من قبل. ستكون كارو الأولى. يوماً ما. كانت هذه العبارة بمثابة تعويذة يرددها في داخله: يوماً ما.

قالت ميليل:"حسناً"، وانتظر أكيفا للحظة، مترقباً ما تقول ما جاءت لتقوله، لكنها بقيت صامتة. النظرة التي رمقته بها كانت تحمل شيئاً من الحنان، وكأنها تفهم ما يدور في داخله دون حاجة إلى الكلمات.

"سأراك على العشاء"، قالت ميليل أخيراً، ولمست ذراعه وهي تودّعه. كان تفاعلاً غريباً بعض الشيء، لكنه تجاهل الأمر وركّز على صياغة رسالته هذا اليوم إلى كارو. لم يدرك غرابة الموقف إلا لاحقاً، عندما نزل من القمة عائداً إلى البيت الطويل في طريقه إلى العشاء. كان ينتظره هناك ما أثار إحساساً أعمق بالغرابة، في الرواق المسقوف بطبقة من القش الذي يمتد بطول المبنى.

رأى الإبريق أولاً، ومنه فهم أن ما تبقى كان أيضاً هدايا. صعد الدرجات ونظر إلى تلك الأشياء التي لم تكن موجودة قبل ساعة. كرسي مطرّز، زوج من الفوانيس النحاسية، وعاء كبير مصنوع من الخشب المصقول مليء بفواكه الجزيرة المتعددة. كانت هناك أطوال من القماش الأبيض الشفاف، مطوية بعناية، وإبريق من الفخار، ومرآة. كان يتفحص كل هذا بدهشة عندما سمع صوت جناحين خلفه، فاستدار ليرى جدته تهبط من السماء وهي تحمل طرداً ملفوفاً.

"أنتِ أيضاً؟" سألها، بصوت فيه نبرة اتهام لطيفة.

ابتسمت له، وكانت ابتسامتها حانية بنفس القدر الذي بدت به نظرة ميليل سابقاً. ما الذي تخطط له النساء؟ تساءل أكيفا، بينما صعدت نايتنغال الدرجات وناولته هديتها، وقالت:"ربما عليك أن تأخذها مباشرة إلى الجزيرة".

للحظة، اكتفى أكيفا بالنظر إليها. إذا بدا بطيئاً في استيعاب ما قصدته، فذلك فقط لأنه كان يحافظ على أمله كما يحافظ على سحره المتطاير، داخل حدود صارمة. وعندما بدأ يفهم ما تعنيه، لم ينطق بكلمة. فقط دفع نحوها رسالة ذهنية، خرجت من عقله كصرخة. لم تكن سوى سؤال، جوهر السؤال ذاته، وأرسلها بقوة جعلتها تومض عينيها، ثم تضحك.

قالت له:"حسناً. أعتقد أن قدراتك في التخاطر تتحسن".

"نايتنغال"، قال بصوت متوتر، يكاد يكون همساً مشوباً بالعجلة.

فأومأت برأسها. ابتسمت. وأرسلت إلى ذهنه صورة خاطفة لشخصيات في السماء: صياد عواصف، وكيرين، ونصف دزينة من السيرافيم، وعدد مساوٍ من الكيميرا. ومعهم شخص كان يحلق بلا أجنحة، ينزلق في الهواء، وشعره الأزرق يتطاير كالسوط في سماء الشفق.

لاحقاً، سيعتقد أكيفا أن نايتنغال هي من جاءت لإبلاغه بالأخبار، ربما لتجنبه استخدام سيريثار دون قصد في فرحة غامرة. لكنه لم يفعل. لقد درّبوه على إدراك حدود الـ"أنيميا" الخاصة به والبقاء داخلها، وقد نجح في ذلك. مع ذلك، شعرت روحه وكأنها أُضيئت كالألعاب النارية التي كانت تملأ سماء لوراميندي منذ سنوات طويلة، عندما أمسكت مادريغال بيده وقادته إلى حياة جديدة، حياة تم عيشها في الليل، من أجل الحب.

والآن، كان الليل يقترب، ومعه، دون توقع، وبصورة عفوية، الحب أيضاً. أسرع مما سمح لنفسه يوماً بأن يحلم.

. . .

كان كارناسيال هو من أرسل مسبقاً لإبلاغهم بوصولهم، لكن النساء تكفّلن بكل شيء آخر. يافث وستيفان من غير الشرعيين، وحتى ريف ورايث من الستيلييين، اعترضوا قائلين إنه من القسوة إرسال أكيفا بعيداً في ذلك الوقت، لكن النساء لم يُعِرن ذلك أي اهتمام.

اجتمعن على الشرفة المطلة من قصر سكاراب المتواضع المنحوت في الجرف، وانتظرن. بحلول ذلك الوقت، كان الليل قد أرخى سدوله، وجاءت معه واحدة من تلك العواصف المفاجئة التي تمطر بلا رحمة، بحيث بدأ القادمون بالهبوط قبل أن تلمع أجنحة السيرافيم بين البرق والرعد.

تم استقبالهم دون أي مظاهر احتفالية. تم فصل الرجال عن المجموعة كما يُفصل القمح عن القش، وتركوا واقفين تحت المطر. تبادل كارناسيال وريف نظرة تضامن تحمل عبء التجربة قبل أن يقودا ميك وزيري، برفقة فيركو، وراث، وإكساندر، وبعضاً من غير الشرعيين الذين بدوا مبهورين

بالأجواء، بعيداً عن العاصفة. أما سكاراب، وإليزا، ونايتنغال، فقد قمن باصطحاب كارو، وزوزانا، وليراز، وإيسا، والظلال الحية عبر غرف الملكة الخاصة، وصولاً إلى حمام القصر، حيث أحاط بهن البخار العطر في استقبال اتفقن جميعاً على أنه كان الأفضل على الإطلاق.

حسناً، باستثناء أمر واحد. كانت كارو قد جالت بعينيها بحثاً عن أكيفا في تلك اللحظات الوجيزة بين الهبوط وبين أن يتم اصطحابها بعيداً، لكنها لم تلمحه. ضغطت نايتنغال على يدها وابتسمت، مما أعطاها بعض العزاء، لكن العزاء الحقيقي لن يتحقق حتى تراه وتشعر أن الرابط بينهما ما زال مستمراً.

كانت تؤمن بأنه كذلك. من دون انقطاع. عندما تستيقظ في كل صباح، كانت تملك يقيناً بذلك، وكأنها قضت الليل معه في أحلامها.

"كيف جئتم إلى هنا؟" سألت سكاراب عندما كنّ جميعاً قد خلعن ملابسهن واستقررن في الماء الرغوي، وحملن كؤوساً فخارية من مشروب غريب في أيديهن. خصائصه المبردة كانت تعوّض الحرارة شبه المحتملة للشلال الحار. "هل أنهيتم عملكم بالفعل؟".

كانت كارو ممتنة لإيسا التي تولّت الإجابة. لم تكن تشعر بأنها قادرة على التظاهر بخوض أي محادثة اجتماعية طبيعية.

أين هو؟

قالت إيسا: "جُمعت الأرواح. وهي الآن آمنة. لكن من المتوقع أن يكون الشتاء قاسياً، والمزيد من اللاجئين يصلون كل يوم. لذا، كان من الأفضل الانتظار حتى موسم آخر لبدء الإحياء".

كان ذلك تعبيراً لطيفاً للإشارة إلى أنهم اختاروا ألا يعيدوا أموات لوراميندي إلى الحياة فقط ليواجهوا شتاءً رمادياً مليئاً بالمطر المتجمد وطين الرماد. لم يكن هناك ما يكفي من الطعام لتوزيعه على الجميع، ولا مأوى كافٍ كذلك. لم يكن هذا ما تصوّره بريمستون وأمير الحرب عندما دمرا الدَرج

الحلزوني الطويل الذي يؤدي إلى أسفل الأرض، ليحبسا شعبهما تحتها. ولم يكن هذا ما ضحّى أولئك الذين بقوا فوق الأرض بأنفسهم من أجله أيضاً— لقد ضحوا لكي يعيش آخرون في يوم من الأيام حياة أفضل وزمناً أرحم. لم يحن ذلك اليوم بعد. سيصبح الوقت ملائماً بما يكفي.

كان القرار صائباً، وكارو تعرف ذلك. لكنها، لأنه أتيح لها فعل ما أرادته أكثر من أي شيء آخر، أبقت نفسها خارج كل نقاش وتركته للآخرين. لم تستطع منع نفسها من رؤية رغباتها الخاصة على أنها أنانية، وكل أملها المخزون على أنه كنز لا يحق لها أن تحمله بعيداً عبر انحناء العالم، لتُنفقه على روح واحدة فقط، بينما الكثير من الأرواح الأخرى تظل عالقة في حالة من السكون.

وكأن سكاراب شعرت بالصراع الذي يدور في داخلها، فقالت:"لقد كان اختياراً شجاعاً، وأتصور أنه لم يكن سهلاً. لكن الأمور ستسير على ما يرام. يمكن إعادة بناء المدن. الأمر مسألة قوة، وإرادة، ووقت".

وعلّقت نايتنغال قائلة:"وبالحديث عن الوقت، كم ستبقين هنا؟".

أجابت ليراز:"معظمنا سيبقى لبضعة أسابيع فقط، لكن القرار قد اتُّخذ"—نظرت إلى كارو نظرة صارمة—"بأن كارو يجب أن تبقى معكم حتى الربيع".

كان هذا أكبر صراع داخلي بالنسبة إلى كارو. بقدر ما أرادت ذلك— الشتاء كله هنا مع أكيفا—لم تستطع التوقف عن التفكير في الظروف القاسية التي سيعاني منها الآخرون، حينما تزداد الأمور صعوبة. الأقوياء لا يأخذون إجازات.

قالت سكاراب:"صحة أنيمياكِ أمر ذو أهمية قصوى لشعبك. لا تنسي ذلك أبداً. تحتاجين إلى الشفاء والراحة". وأضافت نايتنغال:"كما أن الألم يصنع عُشراً فظاً، فإن البؤس يولد قوة بدائية".

وأردفت إليزا، وكأنها تعرف عمّ تتحدث:"في السعادة، تزهر الأنيميا".

أومأت إيسّا موافقة على كل ما قالته النساء، وقد ارتسم على وجهها

تعبير ألم أقل لك؟ بالطبع كانت قد قالت هي نفس الشيء، وإن كان بأسلوب أقل رسمية. "هذا واجبكِ، يا صغيرتي العزيزة"، قالت الآن بنبرة مطمئنة، "أن تكوني بخير في جسدك وروحك".

السعادة يجب أن تذهب إلى مكان ما، تذكرت كارو، ثم غاصت أعمق في الماء وهي تتنهد. بعض الأقدار يصعب تقبلها، لكن هذا لم يكن واحداً منها. "حسناً، حسناً"، قالت متظاهرة بالتردد. "إذا كان لا بد من ذلك".

غسلن أنفسهن، وخرجت كارو من الحوض وهي تشعر بنقاء في جسدها وروحها. كان من الجيد أن يتم الاعتناء بها من قبل النساء، ويا لروعتهن كجماعة. أخطر الكيميرا جنباً إلى جنب مع أخطر السيرافيم، ومعهم ناجا الأفعى، وميك-ميك العقرب الشرسة في هيئة بشرية خادعة بمظهر براءتها، وزوج من الستيليات ذواتي العيون النارية والقوى التي لا يمكن قياسها، وإليزا، التي هي كل الأجوبة. المفتاح الذي يفتح القفل. وأيضاً، مجرد فتاة رائعة حقاً.

قمن بتمشيط شعر كارو ولفّه، وهو لا يزال رطباً، في جدائل مبرومة ومربوطة تنساب كداليات عنب على ظهرها العاري. أخرجن أثواباً خفيفة من الحرير بأسلوب الستيليين، ووضعن أطوال القماش على بشرتها لتحديد الأنسب.

"الأبيض لا يناسبكِ"، قالت سكاراب، وهي تلقي بفستان أبيض جانباً. "ستبدين كالشبح". ثم أخرجت قطعة حرير داكنة كليل، تلمع بتجمعات صغيرة من البلورات تشبه الكويكبات السماوية. ضحكت كارو، ومررت الفستان بين أصابعها كأنها تلامس الماء، وتركت الماضي يتدفق داخلها.

سألت زوزانا: "ما الأمر؟".

"لا شيء"، ردت كارو، وسمحت لهن بإلباسها. كان الفستان أشبه بسارية تلتف حول كتف واحد، تاركة ذراعيها مكشوفتين. للحظة، تمنّت لو كان لديها

وعاء من السكر وفرشاة لتغمر نفسها كما فعلت في ليلة أخرى سابقة. كان هذا الفستان يشبه كثيراً الفستان الذي ارتدته في حفل أمير الحرب، عندما جاء أكيفا ليبحث عنها.

"هل تريدين الاحتفاظ بملابسكِ القديمة؟" سألت إليزا وهي تدفع كومة الملابس المهملة بقدمها.

"احرقوها"، قالت كارو. ثم توقفت فجأة."أوه. انتظروا". مدت يدها في جيب سروالها وأخرجت عظمة الأمنيات التي حملتها معها طوال تلك الأشهر."حسناً"، قالت بعد أن تأكدت من وجودها."الآن احرقوها".

شعرت كارو وكأنها عروس عندما قادتها النساء إلى الخارج مجدداً. كان المطر قد توقف، لكن الليل كان حياً بذكراه؛ بتلك القطرات المتبقية والجداول الصغيرة التي تشق طريقها عبر الأرض، مع أصوات المخلوقات التي تصدح في الأفق وروائح العسل التي تعبق في الهواء المشبع بالضباب والدفء.

وها قد ظهر أكيفا.

جسده غارقٌ بالمطر، والهالة التي تحيط به تتصاعد منها أبخرة حيث كان دفء جسده يجفف الأمطار. عيناه كانتا مشتعلتين، غاضباً من طول الانتظار. يداه ترتجفان وتنقبضان، ثم توقفتا تماماً عندما وقعت عيناه على كارو.

تعثّر الزمن، أو هكذا شعرت هي. لم تعد هناك حاجة إلى تلك الثواني الفاصلة التي لا يكونان فيها متصلين. لقد عاشا الكثير منها بالفعل، وانتهيا من هذه الأخيرة في غمضة عين.

حلّقا معاً. الزمن نفسه قفز بعيداً عن طريقهما. كانا يدوران في الهواء، والأرض تختفي تحت أقدامهما. اختفت الجزيرة. وارتفعت السماء لتستقبلهما، واختبأت الأقمار خلف السحب، تخبئ دموعها لنفسها، وندمها الذي يعود إلى عصر قد انتهى.

شفاه وأنفاس وأجنحة ورقص. امتنان، وراحة، وجوع. وضحك. ضحك يتنفّس ويُتذوّق. وجوه تُقبّل، بلا مكان يُترك مهملاً. رموش مبتلة بالدموع، وشفاه مالحة تُقبل شفاهاً أخرى. الشفاه، أخيراً، تنعم بالرقة والدفء— المركز الناعم والحار للكون بأسره. ودقات قلب لا تنبض في انسجام، بل تمرّ بينهما عبر ضغط الأجساد، كأنها محادثة مكونة من كلمة واحدة فقط:"نعم". وهذا ما حدث. كارو وأكيفا تشبثا ببعضهما البعض ولم يتركا أيدي بعضهما أبداً.

لم تكن نهاية سعيدة، بل كانت لبّ السعادة—أخيراً، بعد كل تلك البدايات المضطربة. قصتهما ستكون طويلة. سيُكتب الكثير عنهما، بعضه في أبيات شعرية، وبعضه في أغنيات، وبعضه الآخر بنثر بسيط، في مجلدات ستُخطّ في أرشيفات مدن لم تُبنَ بعد. وعلى الرغم من رغبة كارو الصريحة، فلن يكون أي شيء من هذا مملاً.

وهو ما ستجده سبباً للشعور بالامتنان مليون مرة، بدءاً من تلك الليلة طيران عبر الضباب المتناثر، أياد متشابكة. جزيرة بين مئات الجزر. منزل على شاطئ هلالي صغير. لم يكن أكيفا يكذب حين قال لميليل إن وصفه بالمنزل كان مبالغة. لقد تخيّل ذات مرة باباً يُغلق على العالم الخارجي، لكن هنا لم يكن هناك باب، وكأن العالم الخارجي كان امتداداً للمنزل نفسه: بحر ونجوم إلى الأبد.

كان البناء عبارة عن جناح: سقف من القش مدعوم بأعمدة، محكم عند منحدر صخري يحميه، وأرضه من الرمل الناعم، مع كروم حية تتدلى من الجرف لتشكل جداراناً خضراء على جانبين. هذا ما كان أكيفا قد أنجزه قبل اليوم. وكانت هناك طاولة وكراسٍ. حسناً، كانت منحوتة من خشب انجرف مع البحر، لكن كان على الطاولة قماش أرقى مما تستحقه.

والآن، كان هناك وعاء خشبي مليء بالفاكهة فوقها، وإبريق جميل أيضاً، مع علبة شاي وكوبين. الفوانيس كانت معلقة على خطاطيف، وأطوال من

القماش الشفاف شكلت جداراً ثالثاً يرفرف برفق، شفافاً كضباب البحر.

هدية نايتنغال قد فُتحت وأخذت مكانها المناسب، وعندما أحضر أكيثا كارو إلى المنزل الذي صنعه من أجلها—مكان بدا كأنه خرج من حلم، مثالي إلى درجة جعلتها تنسى أن تتنفس واضطرت أن تلتقط أنفاسها على عجل—إن أمنيته قد تحققت تقريباً.

على السرير: بطانية لتغطيهما، بطانية تخصهما معاً. في لحظة ما من الليل، التقيا عليها، وجهاً لوجه في الفراغ الذي تقلص بينهما، الركبتان مثنيتان تحتهما، وعظمة الأمنيات مستقرة بين أيديهما.

شبكا أصابعهما حول طرفيها الرفيعين، وشدّا.

النهاية.

شكر وتقدير

نتوجه بجزيل الشكر والامتنان إلى كل من ساهم بجهوده المخلصة وتعاونه المثمر في إخراج هذا الكتاب باللغة العربية إلى النور

نخص بالشكر المترجمين الذين نقلوا هذه الرواية بدقة وأمانة، والمحررين الذين وظفوا خبراتهم ورؤاهم المهنية لضمان جودة المحتوى. كما نعرب عن تقديرنا العميق للمراجعين الذين بذلوا جهداً كبيراً في التدقيق اللغوي والفني، وللمصممين الذين أضفوا لمساتهم الإبداعية لتقديم الكتاب بأبهى صورة تليق بالقارئ الكريم

كما نتقدم بالشكر الجزيل لكل من دعم هذا العمل، سواء عن قرب أو عن بعد. نأمل أن يحظى هذا الكتاب برضاكم، وأن يشكل إضافة قيمة تثري المكتبة العربية

KHAYAT
Publishing

١

Washington, DC
United States

www.khayatbooks.com